JOAN D. VINGE
THE SUMMER QUEEN

WARNER BOOKS

A Time Warner Company

Copyright © 1991 by Joan D. Vinge
All rights reserved.

Warner Books, Inc., 666 Fifth Avenue, New York, NY 10103
W A Time Warner Company

Printed in the United States of America
First printing: November 1991
10 9 8 7 6 5 4 3 2 1

Library of Congress Cataloging-in-Publication Data

Vinge, Joan D.
    The Summer Queen / Joan D. Vinge.
      p. cm.
    ISBN 0-446-51397-0
    I. Title.
    PS3572.I53S8   1991
    813'.54—dc20   90-50521
                                        CIP

Book design by Giorgetta Bell McRee

To the Mother of Us All
To my mother
And to my children

I owe many thanks to many people for their help in making this book a reality, after so long. In particular, I would like to thank Michall Jeffers and John Warner, for bringing *Hamlet's Mill* to my attention; Giorgio de Santillana and Hertha von Dechend, authors of *Hamlet's Mill;* Barbara Luedtke; Jim Frenkel; Vernor Vinge; Brian Thomsen; the Clarion West class of '88; Deborah Kahn Cunningham; Lolly Boyer; Steve and Julia Sabbagh; Merrilee Heifetz; and Richard Plantagenet, King of England, who may be the most misunderstood man in history.

AUTHOR'S NOTE

The following names of characters and places are pronounced as shown:

Ananke (Uh-NON-kee)
Arienrhod (AIRY-en-rode)
Danaquil Lu (DAN-uh-keel LOO)
Gundhalinu (Gun-dah-LEE-noo)
Jerusha PalaThion (Jer-OO-shuh PAL-uh-THY-un)
Kedalion Niburu (Keh-DAY-lee-un Nih-BUR-oo)
Kharemough (KARE-uh-moff)
Kharemoughi (KARE-uh-MAWG-ee)
Kullervo (Kul-LAIR-voh)
Miroe Ngenet (MIR-row Eng-EN-it)
Mundilfoere (MUN-dil-fair)
Sandhi (SAHN-dee)
Tiamat (TEE-uh-maht)
Tuo Ne'el (TOO-oh NEEL)
Vhanu (VAH-noo)

'Do
'You know nothing? Do you see nothing? Do you remember
'Nothing?'
     I remember
Those are pearls that were his eyes.
'Are you alive, or not? Is there nothing in your head?'

                     —T. S. Eliot

There's someone in my head, but it's not me.

                     —Pink Floyd

The mills of gods grind slowly, and the result is usually pain.
                     —Georgio de Santillana and
                       Hertha von Dechend

PART I: THE CHANGE

Do I dare
Disturb the universe?
In a minute there is time
For decisions and revisions which a minute
will reverse.

—T. S. Eliot

TIAMAT: The Windwards

The hand released the bright ribbon of scarf, and it fluttered down. A hundred eager voices made one voice as the cluster of young girls exploded down the shining strand of beach.

Clavally Bluestone Summer sat watching on the cliff high above, feeling the sea wind against her face, feeling it sweep back her long, dark hair. Smiling, she closed her eyes and imagined that it was the wind of motion, that she was running with the others down below. She had run when she was a girl in races like this one, on so many islands across the Summer seas; hoping to be the winner, to be the Sea Mother's Chosen for the three days of the clan festival, garlanded with necklaces of clattering polished shells, fed the best and the sweetest of foods, given new clothes, honored by the elders, flirted with by all the young men. . . .

Her smile turned wistful; she fingered the trefoil pendant that gleamed in the sunlight against the laces of her loose homespun shirt. It had been a long time since she had run in one of those races. She had been a sibyl for nearly half her life now. *How was it possible . . . ?* She opened her eyes, filling them with the endless bluegreen of sea and sky, ever-changing and yet ever constant; the mottled clouds, the shimmering ephemera of rainbows from a distant squall. The Twins smiled down on their gathering today, warming her shoulders with luxuriant heat. Spring was in the air, making her remember with longing her body's own springtime.

She glanced over her shoulder at the sound of footsteps. Her smile widened as she saw her husband making his way up the path with a basket of fish cakes and bread, a jug of beer in his other hand. She saw the gray-shot brown of his braided hair, his own trefoil gleaming in the sunlight.

Her smile faded as she watched him struggle up the steep hill. The stiffness in his joints was getting worse every year—too many years spent in drafty stone rooms, or making cold, wet crossings from island to island for weeks at a time. Danaquil Lu was a Winter; he had not been bred to the hard life of a Summer, and his body rebelled against it. But he rarely spoke any word of complaint or regret, because he belonged here, where he was free to live his life as a sibyl . . . and because his heart belonged to her.

The weather was warming; the Summer Star was brightening in their sky, Summer had come into its own. Perhaps the warmer days would ease his pain. Her smile came back as she saw his eyes, bright and bluegreen like the sea, smiling up at her.

He sat down with the basket of food, trying not to grimace. She put an arm around his shoulders, massaging his back gently as she pointed down at the beach. "Look, it's almost over!" Another shout rose from the watchers below as the runners reached the finish line drawn in the wet sand. They watched a young girl with a bright flag of yellow hair sprint across the line first, watched her being embraced and garlanded and borne away.

"It was a good race, Dana," she said, hearing the memories in her voice.

Danaquil Lu sighed, nodding; but somehow the gesture felt to her as if he had shaken his head. "We're young for such a short time," he murmured, "and we're old for such a long time."

She turned to look at him. "Come now," she said, too cheerfully, because she had been feeling the same way. "How can you say that on a day like this?" and she kissed him, to make certain he didn't try to answer.

He laughed in surprise. They ate together, enjoying the day and each other's company, an hour of solitude stolen from the questions of the festival-goers in the village below.

They came down the hill again at last. A clan gathering was always a joyful time—a time for being reunited with relatives and friends from all across the scattered islands of Summer; for remembering the Sea Mother, giving the Lady the tribute She deserved. This was the annual gathering of the Goodventures, one of the largest clans in the islands. They had been the religious leaders of Summer before the last Change—the clan of the previous Summer Queens—and they still held great influence.

Down by the stone wall of the quay the winner of the footrace, a laughing, freckled girl of no more than fourteen, was tossing the ritual offerings of worshipers and supplicants into the restless green water. Out in the bay, several mers from the colony that shared this island's shores looked on, a sure sign of the Sea's blessing. Clavally watched the girl's face, the sunlight radiant in her hair, and felt a sudden, unexpected surge of longing.

She had made a choice when she became a sibyl. It was a hard, restless life, traveling from island to island, speaking the Lady's wisdom to those who needed her, seeking out and training the ones who would follow after her, to guide a new generation of Summers. They said that it was "death to kill a sibyl, death to love a sibyl, death to be a sibyl." . . . Few if any men who were not sibyls themselves would dare to be a husband to one.

But even after she had met Danaquil Lu, she had gone on taking childbane, because it was too hard a life to inflict on a child, and she had no close relatives to help her raise one. And Danaquil Lu, with his bent back and aching joints, needed more and more of her care. She squeezed his hand tightly, and told her restless body to be quiet. Soon enough her childbearing time would be past, and the questions in her heart would be answered once and for all.

"A question, sibyl—?" A boy came up to them hesitantly, his brown braids flopping against his sleeveless linen tunic. His eyes chose Danaquil Lu to ask his question of; she guessed it was probably a question about girls.

"Ask, and I will answer." Danaquil Lu spoke the ritual response, smiling kindly.

Clavally let go of his hand with a farewell glance, granting the blushing boy privacy. She moved on through the crowd, half-hearing Danaquil Lu's voice behind her murmur *"Input . . ."* as he fell into the Transfer, and the boy's mumbled question.

"Sibyl?" A middle-aged, gray-haired Goodventure woman came up beside her, and Clavally stopped, expecting another question. But before her response could form, the woman said, "Are you going to Carbuncle?"

Clavally looked at her blankly. "To Carbuncle? Why?" she asked.

"Haven't you heard?" The woman looked annoyingly smug. "The new Summer Queen. She has asked all the sibyls of Summer to make a pilgrimage to the City in the North. She claims it is the Lady's will."

Clavally shook her head, expressing her disbelief as much as her ignorance. Carbuncle was the only real city on the entire planet, located far to the north, among the Winter clans. Its name meant both "jewel" and "fester." Tied to the offworlders' starport, it swarmed with their wonders and their corruption during the one-hundred-and-fifty-year cycles with the offworld Hegemony controlled Tiamat. During that time the Snow Queen reigned, the Winters claimed the city and all the lands around it for their own—and sibyls were forbidden in Carbuncle. The offworlders despised them, the Winters hated and feared them. Danaquil Lu had been born in the city, but he had been exiled when he became a sibyl.

But now the Change had come again. The Black Gate that the offworlders used to reach Tiamat had closed; the offworlders had gone away, and taken their technology with them. Even now the seas were warming. Gradually they would become too hot for the klee the Summers herded and for many of the fish they netted at sea. The mers, the Sea Mother's other children, were migrating north, and the Summers were preparing for their own migration as well. Their ways would become this world's ways again, as the Winters relearned the old rules of survival and harmony with the Sea, and the Summer Queens showed them the human face of the Lady's wisdom.

"But why would the Summer Queen—or the Lady—want sibyls in the city," Clavally asked, "and not among the people, helping them to find the way to their new lives?"

"She said that she wanted to tell all the sibyls of a greater purpose, their true purpose, that had been revealed to her by the Sea Mother." The Goodventure woman shrugged and wiped her perspiring face. "But there are those who ask, What possible purpose could a sibyl find, which is better than to do what you do now—?"

"Yes," Clavally murmured uncertainly. "It's a strange request."

"What is?" Danaquil Lu came up beside her, raising his eyebrows.

"The Summer Queen has asked all the sibyls to come to Carbuncle, so that she can speak to them," she said. And she watched her husband's face turn ashen. The scars on his cheek—the cruel legacy of his casting-out from Carbuncle—suddenly stood out like a brand. He took hold of her arm, not-quite-casually, steadying himself.

"Oh," was all he said. He took a deep breath, filling his lungs with clear sea air.

"We needn't go," Clavally said softly, looking up at him. "There will be enough others without us."

"A wise decision. But why do you look like the news brings you no joy, Clavally Bluestone?" A heavyset, weathered woman joined them; Clavally recognized Capella Goodventure, the clan headwoman.

Clavally didn't answer, looking back at Danaquil Lu, who was gazing out to sea as if he were suddenly there alone.

"Or your pledged, either," Capella said, her voice prying like fingers. "What clan is he with—?" Clavally heard the tone in her voice which said she knew the answer, although Danaquil Lu wore no embroidery on his shirt, no token of clan membership.

"Wayaways," Danaquil Lu said flatly, looking back at her. His expression said that he recognized the tone in her voice, too.

"Wayaways? But isn't that a Winter clan?" Capella said, with sour insinuation. The sound of her surprise rang as false as a cracked bell. "I would think you'd be eager to return to your home."

"It isn't my home," he snapped. "I am a sibyl."

"Of course you are." She stared at his trefoil. "A Winter who worships the Lady. Aren't you unusual." She rubbed her arms, looking out at the sea.

Danaquil Lu looked away from her again, irritation plain on his face. He did not believe in the Lady; or in anything at all except his calling. But the Lady believed in him. Clavally looked back at Capella Goodventure, frowning. She had never been fond of the Goodventures' elder. She was becoming less fond of her now with every heartbeat. She opened her mouth to inquire whether Capella had a question to ask, or not.

"I would go nowhere near the City, if I were a sibyl," Capella said, looking back at her. "I was in Carbuncle at the last Festival. It was my duty to oversee the crowning of the Summer Queen—and the drowning of the Snow Queen." She smiled slightly; Clavally tightened her jaw, and held her tongue. "And what I saw then made me wonder whether the Lady has abandoned Carbuncle forever."

"What do you mean?" Clavally asked, her curiosity forcing the words out against her will.

"The new queen claims to be a sibyl."

Clavally's eyes widened. Her hand touched the trefoil hanging against her chest. "But isn't that a good—"

"—But," Capella Goodventure went on, relentlessly, "she's white as snow; she looks exactly like the old queen, Arienrhod." Her voice dripped vitriol. "She forsook the proper rituals of the Change; she speaks blasphemies about the Lady's will. She chooses to live in the Snow Queen's palace—and she went so far as to have me turned out of it when I tried to show her how her willfulness could harm us all."

Ah, Clavally thought.

"The Winter gossip says that she is the old Queen's illegal clone, an unnatural copy of herself, made for her by the offworlders to oppress us," Capella Goodventure went on. "She couldn't possibly be a Summer, even though she claims to belong to the Dawntreader clan—"

"The Dawntreaders?" Clavally said, startled. "I knew a sibyl of the Dawntreaders, about five years ago. Her name was Moon—"

This time it was the Goodventure woman who looked surprised.

"Is she the new Queen?" Clavally asked, incredulous. She read the answer in the other woman's eyes.

"You know her?" Capella Goodventure demanded. "What did she look like?"

"She would be young, and very fair—her hair was almost white. Her eyes were a strange, shifting color, like fog-agates. . . ." She knew again, from the look on the other woman's face, that she had described the new Queen.

"She is a sibyl," Danaquil Lu said abruptly. "We trained her ourselves. And she was a Summer. I would have known if she was not."

Capella Goodventure looked at him, her eyes narrowing; he met her stare, until finally she was the one who looked away. "She isn't right," she said finally, looking at Clavally again. "I will tell you what I have told every sibyl I've seen—I have to return to the city, but you do not. Don't go to Carbuncle." She turned and started away, her angry momentum splitting the crowd like a ship's wake.

Clavally looked at Danaquil Lu, found him already looking at her. "Perhaps the only thing that's truly wrong with the new Queen is that she isn't a Goodventure," she murmured.

Danaquil Lu's mouth twitched with a fleeting, ironic smile; the smile disappeared. "What do you really think?" he asked her.

She brushed at a fly that was buzzing in her ear like doubt, and felt another frown start to form. "I remember the girl Moon Dawntreader that we knew. She *was* different . . . there was something about her . . . but I always felt that it was good. I think that I want to know for myself what the truth is, Dana."

He nodded, his face pinching. "You want to go to Carbuncle."

Slowly she nodded. "But what do you think? What do you feel? . . . What do you want to do?"

He looked out across the sea again, squinting with the glare of light on water, looking north. She saw him swallow as if something were caught in his throat. At last he said, "I want to go home."

ONDINEE: Razuma

"Halt. Who are you?"

He stopped in the inquisitory's shadowed corridor as weapons surrounded him, with cold-eyed men behind them.

"The Smith." They knew him only as the Smith when he came on errands like this; when he wore openly the pendant of silver metal that he usually kept hidden beneath his shirt. He could pass unmolested through circumstances that would be suicidal if he did not wear the cryptic star-and-compass, which stood for so many things to so many people. The star in this particular pendant was a solii, a rare and secret gem born in the heart of dying stars, more precious than diamonds, believed by some mystics to hold powers of enlightenment. In this setting it symbolized all that, and more. "The High Priest sent for me."

The men surrounding him wore the uniforms of the Church Police, with the blood-red badge of the High Priest's elite guard. They looked dubious as they took in his face, his youth; they studied the sign he wore. Their weapons lowered, slightly. They carried plasma rifles, not the stun rifles that most police forces used, that were both cheaper and far more humane. The High Priest's red-badges were called the Terror, and the name was not an empty threat. "Come with us," one of the guards said finally, nodding his head. "He's waiting for you."

The Smith followed them along the dark, echoing corridor, down a flight of steps cut from stone. The steps had been worn into crescents by the pitiless tread of booted feet going down, and up again; by the feet of the inquisitory's countless victims, going only down. Someone screamed, somewhere, as they reached the bottom. The guards glanced at him as he hesitated, measuring his reaction to the sound. *Infidel,* their stares whispered. *Criminal. Offworlder scum.*

He looked back at them, letting them into his eyes, letting them see what waited for them there. "Let's go," he whispered. They looked away, and started on into the inquisitory's bowels.

They passed many closed doors; he heard more screams, moans, prayers in more than one language. The parched heat of the streets was a reeking fever-sweat here. He felt himself sweating, not entirely from the fetid heat. One of his escort unlocked a door, and the noises he had been trying not to listen to suddenly became impossible to ignore. They led him through the chamber beyond.

He did not look right or left, staring fixedly at the back of the man ahead of him; but the corners of his eyes showed him a naked, bleeding body suspended from chains, an inquisitor irate at the interruption; an array of torture equipment ranging from the primitive to the sublime. Nothing ever became obsolete, in this business. The stench was overwhelming, like the heat, the sounds. . . . A rushing filled his head, his eyesight began to strobe; he swore under his breath, and turned it into forced meditation, pulling himself together. He finished crossing the room.

Beyond the far door was another corridor, and at its end another room: a laboratory this time. The air was suddenly, startlingly cool. He realized that this must be where the government kept the research installation he had heard rumors about. No wonder the secret of its location kept so well. He took a deep breath, let it out as Irduz, the High Priest of the Western Continent, came forward to greet him. Irduz was here in person; this was a bigger mess than he'd expected.

"Shibah be praised you've come so soon—"

He shrugged off the touch of Irduz's hand. The High Priest must have his own entrails on the sacrificial plate, to make him touch an unbeliever as if they were friends. "What's the problem?" the Smith asked, his voice rasping.

Irduz stepped back. "That is," he said, and pointed. Behind him stood half a dozen men in lab clothing, some Ondinean, some not. "Our researchers were trying a replication process. Something went wrong."

The researchers moved aside as the Smith started forward, giving him access to what lay behind them. He stopped, staring. Beyond the electromagnetic barrier of an emergency containment shield he saw a seething mass of glittering, cloudlike material. He looked at the display on the wall beside it, just as one more subsystem went critical, and another indicator slipped into the red in a spreading epidemic of crisis. "What the hell . . . ?" he murmured. He turned back to the research team. "What is it?"

They looked at each other, glancing nervously at the High Priest. "We were trying to create a replication process that would restructure carbon into diamond, for a building material—"

He gave a bark of sardonic laughter. "By the Render!" He looked back at Irduz, watching the High Priest's barely controlled anxiety become barely controlled anger, at his blasphemy, at his mockery. "Maybe Shibah and the Hallowed Calavre don't approve of your unnatural methods."

"Our plans for the new temple require large expanses of a material that is both transparent and extremely strong. Diamond veneer will not suffice. The Holy of Holies knows that everything we do in this place is to the greater exaltation of the Name," Irduz snapped. His heavy robes rustled like leaves of steel.

The Smith glanced toward the door he had entered by, and what lay beyond it. He smiled sourly. "Why don't you just evacuate, and drop a nuke on this place? That would solve your problem."

"That is not an acceptable solution," Irduz said, frowning.

"You mean it's too obvious?" The Smith shook his head, turning back to the displays. They had been trying to create a primitive replicator, as limited in function compared to the Old Empire's smartmatter as an amoeba was to a human being. They had wanted something that would mindlessly realign the molecular structure of carbon, transforming it into diamond. They had tried to create an imitation of life; and they had been too successful.

Instead of an army of cell-sized mechanical slaves, whose purpose was endlessly replicating the molecular pattern of diamonds, they had gotten an army of mindless automatons whose only purpose was reproducing themselves. And getting rid of them would require something far more sophisticated and lethal than a dose of disinfectant. The replicators by design incorporated diamond and other materials into their own analog-bacterial structures, making them stronger, more active, and far more resistant to attack than any natural organism.

He studied the displays silently, feeling incredulity and disgust grown inside him as he located the critical error sequence in their programming. He glanced again at the systems monitors, confirming his worst case expectations with one look. "This is eating its way through the shields." He turned back. "It's feeding on their energy output. In about half an hour the whole system is going to crash. Congratulations, gentlemen. You've produced a universal solvent."

The looks on the faces of the researchers turned critical, like the data readings behind him; and he realized that they had suspected it all along. But they had not even dared to speak its name, had been hoping against hope that he would come in here like a miracle and tell them that they were wrong—

"A universal solvent?" Irduz took a step backward, pressing an ebony hand to his jeweled breastplate. "It can't be." It was the ultimate demon of Old Empire technology run wild. "That absorbs everything it comes in contact with. Everything. Nothing can contain it. Nothing can stop it. It's the end of the world. . . ." He looked back at the stricken researchers, his indigo eyes filled with death. "By the Holy—"

The Smith silenced him with an impatient gesture. "Tell me," he said evenly, to the cluster of researchers, "why haven't you stopped this?"

"We can't—" someone protested.

"What do you mean?" the Smith said angrily. "You knew what the problem was. Anybody who knows bacteriology and its analogs could kill this thing. You have the processing power here; and you presumably possess at least the variety of chemical tools available to the average drug dealer. Don't you—?"

"Yes, but—"

"But what, for gods' sakes?" He caught the man and jerked him forward. "What the hell were you waiting for?"

"But—but—we can't get in there." The researcher gestured at the seething mass waiting beyond the transparent wall.

"You what?" the Smith whispered.

"We can't get at it." He wiped his sweating face. "When the emergency shields are up, there's no way to get access to what's contained inside them. But if we open the shielding the solvent will get out—"

The Smith laughed incredulously. "You can't be serious." He looked at their faces. He looked back at the shield displays. "How in the name of any god you like could you possibly set up a system with no emergency access?" *You miserable, stupid bastards—* His hands tightened.

"Isn't there anything you can do?" someone asked, in a voice that sounded pathetically high. "There must be something. You're the expert—!"

"I really don't know. You've done your work so well," he said softly, twisting the knife, almost enjoying the look on their faces.

"What if you can't?" Irduz said thickly. "What will happen to our world?"

The Smith glanced at the data on the displays beside him. "It could be worse." He shrugged.

They looked at him. "What do you mean?" Irduz demanded.

"The term 'universal solvent' is really a misnomer. There are a number of different biotechnical compounds you could call 'universal solvents.' Their interests vary depending on their composition. A few things would actually survive if this escapes containment—"

"What kind of things?" Irduz said. "What—?"

The Smith stared at his feet, rubbing his face, wiping away any trace of sardonic smile. He looked up again, finally. "Titanium spires in some of your monuments."

"What else?"

He shrugged again. "There are a number of things I can think of that would retain their integrity . . . but nothing you'd be interested in; except diamonds. Ships at the starport with titanium hulls, if their locks were completely sealed, might even get off the ground. . . . Carbon-based lifeforms will be the first to go, though; the replicants need carbon to make diamond, obviously. We'll all become diamond— filigrees of diamond frost, on a pond: the human body is mostly water; they don't need water." He glanced at the glittering cloud of doom. "This will spread like a disease. . . . The solvent can't destroy everything as fast as it will destroy human body tissue; some things will take weeks to break down. The whole planet will probably take months to transmogrify. . . ."

"Stop it!" Irduz said, and it took the Smith a moment to realize that he meant the solvent itself. "Stop it and you can have anything you desire—"

The Smith's mouth twisted. "It's not that simple," he said. "Maybe you can bribe your gods, priest, but you can't bribe mine." He gestured at the disintegrating fields, let his hand fall back to his side. "I can probably stop it . . ." he murmured finally, in disgust, looking at their terrified faces. "Personally I'd see you all in hell first, and me on the next ship out of here. But our mutual friends want your ass sitting in the High Seat a while longer, Irduz." He touched the pendant hanging against his shirt. "So the next time you say your prayers, you'll know who to thank. But if I save the world for you. I want you to take these incompetent sons of bitches on a tour of your other facilities." He jerked his head at the door to hell.

"It wasn't our fault!" the researcher beside him said. "Fakl was in Transfer! We were in contact with the sibyl net the whole time, we followed the process exactly! There were no mistakes in our program, I swear it!"

The Smith spun around. "You got this data through sibyl Transfer?" he asked. "I don't believe that. That's impossible."

Another man stepped forward, wearing a sibyl's trefoil. "I was in Transfer during the entire process," he said. "We made no mistakes at our end. We followed everything exactly. The sibyl net made the mistake. It was wrong. It was wrong. . . ." His voice faded. The Smith saw fear in his eyes—not fear of the Church's retribution, or even of the end of the world, in that moment—but instead the fear of a man whose belief in something more reliable than any god had been profoundly shaken.

"That's impossible," Irduz said.

"No," the Smith murmured. "It could be true." *It could be why I'm here—* He shook his head, as the stupefying visions of a realtime nightmare suddenly filled his mind, filling him with incomprehensible dread. He sucked in a ragged breath. *Why—?*

"Do you mean there's something wrong with the entire sibyl net?" Irduz demanded. "How could such a thing happen?"

"Shut up," the Smith said thickly, "and let me work, unless you really want to find out firsthand what it feels like when your flesh cracks and curls, and all the water oozes out of your crystallizing body—"

"You dare to speak to me like—"

The Smith stared at him. Irduz's thin-lipped mouth pressed shut, and the Smith turned away again.

He began to give commands to the control system, going back over the faulty sibyl data; doing his analyses half in the machine, half in his head. The purity of analytical thought calmed him, fulfilled him, making him forget his human fears. The replicators were essentially an analog of bacteria, structured for strength. They could be stopped by the application of appropriate analog toxins. Once he understood their structure well enough, he would know what tools would destroy them. But he also needed heat—a lot of heat, to break down the carbon-carbon bonds of the diamond matrix that made the replicators almost impervious to attack. And then, somehow, he had to deliver the blow. . . .

He crossed the lab to another bank of processors, cursing under his breath at the impossibly inadequate design of the lab itself. He transferred his results, inputting more data, his murmured commands loud in the sudden, perfect silence of the sealed room. "I need access to your toxin component inventory." He gestured at the displays.

One of the researchers came forward. He made a quick pass of his hands over the touchboards, and stood aside again. "You're cleared."

The Smith went back to his work as the accesses opened, searching for the fastest way to create his silver bullet from the simplistic assortment of analog toxins he had available. The solution to this problem was painfully obvious; but it had to be quick, subtle, and right the first time. . . . He was oblivious now to everything but the exaltation of his work—caught up in an ecstasy that was more like prayer than anything anyone else in this room had ever known.

When he had his prototype toxin designed, he activated the sequence that would begin to produce it in large quantities in aerosol form, and heat it to three or four thousand degrees centigrade. He estimated that half that much heat, combined with the toxin, should be enough to turn the seething mass of replicant ooze into useless slag that would harm nothing. This much would also leave their entire system in ruins. Destroying their system wasn't absolutely necessary to this process; but it was better to be safe than sorry, when you were dealing with the end of the world. And besides, he felt like it.

"All right . . ." he said, turning back to his silent witnesses. "Turn off the emergency shields."

"What—?" someone gasped.

"Do it!" he snapped. "I have to get this mixture in there, if I'm going to stop what's happening, and the only way to do that is to shut it down."

"But if the solvent escapes—"

"Shutting off the fields will slow it down, because it's feeding on their energy," he said, as patiently as if he were speaking to someone with brain damage. "That should give my agent enough time to do its work. This is your only chance. . . . You have about five minutes before the replicant mass overloads the barriers anyway, you stupid sons of bitches. And then there will be no stopping it. Shut off the goddamn field!" He went back to his position among the system displays, never taking his eyes off the researchers as they looked toward Irduz; as Irduz nodded, slowly, and someone gave the fateful command.

He watched the data on the screens, barely breathing; timing his own directives to synchronize, to feed the superheated gas into the space at the exact point in time when the shields went down.

Something happened beyond the protective window/wall of the observation room that registered in his eyes as blinding pain; he shut them, as the virtually indestructible material of the window, the room, and the building itself made sounds that no one in this room had ever expected to hear. The Smith felt an impossible heat reach him like the sun's kiss, making his flesh tingle, even here. He stood motionless until he felt the sensation fade, the reaction snuffing out. He opened his eyes. The formerly transparent window before him was opaqued now by a sheen of metallic silver-gray. He could make out nothing beyond it.

He looked down at the displays, where to his relief a new and entirely different pattern of disaster warnings met his eyes, showing him the answers he needed to see. Data feeding in from the black box in the heart of the chamber he could no longer see told him that he had accomplished his goal. The replicant mass had been terminated. He looked away, drained, turning back to the researchers.

He saw in their eyes that they knew he had been successful—even Irduz. *They were safe,* their slack faces said; as if anyone was ever safe.

"You weren't afraid," one of the men murmured, looking at him as if the idea was incomprehensible. "How could you not be afraid?"

The Smith glanced at Irduz. "I'm not afraid of things I understand," he said sourly. "Just things I don't understand."

Irduz's gaze met his own, without comprehension. "It's over, then?" Irduz asked. "It's all right? The solvent has been utterly destroyed?"

The Smith nodded.

"You're absolutely certain?"

"Absolutely." The Smith let his mouth twitch. "Although, if I were you," he added gently, "I'd keep a couple of containers of my brew on call, just in case."

"Did you know all along that this would work, then?" one of the others said, half reluctant and half fascinated.

"The odds of success were ninety-eight percent—if nobody involved fucked up," the Smith said, with a smile that did not spare them. "Have a nice day. . . . And for gods' sakes, when you rebuild this place hire Kharemoughis to do it right." He crossed the room to the High Priest's side. "I'll be going," he said. "I came in the back door; I'm not going out that way. After you—" He gestured, knowing there had to be other ways into this hidden complex, forcing Irduz to acknowledge it.

Irduz nodded, frowning but not daring to object. He led the way out.

The Smith left the Church inquisitory by the main entrance, followed by the High Priest's hollow blessing and many naked stares of disbelief. He pushed the solii pendant back into concealment inside his clothes as he went down the broad steps. He began to walk out across the open square, breathing deeply for the first time in hours as he passed through the shifting patterns of the marketday crowd. The dry, clean, spice-scented air cleared out his lungs. But even the sun's purifying heat could not burn away his fragmented visions of a disaster far more widespread and profound than the one he had just averted. *The sibyl net had made a mistake. There was something wrong with the sibyl net.* And that terrifying knowledge haunted his confused mind as though it were somehow his fault, his responsibility. . . .

"Tell your fortune? Tell your fortune for only a *sisk*?" Someone's hand caught his arm as he passed yet another canopied stall.

He stopped as the dark hand brushed his own, looked down into the woman's deeply blue-violet eyes gazing up at him. "What?" he said.

"Your future, stranger, for only a *sisk*. I sense that you are a lucky man. . . ."

He followed her glance back the way he had come. He had come out of the inquisitory's doors in one piece, walking on his own two feet. *A lucky man.* He was about to refuse her, with a cynicism that probably matched her own, when he noticed she held a circular *tan* board on her lap. Most fortune-tellers used jumble-sticks, or simply the palm of your hand. The intricate geometries painstakingly laid out on the board's polished surface symbolized many things, just as his hidden pendant did: the moves to be made in a game that was probably older than time; the hidden moves of the Great Game, in which he was a hidden player. He had never seen a *tan* board used to tell fortunes. "Sure," he murmured, with an acid smile. "Tell me my future."

He sat down across from her on the pillows in the shade, his curiosity piqued. He leaned forward, intrigued in spite of himself as she cast the smooth gaming pieces out across the *tan* board's surface. They scattered, colliding, rebounding off its rim with the random motions of fate, coming to rest in a configuration that looked equally random.

She stared at the pattern they made, and sucked in a breath. Her night-black hands covered the board with spread fingers, as if to shield his eyes from it. She looked up at him again, with both incomprehension and dread. "Death . . ." she murmured, looking into his eyes as deeply as if she saw time itself there.

He almost laughed. *Everybody dies—*

"Death by water."

He froze, feeling the blood fall away from his face. He scrambled to his feet, swayed there a moment, dizzy with disbelief. He fumbled in his pocket, dropped a coin on her board, not even noticing what it was that he gave her, not caring. He turned away without another word, and disappeared into the crowd.

TIAMAT: Carbuncle

Gods, what am I doing here? Jerusha PalaThion bent her head, pressing her fingertips against her eyes. The feeling that she was a prisoner in someone else's dream crept over her again as the scene before her suddenly turned surreal. She raised her head and opened her eyes as the disorientation passed. Yes, she was really here, standing in the Hall of the Winds; waiting for the Summer Queen, watching over the crowd that waited with her.

But still she seemed to hear the song of a goddess in the air high overhead, feel the living breath of the Sea Mother chill her flesh. The ageless chamber reeked of the Sea; the keening windsong carried Her voice to Jerusha, and to the small gathering of the faithful who waited with reverence and awe at the edge of the Pit for their audience with the Queen.

The Sea Herself lay waiting too, at the bottom of the Pit, three hundred meters below. A single fragile span of bridge crossed the dizzying well, giving access to the palace on the other side. But high above them gossamer curtains swelled and billowed with the restless wind, creating treacherous air currents that could sweep a body from the bridge with terrifying ease. *The Lady gives*, they said, *and the Lady takes away.*

"The Lady."

"The Lady—"

Hushed voices murmured Her name as the Summer Queen appeared suddenly at the far end of the span. Jerusha took a deep breath and lowered her hand to her side, focusing on the Queen, the Goddess Incarnate, as she stepped carefully onto the bridge. Jerusha watched her come, slowly, regally, her milk-white hair drifting around her in a shining cloud, her loose, summer-green robes billowing like grass, like the sea. She wore a crown of flowers and birdwings shot through with the light of jewels, and the trefoil of a sibyl. *The Lady.*

Damn it! Jerusha shook her head: a head-clearing, a denial. She looked at the Queen again, seeing her clearly this time: Not a goddess incarnate, but an eighteen-year-old girl named Moon. Her face was drawn with strain and weariness, her movements were made slow and awkward by the swelling of an unexpected pregnancy that was now near term, no longer completely concealed even by her flowing robes. There was no mystery to her, any more than there was any divine presence in this room.

Jerusha's eyes still reminded her insistently that the Queen wore another woman's face; memory told her that Moon Dawntreader carried another woman's ambitions in her mind, in her heart. It was impossible not to stare at her, not to wonder about the strange motion of a fate whose dance had trapped them both. . . .

She listened to the progression of high, piercing notes that filled the chamber as the Queen touched the tone box she carried in her hand; the sounds that controlled the movement of the wind curtains high above, to create a space of quiet air through which she, and the three people who followed her, could move. The tone box was an artifact of the Old Empire, like the Hall, the Pit, the palace above them and the ancient, serpentine city at whose pinnacle it sat. Technology was the real god at work here, and the Queen knew that as well as Jerusha did. She had come here today to try to reconcile this crucial gathering of her people to that truth, if she could.

Jerusha felt a sudden twinge of compassion for the fragile figure crossing the bridge toward her. Moon Dawntreader had defied the offworlder rule that Jerusha PalaThion had represented, to become the new Queen. And Jerusha had believed her cause was just, had believed in her; instead of deporting her, had let her become Queen. In the end she had even given up her own position as Commander of Police, stopped serving the Hegemony that had brought nothing but grief to her and to this world. She had chosen to stay behind on Tiamat at the Final Departure, and serve its new Queen instead.

But when the offworlders had gone away at the Change, they had gone forever, at least as far as Jerusha PalaThion was concerned. They would not come back in her lifetime; she had exiled herself, and if ever she changed her mind, she still could not change that. *And had she changed her mind—?* Jerusha's face pinched. She rubbed her arms, feeling the rough homespun cloth chafe her skin. Gods, she was so tired, all the time, lately. . . . She wondered if she was getting some disease, or simply getting depressed. She dressed like a Tiamatan even though there were still plenty of offworlder clothes to be had; trying to do the impossible, to fit in, when her dark curling hair and upslanting eyes, her cinnamon-colored skin, marked her as alien. She had never felt at home on this world, in all the time she had served here. She had hated this ancient, musty, mysterious city the way she had hated its former Queen. But in the end . . . in the end it had worked its will on her. In the end it had still been the lesser of two evils.

Someone touched her shoulder. She started, caught off guard; raised her hand in a defense gesture that Police training had programmed into her reflexes. She stopped herself, chagrined, as she realized that the touch belonged to her husband. "Miroe," she whispered, feeling the tension inside her dissolve.

He made a sound that was almost a laugh. "Who were you expecting?"

She gazed at him for a long moment. His offworlder's face looked as out of place here as her own. And yet he belonged here, had lived here all of his life. It was not impossible to learn to love a new world. . . . She only shook her head, and put her hand over his as she glanced away at the Queen. "How is she?" she asked, looking again at the swell of the Queen's belly. Miroe had offworlder medical training, and Moon had chosen him, trusted him over any local physician or healer to attend her; as she had chosen Jerusha to watch her back.

"I think I picked up two heartbeats today. I think she's carrying twins."

"Gods," Jerusha murmured. She shifted from foot to foot, wondering why her hands and feet went to sleep on her so easily lately.

He nodded, with a heavy sigh. "She shouldn't be doing this. I told her that—she ought to let go of it, let the Summers treat her like a goddess. That's all they expect—or want—of her."

Jerusha looked back at him, feeling unexpected irritation rise inside her. "She doesn't want to be a puppet, Miroe. She wants to be a queen. Just because women are the ones who get pregnant—" The sudden thought filled her head like strange perfume: *Am I pregnant—?*

He looked back at her, frowning. "Goddammit, you know that's not what I meant."

She looked down. *Am I—?* Feeling wonder fall through her like rain.

"She's pushing too hard, that's all. She wants it all to change now. She should let it go until she delivers. That's all." The frown was still on his face; concern now, instead of annoyance. "Carrying twins causes complications in a pregnancy; you know that."

Jerusha forced her attention back to his words, saying nothing about what she had just felt, thought, imagined. She wasn't even sure; there was no reason to mention it now. She looked at Moon again, at the swelling curve of her stomach. "If she waits that long, the Summers will smother her in 'worship,' " she said sourly. The Goodventure clan, whose ancestors had been the Summer Queens during the last cycle, had gotten a taste for power, and nursed their hunger for it through a hundred and fifty years, through Tiamat's near-endless Winter. They still believed in the old ways of Summer's conservative outback, and they still believed they held their Goddess's favor, over this heretic upstart who was trying to unnaturally force the Winters' offworlder, technophile ways on them. "She's made enemies of the Goodventures already, by pushing them too hard. But if she doesn't push they'll drown her. She's damned either way."

"The sibyl net is behind her—"

"Who knows what it's really telling her? Nobody understands how it acts, Miroe, or half of what it says." She shook her head. "Who knows if she really even hears it at all . . . or only the ghost of the Snow Queen whispering in her ear."

Miroe was silent for a long moment. "She hears it," he said at last.

She looked away, shifting the projectile rifle's strap against her shoulder; feeling the distance open between them, reminded by the words that he shared a history, a bond of faith that did not include her, with this world's Queen.

She focused on Moon Dawntreader again, as the Queen began to speak. The small crowd of islanders, almost all of them sibyls, shuffled and bowed their heads as the Queen greeted them. They were obviously awed by the trefoil she wore and by her surroundings, even though her soft, uncertain voice barely carried above the sighing of the wind. Sparks Dawntreader, the red-haired youth who was Moon's husband, stood close beside her. His arm went around her protectively as he looked out at the crowd.

Behind them stood a middle-aged woman with dark, gray-shot hair hanging in a thick plait over her shoulder. She wore the same trefoil sign the Queen wore. She gazed aimlessly over the crowd with eyes that were like shuttered windows, as the fourth person, a plain, stocky woman, murmured something in her ear—describing the scene, probably.

"Thank you for coming," Moon murmured, her pale hands clutching restlessly at her robes. The words sounded banal, but gratitude shone in her eyes, a tribute to the people standing before her, whose quiet reverence belied the long and difficult journey they had made to this meeting.

"I . . ." She hesitated, as if she were trying to remember words, and Jerusha sensed her fleeting panic. "I—asked all the sibyls of Summer to come to the City when I became Queen because . . ." She glanced down, up again, and suddenly there was a painful knowledge in her eyes that only the two offworlders understood. "Because the Lady has spoken to me, and shown me a truth that I must share with all of you. The Sea has blessed our people with Her bounty and Her wisdom, and we have . . . we have always believed that She spoke Her will through those of us who wear the sibyl sign." Her hand touched the trefoil again, self-consciously. "But now at last She has chosen to show us a greater truth." Moon bit her lip, pushed back a strand of hair.

Oh gods, Jerusha thought. *Here we go. Now there's no turning back.*

"We are not the only sibyls," the Queen said, her voice suddenly strong with belief. "Sibyls are everywhere—on all the worlds of the Hegemony. I have been offworld, I have seen them."

The rapt silence of her audience broke like a wave; their astonishment flowed over her.

"I have seen them!" She lifted her hands; they fell silent again. "I have been to another world, called Kharemough, where they wear the same sign, they speak the same words to go into Transfer, they have the same wisdom. They also say—" she glanced at her husband, with a brief, private smile, and pressed her hands to her stomach, "that it is 'Death to kill a sibyl, death to love a sibyl, death to be a sibyl.' . . . But they also showed me that it doesn't have to be true." She turned back again, this time to touch the arm of the blind woman, drawing her forward. "Fate Ravenglass is a sibyl, just as you are and I am. But she is a Winter."

"How—?" "Impossible—" The astonished murmurs broke over her again; she waited for them to die down, her hands pressing her swollen stomach.

"It's true," Fate said slowly, as the voices faded. "'Ask, and I will answer.'" She spoke the ritual words, her voice filled with emotion. "For more than half of my life I hid my secret from the offworlders and my own people. The offworlders lied to us all about the true nature of what we do."

"We are a part of something much greater than we ever dreamed," Moon said, moving forward, all her hesitation gone now. "A part of a network created by our ancestors, before we even came to this world."

The sibyls in the crowd pulled their homespun clothes and kleeskin slickers closer about them, staring at her with every face among them showing a different emotion. "But, Lady—" someone began, broke off. "But how can the Lady . . ." He looked down, speechless, shaking his head.

"The Sea Mother is still with you, in you, all around you," the Queen said, forcing into the words a conviction that Jerusha knew she no longer felt. Her time offworld had taught her more than one truth; and it had taught her that no truth was a simple one. "She has blessed your ways, because you serve Her selflessly, as sibyls everywhere do—"

"Stop this blasphemy!"

All heads turned at once, as the voice echoed down the entry hall toward them.

Jerusha stiffened as she saw Capella Goodventure stride into the Hall of the Winds. "How the hell did she get in here?" Jerusha muttered. The Queen had ordered all the Goodventures, and particularly their elder, out of the palace after their last bitter theological argument. Jerusha had directed the palace security guards to make certain it was done; but some of the palace guards were Summers, and the gods—or their Goddess—only knew where their loyalties really lay. Someone had let her pass.

Jerusha took a step forward, her face hardening over, and pulled the rifle strap from her shoulder. Miroe caught her arm, stopping her. "Wait." He looked toward the crowd, as Capella Goodventure showed herself to them. Jerusha nodded, lowering the gun. She moved forward more slowly, only watching now.

"This woman who claims that she speaks as one of you is telling you lies!" The Goodventure elder's voice shook with anger. "She is not a true sibyl; not even a true Summer! She wears Winter's face, and Winter's ways. She has tried to keep me from speaking the truth—but I will speak it!" She turned to face the Queen. "Do you still deny me my right to be heard? Or will you order your offworlders to drag me from the hall? Because that is what they will have to do—"

Jerusha stopped moving, looking toward the Queen.

The Queen glanced her way, looked back at Capella Goodventure. "No," Moon said softly. "Say what you must."

Capella Goodventure deflated slightly, her defiance punctured by the Queen's easy capitulation. She took a deep breath. "You all know of me. I am headwoman of the clan that gave Summer its last line of queens. I have come to tell you that this woman who calls herself Moon Dawntreader Summer has brought you here to fill your minds with doubt—about yourselves, about the Lady's place in your lives. She would strip away the beliefs, the traditions, that make us Summers. She wants us to become like the Winters—miserable lackeys of the offworlders who despise our ways and butcher the sacred mers."

She turned, confronting the Queen directly. "You do not speak for the Sea Mother!" she said furiously. "You are not the woman who was chosen Queen. You have no right to wear that sign at your throat."

"That isn't true," Moon said, lifting her chin so that all the watchers could clearly see the trefoil tattoo that echoed the barbed fishhook curves of the sibyl pendant she wore.

"Anyone can wear a tattoo," Capella Goodventure said disdainfully. "But not just anyone can wear the face of the Winters' Queen. There is no Moon Dawntreader Summer. You are the Snow Queen, Arienrhod—you cheated death and the offworlders, I don't know how. You stole the rightful place of our queen, and now you desecrate the Mother of Us All with this filth!" She faced the crowd again, her own face flushed with an outrage that Jerusha knew was genuine.

But a woman's voice called out from the crowd, "I know Moon Dawntreader."

Capella Goodventure's broad, lined face frowned, as she peered into the crowd.

The Queen stared with her as the speaker pushed through the wall of faces. Jerusha saw a sturdy, dark-haired island woman in her mid-thirties; saw sudden recognition fill Moon's face at the sight of her. "Clavally Bluestone Summer," the woman identified herself, and Capella Goodventure's frown deepened. "I made her a sibyl. She has the right to the trefoil, and to speak the Lady's Will."

"Then let her prove it!" Capella Goodventure said, her face mottling with anger. "If she has the right to speak as she does, then let her prove it."

Moon nodded, looking surer now. "Ask, and I will answer," she said again.

"No," Capella Goodventure said. "A sibyl Transfer can be faked, just like a tattoo. Let her show us real proof. Let the Sea give us a sign of Her Will!"

The Queen stood where she was, listening to the crowd murmur its doubts, her own face furrowing in a frown as she tried to imagine how to lay their doubts to rest. Jerusha stood unmoving, her body drawn with tension as she waited for a sign from the Queen to come forward and remove the Goodventure woman. But she knew that Moon could not take that step now, without losing all credibility.

Moon glanced over her shoulder at the Pit waiting behind her like a tangible symbol of her danger; looked back at Capella Goodventure again. "The Sea Mother is with us here," she said, clearly enough for all the crowd to hear her. "Do you feel Her presence? The waters of the sea lie at the bottom of the Pit behind me. Smell the air, listen for Her voice calling up to you." Capella Goodventure stood back, a faint smile of anticipation pulling at her mouth. But then the Queen held something out in her hand. Jerusha caught her breath as she saw what it was. "This is called a tone box. It controls the wind in the Hall of Winds; it is the only way for a person to cross the Pit safely." She handed the control box to Capella Goodventure, and turned back toward the bridge.

Jerusha swore softly. "No—"

"Moon!"

Jerusha heard Sparks Dawntreader call out to his wife, reaching after her as she left his side.

The Queen glanced back over her shoulder; something in her look stopped him where he was, with dread on his face. She turned away again, raising her arms, bowing her head, and murmured something inaudible that might have been a prayer. Jerusha saw her body quiver slightly, as if she were going into Transfer. The moaning of the winds was loud in the sudden, utter silence of the hall, as she stepped out onto the bridge.

She swayed as the wind buffeted her; froze for an instant, regained her balance and took another step. Jerusha's hands tightened; she felt a surge of sickness as she remembered her own terrifying, vertiginous passages over that span. She fought the urge to close her eyes.

The Queen took a third precarious step, braced against the wind. And then something happened. Jerusha looked up as the Queen looked up: she sucked in a deep breath of wonder. The clangorous sighing of the wind curtains faded, as the wind spilled from the sails, and the air currents died . . . as the open windows high above began to close. Blue and gold sunlight shafted down through the inert cloud-forms of the curtains to light Moon's hair like an aura. "By the Bastard Boatman—" Jerusha whispered, feeling Miroe's hand tighten around her arm with painful awe.

"By the Lady," his voice answered, deep and resonant; although she knew that he could not mean it.

A slow murmur spread through the crowd, and one by one the watchers dropped to their knees, sure that they were in the presence of a miracle, a Goddess, Her Chosen . . . until at last only Capella Goodventure was left standing. As Jerusha watched, even she nodded, in acknowledgment, or defeat. The Queen stood a moment longer, her head held high, her face a mask that Jerusha could not read. The air stayed calm; the ancient hall and everyone in it seemed frozen in place. And then at last Moon Dawntreader moved again, stepping off of the bridge onto solid ground.

She looked back, at the flaccid curtains hanging in the air, as if she were waiting for something. But they did not begin to fill again; the window walls remained closed. She took a deep breath, her shoulders rising and falling visibly, her own face showing traces of the awe that had silenced the crowd. She looked ahead again, with her gaze on her husband's white, stunned face. She returned to his side; Jerusha saw the uncertainty that was almost fear in his eyes as she took his hand. "It is the Lady's will," she said, facing the crowd again, at last, "that I should be here, and that you should be here with me." She gestured at the span behind her, open to anyone who chose to cross it, now that the winds had ceased. "This is Her sign to you that a true change has come; the ways of Winter are not forbidden to us anymore."

She hesitated, looking out at their faces, her own face changed by the emotions that played across it. "We are who we are," she said, "and the old ways have always been our survival. But no one's ways are the only, or the best. Change is not always evil, it is the destiny of all things. It was not the will of the Lady that we were denied knowledge that could make our lives better; it was the will of the offworlders. And they are gone. I ask you to work with me now to do the Lady's will, and work for change—"

Capella Goodventure threw down the tone box and stalked out of the hall. The echo of its clatter followed her into the darkness. But the rest of the watchers stayed, their eyes on the Queen, waiting for what came next; ready to listen, ready to work the Lady's will at her bidding.

"How did she do it, Miroe?" Jerusha murmured. "How?"

He only shook his head, his face incredulous. "I don't know," he said. "I only hope she knows . . . because she didn't do it herself."

Jerusha looked up, her eyes searching the haunted shadows of the heights, her memory spinning out the past. But all the history of this place that she had experienced spanned less than two decades. The layers of dusty time, the hidden secrets, the haunted years of Carbuncle the city stretched back through millennia. Jerusha rubbed her arms, feeling its walls close around her like the cold embrace of a tomb, and said nothing more.

TIAMAT: Carbuncle

Sparks Dawntreader hesitated in the doorway to what had been the throne room, when this was the Snow Queen's palace; suddenly as incapable of motion as if he had fallen under a spell. He stared at the throne, transfixed by its sublime beauty. Its blown- and welded-glass convolutions could have been carved from ice. Light caught in its folds and flowed over its shining surfaces until it seemed to possess an inner radiance.

It had seemed to him to be uncannily alive, the first time he had entered this room and seen her seated there: Arienrhod, the Snow Queen, impossibly wearing the face of Moon, the girl he had loved forever. It still struck him that way, even after all the years he had spent as Arienrhod's lover . . . even now, as he found Moon seated there, wearing the face of Arienrhod; sitting silent and still in the vast white space, in the middle of the night, like a sleepwalker who had lost her way.

He took a deep breath, relieving the constriction in his chest, breaking the spell that held him as he forced himself forward into the room. He crossed the expanse of white carpet as silently as a ghost—his own ghost, he thought. "Moon," he said softly, in warning.

Her body spasmed; she turned on the throne to stare at him. "What are you doing here?" he asked. He heard a knife-edge of anger that he had not intended in the words, and said hastily, "You should be resting, sleeping. . . . I thought Miroe gave you something to make you sleep." After meeting with the sibyls this afternoon—after she had stopped the winds—she had come up the stairs from the Hall below ashen-faced with exhaustion. She had let him support her as they climbed; he had felt her shaking with fatigue. She had no reserves of strength these days; the child—or two—growing inside her demanded them all.

He had helped her to their bedroom, and Miroe Ngenet had given her a warm brew of herbs to calm her, forbidding anyone to disturb her—even him. He had not argued. When he had come to bed himself she had been sleeping.

But he had wakened in the middle of the night and found the bed empty beside him, and had come searching. He had not expected to find her here, like this. "Moon . . ." he said again, tentatively, as if some part of him was still uncertain whether she was the one that he saw on the throne, whether it was not really Arienrhod. "Are you . . . are you all right?"

Her face eased at the words, as if it were something in his face that had disturbed her. She nodded, her tangled, milk-white hair falling across her shoulders. Suddenly she was his pledged again, and barely more than a girl, the porcelain translucency of her skin bruised with fatigue and her hands pressing her pregnant belly. "I'm all right," she said faintly. "I woke up. I couldn't get back to sleep. . . ." She brushed her hair back from her face. "The babies won't let me rest." She smiled, as the thought brought color into her cheeks.

"Two—he whispered, coming closer, stepping up onto the dais beside her. "Gods—Goddess—" barely remembering to use the Summer oath, and not the offworlder one, "we're doubly blessed, then." Ngenet had told him the news, after insisting that Moon should not be disturbed from her rest.

"Yes." She made the triad sign of the Sea Mother with her fingers. Her hand fell away again, almost listlessly, although she still smiled, still shone with wonder. He glanced at the sibyl tattoo at her throat; covered her hands with his own on the swell of her soft, white sleepgown. Once he had believed it was impossible for them ever to have a child together, and so had she. Summer tradition said that it was "death to love a sibyl. . . ." That saying, the fear behind it, had driven them apart, driven him here to the city . . . into the arms of Arienrhod.

But it was not true, and here beneath his hand lay the proof of it. He felt movement; heard Moon's soft laugh at his exclamation of surprise. She got up from the throne, in a motion that was graceful for all its ungainliness. He had always been fascinated by her unconscious grace, so much a part of her that she was completely unaware of it. He remembered her running endlessly along the beaches of Neith, their island home; saw her in his mind's eye climbing the crags in search of birds' eggs and saltweed, never slipping; or darting along the narrow rock-built walls of the klee pens, never falling. He remembered her dancing, held close in his arms while the musicians played the old songs. . . . She was not tall, and so slender that Gran had always said she barely cast a shadow, but she was as strong physically as any woman he knew. Strength and grace were one in her; she rarely doubted her body's responses, and it rarely betrayed her.

Ngenet had told him that carrying twins was doubly hard on a woman's body, especially under circumstances like these, when Moon pushed herself endlessly, relentlessly. He had tried to make her listen, but she would not stop and rest, even for him—as she had never stopped pursuing anything she believed in, even for him. He could only hope that her body would not fail her in this, but see her through until their children were born into the new world she had become obsessed with creating. Her strength of will had always been as much a part of her, and as unquestioned in her mind, as the strength of her body. It had not been easy, sometimes, loving her, when her stubbornness had collided with his own quick temper. But their making-up had always been sweet, back in Summer. . . . "I love you," he murmured. He put his arms around her, feeling the shadows of lost time fall away as he held her close. She kissed his mouth, her eyes closed; her eyelids were a fragile lavender.

"What were you doing here?" He nodded at the throne as their lips parted; half afraid to ask, but asking anyway.

She shook her head, as if she was not certain either. "I wanted to know . . . how it felt when she was Queen." *Arienrhod.* "Today . . . today I was truly the Lady, Sparkie." Unthinkingly, she used his childhood nickname. But there was nothing of childhood in her voice, and suddenly he felt cold.

The Lady is not the Queen. He didn't say it, afraid of her response. The Summer Queen was traditionally a symbolic ruler, representing the Sea Mother to her people.

But from the first ceremony Moon had led as the Lady, she had broken with ritual and tradition. She had claimed that it was the Goddess's will, that this Change must begin a real change. He knew that she did not believe in the Goddess anymore; not since she had learned the truth, that sibyls were human computer ports, and not the Sea Mother's chosen speakers of wisdom. Sibyls existed on all the worlds of the Hegemony, and probably on all the other worlds of the former Empire. They were speakers for the wisdom of an artificial intelligence, not the Sea Mother. But Moon had told him the sibyl mind spoke *to* her, not simply through her; that it had commanded her to bring Tiamat the technological enlightenment that the Hegemony had denied it for so long. He had found the idea as unbelievable as the idea of the Goddess now seemed to him . . . until he had watched her today in the Hall of Winds. "How did you do it?" he asked, at last. "What you did today. How did you stop the wind?"

She looked up at him, her eyes stricken and empty. "I had to," she said, her voice as thin as thread. "I had to, and so I did—" The thread snapped.

"Don't you know how?" he whispered.

She shook her head, looking down; but her fingers rose to the sibyl sign at her throat. "Something inside me knew. It made me do it, to make them believe me. . . ."

His hands released her reflexively. She looked up at him, her pale lashes beating, her agate-colored eyes full of sudden pain. He put his arms around her again; but it was not the same. "Come back to bed," he murmured into her ear. "You should be resting."

"I can't. I can't rest."

"Let me hold you. I'll help you. . . ." He led her down from the dais; she clung to his hand, but her gaze still wandered the room, which was lit as brightly as day. He followed her glance, looking across the snowfield carpet; remembering Arienrhod's courtiers scattered across it like living jewels in their brilliant, rainbow-colored clothing. Gossamer hangings drifted down from the ceiling, decorated with countless tiny bells that still chimed sweetly and intermittently as they were disturbed by random currents of air.

They left the throne room, entering the darkened upper halls that were empty even of servants now. He was relieved to find himself alone with her, jealous of these stolen moments. He had thought when they were reunited at the Change that everything would change for them. And it had . . . but not the way he had wanted. Not back to what it had been. Moon was no longer his alone, his innocent Summer love. And he would never again be the naïve island youth she had pledged her life to; Arienrhod had seen to that.

He tried to lead her toward their room, but she shook her head. "I don't want to go back to bed. Walk with me. Show me the palace—show me all the parts of it."

"What, now?" he said. "Why?" She had promised him, after Arienrhod's death, that they would never set foot in the palace again. He had believed her, believed that she would no more want to be reminded of all that had happened here than he did.

But she had been drawn back to this place, like metal to a lodestone, as if it were somehow part of the compulsion that had seized her at the Change. She did not seem to enjoy being here, any more than he did; he knew she was intimidated by its vastness, its staff of obsequious Winter servants, the alienness of its offworlder luxuries. She seldom went beyond a small circuit of rooms, as if she were afraid that she might take a wrong turn somewhere in its columned halls and be lost forever in time. Only the Snow Queens had lived here, ruled from here, as secular leaders dealing with the offworlders who controlled Tiamat's fate, never a Summer Queen; until now. But Moon would not leave, refusing to make her home among their own people, among the watchful, peaceful faces and familiar ways of the Summers who inhabited Carbuncle's Lower City.

And now, in the stillness of midnight, she wandered the palace's halls like a restless spirit, searching for questions without answers, answers that were better left ungiven . . . forcing him to show her the way. "Why?" he said again.

She touched her stomach, the promise of new life within her. "This," she said softly, looking down.

He nodded, resigned but not really understanding. He started on through the halls, the rooms, one by one, level by level; showing her the places she knew, how they fit into the palace she did not know—the ordinary, the common, the empty; the extraordinary, the exquisite, and the perverse. Light followed them from room to room, at his command, revealing the fluted curves of doorways, the shellform trim that decorated ceiling-edges, the arched convolutions of space and the spiraling stairwells that always made him feel as though he were climbing and descending through the heart of a shell.

The imported technology that had once made the palace seem like a wonderland to his newly opened senses now lay everywhere like the husks of dead insects, an ephemeral infestation. Their components had been rendered useless by the offworlders before the Hegemony left Tiamat. But the palace, like the rest of the city of Carbuncle, lived forever, existing on its own terms, on its own power source, as it had since time out of memory. The palace's nacreous walls were covered with murals, with artwork, tapestries, mirrors. The superficial decorations had been added over the centuries by various Winter rulers, but the palace itself, with its inescapable motifs of the sea, remained unchanged. He had lost count of the times he had wondered who might have built this strange place, and why. Now, moving through these halls that reeked of age, he felt the newness of his life, and Moon's, with a clarity that was almost frightening.

He showed Moon through what had once been his suite of rooms, still filled with the clutter of high-tech equipment that Arienrhod had allowed him for his amusement. All his life he had burned with curiosity about the technomagic of the offworlders who had been his father's people. He had come to Carbuncle seeking something that had been missing from his life. But Carbuncle had not filled that void in him; not the city, not its people, not the endless imported devices he had ruined in his need to learn. . . . He had only learned how well his father's people kept their secrets from his mother's.

He showed Moon through the hidden passageway that led directly from his room to Arienrhod's. Moon looked around the Snow Queen's bedchamber, with its panoramic view of the sea, its furniture that echoed the pale opalescence of the walls—chairs, tables, cushioned seats made of what seemed to be polished shell. He had never known whether they were only a clever imitation, or whether on some world—even somewhere in Tiamat's own all-encompassing sea—there were shelled creatures that actually grew so large.

Moon glanced toward the bed, with its fluted headboard made of the same jeweled-and-gilded shellforms. Arienrhod waking had been like a vision of the Sea

Mother rising from the waves to him; he had never said so, because he had been afraid she would laugh at him.

Moon looked back at him, her eyes filled with dark curiosity. She turned away again, suddenly searching for the way out.

And stopped, in astonishment, staring at the wall in front of her: at Arienrhod, dressed all in rainbows. A portrait—a painting, not a hologram; but somehow it seemed more real to him than any three-dimensional representation of her, almost more real than she was herself. It was as if the artist had trapped her soul there. Even now it seemed to him as if the eyes of the portrait were watching him, watching Moon, all-knowing, pitying, baleful.

Moon moved forward slowly, stretching out her hand until she touched the hand of the woman in the painting, half-fearfully. She stood that way, touching the portrait's hand, as if she were hypnotized. Sparks looked from her flushed, transfixed face to Arienrhod's, which was as pale and coolly prescient as if she had just been told a secret about them, one that even they would never know.

He came forward to stand behind Moon, holding her again as she faced the image that could almost have been a mirror. He felt her tremble, inside the warm circle of his arms that were no protection from Arienrhod's memory—Arienrhod's legacy.

Finally Moon tore her gaze from the painting, and let him lead her out of the room. When they stood in the empty hall again, he murmured, "Are you ready to sleep?" asking it so softly that even the echoes did not waken.

But she shook her head; her purple-shadowed eyes looked up into his. "Where is the room where we . . ." She glanced down at the swell of her stomach. "I want to see it."

"Moon, this is—" He broke off. "All right," he said roughly. "I'll show you where it is. But if you ever go there again, you'll go alone."

She nodded, her eyes filled with apology. He took her back through the halls, moving against his will, against the flow of time, until they reached the door of the sealed room. No one had touched it, opened it, entered it, since Arienrhod's death. He was not even certain how many hands besides his own could make its door respond.

The door slid aside under his touch as if it were avoiding him, and brilliance dazzled their eyes as the lights came up, redoubling from mirrored wall to mirrored wall. The walls and ceiling of the room were filled with mirrors, reflecting back their faces, their bodies from every angle as they entered, multiplying every motion until he stopped, giddy. He had forgotten how entering this room made his thoughts spin.

He looked toward the room's center, toward the bed that was its only piece of furniture. The bedclothes were still rumpled, untouched since the last time someone had lain in it . . . since the night during the final Festival of Winter, when Moon had come to the palace and reclaimed him from his living death. He searched for a single shattered mirror-panel, found it, its cracked surface dulled with dried blood. His blood, from the moment when he had struck out at his reflection, at all that he had become. He remembered how the blood had flowed, red and warm, proving to him that he was still alive, vital, young; that he had not grown old and died, behind the soulless mask of his face.

He remembered how he had made love to Moon, there in that bed, in this room; rekindling their life together, planting the seeds of new life within her. . . .

He looked over at her, in time to see a spasm of pain cross her face. He did not know whether it was physical pain or the pain of memory, but she came with him willingly as he turned back to the door. As he resealed the room behind them, she whispered, "I never want to see it again. I never want anyone to see it. . . ."

He nodded, hoping that this would be the end of all their night's agonizing reminiscences. But she glanced toward the spiral staircase that rose into the secret darkness above. "Where does that go?"

"To Arienrhod's private study," he said. "She never let anyone else up there. . . ." He started forward, surprised to find that he was the one who was eager, leading the way this time. She followed him slowly, carefully up the narrow steps, up through the level of another floor and into the space beyond it.

His breath caught; he heard Moon's small gasp of astonishment behind him. The room they stood in now lay at the peak of the palace—at the peak of the city itself. Its transparent dome rose to a star-pointed pinnacle, and beyond it the glowing forge of the sky surrounded them, fired by the countless separate suns of the stellar cluster into which this footloose system had wandered eons ago. Tiamat's single large moon was not visible tonight, but one star stood out among the thousands over their heads: the Summer Star, whose brightening marked their system's approach to the black hole which had captured the roving Twins and made them its perpetual prisoners.

The black hole was an astronomical object with a gravity well so powerful that not even light could escape it. The offworlders called it the Black Gate, and among the things they had never shared with Tiamat's people were the starships capable of using such openings on another reality for faster-than-light travel. Through the Gate lay the seven other worlds of the Hegemony, some of them so far away that their distances were almost incomprehensible. They were bound to each other because the Black Gates let starships through into a region where space was twisted like a string, tied into knots so that far became near and time was caught up in the loop.

But as Tiamat's twin suns approached the aphelion of their orbit, the unnatural stresses created by their approach to the black hole destabilized the Gate, and the passage from Tiamat to the rest of the Hegemony was no longer simple or certain. And so the offworlders had abandoned Tiamat, as they did every time the Summer Star brightened in its sky.

They had taken their technology with them, forcing Tiamat's people back into ignorance and bare subsistence for another century, ensuring that Tiamat would remain exploitable and eager for their return, when it was finally possible for the Hegemony to come back again. They bound Tiamat to them with chains of need because Tiamat's seas held the mers, and the mers' blood held the secret of immortality. They called it the water of life, and it was more precious than gold, than wisdom, even than life itself. . . .

He looked down, over the city's undulations gleaming in the darkness, out across the sea. He searched the dark mirror of the water for a sign of life, the telltale motion of forms that might be mers swimming. But the ocean surface lay calm and unbroken as far as his eyes could see.

When he could force himself to turn his back on the sea and sky, the room lay waiting. Its rug was made from the hides of pfallas, which were herded by Winter nomads in the harsh mountain reaches inland of the city. Moon moved across the pristine surface hesitantly, her bare feet sinking into the pile as if it were drifted snow.

He began his own slow trajectory through the room, witnessing a side of Arienrhod that he had never seen.

He studied a cluster of dried flowers preserved inside a dome of glass. The blooms were so old that they had lost all color, so old that he could not even tell what kind of blossoms they had once been. He touched a cloth doll, worn and one-eyed from a child's love, dusty now with neglect. There were other things clustered together on the same small, painted table—fragile remains of a childhood spent at the end of the last High Summer.

Arienrhod had been born into a world much like the one that he and Moon had shared in their youth. But then the offworlders had arrived; she had become the Snow Queen, had taken the water of life. She remained young through Winter's one hundred and fifty years, changeless but ever-changing, until she became at last the woman he had known. Arienrhod had told him many times that he reminded her of things she had lost, of memories almost forgotten. He had thought the words were lies, like too many other lies she had told him. He stared at the forlorn mementos bearing silent witness on the table; at last he turned away.

Moon was holding up a piece of jewelry, as he looked at her: a silver pendant on a silver chain, with a jewel catching the light in its center. "That's a solii," he said, in surprise. He had never seen Arienrhod wear the pendant, although it must have been expensive; he wondered if she hadn't liked it. He wondered what the necklace was doing in her private study, instead of with the rest of her jewelry. Moon glanced up at him, and laid the pendant back on the desktop.

Sparks drifted on across the room toward the solitary, ornately framed mirror sitting on another table. It could have been a vanity table, where Arienrhod had studied her reflection to make certain it was still unchanged after a hundred years and more of taking the water of life. But he saw the telltale touchplate in the mirror's base—the offworld electronics that had transformed its silvery surface into something else entirely. He realized, with a shock of recognition, that this silent room was the heart of the spy system that Arienrhod had used to keep her informed of what went on in her city, to keep herself one step ahead of the offworlders who would have taken advantage of her . . . to amuse herself, spying on the private lives of her enemies, of her own nobles, even of the people closest to her, who were the most vulnerable . . . as she had spied on him while he made love to Moon, in the mirrored room down below. . . .

He turned away from his own suddenly grief-stricken reflection. "Moon," he said hoarsely, "we'll never be able to forget, to begin again here. We have to get away from all this—memory. It'll never give us peace. I know we can't go back to Neith, but why do we have to stay *here*? Let's find somewhere else . . . before the babies come."

Moon looked up at him. Her mouth opened, but she made no sound. She held something out to him in her hands, and from the look in her eyes he knew that she had not even heard him.

He took the cube, saw a hologram of a child inside it, a small girl with milk-white hair, bundled in the rough woolens and slickers of an islander . . . a girl he knew. The child moved through a moment's joyful laughter over and over again, held captive forever, never changing.

"It's me," Moon whispered, her voice breaking. "How did she get this? How did it get here?"

He shook his head, staring at the image of the girl he had loved even as a child in Summer.

He looked up again at her sudden sharp cry—not a sound of grief, but of pain. "Moon—?" He reached out to her as she clutched her stomach, doubling over; her face whitened with another spasm. He moved toward her, catching her in his arms, supporting her as he pulled her onto the bench beside the mirror table. Fluid spilled down her legs, wetting her nightgown and the rug beneath her feet.

"Moon, what's happening—?" he cried. "Are you all right? Moon?"

She looked up at him, biting her lips, her eyes glassy. "Find Miroe . . . Sparks— it's time. . . ."

ONDINEE: Razuma Port Town

"Damme, it's Kedalion!" Ravien leaned across the bar, his heavy blue-black hand catching the back of Kedalion's collar and hauling him the rest of the way up onto a seat. "Has it been a round trip already, then?"

Kedalion Niburu straightened up on the high stool, rearranging his coat. "Thank you, Ravien, I think—" he murmured. He leaned on the bar, his legs dangling like a child's over the edge of a seat that was nearly his own height. Being not much over a meter tall in a universe where most humans were nearly twice that height had its drawbacks; among its mixed blessings was the fact that very few people ever forgot him, even after six years. "You've got a memory like a servo. And a grip to match."

Ravien snorted, and poured him a drink. "See if I remembered that right."

Kedalion took a sip of the greenish-black liquid, and made a face. "Ye gods, right again," he said sourly. "You mean to tell me this is still the best thing you have to drink?"

Ravien rubbed his several chins. "Well, you know, we're lucky to get anything at all, what with the stinking breath of the Church Police down my neck all the time. I can get the sacramental wine on the black market, because it profits the Church. . . . But for a certain price, I could maybe find you something special."

"Bring it out." Kedalion pushed the cup back across the bar. "I made all my deliveries on Samathe. I'm feeling worth it."

"Good man!" Ravien nodded happily, wiping his hands down the front of his elaborately formal and extremely unbecoming shirt as he started away toward the back room.

Kedalion leaned on the bar, looking out into the room, absently scratching the astrogation implants hidden in his hair. First a drink, then a room and a shower and some companionship. . . . He felt a pleasant twinge of nostalgia, brought on by the completion of another successful run. Though maybe *nostalgia* was the wrong word for it. *Relief* was probably more accurate. He was a legal trader, but the people he did business with and for usually were not. It was an interesting life . . . and half his time was spent wishing he'd chosen some other line of work. He wondered, not for the first time, if he was trying to prove something to somebody. *Well, what the hell—* As far as he could see, that was what motivated the entire human race.

He let his gaze wander the subterranean room, taking in the reflective ceiling that hid the naked structural forms of someone else's basement. Up above them was the Survey Hall, where offworlders who belonged to that ancient, conservative social group talked politics, gave each other self-important secret handshakes, and generally spent their evenings far more tediously than he planned to. He had wandered through a display of the latest Kharemoughi tech imports in one of their meeting rooms before arriving at the club's hidden entrance; what he had seen of the Hall was severe and stuffy-looking.

The decor here, on the other hand, set his teeth on edge with its gleaming excess. He focused on the dancer performing incredible contortions as effortlessly as he would breathe, to the rhythmic, haunting accompaniment of a flute and drum, and the wild trills of a woman singer. This was the best private club he knew of in Razuma, and that wasn't a compliment. There were no public clubs. The theocracy that was Ondinee's dominant onworld government forbade even thinking about most of the things that went on here, and in other places like this. He had heard that all those things, and worse, went on all the time in the Men's Orders that most privileged Ondinean males belonged to. But places where offworlders were welcome, and permitted to enjoy themselves, were as rare as jewels, and about as hard to find, even in a major port like Razuma.

The irony was that while it persecuted vice among its own people with a fervor that verged on the perverse, the Church also harbored—and let itself be intimidated by—the largest enclave of offworld vice cartels in the Hegemony. A large part of the local population made its living harvesting drug crops and doing whatever else the cartels needed done. The offworlder underworld made an enormous contribution to the Church's economic and political stability.

The relationship was not without its complications, however, like most long-term relationships. Retribution was as much a part of the symbiosis as contribution. A politician or churchman who made too much noise about reform got a single warning—if he was lucky—and then a lethal sample of the offworlders' wares. It was a system which made the cartels' strange-bedfellowship with the Church lords work very well. He should know. He worked for them too.

Ravien came back with a bottle full of something that looked to be a decent shade of amber. He poured it into an ornate silver metal cup, and passed it across the bar.

Kedalion took a sip, didn't gag, and nodded. Whatever it was, it was drinkable. "Better. How's business been?"

Ravien made a noise like clearing out phlegm. "Wonderful," he said sourly. "I could do ten times the business, if I didn't have to be so careful. The bribes I pay would astound you, and still they raid me! But they'd close me down completely if I didn't pay them. At least they've left me alone these past few weeks. . . ." He threw up his hands and stumped away, still muttering.

Kedalion shook his head, even though Ravien was no longer there to see the gesture, and went on drinking, searching the crowd for a familiar face. He'd take a few days off and then it would be time to start hustling for another job. It wasn't that he'd need the money that soon; more that he'd need to get away from here. This world depressed him too much, reminding him more acutely than even Kharemough of how uncomfortable human beings invariably made one another.

The sound of tinkling bells and the heavy fragrance of perfume made him turn in his seat, as one of the entertainers insinuated herself against the bar beside him. "Ah," she said, running slender ebony fingers through his close-cropped brown hair. "Hello, Kedalion. Have you missed me? I've missed you." She let the fingers trickle like water down the side of his jaw.

"Then it's certainly mutual," he said, feeling a grin spread across his face.

She laughed. "I love you lightskins, the way you blush," she said. Her name was Shalfaz, which was the name of the desert wind in the local dialect. She wasn't young anymore, but she could still haunt a man's dreams like the wind. Her body made music with every slightest movement, from the necklaces, bracelets, anklets she wore, heavy with the traditional clattering bangles and silver bells. She did not go veiled, since her occupation, though traditional, was hardly respectable, and her robes were of thinnest gauze, in brilliant layers like petals on a flower. "My room is empty—" she said. Her indigo eyes gazed meaningfully into his own light blue ones.

He scratched his stubbled jaw, still smiling. "Yes," he said, and nodded, answering her unspoken question. "But have a drink with me first; it's the first time Ravien has given me liquor I minded leaving. Let me savor the anticipation a little."

She nodded and smiled too, bobbing her head in what was almost an obeisance. She sat down. "You honor me," she murmured, as she saw what he was drinking.

"On the contrary," he said, feeling uncomfortable as he realized she meant that.

She sipped the amber liquor and sighed, closing her eyes. She opened them again, looking out across the room. "What a strange night it has been," she said, almost as if she were thinking aloud. "It must be a mooncrossing night. See that boy there—" She lifted her hand. "He was with me just since. But all he did was talk. He didn't even take off his clothes. He asked me to show him how I did some of my moves in the dance, but it didn't arouse him. He was very polite. But he just talked." She shook her head. "He always comes in alone, not with friends. I think maybe he's some kind of pervert, but he doesn't know which."

"Maybe he misses his mother," Kedalion said, following her gaze. "He's only a kid."

She shrugged, jingling. "He said he wants to leave Ondinee. That's why he comes in here, he said, to look for someone who would take him on for crew. He's been here every night for a week."

"Oh?" Kedalion kept watching the boy, not certain why he did, at first. He saw a youth with Shalfaz's midnight coloring, dressed in a loose robe and pantaloons of dark, bulky cloth. The boy's long, straight, jet-black hair was pulled back in a ponytail; thin braids dangled in front of his ears. There was nothing about him that marked him as different from any of the dozen or so other local men scattered around the room—probably all hirelings of some drug boss, from their easy mingling with offworlders.

Unease. That was what made the boy different; he looked uncomfortable. It was as if he was uncomfortable inside his skin, uncertain whether it was showing the right face to the universe, or about to betray him. It was a feeling Kedalion recognized instinctively.

"Shalfaz," Kedalion said, leaning back against the bar, "would you ask him to join us?"

She turned to him, her eyebrows rising. "You wish to hire him?"

"I wish to speak to him, anyway." Kedalion shrugged, a little surprised himself. He was not impulsive by nature. "Maybe I wish to hire him. We'll see." He had had a partner when he started out, but they had gone their separate ways a while ago. Smuggling was a business that took its toll on the nerves, and after a while they had gotten on each other's too much of the time. He had worked alone since then, but that had its own drawbacks, especially for a small man in a big man's universe. He suddenly realized that he was tired; and he had never been a loner by nature.

Shalfaz left his side in a soft cloud of silver music. He watched her make her way across the room to where the boy was sitting and speak to him, gesturing at Kedalion. The boy's head came up, and he rose from his chair almost in one motion to follow her back to the bar.

They had almost reached it when a hand shot out from a table full of local youths and caught Shalfaz's clothing, jerking her up short. She tried to pull away without seeming to, and Kedalion could almost make out her murmured half-protests as she explained that her time was taken. The man's answer was slurred and crude. The boy hesitated, looking toward Kedalion, and then turned back, speaking brusquely to the other Ondineans as he tried to take her hand. One of the men pushed him away. Kedalion watched the boy recover his balance with surprising grace, saw his fists tighten with anger. But he didn't reach for the knife at his belt, only stood with his hands flexing in indecision as the drunken youth at the table pulled his own blade.

Kedalion slid down from his stool and crossed the space between them. "My guests would like to join me at the bar," he said flatly. "I'd appreciate it if you would let them do that." He hooked his hands over his weapon belt . . . realized with a sudden unpleasant shock that it was empty, because noncitizens were not allowed to carry weapons in the city. He kept his face expressionless, needing all his trader's skill to ignore the gleaming knifeblade almost exactly at eye level in front of him. "Shalfaz—?" he said, with a calm he did not feel.

"You insult my manhood, runt." The Ondinean with the knife jabbed it at Kedalion's face, this time speaking the local tongue, not Trade. "Leave now, and keep your own—or stay, and lose it."

Kedalion backed up a step as more knives began to appear below the table edge, hidden from most eyes, but not from his. He knew enough about young toughs like these to realize that if he pushed it they'd kill him; but even if he backed off now there was no guarantee they'd let the matter drop. His hands tightened over his empty belt, and he said numbly, "Neither of those choices is acceptable," answering in their own language. He wondered how in seven hells he had managed to get into such a stupid position so quickly. The wine must have been stronger than he thought.

"Kedalion, please go," Shalfaz said softly. "I will stay here." She moved closer to the man who still held her arm, her body settling against him.

"Slut!" He slapped her. "You don't tell a man what to do. I choose, not you!" He shoved her away. She crashed, jingling, into the offworlder who had been leaning against the bar behind them, watching with casual amusement. The bottle the man had been holding fell and smashed, spraying them with liquor and bits of broken ceramic.

Kedalion dodged back awkwardly as the local youth aimed a kick at him. And then his vision seemed to strobe as the man Shalfaz had collided with suddenly exploded past her.

Before Kedalion could quite believe it was happening, the man with the knife was no longer a man with a knife—he was a man howling on the floor, and the offworlder's foot was on his neck. "You want a fight—?" The curved, jewel-handled blade was in the stranger's fist, and he was grinning at the fury still forming on the faces of the other men around the table. He flashed the knife at them. "Come and get it," he said.

Kedalion backed up another step. "He must be mad," Shalfaz whispered. Kedalion, who had caught a flashing look into the man's eyes, didn't answer. Slowly he began to edge away, taking Shalfaz and the boy with him.

"Dopper shit," one of the Ondineans said, "there are six of us, and one of you. Do you want to kiss the sole of my boot and beg our forgiveness? Or do you really want your guts cut out of you with that blade?"

Kedalion glanced back, hesitating as he saw the offworlder's smile grow thin and tight. "Sure," the offworlder said, twisting the knife so that it caught the light. "Gut me. I'd enjoy that; that sounds good. Or maybe use it to peel my skin off a centimeter at a time. . . . But you still have to get this away from me first." He leaned on the edge of their table, waving the blade at them, invading their space with fatal nonchalance. "Well—?"

Their stares broke and fell away from the hunger in his eyes. They looked at each other, their bodies unconsciously shrinking back from him. "The Foreteller has shown us that it is unworthy to kill the insane," another man muttered. The blades did not go back into sheaths, but the men began to get up slowly from the table.

The offworlder snorted and stepped back, looking down at the man still sprawled on the floor. "You kiss my boot, you shit." The bottom of his foot brushed the man's lips in a not-quite-gentle caress. He shoved the man's dagger into his own belt. "Then think twice about being an asshole in such a crowded room."

The Ondinean scrambled to his feet, spitting and wiping his mouth, and joined his friends. "You will die for this!" His voice shook. The others put restraining hands on him, because they were surrounded now by the club's security. Ravien himself stood beside the offworlder, putting a cautionary hand on his shoulder. The stranger shrugged it off. But he only murmured, "Yes. Sooner or later . . ." looking back at them. "Sooner or later we all get what we deserve."

Kedalion joined Shalfaz and the boy at a table as far from the scene of the fight as possible, stopping only to collect his bottle from the bar. As he went he saw the club's security herding the Ondineans toward the door. He noticed with some surprise that Ravien escorted the offworlder solicitously back to the bar instead of having him thrown out with the rest. Well, the man *had* lost a bottle. Or maybe Ravien didn't want his private entrance marked by a litter of corpses.

The offworlder shot Kedalion a curious glance as he passed. Kedalion touched his forehead in a brief, wary acknowledgment, and the stranger gave him a surprisingly cheerful smile. Kedalion looked away from it, and went on to the table. He poured drinks for himself and the two Ondineans; noticed the boy's stare as he handed a drink to Shalfaz. "You ever see that one before?" Kedalion asked her, gesturing over his shoulder at the stranger.

She nodded, still looking as unnerved as he felt. "He comes in often to watch the shows. He never visits anyone's room, male or female. He is usually very quiet, and sits by himself."

Kedalion took a deep breath, shaking himself out, and looked at the boy again. "So," he said, somewhat inadequately, "Shalfaz says you're looking for a way to get offworld." The boy nodded, self-consciousness struggling with hope on his face. "I can't imagine why." Kedalion glanced toward the door and back, his mouth twitching sardonically. "Why?"

The boy also looked toward the spot where the locals had made their forced exit. He made a disgusted face of his own in response.

Kedalion studied him, as unobtrusively as possible. The boy was small and slight compared to the men who'd just left, even though he still towered over Kedalion. Maybe he was tired of being bullied. "What kind of work are you looking for?"

The boy hesitated, and then said, "Anything," meeting Kedalion's stare. Kedalion half smiled, thinking that at least the kid didn't ask for "honest work." He probably knew how much of that he'd find in a place like this.

"What skills do you have?"

The boy hesitated again, his face furrowing. "I'm flexible," he said.

"Physically or mentally?"

"Both." A spark of pride showed in the boy's changeable eyes.

Kedalion laughed out loud this time. "That's unique," he said. "And probably an asset." The boy was wearing the long, curved ritual knife all the local men wore, although his was plain and cheap-looking, like his clothes. He also carried a less common state-of-the-art stun weapon, partly concealed by the folds of his jacket. "You ever kill anybody?" Kedalion asked, wondering suddenly if that was why he was in a hurry to leave. But he remembered how the boy had hesitated, confronting the men who had accosted Shalfaz—not a coward, but not a hothead, either.

The boy jerked slightly, as if he had been insulted. Most of the young Ondinean males Kedalion had met fought knife duels as often as they smoked a pot of water weed together. Those blades weren't for show; they could cut a man open like a redfruit. If it wasn't for modern medical technology, Ondinee would be depopulated inside of a couple of generations. "I don't want to kill people," the boy said. "But I would kill someone if I had to."

There was none of the glazed bravado Kedalion expected in the indigo eyes, but somehow he knew that the boy meant what he said.

"Have *you* killed people?" the boy asked bluntly.

"I don't want to kill people either." Kedalion shrugged. "I'm just a runner."

The boy's glance searched out Kedalion's legs, hidden under the table edge.

"Not that kind of runner. As you can see, I'm not equipped for the odds." For a second a smile hovered on the boy's lips. "Just say I'm a trader. I transport goods from world to world. I travel a lot. I run an honest business. But I can't say the same for most of my customers. My mother, rest her soul, would say I keep bad company. What's your name?"

"Ananke," the boy said, looking down. It meant *Necessity*. He glanced at Shalfaz, and back at Kedalion again. "I would like to work for you."

"Do you have any tech training?" Kedalion asked, skeptical. The boy didn't look old enough to have had much work experience.

"Some." Ananke nodded earnestly. "I've been studying with the university whenever I can pay for an outlet."

He had ambition, at least. Kedalion sipped his drink, noncommittal. "How do you support yourself?"

"I'm a street performer," the boy murmured. "A juggler and an acrobat."

Kedalion reached into the maze of pockets inside his long, loose coat, pulled out the huskball he had carried with him like a kind of talisman ever since he was a boy. He tossed it at Ananke with no warning. Ananke caught it easily, flipped it into the air, over his shoulder; made it disappear and reappear between his hands. Kedalion grinned, and caught it, barely, as the boy suddenly threw it back to him. "Okay," he said. "You work my next run with me, we'll see how it goes. At least it'll earn you passage to somewhere else. I'll pay you ten percent of the profit when we get there. You can make a start with that."

The boy grinned too, nodding. "I have all my things here. I'll get them—"

"Relax." Kedalion put up a hand. "I've still got to find us a cargo. And besides, I just got here; I won't be going anywhere for a while." He glanced at Shalfaz. She smiled, and his bones melted. "Just be here when I want to leave."

Ananke nodded again, looking at them with an expression that was knowing and somehow full of pain all at once. Kedalion remembered what Shalfaz had said about the boy, and wondered. Ananke began to get up from his chair.

"With my compliments," a soft, slightly husky voice said, behind Kedalion's back. "And my apologies."

Ananke looked up, sat down again, surprise filling his face. Shalfaz shrank back in her seat, her hands fluttering.

Kedalion turned in his own seat, to find the offworlder who had challenged the Ondineans standing behind him. The man grinned disarmingly, taking in the tableau of mixed emotions as if he were used to it. He probably was, Kedalion thought. He was tall, but slender; Kedalion's memory of the fight seemed to hold someone a lot larger, more massive. But there was no mistaking those eyes—bluer than his own, probing him with the intensity of laser light when they met his. The offworlder looked away first, as if he was aware of the effect his gaze had on strangers.

He set something down on the tabletop between the three of them—another bottle. Kedalion stared at it in disbelief. The bottle was an exotic, stylized flower form, layers of silver petals tipped with gold. Pure silver, pure gold. . . . Kedalion reached toward it, touched it, incredulous. Only one thing came in a bottle like that: they called it the water of life. It was the most expensive liquor available anywhere in the Hegemony, named for the far rarer drug that came from Tiamat, a drug which kept the absurdly rich young at unbelievable expense. The real thing was no longer available at any price, now that Tiamat's Gate was closed for the next century. Kedalion had never expected to taste this imitation of it any sooner than he tasted the real thing.

"Apologies—?" he remembered to say, finally; he tore his eyes from the silver-gilt bottle to look up at the stranger again. "I should be sending you a bottle." He shrugged, realizing that his own smile was on crooked as he looked into that face again.

The stranger grunted. "Ravien tells me I should have let you settle your own quarrel," he murmured. "I made an ass of myself. I'm not in a very good mood tonight. But then, I guess I never am. . . ." The gallows grin came back; his fingers drummed against his thigh. "Sorry."

"Nothing to forgive," Kedalion said, thinking that if the stranger hadn't intervened, even the genuine water of life wouldn't have been enough to revive him. "Believe me." He looked at the silver bottle again, still not quite believing his eyes. He picked it up, almost afraid to touch it, and held it out to the stranger.

"Keep it," the stranger said. "I insist."

Kedalion looked into his eyes, and didn't argue. He pulled the bottle toward him, his hands proving its reality again, and unset the seal with his thumb. Sudden fragrance filled his head like perfume, made his mouth water, filled his eyes with tears of pure pleasure. "Ye gods," he murmured, "I had no idea. . . ." He passed the bottle around the table, letting the others touch it with awed hands, breathe in its essence; watching their faces.

Kedalion realized that the stranger was still standing beside him, taking it all in, with something that was almost fascination in his own eyes. "Join us—?" Kedalion asked, not particularly wanting to, but feeling that he could hardly do anything else, under the circumstances. The service unit under the smooth onyx-colored table obliged him, spitting out an extra cup.

"Not my poison," the stranger murmured. He shook his head, unkempt fingers of brown hair brushing his shoulders. Kedalion started to breathe again as the man began to turn away; but the man shrugged abruptly, and turned back. He pulled out a seat and sat down. "I'm Reede," he said.

Kedalion made introductions, trying not to look like a man sitting next to an armed bomb. He poured water of life for himself and the two Ondineans, somehow managing not to spill a drop, even though his hands weren't steady.

He stole another glance at Reede, wondering how the other man had come by something like this bottle, and why he was willing to give it up so casually. It was a rich man's gesture, but Reede didn't look like a rich man. He wore nondescript black breeches and heavy dockhand's boots, a sleeveless jerkin dangling bits of jewelry and flash—souvenirs. Not an unusual outfit for a young hireling of some drug cartel. Reede's bare arms were covered with tattoos, telling his life history in the Hegemony's underworld to anyone who wanted to look close enough. There was nothing unusual about that, either; the only thing odd about the tattoos was that there were none on his hands.

Probably he was another smuggler, looking for work, and this bottle was a flamboyant way of advertising his services. Just what they needed; competition. But Kedalion intended to enjoy Reede's generosity anyway. Even though Kedalion didn't advertise, his reputation for reliability was usually enough to get him all the work he could handle. "You a runner?" he asked Reede.

Reede looked surprised. "Me? No." He didn't say what he did do. Kedalion didn't ask. "Why?" Reede asked, a little sharply, and then, "You need one?"

"I am one." Kedalion shook his head.

Reede nodded, easing off. "I knew your name was familiar. Your ship is the *Prajna*. That's a Samathan word for 'God'—?" He raised his eyebrows.

"One of them," Kedalion said. "It means 'astral light,' actually. It's supposed to bring luck." He shrugged, mildly annoyed at having to explain himself.

"It seems to work for you." Reede's mouth twitched. "You have a good reputation. And you had your share of good fortune tonight." He spoke Trade, the universal second language of most people who did interstellar business. Everyone here in the port spoke it; even the boy Ananke handled it well enough. It was easy to learn a language with an enhancer; Kedalion spoke several. It wasn't easy to make a construct like Trade sound graceful. And from what he had seen tonight, Reede was the last person he would have expected to manage the feat. He glanced at Reede again, wondering where in hell somebody like this came from anyway. Reede looked back at him, with an expression that was close to thoughtful. "So 'honor among thieves' is the code you live by?"

Kedalion smiled, hoping the question was rhetorical. "I only wondered how you came by this." He raised his cup of the water of life in a toast; its scent filled the air he breathed. The silver liquid lay in the cup like molten metal, waiting.

Reede shrugged. "I got it at the bar."

"From Ravien?" Kedalion asked, incredulous. "That bastard." He pointed at his own bottle. "He claimed this was the best he had; he's been serving me swill for years."

Reede grinned ferally. "He does that to everyone. You just have to know how to *ask*. . . ." He fingered the expensive-looking jeweled ear cuff that dangled against his neck; jerked it off suddenly, as if it was burning hot, and flung it down on the table in disgust.

Kedalion looked away nervously. "Uh-huh," he murmured. He wondered how old Reede actually was; sitting here he had begun to realize that the other man was much younger than he had thought. Reede had a strikingly handsome face, and surprisingly nobody had smashed it in yet. But it was the face of someone barely out of his teens—hardly older than Ananke, and a good ten years younger than he was himself. The thought was depressing. But maybe Reede was just baby-faced; his punk-kid looks were peculiarly at odds with his manner and his apparent status. Kedalion decided that whatever Reede's real age was, someone who lived like that was not likely to get much older.

Reede sat moodily biting his thumbnail. He noticed Shalfaz staring at his cast-off earring, and flicked it across the table at her. She picked it up with long, slim fingers that hesitated slightly, and put it on. She glanced at him, her expression grave. He smiled and nodded, and slowly she smiled too. Ananke watched them silently; he barely seemed to be breathing.

Kedalion let out his own breath in a sigh, and lifted his cup again. "Good business," he said, offering the toast, savoring his anticipation. The two Ondineans raised their cups.

"Good fortune." Shalfaz gave the answer, still fingering her new earring as she lifted her cup.

As the cup touched Kedalion's lips, a loud sudden noise made him jerk around. The rest of the room seemed to turn with him, a hundred heads swiveling at once, looking toward the club's entrance. And then chairs were squealing on the patterned floor and the crowd found its voice, the room became a sea of shouting, cursing motion.

"Son of a bitch," Reede muttered irritably. "A raid." He leaned back in his chair, folding his arms in resignation, like a man waiting out an inconvenient rainstorm.

Kedalion exchanged glances with the two Ondineans, not feeling as sanguine about the outcome. He had never been present when the Church Police raided a club, and never wanted to be. He had heard enough stories about their brutality toward offworlders—that it was even worse than their brutality toward their own people. The Hegemonic authorities were supposed to have jurisdiction over noncitizens, but the Church inquisitors seldom bothered to notify or cooperate with them.

A half dozen armed, uniformed men stood in the entrance, blocking it off, searching the crowd as if they were looking for someone in particular. Kedalion felt the habitual cold fist of paranoia squeeze his gut; realizing that in a crowd like this it was monstrous egotism to think they were looking for him, but not able to stop the sudden surge of fear.

And then a local man stepped from between the uniformed police—one of the youths Ravien had thrown out of the club. He pointed. He pointed directly at Kedalion.

Kedalion swore, sliding down from his chair as Shalfaz and Ananke rose from theirs. Reede looked toward the entrance as he noticed their panic. "You better get out of here—" He was already on his feet as he spoke, beside Shalfaz, taking her arm. "You know another way out?"

She nodded, already moving toward the back of the club, with Ananke on her heels. Kedalion started after them; hesitated, turned back to grab the silver bottle off the table. He plunged back into the sea of milling bodies like a man diving into the ocean; he was immediately in over his head, battered by the surge of panic-stricken strangers. Cursing, he fought his way through them in the direction he thought Shalfaz had taken, but the others were lost from sight.

Hands seized him around the waist and dragged him back and up. He struggled to break the hold, aimed a hard blow at his captor's groin—

"Goddamn it!"

He realized, half a moment too late, that the man was not wearing a uniform.

Reede swore, doubling up over him. "You asshole!" He straightened with an effort, holding Kedalion under one arm like a stubborn child.

Cursing under his breath, Kedalion let himself be carried ignominiously but rapidly through the crush of bodies, through a maze of dark tunnels, and finally out into the reeking back-alley gloom. The others stood waiting, fading against the darkness. Reede dropped him on his feet.

"Go, quickly," Shalfaz said, waving them on. "I must get back."

"But—" Kedalion gasped, with what breath he still had in him. "Will you be safe?"

She shrugged, her body going soft with resignation. "I am only a woman. I am not held responsible. If I let them—"

"No!" Ananke said. "Don't! Come with us." He pulled at her arm almost desperately.

"The earring," Reede said. "The stones are genuine. Buy them off. You know the customs." She nodded, and he shoved Ananke out into the street. "Get moving." He jerked Kedalion off his feet again.

"Damn it, put me down!" Kedalion swore as Reede began to run. "I can—"

"No, you can't."

"Goddammit, I'm not—"

"Yes, you are. In big trouble. Complain about your injured dignity later," Reede hissed, looking back over his shoulder as he heard shouting. Light burst on them from up ahead, lancing through the mudbrick alleyway between building walls; they collided with Ananke as the boy skidded to a stop. "We're trapped!" Ananke cried, his voice going high like a girl's.

Reede glanced up, at something beyond sight, and grunted, "They're high-tracking us." He turned and forced them into the narrow tunnel between two buildings, out into a small open plaza; all Kedalion could see was mudbrick and shadows, all he could hear was the sound of angry voices shouting at them to stop. He shut his eyes. Any minute Reede would go down to someone's weapon, and this grotesque ignominy would reach its inevitable conclusion—

They slammed through the high double doors in a mountain of building facade, into the vast cavern of its interior, the befuddling darkness barely defined by the glow of countless candles. Up ahead of them a wall of hologramic illumination burst across Kedalion's vision—a thousand views of paradise painted in light, rising to an ecstatic apex, a finger pointing toward heaven like the pyramidal structure of which it formed one wall.

"We're in a temple!" he gasped. "Can we ask for sanctuary?"

"From the Church Police? Who do you think they work for?" Reede muttered. He dropped Kedalion onto his feet again and hesitated, searching the candlelit darkness. There were still a few worshipers prostrating themselves before the high altar and the radiant images of light. He turned back as the heavy doors burst open behind them. "Lose yourselves," he said. "I'll draw them off. . . . Hey! Police!" he shouted, a warning or an invitation, Kedalion wasn't sure.

"Reede—" Kedalion began, but Reede was already bounding away, silhouetting himself against the blinding light. "Gods! Come on." He nudged Ananke forward through the forest of candelabra, hoping that they could fade into the random motion of bodies as people picked themselves up from their prayers and scurried toward the exits. He pulled on the boy's arm, forcing him into the crowd. Ananke followed like someone in a trance; Kedalion felt the boy's body tremble.

Kedalion glanced back as people in the scattering crowd cried out, to see Reede scramble up onto the gold-crusted altar, climbing higher among its rococo pinnacles in an act of unthinkable desecration. Ananke gasped in horror, and Kedalion swore in empathy and disgust as the black-uniformed figures of the police closed in on Reede.

And then Reede leaped—throwing himself off of the altar into the embrace of the light, into the wall of heaven.

Kedalion heard a splintering crash and stopped dead, gaping in disbelief. The image hadn't been a hologram at all—it had been a wall of backlit glass. Now it bore a gaping black hole where Reede had gone through it into the night outside. Kedalion groaned, beyond words to express what filled him then.

He stared on again, but too late. Armored hands fell on his shoulders, wrenching him around and into the embrace of a body manacle; a volley of blows and kicks drove him to his knees, retching.

The police dragged him outside, with curses so graphic that he couldn't even translate most of them . . . or maybe they were promises. Ananke staggered beside him, bloody and dazed. Something was digging into his ribs beneath his jacket—the silver and gold flask of the water of life. *Sweet Edhu,* he thought, *I'm going to die. They'll kill us for this. And I never even got to taste it.* A gasp of hysterical laughter escaped him, and someone slapped him hard.

Behind the temple, in a glittering snowfall of broken glass, the rest of the police were gathered around Reede's sprawled body. Kedalion thought with a sick lurch that they'd killed Reede already. But as he was dragged closer he saw them haul Reede up, his face bloody but his eyes wide open, and knock him sprawling again into the field of glass.

Wanting to look away, Kedalion kept watching as a man who looked like an officer pulled Reede to his feet, shaking him. "You think that's pain you feel, you whey-faced filth? You don't know what pain is, yet—"

Reede stared at him with wild eyes, and laughed, as if the threat was completely absurd. Kedalion grimaced.

"Take him to the inquisitory," the officer snarled, gesturing toward the police ground-van waiting across the square. Reede did not protest or resist as they hauled him roughly toward it. "Take them all!"

Reede looked back as the officer's words registered on him. He stiffened suddenly, resisting the efforts to force him inside. Something like chagrin filled his face as he watched the police drag the others toward the van, and saw their own faces as they were dumped beside him. "Wait—" Reede called out, and ducked the blow someone aimed at his head. "Elasark!"

The second officer, who had overseen Kedalion's capture, turned toward them abruptly, away from staring at the gaping hole in the glass wall of the temple. "You—?" he said, registering Reede's presence with something that looked like disbelief. He swore, and broke off whatever he had been going to say next. He came toward the van, stood before Reede for a moment that seemed endless to Kedalion, before he turned away again, his eyes hot with fury. "Let him go."

The other officer, the one who had knocked Reede down, let out a stream of outraged protest that Kedalion could barely follow. The first officer answered him, in Ondinean as rapid and angry, in which the names "Reede" and "Humbaba" stood out like alien stones. He finished the outburst by drawing his finger across his own throat in a blunt, graphic motion. "Let him go," he repeated.

The other officer didn't move. The rest of the police stood sullenly glaring at him, at the prisoners, as Elasark turned back and released the manacle that held Reede. No one moved to stop him.

Reede climbed down out of the van, shaking himself out. He turned and glanced up at Kedalion and Ananke, looked back at Elasark. "Those two work for me," he said.

Elasark stiffened, and the sudden hope inside Kedalion began to curdle. "The window will be repaired perfectly inside of three days," Reede said. "You will receive a large, anonymous donation to the Church Security Fund." Slowly Elasark moved back to them and released their bonds, his motions rough with barely controlled rage as he shoved them down out of the van. He shouted an order and the police climbed inside, without their prisoners. The doors slammed and the black van left the square, howling like a frustrated beast.

Ananke stood watching silently until the van was out of sight. And then his eyes rolled up and back in his head, and he collapsed in a billowing heap of robes. Kedalion crouched down beside him, glad for the excuse to sit as he lifted the boy's head.

"Is he all right?" Reede asked, looking more surprised than concerned.

"No," Kedalion said, the word sounding more irritable than he had intended. "But he will be. Are you?"

Reede wiped absently at his lacerated face, not even wincing. Kedalion winced. Reede studied his reddened fingers in mild disgust, as if it were paint staining them, and not his own blood. He wiped his hand on his pants. "Sure." A bark of mocking laughter burst out of him as he looked away across the deserted square in the direction the van had taken. "Stupid bastards," he said.

"You just saved all our lives," Kedalion murmured, well aware that the Church Police were anything but stupid; and equally aware that there couldn't be more than half a dozen people on this entire planet who could do what he had just seen Reede do to them. "You don't have to be so goddamn casual about it!" His voice was shaking now. He reached into the numerous pockets of his coat, and found the one with the silver bottle still safely inside it.

Reede looked at him, and shrugged. "Sorry," he murmured. But there was no comprehension in it.

"Goddammit," Kedalion muttered again, still glaring at Reede as he struggled to pull the bottle free. He unstoppered it and took a large mouthful of the silver liquid heedlessly. He gasped as it slid down his throat with an almost sentient caress, bringing his shock-numbed body back to life from the inside. "Gods," he whispered, almost a prayer, "it's like sex."

"I like a man who knows what's really important," Reede said sardonically.

"If you think I was going to miss a chance to drink this, after all that's happened tonight, you're crazy," Kedalion snapped, beyond caring by now whether Reede really was crazy. "Who the hell are you, anyway?" Not really expecting an answer to the question this time, either.

"I work for Sab Emo Humbaba," Reede said, picking his teeth. "Therefore the police and I have a kind of symbiotic relationship."

"A lot of people work for Humbaba," Kedalion said. "I've worked for him myself. But the Church Police don't scatter like cats when I say so."

Reede sighed, and looked pained. "My full name is Reede Kulleva Kullervo. I'm Humbaba's brains. I head his research and development. If anything happened to me. . . ." He shrugged meaningfully. "You know who the real gods are, around here."

The name sounded familiar, but Kedalion couldn't place it. He stared at Reede, trying to picture the tattooed lunatic in front of him at work in a sterile lab somewhere, peacefully accessing restricted information, datamodeling illegal chemicals inside a holofield. "No . . ." he said, shaking his head. "Bullshit. What are you really?"

Reede raised his eyebrows. "What does it really matter?" he asked softly.

As long as he had the power. Kedalion looked back at Ananke, still lying sprawled on the pavement, and took another swig from the silver bottle.

Ananke opened his eyes and sucked in a loud gasp of panic. He let it out again in a sigh as he realized where he was, and registered their faces. Kedalion kneeled down and fed him a sip of liquor from the silver bottle, watched his stupefaction turn into bliss, and grinned at him. Ananke pushed himself up until he was sitting alone.

"You mean," Kedalion turned back to Reede as the realization suddenly struck him, "you could have done what you did here back in the club? We didn't have to run—none of this needed to happen, no chase, no desecrating a temple, no scaring the shit out of the kid here—?" *And me,* but he didn't say it.

Reede shrugged. "Maybe. But in the chaos, who knows? 'Accidents happen,' like they say around here." His bloody grin crept back. "Besides, this was more fun."

"Speak for yourself," Kedalion muttered. He looked away from Reede's molten gaze as he got stiffly to his feet.

"Well, let's go," Reede said, watching as he helped Ananke up.

Kedalion hesitated, suddenly uncertain. "Thanks, but I think we've got other—"

"Other plans? But you work for me now." Reede folded his arms, and the grin grew wider on his face.

Kedalion looked at him, and laughed once, remembering what Reede had told the police. A joke. "I quit," he said, and returned the grin.

Reede shook his head. "Too late. You drank my liquor. I saved your life. You're my man, Kedalion Niburu."

Kedalion went on staring, trying to read the other man's face; suddenly feeling cold in the pit of his stomach as he realized that Reede was actually serious. "You need a runner—?" he asked, his voice getting away from him for the second time tonight. "No. Not until I know what you really do," he said, with more courage than he felt.

"I told you what I really do." Reede lifted a hand. "Ask around. Access it, right now." He shrugged, waiting.

Kedalion felt a strange electricity sing through him, knowing as suddenly that there was no need to check it out. Everything Reede had told him was completely true. "I don't much like drugs . . ." he said, somehow able to keep looking Reede in the eye.

Reede glanced at the silver bottle still clutched in Kedalion's hand, and his mouth twitched. "Everything's relative, isn't it?" Kedalion flushed. "But what I make and where it goes are not the point. I'm looking for a ferryman. I need a personal crew."

"Why us?" Kedalion said. "You don't know me . . . I don't even know *him*." He gestured at Ananke.

"You're a landsman—you're from Samathe, so am I. Maybe I'm sentimental. And I know your reputation. I've already checked you out. You're trustworthy, you have good judgment, and you deliver."

"What happened to your last ferryman?"

"He quit." Reede smiled faintly. "He couldn't stand the boredom."

Kedalion laughed in spite of himself. "What was this tonight? My audition for the job?"

Reede grinned, and didn't answer. "I need somebody I can rely on. . . . I like your style. What do you charge for a run?"

"That depends . . ." Kedalion named a sum that almost choked him.

"I'll double that on a regular basis, if you work out."

Kedalion took a deep breath in disbelief. He hesitated, and shook his head. "I'm flattered," he said honestly. "But I don't think I'm up to it." He glanced at Ananke, watching the mixed emotions that played across the boy's face while he looked at Reede. "Come on, kid." He started away. Ananke followed him like a sleepwalker, still looking back at Reede.

"Niburu," Reede called. "You may find it exceptionally difficult to get the kind of work you want from now on, if you turn me down."

Kedalion stopped, looking back. His mouth tightened as he saw the expression on Reede's face. "We'll see about that," he said, not as convincingly as he would have liked. He turned his back on Reede, and started on again.

"Yes," Reede said, to his retreating back. "I expect that we will."

NUMBER FOUR: Foursgate

Hegemonic Police Inspector BZ Gundhalinu entered his office as he had done every day for almost five years, imitating the precise patterns of the day before; like a robot, he would have thought, if he had allowed himself to think about it, which he never did. He set a beaker of overbrewed challo—the closest thing to a drug he ever permitted himself—down on the corner of his desk/terminal, on the precise spot where the heat of past mugs had dulled the dark cerralic sheen of its surface. He sat down in his chair, turning it to face the view of Foursgate as he requested his morning briefing from the desk. He always took the briefing on audio; it was the closest he came to relaxing all day. The terminal's irritating facsimile of his own voice began a condensed recitation of the file contents. He marked with a murmured word the things to be brought up in more detail, staring out the window at the city shrouded in cold mist. The windowpane was completely dry, for once; but as he watched the rain began again, random fingers tapping restlessly on the pane, droplets running down its face randomly like tears. *Damn the rain,* he thought, rubbing at his eyes. It was too much like snow.

". . . The Chief Inspector requests your presence in his office as soon as possible. . . ."

Gundhalinu stiffened. "Hold," he said to the desk, and turned back, to face the message lying on its screen. *The Chief Inspector.* He stared at the inert forms of the graphics . . . *in his office.* Gundhalinu's hands closed over the molded arms of his seat, anchoring his body in the present while the room around him shimmered as if it were about to disappear, about to leave him alone in the white wilderness. . . .

He stood up, slowly, afraid that his body would betray him; that his legs would refuse to carry him forward, or that when he reached the door and stepped into the hall he would bolt and run. There was only one reason the Chief Inspector could have for wanting to see him in person. He looked down, checking the blue-gray length of his uniform for a speck of dust, a line out of place. When he was certain that his appearance was regulation, he went out of his office and through the Police complex to where Chief Inspector Savanne waited for him.

He stood on the muted floribunda carpet before the Chief Inspector's desk without a single memory of how he had gotten there. His body made the correct salute perfectly, habitually, although he was certain his face was betraying him with a look more guilty than a felon's.

Savanne returned the salute but did not rise. He leaned back in the flexible confines of his seat, studying Gundhalinu wordlessly. Gundhalinu met his gaze with an effort of will. The Chief Inspector was not an easy man to face, even on a viewscreen. And now the uncertainty he found in Savanne's gray eyes was harder to endure than the cold disapproval he had been expecting.

"Sir—" Gundhalinu began, and bit off the flood of excuses that filled his mouth. He glanced down the blue length of his uniform to his shining boots, compulsively, finding no flaw. And yet his mind saw the truth, the real, hidden flaw—saw a hypocrite, a traitor, wearing the clothes of an honest man. He was certain that the Chief Inspector saw the same thing. *Tiamat.* The word, the world, were suddenly all he could think of. *Tiamat, Tiamat, Tiamat* . . .

"Inspector," Savanne said, and nodded in acknowledgment. Gundhalinu felt his own lips press together more tightly, felt every muscle in his face and body stiffen, bracing for an attack. But the Chief Inspector only said, "I think we both realize that your work has not been up to standard in recent months." He came directly to the point, as usual.

Gundhalinu stood a little straighter, forcing himself to meet Savanne's gaze again. "Yes, sir," he said.

Savanne let his fingertips drift over the touchboard of his terminal, throwing random messages onto its screen, as he did sometimes when he was distracted. Or maybe the messages weren't random. Gundhalinu could not make them out from where he stood. "You obviously served very competently on Tiamat, to have risen to the rank of Inspector in so short a time. But that doesn't surprise me, since you were a Technician of the second rank. . . ." Savanne was from Kharemough, like Gundhalinu, like most high officers on the force. He knew the social codes of its rigid, technocratic class system, and all that they implied.

Were. Gundhalinu swallowed the word like a lump of dry bread. His hands moved behind his back; his fingers touched his scarred wrists. He could protect his family from dishonor by staying away from Kharemough. But he had never been able to forget his failure; because his people would never forget it, and they were everywhere he went.

Savanne glanced up, frowning slightly at the surreptitious movement. "Gundhalinu, I know you carry some unpleasant memory from your duty on Tiamat . . . I know you still bear the scars." He looked down again, as if even to mention it embarrassed him. "I don't know why you haven't had the scars removed. But I don't want you to think that I hold what you did against you—"

Or what I failed to do. Gundhalinu felt his face flush, aware that his pale freckles were reddening visibly against the brown of his skin. The very fact that Savanne mentioned the scars at all told him too much. He said nothing.

"You've served here on Number Four for nearly five standards, and for most of that time you've kept whatever is troubling you to yourself. Perhaps too much to yourself . . ."

Gundhalinu looked down. He knew that some of the other officers felt he was aloof and unsociable—knew that they were right. But it hadn't mattered, because nothing had seemed to matter much to him since Tiamat. He felt the cold of a long-ago winter seep back into his bones as he stood waiting. He tried to remember a face . . . a girl with hair the color of snow, and eyes like agate . . . tried not to remember.

"You've shown admirable self-discipline, until recently," Savanne said. "But after the Wendroe Brethren matter . . . It was handled very badly, as I'm sure I don't have to tell you. The Governor-General complained to me personally about it."

Gundhalinu suppressed an involuntary grimace, as he suddenly heard what lay between the words. *The Police had to demonstrate the Hegemony's goodwill.* His eyelids twitched with the need to let him stop seeing, but he held Savanne's gaze. "I understand, sir. It was my responsibility. My accusations against the Brethren's chamberlain were inexcusable." *Even though they were true.* Truth was always the first casualty in their relationship with an onworld government.

Kharemough held the Hegemony together with a fragile net of economic sanctions and self-interested manipulation, because without a hyperlight stardrive anything more centralized was impossible. The eight worlds of the Hegemony had little in common but their mutual access to the Black Gates. They were technically autonomous, and Kharemough cultivated their sufferance with hypocritically elaborate care. He knew all of that as well as anyone; it was one more thing his service on Tiamat had taught him.

"I should have offered you my resignation immediately," he said. "I've had . . . family difficulties the past few months. My brothers lost—" *the family estates, my father's fortune, the sacred memory of a thousand ancestors, all through their stupidity and greed,* "are lost in World's End." He felt the blood rise to his face again, and went on hastily, "I don't offer that as an excuse, only as an explanation."

The Chief Inspector looked at him as though that explained nothing. He could not explain even to himself the dreams that had ruined his sleep ever since his brothers had passed through Foursgate on their way to seek fool's treasure in the brutal wilderness called World's End. Night after night his dreams were haunted by the ghosts of his dispossessed ancestors; by his dead father's face, changing into a girl's face as pale as snow; endless fields of snow. . . . He would wake up shivering, as if he were freezing cold. "I offer you my resignation now, sir," he said, and somehow his voice did not break.

The Chief Inspector shook his head. "That isn't necessary. Not if you are willing to accept the alternative of a temporary reduction in rank, and an enforced leave of absence until the Governor-General has forgotten this incident. And until you have regained some kind of emotional equilibrium."

If only I could forget the past as easily as the Governor-General will forget about me. Gundhalinu swallowed the hard knot in his throat, and only said, faintly, "Thank you, sir. You show me more consideration than I deserve."

"You've been a good officer," Savanne replied, a little mechanically. "You deserve whatever time it takes to resolve your problems . . . however you can. Rest, enjoy this vacation from your responsibilities. Get to feel at home on this world." He glanced at Gundhalinu, his eyes touching uncomfortably on the pink weals of scar at his wrists. "Or perhaps . . . what you need is to look into your brothers' disappearance in World's End."

•

Gundhalinu felt a black, sudden rush of vertigo, as if he were falling. He shook his head abruptly; saw a fleeting frown across the Chief Inspector's face.

"Come back to the force, Gundhalinu," Savanne murmured. "But only if you can come back without scars."

Gundhalinu stared at him. He made a final salute, before his body turned away smartly and took him out of the office.

Without scars. The hallway stretched out, shining and inescapable before him. *Without the past.* He wondered what point there was to having the scars removed. The Chief Inspector would still see them. And so would he. It would only be one more act of hypocrisy. He began to walk. *Life scars us with its random motion,* he thought. *Only death is perfect.*

TIAMAT: South Coast

"Miroe—?" Jerusha called, stepping out of the ship's cabin onto the gently rocking deck. She saw him standing at the rail; still there, as he had been for hours, observing the mers. The sea wind was cold and brisk, rattling the rigging, rudely pushing at her as she came out into the open. But the sky was clear today, for once, and for once the sun's heat on her face warmed her more than just skin-deep.

It was more than she could say for her husband's expression as he glanced up at her. He shut off the makeshift recording device he held, and pulled the headset away from his ears. "Damn it," he muttered, as much to himself as to her, "I'm not getting anywhere—"

She sighed, controlling her annoyance as his frustration struck her in the face. She joined him at the catamaran's rail, looking down at the water's moving surface. At the moment there were no mers visible anywhere in the sea around them. "When you suggested that we go away for a few days, just the two of us, and sail down the coast, I was hoping this would be . . . restful," she said. *Romantic.* She looked away again, unable to say what she felt, as usual, when it involved her own feelings.

"Don't you find it restful?" he asked, surprised. He had insisted that they were both working too hard, after her third miscarriage. Enough time had passed that they could safely try again for a child, and she had hoped that he meant this trip to be for them . . . just them.

"I find it . . . lonely." She forced the word out; forced herself to look at him.

"You miss Carbuncle that much?" he asked.

"I miss you."

His brown eyes with their epicanthic folds glanced away. He put his arm around her, drawing her close. He held her, his nearness warming her like the sun; but his other hand busied itself with the recording equipment, allowing him to avoid answering her. He had always been a man of few words; his emotions ran so strong and deep that they were almost unreachable. She had known that when she married him. It was what had drawn her to him, his strength and his depth. That and his face, golden-skinned and ruggedly handsome when he smiled at her . . . his straight, night-black hair; the absurd stubbornness of his mustache and the way it twitched when something took him by surprise—as she had when she'd told him she was staying on Tiamat, and asked him the question he could not ask himself. . . .

She had always understood his reticence, his guardedness, so well because it was so much like her own. But understanding had not kept the silence from accreting like an invisible wall between them. Sometimes she felt as if they were trapped in a stasis field, that they had been rendered incapable of communication, of motion or emotion. It frightened her in a way that nothing in all her years on the Hegemonic Police force had ever frightened her. This was worse, because she had no idea what to do about it. . . .

"I won't be much longer," he murmured, at last. "I promise you. I'm almost out of recording medium." He smiled, one of his wry, rare, self-aware smiles, and she felt her tension ease.

A mer's face broke the surface beside them, startling her. Another one appeared, and another. Their heads moved with nodding curiosity as their long, sinuous necks rose farther out of the water. Their wet brindle fur glistened; their movements were as graceful as the motion of birds in flight. The mers gazed up at her with eyes like midnight. Looking into their eyes was almost a meditation; a moment's contact somehow gave her a sense of peace that would have taken her hours of empty-minded solitude to attain.

She wondered again about whoever had created them, in the long-ago days of the Old Empire. The mers did not look human, but the human eye saw them as benign, even beautiful. And they seemed to regard humans with instinctive trust; they showed no fear at all, even though humans had slaughtered their kind for centuries. They forgot . . . or they forgave. She could not say which, because she had no idea what really went on inside their minds. Humans and mers shared a genetic structure that was superficially similar; the mers' wide, blunt-nosed faces always reminded her of children's faces—curious, expectant. And yet the ones gazing up at her now were gods-only-knew how old. They were, in profound ways, as alien and unfathomable as they were superficially like anything she recognized.

She watched and listened while Miroe played prerecorded passages of their speech and recorded their responses. Singsong trills and chittering squawks, deep thrumming harmonies filled the air. The mers were a sentient race; their brains were similar in size and complexity to a human brain. The fact of their sentience was recorded in the sibyl net's memory banks, and could be accessed by any sibyl in Transfer. But no data existed about why their god-playing creators had given them intelligence, any more than it existed about why they had been given the gift of virtual immortality. The mers were one more of the mysteries that clung to this haunted world like fog, until clear vision into its past seemed as impossible as looking into the future.

But their intelligence manifested itself in alien ways. The mers had no natural enemies besides humans, and no apparent material culture, or desire to create one.

They lived in an eternal now, in the constant sea; time itself was a sea for them, even as it was a river for the creatures that surrounded them, whose brief lives flickered in and out of their timeless existence; here today, gone tomorrow. . . .

That difference was incomprehensible to many human beings, either because they could not bridge the conceptual gap to an alien way of thought, or because they chose to ignore the distinction. It was far easier to see that the mers made the seas of this world a fountain of youth, one the richest and most powerful people in the Hegemony would pay any price to drink from, even if it meant that they had to drink blood. The silvery extract taken from the blood of slaughtered mers was euphemistically called the "water of life," and if it was taken daily it maintained a state of physical preservation in human beings. So far no one had been able to reproduce the extract, a benign technovirus engineered like the mers themselves through Old Empire processes that had been lost to time. The technovirus quickly died outside the body of its original host, no matter how carefully it was maintained; as the mers themselves died, if they were separated from their own kind and shipped offworld. But a reliable supply of the water of life was needed to satisfy a constant demand. Arienrhod had provided it, as had all the Snow Queens before her, by allowing the mers to be hunted; the Winters had reaped the rewards, growing fat off the flow of trade, and countless mers had died.

But now at last Summer had come again. The offworlders had gone, taking their insatiable greed with them. The mers would have an inviolate space of time in which to replenish their numbers, with painful slowness, righting the unspeakable wrong their creators had done them.

One of the mers ducked back under the water's surface, abruptly disappearing from the conversation Miroe had been attempting to carry on. The two who remained glanced at each other, looked up at him; then one by one they sank out of sight, whistling trills that might have been farewells or simply meaningless noise.

Miroe leaned over the rail, staring down at the suddenly empty sea. He swore in frustration and incomprehension. "What the hell—? Why did they just leave like that?"

Jerusha shrugged. "Did you say something that made them angry?"

"No," he snapped, with pungent irritation. "I didn't. I know that much about their speech, after this long, and it's all recorded—" He had been fascinated by the mers since long before she met him, before either one of them had been certain that the mers were an intelligent race. When she first encountered him he had been dealing with techrunners, buying embargoed equipment that helped him interfere with the Snow Queen's hunts. He had believed in the mers' intelligence even before Moon Dawntreader told him the truth in sibyl Transfer. He had been trying for years to decode what seemed to be their tonal speech, because mers were unable to form human speech.

"Maybe the conversation bored them," Jerusha said.

Miroe turned toward her; but his frown of annoyance faded. He looked down at the water again. "I almost think you're right," he murmured. "Damn it! After all this time, I don't understand them any better than I did twenty years ago." He shut off his recorder roughly. "They don't want to talk, all they want to do is sing. The harmonic structures are there, it's logical and patterned. But there's no *sense* to it. It's just noise."

He had isolated sequences that signified specific objects or actions to the mers;

but those were few and far between in the recordings he had made. What the Tiamatans called mersong was beautiful in the abstract, its interrelationship of tones and sounds incredibly complex and subtle. The mers seemed to spend most of their time repeating passages of songs, as if they were reciting oral history, teaching it to their young, preserving it for their descendants. But the coherent patterns of sound had no symbolic content that he had been able to discover. The mers seemed to have no interest in conversation, in give and take, except to express the most basic aspects of their life. . . . "But isn't conversation, communication what language is *for*—?" he demanded of the empty water. "Otherwise, what's the point? Why have such a complex, structured system, if they don't use it to expand their knowledge, or to change their lives?"

"They *are* aliens," she reminded him gently. "Whoever made them, made them something new. Maybe the meaning of it all died with their creators, just like the meaning of Carbuncle."

He shook his head, looking toward the mers at rest on the distant shore. "If we could only teach them to communicate willingly, we'd have proof of their intelligence that no one could ignore, proof that would force the Hegemony to leave them in peace. If we could even just find how to make a warning clear to them, they could escape the Hunt—" His hands fisted, as memory became obsession.

"Miroe . . ." she said, taking his arm, trying to lead him away.

"Moon should be doing more to solve this problem." He freed himself almost unthinkingly from her hold; she stepped back, away from him. "She told me the mers' survival would be her life's work, when she became Queen. . . ."

"She believes that building up Tiatmat's economy before the Hegemony returns will help both us and the mers," Jerusha said, a little sharply. "You know that. You're helping her do it. Sparks has been doing studies for her with the data we've provided on the mers; maybe you should talk to him about it, get some kind of dialogue going. He might have some fresh insight—"

"Not him," Miroe said flatly.

She looked at him.

"You know why." He frowned, glancing away at the shore. "You, of all people. You saw what he did. You know it's his fault that we had to come out here like this, that we can't be back at the plantation observing a mer colony. . . ." *Because Sparks Dawntreader had killed them all.*

She looked up at the sky, remembering another sky—how she had been certain that any moment it would crack and fall in on them, that day nearly eight years ago at Winter's end, when they stood on the blood-soaked beach together, witnesses to Arienrhod's revenge. They had interfered, unwittingly, with her plans for the Change . . . and so she had sent her hunters to slaughter the mer colony that made its home on the shores of Miroe's plantation; the colony he had always believed was safe under his protection.

But her hunters had killed them all, led by a man who bore a ritual name, who wore a ritual mask and dressed in black to protect his real identity: Starbuck, he was called, her henchman, her lover. . . . And at Winter's end, the man wearing the ritual mask had been Sparks Dawntreader.

Jerusha had never seen a mer before that day. That day she saw nearly a hundred of them, lying on the beach, their throats cut, drained of their precious blood—and then, by a final bitter twist of fate, stripped of their skins by a passing band of Winter nomads. She saw a hundred corpses, mutilated, violated; soulless mounds of flesh left to rot on the beach and be picked bare by scavengers. But she had not really seen a mer that day either, or understood the true impact of the tragedy, the depth of grief felt by the man who stood beside her. It was not until she had seen living mers, in motion, in the sea; until she had heard the siren call of the mersong, or discovered depths of peace in their eyes. . . . Then she had finally understood the hideous reality of the Hunt, the obscenity of the water of life.

And then she had understood why Miroe would not, could not, forgive Sparks Dawntreader—a Summer, a child of the Sea—for becoming Arienrhod's creature . . . Arienrhod's Starbuck. She glanced away from the mers on the beach, facing the emptiness in her husband's eyes. She released her hands from their unconscious deathgrip on the rail; pressed them against her stomach, which was as barren and empty as the look he gave her. She turned away, starting back toward the cabin's shadowed womb; feeling suddenly as if Arienrhod's curse still followed them all, even here, even after so long. She hesitated in the doorway, glancing toward him one last time. He stood motionless at the rail, staring down at the water. She stepped into the cabin's darkness, listening for his footsteps behind her; feeling only relief when she heard no sound.

TIAMAT: Carbuncle

"Well, Cousin, what a beautiful day it's going to be!"

Danaquil Lu Wayaways glanced up, startled, as hands settled familiarly on his shoulders. The pressure sent pain down through his arthritic back, making him clench his teeth. His kinsman Kirard Set, the elder of the Wayaways clan, smiled in sublime anticipation, oblivious to his discomfort; Danaquil Lu frowned. "Are you talking about the weather?" he said.

Kirard Set laughed. "The weather. You're priceless, Dana." He peered at his cousin. "I can't tell whether you're tweaking me, or whether you've simply been so long among the fisheaters that you mean that. But either way you're delightful."

Danaquil Lu, who had not meant it, said nothing.

"I'm speaking of the upcoming decision about the new foundry, of course."

"Then you shouldn't be talking to me about it," Danaquil Lu said flatly. There were plenty of the Winter nobility who were willing to accuse him of favoritism because he was one of only two Winters in the Sibyl College, and a Wayaways; even though the ultimate decision would be the Queen's. He leaned heavily on the tabletop, trying to find a position that would make him comfortable. He could not straighten up fully anymore, either sitting or standing.

Kirard Set grunted. "You not only look old, Cousin—you act old. You should never have left the city." He stopped midway through the motion of sitting down beside Danaquil Lu, and instead moved on around the large, tactfully circular table to find a more congenial seatmate.

"What choice did I have?" Danaquil Lu murmured, to the air. His hand rose, fingering the ridges of scarring down his cheek and jaw. The memory of his casting out from Carbuncle burned behind his eyes, as vivid suddenly as if it had happened yesterday. It was hard to realize now that it had happened half a lifetime ago, to a dumbstruck boy, someone who might as well be a complete stranger to the person he had become in Summer; and almost as hard to believe that he had been back in Carbuncle now for nearly eight years. He shook off the sense of disorientation with a motion that caused him more pain.

Miroe Ngenet, the Queen's physician, was working with Clavally, consulting the sibyl net, trying to recreate some medicine or surgical technique that would help him. In the meantime there was nothing he could do but live with it. He moved like an old man, he felt like an old man; some days it was hard not to believe that he was an old man, especially when he looked at Kirard Set. Kirard Set was old enough to be his great-grandfather, but looked more like his son. Kirard Set had been a favorite of the Snow Queen—and she had given him access to the water of life.

But the Snow Queen was gone, and faint age lines were beginning to appear at the corners of Kirard Set's eyes. Danaquil Lu meditated on that thought, and did not feel so old. At least the physical hardships of life were less severe here in the city. And if they had not come to Carbuncle, Clavally would never have let herself become pregnant, and they would not have their beautiful daughter to delight them, and distract him—and Clavally—from an obsession with his health. Summer had come to the city, and to their lives, at last. It was good to be home.

He glanced up again, noticing with some surprise that Kirard Set had taken the one empty seat next to Sparks Dawntreader, the Queen's consort—a seat he would have expected the Queen herself to occupy. But Sparks had apparently made no protest, and Kirard Set smiled in satisfaction, folding his hands on the tabletop.

"Damnation!"

Danaquil Lu glanced up again as someone else dropped into the seat beside him. Borah Clearwater sat snorting like a klee through the thick white brush of his mustache, rumbling ominously. Danaquil Lu pressed his lips together, controlling his smile as the older man slowly got himself under control.

Borah Clearwater was some kind of uncle to him, on his mother's side, if he recalled rightly; a cantankerous old stone who owned plantation lands far south of the city, and came to Carbuncle only under duress. The duress this time had to do with the Wayaways clan; Kirard Set had been agitating for an access across Clearwater's lands, a shortcut to the sea, as part of his push to get the Queen to grant him the right to have the new foundry built on a landlocked piece of his own holdings. The fact that Clearwater was here suggested he was afraid Kirard Set would be successful.

Danaquil Lu glanced on around the table. There were still a few empty seats. It was some kind of comment on his status that Clearwater chose to sit next to him, and that everyone else apparently chose not to—his status as a sibyl, or his status as an outsider among his own kind. He supposed they were really the same thing.

He fingered the trefoil hanging against his shirt as he glanced to his left, seeing that the seat on the other side of him was still unoccupied. The Greenside headwoman sitting across the gap looked back at him, her expression guarded. The Summer Queen had made the Winters accept what he had never believed they would accept, after centuries of being lied to by the Hegemony: the truth, that sibyls were human computer ports tied to an interstellar information network. She had shown the people of the city that sibyls could give them back the technology they hungered for; that sibyls were not simply diseased lunatics, as the offworlders had always claimed in order to keep Tiamat ignorant and backward in their absence. But a lifetime of suspicion did not fade overnight . . . or even over eight years. . . .

"Well, at least you don't smell like a sugarbath, like most of my kin, Danaquil Lu Wayaways," Borah Clearwater said abruptly, as if he had been reading Danaquil Lu's mind. "And you don't look like a motherlorn offworlder in plastic clothes. Drown me if I wouldn't rather sit with lunatics and Summers than with these city-soft pissants, with their bogbrained ideas about raising the dead." He looked at Danaquil Lu as if he expected agreement, his gray eyes as piercing as a predator's, and about as congenial.

Danaquil felt his mouth inch up into another smile. "Me too," he said sincerely.

Clearwater grunted, not requiring even that much encouragement. "The offworlders are gone, the technology's gone with them; what's gone is gone. I spent my whole life getting used to the idea. Let it go, and good riddance." Danaquil Lu said nothing, this time, thinking privately that if he and everyone else at this meeting table were as old as Clearwater, they might all find it easy to let go of the past and make peace with the inevitable. But they weren't ready to stop living yet, and that was the difference. . . . Although there were days, trying to get up in the morning, when he could almost see Borah Clearwater's point of view. "Goddamn nuisance— this damn woman, this Summer Queen; Kirard Set dragging me halfway up the coast for this—"

Danaquil Lu raised a hand, silencing him abruptly, unthinkingly. "The Queen," he murmured. Clearwater turned, following his gaze as he looked across the room.

"Damnation . . ." Clearwater breathed. It sounded more like wonder than a curse; Danaquil Lu wondered what emotion lay behind it. His own eyes stayed on the Queen as she entered the hall, crossed it under the waiting gaze of a hundred eyes; he found it hard, as he always did, to look away from her. He could not say what it was about her that affected him so. The paleness of her hair made a startling contrast to the muted greens of her traditional robes, which billowed behind her like the sea. Her eyes, he knew, were the color of the agates that washed up along Tiamat's shores; their changeable depths held the earth, the sea, the sky. She was not a tall woman, not extraordinarily beautiful, and still as slender as the girl she had been when he and Clavally had initiated her into the calling of a sibyl. But there was something about her, an intensity of belief, the urgent grace of a drawn bow, that showed even in her movement as she crossed the room; that compelled him to watch her every move, listen to her every word. He knew he was not the only one who felt that way.

He had seen her almost every day in the years since he and Clavally had come to the city. They had been among the first to join the Sibyl College that Moon had established as part of her effort to recreate technology from the ground up. He had watched her grow in confidence and experience from an awkward island girl into a shrewd, determined woman who won her battles more and more through skill, depending less and less on the Lady's Luck for her survival as Queen. If the rumors were true—and he thought they were—she came by her leadership abilities naturally. But where she had gotten the vision that drove her to forge a totally new future for this world, after growing up among the tradition-minded, tech-hating Summer islanders, he could not imagine. That was a part of her mystery . . . which was perhaps part of her power.

Danaquil Lu refocused on the room, on the present, as Moon Dawntreader chose the empty seat beside his own at the table. Still standing, with her hands cupping the totem-creatures carved on the chair's back, she called the gathered men and women to order. Silence fell as she took her seat. Danaquil Lu glanced down at his notepad, seeing the trefoil symbols he had been absentmindedly doodling there. His back was killing him, and the meeting had not yet even begun. Days were long when the College met with the Council. He sighed, wishing that he had the Queen's single-minded resolve; wishing that it had been his turn today to be the stay-at-home parent, and not Clavally's. He covered the symbols with his hand as the Queen began to speak, and Borah Clearwater began to mutter in counterpoint beside him.

There were several members of the Sibyl College here today, including blind Fate Ravenglass, who was its head and still the only other Winter among the sibyls. Jerusha PalaThion and her husband Miroe Ngenet were here too, along with a few Winters who had managed to absorb some technical knowledge from their contact with the offworlders. They were struggling to become the researchers, the engineers of Tiamat's future; asking the questions and working with the sibyls to turn the net's data into measurable progress.

Elders of the various Winter and Summer clans or their representatives filled most of the other seats, and filled the air with give-and-take. They had become the first members of the Council the Queen had established at the same time she had established the Sibyl College. They were already the leaders of their extended-family groups; the Council gave them a forum where they could speak for and vote to protect their clans' interests and holdings.

There had been a Council during the Snow Queen's reign, imitating the offworlders' judiciate government, but it had been strictly for Winters, and dominated by the self-proclaimed nobility who were Arienrhod's favorites. There had never been a Council with Summers on it too, and usually the Summers and Winters mixed like oil and water. He was relieved to see that Capella Goodventure was not here today; he did not recognize the woman whom she had sent as her replacement. It surprised him that she was not here herself. She rarely missed the opportunity to object to any new project the Sibyl College or the Queen proposed.

Making use of the sibyl network and its vast resources of knowledge, the Queen had begun planting the seeds of progress everywhere—and already they were sprouting, like spring grass pushing up through the snow. New resources, new methods of production, new tools and new comforts had already rewarded the hard work of Tiamat's people. It was only the beginning, but already the promise of what the next century could hold was a more tangible incentive to most people than the Queen's constant insistence that they would—must—make themselves technologically independent, so that when the offworlders returned Tiamat could meet them as an equal.

The Winters embraced most of her proposals with an enthusiasm that made up for the Summers' reluctance. Often they were eager to a fault, vying for the opportunity to exploit the mineral rights of their plantations, or have new laboratories and prototype manufactories constructed there. Today they were pressing the Queen for a decision on building a dam and power station north of the city.

". . . that it would allow us to progress much faster if we have adequate power for the new factories—" Gaddon Overhill was saying, speaking with staccato urgency, as usual. "And it won't foul the air or pollute the seas—"

"But a dam will flood lands—mostly Summer lands—that are used for farming and herding," Dal Windward objected.

Overhill waved a hand dismissively. "Those lands are scarcely fit to support either crops or grazing. Small loss."

"To you, maybe, Winter!" the Goodventure representative said. "Someone has to provide food for all you fools while you neglect your own plantations. to play with your new inventions."

"Stick to the sea, then, that you Summers love so much," Sewa Stormprince answered. " 'The Sea will provide,' as you always like to say. And this won't pollute it."

"The Sibyl College has consulted the net on the matter." The Queen raised her voice to silence them, as she frequently had to do. The Summers resisted rules of order, and the Winters would not let the Summers outshout them. "Danaquil Lu Wayaways will give you its findings."

"Rubbish and lunacy," Borah Clearwater muttered, to the room at large.

Danaquil Lu took a deep breath, and a last look at his prepared notes, before he lifted his eyes to the expectant faces of the Council. "The data received in Transfer from the sibyl net indicate that such a project is unfeasible, for a number of reasons—" He pressed on, through suddenly rising protests. "The primary reason we have for recommending against the dam project is that it would, as the Summers claim, render a substantial amount of land unavailable. On top of that, our ability to construct such a dam with complete safety, even with blueprints and material specifications provided by the net, is uncertain at this point in our development. It has to function not only through the relatively mild weather of High Summer, when free-flowing water is plentiful, but also the intense and extended cold of High Winter, when everything is frozen. We don't have a great margin for error, unlike a lot of worlds—"

"Lady and all the gods," Overhill interrupted. "How are we ever going to get past 'this point' if we don't take some chances!"

"The sibyl mind is guiding us." The Queen cut him off almost sharply; something she would not have had the confidence to do two or three years ago. She had become surer in her leadership as she had grown used to being Queen; and as it became clear to everyone that the sibyl net, which she relied on as faithfully as if it really were the Sea Mother's voice, was as omniscient as any goddess when it came to what was wisdom or folly for her people. "It has shown us that our world is barely habitable, by the standards of most worlds human beings live on. We must make technological progress if we are ever to have an easier, safer life here. But we still have nearly a century before the Hegemony returns, and the sibyl mind is showing us the straightest, swiftest course to our future. Without its guidance, we would not have achieved a tenth of what we have done so far. We have to trust it, or we'll end up destroying our world, instead. Therefore, in this matter I support the Summers."

"Then where will we get a new source of energy for our manufactories?" Overhill demanded.

"If you will let Danaquil Lu Wayaways finish his report," the Queen said, with faint impatience, "then you will see that there are alternative solutions." Overhill settled back into his seat. into silence, as she glanced at Danaquil Lu.

"An alternative method of generating power has been offered to us," Danaquil Lu went on, at her nod. "It involves using wind-driven turbines, which can be put up in the fields and on hillsides without spoiling them for grazing or farming. The wind will provide all the energy we'll need for the next decade or so, and by then we may be able to construct tide-driven turbines, and take our power directly from the sea. Carbuncle gets its power that way, and its system has worked perfectly for centuries. . . ."

"You're talking about windmills?" Abbo Win Graymount said. "I've seen one power a pump once or twice, but they could never produce the kind of energy we need to run factories—not if you had half a million of them!"

"You've never seen one with this design," Miroe Ngenet broke in. "I've used them on my plantation for years. They're far more efficient than anything you've ever seen."

Graymount shrugged, dubious.

"We will begin developing detailed plans for the wind-power project, and discuss location sites and materials at our next meeting. We may be able to make use of supplies left behind by the offworlders in some of the city warehouses," the Queen said, looking relieved as the hubbub of discussion faded to murmured speculation among the Winters, grudging silence among the Summers.

Borah Clearwater muttered under his breath as Danaquil Lu settled into a more comfortable position, relieved to be done with his command performance. He was content to let the Queen's other advisors handle all further topics of discussion and debate. He sat, half-listening, half preoccupied by his own pain, through a seemingly endless litany of old versus new.

Kirard Set, who had sat waiting with serene anticipation all the while Borah Clearwater simmered, spoke up at last, inquiring with subtle confidence whether the Queen had considered the matter of his bid for the latest refining operation, and the right-of-way across the Clearwater lands.

The Queen nodded. "Yes, Elder Wayaways," she said, shuffling through her sheaf of handwritten notes. "Your site seems ideal for the foundry, especially since its location is so close to the source of iron ore. Your offer to fund the initial construction work is very generous. I don't see any significant obstacles to granting your request. Does the Clearwater elder have any objection to granting the needed right of way . . . ?" She glanced around the table. Danaquil Lu was not certain that whoever represented the Clearwater clan was even present.

"I have an objection, damn it!" Borah Clearwater loomed up suddenly beside him, glaring at Kirard Set. "It's my plantation, and by all the gods, I won't have any Wayaways touching so much as a speck of dust on it!" He turned toward the Queen as he spoke, bellowing as if she were halfway across the planet, and not almost next to him. Danaquil Lu covered his ears.

The Queen looked up at him with a mixture of alarm and disbelief. "But all that he requested was an easement—"

"Today! And tomorrow he'll bribe you into— Get your hands off me!" The last was directed toward the two city constables who had come in, at Jerusha PalaThion's summons, from their post outside the door. They took his arms and led him forcibly out of the room, still protesting loudly.

Danaquil Lu let his hands fall into his lap. He shook his head, meeting the Queen's astonished stare as the room around them rippled with relieved laughter. She looked away from him again, toward Kirard Set. "Your request is granted, Elder Wayaways," she said, with apparent calm and something like satisfaction.

Kirard Set smiled, nodding his head in what appeared to be grateful acknowledgment. But Danaquil Lu caught the gleam of knowing amusement in his eyes as he looked at the Queen, a secret assumption of complicity that the Queen's expression did not return, or even seem to register. Danaquil Lu looked away, glancing toward the empty doorway. It seemed to him that he still heard Borah Clearwater's voice echoing through the halls of the Sibyl College.

He pushed to his feet, slowly and awkwardly. Murmuring his apologies to the Queen, he left the Council chamber by the same exit.

TIAMAT: Carbuncle

"Motherless blasphemer!" The shout came at her from some shadowed doorway. A fishhead came with it, thudding against her shoulder.

Moon Dawntreader stopped walking and turned back, her eyes burning. "Come out!" Her voice echoed along the almost-deserted street. "If you have a criticism, say it to my face!" But whoever had hurled the insult and the fishhead stayed hidden.

"Lady—?" Jerusha PalaThion asked the question with her motion as she unslung the rifle from her shoulder. She glanced toward the silent buildings gazing back at them with empty eyes.

Moon shook her head, putting her hand on the gun.

"What is it, Moon?" Fate Ravenglass turned toward their voices, her own empty eyes moving restlessly, blindly.

"Nothing, Fate," Moon murmured.

"Just some stinking Summer with fish for brains, losing their mind," Tor Starhiker, the fourth woman in their party, said sourly. She took the blind woman's arm, guiding her steps as they started on again.

Moon raised her hand, pulling down the smile that unexpectedly tried to turn up the corners of her mouth. "The Summers have every right to criticize me, Tor." She felt the smile disappear. "They are my people. Don't insult them for it . . . at least not in my hearing." She looked down, fingered the trefoil pendant that hung like a star against the dappled greens of her robes. "Even when they deserve it."

The stench of rotten fish filled her nose, as inescapable as doubt, or truth. She glanced at the women who surrounded her. There was not a Summer among them. She was not the Queen her people had expected when she was chosen at the Change. And she was not the Lady they wanted—a symbolic avatar of the Sea Mother, who would preside over their sacred rituals and safeguard their cherished traditions. They had not asked for a Queen who needed and wielded real power, one who believed that the ways of offworlders were superior to the ways which had served them for centuries . . . a Lady who did not even believe in the Goddess.

They went on in silence until they reached the mouth of Olivine Alley, one of the countless labyrinthine ways that branched off the rising spiral of the Street, honeycombing the ancient shellform city of Carbuncle. Moon looked down at her feet, shod in soft leather, moving over the smooth surface of the pavement. The pavement was made from some material that never seemed to decay, no matter how many footsteps, wheels, treads, or burdens passed over its uniform surface.

She looked back down the alley, as they turned into the Street, taking a final look at the Sibyl College, where they studied and labored day after day to unlock the secrets of technology. She could still see the alley's end, where the transparent storm walls let in the sunset, the last light of another day. The meeting with the Council had made this day run even longer than most.

One more day was gone in which she had not accomplished all she had hoped to; but still they were one day further along the path to real knowledge, the way to her world's future. She began to walk again, feeling her weariness grow as they made their way on up the Street.

"This is where we get off, folks."

Tor Starhiker's voice startled her out of her reverie, and she nodded. "Rest well, Fate," she murmured. "We have a long way to go tomorrow. Good night, Tor." Their answers were equally subdued, as if her mood had spread to them all. She went on with Jerusha at her side, her head still echoing with the arguments of Winters and Summers, and with doubt.

Tor stood beside Fate with a hand resting on her arm, and watched the Summer Queen go on her way toward the palace at Street's End. "Must have been a rough one," she said, as much to herself as to the woman beside her.

"About as usual," Fate answered, with a sigh. "Council days are always a trial. The ex-nobility's eagerness to build a new world is matched only by their eagerness to be the first and richest in it. . . . They argue endlessly with the Summers, as if everything were some court pettiness over who was the Snow Queen's favorite this week. They don't seem to realize that Moon is *not* the old Queen—"

"Well, she looks just like her," Tor said bluntly.

Fate sighed again, as they started on down the alleyway toward her empty shop. "Yes, I remember. . . ." Tor looked at her. While the Snow Queen ruled, Fate had possessed vision of a sort, using imported sensors; she had been an artist, a professional maskmaker, the one chosen to make the Summer Queen's mask for the final Festival . . . the one who had placed it on Moon Dawntreader's head. But her vision had gone with the offworlders, like so much else that had made both their lives bearable. Now at least Fate had found a new life in the Sibyl College.

And Tor, who had been her acquaintance for many years, had made a new life of a sort as her assistant. But the vacant trances of sibyls, the endless questions that were all but meaningless to her, the stupid wrangling among stupid aristos, still left her feeling cast-adrift. She was glad enough to go on sharing in the lives of the powerful and important people whose destiny she had been sucked into during the Change; what they believed and what they were trying to do awed her, and at least they weren't dull.

But her own life was dull. The present was still too much like what she had expected it to be, inconvenient, narrow, stinking of fish. She had spent her entire life before the Change doing the offworlders' work; she missed the past, with all its excesses and terrors. She had almost escaped this future; nearly married an off-worlder and gone offplanet with him. But destiny had stepped into their path—other people's destiny—sending her lover Oyarzabal to prison with his employers and stranding her like an empty boat when the Hegemony's tide went out.

"Why doesn't Moon get rid of those damned aristos?" she said, feeling irritable as memory pinched her. "There are plenty of other Winters who'd be glad to take their places, and they don't have all the bad habits Arienrhod taught her favorites."

Fate smiled, sweeping the street ahead with her cane, a gesture that let her feel some kind of control over her progress, and maybe her life. "Yes, but they don't own most of the land." The Winter nobility may have been called "noble" by default, but most of them had held their positions at Arienrhod's court because they headed the clans which controlled the most resources. "And they're not all jaded fools: some of them are smart and creative and highly motivated. Those are the ones who will end up as the real leaders . . . I only hope I live long enough to see it." Her mouth twisted with weary irony.

"Right," Tor said. She shook her head, thinking privately that they had more chance of living to see the offworlders' return than they did of seeing all Moon Dawntreader's dreams come true. Looking toward the alley's end, she could see the Summer Star now, the sign that had marked the Change for her people and the offworlders too. As their farewell gesture before leaving, the offworlders had sent down a beam of high frequency energy that fried the fragile components in every single piece of equipment they had left behind, including Fate's vision sensors. Since they had blocked the development of any local technological base, nothing could be repaired.

Then they had gone, secure in the knowledge that the technophobic Summers would move north into the Winters' territory, as they had done since the beginning of their days on this world. The Summer Queen would lead Tiamat's people back—willingly or not—into the traditional ways that had meant their survival for centuries before the offworlders ever set foot here; keeping things stagnant and secure, until the Hegemony could return.

Moon Dawntreader meant to change all that. Tor's admiration for the Queen's goals was matched only by her scepticism about their achievability.

Tor steered Fate sideways, to avoid a Summer striding obliviously down the street with a load of kleeskins on his back. The batch of foul-smelling hides struck her as he passed, and knocked her staggering into Fate. She regained her balance, and caught Fate, barely in time to keep them both from sprawling in the gutter. "Watch where you're going, you crackbrain! You want to knock down a blind woman?"

The Summer swung around without breaking stride. "Watch yourself, Motherless! I've got better things to do than teach you how to walk."

"Like teach yourself some manners?" Tor spat.

"Parasite." He turned his back on them and trudged on down the alley.

Tor flung an obscene hand gesture at his retreating back. Fate's hand reached out, searching for her arm; caught hold of her. Tor forced herself to relax, muttering under her breath. She turned back again, and they went on toward Fate's door. "They should all drown, the fisheaters. Then we wouldn't have any trouble."

"You think not?" Fate said, her voice gently mocking. "Who would you hate, then?"

Tor took a deep breath. "All right, so I don't hate them. They're our cousins. We all need each other to survive. All our sins went into the Sea with the Snow Queen, and now we're all one. . . ." She repeated the litany of the Summer Queen's propaganda, the supposed will of the supposed Sea Mother. "But by all the gods, I don't know who ever said fish was brain food."

Fate laughed, and was silent again, lost in her own thoughts. Tor led her on down the alleyway. The Winters endured the Summers' cyclical invasion, knowing there was no real choice. Winters and Summers had always needed each other to survive, and the ancient rituals they shared gave them enough common ground to get by. Her people waited out High Summer with the patience of exiles, secure in the knowledge that the offworlders would return at the first possible moment, bringing back to their descendants, if not to them, the sophisticated comforts to which they had grown accustomed.

But even though clan ties and traditional religion had left them blueprints for peaceful coexistence, the culture-wide shockwave of the Change still left them with ugly petty confrontations. Winters who had lost all sense of their heritage over the hundred and fifty years of offworlder rule, and newly arrived Summers, wary unwanted guests in the territories of their distant relatives, still cursed each other and had fistfights in the half-empty streets of Carbuncle, even after eight years.

The problem would get worse before it got better, if it ever did, because the new Queen's unorthodox changes heightened all the old tensions. The coming of the Summers was a gradual thing, and that was probably all that saved their world from complete anarchy. In another decade this city would be teeming—in a completely different way than it had been when the offworlders filled its streets, but teeming nonetheless, just like the rapidly thawing countryside beyond its walls. . . .

"Here we are," Tor said. She hesitated as Fate found her way up the single step to her door and unfastened the lock. "Will you be all right if I leave now?" Usually she stayed, and they shared dinner, although she knew Fate was perfectly capable of getting around her home and former shop alone. Sometimes after the meal Fate would play her sithra and Tor would sing, old songs about the sea, new songs about the stars; songs with long memories that carried them both back to better days. Neither one of them liked spending endless evenings alone, although neither one of them had ever spoken of it. But tonight she felt as restless as the large gray cat that wound around Fate's ankles, yowling with impatience. "I think I've got to scratch an itch tonight."

"Yes, I'll be fine." Fate nodded. She leaned down to pick up the cat, stroking its fur, scratching it fondly under the chin. "I think Malkin and I only want to sleep tonight, anyway. It's been a long . . ." She broke off, and didn't say what had been so long.

"You don't need anything from the markets?"

"No, thank you. Thank you for everything." Fate smiled, her sightless eyes finding Tor's with uncanny accuracy. "Let me know whether he's worth losing sleep over."

Tor laughed, pushing her hands into the frayed pockets of her aging offworlder coveralls. "It doesn't matter if he is or not, because I don't intend to remember him in the morning." She stepped down into the street and strode away, heading for her favorite tavern.

Moon sighed, wearied by the steep climb up the Street, the steep upward spiral of life. They had reached Street's End at last; ahead she saw the wide vortex of alabaster pavement, and beyond it the elaborately carven double doors of the palace. Two guards stood at the entrance, as they always did, by Jerusha's order. Moon blinked her eyes clear of the waking dream that had suffused her thoughts as she climbed the hill, as insubstantial as fog, as inescapable as a shadow: the memory of the dark-eyed stranger who had led her once to these doors . . . who had been her spirit guide when she was lost in this strange city, caught up in destiny's storm. The man who had been her lover for one night, before his own destiny had swept him from her life forever. . . .

Moon glanced at the woman beside her, feeling a pang of guilt; afraid that Jerusha PalaThion's shrewd, observant eyes might have looked in through the open window of her thoughts, and seen too much. But Jerusha was gazing straight ahead, lost in a reverie of her own. Jerusha had stayed behind when the offworlders left Tiamat, as much from a sense of betrayal by her own people as from love of her new home. Moon had never fully understood her motives; Jerusha was not a woman much given to discussing her thoughts. But she was an excellent listener, whose friendship Moon had come to treasure as a rare gift. Jerusha was one of their chief advisors regarding the Hegemony's castoff technology—and also her most loyal protector. Jerusha kept the transition peaceful in the restless city, with a cannily chosen security force of Winters who had worked for the old Queen and Summers who were loyal to the new one.

The palace doors swung open before them; Moon's footsteps quickened, forcing Jerusha to lengthen her stride to keep up. Moon began to smile, suddenly filled with eagerness, as two small bright forms came hurtling toward her. She kneeled on the hard pavement, catching the twins, hugging them close; astonished again, as she was every day, by the power of the emotions that filled her . . . still astonished, after all this time, to find herself the mother of two children. She kissed their faces, holding tight to their squirming warmth, absorbing the sweet smell of their hair, the excited clamor of their voices.

"Mama, Mama, Gran is here!"

"—Gran is here!"

Their voices sang together as they echoed the words, each of them trying to be the first to tell her the news. "—Really!"

"Wait, wait," she murmured. "You mean that my mother is here—?" She had not seen her family in all the years since she had left the Windwards for Carbuncle.

Now, holding her children in her arms, her need to see her own mother was as sudden and hot as the sun.

"No, *Gran*—" Ariele insisted, her cloud of fair hair moving across her face as she shook her head. She pushed it back impatiently.

"Gran—" Tammis echoed, pulling on his mother's sleeve.

"Your grandmother, Moon," someone said.

Moon looked up, to see Clavally Bluestone's short, solid figure framed in the high arch of the double doors, the sibyl sign gleaming against her shirtfront, her own daughter Merovy clinging to her side while she watched the twins greet their mother. Clavally and Danaquil Lu had begun to spend less time at the Sibyl College after their child was born, and they had taken on the task of watching Tammis and Ariele as well.

"Not my mother?" Moon repeated, her own voice suddenly thin with disappointment. She wondered why—how—her grandmother had come alone to Carbuncle.

"We'll show you!" Ariele cried, bounding impatiently back toward the palace entrance. "Come on, Mama!"

Tammis stayed by his mother's side, always the quiet one, his brown eyes gazing up at her somberly as he hung on her arm.

"Tammis, I'm too tired—" she murmured, trying to take his hand instead. She broke off, as Jerusha swept Tammis off his feet and up into her arms. "I'll take him," Jerusha said, tickling him until he forgot the protesting squawk he had been about to make.

Moon bit off the protest that came half-formed to her lips, drew back her hands, which had instinctively reached for him. She watched, resigned, as Jerusha strode on ahead, carrying Tammis on her hip, grinning back at him with tender whimsy.

Clavally passed them, leading Merovy by the hand, nodding her head in a formal gesture of respect and farewell as she reached Moon's side. Moon saw unspoken concern in Clavally's glance, and wondered what she knew that she could not bring herself to say. "Danaquil Lu sent word that there is a party being given tonight by his cousin Kirard Set." Clavally's round face pinched slightly. "Dana asked if we would come, to help him get through it. But if you would like me to stay . . ."

Moon smiled, her smile quirking slightly. She could guess, after this afternoon's negotiations among the nobles, what Kirard Set was celebrating. "Go and keep him company. He's like a man who's been in a swarm of bloodflies after he's been with his relatives. He does need you."

Clavally smiled wryly, and nodded.

"Enjoy it," Moon said. "It's in a good cause." She looked down at Merovy, at the little girl's shy, wide-eyed gaze fixed on Tammis. "You have fun too," she added gently.

Merovy nodded soberly as her mother led her on past. She looked back over her shoulder, still watching Tammis. "Bye, Tammis," she called.

He waved, his own expression equally somber, from where he sat perched on Jerusha's hip.

Moon entered the palace, looking up at the frescoed walls as she walked the echoing hallway that led into its heart. The first time she had come into this place, the walls had been haunted by stark scenes of winter. Those murals had long since been painted over at her order with scenes of bright sunlight, green fields, the blues of sea and sky. But still the images of Winter seeped through into her memory, imprinted indelibly on her mind's eye, making her remember all that had happened here at Winter's end . . . making her remember Arienrhod, who haunted the very air here, who haunted every mirror. She forced herself to look down, fixing her vision on her children and the way ahead.

"Mama!" Ariele cried impatiently.

Moon saw her daughter dancing from foot to foot at the edge of the Pit, and her breath caught. "Ariele!" she called sharply, quickening her steps, as Ariele knew she would.

"Hurry up," Ariele shouted, and darted out onto the railingless ribbon of bridge that arced across the shaft. Ariele laughed, fearless, shaking her tumbled, milk-white hair at their dismay.

Moon stepped onto the bridge, her feet soundless in their soft city shoes, and caught her daughter up in her arms. "How many times—" she began, angrily.

"You're too slow! I want to see Gran!" Ariele insisted. She wrapped long, slender legs around her mother's waist, drumming her feet. "You smell like fish—*euw*. . . . Come on, Mama."

Moon sighed and carried her across the bridge, leaving Jerusha to make her way as slowly as she chose with Tammis. The bridge was wide enough that, even railingless, it allowed people to walk its span with no more than a quickened heartbeat, ever since she had stopped the wind. Moon glanced up, resolutely not looking down, letting her eyes find the pale curtains that hung like fog in the vaulting space overhead. A glowing mass of stars was beginning to show through the fading light of day in the tall, starkly silhouetted windows.

Moon stepped off the far end of the bridge and let her squirming daughter down to run on ahead. She stayed where she was, turning back to wait for Jerusha; to stand for a long moment gazing into the Pit, letting the sharp smell of the sea clear the stink of fish from her nostrils. The currents of past and present collided inside her like a riptide, their undertow sucking at her. She swayed a moment, closing her eyes, before she turned and started on again into the palace, her clothes still reeking.

She had defied both Summers and Winters, by crossing that bridge and taking up residence here. The past was no longer an option, not for her, or for anyone. It was unreachable in time, like the sea at the bottom of the Pit. She could only go on, into Summer, changing with the world.

And Gran had come. She tried to recapture the happiness and excitement the news had filled her with.

Tammis slithered out of Jerusha's arms as they caught up, and came to take her hand. She looked down at his hand, so small inside her own, its golden-brownness in such stark contrast to her paleness. She squeezed his hand gently, smiling down at him.

"Where's Da?" he asked. He asked it every day.

"He can't come home yet," Moon said. She gave him almost the same answer, every day.

"Why not?"

"Because there's so much to do," she murmured, as she always did.

"Well, why can't he do it here?"

"Tammis—"

"Doesn't he love us? Doesn't he want to be here?"

"Of course he does." She looked away, seeing the palace walls that Sparks had known for far longer than she had, and which he hated now so much that he spent as little time as possible inside them. She made herself look back at Tammis, and smile. "He loves you very much. He loves us all. He'll be home to play songs for you at bedtime. . . . Someday you'll understand why it's so important for us to finish our work." *Which will never be finished; not in our lifetime.* "Someday I hope you'll help us finish it."

"Ariele too?"

"Yes, Ariele too."

"I want to help." He gave a small hop, hanging on her hand.

"I know." She nodded, looking down.

"Are you happy, Mama?"

She looked back at him, realizing with sudden pain that it was a question which was almost meaningless to her. But it was not meaningless to him, and so she smiled at him, a real smile, filled with the same unquestioning love that she found in his eyes. "Yes, I am. When I'm with you and Ariele."

"And Da?"

"Yes, and Da." She hugged him against her side, looking away again. The Winter staff who took care of the palace and its occupants hovered discreetly at the corners of her vision, waiting for some sign of interest or some command from her as she moved through one vast, purposeless room after another. Their presence still made her uncomfortable, after so many years. She had been born into a world where everyone took care of their own needs, and few people had more possessions, or space in which to keep them, than they could easily use.

Arienrhod's palace—it would never seem like her palace—would have covered a small island in the Windwards, and every room of it was filled with strange and exotic gleanings from all over the Hegemony: the furniture, rugs, and hangings, the exotic playthings and ornaments, glittered everywhere like bizarre deepwater stormwrack.

She had changed scarcely anything of what she had found here, telling herself that she wanted everything for study, just as she wanted whatever other artifacts of the offworlders had survived their leaving. But in the secret places of her soul she knew that she had not touched them because she was afraid of them, afraid of violating the memory of Arienrhod. . . .

Over the years she had grown used to seeing Arienrhod's possessions, just as she had grown inured to the uncertain, overeager attentions of the palace staff; although every time she found herself growing too comfortable with them she felt as if she were startling awake out of a bad dream.

A man in the uniform of a city constable approached deferentially. "Lady," he murmured, bobbing his head. "Commander—" He turned to Jerusha, addressing her by her old title, which had become her new title by default. "The daywatch sergeant asked me to report that a person carrying a concealed knife was arrested trying to enter the palace without—"

"Not here, damn it!" Jerusha whispered sharply, as Moon froze beside her. She gestured him away, leaving their presence with a brusque, apologetic nod.

"What was that, Mama?" Tammis asked, his face filling with concern as he saw his mother's worried frown. "Is somebody going to hurt us?"

"No, treasure," she murmured, stroking his head, hugging him against her. "No, of course not. . . ." She led him on across the hall to the wide, curving stairs, where Ariele was waiting to hurry them upward to Gran.

Jerusha watched the Queen and her children go with a rush of sudden emotion that was almost a physical pain. She turned back to the constable, her own expression settling into anger. "By all the gods, Shellwaters—don't you have sense enough to keep your mouth shut in front of a child, even if you don't have the sense to keep it shut in front of the Queen?"

He grimaced and looked down. "I'm sorry, Commander, I—"

"Forget it." She shook her head, getting herself under control. "Just remember it next time."

"Yes, Commander." He looked up again, relieved; she felt an odd relief of her own as his neutral gaze met hers. He was Tiamatan, which meant that he didn't mind serving a woman; and he was a Winter, which meant that he didn't mind serving an offworlder. At least when she was doing her job she felt less like an alien here than she had in her old life. "You say they got the man—or was it a woman?"

"Yes, Commander. A woman . . . a Summer. She claims she heard the Sea Mother's voice telling her to drive out the impostor pretending to be Queen." He made a disgusted face; something in his voice said that it was no more than could be expected of a Summer. "We have her in detention."

"All right. Good. Give me a full report tomorrow. And for gods' sakes, try to keep the gossip down."

He nodded, and made what passed for a salute among the locals.

She watched him go out of the room. A handful of the palace staff watched him go as well; she knew they were already spreading rumors among themselves. It was an irony that was no more lost on her than it was on the Queen that the Winters of Carbuncle were more loyal than the Summer clans were to Moon Dawntreader. Jerusha tried to spare Moon and her family the awareness of just how many rigid, narrow-minded religious fanatics there were among her people; but she knew in her heart that the task was futile. Moon knew it as well as she did. *She hears voices telling her the Sea Mother wants her to kill the Queen.* . . . Jerusha shook her head. What the hell was the matter with some people—? But then, she remembered that Moon Dawntreader claimed to hear voices that told her to defy her own traditions and change her world. . . .

Jerusha sighed, looking back at the stairway, where Moon and her two children had disappeared into the shadowed upper levels. She felt the mixed emotions hit her again, as she thought of something happening to those children. The sudden, gut-wrenching fear of loss stabbed like an assassin's knife. She loved those children as if they were her own; and if her latest pregnancy ended like the others, they might be as close to her own children as she would ever come. . . . But no, she would not let herself think about that. This time everything would go all right—

If she had left Tiamat at the Change, she could have gotten help; but then, she would not have had Miroe, would not have had any reason to want a child. She would not even have had any reason to go on fighting a system that had never shown her anything but contempt when she tried to lead a full life, the kind any man of her people was free to lead. On Newhaven she had been expected to act like a woman—marry and raise children, but live subservient to her husband forever. Here, on Tiamat, she had thought that at last she'd found her chance to live as a complete human being. But when it was too late to change her mind, fate had played its final trick on her. She had not even told anyone that she was pregnant, this time—afraid that making it real would make her vulnerable.

She started toward the door, trying to shake off the creeping melancholy of her thoughts; knowing they would follow her home, to the empty apartment waiting for her down in Carbuncle's Maze. She would call Miroe, and for a while his voice would fill the silence and drown out her fears. He spent most of his time away from the city, overseeing the plantation, experimenting with the new technology the sibyls and the Winters were creating daily . . . avoiding Carbuncle. *Not avoiding her.* She repeated it to herself again, less and less sure that she believed it, any more than she still believed that remaining on Tiamat had been anything but an act of desperation.

Moon entered the room, at first seeing only the unexpected brightness of the sunset sky through the oval window that filled most of the far wall. Blinking, she found the silhouette of her grandmother's face; blinking again, she filled in its features as her grandmother turned toward her. "Gran—" she murmured, and stopped. *How did you get so old?*

Her memory of her grandmother had not prepared her for this stooped, wrinkled woman, this *old* woman with snow-white hair and skin so transparent that every vein seemed visible. The woman she remembered had gray hair, her face had been lined by time and weather; but she had been strong and vital and full of life, as she watched over two growing children—who had once been Moon herself and Sparks, her orphaned cousin—while Moon's mother went out with the fishing fleet. . . . *It had only been eight years.*

But no. It had been eight years for her; but she had been offworld, and lost five more years in the lives of everyone she loved to the effects of time-dilation during her transit. For Gran it had been almost fourteen years since Moon had left the islands, following Sparks into the unknown.

Joy filled her grandmother's face now, as she saw her granddaughter again, as her great-grandchildren ran to hug and kiss her. "Moon—" She raised her arms, struggling up from the cushioned bench. But as she rose her expression suddenly changed, and she bowed her head. "I mean, Lady—"

"Gran," Moon said again, finding her voice, moving forward quickly to take her grandmother's arms and straighten her trembling body upright again. "Oh, Gran. . . ." Moon held her tightly, feeling the fragility of bird bones, not the remembered solidity of her grandmother's body; the proof of what her eyes had shown her. "It's me. You don't have to bow to me." Suddenly she felt seventeen again, no older than she had been on the day she left home . . . feeling twelve again, or five. . . .

Gran's arms took hold of her with a firm strength that the old woman's body belied, and held her at arm's length. "You are the chosen one of the Lady, you speak for Her," she said, meeting Moon's gaze with eyes that had lost none of the clear intentness that Moon remembered. "And I raised you myself, child. I am proud to have been so honored. You will certainly give me the honor of allowing me to show you proper respect."

Moon nodded silently, still caught in the void of time and distance that had separated them for so long. "I'm so glad to see you," she whispered, feeling the room slide back into focus, hearing the squeals and chatter of her children. She hushed them absently, ineffectively.

Gran hugged them close again, beaming but unsteady under their eager assault. "What a wonderful surprise you and Sparks have given me, to warm my old age, to ease the Change for an old woman."

"Gran, you aren't old," Moon said; hearing the words ring false, wishing she had said nothing, as she guided her grandmother back to the settee. "Are you hungry? How long have you been here? Have they been taking care of you—?" Hurrying on, stumbling through the awkward moment of her grandmother's painful smile.

"Yes, yes," Gran said. "A good Summer woman, a sibyl—"

"Clavally—"

"Yes, she was very kind, bringing the children in. And the—what do you call them, the hands—?"

"The servants," Moon said, glancing down.

Gran's eyebrows arched. "Yes, well, they were very thoughtful, for Winters. Are they all Winters here? Why are you here, surrounded by these people, instead of our own?"

"Winters are just like Summers, Gran," she answered, feeling the prick of impatience. "They're just as human as we are. They're sweet and sour together, just like islanders. They're even sibyls—"

"So Clavally said to me," Gran said, shaking her head. "Her own pledged is a Winter sibyl, she said! I'll believe that when I see it." She folded her knob-knuckled hands in her lap, worrying the folds of her heavy sweater.

"Yes, Gran." Moon smiled again, in surrender, watching her children climb onto her grandmother's lap, giggling and shoving, struggling for position. Seeing herself and Sparks there . . . feeling the memory start an ache inside her. "Gran . . . how is Mama? Where is she? Why didn't she come here with you?" She forced the question out, afraid of the answer, as she had been afraid of it for the past eight years. She had come to hope that her family believed she was dead, and Sparks too; so that they would never know the real cost of this new life, this place of honor she had achieved. But in her darkest nights, she had been sure that somehow her mother did know.

"Moon," Gran murmured, looking up from the two small, contented faces pressed against her, "I don't know how to say this, but badly—"

"She knows, doesn't she?" Moon said, unable to stop the words. "She knows everything, and that's why she wouldn't come here, even to see my children—" Her children looked up at her in surprise, at the sudden change in her voice.

"Moon," Gran interrupted, her eyes filling with a sudden pain that aged them to match her face, "your mother is dead."

"What?" Moon said. She felt her knees give. "What? No. How? When—" She sank down onto the Empire-replica recliner that pressed the back of her knees as she reached out for support.

"An accident, a fall . . . about three years ago. She slipped on the quay while they were unloading the catch, and struck her head on the stones. We thought she was all right, but then at dinner in the hall she grew sleepy. . . . They knew it was a bad sign, and they tried to keep her awake. But they couldn't keep her from going to sleep. And she never woke up." Gran's eyes grew moist with grief, and she held the children closer; they gazed up at her with wide eyes, half-comprehending. "And so the Sea Mother has taken both my children back to Her breast. . . ."

"A concussion?" Moon said, the harshness of her voice startling even her. Now three sets of eyes were staring at her without comprehension. "All she had was a concussion. She could have been saved—"

"It was the Lady's will." Gran shook her head.

"It wasn't!" Her own voice rose, as grief and frustration triggered her anger. "If we had the technology of the offworlders for ourselves, neither of your children would have had to die. Sparks's mother didn't have to die in childbirth—"

"Stop it, Moon!" Gran's frown deepened the lines of her face. "What are you saying?" Her own voice quavered. She shook her head. "So, it is true. . . ." Her face filled with a different kind of grief. "You no longer follow Her will. But you are the Summer Queen, Moon—the chosen of the Goddess. It isn't too late for you to hear Her voice again—"

"You don't understand." Moon shook her head; her hands hardened into fists in the lap of her robes. "Who told you that, Gran? Who brought you here? How did you make the journey here from Neith, if my mother didn't—"

"I brought her to the palace," a voice said calmly, behind Moon's back.

Moon turned, pushing to her feet as she found Capella Goodventure framed in the scallop-form doorway like a portrait. Her graying braids circled her head like a crown, her face was drawn up in a witch's knot of spite and satisfaction.

"I sent my people out into the islands to find some of your clan who might still be able to reach you, and remind you of your proper duty as the Summer Queen."

"They have been very good to me, Moon," Gran said, with gentle firmness, "bringing me here, all this way, to be with you. You should think about her words."

Moon pressed her lips together. "That must have put you to a great deal of effort," she said to Capella Goodventure. "I'm sure the Lady will grant you your just reward." Her gaze was as cold as the sea.

Capella Goodventure's frown deepened. "Perhaps you have already been shown the reward for your heresy committed in the Lady's name."

Moon stiffened. "What do you mean?"

Capella Goodventure bent her head. "Your mother's accident. Perhaps it was a judgment."

Moon felt herself go dizzy as the blood fell away from her face. "My mother's death was not my fault!" Even her grandmother pushed to her feet, leaving the children tumbled wide-eyed on the settee.

"I didn't say that." Capella Goodventure lifted a hand, in protest, in warning. "I only meant to suggest—"

"That it was my fault! Who are you to push yourself into my life, where you're not wanted? Get out! Leave me alone!" Moon's hand found a smooth iceform sculpture on the table beside her; her hand closed over it, and she hurled it at the doorway. It shattered, sending bits of crystal flying. The children shrieked in surprise and fright. Moon turned back, seeing that they were all right, before she looked again at the doorway.

Capella Goodventure was gone. Standing in the hall at the top of the stairs, a Winter servant stood smirking at the Summer woman's abrupt departure. "You get away from there!" Moon shouted, her voice breaking. He turned, his smirk falling away. "Yes, your majesty." He scuttled out of her sight.

She stood staring after him. *Your majesty* . . . He had not been seeing her, but the image of a ghost she wore in her face, felt in her anger— Sometimes they still called her that, the Winter staff, cringing away when she snapped at them, as if she were not the Summer Queen but the Snow Queen, and her anger was as deadly as frost.

But Arienrhod was dead . . . like Lelark Dawntreader, the sandy-haired, sea-smelling woman who had rocked a sleepy child in her arms beside the fire, so long ago. They were both dead. And she was the Summer Queen.

She shook her head, pressed nerveless fingers against her mouth, as she became aware of Ariele and Tammis clinging to her, their faces buried in the homespun cloth of her robes—their voices crying at her like the voices of seabirds that *it was all right*. Comforting her, needing her comfort. She let her hands fall to their slender shoulders, felt the tension begin to loosen in their small bodies and her own, as she gently rubbed their backs. "It's all right, treasures," she murmured, hearing her voice falter as she spoke the words. "Why don't you take Gran down to dinner. She's come such a long way. . . ."

"You come too!" "I don't want to go without you—" The children clung to her hands more tightly than before, their eyes still filled with need, until she nodded. "Yes, all right . . . we'll all go." She looked back at her grandmother; away again from the look in her eyes, her outstretched hand. Seeing her grandmother's sympathy, sorrow, apology, concern, she felt her own tears rise. If she let herself take that hand she would become a child again too; and she could not afford to do that. She turned away, keeping her eyes downcast, watching her footsteps lead her one at a time out of the room and down the hallway, down the echoing stairs.

Sparks Dawntreader Summer—cousin, husband, consort of the Summer Queen—stepped silently out into the night-lit familiarity of Olivine Alley. It had been called "Blue Alley" when Winter ruled, and the blue-uniformed offworlder Police had made its ancient buildings their headquarters. He had avoided this place then; now, he almost made it his home. He began his nightly walk toward the alley's mouth, to meet the long steep spiral of the Street, which would carry him inevitably to the palace no matter how slow he made his steps.

After eight years he still hated the palace, and so he spent as much time as possible outside it. But always he returned there at the end of each day, because Moon was waiting for him and he loved her, as he had always loved her, and always would. She was as much a part of him as his music, as much a part of him as his soul—the things Arienrhod had stolen from him, and Moon had given back to him. Life went on, whether he deserved it or not. And his children, living proof of their love, waited for him there, among the relics and the memories.

"Hallo, Sparks!"

Sparks stopped, glancing toward the brightly lit doorway and the figure limned by its glow.

"We're celebrating! Come, be my guest. I owe you, for your support with the College—"

He recognized the voice now; his eyes filled in the old/young features of Kirard Set Wayaways. Kirard Set stood in the entrance to a tavern called the Old Days, formerly one of the most flamboyant and expensive gaming hells on the Street. Now its equipment lay cold and silent, while the surviving nobility of the Snow Queen's reign sat among its ghosts, drinking to their memories and tossing bone dice—almost the only pleasures left to them now, aside from conspicuous consumption and sex.

"What are you celebrating?" he asked, curious but wary, as he stepped into the light. The old Queen's favorites knew him too well, for better or worse. He became aware of the rich smell of fried meal-cakes, heard other voices calling his name. Talk and laughter spilled past him into the street; he heard someone plucking a mindle with virtuoso skill, and drumming, whistling, voices singing.

He touched the pouch at his belt. He always carried his flute with him; telling himself that he never knew when he would find time to practice or a chance to play. . . . But he wore it more as a talisman now, the way a sibyl wore a trefoil; because it had come to symbolize a higher order which music had first revealed to him—a greater truth which music never betrayed. His work with the Sibyl College had shown him the beauty of mathematics and physics; how they lay at the secret heart of everything, including music itself. Every day new facets of that universal order revealed themselves to him. He had begun to study mathematics in every free moment, experiencing a purity of pleasure he had never found in anything before, except his playing. . . .

The music pulled at him, suddenly irresistible. He stepped into the tavern's brightly lit interior, and Kirard Set pressed a crystal goblet of wine into his hand. "We're celebrating the choice of Wayaways land for the site of the new foundry," Kirard Set said, and he shook his head, smiling. "She's really incredible, you know, the Queen—" He put an arm around Sparks's shoulders. Sparks resisted the urge to shrug it off. "But of course *you* know that, better than anyone. . . . How did she do it, anyway? How did she— But never mind, of course your lips are sealed with a kiss." Kirard Set made a moue with his lips, and nudged Sparks's shoulder.

Sparks took a long drink of the wine, imported offworlder wine, leftover stock. The nobles had hoarded it the way they had hoarded technology, before the offworlders' departure. At least the Hegemony had not been able to spoil its wine the way it had killed its abandoned hardware. Sparks sat down at a table, following Kirard Set's lead without comment. What had once been a hologramic gaming array was covered now by a slab of wood, and a tapestry cloth that had originally draped the window of some offworlder official's exclusive townhouse.

Sparks studied Kirard Set's smiling face, and wondered what actually went on in his mind. Not much, he supposed. He had always found Kirard Set's behavior either unpleasant or unfathomable. But one thing was obvious: Kirard Set, and a number of the other former nobles, actually believed the Summer Queen was the same flesh and blood woman who had ruled Winter; that somehow Arienrhod had cheated the Summers, the Hegemony, and Death itself to go on ruling her world, pursuing the goal she had sworn to achieve: independence from offworlder control.

Sparks glanced away again, with a sigh. Across the room he noticed Danaquil Lu Wayaways with his wife and child, standing apart, looking uncomfortable. Merovy was asleep, held in her father's arms. Sparks felt a twinge of guilt, remembering his own family waiting for him at the palace. He had stayed at the College far too long, later even than usual, caught up in his studies. His own children would be asleep, by now. He shook his head, putting down the wine-filled goblet. "I can't stay." He began to get up.

"Sparks!" A woman's voice called his name, a hand caught his arm as he rose. "Darling, you can't leave us already. We never see enough of you anymore."

Shelachie Fairisle tweaked the laces of his shirt, half pulling it open. He took hold of her jewel-decorated hand and plucked it from his shirtfront like an insect.

She twitched her hand free from his grasp. "Aren't we hard-to-get," she said, matching his frown. He noticed the lines in her face that deepened with her frown.

"You know I don't do that anymore," he said, trying to keep his voice neutral, reminding himself that in the New Tiamat, Shelachie Fairisle controlled ore reserves that would be needed soon for another foundry. He could not afford to insult her casually.

"Yes, sweeting, but I keep hoping. We all used to have so much fun, with *her*. . . . I don't understand—that's one thing I don't understand. Why she doesn't share you with us anymore?" She turned to glance at Kirard Set, spreading her fingers in a shrug. "Do you have a clue, Kiri?" He shook his head, his mouth puckering with suppressed laughter. "She just isn't the same woman, since the Change." She giggled at her own wine-sodden whimsy, at the titillation of not knowing where the truth lay beneath the shimmering water of her fantasies. "Is she, darling?"

"You said it yourself," Sparks snapped, losing patience. "She isn't the same woman. She's my pledged—my wife. And I was on my way home to my wife and my children." He turned away from her, starting for the door.

"*Whose* children, precious—?" The words stabbed him from behind.

He swung back, saw Clavally and Danaquil Lu turn and stare, across the room; saw Kirard Set rise from the table, catching hold of Shelachie with a muttered, "Not *now*, for gods' sakes—"

"Well, whose are they, anyway?" she called out, weaving where she stood, absurdly dressed in the clothes of another world and age. "Where did she get them? They don't look like you! And why didn't she give them special names, ritual names, if she got them during Mask Night? Even the Summers say—"

He didn't stay to hear what even his own people said. *His own people* . . . He reached inside his shirt as he strode on up the nearly empty Street, feeling for the Hegemonic medal he wore, a gift to his mother from the stranger who had been her chosen on the Festival night when he was merrybegotten. . . . His father was an offworlder, and he had never felt at home in Summer, among its superstitious, tech-hating people. When Moon had forsaken her pledge to him to become a sibyl, he had run away to Carbuncle. He had believed that among the Winters and offworlders he would find out where he truly belonged. He had found Arienrhod. . . .

But Moon was his again, in spite of everything, because of it; and his children were proof of it. . . . *Why did she give them those names? They should have had special names, Festival names—* His own mother and Moon's had come to the previous Festival, when the ships of the Hegemonic Assembly paid one of their periodic visits to this world and Carbuncle became a place where all boundaries broke down and everyone lived their fantasies for a night. Children born of the Festival nights were counted lucky, blessed; given special, symbolic names to mark their unique status. He and Moon both bore the names that marked them as merrybegots; so did Fate Ravenglass.

As a grown man he sometimes wished that he could shed the burden of his ritual name, sometimes felt self-conscious speaking it. Yet he had never changed it. He knew that he never would, because it was still the symbol of all he was, his heritage.

It had been Moon's privilege as mother to name their children. But she had not given their Festival-night twins ritual names; instead she had given them names he was not sure any Tiamatan ever used. He had never asked her why—had been afraid to, he admitted angrily, because he knew that during the Festival she had been with another man—an offworlder, a Kharemoughi police inspector, the man who had helped her track him down.

Ariele looked like her mother; so much like Moon that seeing her made him ache sometimes with memories of his childhood, of running on golden beaches with Moon, racing the birds, laughing and alive. But Tammis . . . The boy looked like her too, but he was darker than any Tiamatan child should be . . . dark like a Kharemoughi. Sparks touched the medal he wore again. His own father had been half Kharemoughi—his own skin was dark, by Tiamatan standards. He didn't know what the other man had looked like; he had not seen him, before he went offworld with the rest. But there was nothing he could see of himself in his son's face, no matter how much Moon insisted on the resemblance. He tried not to think about it, tried never to let his doubt show. . . . He loved his children. He loved his wife. He knew they loved him. Together he and Moon were building a new life, a future for themselves, as well as for their world.

So then why did he feel every day that it was harder to climb this hill?

Moon stood alone in the chamber at the top of the palace, at the top of the city—as close to reaching the stars as anyone on this world would come in her lifetime. It was late at night; she had lost track of the time, letting herself drift, aching for sleep but without the strength to release the day and go to her bed.

She gazed out through the dome, looking at the sea. Its surface was calm tonight, a dark mirror for the star-filled sky. Its face turned back her gaze, turned back all attempts to penetrate its depths, or reveal the secrets hidden there. Only she knew the truth: that the hidden heart of the sibyl net lay here, in the sea below her; that the tendrils of its secret mind reached out from here to countless worlds across the galaxy. Only she knew. And she could never tell anyone. . . .

Sudden motion disturbed the balance of sea and sky: she saw mers, a whole colony of them, celebrating the perfect night, as if her thoughts had caused them to materialize. It was their safety the sibyl net had charged her with ensuring; their safety was tied, in ways that she did not fully understand, to the well-being of her own people, and to the sibyl mind itself. She watched them moving with joyful abandon between two worlds, inside a net of stars; their grace and beauty astonished her, as they always did, until for that moment she remembered no regret.

Tiamatan tradition called the mers the Sea's Children, and held their lives sacred; Tiamatans had lived in peaceful coexistence with the mers for centuries, before the Hegemony had found this world. There were countless stories of mers saving sailors fallen overboard, or guiding ships through the treacherous passages among island reefs; they had saved her own life, once.

But the offworlders had come, had been coming for a millennium or more, seeking the water of life. And the sibyl mind had suffered with the death of the mers, until after centuries of suffering it had reached out to her alone, out of all the sibyls in the net—chosen her to stop the slaughter, to save the mers and itself, to change the future for her own people, and perhaps for countless others. It had forced her to obey . . . forced her to become Queen. And then it had left her to struggle on alone, driven by a compulsion that never let her rest; to hope that she was doing its will as it had intended.

She looked down, focusing on the room around her as the night's image suddenly lost all its beauty. All around her she saw the stormwrack of her life: the projects indefinitely postponed or forever abandoned that she had tried to find time to do simply for herself, out of love and not duty. There were piles of books from Arienrhod's library, most of them in languages she did not know, but filled with three-dimensional visions of life on other worlds that she had longed to pore over; there were pieces of toys, fashioned from wood by her own hands but still unassembled; the unraveling body of a half-knitted sweater; clothes for the children with half the smocking done, that she had never finished before they had outgrown them. . . . And there were the fragments of Arienrhod's past, so much like her own past, of which she possessed no mementos at all. Sometimes she began to imagine that those aged, softly fading things were actually her own; or that they were her legacy. . . .

She shut her eyes. The darkness filled immediately with memories of the day, reminding her that she had been standing here alone with her grief for far too long. She had not even been down to kiss her children good night. She had been unable to face her grandmother's gaze any longer, one more word, one more look or murmur of doubt. And still Sparks had not returned, tonight of all nights, to his disappointed son and daughter; to her, when she needed so much to talk to him.

Her hands caressed her stomach, as she thought of her children and remembered the feel of life within her; the joy, the wonder, the doubt. Unexpected motherhood had given her a new perspective on the future, given her the strength to hold fast to her belief against the onslaught of the Goodventures' furious insistence that she was violating the Lady's will . . . against her own doubts, a seventeen-year-old girl trying to imagine how she would rebuild a world, or even a relationship.

She had needed desperately to believe that it was all worthwhile. Feeling the life within her had made her believe there would be a future worth struggling for. She had needed so badly to make Sparks believe it too . . . and yet all the while, she had wondered secretly whether the child she carried was actually another man's.

She rose restlessly from the couch, rubbing her face, as the wraith of a dark-eyed stranger whispered through her mind . . . as a strange sensation began in the pit of her stomach, reminding her of morning sickness. She felt as if something were falling away inside her, turning her thoughts around, drawing her down into another reality— *The Transfer*, she thought; suddenly recognizing the sensation. But no one had spoken, to ask her a question. She caught the sibyl trefoil, feeling its spines prick her fingers; felt her hand freeze in midmotion as the immobility overcame her. *She had been called.* The Transfer enveloped her like a black wind, sweeping her away.

Blinking, she saw brightness again, through a stranger's eyes—*another sibyl, on another world, who saw now through her eyes, gazing out at a sky filled with alien stars.* . . . Her new eyes focused on the questioner who waited for her; she felt her borrowed body start with sudden disbelief at the sight of a face she had not seen for eight years, except in her dreams.

BZ Gundhalinu stood before her like a vision out of the past, his face weary and desperate, his eyes haunted—as she had first seen him so long ago, in the white wilderness of Winter. . . . The man whose need had become her salvation; who had become her sea anchor, her guide . . . her unexpected lover, for one night outside of time. Who had gone away with the rest of the offworlders at the Final Departure, without betraying her secrets. Leaving her to the future he had helped her win, to the man he had helped her win back; leaving her . . .

"Moon?" he murmured, his hand reaching out. "Is it really you?" His fingers brushed her cheek; his dark eyes searched her own wonderingly, as if he were witnessing a miracle.

"Yes . . ." she whispered, feeling her captive body straining with the need to touch him, to prove his own reality. "BZ!" She saw him start and smile as she spoke his name. *How did you bring me here? Where are you? What's wrong—* "What do you . . . want of me?" She forced the words out between numb, unresponsive lips: the only words the Transfer would let her speak to the man she had not seen in so long. "Please . . . give me more information?"

He licked cracked, bloody lips, and mumbled something she could not understand. "I'm . . . I'm here. On Number Four. A place called Fire Lake." He ran his fingers through the filthy tangle of his hair. "I need help. Something gets into my head all the time, and . . ." He broke off, wiping his hand across his mouth, shaking his head violently, as if he could shake free the thing that was inside his eyes. "I'm a sibyl, Moon! Someone infected me, the woman who sees me now for you. She wasn't meant to be a sibyl. . . . She's out of her mind." He swallowed visibly. "And I think . . . I think I am too. I'm trapped here, I can't get help from anyone else. Tell me how you control the Transfer! Every time I hear a question—" His voice broke, and she saw naked despair in his eyes.

"A sibyl . . ." Her disbelief became empathy as she remembered her own initiation, how the bioengineered virus had spread through her system like wildfire— how much greater her disorientation and terror would have been if no one had been there to reassure or guide her. "Don't be afraid," she whispered, aching. "I know you . . . I know that—" her borrowed hands twitched impotently at her sides, refusing to obey her, as the memory came to her of words she had spoken before, gazing into those same eyes, "the finest, gentlest, kindest man I ever met . . . must have been meant for this. That you must have been chosen, somehow . . ."

As I was chosen, somehow. She took a deep breath, fighting to clear her vision of the memory of his face, eight years ago; what had filled his eyes as she had spoken those words to him then. Trying not to remember how his arms had pulled her against him, how he had kissed her with desperate, incredulous hunger . . . how often that moment out of the unreachable past still intruded on her inescapable present. Frantic with frustration as her voice went on mindlessly, relentlessly answering only his question, ignoring her burning need to *ask* and not answer. ". . . There are word formulas for the channeling of stimuli, patterns that become a part of your thought processes, in time—" The flow of words interrupted itself, she felt the sibyl mind stop and search for a meaningful analogy, "—like the adhani discipline practiced on Kharemough."

"Really? I practice that—" Hope showed in his eyes, and she began to believe, at last, in the wisdom the sibyl machinery had forced upon her—the calm, insistent rationality of her response.

"Use it, then," her own stranger's/familiar voice murmured, as she searched her memory for things Clavally and Danaquil Lu had taught her. ". . . There is a kind of ritual to the formal sibyl Transfer; it starts with the word *input*. No other questions need to be recognized. Learn to block casual questions by concentrating on the word *stop*."

"Stop?" he echoed, his voice shaky with disbelief. "That's all?"

"It's very simple; it has to be. But there is much more. . . ." Her words flowed like water as she ceased fighting the tide of compulsion. He repeated every phrase with painful intentness, his eyes holding her gaze, barely even blinking, as if he were still afraid that she might disappear.

She went on until her voice was gone, and the wellspring of her knowledge had run dry. ". . . It takes time. Believe in yourself. This is not a tragedy; it could be a blessing. Perhaps it was meant to be. . . ."

His mouth quivered, as if he held back a denial; his gaze fell away, came back to her face again. "Thank you," he whispered. His hand rose into her vision again, to caress her cheek. She felt her borrowed eyes fill with unexpected tears as he caught her hands in his and pressed them to his lips. "You don't know what this means to me. I love you, Moon. I'll never love anyone else. I've hated myself ever since I left Tiamat—" His voice fell apart. He took a deep breath, still holding her. "I can tell you that now . . . because I know I'll never see you again."

She felt the black tide begin to withdraw inside her, drawing her away, calling her back across the fathomless sea of night, back into her own body. His image began to shimmer and fade. *Never see you again . . . never. . . .* She blinked her eyes, feeling hot tears slide out and run down her cheeks. "I need you—" She heard her borrowed voice cry out the words, did not know whether she was the one who had spoken them, or the stranger whose body she had stolen.

"Moon!" he cried, clutching her shoulders, clutching at her spirit as she began to fade. His kiss smothered the last words that came to her lips: *"No further analysis—"* The black tide drowned her, sweeping her away across spacetime, returning her—

I need you. . . . Her arms were free. She reached out blindly as she began to fall . . . felt arms catch her, circle her, hold her, stopping her fall.

"Moon—?"

She opened her eyes, blinking, dazed, hearing a man's voice, a familiar voice, call her name. She opened her eyes, opened her mouth, tried to speak his name, as her vision cleared. . . . "Sparks." She heard the disbelief in her voice as she put a name to the face in front of her: Sea-green eyes gazed back at her; a blaze of flame-colored hair framed a face she had known, and loved, since forever. . . . *Goddess, was it only a dream—?* Still feeling another man's lips on her own. A small, helpless sound escaped her, as her husband drew her close, holding her in his arms.

"I need you, too," he murmured, against her ear, kissing her hair. "I saw Gran, I heard— Moon, I'm so sorry."

She stiffened against him, almost pulling away. But then her arms closed around him, holding him against her, feeling the tautness of his muscles, his young, strong body hard against hers. She found his lips, began to kiss them with a feverish hunger that she had almost forgotten, as an urgency she thought had died inside her swept her away like the black wind.

This time it was her husband who drew back in surprise. She pulled him to her again, sliding her hands up under the linen cloth of his shirt, pressing her body against his, covering his mouth with hers to stop his questions. He sighed, letting her . . . responding more and more eagerly, answering her body with his own. His hands touched her everywhere with a heat neither of them had known in longer than she could remember.

He sank with her onto the thick white furs that covered the floor. She felt the rug as soft as clouds beneath her as he undressed her, as he explored her with his hands, his mouth, as she pulled him down on top of her, flesh against flesh, and felt him enter her. And as they rose and fell together, their pleasure like the tides of the sea, she closed her eyes, remembering a Festival night, safe in his arms at last . . . remembering another night, in the arms of a passionate, gentle stranger. . . .

ONDINEE: Tuo Ne'el

Reede Kullervo sighed, and sighed again; he shifted from foot to foot, gazing out through the high narrow window slit. The view did not inspire him. From this room near the pinnacle of the Humbaba stronghold, he could see for dozens of kilometers across low, rolling hills and tight valleys, all of them covered by impenetrable thorn forest. Spearbush and hell's needle and firethorn were all that he could see, all of it well-named, and all of it in tones of ash gray shading to brown, looking dead, looking as if it had always been dead. The locals called this piece of real estate Tuo Ne'el—the Land of Death.

But the thorn forest was fiercely, volatilely alive. When it burned, it burned like the fires of hell. The leaves and bark of the plants were loaded with petrochemicals; they burned with furious heat and intensity, until there was nothing left but glassy-surfaced ash on vast sweeps of naked hill. He thought of the thorn forest's life cycle as being like his own . . . except that when he eventually burned himself out, no dormant seed of his, waiting patiently for that immolation to set it free, would germinate and carry on his genetic line.

He began to hum a fragment of song whose words were incomprehensible to him, although he knew them all. Its tune sounded alien and disturbing to his ears, the tonal shifts and intervals made him feel vaguely queasy although he knew they were perfectly precise. He did not hum when he was happy. In the distance he could see other strongholds—fortress towers, sleek needles of self-contained strength rising like defiant fingers through the impenetrable barrier of the forests. He could name the drug and vice bosses who controlled each of them, who ruled the lives of communities of workers, researchers, and henchmen as if they were petty feudal lords. The shielded towers were easily reached only by air. In their business, the thorn forest made for good neighbors. It also kept locals who weren't in their pay out of their hair.

Reede turned away from the twenty-centimeter-thick pane of virtually impenetrable ceramic, moving back and forth restlessly, running his hands through his hair, pushing them into the deep pockets of his lab clothing. He had not bothered to change, because Humbaba had sent word that he was to come up immediately . . . only to keep him pacing out here like some lackey. He hated waiting, hated to stop moving any time when he didn't have to, any time when there was nothing to occupy his mind. . . . He sat down, stood up, his hands tightening into fists; began to pace again, pulling at his ear. "Shit—" he said, and said it again.

The sweet chiming voice of a hundred silver bells whispered his name, behind him. He turned, with the swiftness of a startled animal, as someone's hand circled his arm.

"Mundilfoere—" He stopped himself, as abruptly and lightly as if he had no mass, at the sight of her face. She barely came up to his chin, and her face was veiled; the cloth was a filmy gauze, intentionally almost transparent, so that her features were clearly visible but still a mystery, sensually shrouded. The cloth of her gown, which covered her from neck to foot, was only slightly more opaque. She was Humbaba's First Wife. She said that she was a jewel merchant's daughter from the lands of the south, purchased on a whim to become one of his countless concubines. But she was more than she seemed—which was why she was now his First Wife, and held more influence over him than any of his advisors. And Humbaba was not the only one who had noticed her uniqueness.

Reede's hands rose, trembling; he felt himself overwhelmed by his need for her, which was at once a terrifying physical hunger for the things that her body knew, and was teaching to him, and something deeper that he had never tried to name, let alone understand. His life seemed to have begun the first night that he spent in her arms, the morning that he had awakened to find himself lying beside her. "Where were you last night? I waited . . . I waited until the second moon rose—"

"I was with my lord Humbaba," she said softly. "He required my presence."

"Again?"

She shrugged, expressionless. She had been Humbaba's favorite since before Reede had known either one of them; and as a rule, Humbaba was easily bored.

"I don't suppose you were simply discussing business," he said sourly.

"Not the entire night, no." Her indigo eyes regarded him with mild censure from behind the silvered gauze.

He made a face. "How do you kiss him without vomiting?"

She did not smile. "All men are handsome in the dark, beloved," she said softly. "Just as all women are beautiful."

"You don't believe that."

"I must."

He turned away from her, taking a deep breath. She waited without speaking until he turned back again. He found that she had drawn aside her veil. To see her face suddenly revealed to him was somehow as erotic as seeing her completely naked. He sucked in a breath, as a hundred different images of her face, of her body and his own together, filled his mind . . . a thousand memories of secret moments, hours, nights together in stolen corners of their hermetically sealed world. How long she had been his lover—or he had been hers, chosen by her—he wasn't even sure. His life was all randomness and chaos, except when he was at work in the labs. Time had no meaning for him except when he was in her arms. He kept his hands rigidly open at his sides, afraid that his need would betray them both.

She moved away, as if she sensed his control slipping. "He is an old man, *tisshah'el*," she murmured, barely audible. "Even he says so, so it must be true. He has never made me weep tears of joy. . . . Only you can do that."

"*Tisshah'el*," he murmured. *Beloved stranger.* A word like a sigh, full of so much longing, and so much grief: the word her people used for someone caught in adultery, a crime they sometimes punished with death by flaying, or castration. Sometimes he wished she wouldn't use it, even though she appreciated its poignant irony more than he did.

"What are you doing here?" she asked him, finally.

"Humbaba wanted to see me," he answered, noncommittal.

"Why?"

He shook his head. "I don't know. I've been rotting out here for half an hour—" He broke off. "Why are you here?"

"He asked to see me also."

"Why?" he said, tensing, suddenly feeling afraid. "Gods—do you think he knows?"

"I don't know." There was no concern on her face. There never was. Her thoughts were like the depths of a pool; he was never allowed to see below their surface. Sometimes he wanted to shake her, to force some reaction out of her. Sometimes he was certain her perfect calm was only an act. Sometimes he thought it was just the resigned fatalism her culture bred into its women. . . . And then he wondered if it was his potential violence that attracted her to him; if all she wanted from him was just another suicidal asshole, like the men she had always known. And then he would tell himself fiercely that he was more than that, and so was she—

The doors to the inner chamber opened, with a soft sucking sound like a kiss. He turned, feeling her turn with him; she covered her face quickly with her veil. Stepping back from each other until there was a neutral distance between them, they walked together through the doorway and into Humbaba's presence.

Reede's vision recoiled, as it always did, as his eyes found Humbaba's face—still refusing to believe, after all these years, that what he saw was real. Humbaba came from somewhere on Tsieh-pun, and he'd heard the local customs had merged into and gone beyond the usual underworld tattooing. They had traditionally scarred their faces, the uglier the better, because it intimidated their enemies and their underlings. Cosmetic surgery had given them stomach-turning possibilities far beyond the original, primitive scarring. Ugliness meant strength, power. . . . If that was true, Reede had often thought that Humbaba should have been the most powerful man in the galaxy, because he had to be the ugliest. He looked like he was wearing his intestines on his face.

Reede swallowed his disgust, along with his sudden, unexpected unease, and pressed the heel of his hand to his forehead in a salute. "Sab Emo." Beside him, Mundilfoere made the same obeisance.

Humbaba turned away from them, toward his aquarium, peering in at the fish that moved like glinting shadows through its green-lit depths. Reede could see Humbaba's face reflected in the glass, huge and grotesque, with their own two figures tiny and distorted in the background. Behind the transparent wall, the fish peered back at them curiously; their faces were a wad of distorted flesh that matched their master's. They came from Tsieh-pun too, where for some segment of humanity ugliness had even become beauty. Reede kept the grimace off his face, telling himself that it made as much sense as anything else humans did. And from a bioengineering standpoint, maybe it was even true.

The ever-lengthening moment of Humbaba's silence stretched Reede's nerves like time on the rack. At last Humbaba turned away from the green, peaceful world of the hideous fish and faced them again. "They have given me so much pleasure . . ." he murmured. His voice was perfectly normal, a deep, pleasant baritone; as was the total unselfconsciousness of his manner—another incongruity he used to good effect. "As you have, my jewel." He nodded to Mundilfoere, and she bowed her head in acknowledgment, her bells singing softly.

"And your work has brought pleasure to millions, Reede." His voice took on an ironic amusement. He reached out, his thick, blunt fingers hovering over a long side-table covered with what Reede realized suddenly was a banquet of drugs—all of his creations. Humbaba selected something from the display, popped it into his mouth and chewed it like a sweetmeat. "And put millions into my accounts, which pleases me even more. Our mutual working agreement has served us both well."

Reede said nothing, shifting uncomfortably, sure that this round of empty compliments was not the reason for their being here. He could tell nothing from Humbaba's expression, which was always totally inhuman.

Humbaba turned back to them abruptly. "But something has come to my attention that does not bring me pleasure. In fact, it causes me more pain than anything has since I lost my beloved mother." His small, black eyes seemed to flicker, as if he was blinking rapidly inside the mottled piles of flesh. "How long have you been lovers?"

Reede froze, left groping for words by the bluntness of the unexpected question. "We aren't—"

"Since before I brought him to you, my lord," Mundilfoere said quietly. "Since the day I first saw him." Reede shot a disbelieving look at her as Humbaba moved slowly forward, his massive body dwarfing her.

Humbaba reached out, taking hold of the veil that covered her face, his fist tightening, as if he were about to rip it off. But he lifted it almost tenderly, as he stood staring down at her. "Are you saying you seduced him, in order to ensure his loyalty to me—?"

Reede watched her, unable to take his eyes off her; suddenly needing to know her answer more than he needed to go on living.

She glanced at him; her eyes lingered on his face, before her gaze flickered downward. "No, my lord. That was not why."

Humbaba's fist tightened, muscles bunched in his arm. "Damn you," he said. "Why won't you ever lie to me? I even gave you the lie myself—"

She glanced away, up at him again. "I have never lied to you, my lord. You know that. That is why I have been your First Wife for so long."

He snorted, and wattles of flesh quivered. "I'd like to know what else you never bothered to mention to me, though, my jewel," he said sourly, his hand leaving the veil aside, to close over her jaw until she winced. "I trusted you, in ways I never trusted any other woman . . . and perhaps more than I ever trusted any man—"

Reede's hands tightened impotently; his chest ached from the breath he was holding. "So," Humbaba murmured, "you like pretty young boys the best, after all—? How many other have there been?"

"None, my lord," she answered, with difficulty. "Only him. Only you—"

He snorted again, with derision, letting her go. "You know the penalty for adultery among your people, Mundilfoere. I could have the skin peeled off your face until you looked like me." He shot a glance at Reede. "I could cut off your prick and make you eat it, Kullervo." Reede grimaced. "I always wondered why you had no interest in sex," Humbaba muttered. "I offered you women, all you wanted, or men, or boys—you remember?" Reede nodded numbly. "But you always said no. I thought maybe you were getting it in town. But you were getting it right here. I gave you everything. But you had to take the one thing you were not offered." His heavy fist rose, stopped just short of Reede's face. Reede flinched involuntarily. "Why?"

"Because when I met her she made me forget everything else." Answering only with the truth, too, Reede found the voice to speak; but the voice hardly sounded his own. He felt like a man in a bad dream, trying to wake up. *How did you find out?* He almost asked it, couldn't force himself to. Knowing that the details didn't matter. Knowing it should have happened years ago. Nobody could keep anything a secret in a place like this; it was like living in orbit. It was only his frequent trips around the planet and offworld, and Humbaba's, that had kept them safe this long. He had always let himself believe that even if they were discovered Humbaba would look the other way, because he was indispensable, and Humbaba knew it—

"Yes," Humbaba murmured, "I know you, Reede . . . I know that look. You think you're indispensable. But losing your genitalia won't affect your brains." He looked back and forth between their silent, stricken faces. Slowly he reached into the folds of his long, sleeveless robe, and brought out a heavy blade, with serrations the size of teeth and a tip curved like a claw. "Tell me," he said, "how much do you really love each other? Would you give away your manhood to save your lover's face, Kullervo? . . . Would you give up your beauty, my jewel, to spare him that indignity?" He gestured, the blade echoing his invitation with its smile of steel.

"Yes."

"Yes—" Reede broke off, as he realized that Mundilfoere had answered the same way, at the same moment. He stepped forward, coming between her and Humbaba. He unfastened his belt and dropped his pants. "Go ahead," he said, meeting Humbaba's unreadable gaze above the gleaming knifeblade. "Cut it off."

Humbaba stared at Reede a moment longer. Then suddenly his face began to quake, a landslide of flesh. Deep laughter poured out of the lipless opening that was his mouth. His Head of Research stood glaring back at him with his pants down around his ankles. Humbaba shook his head. "You probably know a way to make it grow back, you crazy bastard." As slowly as he had brought the knife out, he put it away again. "Pull your pants up." He looked at Mundilfoere and shook his head again, his wattles jiggling. "My jewel . . ." he said, almost sadly. He touched her face, a gentle contact this time. "It would have been painful to have ruined that face . . . although in your way you would still have been as beautiful to me, and given me as much pleasure. . . ." He sighed. "But you are growing old, anyway, and that is a form of damage I do not care for." He took her arm abruptly, and pushed her at Reede. "Here. I give her to you, Reede. Have her for a wife. See if she is still as irresistible when the fruit is no longer forbidden."

Reede took hold of her, steadying her against the abrupt motion and his own surprise.

"My lord . . ." Mundilfoere whispered, looking from man to man with stunned eyes. "Is this a joke?"

Humbaba shrugged irritably. "My sense of humor doesn't extend that far," he said, and Reede sensed from his voice what he couldn't tell from his face—that he frowned. "I don't want you anymore. I'm finished with you. You belong to my man Kullervo now, until he doesn't want you anymore." He waved a hand at them, dismissing them.

Mundilfoere fluttered her hands, jingling. Reede put his arm around her, started to lead her to the door; he saw that the expression on her face looked more like distress than joy or relief. "Mundilfoere . . . ?" he murmured. She looked up at him, seeing the unspoken question in his eyes. She reached up, touching his cheek lightly, her face transforming suddenly, giving him his answer. He looked back at Humbaba. "Thank you," he said, for the second time in his life that he could remember.

Humbaba made an unreadable gesture. Reede knew as well as Humbaba did that he could do his work with his cock cut off. But he'd do it better if he was a happy man. Humbaba wasn't an original thinker. He survived because he had a gut instinct for how to keep his people loyal. "That new inhalant you've been developing. I expect to be enjoying it soon," Humbaba said to his retreating back.

"Yes, sab." Reede smiled to himself as the doors slid aside, permitting him to leave with Mundilfoere held close against him, and shut again behind him.

In the outer room he tried to stop, but Mundilfoere kept him moving with a subtle motion of her body. He obeyed her, suddenly understanding her need to put more distance between them and what had almost happened. They went on through the seemingly endless corridor beyond the antechamber. The air was incongruously thick with the scent of flowers, the light was green and dappled, as they entered the lush foliage of a hydroponics area.

He stopped Mundilfoere at last, under the spreading shelter of a fruit tree, and put his arms around her; kissed her with all the depth of need and ravenous hunger of a freed prisoner. He had never kissed her like this, openly, freely, as if there were nothing to fear, nothing to hide.

But her own hands rose, separating her from him with gentle, insistent pressure until he let her go, although his hands still clung to her. "We must be discreet—"

"Why—?" he said.

"Until we have considered the consequences."

He saw the urgency in her eyes, and remembered what she was trying to make him remember. He nodded, barely. "Come to my room with me, then."

"Yes," she murmured, pressing her face against him, her body momentarily fusing to his own. He felt her heartbeat inside his chest like the wildly beating wings of a bird. "I need to weep for joy. . . ."

In his room, in his bed, he made love to her as if the act were a sacrament; though he had no real idea what a sacrament was. He knew only that he would worship her if he could, that her body was the altar of her soul, and that pleasure was the only form of prayer he knew. . . .

Afterwards, lying beside her, the restless motion of his existence stilled at last, he asked, "Why did you seduce me when we met, if it wasn't to make me want to work for Humbaba?"

She looked over at him languorously, her eyes half-closed. He smelled the scent of her, rich with the strange herbs and oils she used on her hair and skin. "To bring you peace," she said, running her fingers across the sweat-gleaming surface of his chest.

He lifted his head, with a single grunt that might have been laughter or disbelief; let it fall back again. "Damn you . . ." he muttered. His hand closed over hers, covering it until it disappeared inside his own. And yet the gesture was that of a child clinging to its mother. "No wonder you kept Humbaba besotted all those years. Even I never know what you really mean. . . . I don't know what anything means, sometimes." He pushed up onto his elbows, looking back at her, touching the silver-metal pendant that lay between her breasts, the solii jewel at its center like a nacreous eye looking up at him. His hand rose to couch the matching pendant that he wore, reassuring himself that it was still there. "Mundilfoere . . . tell me the way we met."

"Again?" She looked up at him, her blue-violet eyes filled with a curious emotion. For a moment he thought that she would refuse. But she only said, as if she were reciting a Story of the Saints, "There are many hidden hands that play the Great Game . . . and the Game controls them all. You were playing the games in the station arcade as I passed, on my way to somewhere else. I looked in because I heard the shouting of the crowd that was watching you play, watching you win and win. I went inside, because I was curious; I watched you too, and I saw you do things by instinct that most players could not even dream of doing. I saw that you had a rare gift, and that it was being wasted in that place. And then you looked up at me, and I saw your face . . . and you saw mine."

"And time stopped," he whispered, finishing it for her. "And you said, 'Come with me,' and I did. . . ." He shut his eyes, trying to imagine the electric feel of winning; the moment when he had looked up, and seen her standing there, waiting for him to look up and see her. Fragments of memory flashed inside his eyes, mirror-shards, puzzle pieces, whirling like leaves in a wind, a storm of randomness. He opened his eyes again, with a grunt of terror, to the serenity and reality of her face, the unreadable depths of her eyes. "Why can't I remember? I can't remember—"

"It doesn't matter," she said softly, and reached up to stroke his hair, smoothing it back from his face, soothing him with the slow, repetitive motion; gentling him. "I love you. I will always love you, more than life itself."

He lay down again, letting the question go, content to let her massage his thoughts into oblivion, where they belonged. He rested his head against her shoulder as she took one of the spice-scented smokesticks from the ebony box on the bedside table and lit it. He breathed in the drifting smoke as she inhaled, for once enjoying the exquisite sharpness of all his senses, the intoxicating awareness of simply being alive. "Was I a virgin when you met me?"

She did not laugh, but turned her head to look at him. "I don't think so. Not physically."

"I was very young."

"Yes," she said, stroking his forehead gently.

"But I feel so old. . . ." He closed his eyes, and fragments of image swarmed through his memory again, bits of glass in a shaken kaleidoscope, a random geometry of light.

"I know," she murmured.

"Mundilfoere, where did I come from—?"

"It doesn't matter," she repeated. She kissed him tenderly on the cheek. "You are here, now."

"Yes. . . ." He opened his eyes again to look at her, and the echoes of a music from no known place or time, that lived inside his memory like a lie, began to fade. He sighed, pressing her hand against his cheek, holding it there. Her skin was soft and cool against his own, like the touch of a . . . of a . . . He let go of the image that would not form, and released her, letting the tension flow out of him, letting his gaze wander. He became aware of the strains of a Kharemoughi artsong still playing in the room, filling the bluegray space, carrying his mind out and into the bluegray heights of the sky beyond the slitted window, out where there were never any questions.

She inhaled smoke, let it out again in a sigh. After a time she said, "Sab Emo has been more than kind to us, in his own way, all these years." She handed him the drugged incense and he inhaled deeply.

"Yes," he murmured, shaking off the past, still not fully believing in the present.

"I'm glad it will not be necessary to have him killed. He has been useful to the Brotherhood, as well."

Reede snorted. "For a minute there, I figured we weren't going to have the chance to think about it, let alone act on it. Gods . . . I thought he was serious. What if he had been—?"

"I would have told him that I was carrying your child."

He pushed up on his elbow again, staring down at her with something close to wonder. "Are you serious?" he said softly. "Are you—"

"Of course not." She smiled at him, a little sadly. "That is not for us. . . . You know that, beloved. It is not our destiny in the motion of things."

He looked away, silent for a long moment, before he said, "I thought you said you never lied to Humbaba."

"It would have been the first time," she answered. "And the last. Although I have not always told him the truth. . . ."

"But if you had, those could be lies too."

"If it's true that I lie." She smiled at him. "One has to know how to ask the right questions . . . and sometimes, how to answer them."

"Have you ever lied to me?"

She looked deeply, unflinchingly into his eyes. "Never."

"But you haven't always told me the truth."

She touched his lips with her fingers. "Don't torture yourself with questions, *tisshah'el*. There is no need. You are my beloved."

Acquiescing, he kissed her again. "You can move into my quarters tonight. Have your things sent over . . ." he smiled, "wife."

She moved restlessly, as if she had not been listening to him. *Or did not want to hear it.* But he would not let himself think that. "The Brotherhood will not be pleased to hear that he has divorced me. It makes controlling him harder."

"Who? Humbaba?"

She nodded. "They may vote to remove him after all . . . and that undermines our position."

Reede put an arm across her shoulders and drew her back to face him. "Don't worry. Humbaba's just barely smart enough to know he's not smart enough. He's depended on you for years for his policy. That's not going to change. Only your sleeping arrangements—" He pressed himself down on top of her, feeling the familiar throbbing warmth between his legs as his chest came in contact with her flesh.

"Yes . . ." she breathed distractedly, between his kisses. "You are wise, my love. But perhaps I should not bring my belongings to you until he has proven that true. Everywhere there are eyes. . . ."

"Damn their eyes," he said, his voice husky, every nerve in his body coming alive with exquisite sensations of arousal. "Do it. Just do it. For me." His arms tightened around her. He felt her hands on him, now, all over him, her nails digging into his flesh as her eagerness began to match his own; felt her legs slide apart to grant him entry. Her hands took hold of him with dizzying insistence, guiding him in. "Oh gods," he whispered, "I love you. . . ."

Reede walked alone through the sterile silences of the lab complex hallways, wearing only a loose robe carelessly wrapped around him. Displays posted every few meters along the walls, beside sealed doorways, above every intersection, reminded him that it was well before dawn by local time. The sky outside his window slit had been as black as death, Mundilfoere had been sleeping like a child beside him, when he awakened and realized why he had—realized what he had left undone.

His body always felt as if electrodes were attached to it, vibrant, jangling, alive. But while he slept the drug had turned up the voltage. He should have realized that the incredible sensations of his wedding with Mundilfoere were more than just her skill, and his desire. He should have recognized the warning signs. But he had been too preoccupied. . . . By the time his body had wakened him from his sodden slumber, every nerve ending was on line, and singing; he could not get back to sleep when his skin told him he was lying on a bed of nails, knowing that by morning he would think it was a bed of hot coals.

Every step he took now was exquisite agony from the pressure on his feet; the light hurt his eyes, every breath he took made his chest ache from the fluid collecting in his lungs. *Stupid. Stupid.* His brain repeated the litany with every step he took, too dazzled by sensation to provide the more graphic epithets his stupidity deserved. He had actually been so besotted with lovemaking that he had not gone back to the lab—

He reached the doorway he was looking for, touched the identity sensor with his fingertip as gingerly as if it were red hot; had to hit it harder when it didn't register him, and swore. The sound made him clench his teeth. The security seals dematerialized and he went inside.

A high anguished keening drilled into his consciousness the moment he entered the room. He stopped, then crossed the lab, not even bothering to order the doors closed behind him.

In a small transparent cubicle was a quoll, the only living thing in the lab besides himself. He had picked it up in Razuma, just one of countless abandoned animals starving in the streets. He never used animals for tests; the results he got from the datamodeling programs were far more precise. But in this case, he had made an exception. In this case, the perversity of his need to know had made him bring the wretched creature back with him to the lab. He had fed it, cared for it, given it the drug. . . . He had watched the quoll grow and thrive as the technoviral had taken over every cell in the animal's body, just as it had done to his own; turning the quoll into a perfect physical specimen. The drug, which he had designed himself, had been meant to do what the water of life did; to keep a body's systems functioning without error—to extend a human life indefinitely. It had almost worked. . . .

The quoll had come to know and trust him, greeting him with eager whistles every time he entered the lab, watching him at work. Sometimes he had even put a hand into the cage when it scratched at the plass, and stroked its soft, tufted fur. . . .

And then he had stopped giving it the drug, and begun to record the results. Its decline had been rapid, and terrifying. The drug had been designed for a human system, but its function—too simplistic, as he had realized, too late—was generic enough to affect a quoll in similar ways. And to kill it in similar ways.

It was the killing he had told himself he wanted to see in detail—not just a computer model, but the real, intimate, bloody, puking symptoms. Because after all, he had such a very personal interest in those symptoms.

He had been trying to recreate the water of life, and he had failed. He had knowingly and intentionally infected himself with the semisentient material he had recreated so imperfectly, even though his test models had shown him what would probably happen to him—what had happened to him. His body had become dependent on the drug as an arbiter of its normal functioning. His body still aged—one more way in which the drug was a failure—but, ironically, it functioned at peak efficiency while it did.

But the substance was unstable. Like the real water of life, it required continuous doses to sustain its effects. Except that the body did not develop a dependency on the genuine water of life. It developed a dependency on his. Without a continuous supply of the drug, virtually every cell in his system would cease to function—dying, running wild; millions of infinitesimal machines all gone out of control.

He stood in front of the cage, forcing himself to look at the agony of the creature inside it; forcing himself to look into the mirror. He watched its body spasming with uncontrollable seizures, the bloody foam flecking its mouth, its soft, spotted fur matted with filth, its eyes rolling back in its head. . . . He had wanted to see it, wanted to know what he had in store— *Then look at it, you fucking coward! You did it; you did it to yourself, because you wanted to.* . . .

The dreadful keening of its torment went on and on, filling his head. Slowly, with hands that trembled from something more terrifying to him than fear, he reached into the cage and lifted out the quoll. He held it a moment in his arms, oblivious to the bites it inflicted on him in its agony. And then, with a sudden, sure motion of his hands he snapped its neck.

He dropped the limp, lifeless form into the incinerator chute, watched it dematerialize before his eyes, cleanly, perfectly, freeing its soul—if it had one—to eternity. *And who will do the same for me?*

He turned away, stumbling back across the lab, the telltale early-stage discomforts of his own body suddenly magnified a thousandfold. He had to stop and inhale a tranquilizer before he could concentrate. He woke up his work terminal, fumbled his way across the touchboard, lighting up the wrong squares as he tried to feed in the security code that would let him get what he wanted. At last he heard the faint sound that told him the proper segment of secured stasis had released. He went to it and pushed his hand through the tingling screen, pulling out an unlabeled vial. The drug had no official designation. It had only one user. He called it the "water of death." He unsealed the vial, and swallowed its contents.

TIAMAT: Carbuncle

"Lady—"

"Lady. . . ."

Voices with a poignantly familiar Summer burr called to Moon as she made her way down the long, sloping ramp at the terminus of Carbuncle's Street. The ramp dropped from the Lower City down to the harbor that lay beneath Carbuncle's massive, sheltering shellform. Workers bowed their heads to her, lifted their hands in greeting, or stared dubiously as she entered their world, which had once been her own world. She wore the drab, bulky work clothes of a deckhand—linen shirt, canvas pants, a thick graybrown sweater her grandmother had made for her by hand. She had come at her grandmother's urging, with Sparks at her side—leaving behind the Sibyl College, the dickering Winter entrepreneurs and the struggling Winter engineers, to remind her people, and herself, of the heritage she had left behind. Gran was with her, pointedly keeping her distance from Jerusha PalaThion, who had also accompanied them, as she insisted on doing whenever Moon left the palace. Standing midway up the ramp was the small knot of Goodventure kin who also followed her everywhere, hounding her and spying on her; one good reason Jerusha was always by her side.

"Lady, what can we do for you?" A sailor came up to her, dragging a ship's line. There was something like awe, but also uncertainty, in his eyes when he faced her; as if he were afraid that she had come down here to pass judgment on her people for their recalcitrance in embracing the new order of things.

But she took the tow rope from his hands, feeling its rough fibers scrape her palms, realizing how her own hands had lost the leather-hardness that physical labor had once given them. "Nothing," she said humbly, "but to let me be Moon Dawntreader Summer for a time, and work the ships, and answer the questions a Summer sibyl has always answered, for anyone who wishes to ask."

He looked at her in surprise, and released his hold on the rope, leaving it in her hands. She tied it around the mooring-post, her hands by habit making knots that her mind had almost forgotten how to form.

Slowly and almost reluctantly, the other Summers began to show her what they were doing. Sparks followed her, self-consciously easing into the pattern of their activities. Their rhythms became her body's rhythms once more, more swiftly than she would have imagined was possible. Gran sat down on the pier and took over the mending of a net from a willing sailor; Jerusha leaned against a barrel, looking uncomfortable, with her gun slung at her back. She had just told them this morning that she was pregnant for the fourth time, after three miscarriages. Miroe had ordered her to avoid any heavy work. Moon knew he would have kept her confined to bed if he dared, but not even he dared that.

No crowd gathered. The other Summers watched her discreetly, still either suspicious or uncertain; but she knew that word of her presence was spreading through the sighing, creaking underworld, where sailors and dockhands loaded and unloaded supplies, scraped, lashed, and refitted hulls, mended nets, all as surely as the cold sea wind moved through the rigging of their ships. She forced herself to forget that there were easier, safer, faster ways of doing most of these things; letting herself remember the satisfaction of everyone working together like one body, each separate part knowing its role. She savored the smell of the sea, its soft, constant, murmurous voice, the feel of a deck shifting under her feet as she loaded cargo.

Sparks smiled at her as he worked, and gradually she saw his face take on a look of ease and peace. It was an expression she had not seen for so long that she had forgotten he had ever looked that way. And in his eyes there was the memory of the unexpected passion that had taken them two nights ago, the fulfilling of a need that was not just physical but soul-deep, and which had not been satisfied in either of them for too long.

She smiled too, breathing in the sea air, remembering a time when each time they lay together had seemed to be all she lived for, when they had been young and free and never dreamed that they would ever be any other way. . . . But the memory of the Transfer, calling her away into the night, suddenly filled her vision with the face of another man, his hand reaching out to her, his mouth covering hers; made her remember the words *I need you.*

She looked down and away, her thoughts giddy. She forced her mind to go empty, as she had had to do time and again these past two days; suppressing the emotion that the memory stirred in her, a feeling as dark as remembered eyes, as desperate, as haunting. *There is nothing you can do about it now. Nothing.* She repeated the words over and over again, silently, letting them flow into the pattern of her work until the helpless grief inside her faded.

She looked up again as a clamor reached her from somewhere up the ramp. She squinted past the crate in her arms, seeing what appeared to be two men arguing with the constables Jerusha had set to question whoever came this way. One of the arguing figures was an old man, the other younger, but painfully stooped. *Danaquil Lu.* And as the voices reached her clearly, she recognized the unmistakable bellowing of Borah Clearwater. "Jerusha," she called over the side of the ship, and pointed with her chin toward their argument. Jerusha nodded and started away.

"Lady . . . ?" someone murmured behind her. She turned back, looking into the face of a tall, brown-haired woman. "I have a question."

Moon set down the crate she was holding, and nodded. "Ask, and I will answer.

Input. . . ." From the corner of her eye she saw Sparks stop his work and move toward her with protective concern as the woman's voice filled her ears, her mind, and she began the abrupt fall away into darkness.

". . . No further analysis." She came back into herself again, and sat down on the crate as a brief wave of dizziness caught her. Sparks put his hands on her shoulders, rubbing them gently. She felt the eyes of the other dockhands and sailors watching her, watching her differently now.

"Thank you, sibyl," the woman murmured, smiling and bobbing her head as she backed away. Moon saw two or three others beginning to cluster near her; knew that they would be the next to come forward with questions.

"Well, what am I supposed to make of this?" A man's voice—Borah Clearwater's voice—carried sharply and clearly up to her.

She pushed to her feet and went to the small trimaran's rail, peered over it. "Make of what, Borah Clearwater?" she said, to his turned back.

He jerked around, away from Jerusha's annoyed expression, to look up at her. He looked blank for a moment, seeing only a plainly dressed island woman with her hair in braids, and not the Summer Queen, answering him. His frown deepened as he recognized her. "If you think you can change my opinion about anything by doing an honest day's work, you're wrong."

Moon laughed, wondering if he actually believed she was here because she was trying to impress him. She felt Spark's impatience like heat as he came up beside her.

"I'm sorry to intrude like this, Lady," Danaquil Lu said, edging his uncle aside with an effort. "But my uncle has been . . . wishing to speak to you about the—uh, right-of-way you granted to our kinsman Kirard Set Wayaways." From Danaquil Lu's chagrin and air of resignation, she guessed that Clearwater had not let him rest until he had agreed to speak to her.

She smiled at him, a brief, reassuring smile, before she looked at Borah Clearwater. Leaning on the rail, she met his stare with a calm centeredness that would have been impossible two days ago—two hours ago. "So you think I arranged this for your benefit, Borah Clearwater? Just as you seem to think I granted that right-of-way to spite you?"

Clearwater snorted, but for just a moment he didn't answer. "Who knows why you do anything? Rot me, this makes as much sense as the other!"

"And who do you think you are," Gran's voice interrupted suddenly, "to come here and speak to the Lady in that tone of voice?"

He turned back to look at her as she stood up, putting aside the net she had been mending. "I think I have more business speaking to her than you have speaking to me," he grunted.

Danaquil Lu rolled his eyes. "Uncle—" he murmured, pulling at the older man's shoulder.

"She's my granddaughter, if you must know," Gran said irritably. "It was my suggestion that she come here and be among her own people and her own ways for a while. She has the grace to respect her elders. Show her the respect she deserves from a Summer, or you might as well be a Winter!"

He glared at her. "I am a Winter, as it happens. But if she acted more like a Summer, and left things well enough alone, I'd be happier to respect her judgment."

"A Winter!" Gran looked him up and down dubiously.

"We aren't all perfumed sissies," he snapped.

Moon looked on, silent with surprise as Gran came to her defense, suddenly and deeply moved by her grandmother's protectiveness. Danaquil Lu stood beside Jerusha, looking bemused. "But as to the matter of the right-of-way across your lands, Borah Clearwater," she interrupted, "why is that such a problem for you, really? It won't interfere with your crops or your fishing rights. You're going to be paid very well for the use of such a tiny strip of your ground. Is it simply the principle of the thing? Or is it because you hate change that much—because you hate me, and my new ideas?"

He snorted again, his mustache bristling. "I'm not fond of you, Moon Dawntreader. I've made that plain enough, and I'm honest enough to admit it to your face, unlike some. But it's my kinsman Kirard Set Wayaways that I hate. He's buying out the holdings all around mine for their mineral rights, for development and building factories. There's metal ores all over my plantation. He wants me to sell out too, but since I won't he's made you give him a toehold on my land. Now that he has that much from you, he's going to keep pushing until he gets it all. Goddammit, you've made him believe it's possible, and now he'll never rest. The whole Wayaways clan is a spot of gangrene, you ask me—excepting young Dana here, he's probably crazy but he's all right. They ought to be cut out, dammit, not encouraged to spread!"

"I hear what you're saying, Borah Clearwater," Moon said gently. "Kirard Set Wayaways is one of the most motivated and effective people I have working with me to develop Tiamat. But I don't intend to do him any favors at anyone else's expense. You've registered your complaint with me. I won't forget it."

Clearwater grunted. "Not until you run short of ores, at least, and I refuse again to let him stripmine my fields."

Moon frowned. "I want to make Tiamat a better place for our people to live. I don't intend to destroy it in the process. No one will force you off your traditional lands against your will. I've given you my word. You'll have to trust it. That's all." She turned away from the rail, not listening to his continued complaint or even the sharpness of her grandmother's voice, at him again for questioning the word of a sibyl, of her grandchild. Moon looked back at the curious stares of the gathered sailors. Slowly another of them started forward with a question.

She answered his question and half a dozen more, before she looked up at last and found no one else waiting. Drained but satisfied, she rose from her seat among the crates and started back to work.

But Sparks took her arm, smiling, and led her to the rail, nodding down at the pier. She started as she saw Borah Clearwater still there, still talking to her grandmother—but sitting beside her now, mending net; speaking agitatedly, but in a tone of voice so normal that Moon could not make out the words through the clangor and shouting of the docks. Jerusha glanced up from where she sat with ill-concealed restlessness, saw where they were looking; smiled and shrugged, shaking her head. Moon went back to work, smiling too, filled with sudden gratitude and surprise at the unexpected rewards of this day; feeling a brief pang as she looked out to sea and did not know where to direct her prayer of thanks.

She heard a sudden pain-cry, and the clatter of something dropping on the pier below. She went back to the ship's rail, saw Jerusha on her hands and knees on the salt-bleached wood, her rifle lying beside her. Moon climbed over the rail, landing on the dock, as Gran and Borah Clearwater pushed to their feet in consternation, as constables came running. Moon saw with sudden bright grief the red stain of blood spreading down Jerusha's pantslegs. "Sparks!" she cried. She fell to her knees, taking hold of Jerusha as the other woman tried to rise, holding her, holding her tightly; feeling the pain that convulsed Jerusha's body as if it were her own; remembering the pain of birth, the pain that had come to Jerusha PalaThion too soon, much too soon. "Find Miroe. Hurry—!"

Jerusha opened her eyes, blinking in a kind of disbelief as she took in her new reality. Her last memory was of the pier, the harbor; the odd sense of peace that had fallen over everyone around her while she watched and waited. She remembered feeling something, as she sat—the slight fluttering movement of her unborn child. Remembered how, for that moment, the world outside her body had ceased to exist, as she became wholly aware of the miracle of life inside her. For that brief moment the peace around her had reached into her and touched her soul, and she had let herself be happy, certain that this time everything would be all right. . . .

And she had felt the baby move again, and then again, restlessly, and a strange restlessness had overtaken her too; she had lost that fragile, precious sense of peace, felt it fly away from her like birds. And there had been a sudden twinge, a pulling tension, that made her rise from where she sat, trying to stretch it out of existence like a muscle kink, trying to make it disappear, because she had felt that sensation before, and she knew what always followed—

Pain had taken her where she stood, as if everything inside her was being twisted and ripped loose, and as the darkness came over her in a terrible, rushing flood, she had been sure that this time, this time she would die. . . .

But she was alive. She was lying in a strange bed, in a strangely familiar room. She recognized its ceiling. She had seen this sight before: the inside of this hospital room, its odd mixture of old and new: modern fixtures and furnishings, abandoned intact by the Hegemony, but with their systems gutted, like hers. She knew the acrid, alien smell of the medicinal herbs that were used for most of the healing that was done here now. She could feel her hands, her arms, her shoulders, although she had no strength to move them. She could feel her toes. But at the center of her body there was nothing, no sensation at all. Numb. And no one had to tell her the reason why.

She moved her head—let it fall, pulled down by gravity as she looked toward the doorway. Someone stirred just beyond her sight, in response to her motion; she realized, from the sudden sensation in her hand, that someone had been holding it. She forced her eyes to focus, expecting to see her husband's face.

Instead, she found the face of the Summer Queen. Moon Dawntreader's pale hand tightened over her own in unspoken empathy, in grief for a loss so fresh she had not even begun to feel it yet. Just for a moment Jerusha remembered a time when their positions had been reversed; when she had sat at Moon's bedside, Moon's hand clutching hers in a deathgrip, in the throes of giving birth. . . . "You shouldn't be here," she whispered. Her throat was achingly dry; she felt as if her body were burning up, a desert. *Barren. Sterile.*

Moon's expression changed, turning uncertain.

"You have duties. . . ."

Moon shook her head. "Time has stopped. It all stopped, until I knew you would be all right," she said softly. "Besides, how can I function, without my right arm?" She smiled; the smile fell away. She looked down, with a knowledge in her eyes that only another woman's eyes could hold—not a queen's, but a mother's; the reflection of the most terrible fear she could imagine.

Jerusha pressed her mouth together, looking away; her lips were parched and cracked. Moon offered her water, helped her drink it. "Where's Miroe?" she asked, finally.

"He took care of you, when we brought you in. He was here before, for a long time . . ." Moon murmured. "He said he would be back soon."

Jerusha nodded, wearily. She looked at the ceiling again, its ageless, flawless surface . . . wishing that her own body could be as perfect, as unaffected by time or fate, as impervious. She looked back at Moon. "I'm all right," she said quietly, at last. "Go home to your family."

Moon rose, her hand still holding Jerusha's tightly, her eyes still holding doubt. She let go, reluctantly. "I'll find Miroe, and send him to you."

"Thank you," Jerusha said.

Moon smiled again, nodded almost shyly as she left the room.

Jerusha lay back, listening to the distant sounds of life that reached her from the corridors beyond her closed door; listening to the gibberings of loss and futility seeping in to fill the perfect emptiness she tried to hold at the center of her thoughts. She imagined the responses of the men she had worked with in the Hegemonic Police, if they saw her now . . . imagined the response of the woman she herself had been to the woman she was now, lying in this bed. They would have been equally unsympathetic. She had spent years trying to force them to accept her as a human being instead of a woman, and all it had done was turn her into a man. In leaving the force, she had believed that she was reaffirming her humanity. She wasn't a man . . . but now when she wanted to be a woman, she couldn't be that either. She felt hot tears rise up in her eyes and overflow; hating them, hating herself for her weakness, physical and mental. She wanted Miroe, she needed him, to help her now. Why wasn't he here? Damn him, he was the one she had needed to see, he shared this loss with her, more intimately than anyone. She needed to share his strength, and his grief—

Someone came into the room. She lifted her head, needing all her own strength, for long enough to see that Miroe had come, as if in answer to her thoughts.

"Jerusha." He crossed to her bedside, his work-rough hands touching her flushed, fevered skin with the gentleness that always surprised her—touching her own hands, her face, her tears. He kissed her gently on the forehead, and on the lips; drew back.

"Hold me," she murmured, wishing that she did not have to request that comfort. "Hold me. . . ."

He sat down on the edge of the bed; lifted her strengthless, unresponsive body and held her close, letting her tears soak his shirt, absorbing them, for a long time. She could not see whether he wept too. The muscles of his body were as rigid as steel, as if he were holding grief at bay. She had never wept before, when this had happened to her; although it had happened to her three times already. And he had never wept, either.

"Why does this keep happening to me . . ." she whispered, brokenly, at last. "It isn't fair—"

"I'm sorry." His own voice was like a clenched fist. "Gods, Jerusha—I've done everything I can."

"I'm not blaming you." She pulled away from him, to look at his face. He would not meet her eyes.

"You should," he muttered. "I can't heal it, I can't make it right. . . . If you weren't here, if you were anywhere else, you'd have healthy children by now."

"No, I wouldn't," she said. "I wouldn't even have a husband. I wouldn't be with you. It's the Hegemony's fault—" A surge of anger and resentment pushed the words out of her throat. But the Hegemony was far away, formless, faceless, unreachable, and she found herself suddenly angry at the man who held her, for making her ask for comfort, for making her comfort him when it was *her* loss. . . . *Our loss. It's our loss!* she told herself fiercely. But she let herself slide out of his arms, as his arms loosened; falling back into the bed's cool, impersonal embrace.

He looked at her, his eyes clouded and full of doubt, looked away again. He reached into a pocket of his coat and took something out: a small jar full of what looked like dried herbs. "Jerusha," he said quietly, "I want you to start using this."

"What is it?" she murmured, straining for a clear sight of it.

"It's childbane." He met her gaze directly at last.

She felt the last embers of hope die inside her. "Birth control—?" she asked numbly; not needing to ask, or to have it explained to her.

But he nodded. "I almost lost you this time, Jerusha. You nearly bled to death. I don't want to take that risk again . . . I don't want you to take it."

"But Miroe—" She tried to sit up, fell back again, as her body pressed the point home. "I'm forty-three. I don't have much longer—"

"I know." She saw a muscle stand out as his jaw tightened. "The risk will only grow, for you or for a child. Maybe it's time we faced the truth, Jerusha: we're never going to have any children. Not here, not in this lifetime together."

She stared at him bleakly. "You know I don't believe in that—in reincarnation, in another chance. This isn't a dress rehearsal, Miroe, it's my life, and I don't want to stop trying!" She broke off, clenching her teeth as something hurt her cruelly inside, through the layers of deadened flesh.

He tensed, and shook his head. "I love you, Jerusha. I love you too much to kill you, or let you kill yourself, over something that's impossible. If you won't use the childbane, I won't sleep with you anymore."

"You don't mean that," she said, her voice thick.

"I do." He looked away, pushing to his feet. "I can't take this anymore. I'm sorry." He crossed the room, and went out the door.

She watched him go, unable to get up, to follow him, to confront him; without even the strength to call after him. She looked over at the bedtable, at the bottle of herbal contraceptive he had left behind. She knocked it off the table with a trembling fist. She fell back again, staring up at the ceiling; felt the numbness at the center of her body spreading, filling the space that held her heart, filling her mind until there was no room left for thought. . . .

"Commander PalaThion! What are you doing here?" Constable Fairhaven straightened away from the grayed wooden railing of the pier, with surprise obvious on her long, weathered face.

"Just doing my job, constable; the same as you." Jerusha returned her salute. Fairhaven's salute was sloppy to the point of being almost unrecognizable, like most of the Summers' salutes were; but she was a calm, shrewd woman, and those were qualities Jerusha had come to realize were far more important than discipline, in a local constabulary where the police and the people they watched over were frequently neighbors and kin. Jerusha leaned against the rail next to Fairhaven, breathing in the heavy, pungent odor of the docks, the smell of wood and pitch, seaweed and fish and the sea. The maze of floating piers was lined with fishing boats and transport craft from all along the coast.

"But so soon—?" Fairhaven said. Her frank curiosity clouded over with concern, at the look Jerusha felt come over her own face.

"I'm fine," Jerusha said mechanically, looking away, down at the pattern of ropes and chains, of shifting light and shadow on the water's surface. She looked up again, at the ships. Miroe had sailed from here yesterday, going back to the plantation, leaving behind the city he hated, and the pain of their shared loss, her pain. Leaving behind the frustration, the recriminations they had shared too, as they had turned anger at the random indifference of an uncaring universe into anger at each other. Avoiding all that: their dead child, their dying dream. Her . . .

"Forgive me, Jerusha." Fairhaven put out a hand, touching Jerusha's arm, a gesture that was somehow both apology and the comfort of one woman reaching out to another. Fairhaven had never addressed her as anything but "Commander" before; the combination took her doubly by surprise. "But I suffered my share of stillborn babes . . . three I lost, out of seven I bore with my pledged. It was hard, hard. . . ." Her mouth tightened, although Jerusha knew her children were all grown; the memories of her losses must be old ones now. She looked up again, sighing. "The Lady gives, and She takes away. . . . We had a saying in the islands, you know, that you should let nine days pass before you took to your work again. Three for the baby's sake, three for the mother's sake, three for the Lady's sake."

Jerusha smiled, faintly. Her head was still buzzing from the native painkillers she had been chewing the past few days. They had used up their own small stock of offworlder drugs, on her previous miscarriages and other small disasters. "But I don't worship the Lady. And as for me, I'd rather work than brood. So I've taken time enough off."

Fairhaven shook her head. Her graying, sand-colored braids rolled against her tunic with the motion. "It's still good advice, you know. To take time to grieve is only right. Otherwise you suffer more, in the long run."

Jerusha forced herself to control the sudden annoyance that filled her. And she remembered, unexpectedly, the face of one of the men under her old command—her assistant, Gundhalinu, on the day he had received news of his father's death. She remembered his stubborn Kharemoughi pride; his refusal even to acknowledge his loss, until finally she had ordered him to take the rest of the day off to grieve. . . . She rubbed her eyes, turning away.

She was saved from having to make a further response by a sound like thunder that echoed through the underworld of the docks. She turned back to Fairhaven, meeting her stare. "A ship's fallen—" Fairhaven said, as the sound of voices shouting filled the stunned silence that followed the crash. They turned together, not needing words; started to run, as others were running now, toward the site of the accident. As they approached she heard pain-cries, before she could even make out what had happened through the wall of milling bodies.

She pushed through the crowd until she had a clear view, taking it all in at a glance: the ship that had been winched up for repairs, the chain that had snapped and let it fall sideways onto the dock, the two men pinned beneath it. As many workers as could press their backs against the hull were already straining to lift it; but one of the catamaran's large floats was wedged beneath the pier, and they could get no leverage.

Jerusha looked from the broken length of chain lying on the dock to the pulley high up beneath the city's underbelly. She looked down again. One of the workers lay unconscious or dead in a pool of blood; the other one, his legs pinned, was still moaning. She tightened her jaw, trying not to listen to the sound, trying to keep her mind clear for thought.

She pulled loose the coiled length of monofilament line she had carried at her belt, ever since her Police-issue binders ceased to function. She knotted one end of the line through the last solid link of broken chain, while the workers looked on, uncomprehending.

She flung the coil of line upward, feeling something half-healed pull painfully inside her; watched with relief and some surprise as it passed through the pulley overhead on her first try. The rope spiraled down to the dock and lay waiting, but nobody moved forward to pick it up. "Come on!" Jerusha shouted. She picked up the rope's end. "Wind it up!" They stared at her, muttering and shaking their heads.

"Commander," Fairhaven murmured. "It won't hold. They know it will snap, it's too thin—" She nodded at the broken chain, as thick around as Jerusha's wrist.

"It'll hold!" Jerusha called sharply, with the sound of the trapped worker's moans grating inside her like a broken bone. "It will! Winch it up!"

Two dockhands moved forward, looking at her as if she were insane, but having no other alternative. She watched them fasten the line to the winch and begin to crank it. Their motions slowed abruptly, their muscles strained, as the line suddenly grew taut. They went on turning the winch; the line sang briefly as every last millimeter of play was drawn out of it and it began to take the full weight of the ship.

Jerusha held her breath, knowing the line would hold, but still instinctively afraid of disaster. The ship began to crack and groan in turn as its immovable mass surrendered to the irresistible force of the winch's power—and finally it began to rise.

Dockhands leaped forward to drag the two trapped workers free as the ship began to lift clear. But the two men at the winch kept cranking, and as the rest of the crowd watched in murmuring awe, the ship rose farther. The float that was wedged under the pier's edge snapped and broke in two, ripping free with a spray of splintered wood. The ship lunged and bucked against the line; gradually stabilized again as the relentless pull lifted it even higher, until it was back in position overhead—and still the line held.

Jerusha tore her own gaze from the ship, to watch the injured workers carried away toward the ramp that rose into the city, toward the hospital. She looked back again as someone embraced her suddenly, awkwardly, before hurrying on past, going after the injured workers.

"Littleharbor's kinsman," Fairhaven said, indicating one of the victims, and the man who had just hugged her. Jerusha nodded mutely, wondering with a familiar, morbid weariness whether the two workers could be healed or even helped in any meaningful way by the primitive medical treatment they had now. Miroe had done his best to share what medical training he had with the locals; but without sophisticated equipment and diagnosticators to back it up, his modern methods were hardly more effective than the herbal-remedies-mixed-with-common-sense the Tiamatans had evolved on their own.

"Commander—?" Someone's voice caught at her hesitantly.

She turned back, finding a crowd of Summers gathered around her. "What is it?" she said.

"How is it possible?" the woman who had spoken asked; asking, Jerusha realized, for them all. "What sort of string is this you carry, that can bear the weight that snapped a chain?"

"It's called monomolecular line," she answered. "It's extremely strong. They say it could lift the entire city of Carbuncle without snapping. It's from offworld." She watched their faces, expecting their eyes to glaze over with disinterest as she said those final words . . . just as they always had, and probably always would. She had come to believe that masochism must be an inherited trait among the Summers; that they were somehow instinctively opposed to making their lives any easier.

But they only came closer, touching the line hesitantly, speculatively, murmuring among themselves about the strength, the lightness, the countless possible uses for netting, bindings, rigging . . . on a farm . . . in a cottage. That this was *better*. All the things that the Queen and her College of Sibyls and the Winter entrepreneurs had been trying to tell them, show them, force on them—forcing it down their throats, when all that had done was make the Summers retch. When they should have been letting those things speak for themselves . . . letting the Summers think for themselves. *Showing, and not telling* . . .

"Is this something the Winters have learned to make?" a large, red-bearded man asked, almost grudgingly.

"Not yet," Jerusha said. "Someday they will." She looked down, trying to conceal the sudden inspiration that struck her. "But—there's a supply of it left in the old government warehouses. If you want it, maybe I could arrange to make it available. . . ." She shrugged, trying not to sound too eager, not to look as though it mattered to her.

The Summers glanced at each other, their expressions mixed, as if they were trying to gauge one another's response: whether the person next to them would somehow be the first to get a quantity of the new line, and an advantage over them, all at the same time.

"What would you ask for it?" someone murmured.

She almost said, "Nothing"; stopped, thinking fast. The Summers made most of their own equipment, and preferred barter to the city's offworlder-based credit system. "We can talk a trade," she said, and saw their faces begin to come alive as she answered them in their own way. "Come up to the warehouse whenever you finish your work. One of my Summer constables will be there to speak with you." She saw them nodding, saw their eyes, and knew that sooner or later, some of them would come. And then, with any luck, more would. *Shown, not told* . . . There were other things in the warehouses, things that she could have put to casual use in the Summers' presence, letting them see for themselves that their way of doing things was not the only way, not even necessarily the best. Lost in thought, she scarcely felt the pain of her overtaxed body as she started back up the ramp toward the city.

NUMBER FOUR: Foursgate

"Wake up, you stinking hero. This is no time for sleep—"

Police Commander BZ Gundhalinu gasped and came awake in utter darkness, the sourceless words echoing in his head like a dream. "Wha—?" *Dreaming . . . he had been dreaming.* But it was a woman's face he had been dreaming of, *as pale as moonlight, echoed in blue, her arms reaching out to him. . . .*

He rolled toward the edge of the bed, groping for the light, the time, the message function on his bedside table; groping for whatever had wakened him so rudely from the sodden sleep of exhaustion. He had not gotten back to the apartment from the latest in the seemingly endless series of fetes and celebrations honoring him until well after local midnight. He could not possibly have been asleep for more than two or three hours. Who in the name of a thousand gods—?

He found the lamp base, slapped it with his hand—but no light came up. He realized then that he could see nothing at all, not even shadows against the night, the hidden form of a window. His hands flew to his face—rebounded without touching it from the polarized security shield locked in place over his head.

He swore, scrambling out from under the covers on his hands and knees; felt strong arms—more than one set of them—lock around him, jerking him back. He heard the unmistakable crack of a stunner shot in the same instant that the hit impacted against his chest, and shut off his voluntary nervous system. He collapsed in the bedding, paralyzed but completely conscious, furiously aware that he was stark naked, because he had been too exhausted to throw on a sleep shirt before falling into bed.

The hands rolled him roughly onto his back; he heard muttered speech distorted by the shield's energy field. *What do you want—?* His slack lips would not form the words that he needed to say—needing desperately to have that much effect on his body, or his fate. He could not swear, could not even moan.

He felt their hands on him again, manhandling him with ruthless efficiency; realized with a sense of gratitude that was almost pathetic that they were wrapping his nerveless body in a robe. They lifted him off the bed, dragging him across the room and toward the door.

Gods, kidnapped—he was being kidnapped. He struggled to control his panic, the only thing left over which he had any control at all; trying to keep his mind working, trying to think. *What did they want?* "You stinking hero," they'd called him. Ransom then, terrorism, information about the stardrive, Fire Lake—? *Stop it.*

No way to guess that, he'd probably find out soon enough. Concentrate. *What do you already know?* He didn't know how many of them there were, where they were taking him—he grunted as he was dumped unceremoniously into the cramped floorspace of some kind of vehicle, and felt his captors climb in around him. He felt the vehicle rise, carrying them all to gods-only-knew what destination.

Trying to use the only sensory feedback he had left to him, he realized that the vehicle had an oddly familiar smell. He recognized the distinctive odor of bandro, a stimulant drink imported from Tsieh-pun. Most of the Hegemonic Police force stationed here were from Tsieh-pun. Police. Could it be Police involvement? That would explain the equipment, the vehicle, the ruthless efficiency of the way they had made him their prisoner, even the effortless way they had walked in on him through the invisible walls of his security system. . . .

But what in the name of all his ancestors would make the Police do this to him—? Maybe it was terrorists; maybe they were going to— *Oh gods, this is insane, why is this happening to me now—? No. Stop it. No.* The stunshock was making it hard to breathe, doubled up in the cramped space. He recited an adhani silently, calming himself, and lay still, because he had no choice. He waited.

They were coming down again. The flight hadn't been a long one. He must still be within range of Foursgate, at least. He tried to feel encouraged by that fact, and failed. The craft settled almost imperceptibly onto some flat surface, and he was hauled out of the vehicle like the dead weight he was. He was carried into another building, downward . . . down a long, echoing hall, into a lift which dropped them farther down. Had they landed on a rooftop pad? Or were they going underground? He had no clue.

At last the sickening motion stopped; he was dropped, dead weight again, onto a hard surface. He felt his leaden hands and feet jerked wide and pinioned, felt a sting against his neck as someone gave him the antidote for the muscle paralysis. He took in a deep, ragged breath of relief as control came back to him, felt his muscles spasm as he tried to move his limbs. And then the invisible hands did something by his jaw, dissolving the security field—letting him see and hear at last.

He raised his head, all he could do freely; let it fall back again. He made a sound that wasn't really a laugh. *I'm having a nightmare. This isn't happening. . . .* What he had seen was too absurd. He was not really lying here like this, inside a cone of stark white light, surrounded by a dozen figures in black star-flecked robes, their identities hidden behind hologramic masks: featureless forms crowned by the image of a Black Gate's flaming corona, its heart of darkness sucking his vision relentlessly down toward madness. *It's a dream, a flashback, stress, nightmare . . . wake up, wake up, damn you—!*

He did not wake up. His eyes still showed him the same figures, barely visible at the edges of the cone of light which shone relentlessly on his own helpless, half-clad body. He watched silently as one of the figures came toward him, stood over him, gazing down at him with infinity's face. He had to look away; he turned his face aside and shut his eyes. Sweat trickled down his cheek into his ear; the itch it caused was maddening, agonizing. His hand fisted with exasperation inside its restraint.

The robed figure reached out, touched his straining hand almost comfortingly. The blunt, gloved fingers closed over his own, formed a hidden pattern as distinctive as it was unobtrusive. He stiffened as he recognized it; returned it with sudden hope.

But then the face of flaming nothingness turned back to his own, and suddenly there was a light pencil in the stranger's hand. The blade of coherent light pricked his throat, touching the trefoil tattoo there; hot enough to make him jump, but not set to burn. An electronically distorted voice asked him, "Are you a sibyl?" The voice gave him no clue to the speaker; he could not even tell if it was a man or a woman.

"Yes," he whispered, with his eyes still averted from the face of Chaos. "Yes, I am—my blood carries the virus." Hoping that the implied threat might prevent his suddenly seeing too much of his own blood.

The voice laughed unpleasantly. "Considerate of you to warn us. But this cauterizes nicely." The faceless figure twitched the light pencil, making the spot of pain dance on Gundhalinu's neck. "What do you know about Survey?"

"*Input—*" he murmured, taking the question as one asked of him in his official capacity; taking the easy way out.

"*Stop,*" the voice ordered, jerking him back into realtime just as his mind began the long fall into the sibyl net. "Answer me yourself. Are you a member of Survey?"

"Yes," he repeated, reorienting with difficulty. His hand tightened over the memory of the other's touch. *But you know that. Why am I here? Can you help me—?* Not asking any of the questions forming in his mind, because he was afraid of what would happen if there were no answers. The silence when no one was speaking was almost complete; the sound of his own breathing hurt his ears.

"What do you know about Survey?" the voice repeated.

He shook his head, more surprised than frightened now by the unexpected turn of the questioning. Of all the possibilities his frantic brain had offered for this ordeal, his membership in Survey had not been one of them. He stared at the ceiling—if there really was one, in the darkness behind the blinding glare. "It's a private social and philanthropic organization. Almost everyone I knew—every Technician—on Kharemough seemed to be a member. There are chapters on all the worlds of the Hegemony." Many members of the Hegemonic Police belonged to it; he had attended meetings on three different worlds. "Look, this is absurd—" He raised his head, with difficulty, to confront the face of nightmare. "What in the name of any god you like do you want from me—?"

"Just answer the question." The voice thrummed gratingly with its owner's impatience. The light pencil traced a stinging track down his naked chest and half-exposed stomach to the vicinity of his private parts. His eyes began to water as he felt the heat concentrate there.

He took a deep breath, letting his head fall back again. "What do you want to know—?" His own voice sounded thin and peevish. "You can find out anything I could tell you down at the local meeting hall!"

"Do many sibyls belong to Survey?" the voice asked, ignoring his response.

He thought about it. "Yes. Quite a few." He had never realized until now what a high percentage of them there were. "But it isn't a requirement."

"Do all sibyls belong to it?"

He shook his head, remembering Tiamat. "No."

"Why not?"

He opened his eyes. "I don't know. I don't even know why so many of them do belong—" he said, exasperated.

"How old is the organization?"

"I don't know. Very old, I think. I believe it originated on Kharemough."

The masked questioner chuckled. "Like everything else of any value?" Gundhalinu grimaced. "How many levels of organization are there?"

"What—? Three, I think. Three!"

"And what level are you?"

"Three. I am—was—am a Technician of second rank."

"There are no higher levels, no inner circle—?"

"Not to my knowledge."

"You've never even heard rumors that such things may exist?"

"Well . . . yes, but that's all they are. People like to see conspiracies everywhere. Some people like to fantasize about secrets. I've seen no evidence—"

"There are no secret rituals involved? No rites of passage which you are forbidden to reveal?"

"Well, yes, but they're meaningless."

"You've never revealed them to anyone, though?"

"No."

"Describe them to me."

"I can't." He shook his head, and felt the discomfort increase as his inquisitor pushed aside his robe, baring his flesh.

"Describe them."

"For gods' sakes!" he shouted, squirming, hating himself for it. "Even you know the goddamn handshake! It's meaningless! It's a stupid, meaningless social club!"

"You're so wrong . . ." the voice murmured. The pain disappeared, suddenly and completely.

Gundhalinu sucked in a loud gasp of relief. "Please . . ." he said, his voice thick, "at least tell me why I'm here—"

"Then ask the right questions."

Gundhalinu swallowed the protests forming in his throat. *Ask the right questions.* . . . He had asked the right questions at Fire Lake, finally, and discovered a treasure of ancient knowledge locked inside the seemingly random phenomena of World's End; discovered a lost source of the Old Empire's stardrive plasma, which made faster-than-light travel between worlds possible. *Was that the point, then?* Was he supposed to discover some secret meaning behind this gathering of madmen? *Gods, I'm too tired for this.* . . . But maybe he had been given the clues—or why all the questions about secrets within Survey, inner circles, higher levels . . . ? "Are you all strangers far from home?" It was the ritual question he had heard others ask, and asked himself, for years in the Survey Meeting Halls of three different worlds.

The hologramic mask above him shifted focus, as if the wearer had nodded. "Very good," his questioner answered. "Now you're beginning to think like a hero."

Gundhalinu bit down on his irritation and was silent again, trying to concentrate on facts and not the incongruity of the situation. "What is the real purpose of this organization, then, if it isn't just what it seems?"

Silence answered him, for a long moment; and then his inquisitor murmured, "There are some things which cannot be said, but only shown—" He reached out and touched Gundhalinu's forehead, in a gesture that was almost a benediction. But in his hand was something that resembled a crown, and it stayed behind, embracing Gundhalinu's head as if it were impossibly alive. Rays of light made a sunburst between the fingers of the disappearing hand; grew, intensified suddenly and unbearably, burning out his vision, throwing him into utter darkness and silence.

He lay that way for a long time, waiting, not trying to struggle because he knew that to struggle was useless; listening to the echoes of his own breathing, until the sound of each breath began to seem part of a larger sighing, as if the darkness itself were breathing around him. He had no sense of physicality at all anymore; of the room or the strangers around him; of the bonds which held him there; of his own body. . . . Cast adrift, he felt the muscles of his body slowly relaxing of their own volition. He began to feel as if he were falling into the blackness, seeing the heart of unlife, the Black Gate opening. . . .

And then, distantly, he began to make out sound again . . . a crystalline music that was almost silence, almost beyond the limit of his senses; the song that he had always imagined the universe would sing (somehow he only realized this now) if the stars had voices.

And as he listened he realized that he had known that song forever, that it was the song the molecules sang, the DNA in his genes, the thought of eternity: the thread of his life, of a hundred, a thousand lives before him, carrying him back into the heart of the Old Empire.

The stars began to wink into existence around him as he listened, almost as if by his thought, godlike, he had placed them there . . . their images lighting the sky in a new and completely strange variation on their universal theme of light against the darkness. The night of another world was all around him, breathing softly, whispering, restless in its sleep.

"Look at the stars, Ilmarinen," someone said suddenly, beside him. "The colors . . . I've never seen stars like this anywhere. This is magnificent. How do you arrange these things—?"

(Where am I—?) He felt himself start to laugh at the comment; felt himself choke it off, still not sure, after all these years *(all these years—?)* whether Vanamoinen was joking or actually meant it. That was a part of Vanamoinen's gift, and his infuriating uniqueness. . . . Vanamoinen had been sitting there looking at the stars for nearly three hours, he estimated, and those were the first words out of him. *(Vanamoinen? Who are you—?)* "I wish I could take credit for the view," he said, (but he was Gundhalinu, wasn't he? Why was he Ilmarinen, answering, letting himself smile . . . ?) "A veil of interstellar dust, that's all." But it was a magnificent sky; he had to admit it. . . . That was the only word for it. The kind of view that reminded him of— *(Of what? Ilmarinen knew, this stranger whose eyes he was looking out of, whose sorrow and urgency he felt tightening his throat, whose life he seemed to have usurped, when he knew he was a prisoner somewhere in Foursgate, strapped to a table. . . .)*

" 'That's all,' " Vanamoinen murmured. His amusement might have been ironic; or maybe not. "They're late—?" he asked suddenly, as if they had not been sitting here for what felt like an eternity, waiting.

"Yes," Ilmarinen said. (And Gundhalinu felt the tension inside Ilmarinen pluck at his guts again. He felt his body move, with old habit, to put an arm around Vanamoinen's shoulders where he sat. He could barely see the form of the man who sat cross-legged beside him on the sandy soil of the highlands, but he knew who it was; had always known Vanamoinen. He surrendered to the vision, letting it take him . . . felt a surge of emotion that was part wonder, part hunger, part need, fill him.) His hand tightened as Vanamoinen's hand rose to cover it. *After all these years . . .* he thought, still amazed by the feeling. Surely they must always have been together; life had only begun when they had met, and discovered the bonds of mind and spirit, the contrasting strengths, that had first made them lovers and then drawn them as a team into the Guild's highest levels. They were at the top of their fields within this sector's research and development—and their fields were information resources and technogenetic programming, which made it just barely possible that they would be able to do what they had set out to do . . . which made what they were doing, their betrayal of the Establishment's trust, doubly treasonous.

(He knew without looking down that he wore the uniform of Survey, the programming of Sector Command; knew it somehow, as well as he knew that no one, no one at all in the Governmental Interface must ever dream of what they were doing here on this godforsaken promontory of this abandoned world—or they would be eliminated like an unwanted thought.)

Goddamn it, where was Mede—? He looked up restlessly at the Towers beyond Vanamoinen's silhouetted form: the massive, organic growths, branching, twisting, reaching for the stars with blunt limbs, no two of them alike . . . still standing like silent guardians, watching over this secret rendezvous. Once they had been home to a race of semisentient, parasitic beings; and then they had been home to the human settlers who had violated Survey's settlement code and decimated the population of their former owners . . . who had been decimated in turn in one of the interstellar brushfire wars that were both a cause and an effect of the Pangalactic's decay.

Now there were only these husks, these silent reminders of life. . . . What was it Vanamoinen had said to him once: "Why did history begin? History is always terrible." He took a deep breath, his chest aching slightly because he was unused to the thin, dry air. It was damnably cold here, too, even wearing thermal clothing. He could not remember feeling this uncomfortable physically for this long since his recruit training. But paranoia made them avoid wearing even foggers, which would have given them the optimal microenvironment they were accustomed to.

"Listen—" Vanamoinen said suddenly, aloud, fingering his ear nervously. They were avoiding the neural comm linkages that were so much easier to monitor from space, even though his own equipment had assured him that there was no one eavesdropping on any imaginable band of the spectrum. . . . He touched his ear, feeling for the absent ear cuff, the dangling cascade of crystal that normally he always wore: the information system made into a work of art, as much a part of him as his skin. Vanamoinen's ear was also empty. It was like being naked . . . no, worse, like being lost in a void. (*Lost in the void.* He felt his identity begin to slide. . . .)

"Damn it all!" a voice said, gasping for breath, as the band of co-conspirators reached their meeting place at last. "Ilmarinen, I hope it's you."

"Yes. It's me," he answered, a little unsteadily. He slid his nightvision back into place with a blink of his eyelids, and smiled at last, as relief flooded through him. He realized as he did that a smile was not an expression he was much familiar with these days. *They had come:* Mede, and six more she had recruited, as she had promised. One more gamble he had won, one more small victory, one more painful step on a journey that seemed impossibly long. . . .

"By all that lives, Ilmarinen, I'm too old for this nonsense," Mede wheezed. She embraced him warmly in spite of the complaint, for old time's sake, and dropped down heavily onto an outcrop of rock. "What are you—and I—doing in this godforsaken place?"

"You know," he answered, even though the question was rhetorical. "Trying to save the future."

She made a sound that was somehow mocking and hopeful all at once.

"How are the children doing?" he asked. He assumed that if they were not doing well, she would have let him know. He and Mede had been together in their youth for long enough to produce three children, before their lives had taken separate turns. They had stayed in touch, and remained friends; their children were grown now.

"Bezai finally gave it all up; she's gone native on Sittuh'. The others are still in the Guild, hanging on, like the rest of us. It's in the blood, I suppose." She shrugged. "You could ask them yourself, sometime." Her voice took on an edge.

He looked down. "I'm sorry. I've been involved in this . . . project for so long. We've had no lives beyond it." When he looked up at her again he saw understanding, and was grateful.

He made introductions; she jerked slightly, showing her surprise as she met Vanamoinen face to face. For years Vanamoinen had been as reclusive as he was notorious within the Guild. Vanamoinen stared at her with a gaze so intense that Ilmarinen always thought of it privately as murderous; though he knew there was no one in existence who had more reverence for life than Vanamoinen had. "You were receptive to my data?" Vanamoinen asked softly, peering at her with naked wonder, as if she were some rare and unexpected insight that had turned up in a random datascan.

She glanced dubiously at Ilmarinen, as if Vanamoinen had asked her something nonsensical. "Of course I was," she said, looking back at him. "I'm here, aren't I? So are they." She gestured at the six other men and women gathered behind her, all of them wearing the uniform of Survey, as she was, with the datapatch of Continuity glowing dimly on every sleeve.

"How many of the people you shared it with refused to come?" Vanamoinen asked.

She looked surprised again. "Three." Her eyes clouded. "When I input your message, I felt . . . transformed. When I knew what it held, I *had* to come . . . we all did." Her voice filled with hushed wonder. "But the others—they got no input, any of them. They said I must be hearing things." She shook her head. "I was sure it was something that they would want to share in. I wanted to *tell* them . . . except that your message forbade it. Maybe there's something wrong with your transfer medium?"

"It worked exactly as I intended," Vanamoinen said flatly. "They weren't suitable for the project. I designed the data medium to select suitable personalities only." He grinned with sudden triumph. "Ilmar!" he shouted, and the empty night echoed. "I did it!"

Ilmarinen smiled. "Again," he said gently, and held up a warning hand.

Mede stared at Vanamoinen for a long moment, and shook her head. "Then I'm flattered, I suppose," she murmured. "It's brilliant, Vanamoinen—a centralized databank with biological ports, as a stabilizing force for the Pangalactic. The Interface is going to hell, and this could make a real, measurable difference. . . ." Her eyes gleamed. "But why not just give the concept to the Establishment? Why this pathological secrecy, for the love of All?"

Ilmarinen frowned, looking up at the stars. (Gundhalinu looked with him, feeling incredulous wonder push his consciousness through the darker mood that now moved the man called Ilmarinen, into the realization of who and where he was, at what fixed moment in time—) "Because I already approached them about it. If they were capable of implementing something like this, don't you think they would have? All they're capable of now is preventing it from happening." He shook his head, hearing the bitterness of years in his voice. "Stupid use of smartmatter has been killing the Pangalactic; we all know it. That's why the Establishment has been trying to root it out of everything nonvital. 'Nonvital' . . . they use the longevity drugs themselves, by the All!" His hands jerked. "We're history, Mede. . . . But smartmatter can save what's left of us, if we're only smart enough—" He broke off. "You know what we think, or you wouldn't be here. Believe me, Mede, we are not two lunatics alone in this." He glanced past her, at the half-dozen other earnest faces, the men and women who stood in a semicircle around her, watching his face in the darkness. "We could never have come this far otherwise. The computer is already functioning."

Mede let out a breath of surprise. "Where?"

He shook his head, as the image began to form in his thoughts; not even letting himself (or the other who held his breath inside him) remember its name. "I couldn't tell you if I wanted to. No one must ever know. It has to be that way, or it will never last."

She nodded. "But at least you can tell me what you want from me . . . us?" She gestured at her companions, glanced around her again, as if she were still astonished to find herself here. But there was almost a hunger in her voice as she asked, "What can we do?"

Slowly he reached into his jacket, and drew out a small container. On its side was the ages-old barbed trefoil signaling biological contamination. "Become sibyls," he said.

She stiffened. "Smartmatter—?"

He nodded, getting on with it before she could form real protests. "You're in Continuity. It gives your people excellent reason to travel extensively. What we need now are outlets—human computer ports able to interact with, and speak for the net. It would be easy for you to spread the word, to recruit them on the worlds you visit, just as we recruited you."

"Ilmarinen, we share a long history. You know I trust you with my life, or I would not have come . . ." she said slowly. "But are we the first you've asked this of?"

He nodded again. "Yes. But you won't be the last." He caught her stare, abruptly understood it. He touched the container of serum. "It's under control," he said, willing her to believe him. "There are no mistakes in its programming. The technoviral that will make you receptive has been designed by one of the few people who truly understands—"

She gazed at the container for a moment longer. "How can we know . . . ?"

"You're not the first to be infected." She looked back at him abruptly, as he drew out the thing that he wore night and day now, hidden beneath his clothing, close to his heart. A trefoil on a chain, the same symbol imprinted on the container; symbolizing how it bound him now to his chosen future. Silently Vanamoinen produced the same sign. Vanamoinen had been the first; he had been the second.

Mede's eyes studied them, searching for—something, or for the lack of it. Then, slowly, she offered Ilmarinen her hand.

(And as he touched her the stars wheeled and died, and . . .)

He was drifting, turning—he watched a spiral of nebula wheel past as he . . . moved. *(Moved.)* He lifted an arm, moved a leg experimentally—set himself spinning again, as if he were in zero gravities. *(Zero gee—)* He looked down; he was hanging in midair, in the pilot's chamber aboard the . . . the interstellar transport *Starcrosser.* Directly below him, through the transparent viewing wall, was a world called T'rast. The *Starcrosser* had brought this group of refugee colonists, survivors of a world decimated in intersystem warfare, here to begin a new life. His crew were in charge of seeing that they began it with all the knowledge, resources, and protection that it was still humanly possible to provide. His crew had mapped T'rast's surface, cataloged its hazards and its resources, seeded it with biogenetically adapted medicinals . . . what they had left of them.

He looked down again at the uniform he wore, the brown/green of Survey. *(Of course,* Gundhalinu thought, *what else could it be; but whose body—?)* The data patches glowed softly against its worn cloth. Still his duty, to serve the Pangalactic . . . to serve its people, even though there was no longer a single Pangalactic Interface controlled by a single Establishment—even though his own ability to obtain supplies or replace equipment had reached critical. He had kept on shaking his fist in the face of Chaos; struggling to do his work, the only work he knew, the only work he had ever wanted to do.

He looked out at the stars. He had known for years that one of these trips would be his last one. He would run out of supplies, or out of luck—Chaos would close its fist on the *Starcrosser,* something vital would fail, pirates would take them. . . . The crew were tired, burned out, afraid. This time—maybe it was right that this time should be the last. That was the way the others wanted it, he knew; to make this their final journey, to settle in here with the rest of the refugees. . . .

He called on the simulators, found himself standing on the surface of T'rast, with warm, azure water lapping his ankles. On the rock-strewn beach behind him, the bleached white boulders had been smoothed by time and tide until they resembled benign alien beings sunning themselves on the peaceful shore. In the distance he could see mountains, snow-capped even though it was summer here. It was beautiful; he could be happy in this place. . . .

But he touched the crystal hanging at his ear, and at his unspoken thought, the simulator changed again. He was living in his memories—deep in the heart of a canyon image, the red-rock walls rising around him until he could not see the sky, only the amber-tinged glow of reflected light pouring down on him, until he seemed to be standing in the heart of a burnished shell, the sensuous undulations of the stone around him like the wind made tangible. . . .

Standing on a glacier surface, in a silence so utter that the sound of his own blood rushing in his veins was like the sound of thunder; watching as the binary twin of his world rose above the black reaches of a distant range of peaks, an enormous, golden globe turning to silver the icebound terrain on which he stood. . . .

Standing beneath the restless, churning sky of yet another world, one where electromagnetic phenomena kept the atmosphere in constant flux like the windswept surface of a sea. . . .

Half a dozen more worlds flickered past, where he had been among the first—to explore, to study, catalog and open to colonization. It had been the life's work of his ancestors, of his Guild, for centuries. Now, at last, all of that had come to an end. Everything had its limits. . . . The world below him filled his eyes again: the last world he would ever see. It would be the challenge of a lifetime, to learn to live on one world, knowing that he could never leave it. He had no choice. *If he only had a choice.* . . . He felt wetness on his face, and was surprised to find that he was weeping.

The voice of one of the crew rattled over the neural link, making his vision light up with artificial stars, because the link was defective and there was no way to repair it. "Yes, what?" he subvocalized irritably, self-consciously.

"An interface from Continuity, sir." Her voice sounded as stunned as he suddenly felt. "I think . . . I think you'll want to input it immediately."

He closed his eyes, although he did not want to, until all that he saw was darkness. . . . And then the sound, that he had always dreamed of hearing . . . the chiming of astral voices, a brightness beyond any known spectrum, and the voice of a stranger calling him. . . .

(Calling him into darkness, falling away . . .)

And he was Derrit Khsana, a minor official in a petty dictatorship that was grinding under its heel the people of a world called Chilber . . . and he was Survey, although he wore no uniform, and the Guild he had sworn to serve above all other allegiances had opened no new worlds in three centuries. . . .

Secure in his secret knowledge, silently repeating a ritual meditation to help him remain calm, he walked the halls of the government nexus as confidently as if he had not just stopped the heart of the First Minister with untraceable poison supplied to him by that same hidden network. The way was now clear for a restructuring of the ruling party. They would insert a moderate in the First Minister's place, and with a few other subtle adjustments of the flow of influence, would release a thousand sibyls from involuntary service to the government's Bureau of Knowledge.

He had done his job well, and he would be rewarded well, as the sibyls' wisdom again flowed freely through the lives of his people . . . as he accepted the influential new post of Subminister of Finance that would be his just reward for this service. . . . He closed his eyes, shutting out the memory of another man's death, feeling it fade into the brightness of the future; feeling everything fade. . . .

And he saw a woman, cowering on the steps of a once-great building below him where he stood. He was Haspa, wearing the crimson robes and the spined golden crown of the Sun King . . . and she wore the spined trefoil of a sibyl. The crowd of faces surrounding her (looking somehow strangely, terrifyingly familiar, as if he were gazing down into the faces of his own ancestors) cried out for her death. And he raised his arm, the curving golden sacramental blade gleaming in the sunlight (he cringed in horror) as he brought it down. But it was not to kill her *(death to kill a sibyl . . .)* but to lay open his own wrist, and, before the gaping astonishment of the crowd, to mingle his own blood with the blood of a sibyl; to become one himself, to end the madness of persecution . . . because he had made the journey to their sacred choosing place, seeking the truth; and he had heard the music of the spheres and seen the unbearable brightness. . . . He felt the mystery of the divine virus take hold of him as their blood flowed together, and he knew fear and awe as the darkness of night overtook the sun. . . .

And he was falling through destiny, vision after vision, until he lost all sense of identity, any proof that he had ever been an individual man, in a structured reality he could call time . . . through centuries of hidden history into the future . . . feared and worshiped and persecuted and revered . . . a sibyl offering the key to knowledge openly, intimately, blood to blood; a member of a once-proud Guild forced into hiding by the secrets it bore, as it guarded its gift to humankind and forged a silent network of its own, a secret order underlying seeming chaos. . . .

And he was BZ Gundhalinu, third son of a rigid, Technocrat father—Survey member, Police inspector . . . traitor, failed suicide. He had gone into the wilderness called World's End in search of his brothers, to save their lives, to salvage the family's honor . . . to salvage his own honor, or end his own life. There he had found Fire Lake, and in the grip of its tortured reality he had lost all proof of his own reality . . . had been taken for a lover by a madwoman, a woman driven insane by the sibyl virus.

In the heat of lust she had infected him. And he had become a sibyl, and it had driven him sane; he had discovered at last the secret order at the heart of the chaos called Fire Lake. . . . And he had brought his brothers back, and given the secret of Fire Lake to the Hegemony. They had made him a hero and honored him, and respected him and kidnapped and imprisoned him and shown him the truth within truth. . . .

"—like he's gone into Transfer, for gods' sakes." Someone shook him, not gently, driving the words through his darkness like lines of coherent light.

"What? How? That's never happened—" Someone else peeled back his eyelid, letting in light; let it go again.

"—got no control, only been a sibyl for a few weeks. No real training either." Their voices echoed blindingly across the spectrum, making his eyes tear, yet so impossibly distant that they seemed unreachable.

"No formal training? It's a miracle he functions at all."

"He is a Kharemoughi—"

A snort of laughter. "He's a failed suicide, too; which meant he was better off dead by your count, until he discovered stardrive plasma in Fire Lake. Neither of those things has a pee-whit to do with why he's here . . . or why he's a Hero of the Hegemony either, probably." The words were clearer now, sliding down the spectrum from light to sound, growing easier to comprehend, closer to his center.

"Kindly keep your lowborn snideries to a—"

"Quiet! Remember where you are for gods' sakes, and what we're here for. We haven't got all night. How can we get him out of Transfer?"

"We can't. Once the net's got him, he's gone."

"This wasn't supposed to happen. Where did it send him? What if he can't pull out of it?"

"By the Aurant! Don't even say it."

"There's got to be a way to reach him. Use the light pencil. Maybe if you really burn him, threaten his life, the net will let him go."

"That won't . . ." Gundhalinu drew in a shuddering breath and squeezed the words out, "won't be necessary." He forced his eyes open, was blinded for his efforts, and shut them again with a curse, turning his face away from the light.

Someone's arm slid under his shoulders, raising him up carefully until he was almost sitting. Someone else held a cup to his lips. He drank. It was bandro; the strong, raw flavor of the spices and stimulant made his mouth burn.

He opened his eyes again, blinking in the glare, and lifted his hands, as he suddenly realized that he could, that he was sitting unaided, freed from his bonds.

The circle of faceless inquisitors still ringed him, at the limits of the light that shone down on him alone. He shook his head, rubbing his eyes, not entirely certain now whether this reality was any more real than the ones he had just inhabited these past minutes . . . hours . . . ? He had no idea how long he had been lost. He was thirsty and he needed to urinate, but that could be nerves, or the drugs they had used on him. He pulled his robe together, covering himself, and fastened the clasp almost defiantly.

"Welcome—home, Gundhalinu," one of the figures said solemnly.

Gundhalinu found himself searching for a hand that held a mug of bandro, anything that would distinguish any one of them from another . . . but even the mug had vanished. "Have I been away?" he asked tightly, his voice rasping.

"You can answer that for yourself," another figure said. "I trust your journey was enlightening?"

"Very," he answered, using the single word like a knife.

"Then you understand who we are . . . and what you have become, now?"

He looked from one flaming, featureless face to another, and shook his head. "No," he muttered, refusing to give them anything, his anger and indignation still fresh and hot inside him.

"Don't lie to us!" One of the figures stepped toward him, with the light pencil appearing suddenly in its hand. Gundhalinu flinched back involuntarily. "Don't ever underestimate the seriousness of our resolve, or of your situation. If we are not certain—now or ever—that you are with us, then you are against us, and you will pay. Sibyl or not, it is simple necessity. The group must survive. You saw how easily we brought you here. Nothing escapes us. Do you understand?"

Gundhalinu nodded silently.

"You went into Transfer during the interface. Was that intentional? Where did you go?"

"It wasn't intentional," he said. He looked down at the reassuring familiarity of his own hands, the skin smooth and brown, scattered with pale freckles. "I wasn't aware that you hadn't done it to me yourself. I don't know where I was. . . . I was—history." He shrugged, turning his palms up.

"You experienced an overview of the origins of the sibyl network, and its ties to historical Survey."

"Yes." He looked up again, facing the flaming darkness of the face before him. "I was . . . Ilmarinen." The archaic name felt strangely alien on his tongue.

"Ilmarinen—?" someone muttered, and was waved silent.

"I see," his questioner murmured; but he sensed from the tone that he had not made the anticipated response.

"I understand now," he pushed on, before they could lay any more questions in front of him like pressure-sensitive mines, "the link between Survey and the sibyls." His mind spun giddy for a moment as the full implications hit him. *If it was all true* . . . And somehow he was sure that it was. "Then it is true that there are higher orders within Survey, inner circles hidden even from our own members?"

"Now at least you're asking the right questions," the questioner said.

Gundhalinu let his feet slide off the edge of the table, so that he was sitting more comfortably, more like an equal. He did not attempt to put a foot on the floor, actually challenging their territory. "I have another question, that may not be the one you want me to ask. . . . Why? Why are you still necessary? Sibyls are no longer persecuted." *Except on Tiamat.*

His questioner shrugged. "In all times and places there are sociohistorical developments which threaten to impede or even destroy humanity's progress. Even before the sibyls, Survey was dedicated to helping humanity grow. To giving our people space, both physical and mental. It has always been that way; it always will be. We are dedicated to doing the greatest good for the most people, wherever possible . . . as unobtrusively as possible."

Gundhalinu rubbed his arms inside the sleeves of his robe. "But you'd kill me just like that if I oppose you?"

The questioner chuckled; the distorted sound was like water going down a drain. "I don't think that will be necessary, Commander Gundhalinu."

The light shining down on him went out, leaving him in sudden darkness, ringed by glowing holes that sucked his vision into the night, Black Gates opening on countless otherwheres or endless nightmare, myriad lights like the stars of an alien sky. . . . He sat motionless, hypnotized, seeing ancient starfields through the eyes of ancient Ilmarinen; the ghost-haunted hellshine of Fire Lake—

And then, one by one, the lights began to go out, until the darkness surrounding him was complete.

Abruptly there was light again, all around him this time; letting him see at last the room in which he was held prisoner—whitewashed, windowless, lined with portable carriers which could have held anything, or nothing—and the three men who remained in the room with him. He had counted nearly a dozen figures before. He wondered where the others had disappeared to, so quickly.

He fixed his gaze on the three who remained, realizing with a start of disbelief that he knew them all. Two were Kharemoughis—Estvarit, the Hegemonic Chief Justice, and Savanne, Chief Inspector of the Hegemonic Police force on Number Four; the third questioner was Yungoro, the Governor-General of the planet. He barely controlled the reflex that would have had the man he was before Fire Lake down off the table, delivering a rigid salute before he had taken another breath. Instead he looked behind himself, pointedly, at the restraints that had held him down. He looked at the men again, forcing himself to remember all he had learned and endured and become in the past months. . . . Forcing himself to remember that he himself was now a Commander of Police, and though he had no assigned command, outranked two of the three men in the room with him. He nodded to each man in turn, an acknowledgment between equals. "Gentlemen," he said. "It's a pleasure to see you again." His voice was steady; his mouth curved up of its own accord into an ironic smile. "Especially as a stranger far from home."

"The Universe is Home to us all." The Chief Justice—the one man who outranked him in the outside world—made the response, with a smile that looked genuine.

"You're a little hard on strangers," Gundhalinu said, and saw Savanne glance away. He got down from the table at last, feeling muscles pull painfully in his stiffened side. His relief and exhaustion left him weak; he supported himself unobtrusively against the cold metal edge of the table.

"I'm sorry, Commander," Estvarit said. "But it is always done this way. It is imperative that we impress upon new initiates both the seriousness of this induction and its grave importance to their own lives. A certain amount of fear serves the purpose." The Chief Justice was a tall, lean man, the tight curls of his hair graying. He had a slow, almost languid way of speaking that put others instinctively at ease.

Gundhalinu felt the iron in his smile turn to rue. "My nurse told me, when I was a boy, that one day when she was a child a winged click-lizard appeared on the windowsill of her parents' house. Her people considered it to be a blessing on the house. When she pointed it out to her father, he knocked her across the room. He told her afterward that an important event should always be marked by pain, so that you would remember it. But she said that she was not sure now whether she remembered the lizard because of the slap, or the slap because of the lizard."

He heard a barely restrained chuckle from the Governor-General. Estvarit quirked his mouth. "I think you have a career ahead of you as a public speaker, Gundhalinu."

"What made you decide all at once that I was material for the inner circles of Survey?"

Estvarit reached into his uniform robes and pulled something out. Gundhalinu started as his eyes registered what the other man held up for his perusal: two overlaid crosses forming an eight-pointed star within a circle, the Hegemonic Seal he had seen reproduced on every official government document and piece of equipment down to the buckle of his uniform belt; but transformed here into a shimmering miracle of hologramic fire. "I'm to be given the Order of Light?" he murmured; stunned, but, he realized, not particularly surprised. He had a sudden memory of the wilderness, of the fiery gem called a solii held out to him in the slender-fingered hand of a madwoman. . . . He shook his head slightly, clearing it.

Estvarit nodded. "For conspicuous courage and utter sacrifice, you are being made a Hero of the Hegemony. You won't be informed—officially—of the honor for about another week. Congratulations, Commander Gundhalinu. This award is usually given posthumously."

Gundhalinu wondered whether there was actually irony in Estvarit's voice. "I'm honored. . . ." He shook his head again, in awe, not in denial, as Estvarit placed the medal in his hand, letting him prove its reality.

"You've shown yourself worthy of the honor, Gundhalinu," Savanne said. "The . . . scars of the past have been erased by your discovery of the stardrive—"

Estvarit turned, frowning, to silence Savanne with a look. The Governor-General coughed and flexed his hands.

"Yes," Estvarit said brusquely, "you have been chosen to join the inner circles because of the discovery you made at Fire Lake, and all that it implies—and I don't mean awards or honors or any other superfluous symbolism. I mean the real, raw courage and the intelligence obviously required of anyone who could survive World's End, and come out of it not only alive and sane, but with the truth about it. The past is meaningless, now, because you've changed the future for all of us, as well as for yourself. I don't have to tell you that."

Gundhalinu passed back the medal without responding. He folded his hands in front of him, feeling surreptitiously for the marks on the inside of his wrists, the brand of a failed suicide, that he had had removed at last after his return from World's End.

"And because, instead of holding your knowledge for ransom, you gave it freely to the Hegemony." The Chief Justice's eyes searched his face. "Gundhalinu, the petty prejudices and the narrow-minded cultural biases of nations or worlds have no place in our organization. We serve the side of Order, against the Chaos that always threatens. I sense that you share that vision. And you have proven that you have the capacity to make a genuine difference."

Gundhalinu hesitated, studying the other man's face in turn, with eyes that had judged a lot of liars, and knew they were too often indistinguishable from honest human beings. But there was no hidden revulsion in this man's eyes, for what he had done to himself in what seemed now like a former life. . . . The Chief Justice was not simply the most powerful man in the Hegemonic government on Four, he was a Tech, a member of the highest level of society on Kharemough, their mutual homeworld. He could not have suppressed his response—would not have bothered to—unless what he said was true.

Gundhalinu had always had a sense that Estvarit was a man who deserved his position, a man of uncommon integrity; but now he actually believed it. "Yes," he said at last. "That is what I feel, too." His ordeal at Fire Lake had taught him many hard truths. But the hardest of them all was the bitter knowledge that what he had believed all his life—what being a Tech on Kharemough had always let him believe—about himself as the ultimate controlling force in his life was a laughable lie. He controlled nothing, in the pattern of the greater universe. And yet that utter negation of his arrogant self-importance, which had made him blame himself for circumstances beyond his control—which had made him believe he was better off dead—had, in the end, freed him. He had witnessed the precarious balance between Order and Chaos in the universe, and realized that, as a free man, he could make his own choices, that he was only himself, and not his family's honor, or his ancestors' expectations.

He had decided then that he and he alone controlled one thing, and that was how he chose to live his life. He had chosen to work for Order, and against Chaos . . . to do the greater good, even in defiance of the laws of the Hegemony, if those laws were unjust. "How did you know?" he murmured.

"Your actions spoke for you."

Gundhalinu sighed, like a man who had finally arrived home, feeling the tension flow out of him—tension that had become so profoundly a part of him that he could hardly believe it had gone. "Thank you," he said, feeling his throat close over the words, "for showing me that I'm not alone."

The Chief Justice smiled, and held up a hand. Gundhalinu raised his own hand, pressed it palm to palm in a pledge and a greeting. Somberly the other men touched hands with him.

Gundhalinu brought his hand up to his mouth to cover a sudden yawn. Without tension driving him forward, fatigue was gaining on him, threatening to drag him down. "Gentlemen, this has been truly unforgettable. I am grateful for all you've shown me. But it must be close to dawn, and I'm expected to be coherent and vertical for a charity breakfast in my honor given by the Wendroe Brethren." Irony pricked him, not for the first time, as he glanced at the Chief Inspector and the Governor-General. "Forgive me, but I am exhausted. . . ."

"Of course." The Chief Justice nodded. "But before you leave us, I must tell you two things: One is, of course, that you must not speak of this to anyone. You know the three of us now for what we are. . . . You will meet others in time, and be taught the ritual disciplines and also certain restricted information as you rise through the inner levels. But, more importantly, before you go there is one thing known only to the inner circles that we must share with you immediately, for the sake of the Hegemony's security."

Gundhalinu forced his weary, restive body to stay still. "What is it?"

"You hold vital information about the nature of the stardrive plasma and Fire Lake. That information must be transmitted to Kharemough immediately. They need lead time in fitting a fleet of ships. They must be ready to maintain order; because once the stardrive gets out, everyone in all the Eight Worlds will have the technology and the freedom to worldhop almost instantaneously, without the time-lags we now face. I'm sure you've already considered the tremendous change that will create in our interplanetary relations."

"You want Kharemough to maintain its control of the Hegemony, then?" Gundhalinu asked. "I am a Kharemoughi, and I love my people . . . but I thought I understood that Survey does not play favorites—"

Estvarit nodded. "But we do play politics, as we said. We try to achieve the result that brings about the most good for the most people. Only the established Hegemonic government can effectively control access to the stardrive, and keep the technology from spreading like a disease, causing political chaos and interstellar war. Because it will spread. . . ." He looked down. "By ordinary means it would take several years for even the news of your discovery to reach any other world of the Hegemony, including Kharemough. But you, as a sibyl, have the means to change that."

"How?" Gundhalinu asked, his hand searching for the trefoil symbol on its chain, which he was not wearing. "If no one on Kharemough even suspects this discovery, they can't . . . ask the right questions, so that I can give them the answers." *And yet* . . . In the back of his mind, he realized that he had done something very like it, when he had been lost in World's End: He had called Moon Dawntreader, and she had come to him—

"There is a way; there always has been, but we have kept it to ourselves. I will give you the name of one of our members, a sibyl, on Kharemough. With the special Transfer sequence we will teach you, you will be able to open a port to this person directly."

Gundhalinu made a sound that was not quite a laugh. "This is incredible! A means of instantaneous faster-than-light communication— Why haven't you shared this?"

"Because if we are to keep faith with the trust of our ancestors, we must have our secrets—keep our edge." Estvarit shrugged. "Now listen to me, and listen well. . . ."

Around them the lighting in the room dimmed and brightened, dimmed and brightened again. "Damnation!" Estvarit murmured. Abruptly the lights went out, smothering them all in pitch-blackness.

Ye gods, not again. The thought formed inside the blackness behind Gundhalinu's eyes. Someone's hands seized him by the shoulders, pulling him around with desperate urgency. "This way. . . ." He recognized the voice of the Governor-General. He let himself be led, fumbling but obedient, across the room and through what felt like a hole in the night—a change in deflected sound, in the quality of the air. He bumped up against a wall two steps farther on.

"Follow the tunnel up," the Governor-General murmured. "Don't worry, don't ask questions. Everything is all right. Just get out. Come to the Foursgate Meeting Hall tomorrow evening. We'll be in touch—"

And then he was alone, closed in . . . sure of it, even though he could see nothing. He stretched out his right hand, keeping his left firmly against the wall; fighting a sinking uncertainty for the second time in one night. He found the hard, slick surface of the narrow hallway's other wall less than an arm's length away. He began to feel his way along it, moving slowly, testing every step. The tunnel led him steadily upward, the air seeming to grow deader and more oppressive as he traveled, until at last he collided with a flat surface, the darkness suddenly made material.

But before panic could take hold of him, the surface gave under his pressure, releasing him into sudden daylight and fresh air.

He stumbled out into the street and the door slipped shut behind him, merging into the surface of the wall, until by the time he turned around he could not have said where it was. He stood staring at the wall for a long moment, breathing deeply, befuddled by the light and the chill, damp air.

He turned away again at last, taking in his surroundings and his predicament. He was still in Foursgate, but in the Old Quarter. Under his bare feet was a narrow stretch of moisture-slick pavement, all that separated the shuttered silent warehouses from the cold, lapping water of a canal—one of the myriad canals winding through the ancient duroplass buildings and out to the sea. He could smell the sea, even though its sharp, fresh scent was wrapped in the reek of stagnant water and rotting wood and other, even less appetizing odors.

The air around him was filled with moisture, as it always was, fog lying like a shroud over the Old Quarter, a fine, incessant drizzle wetting his face. The mottled gray of building walls faded into the wall of fog in either direction within a few meters of where he stood. The fog lay on the surface of the canal until the two became one in his vision, as seamlessly as the door had disappeared into the illusory solidness of the wall behind him. Somewhere in the distance he heard tower chimes begin a sonorous melody, their voices muffled and surreal. It must be barely dawn, and no one else seemed to be up and moving, even here.

He leaned against the building side, too weary not to, pulling his robe tighter around him as he began to shiver. He was all alone, wet, cold, half-naked and lost, without even the credit necessary to hire an air taxi to take him home. The events of the past hours suddenly seemed like an insane dream, but the fact that he was standing here proved their reality. One thing he was not, certifiably, was a sleepwalker.

"What the *hell* is going on here?" he demanded of the walls; heard his own words flung back at him. Why that unexpected, unceremonious exit from the depths of a hidden room? Was this supposed to be one final test—proving himself worthy by making his way home in the rain, creditless and barefoot—? He let out a short bark of laughter, sharp with anger and exasperation. But even as he thought it, he knew he did not believe that. Something unexpected had happened in there, and not just to him. Were there others trying to get at Survey's secrets . . . or were the inner circles of Survey not the haven of order and reason they seemed to be? He shook his head, too exhausted to work it out, or even to feel much concern about it. *They would be in touch. . . .* Then he would have his answers.

"Ferry, sah?" a deep voice called out, resonating eerily off the walls around him.

He looked up, felt water drip into his eyes from his hair. A shallow, high-prowed canal boat was soundlessly nosing its pointed bow in toward the small wooden dock almost below him. The man standing in its stern poled it closer with motions that looked effortless, but probably were not. The boatman wore the shapeless, hooded gray cape they all seemed to wear, *"to keep 'em from molding,"* his sergeant had remarked once.

"Where to, sah?"

Gundhalinu moved forward to the edge of the dock, looking down into the boat. Its outer hull was a silvery gray that made it one with the water surface, the fog, the stones of the quay. . . . But its interior, its single flat, wide seat, the elaborate carving on its prow, were decorated in strident, eye-stunning colors, alive with intricate geometric designs that had been patiently painted by hand.

He looked up again, trying to see the man's face. Most of it was shadowed by the sodden gray hood, but he could see that the boatman was a local—by the golden cast of his skin, the dark eyes with a slight epicanthic fold.

"Sah?" the boatman said patiently, gesturing him forward.

Gundhalinu hesitated, realizing how absurd he looked, and trying not to think about it. "I need to get back to the upper city. But I haven't any money."

The boatman chuckled. "Nor anything to keep it in either, even."

Gundhalinu smiled wearily, and shrugged. "Thanks anyway." He began to turn away, ready to start walking.

"Well, I'll take you up for the company, then," the boatman said. "Business is slow before dawn, and you look to be a stranger far from home."

Gundhalinu turned back, so quickly that he almost slipped on the slick pavement. Moving more cautiously, he climbed down into the boat and settled himself on the seat. He turned to look up again at the man standing behind him. It was no one he knew; he was certain of that. "The universe is home to us all." He murmured the traditional response, still watching the other man's face.

"So it is," the boatman said noncommittally, looking away again as he pushed off from the pier. He propelled the boat on up the canal with brisk, sure motions of his pole. After a time, he ventured, "Must have been quite a night, sah."

"Yes, it was," Gundhalinu said. "It certainly was that." He watched the buildings drift past like fragments of dreams, made rootless by the fog, as if they were moving and the boat was motionless.

"A young lady, sah? Perhaps then an unexpected husband—?"

Gundhalinu glanced back at him, and shook his head, smiling. "No."

"Too much to dream, then?"

"What—?" He broke off, remembering. To the locals that meant drugs. And yet when he thought about it, it made more genuine sense than anything he could have said himself about what he had experienced tonight. "Yes. I suppose so."

That answer seemed to satisfy the boatman, and he fell silent. Gundhalinu kept his own silence, his numb, shivering body hunched over itself, aching for permission to go to sleep sitting upright. But his mind refused to let go, fixating on one thing, the final thing out of all he had learned—*he could communicate with another sibyl.* What had happened to him at Fire Lake was not a fluke. All he needed was to know that sibyl's name. And he knew her name . . . her face, her body, her world. . . . The fog seemed to whiten, like fields of snow . . . *Moon.*

"Here we are, sah."

He started awake; looked up, realizing that he had nodded off, that they had arrived at the Memorial Arch that marked the boundary between the upper and lower sections of Foursgate, between street and canal, land and sea. Here he could find transportation that would accept a credit number, or would at least take him to his own door and wait while he fetched his card to pay for the ride.

The boat bumped adroitly against the pylons of the dock. The boatman held the craft steady as Gundhalinu got to his feet.

"I don't know how to thank you—" he began, but the boatman shook his head.

"No need, sah. Only take some free advice, then, from one who knows this world: Watch out for the ones who did that to you. They'll fill your mind up with too many of their dreams, until you can't think clearly anymore. What they sell you isn't all true, and it isn't all harmless. Be on your guard, when you mix in those circles." He held out his hand, stood waiting to help Gundhalinu make the unsteady step across onto solid ground.

"Yes," Gundhalinu murmured uncertainly. "Yes, I will. . . ." He took the proffered hand; felt an unmistakable, hidden pattern in the brush of the boatman's fingers. He returned it, and felt the grip tighten warmly over his own before he stepped onto the pier.

"Blessed be, sah," the boatman said. "It's a privilege I don't have every day, giving a ride to a famous person like yourself. . . ." He pushed away from the dock.

"Wait—!" Gundhalinu looked up, gesturing the boatman back. The boatman raised his own hand in a farewell salute as his boat drifted on into the mist.

Gundhalinu stood silently, gazing after him until he was lost from sight.

ONDINEE: Razuma

Kedalion Niburu leaned against the warm side of the hovercraft, breathing in the parched, spice-scented air of the marketplace, taking in the color-splashed scene with mixed emotions as he waited for Reede Kullervo's return. He glanced diagonally across the street at a mudbrick wall topped by iron spikes. From behind its heavy wooden gate, he could hear the unmistakable screams of someone in serious pain. The someone in question was not Reede, which meant that the visit was proceeding as planned.

The local dealer behind that gate had been cutting Reede's product with inferior drugs, or so he'd heard. When he was in one of his moods, Reede liked to set matters straight personally, and he'd been in one of his moods today, when he'd kicked Kedalion out of bed at dawn, calling him a lazy son of a bitch.

Damn him. Kedalion took a deep breath. At least it had gotten them out of the citadel for the day. Humbaba didn't like it when Reede did his own dirty work . . . but then, Reede didn't care, and even Humbaba seemed powerless to stop him.

It seemed impossible that it had been less than three years, in subjective time, since he had gone to work for Reede Kullervo . . . since he had, more accurately, come under Reede's thumb. He felt as though he had been Kullervo's private property forever; even though he still remembered as vividly as if it were yesterday the day he had come to work for Humbaba's cartel. Like a near-fatal wound, it was not something he was ever likely to forget: that day when he had finally admitted to himself that Reede Kullervo's power and influence were actually as great as Reede had claimed; that Kedalion Niburu had become a nonperson, who would starve to death on the streets of Razuma's port town before anyone would hire him for any job whatsoever—because Reede had put out the word that he was spoken for. With the *Prajna* impounded for docking fees and the red debit figure on his nonfunctional credit card showing larger each day, he had finally swallowed his pride and sold himself—and a willing Ananke—into this golden servitude.

He sighed, pushing the memory back into a closet in his mind, where he sometimes managed to keep it forgotten for days at a time. He had to admit, in spite of everything, that there were worse jobs, worse positions he could be in. . . . He could be the dealer getting the shit kicked out of him behind that wall across the street, for instance.

He inched farther into the hovercraft's shade. The heat made him dizzy; the sweat on his skin dried almost instantly, but even that wasn't enough to make him feel cool. At least the heat was predictable. Razuma was as close as he had come to a home in a long time, and he was glad enough to be back in town after their latest trip offworld.

His travels with Reede were neither as frequent nor—as far as he could tell—as hazardous to his health as his former solo runs. So far they had been offworld twice in the time he had worked for Reede. And the job paid a hell of a lot better, just as Reede had promised him. But the fact that he never knew what the trips were for—was never given even a clue about what Reede wanted, or got out of, those journeys—preyed on his nerves in a different sort of way; just as being stuck on Ondinee for the majority of his time, playing glorified chauffeur to a manic-depressive, did.

On the other hand, he'd discovered that working for Reede had a built-in cachet that protected him from the locals' harassment, while it gave him access to places and pleasures he'd never dreamed this planet possessed. A world was a big place, and not all of Ondinee was like Razuma. Reede had taken them along to a mountain resort with views he would never forget, to a city on South Island where the sea was as warm as bath water and the color of aquamarines.

And then there had been the orbital habitat, with some of the best gaming simulators he had ever encountered. Kedalion remembered watching Reede play the games one night. It had been like watching free-fall ballet, the way Reede's perfect reflexes and brilliant mind had made winning seem completely effortless. Reede had given them unlimited player-credit, and their losses had almost offset the amount he had won himself. But afterwards Reede had been in a foul mood, as if he'd lost instead of won, or as if, when you never lost a game, winning might as well be losing. . . .

And on the other hand, most of what they saw was still Tuo Ne'el's thorn forest and citadels, or the streets of Razuma.

Kedalion searched the crowds for Ananke, who had wandered off into the square, trying to take his mind off circumstances. He spotted him—surrounded as usual by a squad of street urchins. They shrieked and trilled approval as Ananke juggled anything within reach, contorted his body with an acrobat's absurd grace, and sang nonsense songs. He had taken to wearing a specially fitted leather glove on one foot, instead of his usual sandal; it was a spacer's trick, freeing one foot for use in low-gravity environments. On most of the spacers Kedalion had known it was only an affectation. But Ananke's physical dexterity made the boast genuine: even in normal gravity, he sometimes seemed to have three hands. Kedalion watched him with mildly envious admiration. He saw some of the adults who invariably gathered around toss out coins; Ananke left them lying in the dust for the children to pick up. They all knew that he worked for the offworlders—the money, and his disdain for it, were the proof of his prestige.

Kedalion shook his head, smiling briefly. He reached into a pocket and took out his huskball, tossing it back and forth from hand to hand. Ananke had proved to be quick and flexible, mentally as well as physically, just as he had promised; and knowing that his skill was recognized and appreciated had only made him work harder. Once they'd gotten past the fear that Reede would kill them one day on a whim, he had grown more comfortable with their new employment than Kedalion would ever feel. Ananke had gone from abject terror directly to a kind of blissful hero-worship that was probably a hell of a lot more dangerous. Fortunately his naïve fascination with Reede's volatile mood swings seemed to amuse Reede more than annoy him. This was the kid's homeworld, and having Reede's protection covering him seemed to free him of some of his dislike for living on it.

Kedalion's smile faded, and he sighed again, thinking nostalgically on the false comfort of youth. He straightened away from the hovercraft as his eye caught motion at the distant gate. Reede came out of it, slamming it behind him, and strode through the crowd in the square as if they didn't exist. They flowed out of his path as obligingly as water. Kedalion watched him come, seeing red stains on his clothes and black satisfaction in his eyes. Kedalion felt all expression drain out of his own face. He looked away, calling, "Ananke!"

Ananke turned, catching a handful of various fruits as they fell from the air. His own grin disappeared; he waded obediently through the belt-level protests of the children, tossing the fruit to them as he walked back toward the hovercraft.

Reede reached it first, and nodded at Kedalion with a grunt that meant he was pleased with himself. He leaned against the craft's door, cracking his knuckles.

"Feel better now?" Kedalion said, and regretted it instantly; sounding even to himself like a man chiding a child.

Reede looked at him, and raised an eyebrow. "Much," he said. "Do you mind?"

Kedalion grimaced. "Better him than me, I suppose."

Reede laughed. "Damn right. . . . Don't sulk, Niburu. Ozal will be crawling around on all fours by tomorrow. And he'll never, ever fuck with my product again." He shrugged, loosening the muscles in his shoulders, and pulled at his ear.

"Ananke!" Kedalion shouted again, an excuse to look away, an excuse to raise his voice. He saw with some annoyance that Ananke had gotten sidetracked into an argument with a group of boys who had begun tossing something cat-sized back and forth in imitation of his juggling. Kedalion recognized the shrilling of a quoll in distress; heard Ananke's voice rise above the general laughter as he tried to catch the animal they were throwing like a ball across farther and farther stretches of air. They angled across the square, drawing him away from the hovercraft.

Reede's head swung around as the animal began to shriek in terror or pain. He stood motionless, watching the scene; muttered something to himself about *being a stupid asshole*.

"Ananke!" Kedalion shouted again; feeling his stomach knot with disgust, not sure whether it was the scene in the street or Reede's reaction to it that angered him more. "You bastard," he muttered, looking back at Reede before he started out into the square himself—just as one of the boys shouted, "Catch *this*, juggler!" and pitched the wailing quoll into the air in a long arc. Ananke ran and leaped after it, futilely, crashing into the low ceralloy wall that rimmed the neighborhood cistern. Ananke barely kept himself from falling in as the quoll flew over his head, down into the depths of the spring-fed tank.

Kedalion stopped moving as he saw the quoll go into the cistern. Ananke hung motionless over the wall, staring down into the tank like a stunned gargoyle.

Someone pushed past Kedalion, jarring him; he saw Reede run out across the square to the cistern. Reede climbed onto the wall, stood looking down into the depths for a heartbeat, and then jumped.

"*Edhu—!*" Kedalion gasped. He began to run. Ananke was still hanging over the cistern's rim, staring down into the well in disbelief as Kedalion reached his side.

Kedalion peered over the rim, just able to see down to where the water surface lay in the deep shadows below. He blinked the sunlight out of his eyes, heard splashing and panic-stricken squealing echo up the steep seamless walls. He saw Reede in the water far below, struggling to get ahold of the floundering creature. At last Reede clamped it in both hands and shoved it inside his shirt, kicked his way toward the steps that spiraled down the cistern's interior.

Women and girls with water jugs balanced on their heads stood gaping as he hauled himself up out of the water onto the platform where they had gathered; they backed away as he staggered to his feet and started the long climb up the steps. Kedalion and Ananke watched him come, with the animal held against him, still struggling futilely.

Reede reached the street level at last, his eyes searching the crowd. Kedalion hurried forward, with Ananke trailing behind him. "Reede—!"

Reede turned at his voice, waited at the top of the stairs until they reached him. He wasn't even breathing hard, Kedalion noticed—Reede had more physical stamina than any three men. But water streamed from his hair and clothing, his arms and chest oozed red from the scratches and bites the frantic quoll had inflicted on him in its struggles.

"*Bishada!*" Ananke cried, grinning with awe and gratitude. "You saved it—"

Reede read the expression on the boy's face, and his own face twisted. "No. You saved the fucking thing," he said. He reached into his shirt and dragged the animal out, slung it at Ananke. "Here. You know the rule by now. You save it, it belongs to you. It's your responsibility. Not mine."

Ananke took it into his arms gingerly, keeping its long, rodentine teeth away from contact with his hands, protected by the layers of his robes as he held it against his chest, murmuring softly to it. He glanced up at Reede again, for long enough to murmur, "Thank you."

But Reede's attention was somewhere else already. He moved away from them abruptly, shoving past a couple of locals to pick someone out of the crowd of curiosity seekers. He caught the boy by his robes and dragged him forward, pitched him over the cistern's rim almost before the boy had time to scream in protest.

Kedalion heard the boy's scream as he went in, and heard the splash as he hit the water far below. The motion had happened almost too fast for him to recognize the victim as one of the quoll's tormentors, the one who had thrown it into the cistern.

Reede came back to them, not looking right or left now, his face expressionless as he glanced at the quoll. It had stopped struggling and was burrowing into the folds of Ananke's sleeve, making anxious oinking sounds, almost as if it were trying to become a part of his body. Ananke stroked its bedraggled fur as gently as if he were touching velvet.

Reede moved on past them, the motion signaling them to follow.

"Reede—" Kedalion said, catching up to him with an effort.

"Drop it," Reede said, and the words were deadly.

"—Are we going back to the citadel?" Kedalion finished, as if that were what he had intended to ask.

"No." Reede looked away; looked down at himself and grimaced, shrugged, looked away again. "I have other business to tend to. Drop me in Temple Square. Take the evening off; I'll call you when I'm through."

"You better tend those bites," Kedalion said. "The gods only know what that quoll—"

Reede looked down at him, his irritation showing. "Don't worry about me, Niburu," he said sourly. "I'm not worth it."

"Just worrying about my job," Kedalion muttered, trying to bury his unintentional display of concern as rapidly as possible.

"I thought you hated this job," Reede snapped.

"I do," Kedalion snapped back.

Reede laughed, one of the unexpectedly normal laughs that always took Kedalion by surprise. "If I die I've left you everything I own in my will."

Kedalion snorted. "Gods help me," he murmured, half-afraid it might even be true. He unsealed the doors of the hovercraft.

Reede grinned, climbing into the rear as the doors rose. He sat down heavily, obliviously, his clothes saturating the expensive upholstery of the seat with pink-tinged water. Kedalion got in behind the controls; Ananke climbed in beside him. Ananke was still carrying the quoll, which had buried itself in his robes until all that was visible was its head pressed flat against his neck, sheltered beneath his chin. It still made a constant burbling song, as if it sought a reassurance that did not exist in the real world. Ananke clucked softly with his tongue, and stroked it with slow hands. He glanced up, as if he felt Kedalion's eyes on him; his own eyes were full of an emotion Kedalion had never seen in them before, and then they were full of uncertainty.

Kedalion smiled, and nodded. "Just don't let it shit all over everything, all right?" He took them up, rising over the heads of the streetbound crowd and higher still, until even the flat rooftops were looking up at them. He could see the pyramidal peaks of half a dozen temples rising above the city's profile; he headed for the one that he knew Reede meant, the one near the starport that the local police had driven them into one fateful night. He tried not to think about that night, without much success.

He brought the flyer down again, settling without incident into an unobtrusive cul-de-sac near the club where they had all first met. The Survey Hall still occupied the address above its hidden entrance. Reede often came to this neighborhood, although what he did here was as obscure to Kedalion as most of his activities were.

Reede got out again, saying only, "Do what you want. I'll call you, but it won't be soon."

Kedalion nodded, and watched him move off down the street with the casual arrogance of a carnivore. Reminded of other animals, he turned to look at Ananke; at the quoll, lying against Ananke's chest like a baby in folds of cloth, only muttering to itself occasionally now. "How did you do that?" he asked.

Ananke shrugged, stroking its prominent bulge of nose with a finger. "Quolls are very quiet, really. You just have to let them be." The quoll regarded him with one bright black eye, and blinked.

Kedalion half smiled. "You could say the same about humans."

"But it wouldn't be true."

Kedalion's smile widened. "No. I guess not." He glanced away down the street; Reede had stopped at a jewelry vendor's cart near the corner of the alley.

"I want to go to the fruit seller."

Kedalion popped his door. "Go ahead. You heard the boss: Do what you want."

"You're the boss, Kedalion." Ananke grinned fleetingly, his white teeth flashing.

Kedalion shook his head, not really a denial. "Since when do you have an appetite for wholesome food?" Whenever they were in town Ananke lived on keff rolls—bits of unidentifiable meat and other questionable ingredients, rolled in dough and fried in fat, all so highly spiced that pain seemed to be their only discernible flavor. "Is the fruit seller young and pretty?"

"Quolls only eat vegetables and fruit," Ananke said, glancing down.

Kedalion shrugged and nodded, watched him get out and wander off in the direction of the square, passing Reede, who was haggling with the jewelry vendor. Kedalion had never seen Ananke show any real interest in either a woman or a man, and that was strange enough. The kid seemed to be pathologically shy, to the point of never letting anyone see him undressed—something which could get damned inconvenient in the crowded quarters of a small ship on an interstellar voyage. Maybe that explained his problem, or maybe it was only another symptom of whatever the real problem was. . . . He supposed it didn't really matter what Ananke's problem was, as long as he did his job and didn't go berserk.

He stretched and got out of the hovercraft, securing the doors behind him. He thought about Ravien's club, remembering Shalfaz. He hadn't gone back there for a long time, after what had happened to them that night. And when he had, it had been after two trips offworld with Reede. More than nine years had passed at Ravien's, while only two had passed for him. Someone had told him then that Shalfaz had retired. She'd gone into the somewhat more respectable profession of dye-painting—decorating the hands of wealthy, daring young women with intricate designs for weddings and feast days. He was glad for her, but he missed her. And he sure as hell didn't miss the drinks, or the atmosphere, at Ravien's. Maybe he'd just go get himself some early dinner. . . .

He made his way around the rear of the craft, heading for the square. As he glanced back, checking it over a last time, his eye caught on something that lay glinting in the dust. He went back and picked it up. It was the white metal pendant set with a solii that Reede always wore—he called it his good luck charm. The quoll must have broken the chain in its struggles, and the pendant had fallen out of his clothes.

Kedalion glanced down the street, saw Reede's back turn as he started away from the jewelry vendor's cart. "Reede!" he called, but Reede went on around the corner.

Kedalion started after him down the narrow street, not even sure why; telling himself that handling Reede's lost charm made his own superstitions itch. He reached the corner, ignoring the jewelry seller's singsong wheedling as he looked past the cart at the open square. After a moment his eyes found Reede in the crowd, as the flash of dangling crystals danced across the stark black of his vest-back.

Reede was not moving fast, which meant there was half a chance his own short legs might catch up with Reede's long ones. Kedalion pushed on, keeping to the edges of the unusually heavy crowds. The air reeked with incense. It must be some sort of feast day, for so many people to be out in the square, damn the luck. But he was gaining on Reede, slowly, and he called out his name again. Reede glanced back, but Kedalion was hidden by the crowd.

Reede went on again, walking faster. They were nearing the place where Ravien's club was located. For a brief moment Kedalion wondered if he was headed there—he swore under his breath as he saw Reede turn off suddenly into a passageway between two of the buildings that ringed the square. He kept his eyes fixed on the spot until he reached it, and ducked into the same entrance, below a peeling archway. The shadowy access was so dark after the brightness of the square that he had to stop a moment, blinking until his eyes adjusted. There were ancient flagstones under his feet, featureless walls with no openings on either side of him, so close together that he could almost reach out and touch them. Reede was nowhere in sight.

Kedalion went along the passage, doggedly, unable to stop now until he had found out where Reede had gone. The passageway ended abruptly at a featureless metal door. He pushed on it; to his surprise it let him in.

The corridor beyond it was startlingly clean and modern. Inset glowplates gave him dim but sufficient light as he moved along it, more confidently now, until he reached another set of doors. The doors slid back at his approach, opening on a meeting room. He stopped dead as the people gathered there turned to stare at him. He stared back, taking in the glow of datascreens around a torus-shaped table, the hologramic display at the table's core, the startling contrast among the faces seated around it or still standing together near the doorway.

Half a dozen of them had ringed him in already, looking down at him with the eyes of Death, before he had time to realize he had made a mistake that was probably fatal.

"Are you a stranger far from home?" an ebony-skinned man wearing the robes of a High Priest asked him.

Kedalion glanced down at himself. "I guess it shows, then," he said, and smiled feebly. The smile faded as he watched weapons blossom like deadly flowers, and knew that he had not given them the right answer.

"Kill him," a voice said from somewhere.

"Reede—" he said, "I'm looking for Reede!" raising his voice in desperation.

"Niburu!" Reede's face appeared suddenly, like a vision, among the faces of offworld drug bosses, local police and church officials, other faces he couldn't put any occupation to. Reede pushed into the center of the ring and caught him by the shirt front. "What the fuck are you doing here—?" Reede's fist tightened; the exasperation on his face was as genuine as the anger.

"I thought you'd want this." Kedalion held out the charm, keeping his voice barely under control.

Reede snatched the charm from his hand, and stared at it. "Gods . . ." he muttered, like a man who had lost his soul. As he stuffed it into his pocket, Kedalion realized that two men and a woman standing in the circle around him were wearing the same pendant. One of the men was a drug boss named Sarkh; the woman was Reede's new wife, Humbaba's ex-wife, Mundilfoere.

"Reede—?" someone demanded from behind him.

"He's my man. He saw nothing. Right—?" Reede's hand closed painfully over Kedalion's shoulder. "You saw nothing."

Kedalion shook his head, as Reede pushed him roughly backward through the barrier of bodies until they were both out in the hall. The doors sealed shut behind them.

"You saw nothing," Reede repeated, softly this time, looking down at him with something in his eyes that Kedalion almost imagined was compassion. "Never follow me again." He released his grip on Kedalion's shirt, turned his back on him and disappeared through the doors as if his pilot had ceased to exist.

Kedalion stood a moment longer in the hall, before he had the strength to shake off the invisible hands that still seemed to hold him prisoner. He turned finally and went back along the hall, along the passageway, and out to the street.

"What the hell was that all about?" Sarkh snarled, as Reede reentered the meeting room alone.

"This." Reede pulled the solii pendant out of his pocket and held it up.

The eyes of everyone in the room were on him, now, but he made no further explanation. One by one they began to look away from his gaze, backing down.

Sarkh frowned. "That was a stupid risk. I think we should—"

"Don't think, Sarkh," Reede said. "Why spoil your perfect record?"

Sarkh turned back, his face mottling with anger, and took a step toward Reede.

"I speak for Kedalion." Mundilfoere stepped quickly between them. "Reede— remember where you are!" She held up a dark hand, palm open, in front of each of them; stepped back again, in what seemed to be a single fluid motion. The two men eased off. "Kedalion Niburu has worked for Reede for years," she said, looking at Sarkh. "He saw nothing that he could have understood. And he is perfectly trustworthy. He will do what he is told; and he was told to forget it." She twitched a shoulder, half smiling.

Sarkh grunted and shrugged, turning away as Mundilfoere looked back at Reede. She was not wearing bells and veils now; never did, here. She was dressed in the formless gray coveralls of a starport loader, her long, midnight-black hair pulled back in a pragmatic knot. A perfect disguise . . . or maybe the woman back at Humbaba's citadel was really the disguise. There was no trace of deference in her manner here, nothing but anger in the glance that flicked over him and found his behavior wanting.

"Mundilfoere—" he said, his hand reaching for her almost unconsciously.

"Sit down," she said, and turned her back before he could touch her. Her motion sent out ripples through the figures still standing; they followed her like a wake toward the meeting table. A few of them glanced back at him, at his wet clothes and the fresh scratches on his bare arms and throat, as they took their appointed places.

Reede was the last to sit down, hanging back like a sullen child—or at least, made to feel like one, when he sat down at last at Mundilfoere's right hand.

"Who has called this Brotherhood to meeting, here?" Irduz, the Priest, asked. He always led the Questions, being the sort of pompous bastard who enjoyed repetitious ritual. Reede shut his eyes and leaned back in his seat as the drone of the recitation began. *Gods, get it over with. . . .* He fingered the beaten metal of the ear cuff he had bought from the street vendor, shifting impatiently in his seat.

"I have." Reede recognized the voice of the next person in the circle—Alolered, the Trader, who in the outside world was a dutiful, successful businessman in the interstellar datastorage trade.

"I have." The voice of Mother Weary, one of the few women who had made it big in the drug trade; she headed a cartel that was still growing. She was nearly eighty, and as vicious as firescrub.

"I have." The voice of TolBeoit, who appeared to be nothing more than a seller of herbal cures in a Newhavenese botanery.

"And who has called this Brotherhood into being, and given us our duty, and shown us the power of knowledge?" the High Priest intoned.

"Mede." The progression of voices came inexorably toward him.

"Ilmarinen," Baredo said, next to him. Reede sat motionless, his eyes still shut, paralyzed by the vision of three faces out of memory, three impossible faces. . . . Knowing that it was his turn to speak, but unable to. Baredo reached across the empty seat between them to nudge his arm impatiently. Reede jerked, glaring back at him. "And Vana—Vana—"

"Vanamoinen," Mundilfoere finished the name for him. Her hand brushed his briefly, reassuringly; his own hand felt cold and clammy. He blinked, his eyes burning. *He hated to say that name.* He could never get it out of his mouth, when it came his turn to speak it. The other names were nothing; but that one . . .

"Ho, Smith," Mother Weary snorted, "penis envy?"

Reede glared at her across the table. "Eat it, you dried up hag," he said. She cackled infuriatingly. They called him "the Smith" for the same reason they sometimes called him "the new Vanamoinen"—because if a project involved biotechnology, he was the best at inventing it, producing it, fixing it. He had heard often enough from the Brotherhood that only the Old Empire's last recorded genius could have done it better, faster—or at all, in the case of the water of life, which he had failed so profoundly to recreate. Lately the title had become a mix of compliment and jibe, even though the real Vanamoinen had only been a skillful manipulator of the existing technology, and who had had the resources of an Empire plus the brilliant research data of millennia at his disposal . . . something the Brotherhood would never be able to match, not limited to the Eight Worlds of the Hegemony.

He hated being taunted with Vanamoinen's name, but that was not why it stuck in his throat. . . . He looked down at himself, staring at the raw crystals glinting like rainbow-hazed stars against the black night of his vest; at his hands, his tattooed arms, the muscles of his body, that he had used so recently, together with his superior mind and perfect reflexes, to beat the living crap out of a cheating small-time drug dealer. *Vanamoinen. Vanamoinen.* It caught in his throat, in his thoughts, like an obscene refrain, playing obsessively; when the real obscenity was here, in his . . . in his . . .

Reede stretched the fingers of his bruised hands and forced his mind to pay attention to what was going on around him. The drone of stale ritual was nearly finished—the invocations that supposedly served to remind them all of the greater tradition to which their particular cabal belonged, and from which it drew its real power: *Survey.*

"And dedicated to one thing, for millennia—" Irduz intoned.

"Survival," Baredo answered beside him, as the progression of questions and answers came around the table toward him again.

"And what is the thing that binds us all—?" Irduz asked the last of the ritual Right Questions.

"Blood."

Reede lifted his head, his mouth still half open to speak the response.

Someone had appeared in the empty seat to his right—or something had: A shapeless, amorphous darkness, in which there might have been a human body, somehow twisted or deformed. . . .

Reede swore under his breath, drawing away instinctively from what suddenly inhabited the space beside him. *The Source.* Wondering why in the name of a thousand hells Thanin Jaakola had chosen to occupy that particular seat.

"Beginning without me—?" Jaakola said. If an exhumed corpse could be forced to speak, that was the voice it would have. Reede almost thought he could smell a faint odor of putrescence leaking out of the blackness beside him. But he was probably imagining it; that thing beside him was only a hologramic projection, just like several of the two dozen other Brothers around the table, who, like Jaakola, chose not to attend in person. It was rumored that Jaakola had some wasting, incurable disease. It was also rumored that the darkness was all for psychological effect. The Source could be anyone, do anything, as long as he held that secret. Reede had no idea at what level in the Brotherhood Jaakola actually functioned, which meant that he was powerful enough to be extremely dangerous.

"We begin at the agreed time," Mundilfoere answered, making the response that no one else would make. "You requested this meeting."

He grunted in acknowledgment, or disgust. That he hated women was the only thing anyone seemed to know for certain about him. Reede had never heard why, if there was a reason. He was not sure at what level Mundilfoere's own influence ended, but she dared more against the Source than most of the Brotherhood who gathered here dared. Sometimes he wondered if she antagonized Jaakola specifically because she knew what he thought of her. "I am in time for the real purpose of this meeting, then," Jaakola said, increasing the level of insult a magnitude. "Brothers, news has come to me of something that we have only dreamed of—and in this company, I don't say that lightly." There might have been a smile behind the words. Reede was sure it was mocking; not sure why. Jaakola had the attention of everyone around the table, now. "Someone has discovered a source of stardrive plasma—here in the Hegemony, on Number Four."

Exclamations of disbelief and surprise filled Reede's ears, but his own incredulity drowned them all out. He sat motionless, accessing passively as Jaakola fed data into all their units. The Old Empire had been able to exist in all its far-flung glory because it possessed a means of faster-than-light travel. The stardrive plasma was a form of smartmatter, bioengineered to manipulate space-time, to permit time-like movement by a ship through space without paradox. When the Old Empire had fallen, the technology had been lost to many, possibly most, of its former worlds. None of the worlds that became the Hegemony had possessed a viable stardrive, for a millennium or more. And even though popular wisdom held that the sibyl net could answer any question, there were questions that it would not answer—including any concerning the process for recreating smartmatter. There were those who said smartmatter had caused the Old Empire's fall; that the net's creators had wanted to make sure it didn't happen again, by suppressing all data about it.

The sibyl net also refused to provide its users with a starmap, for reasons no one clearly understood. As a result, it had become virtually impossible to locate other worlds of the former Empire, whether you had a stardrive or not. Kharemough had found the seven worlds of the Hegemony by sending countless probes through their Black Gate, like notes in bottles.

The Kharemoughis' obsessive archaeological work in Old Empire ruins had actually given them a key to the location of a former neighbor in interstellar space as well; one that was not absurdly distant in light-years. They had sent out their fastest sublight ships, hoping to find stardrive plasma still in existence there. The ships had gone out nearly a millennium ago, and the Kharemoughis believed they would return any day now . . . if stardrive technology did still exist on that planet. "Come the Millennium," they said, like a prayer, meaning the day when they regained their freedom in the galaxy. He for one had never expected to see the day when the Hegemony saw a single molecule of stardrive plasma.

But now the Millennium had come, from a completely unexpected direction. One man, out in the formidable wasteland known as World's End, had discovered why the bizarre anomaly called Fire Lake had caused the phenomena that made World's End a realtime Hell: the Lake was actually stardrive plasma run wild, from the remains of an Old Empire freighter that had crash-landed there during the Empire's last days.

Reede wondered what kind of man it was who had made that discovery. He knew the data on World's End; had studied all that was recorded about it in the universal access, because it had fascinated him. There had been details in the data that had seemed to mean something to him, but he hadn't been able to make his mind put it together. The visuals had haunted his dreams like succubi, calling him. He had wanted to go there, to see it for himself, to answer it . . . but the Brotherhood always had plans for him, and none of them included Fire Lake. Now someone had done what he had dreamed of doing—entered the heart of World's End, and actually discovered the secret that had defied centuries of study by the best minds in the Hegemony.

Now that he knew the answer, he saw with sudden, galling clarity that the answer had been obvious all along. But he hadn't asked the right questions. He felt a surge of something that was almost lust when he imagined meeting whoever possessed the mind that had.

Reede glanced into the darkness beside him; looked away again, listening to the mutterings of excitement and concern spreading around the table. He covered his ears, absorbing the datafeed again, trying to ignore the infuriating slowness of it. He hated this system, with its crude combination of inferior technologies. He had never seen a better system; but somehow he knew one existed, somewhere. Just as the stardrive had.

He pulled his mind back into the present at last, forcing himself to pay attention to the discussion that had been evolving around the table.

"—about what this could mean to our trade," someone said, across the table.

"It changes everything," Sarkh echoed, belaboring the obvious.

"It doesn't mean shit if we don't have it," Mother Weary snapped. "And we don't have it."

Noticing Mundilfoere's silence, Reede glanced at her, wondering what was on her mind. She did not look surprised; he found her staring back at him with an indefinable expression. He held her gaze, unable to look away.

"Exactly," Jaakola said, bending the word like a piece of plastic. "And so graciously put. We do not have the stardrive plasma in our possession. And obviously, we must change that."

"Who controls this Fire Lake?" Irduz asked.

"The centralist faction that calls itself the Golden Mean, that wants the Hegemony to exist in more than name only," Jaakola said. "Kharemoughi-dominated, of course, but they are allied with influential cabals on Four. They are already working to ensure that Kharemough gets the stardrive first, so that they can seize military control."

"They will succeed, then," TolBeoit said. "Our influence on Four is not strong. And if we know about this now, Kharemough knows already. We'll have to send someone in—"

"But that will take years in realtime," someone else protested. "By the time we actually get our hands on the stardrive, it may be too late. The Hegemony will be hanging in our skies, ready to obliterate us." The other voices around the table began to rise.

"That need not be so," Mundilfoere said softly. Her words silenced them abruptly. All eyes fixed on her, including Reede's. "Fire Lake is the result of stardrive run wild, perhaps damaged in some profound way—at the very least left to breed uncontrolled for centuries. Even the Kharemoughis have no real experience in dealing with such things. It will take them longer than they think to control it; perhaps it will take them forever. Their own best people are all on Kharemough; they will have to send them to Four. That in itself will give us enough time, if we act."

Reede's eyes widened slightly. *She knew.* He realized she had known all along, even before Jaakola had arrived. The darkness that was Jaakola seemed to deepen, if that was possible. Reede wondered how many of the others around the table had known about the stardrive even before they came here. He knew there were circles within circles, even in this elite; there were things he knew sometimes that the others did not—although usually he only knew them because Mundilfoere had told him. He felt a sharp twinge of annoyance that she had not chosen to share this particular miraculous secret with him; when knowing about it made his head sing. . . .

The water of life and the sibyl virus were the only forms of the Old Empire's smartmatter technovirus still in existence anywhere in the Hegemony—or they had been, until now. And he had never even seen a sample of the water of life; had thought he never would. But now everything was changing.

"Are you sure of that?" Mother Weary said to Mundilfoere. "Or are you just trying to cheer us up?"

Mundilfoere smiled, not even glancing at Jaakola. "My sources are most reliable," she said gently. "Be assured."

"We have to move, then," Irduz said. "We have to put together a team—"

"I'll go," Reede said. "Send me, with Mundilfoere. I'm all you need."

Mother Weary laughed; the sound made him wince. "And modest, too, you crazy bastard!"

Reede twitched with annoyance. "I know more about smartmatter than anybody living. Everybody knows it."

"And you're crazy, and everybody knows that too," Sarkh muttered.

Reede held his gaze. "Only when it suits my needs, Sarkh."

"Yes," Jaakola muttered, beside him. Reede turned toward him in surprise. "He should be the one to go. Let the New Vanamoinen unravel the secrets of the Old Vanamoinen. His very unpredictability gives him an edge, wouldn't you say? He makes a perfect thief. And let him take his leman, if he wishes."

Reede stiffened, sensing more than seeing Mundilfoere tighten with anger beside him. He frowned, suddenly uncertain, and glanced back at her. He thought doubt flickered like heat lightning across her face; or maybe it was just his own paranoia he read there. But she met his stare with a gaze that seemed to him suddenly to hold all of history in it, and he felt her trust, her confidence, her love fill him, like waters rising out of a bottomless well.

"Yes," she murmured, "you are the one who should go, Reede. This is what you were made for, by the higher power that binds us all." Reede opened his mouth to speak, but she shook her head. "But by the same power, I cannot leave certain boundaries unwatched, or projects untended for so long. You will go alone this time." Her eyes forbade any protest. He sat paralyzed, staring at her, while on around the table the others voted agreement, one by one.

TIAMAT: Ngenet Plantation

Moon stood up to her knees in the bright grass on the hill below the plantation house, looking out to sea. She tasted the fresh breath of spring, felt the breeze run cool fingers through her hair, lifting it like wings. For a moment she felt as ephemeral as if she were a cloud-child, about to be swept up to ride on the wind's back, the way Tammis rode now on his father's shoulders on the beach below. Delighted laughter and shrill shrieking reached her ears, as Ariele and Merovy danced around them, grabbing at Sparks's hands and Tammis's flailing feet, begging for rides of their own. She smiled, breathing deeply, imprinting their beauty on her eyes.

Beyond them the sea crashed onto the beach, wave upon wave, reaching northward and southward to the limits of her sight: heavy, silver gray, white-haired with spume, restless with the massive runoff from the melting snows. The sea here still seemed cold and relentless, its enormous breakers battering the steep, rugged foothills that marched down to the shore for miles along the northern coast. No longer snowglazed, catching and reflecting light like a mirror, their new silhouette was a jagged knife-edge against the colorless, fog-burnished sky. But today their massive permanence was suffused with fog until they were only a smoke stain in the lustrous air, a surreal, unreachable dream. . . .

She looked down again at the children and her husband laughing, running, whirling on the beach; all of them suddenly dancing with their shadows, shouting their delight as the suns broke through the haze into full day at last, haloed by sundogs of rainbow. She remembered her own days of laughing on the beach with Sparks, far away, long ago, with a sudden, bittersweet vividness. She stood motionless, caught in a tesseract, watching them, watching the sea brighten and take on color behind them. The turbid northern ocean never showed the limpid greens and blues that she had seen in Summer seas; although perhaps that was only because memory made all skies clearer, dazzled with rainbows, all waters purer, all colors more brilliant and sense-stunning in those perfect sunlit moments. . . . Even if there was no Lady whose spirit brightened the waters, every day the sea was warming here, every day the land was greening, becoming reborn; every day this world and her people took one more step toward a better life. She inhaled another deep breath of the free, restless air, held it, savoring the taste of salt and damp and new things growing.

"Moon," a voice said softly, as if the speaker was reluctant to intrude on her solitude.

She turned, grateful for the thought behind that reticence, even as she was suddenly grateful to have Jerusha PalaThion standing beside her. She had grown as used to Jerusha's presence as she had to her own shadow; to be without it was to be incomplete. "Look at them," she said, pointing toward the beach, where Jerusha was already looking, watching the horseplay with smiling envy.

"I'm glad you came," Jerusha said, glancing away up the hill toward the house, rubbing her arms as if she were cold, even on a day like this one.

"I'm glad you came with us." Moon put her hand on Jerusha's arm, touching her gently through the heavy layers of kleeskin and sweater. She studied Jerusha's face as the other woman looked back at her, witnessing the changed woman that her Chief of Constables became—allowed herself to become—when they were away from the city; an easier, more peaceful woman. Jerusha looked as if she belonged to these lands, this world, in her rugged native clothing, with her dark hair falling unbound down her back or braided in a heavy plait like an islander; just as she herself ceased to be the Summer Queen and became only human, free for a time to breathe and think and move through patterns that had meaning only for her. "Being here heals me, somehow," she said, looking back toward the beach, the sea.

Jerusha turned to watch with her. "Yes," she said. "It always used to make me feel that way, when I was Commander of Police." She sighed, glancing up the hill again. "I knew Miroe was involved with contraband goods. But the best moments of my life for over five years were always here, visiting him." Moon heard sudden longing and disillusionment in the words.

"Not anymore—?" she asked softly.

Jerusha looked back at her; shook her head, looking away again. Moon had wondered why Jerusha did not spend more time here. Jerusha's work in the city, her hours spent administering and consulting, were endlessly demanding; they kept her away from this place, and her husband, far too much of the time. Moon had often told her to take more time for herself. Jerusha had always refused.

She glanced again at Jerusha's face, the deepening lines of its strong profile eased by her smile as she watched the children. Living on a world that was not her own, and living through four miscarriages, had taken their toll on her. Moon felt her heart squeezed, a coldness in her soul, as she watched her own children run and play, and imagined losing even one of them. She looked back at Jerusha, seeing the depths of sorrow below the surface of her smile; realizing suddenly, fully and frighteningly, the toll that Jerusha's losses had taken on her relationship with her husband.

Neither Jerusha nor Miroe shared their emotions easily—not their pain, not even their joy. And the only way for two people to survive a lifetime together was by sharing those things—no matter how painful, how secret, how strange. The more things each one hid, the more a family became only solitary strangers leading parallel lives, blind to any needs but their own. . . .

She did not realize that she had moved, turning away from the sea and the sight of her husband and children, far down the beach now, until Jerusha touched her shoulder. She blinked, startled, found herself gazing inland toward the mountains . . . the remote, fanged peaks still covered with snow, wreathed in wisps of slowly drifting cloud. As she watched, the clouds seemed to take the form of a woman's face and hands, of her blowing hair cloud-white against the blue ocean of sky—and through her hair, scattered by her hands, Moon saw, as she sometimes could on rare, perfectly clear days, a handful of stars, so bright that they were visible even in the daytime sky. She watched the vision of clouds scatter stars . . . remembering how she had watched other stars falling like a vision, above those distant snowfields on a distant night: the ships of the Hegemony arriving on Tiamat for the final visit of the Assembly, the final Festival of Winter. Remembering BZ Gundhalinu, there beside her . . .

"Moon—?" Jerusha's voice pulled at her; she felt the other woman's arms catch her, holding her steady as sudden vertigo overwhelmed her.

"Did you see it?" she whispered, her eyes still on the mountains, the sky. "The Lady . . ."

"What?" Jerusha squinted, following her gaze. But the cloudforms had flowed on, mutating, hiding the ragged scatter of stars, and she saw nothing.

"Nothing," she murmured. "The clouds . . . the clouds were beautiful. It made me think of . . . other skies." She shook her head, avoiding the look on Jerusha's face as she began to turn away. But she turned back, suddenly. "Jerusha—I heard from BZ."

"What?" Jerusha said again, more in disbelief than incomprehension. "Gundhalinu?" He had been one of her inspectors; she had seen him turn renegade out of love, defying her and breaking the Hegemony's laws for Moon's sake. But she had let him go, torn by his divided loyalties, and her own. . . . "That's impossible," she murmured, her eyes asking Moon to prove it was not. "How?" she said finally.

"In sibyl Transfer. He's become a sibyl—" She explained, describing for Jerusha all that she could remember of what she had seen and heard.

"Why was he in World's End?" Jerusha asked, shaking her head. "Was it a Police case? He was assigned to Four—"

"He didn't tell me."

"When did this happen?"

"Months ago." Moon looked away.

"And you didn't tell anyone?"

"No." She shook her head, brushing pale strands of hair back from her face. "I couldn't." She turned, looking toward the beach again, where Sparks and the children were slowly making their way back along the shore. "I couldn't tell him. . . ."

"Oh," Jerusha said softly.

Moon watched Sparks stop on the sand, waving up at her, his red hair catching fire in the sunlight. She felt the heavy pressure inside her chest as she raised her own hand. "I can't stop thinking about it. I gave him all I could, Jerusha, all it would let me give him—" This time seeing not her husband's face but a stranger's, as she had on that night as he took her in his arms. . . . "But I don't know if it was enough. I don't even know if he was able to save himself. There isn't a day since then that I haven't thought about him." She felt her face redden. *And night after night the memory of his final words had haunted her, kept her from sleep, when she needed sleep so desperately. . . .*

"Then you haven't heard anything more?"

"Nothing." She shook her head. "I don't know how to reach him . . . I don't even know how he found me. It isn't supposed to be possible."

"I know." Jerusha glanced at her feet, half frowning. "Damn. I wish I had an answer." She sighed. "But I'm glad you told me." She met Moon's eyes again, and smiled, ruefully. "If anyone will survive, he will. You gave him the gift of survival, before he ever left Tiamat."

Moon looked away uncertainly.

"He was a good man, one of my best. But he was rigid. His pride made him brittle. What happened to him when the nomads had him would have killed him—it nearly did—if you hadn't shown him something stronger in himself. I gave him back his career. But you gave him back his life. You made him human." Her smile widened. "Gods, you should have heard how that man talked about you. I couldn't believe my ears."

Moon turned back, opening her mouth.

"Moon!" Sparks was beside her, suddenly, pulling her close against him as he kissed her. She felt his arms surround her, the warmth and chill of his skin, the tang of sun and sweat. She looked up into his eyes, as green as the new grass, his red hair moving like flame in the wind; his handsome, peaceful face, as familiar to her as her own. She pressed against him, into the solid reality of his embrace, seeing Jerusha's expression turn thoughtfully noncommittal as she watched them together. Moon looked out at the wide water, letting it fill her eyes until it was all she could see; trying to imagine that they had never left the islands, that there had been no lost time, no separation, no bitter secrets between them.

"Mama! Mama!" The twins joined them, and little Merovy—not so little, she reminded herself, looking down at the girl's fair, freckled face and windblown brown hair. None of them were so small anymore. The twins' heads butted her chest as they wrestled for hugging space. She put her arms around them, anchored by their warmth and unquestioning love . . . shaking off the unknowable, the impossible, the past, that was no longer an option.

"Mama, look, I found a carbuncle—!" Tammis held up one of the shining, blood-red stones that washed up along Tiamat's shores: the semiprecious gems that the Winters said had been named for the city, or the city for them. "And look at our shells—!"

"I have one like Da's, he's going to make me a flute!" Ariele waved a slender, pearly corkscrew shell in front of Moon's face.

"No, that's mine!" Tammis cried. "It'll be my flute! I found it!"

"I promised Ariele—" Sparks protested, with faint exasperation. "You wait."

"If he found it, it's his," Moon said, separating small, struggling hands. "You'll find another, and that will be yours, Ariele. You'll have to wait."

"No!" Ariele shook her head fiercely. "I want mine now!"

"I'll let you use mine," Sparks murmured, lifting her chin. "You can use mine."

She gazed up at him, her smile coming out like the sun, as Tammis's smile fell away suddenly. Moon touched his shoulder, soothing and distracting him. "Show me what you found."

"Here, for *you*—"

She laughed and made expected *ohh*s of wonder, holding hands and shells with sudden heartfelt pleasure; refusing to listen to the voice of the past still calling her name, somewhere inside the joyful clamor of the present.

"Well now, well now, what is all this—?"

Moon looked over her shoulder, hearing her grandmother's voice reaching cheerfully ahead up the hillside from the bay. Gran and Borah Clearwater made their way slowly but resolutely toward the gathering on the slope; Miroe paced beside them as host and guide. She saw their small boat, its slack sail flapping, down at the dock, surprised that she had not noticed them coming in. Miroe clearly had, from the house farther up the hill. The children left her side in an abrupt flock and rushed to greet the new arrivals with more gleeful clamor.

Moon smiled, watching them, for a moment imagining that she watched herself, and Sparks. She saw the children's pleasure reflected in her grandmother's eyes; saw in Borah Clearwater, standing beside Gran, the grandfather she could not clearly remember now, who had died of a fever when she was only three. It still amazed her to see Gran beaming like a young girl, as far in spirit from the drawn, aged woman who had come to Carbuncle as the grandmother of Moon's memory had been. Capella Goodventure had done them both a kindness they could never have imagined, on that day when her grandmother had arrived in the city—a fact which Moon silently hoped had caused the Goodventure elder disappointment equal to the pain she had inflicted on them.

It was hard for her to believe that it had taken a Winter to rekindle life's fire in Gran. But over the years she had found that many of the outback Winters had more in common with Summers than they did with the inhabitants of Carbuncle.

"Well, damn it!" Borah Clearwater said, peering with good-natured impatience over the swarming heads of the children. "I see you've added even more of those 'windflowers' to this crackbrained plantation of yours, Miroe Ngenet." He gestured at the windscrews at the top of the hill behind them. "Damn shame it is too, when it was a perfectly fine example before—"

"It ran on hard human labor—and one very expensive offworlder power unit—before, Clearwater, just like yours, and you know it," Miroe grunted, his mouth curving upward under the thick bush of his mustache. "We get twice as much productivity at half the expense with windscrews and generators and fuel made in our distillery, and it frees up my workers to learn trades at the processing plant—"

"Hmph. Sounds like a steaming pile of—"

"Borah!" Gran said sharply. "Watch your tongue. There are children."

"Yes, heart," he murmured, deflating abruptly, without further objection. "But rot me if I want to hear more about processing plants and new trades, new towns, new noise and stink and that miserable pissant Kirard Set . . . Now he's after me again, wanting me to sell him the plantation to develop. It was an unlucky tumble that tossed his genetic code. I can live with the right of way, as long as he pays me well—" He looked at Moon, and she smiled. "But don't expect me to thank you for it. And believe it'll be a hot day in hell before he touches another inch of my lands with 'progress.' Over my dead body! Right, love—?" Gran nodded, her face mirroring his resolution. He put his arm around her, chuckled as she slapped his hand for getting familiar.

"Act your age, you old bull-klee," she said, smiling-eyed; somehow still managing to slide back into his grasp while pushing him away. She accepted more hugs and treasured shells from a half-dozen small hands.

"Ah, but I am, you know I am," he breathed in her ear, and she giggled like a girl. "Where's that nephew of mine, and your mother?" He looked down at Merovy swinging back and forth, pulling on his arm.

"They couldn't come," she said, losing her own smile as she remembered.

"Why not?" He looked up, concerned. "Is his back plaguing him so much, then?"

Moon nodded, pressing her mouth together. Danaquil Lu's back trouble had grown so bad that he could no longer walk upright. The voyage down the coast, even in a motorized craft, was too long and painful; and so they stayed in the city.

"But we're getting close to where I can help him," Miroe said. "The workmanship of our second-generation tool-making is getting finer all the time. Soon we'll be able to produce the surgical equipment I have to have; when I have it, there's a correctional procedure which is relatively simple—"

Borah snorted in disgust. "False hope! Why give him false hope? We can't recreate something it took the offworlders centuries to produce in the first place, in only one century! Let things be, and accept it." He waved his hand, turning away, dismissing them. Jerusha stiffened beside Moon; Moon remembered her childlessness, and how the new technology had not come in time to change that.

"My da will so get better!" Merovy cried indignantly. "Don't say that."

"Of course he will," Miroe snapped, his good humor vanishing like smoke.

"If the Lady wills it," Gran finished, patting Merovy's head with stern resolution.

Moon looked away from them, rubbing her arms inside the loose sleeves of her sweater. Sparks rolled his eyes beside her, and pushed his fists into the pockets of his canvas trousers. "Goddess! He's worse than the Summers," he muttered, so softly that only she heard it.

"Mama, come with us to get more shells!" Ariele pulled at Moon's hand, gazing up at her with bright eagerness.

Moon hugged her, smiling. "Well, I—"

"Moon, I need to talk with you about the newest studies we've been doing on the mersong. I'm running short on inspiration, and I need input." Miroe caught at her with his eyes, nodding toward the house, where they had already spent half the day discussing new ways to encourage Summers to accept the technology that was changing their lives almost daily.

"Come on, Mama." Tammis clung to her other hand.

Moon felt her mouth tighten, seeing the silver stretch of beach waiting, feeling her children's need pulling at her, and Miroe's. "I can't right now. . . ."

"Mama! You promised—"

Moon frowned, caught in a tightening vise of frustration.

"You've played with me half the morning," Sparks said. "You can run on the beach by yourselves a while. Build a city in the sand, like Carbuncle—"

"But Mama promised—"

"You come with us now, children," Gran said, moving forward to pry them loose from Moon's arms. "You haven't been with us, either, and your mother has work that must be done," *regardless of what I think of it,* her eyes said, "like her mother before her, and even I myself, in my day. But now I have time to walk barefoot in the sand! Come on, Borah . . ." She enlisted his support with a jerk of her head. He took Merovy by the hand as Gran pulled Tammis and Ariele half reluctantly away down the hill. "Mama—!" Tammis called plaintively, one last time.

"Nobody's stirring the paddies! Your seahair crop is going to rot, Miroe Ngenet!" Borah waved a hand at the empty fields. "What good will all your technology do when you all starve to death?"

"I've automated," Miroe shouted back. "Wind-powered wavemakers. Worry about your own crops!"

"Automated, you say—?" Borah called, but Miroe was already turning away, waving his hand in disgust.

"Go south around the bay!" Jerusha called. "There was a storm the day before yesterday. There will be wonderful shells along the bay. Maybe you'll even find fog-agates."

"Will we see mers?"

"Not so soon after the storm—" Moon shook her head, waving, a half-hearted, reluctant gesture of farewell. She turned away from the sight of them, her eyes suddenly stinging. "All right, Miroe," she said, to the unspoken apology in his glance, "let's talk about the mers."

Sparks fell into step beside her as they began to walk back up the hill. Miroe glanced at him. "I don't think this is your area of expertise, Dawntreader."

Sparks frowned slightly. "I've been studying the mersong, and I think I may have found a clue to the—"

"Jerusha, why don't you take him down to the factory?" Miroe gestured across the bay.

"I've seen the factory. I want to talk about the mers."

Miroe turned abruptly to face him. "After what you did to them, you have no right."

Sparks stopped in his tracks, and Moon saw the desolation that emptied his eyes like death. She looked back at Miroe, his stare as black and hard as flint, and said nothing, did nothing, as the past breathed on them all with the cold breath of Winter. She followed Miroe on up the hill, gazing at the cloud-hung, distant peaks. Sparks did not follow.

Sparks watched them until they were out of range of his voice. Jerusha PalaThion was still standing beside him; he wondered why he was not completely alone. He took a deep breath at last, and turned to face her. "Why don't you make it unanimous?" he said.

"Because I don't think you deserved that," she answered, meeting his gaze.

"Why not?" He looked away again, feeling something gnawing like worms inside him. "I butchered mers for Arienrhod, so she could sell the water of life, so we could stay young together by committing genocide. You know what I did; you saw what I did—just like him. He's right; I'm guilty."

She looked at him for a long moment without speaking. "That wasn't you . . ." she said finally, "that was Arienrhod. You were only a boy. You were no match for a woman like her. She'd been committing soul cannibalism for a hundred and fifty years. She nearly destroyed us all."

His hands tightened. "Give me more credit than that. I knew what I was doing. You used to believe that, when you hated my guts as Commander of Police."

"I hated Starbuck, the Queen's butcher, just like I hated the Queen. I didn't know Sparks Dawntreader, then, any more than I knew Moon Dawntreader. I thought I did, but I was wrong." She shook her head. "I was a Blue, and I thought I was a good judge of character . . . I still think so. Moon told me you'd never been what you were for Arienrhod, before; she said you'd never be like that again. She made me believe in her because she wore a trefoil. I wasn't so sure about you. But she was right. I've known you for nearly ten years now. You're a good man."

He looked after Moon's retreating back, at Miroe's tall, broad-shouldered silhouette towering over her, making her look small and fragile. He looked back at Jerusha, and suddenly he was not afraid to meet her eyes, for the first time since he could remember. "Thank you," he said finally, softly.

She nodded. "My pleasure."

He looked toward Miroe's retreating back again. "But ten years hasn't changed his mind."

"That's another thing I've learned," she murmured. "He's not an easy man to reach."

Sparks heard the bitter disappointment in the words, and wanted suddenly to reach out to her. He did not, because there was something of her husband's intangible armor about her too. "How can I make him listen to me, at least? Is there any way?"

She shifted from foot to foot, her eyes thoughtful. "He's a determined man; he's self-righteous, and won't be easily shaken out of what he believes. . . . But he respects determination in other people." She looked back at him. "If you want to tell him your ideas about the mers, go and do it. Don't let him shut you out. Stand your ground." A slow smile came out on her face. "It's worth a try. It's how I got him to admit he loved me."

Sparks laughed; he nodded, his smile fading again. "All right. I will." He glanced toward the house. "Are you coming?"

She shook her head, looking toward the beach, where the small group of young and old were gathered in the ageless pursuit of digging miracles out of the sand. "Not me. This is your fight, I'd just be in the way." She stretched her arms. "For once I'm going to the beach." She glanced back at him. "Good luck," she said, and strode away down the slope of rippling salt grass.

Sparks watched her for a moment, until he realized that he was not really envious, and then he began to climb the hill. A dozen windscrews whirled almost silently above him, scattered across the land like surreal flowers, turning the wind's restless energy into energy for humans to use, to keep the water in constant motion in the beds of cultivated sea hair, to provide electricity for light and power in the growing sprawl of the manufacturing plant Ngenet had been constructing on the far side of his small harbor. There was a village growing up around it, where Winter workers had come to live and raise their families; old-style dwellings built in old-style ways to mark a new-style life.

He reached the plantation house that lay at the hill's crest like an immense cairn, its solid, century-old stone and wood construction reminding him of the houses of his youth; reminding him again that the people of this world, Winter and Summer, shared a common heritage because they faced common problems of survival. He wondered why it was so easy for them to forget that. It was the perversity of all human beings, that they forgot their humanity so easily, and nursed their bitter memories for so long. . . .

Sparks went in through the heavy iron-hinged door, found Miroe and Moon sitting at a low table spread with handwritten documents among the uneasy mix of offworld heirlooms and stolid native furniture that gave this house its unique personality.

They looked up at him, Moon in surprise, and Ngenet in something closer to anger. "What do you want?" he demanded.

"I want you to listen to my ideas, Ngenet." Sparks held himself straighter, settling his hands on his hips. "Shut your eyes if you have to, if having to look me in the face makes you sick. But hear me out."

Ngenet stiffened, glancing at Moon. But Moon's eyes were on his own, with a mixture of pride and urgency, telling him he had done the right thing, strengthening his resolve.

He sat down with them as if he had been invited, making them a triad—*Lady's luck,* he told himself, feeling irony pinch him. Ngenet studied Moon's face a moment longer, looked away again with what seemed to be resignation. His glance flicked back to Sparks; he closed his eyes, deliberately. "All right," he said. "I'm listening."

Sparks took a deep breath, finding himself unexpectedly at the center of attention. He glanced away, gazing into the fire that burned in the stone hearth beyond Ngenet's back. "Even when I was a boy in the islands, I used to play the flute. . . ." He touched the pouch at his belt, where he kept his shell flute. "I knew all the old songs everyone sang; but when I played them on the flute they sounded different . . . They reminded me of the mer songs; the way they were constructed, the timbre, the intervals between notes and the tonal slides. I didn't know the terms or understand the relationships then. . . ." He smiled, at Moon's face as she watched him; at the memory of that other time, their lost world. "But my ears knew. After I came to the city, and—" *and Arienrhod found me,* "and I had access to what tech data the offworlders gave us, I began to learn the mathematics of music. How what I'd thought was just . . . instinct, beautiful noise, was actually a matrix, a network of relationships, each note with its own exact resonating wavelength, in a precise location relative to all the others. . . ."

"So?" Ngenet said, impatiently.

"So, I've kept on studying the relationships between the mersong and our songs, even the notes of the tone boxes we used to cross the Hall of Winds, which are actually surprisingly similar." He saw Moon straighten up in surprise. She looked at him strangely, and he could not guess what it was that she was thinking. He forced himself to look away without asking, to go on speaking while he had the chance.

"What's the point?" Ngenet snapped. "Don't waste my time." His weather-beaten face was furrowed with frown lines; his dark, hooded eyes were still pitiless and cold like the wind. Ngenet was the last of a family of offworlders who had gone native in the Tiamatan outback, and he loved this world and all its parts obsessively. He had tried to protect the mers on his plantation from the Hunt. But Arienrhod had sent her Starbuck to his shores at Winter's end for one final, illegal harvesting. All their scattered fates had been brought into collision on that bitter day, on that hideous stretch of beach, by the tightening of the Snow Queen's fist. And none of them had escaped unscarred.

Sparks glanced at Moon, saw his own sudden pain mirrored in her eyes. Their shifting colors were like memories, shimmering reflections on the surface of water. He swallowed the hard knot of his unexpected grief. "I . . . The point . . . the point is that I believe there may be segments missing from the mersong. Parts of it fall into patterns, meaningful enough to be fragments of something greater. But there are gaps. . . ." He had begun to talk with Moon about Ngenet's work years ago, at first out of what must have been a kind of masochistic guilt. But from his need to atone there had come a cleaner, purer interest in the mersong, as it fed his curiosity about the nature of their music, and music in general.

He had studied the recorded data until he was certain the songs the mers sang were something separate from the simple tonal language they used to communicate with one another. The tapes were filled with complex, almost indecipherable polyphonic strands of alien sound, lasting sometimes for hours. But they were songs in the true sense, as distinct and unchanging for each mer colony as they were varied among those separate groups. Each extended family within the colony seemed to possess a different musical strand, passed on by the adults to their small number of young, over countless generations as humans counted time. Blended together the strands comprised something greater, the pattern of which he had only begun to sense in the past few weeks.

"I've been studying the recordings you've made, charting the melodies, and it seems to me that with the—slaughter decimating their numbers over and over, maybe they've lost the purpose of the songs themselves, along with specific passages of them. Even when the offworlders are gone, the mers reproduce slowly; it takes at least the century they have to rebuild their population. It wouldn't be surprising if parts of their songs were lost forever. But if we could somehow reconstruct what's missing, we actually might understand them, maybe even give back to them some of what they've lost."

Ngenet sat forward slowly. Sparks realized suddenly that the older man's eyes were open and looking at him . . . waiting to meet his gaze. "That makes sense," Ngenet said slowly, as if it pained him to admit it.

Sparks bit his tongue, and smiled. He glanced at Moon's face, at the fascination and respect and, suddenly, the unquestioning love he saw there. Her smile widened.

Ngenet leaned forward on the heavy-framed couch, his hands locked together, his knuckles like burls on wood. "Take a look at what we have here. And tell me more about your methods—how did you come to this idea? Do you have your data with you?"

"I can get it." Sparks pushed to his feet, still hardly believing he had heard the other man speak those words, that his own words had been listened to, when he had lived so long with Ngenet's unspoken censure. He had done his solitary research for what seemed like an eternity, seeking the key that would grant him free access to the work Moon shared with Ngenet—grant him the hope, however small, that one day he would not see hatred and loathing, pity or pain, in the eyes of everyone who knew the truth . . . including his own eyes . . . including the eyes of his wife.

He hesitated, as he heard the sound of dogs barking and the excited voices of children coming toward the house.

Ngenet pushed to his feet, with annoyance showing on his face again; but this time his gaze was directed toward the windows, the threatened interruption.

"Mama! Mama!" Ariele burst through the front door, flushed and breathless, barely skidding to a stop in time to avoid a collision with the table below the window. "Da!" she added, seeing her father standing distractedly with the others. "We found mers!"

Mild surprise filled Ngenet's face, momentarily replacing his annoyance at the interruption.

"It's a good sign that you saw mers, Ari," Moon said, getting up, "but we're—"

"On the beach! On the beach!" Ariele cried, as more figures entered the house. Sparks turned as Jerusha entered, her heavy boots clumping on the wooden floor, something heavy and child-sized held in her arms. He froze, until he realized that the other two children were flanking her. "Dead!" Ariele went on. "But look, we found a baby—" She darted back to Jerusha's side, hovering protectively by the bundle held face-high in front of her, her eyes wide as she touched it, stroking it gently.

Sparks stood where he was, suddenly as strengthless as if it had been a child of his in Jerusha's arms, while Moon and Ngenet rose from their seats and moved past him. He watched them go to Jerusha, the conversation they had all just been having forgotten as utterly as he was himself. Ngenet shooed the children aside; they stood back obediently, impressed by his sudden intentness.

"Still alive—?" he asked, answering the question for himself as he ran experienced hands over the merling, and studied its small, unresponsive face. It made a tiny whimpering as he opened its eye; the fragile thread of sound turned Sparks cold inside. He looked away, his hands remembering the velvet soft texture of their thick fur; wanting to move forward, to stand with the rest, but unable to, unnoticed, unwanted—

"We found an adult female too," Jerusha said, "but she was already dead."

"What killed her?" Ngenet asked. Sparks looked back at them, found Moon's gaze on his face; she looked away again abruptly.

"I don't know." Jerusha shook her head. "There was nothing wrong that I could see. Maybe the storm—" The mers had no natural enemies, except their creators.

Sparks let his breath out. Jerusha glanced at him as if she had sensed his response; only then did he realize that he had been expecting to hear her speak his name, blaming him.

Ngenet shrugged, glancing up as Borah Clearwater and Gran came into the house. "Or parasites, or bad food . . . but usually the colony keeps watch when one of their own is in trouble. To find them all alone like that is damned rare. And so is finding a young one, at this time in the High Year. . . ." He reached out to take the merling from Jerusha's arms, but she resisted, rocking slowly, almost unthinkingly, from foot to foot, like a mother rocking her child. Ngenet's expression changed, and he let his hands drop. "Maybe they were separated from the rest by the storm. Or maybe . . ." He shook his head again. "I don't understand it. But this one will starve before the day is out, let alone before we locate the colony, if we don't take care of it right now." He started out of the room, already calling to someone in the kitchen.

"Will a colony take in an orphan?" Moon asked, her own eyes on the small head resting listlessly against Jerusha's shoulder.

"I've never encountered a solitary merling before," Ngenet said. "We'll find out." Mers separated forcibly from their own kind invariably died, but he did not mention that. He paused, giving directions to the startled cook who had appeared in the doorway, sending her off again in search of something suitable to feed a young mer.

"What if the mers don't want their baby back, Uncle Miroe?" Tammis asked, his eyes dark with concern as he gazed at the merling. "Will it be all alone? Who will take care of it?"

Ngenet glanced over at the boy, a smile cracking the shell of his preoccupation. He had studied the mers for a lifetime, but even he knew little concrete about their society, the relationships they formed or did not form, how they raised their young. "Then we'll keep the baby here. But we'll worry about that later. First we'll make the baby strong and healthy."

"Is the baby going to get well?" Merovy asked, pressing forward hesitantly against Gran's gentle restraint.

"We'll do our best to help her," Ngenet said gently, not really answering the question. Sparks saw the doubt in his eyes, and knew the concern that ran like a dark river below it. Ngenet touched the motionless merling again. He had always fought for the mers' survival, with a determination that would have earned him deportation if it had not earned him the love and tolerance of the Hegemonic Police Commander.

"Miroe," Moon said almost hesitantly, her own eyes never leaving the merling, "if you can save her, if you can actually raise her . . . it could be a way of reaching the others. It could help us learn—"

Ngenet looked from Moon's face to Jerusha rocking the merling in her arms. "I'm way ahead of you," he said, with an unexpected smile. "Come on—" He nodded, starting for the doorway, and the others followed.

Sparks watched them go, still rooted where he stood, unable to go after them. Ariele came back through the doorway alone, looking curiously at him. "Come on, Da!" She came across the room to his side.

He put his arms around her, holding her close for a moment.

She squirmed free, tugged at his hand. "Come on, Da, come help the mer—"

"I can't, Ariele," he whispered, barely audible even to himself. "I don't know how." He freed his hand from her grip, and started back across the room to the door. He went out without another word, slamming the door behind him.

TIAMAT: Carbuncle

"Wasn't it wonderful, Mama?" Ariele returned her mother's good-night hug, hanging on her in an ecstasy of excitement. "We had so much fun! Now we can have our own mer to be our pet. I want to call her Silky, because she's so soft!" She squirmed as Moon tried to cover her with blankets.

Moon started in surprise, as the name reflected unexpectedly in her memory. "Our friend," she corrected softly, stroking Ariele's hair. "We don't own them, any more than they own us. Our people, the Summers, call them the Goddess's other children, and say the Sea is the Mother of both our peoples. . . . But I think Silky is a perfect name," she added. "I had a . . . friend once, from offworld, named Silky. He was more like the mers than anyone I knew. I think he would be glad to be remembered this way. And maybe Silky will help us understand the mers better as she grows." She kissed her daughter gently on the forehead. "Lie down and go to sleep."

"It's so early—"

"And you're so tired."

"I want to help learn about them—"

"I know. Shh." She turned away, going to Tammis's bed across the darkened space of the room they shared. There were enough unused rooms in the palace for them each to have one of their own. But the rooms were vast and sterile, and seemed to her always so cold, that she had chosen to keep the twins together in the nursery, close by her own room, until they were old enough to complain, or at least old enough never to wake from a nightmare, terrified to find themselves alone.

But maybe no one ever outgrew those dreams. . . . She still woke at night, feeling lost, terrified, alone; even though she slept next to a man who loved her, a man she had known all her life.

"I want to help too!" Tammis said, propped on one elbow, listening.

"I know." She hugged him, kissed him on the forehead, smelling the scent of sea and wind in his hair. "We'll all do it, together."

"When can we see the mer baby again? Tomorrow?"

"Silky—!" Ariele whispered loudly. "I want to name her Silky, don't you?"

"We just came back." Moon smiled. "We'll go again soon. Not tomorrow. You have lessons to study."

Tammis made a face. "Where's Da? Isn't he going to play his flute for us?"

Moon glanced toward the empty doorway of the room, feeling her face tighten. "Not tonight. He's very tired." He had been impatient and moody through the long, weary trip back up the coast. The only words he had spoken to any of them had stung like nettles; until all that she could do was try to keep herself, and the children, out of his sight. He had not said anything about the reason for his smoldering anger, but she knew. It was the merling. "I'll sing you a song." She closed her eyes, letting go of her frustration; letting her mind carry her back until she was a child in Summer again. She remembered being rocked in the arms of her strong, sandy-haired mother, who came home with the fishing fleet smelling of the wind and the sea; who had sung them songs about the mers like the one she began to sing for her children now. She let herself imagine that they all sat before the fire in a tiny, stone-walled cottage on a tiny windswept island, in a room that had always seemed warmer, safer, more real than any room she ever found herself in these days. She wished, with a sudden soul-deep longing, that she could take herself and her family back to that dreaming island, away from this haunted city.

But that past, of the song and of her memories, no longer existed. The mother who had sung to her was dead . . . and this was where she belonged, whether she wanted it or not, because otherwise what she must do here would never be finished.

She felt with particular heaviness tonight the burden the sibyl mind had laid upon her—knowing that its will would not be done in her lifetime, or ever allow her any peace. She felt her eyes fill with tears as she ended the song, and barely held her voice together to finish it. Tammis looked up at her, his own eyes filling with concern. She smiled quickly, swallowing the hard lump of sorrow in her throat, stroking his hair.

"Will Da make my flute for me tonight?" he asked, as she got up from his bedside.

"I don't know, lovey," she murmured. Sparks had already begun to let Ariele play his own flute, to Moon's annoyance. "I'll remind him about it. Sweet dreams," she said to them both, and went out of the darkened room into the glowlit hall.

Sparks met her at the doorway, glanced at her startled face with an expression that was both apologetic and uncertain, before he went past her into the children's room. She listened for a moment, hearing murmured voices, and then the high, pure notes of flutesong, before she started on.

She walked slowly through the echoing halls, past rooms filled with fragments of the past, or prototypes and plans for the future; heading for her study, where far too many requests and pieces of information waited for her, all of them needing to be considered and answered and dealt with, all of them desperately important to someone. There was no escape from them, no respite. Her work never stopped, even when she tried to . . . had to. When she slept or made love or played with her children, when she fled the city to spend time under the open sky, to see with her own eyes the world she was working to change or the mers whose existence she was struggling to save, still the duties, the demands and expectations followed her, waited for her, relentlessly. And when she returned here, from an hour stolen, or a week, she found the pitiless burden of her work had become even heavier as she took it back on her shoulders . . . until everything she did became a burden, a responsibility; even the things that should have given her joy, that had once brought her pleasure.

She climbed the spiraling stairs to her study at the pinnacle of the palace; stood gazing out at the city's carapace falling away in smooth undulation, gleaming and shadowed. It struck her how precisely the city rested on the terminus between constant sea and ever-changing land, belonging wholly to neither one. She studied what had once been snow-covered wilderness, seeing bare ground, new growth, a scatter of factories and labs, all tapping the city's supply of tidal-run energy. She could see construction going forward on a new manufactory to the south. She turned, gazing inland, seeing the dark, shielded domes of the unoccupied starport complex, the rising hills beyond it, no longer white with snow but green with life.

Farther inland the higher peaks were still icebound, shining like metal among the clouds. Even at the height of Summer most of those mountains were inaccessible, to everyone but a few nomadic pfalla herders. They were uninhabitable now, at their present level of technology, and probably would still be uninhabited when the offworlders returned. She thought of her time lost in those mountains, a prisoner among the nomads—her time alone with one solitary man. . . .

She looked up into the sky, remembering again how they had watched together from the last ridge of those mountains as stars fell over Carbuncle . . . artificial stars made of hologramic fire, lighting the arrival of the Hegemonic Assembly, marking the time of the final Change, the death of Winter, the rebirth of Summer, and an endless circle of futility and hypocrisy.

She watched the Twins setting now in the west; gazed up into the inverted sea of the sky, with its islands of cloud, its deep blue further deepening. Already she was beginning to see the luminous multitudes of the stars, knowing that somewhere beyond that burning sky the Hegemony waited to return; and that somewhere out there the one other man she had loved in her life had reached out to her and touched her across the light-years, impossibly. . . .

She looked down, away from the sky, as she remembered the dream she had had two nights ago, that she had not revealed even to Jerusha: a dream in which she had been drawn out of her body by the Transfer, and into a blackness like the Nothing

Place, the heart of the sibyl computer's lifeless mind. But there had been no question, no questioner. Instead there had been only a voice—his voice, his words becoming a symphony of light as he called her name. He had shown her that he was safe, that he was sane, because of her. He had sworn that he would never forget her; sworn to her that if she ever needed him, somehow he would be there. . . .

She had wakened to the familiar sensations and silences of nighttime at Ngenet plantation—to Sparks, lying peacefully asleep beside her. She had felt dizzy, breathless, as if she had been in Transfer. Except that it never happened that way. What had happened had been impossible; and so it had to have been a dream, even though it was like no other dream about him she had ever had. . . .

Helpless longing seized her, as it had seized her then, while she remembered being held captive in the body of another woman on another world, feeling his hungry mouth on hers. As she remembered now, with sudden, exquisite clarity, the fever that had consumed her on a night long years ago—a desire so hot and helpless that it had turned her soul molten. A need as incandescent as the need of the stranger whose burning body had turned her vows to ashes. . . .

She opened her eyes, focusing on the room around her—the oppressive layers of documents and deeds, the stormwrack of her life. She held herself tightly to stop her trembling; stood motionless with gooseflesh standing up on her arms.

Someone entered the room behind her. She turned to find Sparks standing in the doorway, his own gaze taking in the deceptively passive chaos of her surroundings.

"Moon," he said softly; hesitated, as if he saw something in her eyes that he was afraid to confront. He looked down, and when he looked up again, she knew that it was gone.

"Are you all right?" she asked. The impatience she had felt earlier was gone now; she saw weariness and need reflected in his own eyes. She crossed the room to him, let him put his arms around her, resting strengthless against him for a moment.

"Better now," he murmured, and she knew he meant this moment only, holding her close, and not their return to the city, to these empty, echoing halls. "The twins are wonderful, you know that? They're getting so big, they amaze me, all the time. Sometimes I can't believe they're ours—" He broke off; pressed on again. "Ariele, on the beach . . . she looked so much like you. She's going to be a natural musician. Did you hear her?"

"Tammis is afraid you'll forget to make him a flute," Moon said, managing to keep the words neutral, taking care not to let them cut him. "It isn't fair that you let Ariele use yours, and don't give him one."

"I'm sorry. I will do it." He released her, taking a deep breath as he glanced away out the door. "I couldn't . . . I tried, I know I've been a motherlorn bastard these past couple of days. . . . None of you deserve it. I guess you know why." He looked back at her again.

"The merling?" Not really a question.

He rubbed his face with a hand. "Whenever Ngenet looked at me, I saw Starbuck in his eyes. He didn't want me near her—he acted like my presence in the same room was poison! He'll never stop hating me for what I did as Starbuck, to the mers, to him . . . he'll never let it go."

She put her hand on his arm, feeling her chest ache with misery—his, her own. Feeling the cold breath of Winter again at their backs. "He wouldn't let anyone near the merling until he knew what was wrong, and he was sure that she would live. He wanted to know what you discovered about the mersong—"

"So that he could tell me it was garbage."

"It could be," she said softly, "that he felt envious because you had a new insight into the data, after he had worked on it without any success for so long. But you never really gave him a chance." She let go of his hand, her fingers stretching wide with sudden frustration. "After he told you to leave the room, you didn't say three words to him all the rest of the time we spent there."

"I was afraid, damn it! All right? Is that what you want to hear—?" His own hand made a fist. It loosened, he shook his head. "And I couldn't stand it, to be near one of them; even to think about the mers. I see it in their eyes, too . . . fear, never forgiveness!" He looked away, his own eyes haunted.

"Sparks . . ." she whispered. "Arienrhod is dead! The past is dead. Starbuck is dead. Remember the Change, that last night? The Mask Night . . . and the morning, when . . ." *When we sent Arienrhod into the sea.* "When all of Winter, and all of Summer put off their masks and their sins and their sorrows. We swore that we would begin a new life, we'd renew our life's-pledge again, because everything had changed."

"But the problem is that everything *has* changed. . . ." He glanced away from her at the room, the sky beyond the windows. He turned back, looking into her eyes. He put his arms around her suddenly and kissed her, holding her with desperate tenderness. "Moon . . . let's go to bed. I haven't loved you in the daylight for so long. . . . We haven't made love at all, for so long."

She felt her own desire waken to the pressure of his mouth, the pressure of his body against her. But she pushed away from him, shaking her head. "I can't. I have so much work to do before I can even think about . . . think about . . . anything else—I'm so tired. I can't."

He held on to her. "Moon, please. I need you. I need you now, I need to know you—we—still feel something, still mean something to each other, in the middle of all this—" He jerked his head at what lay around them.

"*You* need?" she said, breaking free of his hold, as the emotion inside her curdled into resentment. "What about *my* needs? You need me, the children need me, everyone in this city, everyone on this damned world, needs me, even the sibyl net—it's always now, it can never wait. Everyone needs needs needs—! No one ever asks me what I need! I need to be left alone for once! Leave me alone, damn it, leave me alone!"

Sparks backed away from her, his face stunned as he reached the doorway again. He turned and went out, granting her wish without looking back, without a word.

Sparks went back down the spiraling stairs, through the halls and the chambers and the chill, empty throne room; not seeing the superficial overlay of the present that still failed to transform them. He saw only the past, memories, Winter. . . . Her: Arienrhod, all in white, on her throne of glass in the white-carpeted hall, with her pitiless purity of beauty, of strength, of control.

He had not understood why they were so alike, then, Arienrhod and Moon; why they both wanted him, needed him, loved him . . . any more than he understood now the things that had come between Moon and himself like a curse, after she had wanted him so badly, come so far and suffered so much to find him, challenged Arienrhod herself for the right to his soul. . . .

He went on, down, out; crossing the bridge over the silent Pit, going on through the Summer-frescoed entry hall and through the massive doors into the city beyond them. He walked, although there were electrified trams now that shuttled people up and down the Street; working off the frustration that clogged his chest until he found it hard to breathe.

He murmured desultory answers to the occasional greetings of passersby, mostly Winters. The Winters clung to their traditional upper sector of the city, where the once-exclusive townhouses still held fragments of the better days they had known when Winter ruled. Most of them were hard at work now, working for the Summer Queen, working toward a day when their useless offworlder luxuries would miraculously function again; when they would be the leaders of the new Tiamat, not by chance or whim, but because they had built its economy themselves, and earned the right to control it . . . for better or worse.

Glancing at faces, looking in through windows as he passed, he saw no one among them to whom he could talk about what he was feeling now—what he had done, and been, and could not ever seem to stop remembering. He went on walking, needing some destination, some human contact . . . drawn by memory into the Maze.

The Maze separated the Winters from the Summers who still inhabited Carbuncle's lowest levels, the spiral of alleys nearest the sea. The Maze had been the heart of Carbuncle, a vibrant neutral zone between those two halves of the world, while the Hegemony had ruled Tiamat. It was the place where most offworlders had lived, plied their businesses, bought and sold their pleasures and vices. It was still mostly given over to the few local-run stores and businesses that existed now.

He glanced down one alley after another: spokes branching off from the Street's lazy downward uncoiling, each of them named for a color, it was said—more colors than he would ever have dreamed existed, even on this water world, whose sky was filled with rainbows every day. He still didn't know what color half of the names actually were, any more than he knew what language they had been in originally, or how the alleys had gotten those names in the first place. Perhaps even the Old Empire builders of this city had been moved by the sight of the sky, with its days of rainbows endlessly forming and fading, its burning nights. . . .

He stopped at the entrance to Citron Alley. It had been some shade of yellow-green; the paint on shutters and doors and occasional building fronts still told his eyes that much. It had been his first home in the city, as a seventeen-year-old boy fresh from the Windwards. Fate Ravenglass, the maskmaker, had lived here then . . . still lived here, as Fate Ravenglass the sibyl. She had heard his music, and taught him how to survive as a street musician; had taken him in and given him shelter, until Arienrhod found him, and claimed him for her own.

Even after he became the Snow Queen's favorite . . . after he became her consort, and then her henchman, her Starbuck, he had returned here. Even after he butchered the sacred mers and drank the water of life, he had returned to this alley seeking sanctuary, when what he had become was too much for him to bear. He had come back to see Fate, whose eyes saw almost nothing; whose soul saw everything, but seemed never to pass judgment on it.

He had never known why she continued to welcome him on her doorstep, any more than he had known that she was a sibyl, the only one in Carbuncle, hiding her secret from Winters and offworlders alike—the way Starbuck had hidden his identify behind a mask and gone all in black. But she had hidden her secret identity to serve a greater good, while he had hidden his reality behind a faceless lie, his only reasons for existence to commit treachery and murder. . . .

He shook his head, driving out the shadows as he started into Citron Alley. He had not visited Fate in a long time—not for the reasons he had visited her in the old days, or for the reason he was about to visit her now.

The buildings nearest the Street were occupied by a mix of new Winter-run businesses and a few Summer shops, although farther down the alley the ancient buildings were shuttered and abandoned, waiting with inhuman patience for someone to return. The transparent storm walls let in the garish colors of the sunset; twilight came late in the northern latitudes, as the lengthening days of the annual spring moved on toward annual summer, adding their warmth to the High Summer of the system's approach to the Black Gate. Fewer and fewer people passed him as he made his way down the alley. By the time he reached Fate's doorstep he was entirely alone, and glad that he was.

He knocked on her closed double-door, lightly at first, and then harder, when there was no answer. Still he got no response, except for the faint yowling of her aged cat telling him impatiently that she was not at home. He swore under his breath, wondering where in hell a blind woman could be at this time of night. Probably she had gone to a tavern somewhere with Tor Starhiker, to listen to music. He knew she did that sometimes. He even thought he knew where. But he did not want to see her with Tor Starhiker, not tonight, with his head too full of the memories of all their former lives, and how they had spent them at Winter's end.

He went back along the alley toward the Street; stopped at the corner looking uphill along its spiral, facing the prospect of his return to the palace. He took a deep breath and made himself start walking. He had nowhere else to go, no one else to talk to, nowhere else to turn. . . .

As he walked he thought of spending the night there, lying alone in the darkness, sharing his bed with Arienrhod's specter, with the chill touch of her ghost arms turning his flesh to carrion, the memories of what they had done together in that place leaving him sleepless. . . . He thought of lying beside Moon, Arienrhod's ghost made flesh—how she would turn her back to him in anger when she joined him, far later, her body cold and tense with exhaustion and resentment. She was held captive not just by her obsessions, but by something even more profoundly inescapable, something he could not begin to comprehend. He thought about its pitiless hold on her . . . the bitter spines of the trefoil she wore, the same symbol tattooed at her throat, inescapable.

He felt a brief surge of compassion, knowing that she deserved more than she had gotten from him tonight, of kindness, of understanding, of love—that she had always deserved more from him than he seemed able to give since they had been reunited. But he also knew that he needed more of her than she could give him ever again. The space around them, the space within their lives, was too small, they had nowhere left to turn; the future had filled it all in with inescapable truths. . . .

His steps slowed as he reached the corner of another familiar alley: Olivine Alley, which held the Sibyl College. His office was there, where he spent his days working with his wife: asking questions that would send her into Transfer, and recording the answers; trying to make sense of what the Transfer told them, as the sibyl net answered queries in its own strange and elliptical fashion.

He realized suddenly that he enjoyed what he did there, was proud of it . . . that when he worked and did research for Tiamat, it was as if he united his two heritages, Summer and offworlder, in a way he had longed to do when he first came to Carbuncle. Discovering the perfect beauty of the mathematics which underlay so many forms and functions, both of human progress and natural order, filled him with a pleasure and satisfaction he rarely found in the randomness and pain of human relationships.

On an impulse he turned into the alley, turning his back on the uphill climb toward home and family. He walked until he came to the entrance to the College; let himself in, moving through its familiar, twilit halls until he reached his office. He turned on a light and sat down at the regulation Police-issue desk, abandoned there by its former owners at the Change. Its useless terminal stared back at him like a sightless eye. Shuffling through the disorder of typewritten papers, handwritten notes, and fiches, he picked up an aging text on fugue theory he had found in an abandoned data shop. He leaned back into the embrace of the shapeshifting chair and put his feet up on the desk. He opened the book and began to read, losing himself in thought.

NUMBER FOUR: World's End

Reede Kullervo rested moodily on a freeform couch in the Port Authority hotel suite, gnawing a hangnail and staring out across the artificial stars of the landing field, into the black heart of the jungle beyond it. He watched another shuttle rise without seeming effort and disappear into the greater blackness of the night. His fist tightened around the bottle of ouvung he had been drinking straight; the cheap plass crumpled under his grip, and viscous ruby liquor oozed out and down over his fingers like blood.

He could hear muted voices and unintelligible noise coming from the next room, where Niburu and Ananke were lost in some time-wasting interactive on the entertainment unit. He sighed, and took another drink from the ruined bottle, staring out at the night. This room stank of newness, like everything here did—of restless molecules still escaping from wall surfaces, fabrics, furniture. Somewhere behind him, if he could have seen through walls, was the sea of light that was the Stardrive Research Project and the prefabricated instant city that had sprung up around it, here in the middle of nowhere, on the edge of World's End..

"By the Render—" He swore and sat up abruptly, felt the couch re-form around him. He took another handful of iestas from the dish on the table and stuffed them into his mouth, chewing them up pods and all. The pods tasted like shit, but they were supposed to have more natural tranquilizer than the seeds themselves. Not that it would do him any good. He washed them down with another gulp of ouvung. No matter how much garbage he put into his system, the water of death annulled the effects. It was virtually impossible for him to get drunk or high, to get even the slightest bit numb, no matter how hard he tried. He kept trying, hoping for a miracle.

He could not have come all this way pointlessly! Damn that stupid bastard Tubiri, who was supposed to have provided the verification that Reede Kullervo had been sent here by the Kharemoughis—who had gotten himself wiped off the face of Number Four so damned inconveniently, so short a time ago. *"Incinerated in an accident with the stardrive plasma."* That was what they had told him. Was it possible that it wasn't an accident . . . ?

No. Accidents happened, even to the Brotherhood. If it hadn't been an accident, it would have happened to Reede Kullervo instead. . . . He was still safe and alive, but he was stranded, with no way to get the access he needed to the research that was going on. If he couldn't get inside and show these shitbrained fools how to contain and control the stardrive material—and in the more than two and a half years of their time it had taken him to get here, they had failed to be successful at either—then he would never be able to get a stable sample of it for himself, to carry back to Ondinee. To Mundilfoere. . . . *Mundilfoere. If only she was here with him, to tell him he had done the right thing, to tell him what to do next. To hold him in her arms.* . . .

He rubbed his eyes, muttering another curse. The Brotherhood had members on Four, but they were few, and he had to be careful about contacting them. They had no one at all on the inside at the Research Project, now that Tubiri was gone. And he knew the security around this place. Between the ruthlessness of the locals and the obsessive technological innovations of the Kharemoughis, this place made the paranoia of the Tuo Ne'el cartels seem like an open market square. He had tried every argument imaginable to make them let him in today, but nothing had worked. And he needed not just the access, but cooperation. Now he would have to go back at least to Foursgate—that was the most cosmopolitan city center on the planet, the heart of their offworld trade. He would have to start all over. . . .

There was a knock at the door. He pushed to his feet, frowning. He was not expecting visitors. He did not want visitors. "Niburu!" he shouted. But the noise and the laughter went on, undiminished in the next room. Swearing under his breath, he crossed to the door; he stopped, reaching inside his overshirt, checking the weapons he had rearmed himself with as soon as he left the Project.

He peered through the one-way panel beside the door, and froze. And then, slowly, his hand fell away from his gun and he released the lock. The door slid open silently. He stood looking out at the local woman, a worker from the Research Project who had tried to speak to him as he left there late this afternoon, and at the stranger standing beside her. She had been a sibyl, he suddenly remembered; and in his exasperation, as they had shown him the door after six hours of useless interrogation, he had shouted, "For gods' sakes, I'm a stranger far from home—"

She and the man with her were both wearing dark, shapeless rain slickers, the hoods shadowing their faces. And yet he suddenly knew beyond a doubt who it was that she had brought to see him. Reede held out his hand to the woman. "Hello again," he murmured, in the local dialect. "I'm sorry I didn't return your courtesy this afternoon."

"I don't blame you." She took his proffered hand somberly, and he felt her answer the subtle movement of his fingers. "I'm Tiras ranKells Hahn," she said; last name first, in the local fashion. "I'm sorry I couldn't be of more help to you then. I'm afraid they don't make strangers welcome easily at the Project. . . . May I present to you the Honorable Researcher Commander BZ Gundhalinu—"

"Yes, yes, of course—" Reede held out his hand to the man who accompanied her, feeling his face flush with unexpected emotion. "Gods, you can't imagine what a pleasure this is." *You can't.* He met the other man's eyes, with a smile that was completely genuine. "Reede Kulleva Kullervo, from the Pandalhi Research Institute."

Gundhalinu offered him a hand, raised palm out in the typical Kharemoughi manner. Reede twisted his own hand quickly, so that their palms met in what he hoped seemed like a natural motion. *Careless, you ass.* He felt the hidden question the other man's touch asked him in turn, and he answered it with silent satisfaction. Of course Gundhalinu was Survey; at a high level too, he was sure.

"I understand you've come all the way from Kharemough to work with us, only to be turned away today by our overeager watchdogs?" Gundhalinu answered his smile with one that looked more reserved. His eyes were so dark they were almost black, and they regarded Reede with frank curiosity.

Reede managed a laugh that might have been rueful. "I seem to have disappeared from your data reality—and they told me my contact has been incinerated. . . . Your security sets a new standard for the entire Hegemony."

"Our bureaucracy, you mean." Gundhalinu shook his head. "I'm truly sorry. This place has always been a godforsaken bottleneck. You should have seen it before there was a research center here, when it was the Company's town. . . . But I wouldn't wish that on my worst enemy."

Reede felt his smile pull. He shrugged, loosening the muscles in his back. "You were here then?" he asked, surprised.

"Our histories have become one, I'm afraid." Gundhalinu's smile turned sour, and he didn't elaborate. Reede realized that Gundhalinu's discovery of the stardrive must have been the catalyst that had precipitated all this change. He had, by his single act, become responsible for the town's transformation.

Reede glanced at the woman named Hahn again, sensing her restlessness. "Excuse my manners. Come in, won't you?" he murmured, including them both in the gesture.

Hahn shook her head. "I can't stay. I have to get back. My daughter . . ."

"How is she?" Gundhalinu asked, turning toward her with sudden solicitude.

"Better . . ." she murmured. "I think she is a little better." She shrugged, in a gesture Reede read as hopeless.

"I'm glad to hear it," Gundhalinu said, with a peculiar sorrow showing in his eyes.

"You're kind to remember her, Commander."

"*Schact!*" Gundhalinu said abruptly. "Don't *you* start treating me like one of your sainted ancestors, Hahn. You know me better than that."

She turned to him in surprise; smiled, and it was a real smile, given to a real man. "Yes, of course . . . BZ." She nodded, looking down again as she did, unable to stop herself.

He took a deep breath. "Thank you for bringing me here. Hahn, if there's ever anything else I can do . . . You know." He shrugged. She smiled at him over his shoulder, and went on down the hall.

Gundhalinu looked back, his dark eyes searching Reede's blue noncommittal ones. "Her daughter is a sibyl," he said, his speech slipping from the local dialect into his native Sandhi, as if he took it for granted that Reede would be able to follow. "She wasn't suited for it. She . . ." He made a brief, futile motion with his hand, and looked away. "Never mind." He trailed Reede into the suite. Reede closed the door behind them. Gundhalinu glanced toward the next room, his attention caught by the light and noise.

"My assistants," Reede murmured in explanation; suddenly, unexpectedly feeling ill at ease. "Have a seat." He spoke in Sandhi now, as Gundhalinu clearly expected him to. He gestured toward the couch.

"Thank you." Gundhalinu dropped his rain gear into an empty side chair. He was wearing the full dress uniform of a Commander of Police, the jacket crusted with the hologramic fire of a dozen medals of honor. And lying against his chest, dimmed to insignificance, was the trefoil of a sibyl.

Reede froze, gaping at him, through a moment that seemed interminable.

Gundhalinu looked at him quizzically, as if he couldn't even begin to guess what was going on inside his host's expression.

"Do you sleep with those?" Reede said.

Gundhalinu looked down at himself, as if he only then realized what he was wearing. He laughed, suddenly, almost in relief. "Ye gods, no." He took off the jacket and tossed it into the chair on top of the wet slicker. "I just came from an exceedingly long and tiresome banquet at the Project. Some visiting dignitaries . . ." He rubbed his neck, loosening his collar as he crossed the room. Reede felt more than saw fatigue overtake him as he settled onto the couch.

"The price of fame," Reede murmured. He ran his hands over his own clothing, glad that he hadn't bothered to take off the neat, conservative overtunic and loose pants he had worn for his interview, or the silver clip that kept his hair reluctantly trapped in a tail at the base of his neck. He sat down on the couch at a comfortable angle from Gundhalinu. He could see the sibyl tattoo on Gundhalinu's throat, now that his uniform collar lay open.

Gundhalinu looked away, his gaze fixed on something beyond sight. "Everything has its cost." His glance settled on the nearly empty bottle of ouvung and the half empty bowl of iesta pods on the clear tabletop beside him.

"Help yourself," Reede said.

"No, thank you. I don't drink." Gundhalinu picked up the dented bottle, turning it around in the light, watching the dead worm swirl past in the ruby liquid. "You must have had an extraordinarily frustrating day, Kullervo-eshkrad," he said, not unsympathetically. Reede recognized the form of address preferred by Kharemough's Technician class; the word meant both *respected* and *scientist*. Usually they only used the term with each other; it was a rare honor when they used it to address a foreigner. He guessed that in this case it simply came with his supposed position as a researcher at the Pandalhi Institute.

"Yes," Reede answered, pricked by annoyance at the implied judgment of his habits.

"This stuff will give you a terrible hangover," Gundhalinu said.

Reede raised his eyebrows. "That sounds like personal experience. I thought you didn't drink."

"That's right. On both counts." Gundhalinu set the bottle down again, and looked back at Reede. "I have to admit, when Hahn told me you had arrived from Kharemough—from the Pandalhi Institute, no less—I expected to meet a fellow Kharemoughi. My people are . . . somewhat resistant to admitting outsiders to their more important institutions. You must be a very intelligent man."

Reede smiled faintly. "I am." He watched Gundhalinu, almost disappointed. This was not the man his imagination had shown him. There was nothing remarkable about BZ Gundhalinu. He was a typical Kharemoughi Tech: medium height, dark and slender, probably in his early thirties. His face was fine-boned and salted with pale freckles, like a lot of highborns. A compulsive, self-righteous, inbred weakling. Who the hell would have imagined that he would have one of the greatest insights history had ever recorded? Not even his own Technocrat arrogance, probably. Kharemoughis thought they ran the Hegemony—and worse, they actually believed they deserved to.

"And a very influential stranger to be so far from home."

Reede nodded again, meeting his gaze with complete confidence this time. "Like yourself."

"Are you a sibyl, then?"

"Me?" The question startled a laugh out of him. "Not me. I'm not . . . suitable material." His hand tried to reach out for the bottle of ouvung; he forced it to lie motionless at his side.

"I never imagined that I was, either." Gundhalinu touched the trefoil dangling on its chain, as if he still had trouble believing he wore it.

"It must be a relief to you," Reede said.

Gundhalinu glanced up at him, curious.

"To have proof you can trust yourself."

Gundhalinu smiled faintly, looking down at the trefoil again. He let it drop. "Kulleva Kullervo . . . is that a Samathan name?"

Reede shrugged. "Yes. But I left there a long time ago. . . ." He looked out the window at the night, as he was impaled on a sudden fragment of memory: *In the turgid undersea twilight a small boy was crying, down between looming tanks where his drug-sodden father couldn't hear him; clinging to the mongrel puppy that he loved more than any human being, while it whined and licked at his tears. Feeling the wetness in its matted fur, feeling the wetness soaking through his shirt, crying because his father had beaten his dog, and then beaten him, and he didn't even know why. . . . Gods . . .* He pressed his hand to his eyes and took a deep breath; held it, reciting an adhani.

"Who is head of the Pandalhi Institute these days?" Gundhalinu asked; repeating the question, he realized, because he had not answered.

Reede leaned back, feeling the couch enfold him like comforting arms. "Tallifaille. Or she was when I left, at least."

"And how is old Darkrad?"

Reede smiled. "Pretty much the same."

Gundhalinu sat up straighter. "Darkrad has been dead for a dozen years."

"That's what I mean. He's still pretty much dead." Reede pushed forward again, letting his grin fade. "If you want to be sure of who I am, Gundhalinu-eshkrad, ask me something important. Ask me why I think I can help you."

Gundhalinu stared at him. "You really believe you can solve this thing," he murmured, and it wasn't a question.

Reede smiled again, and nodded.

"Tell me your ideas," Gundhalinu said, with sudden intensity. "I've been living with this for nearly three years now. In all that time we've barely grasped the smallest part of its complexity. I want answers—" In his eyes Reede saw bottomless depths of disappointment, frustration, failure . . . desperate need. "Convince me you've got the answers, and you can have anything you want."

Reede's smile widened. He settled back into the couch's embrace, satisfied; knowing that Gundhalinu, and the Hegemony, would keep that promise to him whether they liked it or not. "As I understand it, you don't have one problem, you have two. First, the stardrive plasma you discovered suffered some form of integral disruption when the ship containing it crash-landed here. You can't control the function of the plasma. And second, you don't have a way to contain it effectively. They're interrelated, of course. If the plasma was reacting in a predictable, responsive way, you wouldn't need stasis fields to contain it. But unless you can confine enough of it for adequate experimentation, you can't even study it, to learn what's wrong. It becomes a kind of vicious circle for you." Gundhalinu nodded. "My area of expertise is smartmatter."

Gundhalinu shook his head slowly. "Is there really such a thing?" he asked.

"As smartmatter?" Reede said, in disbelief.

"As a living expert in that field. Everybody agrees that the Old Empire created it, used it, existed because of it. The evidence suggests that it even destroyed them. But all that was millennia ago. The technology is lost; only the stardrive and the water of life exist to prove it wasn't just legend—"

"And the sibyl virus."

Gundhalinu stiffened, and nodded. "Yes. And the sibyl virus. We understand in principle how it functions, but no one has been able to successfully reprogram it, let alone reproduce it—or make it reproduce itself. The sibyl network contains no data at all on the process. It's as if they intentionally suppressed all knowledge of it." He leaned back, and sighed. "Damn them. . . ."

"They wanted you to make your own mistakes," Reede said.

Gundhalinu looked up sharply, his eyes questioning.

"Us," Reede murmured. "I meant us, of course."

"Dr. Kullervo—"

Reede looked away, grateful for the interruption, as Ananke stuck his head through the doorway. The boy wore a reasonable imitation of the clothing a serious student on Kharemough would wear—affectedly baggy and unflattering—and spoke in passable Sandhi. Reede had forced both Ananke and Niburu to learn Sandhi and some of the major Four languages on the way from Ondinee, because for once it would be necessary for them actually to understand what was going on. "What?"

"I'm going to sleep now. Do you need anything before I go?"

"Where's Niburu?"

"He went to bed a while ago."

Reede snorted and shook his head. "Turn off that noise. That's all."

Ananke nodded and disappeared; the next room became miraculously dark and silent. Reede glanced at the readouts on the surface of the low table in front of him, surprised by the lateness of the hour.

"Was that a baby your assistant was carrying?" Gundhalinu asked.

Reede glanced toward the empty doorway, and laughed. "Just an animal. A quoll; but he carries the bloody thing around with him in that sling like it's a baby. On Ondinee they have quolls for pets—and sometimes they have them for dinner. Maybe that's why he doesn't let it out of his sight."

"He has a travel permit for it, of course?"

Reede looked back at him, and smiled. "Of course, Commander." He reached out, passing his hand over the table surface to activate its terminal. The port came on line, showing the data he had programmed into it while he was preparing the presentation he had not been permitted to give today. "Take a look at that," he said. "Is this an accurate representation of what you've been trying to do?"

Gundhalinu leaned forward, studying the datamodels, murmuring queries to the system, watching them transform, go three-dimensional, sink back into the table surface again. He did not ask Reede for any clarification, or seem to need any. "Yes . . ." he said at last. "That's a remarkably coherent model of the work we've been doing. But some of this data we've only recently discovered. If you've been in transit, you couldn't possibly have known—"

Reede shrugged. "I made a few educated guesses, to fill in gaps."

" 'Educated guesses,' " Gundhalinu repeated softly, and touched the display of symbols on the table surface. "That's impossible. It's taken us years. No one could casually intuit these—"

"Like I said," Reede murmured, pulling at his ear, "it's what I do, Commander. You made all the classic assumptions about smartmatter. And so I assumed you'd made all the classic mistakes."

Gundhalinu's head came up, his mouth thinning.

"I've made them all myself, Gundhalinu-eshkrad," Reede said gently. "That's why I know them so well."

Gundhalinu's frown eased. The anger left his face empty of all emotion, and drawn with weariness. He shook his head. "All right, Kullervo. Then what next? What—? I've run out of inspiration."

Reede waved his hand over the display, enjoying for once the surreal feeling of being a magician as the constructs changed at his preprogrammed command. "Have you considered this model for the way a technovirus encodes its information?"

Gundhalinu peered at the changed image; his frown came back, half doubt, half concentration. "Interesting . . ." He shook his head again. "But the structural codes become too varied if you carry that to its logical end—" He reached out to the display.

"No, no—" Reede said impatiently, brushing his hand aside. "You're making it too complicated. This isn't life, it's art—the underlying structure is much simpler than that. There has to be some universality, something beautiful in its simplicity, at the very core. Something like this—" He changed the display again, watching Gundhalinu's face almost hungrily for traces of comprehension.

Gundhalinu stared at the image, and slowly became perfectly still. Reede realized after a moment that he had even stopped breathing. "Father of all my grandfathers," Gundhalinu whispered at last. "I don't believe it. Gods—this *is* true. It *is* beautiful . . . more than beautiful, it's goddamned brilliant." He laughed, shook his head, looking like a man who was ready to cry as he glanced up again. "Kullervo, I told you if you gave me a key that worked, you could name your own reward. Name it."

"All I want," Reede said, "is to do what I came here to do—solve this problem, as rapidly as possible. And to work with the man who discovered stardrive plasma in World's End."

"That should be no problem." Gundhalinu said softly, with a self-conscious smile touching his mouth. "No problem at all."

NUMBER FOUR: World's End

"Good news, Reede. We have our clearances. We can go in." Gundhalinu let the words precede him as he strode into the office of Reede Kullervo's private lab.

Kullervo raised his head, startled out of what looked like an early nap. "Come the Millennium!" he said, sitting upright in his seat. Relief and pleasure mixed with surprise filled his face.

"Yes, gods willing," Gundhalinu murmured, with a smile, "come the Millennium." Kullervo understood the irony of those words as well as he did. He had spoken them for years, like everyone else, meaning the day the Hegemony had a stardrive again—and that he never expected he would live to see that day.

Kullervo grinned and cocked his head. "That's the first time I've ever heard you say anything before you said hello."

Gundhalinu smiled and stopped moving as he reached Kullervo's side. "Another unique observation . . ." he said, his smile widening. As usual he was both amused and nonplussed by Kullervo's oblique mental processes. "Hello. Good afternoon. I hope you slept well last night, Kullervo-eshkrad."

Kullervo laughed, pushing up out of his seat. There was an audible smack as he met Gundhalinu's upheld hand with his own; returning the sedate gesture with a greeting that was more like a slap on the back. "I never sleep well, but who cares? Damn . . ." he murmured, "it's coming together. You can feel it too, can't you—?" His hand twitched, as if he wanted to reach out again; but he didn't. Gundhalinu felt Kullervo's unnervingly bright eyes strip his thoughts naked: his eagerness, his aching need to find the answer that would set him free.

But then, abruptly, Kullervo was looking through him again. Kullervo swung back to the desk terminal, to the three-dimensional data model that floated in its surface like an hallucination, a portrait of the information storage within a single microcomputer cell of the technovirus. "You're mine," he whispered to it, as if there were no one else in the room, "and you know it."

He murmured a few more words, unintelligible orders to the terminal, and the image altered subtly. Before Gundhalinu could begin to analyze what had changed, the whole image vanished and the desktop was only an empty surface of impervious graygreen. "No," Kullervo said, turning back to Gundhalinu as if he were responding to some unspoken question, "I was not taking a nap."

Gundhalinu blinked, and forced his brain to take another blind leap of faith as he tried to follow Kullervo's quicksilver chain of thought. He had grown used to the plodding, narrow-focus, too-literal analysis of the scientists who had worked on this project with him before Kullervo arrived. They were the best minds that Four could provide . . . but all the really superior minds tended to emigrate to Kharemough, or to have been born there in the first place.

Once he had believed, like most Kharemoughi Techs, that Kharemough produced citizens superior in every significant way—moral, intellectual, social—to any world in Hegemony. He had learned a painful humility over the years, and he was grateful for it. But his experience here had given him back the belief that he was in fact as worthy of his ancestral name as his instructors at the Rislanne had insisted he was; that he had been given the best education money could buy, and been born with the skill to use it well.

But he had been trapped for nearly three years among uninspired and uninspiring pedants, in a bureaucratic maze of obsessive security and militaristic paranoia. There were only a handful of Kharemoughis onworld, all a part of the Hegemonic judiciate, none of them trained researchers. Once he had transmitted the news of his discovery to Kharemough, he had been promised through the hidden channels of Survey that he would be sent the help he needed to unravel the maddening microcosmic riddle of the stardrive. And for nearly three years he had waited, learning humility once again as he tried to solve the seemingly insoluble, virtually alone.

And then at last his promised aid had arrived. He had expected a dozen top Kharemoughi researchers, two dozen. They had sent him one man, not even Kharemoughi—a total stranger who looked barely old enough to have finished school. Once he had recovered from the shock, he had acknowledged that if Kullervo was their chosen offering, he must be extremely qualified. Many important researchers did their best work when they were in their early twenties. But all that had hardly prepared him for his head-on collision with the brilliance of Reede Kullervo. Kullervo's grasp of how smartmatter functioned verged on mystical, and Gundhalinu was not a believer in mysterious powers. It was as if Kullervo understood the technovirus with his gut, instead of his brain; he didn't so much analyze data as invent it . . . and yet, his undisciplined flights of fantasy were almost invariably, terrifyingly on target.

Gundhalinu had felt his own mind come alive again, felt himself stimulated almost unbearably by his contact with Kullervo. He was pushed to the limits of his perception and past them every day, stimulated into blinding flashes of insight all his own. He had realized almost from the first that his own mind would never be more than a dim reflection of Kullervo's blazing brilliance; and yet, at the same time, he had realized almost gratefully that he had something to offer Kullervo that Kullervo actually needed: pragmatism and discipline. He was not so much a drone, or even a mirror, as he was a stabilizer, a ground, a focus for Kullervo's wild energy. He saw the proof of it sometimes in Kullervo's sudden appreciative glance . . . he saw it in results. These past few months while they had worked together had been like nothing he had ever experienced in his life—a kind of ecstasy that was purely intellectual, but made him wake up every morning glad to be alive, and hungry to be in Kullervo's presence.

And yet in all this time he had learned almost nothing about Reede Kullervo the human being, as opposed to the scientist. When Kullervo had arrived, Gundhalinu had found himself drawn to the other man with an unexpected intensity. His reaction had surprised him, until he thought about it. He realized then that his life had come to resemble the hermetically sealed world of the Project in which he spent all his time. Kullervo was someone to whom he could actually talk as an equal, after so long in this place where he had little in common with anyone. On top of that, Kullervo was unique, with a mind full of brilliant fireworks. He had wanted almost painfully to become friends with the man.

But Kullervo had rebuffed all his attempts at friendship, or even at personal conversation. Finally Gundhalinu had accepted the obvious, and let it drop. He had never been inclined to force intimacy on strangers; and he had realized eventually that Reede's reluctance to meet him halfway was not personal, but instead somehow oddly defensive. Observing Kullervo, witnessing his unpredictable moods and dysfunctional manners, Gundhalinu had realized that the man had problems, which he probably preferred to keep to himself.

He had pushed aside his disappointment, told himself that it didn't matter, they didn't need to be friends to be colleagues. As long as their relationship was focused strictly on research, they communicated flawlessly; they had worked for weeks now in near perfect harmony. But after all this time Kullervo was still an enigma, a cipher, a bizarre mass of contradictions that reminded Gundhalinu every day of the fine line between genius and insanity.

Standing here in Kullervo's office, Gundhalinu remembered with sudden vividness the day of their first triumph as a team, over a fortnight ago. Adrift in the null-gravity chamber, side by side, they had tried yet another recombinant of their key, the encoder that would unlock the molecular structure of the damaged technovirus in the minuscule sample lying somewhere at the heart of the incredibly massive, complex, and expensive array of equipment and processors below them— that would make the stardrive plasma controllable, biddable, sane. . . . They had waited, as they had waited before, side by side but solitary, while the subtle, probing fingers of their fields performed analyses of surpassing delicacy. Waiting for the words that would change history—or send them out of the chamber again, defeated, back to their programs and imagers . . .

We have confirmation. The words had echoed the readouts flashing across his vision inside his helmet. Kullervo's cry of triumph had cut through the monotonal message; the figure beside him, semi-human inside its protective suit and stabilizer fields, jigged in a footloose, impossible dance. "—did it this time, BZ! We fucking did it!" The words became intelligible as Kullervo reached through Gundhalinu's field to catch him in an awkward embrace. "I told you—! Laugh, yell, you overcivilized son of a bitch—we did it!"

He laughed, as belief caught him up at last; he shouted, inarticulate with elation. And then he lunged after Kullervo, who had started down into the depths as if he intended to fetch the sample out of the core with his bare hands. "Reede—!" He had come up under the other man, slammed him to a halt. "Wait for the servos, damn it. They'll bring it up as fast as you could. . . . You may be bloody brilliant, but the fields will still fry your brilliant brain like an egg." He put his hands on Kullervo's shoulders, holding him in place, their merged stabilizer fields glowing golden around them like a misbegotten halo.

Kullervo stared at him, the dazed astonishment on his face slowly replaced by something more recognizable, and yet equally strange. "Ilmarinen—" he murmured.

"No," Gundhalinu said, shaking Kullervo slightly, unnerved. "It's me. . . . Reede?"

Reede blinked at him, shaking his head independently now. "I know," he snapped, brushing off the contact of Gundhalinu's hand.

"Why did you call me Ilmarinen?" Gundhalinu asked softly, curiosity forcing the question out of him against his better judgment.

Kullervo shrugged, "Some of my . . . associates have been known to call me 'the new Vanamoinen.' I guess that makes you Ilmarinen. . . . Bad joke." His gaze broke, and he shook his head, still looking away as the cylindrical servo appeared out of the depths, bringing the now-obedient, quiescent milligram of stardrive with it.

Gundhalinu watched it come, breathless with anticipation. Kullervo hung motionless beside him. And then, with slow, almost deliberate grace, Kullervo turned a somersault in the air. . . .

"Ananke!" Kullervo's voice in realtime pulled Gundhalinu back into the present.

"Yes, Dr. Kullervo." The voice of the Ondinean student who was his lab assistant materialized out of the air.

"Find Niburu for me. Tell him I want to see him. We have our clearance."

"That's great, Doctor! Right away—"

Kullervo turned back to face Gundhalinu. "When can we leave for Fire Lake?"

"Tomorrow," Gundhalinu said, hardly believing the answer himself. "I requisitioned everything we'll need weeks ago." They had perfected the viral program that effectively stabilized the stardrive plasma; they had tested it successfully. The obvious next step was to make the journey to Fire Lake itself, where a vast semisentient sea of stardrive material waited for them to answer its need, to make order out of its chaos. . . . Gundhalinu looked toward the doorway, remembering the touch of its tormented mind, remembering the hot breath of madness, and the chill of winter snow.

"About goddamn time," Kullervo muttered, oblivious. "You'd think somebody around here besides us would want to see this thing work!"

Gundhalinu glanced back at him. "There are plenty who have been aching for this moment as long as I have, believe me," he said. *But not aching like I have.* . . . "You met some of them back in Foursgate, at the Survey Hall." He had taken Kullervo to a special meeting of his local cabal a few weeks back, when he had known that the breakthrough in their research was imminent. Kullervo had been quiet, oddly subdued, during the meeting; even though it had been clear from his responses that he must be at a fairly high level within the inner circles of Survey. "Unfortunately the ones with any vision are all still back in Foursgate. And we are here—out where the bureaucracy is its own reason for existence. The greatest scientific breakthrough in a thousand years becomes nothing but a glitch in the program, to them. They're expecting us in the departure screening area this afternoon for the final certification of our itinerary and proposed goals."

Reede made a rude noise. "Pearls before swine," he muttered. He shut down his terminal with an abrupt gesture, turning back to face Gundhalinu. "Let's get it over with, then." He peered through the doorway into the larger lab space. "Where's Niburu?" he snapped.

Looking past him, Gundhalinu saw Ananke glance up from whatever he had been studying. "Coming up, Doctor." He nodded. "He'll meet you at the usual place out front."

"You're coming too," Kullervo said. "We all have to go." The boy stood up, looking vaguely surprised, or maybe apprehensive. He was not wearing his pet slung at his chest, for once. Gundhalinu glanced around the room, until he found the quoll sitting placidly in a box underneath the desk. He shook his head, imagining the kind of stares that pair must have attracted on Kharemough. He looked back at Kullervo again.

Kullervo swung around, almost as if he could feel himself being stared at. Gundhalinu glanced down, turning away toward the door as Kullervo came back across the room, followed by Ananke. They went out together through the muted hive of research cubicles and labs, through the symmetrical green-lit levels of security, like swimmers rising through the water. They arrived at last in the sudden brightness and noise, the heat and humidity and rank vegetation smell of World's End, which were always there waiting, just outside the Project's doors.

Kedalion Niburu, Kullervo's other assistant, was waiting for them as promised outside the compound, in the noise and heat. He was comfortably insulated from the environment, sitting behind the controls of the triphibian rover Kullervo had requisitioned as soon as he had learned that it was what they used for travel into the wilderness. Since then, Niburu had been learning to handle one in preparation; Kullervo insisted that Niburu could pilot anything, and was the only one he would trust to take them in. Gundhalinu had acquiesced, knowing that he himself was not capable of piloting a rover, and that at least Kullervo trusted this man with his life. It reduced one factor of randomness to have a pilot he at least knew somewhat, and not a stranger assigned by Security. His own gut feeling about Kullervo's other assistant, once he had gotten past the startling visual interference of meeting a man so much shorter than himself, was that Niburu was competent and dependable, and a good deal more stable than Kullervo. And stability was something he valued over anything else, when he went into World's End.

Gundhalinu climbed into the rover, grateful for its shelter after walking even a few meters through the steaming heat of the day. Kullervo and Ananke got in behind him and the door hissed shut, sealing them into its climate-controlled womb. Gundhalinu wiped sweat from his face. The uniform he was expected to appear in during most of his waking hours had been designed for wear in climatized offices, not for practical use in a place like this . . . something he would have to take up with the Hegemony's establishment when he got back to Kharemough. He glanced at Kullervo, who had settled into the copilot's seat next to Niburu. Kullervo's face was flushed; Gundhalinu had never seen him wear anything but a long-sleeved tunic or shirt, even though there was nothing that required him to dress formally. Gundhalinu wondered absently why he didn't use sunblock for protection instead.

Niburu took them up with what seemed to be effortless skill, rising above the nervous dance of ground traffic even though the distance they had to travel was short. Niburu seemed to know his employer's temperament well; Gundhalinu supposed that it was an occupational requirement when working with Kullervo.

Gundhalinu stared out at the crazy-quilt of old and new structures down below. It reminded him of a three-dimensional data model, showing the town's uncontrolled spread like some aberrant lifeform, a runaway virus, the stardrive plasma itself. . . . He forced his mind away from the image, focusing on the concrete fact of the town's explosive growth, for which he was largely responsible. When he had first arrived here to search for his missing brothers, this town had barely existed. It had been the only legitimate access to World's End for prospectors and other riffraff foolhardy enough to dare the wilderness. At that time it was run by Universal Processing Consolidated, the multinational that had controlled World's End mineral rights, and it was more a surreal bureaucratic nightmare than a genuine geographic place existing on real-world maps. It had not even had a name, then. Out here they called Universal Processing Consolidated "the Company," and this was the Company's town.

But he had gone into World's End, and come out of it with news that was still sending shockwaves through the Hegemony. The shock had been felt, the changes had begun first, here, at the epicenter on Number Four. He watched the town pass below, the sullen core of squat, heavyset colonial structures overwhelmed by the gleam of the prefabricated highrise hives the government of Four had dropped here to house the influx of technicians, researchers, and workers who were responsible for the Project and its physical plant.

Down in the warren of its streets, it seemed to be a place completely transformed, reborn, like the future itself. But from up here he could see beyond its perimeter, see the rank frenzy of the jungle that surrounded it on all sides, stretching to the horizon. The jungle was constantly trying to reclaim the earth from this infestation of alien sentience, giving ground slowly, but never willingly. . . . *Chaos against order*. A microcosm of life, of progress, of the human soul.

He shut his eyes for a moment, against the vision, against the resonance it started in his memory. Tomorrow he would be going to Fire Lake with knowledge that, gods willing, would begin to bring the Lake back from the heart of madness, as he had barely brought his brothers back . . . as he had barely brought himself back to sanity, to civilization, the first time. He shifted in his seat, relieved to see that they were already descending again, falling back into the illusion that progress and order were winning.

Not that order and progress had any claim to moral superiority, he thought wearily, as Niburu set them down on the designated spot in the security area of the departure center. Ugliness and banality were all that he could see, rising up on every side, as they got out of the hovercraft and stood on the cercreted landing field. Looking down, he saw the fleshy excrescence of some nameless fungal growth oozing up out of a crack in the inadequately laid ceramic pavement beside his boot, chaos seeping in through civilization's pores. Nothing here had been built to last. *It's frightening,* the sibyl Hahn had said to him once, *how precariously we float on the surface of life.*

He tugged habitually at the hem of his uniform jacket, as the uniformed guard came toward them across the field, bristling with an array of weapons: more a symbol than a threat, a reminder that was easy for the average human mind to grasp of the far more subtle and effective forms of weaponry that now defended the Perimeter, barring the uninvited from access to World's End.

When the Company alone had controlled access to World's End, getting in uninvited had been difficult enough. Now Gundhalinu was certain that it was all but impossible. After word of his discovery had become public, Four's powerful World Enclave had forcibly nationalized them, with the backing of the Hegemonic Police. Universal Processing Consolidated had been one of the major economic forces on the planet; for the world government to take them over under any other circumstances would have been unthinkable. Without the full support of the Hegemony, it would probably have been impossible. But Universal Processing Consolidated owned World's End, where Fire Lake lay. He had found the impossible there, and so the unthinkable had suddenly become the inevitable. . . .

As the security guard approached them, Gundhalinu saw how big the other man really was; not simply tall but massive, moving toward them with the inexorability of a landslide. Something about the guard's broad, bronze face seemed familiar; Gundhalinu wondered if they had crossed paths before. Nothing in the man's sullen expression—or lack of it—suggested anything more than a general resentment of foreigners, which they all plainly were. He wore the uniform of the Enclave's military, but Gundhalinu was sure he had worn the Company's uniform before, like most of the workers here. Their masters had changed, but nothing else had—except that now the totalitarian bureaucracy that had run the lives of virtually everyone on this particular continent for a century had even better tools of oppression, and even less fear of government intervention controlling their excesses; because now they were the government.

Gundhalinu watched the guard raise a callused hand to make him a grudging salute. He returned it, keeping his equal reluctance to himself. Waves of heat reflected up from the pitiless, glassy pavement beneath his feet. He remembered how once he had watched hands like those casually break all the fingers of a would-be prospector, in a bar called C'uarr's.

"Commander Gundhalinu," he said, too brusquely, "to see Agent Ahron."

"And them?" the guard asked, intentionally insulting, as his black, hooded eyes darted at the three other men.

Gundhalinu felt Kullervo frown beside him. "Them too," he said gently. He took a step forward, forcing the guard to take one step back; the guard turned and started away without another word. Kullervo glanced over at him, a brief, measuring glance; but he said nothing as the guard led them toward the administrative complex where Agent Ahron waited.

Inside they were loaded into a secured tram and sent like human baggage through the characterless repetitions of the complex to their destination. The distance was short, but Gundhalinu was still grateful that they did not have to walk, under guard, like criminals. Ananke sat beside him, staring at the identical doorways as if they were a revelation. Gundhalinu looked across at Kullervo, who sat frowning and pulling at his ear, at the crystal-beaded ear cuff that was one of the more obvious manifestations of his unpredictable personal style.

Niburu sat beside Kullervo; his short legs jutted from the seat like a child's. Gundhalinu imagined that Niburu felt more relieved even than he did not to have to walk this distance, since Niburu was always pressed to keep pace, in a body that was constantly inconvenienced by the conventions of others. He had dared to mention the matter to Niburu one day, as he had watched him standing on a chair to access a simple data run that Kullervo had left for him to confirm. Niburu had only shrugged in apparent resignation, and murmured that on board his ship the proportions were to his specs, and not anyone else's.

Gundhalinu stole another glance at Niburu and Ananke. They watched the color-washed walls pass, sitting in an unlikely symmetry of pose. He had wondered to himself whether Kullervo had chosen his staff simply for their shock value. He suspected it was possible. And yet he was almost certain that it was not because of their appearance, but rather in spite of it, that Reede had hired them.

The tram spat them out directly into the mouth of a doorway that was more like an airlock leading into an isolation chamber. The security was hardly this elaborate at the Project itself.

"Overkill," he heard Kullervo mutter to Niburu, behind him. "What do these shitheads think this is saving them from?"

Gundhalinu glanced back at them, his mouth curving slightly. "Spontaneity," he murmured. Kullervo said something unintelligible, as the inner doorscreen dematerialized before them.

A thickset middle-aged woman with golden skin and iron-colored hair looked up at them from across the barren expanse of room. Gundhalinu recognized her as Agent Ahron, who had approved his departure permits and itinerary on several previous journeys to Fire Lake. She wore a variant of the same uniform they had seen on almost everyone they passed, and an expression that was as familiar to him as her face: alert without being at all interested in what she saw. There were three men with her; he knew without having to be told why they were here. "Commander Gundhalinu," Ahron said, managing to give his name a slight querulous lilt, as if she wasn't certain she remembered his face.

"Yes," he said, as ingratiatingly as he could, "back for one more try. For the last time, I hope, thanks to my colleague here." He gestured at Kullervo, who stood stiffly beside him, eyeing the room and its inhabitants.

She said nothing, still gazing at him without the slightest trace of curiosity. The three men stood silently behind her, like afterthoughts.

"We believe we've found a way to control the stardrive. I'm sure I don't have to tell you what that means—"

"Yes, Commander, I've reviewed your documents. Also your permits and supply lists," she said, glancing away at the display surface of the dust-colored desk/terminal beside her. "Everything seems to be in order here, for once. There's no reason that I can see why you shouldn't be able to depart as planned."

He realized with a prick of irritation that the "for once" referred to his input and not Security's response to it. "I'm very glad to hear it," he said, with excruciating politeness. He felt Kullervo begin to relax, infinitesimally, beside him.

"How much time do you expect this expedition to take?"

"It's hard to say. If the tests are successful—"

"I need a precise length of stay." She tapped impatiently at the display.

"Yes, of course. One week." They should know whether Reede's restructuring program worked or not almost immediately. Even with the question of systems setup and the vagaries of time around Fire Lake, that should give them enough slack.

"That's all? You realize that you will have to return in one week, whether your work is finished or not—"

"Two weeks, then," he said, with faint impatience, "make it two weeks."

"All right. But in that case, should you finish your study in less time, you will have to notify us that you are returning ahead of schedule."

"Yes, of course."

"Would you please input your security clearance code, then, to indicate your personal testimony that the data is accurate to the best of your knowledge."

He nodded, touching the remote on his belt, silently transferring the code numbers to the waiting document. After a moment he heard the piercing tone that indicated the security databank had accepted his verification.

"These will be your crew," Ahron said, gesturing toward the three men waiting like stones behind her—her first acknowledgment that there was anyone else in the room.

Gundhalinu nodded, stepping forward as the three government troopers came reluctantly to life. But Kullervo's hand closed over his arm, pulling him back.

"What is this—?" Kullervo whispered, suddenly angry. "You didn't say anything about anyone else coming with us!"

Gundhalinu looked at him, surprised by his vehemence. "It's all right," he murmured, trying to find the right words to make Kullervo ease off. "It's government policy. They always provide the pilot and two troopers for security."

"We've already got a pilot," Kullervo snapped, nodding at Niburu. "And we have all the assistance we need. This is a risk-filled project. We don't need bumbling total strangers getting in the way. You said yourself that the more people we have with us, the more dangerous the Lake is."

"It's a regulation," the agent said flatly.

Gundhalinu watched the expressions harden on the faces of Ahron and the three troopers. If Kullervo lost his temper, they could very quickly lose the clearance he had so painstakingly put together too. "Agent Ahron," he said, sending a sharp glance of warning at Kullervo. "Dr. Kullervo is right when he points out that a larger group would be potentially dangerous, given the unstable nature of the Lake. We've lost several teams out there in the past two years, as you know. We have a full team this time already—"

"It's a regulation," she repeated. She folded her arms. "A certified pilot and two troopers for security."

"It's bullshit," Kullervo muttered. This time it was Niburu who caught at his sleeve and murmured something. "Security from what," he added sourly, "ourselves—?"

Gundhalinu turned back to face him, said softly and swiftly, "This is the way it's done here. I have no problem with this." He put a hand on Kullervo's arm, made Kullervo meet his gaze, and keep it. "What is your problem—?"

Kullervo went rigid under his hand. "I'll tell you very bluntly what your problem will be," Gundhalinu whispered, cutting Kullervo off before he could speak. "If you push these people any more, Reede Kullervo will be permanently banned from entering World's End; or else this entire expedition will end up a beached klabbah, and I don't know if even your gods or mine—" he touched the trefoil hanging at his chest pointedly, "will be able to get it back afloat. A viable stardrive now means nothing to those people over there. It means everything to me. How much does it mean to you—?"

Kullervo stared at him, and Gundhalinu watched the wild light fade from the other man's eyes. Kullervo said nothing more; he shrugged off the contact of Gundhalinu's restraining hand with an abrupt motion.

Gundhalinu turned back to face Ahron, glancing at the three troopers again. He knew the designated pilot from a previous trip inside—a corporal named Ngong, a capable man, but no more enthusiastic about making the journey to Fire Lake than anyone in his right mind would be. "Agent Ahron," he said, "let me propose this. We use our own certified pilot, who is also one of Dr. Kullervo's assistants, but we take the two others. That way our team will be slightly smaller, which somewhat reduces our risk from the Lake; but we will still have adequate security. I don't expect Corporal Ngong will be too disappointed to take some other duty. Will you, Corporal?"

Ngong stole a slightly nervous glance at the sergeant standing beside him, before he answered. "No, sir!"

"I am a Police Commander after all."

Ahron eyed him suspiciously for a long moment, as if she was trying to fathom whatever conceivable plot he was devising against her. "It isn't in the regulations—"

"I know your only thought is for our safety, Agent Ahron, and the success of the project we've all been working on for so long together. . . ." He took a deep breath. "Of all the agents I've had to deal with, you've been the most dedicated and diligent—qualities I value highly." *Gods*, he thought, *lay it on with a shovel, you hypocritical bastard;* hating the taste of his own words. "World's End is a terrifyingly treacherous environment. I know you, of all people, would not want us to risk our lives, or the success of the stardrive project, needlessly—"

"All right," she said abruptly, spitting out her decision like a clot of phlegm. "You may use your own pilot, Commander Gundhalinu. If it was anyone else—" she glanced at Kullervo, "I wouldn't allow it. But you will take Sergeant Hundet and Trooper Saroon with you."

"Thank you," Gundhalinu said, with heartfelt sincerity. He dared to look at Kullervo. "I hope that's a more acceptable risk to you, Doctor?" Kullervo looked at the two troopers with narrowed eyes. Gundhalinu followed his gaze. He had never seen either of the two men before. The sergeant was short and whip-thin, but all muscle, with a narrow, mean face and impenetrable eyes. Gundhalinu disliked him on sight. The private was hardly more than a boy, probably a conscript; he looked right now like the prospect of being sent to Fire Lake was about as appealing to him as his own castration. Gundhalinu sighed.

Kullervo glanced away, down at Niburu. "I guess I can handle that," he murmured. Niburu looked more uncomfortable than relieved; Ananke looked back and forth between them as though they were speaking some language he didn't know. Kullervo looked up at Gundhalinu again. "Thank you, Gundhalinu-*eshkrad*." He smiled, unexpectedly.

Something fluttered and dropped in the pit of Gundhalinu's stomach, as if he were some form of small vermin that was being considered by a cat. He shook off the feeling, annoyed at himself. It was not the first time Kullervo's unpredictable responses had set off alarms in his brain. He had been a Police officer for too long; he read other people's body language almost instinctively. Kullervo's body language was eloquent, and it read all wrong: His volatility and, when he wasn't thinking, his manners and his speech, were better suited to a hotheaded young street thug than to a respected scientist. But he was, undeniably, a brilliant researcher.

Gundhalinu nodded, looking away. He reminded himself that he had grown up with Kharemoughi researchers, the men and women who had been his father's friends and colleagues—scientists whose refined behavior reflected their position at the top of a highly structured, classist society. Kullervo was not a Kharemoughi. Gundhalinu had learned nothing more about his background, perhaps because Kullervo was ashamed of it. That was not an unreasonable response for a man with a mind so superior that it had lifted him out of the gods-knew-what kind of life and dropped him into a nest of elitists. But no one ever left their past behind completely; he knew that, if anyone did.

He looked back at Agent Ahron, at the troopers waiting beside her. "We'll leave from the yard tomorrow at first quarter. I'll expect you to be waiting when I arrive. I believe everything we'll need has already been assembled there—?"

"Everything is in order, Commander," Agent Ahron said. The troopers returned his salute perfunctorily, and he started for the door. Kullervo and the others followed him out without a word. He did not speak again, and neither did they, until they were safely back in the rover, and rising over the town.

"That was impressive," Kullervo said finally. "You're one slick manipulator, Gundhalinu-*eshkrad.*"

Gundhalinu looked up, frowning, as irritation and resentment took root in his festering self-disgust. But to his surprise, Kullervo's face showed him no mockery, no emotion that he could name except perhaps curiosity. "It's not something for which I hope to be venerated by my descendants." He looked away again, out the window.

"You should," Kullervo said. "You should be proud of it. It means you've got a real talent for reading a bad situation. You knew just how hard you could push them . . . and me. It's not something I'm good at, obviously. I'm sorry. Bureaucrats make me nervous . . . World's End makes me nervous." He grimaced, shrugged. "I didn't think you were that perceptive, frankly. It's not a trait Kharemoughis seem to value highly."

Gundhalinu fingered the trefoil hanging at his chest, and said nothing.

"That was a compliment," Kullervo said at last.

"Thank you," Gundhalinu murmured, automatically. He looked down at his hands, at the insides of his wrists, the smooth brown skin that had once been covered with the livid marks of his suicide attempt. His mouth pulled down. "I suppose I've come to deserve some sort of credit, these past few years." He looked out at the jungle, thinking about what lay beyond sight, beyond the distant mountains . . . what lay beyond spacetime, waiting for him.

NUMBER FOUR: World's End

"What are you doing here, at this time of night?" Gundhalinu stopped in the prism of light outside the open door of Kullervo's office, looking in.

Kullervo jerked around in his seat, blinking as if reality made no sense to his eyes. "Gods . . ." he muttered, "you startled the hell out of me." He shook his head, stretching, as Gundhalinu came into the room. "I often work at night, when I can't sleep." He ran a hand through his disheveled hair. "But what are you doing here? I thought you always retired early, and slept the sleep of the just."

Gundhalinu matched his ironic smile unwillingly, and shook his own head. "I can never sleep, the night before I go into World's End."

Kullervo laughed. "So you do have nerve endings, after all, Commander Gundhalinu-eshkrad-sibyl-Hero of the Hegemony."

"Father of all my grandfathers!" Gundhalinu said, exasperated and suddenly angry. He began to turn away.

"Wait." Kullervo pushed up out of his seat. "By the Render, you are on edge. Are you leaving?"

"Yes," he answered, frowning, without turning back.

"So am I. Leaving," Kullervo said. And when Gundhalinu did not respond, "On edge . . ."

Gundhalinu turned back. Kullervo was gazing moodily at the display on the desk behind him. "What are you working on?"

"Nothing," Kullervo said, with sudden bitterness. "A dead end." He ordered the display into oblivion before Gundhalinu could get more than a glimpse of the constructs drifting through its screen. Gundhalinu stared at the suddenly empty desktop; he glanced up at Kullervo's face, expecting to find the same impenetrable surface. But stark, unexpected hopelessness filled Kullervo's eyes.

Gundhalinu hesitated as Kullervo abruptly looked away; knowing that he had seen that look before . . . seen it in the mirror. "Reede, do you want to talk about it?" he said quietly. "Can I help—?"

"No," Kullervo snapped. He looked up again, as if he realized how it had sounded, and muttered, "But I appreciate the offer." Something that could have been gratitude, or even longing, showed fleetingly in his eyes. But he shook his head. "Don't waste your time; it's too valuable. I've wasted enough of my own. There are some mistakes that can't be erased. You just have to live with them. . . ." He turned away, striding toward the door; stopped, looking back at Gundhalinu. Waiting.

Gundhalinu accepted the invitation uncertainly, and followed him out of the room. They went up through the security levels and out into the fetid embrace of the night.

Kullervo hesitated, as Gundhalinu stopped just beyond the dimly glowing screen of the Project's entrance to say a perfunctory good-night. "Share a ride?" Kullervo asked.

Gundhalinu shook his head. "I feel like walking tonight."

"That's a hell of a walk," Kullervo said, looking surprised. "Or aren't you going home?"

"I'm not going home." Gundhalinu glanced away, mildly annoyed by Kullervo's uncharacteristic impulse to camaraderie. He gazed out across the starkly lit artificial landscape, the deceptively open grounds that separated the Project's semi-subterranean fortress from the old Company town. "There's someone I have to see."

"A woman?" Kullervo raised his eyebrows. "Personal?"

"Yes," Gundhalinu said, growing more annoyed by the second. "Not what you're thinking."

Kullervo stared at him, his eyes shadowed by the night. "Then would you mind if I walked with you awhile?"

Gundhalinu hesitated; realized that he was trying to think of a way to refuse. His mind remained stubbornly blank, and so he nodded. "If you like," he said, resigned.

They crossed the gentle vagaries of the parklands together. Gundhalinu looked up at the sky, able to see it for once; seeing an unremarkable scattering of stars on the utterly black face of the moonless night. He remembered Tiamat, where the stars were like glowing coals, where once he had seen his own shadow at midnight. . . . He looked down again, watching his steps as he felt himself stumble.

Kullervo walked beside him, looking down intently, with his hands pushed deep into the side pockets of his loose-fitting blue overshirt. Gundhalinu thought of a boy searching for lost coins; not an image he would have associated with Kullervo before tonight. It occurred to him again, as it had occurred to him before, how young Kullervo was. But then, most geniuses burned their brightest when they were young.

"So it's not a tryst we're going toward. . . ." Kullervo looked up at him, watching him back. "Are you married?"

Gundhalinu shook his head, watching his steps, suddenly uncomfortable again. "Ever?"

"No," he said softly. He glanced up at the sky. "How about you? Are you married?"

"Yes." Kullervo looked straight ahead now, as if he were remembering someone's face. "Gods," he said fiercely, "I want to finish this, and get back to her!" His hands made fists inside his pockets. "She's my life—"

"How long have you been married?" Gundhalinu asked, trying to keep the incredulity out of his voice.

"Not long . . . forever," Kullervo murmured.

Gundhalinu realized that he had never seen Kullervo look twice at a woman in all the time he had been here. He tried to imagine what sort of woman could hold Kullervo's quicksilver temperament in that kind of thrall, when he knew that years would have passed for her before they saw each other again. What kind of woman . . . He looked up again, at the stars. "Is she Kharemoughi?"

Kullervo laughed once. "What? No! She's on—from Ondinee. No offense, but Kharemoughi women aren't my type."

Gundhalinu glanced back at him. "No, I suppose not," he said, a little shortly. "But we're not all of us dead from the neck down, Kullervo."

Kullervo bent his head, meeting Gundhalinu's half frown with a mocking smile. "But you're married to your work. There's really nobody waiting for you out there, somewhere? No lovers—no regrets?"

Gundhalinu felt his throat tighten; he swallowed, and the ache slid down into his chest. "Yes," he said at last. "There is a woman. There was. There is. And a lot of regret . . . Maybe I'll see her again. After all this is finished."

"Where is she?"

"On Tiamat."

"Tiamat!" Kullervo said, incredulous. "Ye gods . . . Tell me that you did all of this just to find a way to get back to her—" He grinned suddenly, waving a hand at the Research Project behind them. "Go on, surprise me."

"I did it all to get back to her," Gundhalinu said, feeling a faint smile turn up the corners of his mouth.

"Liar," Kullervo said, and his grin widened.

Gundhalinu shrugged. "Have it your way." The warm night breeze kissed his face.

They entered the maze of streets that led into the old part of the town, the part that had been there as long as the Company, maybe longer. Cracked, time-eaten walls showed the scars of battle with the inhospitable climate. Here, beyond the protected parklands, mottled graygreen creepers and fleshy, spined shrubs left the jungle's spoor everywhere; its living fingers, working with infernal patience to undo what humans had made. Gundhalinu had found the town and everything about it depressing the first time he had seen it; he still found it depressing. The streets were better-lit at night now, and the nighttime diversions more varied, although they held no more appeal for him than they had three years ago. The streets were noisier and more alive, too, because the credit flowed more freely. More outsiders passed them as they walked than the residents of this place had probably ever dreamed existed, before the Project had come into their lives.

"Who are we going to see?" Kullervo asked, looking from side to side with mild interest.

"Hahn—the sibyl who brought me to meet you."

Kullervo glanced back at him. "Why now? It's late for a social call."

"There's something I need to give her before we leave." Gundhalinu indicated the heavy container he carried in one hand.

"What's in it?" Kullervo asked, when he did not elaborate.

"Something that belongs to her daughter."

Kullervo frowned slightly, either annoyed or trying to remember something. "You said her daughter was a sibyl too . . . but she wasn't meant to be? Does that mean she's—" He gestured, his hand fluttering, touching his head. *Crazy.*

"Yes," Gundhalinu said abruptly, looking down. The sibyl virus caused incurable mental breakdowns in people who were not emotionally stable enough to become sibyls.

"How did it happen? I thought the choosing places rejected anyone who wasn't suitable material to become a sibyl."

"She was rejected; but she wouldn't accept it. Her mother infected her."

"Gods," Kullervo muttered, shaking his head. He looked at Gundhalinu again, glancing briefly, wordlessly, at the trefoil he wore.

Gundhalinu slowed his pace as they reached the corner of a cross street. "This is her street. . . ."

"I'd like to come with you," Kullervo said.

Gundhalinu hesitated. "All right." He shrugged, and entered the side street. It became quiet and residential as they left the main thoroughfare; one- and two-story buildings, some with new, intrusively ornate balconies, rubbed shoulders along the dim-lit, empty sidewalks.

Gundhalinu turned in under the arched entryway to a familiar apartment house. He stopped before the glowing ident plate, touched the proper name, let it register their faces. Hahn's voice answered from the air, sounding surprised, asking him to come inside. The security screen at the building entrance faded.

They went in. Gundhalinu followed the hallway back, found Hahn waiting at the open door of her flat, dressed in a long, loose tunic that might have been sleepwear. Her curiosity was plain, but she gestured them inside without question; her eyes darted at Kullervo's face, and away again.

Gundhalinu had not been inside her home in nearly two years. It looked much as he remembered it, neat and modest, like its owner. The soft, modular furniture she had purchased after he had gotten her a job at the Project still looked almost new.

He set the container he had carried from the research center down on a low table in the middle of a scattering of uncollected dishes. He turned back, answering Hahn's still-unspoken question. "I've brought you something. For Song." He looked again at the box, away from her eyes. He unsealed its cover and took out a globe filled with coruscating fire.

He held it out to her, seeing the small frown of consternation return, furrowing between her brows. "What is it—?" she asked, her voice barely more than a whisper.

"That's stardrive plasma." The answer did not come from him, but from Kullervo. Kullervo stared, his mouth hanging open with utter disbelief. "What the hell are you doing with that?"

"Returning it to its rightful owner," Gundhalinu answered, sounding calmer than he felt.

"You mean you just walked out of the Research Project with that; we just walked out of there with it, together?"

Gundhalinu nodded.

"How is that possible?"

Gundhalinu smiled faintly. "I am the Director of the entire Project. I gave myself permission."

"And the security systems listened to you?" Kullervo murmured. "Just like that?"

"Of course. I programmed them. No one else here was experienced enough with the new system."

Kullervo shook his head. "I need to sit down." He sat.

"Song—" Hahn said suddenly, looking past Gundhalinu; not calling a name, but acknowledging a presence. Gundhalinu turned, following her gaze, as Kullervo looked up from where he sat.

Song stood in the doorway to another room, motionless, with darkness behind her. A long, shapeless sleeprobe covered the painful thinness of her body; her heavy, midnight-black hair hung about her like a shroud. She stared at Kullervo, her mouth open. Slowly she put one hand up to her mouth, pressing it; pointing at him with the other as if she saw a ghost. Or maybe she really was seeing a ghost, Gundhalinu thought. He had seen enough of them himself, at Fire Lake. But her dark eyes moved away again, distractedly, until they met his own. They filled with something that might have been recognition, rejection, hatred . . . or nothing at all, before her gaze fell to the globe in his hands. Her expression slowly changed until he was sure that he was seeing wonder.

She came toward him, holding out her hands uncertainly, as if she was afraid of him, or of his refusal. He put the globe into her hands. She stroked it, held it close to her body; looked up at him, her eyes suddenly gleaming with tears. She half frowned, her quizzical expression making her look momentarily like her mother.

"Yes." He nodded, making no move to touch her or the globe. She looked down at it again, almost as if she were listening with her eyes. He remembered that look; remembered that feeling. "Do you feel it? At peace . . ."

He thought that perhaps she nodded, a tiny spasm of her neck; but she did not look at him again. She turned away slowly, holding the globe close, and drifted like a spirit back through the doorway. The globe's light filled the darkness beyond it with an eerie, momentary radiance.

Gundhalinu turned back to Hahn, ignoring Kullervo's eloquent silence. "I'm leaving for World's End tomorrow."

"I know," she said. "To test Dr. Kullervo's viral reprogramming."

"Yes, we—" He broke off. *Of course; everyone knows.* "I thought . . . whatever happens, whether we succeed or fail . . . in case something should happen to me, I wanted to give you this now. That's stardrive plasma, in the globe."

She nodded again.

"The transformation process was successful on every sample we tested here, including this one. I thought it might help, somehow." He looked down.

"Thank you," she murmured.

"It's the least I can do." He looked up at her again, seeing her lined, weary face, the trefoil tattoo visible on her throat like the one at his own: the reminder that a sibyl was a sibyl even when the pendant on a chain was not there; day and night, waking and sleeping, eating, drinking, making love . . . every moment of one's life. "I wish I knew how to do something more."

She smiled in gratitude, but he saw a world of sorrow in it.

"I'd better be going."

She hesitated, and he wasn't sure whether the hesitation was because she wanted him to stay, or simply didn't know how to talk to him anymore. She turned and led them to the door. "Good night," she said, "and thank you again."

He said, "Good night," in turn, and Kullervo followed him out of the building into the street.

"Explain," Kullervo said, catching him by the sleeve as they began to walk. "You just gave away one third of all the stardrive plasma you've been able to collect in over two years—on a whim?"

"No. . . ." Gundhalinu shook his head. "Hardly a whim." He started back toward the center of town, taking Kullervo with him. "The amount of stardrive we've been able to contain and collect is far less than we need to make even one faster-than-light drive function. We can't even get it to replicate. If what we do at Fire Lake is unsuccessful, that won't change. If we are successful, it won't matter."

"But what's stardrive plasma got to do with Hahn's daughter?"

Gundhalinu was silent for a few steps more. They were nearing the corner of the street, and he gestured Kullervo into a seat at one of the tables of an outdoor tavern. Sitting outside at night had become a favorite pastime for workers from the Project, since sitting outside during the daytime was unbearable. The almost subliminal hum of the sonics employed everywhere to keep insects at bay made a soothing, white-noise counterpoint to conversation.

The tavernkeeper brought them a bowl of heavily salted carrod rinds and two beakers of water. Gundhalinu sipped at the lukewarm liquid, and thought that the tavernkeeper looked annoyed; thinking that he had no right to, since not even a beaker of water was free here—a tradition that still held from his first visit to this dismal town. It surprised him that Kullervo drank nothing stronger; but he had not seen anything that resembled a drug pass Kullervo's lips since the night they met.

"But what's that got to do with Hahn's daughter?" Kullervo repeated, this time holding Gundhalinu's gaze stubbornly. "What have they got on you?"

Gundhalinu laughed. "A hand around my heart, I suppose." He shook his head, glancing away from the look on Kullervo's face. "Nothing more. But the globe that contained the stardrive plasma—that's an original, a relic. A stasis field capable of containing the stardrive harmlessly, without altering its properties, and yet it looks and feels like nothing so much as a ball of plass. I have all the specs on it—we understand it perfectly, in principle—but we have no way to manufacture anything like it . . . yet. Which is why we have to have the plasma's willing cooperation. . . ."

"Damn it, I know all that. What's that got to do with Hahn?" Kullervo insisted. "What's it got to do with her crazy daughter?"

"It belongs to Song. It was the original sample of the stardrive plasma that I brought out of World's End with me. She had it. I brought her out too, along with my brothers. . . . I went in to find them. That's why I was there, in the first place." It sounded like an excuse. He glanced at Kullervo, to see if he had noticed. "I met Hahn here in the town; she asked me if I would look for her daughter."

"And you found all of them, out in that . . . ?" Kullervo jerked his head in the vague direction of World's End, as words failed him. "That's harder to believe than that you found stardrive out there."

"I suppose so," Gundhalinu said, half smiling. "Although at the time I imagined that it would be simple."

" 'The gods take care of fools' . . ." Kullervo murmured.

Gundhalinu grimaced. "Maybe so. As it turned out, by blind luck or otherwise we all ended up in the same place—a place called Sanctuary, by the Lake itself."

"There's a town out there?" Kullervo said in disbelief.

"There was. On an island of red rock in the middle of the Lake. It was built by the survivors of the ship that crashed there at the end of the Old Empire—the one the stardrive plasma escaped from. The gods only know what became of the original inhabitants. It was full of murderers and lunatics when I got there. . . ." His voice faded; he drank water, aware that Kullervo was looking at him strangely. "My brothers were prisoners there—slaves. Song was its queen."

Kullervo laughed, a strangled sound that was more incredulous than amused.

"She was in communion with Fire Lake. She kept the people there protected, more or less, from its randomness." Gundhalinu looked up, facing him directly again. Kullervo only nodded, showing no surprise now. "It was able to communicate with her, after a fashion, because she was a sibyl. I have a theory—"

"That all the forms of Old Empire technovirus still in existence have a single common denominator," Kullervo said. "Their differences are simply a reflection of how they were programmed."

Gundhalinu stared at him. "Exactly," he said.

Kullervo laughed and nodded, his eyes shining. "You're dead right, Gundhalinu-eshkrad."

"You sound like you know that for certain."

Kullervo shrugged and ate a rind. "What we've done here proves it . . . at least to me. I've been working on analyzing and charting the differences to a degree where we can predictably reprogram the basic substance for our own uses. What we've done, and are about to do, with the stardrive is a first step. The options are almost infinite. If only we could recreate the kind of precision they must have had . . ."

"If we're successful at Fire Lake, we'll have proof that more funding and more effort should go into your work when you return to Kharemough."

Kullervo looked back at him blankly, as if the comment were a complete non sequitur; as if his own thoughts had drifted into alien country again. "Yes, I suppose so," he murmured. He rubbed his arms, pushing his sleeves up toward his elbows.

Gundhalinu froze, staring at the profusion of colors and patterns that started at Kullervo's wrists and went spiraling up his forearms. *Tattooing.* The only place he had ever seen tattooing like that was on the arms of criminals. He looked up again, found Kullervo staring back at him.

Kullervo's long-fingered hands twitched, as if they wanted to pull his sleeves down; but he did not. "I got the tattoos on Samathe," he said, "when I was . . . young." He shrugged. "It's not what you think." He held out an arm so that Gundhalinu could see it clearly; see that the intricate geometric designs flowing one into another like music made visible were not the crude pictorials he had seen on underworld thugs. "I liked to look at them. . . ."

"They're very beautiful," Gundhalinu said softly. He was reminded of the fluid patterns of adhani. "I've never seen anything like this. Why do you keep them covered up?"

Kullervo studied the tattoos as if he were hypnotized; but Gundhalinu thought he saw the younger man flush. "So that everybody at the Project won't look at me the way you just did." Kullervo pulled his sleeves down again.

Gundhalinu watched the designs disappear, his embarrassment oddly mingled with regret. He said nothing more, waiting.

Kullervo's attention returned to him abruptly; Gundhalinu read non sequitur again in Kullervo's half frown. "If the Lake communicated in some fashion with Song, what about you?" Kullervo gestured at the trefoil he wore, as if there had been no discussion at all about tattooing a moment earlier.

Gundhalinu forced his mind to retune to Kullervo's sudden change of frequency. He touched the trefoil absently, wonderingly; as he still did often, every day. "Yes. It communicated with me too. It forced me to think about it until I . . . understood."

"What's it really like out there—World's End?" Kullervo twisted the ring he wore on his thumb; a ring of silver metal set with two soliis, that Gundhalinu realized suddenly was probably a wedding ring.

Gundhalinu shook his head. "I can't tell you. I can't explain it. . . . Maybe it's different for everyone who goes out there." He lifted his hands. "Anyway, you'll see for yourself, soon enough. Gods, look at the time. We'd better get some sleep before the night's gone . . . if we can." He smiled and lifted his beaker to Kullervo, for once feeling the kind of comfortable companionship with him that had been almost perversely missing from their relationship these past months. Kullervo raised his own mug, smiling wryly in return, and drained it. "I'll share that ride home with you now," Gundhalinu said.

Kullervo nodded, and used his remote to call a cab. He stood up, stretching, rubbing his neck. "Tell me," he said, "do you still hear the Lake when you go out there?"

Gundhalinu hesitated, nodded. "I still hear it. And I still have some effect on it. Expeditions I head are . . . safer. But the Lake is—insane, for want of a better word. It flows in and out of our particular continuum at will, there's no hard-and-fast reality around it. That's why it's been so damned difficult even to collect a sample." He glanced up, as the cab they had ordered drifted down onto the street beside them. "Reede. . . ." Kullervo looked back at him. "When I'm around the Lake I—get a little disoriented sometimes. It's hard to concentrate, there's so much static in my head." He took a deep breath, feeling himself flush as he went on, "I'm glad you'll be with me on this trip. I'm glad I'll have someone I can count on."

Kullervo's smile came back. "We need each other, on this trip. . . ." He looked down at his wedding ring; his smile quirked oddly. "You can count on that."

NUMBER FOUR: World's End

Reede settled back in his bed in the predawn blackness and sighed. He felt the water of death renewing him, relieving the loneliness and the fear, the countless almost subliminal sensations of discomfort that had been plucking at his nerve endings. It was the closest thing to a drug rush that he could experience anymore. He savored the monstrously deceptive sense of well-being it gave him, the sense that he could do anything, that World's End itself was no match for his intelligence, and the human beings who so trustingly traveled into it with him were no match for his cunning. He closed his eyes, letting go as he felt sleep settle over him like a warm blanket. . . .

The call signal on his remote buzzed loudly in the soft, perfect silence, jarring him out of almost-oblivion. He swore and sat up, dazed, still half dreaming that he had rolled over on some gigantic insect in his sleep. He swore again as he realized where he was, and what the sound meant. By the time he had pushed himself off the bed he was wide awake, seeing dim light through the imperfections of the flimsy window opaquers. He ordered the lights on and groped for the remote lying on his bedside table.

"I'll be right down," he said, and shut it off before Niburu could reply. He pulled on the sturdy, lightweight tunic and pants, the heavy boots, that Gundhalinu had recommended he wear; locked his remote onto his utility belt, and put on the sun helmet he had become accustomed to wearing all the time. He picked up the bag which held everything personal that he owned—because one way or another he did not expect to return to this room—and went out the door without looking back.

Niburu and Ananke were waiting for him in the hired hovercraft. He checked their clothing with a cursory glance; gave their faces a longer look as he got in. They looked tired and nervous, as if they hadn't slept much either, and that worrying about today—or tomorrow, or the next day—was what had kept them awake. "What's bothering you?" he snapped, knowing he ought to feel the same way, but incapable of it when the drug had hold of him.

"Everything," Niburu said glumly. Ananke said nothing, holding the quoll close, stroking its protuberant nose while it burbled mindlessly.

"Lighten up, for gods' sakes," Reede said, frowning.

"You mean, 'it's not the end of the world'?" Niburu asked sarcastically. "Yes it is."

Reede grunted, watching the Project and the town drift by below; wondering whether it was actually the prospect of going into the unpredictable wilderness that was bothering them, or the fear of what they might be forced to do in order to get out again. He did not ask, because he would not be able to give them an answer that would make them feel any better. He looked away from them, shifting restlessly in his seat.

Gundhalinu was, predictably, waiting for them when they arrived at the departure point. Beside him was the insectoid triphibian rover that would carry them all to their fate, and the floating sledge they would tow behind them, which would carry the bulk of their equipment. Reede shook his head and smiled; the smile he saw reflected in the window was not a pleasant one.

Niburu dropped them precisely onto the departure field. Reede climbed out, glancing toward the rover, where the two government troopers were still loading the last of their supplies aboard. Or one of them was, anyway—the kid, Trooper Saroon, or whatever his name was. The sergeant, Hundet, stood hands locked behind his back, watching the kid struggle with loads he probably could have moved one-handed; exerting effort only once, to curse and kick the kid's butt when he dropped a crate.

Reede turned as Gundhalinu came up beside him. "Sergeant!" Gundhalinu said sharply, in Fourspeech. "Give Saroon a hand, not your foot, if you want things to go faster!"

Hundet looked back at him, and Reede saw the black resentment that filled the man's eyes as he slowly and sullenly moved to pick up a piece of equipment. Hundet was the kind who wouldn't forget a rebuke like that, ever. Reede didn't bother to say the obvious, now that it was too late.

"Thank the gods we're making this trip by air," Gundhalinu murmured.

Reede raised his eyebrows. "Why in seven hells would you even consider doing it any other way?"

Gundhalinu shrugged, smiling faintly. "The first time I went into World's End, we did it the hard way, in a broken-down junker with a defective repeller grid. We had to travel overland the whole godforsaken, hellish . . ." His voice faded; something came into his eyes that could never be put into words.

Reede glanced away at Niburu and Ananke, slightly unnerved. "How long did it take you?"

Gundhalinu shook his head. "I really don't know. After a while, even time didn't make sense anymore."

Reede said nothing, unable to think of a response.

"How can we be sure of how long we stay, then?" Niburu asked, half frowning. "What if we stay too long, and your security people . . . give us a hard time?" Reede suspected that was the least of the fears behind the question.

Gundhalinu shook his head. "It won't be a problem this time," he said.

"Because you can talk to the Lake?" Reede said.

Gundhalinu looked back at him steadily. "Yes," he said. "Because I can talk to the Lake."

Reede felt the sudden joint stares of Niburu and Ananke pulling at him, asking him anxious questions, dunning him with silent protest. "You're saying we'll be perfectly safe, then?" he asked, for them.

"No." Gundhalinu smiled ruefully. "No one is perfectly safe, Kullervo-eshkrad. At least, not in this universe."

Reede looked at him sharply; grinned, as suddenly. "I wouldn't have it any other way," he said. He ignored the mixed expressions that were his response.

The last of their equipment was loaded on board, and they chose their seats in the rover's womblike interior. Gundhalinu took the copilot's seat beside Niburu, up front where he would have the fullest view possible of the terrain they were about to pass over. Reede sat diagonally behind him, next to Ananke, relegating the two troopers to the windowless cargo area. Gundhalinu had said the trip should take only a few hours. *If everything went all right.* Reede couldn't keep his own mind from adding that unspoken caveat. He looked out the side port, leaned forward impatiently, peering ahead between the seats for a view through the windshield as he listened with an earbug to Perimeter Control's field clearance sequence.

At last he felt them begin to rise; freed from the suffocating confinement of civilized authority, heading into the wilderness, the unknown, the uncontrollable— chaos made visible. He felt a weight fall away from him, felt as if he were rising himself, uncoiling, being reborn. . . . Ananke glanced at him sidelong, his eyes full of doubt. Reede took a deep breath, and withdrew into his thoughts.

He looked out and down, seeing the bloated gray-green flora of the jungle that lay below like an unwholesome carpet. They followed the sullen yellow ribbon of a river he did not know the name of, like hunters tracking the glistening slime spoor of a whillp. . . . He realized that the only images which came to mind to describe what he saw were vaguely repulsive ones; tried to think of images that were not morbid, and failed. He wondered whether there was something about the physical appearance of this place that a human brain instinctively found repulsive, or whether he was just letting himself be sucked into the mood of the others around him.

"How many trips have you made into World's End, Commander Gundhalinu?" Niburu asked, probably trying to keep his own mind off the view.

"This is my sixth," Gundhalinu murmured, his words barely audible. Something that looked like a refinery flashed by below them, in a sudden, unexpected clearing. Reede felt his shoulders tighten; he relaxed as the obscene overabundance of plant life filled his view again.

"That's the last sign of human habitation we'll see," Gundhalinu said, almost sounding as if he was glad himself to put it behind him.

Reede looked ahead, past Gundhalinu's shoulder, seeing something new in the distance. Up ahead the forest ended, like the shore of the sea, on the lower reaches of a mountain range. The mountains seemed almost dreamlike, silvered by the humid haze of the rainforests. He kept watching them, sure that the image he thought he saw would dissipate at the next eyeblink into cloudforms, mirage.

But it did not. The sun rose higher in the sky, burning away the mists, illuminating the interior of the rover and the silent, pensive faces around him; and moment by moment the shimmering unreality in the distance became more real, became a forbidding barrier, a warning.

As they rose to meet them, the mountains resolved into gigantic piles of rubble, as if some deranged giant had heaped up boulders the size of houses in a futile effort to turn back invaders. "You actually went overland through this terrain?" Reede asked at last, leaning forward again to get Gundhalinu's attention; driven to ask the question by the strength of his disbelief.

"Yes," Gundhalinu said. "Every bloody millimeter of it."

"It must have been a hell of a trip," Reede murmured with grudging admiration.

"Yes," Gundhalinu said softly. "That's exactly what it was." He fell silent again, gazing down at the gray, jumbled ruins of the mountains. "I was the mechanic. I kept the rover running, through that, through everything." He laughed once. "I began to feel like a miracle worker. But World's End teaches you humility—"

Reede sat back, trying to imagine Gundhalinu flat on his back under the guts of a broken-down rover, trying to make it function under conditions like those. He looked out the window again, feeling a sudden eagerness that was almost hunger as he wondered what he would see next, watching the tortured land slip by below.

Beyond the mountains he found the real heart of World's End: an oblate wilderness of stone and sand; mudflats baked by ceaseless heat into pavements of tile; gleaming beds of unexploited mineral deposits. He would not have believed that anything could live here, but he saw clumps of grotesque, stunted plant life scattered across the surface of the ground like excrement. More mountain peaks rose in the seemingly unreachable distance, wreathed in artificial clouds of volcanic smoke.

There was no flight plan in the rover's memory bank. Gundhalinu spoke to Niburu in occasional monotones, altering their course; navigating by sight, or maybe by some arcane sixth sense. He had claimed that any instruments were suspect here, and besides World's End never even looked the same way twice. The warping of the electromagnetic spectrum and the fabric of spacetime caused by the stardrive plasma's compulsive malfunctioning spread out from Fire Lake for hundreds of kilometers on every side. The rational part of Reede's mind accepted the parameters controlling such phenomena in the abstract; another, more primitive part of his brain trembled with terror and awe before the prospect of witnessing its reality.

"What really made you come out here?" he asked, still finding it difficult even to imagine a Kharemoughi highborn doing anything by choice that would require hardship, sacrifice, or manual labor. He knew Gundhalinu had been a Blue before he had discovered the secret of Fire Lake; but becoming a career officer in the Hegemonic Police was hardly an impulsive act. It was considered an honorable profession, even by Techs; it appealed to their sense of order. Being an independent prospector in a broken-down wreck of a rover was about as far from rational as you could get. "Did you already have an idea about what the Lake was?"

"No," Gundhalinu said, not meeting Reede's gaze. "I had no idea what I'd find. I only wanted to find my brothers. I felt it was . . . my duty to my family to find them, if you understand. A matter of honor."

Reede listened in surprise to the stilted reserve of the words, and wondered what Gundhalinu wasn't telling him; what he wouldn't let himself say. He recognized that sudden closing off of communication, that invisible, unbreachable wall of silence. He had used it himself every time Gundhalinu had tried to get close to him. He hadn't cared whether colliding with it had bruised Gundhalinu's ego. The less they felt about each other the better, under the circumstances. He was surprised—and surprised at his anger—at being on the receiving end of a rebuff. "What about the people you traveled with?" he asked, pressing the conversation because he was annoyed. "Who were they? What did they want out of World's End?"

"There were two other men." Gundhalinu glanced at him, and away again, resigned. "Ang was an ex-Company man, a geologist. He'd quit to go out on his own. He thought he knew where a strike was. He thought World's End would give him what he wanted. . . . Spadrin was an offworlder, a criminal; probably in trouble with his own kind, looking for a stake. He thought World's End would give him what he wanted, too. . . . That's what we all thought."

"Did they get what they wanted?" Reede pushed.

"They both died."

Niburu looked at Gundhalinu, and out at World's End again, his face white.

Reede sat back, inside a silence that was suddenly as bitter as the taste of alkali. He watched endless flats of alkali and gypsum pass beneath them like fields of snow. He forced himself to imagine traversing that terrain day after day, in the blistering heat and the nightmarish uncertainty. . . . He glanced at Niburu, couldn't see his expression now, hidden by the seat back; glanced at Ananke, who sat gazing into space, into some private reverie that could have been either bright or dark. Trooper Saroon dozed on the floor with his back against the wall, oblivious with exhaustion. The sergeant met Reede's glance with a sullen stare that didn't have the imagination to look worried. Reede looked away again, and watched the wasteland pass.

Time passed too; how much, he wasn't sure. It didn't seem to matter, here when time as he knew it was a meaningless concept. *Dreamtime,* he thought, feeling oddly as if he were dreaming. No one spoke again, as the dream took hold of them all. At last Gundhalinu roused himself, his muscles tensing as he peered ahead. "There," he said.

Reede looked out through the hazed windshield, his own body tightening. He sucked in his breath as he saw it, suddenly: the unnatural glow on the horizon, the first fingernail of light, the promise. *So soon.* His hands closed, holding on to an emotion that was not elation, or fear, or wonder, but contained parts of them all.

The Lake seemed to come to them, more than they came to the Lake, expanding below them like the surface of the sun: a blinding, shimmering vision of light.

"Shall I set us down along the shoreline there, Commander Gundhalinu?" Niburu asked, his voice sounding dry and uncertain. Reede wondered if it was the hours gone without speaking, or simply awe that made him sound like that.

"Yes," Gundhalinu said, pointing to his left. "There's a canyon mouth over there; I see some green. If there's water, it will make a good campsite."

Reede wondered about the consequences of drinking the water in a place like this; realized with something that was almost disappointment that if Gundhalinu would drink it, it must be perfectly safe.

Niburu brought them down, down, with infinite care into the steep-walled crack in the scarp that bordered the Lake. He followed it inward until he found a stretch of even ground wide enough for their camp, just beyond sight of the Lake's hellshine. The rover settled onto the desiccated earth with a dim crunching sound.

Niburu unsealed the hatch, and a wave of heat rolled into the rover's cab: the wasteland's hot, alien breath touching their faces, their flesh. For a long moment no one moved, as if none of them had the guts to be the first to step outside. Reede looked at Gundhalinu, saw him staring out at the parched canyon walls with his head bent slightly, as if he were . . . listening. There was nothing at all to hear, as far as Reede could tell. Just as he was about to say something, Gundhalinu pushed up out of his seat and left the vehicle. Reede followed him, the others trailing them one by one.

Reede squinted in the glare, flipping down the visor of his helmet. It was hotter here than back in the jungle; but at least it was dry. He turned in the direction of Fire Lake, but it was hidden from his view by a curve of the canyon. He looked down at his feet, felt heat seeping in through his insulated boot-soles from the pale, inert gravel of the canyon's floor; looked up the walls of rock-hard, lithified clay to its rim. Rising like incongruous umbrellas against the glaring ceramic sky he found a stand of giant tree-ferns, their trunks the color of iron, the startling green of their feathery leaves softened by a coat of dust. He wondered at their perversity, growing up there on the plateau when down here in the dying wash was the last of the water, a scattering of shallow, green-rimmed pools set in protected pockets like footprints along the canyon bottom . . . as though Time had come striding down this wash, on its way to somewhere else, leaving everything here frozen in limbo until their arrival had violated an ancient peace.

Someone swore loudly behind him. Reede swung around, abruptly aware of time again, and that he was not standing here alone; that the others were already in more or less efficient motion around him, following Gundhalinu's orders. He watched them setting up camp, in the act of protecting themselves and their equipment from the brutal heat—the only thing they could reliably protect themselves from, here. He turned back, irritated, mostly at himself; gave sharp orders to Niburu and Ananke. He reminded himself that Gundhalinu had seen this landscape, or ones just as strange, half a dozen times; and even if he hadn't, he was compulsive enough not to let the alienness of it distract him from getting the job done.

Reeds wiped a hand across his sweating face, trying to ignore the song of his own blood inside his ears. "Gundhalinu," he called. Gundhalinu turned to look at him, and came back to his side. "Is this place safe? What about flash floods—" He gestured at the stagnant, standing pools, the high, narrow walls of the wash, their image overlain by a memory that wouldn't take form but scraped the back of his eyes with a razor's edge.

Gundhalinu shook his head. "It won't happen while we're here."

"You mean it's the dry season . . . ?" Reede's voice faded before he finished the sentence, as he saw the expression on Gundhalinu's face.

"Yes, of course," Gundhalinu murmured, "it's the dry season." He looked away, calling out directions to Hundet.

Reede started back to the rover and went to work, suddenly wanting it all to be over, to be finished with his real work here as rapidly as possible.

By the time they had fully set up camp the setting sun had all but disappeared behind the canyon wall, giving them some respite from the pitiless heat. Reede found himself still stunned by it, each time he left the access to one of the bubble domes, even though he was no stranger to hot weather. At least the shielded microenvironments they had set up inside the domes would protect their equipment—and incidentally themselves—from as much of Fire Lake's disruptive electromagnetic fluctuation as possible.

Reede exited the dome that held his personal living quarters, certain at last that his own equipment was reasonably functional, and his personal belongings were completely secure. He had spent the entire afternoon checking and rechecking them, running experiments. He wanted to rest; but he could not keep his thoughts off Mundilfoere. Her mystery, her heat, her power over him were as all-consuming, as inescapable as World's End . . . and he was exiled in this bizarre wilderness, unable to return to her until he had fulfilled the quest she had set for him. And he realized now that the quest was going to be harder to complete than he had ever imagined . . . for all the wrong reasons. The knowledge fed his need for her, fed his doubt and sense of isolation, until he could not close his eyes.

"Niburu!" he shouted. Niburu appeared in the arched doorway of the tent that he shared with Ananke, facing Reede's. Reede stared at him, realizing that he needed to have a reason for calling the other man out here, besides simply to prove that he still existed. "What's for dinner?" If anyone could make the rudimentary rations he had seen unstowed from the rover palatable, Niburu could. And at least this was one ungracious request Niburu actually wouldn't resent.

Niburu shrugged. "Shit surprise, probably." He grinned. "I'll see what I can do." He started away toward the supply dome.

"Niburu."

Niburu hesitated, looking back at him with sudden wariness.

"Good job today." Reede nodded toward the rover, fingering his ear cuff self-consciously.

Niburu smiled uncertainly, and went on again. Reede watched as Hundet intercepted his course, imagined the conversation he read into their gestures, as Niburu justified his right to freely access their communal food supply. The two government troopers had taken the rover as their sleeping quarters—for security reasons, he supposed, so that they controlled the communications equipment and the only way of escaping from this hellhole. It amused him to realize that their institutionalized paranoia was perfectly justified. It was also damned inconvenient to his plans; but he told himself that it was only an inconvenience, no more. . . .

Hundet let Niburu pass, finally; momentarily satisfied by another round of petty humiliation. Reede had watched him all afternoon, bullying Saroon, harassing Niburu and Ananke. He did his own work with a sullen disinterest, glaring at Gundhalinu and at Reede.

Reede looked away, wondering where Gundhalinu was. Ananke came around the back of the dome with the quoll draped across his shoulders like a fur piece; started violently as he almost walked headlong into Reede.

"Where were you?" Reede said, more abruptly than he meant to.

"Just . . . looking." Ananke shrugged, looking guilty now. "I wanted to see Fire Lake. . . ." His eyes broke away from Reede's gaze and focused on his feet, which were scuffing gravel. "Did you need me for something, bo—Dr. Kullervo?"

"No." Reede tried to make his own expression more pleasant; every time he looked hard at Ananke, the kid wilted like a plant. Dressed in a loose shirt and baggy shorts, with his hair tied back in a ponytail, he looked almost fragile, in spite of the athlete's muscles that showed along his bare arms and legs. Ananke couldn't be more than three or four years younger than he was himself; but sometimes Reede felt as if the difference between their ages was measured in centuries. "Gundhalinu said not to get too far from camp. It's . . . dangerous." He hadn't tried to explain; World's End's reputation was enough.

"Yes, Doctor, I know." Ananke nodded earnestly, patting the quoll. The quoll burbled contentment, apparently undisturbed by anything as long as it was attached to its owner. "Commander Gundhalinu went with me; he said it was all right."

"Where is he?"

"He's still looking at the Lake."

Reede glanced away down the canyon, and back. "Doesn't that thing ever walk?" he said, gesturing at the quoll, wondering why they didn't both have heat prostration.

Ananke shrugged again, the quoll riding the motion easily. "They like to sit," he said.

Reede smiled in spite of himself, as Niburu returned with an armload of supplies. He left them standing together and walked off between the domes."

He followed the curving canyon in the direction he knew led toward Fire Lake. As he rounded the first bend, shutting away the sight and sound of the camp behind him, he had the sudden, unnerving feeling that if he turned back he would find it was no longer there, and he was all alone. . . . He pushed on resolutely, frowning, listening to the substantial crunch of sand and gravel under his boots, feeling the heat, touching the crumbling mud of the canyon wall as he walked.

Up ahead a flicker of movement caught his eye on the stark, stony ground. He caught up with the thing that floundered there; stared down at it in silent fascination. It was brown, or green, or red, or all of those, and it resembled a fish more than anything else he could imagine, but it was crawling, after a fashion, on things that were more than fins but less than legs. He watched the fish-out-of-water struggle on up the canyon, oblivious to his presence in its grotesque, single-minded urge toward something that was probably forever incomprehensible even to it.

Reede stood wondering what in the name of a thousand gods it was searching for, tortuously dragging itself millimeter by millimeter over the heated stones. He followed its trajectory with his eyes; saw up ahead in the protected curve of the wash another of the moss-green, ephemeral pools that dotted the canyon bottom. A scattering of ferns waved like feathers at its edge, beckoning with their motion in the hot, faint wind. Reede glanced back the way the thing had come, and saw in the distance another pool, reduced now to barely more than a mudhole. *Escape*. He looked again at the fish-thing, in agonizing, floundering progress toward something better. It didn't know that the pool it was struggling toward would be a mudhole too in a few more days; that all its struggles were in vain. He could see that, but the fish-thing couldn't. When that pool dried up, it would struggle on again, until it found another pool, a little deeper, or the floods came, or it died. . . . *Survival.* Maybe it was all meaningless, but that thing would go on futilely struggling to survive. . . . He watched it, feeling wonder, and grudging admiration, and disgust.

And then he kicked it, hard. It went skidding over the gravel for nearly a meter and a half in the direction of the pool. It flopped silently, desperately on its side, its fins waving like flags; righted itself at last and began to crawl forward again toward the pool, as though nothing had happened. Reede turned away from it and strode on down the wash, clenching and unclenching his hands.

He rounded another bend in the canyon, and stopped dead, staring. Fire Lake lay before him, although he had been certain that he could not have come this far already. Its presence was a physical blow against his senses; not simply heat and light, but sensations that his brain could not even begin to quantify. Its presence poured into his mind through every available receptor, eyes, ears, nose, skin—

"You feel it."

It took him a moment to realize that the words, the voice, were not a manifestation of the Lake, or an hallucination; that the shadow-figure suddenly standing before him on the congealed-stone surface of the beach was really Gundhalinu.

Reede blinked, filling in the detail of Gundhalinu's face with dazzled eyes. "Yes . . ." he said, his own voice coagulating in his throat. He was not tempted to ask whether the Lake affected everyone like this; somehow he knew that it did not.

"What do you see?" Gundhalinu asked eagerly. "What do you hear?"

Surprised at the question, and at Gundhalinu's impatience, Reede said thickly, "Light. Noise . . . a kind of white noise. I can't describe it." He shook his head. "As if . . . as if, if I only had *something,* it could tell me, and I'd know . . ." He wanted to spit out whatever was wrong with his mouth, shake something loose that had hold of his brain. "Gods, that sounds like a lot of shit—" he said angrily. "I don't know what I'm trying to say. What do you see?"

"Ghosts," Gundhalinu said, sounding vaguely disappointed, looking out across the Lake again. "The past and the future, flowing in and out of existence; metaspace conduits opening and closing."

Reede laughed uncertainly. "You have a better imagination than I do."

"It isn't my imagination . . . it's the sibyl virus." Gundhalinu focused on Reede's face again with what seemed to be an effort. "It lets the Lake in . . . it's like having a thousand madmen screaming inside my skull, constantly. It makes it very . . . difficult, to be here, and function normally. The adhani disciplines help me; I've learned more biofeedback control techniques since I entered the higher levels of Survey." He ran his hands down the rumpled cloth of his loose pantslegs in a futile neatening gesture.

Reede grimaced. "I don't think I could take that," he muttered. *Not on top of the rest . . . dreams, broken mirrors, the emptiness, the void . . .*

Gundhalinu was still watching him with a strange intentness. "You sense the phenomena more than anyone I've met, except another sibyl. But only with a part of your mind. Another part of you hears nothing; that's what protects you—"

Reede shoved him hard in the chest, knocking him down. "Goddammit!" The pocked, convoluted surface of the shore around Gundhalinu suddenly seemed to be made up of the screaming mouths and mindless eyes of a million faces, souls trapped in an unimaginable hell-on-earth.

Gundhalinu got slowly to his feet. He shook his head like someone who was just waking up, and looked at Reede blankly. "What the hell was that about?" he asked.

Reede forced himself to stop staring at the ground, and met Gundhalinu's querulous gaze. "Don't talk to me like that!"

"Like what?"

"Like you think you know how I feel."

Gundhalinu looked away toward the Lake, and back at him. "Gods, I hate this—!" His voice shook. He rubbed his face, murmuring something inaudible. He said aloud, more evenly, "I'm sorry. It seemed to make sense when I said it. . . . This will get better, as I adjust to it. It's always worst at the start."

Reede made a face, as an unexpected emotion struggled inside him like a fish-thing stranded on burning rock. "I'm not used to being around somebody who seems to be crazier than I am." He began to turn away, wanting to put distance between himself and the Lake, himself and Gundhalinu, himself and the silent, screaming faces of the shore.

"Reede." Gundhalinu gave him a bleak, painful smile as he grudgingly turned back. "Before you go, would you help me find out just how crazy I really am? Do you see an island out there?" He pointed toward the Lake; turned with the motion, as if a kind of yearning drew him.

Reede followed the line of his gesture, squinting into the glare that obliterated everything at first, even the sky. He shielded his eyes, blinking until he could begin to see clearly—see the stark, solid form that rose like the back of some primordial beast from the middle of the molten sea. "Yes," he said at last, his voice as husky as if it had dried up in his throat, as if he had been standing here, listening with his nerve endings, for days. "Yes, something's out there. Looks like an island, I guess."

Gundhalinu made a sound that was a choked-off cry of triumph. "It's come back—! It knows, the Lake knows that this time we've got the answer." He looked at Reede again, his eyes shining; caught Reede's arm as he tried to pull away. "Have you heard of Sanctuary?"

Reede started. "You said it was a place in the middle of the Lake, full of lunatics and 'jacks. . . . Is that where it is?" He looked into the shimmering brightness.

"Where it used to be," Gundhalinu murmured, his own gaze drifting toward the Lake again. "Where I found my brothers, and Song. They came after us when we tried to escape—and the Lake swallowed them all, the town, the entire island. No one's seen it since . . . until now."

Reede half frowned in disbelief. "Gods! You're telling me it just disappeared? And now it's just come back again? Everything?"

Gundhalinu nodded. His fists tightened and he grinned, a grin of desperate hope. "The island has. I don't think we'll find the inhabitants." His voice hardened. "They'd have been swarming on us like deathwatch beetles by now. . . . The question is, what else came back?"

"What do you mean?" Reede asked, caught by Gundhalinu's sudden eagerness.

"I mean the ship the stardrive plasma came from, that created Fire Lake. If the Lake actually knows we have an answer, then it could . . . could . . ." His gaze drifted down to the ground beneath his feet, the screaming faces of the damned. "It must have driven off or killed the people who built Sanctuary. But it's never forgotten them. It dreams about them constantly. It needs human contact, human help . . . it's been waiting for us to come again and end its madness, its randomness—"

"Yeah, right," Reede said, jerking free from Gundhalinu's hold. "Well, we're here to give it what it wants. Then you'll both feel better. Let's go back to camp."

"We have to go out to the island tomorrow," Gundhalinu said, as if he wasn't listening. But his gaze was clear and rational again.

"Why?" Reede asked, still leery.

"That's where the starship is."

Reede's eyes widened. "You mean the actual Old Empire ship, intact?"

"Parts of it, at least." Gundhalinu nodded, and his grin came back. "Imagine, if the drive unit is still there! Having an actual model to work from would give us a tremendous leg up in creating new ones of our own."

Reede felt a surge of excitement that was like some perverse desire. He shrugged uncomfortably, uncertain if the feeling even belonged to him. "We'd better find out if the vaccine works on the real Lake, first," he said roughly. "Let's get out of here." He pulled at Gundhalinu's arm. "Come on—"

Gundhalinu nodded, turning away from the Lake at last in a motion that seemed to take all his strength. They crossed the beach and entered the canyon mouth, hiking back along the sandy wash. Reede saw no sign of the fish-thing. He wondered whether he had ever really seen it at all.

NUMBER FOUR: World's End

With the light of a new day they rose into the sky like the sun, and Niburu took the rover on a long, languid arc out across Fire Lake. Reede watched the displays as their passage spread his fine-tuned nets behind them like the nets of fishermen. The fields of focused energy would selectively excite molecules of stardrive plasma in the matrix of inanimate material with which it had unnaturally mated. Then the secondary fields would draw it in, irresistibly, holding it captive in stasis inside the walls of a containment unit. The methods Gundhalinu had used before had been so hopelessly out of phase with the plasma's molecular structure that it was a miracle the research teams had managed to capture even a milligram of it. But this time they would have a meaningful test sample to vaccinate; he had seen to that. A sample large enough to breed independently, but small enough to carry away, when the time came . . .

But first the vaccination had to work. The plasma they were collecting would stay in stasis forever, frozen in the exact picosecond of time in which it had been captured—until they attempted to manipulate it. Once it had its freedom, if the vaccine did not work almost instantaneously to bring it under control, they would lose it . . . and maybe lose their lives as well.

Reede watched the displays silently registering the amount of plasma they had captured and contained, as it slowly rose; ignoring everything and everyone around him in his elation at proving himself right. For a brief space of time he could ignore the question mark of his own existence, the precariousness of all their lives, the sensations of restless, expectant heat he seemed to feel sucking at him through the rover's heavily insulated hull.

"We're full up!" he called at last. He looked up, jarred by the abrupt presence of the real world around him.

"Good work!" Gundhalinu grinned at him, and raised his fist in triumph. "Come up here and take a look at this, Reede. . . . Take us up over the island, will you, Niburu?"

Reede got up and left his equipment reluctantly, edging past Trooper Saroon, who sat hugging his stun rifle like a religious charm against his chest. Saroon looked up as he passed; the expression in the trooper's upslanting eyes was grim and terrified. His thin, tense face was the face of someone who was hopelessly lost and surrounded by enemies; Reede realized that from Saroon's point of view, that was probably exactly what was happening to him. Hundet had ordered him to go with them on this flight; Reede suspected that it was because Hundet didn't have the balls to fly over Fire Lake himself. Reede enjoyed the brief fantasy that when they got back to the campsite, Hundet would have mysteriously disappeared from their plane of existence, swallowed up by the malign vagaries of World's End.

He joined Gundhalinu and Niburu in the front of the rover, looking out at the hallucinogenic hellshine of the Lake . . . at the monolith of red stone rising up like a dream from its molten sea: the island he had glimpsed from shore. It was larger than he had imagined, easily large enough to hold a small town, although he could see no evidence of a settlement.

"There!" Gundhalinu said, his voice rising. "Sanctuary—"

"Where?" Reede squinted. "I don't see anything."

"Take us lower, Niburu," Gundhalinu said. Niburu nosed the rover down obediently, circling back to cross the island again.

"The town is built from the stone," Gundhalinu said. "A lot of it is in ruins. It's hard to make it out from a height, unless you know it's there."

Reede wondered how Gundhalinu could be sure he wasn't really imagining the whole thing. He managed not to ask, as they arced in toward the sheer cliffs of red rock and his eyes filled with the astonishing vision of a waterfall dropping from the heights of the island into the sea of fire. Clouds of steam shrouded the impact-point of the two elemental forces, filling the air with ephemeral rainbows. They flew on over the plateau, until Gundhalinu said again, "There," and pointed.

This time Reede saw it: the remains of what had once been a town, constructed from the red stone of the island, and then abandoned to decay. But as they closed with it, their altitude dropping farther, he sucked in his breath. The formal grace of its architectural forms had not simply been softened by time, or even ruined by an earthquake—it had been deliberately jumbled, by some wilder, more unimaginable agent of change. Slabs of raw rock lay sandwiched impossibly between building stories, order and chaos, the natural and the unnatural violently re-merged into one.

The city itself was segmented into quadrants, split by two canyons crossing at its center. The deep clefts cut in the rock made waterflow trails that shone into the distance. Reede realized that there must be three more waterfalls like the one he had seen, fed by some impossible wellspring here in the heart of the island, spilling impossibly into the molten Lake from the four corners of this dreamworld.

"*Edhu,* look at that. . . ." Niburu murmured.

"Land us." Somehow he was not really surprised to recognize his own voice, not Gundhalinu's, speaking the command. Gundhalinu glanced up with something darker than concern in his stare, but he only nodded.

Niburu set them down gently in a more or less open square near the center of the town, and released the hatch. Trooper Saroon leaped to his feet, his eyes showing white as reality yawned behind him.

Gundhalinu put a hand on Saroon's shoulder, pushing him back into his seat with gentle pressure. "Watch the rover, with Niburu. We'll be safe enough—there's no one out there anymore."

Saroon nodded in wordless relief as Gundhalinu turned away, starting for the hatch, the glaring brightness beyond it.

"You sure—?" Niburu asked, looking at Reede, looking at Gundhalinu's retreating back.

Reede nodded, realizing that Gundhalinu needed solitude far more than he needed the rover secured or Saroon at ease. "Stay here," he said. He settled his sun helmet on his head and climbed down, following Gundhalinu. The rover sealed shut again behind them as he started out across the plaza to the place where Gundhalinu stood staring up into the city.

As Reede reached Gundhalinu's side, he heard Gundhalinu mutter something; recognized the barely audible singsong of an adhani. Gundhalinu pressed his hands to his face, ground them into his eyes almost brutally, before he let them fall away again. "Gods, yes," he murmured, "I hear you. I see you. I remember you. . . ."

Reede realized abruptly that Gundhalinu was not speaking to him. He gazed up at the rising mass of the ruins, seeing no one, hearing nothing but the whisper of the wind. The stark purity of this place made him think of bleached bones, of a broken vessel, of the ultimate peace of things from which the imperfect soul had flown. He looked back at Gundhalinu, and knew with chilling certainty that they were not having the same vision. And if he listened with the part of his mind that could not even ask to hear, he knew the nameless presence would have spoken to him; if only he could have asked. . . . "Ghosts?" he murmured, his own voice sounding like a stranger's.

Gundhalinu gave an odd, strangled laugh. "Thousands of them . . ." He shook his head. "Everyone I've ever known, or will ever know, among them . . . Do you want to know the future, Reede? If I stand here long enough, I'll be able to tell it to you."

Reede stared at him, stricken with sudden paranoia, until he realized that Gundhalinu was speaking in generalities. "How could you stand to get near this place, the first time, if it was like that for you?" He still found it almost unbelievable that someone as obsessively controlled as Gundhalinu would ever have committed the near-insane act of entering World's End.

"I wasn't a sibyl when I first got here."

"What happened out here?" Reede whispered, not able to keep himself from asking. And, when Gundhalinu didn't answer, "To you. To the others with you?"

"Spadrin murdered Ang," Gundhalinu said hoarsely. "I murdered Spadrin. Multiple stab wounds . . ."

Reede stopped breathing.

"When I reached the Lake, after I'd finally killed Spadrin, I was picked up by 'jacks from Sanctuary. They brought me to her. . . . Song infected me."

A frown narrowed Reede's eyes. "Against your will—?" he asked.

"Yes." Gundhalinu's hand tightened painfully over the sibyl medallion. He turned away and began to walk, picking a careful path over the broken ground. They went on through the abandoned streets, skirting rubble, descending broken steps and corroding metal ladders.

"Why?" Reede said, finally.

Gundhalinu stopped, swung around in his tracks. "Why what—?" he demanded. "Why did I come here? Because I had nothing left to live for. Why did she infect me? Because we were both gone to World's End . . ." His voice cracked. *Gone to World's End* meant *gone crazy* on Number Four. "She wanted a consort. . . ." He looked away, staring at a single tower rising from the city's heights, its middle section replaced by a slab of solid rock. "Maybe she thought if she fed me to the lake, it would give her peace. . . ." Both hands rose now, in a jerky motion that was almost a shrug. "After that, I heard the Lake too, just like she did. It took me . . . it took me a long time to understand what it was trying to tell me. I really believed I had gone mad. And yet somehow, instead, being a sibyl drove me sane." He started on, not looking back to see whether Reede would follow. Reede followed, moving deeper into another man's fever dream. "I almost killed myself, right up there, before I understood." He pointed ahead, toward the canyon rim they were making their way toward. "I couldn't be sure of anything."

"I know that feeling," Reede murmured, feeling his lips drying, cracking. "Gods, yes . . . I know that." Gundhalinu hesitated, looking back at him. "As if you can't . . . you don't even know what questions to ask. If you could just think of the *question,* then at least you'd know what was . . . missing." He felt his eyes burn, suddenly full of tears, as if some bewildered part of him still fought to mourn—even to remember—some unspeakable, forgotten wrong that could never be avenged. He kept his head down, his eyes on the rubble-strewn ground under his feet. "When I work, I always know what questions to ask. But . . ."

"Exactly," Gundhalinu murmured. Looking back as he walked, he stumbled suddenly. Without thinking, Reede reached out to steady him. Gundhalinu nodded; touched Reede's shoulder briefly, gratefully. They began to walk again, side by side. "It's the first thing they teach you, as a Survey initiate: that all the answers are out there already, free for the taking. You only have to ask the right questions." Gundhalinu laughed; the sound was harsh and bitter. "It sounds so simple. You don't learn the price of asking the questions, until it's too late." He kicked a stone; sent it scuttling ahead of them, over the cliff-edge, into the abyss. He began to walk faster, as if he was irresistibly drawn to follow it.

Reede caught Gundhalinu's arm in a sudden restraining hold as they reached the canyon's rim. Gundhalinu smiled, shaking his head, and Reede let him go. Reede followed his gaze; looking down, he felt a rush of fear and exhilaration as his vision fell away, down and down along the sheer wall of rock to the green-veined river running fifty meters below.

Gundhalinu let out his breath in something close to a sigh. "There it is."

Reede let his eyes travel upriver to the place where the two canyons met. He found something there, saw it shimmer, saw it flash as the relentless flow of water rising around it diffracted the sunlight. Something big, something metallic, with a fragmented form that was somehow strangely familiar. . . . "The ship," he said, not making it a question.

"Yes," Gundhalinu whispered, wonder filling his face. "Just the way I remembered it." He crouched down, balancing easily, lucid again as his mind found a focus-point. "We have to get down there as soon as possible."

"It's underwater," Reede said, as the reality of what he was seeing caught up with the vision.

"I know," Gundhalinu said, as if Reede had pointed out something singularly insignificant.

Reede felt the air around him suddenly become viscous, unbreathable. "But . . . it must be twenty or thirty meters deep. You didn't say it was down there like that. We don't have specs on an Old Empire ship. We can't even check it out, to know it there's anything worth salvaging in that wreckage!"

Gundhalinu looked up at him, half frowning in surprise; half smiling as he thought he understood. "We have helmets in the rover, emergency equipment. We can dive down and explore it ourselves. I can use the Transfer to tell us whether we have what we want."

Reede moved away from the cliff-edge, shutting his eyes, pulling at his ear. "Yes, we have to do it. We can't *not* do it. The opportunity is too incredible. . . ."

"You're shaking your head," Gundhalinu said. He stood up. "Reede—are you afraid of water?"

Reede laughed sharply. "No. Why would I be afraid of water?" *Of water, freezing cold, black cold, water closing over my head, blinding my eyes, stopping my ears—*

"Did you have a bad experience?"

"No!" *Water filling my mouth, my nose. . . .* He was staring wildly, trying to find Gundhalinu's face, rising, rising into the light— "There is no problem," his voice was insisting with inhuman calm, as if someone else controlled his responses now, controlled him like a puppet. *Oh gods, what's wrong with me?* But that had never been the right question; and it would never have any answer. "Let's get out of here," he muttered. "I want to get back to camp, get on with the experiment."

Gundhalinu nodded. Exhaustion and doubt shadowed his face now; if he had more questions of his own, he did not ask them. His body was rigid with tension as he turned away. He headed for the rover, moving quickly and surely, not looking back.

The sight that greeted them when they reentered the rover was so absurdly banal that it startled a laugh out of Reede. Niburu and Saroon sat cross-legged on the floor, playing 3-D chama as intently as two schoolboys, as if they had forgotten that they were squatting in the heart of a ghost city in the middle of a lake of molten stone where spacetime tied itself into knots. That it might disappear from under them at any minute, taking them with it.

Niburu looked up, not looking surprised, but faintly querulous at the sound of

Reede's laughter. Saroon twisted around guiltily where he sat, as if he was afraid to be caught enjoying himself. He scrambled to his feet, picking up his gun.

Reede's laughter stopped as second thoughts hit him, and he realized that what he'd seen did not amuse him at all. He glared at Niburu. "Let's go." Niburu shut off the game and slipped it into his pocket. He took his place behind the controls without comment; the expression on his face said one look at their own haunted expressions as they reentered the rover was all the explanation he needed.

They left the island and returned to the campsite, without incident or distractions. Ananke met them as they landed, with obvious relief. Hundet watched, unmoved and unmoving, as Saroon helped them maneuver the containment unit on its floating grid into the confines of their makeshift laboratory.

Reede watched Gundhalinu surreptitiously but carefully, relieved to see that the other man's attention seemed to be perfectly focused on the experiment they were about to conduct. It was almost as if the Lake was letting him breathe, letting him think. Reede had no objection. The unnerving reaction he had had to his own close encounter with the Lake yesterday no longer plagued him much. He wondered if it was extending him the same courtesy, or if they had both simply begun to get used to it, as Gundhalinu had predicted.

"All right," Gundhalinu said, when the containment unit was secure. "Niburu, I want you to take everyone else up in the rover. Circle and wait until we contact you . . . or we don't. You understand?"

Niburu nodded, all the expression going out of his face as the implications of the words registered. "Is it that dangerous?" he asked, with an incredulity that struck Reede as absurdly childlike. "I . . . wanted to watch." He glanced at Reede, habitually checking for his reaction. "I thought the vaccine worked perfectly, when you tried it before."

Reede controlled his impulse to frown, and nodded. "It did. But we only had a fraction of this amount, and a lot more control over the situation. There shouldn't be any problem. But Gundhalinu's seen what happens if there is one." He turned, meeting Gundhalinu's steady gaze. "You know," he said suddenly, "it only takes one of us to do this. Why don't you go with them? You shouldn't risk your neck." He felt Niburu look at him with something like surprise. He felt an odd surprise of his own, as he realized that to some part of him the survival of his work was actually more important than his mission here, or even his own survival. . . .

Gundhalinu raised an eyebrow. "I have complete faith in this process," he said.

Reede did frown, this time. "That's stupid. Don't be an ass. If we were both killed, there'd be nobody who could re-create it."

Gundhalinu smiled. "It's completely documented." His eyes were full of a strange light. "Reede, I've been waiting years for this moment . . . maybe a lifetime."

Reede shrugged, and smiled grudgingly. He had made certain that the documentation of his own work was critically incomplete; no one but Gundhalinu, who had worked so closely with him, would have even a chance of re-creating everything they had done. "All right. I guess I understand that. . . . Niburu, clear the area." He gestured, catching a glimpse of something that might have been admiration, or even envy, in the final look Niburu gave the two of them. Niburu led Ananke and Saroon out of the lab.

When they were gone Reede began preparations. Gundhalinu matched him move for move with calm efficiency, as if they had always worked together. Step by step they sealed the dome inside a field of protective energy, woke the monitors, brought on line the processors that would introduce the vaccine into the containment unit, and double-checked their peripheral equipment. Reede removed a vial of vaccinated plasma from its insulated case and inserted it into the access on the outer shield of the unit.

The all-clear notification came over the comm link from the rover as the last systems check finished running. Reede spoke the commands to the processor, pressed his thumb against the glowing spot on its panel that set the procedure in motion. Gundhalinu stood beside him, and Reede watched as he put a knuckle in his mouth and bit down.

Reede pulled at his ear, waiting instinctively for a feedback that did not come—that never came. He was suddenly aware of the unbearable sensation of not-hearing that had tormented him ever since he could remember; that was not deafness, *that was . . . that was*— Angrily he wrenched his attention back to the displays in front of him, watching as the screen showed him a primitive three-dimensional visual of what was happening inside the unit.

They watched as the vaccine was funneled into place; as the unit followed their precise orders step by step, releasing constraints, dropping shields . . . opening the cage of stasis that held the stardrive plasma precariously captive. Reede's hands opened with a spasm as the vaccine was delivered.

The static mass of light that was the image of what lay inside the containment unit came alive in simulation as the stardrive plasma was set free. He saw it boiling, mutating, diffracting, until the simulation before him became a vision of chaos, utterly incomprehensible to his eyes. Gundhalinu swore, holding his head with his hands.

Reede forced his eyes to stay open when they would have closed, and saw the seething chaos take on a new form—a form that slowly began to alter, until he realized that it was making sense to his eyes, the patterns coalescing into the random forms of flames, of frost, of alien coastlines . . . the rate of change slowing, their mutation slowly, as what lay inside the container surrendered to rationality and order, and came to rest at last firmly connected to the reality stream in which it had been created. *Waiting*. Waiting for their command.

Reede sucked in a breath, let it out in a hoarse cry of triumph. He turned, catching Gundhalinu by the shoulders, embracing him.

"It worked . . ." Gundhalinu whispered, dazed. "It worked! Didn't it—?" His own hands closed over Reede's, still clutching his arms.

"Yes." Reede looked back at the displays. "It's under control. We did it! We got it—we got all of it!" He looked at Gundhalinu again; found his hands somehow touching the other man, Gundhalinu's hands covering his own. He pulled free, stumbling back.

Gundhalinu nodded, oblivious. "Yes, I feel it . . . I felt it happen." His voice was choked with emotion. He rubbed his face, almost as if he were wiping away tears. Reede wondered if it was relief, or pain, or joy that had hold of him now—what a man would feel who had gone through all the hell that Gundhalinu had gone through, for the sake of the Lake, for the sake of his own sanity.

Reede felt happy—pleased with himself, in a clean, matter-of-fact way that he did not feel very often. But the rush of triumph that had filled him as the plasma had come under control had dissipated as suddenly, when he looked into Gundhalinu's eyes; his emotions had gone flat, as if it were all an anticlimax, and he had no idea why.

He shook his head, telling himself that this was only the first stage of his real victory; that he would feel the real pleasure when he had taken what he had come here to get, and returned with it to Mundilfoere. *Mundilfoere, whose love was all the human contact he desired. Mundilfoere, whose touch could make him forget everything, anything . . . even this moment.* He stared at the displays, still telling him just what he wanted them to say.

He looked back at Gundhalinu finally, almost reluctantly. He had what he had come here to get. He should be ready to carry out the next part of the plan immediately, while Gundhalinu and the others were completely off guard . . .

But now there was the ship, the Old Empire wreckage that Gundhalinu had shown him today. If it had anything like an intact drive unit in it . . . He couldn't afford to pass that up. He had to keep things the way they were a little longer; maintain this precarious balance until he found out for certain. He could only study the ship if he had Gundhalinu down there with him, to tell him what he needed to know.

He couldn't kill anybody now. He didn't have to kill anybody now. Nobody had to die, today. . . .

He turned away from the sight of Gundhalinu's face; spoke brusquely into the communicator, calling Niburu and the others back to camp.

"Kullervo, what are the odds," Gundhalinu murmured, his voice still strained, "of our vaccinating the entire Lake? We could do it now. The reprogrammed virus should just keep spreading indefinitely. . . ."

"No." Reede looked back, hearing a hope and a hunger in Gundhalinu's voice that might or might not be Gundhalinu's own. "I mean, let's take it one step at a time, all right?" he said uneasily. "Let's make sure this is completely stable, first." He was almost certain that it was completely stable—and that Gundhalinu was almost certainly right. That would be all he needed—to give the Golden Mean and the Kharemoughis a limitless supply of stardrive. He intended to leave them with exactly what they'd had when he arrived—which was nothing. Less than nothing, if he did the rational thing . . . He glanced at Gundhalinu again, down again, his hands tightening.

"Niburu!" Reede gestured with his chin, summoning Niburu away from the cluster of bodies gathered around the dully glowing solar cooker.

"Try the stew, boss?" Niburu said, shoveling another mouthful into his face as he stopped and looked up at Reede. "It's not bad, if I do say so. I thought we all deserved something spe—"

"What the hell are they doing eating with us?" Reede cut him off irritably, pulling him farther around the side of the lab dome into the shadows.

Niburu glanced over his shoulder at the figures he could still just see. "Gundhalinu eats with us—"

"You know what I mean," Reede snapped. "Those troopers."

Niburu looked back at him, both uneasy and defiant. He shrugged. "I wanted to invite Saroon, so I had to ask Hundet. It's kind of a party to celebrate. . . ." Reede realized that Niburu smelled like beer, that they must all have been drinking the local brew.

"What the fuck do you think this is?" Reede caught him by the front of his shirt and shook him once, hard, spilling stew. "Some goddamn social club? A fucking primitive tour? That is the enemy!" That was all he needed, for Niburu and Ananke to start seeing those expendable pieces of meat as individuals, as friends.

Niburu flushed. "They're not my enemies—"

"Don't playact that naïve bullshit with me." Reede let him go, seeing the incomprehension on his face, wanting to strangle him. "If they knew why we were really here, what do you think would have happened to us all by now?"

"We'd all be dead. And who could blame them?" Niburu said bitterly. "But they're still human beings." The look on his face got dangerously self-righteous. "And it's too late to uninvite them. You want to eat, or not?"

Reede glared at him. The words that would shatter Niburu's fantasy world filled his mouth, but his tongue refused to spit them out. Niburu turned and stalked away. Reede sighed, and followed, realizing that it was already too late for Niburu. But that didn't matter, as long as it wasn't too late for him; as long as his own resolve held.

He followed Niburu out into the open space between the domes. He sat on a sling-stool and ate, smiling an utterly empty smile. The stew was good; full of enough hot spices to burn away any aftertaste of stale freeze-dry. He focused on its texture, the pungent flavors rising up inside his head; relieved that Gundhalinu, who sat next to him, seemed too preoccupied with his own thoughts, or the Lake's, to make conversation. Reede tried not to watch Ananke letting Saroon take the quoll in his lap, not to watch as it crawled up the sweat-damp front of Saroon's uniform shirt to huddle, murmuring congenially, under his chin; tried not to see the first smile he'd ever seen form on Saroon's thin, drawn face, or to feel Niburu's eyes measuring his own reaction. Only Hundet's mood seemed to match his own, and so he watched Hundet.

Hundet's eyes flicked over them one by one, and Reede saw his own alienation mirrored there. Hundet downed the dregs of what was probably not his first bottle of ouvung that day. Hundet hated this surreal wasteland, the strange-looking foreigners, the offworlders controlling his world and his life—anything he didn't understand, and that covered a lot of ground. He hated what he feared; and so he drank until everyone was as much of an animal in his mind as he was himself. If the law didn't give him an enemy, he took it out on grunts like Saroon; on his woman if he had one and on his children, with his foot, with a gunbutt, with his fists. *The kind of man whose hand would hold you under in the black cold water . . .* Reede swore and spat as an unexpected mouthful of spice made his eyes tear. He took a long, meaningless drink from the bottle of cold, piss-colored beer sitting by his boot.

Hundet looked up and caught him staring, read the expression on his face before he had time to make it noncommittal again. Hundet's face darkened; his eyes touched on everyone sitting around him again with obvious disgust. He got slowly to his feet, muttering some insult in his own tongue, and started to leave the circle. He turned back as Saroon laughed out loud, oblivious, reacting to something the quoll had done or Ananke had said to him.

Reede watched with a peculiar feeling of déjà vu as Hundet's booted foot swung out to kick Saroon hard in the buttock. The quoll flew out of Saroon's grasp as he sprawled forward, crashing into the cooker. Ananke caught the quoll in midair with an acrobat's reflexive lunge. Saroon scrambled to his feet, slapping at his smoking shirtsleeve, his face stupefied with pain and surprise. Hundet snarled an order. Reede went on watching, with unwilling fascination, as the pleasure that had animated Saroon's face faded until he had no expression at all. His eyes were like holes in his face, black and empty, as he left the circle of silent, staring strangers without a word, and followed Hundet away.

Niburu swore softly. Gundhalinu began to rise from his seat, his mouth opening to call out an angry protest.

Reede caught Gundhalinu's arm, pulling him back down. "Don't say anything."

Gundhalinu's frown turned to him. "He's going to stop mistreating his man like that or I'll—"

"He's not going to stop," Reede said flatly. "If you call him on it, he'll only wait until your back is turned. And then he'll treat the kid worse because you gave him trouble about it. Leave it alone."

Gundhalinu stared at him, then settled slowly back onto the stool, all his resistance gone. He nodded, tight-lipped with resignation. Reede glanced at the others, saw the resentment fade from their faces, and the helpless anger it left behind. They watched Hundet enter the rover, going inside to sleep it off, leaving Saroon on guard outside, able to see what went on where they all sat, just across the camp from him, but not able to join it.

After an endless moment of silence, Gundhalinu pushed to his feet again. "It's been a long day." He disappeared into his sleeping quarters.

"Saroon is in the army," Niburu said, "because one day a squad came into the village where his family lived and took away all the young men they could find, at gunpoint. He's been in the army three years. He's eighteen."

Reede stared at him. "How the hell do you know things like that?"

"I ask," Niburu answered, meeting his stare.

"There are some things you can't change, Niburu." Reede looked away from him. "Unless, of course, you're willing to kill somebody." He stood up and went toward his own quarters without looking back.

NUMBER FOUR: Fire Lake

Gundhalinu stood in the heart of Sanctuary, on the cliff-edge above the shining river, looking down. Even from this height the water's motion seemed indefinably alien. He stared at the wreckage that lay waiting in the depths like a fallen star. *A fallen starship*. The heat licked at his sweating body with sensual desire; the voice of the Lake was a lunatic choir screaming inside his head. He stood listening to its voice a moment longer, before he turned to look at Kullervo.

Kullervo stood beside him in nothing but a pair of shorts; a delirious profusion of stunning color and vibrant design covered his naked arms to the shoulders. His face showed a stubble of beard; the pale unprotected skin of his back was already burning in the fierce heat. Gundhalinu watched a ghost hazed in red drift heedlessly through Kullervo's slim, well-muscled body and wander back toward town—the energy echo of some former resident of Sanctuary, indelibly trapped in the random memory of Fire Lake. It struck him that Kullervo looked surprisingly strong and fit, for a researcher.

He looked away again. The town behind them was filled with insubstantial forms, to his haunted eyes. They were redshifted into the past, blueshifted into the future, because the Lake existed not only in the here and now but, as far as he knew, in all times. The Lake had even shown him unnerving glimpses of his own future and past. He knew that no one else here saw them. It was no wonder he had thought he was crazy. . . . He envied Kullervo his relative ignorance, even though Reede was not blissfully immune like most people. Kullervo reacted to the Lake in a way he had never seen anyone else react, and he had no idea why.

But he was in no position to figure it out, when the Lake was like a parasite living in his own mind, feeding off him, every single moment day and night while he was within range of its power. Its voice murmured like the sea behind his eyes, louder now as he stood here, preparing to do this thing. Its emotions bled into his own, making him moody and distracted. It took all his self-discipline even to keep a thought in focus.

All his life he had been taught that less than perfect self-control was unacceptable. The Lake had taught him the absurdity of that unachievable ideal. It had made him a better human being . . . but everything had its price. He hated being here; he wished it would end. He wiped sweat from his face, not all of it caused by the heat.

Kullervo glanced up at the glaring blue sky. It seemed never to rain here; just as it seemed always to be raining in Foursgate. As Gundhalinu glanced at him, Kullervo looked down again, staring grimly at the river waiting for them far below, and the narrow path cut into the rockface leading down to it. His entire body was clenched like a fist, and his disturbing blue eyes touched the path, the water, the red rock walls, the water again, with the restlessness of a trapped animal.

Kullervo had barely spoken three words since they had left camp this morning. Something about the water had obviously triggered his paranoia, though he would not admit it. And yet Gundhalinu was aware that on a certain level, Kullervo always felt the way he felt right now, barely holding it together while something inside him tried to eat him alive. He wondered whether it was Kullervo's genius that was also his personal gutworm. . . . And as he thought it, suddenly the voice of the Lake in his own head did not seem so loud.

"Let's get it over with," Kullervo said. His voice sounded strangely distant; Gundhalinu wasn't sure whether the effect was in Kullervo's voice or his own ears. He nodded, picking up the backpack that held his equipment. He slung it over his shoulder, the way Kullervo already wore his, and started down the steep, narrow trail that had been chiseled into the side of the gorge gods-only-knew how long ago. It had been done by human hands, by human design; he was sure of that much. He had seen the redshifted ghosts of memory at work on it. He watched his own footing compulsively, because his eyes kept wandering from the track, toward that gleaming silver mystery far below that he was about to explore at last.

They reached the bottom of the canyon and stood on the red rock of the shore. Gundhalinu watched the river flow past, able to see clearly once again what it was that was so alien about its motion: It did not obey the laws of gravity or atmospheric pressure, like any normal liquid. It flowed in ripples and braids, undulating like a snake; its surface was not perfectly smooth but mimicked the deeper pattern of the stone bed through which it moved. His memories seemed to roll and flow like the motion of the river.

"Ye gods," Kullervo muttered, "what the hell is this stuff—?"

"It's water," Gundhalinu answered.

"Water doesn't do that!" Kullervo's hands jerked.

Gundhalinu crouched down, putting his cupped hands into the flow, lifting up a transparent pool that lay obediently in his palms. He drank it down deliberately. "It's water. I don't know why it looks like that. Some effect of the energy fields, I suppose. Nothing makes sense here. You just have to accept it."

Kullervo said nothing for a long moment, while both of them looked at the water. Then, finally, he asked, "Is it cold?"

Gundhalinu glanced at him. "No. It's quite warm, actually."

Kullervo shrugged the equipment pack off his shoulders. Setting it on the beach, he pulled out the oxygen helmet and lifted it up. "All right, then," he said, as if he were speaking to the river.

"You don't have to do this," Gundhalinu said suddenly, remembering Kullervo's offer to him as they prepared to treat the plasma. "I can get Niburu—"

"No." Kullervo shook his head, frowning. "He's not—qualified. I have to . . . I have to." He settled the helmet over his head, shutting Gundhalinu out.

Gundhalinu stood watching him seal it in place, left effectively alone to wonder whether it was compulsion or only some misguided sense of personal honor that drove Kullervo. *Well, what did it matter . . . ?* He had lived through both those emotions, too. He checked his own helmet quickly and methodically—the small, hard nodule at the back of the transparent bubble where the oxygen pellet and the recycler were located. He took off his shirt and put on the helmet, pressing its seal against his bare skin. The sensation was like something putting its mouth over him; vaguely sensual, vaguely unnerving. He took a deep breath, and was given air. The shadow readouts drifted across his vision like translucent fish, meaningless here, where nothing read true for long. "Can you hear me?" he asked.

"I hear you. . . . You hear me?" Kullervo answered tonelessly.

"Yes. When we get down to the wreckage, you can put me into Transfer and we'll look it over."

"Do a survey . . ." Kullervo said.

Gundhalinu looked at him, laughed mostly in surprise as he realized that Kullervo had intentionally made a joke. "Two strangers, and very far from home," he murmured, staring at the serpentine flow of water while the Lake gnawed at his brain, breathing and muttering inside his head. He started forward, wading into the tepid flow—cool enough to soothe his sweating skin, warm enough to relax his tension-knotted muscles. He thought he felt a tingling in its touch against his skin, wasn't certain if it was some energy force he was sensing or only his overactive nerves. He glanced back to make sure Kullervo was following, and saw him enter the river with stiff, uncertain movements.

Gundhalinu slowed as the water reached his chest; he felt the warm massaging strength of the current, but no sense that it was about to drag him off his feet. Its motion was as random as everything else had become. He took a deep, unnecessary breath as he went under the surface. He kicked his way down into the clear, warm depths, trusting Kullervo to follow now. He saw the red rock falling away below him as he looked down and down through the crystal clarity of the river. He could not gauge how deep the wreckage lay. Its vaguely flower-like, organic form was perfectly visible among the deep-green traceries of plant life embroidering a sinuous pattern across the stone of the river bottom.

Like a dream . . . That was what he had thought, the first time he saw it; what he still felt, every time he returned. It seemed to him that he was damned, destined to return to this dreamworld again and again, until either the Lake destroyed him, or they set each other free.

He stopped his downward motion in midstroke to look up and back, saw Kullervo above him, haloed in filtered light, like the answer to a prayer. He felt himself beginning to drift upward and turned back, kicking his way down again toward the river's wellspring.

The wreckage loomed below him now, reflecting light upward into his eyes, the pieces of the starship as perfectly preserved as if they had fallen there only weeks, and not millennia, ago. He was sure they had not looked that new the first time he had seen them; that before he could solve the Lake's riddle about its identity, it had sent a ripple through time and somehow made the ship young again. He remembered the agonizing ecstasy of the Lake's joy inside him at the moment he had finally recognized the broken form of the ship for what it was. . . . He realized suddenly that right now, as he descended into these depths, his mind was clearer and freer than it had been since he had arrived, as if the Lake had given him space in which to function normally.

They reached the wreckage at last, just as he began to feel that they were suspended in time as well as in liquid. He put out his hand, felt an electric surge of triumph as it closed over the smooth coldness of metal, anchoring him against the water welling up out of some unimaginable depths all around him. He heard Kullervo's grunt of relief as his hand found a grip on the metal.

"It's real after all," Kullervo said faintly.

Gundhalinu nodded, grinning. "Ask me the question. *Input–*" He clung tighter to the metal as he felt himself begin the long fall that would end in utter darkness, or in the mind of a stranger unimaginably far away; as Kullervo's question filled his mind and Transferred him . . .

He was in a place that defied description. . . . Floating, gravityless, in the night-black void of space, he was surrounded by brilliant flashes of light; blinded as the seeming nothingness around him was disrupted by the energy fields of some unseen force. Monstrous skeletal structures lay in space around him, for as far as his eyes could see. They swarmed with clouds of glittering dust in seemingly purposeful motion. *A war, an alien life-form—?* His mind struggled to reintegrate without panicking, to make sense of what it saw, as he realized that the sudden stealing away of this body's mind might have left it, and him, in danger.

Something closed over his arms; he would have jerked with surprise, but he had no control over his borrowed body. Forms swam into his view—human forms, human faces; speaking to him reassuringly from the sound of their voices, although he could not understand the language they spoke. He could hear them, although they did not appear to be wearing spacesuits, and neither did he. . . . He noticed that a hand did not quite touch his arm as he was pulled back under a looming grid, to what he hoped was a safe refuge, and held there. Up above—or down below him—he glimpsed the curve of a planet's arc.

A shipyard. Suddenly the disparate things he had seen fused into a pattern that he recognized: an orbital shipyard, but one that was using far more sophisticated construction techniques than Kharemough used, and building ships with forms like none he had ever seen. *Ships that used a faster-than-light stardrive.* For a moment he wondered if he had been sent back in time to the Old Empire, remembering what had happened to him during his Survey initiation. But no—he was a prisoner in a borrowed body, not an actor in a play; this was a normal Transfer. He must be in some part of the former Empire where they still had the stardrive and knew how to build ships that used it. Some engineer was in his own vacant body now, compulsively explaining to Kullervo how the stardrive unit he was certain must be waiting there functioned, how it could be salvaged, how it could be repaired; borrowing even his brain function, his language, his voice.

And he could do nothing but wait, here at the other end. He struggled in useless frustration against the unresponsing flesh that held him prisoner, unable to ask even one of the countless questions that filled his head, unable to see anything more of all there was to see. *But it's all right. Now, one day soon, this* will *be me, Kharemoughi shipyards, Hegemonic ships ready to cross the endless reaches of night again to any world they choose . . . to Tiamat.* To Moon. He stored in his memory as much of his vision of the future as he was permitted to see. . . .

Until dizzying vertigo began to suck him down once again, and the blackness of space became real, utter blackness . . .

And swimming out the other side, rising into the light . . . *"No further analysis!"* He heard the echo of his spoken words, still rattling inside his head. He shook his head as his own present unfolded around him, as he was free to gape at the cavern of baroque light and shadow that had somehow come to enfold him like tattered wings while he had been out of his body.

Kullervo materialized in front of him, trying to stabilize his motion. Kullervo's fingers brushed the seal of his helmet; Gundhalinu pushed him away reflexively. Kullervo backed off, his hands drifting to his sides.

One look at Kullervo's face gave Gundhalinu the answer he needed before he could ask the question: *Yes.* Yes, the drive unit was there, accessible, salvageable. . . . Yes, it was almost over; *yes,* they could get the hell out of here now at last finally— There was something else in Kullervo's expression, the kind of amazement-that-was-almost-awe he had grown used to seeing in the eyes of others, but had never seen before in Kullervo's eyes. And there was something that might have been doubt. ". . . everything. It's good, come on, let's get Niburu and do it—" Kullervo turned away abruptly, as Gundhalinu became aware that he had actually been speaking, telling him in words what he already knew. "Let's get out of here—"

Gundhalinu looked around him again, his confusion becoming genuine now, as he realized they must be somewhere deep in the heart of the wreckage. Suddenly he ached to explore the ship with his own eyes, for the sheer joy of seeing, touching, learning. . . . But he sensed Kullervo's desperate need to be gone from here, and he nodded. "Which way? How did we get here—?" The oddly refracted light, the reflections and shadows that painted the walls of buckled metal, twisted his vision into knots as he searched for an exit.

Kullervo's face tightened visibly. "You brought us in here. I thought—" He broke off, realizing that it had been someone else guiding them in, that Gundhalinu knew nothing at all of the route they had taken into this place. "Well, we went . . . we came in over there . . . I think. . . ." He kicked off, into a rising arc through the luminous liquid atmosphere. Gundhalinu followed, watched Kullervo disappear through a vaguely doorlike opening, and reappear almost immediately. "No. That's wrong." Gundhalinu could see a trickle of sweat crawling down Kullervo's cheek inside his helmet. "I thought I was sure . . . but the light changed, or something. It must be over there—"

Gundhalinu caught his arm, holding him back. "Wait. Give me a minute. . . ." Gleaming pinholes and fist-sized windows punched through the broken walls let illumination in from somewhere, meaning they were probably close to the outer hull of the ship; but there was no exit that way. He searched the claustrophobic space, trying to collect his wits enough to superimpose the schematics of Old Empire ship design that he held in his memory over what he could actually see; trying to judge where inside the ship's skeleton they were lost. The guts of an Old Empire freighter bore little resemblance to the insides of a Hegemonic ship. All the ships built since the Empire's fall were small and compact, with the compressed disc shape of a coin, the only form that allowed them to survive a passage through the Black Gates. It took an entire fleet of them to carry the goods that one of these freighters could transport. This ship, like most of the Old Empire's starships, had never been intended to pass through a Black Gate—or even to land on the surface of a world, most likely. It had been a huge angular sprawl of storage, environments, drives. . . . "Where's the drive unit?"

Kullervo pointed downward at the unidentifiable excrescence of equipment below him and to the right. As that identification locked into place, Gundhalinu began to recognize the opaque surfaces that had once held data displays, once been alive with the languages of dead worlds . . . to spot repair accesses and broken fragments of equipment. He looked to his left, saw an opening where he needed to find one. "This way." He gestured and kicked off, swimming toward the way out.

Kullervo followed him, so close on his heels that they were almost one person, making physical contact with him every few meters as they threaded their way back through the shifting liquid tunnels, the vast darknesses and pied convolutions of what had once been Fire Lake's reason for existence.

"How much farther?" Kullervo's impatient voice and hand tugged at him, as he squeezed past a buckled section of wall.

Gundhalinu blinked, as a shaft of pure, sea-green light struck him in the eye. "We're there." He pointed toward the gaping rent in the hull wall waiting ahead.

Kullervo's head and arms squeezed past his hip, as if Kullervo couldn't wait long enough for him to move aside, desperate to see the light. He laughed, or something like it. "Gundhalinu—"

Gundhalinu looked down and back as Reede's hand clamped over his arm like a vise. He froze as he saw metal flash in Kullervo's other, rising hand—

Kullervo jerked suddenly, convulsively, releasing Gundhalinu as his hands flew to his own throat, to the clear wall of his helmet. Gundhalinu saw the fine mist of blood from the gash on Reede's shoulder, where a piece of twisted wreckage had ripped his flesh, and ripped loose the helmet's seal. He saw Kullervo's face, stricken with terror, drowning in bubbles as water forced its way in at the broken seal, forcing the air out.

Kullervo floundered, fighting to get past him, knocking him aside as he reached out to staunch the flow of escaping air. Reede's own panicked struggles wrenched the helmet free, sent it tumbling away, carried by the capricious current down into the dark heart of the wreck. Reede lunged after it, following it down to certain death.

Gundhalinu caught him around the waist, dragging him back up toward the light, the opening, survival. Kullervo thrashed wildly; but the water slowed his motions as Gundhalinu got behind him, got an armlock around his neck and dragged him, struggling like a hooked fish, out through the gap and into the open.

Gundhalinu swam up and up through the river's brightening depths, feeling Kullervo's struggles grow weaker. He felt as though he had been swimming forever through the green light that seemed to fill his head like music, like an hallucination, like a dream. His lungs ached; he realized that he had been holding his breath, counting his heartbeats. He sucked in a lungful of air, only half believing that he could. Locked in his grip, Reede had stopped struggling. But somewhere up above him, inside that tunnel of light glowing brighter and brighter, was the open air—

His head broke the surface of the water, and all around him were the canyon walls, the color of the blood rushing behind his eyes. He swam to shore, towing Kullervo's unresisting body after him. He dragged Reede onto the beach and fell to his knees, pulling off his own helmet.

Beside him Reede took a shuddering breath, and his stark blue eyes opened, staring in disbelief. Gundhalinu sat back as Kullervo struggled to roll over, coughing, and retched water onto the warm red stone. He collapsed again, his eyes empty, mirroring the sky.

"Reede . . ." Gundhalinu touched his shoulder tentatively.

Kullervo looked toward the sound and opened his mouth, but no words came out. He pushed himself up onto his elbows, looked down along his body at his feet, still trailing in the water. "He tried to drown me," he mumbled.

"Who did?" Gundhalinu asked blankly.

"I'm going to kill him, that bastard!" Kullervo's hands tightened into fists; he struggled to sit upright.

Gundhalinu put a hand on his shoulder again, holding him back. "Take it easy— You lost your helmet. Your helmet caught on the wreckage." He showed Kullervo the raw scrape on his shoulder, still oozing a thin film of blood.

Kullervo rubbed his eyes, looked up again. "You saved my life," he murmured.

"It was nothing—"

"Don't say that!" Kullervo said furiously. "My life isn't worth shit, and I don't care if I die tomorrow—but not like that. I have dreams about dying like that. . . ." His eyes darkened. "I owe you."

"It was nothing you wouldn't have done for me," Gundhalinu finished.

Kullervo stared at him for a long moment, frozen, and then finally he looked down. He got unsteadily to his feet. He started away along the shore toward the trail that led up, stumbling, supporting himself with one hand against the rock; not looking back or waiting for help.

Gundhalinu stood up and followed, with the Lake's voice inside him like a madman's laughter.

NUMBER FOUR: World's End

"What do you think?" Gundhalinu asked, with eager impatience.

Reede stared at the displays, nodding slowly. "Looks good . . ." They had done minor structural repairs on the salvaged drive unit, under Gundhalinu's guidance but at Reede's urging, and now he had introduced their sample of the stardrive into it. Gundhalinu had wanted to wait until they returned to civilization. But he had pushed, insisted—aware that Gundhalinu's need to know had to be as great as his own; that he could break down Gundhalinu's knee-jerk sense of responsibility if he made the temptation irresistible enough.

He had tried, and he had been right. And now he had fed the stardrive plasma into its intended matrix. They were watching the process imaged on the displays as the plasma settled into its new home—and from what he could see, it was doing fine. The piece of equipment had been in an incredible state of preservation for something buried underwater in a wreck that was gods-only-knew how ancient. But nothing obeyed the rules of the known universe in World's End, because of the stardrive. And the stardrive had wanted this unit saved, as it had wanted itself to be saved. . . . "I think it's happy," he said at last.

Gundhalinu moved closer, staring at the images on the screens. "Then so am I—" He let out a whoop of sheer elation. "Gods, I've never been this happy! Thank you, gods!"

"Neither have I." Reede forced the words out, almost choking on them as elation died stillborn in his throat. He picked up a calibrator. It felt hard and heavy inside his clenched fist, like a stone. He looked back at Gundhalinu. "Because now I don't need you anymore—" He swung, aiming for Gundhalinu's head.

Gundhalinu was already reacting, as if a sixth sense from his years as a Blue had told him something he couldn't have known. He shouted for the troopers loitering outside, lunged backward before Reede's own momentum could catch up to him. He collided with a table in the crowded space behind him.

Reede's fist with the calibrator caught him in the side of the face, slamming him back into a pile of equipment. Gundhalinu fell, crashing down in a rain of electronics gear. He lay still; Reede saw blood.

Reede spun back again as Hundet burst into the tent. Hundet took it all in in one glance; the stun rifle he already held in his hands rose to his shoulder.

Reede reached frantically for the knife at his belt. He flung it without even time to aim, trusting blind instinct and his perfect reflexes. The blade caught Hundet in the chest, stopping his forward motion with the shock of the counterblow. He seemed to hang, agonizingly suspended in midair, through an endless moment before his legs gave way and he sprawled facedown on the floor. Reede crossed the lab in less than a heartbeat to the place where Hundet lay in a spreading pool of red. He rolled Hundet with his foot.

Dead. Hundet's eyes stared up at him in unblinking hatred as he leaned down and jerked his knife from the dead man's body. He wiped the blade on Hundet's tunic impassively, and put it back into his belt sheath. He picked up the rifle, checking its charge. He adjusted the setting to maximum; on that setting it would stop a man cold from a considerable distance, and kill him easily at short range. Holding the gun, he went outside.

Trooper Saroon stood in the open space between domes, clutching his rifle indecisively. His face was tense and worried as he watched Niburu and Ananke, who stood looking toward the lab. The expressions on all their faces changed abruptly as Reede came out of the dome, carrying Hundet's gun.

"Freeze!" Reede said, but he could have saved his breath. Saroon stood frozen already, with the look on his face turning to pathetic betrayal as he grasped what must be happening. He stared at Niburu and Ananke again, in disbelief; his gun wavered.

"Drop it," Reede said, gesturing with his own weapon. Saroon tossed the rifle away and raised his hands. He kept stealing glances at the tent, hoping against hope that someone else would come out of it. "Niburu," Reede said, "Ananke. This is it. We've got everything we came for, and more. Get inside and get started—I want that stardrive unit in the rover now. We're leaving, as soon as I take care of details." He moved a few steps toward Saroon, getting within fatal range, and raised the rifle again. Saroon sat down abruptly in the sand as his knees buckled. Reede adjusted his aim downward.

"No, Reede—!"

Reede lowered the rifle, furiously, as he found Niburu squarely in his line of sight. "Goddammit! Get out of the way, you stupid bastard."

But Niburu stood motionless, placing his body like a shield between the trembling boy and the gun. "You don't have to do this. What's the point—?"

"Yes, I do. Get out of the way." Reede gestured with the gun, feeling his face harden over. "Get out of here if you don't want to watch. But get the fuck out of my way. Now!"

"No. I won't let you kill him." Niburu stood straighter, white-faced and tight-lipped. He barely topped the kneeling trooper's height, but Reede found nothing absurd about his position. Slowly, as if he were hypnotized, Ananke moved forward, ready to add his body to the human shield. Reede's hands tightened over the gun.

But as he began to raise it again, Ananke glanced away, distracted by some unexpected motion. Reede followed his glance, swore as his eyes caught sight of something—someone, disappearing around the bend of the canyon. Someone running like hell toward Fire Lake.

Reede ran back to the tent. A glance inside told him all he needed to know. The far wall of the dome gaped, letting in daylight. Gundhalinu was gone.

Reede went after him down the canyon, leaving Saroon behind, forgotten. Gundhalinu was the one who mattered, the one he had to stop. Because Gundhalinu was heading for the Lake, and he didn't know why. The canyon seemed to go on forever, shimmering with heat, until he began to wonder desperately whether the Lake was shifting reality around him, stretching out spacetime so that he would never reach his quarry. He had almost drowned because the Lake protected Gundhalinu; the Lake loved Gundhalinu. . . .

But he burst out of the canyon mouth onto the open shore at last, and Gundhalinu was there, standing silhouetted by the Lake's hellshine on the barren, tortured stone. Facing the Lake he raised his hand, to throw something—

"Gundhalinu!" Reede raised his rifle even as he shouted the name. He fired.

Gundhalinu staggered as the shock hit him; the impact carried his arm forward. His hand released whatever it had held, as his nervous system went dead and he collapsed on the beach. Reede saw something too small to identify disappear into the shimmering haze.

Reede ran forward, crouched down, rolling Gundhalinu's helpless body onto its back. Gundhalinu stared up at him, bloody and bruised but completely aware.

"What was it?" Reede said fiercely. "What did you throw into the Lake?"

Gundhalinu didn't answer; silent whether he liked it or not, because his voluntary responses had been put on hold. He breathed in ragged gasps. He'd taken a bad hit, enough to affect his autonomic nervous system. But Reede saw triumph slowly replace the fury and the betrayal in the other man's eyes.

Reede kicked him anyway for not answering, out of spite or something darker. Gundhalinu's face spasmed with pain. Reede straightened up, looking toward the Lake; watching, half-blind, for some clue. And then he saw it—a glitch, a ripple, a shimmering transfiguration in the distortion all around him. He could almost *feel* it . . . the vision of his worst fear coming true. And yet something inside him was filled with wonder.

"You did it, didn't you—?" he said, looking back at Gundhalinu. "That was the virus! You've infected the whole fucking Lake with it!" He kneeled down, catching Gundhalinu by the front of his sweat-soaked shirt, and dragged him up to sitting. He held Gundhalinu's bruised face clamped in his free hand so that they were eye to eye. Gundhalinu met his gaze unflinchingly, and blinked once, slowly, like a nod.

Reede slapped Gundhalinu, hard; feeling the other man's pain with the same dizzy sense of terror and pleasure that he felt when the pain was his own. "I was going to kill you because I had to, because you knew too much. . . . But now it's too late for that. Now I'll just have to kill you for revenge." He let Gundhalinu go, letting him fall back onto the mottled surface of the stone. He pushed to his feet.

Picking up the stun rifle, he leveled it at Gundhalinu's head. Gundhalinu's face did not change, could not. But in his eyes Reede saw desperation and fear . . . *grief, betrayal, loss.* The muzzle of the gun sank slowly as Reede's hands lowered, suddenly strengthless; as his mind's eye replayed his waking to a vision of red rock and glaring sky, to Gundhalinu's face hovering above him and the knowledge that the man he had just been trying to kill had saved him from death by drowning.

His rage and resolve drowned in the clear, sweet river of his memories. He remembered all that they had accomplished together, the uncanny way their minds meshed, the knowledge that he had never worked with anyone before who had . . . who had . . . He turned his back on Gundhalinu's naked vulnerability, stared out at the seething, blinding Lake, the face of Chaos. He listened to it screaming, inside his head. But because of what they had created together, already it was transforming into something new, into Order. . . .

He hurled the gun, watched it tumble end over end, arcing out and down until it disappeared into the eye-warping haze, the way Gundhalinu's flung vial had disappeared.

He turned back, his eyes burning with the vision, his hands trembling. "Ilmarinen . . ." he whispered. He fell to his knees, lifting Gundhalinu's hand, pressing it against his face, his lips. He looked down, saw Gundhalinu staring up at him in anguish and incomprehension through the shadow-bars of his nerveless fingers. *Ilmarinen—* And his mind imploded, as the black hole at its heart tore coherent thought limb from limb.

He staggered to his feet, looking toward the Lake and back again with sudden fury. "Why did you make me do that? I have to kill you—!" His hand jerked the knife from his belt as if it had a will of its own; his body kneeled down again beside Gundhalinu's. He pressed the blade to Gundhalinu's throat. His entire body was trembling now. He held himself that way, unable to finish the act, paralyzed as completely as his victim by the anguish of unbearable loss.

He fell back, the knife dropping from his hand to clatter on the hot surface of pitted stone. Beneath his hands he felt the pressure of countless screaming mouths and mindless eyes. "Get up!" he shouted, shouting at himself now. "Get up and do it! Do it! Do it!" He picked up the knife again.

"Reede!"

Reede looked up, feeling something that was almost disbelief as he saw Ananke appear at the mouth of the canyon; as he remembered that he and Gundhalinu were not alone in the universe, the last two men alive.

"Reede! Come on!" Ananke waved his arm, his voice almost shrill as he gestured toward camp.

"What?" Reede shouted furiously, climbing to his feet with the knife in his fist.

"Kedalion says we have to get out of here now!"

"Why?"

"Because he called in the army!"

Reede swore in disbelief. He forced himself to look down at Gundhalinu one last time . . . seeing the trefoil that shone like a star on Gundhalinu's chest, hearing the harsh sound of his labored breathing. Reede touched the solii pendant hidden beneath his own shirt. "Live, then, damn you—" he said, his voice shaking. "It won't matter anyway. We have what we need." He brought his heavy boot back, kicked Gundhalinu in the side with all his strength; felt dizzy with relief as he made Gundhalinu cry out, feebly, involuntarily.

Reede began to run, only stopping when he reached the place where Ananke waited. He struck Ananke's shoulder, jarring the boy out of his slack-faced staring.

"Is he dead?" Ananke asked weakly, still gaping at Gundhalinu's motionless body.

Reede did not answer, forcing him back down the canyon, driving him ahead toward the camp.

"Niburu!"

Niburu stood waiting beside the rover as they reached the campsite, his arms folded, as if this were only another visit to town. He had the second stun rifle slung over his shoulder. Reede didn't believe the expression of calm control on his face for a second. Saroon was nowhere in sight; Niburu must have sent him away somewhere. Reede was beyond caring, now. Trooper Saroon was no more than a nuisance, a detail, a loose end in a net that had suddenly sprung vast, gaping holes. . . .

Reede strode across the camp to Niburu, the knife still clutched in his fist, not caring that Niburu had a stun rifle and he did not. Niburu watched him come without making a move to unsling his weapon.

"Did you call in troops?" Reede snapped, looking down into Niburu's upturned face.

Niburu's body shrank in on itself as Reede loomed over him, as if he suddenly faced an avenging demon made flesh. "Yes," he said, faintly but evenly.

"Why?" Reede shouted, and saw him flinch.

"Because if I didn't, you'd hunt him down and kill him." *Saroon.*

Reede sucked in a breath of burning air. "What makes you so sure I won't kill you—?" he whispered, letting Niburu face his own reflection in the blade of the knife.

Niburu looked away from it, with an effort. "Because I'm your pilot," he said, his eyes clear, his voice calm. "Because you need me."

Reede glared at him, not speaking, not moving.

"Boss, it's time we got out of here." Niburu jerked his head at the rover. "Everything important's on board, except us."

"So you really are willing to die to save that pathetic, puling bastard," Reede murmured. "In fact, you're actually going to kill all of us, just so he can live, and the Four government can go on giving it to him up the ass for the rest of his miserable life."

Niburu stared at him blankly.

Reede smacked him with an open hand, knocking him to the ground. "Did it ever occur to you," he shouted, "in your eagerness for justice, that the Fours are going to track this vehicle and shoot it down?"

Niburu looked up at him, glassy-eyed. "They can't track us here—" He shook his head.

"You don't know that." Reede rubbed his sweating face. "You can't be sure of anything here, you know that—! Gundhalinu vaccinated the Lake with the microviral, you shitbrain! The gods only know what's going to happen here now."

Niburu blanched. "I—"

"How did you propose we survive outside World's End, until we reach Foursgate, anyway—not to mention reaching orbit and our ship, now that you've so effectively drawn their attention to us? Why do you think I wanted no witnesses!"

"I thought—"

"No, you didn't think," Reede snarled. "You miserable cretin, you didn't think, you didn't think at all!"

"But we can still get away. We have the stardrive."

"It's not enough—" Reede broke off, half frowning. They had the actual unit; Gundhalinu had shown him the programming. There was barely enough sane smartmatter plasma suffused through the unit to replicate itself, let alone make the drive function . . . not nearly enough to transport a ship across interstellar space. But if he could get it to respond, then maybe it was enough to get them halfway around one world in a spacetime eyeblink, to a specific track in planetary orbit. . . . He felt the jangling filaments of his mind begin to find harmony as he focused on the possibilities; letting him think with blinding clarity, in the way that only confronting a problem whose answer lay in pure logic ever did.

He dragged Niburu up, shoved him roughly toward the rover's doorway. "You'd better hope you're smarter than I think you are, pilot. Because if you're wrong, you're dead. We're all dead."

TIAMAT: Carbuncle

"Gods, what a relief to eat something ordinary again!" Tor Starhiker sighed as she stepped out of the small Summer eatery only two street levels above the docks. "I never thought I'd get hungry for fish stew again, but after eating Shotwyn's cooking for three years, sometimes I even get a taste for seahair. . . . One step down, Fate."

"That was delicious." Fate Ravenglass found the step with her cane, and then her foot. She took Tor's arm for guidance as they started out into the teeming foot traffic of the alley, most of it fisherfolk and dockhands in drab, heavy clothes, with a few brightly colored Winter merchants among them, picking over produce and goods just in from plantations along the coast.

Tor guided Fate through the milling bodies with a skill born of long practice. Anyone they encountered who noticed the trefoil hanging against Fate's tunic of faded periwinkle-blue gave way of their own accord. Fate clung to her wardrobe of exotic, aging offworlder clothes, most of them made of satin or velvet or other fabrics that were pleasant to touch. She didn't care what they looked like, she said, because she couldn't see them. She only cared how they felt; like old friends.

"But I thought you loved Shotwyn's cooking," Fate said, sounding mildly astonished. "Isn't that why you went into business with him?"

Tor shrugged. "Actually, I think I went into business with him because I thought he was so creative in bed." She laughed. Shotwyn Crestrider belonged to one of the Winter clans that had gotten rich from the offworlder trade, probably from the hunting of mers along their plantation coastline. Like all the rest, he'd been scrambling for a way to hold on to the past in the upside-down world after the Change. Her own restlessness had collided with his when she met him one day at the Sibyl College. He had been intrigued by her history as front-woman for an offworlder gaming hell; she had been intrigued by the seemingly endless variations on the theme of a man and a woman that he had picked up at the Snow Queen's court.

She had also been impressed by his other hobby—imitating the styles of various offworld cuisines, using available native foods. Together they had opened a restaurant catering to nostalgic Winters whose sophisticated tastes had few available outlets left. He had provided the money and the artistry; she had provided the business sense—managing the restaurant, arranging with growers to raise whatever exotic herbs and spices they could reconstitute. She had even gotten Fate to let her use the Transfer to find new ways of creating certain dishes, as Shotwyn's own lifetime supplies of favorite seasonings were depleted. The result had been a perfect marriage of skills, if not personalities.

"Now I know what they mean by 'cookin' lasts, kissin' don't.'" She sighed. "I still like his cooking—and so does everybody else; the place is doing great business. He's got more ways to make fish taste and feel like something else than I ever thought possible, I'll give him that. But I was a dockhand for too long before I ran Persiponë's, I guess; I never realized how much of the food I ate was 'native cuisine.' . . . I just thought it was food, plain and simple, and that's how I liked it. That's still how I like it best. Shotwyn says I'm mired in the mentality of the underclass. Mired! How do you like that one? . . . Tram stop." She pulled Fate to a stop, raising her hand as the tram moved slowly toward them up the street.

Fate chuckled. "I wouldn't have it any other way, myself." The tram pulled in and they got on board.

"Damn right." Tor settled Fate and then herself on a length of wooden seat vacated respectfully by a pair of Summers. "But what the hell, the restaurant gives me something to do with my nights, now that Shotwyn doesn't. I mean, not that we never . . . sometimes we still get an itch, you know—"

Fate smiled. "I think I have some idea, yes."

Tor looked away from the Lower City's warehouses and stalls as they began to fade into the shops of the lower Maze. She looked back at Fate again. "Fate . . . you mind if I ask you a personal question?"

"No—ask me anything."

"Why is it that you never . . . well, you know, with anybody? All these years I've known you, and there's never been anybody in your life that seemed to be special, even for a while."

"Ah. That. Well, I was a sibyl long before I met you. And because the offworlders made everyone in the city believe sibyls were diseased lunatics, I couldn't tell anyone, or I would have been cast out—and half-blind as I was, even with my vision enhancer, I was terrified of that. And I was terrified of accidentally infecting someone, if we were that intimate . . . even though I was never sure how much truth there was in all the lies."

"How did you ever even become a sibyl?" Fate had existed, under her nose and everyone else's, for decades—the only sibyl in Carbuncle.

Fate sighed, folding her hands in the lap of her velvet skirt. "I was not quite twenty-two years old. It was the first Festival after the one when I was conceived, and my family being maskmakers, we had been working on masks for this Festival's Mask Night since I was a child. One day someone came to my shop. He wasn't a Summer, although he claimed that he was, that he had just come to the city for the Festival. . . . He said that he was interested in my masks, and how I made them. He began to come by my shop every day. He'd sit and visit, and help me sort beads. I remember how I began to look forward to his visits, how I began to feel like a bird in flight whenever I heard his voice, or he touched me. . . . We spent the entire Festival-time together. And by the Mask Night, I was his chosen. In the darkness, I couldn't see his tattoo. I let him make love to me . . . and he infected me."

Tor shuddered involuntarily, with a Winter's conditioned horror of contamination by a sibyl. She kept her hand steady on Fate's arm, somehow; hoping Fate would not sense her response.

"He begged me to forgive him, afterwards . . . he claimed it was an accident. But he didn't speak or act like a true Summer. I think now that he was something else—from somewhere else. That he knew the truth about the sibyl network, that they needed someone, a fixed data port here in the city. That he knew exactly what he was going to do to me . . ." She turned her face away, as though she could see the expression on Tor's face, or could not be sure what showed on her own.

"He stayed with me awhile; he taught me how to control the Transfer, just enough so that I could get by. Not the whole truth. And then he left me. He said that he had to go back to Summer before someone discovered what he was. He left me there alone, with my terrible secret, and my masks. And I created a kind of mask for myself, from that day on, pretending that I was not infected. But I was always afraid after that, of . . . physical contact. Of betraying someone else, or being betrayed."

Tor shook her head. "That bastard—" Her fists knotted; she took a deep breath, letting go of her useless anger. "But what about now?" She looked back at Fate, with the ache still deep in her chest. "You know the truth about what you are, and Winters don't hate sibyls anymore. You know how to protect yourself . . . or a lover. You could—"

"No." Fate shook her head. "I've lived alone for so long, too long by now. I've grown to cherish my solitude. I'm not lonely, I'm not sad, my days are full of useful work and good friendships." She smiled in Tor's direction. "I'm content as I am."

Tor grunted. "Maybe you've got a point. I can't say the same about myself. . . ." They had reached the middle of the Maze, near the Sibyl College. "Do you want to stop off and see . . . uh, visit the Shop?" she asked, suddenly regretting the thought of their pleasant lunch ending so soon. Fate was far too punctual for her own good.

"Oh . . . All right." Fate nodded, looking pleased at the thought. "I haven't been there for quite a while." She didn't have to ask which Shop; there was only one that they spoke of that way. It had been one of Jerusha PalaThion's ideas for making their new technological creations more accessible: a block of former warehouses where there were displays and demonstrations and free samples available for whoever was willing to try something new.

They left the tram at the entrance to Azure Alley, where the Shop was located, and made their way through the curiosity seekers to its open-fronted sprawl of stores filled with new or recently salvaged equipment.

"Tor, is that juice seller still across the street?" Fate asked, lifting her head. "I think I smell their fruit—"

"Yeah. Do you want me to get you something?"

"A large cup of the roseberry juice would be wonderful. Suddenly I'm dying of thirst."

"Too much salt in the stew," Tor said, guiding her to a pillar where she could stand comfortably and wait. "I'll be right back."

Tor crossed the alley, noticing with satisfaction that there appeared to be a reasonable mix of Winters and Summers in the crowd. Once they'd gotten past the new idea of a Change that really meant something, the Summers—especially the younger ones—had slowly come around to other new ways of doing things. Not even Summers really liked to go on stirring the seahair paddies by wading through freezing water on stilts, when a simple rig of wind-powered paddles would do it for them, and leave them free to go out in their fishing boats with lightweight, ultra-strong nets that would let them bring in twice their usual catch.

She paid for the drink, went back across the alley and handed it to Fate. They started on, wandering in and out of displays, while she described them as well as she could, guiding the older woman's hands to objects she wanted to experience for herself.

"Well, good day to you, Fate Ravenglass Winter," someone said behind them. They turned together, recognizing the voice of Capella Goodventure, and the unmistakable coldness in it as she spoke the word "Winter." The truth about sibyls—that they were not strictly the province of Summer's Goddess—had not grown noticeably easier for the Goodventures' elder to bear, even after so many years.

"Hello, Capella Goodventure," Fate said, with wry resignation, echoing the Summer woman's formal address but leaving off her clan surname.

"Come to pick up a few handy appliances for your townhouse, Capella?" Tor said, pinched by irritation as she was left entirely unacknowledged.

She immediately had all of Capella Goodventure's attention, and with it her hostility. "No, Winter. I've come to see what new perversions of our tradition are being insinuated into our world in the name of 'the Change' and 'the Lady's Will.'"

Tor matched her frown. "If you love your summer traditions so much, why don't you go live on a plantation—or move back to the Lower City, with the rest of the Summers? You like your townhouse next to the palace well enough."

Capella Goodventure stiffened. "I live where I do because it is tradition that I be near the Lady . . . in case she ever has need of me. And she chooses to live in the Snow Queen's palace." There was bitterness, and something that could have been regret, in her voice.

"So you can keep on interfering in her life, you mean," Tor said sourly. "Why don't you face it—not even Summers want to live worse than they have to. There wouldn't be so many of them here looking, if they did. Even your holy sibyls know that, or they wouldn't all be working for the Queen."

"Tor." Fate reached out to put a restraining hand on her arm. The abrupt gesture knocked over the roseberry juice sitting on the display table. Tor swore as the pink-red liquid splattered onto her pants.

"They work for the Lady because she speaks for our Goddess as Her Chosen . . . and as a sibyl," Capella Goodventure said, "and they owe her their service, whatever they may think of the uses she puts it to."

"Believe that if you want to." Tor turned away, wiping at her clothing, using the accident as an excuse to go in search of a sponge, or better company.

She went back through the tables and displays toward the main entrance, where she knew she would find Danaquil Lu or Clavally. One or the other of them was always here, overseeing the operation—getting the Winters to think of sibyls as symbols of technological enlightenment, and at the same time reassuring the Summers in the crowd with their presence. They answered technical and personal questions for anyone who asked, with a patience that astounded her. But that, she supposed, was why they were sibyls, and she was not.

She saw Danaquil Lu now, standing with his kinsman Borah Clearwater just inside the entrance.

"Well, rot me, boy, I don't believe my eyes!" Clearwater was roaring like a klee in rut, as usual. Tor moved closer, wondering what the cantankerous old bastard was complaining about now. Clearwater put his hands on Danaquil Lu's shoulders, shaking his head. "You're standing straight! It's a miracle—"

Danaquil Lu shook his own head, smiling with his usual reticence. "No, Uncle, it was surgery. I finally had that operation."

"Gods," Clearwater said. "And you survived? They must have gutted you like a fish—"

"No," Danaquil Lu said, in good-natured exasperation. "That's why I waited so long, until— Damn it, Uncle, I wish you'd listen when I try to explain these things to you." He lifted his shoulders in a shrug that would have been impossible three months before; a motion that said he knew further explanation was futile. "Look around you—" He waved a hand at the piled goods and workshops behind him. Tor saw Danaquil Lu's daughter Merovy, who had been stacking boxes with Tammis Dawntreader, put down her load and step between them. "You see, Uncle Borah," she said. "I told you it would happen."

Clearwater looked at her, and at Danaquil Lu. His grizzled beard worked as if he were chewing tough meat. "Well, by all the gods, you look like a miracle to me, Dana. . . . I'm just glad to see you able to look me in the eyes again." He glanced at Merovy. "I'll even grant you that someone's made a difference that matters to me, this time."

Danaquil Lu smiled and nodded, putting an arm around his daughter, holding her close before she slipped away. "It's all the difference in the world," he said softly.

"Where's Gran Selen? Didn't she come with you?" Merovy asked. "If she wants to see Tammis and Ariele, she'd better come here!" She glanced at Tammis, who stood waiting, smiling at her, a half-forgotten box in his grip. Her face brightened, becoming beautiful under his gaze, as she saw his expression.

"Well, you know that woman, she has a mind of her own." Clearwater made a face, his mustache bristling. "Says she doesn't want to see so much *change* in one place. Couldn't convince her to come. Let her spend time with Moon, if she can get it; she gets little enough of that. . . ."

"So, how are the wind-driven paddles doing for your seahair crop, Uncle?" Danaquil Lu said, pointedly changing the subject.

"Good, good . . ." Clearwater raised his head, peering into the interior. "You know, Jakard Homestead was telling me something about a new sort of jury-rig that might get my pumps working again. Not that I believed him, but since I'm here, I suppose I might as well take a look at it . . . just so I can tell him he's wrong."

Danaquil Lu led him away, past a laughing cluster of Winter youths. Tor saw Ariele Dawntreader in the middle of them, the unmistakable fog of her milk-white hair drifting around her. She was, as usual, the supremely confident center of their attention, and not simply because she was the heir-apparent of the Summer Queen. At the moment she was letting Elco Teel Graymount wrap himself around her like a squin, her head falling back in melodramatic rapture.

Tor looked away, unimpressed, back to where Ariele's brother Tammis was helping Merovy with her work. Merovy spent most of her time here, because her parents expected it; Tammis spent most of his time here because of her. But Ariele and her friends were here simply because it was the most stimulating spot in their limited world—just as it was for the other gawking kids who made up nearly half the crowd in the Shop. Tor smiled. "Merovy—" she called. Merovy glanced up. "I need something to mop up a spill."

Merovy disappeared into the back of the store. Tammis nodded in Tor's direction, and went back to his work. He was the quiet twin, the thoughtful one, nothing like his sister. He seemed much happier here with Merovy, who was even quieter, than he ever seemed to be when he was surrounded by a crowd, as Ariele was just now.

Tammis looked up again, at the sound of someone's laughter, and Ariele's voice called out something to him, unintelligible but rude. He frowned briefly as his sister and her friends moved toward him, and past him. Elco Teel looked back as they passed, and blew him a kiss. "Pass that along to Merovy!" he called and rolled his eyes. Tammis stared after them as they went out into the alley. Tor realized that he was still watching Elco Teel, and not his sister, and the expression on his face was not anger; was not one she would have expected to see at all.

She looked away again, pushing curiosity out of her mind as Merovy came back with an armful of clean rags.

"Where is it?" Merovy asked, looking away into the forest of equipment displays.

Tor took the rags from her. "I'll take care of it." She carried them back through the store to the place where Fate waited, still talking to Capella Goodventure. Tor grimaced, feeling vaguely guilty for having left her trapped there so long. The spilled juice had spread in a lurid stain across the floor. She sighed, wishing she had asked for a bucket too.

She opened her mouth to call out to Fate, to let her know rescue was at hand.

Just then Capella Goodventure picked up an electric drill lying in a puddle on the table, gesturing animatedly, her face filled with disgust. ". . . another example of something that no one needs—" She reached for the power switch.

"Don't—!" Tor shouted.

Capella Goodventure turned, frowning, her hand still moving.

Tor leaped forward, reaching Fate first, dragging her aside. They collapsed in an awkward heap, as the Goodventure elder pressed the drill's switch.

Capella Goodventure's scream was high and shrill as the current from the drill grounded itself through her body into the pool of juice. The drill flew from her spasming hands, and she collapsed on the floor.

"Tor!" Fate gasped, as Tor rolled off her. "What happened, what is it—?"

"It's Capella." Tor crawled forward, squatted down beside the Summer woman's motionless body. Capella Goodventure's gray-blue eyes were wide open, staring up at her in unblinking accusation; her face was empty, her lips were rapidly turning blue. "Oh, gods." Tor swore, feeling for a heartbeat, for a sign of breathing; not finding them. She pushed her fingers into Capella's mouth, pulling her slack tongue forward; lifted her chin to clear the air passage. She took a deep breath, put her own mouth over the other woman's, forcing air down into her lungs, counting; sat up, leaning on Capella's chest, pressing, pressing, over her heart. Another breath into the other woman's lungs, more heartbeats, another breath. Dimly she was aware of Fate behind her, still calling, "Tor—? Tor—?" She was aware of the crowd gathering, of Danaquil Lu keeping them back from her. Another breath, more heartbeats, repeating it again and again, but still no response, still the empty eyes stared at her, unforgiving. "Come on—" she whispered. Another breath, more heartbeats. She shook Capella Goodventure's unresponding body, leaned on its heart again, again, forced air in through her open lips. "Come on, you self-righteous old bitch, you can't be this easy to kill! Come on, damn you, ruin my day!"

She forced another breath into the other woman's lungs. A tremor ran through the body under her; it took a sudden, shuddering breath on its own, and the eyelids flickered. Someone was back, behind the staring eyes, looking up at her in amazement, and then in sudden outrage.

Capella Goodventure took in another hoarse, painful breath. "What . . . what are you doing? Get away from me—!" Her hands rose, flailing.

Tor sat back, away from her. Other hands were around the Goodventure elder now: Danaquil Lu, some of her own kin.

"I . . . touched that thing—" Capella Goodventure's eyes focused more clearly, filling with horror, as someone lifted her head.

"She saved you," someone, a Summer, said. "The Winter saved you. You stopped breathing." The man who had spoken turned to Tor incredulously. "I think she was dead. How did you do that—?"

She shrugged. "It's just rescue training. I learned it a long time ago. The offworlders taught it to people who worked on the docks. In case somebody had an accident like that . . ." She saw the Summers look at each other with sudden speculation. She looked back at Capella Goodventure, seeing no gratitude in the other woman's eyes. "It doesn't always work, though."

Capella Goodventure frowned, meeting her stare.

"Do you think . . . could someone show us this?" another Summer murmured, avoiding Capella's eyes.

"It was one of the Winters' 'improvements' that nearly killed me," Capella snapped, gesturing at the fallen tool.

"It was ignorance that nearly killed you," Tor said flatly. "There was nothing wrong with the drill. You turned the thing on when it was wet. If you knew anything at all about electricity you never would have done that. And you wouldn't owe your life to a Winter."

Capella pulled free of the hands that held her, sitting upright on her own. "I am grateful to you, for that," she said, with obvious difficulty. "It would not be fair to deny you the thanks you deserve. But if we used the tools we have always made, ourselves, and kept the ways that have always been our salvation, such a thing would never have to happen. And there would have been no need for your 'offworlder training' to save me." She looked away again, her cold gaze glancing off the faces of her kin.

Tor looked back at the cluster of Summers, seeing their guilt and embarrassment. "I've seen heart-and-breathing work on drowning victims, too."

The Summers looked back at her, then. Every one of them.

TIAMAT: Carbuncle

"Oh-oh-oh! Oh no! You win!" Ariele Dawntreader pressed one hand over her mouth, smothering her ecstatic giggles as she watched the sapphire stone clatter and sing down through the labyrinth of the gaming sculpture and out one of its random openings into her brother's lap. "You have to give Elco heart-and-breathing!" She looked around the circle of their laughing, pointing friends at Elco Teel Graymount, as he flopped back onto the carpet with a bloodcurdling scream and began to twitch. He lay still, eyes staring, arms spread, while the young Winters around him snickered and poked each other, making noises in Tammis's direction.

Ariele could see her brother blushing, Merovy's eyes on him as she sat beside him, clutching his hand. Even though she was some kind of cousin of Elco Teel's, Merovy always looked like a fish out of water when Tammis brought her to one of these parties. Ariele couldn't wait to see how she reacted when the red stone landed in her lap, or the blue one.

"Come *on*, Tammis," Ariele called, unable to resist goading him. "Capella Goodventure's *dying*. You saw Tor Starhiker give her heart-and-breathing. Show us how it's done!"

He pushed up from his place beside Merovy with a peculiar grimace and stepped over legs and bodies until he reached Elco's side. He kneeled down, looking into

Elco Teel's wide-eyed stare and expectant grin. He hesitated for a long moment, with reluctance showing in his own eyes. Ariele wondered what he was afraid of—or if it was only the memory of seeing the real thing that stopped him. He leaned over, lowering his face toward Elco Teel's.

"No, no!" voices sang out. "Not like that—!" "*Do* it—!"

He sat back, looking at them over his shoulder. "That was how she did it!" he said, annoyed, but knowing that wasn't what they wanted. Finally he swung a leg over Elco Teel and sat down on top of his stomach. The act of leaning forward forced his own hips back until their bodies seemed to be joined like two lovers. Whistles and clapping crescendoed around them as he put his hands against the sides of Elco Teel's face, and his mouth over Elco's mouth.

He tried to end it quickly, raising his head; the cheering and laughter turned to mockery and protest. Ariele pushed to her feet. "Get off, Tammis, I'll show you how it's done!" She started around the circle; stopped as Elco Teel's arms abruptly trapped Tammis in an embrace and dragged him back down for a deep, wet kiss. She watched Tammis's body quiver, but to her surprise he didn't fight it the way she'd thought he would. She glanced at Merovy, saw the other girl staring at the two boys, her face confused and half-frowning.

"Well, Tirady, look at this—I believe Elco Teel's found true love."

Ariele glanced up, startled, to see Kirard Set Wayaways and his wife Tirady Graymount standing together in the wide entrance to the room, staring at them. Elco Teel let go of Tammis, who half fell off of him in his desperate attempt to get away. But Elco Teel's father only laughed, shaking his head as he came down the three steps into the room, casually unsealing his shining evening jacket. "Don't stop on my account, children. You know I find it delightful and amusing, when you play with my game set behind my back. And I'm sure it was all quite innocent really. . . ."

"We were just practicing heart-and-breathing, Da." Elco Teel rolled onto his side, propping his chin on his hand with a smirk that attempted to imitate his father's languid smile. "Like at the Shop today . . . I was being the victim."

Kirard Set raised his eyebrows. "You were being Capella Goodventure? Ye gods—or should I say, Lady's Tits—now *that's* depraved. Can you imagine, Tirady—having our child turn into a sanctimonious religious fanatic?"

Tirady Graymount murmured something Ariele couldn't make out, that sounded bored and annoyed. She moved past him without looking at any of them, toward the angular cabinet that Ariele knew held their substantial supply of alcoholic drinks. Elco Teel said they also had a dwindling hoard of more exotic drugs left from before the Change; but even he didn't know where those were hidden. Tirady's movements were not too steady, and Ariele suspected she had had a lot to drink already. Maybe they'd argued, and that was why they'd come back so unexpectedly early.

Ariele looked back at Kirard Set, glanced at Elco Teel, trying to guess whether the father was really angry or only amused; whether the son was actually as unconcerned about being caught in the act as he seemed to be. Their family fascinated her. They were so different from her own that they sometimes seemed more alien than the mers.

But Kirard Set's attention was on his wife. He moved toward her as she pulled a bottle of local wine out of the cabinet, and tried to take it from her. She looked at him, with eyes as cold and pale as glacier ice, and he let his hand drop, shrugging. She moved away from him again, heading toward a doorway at the far end of the room. She stopped as she passed a mirror, and peered into it as if she were seeing into another dimension. She put a pale, slender hand up to her face, pressing her cheek, pulling the skin taut until the deepening line along her mouth disappeared. She took her hand away, frowned, and left the room without a backward glance, as if they had all ceased to exist.

"Your mother is feeling old, tonight," Kirard Set murmured. He took out another bottle, and removed the stopper. He drank deeply, straight from its mouth, and came back across the room toward the now-silent circle of friends. He held the bottle out. Several of the wide-eyed witnesses shook their heads, picking themselves up from where they sat in various stages of embarrassment and awkwardness, saying that they had to go home. One by one the others followed. He made no move to stop them, and neither did Elco Teel. Merovy began to get up, and Tammis followed her.

Ariele put out her hand, still standing where she had stopped when Elco Teel's parents arrived. Kirard Set handed her the bottle with a measuring smile; his glance traveled down her body and back up it again in a way that made her tingle with an odd pleasure—knowing that for once he had not looked at her as if he saw a child. He was a very handsome man, and he still looked young, even though she knew that he was actually very old, and like his wife, was beginning to show signs of it. She took a drink of the wine, careful not to take too much, knowing the burn of it would make her cough. She swallowed it with passable grace, and handed the bottle back to him.

"Well done." Kirard Set smiled again, approvingly. "Ah," he said, "you look lovely in those colors, Ariele. It takes me back to the old days, to see you standing there like that . . . I even remember that outfit, how she looked when she wore it. You look so very much like her, you know . . . more so every day. More even than your mother, because you have more of Arienrhod's spirit."

"Arienrhod?" Ariele said, uncertainly. She glanced down at her outfit. Among the endless possessions in the Snow Queen's closets, she had found things that she had made over to fit her. Her mother had never touched any of those clothes, had never even looked at anything there, as far as she knew. Her mother seemed to hate the thought of it, and frowned when Ariele put them on, even though she never forbade her to wear them. Sometimes, perversely, Ariele wished that they were forbidden, so that she could wear them anyway, and defy her mother's anger instead of her peculiar, distracted sorrow. All her Winter friends wore offworlder clothes, handed down, saved from Before . . . and she had fallen in love with the blazing beauty of their colors, the wonderful fineness and the exotic varieties of the materials. She had wanted clothes like that—and she had found them. But did they actually make her look like a queen? She smiled, looking up again.

"Of course," Kirard Set said softly. "As you should, since she was your grandmother."

"What?" Ariele said. "No, my grandmother was a Summer. She died, I never met her . . ."

Kirard Set's eyes widened. "Gods," he murmured. "You don't know? Is it possible you really don't know?" He looked toward Tammis, who had stopped moving and was staring at him in equal curiosity. "Have you ever seen a picture of Arienrhod?"

Ariele shook her head; Tammis shook his.

"There was one in the bedroom on the third floor . . . a painting of her."

"I remember that. I used to look at it when I was little. But that was a picture of my mother," Ariele said. "She didn't like it, she had the servants put it away."

Kirard Set laughed. "It wasn't your mother. It was her mother. Her real mother. It was Arienrhod . . . That's why she didn't like it."

"That's not true," Tammis said, frowning. "Our mother's a Summer. And Gran is a Summer too."

Ariele waved him quiet. She sat down on the long, narrow reclining couch, pulling her feet up. "Are you making this up—?" she asked, meeting Kirard Set's inscrutable gaze, her eyes begging him to tell her that he was not.

"Oh, no," he said, smiling again as he moved to take a seat beside her on the couch. "It's quite true, Ariele. Would you like to hear the whole, true story?"

She nodded eagerly, looked back at her brother. Tammis hesitated, glancing toward the door. He still wore half a frown, as if he were afraid to hear this. But he sat down again, cross-legged on the carpet beside Elco Teel, who was stretched out with his chin on his palms. Merovy, who had been pulling surreptitiously at Tammis's hand, gave up and sat down beside him. Her habitual look of unease deepened.

Kirard Set leaned back into the sloping corner of the couch, taking another drink from the decanter. "Well, all of this began long ago, long before either of you were even a gleam in your father's eye. . . ." His smile twitched. "Arienrhod had been the Snow Queen ever since the Hegemony arrived at the last Change, and the Goodventures' Summer reign ended with a splash. She'd been Queen for nearly a century and a half, and she knew how the offworlders exploited us, manipulated us, kept us from our rightful equality in the Hegemony. She knew that when the offworlders left she'd be thrown into the sea, and Summer would drag us all back down into the darkness for a century again. So she decided to do something about it."

Ariele nodded, almost hypnotized by the lanquid flow of his words. "What did she do?"

"She used the offworlders' own technology to have herself cloned—to have a perfect copy made of her, only her, with no one else's genes in the mix to weaken her resolve . . . several copies, actually. She had them secretly implanted in the bodies of Summer women who had come to the next to last Festival, who would go home to the islands none the wiser, thinking the child they bore was a merrybegot, the result of a Mask Night fling with a man they would never see again. Out of all the clones she had implanted, only your mother was perfect . . . and grew up raised by Summers, as Arienrhod intended, so that she would understand her people's ways when she came to rule in Arienrhod's place. Arienrhod was willing to die—she told me many times that she didn't want to live on in *this* miserable, half-dead world—as long as she knew that she would be reborn in the body of your mother."

Ariele stared, her mouth open, unable to name the feelings inside her, since disbelief was not permitted to be one of them. "But how could she know my mother would become the new Summer Queen?"

He shrugged. "*She* had become Queen. How could your mother not?"

"How do you know about this?" Ariele said. "Does everyone know—?" *Except me.*

"Of course not, dear child. Most of the Summers don't really know what Arienrhod looked like. Capella Goodventure saw her up close before she died, of course—saw them both together. It's one small reason why she and your mother don't get along. . . . Most of the Winters still think your mother actually *is* Arienrhod—in the flesh, that is—that somehow she cheated death and the offworlders, and lived on and is still Queen. But a few—a very few—people know the real truth. Arienrhod and I were old, old friends. I was . . . an intimate in all her most personal affairs." He raised his eyebrows, and Elco Teel sniggered, lying on the floor.

"Does . . . does Da know about this?" Tammis asked, his voice sounding odd.

Kirard Set chuckled and took another sip of wine. "Oh, he certainly does. Most of it never would have come to pass without him. He and your mother were childhood sweethearts, you know. When she became a sibyl he thought she had rejected him, and he ran away to Carbuncle."

"What's that got to do with Arienrhod?" Tammis said.

Kirard Set waved his impatience aside. "When Arienrhod learned Sparks was in the City, she had him brought to her, thinking she could use him to lure your mother to her, to get her to leave the islands and come to the city. . . . She sent a message to your mother, supposedly from him, saying he was in trouble. Your mother did come after him, because of course she still loved him very much. But she had the misfortune to be abducted offworld by techrunners on her way here—or perhaps the good fortune, depending on your point of view; since she learned the power of her sibylhood, which even Arienrhod never dreamed of. But it took five years for her to get back, and in the meantime Arienrhod thought she was lost forever."

"My mother has been offworld? With pirates—?" Ariele murmured, astonished by the secret lives her parents had led when they were hardly older than she was herself. She had scarcely even wondered what their lives had been like before she was born, imagining they had always been the way they were in her earliest memories: *old,* weary, obsessed with work and not each other. To picture her mother young, passionate, daring anything for her father's sake . . . and not even her own mother's child. *Arienrhod's.* Ariele blinked and shook her head, feeling giddy, tantalized, excited . . . frightened.

"What about Da?" Tammis said again. "Did he think our mother was dead too?"

"Yes, I'm afraid so." Kirard Set smiled again, with a rueful sympathy in his voice that was not reflected in his eyes. "Arienrhod made certain he did. He was almost inconsolable. . . ."

Ariele half frowned, not sure what he was saying, but only that something lay between the words that she did not understand.

Elco Teel laughed. "But Arienrhod consoled him, for five years, right, Da—?"

Ariele saw Tammis and Merovy turn to stare at him; realized she was staring at him too, with sudden comprehension. She looked back at Kirard Set. "You mean, my father . . . and the Snow Queen . . . were lovers?"

Kirard Set's smile widened with what she almost thought was approval, as he saw that she understood. "Oh yes, Ariele . . . it was inevitable. That they would both be Queen—that they would both fall in love with the same man. Arienrhod had fallen in love with him, just as your mother had—he was her favorite for five years. She gave him everything he wanted . . . even the water of life."

"Da . . . drank the water of life?" Ariele whispered. "But I thought . . . I thought . . . he was a Summer." She remembered how the sight of mers always seemed to trouble her father, wondering suddenly if that was why. "And he was pledged . . . with my mother, for life."

"But he thought she was gone." Kirard Set shrugged. "And Arienrhod was there, and so much like her . . . and Arienrhod was very good at getting what she wanted; just as your mother is. Come now, children—" he glanced away from the look on her face, to Tammis's, "surely you can understand, and forgive him, under the circumstances. Even in Summer a marriage—pledging—rarely lasts a lifetime. Everyone has the right to choose. Many Summers never pledge themselves to a single mate at all; they like variety. So do Winters. Arienrhod liked considerable variety, and your father learned to share her tastes. He developed quite a sophisticated palate, for a Summer. You have to understand, it was very difficult not to become intimately acquainted—not only with Arienrhod, but with her other favorites as well, when you were one of them. We were all so close—she encouraged it . . . But of course she was always his first love, and he was hers. Perhaps it would even have been 'only,' under other circumstances."

Ariele took a deep breath, realizing that her mouth had fallen open. She shut it, trying to hide the foolish, gaping incredulity of her expression before Kirard Set, or even Elco Teel, began to laugh at her. "What happened when Mama came back—?" Her voice was almost inaudible; she almost wished that she had never asked the first question, never heard any of this, at all, ever. Almost. "When she found out? What did they say?"

"Only she and your father, and perhaps Arienrhod, know that." He took another drink, and held the decanter out to her. She took it from him, and took a large swallow, almost choking. The hot burn of the wine going down her throat felt punishingly good. "But of course your mother was not really in a position to pass judgment on your father. She had only just learned herself that Arienrhod was her real mother . . . and her exact double. How could she blame Sparks for falling in love with *her,* all over again, when he'd lost her once . . . And besides, they say there was a Kharemoughi Police inspector who turned renegade to help your mother here in the city. You have to wonder what there was between him and her, what kind of hold she had over him, to make an offworlder turn against his own people. Don't you—?"

Ariele nodded, although she did not want to, biting her lip. She looked down, unable to meet anyone's eyes.

"But you haven't asked me what happened between your mother and Arienrhod, when they finally met. That's the best part."

Ariele looked up at him again. "What happened?" she asked faintly.

"Arienrhod had made her new plans while Moon was away; she decided she would live on herself, after all. She'd planned to spread a plague that would kill all the Summers who'd come to Carbuncle for the last Festival—throw the world into chaos, so the offworlders would flee and she could keep her power." Ariele grimaced, but he only smiled and went on. "She didn't need your mother anymore . . . but of course she *wanted* her. How could she not—? She asked Moon to reign with her, share everything with her . . . even Sparks."

"And my mother said *no,*" Ariele murmured.

"Obviously." Kirard Set nodded. "And then Arienrhod ordered her thrown into the Pit." Ariele gasped, in spite of herself. "That was when your mother performed her first 'miracle.' She stopped the winds in the Hall of Winds. I was there, I saw it myself . . . though to this day I still don't know how she managed it. I don't suppose she's ever told you how. . . . But no, of course not . . . Anyway, then the renegade Blue came into the hall and rescued her from the mob. . . . And the rest, as they say, is history. Your mother won the mask of the Summer Queen. Arienrhod went into the sea as planned. Your parents were reunited, you were born . . . and you know all the rest." He lifted his hands in a graceful shrug of denouement.

"What happened . . . what happened to the Blue?" Tammis asked uncertainly.

"The gods only know." Kirard Set shook his head. "He left with the rest of the offworlders, I suppose. Jerusha PalaThion might be able to tell you; he must have been one of her officers. . . . I wouldn't pay any mind to the rumors, though."

"What rumors?" Tammis said.

"Oh, well. More complications . . ." Kirard Set waved a dismissing hand. "Almost no one repeats that scurrilous garbage anymore, anyway. But some people used to point out that . . . well, that Sparks had been taking the water of life at the time of your conception during the last Festival—and of course it does make the user temporarily sterile."

They both looked at him, stricken, through a silence that seemed endless.

He laughed gently, at last. "Ye gods, it's only idle gossip. After all, the water of life was getting hard to come by, by the end of Arienrhod's reign. She'd begun cutting back on how much she allowed us to have—sometimes once a week, not once a day anymore, even for old friends like myself and Tirady. That's how we were blessed with our only son, over there." He gestured at Elco Teel. "He was a complete surprise, unexpected . . . not unwelcome, don't misunderstand me . . . but still an accident. It's quite reasonable to think that your father had become unexpectedly fertile again too."

Ariele nodded dumbly. Kirard Set raised his eyebrows, and offered her the decanter once more. She shook her head this time, and got up from the couch. "I have to go now."

"Us, too," Tammis said, getting up from the floor, holding Merovy's hand with painful tightness. Elco Teel rolled onto his back, his hands folded on his chest, gazing at them with a pale, inscrutable stare as they passed by him.

"Safe home, children," Kirard Set called after them, and Ariele thought she heard laughter as she reached the front door. She frowned, in the darkened hallway ahead of Tammis and Merovy, where no one could see her.

The three of them went out together, gathering in the street as the door of the Wayaways townhouse closed with finality behind them.

"Why do you think he told us that?" Ariele said, her voice sounding thinner and more miserable than she wanted it to.

"Because you asked him to," Tammis said, his own voice heavy with accusation.

"Well, he was the one who said I looked like Arienrhod!" Ariele snapped. "He said she was my real grandmother!"

"Mine too," Tammis said irritably. "Like it or not."

"My father . . . " Merovy broke in, her voice barely more than an insistent whisper, "says that Kirard Set would cut off his own ear, if he thought it would make someone else feel worse than he did."

Ariele stared at her, looked away again. "Are you coming home? Are you going with me now?" she asked her brother, looking uphill toward the palace; trying not to make it a demand, trying not to acknowledge that suddenly she didn't want to go back there, like this, alone.

But Tammis shook his head, his mahogany-colored curls moving against his neck. "I want to make sure Merovy gets home all right." He glanced away, over his shoulder, as if Carbuncle's still-busy Street, with its unchanging artificial day, was suddenly empty and shadow-haunted. He looked back at her. "You can come with us . . ."

She frowned, tossing her head. "No, thanks. Don't let me get in your way—" she said sullenly, even though she had heard nothing but awkward concern in her brother's voice. She turned her back on them, and started on up the street. She didn't look back until she had reached the alabaster-white courtyard before the palace.

Safe home . . . Kirard Set's farewell echoed in her memory like his mocking laughter. She stopped, standing at the Street's beginning—or was it the end?—looking toward the palace entrance that had let pass so much of her world's history; that had opened on the Snow Queen's domain, long before she was born.

She imagined her mother passing through those doors for the first time, in search of her father . . . imagined her father going through those doors for the first time, into the arms of the Snow Queen. *Arienrhod's home.* Her mind tried to imagine her father in Arienrhod's arms, in Arienrhod's bed . . . the two of them doing things to each other she barely understood . . . doing things to each other she couldn't even imagine. Why had her mother wanted to live here, after Arienrhod had died?

Suddenly she didn't want to live here anymore. Suddenly she wished that she had somewhere else to go, that she didn't have to go in through those doors, ever again. But if she went somewhere else there would be questions and explanations to face, and she couldn't bear that, even the thought of it. She looked down at the shimmering red-golds and blue-greens of her soft overshirt and pants, that had once been Arienrhod's own . . . her grandmother's, her other/mother's. *"You have her spirit,"* Kirard Set had said. She lifted her head, straightening her back.

She crossed the courtyard to the palace doors. The two constables who were always there on duty smiled at her and let her pass inside, her own face empty and unresponsive.

She went on into the Hall of the Winds; stopped midway across the bridge that spanned the deep, green-glowing access shaft. *They tried to throw her into the Pit . . . and she stopped the winds.* She looked over the edge, cautious but unafraid, into the green depths that smelled of the sea; looked up again at the curtains hanging high overhead. *I don't suppose she ever told you how—?* Ariele looked back the way she had come. *The renegade Blue came in and saved her. . . . Who knows what there was between them—?* She hurried on, her face pinched with doubt.

She made her way through the palace, oblivious to the servants' greetings; climbed the wide, curving stairs to the upper levels, searched the echoing halls until she found her father, in his study. She stood a moment looking in at him as he worked, stretched out on the segmented couch, humming faintly—an old folk song, she realized—and making notes on a noteboard.

"Da—?" she said softly, at last, from the doorway.

Sparks looked up, startled, and sucked in his breath. He stared at her for a long moment with an expression on his face that she had never seen before.

"Da—?" she said again, uncertainly.

"Ariele," he murmured, "what are you . . . doing here?" He shook his head slightly, as if he were shaking something loose, and sat up on the couch.

She shrugged, looking down, suddenly not knowing what to say.

"Are you all right?" He leaned forward, with concern on his face, putting aside the noteboard.

She shrugged again, and came into the room. She sat down beside him on the sofa with her hands twined between her knees.

"What is it?" he asked, touching her shoulder gently.

She felt tears start suddenly in her eyes; fought them back. "Da . . . " She looked up at him, finally. "Is Mama really Arienrhod . . . Arienrhod's clone?"

He stiffened; his hand dropped away, giving her all the answer she needed. But he took a deep breath, and nodded. "Yes."

"Why didn't she ever tell me?" The words burst out with more force than she had intended. "Why did she lie to me, why did she pretend that she had a different mother, and Gran, and—"

"She didn't lie," Sparks answered, with quiet insistence. "Everything she's always told you was true. She just didn't tell you all of it, the whole truth." He sighed, his eyes growing distant. "She didn't even know it herself, all those years. She couldn't have explained it to you, when you were little. But you shouldn't have had to hear it from someone else." He lifted her chin gently with his fingertips. "What else do you need to know, Ari? I'll tell you anything I can."

"Were you Arienrhod's lover?" She flung the question at him, before she lost her nerve.

He flinched, and forced himself to keep looking at her. "Yes," he whispered. His hands clenched silently on the silver leather surface of the couch. Ariele stared at his whitened knuckles, feeling her own hands tighten like two creatures locked in a death struggle.

"And you drank the water of life with her."

"Yes." The word was barely audible.

"Is that why . . . why seeing the mers always makes you unhappy?"

He nodded; but he looked away, as if there was something in his eyes that he didn't want her to see. "Who's been telling you all this—" His voice was rough.

"Elco's father."

"Kirard Set?" His head came up again; his gray-green eyes were suddenly as bright as emeralds, and as hard. "What . . . what else did he say?"

"That—" Ariele nearly broke off, seeing the stark pain in her father's face. "That Mama loved another man too. An offworlder. And maybe . . . maybe you're not really even our Da."

He put his arms out and pulled her to him, held her close, cradling her head against his chest, so that she could no longer see his expression, and he couldn't see hers. She felt a tremor of anger run through him. But this time he did not answer her.

Tammis stopped in the quiet alley in front of Merovy's townhouse, glancing toward the alley-end, where the smoldering night waited beyond the storm walls, forever held at bay. Merovy followed his gaze; looked back at him uncertainly. "Do you want to come in and . . . and talk?" He had not spoken more than two words to her on the way to her door.

He kissed her suddenly instead of answering her, pulling her against him with gentle insistence. She kissed him back, with no uncertainty now, warming him with her warmth. They had kissed before, often enough, experimenting. But it had never made him feel the way it suddenly did now, her closeness somehow caught in the treacherous tangle of his emotions—the feel of her mouth on his, willing but uncertain, her body against him, the memory of the feel of Elco Teel's mouth and body, all too knowing; the images of his father and his mother, naked with strangers. He had always imagined that the way he was with Merovy, loving her almost since he could remember, had been the way it was for them; but now he wasn't sure, wasn't even sure . . .

He broke off his kiss, letting go of Merovy almost roughly, pushing her back against the wall in the shadow of an overhanging balcony. She blinked her eyes, looking startled and then almost relieved. "Good night, Tammis . . ." she whispered, groping for the door handle behind her. She opened the door, and went inside. Tammis stood staring at the closed door for a long moment. Then he turned and headed back down the alley, pressing his fingers to his mouth.

He walked the whole distance home, needing time to gather his thoughts, needing to walk off the emotions that filled him with a dark heat, like poison. He had tried once to ask his father about the new feelings stirring so urgently inside him; about his confusion, when they were stirred as easily by the sight of a boy's body as by a girl's. But when he had tried to talk about his sexual feelings openly and honestly, his father had lectured him on the ways of the Summer islands, giving him definitions of what was acceptable that he knew from watching his city friends were impossibly rigid. When he had tried to ask if there couldn't be something more, his father had become furious, and ended the conversation.

He had brooded over it, sure that he had failed to understand something his parents had always found obvious. He had told himself that the casual, indiscriminate sex he saw occurring more and more among his Winter acquaintances only mirrored the emptiness of their minds and the aimlessness of their spoiled existence.

He still believed that, in his heart. And yet, tonight Kirard Set Wayaways had told him that everything he knew was wrong. . . .

He reached the palace at last, and went directly to his father's study. He looked in at the door and saw his father alone, sitting on the edge of the silver-gray couch, with his head in his hands, his face buried—sitting as still as stone. Tammis watched him silently for a long moment; and then he turned away and went on down the hall.

He found his mother at work with Jerusha PalaThion in another room. They looked up together as he hesitated in the doorway. "Tammis—" she said, with surprise plain on her face. He saw her glance away at the time, and back at him; saw Jerusha's gaze measure his expression.

Jerusha finished the mug of whatever she had been drinking, and got to her feet. "I didn't realize it was so late. We can try this again tomorrow. Maybe something will come to me in my dreams. . . ." She smiled, weary and wry.

His mother nodded, and looked back at him. Tammis could see the dark fatigue-circles under her eyes, as vivid as bruises against her pale skin. Jerusha went past him, still smiling as she looked at him and said, "Good night." But he knew why she was leaving so abruptly—giving him privacy, for whatever he had to say.

"Tammis—?" Moon said again, her own face growing concerned. She held out her hands to him.

He crossed the room and took them, felt her warm fingers squeeze his, the feel

of her touch, somehow still as calm and soothing as her kiss on his forehead when
he was a child. He sat on the table-edge beside her, careful not to dislodge a pile of
anything.

"What have you been doing tonight?" she asked him, her voice mild; but he
thought he saw a glimmer of doubt in her eyes. He had not disturbed her while she
was working in years.

He shrugged. "We were at Elco Teel's after the Shop closed. . . ."

"Did you see what happened to Capella Goodventure today?" Moon asked, half
curious, half as though she wondered whether that was what was bothering him.

Tammis nodded. "Elco Teel said it couldn't have happened to a better choice of
victims." He smiled, a little guiltily; saw his mother's smile mirror his, equally
guilty.

"I'll never hear the end of it. But thank the Lady Tor saved her, or I'd never hear
the end of *that.*" She shook her head and rubbed her eyes.

"I want to learn how to do that," he said, "what Tor did, I mean. Everyone
thought it was like doing magic." His mother's smile widened, and she nodded.

He pushed up off the edge of the table again, feeling his resolution falter. "I just
wanted to say good night. . . ." He glanced away as he said it, not able to face her
as he spoke the words.

"Nothing else?" His mother's voice caught at him like an outstretched hand,
making him turn back.

He looked at her, seeing her doubled in his mind: his mother . . . the Snow
Queen. "We were at Elco Teel's, and . . ." And he told her, all of it, even about the
offworlder Police inspector; unable to make himself meet her eyes when he repeated
it . . . afraid of what he might find there. She listened, holding herself as tightly as
if she held something that wanted to run away; scarcely interrupting. He saw her
whitening with anger, but knew, from her hand on his and the cold distance in her
eyes, that her anger was not directed at him. "Why do you think Kirard Set told you
all this?" she asked at last, her voice strained.

Tammis looked away, shrugged. "I don't know. . . . Merovy said he'd cut off
his own ear to hurt somebody else."

"Yes," Moon murmured. "I think he would. He did it to hurt you, Tammis, and
to hurt us all. I can't tell you why, exactly . . ." although something in her voice
told him that she could have. "But I can tell you, keep away from people like that.
It doesn't matter why they do what they do; it only matters that you know they will."

She took her hand away from his; looked down at both her hands together on the
tabletop. Her one hand touched the other, almost questioningly. "I am Arienrhod's
clone, Tammis. But I'm not Arienrhod. . . . The woman who gave birth to me was
Lelark Dawntreader Summer. Sparks—your father—" she said insistently, "and I
grew up together on Neith, in the Windward Islands. Gran and my mother were our
family. Maybe I was Arienrhod's clone . . . but Arienrhod didn't raise me or feed
me or sew my clothes or teach me right from wrong. Arienrhod didn't love
me. . . . That's what makes someone your mother, or your father. That's what
family is." She looked up at him, blinking too much. "And as for the rest of
it . . . the Change took care of that, at the last Festival. We all cast our sins into the
sea, and the sea washed them away. That's what forgiveness is."

He nodded, glancing down.

"Do you think you can forgive me?" she asked softly. "And your father?"

He lifted his head, blinking hard himself; but he did not answer. He hugged her, feeling safe and certain for the brief moment that she held him, before he said, "Good night" again, and meant it this time.

ONDINEE: Tuo Ne'el

"Boss, I think we've got trouble." Kedalion Niburu called the words over his shoulder without looking back, not able to take his eyes off the screen in front of him. It showed him the unmistakable expanding diamond of a pursuit pattern forming in their wake—at least half a dozen craft, still beyond sight but closing rapidly with their own.

"Who is it?" Reede dropped into the seat next to him, peering out with bloodshot eyes across the living-death landscape. Tuo Ne'el had been sliding past below them for several hours now; gradually lightening into the visible as they caught up second by second with the day. Kedalion had never thought he would be glad to see that view again; but, until he had done this last scan, it had almost seemed like he was coming home. They had been in flight for nearly twelve hours straight, coming directly off their landing at an obscure shipping field halfway around the planet, flightlagged and exhausted to begin with. But Reede had ordered it, Reede had not explained why, Reede had simply wanted it done, that way, in secrecy with faked codes and no rest at all. . . .

And Reede was swearing now, as Kedalion pointed at the displays, letting him see trouble for himself. "Whose are they?" His own hand moved over the control boards, querying, reconfirming, as if he thought he could somehow find a better answer.

But it was an impossible question. "I don't know," Kedalion said, "except they're not Humbaba's welcoming committee. They don't respond to any of the codes, and they aren't talking. I've tried all the usual frequencies."

"Shit. Shit!" Reede hit the panel with his fist, making some system bleat in protest. "We covered our tracks coming in. How could the Blues have figured it—?" He shook his head. "It can't be the Blues. They'd just nail us from upstairs." He frowned, rubbing his face. "How far are we from Humbaba's?"

"About ten minutes."

"Can we get there first?"

"Don't think so."

"Are we transmitting a distress code?"

Kedalion looked up again, facing Reede's expression with an effort of will. His own face felt paralyzed. "No one's answering it, boss," he said. "Seems like nobody's home."

"That's insane," Reede snapped, reaching for the comm. He stuffed a remote into his ear, sent out the same call, without even looking down. He got the same results: No answer. Nothing at all. Dead silence. His hand fisted on the panel; Kedalion felt his own hands beginning to sweat.

"You think they're jamming us?" Reede touched the images on the screen.

"No. We'd get a reading off their beam."

"By the Render—" Reede tugged at his ear, his eyes searching the featureless horizon for a sign of their pursuit, a sign of salvation. "Get me remote visual on the citadel, as soon as you can."

"Boss . . ." Kedalion hesitated, remembering the mysterious meeting he had stumbled on before their departure for Number Four; remembering that Reede had told him to forget it. "Is there anybody else who can help us?"

Reede looked sharply at him; but then he sat back in his seat, actually seeming to consider the question. "Not close enough. Not that I trust. Not with what we're carrying. Try the citadel again."

Kedalion tried it. No results.

"Try our tail again."

He ran a call all up and down the open frequencies. No answer. "You think they want our cargo?" He glanced into the rear of the hovercraft, where Ananke lay slumped across a seat in blissful ignorance, sound asleep. Concealed beneath the seat there was a heavy, unlabeled container—with the key to the universe locked inside it.

"That's my bet." Reede nodded. "But why—? The only ones who could possibly know I'm here and what we've got know I'm bringing it home for *them*." He shook his hair back from his eyes; a muscle in his cheek was twitching.

"I thought Humbaba sent us—"

"No." Reede looked at him suddenly, with cold disgust. "Humbaba did not send us. Humbaba doesn't know shit. . . . I don't *like* this, gods, I don't. . . . Get the citadel on visual." He pointed straight ahead.

Kedalion could see nothing. Wondering whether Reede actually could, he upped the resolution factor on the forward visual. A segment of their view appeared in abrupt magnification, showing him the distant spire of Humbaba's fortress, rising like a beacon from the gray sea of impenetrable scrub. He heard Reede suck in a long harsh breath of relief, let it out again as he saw the citadel still intact. "Why don't they answer?" he murmured. "Unless someone's cut their entire power system . . . and that means no protection." His knuckles showed white on the panel. "Try them again!" he said. Kedalion repeated the callcode automatically.

As he input the final digit a gout of flame rose from the image on the screen. A ball of white light expanded outward, filling the magnification segment, spilling over into their realtime view, blinding them even through the protected shield of the dome.

Kedalion swore, shutting his eyes. Reede cried out, a sound that was more like despair than pain, as his hands flew up to his face.

An explosion. As his own vision cleared, it let him see that the white light was fading . . . let him see what it had done. Where there had been an impregnable, shining tower on the sullen plain, there was now twisted wreckage, a splinter of ruin glowing cherry-red, flickering with the starpoint flares of secondary explosions.

"What . . . what . . . ?" Ananke groaned, stumbling forward from the back seat. "What happened— Hallowed Calavre!" He stopped, clinging to the seatbacks, gaping in disbelief at what showed ahead. A black shroud of smoke had begun to conceal the ruin, as the thorn forest ignited like a funeral pyre. Kedalion could see the forest blazing up now in explosions of its own as petrochemicals caught fire in bark and leaves, setting off a holocaust that would torch the plain for thousands of hectares in all directions. Beside him Reede stared, motionless, his face devoid of any expression, as if his mind had gone completely somewhere else. He twisted the ring he wore on his thumb. Kedalion looked away from the emptiness of his eyes.

The shockwave of the explosion hit them, the hovercraft shuddered and bucked, dumping Ananke on his butt. Kedalion used voice and hands to reintegrate their stabilizers and speed with desperate efficiency. He looked up and out again—saw one of their pursuers glide forward into visual range, pacing them easily as he pushed the hovercraft's speed to its limit, racing fate toward a destination that had suddenly ceased to have any meaning. He looked down at the specs reading out now on the screen in front of him. Each of the pursuit craft around them was a flying armory.

"Reede Kullervo!" The voice burst out of the comm, through the linkage of Kedalion's headset, making him wince.

Reede jerked as if he had been shocked. Kedalion saw expression come back into his face. "I'm here," Reede said, his voice toneless with barely controlled rage. "Who did this, you shit-eating cowards?"

"We are taking control of your craft's operating systems," the voice said, as if it hadn't heard him. "Tell your pilot to activate override sequence."

Kedalion glanced at Reede. Reede said nothing.

"We are armed. Activate override or we will shoot you down."

"Copy. Activating override sequence," Kedalion said, when Reede still did not answer. Maybe Reede figured this was as good a day to die as any . . . he ususally did. But Kedalion Niburu at least wanted to know who wanted him dead before he took a direct hit.

Reede's expression was like the edge of a blade; but he made no move to stop anything as Kedalion let their escort take over the ship's controls. Kedalion lifted his hands from the board in a shrug of resignation, watching data shift as they changed direction and speed. Ananke was on his feet again, peering over Kedalion's shoulder in stricken silence as they flew on over the thorn forests, the blasted citadel and the raging wildfire falling away behind them like the past.

There was no more radio contact from their escort; they flew on in helpless silence. Ananke didn't ask again what had happened. Kedalion decided that either he'd figured it out for himself, or he didn't want to know. He sat down again in the back, stroking the quoll, staring out at the rearward view until there was nothing left to see.

Kedalion tried a few queries of the boards, the databanks. Nothing at all had been left under his control. He couldn't even change the time on the clock. He drummed his fingers impatiently on the panel; shoved his hand into his pocket. His fingers closed over the huskball. He pulled it out, rolling it from hand to hand, comforted by the motion and its shabby familiarity.

"Can you get a fix on where we're going?" Reede asked.

Kedalion looked up, and shook his head. "Can't get a damn thing out of the banks. And it doesn't look like we're flying a straight course. Reede—"

"Shut up," Reede said. "Shut up, Niburu."

Kedalion shut up.

After about two hour's flight time he began to see the spine of another tower, gleaming like a needle in the late morning sun. He wanted to ask whose citadel it was, but he didn't. If Reede knew, he didn't bother to share the information. A port blossomed in the fortress wall as they approached. Kedalion felt the invisible hand of a docking beam close over their craft, sucking them unerringly, inescapably into its waiting mouth.

Guards were waiting too, as they settled into a dock with a stomach-dropping lurch. Kedalion saw them peering in warily through the dome. The doors popped without his asking: an invitation.

"Let's not keep them waiting . . ." Reede said. His voice was full of broken glass. He got to his feet, flexing his fingers like a man with a cramp; Kedalion was relieved to see that he made no move toward any of the weapons he carried.

"What about—?" Kedalion jerked his head at the rear of the craft, where the container of stardrive plasma lay concealed under the seats.

Reede shook his head, with a *leave it* gesture. He stepped outside.

Kedalion followed, reluctantly, glancing back at Ananke. Ananke was looking at the quoll, looking around, as if he was trying to decide whether his pet would be safer with him, or without him. "Bring it," Kedalion said softly. "The gods only know if we'll ever even see this again—" He gestured at the hovercraft.

Ananke nodded, tight-lipped, and went ahead of him out the door.

Guards moved in on them, searching them by hand and with detectors, with rough efficiency. They had already relieved Reede of an assortment of weapons. Kedalion noticed that Reede's solii pendant—the one he always wore, the one Kedalion had seen once on half a dozen ill-met strangers in a bizarre back-alley meeting—was dangling free. The solii's shimmering, hypnotic light looked strikingly out of place against Reede's nondescript gray coveralls. For once he made no effort to conceal it, wearing it with an almost defiant insouciance. The guards watched him the way they would watch a wild beast, as if his reputation had preceded him. Kedalion felt surprise, and then a wary relief, as he realized they were making no move to put binders on anyone.

Someone entered the docking bay, coming toward them, moving with a ruthless confidence that said he carried some power. The guards looked up at him, and moved out of his path. They were the usual mix of on- and offworlders, wearing the same pragmatic assortment of clothing that Kedalion saw all the time in the streets of Humbaba's headquarters. The man coming toward them now was no more formally dressed. There was no way to guess who any of them worked for; nothing but the new arrival's manner told Kedalion that he was in charge. He was close to two meters tall, and heavily muscled. Dark curly hair, dark upslanting eyes . . . Kedalion figured he was Newhavenese.

He stopped in front of them, looking Reede over while a smile pulled up the burn-scarred corner of his mouth. "Well, Reede Kullervo. Glad you made it." He held out a hand.

Reede wiped his own hands on his pantslegs in response, his eyes glittering. "You're not the Man," he said. "And you're not glad to see me." Kedalion couldn't tell whether Reede actually knew the Newhavener or not.

"I heard you were smart," the big man said, with the same sour smile. He let his hand drop. "Fucking brilliant, in fact. I guess that's why the Man wants to see you about a job."

Reede gave a bark of sardonic laughter. "He wants to work for me?"

Head shake. "He heard you lost your patron. Dangerous, being who you are, and without a patron."

"He maybe have something to do with that?" Reede said.

"Yeah. Maybe." The Newhavener's grin widened maliciously. "You've been offworld a long time, Kullervo. That's dangerous too. Things change."

Kedalion sensed more than saw Reede's breathing become quick and shallow. "Whose cartel is this? Where am I?" he asked, and Kedalion knew it had cost him to ask that.

The big man's expression got uglier. "You'll see," he said. "You're gonna love it here, Kullervo."

"Okay," Reede murmured, his voice rasping. "The Man wants to see me, where is he—?"

"Follow me." The Newhavener turned and started back the way he had come, his boot heels ringing on the catwalk. They followed him, six guards moving with them like their own shadow. Kedalion resisted the urge to look back, at the hovercraft, at the priceless cargo still hidden beneath the back seat, lying in a bucket like yesterday's lunch; at his last glimpse of the open air, and freedom, maybe forever.

The Newhavener took them for the three-credit tour, transporting them deep into the citadel's city-size entrails by ways and means that were guaranteed to ensure they'd never find their way back out again alone. They stepped out of a final dizzying lift ride, into an airy, open space that made Kedalion blink with surprise. One wall let in actual daylight . . . or maybe it was a holo, he couldn't be sure. If it was genuine, they were high up in the air, though he'd been sure they were working their way downward.

"The Man—" their guide said, gesturing across the wide expanse of shining floor toward a sealed door. A small garden spilled out into the open space beneath the windows; he heard the sound of dripping water. Surrounding it was what looked like the waiting room of some successful merchant co-op, filled with incongruously normal seats and tables. "After you, Kullervo."

Reede took a deep breath, and started across the room toward the featureless door. Kedalion followed, with Ananke close on his heels. Midway across the room the Newhavener cut effortlessly between Reede and his men, forcing Kedalion to stop. "Have a seat—" he suggested, looking down at Kedalion.

Kedalion stood where he was and looked toward Reede. Reede turned back, and Kedalion was glad that what showed in Reede's eyes was not directed at him.

Reede looked up at the Newhavener, down at Kedalion and Ananke. "Wait here," he said, his voice coolly arrogant, as if the other man had not even spoken. "This shouldn't take long."

Kedalion nodded, trying to match the confidence of Reede's manner as he moved toward the seats, knowing he was not succeeding. He knew Reede was nervous, even afraid, but Reede was burning now with the murderous intensity that made anyone with a shred of sanity get out of his way. Reede Kullervo might be a madman, but for once Kedalion was glad to be working for him. Maybe they'd even get out of this alive. He almost felt sorry for whoever was waiting beyond that door, planning to make Reede an offer he couldn't refuse. He managed to pull himself onto the couch with something like dignity, managed an encouraging smile to answer the unspoken question in Ananke's glance. Ananke looked away again, through the ring of guards toward Reede. They watched the door go transparent, watched Reede disappear through it. And then they waited.

Reede stepped through the doorway into a featureless box. The security door rematerialized behind him, sealing him in before he had time to realize that there were no other exits. He spun around, getting a mild shock through his hands as they hit the screen, making it spark. Inside of a heartbeat it was as solid and featureless as the other three walls, the ceiling, the floor.

A trap. Reede turned back, searching the room with his eyes. A perfect, featureless cube. He clenched his teeth over the sudden urge to cry out, to throw himself against the walls like a panic-stricken animal. But the part of his brain that always seemed to be under someone else's control held him motionless, pointing out to him that there was light here, which meant that there was probably full life support and fresh air; there had been a way in, which meant that there was a way out. It could even be some kind of lift, although he couldn't detect any motion. They didn't want him dead, at least not yet, and probably not at all. They just wanted him softened up a little.

He leaned against the wall, fingering the jangling piece of jewelry hanging from his ear, and forced himself to relax, in case he was being monitored, which he probably was. *He should be grateful:* They were giving him time to think. He still had no idea who held him. All they'd said to him was, *You've lost your patron,* and that meant Humbaba. They'd talked like he was going to be working here, a simple survivor-claiming, a change of employers, but not careers. They hadn't even asked him about the stardrive. Maybe they didn't know. . . .

Except whoever it was claimed that they'd dropped the lightning on Humbaba's tower, right in front of his eyes, perfectly timed to his arrival. That meant they had somehow been able to shut down all its support systems first, leaving it without even communications, and utterly defenseless against the attack. And they had known exactly when he was arriving, how, from what direction. All of that screamed power, more power than any single cartel involved in a takeover struggle with Humbaba should have access to. It was only the existence of that higher power that let the cartels coexist here as successfully as they did. There were skirmishes, hijackings, ambushes. But when an entire citadel went out, it was something bigger. . . . It meant somebody had tried to cross the Brotherhood.

But he *was* the Brotherhood— He touched the solii pendant that Mundilfoere had given him. He knew its significance, knew why she had told him to wear it always. *Mundilfoere . . .* Not letting himself think about what he would do if she had been in the fortress when it went up, caught inside that blinding ball of light, incinerated . . . *Gods, a man could go crazy trying to figure it out! Go crazy in here . . .* He wasn't going to work for whoever was doing this to him . . . he was going to kill the son of a bitch, with his bare hands. He was sweating; was it really warmer in here, was the air really getting thicker, heavier, harder to breathe, like being underwater— "Come *on,* motherfucker—" he muttered, beginning to twitch. He forced himself to stop it, to curb the insane energy singing inside him. *Save it. Save it, damn you. . . .*

The lights went out. *No—!* He almost screamed it, but the still-sane fragment of his mind that had kept him calm until now closed its hand around his throat, forced him to stand perfectly still in the middle of the utter blackness, his head up, his hands motionless at his sides. *Wait. Wait.* . . . He became aware of his own breathing, the way his heart was pounding, the blood rushing inside his ears. All his senses began to run wild, overreacting to the absence of stimuli. Did he really hear the sound of two people breathing? Gods, what was that smell in the air—not staleness, not his own sweat, it smelled like something rotting. . . . He was beginning to see things, to believe that he actually saw a glow like almost-dead embers on the wall ahead of him. He reached out, stretching his hand toward it—lurched forward as he discovered that the wall was no longer there.

Groping around him, he realized that there were no walls at all anymore; that the room he had been trapped in had disappeared. He was suddenly lost in a much larger room, a formless blackness like the space between the stars. But the glow he had seen was real. It had become barely bright enough to let him believe in it, even though it was too dim to give him any real information.

He started toward it, having no better guide . . . took three steps, and stumbled as his feet caught on something. He sprawled headlong onto a hard, slick surface that felt like ceramic tiles. He pushed himself up on his hands and knees, his body and the remains of his confidence bruised and shaken. Something was still caught under his feet—whatever he had fallen over. He reached around, fumbling blindly until he could touch it. *Cloth.* An odd-shaped, rumpled mound of it, like somebody had kicked aside a rug . . . Like somebody had left a corpse lying there. That smell. Gods, was this—? *Shit—!*

He jerked his hand away, scrambled to his feet, before any part of his body could accidentally discover too much about the mound. And froze, suddenly certain that he had heard faint laughter. "Who's there—?" His voice shook, telling whoever it was too much about how well their plan was working. "Turn on the lights, damn you. Talk to me!" Echoes of his own voice came back at him, were all that he could hear, distorted by surfaces he could not imagine the forms of.

"I prefer the darkness," a voice said, a voice which sounded like something that had been torn physically out ˪ ᶠ its owner's throat, the words striking him like gobbets of flesh. "It's so much more revealing. . . . Everyone is naked, in the dark."

Reede froze, not even breathing; staring into the blackness with every nerve ending of his body. "You . . . ?" he whispered. Trying to make out a form against the dull red ember-glow ahead of him, trying to make himself recognize a human shape in the silhouette he could now barely detect against the light. But he didn't need to, knew already that it would be impossible. He felt his guts turn to jelly. *The Source.* That was what Thanin Jaakola called himself, that was whose citadel he had come to be held prisoner in. Jaakola's cartel was one of the strongest, their drug production and distribution network had outlets on every world in the Hegemony. But Jaakola was more than simply a bigtime narco. He was one of the Brotherhood, and even Reede had no idea how far, how deep, his real power extended.

Reede peered into the darkness again, blinking compulsively. Rumor claimed Jaakola needed the darkness because there was something wrong with him, that light hurt his eyes, that he had some hideous, disfiguring disease. Reede had never believed it, had always figured it was a lie, a disguise, so that the Source could be anybody he wanted to be, and nobody would know. But now, lost here in the darkness, with only that misshapen mound of blackness ahead of him . . . now, suddenly, he wasn't so sure. What was that smell—was it whatever was lying on the floor, was it his imagination, or was it . . . was it— *Stop it! Don't even think about it.*

"Come closer, Reede. There is a seat here by me. No need for you to stand." It was a challenge: Jaakola sensing his fear, daring him to get closer.

Anger and old resentment goaded him forward. He moved with painful caution this time, testing the space ahead of him with each step; afraid of finding another trap, a corpse, a gaping pit. He found an unexpected step up, navigated it without falling on his face, and abruptly encountered the padded outline of what seemed to be a chair. He groped his way around it and sat down, after first exploring the seat and back thoroughly with his hands.

"You must be exhausted after your long, arduous journey," Jaakola's disintegrating voice said. "Congratulations." For a moment Reede actually wondered whether Jaakola meant his journey back from Four, or the journey here to his seat. "You have been completely successful on behalf of the Brotherhood, I see."

"You see?" Reede repeated, picking his words as carefully as he had picked a path across the room.

"We have the container of stardrive plasma that was hidden in your craft. A brilliant coup, how you stole it right out of the Kharemoughis' hands—and you even brought us a stardrive unit! The name of the Smith will soon be legendary among the agents of Chaos. Perhaps you really do deserve to be called the new Vanamoinen. . . . Taking the plasma home to your beloved Mundilfoere, were you?"

Reede felt the hatred inside the words close around his throat and squeeze. "Any reason I shouldn't?" Focusing his own white-hot rage, he managed, somehow, to ask the question without his voice betraying him again. "You know I'm a member in good standing—I wasn't trying to hide anything from anybody but the Blues. I sent Mundilfoere word, I said call a Meeting first thing. Why the fuck am I here with just you? And why shouldn't I want to go home?"

"Perhaps the fact that you no longer have a home to go to . . . ?" The shadow against the darkness moved insinuatingly.

Reede's fingers dug into the chair arms as the fireball went off again inside his memory, incinerating the citadel before his eyes. He let go, abruptly, as something about the consistency of the chair itself made his flesh crawl. "Goddamn you—" He broke off. "If Mundilfoere was—"

"She was not present when we took out the citadel," the ruined voice murmured gently. "Rest assured."

Reede sank back into the chair's suffocating softness, as his rigid muscles let go. "Then, why—?"

"To prove a point, shall we say? To dispose of the middleman. To demonstrate my eagerness to have you as a member of my personal operation. To let you and every little operator out there in the thorn scrub see what real power is . . . and to give the outer world a reason for my claiming you, a tragically patronless biochemist, to do service with me."

"That's crazy," Reede muttered. Nothing he had heard so far made any sense—it only got progressively more maddening. He wondered suddenly if Jaakola was actually insane, or was simply playing with him. "You know Humbaba's was my safehouse, the place where I ran my labs. We had an agreement—I kept him well-supplied and he didn't ask me any questions about my real work. He wasn't even Survey—"

"He was Mundilfoere's pet horror." Jaakola sniggered with sardonic amusement. "We both know who made him as successful as he was . . . who was the real Man at Humbaba citadel. But now that the Brotherhood has the stardrive plasma, our precocious Smith needs facilities appropriate to the task of developing the new technology. What better place than here? The Source and the Smith, in perfect symbiosis. You don't have to play any loyalty games with me. . . . I exist on both planes, just as you do. I have the contacts, the tech base, the resources—everything you'll need. . . . You can call me 'Master.' Everyone does."

"Kiss my ass," Reede said. "You don't tell me what to do. I don't see any Survey meeting here, I don't see any voting quorum. It's just you and me, Jaakola, equal votes."

"There is no need to call a Meeting. This matter was settled among the Brotherhood well before you returned."

"What are you talking about?" Reede snapped. "Mundilfoere would never—"

"You were gone a long time, Reede. Things change—alliances, fortunes, balances of power. And you do not have an equal say in Brotherhood matters. You never did. You weren't Humbaba's possession . . . you were Mundilfoere's."

Reede shook his head, feeling as if he had been expelled into sudden vacuum. "That's a lie."

"Do you actually believe you ever really functioned at the same levels I did? Or even Mundilfoere? Did she actually let you think that? Yes, you were elevated to the inner circles; you were even raised to the tenth level, at Mundilfoere's urging. But you have no idea how many levels there are still above you—or even the slightest idea of what goes on there, far, far over your head. Humbaba was Mundilfoere's tool, she used him well . . . just as she used you."

"Fuck you." Reede tried to push up out of his seat—and could not. He tried again, throwing all his strength against whatever invisible bonds held him there; felt his muscles wrench with the effort, getting nowhere. He fell back again. The pressure eased as he stopped resisting.

"You were always her favorite tool, Reede," Jaakola went on, as if he had noticed nothing. "Her other pet: the clever one, the pretty one . . . She made you herself, Reede—out of stolen pieces. There is no Reede Kullervo. Once there was. But he's gone now. You're not a man, you're a brainwipe: nothing but the biological receptacle for the embers of a great flame. And even that heat is unbearable, it's burning away what's left of your mind. . . ."

"You bastard, damn you—" Reede jerked forward again, into a wall of self-inflicted pain; unable to reach Jaakola, unable even to cover his own ears. Every time he struggled, the invisible bonds tightened.

"You don't believe me—?" the voice said, wounded. "Tell me about yourself. . . . What did you enjoy doing, as a child? What was your family like? Where were you educated? After all, when you came to Humbaba you had knowledge a brilliant master biochemist couldn't have discovered in a lifetime . . . but you were barely seventeen years old. How? How did you do it? Don't you ever even wonder about that?"

"I know who I am!" Reede said hoarsely.

"Then answer the questions. . . ." Jaakola waited, and the silence stretched. Reede's mind echoed with whispers and cries, the stray fragments of a puzzle that had long since been jumbled and thrown away. "Or can't you?" He chuckled, water going down a drain.

"Mundilfoere!" Reede shouted, crying out for her to bridge the pit of bottomless terror that had suddenly opened below him. "I want Mundilfoere here!"

"Of course you do," the Source murmured, "to stroke you and make love to you until you forget, to tell you it doesn't matter, to try to keep you sane until you've served our purpose. You love her more than your own soul, don't you? You should . . . she took your soul away from you."

"She loves me—"

"Yes . . ." Jaakola murmured, "I believe she did. But then, she was a woman—weak, flawed, for all her brilliance. A foolish mistake, to fall in love with her victim . . . an inevitable mistake . . . a fatal mistake. She wouldn't give you to me, even to save herself."

Reede felt his heart stop. "No. You said she wasn't at the citadel—"

"She wasn't." The Source's shapeless bulk shifted. "I said she wasn't there . . . but I didn't say she was still alive."

"I don't believe you." Reede pushed the words out between bloodless lips. Sweat crawled down his cheek, but he couldn't wipe it away.

"Things changed, while you were away—as I said. Power shifted . . . to me. Destiny delivered her into my hands . . . and with her, you. I had waited a long time, for her, for you. She took a very long time to die . . . I saw to it personally."

"I don't believe you," Reede whispered again, shutting his eyes. "It isn't true. Mundilfoere will come for me, she won't let you hold me here. . . ."

"You want Mundilfoere? More than your soul? More than life itself?"

"Yes. *Yes*—" Reede said, grasping at futile hope like a drowning man; not caring what Jaakola wanted in return, willing to give him anything he asked for to make the unbearable untrue. "Anything you want. Anything—"

"Then have her . . ." the Source whispered. "What's left of her."

Reede felt something drop into his lap; something very small. He looked down, blind in the darkness, unable even to move his hands to touch it. He began to tremble helplessly.

A thin beam of brilliant white light lanced out of the darkness in front of him, striking the crotch of his pants, illuminating what lay there. Reede blinked, dazzled by the brightness; forced himself to look down at it, dizzy and sick.

A human thumb. The dried blood crusting it was almost the same darkness as the desiccated skin. And still circling the meaningless stub of flesh and bone was a ring of heavy silver, set with two soliis. The ring he had given to Mundilfoere before he left, a marriage troth.

Reede screamed, a raw soul-deep cry of agony and loss, that went on and on, until at last he had no voice at all left to scream with. And that was when the single beam of light went out.

When there was nothing left in the black silence but the sound of his sobbing, the Source's laughter began.

And when that was finished, the Source said, "I waited a long time for this, too, Reede. To hear you scream like that. You arrogant, strutting piece of garbage, calling yourself the Smith, wearing the genius of the ages in your brain and thinking it was your own. Acting as if you were our equal—*believing* it, when you were nothing but her creature. I only wish that she could have heard you scream . . . that you could have watched me take her apart."

Reede groaned, a mindless, animal noise of grief that echoed in the blackness.

The Source made a low sound of satisfaction. "I knew there was nothing I could do to your body that would hurt you this much, and let you go on living. And you will go on living, Reede. You're my creature now. . . . I have great plans for our symbiosis. You'll breed the stardrive, I'll control its spread, causing the Kharemoughis the most inconvenience possible and bringing the Brotherhood the most influence possible. And when the time is right, you will return with me to Tiamat, and give us the water of life—"

"I'll die first," Reede whispered, his throat, his eyes as dry as dust. "I'll kill myself."

"No . . . I don't think so," the Source murmured. "And you won't break down and go insane either. Do you want to know why? Because already some part of your mind is telling you that if you go on living, you'll find some way to pay me back." He chuckled again, as if he could see every thought in his prisoner's mind. "You'll live a long time trying, Reede. . . . But cheer up. I'll keep you in comfort. You will have everything you need, the best equipment, the best researchers money can buy, plenty of credit to spend as you like—as long as you produce. There's only one thing you had from her that you won't be getting from me . . . unless, of course, you really *want* to share my bed."

Reede's head jerked up, as the Source's obscene laughter ran its fingers over him. He spat, the only form of defiance left to him.

The Source made a wet kissing sound, and laughed again. "I even know the one thing you needed more than *her*. I even have it waiting for you. I believe you call it the 'water of death' . . . ?"

Reede stared, his burning eyes filled with darkness. Something that was not—could not be—relief caught in his chest.

"Oh, yes, Reede . . . I know everything about you now. All your most intimate secrets. You miserable, self-destructive lunatic. You finally found something to do to yourself that frightened even you. . . . And I don't blame you for being afraid. I had the water of death tested on one of my own people. The results were truly unspeakable, simply to witness. I cannot imagine what they must have been like to endure. And incurable—? Oh, you are brilliant. . . ." His voice dripped acid. "You forged your own chains—and now you've handed them to me. You'll have the water of death, Reede; and as long as you are cooperative, you'll have it on time. In fact—" the Source paused, and Reede could feel his smile, feel it like a blade slowly slitting his throat, "I expect you'll be needing a fix soon. That is the real reason you were in such a hurry to get back to Humbaba's, isn't it? Because you'd run short, poor planning, and you were getting desperate. Not even Mundilfoere had that kind of hold on you. . . . You'll find a maintenance dose waiting for you in your new lab. You'll be permitted to make more, as long as you do your work."

Reede said nothing. He swallowed the hard lump of loathing in his throat and took a deep breath, inhaling until his lungs ached.

"Any questions about your new existence?"

Reede said nothing.

"Any last requests?"

"Go to hell," Reede said, his voice breaking.

"Didn't you know—?" the Source murmured gently. "I'm already there, my pet. And so are you." The dull-red glow that revealed nothing, worse than a lie, dropped suddenly, completely, out of Reede's visible spectrum. The darkness around him was utter again, as it had been at the beginning.

Kedalion sighed and shifted position on the couch, glancing at his watch. The couch was not as comfortable as it had looked. He wondered if the perversity was intentional. Or maybe it was just him. *This shouldn't take long,* Reede had said. Reede had been wrong.

Ananke had actually fallen asleep again, curled up with the quoll against his belly. Kedalion envied him his exhaustion. He was tired enough to sleep anywhere, himself . . . except in the middle of an enemy citadel, surrounded by guards. The fact that nobody had been harmed—yet—filled him with relief, but not reassurance. He listened to water dripping like a dirge, somewhere in the garden below the window that might or might not be real: to the distant noises, both strange and familiar, that drifted down the corridors and into the space around him.

The door that had swallowed Reede dematerialized again, abruptly, and someone came through it. The guards turned alert; Kedalion straightened, staring.

At first his eyes refused to believe that it was actually Reede Kullervo they saw. The man who came back through that door wore Reede's face; but the face was ashen-gray, with red-rimmed eyes that registered nothing at all. He moved like a stranger, crippled, broken.

"Reede—?" Kedalion said, keeping his eyes on Kullervo as he reached out to shake Ananke awake. Ananke jerked upright, startled, as Reede stopped moving and turned to look at them. Nothing showed in his eyes except a kind of vacant disbelief. Kedalion was not entirely sure he even recognized them. One fist was clenched tight, as if he held something in it; Kedalion couldn't see what. He had never believed before this moment how young Reede actually was: stripped of his manic arrogance Reede looked like a boy, terrified, terrifying in his vulnerability. Kedalion felt sick to his stomach, wondering who or what had reduced a man like Reede to that, in so little time.

The Newhavener who had brought them all here crossed the room to Reede's side, showing his teeth in a grin as he assessed the obvious damage. "Give me your hand," he said. An order, not a request. Reede obeyed it. The Newhavener's hand closed around Reede's wrist, spread his palm open like a flower. His other hand pressed something down on it, and Kedalion saw a sudden flash of light. A tremor ran through Reede's body, but he made no other response. "Welcome aboard, Kullervo," the Newhavener said, still grinning in cold satisfaction. He turned away from Reede, heading toward the place where Kedalion and Ananke sat waiting. He reached them at the same moment as the smell of burned flesh did. He put out his hand.

Kedalion held up his own hand silently, his jaw clenched; knowing what came next. Most of Humbaba's vassals had worn a brand—although Reede had not, and he had never marked either of his crew as property. Kedalion kept his eyes fixed on Reede, who stood staring at his own branded palm. He told himself fiercely that adoption by the enemy was the best thing that could have happened to them, when he considered the alternatives; kept telling himself that until the iron came down on his own exposed flesh. White-hot pain seared through his hand, went screaming up the nerves of his arm. He cried out, although he had sworn he would not; tried to jerk his hand free, but the Newhavener held it in a grip as inescapable as a vise until he was finished.

He released it, and Kedalion pulled it back, cursing under his breath, dizzy with pain. He forced himself to look at the brand. There was an eye burned into his flesh, staring back at him. He swore again as he recognized the mark. He knew at last whose prisoners they were; and he knew the Source's reputation. He looked away from the livid burn, at Reede again. He looked back as the Newhavener reached Ananke.

Ananke held up his hand, held it steady in the air. His free hand knotted into a fist as the Newhavener spread his palm. He shut his eyes, and bit his lip. The brander came down on him; Kedalion grimaced as he saw the flash of light, saw Ananke shudder and the trickle of bright red that leaked down his lip and chin as the Newhavener let him go again. With his good hand, Kedalion fished a handkerchief out of his pocket, and passed it silently to Ananke. Ananke pressed it to his mouth, covering a crooked grin of desperate pride.

The Newhavener watched them noncommittally, then stepped back, and jerked his head toward the lift. "Come on. I'll show you your quarters." Kedalion hesitated, looked toward Reede; suddenly more afraid for Reede than for himself or Ananke, if they were separated. But the Newhavener moved back to Reede, tried to take him by the arm as if he thought Kullervo was incapable of obeying on his own. "Come on, Reede."

Reede came alive as the Newhavener put a hand on him; caught the man's wrist with his branded hand and pulled it free. The Newhavener stiffened; the anger drained out of his face as he looked into Reede's stare and found no pain registering there.

"Stay away from me," Reede whispered, and for a moment Kedalion saw something he recognized in Reede's expression; something deadly.

The Newhavener backed off with a shrug. "No problem," he muttered, and started toward the lift.

They took another labyrinthine journey through the hive of the citadel. This time the Newhavener took some pains to point out what they were seeing. Kedalion tried to ignore his throbbing hand and concentrate on the view, to get a feel for what he was going to be calling home from now on, whether he liked it or not. But his attention kept flickering back to Reede's vacant face, and every time it did he got queasy again.

At last they reached their destination, deep in the heart of the laboratory complex. The complex covered fifteen stories, the entire south quadrant of the fortress, according to the Newhavener—who had finally told them his name, TerFauw—and it employed close to a thousand workers. By Kedalion's estimate, that made it ten times the size of Humbaba's labs. TerFauw took them up through the general living quarters, pointing out shops and eateries, but they didn't stop until they got to an apartment which seemed to occupy an entire separate level of the complex.

He took them through its rooms, pointing out things with a disinterest Kedalion found remarkable, considering the luxurious elegance of the surroundings. He supposed, a little enviously, that these were Reede's new personal quarters. He tried again to make the relative gentleness of their treatment jibe with whatever had been done to Reede in the three hours that he had been missing. Reede regarded his surroundings with bleak indifference.

"You've got access to your personal laboratories through that door, Kullervo—" TerFauw pointed. "Somebody'll take you the rounds of the whole complex tomorrow. Master's real eager for you to get to work."

Reede turned to look, showing real interest in something for the first time. The door was secured; Kedalion saw the familiar red outline glow of a Kharemoughi stasis lock. "Open it," Reede said.

TerFauw shook his head. "Can't."

Reede turned back to him. "Cancel the fucking lock—"

"Only the Master can do that," TerFauw said. "I can't. You can't. He'll open it when he decides he wants you to have what's in there. . . . It's not up to you, anymore, Kullervo, you understand me?"

Reede glared at him; and then the sudden fury in his eyes turned to ashes, as if TerFauw had said something more than Kedalion had actually heard him say. TerFauw smiled; his twisted lip made a sneer of it. Reede turned his back on them, and went into the next room.

TerFauw turned back to Kedalion and Ananke. Kedalion held his breath, wondering what kind of hellhole TerFauw had in mind to drop them down; sure that they were not going to rate the kind of consideration someone like Reede did. "You two are staying here with him, until we figure out what to do with you."

Kedalion nodded wordlessly, surprised and relieved.

"I'm putting it on you both to watch him till he settles in. He's still a little out of phase right now." The sneer pulled TerFauw's lips up again.

Kedalion glanced at the doorway to the next room, thinking the man had a gift for understatement.

"See that he doesn't do anything to himself." TerFauw met Kedalion's questioning stare. "Anything that happens to him, happens to you. Both of you." He bent his head at Ananke. "I make myself clear?"

"Perfectly," Kedalion muttered. He was suddenly, painfully aware of the throbbing burn on his palm.

TerFauw went out, leaving them alone. Ananke put the quoll on the floor, one-handed, and headed for the bathroom. The quoll snuffled the deep green carpet, decided that it wasn't edible, and began to wander across the floor. It scuttled under a table as Reede came silently back into the room.

Reede's gaze went straight to the locked laboratory door. The seals were still red. He raked the room with his eyes, as if he was reassuring himself that they were finally alone. He sat down on a couch covered with brilliant, flame-patterned cloth, looking like a refugee, saying nothing. Staring at the door. One fist was still clenched over something.

Ananke came back into the room, carrying a can of skingraft in his good hand. "I found this, Kedalion—" he said, and tossed it out.

Kedalion caught it, awkwardly, shook his head as he looked at it. "You put some on already?"

"Yeah."

"Wash it off, or you won't have a scar. The whole point of it is that they want you marked. Unless you want to go through that again—"

Ananke looked sick, and shook his head. He started away down the hall toward the bathroom. "You did good," Kedalion said. Ananke glanced back, and smiled feebly. Kedalion followed him; he took a leak while Ananke gingerly rubbed the bandage off his hand, keeping his eyes averted. Kedalion checked through the supplies in the well-stocked medical cabinet, wondering morbidly if someone had put them there as a precautionary measure, in case Reede tried something drastic. He pushed the thought out of his mind, and took out a tube of ointment. "Here," he said to Ananke. "This'll kill the pain."

Ananke smeared some of it across his palm, wincing; handed the tube back to Kedalion. Kedalion took it with him into the other room, where Reede still sat staring at the door. Kedalion spread ointment on his own palm in full view of Reede, sighed as the pain went out like a smothered fire. Then he approached Reede, offering him the ointment at arm's length. "Boss—?"

Reede looked up at him, down again at his own blistered palm. He closed his fingers over the burn deliberately, and tightened them into a fist. "No," he whispered.

Kedalion moved away from him, swallowing. "Come on," he said quietly to Ananke. "Let's eat." He went into the kitchen, where they could be private enough to talk and still see Reede. Ananke sat on the counter, looking out the doorway, while Kedalion queried the food systems and put in an order.

"What happened, Kedalion?" Ananke said at last. "Gods, I've never seen him like that. What do you think they did to him—?" He touched his own bitten lip, and flinched.

Kedalion shook his head. "I don't know," he murmured, feeling fear knot up his stomach again. "I don't think I want to. But TerFauw's right . . . we've got to watch him like cats."

"He needs more than that," Ananke said, meeting his eyes.

Kedalion nodded, feeling a frown settle between his brows. "I know," he muttered. "I know that. But, damn it, I don't know what to do—" He grimaced, filled with a sense of helplessness as he admitted the truth . . . admitted to himself how much he wanted to help the human shadow huddled on the couch in the next room. The sight of Reede's suffering and vulnerability had gotten to him, in a way Reede's anger and moods never had. It made him feel responsible. He hated the feeling. But he realized, suddenly, that he didn't hate the man. He rubbed his aching eyes, remembering again just how tired he was, how long it had been since he'd had any sleep. He turned back as platters of food appeared on the shelf above him.

Ananke moved them across to the counter and gave Kedalion a hand up onto a stool, before he whistled for the quoll. The quoll came scurrying into the kitchen, greeting Ananke with enthusiastic whistles of its own as he put down its plate of fruit and vegetables. He crouched beside it, stroking its back while it chortled contentedly. Kedalion saw a smile come out on his face.

"Is that thing a male or a female?" Kedalion asked, wondering why it had never occurred to him to ask before.

Ananke straightened up again. He shrugged, stuffing a fishball into his mouth and swallowing it whole. None of them had had a meal in nearly a full day. "Female, I think. It's hard to tell with quolls. They don't look that different." He gulped cold kaff.

"I'm glad I can't say the same thing about humans," Kedalion murmured, thinking with sudden bittersweet yearning how long it had been since he had had an opportunity to really enjoy the difference; wondering when he ever would, now. Ananke gave him a brief stare, folded his arms across the front of his coveralls and looked away as Kedalion raised his eyebrows. "Well," Kedalion said, letting his own gaze drop, watching the quoll eat, "I guess *they* know the difference."

He finished his food, drank down a glass of bitter, double-strength Ondinean tea, hoping it would help keep him awake. "We'd better take turns sleeping. One of us should watch him all the time." He gestured toward Reede.

Ananke nodded. "I'll take the first watch."

"You sure—?" Kedalion asked. "Can you stay awake?"

"Yeah." Ananke shrugged, looked down at his palm. "I don't think I want to go to sleep for a while, you know?" His voice trailed off. He looked at Reede, sitting alone, and his mouth pinched as he picked up the third tray of food.

"Right," Kedalion said. "Wake me up in four hours, then. Sooner, if you get tired." He found his way to one of the bedrooms, dragged himself up onto a bed, and let go. The tea he had drunk was no problem at all.

It felt like he had been asleep for only minutes when he woke up again. Ananke's hand was on his shoulder, shaking him insistently. He looked at his watch, saw that it had been over six hours, and sat up, yawning. "Thanks," he murmured, rubbing his face. "How's he doing?"

Ananke glanced toward the door, his own face tense. "I don't know," he said. "I think something's wrong with him, Kedalion—I mean really wrong. He looks sick." He spread his hands helplessly.

Kedalion slid down off the bed, shook his head to clear it out. "I'll see what I can do. Get some sleep if you can. I'll call you if I need you." Ananke nodded, holding the quoll under one arm. He stared at the bed with mixed emotions. Kedalion went out of the room.

Reede was still on the couch; lying down now, with his knees drawn up and his arms folded tight against his chest. The tray of food sat on the table beside him, untouched. He glanced up, dull-eyed, as Kedalion entered the room; looked back at the laboratory access door again without comment. The locks were still red.

Kedalion looked toward the far wall of the room—transparent ceralloy from ceiling to floor, opening on an uninterrupted expanse of blue sky. A garden with a small waterfall hid the bitter endless gray of the thorn forests from sight. On the other side of the room was a shielded balcony with a spectacular view down the greenery-wall well of a labsec airshaft, onto more greenery in a park space far below. There was a threedy screen and interactive equipment occupying part of a remaining wall, books and tapes. Kedalion wondered why, with all that to occupy his senses, Reede chose to stare at a locked door. He was only sure of one thing—that it wasn't because Reede was eager to get to work.

Reede cursed, so softly that Kedalion barely heard the sound. He turned back, saw a faint spasm run through Reede's body, and his jaw clench. Reede's white face was shining with sweat, even though the room was not warm. Kedalion crossed the space between them, until he reached Reede's side. Reede ignored him.

"Reede," he said. "Tell me what to do. . . ."

Reede's bruised, haunted eyes fixed on him suddenly. "Leave me alone," Reede said, between clenched teeth.

Kedalion nodded mutely, trying to make himself obey and move away. He reached out, touched Reede's shoulder with an uncertain hand.

Reede gasped in startled agony, as if Kedalion had struck him. Kedalion jerked his hand away, backed off as Reede pushed abruptly to his feet. Reede stood swaying, and Kedalion retreated across the room. But Reede only stumbled past him and down the hall. Kedalion heard water running in the bathroom; wasn't certain he heard the sound of someone vomiting. Knowing he should follow Reede and keep watch, he stayed where he was—half afraid of what would happen if he didn't do it, more afraid of what would happen if he did.

After a long time Reede came back into the room, his eyes red and swollen and his nose running, and Kedalion began to breathe again. Reede lowered himself onto the couch, moving as if every cell in his body hurt, and stared at the locked door. Kedalion studied the bookshelves with eyes that refused to read a title; he picked one at random and climbed up into a seat with it. He opened it, and found endless pages of hieroglyphic Sandhi characters, as completely incomprehensible to him as everything else had suddenly become.

He looked up, startled, as a chime sounded somewhere in the room. Reede gave a small, raw cry; staggered up from the couch and crossed the room to the laboratory door. The lock seals were green. He hit the access-plate, swearing with the pain of it, and it let him through into the next room.

Kedalion leaped out of the chair and followed him, as he realized what Reede could find, and do, in a well-stocked lab.

Reede was already at the nearest terminal, voice-querying desperately in some unintelligible language or code. His hands called up displays as if it were something he did in his sleep, moving almost by instinct. Locks unsealed on a series of stasis cubicles; the fields blinked off. He stumbled across the lab, began to peer frantically into one cubicle after another, oblivious to Kedalion's presence. He laughed once, almost hysterically, as he pulled out a container no bigger than his hand. He clawed it open, lifting it to his mouth.

Kedalion swore under his breath. He lunged forward, jerking Reede's arm down. Heavy, gunmetal-colored liquid spilled onto his hand. Reede spun around, faster than he could think, and caught him; Reede's knee slammed into the side of his head, sent him reeling halfway across the room to crash into the metal-drawered base of a work table. Kedalion lay where he had fallen, tasting blood, seeing stars as the astrogation implants in the back of his skull struggled to reintegrate. Paralyzed by pain, he watched Reede gulp down the rest of the silver-gray liquid.

Reede flung the bottle away with trembling hands. Kedalion closed his eyes as Reede looked in his direction suddenly, and started toward him. He felt Reede's hands take hold of his coveralls, jerking him forward through a haze of red, shaking him. "Look at me, you bastard!" Kedalion opened his eyes to Reede's hate-filled stare. "If you ever try to do that to me again, I'll kill you, you motherfucker. I'll break your fucking neck." He caught Kedalion's jaw, jerked it sharply, painfully to one side. "You hear me—? I'll kill you!" He let go. Kedalion fell back against the metal drawers.

Reede turned away from him, swaying suddenly, and staggered back across the open space to the storage shelves. He caught hold of the counter edge, sagged against it, sank to his knees; hanging on, as if his life depended on it. He murmured words in a language that sounded like Sandhi.

Kedalion stayed where he was, dazed and still in too much pain to move. He watched Reede with uncomprehending eyes. *If you ever do that again* . . . How many times could a man poison himself and die? Unless it wasn't poison he'd been after. Not poison, but something he desperately needed . . . In a moment of sudden, sickening insight, Kedalion understood the meaning of everything he had witnessed here today, and more.

Across the room Reede hauled himself to his feet again, shaking his head. He sucked in a deep, ragged breath, looking around him as if he couldn't remember how he had gotten there. He looked down at his hands, one burn-marked, one empty; closed the empty one, opened it again, and swore softly. He got down on his knees, running his hands over the floor, searching for something. He gave a small cry as he found it, and picked it up. He kissed it, sitting on the floor. Bowing his head as he held it against him, he began to rock silently forward and back, like a mourner, his body shaken with hard, uncontrollable spasms.

Kedalion stared, as he realized that Reede was weeping. He watched, completely forgotten, as Reede mourned some incomprehensible loss. At last Reede climbed to his feet again, moving unsteadily past Kedalion to the incinerator chute. He stopped before it, opening his hand; stood looking down at whatever he held there, while tears ran silently down his face.

Kedalion turned, driven by compulsion and pity, pushing himself up until he could see what lay in Reede's hand. What he saw made no sense at all to his eyes: a dark, unidentifiable lump, like a snapped-off piece of stick, circled by a ring of bright metal. *A ring.* Kedalion saw something flash in the light, the eerie brilliance of soliis. *A ring . . . a finger, from a dark-skinned human hand.* Kedalion slid back and down, choking on disgust. He had seen a ring like that before, a ring exactly like that; seen it every single day now for nearly a year. Reede wore it on his own thumb. He was wearing it now. . . . *Mundilfoere.*

He turned back, watching again, hating himself but unable to stop, as Reede gently removed the ring from the severed thumb, his hands trembling so badly that he could barely manage to work it free. He kissed the bloody fragment of his dead wife again, and tossed it into the chute's beam. It went up in flash of light, and was gone.

Reede reached up, caught the chain that held the solii pendant dangling against his chest, and snapped it. The pendant dropped into his branded palm; he looked at it, with the same kind of raw hatred that had been in his eyes when Kedalion had spilled his drugs.

In a fever haze of memory, Kedalion saw that pendant where it lay shimmering in the dust of a Razuma back street, saw it shining at the throats of a group of sudden strangers with his death written in their eyes . . . saw it at Mundilfoere's throat. Mundilfoere, dressed like a man, unveiled, watching as Reede turned those death-filled eyes away from him. . . .

Reede's hand closed over the pendant, his fist jerked with rage or pain as it began an arc toward the incinerator . . . stopped, before the fingers opened, and pulled it back. Slowly, clumsily, he put the pendant onto its chair again; the ring followed, clinking silverly as they met. He knotted the chain around his neck, dry-eyed now.

He lifted his head, and his gaze found Kedalion, still silently witnessing. He came back across the room, moving more steadily, his eyes like a desert. Kedalion tried to get his feet under him; couldn't. Reede bent down beside him and touched his face, looking stupefied. Kedalion saw fresh blood, his own, on Reede's fingertips as they came away again. Reede stared at the blood, almost incredulously, and wiped his hand on his coveralls. He turned away, dropping to his knees, sagging forward, as the fractured glass of his self-control fell apart under the pressure of Kedalion's gaze. He covered his head with his arms. "Oh gods . . . no, no. . . ." The desolation of a man who had been utterly, unspeakably violated laid a blackness between the words as vast as the void between the stars.

Kedalion leaned forward, shaken; his hands made fists as he fought the urge to reach out. "Reede—" he whispered, and broke off, not knowing how to reach a man who had always been impossible to reach, even to touch . . . like quicksilver, shining and deadly. Not knowing how to catch a man who had always walked a frayed tightrope of sanity above a pit of oblivion, now that his line had been cut, and he was falling . . . "Reede," Kedalion spoke his name again, the only word that entered his mind which did not seem as hopelessly inadequate as an obscenity; proving to the man gone fetal beside him on the floor that Reede Kullervo still existed, and was not utterly alone in the hands of his enemies. He repeated the word again, uncertainly.

Reede raised his hand, finally, reluctantly, letting his hands fall away. He stared at Kedalion with nightmare going on and on behind his eyes. But one hand moved, slowly, uncertainly, reaching out.

Kedalion caught it, held on; caught the unexpected weight of Reede's body as the younger man swayed forward and clung to him blindly, like a child. "Reede," Kedalion said again, and, finally, "What happened . . . ?"

Reede pushed away from him, falling back against the side of the table, letting it support him as though he had used up all his strength in the effort of reaching out. "Jaakola . . ." he said, and for a moment the light of coherence began to fade from his eyes. He pressed his hand against his mouth, held it there, finally let it fall to his side again. "Mundilfoere. Killed her, she's dead . . . tortured her to death." He turned his face away, toward the incinerator chute. Kedalion pressed his lips together. Reede stared at him, with his throat working. "And he—he said . . . said . . . I don't know who I am. What I am. I'm just meat. She used me, brainwiped me, put somebody else's mind inside me. . . . I don't understand—!" His fists clenched, his face twisted, spasming. Kedalion waited, until after a time Reede's breathing eased, and he opened his eyes again.

"Who—?" Kedalion murmured.

"Mundilfoere! He said she loved me. . . ." Reede's voice broke. "But I'm just meat."

Kedalion shook his head. "He was lying. He said it to hurt you—"

"No!" The word was a pain cry. "Does your life make sense?"

Kedalion laughed. "Not right now, boss . . ." he said; and regretted it instantly as Reede's eyes darkened with nightmare.

"Do your memories fit together—!" Reede spat out, trembling, "Damn you."

Kedalion offered his hand; Reede's fist closed over it in a deathgrip, holding on. "Yes," he said steadily. "It makes sense. They fit together."

"Mine don't," Reede whispered. "It's like somebody set off a grenade in my brain. Wreckage . . . fragments . . . don't fit together, no way at all. Some of them completely impossible. Working vacuum in deep space, no suit on . . .

worldhopping—worlds that don't exist, on real starships, not coinships. People I don't know, making love to me. . . ." His hand reached up, touching his earcuff. "I had one of these once . . . it let me . . . I'd just *think*, and talk to somebody on another planet, interface like a navigator, access a datanet that makes the sibyl mind seem like . . . like . . ." He tugged on the earcuff, jerked it off, with a curse. "I keep trying to find one like the one I had. . . . I keep thinking if I could just find one like that, I could call them, and they'd come . . . let me out of this flesh prison full of wreckage. . . . But it never works, because it doesn't exist yet, or anymore. . . ." He lifted his hands, staring at them as if they belonged to a stranger. "Ilmarinen—!"

Kedalion bit his tongue, and said nothing.

"It's real!" Reede caught the look that registered on his face; Reede's hand caught him by the front of his coveralls, shook him, shoved him away. "I'm not crazy, I'm not! I'm a fucking genius; how else could I know what I know? I never finished school! Who am I really? What am I—? I tried—tried to ask her . . . but I couldn't remember the questions. I'd get crazy because I was so afraid. . . . And *forget . . . forget*, she told me. She'd put her mouth on mine . . . put her hands on me like that, like that . . . oh gods . . ." His own hands slid down his body, clenched on his coveralls. His head fell forward. "And I'd always forget. . . . Because I was just meat."

"Reede," Kedalion said softly. "You're a man. She loved *you*."

Reede opened his eyes, looked up again, almost sane.

"She loved you," Kedalion repeated.

"But she's dead . . ." Reede said thickly.

Kedalion nodded, looking down.

Reede looked at his branded palm, the eye staring back at him. "He's probably listening to us right now, that—" He broke off, and spat, as if he couldn't find words ugly enough, filled with enough hatred and pain. "Watching me howl, watching me bleed. Jerking my chain—" He ran unsteady hands through his sweat-soaked hair, looking toward the cubicles where he had found the drug. "He told me . . . said I won't kill myself. Won't go crazy. Just go on, holding the pieces together, doing anything he wants . . . because I figure if I live long enough, I'll find a way to get back at him. . . . He doesn't think it'll happen." Reede lifted his head. "It'll happen!" he shouted. "You're my meat, you rotting piece of crud." His hand closed over the ring, the medal, dangling against his heart. His voice dropped to a whisper. "If you're not dead meat now, you will be. I swear it." The man Kedalion knew was looking out of Reede's eyes again, hungry, deadly, and perfectly rational.

"What does he want from you?" Kedalion asked. "The stardrive?"

Reede's mouth twisted. "Oh yeah . . . for a start. Got the plasma already, probably got your ship and the drive unit, too. Wants me to breed plasma so he can sell it. Shit work. That's not my big job. . . . He says when the time's right we're going to Tiamat—"

"Tiamat?" Kedalion said blankly. Realization caught him. "The water of life."

Reede nodded. "Tiamat," he whispered. "The water of life . . ." His gaze faded, as his mind went somewhere else; as if it couldn't help itself, drawn compulsively to the challenge of making the impossible real.

"Can you—?" Kedalion asked.

Reede blinked at him. His eyes filled with fleeting panic, sudden pain, as he remembered where he was again. He held his breath; let it out in a ragged sigh. "We'll see," he said, and shrugged. His hand came up, touching Kedalion's bruised face gently, as he had touched it before. "I hurt you bad—?"

Kedalion thought about it, shook his head. "I've had worse."

Reede pushed to his feet, moving gracefully again. He offered his hand to help Kedalion up. "Niburu," he muttered, looking away. "You know now. Don't ever fuck with me like that again. I will kill you."

Kedalion nodded slowly. "What's the drug?" he asked.

"Don't ask," Reede said. "There's no point." He rubbed his face. "I want to sleep. Got a lot of work to do, tomorrow." His voice turned bitter. "Got a lot of answers to find, before I die. . . ." They started back toward the open door.

Reede stopped abruptly, as they crossed the threshold; caught Kedalion's wrist, turning up his palm. He looked at the eye; met Kedalion's gaze again. "You always hated this job," he muttered. "Why didn't you quit me, years ago, while you had the chance?"

"You wouldn't let me," Kedalion said, looking pointedly at Reede's hand trapping his own.

Reede laughed, and let him go. "You could've quit," he murmured. "I never marked you as property, like this. If you'd hated me enough, you would have gone anyway." He looked curious. "You've had reason enough to hate me, considering all I've done to you. Why didn't you leave?"

Kedalion touched his palm, winced. *Property.* "I don't know, boss." He looked up again, into Reede's dark curiosity. "Maybe because in all the times you swore at me, and even knocked me around, you never once insulted me about my height."

KHAREMOUGH: Pernatte Estate

Gundhalinu stood in the drape-lined alcove of the guest room, dwarfed by the expanse of the windows, which were half again his own height; enjoying the momentary solitude and peace, the momentary lack of motion. It struck him that lately he always seemed to find himself looking out of windows. He wondered just what it was he was looking for.

He told himself it was only the view: The view from the Pernatte manor house was certainly one worth looking at. He watched the setting sun inscribe a trail of molten light on the distant surface of the sea, as if in invitation. . . . He thought suddenly of Fire Lake.

He forced the image from his mind. He was done with Fire Lake. World's End was becoming only an unpleasant memory, for him, for the people of Number Four. His act of desperation when he had flung the stardrive vaccine into the Lake had actually done what he had prayed it would do: It had started a chain reaction that was gradually bringing the Lake under control, and with it the nightmare phenomena of World's End. The Hegemony would have sufficient stardrive plasma to keep it in hyperlight technology from now until eternity, if they used it wisely . . . in spite of Reede Kullervo, and the Brotherhood.

The knowledge of that success had helped him recover from the psychological blow of what Kullervo had done, and been . . . from his anger at his own blindness in ever trusting a stranger, not recognizing that Reede Kullervo was an emotionally unstable killer—and, as he had discovered later, a member of the Brotherhood. Kullervo had not only succeeded in getting a breeding sample of the plasma for the Brotherhood, but the actual, functioning stardrive unit as well.

But even though Kullervo had betrayed him, the Brotherhood had not kept the Golden Mean and the other true representatives of Survey from controlling the major supply of stardrive plasma . . . and they had not killed the only man who really understood everything that Kullervo had done as well as Kullervo himself did.

Gundhalinu had wondered ever since that day why Kullervo had not killed him . . . almost as often as he had wondered whether he would ever have found the answer to controlling the plasma without Kullervo's help. At least in time he had been able to acknowledge that it had been the brilliance of Kullervo's mind that had blinded him to what Kullervo really was. Kullervo's genius had made it impossible to see beyond their potential for actually achieving the goal they both wanted so much, for their separate reasons . . . see beyond the opportunity to watch that genius at work, to work with it, to share in that pure, exalted state of conscious discovery and creation. And in the end, in spite of Kullervo's treachery—because of it, really—he was more of a public hero now than he had been before.

The irony was not lost on him, any more than the mystery of why Kullervo had let him survive, with all he knew. He had all the data that his contacts in Survey had been able to give him about Kullervo's origins—and they did not add up to a logical sum. Kullervo was the man known as the Smith to the inner circles of Survey. Beyond those circles he was only a paranoid rumor, a dark legend in Police halls—fittingly, since he had probably the most brilliant mind since the legendary Vanamoinen. *They call me the new Vanamoinen,* he had said once himself. But according to the available data, he had virtually no formal education. He had begun as a low-order Brotherhood member, and was wanted by the authorities on Samathe for murdering his own father. Supposedly his raw genius was so great that he had risen through Brotherhood circles to a position of key importance, even though he was barely beyond his teens. Gundhalinu didn't believe it. Elements were missing from the equation; had to be. He had sent out more queries, hoping that somewhere he would ask someone the right questions, and be given the answers he needed.

Kullervo had disappeared from Number Four without a trace, although the Four government had been alerted and searching for him. The official account claimed that Kullervo had been killed by the treacherous phenomena of World's End. But the same private sources that had told him—too late—of Kullervo's real associations, had informed him that Kullervo's ship had disappeared from orbit at virtually the same time that he and Kullervo had had their final confrontation. He could only believe that Kullervo's wild genius had found a way out of the trap, a way to force the stardrive to make that infinitesimal blip out into orbit. And that meant the Brotherhood certainly had possession of the stardrive plasma, and a drive unit they could duplicate, as well. He knew that with Reede Kullervo overseeing their program, that would take them no time at all.

Which meant that from the moment BZ Gundhalinu returned to Kharemough, bringing his own specimen of the stardrive plasma with him, he was a prisoner to duty once again. He had been back in Kharemough space for nearly a year, but this was the first time he had actually set foot on his homeworld.

All the meaningful industrial activity that Kharemough carried on was done in its cislunar space, or on the surface of its two moons. He could already see spectral colors painting the Kharemough night, as the sky began to darken. When he was a child, he had thought the colors were beautiful. But as soon as he was old enough to grasp the concept, he had been informed that they were caused by industrial pollutants. It was the price Kharemough paid for its supremacy in the Hegemony, he had been told, as if that were a sacrifice to take pride in. But it had ruined the beauty of the sky for him. He was never able to see its colors the same way again. That had been the first step, he supposed, on his journey to disillusionment.

But still, it felt good, so much better than he could ever have imagined, to be back on the world where he had been born . . . welcomed back into the smaller but equally familiar world of the social class he had been born into. After his disgrace and his suicide attempt on Tiamat, he had thought he would never see this world again, let alone feel welcome in it. But here he was, the Honorable Commander Gundhalinu-eshkrad-ken, Technician of the Second Rank, Hero of the Hegemony, and so on and so on and so on.

All that he had learned, about himself and his place in the universe, during his time away from Kharemough had made him doubt that he would ever want to be a part of Technician society again—of its hypocrisy, its rigidity, its prejudices and injustices. And yet, when he stood in this room, breathing in its rich odor of history, letting the exquisite harmonies of an artsong by Lantheile infuse his senses with the same restrained passion that the artist himself must have felt, as he touched the complex filaments of a saridie . . .

Gundhalinu touched a curtain, let his callused hand slide down along the silken sensuality of cloth which was at once as cool as water and as soft as the skin of a child. He sighed, and looked at his hands. He had never had a callus, in all his years on Kharemough. Stiff muscles and work-hardened hands were for the lower classes, for Nontechs and Unclassifieds, not for the Technician elite, who used their superior minds to guide the Hegemony into an ever more brilliant future. He wondered what would happen now that the real future had caught up with Kharemough the way it had already caught up with him. He suspected that Kharemough's sociopolitical balance, and the Hegemony's, were as fragile as his own emotional balance had been before he encountered the stardrive plasma.

His work with the plasma and the drive unit itself had given him a clue to how very little Kharemough actually knew about real technology, as the Old Empire had practiced it. They prided themselves on their technological superiority, but in fact they were priding themselves on living in the past, within a system that had grown too comfortable, too closed, too smug. The plans for countless innovations still existed in the sibyl databanks, but without the stardrive as a catalyst, no one seemed to have seen any point in pursuing them, because the system worked well enough, and the people in power came to believe they had the best of all worlds possible, given their limited access to the stars. "Come the Millennium" they would say—meaning "come the stardrive." Well, it had come, and the gods only knew what the changes would mean, to everyone involved. The Old Empire had made the Hegemony look like what it actually was—a petty feudal trade network. But the Old Empire had had its own problems; and those problems had proved fatal. . . .

The uncertainty of the future he saw had made him long to be in places like this room, with its sense of permanence and tradition and perfect peace. This room touched his memory, and fulfilled a need in him, in ways he had not experienced in nearly half his lifetime.

But since his return he had spent every single moment of his time up in space, involving himself in every aspect of the new stardrive technology that he had been able to insinuate his presence into—and the leverage his new prestige and his Survey contacts gave him was profound.

Because his Survey-guided sibyl Transfer had informed the leaders on Kharemough about his discovery, they had begun the work of planning and constructing ships that could utilize the new technology, as well as ways of converting the thousands of existing ships to the new drives, before he even arrived. And they had begun work too on the kinds of advanced weaponry that they had formulated plans for, but found small use for, when their only realistic means of control over the other worlds of the Hegemony was economic.

As a result, when he returned home he had been both relieved and disturbed to discover that the new drive units and the fleet already under construction were riddled with errors in design and function. He had seen an actual stardrive unit, had worked with the plasma, and knew things no one on Kharemough could have known. But with their access to the sibyl net, the engineers and researchers should have had flawless design data available to them. The sibyl machinery had shown signs of deterioration over time—hardly surprising, in such an ancient system—but he had been stunned to find error after error in the data he had been shown by the research teams.

The possibility of a major breakdown in the informational system upon which the entire Hegemony depended was almost entirely off his scale of disaster. He had seen the looks in the eyes of the people around him as they discussed the possibility, and told himself fiercely that the sibyl net, at least, was not his responsibility. He was here to build starships, and errors in data were things that could be corrected. The potential problems with the sibyl net only meant that they must make progress with all possible speed, in case a system-wide failure actually was coming. And in trying to bring home that point to the researchers and engineers, he slowly came to realize how the problems with sibyl-net data had become a source of excuses for inefficiency, bureaucratic mishandling, and a lack of rigor.

He had come home to this, hardly expecting to find such problems among his own people. The truth had struck him with the impact of a stasis field. But his hard-earned new perspective had let him look at the technocracy's way of doing things with an outsider's eye, and a stasis field was as good an analogy as any for what was wrong.

He admitted to himself alone the mixed emotions that knowledge had created in him: disillusionment and regret, when he thought of his people, his world's heritage, his own pride . . . frustration, and relief, when he thought of Moon Dawntreader and Tiamat. Every year of delay that kept the Hegemony away from Tiamat gave her more time to do the work she was destined to do. Sometimes he had to fight down his own urge to delay the process he had begun; half believing that that was the way he could best serve the symbol they both wore.

But then he would force himself to remember her face—remember her ghost reaching out to him at Fire Lake, hazed in blue. A memory of the future, a promise of a moment they both had yet to live . . . the words *I need you.* And the realization that every day he was growing older, and she was . . . that nearly nine years had passed for him since they had parted, and sixteen for her, on Tiamat. He could not believe that it had been so long; the years seemed somehow to have dissolved, like the snows of Tiamat melting in the spring. He had not seen her face in all that time, except on a specter. He had spoken to her only twice, and only in Transfer; the first time half-mad with Fire Lake's delirium, the second using Hahn as a medium simply to let her know that he had survived. Sometimes he wondered whether he was deluding himself, clinging to a dream of a love that had no right to exist, that had never existed in the first place. And yet his memories of his time with her—that extraordinary space outside of time, when he had been more alive, more real, than at any moment in his life before or since—were still as vivid as his face in the mirror: his face, which every year showed him new lines at the corners of his eyes that had not been there nine years ago. . . .

And then frustration would drive out longing, goad him to more endless hours of work, of supervision and argument and adjustment. He worked now not only with the top researchers in the habitats, but with the practical engineers and construction hands out in the shipyards. He had come to see that he had as much in common with them now as he did with his own class, and often better rapport. Earning their trust and loyalty had doubled the measurable results his polite suggestions and solicitous modifications of data had won him among the Technicians who oversaw their work.

But his casual fraternizing with the lower classes had caused friction and unease in some quarters, particularly political ones. He was all too aware that he could not afford to offend his peers, particularly considering his clouded background, which was never entirely forgotten even if it was politely unmentionable among the highborns who held the power on Kharemough. He wanted to get back to Tiamat as soon as possible—because that was when the elite wanted to get there, to get at the water of life again. And he not only wanted to get there first, he wanted to get there controlling enough political power of his own to have some effect on what they would try to do to that world, to its people . . . to its Queen. Enough power to help her stop the exploitation. Because if he couldn't, then he would have worked all his life only to betray her . . .

He turned away from the windows, from the dim points of the stars beginning to prick through the light veils on the darkening sky. He would not see Tiamat's twin suns among them even if he tried—they were too enormously distant, at the other end of one of the random spacetime wormholes that joined the Black Gates. The Hegemony was in a sense an empire of time more than space—of worlds that could be reached within a reasonable journey-time, due to the Gates, but which had no meaningful relationship to one another in physical space. But all that was about to change, too.

And he had better change his clothes, he thought wearily, before the party beyond this room's flawless silverwood double doors became a memory, and BZ Gundhalinu, the guest of honor, missed it entirely. He was here to mend offenses, to charm and disarm, ingratiate and manipulate to the best of his ability—and thanks to his years of bureaucratic gymnastics on Four, his ability was now considerable. He knew the social codes, he knew what would flatter whom; and now that the new starships were making more satisfactory progress, his political progress would be measured only by his ability to stomach rich food and his own hypocrisy. This was the first of a number of intimate and large gatherings here on the planet—where most of the wealthy elite still kept homes—as well as up in the orbiting habitats. He was using both his network of old family ties, most of whom were now almost painfully eager to renew his acquaintance, and his network of new Survey contacts to set them up. This was only the beginning. . . .

Which was probably why he found it so hard to overcome his own inertia and move, to cross the room toward the private bath where a solicitous house system had left him a fresh uniform encrusted with all the appropriate honors, insignia, medals, orders, ranks and degrees, including his family crest, which he had not seen since he left home. Technically speaking, he had no right to wear it tonight, since he was not the eldest sibling of his generation. But the most rigid Technicians—the ones he most needed to make a good impression on—put breeding above everything, and this would at least remind them that his lineage was above reproach.

If it was a long time since he had seen that crest, it was equally long since he had been waited on by servants, electronic or otherwise, and Pernatte's estate had one of the most sophisticated household systems he had had the pleasure of experiencing. Even so, after all this time of fending for himself, it made him uncomfortable, at first; but he reminded himself that this was, after all, only a series of servomechs, sophisticated programming. The highest and lowest classes on Kharemough were not even permitted to speak to one another without a formal interpreter; the highborns got around the servant problem by building their own. These were not his fellow human beings treating him as if he were a god—or staring with any interest whatsoever at his bloodshot eyes and unsightly stubble of beard, at the state of his disheveled hair and rumpled worker's coveralls.

He unsealed his coveralls with one hand, scratching his side, wrinkling his nose. He began to move more eagerly toward the bath that was waiting for him in the next room, which he knew would be exactly the temperature and consistency he wanted. The scent of steaming herbs would clear out his head, the massage jets would know just where and how to touch his aching-muscled, travel-weary body to leave him relaxed and energized. . . .

Across the room, the silverwood doors opened suddenly, briefly, letting in a rush of bright noise.

Gundhalinu turned, startled. Someone had closed the doors again, with unseemly haste. And he was no longer alone. The intruder was standing across the room, staring back at him. The glowspot pasted to the palm of her uplifted hand abruptly illuminated the space that had grown almost dark around him without his really noticing it—illuminated the face of the stranger who now shared it with him.

"Oh—" She stared back at him, a momentary reaction of startled dismay fading as she took in the details of his appearance. Her gaze was level and almost painfully open, but there was no recognition in it. He did not know who she was, either. Her features were more striking than classical, but he saw strength and humor there, and intelligence, and unexpected beauty. He broke the gaze of her golden-brown eyes, which seemed to find him so transparent; took in the headdress of pearls that framed her face in luminous strands shifting gently with her motion. She wore a long gown of night-black velvet, its high neckline a collar of pearls, the pearls flowing into the blackness like stars expanding though space until they were lost in night.

"You aren't supposed to be here," she said, with such calm conviction that for a moment he found himself wondering if it was true.

"Why not?" he asked, disconcerted and amused. He was glad that she had not caught him handling the very expensive and very old piece of sculpture he had been admiring earlier; she would have had him feeling like a thief.

"Because I'm not, either." She smiled suddenly, her eyes shining with conspiratorial excitement. "I need a place to be unobtrusive, until enough guests arrive so that I can lose myself among them. You won't give me away, will you—?" It almost wasn't a question; as if she had made some judgment about him on sight.

"Should I?" he asked, uncertainly. He bent his head, inviting her with the gesture to explain.

"I'm quite harmless," she answered, her smile filling with gentle irony. "Truly. I'm only here because I wanted so badly to meet the famous hero Commander Gundhalinu."

Gundhalinu stopped the sudden laugh of disbelief that almost got away from him, keeping his expression neutral. If she was playing a game, it wasn't with him; he was sure that she did not recognize him. "Well," he said, mildly, almost surprised at himself, "you'll have some time to kill until then. Would you like a drink?" He gestured at the clean-lined cabinet beside him; he had been informed that it contained a fully stocked bar.

"Will you join me?" Her smile made him smile with a sense of shared truancy. He nodded. "Something innocuous please," she said. "My senses are quite overstimulated as it is."

Gundhalinu touched the spot on the seemingly solid surface of the tabletop that had been indicated to him earlier. The smooth grain of the wood vanished under his touch as the bar obediently listed its contents for his consideration. "Do you prefer to drink, inhale, or absorb?" The Pernattes had an impressive assortment of mind-altering substances available, all of them perfectly legal.

"To drink, I think." There was laughter in her voice as she crossed the room toward him. "The act is not too active that way, and not too passive."

"Good point." He glanced up at her. "They have the water of life—?"

He saw her face register the same play of emotions that had filled his mind: *Not the real thing . . .* but even the imitation was rare enough. "Oh, yes," she murmured. "Yes."

He spoke an order, looking at her where she stood leaning casually against the cabinet beside him. She smelled of something exotic and heady; he realized that he probably stank of sweat. But she smiled that strangely appealing smile at him, meeting his gaze with unnerving directness. He glanced down, lifting his hand to meet her proffered one in a polite greeting. "How do you do?"

She touched his palm almost playfully with her own glowlit hand. Light and shadows danced as the glowspot flickered. But as he would have let his hand drop she took it in both of hers, keeping it there as she turned it over; illuminating it, running her fingers unselfconsciously across his palm, like a blind woman trying to see. The touch against the sensitive skin made him shiver. "You have calluses. Hands were made to *do* things. I like real hands." She turned his hand over, studying its shape, the length and form of his fingers. "You have beautiful hands."

He took his hand from hers as the drinks appeared, surprised and slightly embarrassed, relieved to have an excuse to free himself. He offered her a goblet grown of synthetic sapphire, with the heavy silver liquid lying restlessly in its convolutions. She took it as he lifted his own in acknowledgment.

"To adventures," she said, with a sudden, glinting grin. The light in her palm shone through the goblet in her hand, illuminating it like some uncanny magic.

"No," he said softly, and shook his head. "Adventures are only tragedies that didn't happen."

She glanced down, considering. "Then to life—" she said, looking at him again.

He nodded. "To life." He sipped the silver liquid they called the water of life, feeling it fill his head with the bittersweet taste of memories. The last time he had drunk it he had been hardly more than a boy, still living in his father's house, on the ancestral estates. . . . He remembered his home, the beauty and peace of the land, his father's voice. He took another sip, and remembered the future—remembering Tiamat, the source of the genuine water of life, and suddenly, vividly, Moon, her face as pale as the endless fields of snow, her body warm with life against his own. . . . He took another sip, and forced his mind back into the present, forced his eyes to register the astonished pleasure on the face of the elegant stranger standing beside him now.

She sighed. "Oh, this is well-named."

He smiled, and nodded again. They shared a space of silence, savoring the guilty pleasure of each other's company. At last, moved by his own curiosity, he asked, "You truly weren't invited to this party?" He could see nothing about her that would make her an unwelcome guest. He thought, rather surprised at himself, that if anyone consulted him right now, he would put her high on the list of people he would like to share the evening with. He blinked, forcing his eyes away from her face.

"No." She lifted her head, the pearls whispering against her neck. "I was specifically excluded."

He opened his mouth, about to ask the obvious question, when there was a knock at the silverwood doors. She turned, startled, her face betraying barely controlled panic.

Gundhalinu gestured her to silence, urging her aside as he moved toward the doors.

The doors swung inward before he could even reach them. He stopped, blinking, caught like a moth in the flood of light and noise. He stole a quick, cautioning glance at the dark angle behind the left-hand door, which now concealed the uninvited guest from view. She had closed her hand, stopping the light from the glowspot.

"Excuse me, sir—" The new intruder wore the formal clothing of a party guest, but Gundhalinu recognized the discreetly disguised communicator worn by house security personnel. She shifted slightly, trying to see past him into the dim-lit corners of the room.

"What is it?" he asked, his awkward discomfort sounding to his own ears like impatience.

"I'm sorry to disturb you, sir," she said, "but I had a message that an unauthorized visitor had come into this room."

"Not while I've been here," he said, amazed at how easily the lie came out. "I've been trying to catch a few minutes of rest—" He nodded at the darkened space behind him in explanation.

"No one at all has been here?" She gave him the kind of look that he had once given to suspected conspirators.

"Someone did stop in for a moment to ask whether I needed anything." He shrugged, all too casually. "Perhaps that was what it was."

She nodded, looking relieved. "And do you need anything, sir—?"

"Only to be allowed to clean myself up and change in peace," he said.

"Of course, sir." She nodded again, chastened. "I'll see that you aren't disturbed." She backed out of his presence, closing the doors after her.

Gundhalinu sighed, feeling giddy, as the woman in black stepped out of the shadows and opened her palm, releasing light into the space around them again.

"Thank you." She smiled, bowing her head in gratitude, pearls whispering against her neck.

Gundhalinu opened his mouth to call on the room lights; hesitated, suddenly realizing that he preferred the shadows, the subtle mystery of this shared conspiracy. "Tell me," he said, "what made you so certain that you could trust me?" He had thought for a moment that she had seen his sibyl trefoil; but it was inside his clothes, and he doubted that she could see the tattoo on his throat in this dim light.

"You have clear, deep eyes," she said softly. "When you looked at me, I saw that you have an old soul."

He almost laughed, taking it for fatuous nonsense, until he heard what she was really saying—paying a tribute to the ancestors he had been taught in youth to venerate, and emulate. He had never heard it put that way before. Instead of laughing, he smiled.

"And so I sensed that you would be an honorable man."

It struck him as ironic that she considered it honorable to help a total stranger crash an exclusive party. He said, "I've never done this kind of thing before." And yet he had, he suddenly realized. On Tiamat. But this time the results of his impulsiveness would hardly change the course of a world. Or even his life.

She bent her head, pearls whispering. "Then tell me why you trusted me."

"I don't think I can." He glanced away, suddenly reluctant even to try putting it into words.

"Perhaps because you sensed that what I wished to do was, in truth, honorable."

"Perhaps," he murmured, looking back at her. "You know, you needn't be here under false pretenses. I can speak to someone. . . ." No one had consulted him about the guest list—assuming, he supposed, that he had more important things on his mind, which was true.

But she hesitated. "You're Technician, aren't you?"

He nodded, thinking that she seemed surprised. But then, he hardly looked the part, the way he was dressed. Perhaps she had taken him for some hired worker.

"Do you know Commander Gundhalinu personally?"

"Yes," he said, not sure why he didn't simply tell her the truth. But then, he was not quite sure of anything just now, except that he was enjoying this game far too much. "Since childhood."

"Then, no thank you. It wouldn't be fair to compromise you with such an old friend."

"It will hardly—" He broke off, as he remembered what she had been saying when they were interrupted. "Did you tell me that you were specifically excluded from attending this party?"

"Yes," she said, less certainly than she had said anything since they met; as if she were regretting the confession now. She glanced away. "At his own order, I expect."

"Really?" Gundhalinu said incredulously. "Does he know you, then?"

"No." She looked back at him and there was sudden anger in her eyes. "He does not. Nor does he wish to, obviously."

Gundhalinu blinked, wondering what odd quirk of social scandal he was inadvertently taking the blame for. He thought of his brothers, wondered suddenly whether she had had some unpleasant dealing with them. It would be like them to blame him for it. "Well . . ." he said self-consciously, "he's been away, you know, for some years. He's changed a great deal. . . ." He smiled earnestly. "He used to be an insufferable little snot, I have to admit, but he's become almost human, actually. If there's been some misunderstanding, he'll want to put it right. What was the problem—?"

She shook her head; the fall of pearls rustled with her refusal. She looked away from him again. "It's nothing that should concern you . . . and I don't want to talk about it. Besides, I don't want that to be what you remember me by." She smiled, a little sadly this time.

He sighed, and nodded in resignation. "Then, if you'll excuse me, I have to change my clothes or they'll be evicting me instead." He gestured ruefully at his filthy coveralls, and toward the lighted doorway of the suite's bath and dressing rooms. "Stay as long as you like, until you feel comfortable about joining the party."

"Thank you." Her smile widened. She put out her hand suddenly, as he began to turn away. "Who are you—?"

He shook his head. "No names. That would spoil it. The next time you see me, ask me again."

Her mouth opened, and closed. Her smile turned ironic as she acknowledged his request, realizing that he had bested her at her own game.

He went on into the next room, carrying the half-empty goblet of liquor with him, not letting himself glance back. He locked the door behind him. He bathed and changed into his formal clothing, completing his transformation into a shining shadow of himself. He finished the water of life in the sapphire goblet slowly, savoring it, fortifying himself for the ordeal to come. And then he left the suite by a different door, without looking in to see whether his mystery guest was still waiting.

He stepped out into the bright splendor of the Pernattes' manor house, entering a shifting sea of bodies; colors swirled like oil on water, music and the sound of voices filled his senses. He stopped moving as the door closed behind him, trying to remain unobserved for long enough to orient himself, waiting for the surge of adrenaline he needed to face the crowd. He had never been naturally outgoing, and he realized by now that he never would be, no matter how many parties he attended, or how many speeches he made. Entering a crowded room would always be like walking head on into a closed door.

"Commander!"

He looked up as NR Vhanu, his chief aide, materialized out of the crowd beside him. "Vhanu," he said, smiling in relief as he returned a salute. Vhanu had been his liaison while this affair was being planned, and, he trusted, knew everything about it that he did not.

"There you are, sir—" Vhanu brightened, and a certain amount of relief showed on his own face. "I was beginning to wonder if you were all right."

Gundhalinu glanced at him, mildly annoyed, but could detect only eagerness and concern in the younger man's expression. "Worry about me when I seem to be enjoying one of these affairs too much," he said.

Vhanu looked at him, his incomprehension barely concealed. "But sir, I thought you wanted this party. The honor that is being paid to your family tonight— deservedly, of course . . . that is, this is probably the social and political event of the decade. I've never seen such a gathering anywhere but at a visit by the Assembly. . . . Have you met with the Assembly, sir?"

"Yes, I have," Gundhalinu said, and didn't say anything more. He had met with the Assembly, while he was serving on Tiamat. And they had all but spat in his face, calling him *coward, failed suicide.* Just as anyone in this room would have done, had they been there. He had believed, in that terrible moment, that his life was over. And yet here he was, a Hero of the Hegemony. If any of these people knew of his former disgrace, he doubted they would ever have the nerve to refer to it now. . . . He took a deep breath, as he realized that his chest ached.

He looked back at Vhanu, who was gazing out across the crowd again, probably tallying famous faces, with a look that was at once complacent, slightly dazzled, and completely unselfaware. . . . It reminded Gundhalinu of himself, ten years ago. Like himself, Vhanu had as honorable a family history as anyone in the room—he was the younger brother of JM Vhanu, an old school friend who was now a respected researcher at the Rislanne. And like himself, Vhanu had chosen a career in the Hegemonic Police—a common profession for a younger son forced out into the world by the rigid Kharemoughi inheritance laws, which gave family title and any wealth to the eldest child.

He had encountered Vhanu on his return—remembering him (although he had not admitted it) only as a small, shrill, rather obnoxious presence on the perimeter of numerous earnest discussions about datamodeling, conduit physics, and the Meaning of Life. But the Vhanu he had found on his return was a responsible career officer, already a Captain, capable, likable, and politically aware, if somewhat conservative and status-conscious. But then, Gundhalinu had discovered to his regret that most Kharemoughis of his social rank now struck him as conservative and status-conscious. At least, with everything else, he had gained the perspective to realize that it was he who had changed, and not his world. He had first met Vhanu in the relatively egalitarian setting of a Survey Meeting Hall, and they had hit it off. He had needed assistants he could rely on, and Vhanu had quickly made himself indispensable.

"Sir, there are the Pernattes. Let me introduce you to them first."

He nodded, and let himself be guided with faultless grace through the murmuring curiosity of the crowd, on into the next room.

This room was even larger than the last, with the same severe, almost monolithic grace. The walls were of unadorned gnarlstone, polished to a glassy sheen. Gnarlstone was another legacy of the Old Empire; they had found its strange, fractal-patterned strata all over the planet. Gnarlstone was dead smartmatter sediment, lithified by the volcanic heat of its own catacylsmic failure. The most prized varieties contained lacy deposits of calcium, from human remains. The burl-like complexity of the matrix reminded him of the beach at Fire Lake. He looked away from it.

"Sir—" Vhanu touched his arm, catching his attention.

He turned, and saw the Pernattes progressing toward him, saw guests stepping aside discreetly to let them pass. He recognized them both easily: AT Pernatte had been prominent in Kharemoughi politics for as long as he could remember; he had seen the man's long, slightly morose face on the threedy, and occasionally at parties before he had left Kharemough—though only from a distance. Pernatte had aged imperceptibly in the sixteen realtime years that Gundhalinu had been away from Kharemough—just as Pernatte had seemed never to age at all before, or his wife either. Their marriage had combined two of the wealthiest and most influential Technician lineages on the planet.

Gundhalinu had dealt more directly with Pernatte's wife, though not in the flesh—CMP Jarsakh held the controlling interest in the shipyards which were endeavoring to build the new faster-than-light fleet. She was looking back at him now, showing the recognition her husband lacked. It was widely, if privately, held that she was the mind behind the ever-growing success of their already vast mutual holdings, that she put into Pernatte's mouth the words that he spoke before the Council. Having dealt with her himself, Gundhalinu could see where there might be truth in it. His experience with his own brothers had made him painfully aware that being the firstborn child of a Technician family did not necessarily confer intelligence along with inheritance; but he would not make the mistake of underestimating either of the Pernattes.

He gathered himself to make the expected bow as the couple stopped before him and Vhanu began to formally present them. Vhanu was a relative of the Jarsakhs, not close, but not too distant to use the familiar form of address or to speak with them easily and comfortably.

Gundhalinu caught himself just in time, as the Pernattes bowed first to him, extending him the greater honor. He returned the bow, and touched each proffered palm.

"A great honor, Gundhalinu-eshkrad," Pernatte murmured.

"The honor is mine, Pernatte-sadhu," Gundhalinu answered, more sincerely than he had said anything in public in a long time. He was secretly pleased that of all the assorted titles he now bore, Pernatte had chosen the one which marked him as a scientist. He sometimes found himself groping among the complexities of honorary titles in Sandhi for the correct forms of address for his peers, after having spoken nothing but foreign languages for so long; just as he had almost forgotten the use of the personal *thou,* after so long among strangers. But then, he had not used *thou* with anyone since he had returned, either. Most of his old school friends were scattered among the stars; the few he might hope to see tonight he probably would not even recognize.

"You look splendid in your rightful uniform, Commander," Jarsakh said, looking him up and down, her eyes assessing his assortment of honors, medals, and crests with an almost predatory interest. "It's much more gratifying to see you in the flesh. . . ." She raised her eyebrows, and smiled.

"Thank you, Jarsakh-bhai." He nodded in self-conscious acknowledgment, keeping a straight face and using her family name, as he had become accustomed to doing when he dealt with her as an industrialist. It was an unexpected side effect of his position that when he wore his full military uniform and honors—or sometimes just spoke his name—women he had never met or who had barely acknowledged his existence suddenly began undressing him with their eyes. He found it more embarrassing than flattering. "It's an honor and a relief to hold a conversation in such magnificent surroundings."

The Pernattes exchanged a look of mutual satisfaction that might even have been fond. They both wore the uniforms that were their right and duty as the heads of two important lineages; but no expense had been spared on subtlety of design, use of color and embellishment, to transform the spare lines of a robe and slacks into something unique and beautiful.

Gundhalinu found his own eyes glancing from one youthful, perfect face and fit, flawlessly dressed body to the other in helpless fascination as he went on making small talk. He deftly answered the kinds of questions about his career and discoveries that everyone seemed to ask, feeling vaguely surprised that even the Pernattes would ask the same things.

While he was growing up his family had been well-off financially, the bearers of a family line whose ancestry was unimpeachable and whose contributions to technological progress stretched back through Kharemough's history for countless generations. But the Pernattes were *rich;* so rich that they had been able to afford the water of life. Their bodies wore the unmistakable proof of it as unselfconsciously as they wore their clothes—Pernatte was at least as old as Gundhalinu's father, who had married late and been an old man when Gundhalinu was born; but he looked scarcely older than Gundhalinu himself. Pernatte's wife looked younger; her skin, a glowing mahogany color dusted with pale freckles, was almost completely unlined.

". . . and my wife says that you are progressing very well with the new technology," Pernatte said.

"Yes." Gundhalinu glanced at Jarsakh; she smiled a professional smile at him this time, meaningless and full of steel. They had collided often enough over his impatience with errors and delays in production. "There have been some setbacks in getting our new equipment up to specs, but there is no question that we will have our fleet, and the base for equipping all the Hegemony's ships with stardrive units within the decade."

"The sooner the better, eh?" Pernatte said. "We must maintain our rightful place as leaders of the Hegemony—and we will, thanks to all you've done. As well as establishing permanent ties with our 'lost colony,' Tiamat. We're not getting any younger, you know." He laughed, with the casual thoughtlessness of someone who assumed the listener would both get and sympathize with his jest.

"You served on Tiamat in the Hegemonic Police, didn't you?" Jarsakh asked.

Gundhalinu nodded, with a meaningless smile of his own. "Until the final departure."

"That must have been a sight. Did you see the sacrifice of the Snow Queen?"

"No." He glanced down. "I was in the hospital with an illness, at the time."

"Dreadful, backward place—you're lucky you didn't die." She shook her head. "That would have been a terrible tragedy for all of us."

Gundhalinu made no comment.

"Young Vhanu here tells me you've expressed an interest in entering politics, once the starship technology is fully established," Pernatte said.

"Yes, in fact I have been considering that." Gundhalinu glanced at Vhanu, letting his pleasant surprise show, and Vhanu smiled, looking down. "My family has never been active in politics, however. I'm afraid I have a lot of process to learn. . . ."

Pernatte's smile widened, as Gundhalinu had been hoping it would. "It would give me great pleasure to serve as your mentor. As you know, I have more than passing knowledge of the occupation."

Thank you, gods! Gundhalinu bowed once more, to hide the unseemly rush of elation rising inside him. "I would be most grateful, Pernatte-sadhu."

"Then you must allow CMP and myself to guide you to some of our more influential acquaintances tonight. It would be a shame to waste such an occasion on gossip and hero worship. Have you given thought to what sort of service you would be interested in? Something in the world government, perhaps, or the Hegemonic Coordinating Council. Even an Assembly seat would not be out of the question for a man of your reputation and family, if there was an opening. . . ." He touched Gundhalinu's arm, guiding him with the motion.

Gundhalinu gave a faintly incredulous laugh and shook his head. "My aspirations are more down to earth. Actually I had thought of something in the judicial branch or the foreign service . . . in fact, perhaps the Chief Justiceship of Tiamat, when it's reopened to contact."

Jarsakh's luminously calculating eyes widened with a surprise that looked genuine. "Father of all my grandfathers! You actually *want* to return to that backward, unfortunate world? But you said you almost died there—"

He remembered saying nothing of the kind, although actually it was true enough. "Perhaps that's why I want to go back, bhai. . . . To oversee its development into a modern society, one which can be a full, contributing partner in the Hegemony, seems to me to be a worthy career, and one that ought to take a lifetime—" He smiled carefully, not sure himself what the words meant.

"Modernize those barbarians?" Pernatte shook his head. "A selfless goal, but I daresay it's a hopeless task, trying to uplift a people who practice cannibalism—"

"Human sacrifice, best beloved," Jarsakh interrupted gently, "not cannibalism."

"Whatever," he murmured, annoyed. "Better simply to find more permanent ways to control them, I should think. After all, the damn world is all but uninhabitable anyway, by anything but savages. All they have that's worth the trade is the water of life."

"But of course that's worth the ransom of worlds," Jarsakh said dryly.

Gundhalinu bit his tongue. Vhanu was still at his side, gazing at the Pernattes as if he were hearing the voices of his ancestors—which he was, in a way, Gundhalinu supposed. "All the more reason to have someone in charge who can monitor the safety of the supply," he said, choosing his words with the painstaking care of someone picking up shards of glass. *To see the path of Light clearly,* they said on Four, *you must walk in the shadows.* "I'm very interested in undertaking a thorough study of the water of life. I have a theory that it may function by the same technoviral mechanism as the stardrive plasma. And now that we are learning how to deal with that—"

"You mean you might find a way to reproduce it?" Jarsakh said, meeting his gaze almost hungrily. "An unlimited supply—?"

He glanced down. "That would be my hope. . . . It's certainly within the realm of possibility." He had no idea whether it was possible or not. But if it would save Tiamat, he would try . . . he would lie, he would—

"Forgive me—" a voice interrupted, in a tone that was deferential but not to be denied. "I couldn't help overhearing your discussion of Tiamat, Commander Gundhalinu."

Gundhalinu turned, found himself looking down into the face of a frail-looking old man in a sedate ceremonial uniform. "KR Aspundh," the man said, offering his hand.

Gundhalinu met Aspundh's dry palm briefly with his own; felt a shock of recognition that was almost subliminal. He had known the Aspundhs slightly, years ago—he would not have recognized KR without an introduction, after so long. But there was something else: an odd bright bit of random memory, in which a native girl named Moon told a Kharemoughi Police inspector named Gundhalinu tales of her visit to his homeworld, *". . . and we visited KR Aspundh, and we drank lith, and ate sugared fruits. . . ."* The vision almost kept him from noticing the brief, hidden fingersign that told him suddenly why Aspundh had had the temerity to interrupt this conversation. Aspundh was Survey. Gundhalinu's eyes registered the sibyl trefoil the other man wore, the only visible symbol of status besides an unobtrusive family crest. "Yes," Gundhalinu answered. "I served there for several years."

"He wants to go back there, if you can imagine, KR," Jarsakh said, apparently not offended by the interruption. KR Aspundh was a first-generation Technician; his lineage was irrevocably Nontech . . . but his father had been posthumously raised up, due to the creative innovations in long-distance EM sensing apparatus that had come out of his independent work with production methods. He had not gotten the credit he had deserved in his lifetime, but his children had benefited from it.

KR Aspundh was respected by Techs of old lineage because of the sibyl sign he wore, but also because it had been their decision that he was deserving of respect—unlike nouveau riche upstarts who bought their way into respectability by purchasing the estates and ancestors of deserving highborns who had fallen on hard times. KR Aspundh, as far as Gundhalinu knew, was a staunch supporter of the status quo that had put him where he was. And yet, his interest in Tiamat could hardly be casual curiosity. . . . "Have you ever known anyone who would willingly give up Kharemough for a lifetime on Tiamat—?" Jarsakh asked, bemused.

"Only one person," Aspundh said mildly, glancing at Gundhalinu. "And that was years ago."

"And did she?" Gundhalinu asked, trapped again inside a moment of double vision.

Aspundh looked back at him in sudden surprise. His gaze turned measuring, and his face became expressionless. "I believe she did. But then, she was not, of course, a Kharemoughi." He smiled slightly. "I have never been to Tiamat myself, but I've felt a fascination with the place ever since, wondering what could have obsessed her so about it."

"It does get under your skin, somehow," Gundhalinu said, feeling a faint smile turn up the corners of his own mouth. "I had always wanted to see the place, when I was young."

"Where are you staying while you are planetside, Commander? At your family estates?"

"He's staying with us," Pernatte said. "Right, BZ? I may call you BZ—?"

"Please." Gundhalinu nodded and his smile widened, barely covering his surprise. He wondered whether Vhanu had forgotten to tell him about his accommodations, or whether he had merely forgotten that he had heard about them. He glanced at Vhanu, whose own expression looked slightly disoriented.

"Call me AT, then," Pernatte said, and his wife echoed him, "CMP—" When the Pernattes took an interest in someone's life, their interest was, it seemed, peremptory. He took a deep breath, remembering that it was not BZ Gundhalinu, a complete stranger with a past they would find reprehensible and future plans they would consider treasonable, whom they were taking into their lives like an orphaned child; it was a construct, an image, a Hero of the Hegemony—a glittering, fame-encrusted shell, bright enough to blind even them. *Ride it, just ride it.*

". . . is not so far away, then," Aspundh was saying. "I realize your schedule must be extremely tight, Gundhalinu-ken," using the title that marked him as a sibyl, "but perhaps you might find space in it for a quiet meal at my home? I would very much like to talk more with you about our mutual interest."

"Thank you, Aspundh-ken." Gundhalinu nodded, reading what lay in the older man's eyes. "I would enjoy that." He glanced at Vhanu. "Make rearrangements, will you, Vhanu?" He smiled apologetically. There seemed to be no natural breathing spaces in his life at all, anymore.

Vhanu nodded, looking both surprised and resigned. "Yes, Commander."

"I'll make arrangements with your aide." Aspundh bowed graciously, as if he sensed the growing restlessness of his hosts. "I know everyone here is eager to make your acquaintance."

Gundhalinu damped his curiosity and let himself be led on through the crowd, from one introduction to another, gradually progressing from one room to another. He realized with a kind of surprise that he was actually beginning to enjoy himself; because for once the people he was being forced to meet were his own people— people who spoke his language, not simply figuratively but literally—who looked like him, acted like him, responded predictably to his jokes and stories. More than predictably—enthusiastically. Old and new acquaintances, the best and brightest of the people he had admired for a lifetime, were all around him now, proclaiming their admiration for him. And after all, it was not as if he had done nothing to deserve it; he had. He could let himself acknowledge that now, let himself begin to believe that he truly had expunged his dishonor in his people's eyes.

Vhanu rejoined them after a time, relieving Gundhalinu of having to remember the names and credentials that went with every face he saw, and making him remember again his odd brief encounter with KR Aspundh. He checked his calendar unobtrusively and found the requested dinner date there. He ate another pastry, listening to the silent reminder in his brain that said nothing was what it seemed.

But the cool, fluid strains of music moved with him like a sense of ease from room to room. The music was always changing, because there was a different group of musicians, with different instruments, in each new hall—and yet it was always the music he remembered from his youth, the classical refrains with their hidden mathematical secrets of structure and counterpoint that he had studied in school. Music was a form of mathematics made tangible, and so it was everywhere in the world of the Technician class, reminding them always, gracefully, of their place. The food and drinks circulating through the crowd were a movable feast, all his favorite delicacies of boyhood, beautifully prepared, exquisite to look at, tasting even better to his heightened senses than he remembered.

The Pernatte manor house had been decorated with the same relentless sophistication as the Pernattes themselves, furnished in what he assumed was the most modern fashion, since he did not see any furniture that seemed to be in a style he remembered. There were vast islands of low modular couches in intense but subtle combinations of colors, and flat, slab-like tables that probably contained hidden functions he couldn't imagine. The polished stone walls were empty of any decoration unless it appeared to be functional; the works of art scattered on stone pedestals among the bright settee islands were all historical—archaeological treasures, remnants of the Old Empire's glory. The effect in the vast space of the rooms was striking but austere, almost monolithic, even when the space was cluttered with bodies, as it was now. From time to time he became aware that his eyes were searching for the mystery woman, but he did not see her. He hoped that he would find her before the evening was through, enjoying the prospect of the encounter with guilty pleasure.

"Ah—" Jarsakh said, beside him, as a gleaming servo murmured a few inaudible words in her ear. "I believe our entertainment for the evening is about to begin. We've reserved the best viewing spot for you. I hope you enjoy art." She took his arm.

"Very much," he said. "And frankly I haven't had much of an opportunity to view it, in recent years."

"You'll have an opportunity to do more than that, tonight. You'll have a chance to interact with it—"

He smiled, intrigued, as she led him outside through the sighing breath of a door onto a patio open to the sky.

"BZ—!"

His smile faded abruptly. He turned, peering across the shifting dance of the crowd. He almost swore, remembered himself in time, swallowing the bitter words like vomit. "Excuse me, CMP," he said to Jarsakh, and left her side. "Vhanu," he murmured, keeping his voice down with an effort. "What are they doing here?"

"Who, Commander?" Vhanu tried to follow his gaze.

"My brothers." Gundhalinu felt every muscle in his body tense as if he were about to be attacked, as he watched his brothers make their way inevitably toward him.

Vhanu registered his answer, looked back at him uncomprehendingly. "Your family, sir? Didn't you want them here?"

"No," he said gently, "I did not want them here. I do not want them here. They—" *They tried to murder me.* "We do not get along."

"I'm sorry, Commander." Vhanu shook his head, his expression caught between embarrassment and curiosity. "But they are your only close relatives, I believe—? Your eldest brother is the Gundhalinu head-of-family. We could hardly have excluded them, if you wanted this occasion to be—"

Gundhalinu waved him silent as Jarsakh rejoined them, with her husband at her side. "Is everything all right, BZ?"

"Yes, fine," he answered, a little too abruptly.

"BZ—" His oldest brother, HK, reached him first. HK had regained all the considerable weight World's End had stripped off of him. He wore the proper family uniform; it was loosely tailored and carefully draped to make the least of his soft, fleshy body. "Gods, it's like a miracle—to have thee back home, and the family reunited. I can't tell thee how proud it makes me feel to share tonight with thee—" He went on babbling inanities as he pressed Gundhalinu's automatically raised palm—held up as much in a warding gesture as in greeting—with too much force. Gundhalinu watched his brother's glance touch his wrist, checking surreptitiously for the scars that had once been there, the brand of his dishonor. But the scars were gone—along with any illusions he had had about the relative worthiness of his brothers' lives, and his own.

SB, their middle brother, drew up behind HK like a shadow, regarding Gundhalinu with a measured silence that was the antithesis of his brother's diarrhea of well-wishes.

"SB . . ." Gundhalinu said, with a curt nod, not even offering his hand this time.

"How are thou, little brother?" SB murmured, his voice toneless, his eyes alive with envy.

"Fully recovered, thank you," Gundhalinu said, meeting the bitterly cold stare with his own. The mark his brothers' treachery had left on him, after he had brought them alive out of World's End, had been far more difficult to erase than the damage he had done to himself.

"So I see," SB murmured. "How nice for thee. Wearing the family crest tonight, are thou? That's a little premature."

Gundhalinu turned away from the insinuation, from SB's eyes, as HK's obsequious chatter finally, mercifully ceased. "It's good . . . to be back," he said, struggling with even those empty words; not having become a skillful enough liar yet to attempt something more personal. He made perfunctory introductions between his brothers and the Pernattes, because not to do so would not only have been socially awkward, but inexplicable. The Pernattes were already looking uncomfortable; Vhanu looked as if he were watching for hidden weapons.

"And is this the first time you've seen each other since you left Kharemough—?" Jarsakh asked, in mild astonishment. "Haven't you even paid a visit to your family shrine, to venerate your ancestors?"

He looked down. "I am afraid I have been remiss, CMP," he said quietly. "I haven't even been planetside before today, since my return. The urgency of our concerns upstairs claimed every moment from me until now. It has been . . . a profound oversight, as you so rightly observe." Realizing as he said it how shamefully true it was—realizing the painful, overwhelming array of reasons why he had not even let the possibility of a visit enter his mind until now. Not the least of them was the fact that his brothers controlled the family estates, where the remains of all their ancestors, including the father who had died during his absence, lay. "I shall rectify it as soon as humanly possible." He bent his head in acknowledgment.

"CMP—" Pernatte chided.

Gundhalinu raised his head again; saw her smile with something which for once looked like rue, or honest sympathy. "Please," she said, "let me apologize, not you. It was not my place to criticize you, when your unselfish service to our people has all but robbed you of a life."

"Come on, BZ, the entertainment's going to start without us if we don't pay a mind to it," Pernatte said, "and by my sainted ancestors, we paid enough for it that I don't want to miss a minute. Bring your brothers. I'm sure you must have a lot of catching up to do."

Gundhalinu nodded, helpless to do otherwise; knowing without looking behind him that his brothers would not leave him alone. He was guided to his reserved spot among the guests who were standing patiently, or perched on an astonishing assortment of cushioned antique leaning-posts arranged over the wide expanse of patterned stone.

In their midst was an open space, on which sat an unremarkable chest that appeared to have been hand-fashioned. Overhead the pollution aurora was a symphony of color rippling across the perfectly clear autumn sky. He thought fleetingly of other skies—a sky hung with colored lights, in the something-like-a-dream of his initiation into the inner reality of Survey; the emberglow of a Tiamatan sky. The air was crisp and pleasant, the anticipation around him was almost tangible, and the scent of night-blooming aphesium filled his head with pungent nostalgia.

The nostalgia pushed unpleasantly into realtime as his brothers settled onto the ornate bench beside him. A servo deferentially offered him a finely filigreed head-set—a work of art in itself, he thought—along with brief droning instructions for its use.

"The artist is a biochemical sculptor—perhaps the most highly acclaimed one in her field," Jarsakh said, as if she had also prepared a lecture. "Her works are interactive, rather than preprogrammed, which accounts for her remarkable popularity, I'm told. She calls them mood pieces; supposedly they mirror the emotions of the user so that they are always appropriate to the occasion, and satisfying to experience."

"It must be extraordinarily difficult to create the kind of programming something like that would require," Gundhalinu said.

"Yes, I'm told that it is. The sculptor has several degrees in the advanced sciences, even though she is merely an artist," Jarsakh said. "We support the arts whenever we can; I have always believed that one cannot be well-rounded without an interest in the nontechnical areas . . . but we try to support only artists who show a particularly strong design sense, or an imaginative use of technology."

"You seem to have a taste for antiquities, as well," Gundhalinu remarked, remembering the art he had seen displayed inside.

"Well, yes, traditional static art is of interest mostly for its sense of historical perspective, don't you think?" Jarsakh shrugged. He wondered suddenly whether she had ever taken more than a superficial look at anything in the house. Any sense of real history in this place had been buried long ago.

"Is the artist who designed tonight's work here? What's her name—?" He wondered whether it was anyone he had heard of before he left. He saw Vhanu murmur something to Pernatte, behind her.

"She wasn't able to attend," Pernatte said, interrupting and ending the conversation all at once, in a way that left Gundhalinu wondering.

"Her name is Netanyahr," SB said suddenly, sourly. "I recognize her work. She's the one we lost the estates to, until thou took them back, BZ. No wonder they don't want her here in person."

Gundhalinu turned where he sat, feeling anger and humiliation burn his face like a slap.

"SB," HK muttered, "hush up, will thou? He'll never—"

SB snorted, shrugging HK's warning hand off his shoulder. "Why should I? If they had the bad taste to hire her to display a work here, why shouldn't I have the bad taste to mention it? We're all friends here—" He met Gundhalinu's withering stare with a look of empty mockery. "True, little brother?"

"If you will excuse us, BZ—" Pernatte said, visibly chagrined. "We must join CMP's honorable relatives over there for a time, or they will be unforgivably insulted. And I'm sure you have much to talk about with your brothers. . . . But when everyone is settled, please, be the first to use the headset, and begin the entertainment for us."

Gundhalinu looked down at the circlet of filigreed silver in his hands, feeling his brothers' eyes on him. "Delighted. Thank you so much," he murmured, with an inane smile. He watched the Pernattes move away through the gathering crowd, discreetly taking Vhanu with them; saw Pernatte say something to his wife and gesture at the waiting piece of art. He wondered how in the name of a thousand ancestors they had come to choose the work of someone so intimately associated with the humiliation of his own family name. He was sure it had not been intentional. But if they hadn't known of his family troubles before, they certainly knew now. If SB had only kept his goddamned mouth shut—

"How long are thou going to be down here, BZ?" HK ventured, beside him.

"No longer than I have to be," Gundhalinu snapped, not looking at them, struck by the irony that the only people he was required to address with the personal *thou* were the ones he felt least close to.

"Thou are welcome at the estates," HK went on, with awkward insufferability. "That is, if thou want to visit father's ashes, and make an offering. Thou are even welcome to stay, if—"

"I have a place to stay." He forced the words out, still looking away, amazed at the blackness inside him, the welling up of bitterness and bad feeling that came with the rush of memories he had tried to suppress. Their rigid, tradition-bound father had tried, before his death, to get him to displace his brothers in the line of inheritance. But the youth he had been then had been unable to violate tradition so profoundly, when his own father had lacked the will to do it. . . . And so his brothers had ruined the family's fortunes, just as his father had feared—weak, self-indulgent HK led willingly into disaster by SB, who should have made a life for himself decades ago, if he had had any shred of self-respect or character.

And after they were done ruining their heritage they had come to Number Four, where he was stationed, to deliver the final blow to his crumbling facade of control—to tell him how they had lost the estates, sold the family name to some social climber with money for honor. Until then, he had been able to go on functioning, as long as he kept his own dishonor hermetically sealed; believing that his family was unstained by his humiliation as long as he stayed away from Kharemough. But his brothers had destroyed that last hope, and had come to Four to tell him that they intended to buy back the estates by striking it rich in World's End. He had warned them off, warned them about making what the Fours called the Big Mistake . . . watched them go anyway. And then when they did not return, he had gone after them; not because he cared about them, but only because there was nothing he cared about anymore, not even his own life.

He had found them . . . and the stardrive. World's End had changed his life forever. But it had changed his brothers, too. He had brought them alive out of that soul-eating hell . . . and then they had ambushed him and stolen the stardrive plasma he had brought out with them, leaving him for dead in a back alley of the Company town.

But he had not died. He had lived, to see them arrested, see that the plasma was delivered into the rightful hands of the Hegemony, and not held for ransom. And then he had used the sudden influence that his "selfless patriotism" had thrust upon him, to reclaim his family's estates and name.

He had sent his brothers home under a kind of glorified house arrest, with enough money doled out to them by a trust fund—and enough threats of retribution—to keep them comfortably under control. Because blood was still thicker than water. He had told himself the stress of their ordeal in World's End had made them turn on him; that even though he had never gotten along with them, they weren't murderers, only fools—and someone had to oversee the estates. . . .

But now he was back on Kharemough, and the very sight of them was enough to paint everything within his vision black.

"BZ—?" HK said again, and Gundhalinu realized that his brother had gone on speaking, even though he had stopped listening. "Why did thou refuse to let us do it?"

"What?" he said, frowning. The crowd around them seemed settled now; an expectant silence was falling. He realized they were waiting for him to begin the entertainment. He looked at the headset, like a silver crown, clutched between his clenched fists. He forced his hands to loosen, afraid of crushing it.

"The opportunity we had to invest in lightspeed shipfitting? Now that you've— now that thou have returned, and the new fleet is almost ready . . . well, there's no going back is there? It's a sure investment. Since thou're on such good terms with Jarsakh-bhai, thou could still put in a word, couldn't thou?"

"No," he said, cutting off the flow of HK's speech. "Thou get more than a sufficient stipend to cover thy needs. I told thee, if thou ever tried to profit off the stardrive again, in any way at all, I'd have thee up on charges. I meant it. And I'm here, now."

"Yes, but, BZ, I'm head-of-family—"

SB caught HK's arm, jerked it, silencing him again. "Drop it," he said, speaking to HK but looking at BZ. "He's not interested. He thinks he's some kind of god. We'll do it our own way."

BZ frowned. "If thou cause me any embarrassment, thou will be stripped of all rank and rights. Push me further and there will be charges of attempted murder. Just remember that." He looked away, and settled the headset carefully onto his head. SB sniggered as if he were crowning himself. Gundhalinu swore under his breath, pressing the contact points until he felt the tingling sensation of on-line seep in through his ears. Whatever was in the box would respond to his emotions, translated into some sort of electronic stimuli, he had been told. *Then gods help it,* he thought. He shut his eyes, concentrating.

Red-gold incandescence exploded into the air, to the gasps and startled cries of the waiting crowd. Wave upon wave of it spilled out of the box and fountained into the sky like erupting magma, congealed as it struck the stones, thickening, darkening, struggling like vague semi-human forms wrestling to the death, filling their collective vision with fire and blood, *Fire Lake—*

BZ slammed the controls down on his emotions, astounded and appalled; was relieved to hear a chorus of sighs and a patter of applause from the unsuspecting watchers. He pulled himself together, watching the colors fade and soften as the violence of the exploding material died back into a sinuous outpouring that made him think of fog, smoke, water falling into that molten sea, rising up again in clouds, filled with rainbows, filled with ghosts. . . .

He concentrated now on the artsong he could hear still being played somewhere inside, its graceful, poignant measures and counterpoints like a dance between would-be lovers, stepping forward, moving back, filled with hesitancy and yearning. . . . He saw the music and his vision of it suddenly begin to appear, in front of him, not quite real, not quite imaginary, like the ghosts he had seen in Sanctuary, like the face he saw in dreams, her face, hazed in blue. . . .

She was there, forming out of the not-quite-matter, not-quite-fog, always re-forming and melting away at the same time, her hand held out to him, as he remembered her, as he had wanted to believe she was, waiting for him. . . .

He rose from his seat, lifting his own hand, oblivious to his brothers' stares or the murmurs of the crowd as he stepped forward into the vision, to gently mime the touch of his hand on hers, feeling the cold, faint tangibility of the mist from which she took her form as he began to lead her with his thoughts, and with his heart, through the precisely patterned motions of the dance that matched the music. And she smiled and met his gaze, with her eyes the color of mist and moss agate, filled with yearning like his own, and her long, pale hair tendriling about her like fog. . . .

They danced until the music began to fade away; he bowed to her with its final strains, letting her fade back into the mist, into formless swirls of color like a rainbow, like the ribbons of light in the night sky overhead. He turned back to his seat, through a starswarm of applause, already reaching up to lift the crown from his head and pass it on. . . .

He stopped dead, staring, as his eyes cleared of one vision and he saw, standing before him like another, the mystery woman he had given sanctuary to this evening.

She stood before him, shimmering in pearls and black velvet, staring back at him with equal astonishment—and an upraised pitcher, in midswing through an arc, its contents aimed straight at him.

He flung up his arm in a defense gesture—saw her expression already changing from disbelief and recognition to horrified dismay: Her arms jerked as she tried, too late, to stop the motion. He lowered his guard just in time to watch the contents of the pitcher spewed squarely onto his brothers' heads. HK bellowed in surprise and SB fell off the end of the bench. Whatever had been in the pitcher was all over them now, and looked like liquefied garbage. Smelled like it, as the odor hit him.

The space around him was absolutely silent then, for an endless moment, except for the gasping and cursing of his brothers, and his own sudden, wildly heartfelt laughter.

The aghast crowd of partiers sat gaping a moment longer. And then household security appeared, human and otherwise, surrounding the woman in black where she stood motionless and unresisting, staring back at him with a look that he suddenly understood perfectly. His laughter fell away, and he opened his mouth.

"BZ, ye gods, are thou all right—" Pernatte was beside him, putting an arm around him; not even looking toward his brothers. Vhanu was at his other side, frantically asking him something he ignored, as Pernatte gestured at the waiting security staff, "Take her away, for gods' sakes! Have her arrested!"

"Wait!" Gundhalinu put up his hand, stopping them in midmotion as they began to lay hands on the woman. "Let her go," he said, walking toward her, and the armed guards, with a calm authority he didn't quite feel. They looked past him at Pernatte, who must have given them a signal, and then backed off. "There's been a misunderstanding here. It was . . . just a part of the art experience. No harm."

He held up the silver circlet of the headset in both his hands, and as he reached her he set it on her head. "This belongs to you." Not even making it a question. He took her hand and she followed him like a sleepwalker out into the open center of the patio where the box lay, the creative medium tendriling faintly, aimlessly, or whispering like ashes beneath their feet. He turned back to the crowd, glancing at his brothers just long enough to catch SB's murderous glare as the security guards helped them up and away, through a ripple of disgusted faces.

"Sadhanu, bhai," he said, raising his voice to catch the watchers' attention. "This is the artist who is responsible for tonight's entertainment. Please show her your appreciation." There was more applause, some of it uncertain, some of it punctuated by small noises of approval. "Through an oversight, she was not invited to attend this evening's affair." He turned back to her, saw that the expression on her face was utterly lost. "If you will allow me to rectify the matter right now—" He looked back at Pernatte, saw the flash of awkward alarm in Vhanu's gaze as he said, "I would be most grateful to have you welcome this woman as my honored guest."

"Of course," Pernatte murmured, staring at him and at the woman, clearly remembering what had been said about their relationship. Pernatte's expression suggested that he thought someone had had too much to drink, but he wasn't sure who. "Delighted. And sorry about the misunderstanding." He looked at the woman again. "I suppose we shall just have to toss that bit of business off to artistic temperament, eh? We all make mistakes, eh—but please, my dear, be more circumspect in the future about how you express your . . ." He grimaced, attempting a smile.

"Of course, sathra." She bowed to him, with a grace any Technician would have envied, her flawless mask of composure securely back in place, and the perfect image of a chastened smile on her lips. She looked up again, and took the headset carefully from her head, offering it to Pernatte. "It would give me unforgettable pleasure if you would take the next turn, sathra." He accepted the headset, somewhat mollified by her show of manners, and eager to get the party flowing again. He put it on. She looked at Gundhalinu, and raised her eyebrows.

He nodded and touched her elbow, asking her wordlessly to follow him.

"Sir—?" Vhanu said, his own face uncertain, his body twitching with conflicting signals.

"It's all right, Vhanu. I'll call you when I need you." He led her through the edge of the crowd, which had begun to *ooh* and *ahh* again as their host tried his hand at guiding her creation. She did not look back, and he suspected she did not really want to see it. He wondered what she had thought of his own performance. Not much, probably.

He led her along the neatly trimmed hedges of the maze that protected the Pernatte family shrine, until they reached a cushioned waiting-seat of the sort that were always located in spots like this, lying in the half illumination of the mansion's windows. They sat down and looked at each other. Sweet a capella voices singing a song whose words he could not make out drifted across the lawn, filling the empty silence that neither of them seemed able to break.

At last she said, "You told me I could ask your name when we met again. But I guess that really isn't necessary."

"I guess not." He looked at his hands. "But at least I can ask yours. Netanyahr, I believe my brother said—?" He looked up again. "They said that you owned our estates?"

"Pandhara Hethea Netanyahr," she said, and met his uncertainly upraised hand. "Although for a brief, beautiful time I was PHN Gundhalinu." She met his gaze, unflinching, and he saw the embers of anger in her eyes, saw too the pain and humiliation that had driven her to the act of absurdist revenge she had committed tonight.

He felt the painful heat of his own chagrin; remembered his humiliation at his own loss, how it had made him willing to do anything to get back what was his by right. "Now I know why you thought I'd personally forbidden you to come tonight. But I hadn't. I had no idea—" But someone must have had, and it made him feel peculiar to have taken the blame for it.

"I know." She nodded. "If I hadn't met you earlier tonight, the way I did, I don't know if I would believe you. But . . ."

"I don't even know how someone had the temerity to ask you to provide entertainment for tonight . . . although the quality of your work is spectacular," he added hastily. "I don't mean to—"

"Thank you," she said, and actually smiled. "What you chose to do with it was quite wonderful. I actually forgot myself, watching you dance with that beautiful vision. . . ."

"Really?" He smiled, hesitated. "I . . . have become a believer that certain meetings aren't by coincidence, Netanyahr-kadda. Perhaps this is one of those." He glanced down. "At least it gives me a chance to apologize to you. You see, when I heard that my brothers had lost the family name, I—my own life . . . was not going well. To hear that . . . It seemed . . . it seemed as though my lifeline had snapped." His hands made fists in the shadows. "I was desperate to get my birthright back. And when the—opportunity came, I took it. I never even thought about the person at the other end, whose new life I was disrupting." He looked up at her again, with an effort. *Except to imagine some crude profiteer with money for honor.* Her expression said that it was exactly the attitude she would have expected of an arrogant, classist Technician. "If that's what you think of us all," he murmured, "then why did you want so badly to be one of us?"

The pearls whispered as she looked away. "It's not 'becoming one of you' that I desire, Gundhalinu-sathra. You are all just as human as the rest of us, and if you ever had to face that, you might even realize it." She looked back at him, as if she were expecting him to object; looked surprised, looked away again. "It's . . . it's the sense of *tradition*, the achievements of the families. I . . . you will think it presumptuous, but in school I studied the Dark Ages, and I dreamed of what it would have been like to have been alive then, helping to bring a return to the light. Sometimes I even imagined that I had been a part of it, in some former incarnation; I felt it that strongly. And it was your own family's history that I became obsessed with—your ancestors' intelligence and courage, their refusal to compromise their humanity in the face of persecution and terror. When I heard that the Gundhalinu name was actually for sale—"

His own surprise fell away; he grimaced, involuntarily.

"I'm sorry . . ." she murmured. "I know now how very painful it must have been for you. I only meant to pay you the honor your achievements, and your true kindness toward me, deserve."

"Perhaps we have both been guilty of the same oversight, Netanyahr-kadda," he said softly.

She nodded. "Yes, Gundhalinu-sathra."

"Then let me do what I can to set things straight. There are always other names and estates available, if you know where to ask."

"No," she said, almost sharply. Her hands knotted in her lap.

"Why not?"

"In order to take your estates away from me again, when they were legally mine, the litigators you hired filed a proscription. I am ineligible for the rank of Technician forever."

"What were the grounds?" he asked, in disbelief.

"Genetic insufficiency."

"But that's absurd—" He broke off. Genetic insufficiency meant that someone was a certified mental defective. "You have several high technical degrees, and demonstrable creativity—" *And humor and beauty and social grace—* He stopped himself before he said that.

"But still I couldn't earn my way into your estimable class, sathra, with all that. I had to buy my way in. Do you really find it so absurd that I could be judged defective—?"

He looked away.

"The heritage that I truly wanted to be mine was yours, Commander—for the sense of continuity it would have given me, for myself and for my children, into the future. . . . But the honor of the Gundhalinus lies in deserving hands, and there is no other Technician lineage that meant as much to me. So perhaps I am content, after all." She shrugged, glancing away.

He thought of his brothers, and said nothing. He listened to the voices begin a new song, and the sudden flurry of appreciative noise from the patio crowd. "So you would have done this in part for your own family . . . for your children? How many do you have?"

"None, yet. But I shall."

"You're married, then—"

"No. Do you consider that one must follow the other?"

He looked back at her. "Many people don't, of course," he said.

She stared at him, as if she were trying to decide whether he was being sarcastic, or possibly about to make a pass at her. "And what about you?"

"Married to my work, I'm afraid." He thought suddenly of Reede Kullervo, walking beside him through a park on Number Four: *Married to your work—?* Kullervo had asked him.

"And so am I." She smiled, still looking at him that way. "But not monogamously . . ."

"Netanyahr-kadda," he murmured, "would you ever consider—"

"Yes—?"

"Consider . . . consider showing us what you can do with your own creation, here tonight?" he finished, gesturing toward the patio as an excuse to look away; feeling like a man who had almost stepped into quicksand.

Her face became expressionless. Her own hands, held tightly in her lap, twitched. "If you would like me to, Gundhalinu-sathra."

"I would like it very much," he said weakly. He felt oddly giddy, as though he had drunk too much, which he had not.

She led the way this time, back to the partiers, and took the headset as it passed by, putting it on without hesitation. What she did then with the sensuous luminous cloud of matter from the carven box made him exceedingly glad that he had been a coward two minutes before.

And far later that night, when the party had ended and he lay alone in his bed, he was painfully sorry. He spent what was left of the night wide awake in the unfamiliar room. Only after dawn did he manage to sleep. He woke in the late morning to a spot of wetness on his nightshirt, and knew that it had not been the old dream, the usual dream, that had haunted his sleep this time. . . .

He reminded himself that today he would see KR Aspundh; that in a few hours more they would talk together about Tiamat. He needed suddenly, desperately, to talk to someone about Tiamat.

KHAREMOUGH: Aspundh Estates

Gundhalinu arrived, alone for once and precisely on time, at KR Aspundh's front door. Flowering vines spilled down from the roof of Aspundh's manor house, which blended with studied artistry into the rolling land around it. Aspundh met him in person. The silver trefoil was prominent against his dark, silver-threaded robe, and as they touched hands in polite greeting Gundhalinu felt the brief, hidden handsign that told him he was welcomed as a stranger far from home.

"Good of you to come," Aspundh murmured, and beckoned him into the house.

Gundhalinu slowed the barely suppressed urgency of his own strides to match the older man's gait, forcing himself to appreciate the artful use of light, the play of shadows on a wall, the subtle inlays of the carpet as Aspundh led him through the seemingly endless house. "You live alone?" he asked.

"Yes, except for the staff. My children visit me, and my grandchildren, of course." Aspundh did not say whether his wife was dead, or simply out of his life. Gundhalinu thought of his own mother, an archaeologist, who had abandoned her family out of unhappiness when he was five. He had thought, after all these years, that while he was on-planet he would go to see her, now that she could be nothing but proud of him. But Vhanu's search of records had told him she had died, three years before his return. Classical archaeology as a profession lay somewhere on the scale of risk between microsurgery and the bomb squad. Her research team had unearthed some Old Empire system that had utilized smartmatter, only to discover, too late, that it had decayed disastrously. The resulting catastrophe had obliterated the entire site, and everything else for kilometers around. There had been no survivors. . . . He walked on in silence, suddenly unable to make small talk.

At last they reached a sitting room where a wide expanse of window framed in colored glass looked out over Aspundh's exquisite ornamental gardens. Aspundh settled himself on a low cushioned seat beside a table inlaid with amethyst, which already held a set of frosted glasses and a pitcher of drinks. Gundhalinu had a sudden disconcerting flash of déjà vu, staring at the table and out at the view. Aspundh looked up at him curiously, waiting.

"I feel as if I've seen this room before." Gundhalinu shook his head, attempting a shrug; surreptitiously his fingers proved the reality of the table's inlaid edge.

"Odd how that happens, isn't it?" Aspundh said, and smiled. "I chose this room because it always makes me think of Tiamat. The last time I sat and talked about Tiamat with anyone, it was in this room.

"*. . . the gardens. And we drank lith, and ate sugared fruits. . . .*" The words echoed in his memory. He realized that Aspundh was still staring at him, waiting, expectant. He found his voice again. "The people you were speaking of it with, KR . . . was one of them a sibyl named Moon Dawntreader?"

Aspundh sat studying him for a long moment. Gundhalinu realized that Aspundh was weighing whether to trust him with a secret that could easily be considered not only dishonorable but treasonous. "Yes," Aspundh said finally.

Gundhalinu sat down at the table as his knees suddenly felt weak. "Gods . . ." he murmured. He looked up again, meeting the older man's wary gaze. "Some techrunners brought her to you. Moon described this room to me—every detail. What you all drank, even about seeing old Singalu raised to Tech on the threedy just as you entered." Aspundh's eyes brightened, but he said nothing else. "And I wondered why in the name of a thousand ancestors the honorable KR Aspundh would have techrunners to tea—" he laughed, "let alone commit treason, to help a proscribed sibyl get back to Tiamat, where she could tell her people the truth about what we were doing to them." He leaned forward. "You knew," he said softly. "That she had to go back. Didn't you—?"

Aspundh touched the trefoil sign; his face furrowed suddenly with guilt and memory. "I told her then that I had to answer to a higher authority. She said that she had had a sending from the sibyl net. She wore a trefoil—which made her a stranger far from home, who had the right to claim a higher justice, even though she did not know it." He looked up again. "You know what became of her." It was not a question.

"She's Tiamat's Queen."

Aspundh froze; shook his head, slowly. "It was true, then."

Gundhalinu nodded.

"And what have you to do with all of this, and her, BZ Gundhalinu? I remember you as a boy. You were not the kind I would have expected to—" He broke off, as if he realized how it sounded.

Gundhalinu smiled ruefully. "Nor I . . . until I met Moon. I was a Police inspector at the time, I had been taken prisoner by a band of nomad thieves we were pursuing. They treated me . . . badly. I felt . . . I attempted suicide, as my family's honor demanded . . . but I failed." He faced Aspundh's stare, baring his own painful secret. "They captured Moon too, on her way to Carbuncle after her return. When I met her I'd given up all hope of rescue . . . of any future at all. But she made me see that my life was a sacred gift, not a soiled rag to be thrown away. Together we escaped. And then, when we reached the city I helped her find her . . . helped her become Queen. I could have—I *should* have—arrested her. I knew where she'd been, what she was, what it meant . . . probably better than you did. I knew my duty. But I couldn't do anything else. . . ."

"Because you both wore that?" Aspundh asked gently, indicating his trefoil.

Gundhalinu shook his head. "I wasn't even a sibyl, at the time. It was because I'd become her lover." He looked down, away from the expression that followed realization onto Aspundh's face.

"I see," Aspundh said, but he did not. Gundhalinu waited, staring at his hands, wondering if he had made a mistake in coming here. But after a moment Aspundh sighed. "You wear that sign now, and you are the same man you were then. If you hadn't helped her, she wouldn't be Queen. . . . If I hadn't helped her, and she hadn't helped you, you'd be dead now, or stranded for life on Tiamat. Instead, you've become a leader among your own people, and given us back the stars. So who is to say, really, whether either one of us committed an act of treason in helping her, or an act of profound patriotism?"

Gundhalinu looked up again, and smiled. "Thank you, Aspundh-ken."

"Thank you, Gundhalinu-ken. For letting me know, after all these years, that in the Great Game, the gains have outweighed the losses for once." He shook his head, looking down. "I used to find the conflict between loyalty to my people and loyalty to Survey burdensome, at times. I have become somewhat more philosophical in recent years, due to greater—insight, or simply to age. My perspective on the purpose of the Game has shifted. But still, it's good to know. . . . Tell me, was it true what you said about wanting to return to Tiamat?"

Gundhalinu nodded. "Yes. I very much intend to go back when contact is reestablished, as the new Chief Justice."

Aspundh half frowned. "Why?"

"Because I am responsible for what's about to happen to that world, and its people . . . and they are not going to be given any kind of justice unless I'm there to enforce it."

"That's a large judgment for one man to make," Aspundh said mildly. "What makes you believe it?"

"I have ears. The power factions that are pushing for an early return to Tiamat want one thing from it—the water of life. Even people like Gelvasthan and Pernatte think Tiamat is backward and barbarous, with marginal resources—not worth the effort otherwise. No one else will pay attention to its fate until the damage is done—they'll have too much else on their minds. Their shortsightedness will crush whatever progress its people have made under the Summer Queen's guidance, because the Hegemony won't want the Tiamatans able to interfere with its exploitation, any more than they did before."

Aspundh nodded. "I begin to see your point. Have you brought this matter up at a Survey meeting?"

Gundhalinu shook his head. "I'm still feeling my way. I know what I have to do. But as you say, choosing between loyalty to one's people and loyalty to what seems the greater good can be . . . treacherous and painful. And not just for you or me. I don't yet have a feel for the motion of the wheels within wheels that I sense in the inner circles of the Golden Mean here."

"So the power factions you spoke of are not simply confined to the halls of the Hegemonic government."

"No."

"Then my estimate of your judgment rises." Aspundh smiled faintly. "There are indeed wheels within wheels, because there are many opposing views on how best to play the Game. And I think I can help you there. . . ."

Gundhalinu rubbed his eyes, slumping back among the cushions. "Gods—I'm so tired of trying to figure it all out." He looked down at his hands. "I've carried this thing inside me for so long, and there's never been anyone I could share it with. Sometimes it begins to feel like a delusion, and I wonder if I'm living a lie, gone mad with greed and power, all the while believing that I know what's best for everyone else; just like all the rest of the manipulators. . . ."

"Rest assured, sibyl, you sound quite sane to me," Aspundh said. Gundhalinu looked up again, with gratitude in his eyes. "Tell me, though—what made you so certain you could trust me to judge this guilty secret of yours? I did not think I had a wide reputation as the most understanding or liberal-minded of men."

"Moon." Gundhalinu shrugged, and smiled briefly. "That was enough."

Aspundh nodded, his own expression still wry. "By the way," he said, after a long moment, "do you know what happened to the techrunners who brought her here, and took her back?" He hesitated. "One of them was my sister-in-law."

Gundhalinu choked off a laugh of disbelief, as he saw the expression on Aspundh's face. Dimly he remembered that KR had inherited these estates from a dishonored older brother, who had been stripped of his rank for some scandal. "The Police spotted their ship on entry and shot it down; Moon said a woman named Elsevier died in the crash."

Aspundh grimaced, and looked away.

"I'm sorry," Gundhalinu murmured, no longer wondering about why KR Aspundh had techrunners to tea; wondering again how it had been possible for him to have believed, for so many years, that everyone else led exactly the perfect lives their perfect public faces had suggested to him.

"The end of a long story." Aspundh sighed, and Gundhalinu saw the lines deepen in his face before he looked up again. "And while we are speaking of unfinished business—what about you, and Moon? What is it that makes you feel such a compulsive responsibility for her fate, and her world? Are you still in love with her?"

"Yes." Gundhalinu's hands tightened into fists on the tabletop. "I mean, I think so. . . . Ye gods, it's been nearly nine years—sixteen, for her. And she was married to another man." His voice faded. "But I saw her once, in Transfer; I spoke to her. She said she needed me—" He felt heat rise into his face.

"She does, from what you've told me," Aspundh said mildly. "But what you really want to know is whether she still *wants* you. Isn't it?"

Gundhalinu nodded, as sudden longing closed his throat.

"What if you get there, and she doesn't?"

Gundhalinu took a deep breath. "As you say . . . at least she'll still need me." His mouth twitched up.

"Does she know about your discovery? Or that you're coming back—that the Hegemony is, for good this time?"

"No." He looked down again. "I—wanted to make sure it would happen, first, before I . . . before I . . . " He broke off. "And . . . I needed to find a medium I could trust—" Another sibyl, to form the triad that it took to initiate directed contact.

"Sensible," Aspundh murmured, as if his guest had not suddenly turned into a stammering brainwipe.

"I think I've found one." Gundhalinu pulled his voice together, and faced Aspundh's measuring state. "Have I?"

Aspundh smiled, and something that might have been sympathy filled his eyes. "Then perhaps now is not too soon to let her know."

Gundhalinu sucked in a breath of surprise. "You're willing—now?"

Aspundh nodded. "Are you ready? Ask, and I will answer."

Gundhalinu swallowed his disbelief and nodded, realizing that he had been ready for this moment for years, rehearsing what he would say to her, and how he would say it, to make her understand. He began to speak the words that would put them into a mutual Transfer, opening a line of communication that would finally give both Moon and himself the freedom to ask, and to answer. . . .

TIAMAT: Carbuncle

Moon began to fall, drawn down into the helpless, vertiginous spiral of the Transfer; taken by surprise, because there had been no question asked. *She was being called*—to someone else, somewhere else. Her vision of the room and the face before her faded as reality began to turn inside out; she fell into the timeless moment, expecting in another moment to find herself captive inside someone else's reality, looking out through the eyes of a sibyl on some other world. . . .

But this time the blackness remained. She drifted inside it, formless, like an embryo. She waited, calm because she had been here many times before, in what the sibyls called the Nothing Place, which the offworlders had taught her was the lifeless heart of the sibyl computer itself. . . . But she had never been called to it like this; only in answer to someone's direct question.

Her confusion began to slide into a darker emotion, her fear quickening with every measureless second. The sibyl mind had touched her, murmured its will to her own mind before—goading her on to achieve its goals—but never like this. Its guiding voice had rippled through her subconscious, leaving impressions of rightness, visions, compulsions to *do* that could have come out of her own thoughts, until in her worse moments she had sometimes wondered if they had. It had never called her here. . . .

(Moon . . .) Her name came singing through the void, and suddenly a golden wind enfolded her, and swept her beyond the heart of absence. She shimmered through an infinite spectrum of sensation that fired all her nonexistent nerve endings, into a rippling symphony of light.

(Moon—?) The vision of her name filled her, she watched it transform the darkness again, wave after wave of opalescent music echoing, fading fading fading. . . .

(Here—) She tried a response, with sudden urgency as the sensation diminished; watched as her own thought charged the unspeakable emptiness with a flare of brilliance.

(Moon . . .)

Once more the sensory song of her name touched her, this time caressing her impossibly, like the gentlest lover's hand. Impossible, improbable longing filled her, and with it, fear. (Who . . . What? What do you want?)

(Moon, it's BZ. BZ Gundhalinu—) There was an odd, shadowy hesitation in it, as if the voice imagined that she might have forgotten the name, forgotten even that she had ever known the man who bore it.

(BZ . . .) Her astonishment flowed out into the darkness and silence like bright waves, overlapping the radiant music of his words. (BZ. How? Where are you—we—?) Not understanding why she could not see him, or why she was able to speak freely.

(In Transfer. A special kind of Transfer.)

(Are you in the Nothing Place? I *feel* you. . . .) Feeling herself lifted, raised, exalted by light, by the sensation, the realization . . . Realizing, in that moment, that the years had not diminished her need to know his fate, or her memory of the sacrifices he had made for her in the name of love. Or the memory of all they had shared, so fleetingly, so long ago . . .

(I'm not sure where we are. . . . I feel it too, but it's completely indescribable. Moon, I . . .) Dark-bright, the sound of his sudden silence lapped her consciousness.

(BZ?) She called out his name. (Oh, BZ, I dreamed once before that you spoke to me like this. Was it a dream? Is this a dream?)

(No,) he answered softly, the word touching her like a sigh.

(Then why haven't you done this before . . . since . . . if you can control the Transfer? I've wanted—) She broke off, as the radiance of her sudden longing warmed her like the dawn sea.

(Have you—?) he whispered. Again, the shadow of his silence lengthened across the waters of her thought. (I couldn't,) he answered at last. (I couldn't, because I wasn't certain. . . . Certain you'd want that; certain that there was any point in torturing myself, or torturing us both, when there might never be a future where we would ever meet again.)

She absorbed the radiance of his words, her double vision falling through them into their deeper meaning. (Are you saying . . . that we will?)

(Yes.)

(How . . . ?) Feeling something within her catch fire, burning her with an exquisite pain that was as much fear as wonder, as much desire as dread. (It isn't possible. It can't be possible—)

(It is now. It will become a reality very soon. Moon, after I contacted you in Transfer, at Fire Lake—I found out that the Lake was made up of stardrive plasma. I brought it back to the Hegemony. I'm on Kharemough now. They're building starships.)

The exquisite pain inside her turned suddenly to fear as cold and inexorable as glacial ice. (The Hegemony is returning to Tiamat?)

(Yes.) One word, falling out of the brightness like a sword.

(Soon—?) She was barely able to ask it.

(As soon as they can. I'm overseeing the construction project. In three or four years, I estimate, it will be possible to reestablish contact.)

(And you—made this happen? Why—?) she asked, her disbelief metamorphosing. (Why are you telling me this? To make me afraid? Because you've changed your mind about Tiamat's right to a future?)

(No! Because . . . Damn it, I don't know how to . . .) His voice strobed in the darkness. (Moon, if I could only see your face! Do you remember what I told you, when I called you to me in Transfer at Fire Lake? What I . . . felt, when I thought that I would never see you again?)

(Yes.)

(That hasn't changed . . . this doesn't change it. When I realized the truth about Fire Lake, I realized it couldn't be kept secret. I knew the stardrive plasma had to be given to the Hegemony, for the future. And I knew . . . I realized a stardrive would make it possible for me to see you again. But I also knew what it would mean for Tiamat. And I knew that because I would be responsible for that, I would owe you a debt I could only repay in one way. I'm coming back with the Hegemony, I'm coming back in charge, if I can manage it—to stand between your people and mine, to make certain we don't destroy you. I didn't know . . . can't know . . . whether you even want to see me, after all this time—)

(I—) she began, not knowing what answer she would make; feeling as if the words had swept her up into a whirlwind, leaving her centerless and without refuge.

(It's all right—you don't have to answer.) As if he were trying to convince himself, he repeated, (It's all right. . . . I'm not coming there to force myself on you. I believe in what you're doing for your world, and I mean to preserve that. But to help Tiamat we will have to work together. That's why I'm warning you now—not to make you afraid of me, but to give you time to prepare. That's also why I didn't contact you sooner . . . because until now I wasn't absolutely certain that nothing would go wrong; there was still doubt in my mind that everything would happen as I believed it would.)

(And there is no doubt in your mind now—?)

(I know that the Hegemony wants Tiamat back; they want the water of life. I'm not certain yet of how high I can climb before it happens. But my prospects are good. I hope to be the new Chief Justice by the time I get there.)

She was silent, filled with brilliant noise, filled with the future his words had painted inside their spectral prison of light.

(Moon—?) He called her name again, as softly as rain, when she made no answer. (Are you still Queen? Have you been Queen all this time? Have you done what you set out to do—shown your people the truth, and begun to rebuild?)

(Yes . . .) she murmured, as realization rose inside her, wave upon wave in a blinding flood. All she had done to create a new, independent technological base for Tiamat would be useless. She had believed Tiamat had a century in which to reach a level of development where they could protect themselves, and the mers, from the Hegemony. They had come so far . . . but nothing like far enough. Even if she had known from the beginning, there would not have been enough time. It had been an impossible task . . . futile from the start. The Hegemony would come, and they would slaughter all the mers in their blind greed. (But why—?) she said, asking it of the sibyl mind itself, the invisible Other whose presence must be all around them. (Why did I begin this, if there was never going to be time to finish—?)

(But you'll still be the Queen. And I will be Chief Justice.) It was BZ who answered her, with words like the light of stars falling. (Have faith in what you have done already, have faith in me. I believe now what you always believed, that there is some reason for all of this, and for what our lives have become. It doesn't mean we'll win. But it means we have a chance. . . . Moon, when I left Tiamat, I left it feeling as if I was a moth that had been caught in a flame. I've come so far since then, along stranger paths than I ever dreamed of, because of what I shared with you—)

(Yes,) she thought, feeling an infinity of clear skies suddenly illuminate her soul. (Yes, we both have. I would have had nothing, no past at all, all these years, if it weren't for you. . . . And it will come to nothing in the end, without you.)

(Are you still . . . with Sparks?)

(Yes,) she said again, and there was a dark silence. (BZ, there is something you don't know,) she pressed on, forcing brightness, (about Tiamat, about the mers. Something more important than you are or I am, more important than you ever imagined. The mers are sentient.)

(What?) he murmured. (No . . . how is that possible?)

(The Hegemony knows—on some level they must know; because the sibyls know. The Hegemony has been slaughtering an intelligent race for centuries.)

(But, it makes no sense . . . he protested.) (The mers were an experiment left over from the Old Empire; they're only animals. It couldn't be that the Hegemony would knowingly—)

(Ask, and you will see.)

(But why? Why make the mers intelligent, and then abandon them on a lost world like Tiamat? What purpose could there possibly be for such a thing?)

(The most important purpose imaginable, BZ, and it will be lost, destroyed, if the Hegemony is allowed to go on killing them. Because . . . because the mers . . .) She became aware that the luminous lightmusic was beginning to dissipate, the waves of limpid sound breaking up into static, into the rush of rapids, flickering geometric patterns of lost image. (BZ—)

(I'm losing you. . . . It's breaking up. . . .)

(BZ . . . the mers, ask . . . BZ—) But only silence answered her, and she felt herself falling again, back through the conduit of night. . . .

Coming to in the reality she knew, she found herself still clutching the cold marble table-edge, blinded like an insect by the artificial lamplight of her office. Gradually her vision cleared, and her eyes registered the concerned face of her husband gazing back at her across the cluttered desk.

"Moon—?" Sparks murmured. "Are you all right?"

Moon nodded, slumping forward, propping her head in her hands. "Yes."

"A Transfer?" he asked, with a matter-of-factness in his tone that his expression did not quite support.

She nodded, lifting her head again as strength began to come back to her. Her time in that nameless otherwhere had drained her more than the Transfer normally did; she wondered whether the contact had broken because their physical bodies—or their sanity—had reached some limit of endurance. "How long was I—like that?"

Sparks shook his head. "Maybe five minutes."

She felt a brief pang of disbelief. "Only that long? Did I say anything?"

He looked surprised. "No. It was like a trance. You didn't move the whole time." Something passed across his face that suggested he had not been particularly comfortable during the wait.

Moon sat silently for a moment, as all she had experienced, and felt, rose into her conscious mind. "It was BZ Gundhalinu, Sparks," she whispered.

"Who?" he asked, uncomprehending. And then his face changed. "Him," he said, and his voice was curiously flat. "Why—?"

"He told me the Hegemony has found a source of stardrive plasma," she answered, the words dropping like stones between them. She stood up, suddenly too restless to remain sitting.

"What?" Sparks actually laughed, his disbelief was so complete. "That's impossible. There's no source of stardrive plasma within a thousand light-years—"

"He said that Fire Lake is made of stardrive plasma."

"Fire Lake? I've heard of that. But that's . . ." He shook his head, looked up again. "It's actually true?"

Moon nodded, folding her arms against her stomach. "The Hegemony is building starships."

He jerked as if he had been struck. "So they can come back here."

"Yes."

"How soon?"

She let her hands fall. "He thinks no more than three or four years."

"Three or four years—?" His face filled with the stunned disbelief that had torn the center out of her own existence only moments before. His eyes went on gazing at her, but for a long space they did not seem to register anything at all. "I thought we were safe." He looked away.

I thought we were safe. Moon looked down at her own hands, saw them clenched, white-knuckled, on the table's littered surface.

"You learned all this in Transfer?" He glanced up at her finally, half frowning. "From Gundhalinu himself?"

"Yes." Moon sat down in her seat, brushing a loose strand of hair out of her eyes. "It was like nothing I've ever experienced. It was as if I'd been drawn into the Nothing Place—the mind of the computer itself. And yet somehow he was there too; not physically, but like a . . . spirit. We could speak freely. . . ."

He shook his head, still half frowning. "You're sure it was really him?"

And not the sibyl mind. "The net has never spoken to me like that. . . . It hasn't spoken to me at all, since it made me Queen." She heard something that was almost forlorn creep into her voice. She looked up again, at his dark surprise. "I'm sure it was him." She went on, telling him the rest of it, watching him; feeling herself watched, in turn. ". . . He said that he intends to come back with them. As the New Chief Justice."

Sparks stared at her, his entire body suddenly rigid. "Why?" he asked at last.

Moon looked down. "He wants to help us. He feels responsible for what he's done to Tiamat, by making it possible for the Hegemony to return."

"Why?" Sparks asked again, roughly.

She raised her head. "He said . . . he said that he still loves me."

Sparks sucked in a small breath, and did not ask the question that Moon saw come into his eyes.

She did not answer it. She glanced away, across the room; saw her own face looking back at her from a mirror on the wall. Seeing another woman there, in her memory—one with the face of a young girl. Not even certain whether it was herself she was remembering, or Arienrhod . . . She looked away. "We need his help," she murmured. "Tiamat does. You know what this means. The Hegemony will want to control Tiamat full time. And we won't be able to stop them."

"I know," he said, his voice strained. "The water of life . . . they're going to want it. They'll take it, if they can." His jaw tightened. "And I don't see how even Gundhalinu can prevent that."

"I told him the truth about the mers. That they're sentient." She wove her hands together on the tabletop, finger by finger, tightening. "I don't know if he believed me. . . . But the information is there for anyone to see, in the sibyl network. If he can make the Hegemony acknowledge that—"

"He can't," Sparks said angrily. "Lady's Eyes, Moon—they don't want to know!" His voice hardened. "The ones who want the water of life don't care about anything but what it can do for them. They don't have to—they're the ones with the power. They don't give a damn about anyone's suffering; as long as it doesn't hurt them. And mers aren't even human. You're talking about the ones who run the Hegemony, and they aren't going to listen."

Moon rose to her feet, staring at her own reflection across the room. "They will listen, this time." She touched the trefoil dangling against her linen shirt. "Because there's more. It's not just about the morality of committing xenocide; it's about enlightened self-interest." She turned back to him, leaning forward on the table. "Because the mers are the key. They have to survive, or the . . . or . . ." Something was happening behind her eyes, like the beating of dark, enormous wings. They tumbled her thoughts into chaos, stopping the words in her throat.

"They're . . . they're the . . ." She pushed away from the table, falling back into her chair.

"Moon—?" Sparks reached out to her.

"I . . . can't. . . ." She shuddered, as something inside her collided with an impenetrable wall. "I can't . . . tell you. I can't . . . ever tell anyone." She shook her head. Her thoughts began to clear, the black wings slowly furled, as she surrendered to the sibyl mind and its compulsion, still controlling her, holding her under its geas. *That Carbuncle is the pin in the map. That the computer itself lies here—the secret heart, the hidden mind, of the sibyl net.* No one could ever be allowed to know its hiding place, because that would make it vulnerable, and its reason for existence would be lost, along with its secrecy. The people it had been created to serve could not be trusted. And so she could not be permitted to reveal its existence here; or the mers' reason for existence, even if saving them meant saving itself.

It had chosen her to do its work . . . but now she suddenly understood that it did not trust even her completely. She would not be allowed to share her secret with anyone, no matter how vital it was to the success of her task, to saving the mers, to saving the net itself. She had to save them, somehow, without letting the enemy know the one thing that might make them willing to compromise. *Because she could never tell anyone why.*

She turned away from Sparks's confusion, the sound of her name being spoken again in urgent concern, and went wordlessly out of the room.

TIAMAT: Goodventure Holding

The small trimaran nosed in toward moorage at the docks, its engines tactfully silent. Moon Dawntreader stepped down onto the mortared stone surface of the landing wearing the heavy woolens and kleeskins of a Summer sailor, with her hair in braids. She knotted the forward mooring rope to an iron post in the chill shadows below the cliff-face; turned, with her cold-stiffened hands resting on her hips, to gaze at what lay waiting for her.

There was no one else on the pier, or on the ancient steps that zigzagged up the dun-colored sandstone slope to the town above. Here and there the steps showed the near-whiteness of fresh patching. A basket attached to a winch-rope, for hauling the day's catch and other goods up the cliff, sat empty on the stones. Up above was the Goodventure clan's ancestral claim, which lay a day's travel north of Carbuncle. During High Winter it had been completely inaccessible, permanently buried under snow. But with the coming of spring it had been reborn; she could see the green of new grasses spilling over the cliff's edge, limned by sunlight against a rare, perfectly blue sky. Seeds that had lain dormant beneath the snow had neither failed nor waited in vain. . . . The sight of green high above the bleak, barren shore was a testament to faith and change.

Moon took a deep breath, looking down again. There were thirty or forty other craft clustered at the docks, bobbing offshore, tied up along the pier or pulled up onto the narrow, stony beach below the cliff. Hers must be among the last to arrive for the triad of festival days. To find mooring space had not been the Lady's luck: a place had been reserved for her, as Summer Queen.

Tradition dictated that she should be the one to oversee these annual celebrations. By rights they should have been held on ancestral Dawntreader lands, because she was the Queen. But the Dawntreaders were an obscure clan, whose few members had been scattered across the far islands of Summer. They did not even have a meaningful holding here in the north, but lived randomly spread among the other Summer families, as they always had. And she had neglected her traditional duties more and more over the years; she had always been too busy defying her heritage to make the time for them.

And so Capella Goodventure had come to oversee the festivals that were held every year at the annual midsummer of Tiamat's orbital passage around the Twins—the ages-old festivals that must have given rise to the Festival of the Change, when Winter and Summer changed places in the revolving cycle of time. The Great

Festivals of the Great Year had become tied to the cycle of offworld exploitation and onworld ignorance only after the Hegemony began coming to Tiamat. Remembering those things, she felt her resolve strengthen, and her belief that she was doing the right thing.

Behind her Moon heard Ariele and Tammis come out of the small trimaran's protected cabin onto its deck. Ariele looked sullen and annoyed, as usual. She shielded her eyes, gazing out across the sea to avoid having to acknowledge her mother. Tammis simply looked glum and uneasy. There was no one else on board. She had brought them here herself; had wanted to feel her own hands on the ropes and tiller, needed to prove to herself that she had not completely lost touch with her past.

Beyond the bright forms of her two children she saw another ship coming in, on a course that would ease it in beside her own craft to a precariously tight moorage. Miroe and Jerusha had followed her up the coast, at her request; not just as guardians, but to help her in what she had to do.

Ariele crouched down suddenly at the stern of the boat's deck, watching intently until a familiar brindle-furred head broke the water surface. Ariele whistled shrilly and the merling swam toward her, meeting her outstretched hand with a sleek, wet caress. "Silky!" she murmured. "You came. I knew you would . . . beautiful Silky." The young mer regarded her with rapt attention as she slid into a series of hums and whistles. Tammis stood behind her, watching silently, listening for the mer's response.

Moon felt wonder strike her, as she watched her daughter and the mer. The merling had followed Ngenet and Jerusha up the coast all the way from their plantation. It was a triumph of sorts, and not a small one, that they had successfully communicated their request. And beyond that, Silky had trusted them—loved them—enough to leave her home in Ngenet's bay, and the mer colony that had adopted her, to journey this far with them.

But in this moment Moon was not sure whether the mer's presence here, or Ariele's gentle joy as she touched the face of her sea-friend, astonished her more. In the city, in the palace, Ariele showed her nothing but defiance and thorns; until there were times anymore when she looked at her daughter's face and could not remember any emotion but anger or pain. When all she saw in that face so like her own was Arienrhod. *Arienrhod.* But in this fragile, unguarded moment she had glimpsed the beautiful spirit of the child she remembered: it was still there, only hidden, like a bud beneath the snow, waiting for spring to come in its own time.

Moon turned back as Jerusha and Miroe came along the pier toward her. She crossed the dock to meet them, smiling.

"We made it," Jerusha said, her own pride and relief reflected in her husband's face.

Moon nodded, gripping their hands. "We've come two thirds of the way. The third part is the hardest." She glanced at the steps leading up the cliff face. "I hope we haven't come this far for nothing."

Jerusha smiled faintly. "Well, there's strength in numbers." She gestured toward the way up.

Moon looked back at them, hesitating, and shook her head. "First I have to go alone. I have to show the Goodventures that I've come in humility and without arrogance . . . or there's no point. It will be hard enough to make them hear me out as it is, without—" She broke off, looking down; looked up again into their faces:

offworlder faces. The faces of the Enemy, even more than her own was, to Capella Goodventure. She had long since stopped seeing anything unusual about the appearance of either of them. But she saw now, with sudden clarity, how they would stand out among the tradition-bound Summers up on the plateau. "Let me bring her here to you . . . and Silky." She glanced away at the water.

"It isn't safe for you to go alone," Jerusha protested, with the habitual concern of years spent guarding the Queen's back.

"Tammis and Ariele will be with me." Moon nodded toward her children. "We'll be safe. Not entirely welcome, but safe. Capella Goodventure may hate everything I stand for, but the duty and honor of her clan are at stake. She'll guarantee my well-being."

Jerusha glanced at Miroe, who made no protest, and nodded her head grudgingly.

Moon began to strip off the layers of slicker and knitted wool that had kept her warm on her journey. "I'll bring Capella back here as quickly as I can." She called Ariele and Tammis away from the ship's rail. They came to her side, resigned, dressed as she was now in traditional Summer festival clothing—loose linen shirts and pants dyed in shades of green, decorated with shells and embroidery. Tammis looked self-conscious but expectant; Ariele looked resentful as she left Silky's side. Neither of them had wanted to come. But they had, at least. Her eyes filled in the image of Sparks's absent face, behind them.

Days had passed, after she had learned the news about the Hegemony and the stardrive, before she had told anyone else about it. She had moved through those days as if she were still outside reality, endlessly considering the consequences of what she knew but could not share, and what she must do about them . . . and waiting for a sign, from the sibyl mind, that had never come.

At last she had told the Council about what she had learned, and what it would mean for Tiamat. And she had told them that she had decided to turn all her efforts and the resources of the Sibyl College to finding a way to protect the mers.

The news had been greeted with shock and disbelief, and then, in a flood, the reactions she had anticipated and dreaded. She had seen the hunger come into the eyes of too many Winters, and even newly tech-proficient Summers, for a future like their past—a life of golden subservience in which all their needs were taken care of by the Hegemony, and the only measurable price they paid for it was the water of life.

Some of the new industrial leaders and even the sibyls had argued against abandoning the push to raise their technological level, saying that instead they should do everything possible to make what progress they could . . . that they should turn their efforts to weapons research.

She had rejected that outright, knowing from all Jerusha had told her that they would only be creating the weapons of their own destruction. But she could not reveal to the Council the reason why the mers' survival was ultimately the key to their own survival, and even the Hegemony's; why protecting the mers had to come before anything else . . . any more than she could explain to her husband why BZ Gundhalinu wanted to return to Tiamat, and save their world from his own people.

She could no longer rely on the people she had always relied on. And so she had turned to the traditional elements among the Summers for help and support; for their knowledge about the sea and the mers . . . which had meant even more resentment, more resistance, from the people in the city, who had always been her strength.

And it had meant that somehow she must heal the long enmity between herself and the Goodventure clan.

She and Sparks had argued over every aspect of her decisions, even though she knew that for his own reasons he wanted to protect the mers as much as she did. He had refused to accept any changes in their plan for progress, even though for sixteen years he had spent as much time studying the mers as he had spent working with her on the task of building a new Tiamat. The reasons for his anger and his intractability had been as clear to her, through all their bitter words, as she knew they must be to him. But neither one of them had dared to speak the truth that might have freed them . . . or made it impossible for them ever to look into each other's eyes again.

And when she had asked him to come with her to meet Capella Goodventure, he had refused to leave the city.

She sighed, pulling her memory and her fears back into the present, back under her control. She looked at her children, who stood nearly as tall as she was, waiting for her. She had been with Sparks through all the years that she had been Queen . . . and that was nearly as long as she had been with him in the islands before that, before the separation that had changed them, their world, their place in it. It was hard to believe so many years had passed so quickly—and yet so endlessly. Almost as hard to believe as the sudden image in her mind of the people they had become: such strangers that the innocents they had been in Summer would scarcely recognize themselves . . . such strangers to each other.

She shut that thought out of her mind with finality, not letting herself even begin to wonder whether the distance that had grown between them had become unbridgeable. Or what it would mean to them—to all three of them—if BZ Gundhalinu returned to this world . . .

She started toward the flight of steps that would lead her into a future that was not the one she had wanted, or intended. Silently she reminded herself that neither was the future she had now one she wanted, or intended.

She climbed, Tammis and Ariele trailing behind her. Her breath came hard by the time she reached the top. She wondered whether it was the years, or only her body's enforced inactivity that had left her winded. But waiting for her was a sight that made her sudden sense of mortality fall away—a sea of Summer, of sea-greens, grass-greens . . . fair, sun-reddened faces, young and old, laughing, wrestling, eating, at play. A picture out of time.

She moved among the ancient stone-walled houses with their newly rethatched roofs of dried seahair, moving forward into the past as she searched the crowds for a face she recognized. Curious strangers looked back at her, smiling as they saw the trefoil shining against her shirt, and called her "sibyl." Some of them looked hauntingly familiar; she was not sure if she had seen their faces before, perhaps even dealt with them in the city . . . or whether they only reminded her of people she had known in her former life. Most of them gazed at her without recognition; but one or two bowed their heads, murmuring, "Lady . . ." in surprise, before they turned away to spread the news.

She realized then that word of her arrival would travel; that Capella Goodventure might even find her first. She slowed her random motion, forcing herself to be patient, letting herself become accessible, as a sibyl should be. Ariele and Tammis stayed close beside her as she moved out into the open meadow beyond the village, and she realized with fleeting sorrow that they felt far more alien here among their own people than they did among the Winters of the city, with whom they spent nearly all their time. And she realized that, after so long, she did too.

A small voice that was never entirely still inside her reminded her that she was Winter by blood: Arienrhod's clone. But they were all the same people, the Winters and Summers. They belonged to the same world, and its heritage belonged to all of them. The name she bore, *Dawntreader,* and the name *Goodventure* were two of the original shipnames, passed down over the centuries from their refugee ancestors. She and Capella Goodventure were alike, at least in their love for this world. If they could only both remember that . . .

Tammis passed her a warm fish pie, as Ariele was drawn away, semi-reluctantly, by a handsome blond boy. Ariele disappeared into a group of young Summers who were practicing a triad dance under the guidance of an older woman. Moon's feet remembered the steps of that dance as she heard its music, and her body began to sway to its rhythm. Her flesh might be Winter's, but Summer was in her blood. . . . She smiled at Tammis, who stood beside her watching the dancers. "Do you want to try it?" she asked.

He shook his head, looking down. "No. I'd rather just listen. You need someone with you—" He looked up at her again. She saw both his concern and his instinctive reticence; knew that he was right, and that he would be happier where he was. "I used to dance like that," she said.

"Do you want to join them?" he asked, curious and surprised, as if it had not really occurred to him that she had ever known any reality besides the one they had always shared in the city.

"No," she said softly. "It's a dance for the young. A lovers' dance." She watched Ariele step into the circle, swirling with unselfconscious grace among the other dancers, and felt an odd sense of déjà vu.

"Lady," a voice said behind her, its familiarity startling her. Capella Goodventure stood waiting, her expression guarded and suspicious. She nodded in grudging deference. "I was not expecting you to come."

"There was a place for my boat at the dockside," Moon said.

"There is always a mooring-place left empty for the Lady, in hope that she will come. It is tradition. But I did not expect you to come." A slight emphasis on *you.*

"But I have . . . and I thank you for remembering me, even in my absence, Capella Goodventure."

The Goodventure elder looked at her a little oddly, as if she wondered whether Moon meant the words or was mocking her. "And you brought your children to witness their heritage—for the first time," she said, in the same tone. "But not your pledged." She raised her eyebrows.

"He had too much to do . . . in the city." It sounded evasive, and was. Moon wondered whether Capella Goodventure believed that he had not come because he had become too corrupt, too much of a Winter—or whether Capella knew more about his past than she thought. The words did not sit well, either way.

"I came because I wanted to feel what it was like to be in Summer again. I have spent much too long in the city myself, as you have rightly pointed out." Moon felt her speech falling back into the outland cadences of the voices around her. And this time the words were true, she realized suddenly. She had fallen so easily into the pursuit of technology to the exclusion of everything else, telling herself that it was the will of the sibyl mind, the only way to save her world. But the revelation of the

Hegemony's unexpected return had shown her suddenly and profoundly that she had been wrong, all along. She had been thinking like Arienrhod; repeating Arienrhod's mistakes. It had to be for the ways in which she was different from Arienrhod that the sibyl mind had chosen her. She was the sibyl, not Arienrhod; she was a Summer, and she must forget now that she was anything else. . . .

Capella Goodventure continued to look at her skeptically, without comment. "And I came . . ." Moon pushed the words out before they could wither on her tongue, "to make my peace with you, if that's still possible."

Capella Goodventure stiffened, as if she was sure now that this was some sort of trap. "What do you mean?"

"I know that we have never seen eye to eye, all these years," she said, carefully, "not simply in matters of tradition, but also on the most basic questions about what kind of future this world should have. But in spite of our—differences, I believe that you are a good woman, and that you have only been trying to do the Lady's will as you see it. And although you find it hard to believe, the same is true of me. Both of us have been trying to preserve the Tiamat we love, and protect both its peoples, the humans and the mers."

Capella Goodventure half frowned, and twitched her shoulders in an impatient gesture that Moon couldn't read. "I suppose that's true enough. I'll grant you that. But I don't see anything we have in common beyond that, Moon Dawntreader. Your ways will never be Summer's any more than your face will be anything but that of the Snow Queen."

Moon felt her face flush with sudden heat. She swallowed the angry response that filled her throat; aware of Tammis watching her, and Capella Goodventure glancing at him with sharp suspicion. Moon put a hand on Tammis's arm, urging him with a look to let them have privacy. He left her side reluctantly, frowning as he looked back at them. "I won the mask of the Summer Queen fairly, by the Lady's will. Do you question Her will—?" She felt every muscle in her body knot in anticipation of Capella Goodventure's response; afraid that the sudden emptiness inside the words would betray her.

But the other woman only looked down, with her lips pressed together. "The Lady works in strange ways," she murmured. "Even people of my own clan seem disposed to accept the changes you have forced on us in Her name. But I don't understand this, and I never will." She began to turn away.

"Wait," Moon said, hearing the unthinking edge of command come into her voice, watching with surprise as Capella Goodventure obeyed her automatically. "There is much more at stake here than you know—more than my pride, or yours. I have something to show you. And something to tell you."

Capella Goodventure hesitated, looked back at her, waiting again.

"Will you walk with me to the steps?" Moon asked.

Capella Goodventure nodded slowly, and followed her. "What is this about?"

"It's about the one thing that we both believe in with our whole hearts—the protection of the mers."

The Goodventure elder looked up, startled out of watching her shadow precede her across the grass. "How are they in danger, now that the offworlders have left us in peace? They will increase their numbers while Summer is here; they always do. This is their time of mating and rebirth, when the Summer colonies migrate north, and join the Winter colonies."

"Is it?" Moon said. "Are you sure?" She had heard it as casual lore, but she had no records to compare it to.

Capella Goodventure looked disdainful. "It is part of the common knowledge about the mers. You should have spent more of your time studying the ways of your people."

"I intend to, from now on," Moon murmured, as sudden urgency took the sting out of the other woman's sardonic reprimand. She was not sure how accurate the Summers' knowledge was; but any new resource they could add to what they had already observed could only help them.

"What makes you say they are in danger?" Capella Goodventure repeated impatiently. "The offworlders won't be back for nearly a century. And even you have not dared to suggest we begin murdering the Lady's Children ourselves and drinking their blood to stay young."

Moon flushed again, and bit her tongue. "We don't have a lifetime or more before the offworlders come back," she said flatly. "We have maybe three years."

Capella Goodventure looked at her as if she had suddenly gone insane.

Moon rubbed her arms, inside the loose, shell-clattering sleeves of her shirt. "I have learned in sibyl Transfer that the offworlders have discovered a source of the stardrive plasma the Old Empire used. They're building starships right now that can reach Tiamat without using the Black Gates. They don't have to wait. When the starships are ready, they'll come."

Capella Goodventure's stare turned incredulous, and then disturbed, as she absorbed the full implication of the words. "Lady's Eyes—" she murmured, walking a few more steps lost in thought. And then she looked up again. "So," she said. "This was the Lady's plan." Moon hesitated, wondering against hope whether the Goodventure elder had finally understood what she had been trying for so long to make her see. But then the other woman smiled bitterly. "You strove to make us like the offworlders, to make us forget our old ways and be like them. And now that blasphemy has brought the Lady's curse down on you—perhaps on all of us. The offworlders will return with their technology, which you wanted to possess so badly. And they will put the Winters back into power and throw you into the Sea, like the Motherlorn, unnatural creature you are—"

Moon caught the Goodventure woman's sleeve, jerking her around as they reached the edge of the cliff; as she heard her own unspoken fears mock her from the other woman's lips. "Are you blind as well as deaf, Capella Goodventure? Goddess! Why can't you see that all I've done to change Tiamat has been to keep us from losing everything to the offworlders when they come back again? Not because I love what they are that much more than what we are! They have things, and ways of doing things, that we can profit from—just as we have things they could profit from understanding, like . . . reverence . . . for the mers. Even your own people know that, or they wouldn't be using that synthetic silkcloth as a tent to shade food that's been stored in those insulated coolers for the festival!" She gestured fiercely back the way they had come. "But that isn't the point. The point is that I've done everything that I've done for the single purpose of protecting the mers."

Capella Goodventure snorted. "You can't make me believe that."

"The . . . Lady told me that I would have to save them. That it was more important to Her than anything else. That I was Her tool, that I must do anything that was necessary to help the mers, because they . . . they are . . . sacred to Her."

She stumbled over the words, hearing them fall awkwardly on her own disbelieving ears. She hoped that Capella Goodventure would not hear her doubt, but only her desperate urgency. She looked up again, realizing that she had always had a genuine reason in her heart for protecting the mers, one which needed no deeper explanation: "The mers saved my life, once. I would do the same for them, if I can."

Capella Goodventure was silent now, her eyes hard but clear, her face expressionless; listening, at last.

"I have worked all these years to give us independence, so that the mers would never be slaughtered again. But now everything has changed again—for all of us, like it or not. The offworlders are coming back too soon, we aren't ready, and they will slaughter the mers before the mers have had a chance to rebuild their colonies. They'll go on killing them, in blind greed, until they've killed every single one. And that will be a tragedy beyond imagining, not only for us but for them. We will all be . . . under the Lady's curse. Unless I can find some other way to prevent it."

"And how do you think that can be done?" Capella Goodventure asked finally, with doubt still in her voice, but at least without hostility.

Moon started down the steep, narrow stairs, watching her feet; glancing back as she beckoned Capella Goodventure after her. "The Lady has shown me the truth about the mers: that they are . . . intelligent beings, just as we are."

"You believe this?" Capella Goodventure asked. Moon realized her incredulity was not for the words themselves, but for hearing them spoken by someone she believed had turned her back on the tradition that held the mers sacred.

"I believe it as profoundly as I believe in my own existence," Moon answered. "They have a language of their own. One of the things that I have been doing—with the sibyls of the College—is studying their language, so that we can find a way to communicate with them. If we can do that successfully, we may be able to warn them of their danger, at least."

Moon had reached the foot of the steps now. She nodded to Jerusha and Miroe, who stood together on the pier. Behind her she heard Capella Goodventure's footsteps stop suddenly.

"What do they want?" Capella Goodventure asked. "Why have you brought them here? They're not welcome—"

Sudden motion in the water interrupted her, as a mer's head and long, sinuous neck appeared suddenly beside the two waiting figures. Silky looked quizzically at Jerusha and Miroe, away at the new arrivals, and back at them. Jerusha crouched down, murmuring something inaudible, stroking the merling's head. The Goodventure elder watched as if she were hypnotized.

"I asked them to come because she is theirs," Moon said softly.

"No one owns a mer," Capella Goodventure snapped. "And certainly no offworlder has the right—"

"They raised her," Moon said. "They found her orphaned on the shore about seven years ago. They are her family. She left the bay at Ngenet plantation, where she has lived all her life, and followed them here . . . because they asked her to. That's why they've come. To show you that I've spoken the truth."

Capella Goodventure went slowly past her, moving toward Jerusha and Miroe. She moved as though every muscle in her body resisted it, as if she was helpless, under a compulsion. "Did you raise this merling?" she asked.

Miroe nodded. "We did." Jerusha still crouched down, holding on to a mooring post for support as she coped with Silky's head-butting caresses.

"How is that possible?" Capella Goodventure said bluntly, unable to reconcile what her eyes showed her. "You aren't Tiamatan."

"My family has lived on Tiamat for three generations," Miroe said, looming over her, matching her irascibility with his own. Moon remembered her own first meeting with him, and felt a brief flash of pity for Capella Goodventure. "My wife chose to stay on Tiamat when the rest left here for good, because she preferred this world to anything she'd seen out there. How can we belong here less than you? Your own people came here as refugees from somewhere else, on a ship called the *Goodventure*. Only the mers are truly of this world." He glanced over his shoulder at Jerusha and Silky. "I've studied the mers all my life. My life was protecting them in any way I could, until Winter's end. . . . But it wasn't enough. I don't ever want to see again what I saw on my own shore—" He looked back at her.

Capella Goodventure studied their faces a moment longer, then turned back to Moon. Moon met her stare; felt as though the Goodventure elder looked at her and really saw her for the first time in sixteen years. "I feel as though I must be dreaming," Capella Goodventure murmured, as she looked out at the sea. "Perhaps the Lady has spoken to us all, in Her way." She looked again at Moon, at Jerusha and Miroe. "You claim that you can actually talk to this merling; that she followed you here at your command?"

"Request," Miroe corrected.

Jerusha nudged him into silence. "It was as much out of trust as real communication," she said. "There seem to be very few concepts we have in common . . . we don't even know how to ask them questions. So much of what they do seems to involve mersong—and the mersong is incomprehensible to us."

"The mersong is how they worship the Lady," Capella Goodventure said flatly. "No more, no less. It wasn't meant for us to understand."

"But we've found patterns in the mersong that are like those in traditional Summer music," Moon said, forcing patience into her voice. "We would like to speak with people at the Festival today and record songs they remember, especially songs about the mers—and any lore they know, stories, superstitions. If you would help us, then all of Summer would begin to understand that what we're doing is vital to everyone on this world."

Capella Goodventure hesitated again, looking uncertain.

Moon glanced away from her, as unexpected motion on the steps caught her eye. She realized, surprised, that it was Ariele and not Tammis coming down to them. Ariele was trailed by three Summers, two boys and a girl; she swept past the four adults on the pier like a warm breeze, calling out to Silky with a series of trills. Silky came obediently back to the pierside, and she presented them to the merling with the obliviousness of youth.

Capella Goodventure watched them, and Moon watched all that the other woman saw: Ariele, so much like her mother, growing up in the city and yet somehow in her element, here with the mers. The Goodventure elder shook her head in something that could only be resignation. "Very well," she said slowly. "I never thought I would live to see this day; but I have." She looked back at Moon. "You and I have one goal from this day forward, Moon Dawntreader. We will do the Lady's work together, from now on. I only hope that we can do it well enough."

KHAREMOUGH: Orbital Habitat #1

"How did it go, Commander?" Vhanu rose from his seat, putting back the headset he had been using to pass the time as Gundhalinu stopped beside him. The conference had run overlong, as usual, and Vhanu had arrived here promptly, as usual.

Gundhalinu smiled. "It was just what Faseran and Thajad wanted to hear. I think everything is going to work out exactly as Pernatte predicted." They began to walk, threading their way through the workers, human and servo, who were laboriously fitting a new series of murals into place in the hallway of the Hegemonic Coordinating Center. "It will still take almost two years of preparation before they send the expedition to Tiamat—that's if the ship production continues on schedule too, of course—" He looked back over his shoulder as they were forced to go single file. "But Faseran actually told me today that I can have the Chief Justiceship if I want it."

Vhanu started in surprise. "Father of all my grandfathers! That is good news. . . . I do hope you'll consider my application for a place on your provisional staff, Commander. That is, as you know, I—"

"After all you've done to help make this happen, NR," Gundhalinu said, "you can name your position in the new government." He smiled. "Even Commander of Police, if you still want it." His smile widened as he saw sudden pleasure light up Vhanu's face.

"Yes, sir. Very much—" Vhanu's own smile widened; his fist tightened at his side like a surreptitious shout.

"Then consider it a—" Gundhalinu collided with the body that backed suddenly into his path. Hands flew up to steady him; the youth he had run into met his gaze with urgent gray eyes, and he felt the brush of a familiar hand-sign as a piece of paper was pressed into his palm.

His fingers closed over it, he opened his mouth—noticing just in time the registry numbers printed on the young worker's forehead, that marked him as an Unclassified. Gundhalinu swallowed the words he had been about to speak as the day-laborer's expression became deliberately abject fear. The worker flung himself flat in an abasement. Gundhalinu looked down at the dark, unkempt curls of the youth's hair, and kept silent. By law Technician and Unclassified could not even speak directly, without an interpreter of intermediate rank. Even an apology was impossible, on either side. And no matter who was right, the Unclassified was always wrong.

"Look out, you dumb bastard—" A Nontech foreman caught the laborer by the neck of his coveralls as he began to rise, hauling him out of Gundhalinu's path. "He begs your pardon, Commander-sathra—" the foreman said, shoving him; the worker grunted as his face collided with the chiseled stone images of their mutual ancestors on the wall.

"It was my fault," Gundhalinu said, feeling the paper crumple as he tightened his fist. The laborer turned to look at him, with one cheek red, leaving a red smudge on the wall as he turned away from it. There was no expression at all in his eyes now.

"No, sathra. It was his fault." The foreman shook his head. "You—!" The worker flinched as the foreman's voice caught him. "You're fired." He nodded, head down, and started away without looking back. "Sir," the foreman said, pleased with himself. He bowed and backed out of their way.

"Thank you," Gundhalinu muttered as he started on, because it was expected.

"Gods," Vhanu said, glaring at the laborer's retreating back, "why do they even let these people work on such an expensive project?"

"Because they work for almost nothing," Gundhalinu answered wearily, looking straight ahead as they went on toward the tram stop. "Vhanu, did you ever imagine how it would feel to live as a lowborn?"

Vhanu glanced at him. "Certainly not."

Gundhalinu touched a sequence on the glowing plate of the tram's callbox. "What if it had happened? Do you think you'd like it?"

Vhanu laughed. "I think I'd rather die."

"That's what I always said." Gundhalinu smiled ruefully, remembering when his own convictions had been as rock-hard, and as simplistic. He turned away as he opened the crumpled piece of paper the worker had pressed into his hand. He swore.

"What is it, Commander?"

Gundhalinu turned back, handing him the note. Vhanu read it, reacting as he saw the cryptic symbol scrawled at the bottom. "Survey . . . ?" He passed it back again, uncomprehending. "What does it mean?"

"Trouble."

Vhanu looked back down the hallway, where the day-laborer had already disappeared. "Do you want me to notify security—?"

"No." Gundhalinu's fist tightened, crumpling the paper again. "This is a family matter. Call ahead for a shuttle. I have to get across to Hub Two."

"The starport complex? But what about the meeting with Jarsakh-bhai and the board, and the inspection of the—"

"Cancel everything." The tram arrived, he held the door. "Say . . . say it's a family emergency. You won't be lying." He got on board. "I'll be in touch."

Vhanu stared at him; pushed forward suddenly, boarding the tram just as the doors squeezed shut. "Commander." He glanced down, up, touched Gundhalinu's arm briefly. "I don't understand what this is about, but you shouldn't go alone."

Gundhalinu nodded, not sure whether he was grateful or only annoyed to have that pointed out to him.

"Is it your brothers, again?"

"Yes." Gundhalinu sank into a seat as the tram began to move.

"What have they done?" *This time.*

"I don't know yet, but it's bad. I don't even care what it is—by all our ancestors, this time is the last time. I won't bury any more 'mistakes.' I'll have them arrested, stripped of rank—" He looked up, bleak-eyed, into Vhanu's stare. "I don't mean that, do I?"

"You never have before," Vhanu said quietly.

"It's not even the memory of our ancestors that stops me anymore, NR. It's politics . . . 'how would it look.' . . ."

"Soon it will be over," Vhanu murmured. "You'll be where you want to be, in your Chief Justiceship. And then it won't matter, you can let them go hang."

"I'll leave them plenty of rope." He shut his eyes.

The waiting shuttle carried them between artificial worlds, backtracking across Kharemough's cislunar space, which was dotted with the false stars of other habitats and industrial hubs. Gundhalinu spent the trip in silence, imagining scenarios of shame, scenarios of furious outrage, a hundred different gut-knotting confrontations, until the vast, whitely-gleaming torus of the starport slowly filled their view. A wheel of habitat connected by transparent access spokes to a central island that was the port itself, Hub Two was the largest of all the orbitals. He stopped brooding long enough to stare out at the chains of coin-ships where they lay strung across the vacuum, in safe harbor within the wheel—at their flattened forms designed for Black Gate transit. Already they looked alien, almost primitive to his eyes, which had grown accustomed to visualizing the organic forms of the new hyperlight fleet that was taking shape; even though he knew coin-ships with converted drives would continue to be the foundation of interstellar trade into the indefinite future. *The future* . . . He sighed, watching as they closed orbit with the station below.

Three figures stood waiting for him inside the access as the small, manually operated lock cycled discreetly behind them. He recognized Donne, one of his on-line metallurgists from the shipyards, and two other workers—a chief rigger and a powersuit operator, from the datapatches on their coveralls.

Vhanu frowned as they came forward, with incomprehension and annoyance. "Why are you—?" He broke off as Gundhalinu gestured him silent.

"I'm grateful for your message. Can you tell me what's happened, Donne?" Gundhalinu touched the woman's upraised hand briefly, in a silent acknowledgment between equals.

She nodded. " 'Fraid so, Commander. But we've been waiting here for you a long time; we'd better move, if you don't mind. You know Zarkada and Tilhen—?"

Gundhalinu nodded, looking from one man to the other. Both were offworlders, he realized, and appreciated her discretion once again—two big men, who looked as if they solved most of their problems the hard way. But they were reliable and steady on the job, from what he remembered. "Gods. Is it that bad?" he asked Donne.

She grimaced, and nodded again. "We're headed for a low-gee neighborhood."

Gundhalinu looked back at the two men, feeling as though he had swallowed stones. "Thanks for coming." They ducked their heads. Tilhen showed a trace of smile, and shrugged. "Sorry to hear you need us, Commander."

"Right," he said.

Donne led them to an anonymous-looking hired van. They climbed in and she activated the controls. A map grid came up on the display; Gundhalinu saw two red lights blinking, side by side, somewhere deep inside it; realized there must be a trace acting on his brothers. He watched the light that was their own vehicle start to move as he felt motion around him; they appeared as a spot of green, entering the grid.

"There's work clothes in the back, Commander. You ought to put them on,"

Donne said. "Half the people where we're going will be afraid to speak to you dressed like you are, and the other half will want to cut your throat. No offense," she added, as Vhanu glared at her.

"None taken." Gundhalinu urged Vhanu ahead of him into the back of the van, and pushed faded coveralls into his hands.

"Commander," Vhanu murmured, clutching the coveralls as if they might be alive, steadying himself as the van rose suddenly and steeply. "This is madness. We can't do this; call in the Police—"

"We are the Police, Captain Vhanu." Gundhalinu shrugged off his uniform jacket and held it up, dropped it. He unsealed his tunic and stripped it off.

Vhanu looked down; began, self-consciously, to take off his own jacket.

Gundhalinu turned his back, remembering a time when he had been equally prudish. He pulled the coveralls on in awkward silence and semidarkness as the van banked sharply. Vhanu turned back at last, self-consciousness warring with discomfort on his face.

"NR—" Gundhalinu said gently, to the look, "thou're not under orders. Thou don't have to get involved in this. Thou can leave us anywhere, with my gratitude. . . . My brothers may be stupid but they've never been suicidal; this will ruin my day, but it's not going to kill me either." He settled a battered dockhand's helmet onto his head.

Vhanu glanced toward the three semi-strangers waiting for them, forward of the partition wall. His expression did not improve. "Damn it—"

"They're all Survey. So was the one who passed me the note. All doing me one hell of a favor."

Vhanu looked back at him, incredulous. He nodded, accepting it, and sighed. "At least it makes more sense that way."

"More sense than what?"

Vhanu's mouth twitched. "Than that you let Nontechs and laborers address you as equals for no reason at all." He finished fastening his coveralls and put on a helmet.

Gundhalinu went forward again, stood behind Donne's seat. "Tell me about it. What in seven hells have they got into, to drag them into a place like this?"

Donne glanced up at him in a brief moment of understanding. She looked out again at the featureless artificial terrain of the lower level warehouse district, rubbing her cropped, graying hair. "It's not pretty, Commander. It looks like your brothers are trying to sell restricted program codes, giving access to classified production specs on the starship fleet—"

"Damnation!" Gundhalinu's hands tightened on the seatback. "How could they even get such a thing? They have no clearances—"

"Looks like your brother SB hired someone to deepsearch your family codes, and got a key on you. Used one of your security clearances to fool some program here upstairs, just long enough."

Gundhalinu swore, feeling as if someone had kicked him in the stomach. He shut his eyes against the awareness of everyone else's eyes on him, like spotlights. "Who? Who are they dealing with . . . ?"

"Certain factions whose rules you also play by, but who are playing an entirely different Game with them."

Gundhalinu forced himself to take a deep breath, hold it; forced himself to concentrate. "It won't do them any good. The codes won't work—they all change automatically, every shift."

"I know that, Commander." Donne nodded. "But I guess your brothers didn't."

His deathgrip on the seatback loosened. *No damage done. No real damage. But there could have been.* This time it had gone too far. This time he could not afford to ignore it, rationalize it, forgive it . . . cover it up. What they had done was not simply a betrayal of him, but betrayal on an entirely different scale. This was greater than any personal humiliation, private or public—

Donne stopped the van; Gundhalinu saw a blinking barrier ahead, the drift symbol of a low-gravity environment. "We'll have to walk it from here, Commander," she said. "It's not far."

He glanced at the twin lights on the display that marked his brothers' position. He touched them with his hand. "They haven't moved," he said.

"Probably waiting. With any luck, they've been stood up, their contacts found out the codes were worthless and didn't even bother to show."

"You're sure there's no one else there?"

"No one's registering, Commander." She shrugged and got up; passed him a handgun. "Rough neighborhood." He checked the charge automatically, and pushed it into an easy access on his coveralls, as she silently handed out more weapons. Vhanu put his own weapon into a pocket, looking uneasy.

They left the van behind and walked toward the barrier, no one straying too far from the others; went past it, into the vast, slowly rising curve of the low-gee area. Gundhalinu felt his footsteps begin to slide and drift, changed the way he was moving in response as his weight suddenly dropped to a fraction of what it had been. The gravity here changed from place to place, moment to moment, depending on what was being done in the factories and warehouses. He had become accustomed to moving in low- and zero-gee environments since coming to the shipyards. He let his body function on habit, thinking ahead, watching the red lights burn steady on the map display he had called on inside the shield of his helmet.

Vhanu swore beside him, obviously lacking similar experience with variable gravity. Donne and the two men watched him flounder without comment. They kept moving, in long, arcing strides, forcing him to make the adjustment. Vhanu was about to get an education, Gundhalinu thought, and it was one he could use, if he bothered to remember it afterward.

The low-gee areas existed like knots in the intestines of the starport's habitat ring; they were used primarily for storage and processing of materials that would be impossible to work with otherwise. There were warrens of living quarters here too, climbing the walls, jammed into crannies among the looming warehouses, the cranes and machinery in this gray, echoing, twilight world. They were housing for the lowest of the lower classes. He saw the eyes of a child peering out at him from a makeshift doorway as they passed, and looked away again, with an ache in his gut. Kharemough supplied most of the Hegemony's high-grade technological equipment, and did most of its manufacturing out in space; which meant that most of its population and thousands of immigrant workers were out here too, crammed into too little space, sometimes under conditions no sane person would want to think about. Only the most wealthy, the most powerful, still lived down on the planet's surface—or could afford to.

Gundhalinu rubbed his arms, remembering the pernicious chill in these places, as they stopped for an automated gateway and Donne punched in a code. A tow drifted by over their heads, the deep throb of its engines echoing eerily off the hard surfaces everywhere around them. Other noises invaded his consciousness: distant shouting, the sound of heavy machinery grinding, the whine of cutters, some vibration so deep that he felt more than heard it, that made his teeth hurt. The work here never ceased; neither did the noise, always changing but eternal, echoing and distorting in ways he never heard anywhere else; as if sound was somehow warped and dysfunctional too, like gravity.

They moved on again like awkward swimmers, passing workers who drifted like shadows across their vision, in small groups or alone, variously empty-faced, wary, dull-eyed. The meter-thick rails of a transport track rose up across their path, leading toward the access door of an airlock that could have admitted half a ship. Gravity increased abruptly, and they stumbled the succession of painfully clumsy steps to the other side, only to drift and collide with each other when the gravity faded again. Gundhalinu righted Vhanu, saw the disorientation growing into panic in his eyes. "It gets easier," he murmured. Vhanu nodded and took a deep breath, starting on unaided.

A gang of Unclassified workers came up alongside them; Gundhalinu heard mocking laughter and muttered insults. "Hey, fresh meat," a voice called out. "Maybe you need a little *help*—" Someone's elbow struck Vhanu, sent him caroming into a wall.

Vhanu recovered his balance; his hand darted toward the pocket that carried a concealed weapon, his face full of sudden fury. Gundhalinu caught his arm, held him back as Zarkada took hold of their harasser, towering over him, and shoved the man away into his companions. "Maybe you'd like me to help you find out which way you bend, scumbag . . . and which way you don't." Tilhen moved forward until they were shoulder to shoulder.

"Hey, just having a laugh, that's all," the worker said, raising his hands, dancing backwards away from them. "Welcome to Kharemough, you miserable assholes. Hope you like it here. Foreigners—" He spat. The rest of his group was already moving on, getting out of range.

Gundhalinu watched them go with his hand casually deep in his pocket, feeling the comforting solidness of his own stun weapon. Their voices already seemed to reach him from some unimaginable distance; their laughter drifted on down the tube, always echoing, and was gone.

Donne started on again. The others followed, silent now. Vhanu stared at the faces of the people they passed, as if he were looking for something he didn't find. Gundhalinu realized he was still expecting the strangers to somehow perceive an indefinable difference in Gundhalinu's appearance, or his own. Something which set them apart. None of the workers glanced at him twice.

"How much farther, Donne?" Gundhalinu asked, his unease increasing with every stranger who passed.

"That warehouse section right up there, Commander." Donne pointed.

Gundhalinu pushed off from the building wall beside her, taking the risk of a faster, longer move. He pushed off again, not looking back to see how well the others managed to follow; focusing on two small pinpoints of red that still had not changed, on the motion of his own body closing the distance to them.

He could not believe it had come to this, that he was about to confront them in a place like this about an act of such obscene stupidity. He felt his anger come back, a blind, murderous, fever heat that seared everything from his mind but the need to find them, confront them, give them what they deserved. This time nothing would stop him, nothing would change his mind. He had warned them over and over again, those ingrates, those shitbrained, honorless fools—

He reached the base of the warehouse. There were no workers anywhere near it, no sign that anyone had made any regular use of this place in months. He looked up the looming face of the building, seeing the designation codes, most of them meaningless to him, glowing red and yellow on its grimed, metallic skin. Before him was the five-story door of the cargo entrance, solidly sealed shut; but like a rat hole in its base there was a narrow door sized for human access. He took out the stunner, checked its charge again with compulsive care.

He felt more than saw Donne and the others come up beside him. Donne made a move to stop him as he started forward; suggesting with a look that he should let someone else go in first. He shook his head. The control panel beside the door said that it was unlocked. He pushed the black-painted metal inward; the door gave with a grating screech, opening on shadows. He stepped inside, wary but unhesitating now, aware that his heart was beating too hard, his brain singing with adrenaline; and that the emotion causing the reactions had nothing to do with fear. His own slow, drifting footsteps echoed hollowly, overlapping the sounds his companions made like ripple rings on dark water.

"HK!" he shouted, seeing no one, hearing nothing else. "SB!" The others followed him, through a cavernous storage area half full of cryptically labeled bins, and then another, half full of house-sized crates. The green lights that marked their presence on his map closed inexorably with two stable points of red. He shouted his brothers' names again, still getting no response. He wondered what in the name of a thousand ancestors they thought they were doing. Why didn't they answer . . . why didn't they run—? Instead they were just standing there: silent, waiting; caught red-handed but still humiliating him, forcing him to come to them.

He pushed off, too hard, trying to reach the access to the next storage area. He collided painfully with the metal doorframe; steadied himself, blinking his vision clear. His hand was slippery on the butt of his gun as he pushed through into the next room, and the pinpoints of light on the map converged.

In front of him the floor of the room was red: a lake of red, wet, shining, as if someone had spilled a vat of paint. He wrenched his body with his sudden attempt to stop moving; still landing with both feet in the spillage. A drop of red hit the sea of redness in front of him, from somewhere above; and then another. The gun slipped from his nerveless fingers, hit the floor, splattering his pantslegs with red. He raised his head, moving in slow motion, as time itself seemed to redshift around him, as compulsion closed its inexorable fingers around his throat, forcing him to look up.

His brothers were up there. Hanging from the ceiling, suspended high out of his reach. They hung from a chain like meat, the spine of a grappling hook driven clear through each of their chests, stone dead. He watched as two more drops fell, watched them hit the sea of blood in front of him like silent tears.

He turned, stumbling, collided with the mass of bodies directly behind him. He saw their faces—the stunned disbelief of Donne and Zarkada and Tilhen, the horror in Vhanu's eyes. Vhanu turned and bolted back through the doorway.

"Get them down," Gundhalinu muttered, forcing his eyes to stay on Donne. "Find somebody . . . get them down."

Donne nodded, gesturing to Tilhen and Zarkada. They went out. Her eyes left his face fleetingly, glanced upward, fell again. Gundhalinu pushed past her. She followed him out; following the blood-red tracks his boots made every time his feet came down.

They were outside. He stopped moving, staring in surprise at the unchanged light, the unchanged view his eyes found in front of him. Vhanu stood against the building wall, wiping his mouth, his eyes red-rimmed. Gundhalinu looked away from him. His own eyes felt as dry as sand. He couldn't blink. "Why—?" he murmured to Donne.

Donne pressed her hand against her mouth, shook her head once, before she could meet his gaze. "Don't know, Commander. . . ." Her voice was matter-of-fact, when she answered. "My best guess would be, they did it to make a point."

He frowned. "Because the codes my brothers had were useless?"

"Or because they were your brothers," she said. "Maybe the whole thing was a setup. To prove that even if the Brotherhood doesn't dare lay a hand on you, they can still . . . hurt you. I'm sorry, Commander. . . ." Her voice faded to a whisper.

Gundhalinu took an unsteady breath, watching his own hands become fists. The sound of process and progress boomed and reverberated and clattered and whined, nearby, far away, echoing echoing hollowly all around him, through him, inside his head where no meaningful thought would form.

"BZ—" Vhanu said hoarsely, and came back to his side; he was aware of Vhanu's hand laid hesitantly on his shoulder, although there seemed to be no feeling at all anywhere in his body. "I'm going to call for help. I'm going to—"

"No," Donne said. "We'll take care of it, Vhanu. No Police involvement. No scandal. No one wants that for the Commander. It will all be taken care of. You understand?"

Vhanu stared at her for a long moment, his jaw set. At last he nodded. "Understood," he murmured.

Gundhalinu turned back to Donne, trying to find words adequate to thank her, and failing. He put a hand on her arm, meeting the gaze of her clear, dark eyes. "In your debt . . ."

Donne smiled briefly. "Let's go, Commander. We'd better go."

He turned away from them, from the warehouse door still gaping like an open wound, and started back toward the streets.

KHAREMOUGH: Gundhalinu Estate

Gundhalinu watched the last of the mourners depart, moving away through the passionate colors of the gardens dressed in somber gray. He stood where he had stood all through the memorial service, motionless, emotionless, the perfect model of gracious, civilized inhumanity. *Waiting* . . . he wasn't sure for what. *Waiting for it to be over. Waiting to feel something.* Waiting.

He knew what he must do now: what he had avoided doing during the entire week that he had been home, keeping himself too busy with details and arrangements that could have been handled by others, too busy communicating with the people he had left in charge of the shipyards up in orbit, to do this one thing. . . .

He glanced back at the manor house rising behind him, as servos began to move among the clustered seats, clearing them away. The vine-traced wall, fitted together out of blocks of native stone, still stood as solid as he had always believed his family's reputation to be. Its windows gleamed with the sun's reflected light, making him squint, the brightness making his eyes burn until the colors of the gardens swam, like colors in an oil slick.

He turned back again, starting across the smooth stones of the patio with a lump in his throat . . . stopped.

One final guest stood limned by garden colors at the far side of the open space: a woman, in a characterless gray robe, her hair swept up and back, twisted and pinned in deft, fluid folds that made him think of wings. He changed his trajectory to intersect her. She did not move, making him come to her—although he sensed that it was not arrogance but uncertainty that held her there.

His footsteps slowed again as he saw her face clearly. "Netanyahr-kadda," he murmured, in surprise, as he recognized the woman who had once owned his estates.

She bowed, lifted her head again as he crossed the final distance between them. "Gundhalinu-sathra," she said, and for a moment he could not think why there was such sorrow in her voice, such compassion in her gaze. "I imposed upon an invited guest to bring me with her . . . I hope you will forgive me, for committing trespass upon your goodwill again. I did not wish to embarrass you, but I wanted to—to see you again. To offer my condolences—" she went on hastily, as he felt his own expression change. "I was so terribly sorry to hear about your brothers' accident."

Don't be, he almost said, didn't.

"I wanted you to know that after all this time I hadn't forgotten you—your extreme kindness to me. Simply to send you a meaningless message of sympathy, among thousands of others, was not enough. But I was unlikely to meet you by chance. So I came, to tell you that." He nodded acknowledgment, saying nothing. "And now I will leave you alone." She bowed again, and after a moment's further hesitation, turned away.

He watched her begin to disappear among the flowers; she was almost lost from his sight before he could free his body from its paralysis and call her name.

He entered the path between rows of shrubbery massed with golden blossoms, walking quickly; found her waiting for him beside the octagonal, blue-and-gold tiled fountain. "Thank you for coming," he said, before he even reached her. He stopped, meeting her gaze, and suddenly was struck speechless again.

She looked at him expectantly; he looked away. "Netanyahr-kadda . . ." he said at last. "I was about to go down to the family shrine and pray." *Try to.* "I would be pleased if you would care to accompany me."

Her face registered surprise, but she nodded. They walked together through the gardens, making meaningless, innocuous conversation about the plants and the weather. Surreptitiously he watched her face as she took in the view, saw the longing she could not quite conceal. He could never keep his own eyes off the view for long. The manor house sat at the peak of a narrow pinnacle of limestone, one of dozens scattered across the ancient, eroded terrain. He could see many of the others from here, rising like gnarled chimneys from the lush green of the plain, most of them bearing estates like his own. *My own—* He looked back suddenly, at the house on the rising slope behind him, and out at the view again; feeling a rush of vertigo.

The family shrine lay ahead of him, gleaming whitely on an outcrop at the edge of the sheer drop. There was no maze of shrubbery concealing it; the promontory itself offered a privacy that most estates did not have. Pandhara Netanyahr stopped as they reached the waiting-bench beside the path. She glanced at him, her fingers brushing the filigreed seatback; uncertain whether he wanted her to wait, or to stay at all.

"This is the first time I've seen the estates since I returned to Kharemough . . . the first time I've set foot on this path since I left home to join the Police, years ago," he said. He turned back to her; she settled onto the bench, looking up at him. "When you . . . when you came here to pray, what did you say? I don't know what to say, anymore."

She shook her head, glancing at the shrine. "I didn't know what to say, either, Gundhalinu-sathra."

He nodded, and went on along the path alone. He went in through the always open door, into the cool, echoing interior. He paused, startled by the quality of the light. He had forgotten how the light . . . forgotten so much. There were no windows at all, but daylight shone through the translucent ceramic of the walls, silhouetting the countless barely visible names inscribed along their luminously glowing planes: the actual names of members of his family for every generation, for as far back as anyone had ever been able to remember and record, in a record that began well over a millennium and a half ago. He noticed, with a sense of dim surprise, something that he had never realized before—that his family actually claimed to be descended from Ilmarinen. He touched the name, feeling an odd electricity run up his fingers, wondering whether it was true.

He moved on along the walls, running his hands over the names, following them up through time into the present . . . stopping at last by the names of his parents, his brothers, himself. His own name was the only one with a red stain, coloring rubbed into the letters . . . he was the only one left alive. He stared at his own name for a long time.

At last he turned away, facing the small bench in the center of the room—a simple surface of gleaming white, mottled now with the dust of neglect. Still beside it were the cylindrical covered urn of the same perfect whiteness, and a container holding incense. He moved to the bench, sat down, with a peculiar reluctance. He took a stick of incense and held it between his hands like a flower, before he struck it sharply with his thumbnail, kindling it. He blew out the sudden flame, left it smoldering, watched as it perfumed the air with its bittersweet smoke. The old familiar scent brought the past flooding into his mind: memories from his childhood of sitting silently on this same bench while his father, his First Ancestor, head of the Gundhalinu family, prayed.

But his father's prayers were silent, he had never known what they said . . . they didn't help him now, as he tried to form something like a coherent thought. He looked up at the walls again, rolling the incense stick between his palms, the smoke making his eyes sting with artificial grief. This was the place where you came to feel pride, and tradition, to meditate on your family's accomplishments; to worship the perfect order in which everyone knew their place, and yours had always been on top . . . to call it justice.

But he no longer believed that, had not believed it for a long time now. What was he supposed to do now? Ask forgiveness—? *For whom?* For himself, for losing faith, or for seeing the truth? For his father's failure to act, for his brothers' cravenness and venality and greed, for the ultimate degradation and humiliation of their deaths? His hands dropped the incense, left it smoldering between his feet. *He should weep*. He was the last of his line, and he was living a lie. And he could not weep, could not grieve, could not feel anything at all. He made himself remember the moment he had learned of his father's death—when he had been far away, on Tiamat. Made himself remember his mother, her face blurred by time, as she kissed him goodbye and abandoned him in the rose-colored light of dawn. He pictured how his aged father had stood, leaning against the carven mantel in the main hall, his eyes like garnets as he urged his youngest son to usurp his brothers' place, to spit on the ideals he had been raised to revere. . . . Forced himself to see his brothers suspended like meat in an abattoir.

He realized that his face was wet, that there were real tears on it, this time. Tears of self-pity. He wiped them away, disgusted. *Gods . . . I'm so tired.* Slowly he got to his feet, and slid aside the top of the urn beside the bench. It was filled with ashes—the ashes of his ancestors, a pinch added at each death, before their remains were scattered into the wind. He sank a finger into the surface of the ash, and painted the requisite smudge of grief on his forehead.

He left the shrine, taking a deep breath to clear his lungs as he started back along the narrow path. Pandhara Netanyahr was still sitting alone on the waiting-bench, gazing out across the valley. She did not even look up as he approached, until he said, softly, "Netanyahr-kadda."

She started, looked up at him with a slight shake of her head, as if she had been completely lost in the view.

"Yes," he said, answering the look, "it is beautiful here, isn't it?" He sat down on the bench beside her.

She looked at him a little oddly; he realized, embarrassed, that she was searching for some intentional slight. But it was not there for her to find, and her expression eased again. "Thank you for letting me have the pleasure of its company awhile. I feel as if this place and I are like old lovers, in a way. The parting was painful, but there will always be something special between us."

He heard the melancholy in it, and glanced down. "Yes, I think I know what you mean." He looked toward the house, where it rose above the gardens like an extension of the peak itself. "I've felt the same way, since my return home."

"But you are the head of family now, aren't you?"

Head of family. He sat down, wondering dismally what he was going to do, now that he was . . . now that everything he saw, every fond detail, with all the painfully bright memories of his former life they evoked, only rubbed salt in the wounds of his bitterness. Even if his only memories had been happy ones, there was no way that he could possibly stay here more than a few days longer. Then it would be back upstairs—to the shipyards, to the halls of the government centers and Police headquarters. There could only be brief, stolen visits to this place, at long intervals if at all, once he was back at work. And then there would be Tiamat waiting, and the gods only knew when, if ever, he would return from there. . . . He pressed his hand to his eyes, resting his arm on the seatback.

"Gundhalinu-sathra . . ." Netanyahr rose from the bench beside him as though she thought somehow her words had been to blame. She touched his shoulder briefly. "I should not have stayed. I'm sorry—"

"Don't go." He caught her hand, when she would have started away.

She turned back, sat down again, looking at him silently.

"I'm glad for a little companionship that has no deadlines attached to it," he said, forcing a smile. "I don't want to go back up to the house. It's full of guests and messages of condolence, all with frantic inquiries about my return attached to them—"

She raised her eyebrows. "Are you truly so indispensable that they can't leave you in peace even to mourn?"

He laughed sharply. "Not as indispensable as I've made them think I am, I'm sure. . . . Vhanu tells me I have problems delegating authority. So I suppose I can only blame myself."

She tucked back a strand of dark hair that the wind had freed. "Is that why this is your first visit home, then—because of your work?"

He glanced away. "Partly . . . You may know that my brothers and I never got along particularly well."

She nodded, and he saw her mood shift.

"Did you know my brothers?"

Her hands knotted in her lap; he sensed her sudden embarrassment. "I met them when I bought the estates. And of course I saw them again after they returned to Kharemough from Number Four. When I was forced to give everything up, they . . . I . . ." She shook her head. "I knew them only slightly." She folded her arms, hugging herself as she looked out at the view.

"What did they do to you?" he asked, forcing her with his voice to look at him again.

Her golden-brown eyes regarded him steadily. "Your brother SB told me that I could stay on at the estates, live here and do my work—if I was willing to sleep with them both, and do whatever they asked me to. I actually tried it . . . until I found out what sort of tastes they had." Her hands closed over her arms, squeezed.

Gundhalinu looked away, swearing under his breath.

"It wasn't your fault, Gundhalinu-sathra," she said quietly. "Although . . . at the time I confess that I thought it was."

He looked back at her. "Do you remember my reaction when your pitcher of slops hit my brothers instead of me?"

"You laughed and laughed," she said, and something like understanding came into her eyes.

"My brothers tried to kill me, on Number Four."

She stared at him, blinking.

"Do you know anything about World's End?"

She nodded. "The place where you found the stardrive plasma. Yes, information about it was all over the newsnet when you returned. It was incredible . . . terrifying."

"My brothers got themselves lost out there, trying to strike it rich." He looked up at the milky greenblue dome of the sky, wondering suddenly whatever had inspired his brothers to think of such an insane scheme in the first place. Wondering whether it had really been chance; as he wondered about everything, lately. "I went out there to find them. I brought them back. But the things that had happened to them—to all of us—" his voice roughened, "out there, changed them. It twisted them. All the things I'd always disliked and resented about them—being out there made those things worse. My brothers wanted to hold the stardrive plasma for ransom. I didn't. They ambushed me and left me for dead. But I stopped them. That was probably all that kept me alive: needing to stop them. . . ."

He was seeing her face again, suddenly, at last. "After I recovered, I made myself believe it was the trauma of what they'd been through that had pushed them over the edge. That they'd be all right again, if I gave them back their old life. I'd been through so much myself . . . I thought I'd learned all the lessons I'd ever need to learn. My mistake." He shook his head. "My brothers' death wasn't caused by a hovercraft accident. They were murdered, when they tried to sell restricted data to criminals—data they stole using filecodes they stole from me." Suddenly it hurt to breathe. "I hated my brothers. I'm glad they're dead. May they rot in hell—!" He shut his eyes. "Gods, I needed to say that to somebody . . . somebody who would understand. May my sainted ancestors forgive me."

"They say," Netanyahr murmured, "that the difference between friends and family is that one can choose one's friends . . ." He felt her smile touch him, tentatively.

He made himself look at her again—was startled to see that her eyes were gleaming, too full. She held herself perfectly still, as if even an eyeblink would set free emotions she did not want to let go of. She took a deep breath, finally, and smoothed the folds of her robe. And the world settled back into place, and he realized again that it was a beautiful day in spring. He felt the warmth of the sun on his back, watched the feather-light silver petals of her single simple earring move in the breeze, below the graceful seaform waves of her hair. The sound of leaves rustling, of birds calling, filled the air. She looked out again at the view.

"Netanyahr-kadda . . ." He pressed his lips together over the urge to call her by her first name. He looked toward the house above the gardens, as the seed of an idea that had lain in his mind since their first meeting took root at last in conviction. Groping for the right words, the right order in which to speak them, he said, "I have a proposition for you, regarding the estates—and myself."

She looked back at him, her expression caught between two utterly conflicting emotions. She rose from the bench. "Is that why you think I came here—? To see if you were like your brothers?"

"Why exactly did you come, then?" he asked, hating himself for asking.

She bit her lip, staring at him. "I thought . . ." She broke off. "I came here because I knew you were not like them. I thought I came for the reason I gave you. But who knows . . . ?" She looked away, filling her eyes with beauty. "Who knows why we do anything, really?"

"Pandhara—I want you to marry me."

Her mouth dropped open. She gave a small laugh, a sound of disbelief.

"Strictly a marriage of convenience," he went on, before she could speak. "That's all I'm asking . . . that's all I require."

"I don't understand," she said weakly. She sat down again. "You're head of family now. Why—?"

"Because it's impossible. I don't want the responsibility, I don't want the—memories." He shook his head. "Gods . . . I still love this place, in spite of everything. But I don't have time for it. I can't live here. My life is up there." He glanced at the sky. "When the first ships are ready, I'll be going to Tiamat. And I don't think I'll ever come back." He looked down at her again. "I need someone to take care of things for me: my inheritance, my heritage . . . my name."

"What about the proscription? I'm ineligible even to marry a Technician." A glint of remembered anger shone through the words.

"The charges were false, the evidence was incorrect. . . . I'll have it taken care of." He glanced away.

"You barely know me," she said, her voice turning cool. "Surely you must have friends, someone of your own class—"

He shrugged. "No one to whom this place matters, the way it matters to me . . . or to you. I know more about you than you think, you see. I had you researched, after I met you, because I was—curious. You are intelligent, highly educated, creative, and your manners are, for the most part—" he smiled, "above reproach. You seem to me completely worthy to carry this family's name. I long ago stopped believing that class and rank meant anything at all. I didn't have to look any further than my own family to see that."

"You mean that . . . ?" She stared at him. "You actually mean that, this isn't some . . . some . . ."

He nodded. "There are absolutely no strings attached."

She pressed a hand to her mouth, shaking her head; her hands dropped into her lap and lay motionless. "I don't believe this is happening." Her voice was unsteady.

"That's because justice is so rare," he said softly.

Her eyes flickered up, fixed on the trefoil hanging against his robe, before she met his eyes again. "Gundhalinu-ken . . ." she murmured.

He smiled.

"You said that this would be strictly a marriage of convenience?"

He nodded. "I would ask only the use of a spare room for an occasional night, if I can find the time to visit the house now and then, until I leave for Tiamat. Nothing more. You will be free to live your own life."

She looked at him speculatively. "I would not find it at all—inconvenient to share a marriage bed with thou," she said. Her hand settled on his arm. "If thou would like it."

He turned away, feeling his face flush. "No. It's all right. You—thou honor me, but I can't."

"Is it this—?" Her fingers brushed the trefoil. "I thought there was no danger of infection, if one is careful—"

He shook his head. "It's not that."

She let go of the sibyl sign. "I see," she whispered, glancing away; although he knew that she did not.

Seeing her chagrin, still he could not bring himself to confess the truth to someone he barely knew. "But I would like very much for us to be friends," he said. "Would that be possible?"

She looked back at him, and smiled. "Suddenly I feel as if anything is possible," she said.

She took his hand as they rose from the bench, kept it held tightly in hers, as if she had to prove his reality through the long walk back to the house.

TIAMAT: Carbuncle

Tor Starhiker came down the steps from her private apartment, into the rear of the Stasis Restaurant, which occupied the entire ground floor of the townhouse. Dressed in a sensuous, sensual jumpsuit—one of the endless supply of garments from the old days that Shotwyn unearthed so effortlessly, from gods only knew whose closets— she could almost convince herself that these were still the old days in reality. The time when she had run Persiponë's Hell had been the pinnacle of her existence, no question. . . .

She glanced at her reflection in the mirror that hung discreetly at the bottom of the stairs: confronted by the present wearing her face. Her once stolid body had changed, rounding out with the years and Shotwyn's rich cooking. But to her surprise she found that she liked the changes. Maybe it was because Shotwyn, in his better moments, referred to her as voluptuous; or maybe it was just that the wider, softer curves filled her clothing in a way that made her feel elegant, and not fraudulent.

She forced herself to admit again that while this might not be all she could ask of a future, at least there had been a future after all, and at least she was here to see it. And now they were even saying that the Millennium had come, that the offworlders had gotten their legendary stardrive and would be back on Tiamat within a matter of years. Never in her wildest dreams had she expected she'd live to see that day. Life hadn't turned out to be nearly as dull and fish-stinking as she had imagined it would be.

In fact it felt, and smelled, extremely good as she drifted on past the mirror. She took a deep breath. Between her own perfume—which Shotwyn had concocted from a blend of herbs and flowers on a passionate whim, too long ago—and whatever he was putting in the sauce and soup tonight, the warm, heavy air around her smelled like heaven. She looked out into the dimly lamplit room, at the scattering of early evening guests. The lampglow was not exactly a high-tech environment, but the light was more flattering to all those aging faces; and even the offworlders had liked a few rustic touches, that let them feel like they were experiencing something exotic, here on this strange backwater world.

She picked up a copy of the evening's menu and glanced at it as she started into the kitchen. The florid names riddled with words in barely pronounceable languages always annoyed her, even though she knew they were necessary; a part of the ambience, as Shotwyn would say. She had to ask him for a functional description of each dish every evening, because most of their clientele could no longer speak any of those languages fluently, if they ever had.

"Ye gods—"

She heard Shotwyn's slightly nasal voice rising in exasperation as she let the kitchen doors slip shut behind her. He stood across the room, oblivious to her arrival, gesturing expressively as he berated one of the cook's helpers for some inadequacy or other. The hapless recipient of the abuse was Brannod, one of the two Winter nomad brothers she had hired to wash dishes and clean up.

The City was filling up with nomads these days; aimless, ignorant, and likely to starve to death unless a soft touch like her took pity on them, and gave them some menial job. The worst part was that they had no idea even of how ignorant they were, which made them worse than the Summers. Many of them had become dependent on the offworlders through trade and thievery during the hundred and fifty years when the Snow Queen and the Hegemony had ruled; but they were only superficially knowledgeable about technology, unlike Winters from the city or the coast. The nomads tended to be as insular and superstitious as the Summers, but unlike the Summers they had let their traditional customs slide, until they no longer knew how to survive off the land when they had no choice. And so they wandered down to the shore with the melting snow, and eventually found their way into the city.

This pair were all right—not too bright but not too stubborn, and they'd been hungry enough to become loyal, if limited, employees. She hired city-bred Winters for work that required more skill, or more social grace.

"What's the matter, Shotwyn?" She strolled up behind him, saw him start and turn to look at her; saw the relief in Brannod's pale blue eyes at her appearance.

"Everything!" Shotwyn snapped, planting a flour-covered hand in the middle of Brannod's chest and shoving him away. "Go, and get me another one! Then clean up this mess! Imbeciles . . ." Brannod wandered away glumly, in search of another whatever. Showtyn ran the floury hand through his hair, whitening the gray-shot auburn. "I'm going to disembowel myself if this goes on—"

"Only Kharemoughis disembowel themselves, Shotwyn," she said mildly. "Don't carry nostalgia for the past too far."

He sniffed. "That's what's paying the bills, my dear."

"Well, we won't pay many more bills if you kill yourself over broken crockery. So what are we eating tonight, anyway?"

"Cream of crockery soup."

"We'll charge extra," she said, and saw him smile, grudgingly. His long, saturnine face looked ten years younger when he smiled, which wasn't often—because, he insisted, he was an *artist*. "And explain this menu to me, will you? What's this?" She gestured at something which contained a hieroglyphic character.

"It's Sandhi," Shotwyn said, with irritating superiority. "The primary language of Kharemough."

"I *know*," she replied, with exaggerated patience. "But what *is* it?"

" 'Fish,' of course," he muttered, frowning as he turned away. "It means 'fish,' that's all. Everything means 'fish.' Pronounce it any way you like." He waved his hand in despair and dismissal, as Brannod came back reluctantly into his line of sight, carrying a bowl and a broom.

Tor sighed and went back through the doors into the dining room. There was no use talking to him when he was in one of those moods; which was most of the time, she thought irritably. She fixed a serene, welcoming smile on her face as she moved out into the room beyond, to mingle with the early diners, most of whom were regulars she knew personally. She had been forced to develop a reasonably gracious manner as the proprietor of Persiponë's, had worn it like the bizarre persona its real owner had forced her to wear—the image of a dead woman, whose holo he kept with him always, in the blackness he had inhabited like some night demon. Having to play Persiponë was the one thing about her job she had hated. When the Change came, she left behind everything that even reminded her of that unwholesome imitation of someone else's life.

But you never really unlearned a skill, even the skill of smiling graciously when you didn't feel like it, and speaking empty pleasantries to empty-headed guests. She made her way among the tables, saying hello, making certain that the servers were doing their jobs.

She stopped suddenly, as she noticed Sparks Dawntreader sitting at a table in the far corner of the room, by the diamond-paned windows that faced on the alley. It was the third night she had seen him here in the past week. He had been here only one time before this, under duress, she suspected, at the party they had thrown when they opened the place.

He sat at the same corner table each time, isolating himself as much as possible from the rest of the crowd eating here, keeping company with a book or a tape reader. And yet he watched the others, the Winters who had once been his constant companions, while trying to pretend he wasn't watching them; just as she watched him while pretending not to.

She wondered why he was here, since it wasn't out of fondness or loyalty. She wondered why he wasn't home with his family . . . wondered if he and the Queen weren't getting along. It wouldn't surprise her—it surprised her that they'd gotten along at all over the years, after all that had happened between them.

Moon had believed she loved him more than life itself when she'd come to the city hunting him. She had dragged everyone she met, including one Tor Starhiker, into her quest to save him and her confrontation with Arienrhod. There had been something about her that defied reason—maybe the intensity of her passion, or maybe just her uncanny resemblance to the Snow Queen—that had compelled Tor to defy her own better judgment and help a naïve girl fresh from the outback, full of impossible, romantic dreams.

Just because Moon had actually made those dreams come true, it didn't mean that in the long run she wouldn't come to realize that getting your heart's desire was sometimes more of a curse than a blessing. Tor wondered if Sparks Dawntreader had come to the same conclusion; whether he was sitting there now moodily watching what went on across the room because he felt guilty, or because he missed the old days . . . whether once you began living on the dark side, you got a taste for it that would never go away. She sighed, turning away as a crowd of half a dozen new customers entered the restaurant.

She saw Kirard Set Wayaways at the front of the party, and his wife Tirady Graymount. They ate here almost every night—old friends of Shotwyn's, who liked pretentious, nostalgic food.

As she started forward to greet them and show them to a table she saw them notice Sparks Dawntreader; watching their faces, she read their amusement and interest. They murmured inaudibly, nudging each other. Tirady and another woman split off from the group—at Kirard Set's urging, Tor noticed—and went to Dawntreader's table.

He looked up from his reading; startled but not surprised, Tor was sure. She greeted the rest of Kirard Set's colorfully dressed party, still watching from the corner of her eye as she led them to their seats. She saw the women flank Sparks, putting their hands on him familiarly, kissing him in a more-than-polite greeting as they gestured toward their own table. Sparks shook his head, at first noncommittal, and then frowning. He stood up abruptly, shaking them off, and left the restaurant.

Kirard Set *tsk*ed audibly. He looked up at Tor looking back at him. "I guess poor Sparks didn't like what was on the menu," he murmured, with a smile she didn't know how to read. "Please give my compliments to the chef."

"I'll tell him you're here," Tor said, keeping her own expression neutral. She had never liked Kirard Set much, particularly because she sensed that he didn't like her. When he watched her, listened to her, she knew he never forgot for a moment that even if he was no longer a noble at the Queen's court, he was still a rich, highly educated landowner, and she was and would always be an ignorant dockhand, no matter how many restaurants she owned, or expensive jumpsuits she wore. She turned away, trying not to listen to the tittering laughter behind her, or to wonder whether any of it was at her expense.

Shotwyn came out of the kitchen at her call, looking like a reprieved prisoner, his hands red and his face despairing. He might be an elitist, but at least he wasn't a snob. She smiled at him almost fondly.

She visited the tables of other new arrivals, exchanging gossip about the offworlders' pending return with Sewa Stormprince, her old boss from the docks. Stormprince had built herself a whole new career too; like a lot of other Winters, and even Summers, who hadn't started out with land or money, but had sufficient guts and brains to make up for it. And like all of them, she found the sudden change in their future to be a subject of obsessive interest.

Sewa Stormprince came here to eat not because of the food so much as the old acquaintance, and Tor appreciated the distinction. But she forced herself to end their conversation and head back toward the table where Shotwyn was still standing with Wayaways and his friends. If he didn't get back into the kitchen soon, they weren't going to have enough food prepared to feed themselves dinner, let alone several dozen other people who were all ready to spend a ridiculous number of imitation offworlder-style credit markers on it.

"Well, you know, I don't have anything against Worin's parents, and neither does he, but I just wish they'd hurry up and *die*, so that we can add the coastal rights to our own plantation before the offworlders want to start hunting mers again—"

Tor managed somehow not to wince as she heard Kima Tartree's high-pitched, strident voice announcing to the entire room something that anyone with half a brain would never even whisper in someone else's ear. She saw the others around the table snigger in a combination of empathy and barely concealed disdain.

"Well, that's calling it as you see it," Shotwyn drawled, as she came up beside him and put a hand on his arm in an unobtrusive signal.

"I'm sure we've all felt equally frustrated by something that stood in our way, at some point," Kirard Set said, dryly but with a peculiar vehemence. "In fact, my kinsman Borah Clearwater has been refusing to sell his plantation to me for years, although I've quadrupled the price of my offer and done everything but clean out his cesspool to try to change his mind."

"Then why not forget about it?" Tor said.

He looked at her, looked away again. "I begin to think he has no mind to make up," he said, with a heavy sarcasm that was not lost on her. "And he's living out there with the Queen's grandmother, so I get no help from her. It wouldn't break my heart if the Summers' beloved Sea Mother decided to take both of them to her watery bosom. . . ." His mouth curled. "In fact, I make a little offering to Her every night. If She doesn't hurry up and do something for me, I may have to turn my credit to some more responsive god, like Arienrhod did."

The laughter that answered him made Tor's skin crawl. Kirard Set glanced up at her again, raising his eyebrows. "Don't you agree?" She jerked more urgently on Shotwyn's arm, until this time he responded, following her away, back toward the anonymity that waited beyond the double doors.

TIAMAT: Ngenet Plantation

Ariele Dawntreader burst through the surface of the bay into the open air, inhaling deeply, with a gasp of relief. Her dripping hair clung to her face like seaweed. She pushed it back, blinking her eyes clear until she could locate the plantation house high on the hill, above the distant docks. Treading water, she made no move to start swimming toward shore. Her lungs ached, her body was numb with cold, but all she could feel that mattered was the transcendent joy of her stolen existence in the sea.

Beside her Silky surfaced, still moving in tandem with her, although the merling could stay submerged for twenty minutes without surfacing to breathe. She had never been able to stay down herself for longer than two minutes, even though she practiced holding her breath whenever she had a chance, any time that she had an undisturbed moment.

Using underwater equipment, she could stay down for an hour or more. She used diving gear whenever anyone was watching; or when the mers of the local colony were in the bay and she was trying to record their song. But whenever she put on a thermal suit and air tanks she became an alien, separated by an inescapable membrane of life support from the reality of their world.

To swim this way, relying only on herself as the mers did, was what she had always longed to do—what she had done in her dreams, since she was a child. The difficulties, the physical discomfort, were nothing compared to the freedom she felt here in the sea.

She took a last deep breath and ducked beneath the surface, sensing more than seeing that Silky followed her. She pulled herself down through the liquid depths with long, precise strokes, kicking to propel herself faster. The molten atmosphere of the ocean yielded to her passage, as Silky spiraled around her in ecstatic loops. Without her equipment she could not speak; could not hear when Silky sang, or spoke to her. But she could feel it, a strange susurration against her skin. She let her imagination fill in the wild, poignant music of whistles and wails and bell-like chimings, the siren song of legends and dreams that defined the mers' existence. To be with Silky was to be with her truest friend, the one being in her life who accepted her without question, without demands. It didn't matter that their lives interfaced as narrowly as their worlds did; when they were together the circle of their understanding was complete, and required nothing more.

The water of the bay was clear today, and occasional shafts of sunlight penetrated the bluegreen depths, illuminating the crazy-quilt crenolids and bright-colored crustaceans patterning the bottom sand. She was sorry that there were no other mers in the bay; it was a perfect day to watch them in motion, suspended by the Sea's unseen hands. Their effortless grace and heart-wrenching beauty were like a glimpse into the eyes of love; whenever she was among them she felt herself embraced by the eternal mystery of their existence, and the sea's.

Being in the sea among the mers, confronted by her own profound limitations, she had gained a poignant empathy for the time that they spent on land, where their bodies were at a disadvantage, awkward and ill-equipped for motion. On land Silky could share with her the beauty of the rain and the sun, the pleasures of warm sand and soft grasses, the ever-changing seasons that charted the endless days of existence, but the mer's real home would always be the sea. Like the humans, who belonged to the land, the mers could only balance precariously on the thin edge between their separate worlds.

She had often wondered if Silky longed to be a permanent part of her adopted family's world. She would probably never know, any more than she could really be sure of how the merling perceived anything else; probably she would never even be able to ask her. But ever since the merling had become a part of her life she had ached to become a part of this water world, shedding her skin for one with thick, brindled fur, so that she would never have to leave the sea . . . as she would have to do now, all too soon. Her lungs were burning with the need to breathe, and she propelled herself upward again. Exhaustion and the relentless cold were forcing their way back into her consciousness. Soon she would have to surrender, returning to the world in which she really belonged, the world that she was far less at home in than she ever was in this one. . . .

Jersusha PalaThion stood beside her husband on the graying, ancient dock at the bayside. The tide lapped the ankles of their high kleeskin boots as restless wavelets spilled onto the pier. Behind her, farther up the hill, plantation workers were constructing a new pier, one that would float on pontoons, adjusting as the water level rose. It still astonished her that the level of the sea had risen four inches in the time she had been here, fed by the dissolving sea ice, the massive runoff of melting snow.

It astonished her to think that she had been here for all those years . . . that she had been on Tiamat for over thirty altogether. For the better part of her life; so long that she had actually begun to measure her life by the alien rhythms of this world, so long that her body was no longer restless for the circadian rhythms of Newhaven. Now she had come to think of a day like this as so warm that she could walk out into the wind without bundling herself up in sweaters.

Now, this cool green sea no longer oppressed her with the relentless omnipresence that had led the Tiamatans to worship it as a goddess. She moved to the rhythms of Tiamat's tides and twin suns, looked up into night skies nearly as bright as its lengthening days without amazement. Her memory no longer dwelled on New-haven's endless honey-colored days of heat and blinding sky, its cool soothing nights when the courtyards were filled with the scent of night-blooming flowers. Some impatient part of her mind had even stopped asking her, day after day, when she would give up the foolishness of pretending to live on this alien planet, and go home. Now, after years of insomnia caused by Tiamat's different-length day, years filled with doubts and regrets, she even slept at night. She pressed closer against the solid comfort of her husband's side, felt his arm go around her, holding her there with fond insistence.

Her thoughts pulled back to the present moment as Miroe pointed suddenly, and she saw the water begin to roil with bubbles in front of her, below her feet. She leaned on the rail, peering down into the green depths, as two heads broke the water's surface suddenly—one human and one not: Ariele Dawntreader and Silky. Ariele shook back her hair, laughing in delight as she sucked in a long breath of air, and saw them waiting.

"Ariele!" Miroe said. "By all the gods—you're not using any equipment!" He gestured at the pile of her belongings lying heaped where the dock made a sudden right-angle turn. "Damn it, girl, I've told you before, you're going to freeze to death or drown down there."

"No, I'm not, Uncle. It feels wonderful! Anyway, Silky would never let me do that, would you, sweet Silky, my love—?" She broke into a trilling whistle, repeating a fragment of mer speech that had become as familiar to their ears as human speech. Her arms circled the half-grown merling's neck. Silky nuzzled her, nose to nose, and sneezed abruptly. Ariele laughed again, letting Silky go. She pulled herself out of the water onto the pier in one supple motion; she was wearing nothing but a sodden suit of long underwear.

Jerusha covered her face with her hand to avoid seeing the look on her husband's face, to keep him from seeing her smile. "I'm working on my endurance, Uncle Miroe," Ariele said, her own voice stubbornly chiding. "The others aren't in the bay anyway, so there was nothing to record." She strode away to the corner of the pier, blue-lipped, trying to disguise her shivering as she pulled a thick sweater and heavy pants from the railing and put them on over her wet underwear.

Miroe shook his head, his disapproval plain on his face, but he said nothing. A warm current ran north along the coast past Carbuncle, helping to keep these lands habitable even in the depths of Winter. And as Summer progressed, the average water temperature had risen, although it was still hardly comfortable. He looked out across the empty bay; it had been obvious to both of them already that the mers were not here. After all this time, their comings and goings were still a mystery to the humans trying to understand them.

"Hello, Silky." Jerusha whistled a now-familiar singsong melody, crouched down, holding out her arms as Silky swam toward her. The young mer pushed her neck through the space between the worn railings on the pier, pressing her face against Jerusha's and crooning softly as Jerusha embraced her. The dense softness of the merling's fur was like thick velvet, whether wet or dry, with a clean, fresh smell of the sea always clinging to it.

Miroe kneeled down beside her. Jerusha gave up her place to him reluctantly as Silky gave him a wet, thorough nuzzling, her bristling whiskers scraping against his mustache until he laughed. The merling looked back and forth between them, still crooning in contentment, and Jerusha caught fragments of songs in her humming that they had sung to her when she was still small enough to hold in their arms.

She had long since grown too large to hold that way, even though mers matured at least as slowly as human beings. But she still depended on them as if she were their own child; still made the long, arduous trek up the hillside to their home each evening; still slept in a pile of pillows at the foot of the bedroom stairs she could no longer climb. She had filled a void in their lives at least as profound as the one they had filled in hers. They had become her family . . . because her presence in their lives had made them a family, taught them how to share themselves with her, with each other. Jerusha knew that one day Silky would not make the climb to the house; someday she would leave them, and return to the sea for good—as was only right, she told herself for the thousandth time. As any human child would one day do . . .

Silky could have left them long before now. A colony of mers had ventured into this harbor several years ago, and had found one of their own already here, in strange symbiosis. She would not leave and so they had stayed, taking up semi-permanent residence in the inlet farther north along the plantation's shore, where once a Winter colony had lived. They had accepted Silky into their extended family, and she was learning to sing their individual skein of the mersong. She spent more and more time with them; but her ties to her adopted family were still stronger than the ties of blood, to Jerusha's profound relief. Eventually the colony had seemed to comprehend that, and welcomed the humans who put on diving gear and recording equipment and intruded on their hidden world.

But someday it would not be enough for her, and that was how it should be. There were few enough mer colonies left by the end of Winter; they had been fortunate that one had decided to visit this shore. These waters had been empty of anything but memories for far too long, until these mers, swimming north from the Summer islands, had changed things for the better.

And now the offworlders were coming back, to change everything for the worse. The thought was suddenly there in her mind, as it was at least once every day, to make her feel cold and afraid. She touched her face, touching the years, their mark upon her; rubbing her forehead as if she could brush the lines away like cobwebs. The Hegemony that she had turned her back on was coming back, and BZ Gundhalinu was coming back in charge, or so he had told Moon . . . and she had no idea what that would mean, for any of them.

Ariele came back to them, crouching down by the merling, making whistles and trills. Jerusha pushed the future and the past out of her thoughts for one more day, watching Ariele in fond amazement; the girl was a natural mime, and could imitate the sound of mersong better than anyone Jerusha had ever heard attempt it. But more than that, she had an instinctive sensitivity to the way other creatures viewed the world. She sensed their fears, their pleasures and interests, in a way that was almost uncanny.

Jerusha had been struck by it from the time Ariele was a child, watching her with orphaned Silky, her gentleness and her rapt attention, the way she would not be separated from the merling night or day after they had found her, until they were sure she would survive. She spent as much time out here as anyone would permit her to, among the mers, in the sea.

"The mers saved your mother from drowning, once," Miroe said, looking at Ariele, and out across the water. "Though I don't say it as a promise that you'd be so lucky."

Ariele looked up at him. "You mean back in the islands? Did she fall off a boat?" She gave an odd laugh.

"No . . . not exactly. The techrunners who took her offworld were shot down by the Hegemony, trying to reach my plantation. They crashed at sea. The mers found your mother, and kept her from drowning until I could reach her."

"Really?" Ariele sat back, lanky and sun-freckled, pulling her knees up. Jerusha was struck suddenly by the memory of the girl's mother, not much older at the time than her daughter was now; she realized how much more strongly Miroe must remember that other girl, as he stood looking down into the face of Moon's daughter. "Uncle Miroe, were you a techrunner?" Her eyes brightened. "I thought you knew my mother because of Aunt Jerusha. Was it exciting—?"

"Your mother never told you?" he asked, mildly incredulous.

She shrugged. "I don't know . . . all she ever talks about is how she has to do things because she's a sibyl, and she's not like Arienrhod. . . . I don't like to hear about that." She looked away, her face furrowing with something darker than impatience. "And Da hates to talk about the old days." She tossed her head. Silky pressed her chin against Ariele's bare foot, and slid back into the water with a trill of farewell.

"Well, in fact I was involved with techrunners, and that's how I met Jerusha. She nearly arrested me . . . but I charmed her out of it." Miroe glanced up at Jerusha, and she met his smile with a laugh of pleasant disbelief. "Well, how else would you explain it?" he said. "You had me dead to rights." He looked back at Ariele. "I'd given your mother a ride when she decided to set out to find your father, who'd gone to Carbuncle. I was on my way to buy embargoed goods, and there was a little mixup, and your mother got taken to Kharemough instead of Carbuncle. . . ."

He shook his head, as other memories filled his mind. "She got back again because the sibyl network wanted it to happen, as near as I can tell, but the Hegemony nearly had the last laugh on us after all. Only the mers saved her. But she couldn't save them from Arienrhod . . . that's partly why what she does is so important to her now. She wants to make sure that when the Hegemony comes back, they won't be able to slaughter the mers again."

"You mean like Arienrhod did?" Ariele said, her voice both sullen and grudgingly fascinated.

"Arienrhod wasn't that simple," Jerusha murmured.

"Arienrhod is dead!" Ariele said, pulling herself to her feet in sudden anger. "Years and years ago, before I was born! Why does everyone have to keep talking about her—?" She looked out across the water.

"Because she's still alive, for us, in us . . . even in you," Miroe said flatly. "You have to understand that. She made us what we are. She did everything she could to break us, to destroy us—Jerusha and me, because we were responsible for your mother being taken away from her . . . your mother and your father because they both defied her. She nearly destroyed Jerusha's career, and she killed the mers who lived on this plantation, to get at me. . . . She ordered the Winters to throw your mother into the Pit, she tried to take your father with her when she drowned—"

"Da?" Ariele looked back at him suddenly. "But I thought it was Starbuck they drowned with her, the offworlder who killed the mers."

"It was," Jerusha said abruptly, putting a hand on Miroe's arm. "He did."

Ariele looked at her, and at Miroe's tense, closed face, half frowning. "Da said he used to play his flute at the Snow Queen's court."

"Yes," Jerusha said, "that's right."

"And he used to sleep with her, too."

Jerusha looked down. "I don't know."

"He says so," she whispered. "Is that why Mama hates Arienrhod?"

"No. Not entirely." Jerusha rubbed her arms. "They both loved your father. They couldn't help it."

"Because they're the same person," Ariele said, her voice turning flat and strained.

"It isn't that simple," Jerusha repeated. "They wanted the same things—your father, and this world's freedom from the Hegemony—but not in the same way."

Ariele shook her head, her face twisting with disgust, and Jerusha knew that they had lost her. She started away down the pier, her bare feet splashing. As she reached the shore she began to run, disappearing down the diminishing strand of beach.

Ariele slowed again when she knew that she was beyond earshot of anyone calling after her. She stopped, looking out at the bay, waiting for the sight of Silky's head. She whistled shrilly, calling the mer to her. Silky came out of the water, moving awkwardly up the beach on her wide, flat flippers, her neck weaving in curiosity. Ariele leaned down, nuzzling her; feeling the cold space inside her heart fill with warmth and love, feeling her mind fill with thoughts that held brightness and promise, a future not bound up in anyone else's past.

"Come on, sweet Silky, you hear that?" she asked. "My fishbrained brother trying to make your music with his flute. Let's go sing him some real music—" She began to walk again, slowing her pace this time so that the mer could keep up with her. She watched the shining sand under her feet, stooping to pick up an occasional agate pebble from the flotsam of stones and weed and shells underfoot.

Ahead of them was a steep hummock of eroded sandstone, almost like a castle. They had always called it the Castle, pretending it was something out of the stories that Jerusha had told them when they were children. Tammis still liked to sit up there in its sun-warmed crannies (and sometimes even she did) and play his flute, the way he was doing now. Merovy was probably up there too, hanging on every note, on his every word, like the infatuated little idiot she was.

They had all been happy enough as playmates when they were children. But Ariele had long since lost patience with the younger girl, just as she had lost patience with her cautious, moody brother and his obsession with his music. She was sure he only played to impress Da, but he would never impress Da, not until he stopped being such a whining bore.

She stopped at the foot of the Castle, listening to her brother's music, which reached her purely and clearly now: a mix of old traditional Summer tunes and freeform improvisation on some of the mersong fragments she had taught him, all of it flowing together into a surprisingly coherent and—though she hated to admit it—beautiful whole. Silky raised her head and began a low singsong in response; breaking off, her head swaying, starting up again, as if she wanted to continue the music, but was uncertain of its pattern.

Ariele began to sing and whistle, encouraging her, until a head peered over the top of the rock far above them. Ariele looked up, seeing Merovy's long, curly brown hair, her pale face and gray eyes framed by its thick waves. Her face disappeared again, and the music stopped.

Tammis looked down now, the sunlight glinting red-gold off the highlights in his darker brown hair, his expression caught between annoyance and concentration as he listened to their music. The expression turned completely annoyed as he realized she was only parroting back his own song. "Go away," he said. "You're interrupting me."

"Oh—?" Ariele cocked her head. "Really? And I thought you were just playing with your *flute*." She laughed, making her own face into a travesty of romantic longing, wriggling suggestively. "Come on, Silky, we'll leave the lovesick birds in their nest. . . ." She sauntered away down the shore, picking up agates and carbuncles, with Silky trailing reluctantly behind her.

"Lady's Eyes!" Tammis settled back into the warm palm of stone where he had been lying beside Merovy with his head in her lap, playing his music for her. He felt his face burning with anger and embarrassment as he looked away from his sister's retreating back; back into Merovy's gray, calm gaze. "Sorry," he said, looking away again. "I just wish she'd leave me *alone*. She always has to ruin everything." He looked at his flute, with the memory of how she had tried to take it from him, years ago, still as fresh as the way she had taunted him just now. The memory of how their father would have let her; how, when their mother had stopped it, Da had given her his very own flute. She had hardly touched it since, as far as he knew; while he had practiced and practiced. But the only time his father listened to him was when he had discovered a new fragment of mersong to play. . . .

He dropped his flute irritably, heard it clatter on the stone behind him.

"Oh, don't—" Merovy leaned over and picked it up with quick hands, brushing off the sand, checking it for fractures. She held it out to him. "Here, it's all right. . . ."

He grimaced, shaking his head. "I don't care—nobody else does."

She looked at him.

"Sorry." He sighed, sitting back down under the gentle censure of her gaze. He took the flute from her; held on to her hands as he did, drawing her close. She settled into the curve of his body, putting her arms around him, kissing him on the cheek. He stroked her hair, turned his face to kiss her on the mouth, a little self-consciously; feeling the sudden giddy rush of heat inside him, the sudden uncomfortable pressure against the fastenings of his pants. He pulled back, catching his breath, still half-afraid of his body's unexpected and unpredictable responses to things that excited it. But at least this time it was a girl's body he was excited by, and this time it was not simply because she was a girl, and touching him, but because she was Merovy. . . .

What he felt for her ran far deeper than newly awakened sexual desire, far beyond the shared memories of old friendship. Because when he looked into Merovy's eyes as he did now, he saw only himself reflected there, and not the son of the Summer Queen; not prestige or power or superstition or anything else. Only deep, unquestioning trust, and unspoken yearning. Shy and soft-spoken, half Winter and half Summer, she was lost in the casual wit and flash of their usual crowd of city acquaintances. But out here in the peace and silence, he saw her real beauty.

And, trusting her as she trusted him, he drew her down beside him into the warm hollow of the rock. He kissed her again with sudden longing, his hands touching her, cupping her breasts through the soft cloth of her shirt with gentle insistence. She let him, as she had let him before, only kissing him more passionately, her lips soft and open against his. She made no move to stop him as he loosened his shirt and then her own, slipping his hands up under it, dazzled by the softness of her skin, while her own hands caressed his face, his chest, the muscles of his back; never daring to wander below his waist. He felt himself aching for her to do it, to touch him there. . . . He let his own hands leave her breasts and slide down, loosening her pants, curving around the soft lines of her thighs and hips, in between, as her knees tightened, resisting, then loosened again.

They had done this much before, exploring each other tentatively, achingly; but always she had stopped him from going further, and always, afraid of hurting her or driving her away, he had been content to stop. There were girls he knew in the city who were more than ready, who had tried to make him feel what he suddenly felt now, as Merovy's hands abruptly tried to push his own away. He had not given in to them, wanting it to happen with her, only with her; an act of love, not just the impulse he felt when he had looked at those other lithe, willing young bodies, both the girls and the boys. . . .

He pushed her hands aside, pulling open the fastenings of his own pants. "Come on, Merovy, please, let me, let me. . . ."

"Tammis—" She pushed at his chest, turning her face away from his kisses.

"I love you so much, Merovy. I don't want it to happen with someone else. . . . It's only you I want, forever; I want to pledge my life with you—"

She turned her face back again, her eyes wide with amazement, and he found her lips, kissing her long and deeply, smothering her attempt at words. He felt her hands give way, and her arms go around him then in answer. He freed himself, freed her, from the confinement and the protection of clothing, until there was nothing between his eager body and what waited to receive it. He slid in between her legs, felt her tremble beneath him; hating his clumsiness and confusion in the middle of his desperate need. She whimpered as he found the place where he was meant to be and began to push; cried out, like a seabird crying, as the membrane that held him back abruptly tore, and he entered her.

He froze as her arms tightened around him; held her tightly, kissing her with passionate tenderness as he saw the tears shining on her cheeks. And then, astonished by the sensation of being within her, he began to move, slowly and tentatively at first, and then more deeply, as her body began to respond to him, and he realized that the sounds she was making were muffled sounds of pleasure. His body controlled him now, carrying him like the sea through wave after wave of pleasure, until at last his pleasure crested and the tides flowed out of him. She gasped and sighed, and then she was kissing him wildly, gratefully. "I love you," he whispered again, wonderingly, as he understood at last how a lifetime together with someone that you loved could seem like eternity, and yet not be long enough.

KHAREMOUGH: Aspundh Estate

BZ Gundhalinu stood smiling at the edge of the perfectly manicured expanse of lawn, as his wife began the introduction to her latest work. The lawn rolled like a wine-red sea into the twilight, toward the distant shore of trees, with KR Aspundh's invited guests scattered over it in expectant silence.

"The performance is about to begin—?" Aspundh came up beside him, and Gundhalinu turned, with his hands in his pockets, to acknowledge their host.

"Yes." He removed a hand to glance at his watch. "In precisely two and a third minutes, at sunrise. I wanted to thank you for your kindness in inviting my wife to debut the performance of her new work here, Aspundh-ken. The gods themselves couldn't have picked a more perfect setting for it. Our own knob of rock would never accommodate such a display, even though it is a celebration of our marriage."

"Yes, so Gundhalinu-bhai told me. She is a unique and charming woman."

Gundhalinu smiled, glancing down. He looked away again at the view, as dawn's lavender-blue sky brightened with rose and peach, as the last fragile vestiges of the night's auroras began to fade from the zenith. He stifled a sudden yawn.

"Dear me," Aspundh chuckled. "Is it the hour, or the company?"

Gundhalinu shook his head vehemently, feeling his face flush. "Neither, I assure you," he murmured. "Well . . . the hour, perhaps; but Dhara insisted that the work had to be presented exactly at sunrise. And I've been on stims for three days straight; my body doesn't take it as kindly as it did in my student days." He touched the skin patch pasted unobtrusively on the back of his neck. "Production schedules up at the shipyards were lagging behind. It was only a run of last-minute serendipity—call it a miracle—that I was able to get down here for the performance at all. I really thought I wouldn't make it. I would have hated that."

Aspundh smiled, with fleeting, inscrutable amusement. "Your presence here is a provident miracle indeed, then," he said.

"Dhara was pleased and honored at your offer to sponsor her performance, and so was I," Gundhalinu added, sincerely. "It's good to see you again, Aspundh-ken."

Aspundh shrugged modestly. "The honor is mine. I've been an admirer of her work for years—and yours. And also I have felt it was time—past time—that we spoke together again, Gundhalinu-ken; in light of our mutual interests. I know that your private time is nearly nonexistent, but there are some strangers far from home who share our concerns—" He glanced over his shoulder toward the manor house. "They would like to speak with you too."

Gundhalinu followed his glance, startled by the unexpectedness of the invitation. He looked back at the place where Pandhara stood, about to begin.

"She won't notice that you've gone," Aspundh whispered, apologetically but urgently. "We'll be back before the work is over."

"I—" One look at Aspundh's face told him that this was not an invitation made lightly, and not one that he could refuse. He nodded once, and followed the other man inside.

They made their way through the now-empty rooms until they reached one which overlooked the silent, enclosed inner courtyard. Five people were waiting there, three women and two men, reclining around a table. They were playing *tan* on the sunken table-surface. The table had been inlaid with patterns of semiprecious stones to form the geometric intricacies of the game board; the entire piece appeared to be very old.

He glanced up again, looking in curiosity from face to face. One man and one woman were offworlders; the two other women and remaining man were Kharemoughi. Aspundh made introductions: One of the Kharemoughi women was TDC Dhaki, a researcher he knew by reputation. The other was a Police inspector; the datapatch on her uniform read *Kitaro*. She was wearing a trefoil; he looked at her a moment longer, because there were not many sibyls on the force, and not many women either, as a rule. He glanced away again, as he realized suddenly that everyone in the room was not only Survey, but a sibyl.

Aspundh beckoned him to a place at the table. He settled onto a cushion, as Aspundh sat down beside him with the obvious difficulty of age. The others around the table assessed him in turn.

"We will dispense with tradition today," Aspundh said, leaning forward to gather up the colored-crystal gaming pieces scattered on the table surface. "Time is limited, and we have important matters to cover." He turned to Gundhalinu. "You said to me the last time we met that you were unsure who to trust, that you sensed there were factions and rivalries even within the Golden Mean itself."

Gundhalinu smiled ruefully, and nodded. "The man who helped me control the stardrive plasma turned out to be working for the Brotherhood." He glanced from face to face again. "That was my first, rudest awakening. But since my return home I've come to feel more and more that when they speak of the 'best interests of the Hegemony' at the Meeting Hall, they mean 'the best interests of Kharemough.' And frankly I for one do not believe the two are necessarily synonymous."

"A lesson brought home to me some years ago, by our mutual acquaintance from Tiamat," Aspundh murmured. "It was a hard lesson, but one that made many things clear for me. I have always loved Kharemough fiercely, and believed in our way of life, perhaps to a fault, because of my own family's experiences. But I have come to see that as a limitation rather than a virtue of mine . . . one of many insights I have gained, along the way to enlightenment within this order." He shrugged. "The reality of things is infinitely more complicated, and yet simpler, than any of us will ever know. It's a lesson you grasped much more quickly than I, Gundhalinu-ken."

Gundhalinu glanced down. "I had some formidably insistent teachers, Aspundh-ken," he said softly. "Sometimes I think the words we live by in Survey should not be 'Ask the right questions,' but 'Trust no one completely.'"

"Both of those are sound advice," IL Robanwil, the other Kharemoughi, said.

Gundhalinu looked up at him. "And what questions about my trustworthiness do you want to ask of me, then?"

"You believe that you know, better than the people who run the Hegemony—and possibly Survey itself—what is good for Tiamat." Robanwil smiled faintly. "I suppose that I for one would like to know how much you trust yourself . . ."

Gundhalinu almost laughed, although he knew the question was not in the least frivolous. "If I don't trust myself completely, I probably shouldn't be attempting any of this," he said slowly. "But if I don't constantly question my motives, I'm probably a lunatic. . . . I guess I believe that I've earned the right to trust myself as far as I have to."

"You have earned the right to be trusted further than most people, Commander Gundhalinu," DenVadams, one of the offworlders, said. "That's why we're here. . . . Your accomplishments are impressive. Tell me, do you believe the remarkable things that have happened to you in your life are due to your own effort and intelligence, or random fate . . . or is it possible that you are actually part of a plan so great and complex that even your full part in it is incomprehensible to you?"

Gundhalinu's mouth quirked. "I've believed all those things, at one point or another. But if I believed any of them completely, I expect you'd have every right to kill me."

"Frankly, Gundhalinu-sadhu, we prefer conversion to coercion, whenever possible," Robanwil said. "If someone were truly a madman, they would not present a meaningful danger to us. Someone who is influential and intelligent enough to create a major change of course in the flow of human history for our corner of the galaxy, on the other hand, must be reckoned with. To play god by deciding whether someone like that should live or die would not only be immoral, it would be a terrible waste of resources. We wouldn't kill them, we'd recruit them."

"And work to convince them that your version of universal truth is the only real one, and that you are on the side of right in the Great Game—?" Gundhalinu finished it for him. The ironic smile stretched his mouth again.

Nods and smiles that were equal parts irony and acknowledgment answered his, around the table.

He glanced at Aspundh again, suddenly feeling like a man in a hall of mirrors. "Are all of you truly sibyls, or are you only wearing trefoils to make me trust you?"

They glanced at each other, and one by one spoke the words, "Ask, and I will answer."

He asked. Each in their turn went into Transfer, and gave him the answer he anticipated to the question he asked of them. He looked back at Aspundh, expectant this time.

"The Survey that you know well, that calls itself the Golden Mean, is dominated by Kharemoughi interests. A number of cabals on other worlds of the Hegemony ally themselves with it, either because they want its strength behind them, or have reason to support the status quo," Aspundh said. "You know that Survey exists on as many worlds as sibyls do, inside and outside of the Hegemony. It has existed for a long time, and it has a great deal of influence in some of those places. There are nearly as many factions of Survey as there are Meeting Halls in the Eight Worlds. They acquire local personalities, they change . . . power corrupts, as it always does.

What was done to your own brothers is a graphic example of the dangers we face when a cancer such as the Brotherhood occurs. And such mutations occur more and more frequently, in an organization so ancient and far-flung."

"You speak of all these—arms—of Survey as if you belong to none of them," Gundhalinu said.

"We are all cells of its nervous system," Aspundh said, touching his trefoil briefly, "for want of a better definition. We each belong individually to different cabals of the order, but at the same time we in this room are part of a still greater level of organization. Not all sibyls reach this level, but everyone who reaches this level is a sibyl."

"Gods," Gundhalinu murmured. "Wheels within wheels. And where is the brain . . . or am I permitted to know that?"

Aspundh shook his head. "I don't even know the answer to that. . . . I don't believe any of us do." He looked from face to face. "Can the sky be said to end?"

Gundhalinu remembered the Parable of the Sky, which he had been forced to learn along with a vast number of other seemingly random bits of information that, little by little, he was beginning to see the point of. " 'I lived below the clouds,' " he recited softly, " 'never suspecting that anything lay above them. And then I rose until I was among the clouds, and thought I understood the sky. And then I rose above them, and realized that the sky was infinite.' "

"If you need someone you can depend on, this sign is as reliable an indicator as you'll find in this universe, Gundhalinu-ken," Aspundh said.

"Thank you," Gundhalinu answered, feeling his own fogged-in vision of the future slowly brightening. "Thank you all." They nodded again. He got up from the table, offering Aspundh a hand as the older man got up in turn.

"Good luck in your endeavors far from home, Gundhalinu-sadhu," Robanwil said suddenly. Gundhalinu hesitated, looking back at him. "Tiamat has been a world underappreciated by everyone, including Survey, for far too long. That will only make your future there all the more difficult. May the blessing of your ancestors go with you."

He nodded in turn, not smiling now, and followed Aspundh out of the room.

They reached the outside again just as the applause and cries of appreciation began to fade. Gundhalinu realized, chagrined, that he had missed the entire performance of his wife's new work.

Pandhara came toward him through the crowd's admiration, shining with pleasure. Her expression did not change as she saw him; he realized, relieved, that Aspundh had been right. She had been so preoccupied that she had not even noticed his absence.

She held out her hands to him. "Well, BZ—?" she said, with eager anticipation. "What do thou think of thy wedding gift?"

He took her hands in his, held them, smiling back at her with sudden, profound gratitude. "Unforgettable," he murmured.

TIAMAT: Carbuncle

Sparks Dawntreader pushed up from the bench as his wife appeared suddenly in the doorway to the back room. He had been waiting with the patience of the damned there in the crowded, noisy, lower-city tavern for her to emerge from her latest in an endless round of meetings with Summers who had knowledge about the mers.

She stopped in the doorway, wearing the sea and earth colors, the rough handspun and knitted clothing of the fisherfolk, as if she had just come off a ship. She stared at him for a moment as if she had completely forgotten his existence, even though he had come here with her, and she had known that he would be waiting, no matter how long it took her to grant him his due share of her time. "Moon, we need to talk."

"Yes, of course," she murmured, with the cautious reserve he heard in her voice when she answered strangers. Jerusha PalaThion, who had been sitting with him, looked up at Moon, over at him, and away again uncomfortably.

Because, damn it all, that was what they had become since she had had a vision, heard a voice—the voice of her old lover—speaking to her in Transfer, telling her the world as they knew it was coming to an end. The offworlders were coming back, and BZ Gundhalinu was coming back with them, if what she believed was really true, if it had really even happened. Sometimes he wondered whether she had only dreamed it . . . or wished she had. She had sworn to him that nothing would change between them if it all came to pass; that he was still her husband and she was still his wife. That BZ Gundhalinu was the man who had made it possible for them to be reunited; that he was coming here only to help them, not to steal their world, or her heart. . . .

And then she had turned her back on everything they had worked to achieve, all these years; buried herself in this sudden obsession with the mers. He had long since reached the conclusion that without the use of a computer network at least as sophisticated as the one the offworlders had had in Carbuncle during their time here, it would be virtually impossible to integrate all the diverse data they had collected, or to reconstruct what he was sure were critical missing segments of the mersong. Without a complex analysis program, it would take far more time than they had left, if what Moon believed about the offworlders' return was true.

The sibyl net should have been able to give them the data—even manipulate it for them. But it seemed . . . incapable . . . of helping them. He would almost have said "unwilling," because of its eerie, utter absence of any response. Jerusha had told him the system had been notoriously eccentric for as long as she could remember. She had heard claims that it had grown worse over time, although she said no one was really sure that it had. But even she shook her head in exasperation lately at the number of incoherencies it generated. And for all the precise guidance it had given them, he had still seen enough examples of its flaws to feel both confounded by and suspicious of its function. Only last week a sibyl at the College had been seized by a fit as he attempted to go into Transfer; he still was not fully himself. Ngenet had said it was a coincidence, but the evidence suggested otherwise.

He had pushed the whole subject of the mers to the back of his mind as futile, even as Moon had made it the center of her ambitions. He had done what he could to continue the progress of their technological development, working with the others at the College and on the Council who felt the same way, because whether the Hegemony came back in a matter of years, or never in his lifetime, he could not see any point in giving up now on what they had begun. The further they progressed, the harder it would be for the Hegemony to dismantle and dismiss their work, if that was what it intended. And if not—if the gods, or the Goddess, chose to smile on this benighted world for once—then all the better.

But recently, even the slow-but-steady progress they had been making in their production and manufacturing had hit a snag. They had tapped into Carbuncle's independent power supply early on in their development. The city's self-perpetuating, seemingly endless supply of power came from a system of immense turbines located in caves cut from the rock below the city, that turned the massive, relentless energy of the tides into light and warmth, into survival for Carbuncle's systems and its inhabitants. By their own estimates there should have been power to spare for the new needs they were generating locally.

And yet they had been experiencing power outages, brownouts, lapses and lags that were causing critical complications in their productivity. And he had been able to think of only one possible way to determine where the problem lay in that ancient, unexplored system.

"What is it?" Moon said, with a flicker of impatience. "What is it we need to discuss so badly that it can't wait until—" She broke off, as if she had realized that whatever she had been going to say was meaningless. He wondered what nonexistent moment in the day she had been thinking of; what time they had once reliably shared, and no longer did. There was none that he could think of. "What is it?"

"It's about the Pit," he said. She looked at him uncomprehendingly. "I want to go down into it—to explore it. If there's any way to work around the power problems we've been having lately, the key has to be there."

Moon put her hand up to her face, blinking, as if what he had just said was somehow appalling, or terrifying, to her. Her hand dropped away, as coherence came back into her eyes. She touched the sibyl pendant hanging against the drab cloth of her shirt. "No," she murmured. "I don't think that would be a good idea."

"Why not?" he snapped, in reflexive anger; unable to stop it, because his anger had so little to do with what she had just said, and so much to do with something that ran much deeper. "The Pit is the access shaft to Carbuncle's operating system—there's no other way to affect or change it. That's what the Pit is there for—to give access for repairs and adjustments." While he had been at the palace with Arienrhod, researchers from offworld had come there many times; they had gone down into the access well to study its function, apparently without any noticeable success. The system had never required any adjustment that he knew of—until now. But while the offworlders had been here the storm walls had still stood open in the Hall of the Winds, causing tremendous updrafts to form inside the shaft. Anyone who descended into the Pit would have had to stay sealed in the system's elevator capsules or be swept to their deaths. Maybe that had even been the reason for the whole bizarre setup—a kind of perpetual security, to protect the system from tampering.

But Moon had sealed the Hall of the Winds. The Pit was still the Pit, a green-lit well dropping down and down until it met the sea. But without the treacherous winds, it should be possible to actually explore the catwalks and ledges, the outcroppings of display and hardware visible down there.

"But you don't know anything about how the Old Empire's technology functions," Moon said.

He shrugged, an abrupt, barely controlled gesture. "And how will we ever learn, unless we study it? There are certain basic rules which everything that functions obeys, on one level or another. But until we can get a closer look at the system, we can't even begin to study it."

She shook her head, and he saw something unnamable come into her eyes. "It's too dangerous. I don't want you to try it. I don't want you to go down there. I don't want it to . . . want you to get hurt."

"It's not dangerous, without the wind. Nothing will happen to me. It's an access well—"

"You don't know how dangerous it is."

He frowned, his exasperation growing. "Do you know something about this you aren't telling me?" He remembered again how she had stopped the winds.

She looked at him with anguish and frustration, but she only shook her head.

"Even Ngenet agrees with me about this. He wants to go down with me."

Moon turned in surprise to Jerusha. Jerusha nodded her confirmation. "And do you agree too?" Moon asked.

Jerusha shrugged. "I think Miroe's too old for this kind of thing," she said. "But I expect I'd let him break his neck before I'd say that to his face." A weary half smile of resignation showed on her own face. "As to whether I actually believe that what they want to do is necessary and useful . . . yes, I do." She glanced down, looked up again. "Protecting the mers has become more important to me than anything else, too, Moon. But everything else hasn't ceased to be as important as it ever was. We need to do more than we've been doing for the people who've followed you this far. The problems they've been experiencing are too important to ignore."

"Yes. Yes, I suppose . . . I . . ." Moon lifted her hands in a gesture that looked almost helpless, hopeless. She glanced back at him, her face pinched as if she were in pain; but her eyes showed him something like understanding at last.

"Danaquil Lu Wayaways said he would go too; we can ask questions—"

"No!" Moon caught his arm, suddenly white-faced with anger, or terror. "With his back—?"

His frown deepened. "Well, someone else then, another sibyl—"

"No." She stood face to face with him, clutching her elbows. "No sibyls are to try a descent into the Pit."

He stared at her. "By'r Lady, why not?"

"It isn't safe. There are . . . I've felt . . . there's *something* there. . . ." She looked away, her lips pressed together. "Not a sibyl. No sibyls. I forbid it."

"All right. Then we'll map it with recordings and instruments," he said, hearing the coldness in his own voice. He folded his arms, echoing her unconscious gesture of self-defense. "If you have no objection to that."

She looked at him for a long moment, still holding herself tightly, and he saw—thought he saw—a tremor pass through her. "Do what you must," she said faintly.

His anger turned to ashes, as he saw what filled her eyes. She stepped back as he reached out; eluding him when he would have touched her, when he wanted suddenly to take her in his arms. "But it won't do you any good," she said, turning away. "You won't learn anything. It's impossible." She went on across the room, moving toward the light, the doorway; escaping, leaving him there to meet Jerusha's uncomprehending gaze with his own.

"Da—?"

Sparks looked up, surprised by the sound of his son's voice calling his name. He straightened, looking past Ngenet's shoulder, to see Tammis coming toward them across the Hall of Winds. "What is it?"

Tammis stopped a short way from the two men, staring at the small pile of equipment they had been going over. He glanced at the half-dozen assistants, including Danaquil Lu Wayaways, who waited nearby to monitor their descent.

"You're really going to explore the Pit?" Tammis asked.

"What does it look like?" Sparks jerked his head at their preparation. The words sounded harsher than he had intended, and he felt Ngenet glance up at him. He told himself that his nerves were simply on edge.

"You didn't tell me—" Tammis's own voice took on an accusing tone; but Sparks saw him swallow his anger, as if he were afraid of it, or of the worse response it would bring down on him. "Nobody told me. I overheard Aunt Jerusha talking about it. Did you tell Ariele?" He tried to disguise the jealousy in his voice, with less success.

"No," Sparks said, truthfully, realizing why his son had asked the question.

"Why didn't you tell anyone?"

Sparks sighed. "We did." He nodded toward the small gathering near the edge of the Pit, where the access to the elevator modules lay.

"It wasn't a secret," Ngenet said, fastening his equipment belt, lifting a pack. "But an experiment like this is not something that you want a big crowd for, either." He shrugged. "Probably just be a bloody anticlimax, anyway."

"Are you going to repair the city's power system?"

"We're only going to look at it," Ngenet said patiently. "This is our first try. The gods only know if we'll be able to make any sense out of it. If we can we'll decide from there what our next move will be."

Tammis looked away, toward the rim of the Pit, and the span that bridged it. He had been crossing that bridge all his life, but Sparks knew he had always been afraid of it. Even now, he could see the shadow of fear in his son's eyes. Sparks looked away from it, picking up his own pack.

Tammis turned back to him. "I want to come with you."

Sparks looked at him incredulously. "Why?"

"I know I've always been afraid to look over the edge," Tammis murmured. "But I've always wanted to know what was down there." The only fear in his eyes now was the fear of rejection.

Sparks reached out, feeling an odd surprise, and put his hand on his son's shoulder. "Maybe next time," he said. "It could be dangerous; we just don't know enough about it."

"You're not worried about getting hurt," Tammis protested.

Sparks laughed. "On the contrary. I don't want to have to worry about you too. That would cause me twice the pain of something happening to myself."

Tammis blinked as the words registered, and then he smiled. It was not an expression Sparks saw on his face often. "I'm seventeen, Da," he said softly. "Can't we watch out for each other?"

Sparks began to shake his head, but Ngenet said, "Let him come. Originally we'd planned on taking a third person. He'll be safe enough, between the two of us."

Sparks glanced toward the rim of the Pit, remembering how it had been before . . . remembering the moaning of the winds, the way he had always heard them long before he reached this place. Then, this had been a place hungry for death. He had a sudden strobing vision of himself at seventeen, standing alone on that bridge facing Herne, the Snow Queen's Starbuck, in a duel to the death over Arienrhod. . . .

"All right," he said at last, aware again of where he was now, of when, and with whom. . . . "All right, he can come." He looked back at his son; telling himself that perhaps at least Tammis might not walk like a condemned man every time he crossed the bridge if he saw what was really down there. That maybe after a willing descent into that green-lit darkness, neither of them would have to feel that way ever again. He met Tammis's half-eager, half-uncertain stare. "You stay between us," he said, "or you stay in the car, if it makes you dizzy to step out."

Tammis nodded, his face resolute. "I will."

Sparks looked into his son's eyes for a long moment—eyes that were the clear windows to a soul untouched by bitterness and disillusionment; as clear as his own eyes must have been, when Arienrhod had first looked into them. He turned away, not saying anything. He led Ngenet and Tammis toward the waiting car, toward the people waiting beside it. The one person he had needed to see was not there: *Moon.*

He wondered what it was that made her avoid this place. Was it her own memory of the things that had happened here? Or was there something else, something more, some secret hidden in the way those windows high overhead had closed miraculously at her command?

But he didn't believe in miracles, any more than he still believed in the Sea Mother. It was easier to believe that something had gone wrong with his wife's mind, as Kirard Set had muttered at the last Council meeting; that the sibyl net had done something to her on the night he had seen her seized by the Transfer. He thought of the sibyl he had seen stricken by a fit. He looked up at the wind-curtains where they hung still and dust-softened in the space where they had once held clangorous sway. They reminded him of corpses.

He looked down again, hastily, as the morbid image formed in his brain. He searched the stairway leading up to the palace, finding it still empty; tried not to follow the other images that spread like ripple-rings deeper into his mind, of other kinds of death, the death of innocence, of love and trust between two people, all rippling outward from this haunted place, from that long-ago time. *Moon, where are you? I can't reach you anymore.*

He looked back again, at the expectant faces waiting for him. He saw the others move aside to reveal the open hatch that gave access to the car.

Jerusha PalaThion glanced past him at Tammis, and looked a question at her husband, who shrugged and nodded. "Does Moon know about this?" She turned, inflicting a look full of official scrutiny on Tammis. He shook his head, and her mouth pulled down. "Be careful," she murmured, looking at no one in particular.

"We'll keep the comm link open all the time we're down there," Ngenet said, touching her shoulder briefly, reassuringly.

"You're sure the link will work down there, in all that EM noise?" She frowned; lines of concern deepened around her eyes.

"It did when we sent equipment down in the capsule yesterday as a test," he said. "No reason why it shouldn't today." No one said anything more, but Sparks knew every one of them felt the need for that fragile link between the capsule and the people waiting above; the need to preserve that tenuous psychological bond, even though there was no way anyone could help them if they ran into a problem. Ngenet looked toward Danaquil Lu. "I wish I could say the same for the visuals. It just isn't sophisticated enough."

Danaquil Lu nodded. "We'll work with whatever data you manage to bring up, and your observations. It will be a start." He smiled; Sparks felt some of his own anticipation come back as he saw the hunger for new knowledge fill the other man's eyes.

Ngenet pulled Jerusha into his arms and kissed her with sudden, unexpected passion, before he moved to the hatchway, the first one to enter. Jerusha smiled crookedly, smoothing the collar of her shirt.

Sparks gestured Tammis ahead of him, watched the boy climb down after Ngenet and disappear. He glanced again at the empty stairway; looked down, avoiding Jerusha's gaze. He went to the hatch and started down the ladder, seeing the faces of Ngenet and his son look up at him expectantly.

Hesitating in that last moment, he could not help looking up, one last time. And he saw her appear suddenly at the limit of his sight, at the far side of the hall, looking on. He lifted his hand; thought she raised hers in response. He went on down the ladder, heard the door seal shut above him. He glanced up. It had merged so perfectly into the ceiling that he could no longer see it.

There was standing room only inside the car. The surfaces around them were smooth and deceptively simple, almost austere. The proportions felt right to his senses, reminding him that this space had been designed by and for human beings, even while the subtle alienness of its forms nagged at his brain. He moved to the control panel below the wide window, glancing out at the Pit's darkly gleaming walls.

He looked down again at the arrays of symbols before him—ideographic illustrations of available functions, intended to be clear enough in form so that anyone could operate this car, no matter what language they spoke. He had questioned the occasional offworld research teams that had been sent by Arienrhod to study the city's operating system during her reign; learning from them how to operate the access car. He touched a symbol on the board, and another; a new sequence lit up, and he made more choices, aware of Tammis and Ngenet watching intently over his shoulder. Ngenet made no comments or suggestions. Even though they had agreed about the need for this experiment, the best thing he could call their working relationship was a truce. There was no room in it for small talk.

The car began to move downward. The knowledge that they were actually descending filled him with a giddy vertigo that was equal parts elation and fear. "We're underway," he murmured into the speaker of his headset. "Are you receiving us all right?"

"We hear you fine." Jerusha's voice answered him, abruptly and clearly. "Take it easy down there. The first step is a long one."

"Right," he said, seeing his ghostly image in the darklit glass smile faintly. He looked through himself, gazing out in fascination as they descended into the ancient, human-made neverland, the axis of Carbuncle, the access to unimaginable secrets of Old Empire technology. The car circled the inner wall of the Pit, spiraling slowly downward, just as somewhere outside the Street spiraled down through Carbuncle's shellform city, the real-world avatar of this inner mystery. Tammis and Ngenet stood beside him now, their hands clutching the shining rail at the edge of the control panel, their own eyes mirroring the wonder of their descent.

After a time that seemed measureless to him—although it registered with meticulous precision on the ancient instruments before him—the car whispered softly to a stop, at the first checkpoint on its programmed rounds.

The rear wall of the car opened almost silently behind them this time, giving them access to what lay outside. They turned, all of them staring in wonder at the sudden opening. Sparks had the uneasy thought that the entire car might somehow be malleable, an artifice; that it might open wherever it chose, wherever was required. It occurred to him that this entire capsule had been extraneous, even an afterthought, to the original builders of this place; put here for the benefit of their less-blessed descendants, intended for times like these. . . .

"We've made our first stop." Ngenet spoke into his headset, reporting to Jerusha and the others up above as he started toward the open door. Sparks glanced at Tammis, who still stood at the window, gaping as if he were hypnotized. Sparks left him standing there, and followed Ngenet out.

A narrow catwalk waited for them, curving away from the car in either direction, rimmed by a low rail of what appeared to be pure light. He touched it—tried to—as he moved away from the capsule's protective solidness. There was nothing, under his touch . . . and yet his hand would not move through or past that point. He tried the pressure of his body against the barrier, holding his breath—to find that it held him.

"Gods, this is incredible," Ngenet murmured, looking up and up along the wall's impassive, glowing face. He turned, looking down over the rail of light with casual unconcern, as if the vertiginous drop did not affect him at all. "Come on, Dawntreader," he said, half eager and half impatient. "It doesn't bite." He went back to his murmured commentary over the comm link, describing his view to the listeners at the other end of their lifeline.

Sparks let himself become preoccupied with adjusting the jury-rigged recording equipment he carried slung over his shoulder, granting himself a few more stolen moments to get his vertigo under control. They both carried monitors that recorded not just video images but also as much of the EM spectrum as they could capture, stretching their erratic technological expertise to its limits. What they would actually get, and what they would be able to make of it, remained to be seen.

He looked up, as Ngenet had, seeing the lip of the Pit limned by the cold glow of lights, his view of its perfect silhouette broken by dark outcroppings of unidentifiable machinery. It was one of those outcroppings that had broken the fall of Arienrhod's lover Herne, in their combat on the bridge—and broken Herne's back.

And yet in the end, at the Change, Herne had reclaimed his place by her side; had willingly put on the black executioner's mask of Starbuck one final time and gone to his death with Arienrhod, in the ultimate act of love and revenge. Arienrhod had that effect on people . . . and so did Moon. It had been Moon's idea, her own revenge of a kind to save him from Arienrhod by using Herne . . . Moon had convinced Herne to do it.

Sparks looked down, feeling dizziness overwhelm him again as the past and the present collided inside his memory. He stared at the incomprehensible instrumentation before him, forcing himself to concentrate . . . noting that here the lights were not actually green, as they appeared from above, but various colors and shades, making him think of star maps; the sum total of their spectra only struck the eyes from a distance as green.

He looked cautiously over the rail. The dizzying whorls of light spiraled downward toward a point of blackness at the bottom of the shaft: the dark eye of the Sea observing their intrusion, coronaed in unnatural light. He could smell the sea here, much more strongly that he could up above. He thought he could even hear it; or maybe it was only his imagination, or the rush of blood inside his head.

Sparks glanced back at the car. Tammis was still inside. Both disappointed and relieved that he had only himself to look out for, Sparks went on along the catwalk, following Ngenet, who had stopped up ahead to study a portion of the wall.

"Gods, where do you begin?" Ngenet murmured, muscles in his face twitching with frustration and incredulity. There were symbols on a smooth, narrow stretch of the wall, among sinuous tendrils of equipment, none of it resembling anything that he remotely knew the function of, any more than he could be sure the symbols actually stood for something in an Old Empire language. He reached out toward the shining, inviting surface, wondering what would happen if he touched this the way he had touched the instrument panel in the car; if one sequence would lead to another—

"Don't touch that!" Ngenet snapped. "We agreed we wouldn't try to activate anything. You could send the car on without us, and strand us here—"

Sparks lowered his hand, frowning. He looked at Ngenet. "This has nothing to do with the car."

"You can't know that." Ngenet waved his own hand.

"There are controls for the car back there where we stopped."

Ngenet stared at him. "How do you know that?"

"I was told about it by the ones who used to come down here for Arienrhod. And I saw the display; the symbols match the ones used in the car."

Ngenet's frown eased slightly. He looked away, as if he couldn't bring himself to apologize.

Sparks made no response, either, to Ngenet's turned back. They had no idea what this display did control, if anything. He admitted to himself that they had agreed only to gather information this time; that a sibyl could translate symbols like these, if they were in some Old Empire tongue. He rubbed his neck, controlling his impatience with an effort as they started on along the catwalk.

Moving along this precarious pathway, with the sheer wall on one side, the sheer drop on the other, the presence of the sea far below, reminded him of something. Another place, another time . . . half a lifetime ago, when he and Moon had made their journey across the sea to the sibyl choosing place.

He wondered what would have happened if Moon had turned back, and never became a sibyl; if they had never gone to the choosing place at all. If Moon had never seen Clavally Bluestone on the beach one day when they were still children, and fallen in love with the mystery and power of sibylhood. If she had been the child that Gran and everyone on the island had always believed she was: the child of her mother's blood. If Arienrhod had never had herself cloned, never become Queen, never existed . . .

They were almost halfway around the circumference of the Pit. He looked back across its empty expanse at the car. Tammis's face was barely visible inside it, dimly lit by the glow of the instrument displays where he stood watching them. *His son.* . . . Sparks looked down at his feet again, watching his step. Wondering whether if one link in that long chain could have been broken, it might all have been different—whether he and Moon might have shared the peaceful, unremarkable life together that they had always imagined they would have, secure in tradition and their love. Or whether the course of his life and hers had really been as inevitable as the long, circular track he followed now, like an orbit, with only room for one step and then another, no turning aside . . . and never any turning back.

They completed the long circuit of the well's inner surface, returning at last to their starting point, to the waiting car. Sparks stepped inside first, with a sigh of relief. Tammis stood waiting for him, still clinging to the edge of the instrument panel as if he had lost gravity and was afraid of drifting away. There was something more uncanny than simple wonder in the boy's eyes; something that was somehow familiar. . . .

"Are you all right?" Sparks asked, half concerned and half uncertain.

Tammis nodded vaguely. "It's more beautiful down here than I ever imagined. The light—" He half turned, gesturing at the window behind him.

Sparks nodded, glancing out at the subtly changing jewel patterns in the darkness, unable to disagree, unable to put a name to the echo of something else that he heard in his son's voice.

Ngenet reentered the car, and Sparks listened to Jerusha's response over his headset as she answered what Ngenet had been reporting to her. Sparks knew that Ngenet had studied the display on the wall behind the cab, reaffirming for himself what Sparks had told him. Sparks smiled, a brief, tight smile that did not touch his eyes, as Ngenet's head bobbed once in acknowledgment.

Sparks passed his hands over the touchboards on the instrument panel and the car resealed, becoming whole around them again. They went down, describing as they went all that they had seen and experienced to the listeners who were growing more distant with every heartbeat. Questions came back at them from Jerusha and Danaquil Lu, and occasionally from someone else, but never the one voice he listened for. He wondered whether Moon had joined the others at the Pit's edge; or whether she was still standing apart, keeping her distance from him and everything about this expedition.

They made another programmed stop, another circumnavigation on foot of the wall; recording every aspect of their environment, the visible and the invisible, because they had no way of knowing what had been important to the human gods of the Old Empire, or what might give them the key to their own unlocking of its potential. Tammis stayed in the car, and Sparks was relieved that he did, still not sure whether it was fear or fascination that held his son immobilized.

The third stop occurred at nearly half the well's depth. There were no units of measurement that he recognized on the panel before him, to tell him exactly how deep they were.

He followed Ngenet out onto the catwalk, this one exactly like the others. The process was beginning to seem almost ritual-like. Looking up, he could barely make out the Pit's rim through the glare, past the outcroppings of machinery; but he could see the bottom of the well clearly now. He realized that the well must widen gradually as it deepened.

The light seemed brighter here, perhaps because they were inside a greater concentration of it. It made him think of the Black Gates, with their flaming halos of light, waiting to suck the unwary down into a place where space and time changed partners, and changed partners again. Moon had seen that vision, as she passed through the Black Gate to another world; seen it again when she returned, armed with the sword of knowledge. He wondered if she had felt equally mesmerized, equally terrified, falling toward the heart of the unknown. . . .

Ngenet's hand was suddenly on his arm, putting painful pressure on it, pulling him back from the rail, and around. "Be careful. Don't look down too long."

Sparks stepped back into the narrow alcove between outcroppings of machinery, reassuring himself of the solid reality of the wall, the forms of alien equipment behind him. "Doesn't this bother you at all?" he asked, a little more sharply than he had intended.

Ngenet shrugged. "Things don't get on my nerves. People do."

Sparks felt his hand tighten. He bit his tongue and managed to keep from making it personal, whether it was meant to be or not. He pushed past Ngenet heedlessly, feeling his throat close with fear as his hip brushed the light-rail, and he swayed out over the abyss momentarily. He went on, forcing himself to walk with a confidence he did not feel.

He did not look back to see whether Ngenet had followed until he was nearly halfway around the circuit. He slowed, seeing Ngenet about midway between his position and the car. Ngenet was studying some exposed infrastructure they had not seen before. And beyond him, Sparks saw another figure. The tentative silhouette of Tammis moved slowly along the catwalk in their direction. Sparks frowned, wishing that the boy had had the Mother-wit to stay inside where he was safe, and not come out here. "Ngenet!" he called, and pointed as the other man glanced toward him. Ngenet looked back, following his gesture toward Tammis.

Sparks stood watching a moment longer, almost but not quite confident enough to continue on his way. And then, not sure why, he started back the way he had come.

He watched Tammis stop, staring up along the glowing wall just as they both had done. And then he turned, leaning against the rail of light, looking down; leaning out over it in a way that made Sparks's heart stop. "Tammis!" he shouted. Ngenet broke into a run. Sparks began to run too, heading back around the rim.

Ngenet reached Tammis's side first, pulling the boy back, holding on to him. Sparks heard their mingled voices, made unintelligible by distance and echoes. He pushed himself, not thinking now about the narrow track or his own precarious progress along it. As he closed with them, he heard Ngenet's voice asking Tammis questions; saw Tammis's eyes, the dazed look he had seen there before grown nearly opaque, as if the boy were in a trance.

He pulled up short as he reached them, because there was no room to maneuver on the narrow walkway. "Tammis," he said, the concern in his voice hardening into irritation. "Get back in the car. I don't want you out here."

Tammis looked at him. "But I had to come out. I have to be here. . . ."

"You don't have to be anywhere, but safe," Ngenet said, with surprising gentleness, his hands still firmly on Tammis's shoulders. "It's all right; you're just a little shaken up. It's too much for anybody out here—"

"But it's so beautiful here," Tammis murmured, and there was something eerily like the manner of a sleepwalker about him. His eyes drifted away from them as he spoke; he strained toward the rail again. "The light—it keeps getting brighter. And there's a kind of music here, do you hear it? I had to come out."

"What are you talking about?" Sparks snapped. "Tammis! Damn it, look at me—"

But Tammis turned toward the void again, staring down into it as if he were looking for the sea, his straining body silhouetted by whorls of light.

"What's happening down there?" Jerusha PalaThion's voice interrupted suddenly, through the earjack of Sparks's headset. "Is everything all right?"

"No problem," Ngenet grunted, pulling the boy back again. "He's all right; I think maybe there's a kind of effect the light down here has, a kind of rapture. . . ."

"Sparks—"

Sparks started, as Moon's voice suddenly filled his ears. "Sparks, I don't like this. Bring him up, it isn't safe. Bring him up now!"

"He'll be all right. He's just got a case of vertigo." Sparks felt himself frown again. "We're not finished here."

"I can't leave," Tammis echoed, not looking at them. "I have to get down there—"

"Come on, Tammis," Ngenet said, more insistent, trying to pry him away from the rail, pulling him around. "Come on, boy, let's get back."

"No, I don't want to get back in the car. I have to be near it; I have to go to it—"

"Tammis—!" Moon's shrill, panic-stricken voice made Sparks wince; he jerked the jack out of his ear. He pushed forward, his exasperation giving his movements too much force as he caught his son's shoulder, trying to propel him in the direction of the car.

Tammis twisted, resisting as he was caught between the movements of the two men, trying to break free. He lost his balance, and stumbled into Ngenet. His hands flailed wildly as he began to fall outward; as behind him Ngenet lost his own footing in the middle of a move to stop the boy from pitching over the rail. Tammis's cry of surprise was drowned in Ngenet's sudden, louder cry, in Sparks's shout of warning as he lunged forward—colliding with Tammis, knocking him down, as Ngenet struck the rail and went over the edge.

"No—!" Sparks's scream filled his own ears, as his frantic lunge grasped nothing but air, too late. "Ngenet!" He hung against the rail, his body strengthless as he looked over and down, at the tiny speck of black falling downward through the pinwheeling light, still falling and falling toward the black depths. Voices clamored in his head, through the headset, out of the mouth of the pathetic figure clinging to his feet, beside him on the catwalk. But he had only eyes, no other senses; only eyes to watch that spot of black growing smaller and smaller, until it was lost at last in the utter blackness below.

TIAMAT: Carbuncle

Tammis . . .

Tammis spiraled up through an endless tunnel of darkness shot with light, rising like a swimmer, knowing only that he fled from some horror in the bottomless depths. It howled after him like a lost soul, like the sound of his own madness gibbering, calling him by name. He felt it gaining on him; knowing that if he looked back, if it caught his gaze and forced him to put a name to it, it would drag him down into madness forever. . . .

"Tammis—"

He woke, hearing his terrified cry half-drown the sound of someone calling his name. He jerked upright, felt hands press his trembling body back against pillows. He opened his eyes, staring in disbelief at the ceiling of his own room. His gaze slid down over the line of molded trim onto the wall's long sky-blue expanse, found the familiar triptych painting of the sea. His hands rediscovered the heavy quilts and woolen blankets of his bed.

His mother's face hovered above him, her hands still pressing his chest in gentle restraint. "What . . . ?" he said, his voice a broken whisper. "What am I doing here?"

As he spoke the words, he felt himself begin to fall away, back down into the blackness without bottom. . . .

"*Stop—*" Moon said, and there was something in her voice that he had never heard before. Abruptly the compulsion that was suffocating his thoughts began to dissipate like fog. Her hand brushed his hair gently away from his eyes. "Whenever you feel yourself begin to slip away like that, you must say *stop*," she murmured. "That's all . . . *stop*. And it will."

He nodded, staring at her for a long moment, uncomprehending. His eyes caught on the white bandage wrapping her wrist, the matching strip of bandage around his own. He frowned, trying to remember why the sight of those bandages filled him with such awe and terror and grief. He closed his eyes, looking inward, trying to make sense of the images as they began to take form.

The Pit. At first it seemed to be the last thing he remembered: the descent into the Pit with his father and Miroe Ngenet . . . the hypnotic kaleidoscope of light and darkness swirling upward around him. The light had been made up of all colors, and yet it had seemed to him to become greener and greener, and to have music in it, like no music he had ever heard or could ever possibly hear, outside of his own soul, or the song of the mers.

He remembered nothing more, nothing except the terrible need to join that calling beauty. . . .

And then somehow he had found himself in the Hall of the Winds again; with hands holding him up, holding him back when he would have gone to the edge—

And as his head began to clear, he had heard the cries and the questions, seen Jerusha PalaThion's stricken face, heard her voice repeating endlessly, "It can't be! He can't be—" And Miroe Ngenet had been nowhere.

He had searched every face around him; seeing only a strobing nightmare of a figure falling, black against night, that couldn't be real, couldn't be his fault, couldn't be. . . . He saw his father's face, with eyes as hard as emeralds, turning back his confusion with grief, and his sudden fear with fury.

"What is it?" he had asked, almost desperately. "What is it—?"

The others had looked at him, and their faces gave him no comfort. "Miroe is dead," his father had said flatly. "He fell. He fell because of you—"

And then his mother the Queen had been there beside him, putting her arms around him protectively, saying, "He doesn't remember! He doesn't understand."

He had followed her away, up the stairs, moving as clumsily at first as if he were newborn, stumbling over his feet. His mother led him to a small, quiet study, a room he had always felt comfortable in, and settled him on the couch.

She sat beside him, looking at him for a time without speaking. He saw compassion in her eyes, and something that might be understanding—although he could not believe she understood something which was so incomprehensible even to him. "I killed Uncle Miroe . . . ?" he said, his voice breaking with his own disbelief. "I killed him?"

"No!" Moon reached out, covering his fists with her hands. "No . . ." she said again, softly. "You were called. There in the Pit. It's a choosing place. You were meant to be a sibyl, and it chose you, then and there—as I was chosen, when I was barely older than you are."

"But . . ." He looked away, at the walls lined with books and other more arcane forms of datastorage; at the strange collected whimsies of his real grandmother, Arienrhod, the Snow Queen. His gaze caught on an emerald egg, the shadowy form he could not quite make out trapped in its heart. . . . "But didn't he fall—?" He remembered it now, as if it were a dream: the falling form, the scream that went on and on. . . . "Because of me." He looked back at her, felt himself trembling. "I made him—"

"He tried to help you," his mother whispered, and he saw her eyes fill with sudden, unshed tears. "And he fell. It was an accident . . . not your fault."

"Da . . . Da was there," he said thickly. "He saw it. He thinks it was my fault. I saw it in his eyes when he looked at me."

"He didn't understand," Moon said, her voice strong with feeling. "He will. He saw it happen to me, too. . . ." She broke off. "When it happens, it takes you, and there is nothing you can do to stop it, nothing at all." She looked away briefly, before she drew him close and held him, rocking him in her arms as she had done when he was a small child.

She let him go again, at last, as someone else entered the room. Tammis looked up, to see Danaquil Lu looking back at them, with the same unspoken understanding that he had seen in his mother's eyes.

"He was called, wasn't he?" Danaquil Lu said to Moon. "I know the signs."

She nodded, straightening away from Tammis's side. "Yes."

"The Pit is a choosing place?" Danaquil Lu asked, incredulous. "How is that possible?"

Moon shook her head. "I don't know." A look that almost seemed to be pain passed over her face.

Danaquil Lu hesitated. "You stopped the winds, there. . . . Does that have anything to do with it, do you think?"

"I don't know," she said again, as woodenly as before; as if she could not say anything else, caught in a trance like he had been. Tammis touched her arm tentatively. She started, glancing at his hand.

Danaquil Lu came on across the room, stood looking down at them both. Tammis stared at the trefoil hanging against his shirt; at the one his mother wore. He felt his hands begin to perspire.

"It's a great honor that you have been chosen for, Tammis," Danaquil Lu said softly. "And a great responsibility. The very act of being chosen proves that you are deserving and capable of it—"

"I don't want it!" He flinched at the rawness of the words. "I killed someone because of it! He's dead—" He broke off, as someone else hesitated in the doorway. Merovy. She crossed the room, passing her father with barely a glance, to settle beside him on the couch. He fought the urge to move away, feeling unclean, untouchable. But she put her arms around him, and he saw that his image in her eyes had not changed. Hesitantly, painfully, he put his arms around her and pulled her to him. She rested her head on his shoulder.

"Nothing is free, Tammis," Danaquil Lu said, gesturing at the scars still visible down the side of his face, his throat—the marks a witchcatcher lined with iron spikes had laid on him. Tammis remembered how Danaquil Lu's own people, driven by prejudice and fear, had cast him out of Carbuncle. "There's always a cost—a life . . . a death."

Tammis looked at his mother. She nodded, slowly. "If your father had been chosen, along with me . . . or if I had been turned away, along with him . . . we never would have been separated, back in Summer, or come to Carbuncle, or . . ." She looked down, her body moving slightly, in a shrug. "Nothing was the same for us, afterward, as it had been before. But I wouldn't change it back," she said, seeing the look in his eyes. "Once you know, nothing is ever the same again, anyway." She shook her head. "Oh, Tammis, don't deny the gift you were given today. Miroe wouldn't want that . . . Jerusha wouldn't. Accept the gift, or the cost will be that much harder for everyone to bear."

Tammis looked down, away from the sudden insistence in his mother's eyes. He turned back to Merovy. "What should I do?" he murmured. "Should I—?"

She nodded, touching his face. "You must," she said, and it was not so much a command as an observation, as if she had seen in his eyes what he refused to see himself: that he had no choice, now that he knew.

"Clavally and I initiated your mother," Danaquil Lu said. "We would be honored to do the same for you."

He hesitated, unable to speak, caught between fear and desire. *Nothing will ever be the same.*

Moon took his hand, holding it in her own. "Let me be the one who gives the . . . the Lady's Gift to you." She used the old Summer term, not "the virus" or "the sibyl net," as if those words were too hard and literal, not possessed of enough mystical awe to express the power of the life change that a human being underwent in becoming a sibyl.

He nodded, at last, and held out his hand, offering his wrist; wishing his arm was steadier. "Then let's do it now."

Danaquil Lu hesitated, glancing at Moon. "It isn't usually done that way. . . ."

"Everything's already changed, because I was chosen," Tammis said. "If I'm going to become a sibyl, I want to do it now. The sooner I can start helping people, the sooner I can start making up for what happened today."

"Very well, then," Danaquil Lu said quietly, as Moon nodded. Merovy clung to him more tightly as he offered his wrist again.

Danaquil Lu reached into his belt pouch and took out one of the crescent-shaped ritual knives that had only one purpose, on Tiamat. Having grown up among sibyls, Tammis knew enough about them to know what their use was. Danaquil Lu began to sing a prayer-song; one of the few Summer songs Tammis had never heard all the way through. There were no Winter rituals for entering sibylhood, and no one here knew how the offworlders did it.

Moon joined in the singing midway through. In the years since his childhood, he had rarely heard his mother sing. He had forgotten how beautifully she sang. Her voice was high and clear; her eyes were suddenly full of tears again.

When they had finished the song, Danaquil Lu made a swift, deft pass with the blade over Moon's wrist. Tammis saw his mother's mouth press together, saw the bright blood well out of her arm. Danaquil Lu took Tammis's wrist then, and before he had time to think, the blood he saw was his own. Danaquil Lu took his hand, and his mother's, pressing the wounds together, reciting another prayer.

Tammis waited for what seemed like an eternity, feeling nothing except the dull, stunned pain in his arm. And then, suddenly, a chill ran up his spine; burning heat poured into the channels of his nerves. There was a rushing in his head, the voice of the Sea. . . .

Darkness closed over his head like the waters of the sea, and he remembered nothing more—

Until now, as he woke again out of vague, terrifying dreams, to find himself in his own room. He stared at his wrist, wrapped in bandage like his mother's. Danaquil Lu was there with them, and Clavally as well, this time. And Merovy, her hands knotted tightly in her lap, the concern on her face turning to relief as she saw recognition come into his eyes.

Where's Da? He almost asked it; didn't, afraid of the uncontrollable response it might trigger in his altered brain . . . afraid of the answer he might hear, remembering the look he had seen in his father's eyes. His mother offered him a cup of sweet tea; he drank it gratefully, felt the warmth and stimulating herbs start his sluggish body tingling. "You'll be fine now . . ." Moon whispered, stroking his hair with an almost-forgotten gesture that carried him back to his childhood.

But then she rose to her feet, glancing toward the doorway, before she looked at him. "I have to go."

He sat up clumsily, reaching out to her. She touched his hand, but shook her head. "I have to, Tammis . . . Clavally and Danaquil Lu will teach you how to control the Transfer, all that you need to know as a sibyl—beginning now, if you feel strong enough." She let go of his hand again, with a forced smile. "I'll come back to see you as soon as I can." She turned away from the question in his eyes, and went out of the room.

TIAMAT: Carbuncle

"Well, cousin, this is a fine party. You should give one more often."

Danaquil Lu turned, still smiling even though it was Kirard Set who was speaking to him, and that was usually enough to ruin his mood. "I only have one child to celebrate a marriage for, unfortunately. But one is better than none." His smile widened as he looked past Kirard Set and saw his daughter's face across the room, radiant with happiness as she danced to the traditional wedding music. Merovy had told him that she and Tammis had pledged with each other last year. He had lived long enough in Summer to be at ease with its customs, and he had not minded when she had moved out of their townhouse and into Tammis's rooms at the palace. He and Clavally still saw her almost every day.

But now she was seventeen, old enough for the more formal wedding oath the Winters made, following the offworlders' customs. He had found himself feeling a sense of tradition that was as strong as it was unexpected, wanting to mark his daughter's rite of passage in the way his family had done for generations. He sipped at the offworlder wine in his crystal cup, savoring it. Both the cups and the wine had been among the things the Queen had donated from the remaining Winter stores at the Palace, to make the wedding feast of her son and his daughter so memorable that it had impressed even Kirard Set. "Excuse me," he said, spotting Clavally waving at him from across the room. "Enjoy the party."

He moved away, grateful to be out of Kirard Set's orbit; letting his shoulders slump as his cousin wandered on through the crowd. His back was beginning to trouble him again, as Ngenet had predicted it would. He pushed the thought out of his mind, focusing on the present, and said a silent prayer to the Lady—to whom he had always directed the few prayers he made, since his exile to Summer—that they might all be as happy in the future as they were today.

Clavally was standing with Moon and Sparks in front of the enormous box decorated like a boat, which was piled with householding presents for the newly-weds. She gestured again, impatiently, as he approached. "Come on, old heart, we're posing for a picture!"

"What, in the middle of all this?" He looked around, surprised, not seeing anyone with paints or charcoal; only Tor Starhiker and Shotwyn Crestrider, consulting furiously over some sort of vaguely familiar mechanical device. "Mother of Us All, is that a camera?"

Moon nodded, her expression caught somewhere between amusement and impatience. She pressed something into his hands. "They've made it work somehow with a battery pack. Come on, Shotwyn!" she called. "I'm late. I have to go—"

"Go?" Sparks said. "Go where, in the middle of Tammis's wedding?"

She looked at him, all the pleasure disappearing from her face. "I told you. I have a meeting with Capella Goodventure."

"Lady's Eyes!" he said, frowning. "Why can't she come to the wedding; then at least you could pretend your mind was on this."

"She won't come to a Winter ceremony," Moon said.

Danaquil Lu glanced at the Queen as he moved into line beside his wife; seeing an unhappiness in her eyes that her voice did not reveal. He looked away again, down at the thing she had pressed into his hand—a startlingly lifelike three-dimensional image of Merovy and Tammis kissing, caught in some enchantment that held them perpetually in that moment of joy. He touched the image hesitantly, finding that his finger passed through it as if it were a hallucination, touching only a flat surface he could not see.

"Smile!" Tor called, her voice slightly slurred.

He looked up at the camera, but he was already smiling.

Sparks looked away from the camera's pitiless eye as Tor finished trapping their souls inside it. (Some part of him would always think of it that way, the seed of superstition from his childhood, transformed by time into an uncomfortable pearl of irony.) Moon touched his arm briefly, as if in apology; but when he turned to look at her she was already disappearing into the crowd, on her way out.

He frowned, looking back at Danaquil Lu and Clavally, who were head to head over the holo of their daughter and his son, as Tor passed them the one of themselves. Suddenly not wanting to see the picture, he moved away. The band on the other side of the room began to play another traditional song, and he reached into his belt pouch for his flute. He had taken it back from Ariele, because she seemed to have no real interest in it. Now, hearing the band play, he thought of joining them. It was one of the few privileges of his position that actually mattered to him—that when he asked to play, almost no one would refuse him. The awareness that he would not disgrace himself by his musicianship if he did was one of the few things in his life that he still felt justifiably proud of.

"Da—"

He turned, surprised by Ariele's voice behind him. He looked at her, her clothing wrapping her like rainbows in bright arcs of fabric, her long hair bound up in an attempt to imitate an elaborate offworlder style. She had always reminded him of Moon when he looked at her, in a way that pinched his heart; but today she reminded him suddenly, strikingly, of someone else. *Arienrhod*. He blinked, forcing himself to see only his daughter, in love with the offworlders' legacy, the way he had been once, in his youth. "What?" he asked.

"Where did Mother go?"

"To meet with Capella Goodventure."

Ariele made a face, and sighed. "Where's Gran? Tammis said she was coming to the party with Borah. She was bringing me some tiller shells to make into combs. Isn't she here yet?"

He looked away, searching the crowd, surprised again as he realized that he had not seen either of them here, when he knew they had been expected. "I don't know," he said.

"Well, they should have left earlier, then," she said, with an impatient shake of her head. "They're missing everything."

"A storm could have delayed them." Elco Teel Graymount came up behind Ariele, putting his hands on her familiarly, smirking as he glanced at her father.

Sparks felt himself begin to frown; made no comment as Ariele only smiled and sidled closer to the boy. At least she showed no signs of taking a special interest in him, or anyone, yet; although Elco Teel was at her constantly, like an insect at a flower. Sparks had wondered more than once whether Elco Teel would have been half as interested in his daughter if she were not going to be the next Summer Queen. The prospect of having Kirard Set's only son for a son-in-law did not appeal to him. "What are you talking about?" he asked. "The weather report said that the weather down the coast was fine."

Elco Teel shrugged. "There could be a storm. Squalls come up suddenly all the time, and swamp small boats. Especially when the ones sailing it are getting old . . ."

Sparks glared at him, about to chastise him for speaking ill-luck about a journey. But he saw Merovy come up behind Ariele, her hair garlanded with flowers, her gray eyes glancing curiously from face to face. Sparks smiled instead, the way her father had smiled as he looked at her picture. Ariele and Elco Teel turned as they saw his smile, to stare at her with unreadable expressions. "Have you seen Tammis?" she asked.

Sparks began to shake his head. "Not in a—"

"I saw him," Elco Teel said, and Sparks thought he heard a hint of malice in it. "He went upstairs. Brein wanted to congratulate him on his marriage." He glanced at Ariele, raising his eyebrows, smiling as Merovy's face pinched with some emotion Sparks couldn't name.

Ariele looked back at him, but she did not smile, this time. She pulled her arm free from his grasp. "I don't care," she said. "I want to dance." She started away, leaving him behind. He scrambled after her through the crowd to the space where others were dancing already—old dances, offworlder dances, to music that had over time become a unique mixture of different heritages; like their world.

Sparks looked back at Merovy, seeing something secret and forlorn fill her face as she watched them go off without a word. Sensing that there was more to it than simply the casual rudeness of youth, he touched her arm gently. "I'll find him, and send him to you."

She nodded, smiling.

He made his way through the party toward the stairway at the back of the room. Kirard Set intersected his course, leaning against the banister at the foot of the stairs as he reached it. Kirard Set's smile was annoyingly like his son's. "The facilities are free down here at the moment—" He gestured at the bathroom.

Sparks felt his frown come back. "I'm looking for Tammis. Is he up there?"

Kirard Set shrugged. "Yes." He stepped aside, leaving the stairway clear, but his expression changed subtly. Sparks knew, with a sudden coldness in the pit of his stomach, that he should turn and walk away. But Kirard Set's smile held him, gently mocking.

Instead he climbed the stairs to the second story of the townhouse, hearing the sound of voices speaking softly, growing more distinct, until he recognized one as Tammis's. He reached the top of the stairs and saw two figures embracing in the dim light. They broke apart, startled by his sudden appearance, so that he saw them clearly—Tammis, with his bright wedding shirt hanging open, and Brein, a Winter boy from the crowd he was always with, stroking his bare chest.

He saw the sudden guilt, the sudden despair in Tammis's eyes as son came face to face with father on his wedding day. Brein backed away, looking everywhere but at the two of them, and disappeared down the stairs.

"Tammis," Sparks said, and Tammis flinched as if he had been struck. "What was that—?" He gestured at the empty spot where Brein had stood.

"Nothing. He was just . . . I . . . ." Tammis flushed, pulling his shirt together, and hung his head. His trefoil was lost in the tangle of his clothes.

"By the Lady and all the gods!" Sparks caught him by the shoulders, slamming him up against the wall. "You miserable— On your wedding day? When you have a beautiful wife who loves you searching for you downstairs? Why—?"

"I couldn't help it," Tammis murmured. The words were almost inaudible. He fumbled with the laces of his shirt, trying to fasten them.

"Damn it!" Sparks slapped his hands away. "Look at me when I'm talking to you!"

"Oh, don't be so hard on the boy, Dawntreader," Kirard Set's voice said, behind him.

Sparks turned, his own face flushing with anger and humiliation as Wayaways joined them at the top of the stairs.

"You Summers are so narrow-minded about everything. You act as if there's only one right answer to every question." Kirard Set shook his head. "It's only a little harmless flirtation. A boy's got to be sure he's not missing anything, you know."

"Leave us alone, Wayaways." Sparks turned his back on the other man, infuriatingly aware that Kirard Set made no move to depart, still hanging on every word and motion like a voyeur. Sparks caught Tammis by the jaw, forcing his son to look him in the eye, beyond caring what Kirard Set saw or heard or thought, now—sure that he had known it all along. "You are a Summer, a sibyl, by the Mother's Will! Not some buggering Winter pervert, trying to make yourself smell like the offworlders by wallowing in shit!"

"Like you—?" Tammis said, suddenly and furiously, his dark eyes burning. "Like you did, at Arienrhod's court, while you were supposed to be pledged to my mother—?"

Sparks froze, speechless, feeling the ice-taloned hand of the past reach into his chest and stop his heart. "Who . . ." he said at last, "who told you that about me?"

Tammis's eyes flickered away from his face, briefly touching on Kirard Set still watching and listening behind them, and back again. "He told me you liked it both ways. He said you used to laugh at Summers for being narrow and stupid, that you did things for Arienrhod that—"

Sparks's hand shot out, slapping his face, stopping the words. "Believe that if you want to," he whispered, his mouth filled with bitterness. "But don't ever use it as an excuse. Especially not with me." He turned away, turning his back on his son's anguish. Kirard Set shrugged as Sparks met his amused gaze. "Like father, like son . . . ?" he said softly, and pursed his lips. He shook his head. Sparks moved past him, pushing him aside with a heedless elbow.

Heading back down the steps, he barely registered the sight of Merovy, standing midway up the stairs, or the expression in her eyes as she watched him pass.

TIAMAT: Clearwater Plantation

"I can't believe it." Moon shook her head, standing knee-deep in water beside the canted hull of the abandoned boat. "I can't." Her mind refused to accept the obvious truth: that her grandmother was dead, as suddenly and as irrevocably as a wave broken against the shore. She ran her hand along the totem-creature on the boat's prow, touching the third eye carved on its forehead above the other two in the Summer fashion. The Weather Eye, they always called it. Selen, her grandmother's name, was painted on the stern; a boat was always called after a woman, because it pleased the Sea Mother. . . . But this time the Sea Mother had not been pleased, and the name on the stern of the abandoned craft left no doubt who had been taken away by the sudden, elemental sweep of Her hand.

Moon turned back again to Sparks, who stood between her and the small cluster of plantation hands. The workers had been led to the boat by mers from the colony that sheltered along the plantation's shore. There had been no sign of any bodies.

Mers hovered near them in the water even now, or squatted on the beach a short distance away. Sparks shook his head, meeting her gaze, before his own gaze moved out across the sea. He squinted into the sun's light, mirrored by a million chips of brilliance and thrown back again into his eyes by the changeable water surface. "Elco Teel said something about there being a storm down the coast, when we were at the wedding."

Moon saw the wedding feast suddenly in her mind's eye; the happy faces, the happiness she had felt in her own heart— She looked back at the workers. "Was there a storm, after they set out?"

They glanced at each other, murmuring and shrugging. "No, Lady, there wasn't a storm," a woman said. "The weather's been clear down this way, for most of a week now."

Moon looked at Sparks again. "Elco Teel said that? Why would he say that?"

Sparks shook his head again, and she saw his mouth pull down. "To make trouble," he said sourly, glancing away. "To spoil someone's moment. It's what he lives for; like his father."

"It's as if he knew something was going to happen."

"But there wasn't a storm," Sparks said.

"No," she murmured, and fell silent; feeling suspicion like a sudden spear of glass, puncturing the stupefaction of her loss. "There wasn't a storm." She looked away at the mers, their long necks pushed out of the water, their obsidian eyes fixed on her as she waded deeper, running her hand along the boat's rail. There was no sign of damage to the craft, no evidence of anything at all. It was as if her grandmother and Borah had simply vanished. She looked at the mers again. "You saw, didn't you?" she said. "If you could only tell me what you saw—"

Sparks hesitated. He pulled the flute out of his belt pouch and put it to his lips. The workers looked at him, as she did, nonplussed. But as the odd run of notes he began to play registered on her ears, she realized that he was mimicking mer speech. The mers swiveled their heads to listen, obviously realizing the same thing. The workers murmured in surprise. The mers looked at each other once more as he finished, and trilling runs of sound passed between them.

After a moment, something landed with a sodden thump near Sparks's feet. It had come so quickly that Moon had not been able to track its course; but it had come from among the mers.

Sparks picked it up, frowning in concentration, as Moon waded ashore. It was a wad of monofilament netting, the kind of Winters had taken to using to trawl for fish. He shook it out, tossing it to the workers.

"Did this come off the *Selen*?" Moon asked; suddenly, presciently sure that it had not.

The Winters passed the piece of net among themselves, fingering it, tugging on it. "No, Lady," a man said. "Borah Clearwater wouldn't let a piece of this stuff on his property." He shook his head, with a rueful grimace. "The old man was stuck in his ways, gods rest him. He always says—said, he'd hang himself with monofilament before he'd use it on fish."

Moon felt her own mouth twitch with wry acknowledgment. "Yes," she murmured, "that sounds like what he would always say. . . ." Her smile fell away. "Then it means there was another boat—probably crewed by other Winters."

Sparks shrugged, coming back to her side. He put his hand on her arm. "Maybe. Maybe it's only something the mers found drifting. I asked them where the people in the boat are . . . but only the Sea knows if that's what they heard."

"It could mean that someone used nets to drown them, too," she said, her voice thickening. "You know that Kirard Set Wayaways has been after the Clearwater holdings since before Gran came to the city. Borah Clearwater would never sell them to him while he was alive—"

"Moon," he said gently. "You have no proof. I know what you think of Kirard Set. It's no better than what I think. But murder—?"

She looked toward the boat. "I never had a chance to say goodbye. I never even told Gran how much I . . ." Her voice broke. She shrugged his hand away, feeling her helpless grief hardening into anger, feeling its focus crystallize, as the memory of her grandmother's face was overlain by the image of Kirard Set Wayaways. "No, I can't prove that he bears the blame for anything, except the ill will to wish it would happen. But simply for that, I'll keep my promise to Borah Clearwater, to protect his lands for as long as I live." She turned away, starting back along the beach to the place where their own craft waited to carry them north to the city.

KHAREMOUGH: Gundhalinu Estates

"Pandhara!" Gundhalinu called, striding into the front hall, hearing his voice echo through the house. He draped his uniform jacket over the servo that had come to meet him at the door, settled his helmet onto its faceless head, grinning as it informed him lugubriously that it was not a hatrack. "Well, *find* one!" he said, laughing. He went on into the room, shouting his wife's name again.

"Gundhalinu-bhai is in the cutting garden, sir—" the servo droned behind him.

He turned right at the dining room, went down through the study and the sun room and out onto the south wall patio. Pandhara climbed the steps from the cutting garden with an armload of flowers and stopped, her face filling with astonished delight. "BZ! Are thou here already? I wasn't expecting thee until tomorrow."

He stopped too as he saw her expression, surprised and bemused by its bright eagerness. He was secretly relieved that the look on her face was not dismay; and that he had not interrupted her with a lover. "I wasn't expecting to make the shuttle, but I did—by the skin of my teeth." He started forward again, smiling. "The thought of two peaceful nights of uninterrupted sleep instead of one was enough to make me push it."

She lifted a hand to meet his upraised one, dropping flowers as they touched. He leaned down, picking them up and piling them carefully back onto her armload.

"I picked them because thou were coming home," she said, breathing in their fragrance. "I know how thou love them."

His smile widened; he held the doors for her as she carried them inside. She handed them over to a servo, sent it away with a "You know what to do—" She stood before him in baggy coveralls, smoothing back the dark strands of hair that had escaped from under her scarf with color-stained hands. "Oh, damn it all, BZ, nothing is ready! I have it all planned; everything was to be the way thou like it when thou arrived. . . . But I've been setting biosculpture all day. I haven't even cleaned myself up."

He caught one of her gesturing hands, turned it over, studying the rough palms and the pattern of stains. "I like real hands . . ." he said, and looked up at her, to see if she still remembered their first meeting.

Her look of blank surprise blossomed into sudden comprehension, and she grinned back at him, tilting her head.

"It doesn't matter. There's always tomorrow. All I want tonight is normal conversation, and maybe a game of chama." He let go of her hand, turned away to survey the room as he felt himself beginning to look at her for too long. "What's new? Thou've done something to this room; it's brighter."

"The walls are yellow, instead of gray, over there, and there . . . I bought some new settees and restored that reclining couch. I hung some of my statics. . . ."

"I like it."

She searched his face as he looked back at her. "Truly? I've been very careful: I haven't touched the things that are timeless." She gestured at the ornately carved mantel, which had been a part of the original house. He knew it was at least a millennium old. "I would never do that—"

"I know," he said. "I've seen everything else thou've done here. I trust thy judgment implicitly."

"But it is thy home—"

"It's thy home." He put a hand on her shoulder. "Thou live in it; I'm only a visitor. The gods know, my father kept it like a museum; he never allowed a damn thing to change in this entire place, for as long as I could remember. And HK and SB ran it into the ground. . . ." His mouth twitched. "Make it thine, Dhara. It is thine."

She shook her head, putting her hands on her hips; her smile struggled with something that looked like exasperation. "Gods! Must thou always be so insufferably good-natured and kind?"

He laughed. "Thou think so? Ask my programmers and crew chiefs, when they glitch on me or fall behind. . . . Ask Vhanu, when his staff double-schedules me with the High Command and half the Coordinating Committee—"

"Well, all I know is, thou make me want to—"

His remote began to beep. He looked down and swore, clapping his hand over the noise. He crossed the room in half a dozen strides, ordering the side-table terminal below his wife's newly hung painting to take the call.

Vhanu's face materialized, looking urgent. "Goddammit, Vhanu," Gundhalinu snapped. "It can wait—I said I'm off-line. No exceptions!"

Vhanu's imagine said evenly, "We've got the departure date, Commander. It's been approved."

"Tiamat—?" Gundhalinu breathed.

"Yes, Commander. I thought you'd want to hear that." Vhanu hazarded a wary smile.

Gundhalinu nodded. "Yes . . . thanks, NR."

"My regards to Gundhalinu-bhai. Have a good visit, BZ." Vhanu cut contact, the table top went opaque. Gundhalinu stood a moment longer, gazing at the painting, at its cascading golds and shadow-greens, a distant haze of blue. He turned away at last, facing his wife.

"Thou're leaving," she said. "For Tiamat. Soon."

"Yes," he said.

She looked down, folding her arms, hugging her chest. "Ah, well." She looked up again, smiling at him. "Congratulations, BZ . . . I know what this must mean to thee, after thou've waited so many years; after all that thou've done to cause it to happen—"

"I make thee want to—what?" he said.

"What?" she repeated.

"Thou started to say, that when I'm insufferably kind, I makes thee want to . . . ?"

" 'Rip thy clothes off,' " she said, expressionless. "Thou make me want to rip thy clothes off and make love to thee right here on the floor." She turned on her heel and went out of the room.

He stood motionless, staring after her, for a very long time.

Gundhalinu sat on the warm, solid wall of the western wing balcony, sipping a drink that seemed to be completely tasteless. He looked at it, looked at the pitcher on the low, random-edged table made from a slab of polished gnarlstone, and remembered that he had told the servo to bring him water. He sighed, and looked out across the dusk-blue valley again; feeling the wind ruffle his hair with a casual hand, listening to the screel of white-winged sikhas circling high in the air overhead. The western edge of the house sat closest to the rim of the pinnacle on which it had been built; from here his view was unobstructed, and he could actually see the ocean when the weather was clear. It was clear today, as it had been yesterday, so clear that he could count the offshore islands.

He had called KR Aspundh and asked him to come to dinner, after he received the message from Vhanu. Aspundh would be arriving from somewhere across that sea very soon. It would be doubly good to see him now, considering the news. Because it would probably be the last time they would ever meet . . . and the last chance he would have to contact Moon, before he arrived on her doorstep with the sword of the Hegemony's might hanging above him in Tiamat's sky.

He heard someone come out of the house, and turned where he sat. His breath caught as he saw Pandhara crossing the balcony, formally dressed for dinner. Suddenly he could not take his eyes off her; he felt as if he had never really looked at her before. Her hair was elaborately styled with carven combs and glittering pins; a loose, fluid robe of red moved around her as she walked, covering her conservatively from neck to foot, and yet clinging to her body everywhere, changing what it revealed from moment to moment. . . . He looked away, finally, before she reached his side; struggling against frustration and sudden arousal, wondering if she had done this to him deliberately. But he remembered her on the night they had met; remembered that she was simply a beautiful woman, with the sensibilities of an artist.

It was only a joke, she had said to him, last night, when she had finally come back into the room, clean, neatly dressed in robe and slacks, and perfectly composed.

She had only meant to make him laugh; it had happened at the wrong moment, she was dreadfully embarrassed. . . .

He had assured her that he understood; but it had taken him nearly an hour to turn her back from an excruciatingly polite stranger into the quick-witted, laughing woman whose pungent humor and chameleon moods he had been looking forward to sharing for weeks. She had shown him her latest works-in-progress; they had played two games of chama instead of one.

And then, as they sat together drinking lith on the west wing balcony, watching the shifting colors of the night, he had told her about Tiamat. She had not asked him to, but he had seen in her eyes her need to understand, and knew that he could not leave her without any explanation at all.

And so he told her about the sheltered young Tech who had gone to Tiamat full of romance and arrogance, certain of his place in the universe, and its justification. He told her what Tiamat and its people had done to him, to teach him that pain and brutality and futility were his real fate. *Death before dishonor.* He had sworn the blood oath with his companions at school, never believing that he would ever come to such a place; that, held captive by nomad thieves, caged like an animal, he would take the sticky lid of a food can and slash his own wrists, praying to die. . . .

But he had not died. And then his captors had given him Moon—another dazed hostage battered by fate, a hapless Summer girl caught up in the motion of a Game beyond her comprehension. . . . Or at least that was what he had believed, then. An illegal returnee who claimed the sibyl net itself had sent her back to Tiamat, on a kind of holy quest. He had thought she was slightly mad. Only afterward had he come to realize how much more she really was . . . after she had won their freedom, his grudging respect, his unwilling heart . . . after he had lied to and betrayed his own people to help her reach Carbuncle; after he had become her lover, and led her to the man she was desperate to save, the man she was actually married to . . . only after she had become the Summer Queen, and he had left Tiamat without her, without betraying her. Leaving forever, or so he had thought.

Only then, trying to rebuild his own life and career, had he realized fully what he had only sensed about her before: that she was right about everything she claimed. And he had believed then that he had been nothing but a meaningless pawn in the Great Game he had not even known the rules of himself.

"And that's what drove me into World's End." He shook his head, gently touched the trefoil sign. "And suddenly I was no longer only a pawn. I was changing history."

His wife sat silently for a long while after he stopped speaking, her arms wrapped around her knees, staring up into the sky. At last she looked down at him, and shook her head slowly. "Thou are worthy of thy ancestors," she murmured, and took his hand, lifting it to her forehead in a gesture of admiration.

He pulled his hand from hers in sudden impatience, and said, "I haven't told thee everything."

She raised her eyebrows. "Do thou think thy ancestors told the world everything—every single, terrible part of the truth?"

He looked at her.

"'History' is merely what someone thinks happened, Gundhalinu-ken," she said softly.

He stared at her, while behind his eyes he remembered being Ilmarinen, in the beginning: Ilmarinen his ancestor, who had committed treason for the greater good, and set the Great Game in motion. . . . He sighed. "Why is it that the obvious things are always the most difficult to see?"

Pandhara touched him again, hesitantly; her hand slid down his arm and fell away. "Because if it weren't so, life might actually begin to make sense." She met his gaze, glanced away again as if it were painful. But her voice was cool and dry as she said, "And we couldn't have that, could we?"

And somehow after that there had seemed to be nothing more to say; so he had bid her good night, and gone off to his room. Even though he had gotten to bed far later than he had intended, he slept as poorly as a man on the eve of execution.

This morning they had gone to Serakande Center, where the Art and Science Museum was featuring a show of her works. He had worn nondescript civilian clothes, and few people had looked at him twice. Pandhara had been the center of attention; he had enjoyed the luxury of standing unmolested in someone else's shadow, watching the world interact with her, observing her grace and intelligence, the way her pleasure made her shine, the way it drew them to her.

Afterward he had taken her to his favorite restaurant; the owner had brought them a bottle of imported Lilander, from her private stock. Later they had discussed art and politics in the comfortable darkness of a back-street tea shop, sitting with a handful of Pandhara's old friends. They were all creatives, Nontechs who sat smoking spicesticks and making no concession to her new highborn status, or even to his. They had called him "sibyl," and he had known that, coming from them, it was honor enough.

And now the sun was going down on the last day he would ever spend on his homeworld; and as faint music drifted out through the open doors, he sat gazing up at the wife he would never see again, feeling as though he had never really seen her before. "Thou look beautiful tonight," he said, with difficulty, as she lifted her hand to him in greeting. He touched it with his own, feeling the warmth as their palms met, his eyes never leaving her face as the words brought out her smile. "I am grateful to thee, for today." He looked away at last, toward the sea. "I'll carry it with me for a lifetime, after I'm gone."

"As will I," she said, turning her own gaze to the sea. "BZ . . . last night I thought a great deal about all the things thou told me. And about things thou said thou had not told me—"

He looked back at her.

"Some of the things," she said carefully, "I think were there all along, between the words. But—"

"But thou need to know the rest."

She nodded.

"I—" He pressed his mouth together. "Ask me. I'll tell thee everything I can." Realizing that what he did with the rest of his life could very well affect her, even half a galaxy away.

She rested her hands on the stone-capped top of the wall; he saw the fingers tighten. "When thou asked me to marry thee, thou said thou did not want a—a marriage in fact, but only in name. Was it because of this woman on Tiamat, the one who became Queen? . . . Are thou still so much in love with her, after so long? Is that why thou're going back?"

"Yes," he whispered, looking down.

She leaned against the wall, her eyes still on him, her face uncertain. "Thou said that she had a husband?"

"Yes."

"That thou had only one night with her?"

"I only slept with her once. But it was more than that—"

"I know. I . . ." She glanced away, lifting her chin. "But thou haven't seen her since. It must have been—"

"Twelve years. More than eighteen, for her." He looked up again. "How do I know she still wants me? I can't know, for certain. But Fire Lake showed me glimpses of my future . . . it showed me her. And—" He took a deep breath. "I've spoken with her, since I left Tiamat."

She stared at him, incredulous. "How? No one can even send a message—"

"She's a sibyl, and so am I. It's possible . . . and that's all I can tell you. I shouldn't even say that much." He glanced down. "I've communicated with her several times since I left. She knows what's about to happen. She's afraid of it. And she has every right to be. The Hegemony wants only one thing from Tiamat—the water of life. The Summers consider it a sacrilege to kill the mers, and the mers have been hunted close to extinction as it is. There is even evidence in the sibyl net that the mers may be sentient. . . ."

"What?" she said, in disbelief. "But that means—"

"Genocide." He nodded. "If it is true, we've been committing genocide for centuries."

"Have thou told anyone about this?"

He laughed bitterly. "I tried. No one on the Central Coordinating Committee wants to hear it. Pernatte made it very clear to me that further argument, or any public protest, could ruin my career. . . ." He shook his head. "If the Queen resists new hunting, which she will, that will give the Hedge the excuse it needs to trample them into the mud, the way it's done for a millennium. That's why I had to become Chief Justice. I have half a chance now to keep control of the legal system, to draw the line between government and exploitation."

"Are thou so sure that will happen, without thee?"

He nodded, tight-lipped. "The signs are all there. Everything I hear. No one's talking marriage upstairs, they're all talking rape. The pols want easy profit, the Blues want an excuse to flex their new weapons technology, and everybody wants more power. The time lags were all that kept them from doing anything about building a new Empire, until now. Exploiting Tiamat is a perfect first step."

"But with the stardrive, the Hegemony will become a meaningful political and economic unit anyway." Pandhara gestured with her wine glass, glancing up at the sky. "Even a marginal world like Tiamat will become a valuable resource; there simply aren't that many habitable planets. Without the Old Empire's starmap data to show us other inhabited systems, it could take generations to find even one world we aren't already in contact with."

He nodded, pushing restlessly to his feet. "I know that. I make that point at every opportunity, upstairs. But it may take years before the Hegemony's leaders see the big picture clearly. By then it will be too late for the mers, and maybe for the humans on Tiamat as well."

"Does Moon know that thou're returning?"

"Yes."

"How does she feel about that?"

"I think . . . it makes her afraid, too."

"And thou—?"

He looked back at her for a long moment without speaking; turned away, averting his eyes to the view of the land falling into shadow, the distant, gleaming sea. "I'm afraid," he murmured at last, "that I don't want to give this up, Dhara. I'm afraid that, after all I've gone through to reach this point, I don't want to go back to Tiamat."

He felt her come softly up behind him where he stood, felt her arms slip beneath his and circle his chest, holding him; felt her warmth against his back, her hair gently brushing his neck as she rested her head on his shoulder. She said nothing more, did nothing more, only held him.

Slowly, uncertainly, he lifted his own hands to cover hers. "I could stand here like this, looking out at this view, for the rest of my life," he whispered, "and be perfectly happy. . . ." Thinking that he could run for the World Parliament, and be elected: work to redirect the fate of this world, his own world, instead of one whose people would probably only hate and resent him for it. "Right here, right now, I have everything that I ever dreamed of having—more. I feel respected, honored . . ." He moved inside the circle of her arms, turning until he faced her. "Even . . . loved?"

Her arms tightened around him, as his own arms closed her in.

"Sathra, bhan, your guest is coming in—"

Gundhalinu jerked guiltily as the estates manager stepped onto the balcony with a brief bow, found him embracing his wife, and hastily departed. Gundhalinu took a deep breath, realizing that he had every right to be found embracing her; realized that somehow he was no longer touching her at all.

The compassion in her eyes as she took his arm to go in and greet KR Aspundh was, for the moment until she looked away again, more painful than the sorrow that lay below it.

Aspundh looked at them both a little oddly, when they greeted him like a pair of mourners; but he made pleasant, innocuous conversation as they waited for dinner, and gradually Gundhalinu felt the tension leaving the air, letting go of his body. They all drank a great deal of lith, and somewhere in the middle of the main course Pandhara began to tell off-color jokes, which Aspundh unexpectedly found hilarious. Gundhalinu watched Aspundh laugh, in silent astonishment, too preoccupied to find anything amusing himself except the sight of the old man's obvious pleasure.

"Delightful, PHN—" Aspundh gasped, still short of breath. "And my compliments to your chef, my dear." He lifted his glass to her, and washed down the last of the spicy, unfamiliar stew with another swallow of lith. "Best meal I've had in years."

"Thank you—" she said, and pressed her hand to her mouth, giggling as though it reminded her of another joke. "Did thou enjoy it, BZ—?"

He nodded, feeling mildly out-of-focus. He had hardly been aware of eating at all, but his bowl was almost empty. "Excellent," he murmured. "What is it?" He ate another mouthful.

"Grisha," she said, beaming. "My mother's recipe."

"*Grisha—?*" He swallowed convulsively, and began to cough. "You mean we're eating rat meat?"

"BZ! How dare thou suggest it." She looked at him in disbelief. "We are not eating rat meat. Don't be such a bloody snob." But she began to giggle again, helplessly. "Thou've never eaten grisha. . . ."

"My father used to make it all the time," Aspundh said. "I loved it."

Gundhalinu stared at him. "But grisha is . . . is—" Remembering a beat too late that KR Aspundh's father had been a Nontechnician.

"So 'common' . . . ?" Pandhara reached across the wide table to pat his hand, reaching to his rescue. "Of course it is. 'Common' only means that everyone eats it."

He looked back at his dish, shaking his head. "My nurse . . . told me when I was a boy that Unclassifieds ate grisha made out of rat meat and spoiled vegetables."

"You make do with what you have," she said gently.

He glanced up, down again, remembering Tiamat, remembering World's End, remembering the stranger things he had eaten, and would soon eat again. . . . He ate another mouthful, and another, under their watchful gazes, and smiled, slowly. "We grow or we die, don't we? It really is very good, you know."

After dinner they settled into the deep cushions of the sunken meditation room. A servo left them a drifting tray of sweets. Pandhara lit a spicestick, inhaled and exhaled; the incense-heavy smoke curled languorously into the air over her head. He had never seen her smoke one before today. *So many things that he did not know about her; that he would never know, now. . . .*

"Those are very unhealthy, you know," Aspundh chided her mildly.

She looked at BZ; he saw something that was more than a simple question and less than grief in her gaze. "Tonight I feel reckless, KR."

Aspundh glanced from face to face, and said no more about it. Instead he turned to Gundhalinu. "So the time has finally come. The way is open to Tiamat once again. And you are going back, as Chief Justice. It has all worked out just as you said it would, years ago."

Gundhalinu almost nodded; but his neck resisted the lying motion. "No," he said softly. "Not exactly as I planned, KR."

Aspundh said nothing, waited.

The tray of sweets drifted up to Gundhalinu's side; he picked up a small, ornate cake. He held the cake in his open palm, studying it; put it back and pushed the tray away. "You'll probably think I'm mad, but . . . I don't know if I'm doing the right thing." He put his hand over his eyes, unable to go on looking at them for a moment. "Suddenly I'm full of doubts—about why I'm really going, what I can possibly achieve there . . . about whether there's even any point to all of this. I've been living with this obsession for years; and now, suddenly, I find myself wondering *why*. Was it only because for so long I had nothing else to hold on to? Since I've come back to Kharemough. . . ." He shook his head, looking up at them again. "Gods help me . . ." he whispered, "I don't want to leave."

Aspundh frowned; but there was sympathy, not censure in the older man's eyes. He glanced at Pandhara. "How much of this have you discussed with PHN?"

"Enough," he said, his own eyes meeting hers.

"And how do you feel about what he has told you, PHN?"

Pandhara moved restlessly among the cushions. "I want him to be happy. . . ." She jerked her head, almost angrily. "I want him to stay—" She looked at BZ again, and the look made him ache. "Thou have been such a solitary man, BZ. . . . All these years, thou've worked on this dream, and not until now have I understood even the smallest part of why . . . only that thou were not at peace, and could not be, I thought, until thou saw it through."

Gundhalinu shut his eyes, pressing his face with his hands again. "Damn it all! After I survived World's End, I knew I could face anything that came between me and what I had to do—" His hands dropped away, lay motionless in his lap. "Anything but this." *Anything but happiness.*

"Then we must let Moon know that the fleet will be arriving within months . . . but you will not be coming with it," Aspundh said.

Gundhalinu's head rose; he felt his face flush. "Moon told me," he murmured, "after she came back to Tiamat . . . that even she could have been happy staying on Kharemough. But she *felt* something, that forced her to go back. The sibyl mind spoke to her somehow, made her know what she had to do. I've never felt anything like that. If I could just be half as certain as she was that I was doing the right thing—"

"Perhaps you haven't heard 'voices' because you haven't required them. Your own desire, your own belief in what was right, have carried you this far on your own," Aspundh said. "Perhaps she was never as certain as you were—or even as you believe she was. Have you seen or heard anything, in your dealings with the Police High Command or the Central Coordinating Committee, to make you believe your opinions of them are unjustified?"

Gundhalinu's eyes darkened. "No."

"And do you still feel at all responsible for what will happen to Tiamat . . . ?"

"Yes." He looked down. "Yes, damn it! You know I do."

"And what about Moon Dawntreader?"

BZ looked toward Pandhara, helplessly, knowing that she could read in his eyes what his own pain and confusion would not let him say.

"Have you considered," Aspundh asked, almost reluctantly, "what may happen to the Summer Queen when the Hegemony returns to Tiamat?"

Gundhalinu felt a cold fist close around his heart. "Gods . . . No, they wouldn't order her sacrificed! It isn't the time . . . Summer has scarcely begun there. It would be a total violation of the Change rituals."

"This return of the Hegemony is already a total violation of the pattern, on Tiamat. I'm not saying it would happen. I don't know that. But what if it did—?"

Gundhalinu sagged back into the elusive support of the cool, satin-surfaced cushions. Moon Dawntreader was not the ruler that the Hegemony would be expecting to find when it got to Tiamat. If she defied them . . . most of the old Winter power structure was still alive, and would be more than willing to sacrifice Summer to the sea. He looked toward Pandhara again, his throat aching with the sight of her; realizing he had known all along that he could not stay, could never be free of his memories, or the truth.

"BZ," she said, and her own voice was stronger now, more certain. "When thou told me all the things I did not know about thy past, all that thou had endured and overcome . . . and how because of Tiamat thou had become all the things thou are . . . I felt as though the spirit of this place, and thy ancestors, had touched my soul through thee. That whatever it was thou felt thou must do, it was right, and thou would achieve it. I saw it in thy eyes then, even when thou embraced me. I see it now . . . thou are only a ghost. Thou are not truly here, and will never be, while all the answers to what thou are still wait for thee on Tiamat. Go back to

Moon . . . and the gods go with thee." She reached out, only to touch his fingers with her own.

He closed his hand over hers; her hand felt more substantial, more real, than his own flesh. He looked back at Aspundh almost reluctantly. *Moon.* He must do it now, one final Transfer, one final message, to let her know. . . .

Aspundh nodded, understanding, and rose slowly, stiffly to his feet.

BZ rose with him. "I'll show KR to his rooms, Dhara—"

She let go of him, remaining where she was; used to this arcane ritual of her husband and his guest, accepting his explanation that they had confidential policy matters to discuss. "Thank you for coming, KR."

Aspundh nodded again. "I'm glad I could be here." They both looked at Gundhalinu.

He hesitated. "Will thou wait here for me, Dhara? I . . . need to discuss something with thee."

She nodded. Surprise drove the brooding sorrow out of her gaze for a moment as she watched them go out of the room.

"BZ . . ." Aspundh said, settling himself in a comfortable chair as Gundhalinu closed the door behind them.

Gundhalinu glanced back at him, unsure of what was in the older man's voice, just as he was unsure of his own expression. He crossed the room, sat down in the chair's mate. "Yes," he said softly, "I'm ready."

"To go into Transfer?" Aspundh asked. "Or to go back to Tiamat."

"Both," he said, looking down.

"Then let me tell you something that may help to ease the pain of this transition."

Gundhalinu looked up again in silent curiosity.

"There is some evidence," Aspundh murmured, holding his gaze, "that the situation you find yourself in now may have been set up intentionally, to fill you with exactly the kind of doubts you are feeling now."

Gundhalinu stared at him. "What are you saying? Are you saying that Pandhara—"

"No . . . your wife is completely innocent in this matter. But it appears certain factions made sure that the two of you would meet in the first place, and that you would continue to encounter each other; that eventually you would find yourself in your present position—too comfortable, too happy . . . even falling in love," Aspundh said gently. "Doubting yourself, doubting your choices. There are those people who would rather not see you return to Tiamat."

"Do you mean the Brotherhood?" Gundhalinu asked, remembering his brothers' death with sudden appalling vividness.

Aspundh nodded. "Yes. But not the Brotherhood alone. . . . You are at the center of too much power now for anything to be that simple. Your position may protect you from direct attack, but it also makes you a lodestone for subtler forms of betrayal."

" 'Ask the right questions' . . ." Gundhalinu muttered, " 'and trust no one.' "

"Exactly." Aspundh's smile was full of sorrow. "Not even yourself."

Pandhara was still sitting where he had left her when he returned to the meditation room . . . sitting perfectly still, with the lights dimmed and her eyes closed, meditating on an adhani, as he had shown her how to do. She had picked up the skill very quickly. He had been pleased when she had told him that it helped her focus while she worked.

She opened her eyes as she heard him come back into the room; looked up at him expectantly, folding her hands in her lap.

He dropped down to sit cross-legged facing her, exhausted by the unnatural stress of the Transfer. He looked away for a long moment, with no idea of how to begin. At last he made himself look at her again. "Dhara . . . you told me once that one of the reasons you wanted my family's heritage was for your children. That you wanted to have children . . . ?"

Her eyes widened slightly, and she bent her head. "Yes."

"I . . . Gods—" he whispered, and his hands fisted. He looked up at the diamond-within-diamond pattern of the ceiling dome, an infinity of blue-on-blue. "I don't know how to explain this so that it doesn't . . . When I go, where I'm going, with what I'll have to do when I get there . . . thou know I won't be coming back. And . . . the gods know, if it goes far enough, there may be trouble . . . enough trouble, focused on me, that it might have repercussions even here, for thee and the estates. I don't want what happened to thee ever to happen again." She watched him, her eyes dark, saying nothing. "I've given it a lot of thought these past two days—" pushing on before he lost his nerve. "How to secure thy position, and protect the estates from any possible attempt at confiscation. . . . Dhara, would thou consider having a child by me?" The final words were barely audible.

"I—" Her hand rose to her breast.

He looked down, said hastily, "I would set up the necessary sperm account before I leave. I'll see to everything. The procedure could be done at thy convenience, that way, quite easily. . . . With an heir, a child who belongs genetically to both of us, there can be no question to whom the Gundhalinu family holdings belong. . . . And I would know . . . would know that I have honored my ancestors in the only way that holds any real meaning in my heart, anymore."

She was silent for a long moment. "Thou have thought this out very carefully, very considerately, as always, I see." She waited for him to look up again, finally. "It would give me great joy to bear thy child, BZ . . . I could not imagine a more beautiful thing."

He began to smile, with relief and release.

"On one condition. Will thou give me one thing, in return?"

Surprise stirred in him. "Whatever thou want, that I can give thee."

She looked steadily, deeply, into his eyes. "Give me tonight, BZ. Give me a child with thy own body."

He stared, feeling himself flush again, feeling his heartbeat quicken. "I . . . Are thou at the . . . I mean . . ."

"I will arrange it." She whispered the same words he had spoken so many times to her. "I will not do it any other way. A child is a human being; to create one is not as simple as mixing sperm and egg in a bottle. Thou will give this child life—but thou may never see it again, for as long as either one of thee live. Thou can't do that; it isn't fair. Let our child's life begin as an act of love . . . so that when I tell our son or daughter of it, I can tell the truth. Be a husband to me . . ." She leaned toward him, her taut body clearly outlined beneath the fluid cloth of her gown, and put her hand on him. He got an erection, so quickly that the pain was like a shock. "Just for tonight."

He felt his sudden understanding of the truth she had spoken drown in a wave of need, as the rush of heat rose up through the aching emptiness inside him from his aching loins. "Yes—" he whispered. He found her waiting mouth, soft and wet and warm, drank her kisses like a man dying of thirst. His hands slid down her body, feeling her warmth, her womanliness, the pressure of her breasts against him as his arms circled her back and began to unseal her gown.

He slid her gown down her body, revealing her shoulders, the exquisite curve of her back, her breasts. Her deft fingers unfastened his jacket, opened his tunic, undid his pants—were down inside them, doing things to him that made novas of his nerve endings. He gasped in ecstasy and anguish as he felt himself slide over the edge of control. Unable to stop it, he pushed her back and down, found his way inside her, spent himself, in an act of desperation, hearing her feeble cry of protest drown inside his own cry of release.

He lay on top of her, his heart pounding, dazed and humiliated, until he could find the strength to push himself up off of her again, so that their bodies were no longer joined together, or even touching. "Gods . . ." he mumbled, "oh gods . . . I'm sorry. It's been so long—"

She reached up, drawing him back down beside her. She stroked his hair, touched his lips like a kiss. "Hush, I know—I should have realized. . . ."

"Did I hurt thee?" he whispered, and remembered his brothers. He shut his eyes, sick. "Oh, Dhara, thou must think I—"

"It's all right— It is. . . . Hush. . . ." She drew him into her arms, rubbing his back, holding him close. "We have all night."

He breathed in the scent of her, absorbed the sensation of her skin against his own. And then he raised his head, finding her lips, kissing her again, deeply, lingeringly, as if *tonight* meant *forever*. He used his mouth, his hands, the touch of his weary, contented body pressed close against hers, to give her all the pleasure he had meant to give her, to make love to her as he had wanted to make love to her, to give her the release he had taken from her so unexpectedly. . . . Until at last he knew from her sighs and her cries and the way she clung to him that she had found her own joy at last.

He held her for a while, until her breathing slowed, falling into the rhythm of his own. And then her knowing, skillful hands began to do their work again, caressing him, guiding him with a sensual skill that he had never known before, exploring him more eagerly as he began to respond. . . . But there was no urgency this time; the pleasure of their intimacies went on and on, rising to meet in a peak of dizzying sensation, falling away again into warm dreaming valleys, and finally into sleep.

The sun rose, the light of the new day shone in on two sleeping forms, husband and wife twined together into the illusion of one; and in their separate dreams, for a time, a separate peace.

TIAMAT: Carbuncle

Moon Dawntreader sat gazing out across the circle of gathered sibyls, entrepreneurs, and landholders, holding the expressionless mask of the Queen firmly on her face. She had had to face these people, or others like them, virtually every day for over eighteen years, listening as she did now to the cacophony of their voices as they settled into their seats. Once most of the voices had been full of enthusiasm and new ideas. The arguments had been petty and annoying then, and the sense of hope and progress has always outweighed them.

The arguments had gotten louder and the complaints more bitter in the years since she had turned her back on the pursuit of progress, to devote her time and resources to the mers. Because she could not tell anyone the whole truth, most of the Council members reacted as though she had gone slightly mad . . . until sometimes, facing them like this, even she had wondered if maybe they were right.

BZ— She closed her eyes, silently reciting the name like an unwilling prayer. Remembering his voice speaking to her, as it had done again yesterday; calling her away into the shimmering sea of light/sound/absence that had been their secret meeting place for nearly four years now—calling her away for what would be the last time before he arrived on Tiamat in the flesh, with the Hegemony. Their fragile, fleeting contact, his encouragement and reassurance, her memories, had given her solace and strength through these increasingly difficult bureaucratic ordeals, the endless testing of her resolve and her faith. And now, at last, he was returning—

And what did she want . . . hope for . . . expect, when they met again . . . ? She let her mind fall inward, the cacophony fading around her as she tried to picture his face, imagine how it had changed, in what ways; wondering whether she would even recognize him when they met again. She had known him for such a short time, so long ago. It was hard after so long to remember his face, even though—or perhaps because—it had been so unlike the faces that had surrounded her all her life, and through all the years since then. His voice, his smile, the gentleness of his touch . . . did they belong to a real man or only the dream of a shadow? When his return had been impossible, or even years away, his memory had been a refuge from the burdens and disappointments of her life, her secret fantasies of remembered passion had been a release and an escape. But now that he was about to become a part of her reality, suddenly she found that she had no refuge left. . . .

She shook her head, shaking free the images that were choking out the present of things that must be faced down and lived up to and dealt with today, whether she had the strength to deal with them or not. Sparks turned in his seat to look at her, his eyes questioning and impatient. She met his gaze, as the last tendrils of someone else's image faded across his face. Looking at him she felt a final, disorienting slip of perception, as if his face was the stranger's, as if she barely remembered who he was.

She looked away again, realizing with sudden sorrow that it was not her imagination that had made her husband into a stranger, or driven her to seek solace from a shadow. The tragedy in the Pit had only been the blow that had finally opened the fractures in something that had once been whole and perfect, and as precious to her as life. She did not understand how they had let this happen to them . . . even though she had watched it happening, for years. She did not even know at what point this moment had become inevitable—or whether it had been inevitable all along, from the moment she had heard the sibyl voice calling her away.

She looked at Tammis sitting across the room beside Danaquil Lu, his new father-in-law; at the trefoils that lay against their shirts like shining eyes, gazing back at her. Tammis's tragic calling had not only split the cracks of her marriage, it had done something equally painful to the son's relationship with his father. Even Tammis's wedding to Merovy had done nothing to help the situation; afterwards Sparks had seemed more remote and unapproachable than ever. His eyes had turned her back when she would have asked him why; and so had her son's.

She glanced at Jerusha PalaThion, sitting on her left; sitting with an empty seat beside her, as she always did, marking the absence of the man they both still missed so often, and so deeply. Moon saw in Jerusha's face the price of her loss, the loneliness and doubt she still held fiercely inside. Jerusha had never shared her emotions easily, after a lifetime spent among strangers—first her own people, and then the Tiamatans. Moon studied the depths of sorrow in her eyes; wishing that there was something she could do for the woman who had been her steadfast and unexpected friend for so many years . . . wishing there was something she could do to help herself. Jerusha looked up and smiled, more a grimace, as Moon gathered herself at last to speak the unavoidable words that would open the Council meeting.

"Summer and Winter—" she said, her voice surprisingly even. She folded her hands on the tabletop before her in a white-knuckled imitation of control, waiting for their silence and attention. "I have received another message through the Transfer. Preparations are complete for the offworlders' return to Tiamat. They are ready to send their ships—and a new Hegemonic government—here from Kharemough." She waited again as the flood of excitement, wonder and consternation rose around her, and drained away; waiting until at last there were coherent questions to be answered.

"How long will it be, then?" Sewa Stormprince asked, asking for them all. Moon saw the mixed emotions on the woman's face, a reflection of the expressions all around the room.

"A matter of weeks," she said, feeling the spin of her own disbelief make her dizzy, as if hearing the words spoken aloud had somehow made them more real. "I can only tell you that I believe the new government will be more just toward us, and that all we have done to develop our resources has not been an exercise in futility. But there is the matter of the mers—"

She broke off, as the faces that had brightened with relief and sudden interest turned annoyed, or turned away, already lost in speculation about the Return. The resentment against the changes she had made, redirecting the resources of the Sibyl College toward her study of the mers, had cost her a loss of support that Capella Goodventure and the traditionalist Summers had scarcely made up for. She had angered and alienated the Winters and even the Summers she had fought so hard to win to her original visions of a new Tiamat. She had done her work too well, all those years, driven by the same compulsion that now drove her to redirect her vision; so that redirecting it had proved twice as difficult.

If the future meant the death of every mer on Tiamat in exchange for the easy comfort of citizenship in the Hegemony's new empire, most of the people sitting in this room would make that sacrifice—some guiltily, but most without hesitation. "The problem of the mers has not been resolved," she said, raising her voice. "And that is important, to your future, and to the Hegemony's future as well!" She was almost shouting, to make herself heard above the rising murmur of voices. "If the Hegemony destroys them, if we allow that to happen, in the end we will be losing everything we thought we had gained—"

"Why?" Flan Redstone said flatly. "Because they're an intelligent race? Then let them look out for themselves."

"If they're so intelligent," someone else murmured, "why have they let the offworlders kill them for so long, anyway? How smart can they be?"

"They are the Lady's Children!" Capella Goodventure called out. "If you abandon them, she will abandon you—"

"She never took as good care of us as the offworlders, anyway," Flan Redstone answered.

"It's wrong to stand by and allow the mers to be slaughtered, whatever you believe," Clavally Bluestone said sharply. But she looked back at Moon. "But what can we do to stop it, Lady? You said yourself that we can't fight the Hegemony and win."

"That's true. So we have to find some other answer." Moon rose to her feet, leaning on the circle of table.

"Well, you keep saying that this is bigger than all of us, that the future depends on it," Sewa Stormprince said. "What does that mean? It's only a tragedy for the mers—and they don't seem to be concerned about it. What difference can it make to the future of Tiamat or the Hegemony if they kill all the mers? Then a few ultra-rich offworlders won't be able to live longer than all the rest of us. That hardly seems like a tragedy to me."

"That isn't the point." Moon shook her head, feeling the heavy plait of her hair slide against the back of her robe. "They are part of something far more important. I know that . . . I know that—" She felt her face convulse with frustration, felt her throat close, paralyzed, over the words that could never be spoke. "I know . . . what I know," she finished, looking down, her voice faltering, defeated. She sat down again, feeling too many eyes watching her with morbid curiosity, filled with doubt—even Jerusha's, even her husband's.

Her hands clenched together on the table surface. She studied the pattern they made, clinging to one another; feeling isolated in a way that she had never imagined possible—surrounded by people, people she knew and trusted and even loved, but people who could not help her. . . .

"Maybe we should all consider this," Jerusha said abruptly. "The Hegemony functions on trade. They'll give you what you want—but not for free. They'll want the water of life in return. But if you let them kill all the mers, there won't be any more water of life. And what will this world have to offer them, when the mers are all gone—? Think about it."

The tone of the muttering around the meeting table changed, more thoughtful now, but still querulous.

Moon looked up again, glancing gratefully at Jerusha, but still aware of the growing restlessness and noise. Surrendering, she opened the meeting to general questions about the Return and spent what seemed an eternity attempting to answer them all, hoping that her mind would stay focused on the matters at hand for long enough to provide a coherent answer when one was needed. Her gaze drifted to Kirard Set Wayaways, and she felt her face freeze as the images of her grandmother and Borah Clearwater blurred his face into an inhuman mask. *Inhuman—*

He looked up suddenly, as if he felt her gaze touch him. He looked mildly curious as her expression registered; but then something came into his eyes that looked like recognition, and he smiled. She felt herself turn cold inside as she realized that it was someone else's expression that he was acknowledging . . . the Queen he had known in Winter.

"Lady," he said, with the irritating, slightly mocking drawl that most of the former Winter nobles—even the ones she liked—seemed always to have, especially when they spoke her Summer title. He leaned forward, with a sudden intensity showing in his eyes. *It's coming now,* she thought, feeling tension pull her taut as she waited for his words. "I think we have said all that can be said about the subject of the offworlders' return. I would like to touch on local matters, if I may. . . . Specifically I would like to pursue my bid to buy out the rights to the Clearwater plantation, now that . . . the required time has passed since the tragic accident that claimed the life of my kin and yours—" He dropped his voice, and his gaze, in a show of regret and loss. She sat silently, her own face settling into a rictus. "As no relation has laid any first claim on it—"

"You're wrong about that, Kirard Set Wayaways," she said softly, and watched his own face freeze, midway into a look of smug anticipation.

"What do you mean?" he asked, in the sudden, perfect silence that fell around the room.

"I have decided to place a kin-claim on the land myself, as nearest surviving relative."

He stared at her. "What?" he said again, and then, "Gods. . . ." His eyes darkened. "You're a Summer. You're no kin of his or mine!"

"He was pledged to my grandmother." *Who died with him. And was it because of you? Was it—?* She pressed her mouth together, holding back the words—the accusations that she could not prove, the loss and the suspicion that still burned insider her like live coals.

"'Pledged'?" he said, his voice thick with anger and scorn. "That means nothing. It isn't legal marriage; there's no record of it—"

"A verbal pledge is accepted as binding in Summer," Moon said calmly. "And you are in Summer now. Their shared property is mine to claim, if I choose."

"What do you want with a stretch of underdeveloped coastline three days' travel from the city?" he snapped, glaring at her.

"I'll decide that in due time."

"Then why not sell it to me, for gods' sakes? You've been pleased enough with the way I've developed my other holdings. You know I've wanted this piece of land for years, but the . . . my late kinsman . . . wouldn't sell."

"I won't sell it to you because I swore to him once that I would never let you have it."

His disbelief shifted focus. He shook his head. "Fine," he murmured, controlling his voice with an effort. "So I presume to please your old grandmother, you kept your promise. But she's dead now, damn it. They both are—"

"And I have heard it said that you wished aloud on more than one occasion that your kinsman would disappear, so that you could get hold of his lands." She met the sudden gleam of knives in his stare. Seeing only the capsized boat adrift in a deserted inlet under a clear sky, on a peaceful sea; and no sign anywhere of the two people who had been sailing to Carbuncle, their shared experience with the sea equaling more than a century, with no storms reported.

"Are you accusing me of causing their deaths?" he said indignantly. "They were old. Maybe his heart stopped. Maybe she fell overboard—"

"I have no proof that their deaths were anything but an accident," she answered, hearing the toneless lack of belief in her voice. After the news had reached the city, Tor Starhiker had come to the palace, uneasy but unable to keep silent, and reported what she had overheard at her restaurant . . . and that she had seen Kirard Set down in the marketplace, where she had never seen him before, holding money under the noses of certain Winters of bad reputation, not long before Tammis's wedding day. Moon had asked Jerusha to investigate; but no bodies had been found, and no evidence beyond hearsay. "But you Winters have a saying: 'Today's word is tomorrow's deed.'"

He made a disgusted noise.

"I'm not accusing you of any crime. But your ill will toward your own kin and mine is enough to make me choose to see that you never hold those lands."

"Rumors and lies—" He pushed to his feet, glaring at her. "It's bad enough that we've had to put up with this half-assed religious fanaticism about the mers! But now this— This is too much." He waved an arm at her, as if he could dismiss her with a conjuring wave of his hand. "The Hegemony isn't going to see it that way when they get here. And if you don't start to see this world the way Arienrhod did again, don't expect to see it for long, after they get here." He turned and left the chamber.

TIAMAT: Starship *Ilmarinen,*
Planetary Orbit

"Commander Gundhalinu—"

"Captain." Gundhalinu returned the half-surprised salutes of CA Tabaranne, the *Ilmarinen*'s captain, and the handful of officers standing with him on the starship's bridge. They went on staring at him as he crossed the control room, his own eyes riveted on the viewscreens and displays. "Tiamat—" he whispered, more to himself than to the others listening.

"Yes, sir," Tabaranne said, coming up beside him. He eyed the displays with justifiable pride, and what Gundhalinu suspected was palpable relief. "There it is. Congratulations, Commander."

Gundhalinu smiled fleetingly, as the brilliant blue orb of a water world filled his vision. "Thank you," he murmured, a prayer of gratitude to unseen gods, carried inside a polite acknowledgment. Remembering himself, where he was and how he had come to be here, he looked back at Tabaranne and raised his hand. "Congratulations to you, too, Captain. To everyone aboard."

Tabaranne's smile widened, as he met Gundhalinu's palm with his own. He glanced away at the view of Tiamat. "Unbelievable," he said softly. He looked back again. "How are you holding up, Commander?"

Gundhalinu shrugged. "Tolerable. Still a few aches, and nauseated." Tabaranne nodded, with an expression that suggested he knew exactly how Gundhalinu felt. His own face was haggard enough, Gundhalinu noted. The distance to Tiamat had been so great that it had taken six hyperspace jumps, with real-space stopovers in between, to get them here. The stopovers had not been due to any limitations of the stardrive, or even of the *Ilmarinen* itself, which had been built as precisely to the Old Empire's specifications as was now humanly possible. The ship had borne the stresses of hyperlight transit with virtually no problems. The problems and limitations lay in the human bodies of its passengers and crew.

The transit time of a jump in hyperspace was not instantaneous, and their first brief experimental jumps in the *Ilmarinen* and its sister ship the *Vanamoinen* had demonstrated that the effects on a human body and mind of time spent Between were profoundly unpleasant. There were limitations on how long a human being could tolerate hyperspace transit without severe physical or mental problems. Further Transfer queries had shown him that the Old Empire had used serial jumps to cover long distance safely; he had managed with his research staff to work out programming for the stardrive unit that would let them automatically make stopovers in deep space, giving them the necessary recovery time.

The actual transit they spent drugged into oblivion—even the crew, who had no function anyway, during that interdimensional leap of faith, when everything was beyond human control. Still, when they recovered from the drugs, their bodies relived vividly, in pain and sickness, what their minds remembered only dimly, in haunted, half-formed dreams. They sat in uncharted space for long enough to recover to the point where they could face another span of transit, and then jumped into the unknown again, never completely sure that they would ever reach their destination.

"This trip has been a lesson in humility for a number of people, I'm afraid," Gundhalinu said wryly. "And I doubt anyone will thank me for that." He glanced toward the doorway he had come through; no one else had followed him up here yet. He had pushed himself, he knew, wanting to be the first, trying to shake off the drugs' effects quickly, helped by the adrenaline of his need to know, to see this sight . . . wanting, needing to see it without the interference of a dozen observers at his back.

Tabaranne grinned. "If that view doesn't make them forget their troubles, then they should have stayed home. That's the trouble with these bureaucrats—they travel across half the galaxy, but they want it to be painless, and they want it to be just like what they left behind when they get there. What's the point of that? We've accomplished something no one in the Hegemony has ever done before . . . and there's not a body in this ship's crew that wouldn't have gone through twice the hell to be here when it happened. That's why we're here—not lying in a bunk with a hangover. That's something those civilians will never understand."

Gundhalinu smiled at the truth in it, at the implicit compliment of being included in Tabaranne's inner circle. He had not known Tabaranne well before this singular journey, but he had been impressed by the other man's courage and dedication in heading the test voyages of the new ships. Tabaranne was a career Navy man, a seasoned enforcer in an arm of the Hegemonic Forces that Gundhalinu had never had much contact with before. Gundhalinu had come to like and respect him, and most of his hand-picked crew—almost reluctantly. Tabaranne was a hard-line militarist, and Gundhalinu knew that someday they might find themselves on opposite sides of an impassable ideological barrier.

But for now he felt more at ease with Tabaranne's sense of purpose, his sense of wonder about this mission, than with the endless complaints and overwrought physical symptoms of his own staff. He wondered fleetingly if he would have been as unpleasant to be around as the rest of them if he had not had World's End to compare this to. He liked to think not.

"We'll have to look into some kind of stasis field suspension for future journeys, like they use on the coin-ships. . . ." He felt a part of his mind slide into a now-habitual problem-solving mode. He realized that the Old Empire must have had some better solution, wondering why it had not been given to them in Transfer, along with the basic specs of ship design. There had been nothing at all about easing the passage for the human beings who were the sole reason for the ships' existence. He was suddenly certain that it was one more example of the sibyl net's disturbing deterioration.

"Would you like to take a look at the big picture, Commander?" Tabaranne gestured toward the viewscreen.

"Very much." Gundhalinu nodded, pushing the unpleasant train of thought to the back of his mind, glad that it was no longer his concern.

Tabaranne ordered the navigation displays to expand focus. Tiamat's disc shrank and spun away on the screens before them: Gundhalinu watched as the double-diamond of the Twins, Tiamat's binary sun system, gradually filled his vision until he viewed them close-up for the first time. They were a mismatched pair, one tiny and actinic-blue, the other vast and bleary-red, mated by a yoke of incandescent gases—the outer atmosphere of the red giant, siphoned off by the insidious gravitational drag of the tiny blue dwarf.

Gundhalinu stared at the spectacle of the double suns, marveling, both at the sight and at the power of the ship's Old Empire-design navigational sensors. He watched as the image changed again. This time the binary Twins fell away, and the ship's far-seeing eye turned toward two points of light even farther away. He watched them come, reeled in by an invisible magic thread; watched the simulation whirl past the blinding, tormented face of the yellow sun the Tiamatans called the Summer Star, whose appearance in their daytime sky marked the Change from Winter's reign to Summer's.

The Summer Star was held captive, like the Twins themselves, by the thing that was swelling across the screen now: the Black Gate, the revolving black hole at the heart of this stellar cluster, which for a millennium had given the Hegemony its only access to Tiamat.

Utter blackness became the focal point on the screen, limned by a flaming halo of energy as countless particles of matter were sucked down into the insatiable maw of the black hole's gravity well. He felt a prickle of terror, gazing at it, even knowing that he was actually far away, safely out of reach; that this monstrous whirlpool in the sky was only a data simulation. He thought of the times he had calmly and acceptingly let a coin-ship carry him into that maelstrom, always confident that he would emerge from the other end of the wormhole through space unscathed. He had taken that leap of faith far more casually than he had taken this one. But then, no one had ever shown him this sight before. . . . *Ignorance is bliss.* He remembered passing through the Black Gate one last time, leaving behind an impossible love; believing that it was forever, and believing that there would never be a way for him to change his mind . . . or to change anything else. He shook his head, and sighed.

The image of the Gate began to shimmer, transforming back into an image of Tiamat as suddenly as if his own thoughts had willed it. The world was larger now, its details clearer. The assistant navigator said, "Locking into stable orbit now, Captain."

Tabaranne murmured acknowledgment, turning with Gundhalinu as half a dozen more people entered the bridge.

Gundhalinu kept his face expressionless as he observed the various states of distress of Vhanu and the other ambulatory representatives of the provisional Hegemonic government. He watched their faces change, saw the same play of wonder and relief that he knew had filled his own, as they took in the reality of Tiamat on the displays before them. It had already been announced through the levels of the ship that the *Ilmarinen* had reached its destination. That was why they were straggling up here now like the walking dead. But the difference between hearing it over an intercom, and actually witnessing it with one's own eyes was unimaginable.

He let them congratulate him, a part of him savoring their praise, unable to resist the admiration of a people whose respect was not easily won, and somehow meant so much to him even now. . . . But always there was a part of him that kept its distance, a still, small voice reminding him that in his heart he was no longer completely one of them.

He had tried to use his influence to surround himself with people he thought he could trust, who were at least flexible enough to bend his way when he tried to set policy, to listen when he tried to explain that there was a larger picture to consider . . . who understood the real parameters of the Great Game, whether they were Survey or not.

But every favor had a price; every faction had its influence and its own agenda. In trying to negotiate who would be on his staff, he had been forced into compromise after compromise, until he felt like a highborn bridegroom trying to decide who would attend his wedding. He thought suddenly, with poignant regret, of Pandhara— how she had insisted on an automatic notary marriage, scandal or no scandal, as soon as he had given her the first hint of what they would face if they so much as announced their intentions publicly.

But he had had no choice, in this matter. . . . He looked around him, seeing Vhanu, who was his new Commander of Police, the only one on his staff whom he knew well enough to trust completely; and HM Borskad, a Survey colleague, but one who believed more strongly than he liked in a Kharemoughi-centered vision of order. Behind Borskad was YA Tilhonne, a grandnephew of Pernatte's, of unproven competence and loyalties; and beside him stood VX Sandrine, a Foreign Service career man who had spent time on a number of worlds but did not seem to have learned much from any of them. They had in common right now only their various expressions of awe and discomfort.

Another small clutch of officials entered the bridge, as he watched. Still more remained below, recovering from their ordeal. They had all made this journey willingly, but he could only begin to guess their individual motives for it. If a quarter of them had the vision and flexibility he had hoped for, he would be lucky.

Women were a distinct minority among them. Equality depended less on sex than on social standing for Kharemoughis, who valued brain over brawn, unlike most of the cultures of the Eight Worlds. But he had forgotten, until he returned to Kharemough—if he had even realized it before—how the Foreign Service seemed to attract the most rigid and inflexible of his own people. He had wanted a higher representation of women, because Tiamat was more egalitarian and more matriarchal than any world he had ever been on; understanding and cooperation would be more likely on both sides if his own representatives were equally divided between the sexes. But because of the biases and restrictions built into the Foreign Service, there had been few women even qualified for the positions he had needed to fill.

The *Ilmarinen* carried not only the staff of the new provisional government, but also a squadron of Police, the backbone of the new government—virtually all of them Kharemoughis as well, most of them Nontech, all volunteers. They were all Kharemoughi because it was both convenient and efficient; but it also meant another link in Kharemough's chain of control. It meant that he would understand the mentality of the police working for him better than he had understood the largely

Newhavenese force he had served with on Tiamat before. Whether they would understand the people of Tiamat any better than the Newhavenese had was the question he could not answer. He had had them working with cultural indoctrination tapes, learning the language with enhancers, even before they boarded the ships. But he remembered how much good that had done him, in his smug, self-satisfied youth. . . .

He realized, with a pang of irony, that he had finished the last of his gracious, automatic responses to the congratulations of the new arrivals. Their comments had barely even registered in his mind. He looked out at Tiamat, watched the planet's cloud-whorled arc of blue move slowly from day into night. He looked away, shaking off the vision, refusing to read any symbolism into it.

"This time tomorrow, Gundhalinu-sadhu," Sandrine said, beside him, "all this will be ours."

Gundhalinu looked at him, and said nothing.

"Excuse me, Commander," Tabaranne said, coming back to his side. "I thought you would want to know that we've completed one orbit of Tiamat. We're about to begin positioning the high defense weaponry."

Gundhalinu turned back to the image of the world on the screens before them, unable for a moment to make a response. "Thank you, Captain."

Tabaranne moved away to his station, and input a brief, irrevocable series of codes into the waiting systems. Gundhalinu tried to concern himself with the conversations and speculations going on around him for the time it took to make another complete orbit of Tiamat; knowing that at preset intervals they were dropping the components of an orbital weapons system into place—weapons that could be turned on potential invaders, illegal entries . . . or any rebellious activity occurring on the planet's surface.

"We have verification, Captain," one of the crew reported. "Systems are completely deployed, and coming on-line." Images of the new defenses came and went in the corners of the display; he watched them spread arrays of microwave lasers and plasma weapons.

"Good," Tabaranne said. He looked back at Gundhalinu and the silently attentive audience behind him. "Tiamat is secure, sadhanu. You can sleep easily in your new beds tonight." A murmur of appreciation filled the space around him. "I'm bringing the starport on-line . . . now."

The view behind Tabaranne changed as the ship's remote sensors brought the surface of Tiamat spiraling up suddenly, disconcertingly, toward their eyes. "We're passing over Carbuncle right now." And Carbuncle appeared, pushing the image of Tiamat aside, like a split-screen hallucination. It was barely more than an outline of lights against the burning sky on Tiamat's nightside . . . but still it looked the way he remembered it, an immense shellform, like some incongruous jetsam cast up on the shore of Tiamat's omnipresent sea. "Send the signal to activate."

Gundhalinu watched, searching the inland darkness for a sign of the starport that lay in hibernation there, its systems dreaming of peace for another eighty-odd years. While he watched, new lights blossomed suddenly against the darkness: The starport answered, rudely awakened but responding to their commands. "Will the natives know we're coming?" someone said behind him. The spot of brightness grew as if he were watching a signal fire, a beacon lit to mark their landing place, the location-point of their new home . . . announcing their arrival to the city of Carbuncle, from which it was very visible.

"They will now," he murmured. Although it would hardly be a surprise, at least to their Queen. He wondered fleetingly what Moon had told her people—if she had told them anything, warned them, prepared them. Not, he supposed, that it would matter much one way or the other, in the end. . . .

More displays began to appear, overlapping the image with readouts and simulations.

"Starport systems are intact, Commander," Tabaranne reported. "The landing grids are powering up according to schedule. We can begin sending down shuttles after another pass." Unlike the coin-disc ships of the old technology, which were individually small and made the transit to Tiamat in groups, the *Ilmarinen* was too massive, and its hull too fragile, for a planetary landing. It would remain in orbit until their arrival was secured, and then begin its return trip to Kharemough, to come back again with the first group of civilians, who would begin the process of turning Carbuncle once again into an interstellar port of call.

"Do you still want to make the trip down using the traditional hologramic displays, Commander?" Tabaranne asked him.

Gundhalinu nodded, staring at the images of Tiamat on the screen. Remembering how he had stood with Moon Dawntreader in the hills above the city, watching as the Prime Minister and the Assembly made their descent from the starry heavens like gods, in a flaming cascade of hologramic imagery. Their magic fires had told him that he had returned from the wilderness to civilization in time for the Final Departure; that he had not come too late, that he was really free to leave Tiamat and never come back . . . the thing he had believed he wanted more than life itself, until it was too late to change his mind.

The hologramic show had been a hollow display, as empty of real magic as the Hegemonic Assembly had been empty of real power. But he had been blind to that subtle irony, as awe and wonder transformed the face of the beloved stranger beside him; as Moon Dawntreader watched them fall like stars. All he had seen was their promise—of freedom, of safety, of a return to the life he'd believed he had lost forever. A life he had regained, by a miracle, because of her.

If she was watching—and he was certain she would be, now—she would see that same display, and perhaps remember that night, and all it had meant to them both. . . . "Yes," he said at last, remembering to give an answer. "Yes, I want the full display. There won't ever be another night like this one."

Moon Dawntreader stood alone in her study at the peak of the city, sleepless now since word had reached her that the starport had come back to life. She stared out at its brilliant beacon astonishing the night, unable to look away; knowing that it was only a matter of time until she looked both the future and the past in the face. . . .

She turned away at last as her husband entered the room behind her. It had been a long time since he—or anyone else—had sought her out here. This had always been her private space, separate from the meeting rooms and audience halls down below. She had never made it forbidden ground, as Arienrhod had, but as the years passed she had found herself alone here more and more, inviolate, isolated; not even certain why, but only certain that she had no one else to blame for it.

She met Sparks's gaze, feeling relief fill her as he broke her silence . . . feeling the smile that began to fill her face fade as she saw the look on his own face.

"Are you still awake?" he murmured, asking the obvious, as if he suddenly didn't know what to say to her.

"I couldn't sleep." She answered with the obvious, because there was nothing else that she could bring herself to say.

He hesitated for a moment, before he crossed the stretch of time-worn rug that had once been as white as new-fallen snow, to stand beside her and look out at the starport glowing like a buried sun half a kilometer inland. He did not put his arms around her, or even touch her. She suddenly wished that he would; but she did not ask him to. "So they've really come," he said.

She nodded, folding her arms around herself, clutching her elbows tightly because she wanted to tremble, feeling something break loose and spin away inside her, leaving her sick with nameless fear. *Oh, Lady,* she murmured silently, a plea but not a prayer.

"And he's come with them," Sparks said.

"I suppose so," she whispered, helplessly noncommittal.

"What does he want?" Sparks asked, still softly. He turned to face her, to face the unspoken truths within the truth they knew. She was surprised that this had not happened before, even while she knew why it had not.

"I told you," she said numbly. "He feels responsible for the return of the Hegemony. He wants to help us."

"And what else does he want?" Sparks's eyes darkened. She felt him pushing her, felt the pain inside the pressure; knew that it was hurting him as much as it was hurting her.

"He's become a sibyl," she said, hoping that after all this time he would understand what that meant, about a willingness to put the needs of others before oneself. But she saw his mouth tighten, and realized that after all this time it still meant only one thing, to him: She had become a sibyl, when he could not. She had chosen it over his love. And now even this stranger, who had once tried to take her from him, had become a sibyl too. "He's become a sibyl," she went on, hopelessly, insistently. "That means he understands now that . . . there are things which are more important than . . . individual feelings."

"More important than his loyalty to his own kind?" Sparks asked bluntly, asking her for the truth; asking her—

"Yes," she said, meeting his eyes.

He looked away from her, out at the glowing, waiting starport. "There's one more question I have to ask you—" He kept his eyes averted; she watched his profile, seeing his throat work as he tried, and tried again, to speak it. He looked back at her, his eyes as green as emeralds, shining, too full, and the question went unasked.

She reached out to him; put her arms around him, holding on, pressing her face against his shoulder as she felt his arms go around her almost reluctantly. And his unspoken question went unanswered, as they stood locked in an embrace; holding each other like lovers at a crossroad, unable to speak a farewell.

At last she turned slowly inside the circle of his arms, to look out again at the night. She lifted her hand suddenly, pointing. "Look."

Sparks followed her gaze; seeing what she saw, and knowing as well as she did what it meant. Stars were falling out of the sky . . . hologramic stars, their perfectly controlled trajectories crossing and recrossing, to form one stunning congruence and then another as they fell to earth. She had seen this sight only once before, and that time she had had no idea what they were, what they stood for, what they meant to her world. Then, it had been the sign that the offworlders' days on Tiamat were numbered. Now they were a sign that its future days here would be numberless, unending. And what of her own future—? She clung to her husband's arms; a woman caught in an invisible storm, afraid of being swept away.

TIAMAT: Carbuncle

BZ Gundhalinu gazed out through the mirrorshielded windows of the hovercraft as it made its slow progress up Carbuncle's Street—moving slowly for effect, and for the sake of caution. He shared its insulated space with Vhanu, who made desultory conversation and asked an occasional innocuous question, which he answered absently, and with Echarthe, the new Minister of Trade. A well-armed Blue in a regulation uniform piloted the craft, doubling as security. Two more craft followed, carrying other officials and other security personnel, all equally equipped with shields and weaponry, at Vhanu's insistence.

Gundhalinu studied the clusters of Tiamatans who lined the Street to watch them pass. Some of the natives looked hostile, but most simply looked unblinkingly curious, probably more interested in the strange vehicles than in their nearly invisible occupants. A few actually waved and made gestures of triumph—Winters, he supposed.

Even before the first shuttle had set down on the starport grids, the *Ilmarinen*'s sensors had begun to pick up data about Tiamat that had made everyone on board—except himself—abruptly paranoid. Their routine EM scans had turned up evidence of widespread, if primitive, use of electronic equipment where there should have been complete EM silence; evidence of factories and new construction: real progress, instead of the primitive lifestyle and cultural stagnation they had been told to expect.

He had kept his own responses muted and cautious—downplaying the concern of everyone around him as much as he could without revealing too much, second-guessing every word that came out of his mouth for fear some casual comment would reveal that he knew too much, about the past, about the present . . . about the Summer Queen.

He had sent Vhanu as his emissary to the palace yesterday—since that was where the local constabulary said that Moon Dawntreader made her home now—but

Vhanu had not seen the Queen. He had been met by her representatives, led by a blind woman named Fate Ravenglass, who was a sibyl . . . and a Winter. Vhanu had not remarked on it, still too unfamiliar with the social situation here to comprehend the significance of that fact. They had formally set the time of the meeting he was about to attend, and that was all.

He let his eyes shift focus, no longer registering the gaping natives or the strangely familiar forms of the hive-like buildings behind them, half as old as time . . . seeing instead his own reflection. His tense, expectant face looked back at him, as insubstantial as some ancestor's spirit. But he saw in his mind's eye the unlined, unremarkable face of twenty-five-year-old Inspector Gundhalinu, whose memory still haunted this city that he had not seen in nearly twelve years.

"There seems to be remarkably little change in the city itself," Vhanu said beside him, "compared to the data we have, at least."

"Superficial changes are all anyone, including the Hegemony, has ever made on Carbuncle," Gundhalinu murmured. "Carbuncle is . . . almost mythic, in its way. A functioning relic of the Old Empire. That was what made me choose it for my first duty post, when I joined the Police. I wanted to see it for myself, before that became impossible."

"And were you disappointed by the reality?"

Gundhalinu's mouth twitched. "By its superficial realities, yes—I suppose I was. But there is a deeper level of reality here, a depth to this place, and that did not disappoint me at all. I found it unforgettable." He smiled self-consciously. "I suppose that sounds like a lot of mystical drivel, doesn't it?"

Vhanu laughed. "Well, yes, actually. . . . But then, I wasn't here. You were."

"Yes . . . I was." Gundhalinu looked out the window again, taking a deep breath to ease the aching tightness in his chest.

"Tell me," Echarthe asked, "did you ever meet the previous Queen?"

Gundhalinu grimaced. "I had that misfortune, on more than one occasion. Everything the reports said about her is true. She was a soul-eater."

"Did you meet the new Queen?"

"I . . . Yes. Briefly. But before she had become the Queen." He felt Vhanu glance at him in surprise. "She had come to the city looking for her pledged—her husband. I helped her find him." He glanced at Echarthe, away out the window.

"How did she strike you?"

Gundhalinu looked up again, said carefully, "Determined. Smart. Deserving."

"She bears an uncanny resemblance to the Snow Queen, in the holos I've seen," Echarthe said. "There were questions about it in the departure records. In light of what we've seen so far, this push toward technological development, it raises some serious questions in my mind—"

"Many Tiamatans bear a striking resemblance to one another," Gundhalinu said abruptly. "The population is small and isolated; that means a concentrated gene-pool." He gestured at the window. "Just look out there along the Street. You'll see what I mean."

"Do you think the Queen remembers you favorably?" Vhanu asked. "It could help us in establishing the new government here, if she does."

Gundhalinu shrugged; the corners of his mouth turned up slightly. They were nearly in the Upper City already, almost to Street's End. "We're about to find out," he said.

They came to Street's End at last, and the wide, alabaster courtyard before the palace entrance. Gundhalinu felt a strange sense of déjà vu as he discovered workers there, sweeping, scrubbing, keeping the surface pristine—just as they had nearly two decades ago, in local time, the last time he had laid eyes on them. He wondered if any of them were actually the same people, still at their same task after all these years, their lives that stable and unchanging. He saw the local constables on guard at either side of the palace doors. They no longer wore the imitation offworlder uniforms of Arienrhod's security force, but plain everyday clothing instead. An armband and a crested hat were all that set them apart as peacekeepers.

The hovercraft he rode in, and the two craft accompanying it, settled without noticeable impact onto the alabaster pavement. The high carven doors of the palace began to open toward him, like outstretched arms, across the square.

He shook off the image, as the door of his hovercraft unsealed and rose, letting in the breath of the city, rich with exotic smells that were both strange and strangely familiar. He climbed out, flanked by a phalanx of guards in the dusty-blue uniform that he knew so well, but no longer wore himself. Any of them could have been his companions, in the former time . . . could have been himself.

He felt the years fall away from him in a sudden, almost dizzying rush. From a distance, as if from that other world, he heard faintly echoing voices speaking Tiamatan. The workers had gathered at the far side of the courtyard, pointing and murmuring. He had recovered his skill with the language, using the same indoctrination tapes he had made everyone else study. But here, confined inside the echoing city walls, the words sounded different in a way he could not define. More real, in this three-dimensional context of real place and real people.

He turned, forcing his body to move, looking toward the palace. Its entrance stood open, but no longer empty. As the small crowd around him began to step aside, making way for him, he saw clearly who it was who waited for him there. He stared, all other motion suddenly impossible, every other human being around him ceasing to exist. It was only himself . . . and her, inside a moment where time had stopped. He went on looking at her, sure that he must be dreaming, because he had dreamed of this moment so many times.

But he did not wake, and still she did not disappear . . . still she looked the same as he remembered, after all these years . . . exactly the same, not a day older. He looked down suddenly, almost expecting to find himself transformed by the same spell, the dark magic of this haunted city—still wearing his old uniform, still hardly more than a boy.

But he wore the stark, unadorned black of a Chief Justice. The fishhook-barbed star of his sibyl trefoil rested in silent affirmation against his chest. He looked up again, wondering if he had gone half-blind, or insane.

He felt Vhanu's hand on his arm, surreptitiously urging him to make some response. He turned slightly, to Vhanu's curious glance. "They're waiting for us; whenever you're ready, Justice—"

"Yes, of course." Gundhalinu ran his hands down his clothes in a compulsive gesture, looking toward the waiting figures. He looked back at the guards surrounding him. "You three," he gestured at the three men closest, "will come with us."

"But Justice—" Echarthe protested. "Don't you think—"

"We'll be safe enough," Gundhalinu said impatiently. "Let the others guard the hovercraft—the vehicles are in more danger from the curiosity of the locals than we are." He started forward, walking with even, controlled strides that seemed to belong to someone else. He watched the woman before him growing clearer, every detail about her more real—and yet still she did not age. "She hasn't changed . . ." he murmured incredulously, to Vhanu. He had counted the years elapsed, his time, her time, knowing that she should be at least as old as he was now.

"Then she's using the water of life," Sandrine said, with sudden, unpleasant obviousness. "It's the only way she could have stayed that young."

"That's impossible," he murmured. And yet he could see that she was unchanged, untouched by time. She was looking back at him, watching him come—but he saw no flicker of recognition in her strangely colored eyes. She still wore her hair long and loose, falling nearly to her waist; her clothing was made of what looked to be bright-colored offworlder cloth, vintage clothes recut to look more like the Tiamatans' own shapeless, pragmatic garments. Her gaze took in his face, his uniform, his trefoil, his companions, all with equal fascination, and equal lack of emotion.

He stopped before her, wondering at what point this would cease happening to him; whether if he tried to reach out and touch her she would disappear. Swallowing to ease his throat, he made a brief, formal bow. "Lady," he said, careful to use the proper form of address for the Summers' Queen. Hearing his own voice speak Tiamatan was more disorienting than hearing strangers speak it. "I am the new Hegemonic Chief Justice."

"I'm not the Lady," she said, and giggled, abruptly and disconcertingly.

He blinked, staring at her with an incomprehension so complete that it made her laugh again.

"I'm Ariele Dawntreader." She made something that vaguely resembled a bow in return. "The Queen is my mother. She sent me out to greet you."

"Oh," he said, inadequately. He gazed at her in astonishment, realizing belatedly that she was not wearing a sibyl trefoil—did not even have the tattoo at her throat. He was aware that he went on staring at her, but he was unable to stop. "I didn't know. . . . You look so much like her. I thought—"

"He thought the Queen had been using the water of life," Sandrine said bluntly.

Gundhalinu frowned and gestured him silent as he saw sudden anger come into the girl's eyes, and disgust.

"We don't kill the mers anymore," she said, looking back at Gundhalinu, and he heard the defiance in it. This time it was one of the people behind her who put a restraining hand on her shoulder. He realized—for the first time in a meaningful way—that there were others waiting with the girl, observing him; left unacknowledged by his disbelief at finding so much of a lifetime had passed in a heartbeat, that the woman he had been expecting to see had a daughter who was as old as she had been when he had left her—maybe older. *A daughter. A husband* . . .

He nodded in belated acknowledgment to the others in the welcoming committee—three older Tiamatan women, two of them wearing sibyl signs, one of them quite obviously blind, probably the woman Vhanu had spoken to. The third woman stared back at him as though she seemed to recognize him, although her face did not look at all familiar to him. The dichotomy between the group in front of him and his own group struck him suddenly—one all female, the other all male. He wondered whether Moon had done it intentionally, wondered what reactions the others around him were having to the situation.

"Please come with us," the girl said, turning her back on him with unconscious arrogance. The other women stood aside for her, more tolerant than obedient, and followed her inside.

He followed too, flanked by his own people, like night following day. He wondered what Moon's motive had been in sending her daughter to greet him; if she had meant to remind him of all the things that it had reminded him of . . . time, mortality, all that had passed in their separate lives since the day of his departure. Or whether she had simply meant it as an honor to her daughter, as an answer to a child's curiosity. *Her child* . . .

He glanced from side to side as they moved along the entry hall, seeing the scenes of Summer's bounty that had replaced the Winter murals of storms and snow. He remembered walking this hall before, more than once; the details came back to him with startling vividness. He realized suddenly that there was another face he had not seen yet, one he had been expecting to see among the greeters at the gate: Jerusha PalaThion, who had saved his career when he had broken Hegemonic law to help Moon—and then given up her own career to stay on Tiamat.

He had walked these halls with her, more times than he had liked, during his years on Tiamat. He had been stunned by her abrupt decision to remain here, even though he had thought he understood her disillusionment well enough, by then. And now, remembering the treatment she had received from the Hegemony she had served bravely and loyally, perhaps he shouldn't be surprised that she was not eager to see an offworlder's face at her door again . . . even his.

He realized that a part of his mind had been listening as he walked for the sound of the Pit—the hungry moaning that had filled the Hall of the Winds, and filled his heart with secret terror. Crossing the bridge that spanned the Pit had been an ordeal that had never gotten easier for him . . . that probably never did for anyone with a shred of imagination.

But this time there was no sound except the clatter of bootheels and the softer shuffling of leather-soled city shoes on the dark, polished floor, even as the corridor opened out suddenly, revealing the Hall.

Still there was only silence. Gundhalinu almost stopped short, looking up to find the wind-curtains hanging slack. He forced himself to continue on, crossing the bridge in the Tiamatans' wake, listening to the incredulous mutterings of Vhanu and Echarthe as they followed him across that perfect, railless span above the glowing green-blackness. He wanted to tell them about the wind, how much more terrifying it had been before . . . that by comparison what they saw now was completely harmless. He didn't.

He remembered the last time he had stood in this hall, a dumbstruck witness as Moon Dawntreader stopped the winds. He wondered if she had been responsible for stopping the winds for good. How, and what it meant if she had, he could not even imagine. *So many questions* . . . He forced himself to keep his gaze fixed on the way ahead; seeing the milk-white of Ariele Dawntreader's hair, his mind unable to stop seeing someone else in her place. He had imagined this day of reunion so often . . . there had barely been a day since he left Tiamat when he had not imagined it. But he had never imagined it would be like this. He realized it would have been impossible to picture the reality, to imagine the absurd ordinariness of it all.

They reached the far side of the Pit at last, although it felt as if they had been walking suspended above it forever. They went up the broad stairway beyond, which he remembered with a peculiar fondness because it always followed that excruciating passage. At the top of the steps had been Arienrhod's throne room, its carpet always as flawless as untrodden snow, bejeweled with brightly colored courtiers. There the Snow Queen had waited for her visitors—her victims, still sweating from their ordeal with the Pit—clothed in white, sitting on her crystal throne; pretending to be immortal, an elemental, Winter incarnate, as pitiless and cold as ice. . . .

But it was not Winter that waited for him now. The throne room, which had once been as starkly white and silver as a crevasse, had melted into a place of random earth tones, the fresh colors of spring, greens of all shades, rust and clay, earth brown, a startling flash of blue.

The convoluted crystal throne still sat in the center of the dais at the center of the vast, suddenly silent room. It was surrounded by a small group of attentive, expectant faces, which had all turned in his direction. And at their center on the throne sat a woman, her hair the color of snow, her eyes like mist and moss-agate. But she was dressed like the room in the colors of Summer, in silks and tapestries and homespun, the contrasts of texture and cloth somehow not absurd but perfectly in harmony. She wore a simple circlet of gold on her hair, set with a blood-red stone: a carbuncle.

This time the face written into his memory had aged like his own . . . still unmistakably her face, but undeniably mortal, changed by time. And yet as he looked at her she struck his inner eye with such beauty that he had to look away or be paralyzed. His heart constricted. *Moon,* his heart said, his mind, his body . . . every part of him but his throat, which he would not allow to speak the word.

He took a deep breath as he started on into the room. He forced his eyes to glance over the small group of people gathered around her, to do anything but touch her face again; suddenly afraid, after all these years, all the rehearsals of this scene he had played out in his mind, that he would lose control at this critical moment and destroy everything. Searching the crowd around her he found Sparks Dawntreader—remembered him, struck by his red hair, even though he had seen him only once, a mugging victim freshly arrived in the city from Summer, dazed and defiant at Jerusha PalaThion's attempts to help him.

He had never laid eyes on Sparks Dawntreader again—although Dawntreader was a figure more real in his mind than any number of people he had seen constantly for years in the time since then: Moon's consort, her lover; the father of the girl who had already reached their side and turned back to gaze at the approaching strangers. Sparks looked past her, meeting Gundhalinu's stare with eyes as green as envy, his gaze full of suspicion.

Gundhalinu glanced away again into the crowd—stopped suddenly as he found the one face that stood out for its alienness the way his own would have, within that gathering of pale, sky-eyed figures. *Jerusha PalaThion.* He was stunned to see how her years of exile had aged her. He wondered with sudden empathy how much she had regretted her choice—if she had truly regretted it as much as her face said she had. But as she saw recognition in his eyes she smiled at him, a fleeting smile full of satisfaction. She nodded her head slightly, in acknowledgment.

He let himself smile, barely, acknowledging her in turn before he had to look away again. Carrying her smile with him, he felt the room and everything in it suddenly stabilize.

"Who is that woman?" Vhanu whispered in Sandhi. "She's not Tiamatan."

"My former commanding officer," Gundhalinu said softly. "Your predecessor; the former Commander of Police."

"Why is she here?" Tilhonne said blankly; as if the idea that she might have chosen to stay was incomprehensible to him.

"Because the idea of seeing a Police uniform or a Hegemonic representative ever again for as long as she lived did not appeal to her," Gundhalinu murmured, remembering the day of their parting, and the Commander's badges Jerusha PalaThion had taken from her own collar and pressed into his hands.

He reached the edge of the dais, below the foot of the throne, and stopped, making a formal bow once more in acknowledgment of the woman who sat there. He lifted his head, meeting her gaze at last. "Lady," he said softly, evenly.

"Your eyes . . ." The words were barely audible; her eyes held him riveted. "I had forgotten your eyes . . . how they—" She broke off, but her face, which until that moment had been as rigidly expressionless as his, colored suddenly, betraying the strength of her hidden emotion. "Inspector Gundhalinu," she said at last, speaking clearly and calmly. "Welcome back to Tiamat. I never expected that I would live to see . . . to see you again." She smiled, a smile that touched him tenderly, without seeming to.

Gundhalinu felt the cloud of tension in the group of men at his back dissolve; felt his face, which had seemed to him a moment ago to have frozen to death, actually begin to smile. "It's Chief Justice Gundhalinu now, Lady. But I'm honored you still remember me, after so long." He kept his eyes on only her, afraid now to look away and encounter any of the others witnessing what passed between them.

Moon rose, moving forward until she stood at the edge of the raised dais, facing him directly. "It would be difficult to forget, even after so long, the kindness you did me then." She held her hand out to him, and to his surprise met his own hand palm against palm, Kharemoughi-fashion, not clasping wrists as he remembered the Tiamatans doing. "It is good to see you again."

He let his hand fall away, feeling as if her touch had seared it, wondering if she felt the same thing. "I hope that . . . our relationship," he stumbled imperceptibly on the word, "will be as mutually amicable in the years to come."

"So it has truly happened, that you've come back to Tiamat . . . that the Hegemony has. To stay." Her glance flicked past him, touching the faces of Vhanu and the others in brief acknowledgment, and assessment. He looked past her at Sparks Dawntreader; looked away again. "The Millennium has finally come, as your people used to say."

He smiled, and nodded in wry amusement. "Yes. We have the stardrive again. It means a great change for both our peoples."

"For better or worse," she murmured. Her eyes were dark, as if she had not been reassured by what she found in the faces of the men behind him. She turned away, moving back to her throne; but she did not sit down. She stood, with her own people flanking her. "The stardrive means that the relationship of the Hegemony and Tiamat will be permanent, from now on," she said. "I hope that means that you intend to deal with us as you deal with your other member worlds. We deserve and desire equal citizenship with the rest of the Hegemony—equal right to leave and return, equal access to technology, equal treatment under your laws. We want a relationship based on autonomy and mutual cooperation. I hope that is the sort of change you mean. We've waited a millennium of our own for that to happen. I think we've waited long enough."

He stared at her, pressing his lips together to keep his smile from becoming a sudden grin of pleasure and admiration. "Your point is well taken, Lady," he said, and nodded. "I think you'll find that our vision of Tiamat's future is more like your own, this time." He hesitated, sensing the restlessness at his back. "We have observed that you've brought considerable change to Tiamat yourself, in the years since the Departure," he went on, carefully. "Some of my people were surprised to find that you had made so much technological progress. That had not been our experience with previous Summer Queens. I told them that perhaps the gods . . . including your Sea Mother . . . have given both our people a gift." He spoke the words reluctantly, knowing that he could not afford to ignore the obvious.

Moon nodded serenely, although he was not really certain her confidence ran any deeper than his own. "Yes," she said. "You have been given the stardrive, and we have been given the use of the sibyl network."

Gundhalinu felt the words pass through the listeners behind him like a sword. Mutterings of disbelief, questions in Sandhi, filled his ears. He heard a low, querulous voice accuse "that renegade bitch"—Jerusha PalaThion—of treason, of handing over the forbidden secret of enlightenment to the miserable primitives of Tiamat.

He turned, taking a step up onto the dais so that he stood looking down on his companions as he ordered them sharply into silence. "Listen to me," he said softly, in Sandhi. "How the people of this world learned the truth about the sibyl network is unimportant—it's meaningless, it's in the past. Do you understand me? Recriminations are pointless—the secret is out. Nothing can change that." He held them with his eyes. "And frankly, I believe it no longer matters. As the Queen said, everything has changed about our relationship with this world. We no longer need ignorance as a weapon to control them during our absence—because there will be no Hegemonic absence, ever again. To keep the truth about the sibyls secret would be immoral—and not only that, it will be impossible, now."

There were more muttered protests, dark looks, abrupt angry motions; but the patch held. He stood his ground, staring them down until all protest subsided. He turned back to face the waiting Tiamatans, wondering how much, if anything, they had understood. He remembered that Moon knew some Sandhi, and so did Jerusha PalaThion. From Moon's expression, she had at least guessed what the reaction to her words had been.

And he realized, and suddenly appreciated, the intent behind her blunt revelation—the risk she had taken to deliver the message that she was neither ignorant of the truth, nor of their part in suppressing it. That she was in charge of her people's future; that she was not afraid. And he recognized the other message that lay hidden within the words: That she trusted him . . . that she was not afraid to test him, or to rely on him. He smiled inwardly, and was suddenly aware that he was still standing on the dais—standing on her ground now, and not with his own people. He stepped down, still keeping her gaze. "Then both our peoples must learn to accept that the inevitable has come to pass for us, Lady—and make the best of it."

"Yes," she said, and sat down, the motion full of control and grace. "So it seems." Her hands closed over the convolutions of the throne arms.

"There will be far too many other questions about every aspect of the reopening of Tiamat to begin addressing them here," he said, pressing on. "Perhaps we can set up a schedule of preliminary meetings, with our advisors. But first I'd like to present my staff, with your permission."

She nodded, leaning back as she did, as if some part of her were instinctively shrinking away from contagion.

"NR Vhanu, Commander of Police for the Tiamat sector . . ." He went on through the introductions; listening, watching, trying to gauge the responses of her people and his own as each of his administrators made a brief bow, and spoke a few awkward words in Tiamatan.

Moon replied with guarded solicitude, her eyes frequently glancing away from the face of yet another alien-looking stranger to his face. When he had finished she rose from the throne again, and introduced the small gathering of advisors who surrounded her on the dais. She named Jerusha PalaThion as her Chief of Constables, and the blind woman, Fate Ravenglass, as the head of something she called the Sibyl College. There were a handful of civic leaders, both Winters and Summers—Tor Starhiker, the woman who had stared at him as if she knew him, among them. There were other sibyls, including a man with a Winter clan affiliation.

". . . and my family—" she said at last. "You have met my daughter already, I think." She smiled briefly at Ariele, who shifted from foot to foot beside the throne, looking restless and uncomfortable as she met Gundhalinu's eyes. "And my pledged—" he felt her almost self-consciously using the Tiamatan word, and not the offworlder term "husband," "Sparks Dawntreader Summer."

Gundhalinu met Dawntreader's gaze, realizing as he did that he had been avoiding it. Dawntreader's expression was neutral now, under control. There was no real recognition in his gaze to match the suspicion.

"I believe we've met," Gundhalinu said, unable to stop the words.

"Where?" Dawntreader asked, taken by surprise.

"In a dark alley."

"I don't remember you," Dawntreader said flatly.

"Do you still play the flute?"

Dawntreader's expression changed suddenly, as realization filled his eyes. He glanced at Jerusha PalaThion, away again as she nodded. He grimaced. "Yes," he said finally.

"My son also plays the flute," Moon said, gesturing someone else forward from behind the crystal throne.

A boy stepped up beside her almost reluctantly; it was difficult to tell, looking at him, whether he was younger or older than the girl. Gundhalinu struggled to control his response, seeing a second nearly grown child of the lover he had left behind so long ago; yet another reminder that she had been someone else's wife through all these years, and not his own.

But as the dark-haired boy stopped at his mother's side and raised his head, Gundhalinu felt astonishment pass through him like light through a prism.

"This is my son. . . ." Moon said. "Tammis." And all at once her voice seemed oddly changed, distorted by the same emotion, and he knew that she saw what he saw, as he met the boy's stare—met eyes too much like his own looking back at him from a face where they did not belong, the face of another man's son.

"A pleasure," he murmured; seeing curiosity and uncertainty begin to seep into the boy's expression, as if he almost realized the same thing. Gundhalinu glanced at Sparks Dawntreader, saw that the sudden surprise had spread to his face; saw his surprise darken. Gundhalinu looked back at Moon again; at the change that had come over her own face, at once anguish and wonder, as she looked at them both; looked at them, all three. . . . *I had forgotten your eyes.*

He looked from face to face again, suddenly comprehending the real change he had forced on all of their lives, including his own . . . and that it was far more irrevocable than he had ever imagined.

PART II: THE RETURN

After such knowledge; what forgiveness?
            . . . Unnatural vices
Are fathered by our heroism. Virtues
Are forced upon us by our impudent crimes.
These tears are shaken from the wrath-bearing tree.

—T. S. Eliot

TIAMAT: Carbuncle

"Jerusha PalaThion to see you, sir," the disembodied voice of his aide informed him.

"Send her in." BZ Gundhalinu rose from the chair behind his desk/terminal, where he had been sitting for what his body told him was far too long. He stretched, hearing joints crack, shaking the fog of data and fatigue out of his head.

His aide, Stathis, showed Jerusha PalaThion into his office. Nearly six months had passed since his arrival on Tiamat, and this was the first time she had entered this room. She paused just inside the door, taking in her surroundings with the unthinking glance of a trained observer before she looked back at him. "Justice Gundhalinu," she said, with a nod and a sudden, slightly bemused smile. Her hand moved almost imperceptibly, as if she had felt the urge to salute him, and he read incredulity as well as pride in her gaze.

"Commander," he murmured. He made a formal salute, giving her the acknowledgment of her old Police rank even though, in her present position as head of the local constabulary, it was hardly what it had been.

Jerusha returned the salute solemnly, perfectly; irony widened her smile. "It's been a long time since we stood like this, BZ," she said. "The last time it was to say goodbye."

"I still have the Commander's badges you gave me off your old uniform." He smiled too, remembering. "You said then I'd need them someday. I hardly believed you. But you were right." He shook his head.

"And now you've outgrown them." She nodded at his trefoil.

He glanced down; gestured her toward a seat. "Help yourself to some food. I haven't had lunch yet." He looked at his watch, and realized that it was nearly time for dinner. A platter with an untouched meal on it still lay on the low, rectangular greeting-table. He sat down across from her in one of the solid, wood-framed native chairs. They were all the furniture to be had, until the flow of imported goods had satisfied the new government's vast and immediate technological needs, and ships had space in their holds for less vital commodities. "It'll take me a minute to clear out my head, anyway. I've been reviewing data the hard way for most of the afternoon. Gods, I'd forgotten the kind of aggravation we had to put up with in the old days here—" The embargoes and restrictions that had existed when he served here before had meant that even the Police were forced to make do with outmoded, inadequate data systems.

"You didn't know the half of it, then," Jerusha said, taking a piece of cold fish.

"You were only an inspector. When I became Commander of Police, I found out what real red tape was. I expect you know what I mean now."

"For several years now, unfortunately." He nodded, matching her grimace. He chose what appeared to be a vegetable fritter, and began to eat it. It was cold and greasy, but he was hungry enough not to care.

"It's a lot of water under the bridge since we said our goodbyes. What have you been doing all these years, BZ? I've heard—well, call them rumors." She glanced significantly at the walls, the air. She looked back at him for a moment, before she casually touched her ear. He nodded. Their conversation was being recorded; everything that happened here was on the record.

"Developing the stardrive technology, on Number Four, and back on Kharemough." He shrugged slightly. "Two excellent training grounds in bureaucracy."

Her gaze met his, reading what lay behind the self-effacing words. "I thought you said you'd never go back to Kharemough again, after . . . what happened here."

He glanced away, remembering the scars he had borne then—the marks of his suicide attempt, the crippled image of himself. "I said then that there were two worlds I never expected to see again—that one, and this one. Kharemough and Tiamat. And I believed it, then. But what happened on Four changed both those things for me."

"You discovered the truth about Fire Lake." She shook her head. "I know that part. And you became a sibyl." She smiled again. "I suppose that's all the explanation I really need."

"What about you?" he asked. "The last time we spoke together I was getting on the last ship going up from here at the Final Departure—and you weren't. I'm still not sure what gave you the courage to stay, when you believed it would be forever. I didn't have that kind of courage. . . ." He shook his head.

"It was as much desperation—or pride—that made me stay, as it was courage," she said. "And it was love. . . ." He realized that she did not mean a love of justice, or some noble ideal; she meant human love. He felt himself flush, as if she had somehow spoken his own deepest thoughts. He reminded himself fiercely that she was telling him about her life, not his, in the years since the Departure; and he felt incredulity fill him again.

"Really—?" he said softly. She had always seemed to him to wear self-reliance like body armor, when she had been his commanding officer and the only woman on the force. He found it almost impossible to believe someone had gotten through her defenses far enough to capture her heart . . . that it had somehow happened right in front of his eyes, and he had never even noticed. "Who?" he asked.

"Ngenet ran Ahase Miroe."

He scratched his nose, searching his memory. "Gods—" he said suddenly. "Him? That one? The smuggler—?"

Her smile filled with unexpected sorrow as she nodded. "That's the one."

He shook his head. "Strange bedfellows," he murmured.

"More alike than you know," she said, again with the strange sorrow in it. "For better or worse."

"So that was why you stayed, then."

"Not entirely." A flicker of the old defiance showed in her eyes. "I told you then, I wasn't a quitter. What gave me the courage to . . . trust my heart, was knowing the truth. About what Moon Dawntreader was. About what she wanted to do, making the Change mean something. Miroe wanted that too. I knew it was work we could both give our lives to, willingly."

He smiled, nodding; his smile faded as the animation went out of her face. "Are you still married?" he asked, carefully.

She shook her head. "Miroe died, a little over a year ago. An accident. A fall."

His face pinched. "I'm sorry," he said, understanding now what had changed her so painfully and profoundly. The measuring intelligence was still there in her eyes, but something was missing. Since he had last seen her, she had spent close to twenty years, hard years, on a hard world; but it was not so much that her body had aged. It seemed to him that what had been lost was the thing he had always admired most about her: her stubborn resistance to fate.

"So am I." She looked up at him again. "Every day."

"Do you have any children?" he asked, to fill the awkward silence.

She shook her head, and her expression then was too mixed to read. At last it became curiosity, as she looked back at him; but she did not ask the question he read in her eyes. She picked up a piece of pickled meat, elaborately noncommittal. "But the past is behind us, now, anyway," she murmured. "History. The Change has come, and we're supposed to cast off our old lives, try on new ones."

"I thought that only applied after the proper rituals, when the Sea Mother gave her blessing," he said, with a smile.

Jerusha raised her eyebrows. "Don't tell me you believe in that, now—"

He shook his head. "Don't tell me that you do."

She shrugged. "But things have changed, whether we want them to or not—haven't they?" She looked at him speculatively. "Everyone was afraid, on some level, that the Hegemony's coming back would mean we'd be crushed under its boot again."

We'd. His mouth quirked as he heard her include herself with the Tiamatans. *Well, why shouldn't she?* She'd spent most of her life here. Newhaven, her homeworld, must be barely even a memory to her now. He studied his boot resting across his knee. "The Hegemony still has a heavy foot. I'm trying to keep them from setting it down in the wrong places too often. That's why I asked you to come, actually. I wanted feedback from someone who knows Tiamat, but has a sense of the Hegemony's perspective as well. Someone I know I can trust. I want to know what the mood in Carbuncle is; what sort of effect our presence is having, for better or worse. Anything I can do to make it better—"

They had been here for nearly half a standard year, and the demands on his time and attention had been unending. But they had made unexpectedly good progress in reestablishing their base of operations, because so much of the technology they had left behind still remained intact—because unlike all the Summer Queens before her, Moon Dawntreader had not ordered everything dumped into the sea. All they had had to do on many of the surviving systems was replace the microprocessors that the Hegemony had destroyed by high-frequency signal transmission at the Departure.

That had meant that more of the equipment they'd bought here with them could be spared to make their lives comfortable, more like what they had been used to back on Kharemough. That hadn't hurt morale any among his staff and advisors. He was sure it had helped him push his arguments that the technological progress achieved in their absence should be allowed to continue: that besides creating good will, it made economic sense, that it pushed all their own plans ahead of schedule.

"I'm engaged in a precarious balancing act here. It's going to be vital to keep as much cooperation as I can going on both sides." *If it isn't impossible.*

"So far it seems to be going all right," Jerusha said. "Moon . . . the Queen, and most Tiamatans are reassured because you haven't suppressed what they've done. But so far it's been simple, because there aren't that many offworlders here. Things are going to start getting more complicated as you open Tiamat up. When are you going to start permitting unregulated civilians back? When do the flood gates open on trade and contact—?"

He wiped his hands on the sponge beside his plate. "Because we're ahead of schedule, I plan to start letting a trickle in as early as next month. We'll gradually expand the flow, to try to keep things stable. I want to keep underworld elements out for as long as possible; I don't want Carbuncle to become what it was before—a convenient resort for the scum of the galaxy."

"That was Arienrhod's doing, mostly," Jerusha said. She leaned forward. "She let them hide under the wing of her 'independent rule' so we couldn't get at them, because she enjoyed watching the Blues squirm. You won't have that problem with the new Queen."

He nodded, swallowing down a glass of juice, startled by the sudden, pungently familiar flavor of a fruit he had not tasted in over a decade. "I know, thank the gods. But there are other ways of gaining influence and control, even when your influence isn't welcomed with open arms . . . you know that as well as I do, and better than the Queen does." *Ways and means even Jerusha PalaThion had never dreamed of.* He looked up again. "I want to minimize the kinds of culture shock we're going to have when access to trade goods becomes easy, and real greed sets in—"

"Are you talking about Tiamat, or everybody else?" Jerusha asked.

"I'm talking about everybody—including the Tiamatans. That was the other reason I wanted to meet with you today. I wanted to ask you whether you'd consider becoming my Chief Inspector."

Jerusha straightened up, staring at him in disbelief. "Are you serious?" she murmured. She laughed abruptly. "Of course you are. You wouldn't ask me that for the hell of it. But, why?"

"Because of all the things we've just been talking about," he said. "We go back a long way, you and I. We know where we stand with each other." He smiled briefly. "You'll never be afraid to give me a straight answer. . . . Too many of my people are unknown quantities to me, or not the ones I would have chosen to fill the positions they hold. I need people around me—at my back, if you will—that I can trust and rely on, in order to make this work." *In order to survive.* "I need the kind of help only you can give me. This police force is inexperienced in dealing with Tiamatan society. I trust Vhanu, my Commander of Police, with my life; he's worked with me for years. But he doesn't know Tiamat yet. . . . And frankly, in some ways, he reminds me of me." He smiled, ruefully; remembering his service on Tiamat, how long it had taken him to learn this world's lessons.

Jerusha nodded, and he saw that she understood. "I've met with him several times," she said. "I've seen the resemblance."

"Then you can see why you'd be invaluable, not only to the force, but to him."

She leaned back again in her seat. She was silent for a long moment. "Have you discussed this with him?"

Gundhalinu nodded.

"How does he feel about it?"

"He's against it," he said, giving her the truth.

"And how do you think the force is going to tolerate having a woman—a renegade, a traitor, no less—forced on them as Chief Inspector?"

"Are you a renegade, or are you a retired Police Commander with years of invaluable foreign service experience? . . . Am I a failed suicide, or a Hero of the Hegemony? It all depends on what kind of spin you put on it, Jerusha." He smiled slowly, and shrugged. She looked at him, mildly incredulous. "As far as your being female, Kharemoughis will give you less grief about that than your own people did. There are several women on the force, and I hope to recruit more, in time."

She looked down, biting her lip absently, considering.

"You've never been someone who walked away from a challenge." He pressed her, driven by the urgency of his need to have her support.

"True enough," she murmured, with some of the steel he remembered showing briefly in her grin. And he saw her eyes come alive as she thought about it. But she looked down again, shaking her head. "I can't. Thank you for asking me, BZ. But I can't do it."

"Why?" he asked, controlling the sudden frustration that made him want to shout it. "Why not?"

"Because the Queen needs me. She depends on me. . . . For all the same reasons you want me working for you. I can't be loyal to both of you. You can't rely on someone with divided loyalties."

He leaned forward, his hands twined between his knees, tightening. "Work for me, Jerusha," he spoke each word like a solemn pledge, "and you won't have to have divided loyalties."

She stared at him for a long moment; while he realized, suddenly and gladly, that this was not simply something that he needed . . . it was something that she needed, too. "Gods . . ." she murmured. "Let me sleep on it, BZ. I can't accept something like this without having time to think it through."

"Take whatever time you need." He nodded, feeling the tension loosen in his shoulders. "Just tell me you won't reject the idea out of hand."

"No," she said, rising from her seat. "No, I won't."

"Will you be speaking to—to the Queen?" He barely kept himself from calling her by name. He got up from his own seat.

"I expect so." She nodded, looking at him curiously.

"Tell her for me that I've gotten my people to accept a temporary moratorium on the hunting of mers, while we conduct further studies. I don't know how long it'll hold. The Central Coordinating Committee back on Kharemough is giving me hell about this; tell her it's the best I can do for now."

"She'll be glad to hear it. I am, too. Thank you. I know the kind of pressure you mean—gods, it must be worse when there's hardly any time-lag on interference from the home office. I know how much they want the water of life; I know how hard it is to stop them from getting what they want. I know . . . I tried it myself, once."

He grimaced. "I wish the Queen understood that. She's been pushing hard for rapid change, and for a ban on the hunts at the same time, in every meeting we've had at the palace . . . too hard. I've tried to make her see that we have to take this a step at a time; Tiamat has to be lifted up to a certain level of technological competence before it can qualify for full equality among the Hegemony's worlds. Change just for the hell of it will only leave everyone worse off then before. And the Hegemony doesn't like something-for-nothing trade, any more than Tiamat does."

"She understands that," Jerusha murmured. "But she also understands that the Hegemony came here thinking of her people as barbarians—and they aren't. She's willing to compromise, and meet the Hegemony halfway with her demands, if they'll meet her there. She only wants to make sure the Hegemony understands that her viewpoint and theirs are not the same one. The Hedge has always had a 'what's mine is mine and what's yours is negotiable' attitude about this world. . . ."

"I'm doing my damnedest," he said, a little impatiently. "She's got to watch her step. I wish she could just . . . If we could only—" He looked away abruptly. "Damn," he whispered. *Damn. Damn.*

"I know, BZ," Jerusha said, with sudden understanding in her eyes. "She wishes that too." She smiled. "I suppose we all wish it."

He looked away; looked back at her finally. "There's an old saying on Kharemough: 'There are two tragedies in life. One is never getting your heart's desire. The other is getting it.'"

She laughed softly. "On Newhaven, when you curse someone, you say, 'May you get everything you wish for; may you be noticed by people in high places; and may you live in interesting times.'"

He felt himself smile, relieved to find that at least he had not lost his sense of the absurd. "Then there's no hope for me, clearly." He held out his hand to her. She shook it, gripping his wrist like a native. "Let me know what you decide. Give my regards to the Queen. And . . ." He broke off, seeing the faces of Moon's children in his mind. "And to her family."

She nodded. "I will," she said gravely. "I will, BZ."

He watched her go out of the office. His intercom began to buzz as soon as the door closed. He ignored it; listening to something else entirely.

TIAMAT: Carbuncle

"Jerusha, I'm glad you're here—"

Jerusha felt her face quirk as the Queen turned to smile at her with uplifted hands. She nodded, attempting a smile in return, as Moon gestured at the data-filled screen lying like a magic pool in the surface of the desk/terminal behind her. "I've been working on this all afternoon, and now suddenly it's refusing all my commands.

I told it I was the Queen, but it wasn't impressed." She laughed, half amused and half exasperated. "And all the help files are in Sandhi."

Jerusha leaned past her shoulder to study the screen. "I don't remember enough written Sandhi to find my way to the bathroom, let alone pick a computer's brains." The written language was ideographic, and bore no resemblance to the spoken tongue. "I never did know it well. . . . Is your data safe?" Moon nodded. "Then just shut it down, and start it up again. It's a nuisance, but it always works for me."

Moon looked mildly aghast, but she shrugged, and nodded. Jerusha watched her do it.

"Ah. Better! Thank you. . . ." Moon swiveled her chair around, leaning back in her seat. "Was that simply your uncanny sense of timing, or is there something you wanted to talk about?" The look in her eyes suddenly made Jerusha wonder about the Queen's own uncanny sense of things.

"Well . . . yes, there's something." She sat down in the corner chair next to the desk, studying her hands—the lines, the thickening knuckles, the calluses that seemed to have become a part of her being after so many years.

"How is it for you these days?" Moon asked softly. "Has it gotten any easier without Miroe, now that the Hegemony has come back? Or has that made it harder?"

Jerusha looked up at her again, realizing that they had not had even a few moments to spend like this, a stolen space of private time to speak to each other as human beings, in weeks. "Both, I think," she said.

"Yes." Moon's eyes turned distant, as if her thoughts were blown smoke. "That's about right. . . . Both." She twisted a strand of pale hair between her fingers, absently knotting and unknotting it. "The Hegemony's presence here has given everything double strength." She glanced at the terminal, part of a system that had lain useless and inert through her entire reign, until now. She had been computer-literate in a meaningful way for only a few weeks, a fact that Jerusha still found almost unbelievable. "And double meanings . . ."

Jerusha saw BZ Gundhalinu inside the words, like an image in a mirror. "You should talk to BZ, Moon," she said.

"I have," Moon said. "I see him several times a week. . . ." Her gaze broke. "But not alone. I can't, Jerusha."

"What do you expect he'd do?" Jerusha asked, raising her eyebrows.

"It's what I might do." Moon's face reddened. "When I watch him, whenever he speaks— Over the years I thought I'd become immune to those feelings . . . numb. That after all Sparks and I have—lost, of what we had, all I really hoped for from life anymore was to finally, someday, be left alone. Peace." She shook her head. "I hardly knew BZ, Jerusha . . . all those years ago. And yet now, when I watch him I want him—" Her hands clenched. "I don't understand this. I don't even know if it's him, or me. But I can't trust myself. . . ." Her voice faded.

"That's the most unbelievable thing I've heard you say in nearly twenty years." Jerusha shook her own head. "You owe it to him to see him alone. You have to talk, about the children." Moon's face pinched with denial. "You think he doesn't know? He knows. . . ."

Moon looked back at her suddenly. "You've talked to him, haven't you?"

Jerusha nodded.

"How is he . . . ?"

"Up to his ass in bureaucracy. But I don't think he regrets it. Yet."

"What were you talking to him about?" Moon's expression changed abruptly. "Jerusha, are you thinking of leaving Tiamat?"

"No." Jerusha almost laughed, the question was so far from what was in her mind. "No. . . . He asked to see me." She took a deep breath. "He offered me a job, Moon. Chief Inspector."

Moon stared at her in silent speculation. "You'd be working for the Hegemony, then—?"

Again. Jerusha heard the real question she was being asked, had been expecting. When she had worked for the Hegemony before, she had been the enemy of this world, although she had not seen it that way. "I'd be working for BZ," she answered.

"What about your position as my Chief of Constables?"

"If I accepted the Chief Inspectorship, there would be several people I'd trust to take over my position. I'll make sure it's taken care of."

"Have you made your decision, then?"

Jerusha almost shook her head. She hesitated, realizing that she had. "I think I can do more good there," she said slowly, "for all of us. I know both sides. BZ needs people behind him who have that kind of experience. . . . He needs someone to watch his back."

"And who'll watch my back, then?" Moon murmured, a little sadly.

"BZ will." Jerusha smiled. "We both will." She looked down at her hands again, and stopped smiling. "Moon, ever since Miroe's death, I've felt as if my life has been sinking into a rut, deeper and deeper. Everything I am, and have, and do, isn't enough. . . . I think I *need* this. I need the challenge, the headaches, the confrontations, the problems—I need a good heavy jolt of culture shock to get my life started again." She glanced away at the terminal, still waiting behind the Queen like an unblinking eye. "And after nearly twenty years, I still miss the action."

Moon nodded, with her lips pressed together. Jerusha saw understanding in her eyes; and depths of disappointment and loss.

"Only the surface of it will be different," she said; not certain who she was really trying to reassure. "We're all on the same side, working toward the same goals. We always will be."

Moon turned to look at the desk/terminal's deceptively warm, bright eye. "The only thing that ever really remains the same," she said, "is change."

TIAMAT: Carbuncle

"You're early, Justice Gundhalinu," the blind woman said.

Gundhalinu stopped just inside the shellform doorway of the palace meeting hall, nonplussed. Fate Ravenglass, the blind woman who was the head of the Sibyl College, sat alone at the large circular table in the center of the room. Her shuttered gaze was fixed on him, on his general presence, not meeting his eyes. There was no one else present to have told her he was the one who had come into the room. "How did you know it was me?" he asked, curious, as he started toward her.

"You have a very distinctive walk," she said, smiling, and did not elaborate.

"Oh." He smiled wryly, hoping she could hear the smile in his voice. He stopped in front of her, not sitting down, folding his arms as he leaned against the high, hard back of a chair. "You seem to have come early, too, Fate Ravenglass." He did not know where to look when he looked at her face; he was not used to speaking to someone who was sightless. It made him self-conscious.

She nodded. "So I did. Tor dropped me off before she went to a business association meeting." She cocked her head. "But you didn't come here early, and alone, because you expected to meet me," she said, with an odd gentleness.

"No," he murmured, glancing away, at the empty room with its several empty doorways. "Tell me," he said, changing the subject, "how did you come to be a sibyl, in the heart of Carbuncle, all those years ago? And how did you keep it hidden?"

"Someone infected me on Mask Night, during a Festival, many years ago." Her fingers moved restlessly over the tabletop beside her.

Gods. He considered the implications. "Was it an accident?"

"No." Her sightless eyes rose, finding his own this time with unnerving accuracy. "It wasn't. Why do you ask, Justice Gundhalinu?"

He sat down, slowly, in the seat next to hers. "Something very like it . . . happened to me," he said, not really answering the question.

"Then you are a sibyl too—?"

"Yes," he said, surprised, until he remembered that she had no way of seeing his trefoil, or his tattoo; surprised again to realize that no one had even thought to tell her that.

"Did it terrify you when it happened?" she asked.

"Yes," he said again. "I thought I'd lost my mind."

She made a small, sympathetic noise, bowing her head.

"Was it an offworlder who infected you?" he asked.

She nodded. "I believe that it was. But he claimed he was a Summer. . . . I kept what had happened to me a secret, for years, because I was afraid of what would happen to me if I was discovered, and cast out of the city."

Gundhalinu pressed his mouth together, wondering what motivation a sibyl could possibly have had for knowingly infecting a blind woman with the virus, and then abandoning her, in a city where sibyls were hated and feared. "And so you never used the Transfer until M—the new Queen told you the truth?"

"Yes, I did—"

He looked up, surprised. "How . . . ?"

"There were people who would seek me out, sometimes, to ask me questions. I'm not sure how they found me. They were always offworlders, but they never betrayed my secret. I always knew them because they said that they were 'strangers far from home,' and by their handshake."

"Handshake—?" Gundhalinu stiffened. "Do you mean . . . like this?" He reached out, taking her hand, his fingers forming the hidden Survey sign against her palm.

Her hand jerked from his grasp. "Yes! How did you know that?"

"There is a secret order which works to change things for the better in the Hegemony, and in other parts of the Old Empire, as well. . . ."

"And you belong to this group?"

"Yes."

"And they work for the greater good—?"

"Yes," he said again, more uncertainly.

"By infecting unsuspecting and unwilling people with the sibyl virus?"

"No." He grimaced. "There must have been an extraordinarily important reason for a sibyl to have done that to you. . . . I'm sorry," he said, inadequately.

"Is that what was done to you, too?" she asked, after a long silence.

"No." He took a deep breath, exhaled it in a sigh. "There was no reason at all for what happened to me." And yet, if it hadn't been done to him, he would never have learned the secret of Fire Lake, or brought back the stardrive. . . . Song was mad, had been driven insane by the virus. But her mother Hahn, who had asked him to find her, had been a member of Survey. Had she been at a much higher level than he ever suspected? Had there actually been a hidden pattern inside the seeming randomness of his fate, all of it destined to pull him back here to Tiamat? Gods—he could go crazy with suspicion, once he started to let himself think about the possibilities. . . . "It was a random act."

Her brow furrowed slightly, as if she heard doubt in his voice. But she only said, "I'm glad you told me this. I always wanted to believe that there was some meaning to what had happened to me. I only knew what the Summers claimed about their sibyls, and what the Winters claimed about the Summers, for so long. But still the offworlders would come to me. And sometimes I would be called away into Transfer from the other side; I was the only one, for years, who could answer questions about Carbuncle through the Transfer link. I always wanted to believe that what I had become mattered, somehow; that it was important. . . ."

"It was," Gundhalinu said. "More than you'll ever know." He glanced down, and up again at the eyes like darkened windows in her lined, patient face. "So you never saw the people who came to ask you questions?" He wondered if that had been intentional on Survey's part.

"Oh, I saw them—after a fashion. I wasn't completely blind then—I had a vision sensor band from offworld. It gave me enough vision to ply my trade. I was a maskmaker; I made the mask of the Summer Queen, for the last Festival."

"I remember it," he said; remembering it like a dream. Moon had come to him where he lay, delirious with fever in a hospital bed. She had carried the mask of Summer in her arms, to let him know that she had won. . . . He blinked the present back into focus. "You lost your vision when we deactivated all the tech equipment we were leaving behind at the Departure, then."

She nodded.

"I'll make it a point to see that you receive new vision sensors as soon as possible."

"Thank you," she murmured, surprised.

He nodded in turn; realized that she couldn't see the gesture. He touched her hand, making a certain sign with his fingers.

She smiled; her own hand closed over his as he would have withdrawn it. "May I touch your face?" she asked.

Comprehension overtook his surprise, and he lifted his hand, guiding her fingers until they touched his cheek.

Moon watched the two figures sitting side by side in the room beyond the hidden window. She saw Fate's fingers trace the face-map of the man who sat perfectly still beneath her touch, sensing a portrait of him for her mind with her artist's hands.

Moon closed her own hands, when they would have begun to tell her the feel of his skin, the gentle, insistent touch of his mouth against her palm, her lips. . . . She began to turn away, feeling her face flush; angry at her body's tingling betrayal, the arousal that played like silver music through her nerves—at the fact that she had come here to stand, behind this one-way window in this hidden hall, waiting, watching for the first glimpse of that face. . . .

This was one of Arienrhod's secrets, hidden from the room beyond behind what appeared to be an imported mural. Arienrhod had had observation points all through the palace, so that she could watch anyone she chose, whenever she wanted to. That had been one of her tricks, to hide like this, living a lie, betraying herself and whatever unsuspecting person she observed.

But— She turned back again, unable to help herself. She needed to see him, she needed this time. . . . She could not keep her public mask of calm indifference perfectly in place, unless she first took this secret moment alone to gaze at him. He had come early to this meeting, not waiting for any of his own people; arriving even before any of hers should have been here. He had come early; she was sure that he had done it for one reason, and that it was not Fate Ravenglass he had been looking for. . . .

Three other people entered the room—all members of her Council. Fate and BZ turned away, and she could no longer see his face. She pressed her hand against the window, wondering how long it would be before she no longer felt this piercing urgency, this desperate need for even the sight of him. She had never expected to feel this way; not after so many years. But when she had seen him again—and realized that she had seen his face every day through the long years of their separation, in the face of her son . . . his son . . .

She bit her lips. Had that been the reason he had been in her thoughts so often, for so long? Or had it really been the memory of the one night they had spent together? Perhaps it was only because she could never resolve them that her feelings for him obsessed her so, now that he had come back. For the sake of her marriage, her children, her world's future . . . herself, she must not weaken; must never meet with him unless they were not alone, until she was certain that she could control her emotions completely. . . .

She turned away from the window, the spell broken as more people, offworlders now, arrived for the meeting in the room beyond. She started back toward the hidden doorway; stopped suddenly, as her husband blocked her path. "Sparks—"

His gaze flicked past her, to what lay beyond the windows; lingered there, for an endless moment, before it came back to her face. She felt her face redden under his stare; unable to speak, to answer the accusation in his eyes, because there was no possible excuse she could make for what she had been doing here, when the truth was so obvious.

"Why bother with this?" he said, in disgust. "Have him for a lover, if after twenty years you still find him so irresistible."

"I don't want him—"

"Then what do you want? You don't seem to want me." His hand struck his chest, hard. "For twenty years I've been trying to win you back, your love, your respect; running after you, begging you for every touch, every bit of proof that you still cared. And all the time you just kept getting further and further away from me. . . ." He shook his head. "All that time, you were still in love with a memory. I always suspected it. But I could live with it, as long as that was all he was—" His hand jerked at the window. "I can't live with this. Seeing him. Seeing how you look at him . . . Seeing the truth: Even Ariele and Tammis aren't mine. They're his!"

He turned away from her, and she felt her face convulse with pain. "That's not true. They've always been your children! I've always been your wife. I love *you*—"

He turned back, his eyes burning. "Do you think I'm blind? Stupid? They're not my children! And you're not my wife—not in any way that means anything." His anger turned to ashes. "I can't take it. Do whatever you want . . . just don't lie to me about it anymore." He turned and left her without a backward glance.

She stood alone, unable to move, as if she had been turned to stone, until she could no longer hear his footsteps.

She moved again at last, taking in a long, tremulous breath. She looked away from the empty corridor toward the hidden window; saw the faces beyond it looking toward her as if they could see her. She realized that the sound of arguing voices had carried into the meeting hall. But they were already turning away again, their expressions uncertain. She wondered how much they had actually heard.

She clenched her fists until her hands spasmed; released them again, her fingers white and cold, as she made her way back out of the hidden space. She entered the large chamber beyond, where a dozen people waited for her now, waiting to begin a meeting that would shape the future of her world. She saw BZ's eyes on her; resisted meeting them. She wondered how she would get through this next hour, this next day; where she would find the strength she needed to be the Queen, and not a woman. In her mind she pictured the mask of the Summer Queen that Fate Ravenglass had placed on her head one fateful day, half a lifetime ago. She built an image of its serenity and calm, superimposing them on her own features as she walked toward the expectant representatives of the old and new.

TIAMAT: Carbuncle

"Oh, Tor, this is off the scale! I can't *believe* it—" Ariele Dawntreader draped her sinuous, slender form across the transparent table surface, looking down into the depths below her. She clattered as she moved, wearing a bodystocking covered with tiny, glittering silver plates. "Is this exactly what your club was like before the Change—?" Around her, the voices of her friends made a song of delight. It was opening night at Starhiker's, the first offworlder-style gaming club to open, or reopen, in the Maze.

Tor had bought up the remnants of club technology wherever she could find it, used or abused, buried in storage around the city; had everything refitted and all their burned-out entrails repaired with suddenly available microprocessor replacement parts. With the Queen's blessing, she had gotten in ahead of all the offworlder entrepreneurs who had been clamoring at the palace gates, and down in Blue Alley, petitioning the onworld and offworld governments for permission to start filling half-empty buildings of the Maze with stores and places of entertainment. The new Chief Justice had kept a chokehold on the influx of offworlders and their technotoys, the changes that her own people awaited with what seemed to be equal parts eagerness and dread. So far, tradespeople and technicians were given heavy preference over those in less functional occupations.

Ariele felt only the eagerness and awe, not understanding why anyone, including her mother, could feel any other way about the dazzling possibilities of their changing city. She had lived all her life with a hunger for these wonders, never realizing until they actually began to appear what it was she had been hungry for.

"Glad you like it, sweeting." Tor reached across the tabletop, patted her cheek fondly with a jewel-gloved hand. "Enjoy yourself, it's on the house tonight for you and your friends. But this is only a pale imitation of what my old place was like. The difference is that it's *my* place, this time. . . . Wait till the technology really begins to flow—this place will turn your eyeballs inside out. The Maze . . . gods, I never thought I'd live to see it come alive again!" She shook her head, her gray-shot hair scintillating, netted in silver.

Ariele looked at her, feeling another kind of wonder; feeling as if she had never really seen Tor Starhiker before, although she had known her forever . . . that she was seeing Tor now in her element, where she had always belonged. She hoped she would have that kind of light in her own eyes when, after some inconceivable length of time, she was as old as Tor was now.

"Ye gods, Ariele—" Tor straightened suddenly, peering back at her as she passed a round of drinks and gaming pieces into the waiting hands of her friends. "What happened to your hair—?"

"I got it cut like the offworlders." Ariele shook her head, feeling the giddy lightness of the motion, as if a weight had been lifted from her soul, along with the weight of her waist-length hair, which she had left on the floor of an offworlder's shop only this afternoon. What was left was bare inches long, and stood out all over her head like cat's fur. Elco Teel had dared her to do it; but once she had gone ahead, none of the others had dared not to follow her lead. Most of the crowd of bobbing heads behind her sported newly shorn hair, one cut more bizarre than the next. "Don't you love it—?"

Tor raised her eyebrows, and then nodded, smiling. "I think it's perfect. Your mother will hate it."

Ariele grinned. "I hope so," she said, feeling her own smile pinch. "At least I don't look like her anymore." She shook her head again, pushing back off the table surface, taking a drink with her. She sipped it, pleased and a little surprised to find that Tor had actually given her a drink with alcohol in it. "Thanks, Tor."

Tor lifted her hand in good-natured dismissal, moving away from the table, which suddenly came alive with a hologramic vision of an alien city.

Ariele's gasp of astonishment was lost in the murmurs of amazement around her. She stood between Elco Teel and Tilby Atwater, watching as eager offworlders materialized out of the crowd, elbowing her friends aside, flocking to the display to try their hand at a new game which was probably long since an old game to them.

She watched, trying to get a feel for the way it was done, murmuring observations, gasping and pointing with the others; all of them, all the while, still trying not to look as though they had never seen anything like it before. Music filled the air around her with loud, insistent rhythms, the imported heartbeat of some other world. They moved on after a time, drifting from one table to another, sipping their drinks, surreptitiously staring at the astonishing varieties of humanity who filled the space around them—all shapes and sizes, with hair that came in every conceivable style and texture, with colors of eyes and skin that she would have laughed at the very idea of, a year ago. She loved the sight of them, the sense of diversity that they symbolized, the living proof of life's endless possibilities.

"Gods." Tilby's sister Sulark spoke the offworlder oath self-consciously behind her. "How does anyone ever get enough points even to call it a truce? These games are impossible. . . . Even the offworlders can't win." She pointed as a red-faced player turned and stalked away from the jumbled ruins of a world shimmering in front of them.

"That one can," Ariele murmured, nudging Tilby with her shoulder. She had been watching the man two tables away, who was doing something that seemed completely incomprehensible to her, but doing it brilliantly, from the awed cries and laughter that surrounded him. The crowd followed his every move, as she had done, ever since she glanced his way. "Look at him, Tilby, oh Lady's Tits, I'd like to see the rest of that one, wouldn't you—?" He was fair enough to pass for Tiamatan; but she was sure he was an offworlder, by the bizarre swirls of decoration that spiraled up his bare arms to his shoulders. She could barely take her eyes from the burning beauty of his face, the intent, perfectly controlled dance of his hands inside the showers of phantom gold that rained down on him, even to take in what she could glimpse of his body through the shifting crowd.

"Mmm," Tilby said, ruffling her hair with a hand. "I sure would."

"But I saw him first," Ariele said peremptorily, pulling Tilby back when she would have started forward.

Tilby pouted, and Elco Teel said, "You're depraved, Ariele—how can you want to do that one? Look at his skin. Do you think he was born mottled like that, or does he have some kind of disease?"

"It's tattooing," she said, impatiently superior. "You know that. Like a sibyl—"

"Hardly." He made a face.

Ariele lifted her middle finger, let it droop, significantly, in front of his face.

"Do you suppose he's tattooed *all over*—?" Tilby asked, with wide eyes.

"Let's find out." Ariele pushed between them, making her way on across the crowded floor. But as she reached the gaming table where the offworlder was playing, she saw him withdraw his hands from the golden hallucination, saw it beginning to fade from the air. She squeezed in beside him before he could back away through the crowd, edging aside a youth with night-black skin and hair, and a man whose head barely topped the height of the table. She saw startled surprise on both their faces, and utter boredom in the piercingly blue eyes of the player himself. Intentionally she brushed up against him, letting the curve of her body slide along his hip as her hand grasped his arm. "Teach me," she murmured, to his face.

He stared at her with what seemed to be incomprehension, for a moment. She held him pinned against the table with the subtle, suggestive pressure of her body.

"Boss—?" the short man said, behind her.

The player gestured sharply with his hand, and the short man fell silent. The offworlder shook his head slightly, but it was not a refusal; a smile that was nothing but amused pulled up the corners of his mouth. His eyes remained expressionless. "Sure," he said. His own hands rose, circled her, slid down her back to her metal-jangling hips. He turned her where she stood until she was facing the gaming table in front of him. She felt his body move up against hers now, not so subtly; felt the pressure of his sudden erection against her spine.

He held her hands inside his, slipping filigreed mesh over them, lifting them as if he were about to play music on an instrument. The swarming fireflies began to fill her eyes. She was only vaguely aware that her friends had gathered around her, watching her with varying degrees of amusement and envy as the game began.

He began to force her hands to move to his rhythms, murmuring explanations and encouragement in her ear as she struggled to match his artless grace. "Let go," he said softly. "Winning means nothing. Only the act, only the flow, let it carry you like a river—"

She let go, and felt herself swept away by the flow of motion, the overflow of her senses. The light, the music, the warm pressure of his body fed the hunger inside her; the proof of his desire was a dizzying torment against the small of her back. She dissolved into the sensual heat and flow until she became one with them: her movements were his movements, she saw with his eyes, and as the gold rained down on them, she felt herself winning, and winning, the crowd's awed cries, their applause and laughter, the shining faces of her friends, the shining gold. . . .

And then the faultless motion of her hands began to fail; she missed the capture of one golden trajectory, and then another and another. The spell that had held her was broken, and all at once she became aware that the hands which held hers, guiding them through the arcane ritual of control, were gone as well. Startled, wondering, she watched the light fade; the crowd began to murmur and drift apart. She peeled the golden filaments from her nerveless fingers. There were no fantastically decorated arms caging her, no warm insistent pressure against her back.

Turning, she found that the offworlder was gone; that she had no idea even of how long he had been gone. He had slipped away and left her without a word.

Her friends surrounded her, their mindless, taunting envy and praise raining down on her, as insubstantial as the rain of gold. Elco Teel was beside her with a smile of knowing mockery as he saw the look on her face. "He's too slick for you, my little Motherlover." It was a term of insult the offworlders used for Tiamatans, and she frowned. "Caught you in your own trap, didn't he?" he murmured, with smug satisfaction. She brought her knee up sharply, hitting him in the groin—not hard enough to double him over, but hard enough to make him swear.

"You bitch," he muttered. But he smiled.

"And don't you just love it?" She kissed him, then, letting him into her mouth, closing her eyes so that she could imagine the offworlder kissing her instead.

They wandered on through the crowd in a group, finding strength in numbers among the growing press of offworlders; playing at games, watching and learning, groping after a sophistication that suddenly made their own behavior seem like childish, provincial pretense. At last, when Tor refused to let them have anything beyond three drinks, they drifted out of the club and on down the Street in search of simpler, more familiar pleasures.

As they passed the entrance to Olivine Alley, Ariele stopped, peering down its throat. For most of her life its strangely baroque hive of buildings had been the home to the Sibyl College her mother had founded. But now it was called "Blue Alley" again; it had become what it had been before—the official home of the offworlders: their government offices, their ground, not to be casually wandered into, as she had done all her life since she was a small child. There were still people moving along it, even though the hour was getting late; most of them wore the uniform of the offworlder Police. This ground had been hers to walk on, to play on, by right. But now if she entered it she knew she would be stopped, questioned, driven off—politely, because she was the Queen's daughter, but peremptorily, as if she were a nuisance or a threat.

"Come on, Ari," Brein said, impatiently, tugging at her arm when she still did not move.

"Wait." She shrugged off the hold, watching the three figures coming toward the alley's entrance. They were deep in conversation; not a pleasant one, from the look on their faces. The one in the middle was BZ Gundhalinu, the Chief Justice; on his right was the Commander of Police. At his left was Jerusha PalaThion, wearing the same dusty-blue uniform, with the insignia of a Chief Inspector.

She still had not gotten used to the sight of it, or to the sight of Jerusha among those strangers with their alien faces . . . making her see with painful clarity the alienness of Jerusha's own face, a thing she had never recognized through all the years before. The three of them reached the corner and started downhill. Only

Vhanu, the Police Commander, glanced her way; he frowned and looked ahead again.

"Hello, Aunt Jerusha," Ariele called out, hearing the mocking echo of her voice come back at her from the building walls.

Jerusha stopped; she turned back, the others turning with her. She searched the faces of the cluster of gaudily dressed Tiamatan youths in wary surprise. Ariele moved forward slightly, waiting through the endless moment until Jerusha picked her out of the crowd.

"Ariele—?" Jerusha came toward them, her expression half curious and half incredulous. Ariele leaned close to Elco Teel, murmuring instructions in his ear. He nodded, and grinned.

"Ariele," Jerusha said again; Ariele read dismay in the older woman's stare. "What have you done to your hair?"

The Chief Justice followed Jerusha toward them, as Ariele had hoped he would; only the Police Commander remained where he was. She saw Gundhalinu's belated, barely concealed start as he recognized her. She had not seen him close up in months. She heard Elco murmur something behind her, and snickers of laughter: *He was the one.* The Blue who had slept with her mother, before she was born. The one who had made the father she loved suddenly look at her as if she were a stranger, and turn away from her without a word. The one who had come back to Tiamat to tear her family apart. . . .

She thought she caught, again, the look she had seen in Gundhalinu's eyes before—the strange mix of uncertainty and longing. It was not sexual, but an emotion that ran equally deep and strong . . . the kind of look a man might give to his long-lost child. The thought made something twist in her stomach. "Hello, Ariele," he said, in Tiamatan; his voice was soft and faintly accented.

She looked away from him deliberately. "I wanted it to look offworld—" She touched her hair, answering Jerusha's question instead; ignore Gundhalinu entirely now. "We love everything offworld." She put her hands on her hips, flaunting her glittering clothes, the flamboyant circle of friends all around her.

"Except the offworlders," Elco Teel said, with perfect venom, just as she had told him to.

"Yes," she murmured, leaning her head languorously against his shoulder, smiling with satisfaction. "Too bad they can't just all stay home where they belong." She let her gaze meet Gundhalinu's again, raking him with spite.

He looked down. "Good night, Jerusha," he murmured, to his Chief Inspector. He glanced back at Ariele, and she thought he was going to say something more to her. But he only gazed at her a moment longer, as if he were taking her picture with his mind. And then he turned away, back to the other Kharemoughi, who was still pointedly keeping his distance, his dark face closed and suspicious. They went on down the Street.

Jerusha watched them go, before she looked back at the small cluster of Tiamatans. Ariele read disapproval and annoyance in her glance. Jerusha opened her mouth—changed her mind, as Gundhalinu had, before the words could form. Instead, she said, "You look like a hooker."

"What's a hooker?" Ariele said.

"A whore," Jerusha said flatly. "You look like a whore in that outfit."

Ariele frowned, feeling her face redden. She had never heard the term before the offworlders had come back. "So do you," she said sullenly. She jerked her head, the abrupt motion signaling her friends to follow her. She felt their hands stroking her, their voices in her ear congratulating her, giggling and muttering like the empty cries of sea birds as she started on down the Street, leaving behind the woman who had once been her mother's loyal defender—and perhaps her own.

Gundhalinu sighed heavily, rubbing his face, as Vhanu fell into step beside him and they continued on their way. Vhanu glanced at his expression, and away at the crowd of Tiamatan youths who were already passing them by, accompanied by rude remarks and catcalls. Vhanu made an audible noise of disgust. "Delinquents," he murmured, in Sandhi.

Gundhalinu did not respond, watching the crowd of teenagers, his eyes following a white-blond crest of hair bobbing in their midst; watching to see whether Ariele Dawntreader looked back at him. "Sorry, NR—what was that?" His mind snapped back into focus as he realized that Vhanu was still speaking.

"I said that—" Vhanu pointed at the Tiamatan youths disappearing into the crowd ahead of them, "is exactly the kind of thing I mean. They laughed at us! That pack of miserable—"

"In Tiamatan; please, NR—" Gundhalinu said abruptly, in Tiamatan. "Speak Tiamatan, not Sandhi. We all need the practice."

Vhanu glanced at him, and controlled his sudden, obvious irritation. "Very well. Those miserable little—" He broke off, at a loss for a satisfactory term in a foreign tongue. "They put on our clothes and cut off their hair, but that doesn't make them our equals. They still behave like . . . like . . . *dashtanu.*" He fell back into Sandhi in exasperation. *Barbarians.* "Damn it, PalaThion keeps putting all of us through these indoctrination sessions along with the new recruits— By all the gods, even you and I have been fed the tapes half a dozen times ourselves. I can recite the information word for word—"

"It makes a good impression when the force sees us studying the material as well," Gundhalinu said, keeping his voice neutral; wondering to himself a little wearily when the information would actually begin to have any effect on Vhanu's attitude.

"But the real point—which PalaThion seems incapable of understanding—is not that we need to learn the way the Tiamatans live and speak and think. They need to learn our way of doing things. Until they do, they'll go on being *dashtanu* in fancy clothing, unqualified to be citizens of the Hegemony, and undeserving of its full privileges. Look at that little *yiskat*"— slut—"we just saw. The Queen's daughter, and she has the manners of a *mekru.* She ought to be publicly thrashed; that would make the point more effectively than—"

"Vhanu!" Gundhalinu bit down on his sudden anger, as Vhanu looked at him in surprise. "The real point, NR," he murmured, not looking at his old friend now, "is that both sides need to understand the other's point of view. Jerusha PalaThion not only knows that, she's done it. That's why I wanted her to work with you in training the force. If we want more cooperation and less catcalls from the locals, we have to do it too. You do see the point of it—?"

Vhanu nodded once, stiffly. "But by all my ancestors—" he said, his voice taking on an edge, "you heard what she told them tonight, after the meeting: She was sure everyone there could see now why all intelligent beings deserved equal respect and equal treatment . . . but just in case someone couldn't, she wanted them to know that anybody who so much as called a native a Motherlover could pick up their pay and turn in their uniform. She can't enforce that."

"Why not?" Gundhalinu said. "Her new policy has the backing of my office—and, I hope, yours."

Vhanu looked at him again, searchingly. He shrugged his shoulders. "Yes."

Gundhalinu glanced away at the passing crowd. "If there's one thing I've learned over the years, NR, it's that enlightened self-interest is a more effective motivator toward good than mere understanding of the situation."

"I suppose so," Vhanu said, somewhat glumly. He glanced away again, as someone shouted drunkenly; a fishhead flung from somewhere down an alley struck the invisible field of his bodyshield, and dropped at his feet. "Perhaps she should be encouraged to try the same methods on the natives she knows so well."

Gundhalinu stepped over the offal. "How difficult have you found your interactions with the local constabulary to be?"

"Surprisingly easy, all things considered," Vhanu admitted. "They seem glad enough to have our help in dealing with the increased population in the city. They're competent and efficient, but they know their limits."

"PalaThion trained them," Gundhalinu said. "Give her a chance to prove what she can do for us. The rules are different than they used to be, for us, for the natives. If they don't understand that we exist as a buffer, to protect them from our own people, then the hostility won't stop with catcalls and fishheads; it will keep on escalating."

"You said that PalaThion was in charge here during the Snow Queen's reign, as Commander of the Police." Vhanu gestured at the city around him. "Are you telling me it's worse with the Summer Queen running things?"

"Different," Gundhalinu said, shaking his head. They stepped aside to avoid the sudden, almost silent approach of a passenger tram. "Most of the force were Newhavenese, hard-nosed and pig-headed. They never did understand. And the Snow Queen had her own reasons for giving us hell. She did it very well. She actively protected the underworld elements on-planet, because she knew the legitimate government was exploiting her people. We have a chance to prove to the new Queen that it isn't like that anymore—that both sides have something to gain from the new relationship."

"Frankly, BZ, what does Tiamat have of any real value to offer us, besides the water of life? I haven't seen anything—"

"A good point, Commander Vhanu," a Tiamatan voice said behind them.

Gundhalinu looked back, surprised that anyone, let alone a local, would intrude on their conversation so casually. He recognized Kirard Set Wayaways, from the City Council—remembered him from the old days, vaguely, as one of the Snow Queen's Winter favorites. He recalled an impression of mocking superiority whenever Wayaways had looked at him, or at anyone who did not share Arienrhod's favor. Wayaways had appeared to be barely older than his own twenty standards, at their first encounter; although the wardroom gossip had it that he was closer to sixty. But without the water of life, the years since the Departure had left their mark on Wayaways. Gundhalinu observed the signs of aging in the other man's face with silent satisfaction.

"Are you walking, when you could be using our new public transportation?" Wayaways gestured at the tram, which was moving past them again.

"We haven't far to go," Gundhalinu said, glancing on down the Street. "After a long day of sitting in meetings and interfacing a dataport, I prefer to walk."

"Good idea. They say exercise is one way to keep young," Wayaways remarked, showing a trace of the sardonic smile that Gundhalinu still remembered with distaste.

"It's the one I prefer." Gundhalinu began to turn away, eager to put an end to the conversation.

"Is that why you suddenly chose to get off the tram and join us?" Vhanu asked Wayaways, with a sharp curiosity that was more professional than personal. For once Gundhalinu regretted his friend's unshakable attention to duty.

"No, actually." Wayaways took the question as an excuse to continue with them as they began to walk again; Gundhalinu frowned. "I was just curious to see two of the top officials of our new Hegemonic government walking in the Street like anyone else. I was pleasantly surprised to see that you weren't in a hovercraft."

"Then I hope we've satisfied your curiosity," Gundhalinu said shortly. "Now if you'll forgive us, Elder Wayaways, we were having a private conversation—"

"About the water of life." Wayaways nodded. "Commander Vhanu was remarking that he didn't feel our poorly endowed planet had much to offer the Hegemony, in return for all the benefits you bring to us—except for the water of life. I think that's absolutely true. Which is why I felt compelled to behave so rudely, and intrude on your privacy."

Vhanu glanced at Wayaways, his initial look of distrust fading. "Who did you say you were?"

"I didn't, actually. I believe we've met before, but we've never really spoken. I'm Kirard Set Wayaways Winter. I'm one of the Queen's advisors." He held out his hand, palm up; Vhanu touched it briefly with his own palm. Wayaways looked back at Gundhalinu. "I was very surprised to hear that you had declared a moratorium on the hunting of mers, under the circumstances, Justice Gundhalinu. I'd think you'd be eager to start demonstrating to the Hegemony, as soon as possible, that its return to Tiamat is economically profitable as well as technologically feasible."

Gundhalinu looked at him. "I don't know why you find it surprising, Wayaways, since I'm doing it at the Queen's request. A full study is being made on the question of whether the mers are actually an intelligent race, before the hunting begins again. As a member of the City Council, I'd think you would know that."

Wayaways shrugged. "Certainly we all know about the Queen's recent . . . obsession, for want of a better word, with the mers. Being a Summer, she is rather more conservative in her beliefs than her predecessor. But we don't necessarily all agree about the wisdom of this move . . . just as I'm sure your people don't all agree about it." He raised his eyebrows.

Gundhalinu frowned slightly. He wondered how much Wayaways really knew—if he really knew anything—about the struggle with his own Judicate members and chiefs of staff, including Vhanu, to win their support and gain even that grudging concession from the Central Committee. "There is also the matter of whether continuing unrestricted slaughter of the mers, sentient or not, will cause them to become extinct . . . and a study needs to be done concerning the feasibility of synthesizing the water of life . . ." He let his voice run on through all the arguments he had used to sway his own council, not sure why he felt compelled to justify himself, except that something in Wayaways' tone put him instinctively on the defensive. He didn't like the feeling, any more than he liked the man. "Do you have some personal interest in this matter?" He took the offensive again. "I seem to remember reviewing your applications. You were the first to request that your holdings be hunted—"

Wayaways made an unreadable gesture. "Is that against the law?"

"No," Gundhalinu said, aware that Vhanu was looking at him sidelong.

"Then why shouldn't I put in my application? It's no more than what I've always done. . . . Well, of course, you're too young to remember that far back . . ." He shrugged again. "You were only on Tiamat for . . . what? About five years, before the Change. I seem to remember seeing you at Arienrhod's court, along with Commander—Chief Inspector—PalaThion, when she was only an inspector. In fact, I remember an amusing incident. . . ." He broke off, as Gundhalinu's expression darkened. "But you've probably forgotten that encounter with Starbuck, long since. I remember much more vividly that spectacularly heroic moment during the final Festival, when young Inspector Gundhalinu burst in on the mob in the Hall of the Winds, as Arienrhod was trying to have Moon Dawntreader thrown into the Pit. You single-handedly saved the woman who became the new Queen."

"Ye gods," Vhanu murmured in Sandhi, looking at Gundhalinu as if he had never seen him before. "Thou never told me about that, BZ."

"He exaggerates," Gundhalinu said abruptly, answering in the same language. "Moon Dawntreader saved herself, Wayaways—" switching back to Tiamatan, "or don't you remember how she stopped the wind, when you were in the hall with the rest of the mob?"

"Yes, I do remember." Wayaways shook his head. "Incredible. How does she do that? Did she ever tell you? . . . But you're too modest, Justice. The mob would have had her anyway, if you hadn't shown them your Police badge and faced them down."

"Father of all my grandfathers," Vhanu said. "Why would the Snow Queen want to kill Moon Dawntreader in the first place? Arienrhod surely couldn't know that she would become Queen."

"Well, because Moon was—" Wayaways hesitated, glancing suddenly at Gundhalinu, his gaze like a spotlight, "a sibyl. You know, Commander, how stupidly superstitious we used to be about sibyls, before the Summer Queen enlightened us." He laughed. Gundhalinu pressed his mouth together. "But there was more to it, there was Sparks Dawntreader, Moon's pledged. The Queen had him for a lover, and Moon wanted him back. Jealousy is one of the great random factors in history, you know. But I probably don't need to tell you gentlemen that, considering the positions you find yourselves in." His eyes danced speculatively from Gundhalinu's face to Vhanu's, and back. "It's no wonder the Queen is so fond of you, Justice. She must have been someone special to you back then for you to risk your life for her."

"I was doing my sworn duty as a Police Officer." Gundhalinu looked straight ahead, frowning again. "That was all."

"But you chose to come back to Tiamat, after all this time, knowing she was Queen. And the way you've supported her policies—"

"That has nothing to do with the present."

"I say, BZ, how did you come to know Moon Dawntreader?" Vhanu asked. The faintly scandalized fascination still showed in his eyes.

"Really, he never told you—?" Wayaways exclaimed, in mock surprise.

"It's a long story, and exceedingly unremarkable," Gundhalinu said, his voice grating.

"Not the version I heard," Wayaways protested. "Something about techrunners, and nomad thieves up in the interior; that the two of you were lost together—"

"We're here." Gundhalinu stopped abruptly, cutting Wayaways off. He looked up at the newly installed sign above the ancient doorway, which marked the reopened Survey Hall. He turned back to Wayaways, meeting the Tiamatan's gaze with a stare of cold warning. "Some other time," he said. He looked back at Vhanu, putting a hand on his shoulder.

Wayaways nodded and shrugged. "Until then," he said, gracefully retreating. "Have a pleasant evening. The Survey Hall must seem like a haven of peace and respite for strangers like yourselves, far from home." He raised his hand in farewell, turning away, disappearing into the crowd even as he spoke the words.

Gundhalinu stared at the Tiamatan's retreating back; his body quivered, caught between the urge to go after Wayaways, and the urge to be rid of him. He looked back at Vhanu, finally.

"A chance remark?" Vhanu murmured. His expression said that he doubted it.

Gundhalinu shook his head. "No."

"I thought there were no Tiamatan members of Survey," Vhanu said.

"So did I." Gundhalinu turned back, looking toward the dark, shadowed rectangle of the building entrance, below the static image that displayed only a single data figure, the ancient star-and-compass symbol of the order. He had never seen a Tiamatan face inside this building, when he had visited the Hall during his previous tour of duty on Tiamat. He had been told that the locals were excluded from membership, and he had simply accepted it. But back then he had thought that this was merely a social club. He had not known then anything of what he knew now . . . about the secrets this building held, even from the majority of its membership; or the secrets within secrets signified by that symbol above its door. He looked back at the crowd eddying past along the Street. Wayaways had disappeared.

"He must have picked up the expression during the previous occupation. He seems to have collected a great deal of unexpected information. . . ." Vhanu glanced at Gundhalinu again; curiosity still glinted through his doubt and concern.

"He was a user. . . . I suppose anything is possible," Gundhalinu said, still frowning. *Even that he is Survey.* But not the one they knew and served.

"A user—of people?" Vhanu asked.

"Of the water of life." Gundhalinu's mouth pulled down. "Of people too. I wouldn't trust anything he says, if I were you."

"I'll keep that in mind." Vhanu nodded. But Gundhalinu felt Vhanu's eyes linger speculatively on him a moment longer.

He shook off his unease, cursing Wayaways under his breath for making him doubt the one man he really depended on, for making that man doubt him, even for a moment. He went in under the overhang, into sudden darkness; pushed through the ancient, windowpaned doors and on into the light.

Superficially the Survey Hall was just as he remembered it from before: one large main room for social functions, with smaller offices and meeting rooms above it. Now he knew there were rooms within the rooms, hidden inside each other like

Samathan votive-boxes. The main room was still rather spartan, with few of the odd souvenirs of other worlds that had formerly decorated its walls and native-crafted shelves, an accretion of mementos that had been left there by visiting members over a century and a half. He wondered what had become of the old collection; supposed the things had been carried off by the locals, or thrown away.

The room was sparsely populated tonight, even though this was the night of a scheduled meeting. There simply were not enough Survey members on-planet yet to fill the Hall. It was late enough for them to have missed the somewhat tedious pattern of rituals that had opened this evening's gathering, at least. Most of the men and few women stood clustered together in small conversational groups, eating and drinking desultorily, or huddled on the clusters of cushioned benches in the ghostly light of their dozen gaming tables.

The air was rich with the mingled odors of various recreational drugs—none of them on the prescribed list, since the majority of people in this room were wearing the uniform of the Hegemonic Police. He wondered what they would think if they knew what kind of mind-altering substances were sometimes used in the hidden rooms just behind these walls—just beyond their knowledge. It astonished him to think of some of the drugs he himself had been forced to take, under strict supervision, to guide him toward deeper levels of insight and strengthen his concentration.

There were a few random non-uniformed figures, dressed in the melange of styles typical of the Hegemony's disparate cultures. Out of habit his eyes took in each outsider, seeing loose robes, pragmatic coveralls, lace-edged funeral foppery. . . . His gaze caught on a figure standing across the room, leaning against the wall beside the mantel above an artificial hearth. The figure wore loose pants and robes of a deep midnight blue; face and head were almost entirely covered by the serpentine folds of a night-blue length of scarf. All that he could see were eyes, gazing back at him through a narrow window of exposed flesh. He felt vision and memory make a connection abruptly: *Ondinee*. His immediate image of a traditional Ondinean was that the women covered their faces among strangers, not the men; but this one wore a man's garments. He remembered hearing about a perversely independent cult that defied the dominant theocracy; where the women went unveiled and were not treated like slaves, where the men covered their faces instead, probably as much to escape persecution by the government as to preserve their spiritual essence.

The man looked away abruptly, just as it struck him that he was being studied in turn, and began to inspect some object on the mantel.

Gundhalinu turned back to Vhanu, telling himself that he had probably imagined the man was staring at him; that his nerves were on edge. Vhanu had drifted away into a conversation with YA Tilhonne, Pernatte's grandnephew. Mithra Kitaro, the Police inspector he had first met at KR Aspundh's, approached him to ask whether he needed anything. He requested lilander, allowing himself that indulgence. He sat down on a bench and activated the gaming table in front of him; not really in the mood to play games, but needing some semblance of social activity to cover a few moments of uninterrupted thought.

He was not sure what Kirard Set Wayaways had wanted from their unexpected encounter, but he was certain that Wayaways' intent had been neither harmless, nor casual. He decided that he would speak with Jerusha PalaThion about it, privately, tomorrow. . . .

He glanced up again, realizing that it was not for the first time, to check on the Ondinean. The other man had moved a short distance away, and was talking to a Kharemoughi whose back was turned to Gundhalinu. The Ordinean glanced past the other man's shoulder at Gundhalinu, as if he felt himself being looked at.

Kitaro returned with a tall lilac-tinted glass of lilander. He touched Kitaro's arm as she handed him the drink. Gesturing unobtrusively at the Ondinean, he asked, "Do you know that man?"

Kitaro glanced away, and back. "Only that he's a stranger far from home."

"You're sure of that?"

Kitaro looked at him, surprised. "Absolutely, Justice. He wouldn't be inside, otherwise." Not only human intervention, but also certain hidden surveillance checks made certain of it. "I remember seeing him before. Is something the matter?"

"No." Gundhalinu shook his head. "Just curious. I suppose I wore that uniform," gesturing at Kitaro's blue tunic, "for too long. A man who hides his face makes me nervous." But he knew, in his gut, that what bothered him was not so simple. It wasn't the man's hidden face. Something about the way he carried himself, the way he moved, was familiar. Gundhalinu knew that body language, in the same way he might have recognized the work of a familiar artist, deep in the nonverbal sectors of his brain. But the part of his mind that thought it knew could not speak, and the part that could, couldn't remember.

He sipped the lilander, letting its pungent sweetness fill his senses and still his impatience. Maybe it was only his imagination, after a day full of nerve-racking, tense debates, and an evening's walk filled with unpleasant innuendos. . . . But he found himself on his feet again, moving not-quite-casually across the room in the direction of the Ondinean, who seemed to drift away with equally deceptive randomness . . . or was he just imagining that too? But the part of his brain that was still taking the measure of every movement the stranger made told him he was not.

He reached the mantel, with its dark, fancifully carved supports and its litter of small, foreign oddities. He picked up the thing he had seen the Ondinean handle. It was a silver vial, almost like a perfume bottle. He studied it for a moment, trying to remember where he had seen such a thing before. Recognition caught him suddenly, painfully: It was a container for the water of life. Not the liquor, but the genuine water of life, the extract from the blood of mers.

He turned it around in his fingers, handling it carefully, cautiously. It had not been here a few days ago. Where had this come from? Who would have left such a thing here? He looked up, searching the room. *Or had the Ondinean put it there himself?* The Ondinean had his back turned now, as if he were oblivious to whatever Gundhalinu was doing; although Gundhalinu was certain he was not. *The water of life* . . . It had been on his mind ever since he had arrived here. It had been in his thoughts and on his lips constantly for the past weeks, as he had hammered out his compromise with the Judiciate and the representatives from the Central Coordinating Committee. Finding this here, now, he felt as if he had conjured it up out of his own preoccupation.

But he had not. Someone had left it there, intentionally—and in this Hall, there were no coincidences. He reached into the belt pouch underneath his jacket and pulled out a scanner, part of the Police-issue equipment he still habitually carried with him. He ran a full scan on the vial, measuring and recording everything that could be known about its age and previous provenance, including the fingerprints of anyone who had touched it.

He put the scanner back into his belt pouch, placed the vial back on the mantel. Then he glanced away into the room, to see whether anyone had been watching. Only the Ondinean was looking back at him, standing perfectly still at the opposite side of the room. Gundhalinu started toward him, keeping eye contact; unable to see anything about the other man's expression. VX Sandrine caught his arm as he passed; he murmured an abrupt excuse and moved on, willing the Ondinean to stay put. The stranger stood unmoving, still gazing back at him, until he had almost closed the distance between them. And then the man turned suddenly, and disappeared through the darkened doorway behind him.

Gundhalinu started after him; stopped, looking down suddenly, as the call beeper sounded on his belt remote. He swore, knowing that the only message he would be getting at this hour would be an urgent one. He glanced over his shoulder at the room behind him, knowing that he should find a place to take the call—looked back, to find that the dim-lit hallway ahead of him was empty. He swore again, in disgust. Standing just inside the hall entrance, he put the call through on his remote.

"Judiciate," a disembodied voice said.

"This is Justice Gundhalinu," he said, as the link came alive. "You have a message for me?"

"Justice Gundhalinu—?" The voice that answered him sounded nonplussed. "No, sir. No message."

"You just called me," Gundhalinu snapped. "There must be a message."

"No, sir—" He could hear the embarrassment in the voice that answered him. "There must be some mistake. No one called you. There's no record of any call here."

"All right," he said brusquely. "Thank you." He shut off his comm link with an angry motion of his hand. He went back into the main hall, crossing it to where Vhanu stood in conversation with JK Wybenalle, one of the Central Committee representatives. Beside them was a table that held a buffet of native foods, prepared with surprising skill by a local restaurant called, oddly, Stasis.

". . . And what do you suppose this is?" Wybenalle was saying, in Sandhi, as he prodded a flaccid, glistening piece of meat with a silver-pronged pick.

Gundhalinu reached past him and speared a slice off the plate. He put it into his mouth and chewed. The taste was indescribably spicy, the texture chewy, just as he remembered it. "Try some," he urged, speaking Sandhi, as Wybenalle always insisted on doing. "It's quite good."

Wybenalle accepted the slice he proffered, looking at him with raised eyebrows and so missing Vhanu's look of disbelief, which was plainly visible to Gundhalinu. Gundhalinu smiled.

"Interesting," Wybenalle said, chewing gamely. "What do they call this?"

"It's pickled *squam*," Gundhalinu said. "A kind of indigenous sea slug, I believe."

The scattering of pale freckles on Wybenalle's brown, narrow-featured face turned a sudden, anemic white. He swallowed the mouthful of squam like a man swallowing poison.

"Try some of this—" Gundhalinu gestured at a platter of small cakes heaped with fish eggs.

"Excuse me . . ." Wybenalle mumbled, beginning to turn away, searching the room with desperate eyes.

"We grow or we die . . ." Gundhalinu said, smiling pleasantly as Wybenalle left them abruptly, heading for the bathrooms. "Right, Vhanu?" He looked back at his Commander of Police, letting his smile widen.

Vhanu grimaced. "Do thou really think that was wise?" he said, still speaking Sandhi.

"No." Gundhalinu shook his head, still smiling. "It wasn't kind, either. But by all my sainted ancestors, that man has given me enough grief for a lifetime in the past weeks. Allow me the privilege of being petty." He shrugged, trying to loosen the tense muscles in his shoulders and neck. He reached into his belt pouch, and pulled out the scanner. "I have some data I'd like you to run a check on for me, NR."

Vhanu produced his own scanner, and let it replicate the readings Gundhalinu had taken off the vial. "I should have the analysis for you some time late tomorrow. Will that be soon enough?"

"Fine." Gundhalinu nodded. "It's nothing pressing," he said, answering Vhanu's unspoken question. "Just my curiosity about one of the objects on the mantel over there." He gestured casually, leaning against the table, looking toward the doorway the Ondinean had disappeared through. He was not sure why he didn't say more; whether it was simply the fear of seeming absurd, or something deeper. Maybe tomorrow he would know.

Vhanu looked up as Kitaro approached them. "Excuse me, *sathranu*," she said. "That friendly cycle of *tan* is about to begin on the upper level, if you care to join us?"

Gundhalinu nodded; answering both a spoken and an unspoken question.

"*Tan?*" someone said behind him. "May I join you?"

Kitaro shook her head. "Sorry. We already have our set. Next round—?" He shrugged, and drifted away. They followed her to the back of the room, and up the curving stairway. On the second floor they entered the gaming room, where five others waited expectantly, sitting cross-legged on floor mats around the circular game board. Gundhalinu looked down at the complex pattern of geometries on its surface. The board had been hand-crafted somewhere on Tsieh-pun from perfectly fitted inlays of colored wood. He admired its workmanship as he took his place in the circle. Vhanu sat down across the board from him; Kitaro closed the door and sat down on his left. To anyone looking in on them through the single window they would appear to be doing exactly what they were doing.

But they were doing something else, playing games within games, playing the Great Game, in this private room within the walls of the Survey Hall. He looked around the circle of faces, all but one of them Kharemoughis, and familiar to him. The one offworlder was a businessman from Four; the only woman was Kitaro, who was the only other sibyl besides himself. He looked down at the *tan* board again, the glittering colored-crystal gaming pieces, the almost hypnotic patterns of the wood. There were subtleties hidden within subtleties among the interlocking geometries of the board; he had learned to seek them out visually in all their permutations, as one of the disciplines he had been forced to master to reach the Seventh and the Fourteenth levels within Survey . . . discovering, the second time, all that he had missed the first, and wondering how he could have been so blind.

Tan was rumored to be nearly as old as the Great Game, if not older. There was an entire twelfth-level adhani made up of meanings ascribed to the crossings and combinations of the various forms, as if it were a kind of mystical genetic code. Some of the numerical symbolism had a relation to patterns occurring in the real world; some of them were completely obscure to him, and yet seemed to be utterly consistent within themselves. Others seemed to him to be nothing but accumulated superstitions . . . so far. He had yet to learn whether he would ever be required to study the game of *tan* again, at some future stage of his ongoing initiation into some unknown heights of perception, from which he could look down more clearly on the endless complexity of the human condition, on the interfaces of Order and Chaos.

Kitaro gathered up the colored fire of the gaming pieces and scattered them casually as she began the Recitation of Questions, taking on herself the role of Questioner. He marked in his memory where the pieces came to rest, randomly scattered across the board, but showing a heavy concentration of single-figures. The businessman from Four gathered up the crystals, tossed them out again, as he gave the first response. The sine wave of question and answer moved on around the circle, touching Vhanu, touching the official who sat next to him; the game pieces clattered against the edges of the game board and regrouped.

Gundhalinu made himself remember the outcome of each throw, searching for the greater pattern that would inexorably take shape out of the random motion; forcing himself to comprehend it, whether he believed it had any significance or not. The question-and-answer pattern of ritual response was the same one they used in the larger meeting hall below, at the formal social gatherings held there. But the questions asked here were not the same ones; nor, more importantly, were the answers.

He had found the rituals of the Survey he had known in his youth to be excruciatingly empty of meaning. But this ritual sang in his brain: Order and Chaos, the random workings of fate precariously balanced by the laws of universal motion. He found himself thinking of the Ondinean. His eyes wandered away from the game board toward the wide window looking out on the hall, as a pattern began to take form in the motion of falling stones, and fell apart again.

"And who has called this fellowship into being, and given us our duty, and shown us the power of knowledge?" Kitaro asked.

"Mede," Abbidoes answered, beside him.

Gundhalinu looked down at the game board again, and gathered up the crystals. "Ilmarinen." He spoke his ancestor's name as he cast the stones. He watched the pieces fall, stared at the sudden, subtle shift in the pattern he held inside his head. "Vanamoinen—!" he murmured, echoing Kitaro's voice as she spoke the response in proper progression beside him.

Gundhalinu looked away at the window again, not even noticing the sharp looks of annoyance several people directed at him; half expecting to see a face staring in at them, at him, disguised by a fold of cloth, by skin dyed black, eyes darkened to indigo—but still with a gaze as insistent as a madman's.

The window was empty. But he *had* seen Kullervo: *Kullervo. Kullervo was here.* He bit his lip to keep himself from shouting out the name, interrupting the pattern again, inexcusably. He forced his emotions back under control, recognizing the significance of the pattern, the importance of not breaking the surface tension of the group's concentration. . . . Holding to his own place in the ritual, while at the same time his mind scattered clues like gaming pieces and read their pattern. . . . Kullervo had been here tonight; had been here before, disguised. But Kullervo was in the Brotherhood . . . Survey corrupted by the power of knowledge, using its secrets and its influence to destabilize and poison societies, feeding off the chaos they created, profiting off of it. The ones who had turned the values and beliefs of the guild's original members inside out . . . who had murdered his brothers, and tried to keep him from returning to Tiamat.

Why had Kullervo come here tonight, and deliberately—he was sure of it—tried to attract his attention? He remembered the vial on the mantel suddenly. Even if Kullervo had not put it there, he had made Gundhalinu notice it. *Why?* Kullervo worked for the Brotherhood; Kullervo was a bioengineering genius, who knew more about technovirals than any living human being in the Hegemony. . . .

And suddenly he understood: *It was about the water of life.* The Brotherhood was already at work here, insinuating itself into the fabric of the new society, as if he had set up no safeguards at all to prevent it. They wanted the water of life for themselves. . . . and Reede Kullervo was here to give it to them.

But then, what had Kullervo been doing here tonight? Spying, possibly; gathering data on the strength and organization of his enemies. Except that he seemed to have been deliberately drawing attention to himself, intentionally placing clues in the path of the one person who would understand them. . . .

The gaming pieces rattled for the final response; Gundhalinu stared at the element that completed the pattern, the forms which he had graven on his mind.

"Are there any questions which must be asked to be answered?" Kitaro murmured, glancing around the circle of pensive faces.

"Yes," Gundhalinu said. "There was a man here tonight, passing as one of us. I just realized who he is. He's one of the Brotherhood—the man who stole the stardrive from me at Fire Lake. His name is Reede Kulleva Kullervo."

Vhanu started, across the table from him. "The Smith?" he murmured. "Ye gods—they say the Smith's responsible for everything from the illegal stardrive market to half the drug trade coming out of Ondinee. He's linked to Thanin Jaakola—"

Gundhalinu stiffened. "I hadn't heard that. For how long?"

"Since the stardrive incident," Vhanu said.

Gundhalinu grimaced, and frowned. "Vhanu, you have scanner data on his bionomes. . . . I had him investigated through official channels once; what I got didn't satisfy me. I would like to put our resources to work on revealing who and what he really is. I think it could be vital to us to know exactly what he wants."

"Let the Police pick him up, then, BZ," Vhanu said with sudden eagerness. "Deactivate him, put him through deep questioning. Gods, to capture the Smith! It would be a phenomenal victory for us—for the Golden Mean."

"No," Gundhalinu said, filled with sudden repugnance. Vhanu stared at him. "No, NR," he said again, less abruptly, and shook his head. "I think . . . I think the consequences would be too unpredictable." Because Kullervo was too unpredictable. He tried to imagine the effect deep questioning would have on Kullervo's unstable personality. It could easily cause him to have a complete breakdown. He wasn't even sure exactly why that mattered to him, after what Kullervo had done to him at Fire Lake. Only that he wanted that mind intact . . . and, perversely, the soul of the man it was attached to. "We're better off just watching him discreetly, now that we know he's here; seeing where he leads us. There's time enough to short-circuit him, if that becomes necessary. He isn't going anywhere. I'm sure of that much."

Vhanu nodded reluctantly.

"We'll run a search on him, then," Kitaro said. "As soon as possible."

Gundhalinu nodded, barely listening as the next question was brought up by Abbidoes . . . as his mind sank into memories of Reede Kullervo, the mystery, the contradictions of the man. Realizing suddenly how deep his need to have the answers was . . . how deep his need to see Kullervo again, and confront him, really ran. The pattern between them was incomplete; they had unfinished business. . . .

TIAMAT: Carbuncle

Sparks Dawntreader entered Tor Starhiker's new gaming club, feeling an unnerving flicker of déjà vu. Nothing had changed. His memories told him so, even though his eyes said that this club did not really resemble anything he had seen in the old days, when he had roamed the Street with a bottomless credit rating, playing the decadent jade as if his life depended on it; secretly Starbuck, sniffing out information to help Arienrhod keep on top of the offworlders.

But the *feel* was right; his inner eye knew this place. Tor Starhiker had once run the best club on the Street, and she had the best club now, even it was only by default. He saw her across the room—recognizable, at least, not transformed completely as she had been in the old days. Then she had been decorated like a puppet, to suit the bizarre fantasies of the offworlder who had really owned the club, the living nightmare they had called the Source.

Tor lifted a hand, acknowledging him. He nodded, but stayed where he was. He had not wanted to come here, had told himself he would not come. . . . But still, like a man sliding helplessly down a muddy slope, he had found himself stepping through the doorway. . . .

"Hello, Sparks." A hand took hold of his arm, drawing him around.

"Emerine," he said, only half surprised. She smiled at him, and he saw the age lines that bracketed her full-lipped mouth deepen. He hadn't looked at her closely in a long time—the changes in her face were startling; unlike the changes in his own, which had crept up on him day by day over the years. But she was still a beautiful woman, with her hair dark and long, her eyes the color of the sea. "All alone—?" she said, with gentle reprimand. "Join us, and you won't be." She drew him after her.

He followed her willingly across the room to the secluded corner where Kirard Set Wayaways and half a dozen of his other friends from the old days were sitting. He noticed without really thinking about it that Kirard Set's wife was not among them.

He sat down with them, feeling his sense of having slipped outside of time deepen as he sank under the weight of their welcoming hands, the spell of the hypnotically strobing lights and bizarre sound effects of the games that were the backdrop to their spoken greetings.

"Have some of this." Kirard Set pushed a bottle of tlaloc at him, and a cup. "A survivor of the time before, just like we are. Hard to believe, isn't it?" He gestured, filling the air with a cloud of cinnamon-scented smoke. "Seems just like old times. . . ." His smile turned rueful, and genuine. "I feel young again—reborn. Gods, I never realized how miserable I was, lost in the void, until now, when I have something to look forward to again besides my own death."

"Yes." Sparks nodded, feeling an unexpected pang of empathy as he echoed the murmured sentiments of the others around the table. He sipped the tlaloc, its bittersweetness vaporizing as it touched his tongue, filling his head, matching his mood. He sighed.

"Tor Starhiker has done all right for herself, for a common dockhand, I must say." Kirard Set raised his head again, looking away into the room. "She's made good use of the Queen's favor, and a certain native shrewdness." He rested his chin on his palm.

"What about the restaurant?" Sparks asked, leaning back in his seat.

"She's still part-owner, but she leaves the running of it to Shotwyn now. Business is better than ever, I hear; but dealing with practical matters is not Shotwyn's strong suit. He's fit to be tied." Kirard Set chuckled.

"I suppose he'll just have to find someone else to tie him up, from now on . . ." Cabber Lu Greenfield said, smirking.

Laughter spread like ripples over water around the table, until Sparks found himself unexpectedly laughing.

"Good!" Kirard Set said, his eyes shining. He reached out, squeezing Sparks's arm. "That's what I like to see. We've all missed your company, you know."

Sparks looked back at him, waiting for the usual venomous coda; surprised when it didn't come. There were only nodding heads, smiling faces all around him. "I guess I'd forgotten how much I missed the old days too," he murmured. He looked away from the too-curious scrutiny of his former friends, feeling suddenly as if he sat in a room with mirrored walls. He let his eyes wander, taking in the random stimuli of light and noise.

"Look," Emerine said, pointing. "Isn't that your son? Tammis!" she called.

Spark found Tammis's face in the crowd as the boy turned, startled at hearing his name. Tammis looked back at them, and his expression was stark with guilt. He turned away again and disappeared.

"Well, what was that all about?" Emerine murmured. "I thought your son was a happily married man, Sparks. What's he looking for here, looking so guilty, and all alone . . . ?"

Sparks frowned, his hand tightening around his cup; hearing implications inside the implications. "He's not my son." He took another sip of tlaloc, tasting only the bitterness.

"Come now," Kirard Set said gently. "That's a little harsh, isn't it? Just because he's out wandering the night with the rest of us lost souls, troubled in his marriage and looking for something he can't get at home . . ."

Sparks looked back at him in sudden anger, remembering the wedding feast, the upstairs hall. "He's not my son," he said flatly. "I have no children." He saw Ariele suddenly in his mind, the expression on her face as he had almost collided with her, outside the hidden alcove where he had caught his wife watching BZ Gundhalinu like a voyeur. The look on her face, always so much like her mother's face, told him she had heard everything that had passed between them: *Even Ariele and Tammis . . . They're his!*

"Da?" she had said, reaching out to him, catching at his sleeve. "Da—!" she had cried, as he jerked his arm free and pushed past her without a word, unable in that moment even to bear the sight of her. From that moment on he had not spoken to her or her brother again.

Kirard Set raised his eyebrows. "You mean the rumors really are true? About Moon and that offworlder—the one who's come back as Chief Justice? Is he really what's come between you and her? Is that why he supports her every whim so passionately?"

Sparks shrugged, a knotted, jerky motion. "Yes," he murmured.

"I'm sorry to hear that," Kirard Set said, as if he actually meant it. Sparks glanced at him dubiously, and wondered how many of those rumors Kirard Set had set in motion himself. "Are they actually . . . seeing each other, in secret?"

Sparks shook his head, studying his hands with sudden intentness. "No. She won't let it happen. It would compromise her position too much. But they make love to each other with their eyes, whenever they're in the same room. . . ." He shut his own eyes, but still he saw them, gazing at each other.

"My old friend," Kirard Set said, touching his arm again, "this battle was lost a long time ago, even if you only bleed from it now. Moon has not been the woman you loved, and I respected, for years. You know that. Leave her and that tightassed Kharemoughi to their sterile futility. There are layers within layers here, ways that were closed that are now open again, and will lead you to satisfactions you never dreamed of—"

Sparks met Kirard Set's gaze, as curiosity forced its way up through his darker preoccupation. "What are you talking about?"

"We are part of a . . . secret order that has members on all the worlds of the Hegemony, and an ancient lineage, independent of any government or group— including the Hegemony itself. We have our own rules, and our own goals, and our own rewards, which have the potential to surpass anything you could imagine. . . . Does this interest you?"

Sparks looked away from the sudden intensity of Kirard Set's eyes, searching the other faces around him at the table. They were all people he knew—or had thought he knew, years ago, in Winter. Then, green from Summer and longing for acceptance into their shining, sophisticated dreamworld, he would have done anything to be one of them. . . . He had done anything, whatever they asked, until finally he believed he had seen and done everything, that nothing would ever surprise or repel or humiliate him again. That he was shockproof.

He realized suddenly that he wanted to feel that way again; to feel nothing at all, except sensation. . . . "Tell me more about it," he murmured.

Kirard Set smiled. "Before we can do that, there is the matter of your initiation." Someone's hand settled on Sparks's knee beneath the table as Kirard Set spoke. Sparks jerked in surprise as the hand squeezed his thigh, slid inward along his leg. "A demonstration of your sincerity in wanting to join us," Kirard Set went on evenly, "a series of tests designed to prove your trustworthiness . . . your devotion, your receptivity, your flexibility . . . your endurance."

Another hand joined the first under the table, sliding in between his thighs, moving with brazen confidence to cup the sudden painful bulge that strained his pants. More hands roamed his hidden lower body, massaged him, caressed him, while his own hands tightened spasmodically over the table edge; but he made no move to push them away.

Kirard Set's eyes never left his face, intent and knowing. "I think you'll enjoy the challenge. I know you'll succeed admirably." He gestured toward the door. "Shall we go?"

Sparks finished his drink; his hand trembled, the tlaloc exploded his senses with bittersweetness. "I'm ready," he whispered. He pushed to his feet, the hands falling away from him, a press of bodies surrounding him now. He could feel their heat, dizzy with it, as they laid hands on him again to guide him toward the door.

TIAMAT: Ngenet Plantation

"But, boss, it's at least an hour's flight time back here from the city—"

"I said go back!" Reede gestured angrily northward along the bleak coastline. "Goddammit, the hovercraft will stand out like a flare on any surveillance. Nobody's supposed to be on these lands, not even Gundhalinu's study teams. This plantation belongs to PalaThion."

"The Chief Inspector—?" Niburu half frowned in incomprehension.

Reede nodded, his exasperation growing. "Yes, shitbrain. She inherited it from her husband. They both went native out here."

"Then what are we doing here?" Niburu stared around him at the empty, rocky shore, the green, sloping hills above them, the cold gray sky, as his incomprehension became incredulity.

"Because this is where the Source wants it done," Reede said, tasting each word like blood. He watched Niburu blanch. "Now get the fuck out of here." He shoved his pilot back toward the waiting hovercraft. "I'll call you when I want you."

Niburu climbed back into the hovercraft without further argument, but Reede saw the mixture of concern and doubt in Niburu's eyes as he sealed the doors. Reede looked away from it. He stared down at his feet, at the piled equipment, at the coarse quartz-glittering sand; stared at the ground, and his irrevocably fixed place on it, until the hovercraft had risen from the beach and was disappearing northward.

He looked up again, when he was sure that there was no one at all anywhere near him. The sound of the surf breaking against the shore seemed unreal to him, as if the sound must actually be inside his head, as if he were in a silence so complete that it was deafening. He took a deep breath, inhaling the chill sea air; held it, as he turned slowly, studying the fog-lidded hills that closed him into this two-dimensional universe on a strip of wet sand. He looked down at the sand again, on along the rocky outcroppings of the beach until the fog stopped his vision.

At last he turned to face the sea. It stretched like a taut silver curtain to the formless horizon, where it bled into the sky until they became a single entity. The Tiamatans worshipped the sea as a goddess, all-powerful, all-consuming. *"The Lady gives,"* they said, *"and the Lady takes away."* . . . He hugged his chest, telling himself that it was the wind that made him shiver as he took three stumbling steps toward the white-edged advance of the waves. "Tiamat . . ." he whispered.

He ventured farther down the shining incline. The tide was out, but turning. He forced himself to keep moving until he reached the point where the sea met the land; let the next incoming wave roll boiling and hissing up the sand toward him and break against his legs, wrapping its formless fluid arms around him like a living thing. The icy water smashed against his shins, soaking the cloth of his pantslegs.

He turned and ran back up the beach to the place where he had left his equipment, collapsed beside it on the elusive stability of the sand, gasping. His hands clenched and loosened, clenched and loosened, buried in the shifting grains. He sat huddled inside his heavy parka like a child huddled inside blankets, hearing unknown noises in the night. He watched the sea advance toward him and withdraw again, endlessly.

Eventually his breathing eased. He shook his head and got to his feet, empty-eyed, flinging away a fistful of sand with a curse. The cold, damp wind found every vulnerable gap in his heavy clothing, making his misery complete. The Motherlovers called this spring, and went out in their shirtsleeves, but he was freezing his ass off. He had to start moving; it would warm him up. The mer colony he had marked from the air as Niburu flew southward was back the way he had come a kilometer or so. He had not wanted to land any closer, and attract unwanted attention from humans or mers. He pulled on his equipment pack, slung the heavy-gauge stun rifle over his shoulder, and began to trudge north.

He had been on Tiamat for over three months now, and this was the first time he had been out of the city. He had been sent to Tiamat as soon as it had become feasible, just as the Source had promised him he would be, to begin his work on decoding and recreating the technovirus they called the water of life. TerFauw, the Newhavener who had branded him as property, had come with him, his overseer, relaying the Source's wants to him, rewarding him with access to the water of death each night, for having survived another day. Niburu and Ananke were still with him; they had been allowed to stay together, although he was not certain why.

He had been disturbed, but not really surprised, to find Gundhalinu here before him. Somehow, when he thought about it, it had seemed inevitable that they would meet again. But BZ Gundhalinu was the head of the Hegemonic government this time; and Reede Kullervo was a slave. He considered the irony of that, letting it gnaw at his guts like worms as he walked along the shore. Even though he walked like a free man in Carbuncle's streets, the unsleeping eye that looked up at him every time he opened his hand reminded him a hundred times a day that he had lost all control over his own life.

He had not been surprised to find that Gundhalinu was conducting his own investigation of the water of life, using studies and data given to him by Tiamat's Queen, who was said to be some kind of fanatic on the subject of the mers. The Queen had forbidden all killing of mers, even for research, and so the Hegemony must be desperate to get the water of life some other way. They must be looking for a way to synthesize it, if that was possible, just like he was . . . and Gundhalinu knew more about smartmatter than anyone alive, except himself. He had taught Gundhalinu well, and then he had let him live, to make use of what he knew. . . . It should have been the worst mistake he had ever made.

But Gundhalinu wasn't just here to do research, this time. He was trying to run a world. He had been forced to delegate his responsibilities—he was no longer Head of Research. And so Reede had made use of the data Gundhalinu had unsuspectingly begun collecting for him again; secretly this time, using the Brotherhood's hidden hands to help him gain access to it.

He could not approach Gundhalinu directly . . . could not afford even to let the new Hegemonic Chief Justice of Tiamat know he was within light-years of this world. But still, some perverse part of him had been drawn as if by a compulsion to seek Gundhalinu out: watching him, hinting to him, leaving him clues. Playing a treacherous game of tag with the Golden Mean and the Brotherhood—further proof, to himself and anyone who caught him at it, that he was thoroughly and completely insane. He felt inside his clothing as he walked for the chain he still wore around his neck, for the pendant mated with a ring that lay warm and protected against his heart.

To begin his own work, he had used the data he had siphoned away from the Hegemony's researchers. But much of the data had seemed either unfocused or completely meaningless. There were endless linguistic analyses and theoretical studies of mersong, details of mer lore, woven through the braid of information—things which he should simply have discarded as useless. And yet he had found himself lost in a kind of rapture whenever he listened to the recordings of their songs, filled with joy and melancholy and bitter grief in turn, caught up in a pattern of stimulus–response he had no control over, or understanding of.

He had pored over every bit of the data until he knew everything that anyone on this world knew about the mers; until they haunted his dreams with their singing. . . . And all along, some part of his shattered mind had kept screaming at him that he already knew more than anyone living, not simply about the technovirus that made the mers what they were, but about the mers themselves; if he could only remember . . . *only remember, only* . . .

He blinked himself out of his waking dreams, finding himself still alone with the sea, trudging along the endless narrow strand, the knife-edge between the water and the land. He listened to the roar and hush of the waves, the skreeling of birds, the absence of any other human sound. Ahead of him now a sudden wall of stone loomed out of the fog: an old rockslide that had tumbled down onto the shore long ago, forming natural breakwaters, shielding the crescent of beach between its arms. The colony of mers he had come to find had made its home there. The fall of rocks reached out into the sea; he would either have to wade around it, or climb over it. He knew, resigned, which it would be. He looked down again, watching the endless progression of sand and seawrack pass beneath his feet.

He had played with the data about the mers, making no real headway but finding plenty of excuses to postpone the inevitable—the day when he would find himself here, cast out of Carbuncle's shellform womb, sent to hunt down the mers and kill one for its blood.

He knew that it had to be done; no analysis of the technovirus could be successful without studying an actual blood sample. He was surprised that there had not been one blood sample among all the data he had gotten from Gundhalinu's work. Even if the Queen's ban on killing mers extended to researchers, there must be some way that they could get blood from a live one. From the accounts he had read, a mer colony would come to the aid of any mer that was under attack, or in some kind of distress. That was why the hunters had always simply killed them, and drained their blood. It was easier, more efficient that way; and they'd always counted on the mers repopulating during the century they were gone.

But there must be some way, with the resources Gundhalinu had available to him, to pick a single mer out of the herd, stun it, and get a blood sample. He wondered again why it hadn't been done. The oversight was so obvious, it was almost as if Gundhalinu was intentionally stalling the research—or looking for something else. . . .

Reede considered the pseudo-linguistic gibberish of the mersong again. There *were* flawed but meaningful patterns there; he didn't have to be told that by the studies, he felt it in his gut. *And their meaning was important*— Something helpless and hopeless rattled its cage inside his brain, and he swore. "Not to me!" he shouted furiously. The wall of rock flung his words back at him, and the fog swallowed them up.

Maybe Gundhalinu was only stalling the research because he was afraid that reintroducing a smartmatter drug into human society on a large scale would do to the Hegemony what it had done to the Old Empire. Gundhalinu always worried too much about the big picture—as if he could control anything, anyway. If he didn't do this, someone else would; there was always someone who would, and damn the consequences. That was Gundhalinu's flaw, it muted his natural instincts; he didn't trust even himself enough. Reede remembered the look of exhilaration and release that filled Gundhalinu's eyes sometimes when they had worked together . . . the look that had always been one step away from terror. But he had never stepped over the edge, and with Reede forcing him to face his own potential, he had never stepped back, either. And together they had made a miracle happen once, against the odds. . . .

He stopped abruptly, as the black wall of volcanic rock rose in front of him, blocking his way. He moved forward to it, putting out his hands until they touched it; feeling it support him, feeling the rasp-sharp, porous surfaces scrape his flesh as they stopped his forward motion. He could not turn back, he could not go around it—he could only go over it, flaying himself against its inevitability.

He began to climb, because there was nothing else that he could do, picking his way from broken surface to broken surface, pulling himself upward heedlessly, mindlessly, with bleeding hands; scrambling, leaping, letting his perfect reflexes carry him instinctively to safety from one jagged ledge to the next. Somewhere above him water geysered upward, exploding through a natural funnel in the rocks, showering down on him. Far below he glimpsed shadowy motion as the sea insinuated its way beneath the seeming solidity of the stones, relentlessly undermining their stability; waiting for him to make one misstep. . . . He felt the stone beneath his feet begin to shift under his weight; he leaped again, scrambled up another steep, angled surface, breathing hard.

He had reached the crest of the rockfall. He raised his head, stabilizing his balance as he looked out across an unobstructed view, and saw them at last, waiting for him. *The mers* . . .

He watched them moving below him, dozens of them; heard their voices dimly through the voice of the sea. He made a sound that was half laughter, half incredulity, as a nameless, sourceless joy filled the emptiness in his mind and soul. "I know you . . ." he whispered, "I know you. You're mine."

He swore and shook his head, frightened by the incomprehensible words. The wild, profound joy he felt was crushed beneath sudden despair as he reached back over his shoulder, reaching for his gun. Knowing what he was about to do, he knew suddenly that he was committing an obscene crime, the ultimate act of self-denial and perversion that would damn him forever. . . . But he did not know why, didn't even know how he knew it.

He had been sent here by the Source to get answers. He had been sent here by the Source to kill a mer, and bring back its blood for study. If he failed, if he resisted, he knew what his punishment would be. Desolation filled him, and hopeless grief, as if he were about to murder one of his own children. The sound of the sea was like the black laughter of the gods, and he knew that he was the butt of their joke.

"They're fucking animals, damn it!" His own blinding, animal fury rose up in him, consuming the fear, the grief . . . the other fury that would have stopped him from what he was about to do. He had been ordered to kill, and he would. All he needed to let him do it was to see in his mind's eye that faceless, soul-eating mound of corruption who had sent him here. And then he wanted to kill something, anything; needed to, had to—

He began to work his way down the far side of the rockfall, moving single-mindedly now; taking care not to make his movements sudden, or do anything that would attract the attention of the mers before he could get within range. He had to be close enough to kill one with his first shot, because he had no way of knowing how they would react when he started shooting. He would kill one, and if the others didn't flee, he had come equipped with the kind of sonic scramblers the mer hunters had always used, to drive them into the sea in a blind panic and leave him alone with the corpse.

He was close enough now to make out the colors of their fur clearly, the brindled brown backs, the V of golden fur on the chests of the females. Their heads nodded gently on long, slender necks; their eyes were filled with peace. Their flipper-footed movement on land was hardly graceful, but its pragmatism and dignity struck him as oddly poignant. *He had done well, he had made them strong. He had made them—*

He swore again, unslinging his gun; forcing himself not to see the vulnerability of the unsuspecting creatures below—to see only the formless shape of his rage. He pushed to his feet, balancing on the canted surface of the rock, raising the rifle. He took aim, letting his gunsight range randomly over the herd; let it lock in on a single mer chosen by chance. He took a breath, held it, trying to make himself fire.

Wave-driven water exploded through the blowhole on his right, showering down on him. Drenched and blinded by icy spray, he felt his feet go out from under him on the wet ledge. He dropped his gun, heard it clatter down through the rocks as he scrambled frantically for a handhold. He caught a lip of stone behind him, felt his arms wrench as they took the full weight of his body. And then he felt his fingers lose their grip on the algae-slick surface, letting him fall free, following his gun down into the throat of stone.

He cried out as he fell; cried out again as his fall abruptly stopped. He shook his head in stunned disbelief; tasted blood from his bitten tongue. As his eyes cleared he saw black stone in front of his face . . . black stone all around him, like the shaft of a well. Far above was a slit of blue, all he could see of the sky. Blocking his sight were his own upflung hands, flailing like insect wings. Pain screamed along the length of his left arm, down his side, up through his jaw as he tried, futilely, to pull them down. He was wedged like a bug between pincers of rock. His feet were not touching a solid surface; his legs were not free to kick or even move more than a few inches. They were numb. . . . He looked down, straining to see past the angles of the rock, and found the restless gleam of light reflected on water. A wave rolled into his prison, breaking against his hip, chilling him to the bone a few centimeters farther up his body. He was nearly waist-deep in water . . . and the tide was coming in.

He lost control as the realization took him; as if he had fallen into a sea of acid, and it had already begun to eat the flesh off of his bones. His panic-stricken struggles wrenched his arm until pain blinded him, and only drove him deeper into the water. Terror rose in his throat; he swallowed it down, fighting himself for the right to stay sane. There was a remote in his backpack; he could call for help, if he could only get to it. Niburu would come for him, pull him out of here, save him. There was still plenty of time, if he could only reach his pack—

He tried again to shift position, moving cautiously this time, groping along the slippery, unyielding walls for leverage, for a hold that was never there; punished by pain every time his desperation grew and he struggled too hard. He tried for a foothold, somewhere in the cold, surging water below, but there was no foothold to be found.

He went on trying, for an hour, two, three, mindlessly; refusing to accept what a part of him had known from the beginning: that it was impossible. The digits changed on the watch strapped to his right wrist, more accessible and more clearly visible to him than anything else in the universe. Marking time . . . his time, running out. His entire body was trembling convulsively, but it seemed to have lost all sensation; even his battered, aching hands had grown numb with cold and restricted circulation. Only his mind was still clear, still registering every excruciating, humiliating second of his last moments of life. He could not get to his remote, and even if he could, there wasn't enough time left now for Niburu to get here before he drowned. The cold, inexorable sea was lapping against his throat.

He groaned softly; his helpless hands made fists in the air above his head. Another sea swell rolled into his prison; for a moment water lapped his chin. Something gray-green and tentacled clung to his parka, groped his face with a pink, pulsing extrusion from its body, before it slid off him again. He shut his eyes, feeling his mouth begin to tremble. . . . Feeling something jar his dangling foot, jar it again. He swore and struggled, panicking, until pain shocked him into immobility.

Something broke the water surface beside him. He jerked his head around, breathing in ragged gasps—found the dark, impenetrable eyes of a mer staring back at him. He cried out again, in surprise, and the mer cocked its head. It pushed its face toward him, snuffling at his exposed flesh, nudging him curiously.

"No—!" He swung his own head, hitting it in the face, his feet flailing under the water. "Get away from me! Goddamn you, don't touch me, don't touch me!"

The mer jerked back, startled, and disappeared under the water surface. He felt it jar his legs once more, hard; and then nothing.

Alone again, he felt the sea swell kiss his chin with cold hunger, as if he were Death's chosen lover, and Death was growing impatient. . . . He felt the stunning heat of his own tears spill out and down his face; tasted them as they ran into his mouth, salt water like the sea. He went on weeping, as the sea reached up to wash away his tears.

"Hello—"

The sound spiraled down to him, echoing from the walls of rock, some freakish turn on the crying of sea birds, or the distant voices of the mers. But he raised his face toward the sky far above him, gaping into the light. Another wave washed over his head, catching him unawares; he inhaled water, choking and coughing.

". . . help you . . ."

This time he was sure he had heard it: a high, clear voice, speaking Tiamatan. He shook his eyes clear, and now he could see what seemed to be a woman's form, surreally limned with light, peering down at him from above. She seemed to be made of light, impossibly shining. The Tiamatans called the sea a goddess, the Mother, *the Lady, who gives and who takes away.* . . . "Help me," he gasped, echoing her, in Trade, and then in Tiamatan. "Please help me. I'm sorry. Forgive me. Save me. . . ."

"I'm coming down," she called. "I'm coming—" The radiant vision of a woman's form took on sudden substantiality as she moved, blocking and unblocking the passage of light. He watched her bare feet, the strong muscles, the paleness of her legs, as she eased herself deftly down between the precarious walls of the cleft until she was kneeling on a shelf of rock just above his head, with the cold stone pressing her rainbow-lit shoulders. Her hair was silver, splintering light, as she leaned toward him, reaching out.

Another wave broke over his head, drenching him, filling his eyes and his mouth with water; he gagged and spat.

Her hands closed over his, he felt the contact of her flesh warm and firm against his own cold-deadened fingers. "It's all right," she said, and he became aware that he was sobbing again. "It's all right, I'll get you out. . . ." She reached down, one hand touched his face briefly.

"I'm stuck," he said; his voice sounded like a stranger's in his ears. "I'm stuck. I can't move—"

"If I take your hands, if I can pull you up, maybe you can reach the ledge." She had hold of both his hands again; he clenched his teeth against the coming pain as he felt his arms stretch taut, as she slowly climbed to her feet on the narrow ledge. She straightened, pulling harder, and he screamed as the agony in his shoulder suddenly became unbearable.

She dropped to her knees, releasing the pressure, still holding his hands. "You're hurt—?"

He clung to her, his own grip tightening spasmodically. "I can't do it. . . ." He spat water, coughing, sucked in a long, deep breath of air that reeked of the sea. "Need . . . need a rope. In my backpack—"

He felt her shift, searching, reaching past his shoulder. "I can't reach your backpack!"

"Oh, gods . . ." he moaned, not even sure what language he was speaking. "Not like this . . ."

"We'll get you out," she said fiercely. "We will! Silky—!" she called out, following the words with a series of strange trills and clicks.

The sounds were incomprehensible to him—and yet something stirred inside him, profoundly eager, ready to answer— He opened his eyes, only realizing then that he had closed them. He turned his head, following her gaze; jerked in startled surprise as he found the mer's face beside him again in the pool. "No!" he cried. "No—"

"Let her help you!" the woman said, pulling him back with her voice. "We're here to help you. Let us—!"

He looked up at her again, his eyes burning.

"You're wedged in. She's going to push you up from below, if she can. You understand? Hold on, be ready—"

He nodded, as the mer disappeared below the water surface. He felt something moving, beneath his feet, the mer butting experimentally at his legs, as it had before. Grimacing, he forced his legs to stay still, held his numb limbs rigid against the overwhelming need to fight off the contact. The mer's body collided with his own, harder; jarring him from below. He cursed as the shock rattled his teeth, rattled all through his aching body. But he realized that he had felt something move—felt his body move, against the rocks.

The mer butted him again; its back heaved upward under his feet. Ready for it, this time, he stiffened his legs against the blow, giving it extra force, just as another swell came rolling into the cleft. He felt his body grate, slip against the rocks, and rise, suddenly buoyant, suddenly free.

He shouted in elation. The woman scrambled to drag him onto the ledge where she was crouching as the mer heaved him upward, ignominiously, from below.

He lay on the ledge taking long, shuddering breaths; feeling the solidness of stone supporting him now, safely above the level of the water, and no longer holding him in a deathgrip. He clung to it, his mind a singing emptiness, oblivious to the pain in his body, even to the woman who had saved him. She searched in his pack for the length of line, tied it around his waist, tied the other end around her own. At last, getting carefully to her feet, she helped him pull himself up until he was kneeling beside her. "Do you think you can climb? I can call for a rescue—"

He looked up, studying the steep, erratic walls of the cleft, and down again, tight-lipped. "I can make it," he said. "You lead."

She nodded, glancing at him for a moment as if she was uncertain; but she turned back to the rock face and began to climb up it. He watched where and how she chose every handhold, every foothold. As the slack began to disappear from the line between them, he pushed to his feet, swaying. Sudden dizziness took him, and he rested for a moment against the wall of rock, steadying himself. And then, grimly, he began to climb.

His body did not betray him. Bruised and stiff and trembling with cold, it made the climb, compensating with balance and skill for the one arm that he could barely use. For once in his life, he was grateful to the water of death.

They reached the top of the crevice at last. He laughed once, in triumph, in amazement at the beauty of the day, standing now in the spot where he had stood before, and known nothing but the need to kill.

The woman had already begun to make her way on down the rock slope toward the beach. He hesitated; felt the rope pull taut around his waist. Too spent to resist, he followed her down.

She stood waiting for him on the dark gravel among the mers, the waves breaking like glass around her; bare-legged, with foam swirling over her ankles like lace skirts billowed by the wind. He sagged against a boulder as exhaustion hit him; unspeakably glad to be on solid ground again. The mers lay on the beach around him, regarding him without concern or apparent curiosity. But the woman was staring at him now, her intentness making up for their lack of interest.

He stayed well away from the waterline, and as far from the mers as the rope would let him, gazing back at her. She was very young, he realized; not much more than a girl. He felt an odd surprise, realizing that he had barely gotten past believing that she was not the Goddess. At least, now that he saw her clearly, she was not actually haloed in silver, and casting off rainbows. It was only that her hair was so pale it was almost white; she had the exotic coloring he sometimes saw among the locals, blindingly fair, beautiful in a way that was unnerving to him. Her imported wetsuit had a vaguely opalescent sheen, giving off faint echoes of color when the sunlight struck it. He realized that the sun was out now, wearing a corona of rainbow behind the burnished haze of the sky.

He looked down at the rope around his waist, still binding him to her like an umbilical; looked up at her mutely, hearing the mers around him, hearing the song of the sea. He put his hands on the line, holding it but making no move to untie it.

"What are you doing here?" she asked, when he did not speak—asking him the question he could not force himself to ask her.

He hesitated. "I'm, uh . . . a researcher."

"You came to study the mers?"

"Yes," he said finally, his fatigue-deadened mind refusing to come up with a better answer.

"For the Hegemony?" She half frowned.

Something in her expression and the tone of her voice told him to answer, "No."

"For my mother, then?"

"Who's your mother?"

She looked at him oddly. "The Queen."

The Summer Queen. Gods— He bit his tongue. "You're her daughter?" he repeated, hearing his own incredulity. He remembered hearing that the Queen had a daughter. But he had heard that she was a sullen, spoiled brat.

"She's my mother. I suppose that makes me her daughter." The girl began to move toward him. "I'm Ariele Dawntreader." She stopped in front of him, gazing up into his face with disconcerting fascination. He stared back at her, trying to decide what color her eyes really were. "Are you all right?" she asked, and he felt her hand touch his aching shoulder.

He winced. Her hand fell away, although it had not been pain, but only memory that had hurt him then. He glanced down, avoiding her eyes as he remembered how she had found him, helplessly drowning in his own stupidity and crying like a baby. Looking away, he saw a mer nearby that seemed to watch him with an interest the others did not show. He remembered the one that had found him in the cleft. He wondered if this was the same one. He couldn't tell; they all looked alike.

"I know you . . ." Ariele Dawntreader murmured suddenly. "Don't I?"

He looked back at her. "No," he said hoarsely, even as his eyes searched her face, looking for some feature he recognized.

"You were at Starhiker's the night it opened. You helped me win at Starfall. . . ." A strange look came into her agate-colored eyes. She moved a little closer.

"I don't remember you," he said bluntly, telling the truth. He put his own hand up to his aching shoulder.

Her gaze flickered down, broken by his stubborn lack of response. "You're not Tiamatan," she said, changing the subject with reluctant resignation. "Where do you come from?"

"Offworld."

She looked up at him, raising her eyebrows. "Don't you have a home?"

"I've lived a lot of places," he said. He shrugged, and was sorry he had.

She stared at him, unblinking.

"What are you doing here?" he asked, finally. Emphasis on the *you*.

"Studying the mers too. We've been working on communicating with them since long before you arrived." Pride mixed with challenge in her voice.

"I know," he said. He wanted to ask her why in the name of the Render communicating with the mers was such a high priority for the Summer Queen, when doing blood research on them was on her forbidden list. He didn't ask, afraid that he was expected to know that too. Maybe it was all a part of the mystical religious bullshit she was supposed to be obsessed with.

He glanced at her daughter again, standing in front of him, bare-legged and stringy-haired, looking all of fifteen. In her resolute, perfect innocence she seemed to belong here, to this place, like the mers, the stones, the sea. He had a sudden, strobing memory of her in a silver-spangled bodysuit, appearing in front of him like an hallucination in the eerie, shifting shadowplay of a gaming hell; of her pressing her body against his, and his own body unexpectedly responding. . . . He shook his head, and she looked at him in confusion, as if she thought he meant something by it. She seemed to him all at once to be as unfathomable as the creatures gathered around her . . . like most Tiamatans did; like most human begins did.

He rubbed his face with cold-whitened fingers. "You spoke to that mer, down in the hole, when I was trapped . . . or did I imagine that?" He realized that he had not thanked her for rescuing him. He did not thank her.

She turned away from him, calling out, "Silky!" A series of the same trills and clucks he remembered followed it out of her mouth, as naturally as human speech.

The mer he had imagined had been staring at him swiveled its head at the sound, and began to waddle toward them across the beach. It was a young one, he realized, smaller than the adults, and female, from the golden V on its chest. He watched it come, pulling at his ear, part of him suddenly trembling, wanting to bolt from its alienness. And yet his hands ached with the need to feel its heavy, brindle fur, knowing somehow exactly the depth and incredible softness of its silken undercoat. . . . "You own this mer?" he asked.

She looked at him as if he had suggested something obscene. "No one owns the mers. She's a—friend. Aunt Jerusha—Commander PalaThion—raised her, she was orphaned. . . . This is Silky." Ariele held out her hand, indicating the mer, and made more merspeech. The mer whistled back at her, and sneezed abruptly. Ariele laughed, and put her arms around the slender neck as the mer butted her gently. "She says, 'And what is *your* name?'"

"No, she didn't," Reede said. He came forward, and the mer's head moved toward his outstretched hand. As he touched its body, he felt his own lips and tongue come alive and make the same kind of alien speech, in answer to it.

Ariele Dawntreader gaped at him. "You really do know their language," she said, almost in disbelief.

He broke her gaze almost desperately, because he had no idea what he had just said, why he had known how to shape the words, why he had needed to make contact with the mer, feel that strange, cloud-soft fur against his skin. . . .

He sank to his knees in the sand, not even sure if the motion had been voluntary, or if his half-frozen body had simply given way; not caring. The mer pulled free from Ariele Dawntreader's grasp to explore him with its face, snuffling, lipping, butting him, making murmurous conversation all the while. He shut his eyes, letting his mind go, and heard his own voice answer, like someone speaking in tongues.

How long their communion went on he did not know, because time as he knew it ended and began in that moment, and contained eternity. He only knew, when the merling left him at last, turning its back on him to make its ungainly way toward its own kind again, that for that single moment he was real. . . . And that inside his wasteland of violence and pain he rejoiced in his captivity, because it had given him this moment in which the circle was completed, in which he was made whole, one with his dream of the future . . .

"You really understand," Ariele was saying, over and over, or maybe it was simply an echo in his nerve circuits. "You really understand them . . . you can teach us. . . ."

He shook his head, unable to form a single word of human speech; unable to tell her the truth, even if he could have spoken. He tried to get to his feet, needing to get away—from her, from here, from himself, before he lost control completely.

He fell back again onto the sand, sat among the pebbles in a kind of stupefied disbelief as his body refused to respond. Ariele kneeled down beside him, still speaking although he could not understand anything she said now. She began to pull at him, trying to force him up again.

Unwilling, but suddenly without any will of his own, he did what she wanted him to do, and this time he succeeded in standing. She went on asking him questions, and slowly he began to comprehend what she said.

". . . get here? Where is your boat? Your boat—?" she repeated, her face filled with concern.

"I don't have one," he muttered, finding his voice again in a forgotten coat pocket of his mind. "No boat."

She looked uncomprehending, now. "How did you get here?"

"I walked. . . ." He felt her body close against his, half supporting him; remembered the gaming tables and the sudden, unexpected, undesired hunger of his unruly body for the feel of a woman's flesh against his own. . . .

"From Carbuncle?" she said, in disbelief.

"No." He frowned. "Down the beach. Flew in." He looked over his shoulder. "I sent it away."

"Then I'll take you back to the city in my boat. Come on. You can't stay here longer; you're freezing to death, and your shoulder needs treatment." She pointed on along the shore, tried to lead him after her in that direction.

"No," he murmured. "I'll call my own pilot." He let his backpack slip from his shoulder, wincing; fumbled for the remote among its sodden contents. He pulled the remote out at last, dripping; called it on, and got no response. He shook it, and drops flew; but it stayed silent, dead. He dropped it, kicked it away. Still looking down, he saw the rope knotted around his waist; he jerked at it in sudden fury, as if it had become the cause of all his confusion and humiliation, or its symbol. Even his fingers would not obey him; he seemed to be inhabiting a space where he did not function in realtime. He swore in frustration, seeing the other end of the rope attached to Ariele Dawntreader's body.

Calmly, she gathered up the length of cord that lay trampled in the sand between them, looping it over her hand, until she had left him no slack. "It could take days before anyone comes back to look for you. You'll be sick or dead from exposure by then. Come on . . ." she said gently. "I have dry clothes on the boat, and some wine. Come with me—" Her fingers slid under the rope around his waist, tugging slightly; but she only untied the knot, with deft fingers, setting him free—as if he had some choice—before she untied the rope around her own waist. "Let me take you back to the city. We can talk about the mers, on the way. . . ."

"All right," he mumbled, feeling a strange fatalism creep over him. He let her arm circle his waist, to lend him support as she guided him on up the beach toward the boat waiting with furled sails in the distance. "Yes," he said, and he knew somehow that his voice was not his own. "I need to talk . . . about the mers."

TIAMAT: Carbuncle

". . . And get another keg of the kelp beer while you're back there, and hook that up too, all right, Pollux?" Tor Starhiker paused, turning away from the bar to look expectantly at the shining, semi-human body, the faceless face of her newly leased servo.

It nodded, the twin red lights of its visual sensors meeting her eyes with an unreadable stare. "Yes, Tor," it said.

She sighed, indefinably disappointed. "You do know how to do that?"

"I do."

"Then go do it." She waved her hand and it started away, emotionless and inevitable. She watched it disappear through the doors into the storage area. "Shit," she said, and sighed again.

"What's the matter?" a voice asked behind her. She turned back to the bar, only mildly surprised to discover who it was that had spoken to her. He'd been a sometime regular since the beginning, and in here almost nightly for the past couple of weeks. He was from offworld; he had some foreign-sounding name she kept forgetting, although lately he had sat at the bar and talked to her every night. *Niburu,* that was it. *Kedalion Niburu. "Call me Kedalion,"* he'd said.

She shrugged, and pulled an elusive strap back onto her bare shoulder. "It's not the same," she said, glancing toward the doorway the servo had disappeared through. "I had one of those before the Departure. But this one's not the same. It looks the same. It even has the same name. I thought it might be the same one. I thought . . . this probably sounds stupid, but I thought maybe it would remember me. We got . . . we got real attached to each other. It had a lot of personality, for a machine."

Niburu laughed, but it wasn't unkind laughter. "How can you tell that it doesn't remember you?"

She leaned on the bar, watching his blue eyes crinkle at the corner with his smile. He had a nice smile, and when he was sitting at the bar it was easy to forget how short he was. She wasn't tall herself, but he didn't clear her shoulder. The first time she'd seen him in the club, she'd thought he was a child, and almost had him thrown out. "The usual?" she asked.

He nodded. "And one for my friend—" He gestured over his shoulder; she saw the young Ondinean who usually came in with him standing at one of the gaming tables.

She poured out drinks, and pushed them toward him. The servo came back from the rear of the club, carrying an assortment of full kegs and containers as easily as if they were empty. She watched it begin to hook them up to the dispensers. "I know it's not the one because it doesn't get the joke."

"What joke?" Niburu asked.

"The one I used to work with could do anything . . . gods, he—it, I mean, it was incredible. I used to let it pick out my clothes. But all it ever said, for years, no matter what I did to it, was 'Whatever you say, Tor.' It was making a joke; it was our little personal joke. . . . I only knew that for sure when it was leaving, and it finally admitted it."

"I've heard they get like that." Niburu sipped his drink. "I've never spent time around one, but I hear their programming's so interactive they begin to evolve personalities of their own. That's why they get overhauled and reprogrammed at the end of every contract, and have to start all over from zero."

She felt her face pinch. "I know. He . . . it didn't want to go. It didn't want to forget. I think it was afraid, of disappearing. . . . But that's impossible, isn't it? That it could feel anything like that?"

He shrugged. "Yeah. I would think so. It's only a machine, after all. The Kharemoughis like things that don't talk back."

"Well anyway, when I saw they had this model available, I thought . . . well, maybe what if it did remember? If it wanted to come back." Her mouth pressed together.

He studied her for a long moment, with what looked like genuine understanding. He looked down again, at his drink. "It's probably not even the same one, you know. The Pollux units make up a whole line of heavy-work servos, with several specialty modes."

"I know that," she said, a little shortly. "I used to work on the docks. But it was the same one . . . the same model, anyway. Only it doesn't remember anything. I sure as hell wouldn't let it dress me. It's just a machine." The servo came up to her, stood motionless, waiting for further orders. "Mix drinks," she said, gesturing at the patrons who had begun to line up along the bar while she had been talking. It did what she told it to, without comment.

"You just got it?" Niburu asked, watching.

She nodded. "Picked it up yesterday."

"Well," he smiled, "give yourself some time to get acquainted. Give it some time, too. You only just met."

She looked at him, and felt her own mouth curve upward in a reluctant grin. "Maybe you've got a point. I will."

The Ondinean, whose name seemed to be Ananke, came up to the bar beside Niburu, and picked up the other drink.

"Here," Tor said, pushing a bowl of toasted seeds across at him. "For the quoll."

"Thanks." He nodded at her, with a shy grin. He rarely said more than two or three words to her, but he seemed like an all right sort, and she liked his pet. He lifted the quoll out of its sling and set it on the bar. It buried its nose in the seed dish, making chortling noises as it began to eat. The Ondinean helped himself to a handful of seeds, chewing contentedly.

Tor stroked the quoll's back, and it purred more loudly. She'd had a few complaints from customers who didn't like sharing a drink with something hairy; but this was her place, and she didn't care. There were other gaming hells on the Street now, and always plenty of other customers. "Where's the Mystery Man tonight?" Usually Niburu and Ananke came in with another offworlder named Kullervo. She knew they worked for him; and she knew who he worked for. She'd seen the brand they all wore on their palms often enough, seen it all the time, back before the Departure, when she had run Persiponë's Hell for the Source. The sight of the brand had almost made her sick, the first time she'd seen it on somebody again, here in her new place. But she'd realized that just because they'd come into her club, it didn't mean the Source had any interest in her anymore—didn't even mean he was actually here at all, in the flesh. Things were different now, the Source couldn't use a Tiamatan to shield his business from the law; because the law had changed with everything else.

She didn't know what Kullervo did for the Source here on Tiamat; she didn't care, as long as he didn't do it to her. Just because any of them worked for a criminal didn't mean she had anything against them personally. She'd almost married a man once who worked for the Source.

All she'd ever seen Kullervo do was win at her tables—and win and win, at almost anything he chose to play, when he bothered to play. She would have minded that, except that he didn't play much, and he gave all his table credit to his two men, who invariably lost it all again. And it gave her other customers a thrill.

"He said he'd meet us here." Niburu shrugged, and smiled a little. "Why? You miss him?"

Tor laughed. "Not me. Ariele Dawntreader's been asking."

"There he is now." Ananke poked a thumb over his shoulder.

Tor followed his motion, and saw Kullervo making his way in their direction through the surreal patterns of light and darkness. Tor's eyes stayed on him a moment longer than she wanted them to, as they always did—partly because she liked to look at his face, and partly because he always unnerved her. There was something about his eyes that wasn't entirely sane. Seeing him always sent an irrational frisson of terror and pity through her, even though he had never so much as raised his voice to her. His strangeness, more than anything he'd actually ever done, was why she thought of him as the Mystery Man.

She glanced away toward the table where Ariele Dawntreader was sitting with some of her friends, to see if the girl had noticed him coming in. She'd noticed, all right. She was on her feet already, about to intersect Kullervo's course. Tor saw Elco Teel Graymount get to his feet beside her, catching her arm, saying something into her ear that she didn't seem to like much. She shrugged him off, frowning, and came on across the crowded, noisy room. She caught up with Kullervo just before he reached the bar, and spoke his name.

Tor saw the look on her face as he stopped and turned toward her—the brightness of her eyes, the flush of her cheeks; saw the breathless anticipation singing through every millimeter of her body. Tor had never seen Ariele look that alive, not since she was a child. She knew what that look meant: Ariele was in love. She wondered if it was the mystery Ariele was infatuated with . . . that wildness, the danger she had sensed in the man. Tor sighed. She hoped not. Maybe it was just his face. Thirty years ago, a face like that would have been enough to turn her own senses inside out. She wondered whether the Queen knew about this.

She couldn't see Kullervo's expression as he and Ariele talked together; his back was turned. But she knew that lately he had been in here almost every night, and so had Ariele . . . and that almost every night they had ended up in one of her private rooms. Kullervo nodded once, and they started away together. But Tor noticed, surprised, that he didn't touch the girl, and Ariele didn't touch him, even once, before she lost sight of them.

She looked at Niburu and Ananke again, as they turned back from watching the same scene. She saw Niburu meet Ananke's stare and shrug, shaking his head. "Go figure," he muttered.

Tor leaned on the bar. "Listen," she said, "is she safe with him?"

"Safe?" Niburu repeated blankly.

"She's the Queen's daughter. And more than that, I've known her since she was a baby. She matters a lot to me. I don't know anything about your boss, except I've seen his tattoos. . . ." *And I've seen his eyes.*

Niburu nodded. "The tattoos aren't what you think." He hesitated. "And neither is Reede. She's safe with him. He's not like that . . . like what you mean. In fact—" he turned to Ananke, "you know, he's been in kind of a good mood lately."

"Yeah," Ananke said ruefully. "He hasn't called me a dumb shit in days." He slurped his drink, and reached for another handful of seeds. The quoll nipped at him, muttering irritably. "Sorry," he murmured.

"I've never seen Ariele look at anybody like that, before. The gods only know what the Queen's going to think if she finds out her daughter's getting personal with one of the Source's brands."

Niburu started visibly as she spoke the name. But he said, "Reede's not just some thug," sounding defensive.

"Oh? What is he then?"

Niburu frowned, but she could have sworn there was uncertainty in his eyes. "He's a biochemist. He's Jaakola's Head of Research."

She put her hands on her hips. "And I'm the Summer Queen. Come on, shorty, I know what that eye burned into his palm means. The Source doesn't brand his chiefs."

Niburu opened his mouth to answer her, but Ananke put a hand on his arm, with an urgent grimace. Niburu let his breath out in a sigh, and muttered, "Have it your way, Tor." He shrugged and finished his drink in one swallow, wiping his mouth. A branded hireling of some underworld cartel wasn't much better than a slave. She supposed her comments about Kullervo had hurt Niburu's pride by association; he probably wanted her to think his boss was something better because that made him something better too. "The Queen doesn't have to lose sleep over Reede, anyway. Because he's not sleeping with her daughter."

Tor stared at him. "Then what the hell are they doing in one of my private rooms almost every night?"

Niburu shrugged. "He says they talk."

Tor made a rude noise.

"He says they talk about the mers. They share an interest. That's all."

"You believe that," she said. Not a question.

He nodded. "She isn't his type. His wife was Ondinean."

"Wife?" she asked. "Was?" Thinking that Reede Kullervo hardly looked old enough for that much history.

"She died . . . in an accident." He looked down. "Since then I've only seen him with Ondinean women. Even here. And never with the same one twice."

Tor felt herself frown again; with concern this time, because the longing look she had seen in Ariele's eyes had nothing to do with a need for stimulating discussion. "Well," she said at last, "I don't know if that's good news, or bad news. . . . But all I can say is, much as I care about that girl, I never thought of her as a spellbinding conversationalist."

"It is kind of unusual, Kedalion," Ananke said, glancing away into the room. "We've been in here practically every night for a couple of weeks straight, now. He's never done anything like that before."

"That's true. . . ." Niburu nodded thoughtfully.

Ananke picked up the quoll, which had surfeited itself on seeds and begun to wander beyond reach. He tucked it back into the sling at his side. "You want to play the tables?"

"In a while." Niburu waved a hand at the action. "You go ahead; I want to finish my drink."

Tor glanced at his glass, which was empty. She saw Ananke glance at it too; a smile twitched the corners of his mouth as he looked up at her. He shrugged and started away, losing himself in the crowd.

Tor looked back at Niburu, and caught him looking down her cleavage. She straightened up, with a wry smile pulling at her own mouth, and casually ran her hands down the silken curves of her gown. Niburu raised his eyebrows, and she supposed she should be glad the light was dim, and that at her age she still had anything somebody wanted to look at. "Refill?" She gestured pointedly at Niburu's empty glass.

"Yeah, thanks." He grinned sheepishly.

"Pollux!" She stood back while the servo came, and watched it refill the drink. It moved away again without speaking, to take another order down the bar. "Well, it does the job, anyway. At least it'll give me a break when I want to talk to the customers. Everybody wants to talk to the bartender. . . ." She took a drugstick out of the box below the counter and lit it, inhaling the spice-scented smoke that curled lazily from its tip.

"Yeah," Niburu said again, still smiling. "I know." He lifted his drink to her, and glanced away along the bar. "I hear you used to have a restaurant. . . . I like to cook," he added, with a shrug.

"What kind of cooking?" She looked at him with genuine interest.

"Home-style. Plain but filling. A lot of spice—" He looked up again, into her eyes.

"My partner was the creative one. . . ." She smiled at what she saw in his gaze. "I just like to eat. But I got tired of his cooking; too complicated." Her mouth quirked. "I find running a club more satisfying, these days."

"I like your style," Niburu said. "Yours is the only place in the Maze where a real person does anything personal. It's a nice old-fashioned touch. Customers feel like maybe you enjoy their company as much as you like their credit." He looked at her as if he hoped she'd tell him it was mutual.

"Thanks." She rested her elbows on the counter again, letting him have another look down her cleavage as the drug smoke began to make her feel good. "Nice of you to notice. . . . I used to have a real bartender when I ran a place for the Source. It always seemed to work out."

He looked surprised, as if he hadn't believed that she'd known what she was talking about, when she'd named the Source before. "You really worked for Jaakola? Here?"

She nodded. "As a front, in the old days. Not now. Never again . . ." She glanced at his hands; she couldn't see his brand. She looked at her own unmarked hands, feeling perspiration prickle her palms.

"It must be nice to have a choice," Niburu muttered, and one of his hands made a fist.

"How'd you get to be a brand?" she asked, feeling a sudden empathy as she looked at him.

"It was a package deal. Me and Ananke, with Reede. We worked for him before he worked for the Source. I'm his ferryman," he said, with a kind of stubborn pride.

She raised her silver-dusted eyebrows; knowing common brands didn't have personal ferrymen, even if they worked for the Source. Only a chief rated that kind of service. She wondered if it was actually possible that Niburu had told her the truth, and hadn't simply been trying to impress her with big talk. And she wondered what motive the Source could have had for mutilating one of his top men like a common vassal, humiliating him like that and still expecting loyal service from him. She shook her head, never doubting for a second that the Source was capable of any cruelty, whatever his reasons were for ordering it done. "Look, I don't want anything to do with the Source anymore, you understand me?"

"Perfectly." Niburu nodded. "Don't worry about it. I wouldn't wish that on anybody. . . . So anyway," he said, taking a deep breath, shaking off the mood, "what are you doing after you close up for the night?"

Her mouth twitched; she straightened up again. "Sleeping."

"Alone—?"

She looked at him. "Yeah, if that's any of your business."

He lifted his hands. "I wondered if maybe you might want some company."

"Why me?" she asked suspiciously. There were plenty of other available women around, younger and prettier, amateurs and professionals.

"Because I only sleep with women I like."

"I could be your mother. Almost."

"You look nothing like my mother."

"What about your wife?"

"I'm not married. Never been married."

"Why not?"

"I travel too much. What about you?"

"I stay in one place too much," she said, beginning to get impatient. "I called you 'shorty'—"

"I've been called worse." He shrugged. "Besides, where I come from that's a compliment."

"Look," she murmured, flattered in spite of herself, "you're too short for me."

He leaned back on his stool. "You mean you're too old for me."

She flushed. "I'm not old where it counts."

"I'm not short where it counts."

She grinned, in spite of herself, and knew the cause was lost. "All right," she said. "Why the hell not? The place closes at three. If you're still around here then, we'll see what happens. . . ."

Tammis Dawntreader entered Starhiker's alone; sleepless, aimless like the crowd around him. He scanned the faces he passed as he wove his way deeper into the labyrinth of hallucinatory illusion, illusory pleasure, where seduction and destruction coexisted in a delicate balance. He searched for anyone he knew; ready to escape again into anonymity before they could call his name.

To his relief he did not see his sister, or any of the usual Winter crowd. They generally started their nights here; they would have gone on to other clubs by now. He stayed away from the bar, where Tor was holding forth; not able to face her tonight, even though he knew he would not find anything in her eyes but sympathy. Sympathy was more than he deserved, and more than he could bear.

He didn't feel like playing the games either; their futility and emptiness mirrored his own mood too accurately. He wandered like the damned through the crowds, watching strangers play the tables, playing with each other's heads, in the disorienting shadowplay of random light. Blaring music and the cloying heaviness of perfumes and drugsmoke saturated his senses, until he could forget for a time that he was an individual human being, filled with grief, and love, and confusion; that he had any need to think at all.

He stopped moving after a span of time he could not judge, finding himself in the rear of the club, where the density of milling flesh was less. Across a momentarily empty space of floor, he saw someone sitting in a booth, alone like he was. He had seen that night-black offworlder face before, that slight, slim figure with hair like shining jet, and indigo eyes. The offworlder was Ondinean, he'd been told; not much older than he was, and always part of a striking triad. Its second member was the shortest man he'd ever seen, and the third was the one with the tattoos and the uncanny skill at the interactives, the young offworlder his sister was trying to add to her collection of trophies.

The Ondinean was leaning back into the corner of the booth with one foot up on the bench; the foot wore an open-toed leather glove instead of a boot. He was juggling berries one-handed, with a look of resignation on his face. Occasionally he let a berry fall—always intentionally, because there was always another that replaced it—and something the size of a cat that wasn't a cat would scuttle forward on the table to eat it.

Tammis started toward him, dodging random bodies, drawn by curiosity and something stronger to stand before the booth, watching the Ondinean perform his solitary juggling act. At last the Ondinean glanced up, startled to find that he had an audience.

"You're very good at that," Tammis said; suddenly, equally self-conscious. "I wish I could do that."

The Ondinean nodded, with a hesitant grin coming out on his face. "You're a sibyl. I wish I could do that." He caught the berries one by one, and dropped them into a bowl.

"You mind if I join you?" Tammis gestured at the room behind him, where there were no empty tables.

The Ondinean shrugged, as if it didn't matter to him either way. But he watched intently as Tammis slid onto the bench across from him. The look was one that Tammis knew, and it was not indifferent.

"What kind of animal is that?" Tammis asked, as the creature on the tabletop between them rearranged itself to study him. It had eyes like the bright black buttons on a child's toy.

"A quoll," the Ondinean said, stroking it gently, still looking at him with uncertainty and speculation. The quoll burbled and chittered, sidling closer to its owner on nearly invisible legs.

"Did you bring it from Ondinee?"

The Ondinean nodded, and reached for another berry; the quoll scuttled forward eagerly. The berry slipped out of his fingers and dropped under the table. He glanced down, did something casually with his gloved foot. A moment later the foot appeared briefly on the bench beside him. He held the berry between his toes, so deftly that the fruit was not even bruised. He took the berry in his hand and fed it to the quoll, watching Tammis again, as if he were trying to see whether his lithe grace had made any impression. "That's enough," he murmured, when the quoll looked around for more. He ate one of the remaining berries in the bowl, in slow bites that revealed his even white teeth. He pushed the bowl across the table to Tammis, offering him the last one. Tammis took it, savoring its sweetness.

"What's its name?" Tammis asked, nodding at the quoll.

The Ondinean shrugged. "It's never told me."

Tammis smiled.

"I know you," the Ondinean said slowly. "I've seen you in here a lot. You're the Queen's son, aren't you? Her brother?"

Ariele's. Of course he would know Ariele. . . . Tammis felt surprise stir in him, almost pleasure, as he realized that the Ondinean had noticed him. He nodded. "Tammis."

"Ananke," the Ondinean said, suddenly self-conscious again. He turned his hand palm up on the tabletop, staring at it. "You're a sibyl too, like the Queen. Are you going to become king someday?" he asked softly.

Tammis saw the scar, like a strange eye, staring back at him. "No." He shook his head, sensing Ananke's unease, wanting to put it to rest. "My sister will be Queen, if she wants it. How did you get that—?" He risked the intimacy of pointing at the scar, livid against the paler skin of Ananke's palm.

"It means I work for somebody called the Source." His voice turned flat.

Tammis blinked, and changed the subject. "Where are your friends tonight?"

Ananke looked up at him, surprised or confused for a moment. "Kedalion's over there—" he pointed toward the bar, "making time, I guess. He claims the owner's going to take him home later. Reede's with your sister." His voice was toneless, and he didn't meet Tammis's eyes.

"What about you?" Tammis asked.

Ananke shrugged. "I'm here. I've got to wait for Reede."

"You've got to?"

His mouth quirked. "Taking care of Reede is what we do." He glanced up, shaking back his long, shining hair. The gesture was almost feline in its unconscious sensuality. "You worried about your sister?"

"No," Tammis said.

Ananke looked at him a moment longer, and then shrugged again. "Then why are you here?"

Tammis met his eyes; eyes so deep a blue that they were almost black. "Because I didn't feel like being alone tonight," he said softly.

Ananke's hand hesitated, in the act of reaching out to stroke the quoll. He continued the motion as if he had not meant to betray himself with that hesitation, as if the meaning of the words was lost on him. But he did not look away. "I guess nobody wants that," he said. "I guess everyone gets tired of being alone." He looked down, finally, with an odd spasm working his mouth.

Tammis put out his own hand, stroking the quoll's back; letting his fingers stray until they made tentative contact with Ananke's hand. "We could go somewhere . . . somewhere else."

Ananke froze, staring at the interface of pale and dark fingertips. And then slowly, almost painfully, he took his hand away. He shook his head. "I can't," he murmured. "Got to stay here. Got to look out for Reede." He shrugged, as if he were trying to shake something free from his back. "It's what we do."

Tammis hesitated, seeing depths of fear in Ananke's eyes; but the eyes clung to his face with sudden, helpless longing.

Ananke shook his head, his midnight hair moving across his shoulders in a way that made Tammis ache with sudden need. He looked down. "I can't."

"Another time—?"

"I can't." His head came up again, to meet Tammis's gaze. "I can't, ever." A tremor ran through him. His long, slender hands made fists, and he withdrew them below the tabletop.

Tammis stared at him a moment longer; certain all at once that for once he understood exactly what someone else was feeling. He took a deep breath, forcing the heat inside him to subside, until all that was left was the unexpected warmth of a different kind of contact. "That's what I always tell myself . . ." he said at last. "But I never mean it. That's why I'm here tonight, and not at home with my wife. Because I don't know what I want."

"Your wife—?" Ananke murmured.

Tammis looked down. "I can't explain it to her—why I feel these things. I can't explain it to anyone I care about. I can't even explain it to myself."

Ananke nodded. Understanding and amazement filling his eyes like dawn. "Yes," he said softly. "It's like that for me. No one ever understood. There's no one that I can ever share it with. Kedalion and Reede . . . they're all the family I've got. But if they ever found out, I'd lose them. . . . I hate the way things are, the ideas about men, and women, and what makes them different; what they can do and can't do about it. I hated it on my homeworld, I thought if I could get away from there, there must be a place, somewhere, where it would be better for me. But I'm still afraid—of what would happen if anybody found out what I really am—"

"—or afraid you'd see they're really right, and you're wrong. Or that even if you could have what you thought you wanted, it wouldn't make you happy, because it's not the real problem . . . because there's no real answer." Ananke nodded slowly; his face reflecting the impossible sorrow that squeezed Tammis's own heart. "And so you never . . . ?"

Ananke shook his head, glancing down. He brought his hands back onto the tabletop, and locked them together in front of him, intertwining his fingers.

"Not even—?" *With someone who understands . . . with me?*

Ananke looked up again, his eyes gleaming too brightly, full of precarious grief. "No," he whispered.

Tammis stared at him, watching him struggle to bring his emotions under control. "But why not?" he asked at last, gently.

"Because it's not really the problem. . . ." Ananke leaned back against the hard, mirroring wall of the booth, hugging himself with mournful resignation. There was no brightness in his eyes at all, now; no tears, no hope.

"Do you want to talk about it?"

Ananke shook his head. "It wouldn't change anything," he said.

Tammis nodded, numbly. "Then I guess there's nothing else to say. I guess I'd better be going." His hand rose to the sibyl sign hanging against his shirt.

Ananke nodded, and broke his gaze.

"I'm sorry. . . ." Tammis pushed to his feet, sorry that there was nothing he could do to ease anyone's pain tonight . . . anyone's at all.

TIAMAT: Carbuncle

"Gods, I miss the open air! This place gives me claustrophobia: the mustiness, the *ancientness*, of it, the smells and the echoes. I keep thinking I'm seeing things out of the corner of my eye. The way it surrounds you . . . it's unnatural."

Gundhalinu pushed the simulator headset up from his eyes, startled out of his reverie as Vhanu dropped into a seat next to him, followed by Kitaro and Akroyalin, one of the Associate Justices. Gundhalinu blinked the main room of the Survey Hall into focus, and then their faces. "Here, NR, try one of these." He stretched and pulled the headset off, holding it out. "They just arrived. Take a vacation without ever leaving your chair." He had been enjoying a full-sensory re-creation of the desert retreat his father had taken them to back on Kharemough. They had gone to the Springs every autumn in his childhood, because his father believed that the ascetic conditions, the heat and solitude, were good for body and soul.

Gundhalinu had never particularly enjoyed the place, in his youth. He had been surprised to find that spot among the selections on the headset's menu. But he had discovered that after all these years he had finally come to appreciate his father's wisdom. Even the illusion of sitting up to his chest in bubbling, mineral-tinted water had energized and relaxed him as utterly as if he had actually been there. He savored the faint reek of copper and sulfur filling his head, the bizarre wind and water-carved undulations of the red sandstone all around him, completely filling his vision. *Like the undulations of a shell, glowing with reflected light . . .*

He jerked out of the insidious daydream, the echo of the headset program . . . of a stolen memory, of a vision of history force-fed to him during his Survey initiation by a process he still did not really comprehend. Had it actually been his own world he had seen then, through some other man's eyes, in a time before it had even been colonized? . . . Through the eyes of one of his own ancestors—? Had that image really appeared on this program by chance? Or was someone trying to make him think, remember, realize . . . ? *Coincidences happen, damn it!* He shook his head, annoyed at the thought; realizing that Vhanu had gone on speaking and he had no idea about what. "Pardon?" he said.

"It must be a good one," Vhanu said, smiling as he took the headset. "You hate to leave it."

"Kharemough," Gundhalinu murmured, returning the smile.

"The only place worth looking at for long," Akroyalin remarked.

"Carbuncle is no more confined than the Hub cities back home," Gundhalinu said. "There's a lot worth seeing and doing here—more things every day. And you can always travel down along the coast, if you want to get out of the city."

"I tried a day trip. Nothing exists outside Carbuncle but fog and fish and superstition. It's as if time has stopped on this planet." Vhanu shook his head. "And all that water . . . I found it oppressive."

"Oh, come on," Kitaro chided. "Where's your sense of adventure?"

" 'Sense' and 'adventure' do not belong in the same sentence, if you ask me," Akroyalin said, dismissing her comment with a perfunctory glance. The ideal of the Survey Hall was that outside rank and status were to be left at the door; Gundhalinu had noted that some members lived more easily with those tenets than others. Kitaro's mouth tightened, but she said nothing more. Akroyalin pushed up out of his seat and moved off across the room.

"Well, at least these things will be a welcome addition to our limited recreational options," Vhanu said, holding up the headset. "Although now that one can actually take a ship to another world—or go home—and return again without losing years, even this isn't the same anymore."

"It'll be years before taking a casual vacation on another world will be as easy as putting on that headset," Kitaro said dryly. "Especially for poor underpaid wretches like myself. You might as well take even vicarious pleasure while you have it, before everyone else hears about it—"

Vhanu glanced at her, raising his eyebrows. But he shrugged, and put on the headset. Gundhalinu watched him stiffen and then sigh involuntarily, as his chosen vision took hold of him.

Kitaro smiled in satisfaction, and leaned across the low table between them. "I have something for you," she murmured, her smile falling away. She glanced around them, making certain that they were unobserved, and passed him a data button. He looked at it, as small and featureless as a nut in his hand. It had no governmental seal, no identifying marks on it at all. It might have been blank. He looked at her with sudden eagerness.

She nodded. "The information you wanted. Just make sure you get everything you need from it the first time. It's a read-once database."

He glanced down at the thing in his hand, over at Vhanu, lost in another world; back at her, questioning.

"Only you are at a level to be given access to this information," she said.

He nodded, surprised for the second time. He pushed to his feet, slipping the data button into his pocket. "Tell me, Kitaro . . . do you know what's on this?"

She went on smiling, her expression completely unreadable. "I think it only matters that you do, Justice."

He returned her smile, before he excused himself and went in search of real privacy. He found an empty meditation room and shut himself into it. Settling cross-legged among the pillows, he pushed the button into the remote at his belt. He pressed a contact to his forehead, like a third eye above his other two.

He closed his eyes and called the link on. He felt the vaguely dissonant tingle as images began to form . . . more and more of them, until within seconds there was a blizzard of random information burying his mind in snow. He felt sudden panic as he realized that he had been given an entire database to study: far more information than he could absorb in one session without neural damage, and the vast majority of it only obliquely related to the subject of Reede Kullervo.

Whoever had sent this to him must have known that he could not possibly get through it at one sitting. He wondered frantically why they had done this—unless perhaps they had simply not been able to guess what he really needed. Like an oracle, they had left it up to him to ask the questions. . . .

Ask the right questions. Somewhere among the pandemonium of datafiles was a processor that would let him route queries to access the information he needed. He used the techniques Survey had taught him to bring his spiraling physical and emotional responses under control; to gradually narrow his focus until there was no blizzard raging in his mind, nothing at all in his conscious thoughts but the vision of what he needed: *"Query: Reede Kulleva Kullervo."* He subvocalized the request, and waited.

The information had been hologramically coded; it unfolded like a memory, as if the images had lain hidden in his mind all along. . . . Reede Kullervo's face formed with perfect clarity inside his eyes, and he felt a pang as sharp as the pain of a booted foot cracking his ribs, the pain of trust and friendship betrayed . . . the pain of longing for the hyper-real, sweet-and-sour chemistry of their time together on Four as they had struggled to make order out of chaos.

Gundhalinu held himself perfectly still, restraining the sudden surge of his emotions. Normally, the only times he experienced an extended oblique feed were during his inductions into higher levels of Survey; the intensity of his responses always astonished him. *"Query: Known history of Reede Kullervo."* He requested, waited. . . . Again it seemed as though he simply, suddenly remembered what he had gotten from the Police databanks: That Kullervo was a native of Samathe, born and raised at one of the undersea mining stations. That he had a record of delinquency, and a reputation for being uncanny at the interactives in the local gaming nucleus. He had been permanently expelled from the station school; he had never finished the required course of study. When he was seventeen, he had murdered his father, and disappeared, probably into the Brotherhood.

"Query: Why did he kill his father?" His mind produced an image of Kullervo's father—a hard-eyed face with a thin, bitter mouth, and no visible resemblance to his son's face. A miner, semi-unemployed because of recurrent drug abuse; accusations

on record that he also abused his wife and children. The accusations were always retracted or denied by his wife.

"Query: How was the father killed?" Death by drowning. . . . He saw the body, as someone had recorded it then, drifting, wide-eyed with astonishment, in an undersea access well. . . .

He tried to drown me, the bastard. I'll kill him— It was his own real memory this time, of Reede coming to on the shore beside the river that ran through Sanctuary, his eyes furious with terror. Now, at last, he really understood what Reede had been talking about, who, and why. *Extenuating circumstances.* . . . Not sure if that was the datafeed, or his own judgment.

But still none of that explained how Kullervo had become a brilliant biochemist. On the contrary. . . . *"Query: What happened to Kullervo after he left Samathe?"*

His mind abruptly went blank, and then a voice was murmuring inside his head, asking him a certain question. There were three different responses to it, all correct, but each truer than the last. He had learned them at three different levels within Survey. He gave the truest answer that he knew, and waited.

He felt data begin to feed into his mind again: Kullervo's image haunted the space inside his eyes. As he watched, the image seemed to blur and mutate, as if all of Reede's changeling contradictions were being made visible . . . until he seemed to be two people, and neither of their identities was clear. *Gods* . . . Gundhalinu murmured silently. Because somehow the other face that overlay Kullervo's now was almost familiar; he could almost name that other. . . . But this time he kept silent, letting the datafeed unfold its story in its own way.

He saw a woman, with the exotic midnight beauty of an Ondinean, a powerful figure in the shadow world of the Brotherhood—saw her with Reede, saw her embrace him, saw her power close around him like the shadows, drawing him with her into the darkness of the interstellar underworld . . . swallowing him up.

And then the vision opened out suddenly, unexpectedly. Like a soft explosion he saw the larger pattern—the macrocosm of Survey itself, extending back through time, across all the scattered worlds of what had once been the Old Empire. He watched the pattern fragment, as the Empire's failure isolated its former worlds. New petty leagues of planets struggled to cling together and recapture lost contacts, isolating severed limbs of Survey, which further fragmented with time as disagreements over policy and purpose lost focus, the temptations of power led their members to fallings-out . . . to perversions of the sacred trust, to the Brotherhood, which practiced power for its own ends, for greed, for profit and pain, in the name of Chaos.

But at the highest levels an inner core of Order survived, its original purpose still intact, and incidents were set in motion which could affect the future of not just single worlds, but the farthest reaches of the Old Empire itself. He had glimpsed something of that higher plane, with Aspundh . . . realized suddenly that he was glimpsing it again now.

At a time when he had still believed that Survey was no more than a harmless social club, data had been leaked by the matrix of the sibyl mind to those innermost circles, revealing that Vanamoinen, its creator, still existed. . . . *Vanamoinen.* He remembered Vanamoinen's face gazing up into his own, smiling; heard his voice, *"Look at the stars, Ilma. . . ."* Vanamoinen had died, millennia ago; but the imprint of his mind had been preserved, somewhere inside the sibyl matrix. And now, by its own inscrutable logic, the sibyl mind had chosen, after millennia, to resurrect him.

Father of all my grandfathers. Gundhalinu shook his head, wondering. The secret knowledge had not been granted to any single chosen faction of Survey, but had spread as if by osmosis through the numerous cabals that were Survey's inheritors inside the Hegemony—regardless of where those groups lay along the sequence of chaos and order. *"Query: Only within the Hegemony? But why? Why not somewhere else? Or was it elsewhere too?"*

But no insight filled his thoughts. Only the knowledge that a power struggle had ensued, one which he had never even suspected was occurring all around him, as he sat obliviously playing at games of chance in the Survey Hall. He saw the struggle for control of Vanamoinen's brain/soul spread across the worlds of the Hegemony . . . saw the shadowy figure of a woman, with Vanamoinen's soul in her hands, in the hands of the Brotherhood. He saw it poured, like liquid light, into the neural pathways of a living man, a man with a mind and soul of his own, a man whose face he knew . . . *Reede Kullervo.*

Reede's image in his sight altered again, and this time he felt it drive into the depths of his consciousness like a spearthrust. He knew, this time, what that mutating vision meant, as he watched one face overlay the other until what remained was neither Vanamoinen nor Reede Kullervo, but something unrecognizable, blurred beyond recognition. Not one man, or the other, anymore. *The Smith:* Part human being, part legend. He watched the image bleed and dissolve until it was not anyone at all, until all that remained was naked light, the blinding brilliance of a genius whose knowledge and insight had been set free to solve some unknown task. . . .

Gundhalinu remembered tales of the Chained Gods of Tsieh-pun, elemental spirits who, if freed, could take possession of a human being, driving their unwilling avatar to feats of impossible courage or unspeakable evil. . . .

Gods . . . he thought again, and this time the image resonated through his consciousness to the bottom of his soul. He tried to pull his reeling thoughts together, suddenly not knowing which way to turn. *"Query: Why?"*

There was no answer. No test this time of his right to know; no refusal of it. His mind stayed completely empty. He shook his head in frustration and disbelief. Had Vanamoinen been brought back simply to help him solve the riddle of Fire Lake, to give the stardrive back to the Hegemony—or to its secret substructure? But he rejected that even as he thought it. Vanamoinen's soul had slept for millennia. It would require something far more significant than the expansionist dreams of Kharemough to cause the sibyl mind to recall him to the realtime plane, and subject him to this tormented existence, sharing another man's brain space. But still there was no answer.

"Query," he murmured, after a long silence. *"How was it done? Smartmatter?"* Again nothing happened in his mind.

"Query: Was this occurrence an accident—?" He pressed the remote against his skin, beginning to wonder whether the link was defective.

No. He saw that clearly, suddenly. Vanamoinen's return was not an accident. But his mind told him nothing more: no confirmation or explanation of why, out of all the possible choices, Reede Kullervo had been the receptacle for Vanamoinen's memories.

"Query: Am I restricted from knowing this?"

No answer. He swore in frustration, having no idea now whether his source would not tell him, or could not. *"Query: Is Reede Kullervo on Tiamat now? What does he want? Tell me that much, for gods' sakes—"* The last of it was born out of his own exasperation, more than any hope that he would get an answer.

Affirmation. He was seeing visuals again: Reede here, in the streets of Carbuncle. Gundhalinu saw him with the two men who had been with him on Four; saw him arguing with a big Newhavenese . . . saw the brand-scar on the palm of his hand, the open eye staring back at him.

Gundhalinu swore aloud. He knew that brand—it marked the property of the Source. *Property,* not an equal, or willing, partner. He had seen that symbol often enough, when he had served on Tiamat before the Departure. Thanin Jaakola had been here then, manipulating the ebb and flow of his Hegemony-wide drug interests from Carbuncle, the closest thing the Eight Worlds had had to a central stopover point. He had sold Arienrhod the virals she had tried to use against her own people, in her final desperate attempt to remain Queen. She had not gotten away with it . . . but the Source had.

Now Gundhalinu understood how, and why: Jaakola the drug boss had been only the exposed tip of an evil whose weight and depth he had never suspected in his days as a Blue. Jaakola belonged to the Brotherhood at a level so high it was uncertain how far his influence really reached. His presence in the Hegemonic underworld was like a gravity well, drawing everything and everyone who got near him down into his irresistible darkness. Even his image in Gundhalinu's mind was only darkness.

And now he had the Smith. Jaakola had won a power struggle within the ranks of the Brotherhood . . . had won Kullervo's flawed brilliance, and with it the new stardrive technology. He had wasted no time exploiting the potential of either one. Reede was here on Tiamat for one reason: to do for the water of life what he had done for the stardrive plasma.

The water of life . . . Gundhalinu let his concentration slide, wandering into his own speculations, considering the implications of Kullervo's presence here, forgetting that he had asked one more question—

Reede Kullervo appeared suddenly inside his thoughts, scattering images like mice, and in his wild, translucent eyes Gundhalinu read a look that he understood: a look he had seen once in the mirror. . . . *What does he want?* had been the question. And the answer was *Death.*

Gundhalinu ripped the contact from his skin—put it back, as suddenly. But there was no response at all. He remembered, too late, that Kitaro had warned him he would have only one chance. The data was gone.

He got up, only to stand motionless in the center of the room for a span of heartbeats. There seemed to be only one concrete thought in his brain now, and it was entirely his own: *Find him.*

He would put Vhanu on it— But, no. Vhanu would want, justifiably, to know everything; and Gundhalinu knew by now that he was not the kind of man who could simply take a matter on faith. Vhanu would demand to know why Kullervo could not be picked up openly, questioned and sentenced under the laws of the Hegemony, like the criminal he was. But that was a solution that served nothing, helped no one. Kullervo couldn't simply be negated—he was too valuable. *If he could be converted* . . . Vanamoinen would choose to serve Order, rather than Chaos: he would ally himself with the Golden Mean, given a choice. If the Golden Mean was wise enough to give Kullervo a choice, as well. . . . But Gundhalinu was not entirely certain that they were.

He frowned, still thinking as he moved toward the door. Kitaro had come through on this information for him; he could ask her to search for Kullervo, have Reede brought to him in secret, avoiding conventional Police channels. He didn't like doing it; didn't like to create any kind of rift between himself and Vhanu. But in this he had no choice.

He returned to the main hall, to find Vhanu still lost in the headset's sensory pleasures. He half smiled, knowing from experience how hypnotically addictive they could be, although they were only emotionally interactive, not like the neural taps in some of the gaming clubs. The lure of familiar scenes from home was hard to resist . . . and sometimes, the lure of the strange was even harder to shake off. He remembered experiencing Tiamat in his boyhood, carrying the exotic flavor of its scents in his head for days, hearing echoes of its people's musical speech; being haunted by a shimmering vision of Carbuncle, the City in the North, viewed from the sea. . . .

Kitaro was leaning back in her seat, with one boot up on the low table, engaged in what appeared to be a policy argument on trade restrictions with an offworlder merchant. Gundhalinu was mildly surprised to find her still in the same spot, until she looked up at him. She broke off her conversation, sent the merchant scuttling with a word, and Gundhalinu realized that she had been waiting for him. "Were all your questions answered for you?" she asked.

He smiled faintly. "The day all my questions have been answered will be the day I die . . . I hope. But it gave me enough to let me understand how little I know about what's really happening here." He shrugged, and explained to her what he needed done, glancing uncomfortably at Vhanu's oblivious presence.

Kitaro listened, her gaze steady and her face noncommittal. "I'll get on it right away, Justice," she said. "Arranging the kind of meeting you require will take time. Kullervo's too deep in the Brotherhood's quicksand to be easy to reach."

He nodded. "I understand. If you need assistance, I'll tell PalaThion to see that you get it. You can trust her."

She glanced away as Tilhonne, the Minister of Communications, approached them, trailed by Akroyalin and Sandrine. Tilhonne's boyish face shone with the eagerness of someone bearing news. He put his hands on Vhanu's headset, shutting off the feed as he came up behind Vhanu's chair.

Vhanu jerked spasmodically and swore; he pulled off the headset, glaring over his shoulder.

"This is something you'll want to hear too," Tilhonne said, before he could begin to complain. Tilhonne looked at Gundhalinu again, with a smile Gundhalinu read as unintentionally smug. "I've just received word from my uncle that the Assembly will be paying its first official call on the new Tiamat—"

Gundhalinu started. "When?" he said.

"The Assembly has only just returned to Kharemough. Their ships will have to be fitted with the new stardrive units. The Central Coordinating Committee estimates as little as half a year. They're departing from the usual itinerary—an acknowledgment both of our status here, and the importance of the new freedom and power the stardrive has given us."

"And their eagerness to get hold of the water of life. By the Boatman!" Gundhalinu muttered—a phrase, he realized absently, that he had picked up from Jerusha PalaThion.

Tilhonne laughed. "Ye gods, BZ, you'd think I'd brought you bad news. Come on, old man, accept it as a compliment!" He clapped Gundhalinu on the shoulder.

"I'm flattered, truly," Gundhalinu murmured, glancing at the measured speculation on Vhanu's face, and away again. "I was just considering the implications." *The complications.* His hands twitched restlessly at his sides. "This is a major event."

"I hear the Tiamatans used to throw one hell of a party in honor of the Prime Minister," Sandrine said. "That sounds to me like a tradition we should reinstate. We could use a little entertainment."

"Within limits," Gundhalinu said dryly.

"You mean the practice of sacrificing the Queen?" Vhanu asked.

"Yes." Gundhalinu looked away uncomfortably.

"Well, by my sainted ancestors," Vhanu said, "it seems to me that's one very efficient way of effecting change. And wasn't that the point of it? Don't they call it the Change?"

"If they'd thrown the Summer Queen into the sea when we came back this time, we wouldn't have had so damn much trouble over this mer-hunting question," Tilhonne drawled. "The Winters are already beginning to push for a return to power. They want her out—"

"Who does?" Gundhalinu said, frowning. "Who's been saying that?"

Tilhonne shrugged. "Gods, I don't remember names—they all sound alike. But I've heard it from more than one Winter's mouth."

"Was one of them Kirard Set Wayaways?"

Tilhonne nodded. "Wayaways. Yes, he's on the City Council, isn't he? Smart man, for a provincial. Ambitious. Knows which way the smoke is blowing. He's been in to see me several times, with this delegation or that, about various local matters."

"Yes, I know him," Akroyalin said.

"He's the one we met on the street a while back, isn't he?" Vhanu asked.

Gundhalinu nodded, tight-lipped.

"Intelligent, yes, and well-informed. Maybe too well-informed . . ." Vhanu looked at Kitaro, and back at Gundhalinu. "Someone to take seriously, in any case." His eyes turned thoughtful.

"There is only one thing about this conversation that I want taken seriously," Gundhalinu said abruptly. "The subject of human sacrifice is not to go any farther than these walls. Understood?"

They nodded, and shrugged, looking at him with varying degrees of resignation and incomprehension.

"I wish you all a good-night, then." Gundhalinu turned on his heel and went out of the room. But the awareness followed him like a shadow, that he had not heard the last of this, any more than he had heard the last of Reede Kullervo.

TIAMAT: Carbuncle

Sparks Dawntreader made his way through the gaming hell called Persiponë's, following Kirard Set Wayaways with his usual sense of walking backward through time. There had been a Persiponë's Hell in Carbuncle before the Departure, run by the Source; and he had had business with the Source then, as he did now. Sometimes it seemed to him as if he had begun to live his life in reverse, as if tomorrow had become yesterday, and his memories had turned back into reality, while reality faded further and further into a dream.

But no— He couldn't let himself start seeing it that way. He reached up, feeling the faint outline of the pendant he wore beneath his shirt; wore always, as he had once worn the medallion that had belonged to his offworlder father. It had a shape strikingly similar to the symbol above the entrance of the Survey Hall that BZ Gundhalinu frequented, farther up the Street—except that this one had a solii at its heart, one of the most valuable gemstones in existence.

The resemblance was not a coincidence. He had learned that fact, along with many other things, since he had become a member of the Brotherhood—and of Survey. Gundhalinu had caused the local Survey Hall to induct Tiamatan members; he had been one of the first of its new members, along with Kirard Set. Those things had changed his life forever.

Once he had understood the existence of the Great Game, and had become one of its players, he had felt his perception of the universe and his place in it expand a thousandfold. He sensed the entropy going on at all levels, the endless struggle between Order and Chaos—and how easily Chaos could overcome Order with a single touch, no matter how the stars in their courses and human beings in the course of their lives struggled to maintain their bearing. Chaos had constantly driven a random finger into the motion of his own life, destabilizing him at every turn. Now, at last, he had stopped struggling against entropy's flow, and had chosen to embrace it. At last he saw clearly, even in the darkness.

They entered a darkened hallway at the back of the club; the garish noise of the club's nightlife faded as if they had passed through some kind of field, which maybe they had, although he had sensed nothing beyond the sudden chill of anticipation he always felt when he reached this point.

They took the lift at the end of the hall—a box so amorphous that it could have been an empty closet, and probably passed for one. There was a sense of motion after the door/wall sealed; upward, he thought, though he could never be sure, even of whether it was the same motion, or for the same length of time, from one visit to the next. It could all have been random—which suited.

The featureless wall/door in front of him opened, revealing a meeting room. It was not the one he had always seen before, large enough to contain a gathering of two dozen or more members of the Brotherhood. This room was smaller, although it was otherwise almost identical, with walls whose colors shifted in a slow, almost hallucinogenic way. He looked away from them uneasily, focusing on the lone man who sat waiting at the table.

"Good day to you, Reede Kullervo," Kirard Set said.

Kullervo laughed once, as if Kirard Set had said something incredibly stupid. He looked away from them in disgust, his knuckles drumming on the tabletop with a hard, insistent rhythm. "You're late," he muttered, to the wall.

Sparks wondered whether he was speaking to them. They were not late; although this was not the Brotherhood meeting he had been expecting. His resentment of Kullervo's attitude tightened another notch. He had disliked Reede Kullervo from their first meeting; Kullervo was by turns sullen and hostile, and always arrogantly superior. And more than that, Sparks had the uneasy feeling that he was not simply moody, but actually crazy. Kullervo appeared to be nothing more than one of the Source's brands; he was the last person Sparks would have thought to find included in this unexpected intimacy. "What happened to everyone else?" he asked.

"There was a change in plans," a voice said, seeming to come at him out of the walls. *The Source.* The sound of that voice made his flesh crawl, even without the physical manifestation of it, which was beginning now across the room. He watched darkness begin to gather at the head of the table, impossibly, out of nothing. The shadow deepened until there was a formless but undeniable presence among them. Sparks told himself that it was only a projection, a hologram. But he knew the reality behind it existed, here somewhere. . . . He forced himself to sit down with Kirard Set and Reede at the table.

"There was a situation," the Source's corroded voice went on, expressionlessly. "The meeting was postponed. But the Brotherhood wished to hear about your progress in your various activities, and so I am here to receive your comments. Sparks Dawntreader—"

Sparks pulled his attention away from Kullervo, from watching the sudden, feral hatred in the other man's gaze as he watched the darkness take form. A trickle of sweat ran down Kullervo's cheek; his mouth quirked as the drop passed it.

Sparks nodded, trying not to focus as he faced the darkness.

"How is your exquisite wife, the Queen? And have you had any success in your attempts to convince her that she would stand to profit from extending her protection to certain of our interests, and opening this port to a . . ." the voice smiled, "wider spectrum of trade, as her mother did?"

Sparks shook his head. "Not much," he said.

The Source made a disgusted noise. "So your wife is still besotted by her ex-lover, the new Chief Justice—?"

Sparks felt his mouth thin; feeling Kirard Set's eyes on him, and Kullervo's. "The Queen, my wife," he said, "is getting everything she needs from the Hegemony." He twisted the tight line of his lips into a smile. "So, unlike Arienrhod, she really doesn't need either one of us." He shrugged. Kullervo snorted with amusement; Kirard Set's mouth inched upward in grudging respect.

"How unfortunate." The darkness at the end of the table seemed to transform in a way he could not define. "Well, in the real world there are always several answers to any given question. . . . Kirard Set Wayaways—how is your charming family?"

Sparks shifted in his seat as the Source's indefinable attention moved away from him.

"My son is lusting after Ariele Dawntreader, as usual. My wife is lusting after anything that can make her feel younger. This week it's a cosmetic surgeon, I believe."

"And what progress has been made in spreading the idea of the return of Winter to power at the Assembly's visit?"

"Good progress," Kirard Set murmured, with a faintly superior smile. "Most Winters are for it. Even the Summers are so infected with an itch for progress that they might accept a transfer of power, if the Queen keeps the balance of trade skewed by refusing to allow exploitation of the water of life . . . as long as the Change is brought about in the traditional way. Which suits our purpose admirably—"

"What do you mean, 'the traditional way'?" Sparks demanded, leaning forward.

"By drowning the Queen, of course," Kirard Set said.

Sparks froze, staring in disbelief, one part of his brain perversely aware of how absurd the expression on his face must be. "You motherlorn bastard. You sit here and tell me to my face you've been plotting to sacrifice my wife at the Festival, like it's a matter of changing your tailor? Do your plans include drowning me too, like Arienrhod's did—?" He pushed halfway out of his seat.

"Ye gods," Kirard Set said, wincing and putting up his hands. "As hotheaded as ever, after all these years. Sit down, Sparks, and let me explain."

"There is no real danger of the Queen being sacrificed . . . or, more pragmatically, yourself, Dawntreader," the Source said coldly. "That is not the point of this exercise. You must learn to stop taking everything at face value, if you are ever to rise within our circles. You will never see the opportunities here, any more than you see them in your own life, if you assume everything is exactly what it appears to be."

Sparks settled back into his seat, managing somehow to keep the betraying rush of blood from reddening his face. "Forgive me," he murmured. "Enlighten me."

"This is about the Queen, yes; but it is more about your rival, BZ Gundhalinu. He is in love with your wife—and only he has the power to override her wishes in the matter of releasing the water of life. We want him in the position of being forced to choose which is more important—protecting her, or protecting the mers. Either choice will cause him considerable difficulty and grief. . . . If he is caught in the bind between sacrificing the Queen, and violating her obsessive protection of the mers, which do you think he will choose?"

Sparks was silent for a long moment. "I think he'll choose to let the mers die. . . . But that's exactly what the Golden Mean wants him to do anyway. Then they'll control the water of life, not the Brotherhood. What do we get out of that?"

"In the short term, until we achieve our own independent supply, it gives us simple availability. As long as the drug is actually being made, we have ways of getting our share. In the long run, the benefits of forcing this choice on the Chief Justice and the Queen are many, and not all of them are necessarily obvious to someone like yourself. For your own part, as a loyal Brother, be satisfied with the knowledge that this will cause no pain to you, and considerable pain to the man who is trying to steal your wife."

"And even your children," Kirard Set murmured, raising an eyebrow. "How are Ariele and Tammis bearing up under all this?"

Sparks looked at him, cold-eyed. "I told you before, I don't have any children," he said. "So you'd know that better than I would."

Kirard Set grimaced, in what Sparks supposed was meant as apology. "Well, I suppose Kullervo knows more about Ariele's intimate emotions than any of us, these days. How would you describe her, Kullervo?"

Sparks turned to look at Kullervo, feeling disbelief hit him in the chest as he imagined his daughter—*not his daughter, but*—his daughter in the arms of that walking deathwish.

Kullervo froze, caught by their mutual stare in the act of biting his knuckle. He lowered his hands to the tabletop, knotting his fingers together. Sparks saw the livid marks his teeth had left on his own flesh. "Did you ever have intestinal parasites, Wayaways?" he said, looking at his hands.

"No," Kirard Set answered, nonplussed.

"Too bad," Kullervo said.

"Yes . . ." the Source murmured, "do tell us about your relationship with Ariele, Reede. You've been with her almost every night, for some time now. This is a first, since Mundilfoere. . . ." His voice trailed, and Sparks saw Kullervo stop breathing. "Does she remind you of your lost love—?" The words were dark with insinuation, and threat. "Is she perhaps responsible for your failure to produce the blood sample you require for your research?"

"No." Kullervo's face went gray, as if he were suddenly in such terrible pain that he could not even cry out. He took a deep breath. "I told you what happened," he said thickly. "I fell. I lost my weapon. . . . Ariele Dawntreader knows a lot about the mers. She spends a lot of time with them. I've been stringing her along because I want what she knows. She's not my type." He looked up again suddenly, almost defiantly, at the waiting darkness. "I've never even touched her." He glanced briefly at Sparks, and away again.

"So you've only been collecting her data, that's all?" the Source repeated, with heavy amusement.

"Yes," Kullervo said.

"Yes—?" the Source chided gently.

Kullervo's mouth tightened. "Master." He looked down again. Somehow on his lips the Source's chosen form of address sounded more like a curse than a lackey's obeisance.

"Dawntreader—" the Source said suddenly; Sparks looked toward the darkness. "I understand that you have produced something else which my man Kullervo would find interesting."

Sparks felt his own mouth tighten. "What do you mean?"

"You also have a large accumulation of data about the mers, having studied them for years since your retirement, I understand."

"My retirement?" Sparks repeated slowly.

"From being Starbuck for Arienrhod. From killing them," the Source said. "Is that true?"

Sparks felt anger corrode him like acid, wondering why he had been brought to this meeting, unless it was to see how much abuse he could take. His paranoia began to spread, cancerous; until suddenly he remembered what the Source had said to him: that he would never succeed, here, until he learned to see beyond the obvious. Maybe they *were* testing him: his loyalty, his ability to restrain his mercurial temper, his potential. He gazed at the hypnotic flow of color on the wall across the room until he was under control again. "It's true," he said steadily. "I suppose you could call it a love-hate relationship." He looked at Kullervo. "What's your interest in the mers, Kullervo?" he asked, keeping his voice neutral, forcing himself to take nothing for granted, even the unlikely possibility that Kullervo had a brain.

Kullervo's restless hands had begun to tremble visibly, even though he held them prisoner on the tabletop. The heavy ring set with soliis that he wore on his thumb rattled suddenly, loudly on the hard surface, and he pulled his hands into his lap, hiding them from view. "It's a love-hate relationship," he muttered.

"You're too modest, Reede," the Source said. "My man Kullervo is a bioengineering genius . . . he is the one you have heard called the Smith. He knows more about smartmatter than anyone living . . . including himself." He chuckled sourly. "He is applying his—unique mind to the problem of synthesizing the water of life, just as he did with the stardrive plasma. Without his help, BZ Gundhalinu would never have succeeded in reprogramming it."

Sparks stared at Kullervo; Kirard Set stared with equal disbelief, beside him. He almost laughed, sure that it must all be a bizarre joke, and unable to imagine what the point of it was.

"Isn't that right, Reede?" the Source urged gently.

Reede straightened up in his seat, raising his head in what could have been pride, or defiance, as he faced down their stares. His trembling hand rose to his ear, making the crystals of the elaborate jewelry he wore ring sweetly, incongrously, in the sudden silence of the room. "Yes," he whispered.

For a moment Sparks had the unnerving feeling that a total stranger looked out at him through Kullervo's eyes. In that moment Sparks felt his incredulity turn to belief, and a dark, bottomless terror filled him, the way the Source filled his vision, seeming all at once to inhabit the entire room. "I'll get the data together for you as soon as possible," he said, to the prisoner inside Kullervo's eyes. "I don't know how much use it will be, but it's yours."

Kullervo nodded, abruptly; he looked down and away, with a muscle twitching in his jaw.

"Don't belittle your own achievements, Dawntreader," the Source murmured. "You have quite a remarkable mind. You've been wasting your life here, among these illiterates on this backwater world. But finally you are among people who appreciate your gifts. Your years of work and study will be put to profitable use at last. . . . Why don't you go now, and see that it happens."

Sparks looked back at the darkness in surprise. "Then the meeting is over?" he asked, trying to make the Source's unexpected praise and his equally unexpected dismissal form a coherent whole.

"It is," the Source said, in a tone of voice that made him sorry he had asked, "as far as you are concerned." Sparks looked down. "There are certain Brotherhood matters which do not concern you, which require the attention of Wayaways and my man Reede. You have fulfilled your part in the process, Dawntreader. Rest assured."

Sparks pushed to his feet, avoiding the eyes of the other men in the room. He nodded, and left the table. The lift doors opened, as if they had been waiting for him.

"Reede . . ." the Source's voice said, as Sparks Dawntreader disappeared into the lift.

Reede pulled his gaze back unwillingly, a part of his mind caught in a daydream of changing places with the man being sent away. His eyes glanced off of Wayaways, registering the satisfaction on the Tiamatan's face as he watched Dawntreader banished while he stayed behind; sitting here as if he knew everything, as if he knew anything. He had been a member of the Brotherhood for years during the Snow Queen's reign, but he still had no idea what kind of mire he was sinking into. Reede met Wayaways's stare, watched its smirking arrogance falter as it collided with his own unshakable despair.

Reede turned to face the darkness again, forcing his eyes to see the vague suggestion of a humanoid form within it, and not to look away. "What?" he said, his voice rough. He knew that the Source was actually here on Tiamat now; that whatever was on the other side of that projection saw him clearly, saw him sweating and hurting, the telltale signs of deterioration because he had been kept waiting too long for the water of death. He didn't know whether this delay in his scheduled dose was meant as punishment or persuasion; he only knew that it was intentional. And that at last he was about to know why.

"Ariele Dawntreader," the Source murmured.

"What—?" Reede said again, uncomprehendingly.

"I know that nothing more . . . intimate has occurred between you and the Queen's daughter than simple conversation. But she wants more than conversation. She wants you, Reede."

Reede froze. "So what?" he muttered. "It keeps her talking about the mers."

"What she knows about the mers is useless, for your purposes. You know that as well as I do. Why do you keep seeing her?"

"It's not useless," he said stubbornly. "I need all the data I can get."

"You need a blood sample! She saved your life . . . and she stopped you from getting the one thing you really need to develop a replication of the technoviral. She has been a hindrance, not a help, in your work: she's actually made you wonder if you have a conscience, hasn't she?"

Reede felt himself flush. He glanced at Wayaways, realizing the Tiamatan was probably the one who had told the Source everything. "You want me to dump her? Okay, I'll dump her. No problem."

"No," the Source said softly. "That is not what I want. What she knows about the mers is nothing . . . but she is still important to us."

Reede glanced toward the lift again, suddenly understanding why the Source had gotten rid of Dawntreader. He kept his gaze fixed on the wall, letting the fluid motion of the colors fill his eyes. A hard lump of tension filled his throat as the silence stretched. *But he would not ask; he would not, he would not—*

"What did you have in mind?" Wayaways murmured, asking the question for him.

"My man Reede is going to seduce her."

Reede's head snapped around; he saw Wayaways' amusement turn to sudden surprise at the sight of his revulsion.

"It should be simple for you, Reede. From what Wayaways has told me, Ariele has far more in common with her grandmother, Arienrhod, than with her mother . . . and she's already infatuated with you. All you have to do is let her have what she wants. I'm sure she won't be disappointed. You never disappointed Mundilfoere."

Reede swore, pushing to his feet. Dizziness made him lean on the table; he sank into his seat again. Wayaways' eyes were on him like a voyeur's. Reede shook his head, in disbelief more than denial. "Why . . . ?" he said, uncomprehendingly.

"Because it will bind her to us. It will give me power over her . . . and over her mother."

He shook his head again. "What's the point? Drop a dose of something in the Queen's soup, if you want her to cooperate. Why bother with this game—"

"Because it's my game, and you are my pawn," the darkness said. "And I want you to make her fall in love with you. That is your penance; for lying to me, for failing to make meaningful progress in your research on the mers because of your infatuation with this girl."

Reede felt nausea rise like a living thing inside him, barely able to control it. "I'm working on it, you bastard! I'll get the blood sample—I'll kill the fucking mer with my bare hands if that's what you want. I'll give you what you want. But not her. It's not going to happen. Not with me."

"I thought she didn't matter to you."

"She doesn't—"

"—Or is it Mundilfoere?"

Reede jerked with impotent fury. Wayaways flinched back as he rose to his feet again. He started away from the table, heading blindly for the lift, although he knew that he was a prisoner, that it would not even answer his call unless the Source ordered it to.

"Reede." Something in the Source's voice stopped him dead. "I have what you need."

He turned back slowly, willing his eyes to see what they saw waiting for him on the table. He flung himself across the room, catching up the vial before it could disappear, and emptied it into his mouth.

His throat closed suddenly, as he would have swallowed—as his lips, his tongue, registered something wrong. He spat; a mouthful of warm blood crimsoned the front of his clothes, his hands, the tabletop, like gaudy vomit. "Shit!" he gasped. "Shit—!" Droplets of red splattered on Wayaways as he shook his dripping hands. Wayaways swore in furious disgust.

"Whose was it?" he shouted at the darkness. "Whose? Whose?" He wiped his mouth on his sleeve, leaving a smear of red. He spat again.

"Mer blood," the Source said. "What you need to continue your research . . . as I said. Since you failed to get it yourself, I have obtained it for you, with the cooperation of Wayaways here. You'll find the rest of the sample waiting for you in the labs. I want you to go there now and do your work."

Reede looked down at his trembling, bloodied hands, at the empty vial lying on the tabletop. "I can't. I can't work when I'm like this! I need—"

"I know what you need," the Source said softly. "You'll find that too, waiting for you. . . . Now go."

Reede wiped his hands on his shirt, swallowing bile. He glanced at Wayaways as he raised his head again. The Tiamatan was staring back at him with morbid fascination. Reede leaned forward suddenly, and hit Wayaways a blinding slap across the face with his open palm. He pushed back again and went on across the room toward the lift. This time its doors opened to him, and took him inside.

Kirard Set Wayaways rubbed his face, frozen somewhere between outrage and disbelief as he watched Kullervo step into the lift and disappear from sight. Finally he looked toward the formless blackness that claimed to be the Source, realizing that he was suddenly quite alone with it. He had never been alone in the Source's presence before, and remembering what he had just seen, he was not sure whether to be flattered or unnerved by this unexpected audience.

"Wayaways . . ." the Source's ruined voice said.

Kirard Set attempted to hold an expression of calm anticipation on his face.

". . . you show great potential. I commend your work so far. You seem to accomplish your goals with alacrity. I expect you will continue to rise within the Brotherhood, and enjoy its rewards."

Kirard Set smiled in acknowledgment; but his hand rubbed his still-smarting face.

"Don't take Kullervo's insufferable behavior to heart," the Source murmured. "He has a lot on his mind. And he will have more, before long. Perhaps you would like to help me see that he does. I want his relationship with Ariele Dawntreader consummated. It won't happen if I leave it to him. He belongs to me . . . but he still likes to pretend he has some choice in the matter." He made an amused sound. "This star-crossed romance will need additional effort. You can help me see that it takes place."

Kirard Set nodded, more eagerly this time, with his hand still pressing his cheek.

"This is what I want you to do. . . ."

TIAMAT: Carbuncle

Moon arrived at Fate Ravenglass's doorstep with Clavally Bluestone, and knocked on the closed upper half of the door. She heard footsteps approaching and a familiar voice, heard a cat squawk as it inadvertently got underfoot. The upper door swung open, and Fate's unseeing eyes looked out at them. She smiled as if she could actually see their faces, because she had been expecting them.

"Come in, come in—" She opened the lower half of the door as they spoke their own greetings, and two spotted cats were suddenly under their feet as they stepped inside. Fate's old gray tom had finally died, some years back, and Tor had supplied her with not one, but two replacements, when the restaurant's cat had kittens. "What's this? You've brought lunch?" She sniffed pointedly. "Does this mean you're here for more than simply to discuss College business, then?"

"Well, we all have to eat, and why not gossip a little over lunch, then?" Clavally said cheerfully. She set the covered basket down on the table in the front room, which had been a workshop in the days when Fate had been a maskmaker. Now that the College had moved up the long spiraling hill to the palace and the city had begun to fill up with foreigners, Fate got out less and less, and they both knew it. With the years slowing her body and making her less sure on her feet, the accumulation of difficulties had been gradually conspiring to make her housebound.

"Well then, tell me what's new?" Fate found her way to a seat, moving confidently within the confines of her home. She gestured to them to sit down. "Have either of you been to Tor's club yet? I hear that it's thriving. I'm very happy for her, I know it's what she was meant to do. Although I virtually never see her anymore, and that's a shame." Moon heard the vast loneliness and regret inside the resolutely positive words.

"No," Moon answered, hearing Clavally's "No" echo her own. They glanced at each other, smiling ruefully. "Too busy," she said.

"Too much noise," Clavally said. She opened the basket, passing around meat pies. "It's for the offworlders, who don't know what silence means, and for the young ones, who don't want to know."

"For shame," Fate said, clucking, as she accepted a pastry, its wrapper covered with unintelligible offworlder script. She breathed in the smell of the food, took a tentative bite, and sighed, nodding approval. "Well, this is not bad, you know. . . . You should go to the club. Make the time! You're young yet, you should enjoy yourself. Try something new. I'd like to hear about it."

"I'll send Ariele to give you a complete description," Moon murmured. "If she ever speaks to me again. She lives there, or would, if Tor would let her."

"Oh, now," Clavally said. "It isn't that bad. She's still out at the plantation with the mers as much as she is down in the Maze with Elco Teel and that lot. She'll stablize. All the young ones are gorging themselves on the offworlders' sweetmeats, because they've never had anything like it. Eventually they'll grow tried of it."

"How, when there's something new every week—? They're lost at sea, with nothing to navigate by, and no anchor." Moon heard her own voice sharpen; knew that it wasn't the temptations of the Maze, but Ariele's response to them that galled her. "At least your Merovy has a sense of purpose; the future isn't an infinite present to her."

"How is Merovy?" Fate asked. "Has she finished her medtech internship yet? And how is Tammis? I miss his voice too, and his music, without my days at the College. And Dana—?"

"Dana is doing well. With the new medicine he's been taking, his back is much improved again; his arthritis is virtually gone. Merovy will be licensed in a fortnight," Clavally said.

"Wonderful." Fate smiled. "And Tammis—?" she prompted, when no one said anything more. "They make such a good match, it gives one hope for the future."

"They're fine," Clavally said, but the animation went out of her voice. Moon looked at her in surprise. "Their work keeps them both so occupied . . . she complains that they don't spend enough time together anymore."

Fate's expression altered. "That will change when her studies are finished, I imagine."

"I don't know." Clavally glanced down. "Perhaps. I hope so. Maybe it will."

"I didn't realize they were having problems," Moon said softly, self-consciously. "Tammis hasn't said anything about it to me. . . ." He said almost nothing at all about what was going on in his life, and she hadn't even been aware of it. They talked about the mers, or research, when they saw each other these days; nothing personal. Ariele avoided her as if she had a contagious disease.

Tammis did seem moodier than usual, she realized, just as Ariele seemed even more willful. But until now she had not thought about why—any more than she had thought about why neither of them had asked her the question she had been anticipating for months: The question of who their real father was. They had never asked . . . and her only emotion had been relief.

It had been her responsibility to bring it up, not theirs. But she had been too preoccupied with the Hegemony . . . with her own troubled feelings for the two men who had equal claim to the title "father." Too self-obsessed . . . too much like Arienrhod. Guilt writhed like eels in her stomach. She picked at her food, suddenly without appetite. "I'll try to speak to him," she said. *Try.* She had been trying for weeks, months now, without success.

"And how is Sparks?" Fate pressed on, with determined good-naturedness, through their awkward silence. "He hasn't been by in some time. Is he still working on that program to recreate segments of a damaged fugue structure? What was it he said: 'It was like mending mathematical lace.' His mind amazes me. . . ."

Moon traced the rough, random patterns of ancient glue-lines on the table surface, as she considered the fact that she had no idea Sparks had even been working on such a project. "I don't know. He isn't at the palace much these days. He's . . . he's involved in some . . . business venture, with some of the Winters he used to be . . . close to, when he was with Arienrhod." Her voice faded until it was barely audible.

"Ah," Fate said, and that was all. She glanced away, her eyes moving randomly around the room. Moon wondered what she was seeing, inside her thoughts.

"But we didn't come to spoil your day with dreary moments of our lives that probably mean nothing," Clavally said, forcing a smile. "Everything changes, today's tears are tomorrow's absurdities, after all."

"And speaking of change—" Moon matched Clavally's tone with resolute lightness. "I've been informed by the offworld government that the Prime Minister and the Assembly will be paying one of their traditional visits to Tiamat, in only a few months."

"A few months?" Fate said, her disbelief showing. "Isn't that early? They used to come every . . . twenty-two years, wasn't it—?"

"It would have been a hundred years, if they hadn't got the stardrive back, remember." Moon smiled. "They are so pleased to have us as a new jewel in their crown that they are breaking with their own tradition, and visiting us out of sequence." Her smile, and her voice, turned faintly ironic.

"Is that so?" Fate said, her own voice still full of incredulity.

"So they say," Moon answered. "What they mean may be another matter. But the offworlders are encouraging us to put on our traditional Festival for the arrival, to celebrate 'the new union of our cultures,' as they put it. I've said we'll cooperate. . . . Why not, after all?" She felt something stir inside her, like spring. "We might as well embrace change gladly, as we've always done, in our way; because it will have its way with us whether we like it or not. That's what the Festivals mean; that's what they've always been there to symbolize: to greet change with rejoicing and celebration, make something beautiful and alive of the moment, to hold in our memories."

"Will there be a Mask Night?" Fate asked, leaning forward on the table.

"How could there not be?" Moon touched her hand, remembering the mask of the Summer Queen. "We need to cast off our old lives with the proper ritual, because we've been handed our new ones already."

"But it takes years—decades—to make enough masks for everyone. We used to work from one Festival to the next, whole families of maskmakers, to make them all. . . ." Moon saw the sudden realization and loss that filled Fate's face. She would not be among them, this time.

"We have manufactories now," Moon said; her hand tightened over Fate's. "They can do a great deal of the repetitive work. . . . The masks may not be such works of art this time; but they can be ready. And by the next Festival, they can be both. Tor has recommended a man named Coldwater to me; she thinks he would be willing, and his production complex is suitable, with some minor alterations. She also said it would be a way to reuse some of the vast quantities of trash the offworlders have been making us such a present of. . . ." She flicked the plass wrapper from her meat pie. "The rubbish can be turned into raw material to produce mask forms. She thought that if you were willing, you might advise Coldwater about supplies, and designs. . . ."

Fate's face eased as she listened, as she adjusted her expectations and considered the possibilities that change had set before her. "Yes . . . yes, I could do that, I suppose. I—"

There was a knock at her door. They all turned, startled by the sound. "This day is full of surprises," Fate said.

Clavally started to rise from her seat; Moon stopped her, getting up in her place. The other women let her go to the door, their surprise unspoken but palpable. She reached for the handle, somehow certain that it was Sparks who had come here to see Fate, to share with her all the things he had not shared with his wife. Suddenly eager to tell him that another Change was coming, that there would be another chance for them to cast off old lives and try again. . . . She opened the door.

She sucked in her breath, staring at the face she found there, so unexpectedly. "BZ," she whispered. She saw his stunned disbelief, as plain as her own.

"Moon—?" He glanced away, at the house-front; past her into its interior, and finally back at her face. "Is this the home of Fate Ravenglass?"

She nodded and moved aside, opening the bottom half of the door to let him in. He was alone, without bodyguards, and not in uniform. He wore a loose-sleeved tunic and pants, a dark cloak and a wide-brimmed hat; everyday clothing for a Kharemoughi businessman or trader. She would not have glanced at him twice, in the street. He looked at her in equal wonder, seeing her wearing the native clothing that she still preferred, when the requirements of politics and ritual did not force her to dress to meet the expectations of others.

He stepped into the room, blinking as his eyes adjusted to the light, and to sharing the room with her. He looked away from her finally, taking in the presence of Clavally and Fate.

"Justice Gundhalinu," Fate said, her own voice remarkably calm.

He smiled wryly. "You recognized my footsteps."

"You aren't in uniform. You're wearing different boots," she said. "But I knew you. Welcome. What brings you here to my home?"

"A special delivery, Fate Ravenglass." He started on across the room. Moon followed him, avoiding cats. She watched silently as he produced something from inside his cloak, and set it on the glue-scarred tabletop. He opened the container and took something out of it, very gently—a glittering mesh web that resembled headsets Moon had seen the offworlders use. But she had never seen one like this. "Here. . . ." BZ laid it against Fate's forehead, spreading its tendrils with infinite care; Moon watched in fascination as the spreading filaments seemed to take on a life of their own, conforming to the shape of Fate's head.

Fate, who had sat motionless even while he touched her, gasped suddenly and stiffened, her hand rising—not to pull the thing away, or even touch it; but instead reaching out, to touch Gundhalinu's chest. She rose slowly from her chair as he took hold of her hand, steadying her until she stood before him, staring up at his face. Her own face filled with wonder. "Justice Gundhalinu . . ." she murmured, "I can see you!" And now her hand rose to his face, touching its features, verifying its reality.

"Good," he said softly, in his faintly accented Tiamatan. "That's good . . . that's as it should be." He smiled.

Fate turned away from him, moving uncertainly as she matched the sudden input of her eyes to the feedback of her other senses. She faced Moon, gazing at her for a long moment, and although her eyes were still like shuttered windows, Moon knew by the expression on her face that she saw. Fate's tentative smile widened, growing strong with her belief. "Lady . . . Moon . . . I remember you," she murmured. "Oh, yes, I do, my dear. . . . I remember the moment when you came to my door, like a lost child. . . . I remember the moment when I placed the mask of the Summer Queen on your head." She moved forward to touch Moon's face in turn, almost caressingly, and Clavally's, which she had never seen. "You are much as I imagined you, Clavally Bluestone," she said contentedly. Clavally's hand squeezed hers.

Fate turned back to Gundhalinu again, and this time her hands rose to touch the shining filaments that lay against her skin. "I see so much more clearly, this time. I never saw this clearly, when I had my sight before the Departure. Even my dreams of how clearly I saw are not like this—" Her hands trembled faintly.

"This is the best sensor system available that doesn't require surgery."

"Thank you," Fate murmured. Her restless eyes held his for a long moment. "I had forgotten. . . ."

"My promise?" he asked. "I didn't. But it took some time to get a special request through the maze of bureaucratic red tape, I'm afraid."

"Justice Gundhalinu," Clavally said, asking the question Moon's lips refused to form, "why did you do this?"

He looked at her, as if for a moment he couldn't imagine why she would even ask such a thing. And then he glanced at Fate again, at her gaze moving everywhere with glad distraction. "To right an old wrong."

"Do you mean the Departure?" Moon asked; thinking he meant all the things that they had lost, that had been taken away from them like Fate's sight when the Hegemony abandoned them.

"Oh, you beauties!" Fate leaned down to stroke the cats that were winding around her legs. "Look at you, I never dreamed you were so many colors. . . ."

BZ shook his head, his own eyes holding Moon's, but filled with a secret he did not share with her. "An older wrong than that—and a more personal one."

Fate straightened up again, with a squirming cat under each arm. "You are a sibyl, Justice Gundhalinu," she said, gazing at him, at the trefoil hanging against his shirt. It was not a question. But he said, "Yes," his voice oddly strained.

Moon's fingers touched her own sibyl sign, as she realized all at once that everyone in this room was a sibyl. She watched BZ's eyes flicker from face to face, as if he had suddenly realized the same thing. His gaze came back to her again, touching her face, her pale, plaited hair; glancing down at her pragmatic native clothing. His hands tightened unobtrusively over the deep-blue fabric of his simple, ordinary shirt. She saw in his eyes then no Queen, no Chief Justice.

She remembered with sudden clarity a moment half a lifetime ago, when she had been a stranger lost in this strange city-world at Festival time. How his eyes had gazed at her then, and pierced her heart like light through windowglass. . . .

He looked away abruptly. "I have to be getting back," he murmured. "My staff thinks I'm on my lunch break."

Fate smiled at him, letting go of her cats. She held out her hands in wordless farewell. He touched them briefly, as Moon watched in silent envy. "Bless you," Fate said.

He smiled back at her. "Fate's blessing is what I'll need, to accomplish my work here," he said. He nodded to them all, not meeting Moon's eyes again as he started toward the door.

"Wait—" Moon said. He turned back, waiting as she picked up her untouched meat pie from the table. "Don't leave without something to eat on the way . . . Justice Gundhalinu." She put the food self-consciously into his hands, an excuse to reach out and touch him, for even a moment, across the impossible distance that separated them. His fingers closed over hers briefly, warmly, as he took the food from her hands. He smiled at her, this time looking directly into her eyes. She saw the hunger there, before he turned away again. He looked back at her once more as he went out; he was still looking at her as the door closed between them, cutting off her view.

She turned back again, slowly, to find both Clavally and Fate watching her. She felt her face redden; looked down, away from their unspoken curiosity.

"He is a good man," Clavally said at last, with what sounded like surprise. "I wouldn't have thought it was possible, especially in an offworlder who has so much power."

"They really aren't so different from us," Moon murmured. She pushed at her sleeves, raising her head again. "They're only human. They want the same things we want. . . ."

Fate shook her head, her face caught in a strange expression as she looked at Moon. But then she looked down at her own hands, turning them over and back, over again. She moved away, going cautiously across the room to the painted wooden storage chest below the diamond-paned window. She raised the lid and began to search through its contents. With a soft exclamation she pulled something out, and held it up. Light flashed, the random beam spearing Moon's eye. She realized that it was a mirror Fate was holding.

As she watched, Fate turned toward the light to look at her own reflection, which she had not seen even dimly in almost twenty years. Her hand rose slowly, visibly trembling, to touch the deep lines of age on her face, the whiteness of her hair, that had not been that way when she had last looked into a mirror. Her hand fell away again. Still slowly, carefully, she placed the mirror back in the chest and closed the lid. Turning to face them, she found in their eyes the affirmation of what she had seen with her own. "I still feel like the same person I was before. Where did this body come from . . . ?" She spread her hands helplessly.

Moon glanced down; felt Clavally do the same beside her. She made herself look up again, seeing the woman she had always known, standing suddenly in a different light. "Fate," she said, as realization struck her. "Mask Night—"

Fate straightened, her face brightening as her thoughts left the last Festival, coming back into the present, and reaching toward the future. "Yes, of course—" she said, starting back toward them across the room, holding up her hands. "I can work again, on my own. Only a few masks, but very special . . . My dear, you shall have one fit for a Queen."

TIAMAT: Carbuncle

". . . as you can see on your displays, the record clearly supports Citizen Wayaways. The data shows both a desire among the people and an historical precedent for replacing the Summer Queen with one chosen by the Winters on our return. This is usually done during what they call the Festival, when they celebrate the Prime Minister's visit. . . ."

Echarthe's data flashed on the screen in front of Gundhalinu where he sat, surreptitiously folding a scrap of food wrapper into smaller and smaller triangles. He looked up, his hands hidden below the edge of the torus table that dominated the council chamber. His eyes touched briefly on the members of the Judiciate and his government staff seated around him; he pictured the Summer Queen's Sibyl College and the Tiamatan civic leaders who had once occupied those same seats. Only one figure was unchanged from that image to this one . . . Kirard Set Wayaways.

He found Wayaways looking back at him, as if the Tiamatan had had him under observation all the while. Wayaways smiled faintly, knowingly; that smile which he had come to detest more than any expression he had ever seen on a human face, because it had the ability to blind him like a beam of light with his own irrational, gut-knotting rage. . . . He forced himself to meet Wayaways' stare unflinchingly, closing the fist of his concentration around his anger, suffocating it with self-discipline.

Wayaways had insinuated himself into the awareness of everyone in this room, become a constant presence in their halls. He was the official representative for the City Council, lobbying for the return of the mer hunts—working against the Queen whose most loyal supporter he had once been, according to rumor.

He had come to Gundhalinu's office a few weeks past, oozing charm and secret knowledge, hinting with barely concealed malice that if the Judiciate did not grant permission for the mer hunts to begin again, he would provide the Council with certain information about the real nature of the relationship between the Hegemonic Chief Justice and the Summer Queen.

Gundhalinu had listened in silence, and then played back to Wayaways the record of everything he had said, which Gundhalinu had discreetly edited even as he spoke, eliminating all the potentially incriminating details, leaving only a damning litany of attempted bribery and coercion. "I know you have friends," he had said softly. "I have friends too. Leave now, while you're still free to do it."

Wayaways had taken him at his word; there had been no more direct attacks. Instead, Wayaways had simply gone around him, gotten to the other members of the Council behind his back. He no longer pressured them directly to reinstate the mer hunts, because Gundhalinu had overridden the Council's vote and ruled that it was traditionally a matter of Tiamatan law, and under the Summer Queen's control. And so Wayaways had followed him doggedly down that path of argument, and turned Tiamatan law back on him, in one swift, vicious thrust.

"I question the claim that a majority of Tiamatans are dissatisfied with the Queen and want her replaced," Gundhalinu said. "This data is hardly proof of that. And even if it was, we are not in a position to rule on deposing her—"

"We aren't talking about deposing her ourselves, Justice," Echarthe interrupted. "Their own traditions will take care of that. I'm only recommending we see to it that they carry those traditions out, when the Assembly finally arrives."

"Then we'd really have cause to celebrate," Sandrine said, with a sour smile. "If that Motherloving bitch was gone, and Winters were running things, it would solve our whole problem with the local government giving us the access we need to the water of life." Laughter and murmurs of agreement spread around the table.

"Bigotry and threats against a local head-of-state are not something I consider a subject for humor," Gundhalinu snapped. Beside him, Vhanu raised his eyebrows.

Sandrine frowned, his irritation showing. "I wasn't aware that I was saying something humorous."

"Either that, or treasonous," Gundhalinu said, feeling himself frown. "I've made it plain that prejudiced behavior toward the people of Tiamat is not acceptable from our Police force. It is not acceptable from members of my government either."

"BZ," Vhanu murmured in Sandhi, gently nudging Gundhalinu's arm. "We're among friends here, after all. We're all Technician, we understand each other. A situation like this is difficult enough, under the best of circumstances, and the circumstances are hardly the best. Allow us a little slack, won't thou?"

Gundhalinu took a deep breath. "I suppose thou're right," he said softly, answering in Sandhi. The language of his own people was beginning to sound alien to him again, he realized. He had even begun to think in Tiamatan.

"You have defended our rights as a people eloquently since you've come here, Justice Gundhalinu," Wayaways said. "My people are deeply grateful to you for that." He lifted his hands in something like a shrug. "Why are you suddenly against something like the Change, which has been a tradition of ours far longer even than the cycle of your departures and returns?"

"Precisely because it is such an ancient tradition," Gundhalinu said, under control again. "There is a new order here now, and the laws of the Change no longer serve any useful function. It has become an act of barbarism. I've supported most of the innovations that your Queen made during our absence, because they were positive, and in keeping with the kind of relationship I want to build between our peoples, now that our relationship has become permanent. But human sacrifice is something which has become indefensible—"

"But it's a part of our religious system." Wayaways pointed at the data on the screen, his voice taking on an indignant edge. His eyes mocked Gundhalinu, coldly knowing. "You defended the Queen's protection of the mers on those grounds, did you not? Shouldn't we be the ones to determine whether the Change rituals still have a meaningful function for us? Do you have some particular personal interest in the Summer Queen's well-being, that makes you resist anything that might threaten her?"

Gundhalinu felt Vhanu's eyes on him suddenly; heard the other officials around the table begin to murmur among themselves. "I've stated my reasons for restricting the practice. I don't need to defend them further," he said flatly.

"The fact remains, Justice," Vhanu said, "that removing the Summer Queen would be in our best interests. She's an intractable fanatic. She reigns for life, and she's not likely to die of natural causes any time soon. I think we should seriously consider this opportunity to get rid of the Queen."

Gundhalinu looked at him, away again quickly, unsure of his own expression.

"The Prime Minister and the Assembly are going to raise bloody hell if they don't find the water of life waiting for them," Borskad, the Minister of Trade, said.

"And riots instead of celebrations," Wayaways murmured. "I can guarantee that feelings will run high, that there will undoubtedly be public protests and even incidents of violence, if you attempt to suppress a ritual which is such a fundamental part of our culture."

"Are you threatening the Hegemony, Citizen Wayaways?" Gundhalinu asked, his voice brittle.

Wayaways stiffened, and settled back into his seat.

"The Prime Minister and the Assembly are figureheads, with no real power," Gundhalinu said impatiently, meeting other stares around the table, "and absolutely no understanding of the complexity of the issues involved here."

"But the Central Committee has plenty of influence," Tilhonne said. "My uncle has already threatened to come here himself and find out what in the name of his sainted ancestors is going on, if we don't reach some kind of compromise with the Queen. If we have riots when the Assembly comes, that will be all he needs to start an investigation. And that could ruin all our careers." He looked exceedingly unhappy at the prospect.

Gundhalinu barely controlled a frown, aware that Tilhonne's concern was well-founded. He had autonomy here only as long as he did nothing that attracted too much negative attention. He stared at the Hegemonic Seal, the Eight Worlds symbolized by a sunburst on the wall across the room.

Other voices around him were rising now, impatient, full of concern—all of them anxious about one thing, he was sure, and it was not the well-being of Tiamat's Queen.

"I move that we vote to accept the petition brought to us by Citizen Wayaways," Borskad said, registering the motion on his screen. "That there will be a full Change, including the return of Winter to power by the traditional practices of their own theocratic rituals."

"I won't allow it," Gundhalinu said. His hand moved to his touchboard, clearing the screen with an automatic veto.

Echarthe touched his own board again; one by one the others around the table did the same, as Wayaways watched, smiling, hands in his lap. Gundhalinu watched their feedback tally. As the votes became unanimous against him Borskad's motion reappeared, inexorably, on all their screens.

"Overridden, Justice," Borskad said. He cracked his knuckles complacently. "The Tiamatans must be permitted to control their own government."

"I won't allow it," Gundhalinu repeated tonelessly. "I'll have the Police stop them."

"You can't do that, BZ," Vhanu murmured, beside him. Gundhalinu turned, looking into his eyes. "Only I have that authority," Vhanu said. Gundhalinu saw regret and discomfort in his gaze, but no doubt at all. "You can't stop it."

Gundhalinu turned back, seeing the resolve and determination in all their faces. "Damn it, I will not permit the Queen to be sacrificed!"

"There's no other choice, Justice," Borskad said bluntly. "The Hegemony wants the water of life. We have to get it for them, one way or another, or they'll find someone who can."

"There's no other way." Vhanu shook his head. "That woman and her troublesome demands are going to cost all of us our positions here—including your Chief Justiceship, BZ. I would rather see the Queen sacrificed than our entire government, wouldn't you? After all the years of effort we put into achieving this goal, I for one am not ready to lose everything. But that is what will happen."

"Unless—" Wayaways dropped the single word among the rest, let its ripples spread until there was complete silence.

"Unless what?" Gundhalinu forced himself to ask, knowing that his visible humility and hidden humiliation were required elements in Wayaways' equation.

"Unless you change your previous ruling and permit the mers to be hunted. Then we can all have what we wanted in the first place—the Hegemony gets the water of life, Tiamat profits from it, and you get to save the Queen. That way everyone is happy . . . except the Queen, perhaps, but I expect even she would prefer disappointment to death. I'm sure the people would agree to let her continue as Queen as long as we get what we want. She was actually quite an enlightened woman, for a Summer, until she developed this unfortunate religious fixation on the sacredness of the mers. . . ."

The mutterings began again around the table; their tone was positive this time, urging him to agree. Wayaways sat in their midst without speaking, staring directly at him cross the torus of burnished native wood.

"It makes a lot of sense," Vhanu murmured in Gundhalinu's ear, his voice both encouraging and conciliatory.

Gundhalinu looked away from him, tight-lipped, and back at Wayaways again. *The mers die or the Queen dies,* Wayaways' eyes said to him. *You choose.*

"All right. . . ." Gundhalinu looked down. "All right," he said again, his voice stronger, as if he were actually in control of the situation. "I'm rescinding my ban on the mer hunts. But there will be no more sacrifices, no more Changes in the old way. Summers and Winters will have to work out some other way of doing things from now on."

"You are as wise as you are fair, Justice Gundhalinu," Wayaways said, and smiled.

"The Council meeting is adjourned." Gundhalinu blanked his screen, and crushed the food wrapper into oblivion in his hidden fist.

TIAMAT: Carbuncle

"The Queen, sir."

Moon moved past the uniformed aide as he stepped aside for her. She glanced away self-consciously as he caught her staring a moment too long at his face. The alienness of his offworlder features, of every person's features since she had entered the Government complex, only made her feel more strongly that she had stepped outside the safety of her own world, and into the unknown. She tried not to think of it as *enemy ground,* but the image formed anyway in her unwilling thoughts. The aide glanced down, too quickly, from staring at her own face a moment too long; she saw only curiosity in his gaze, nothing more.

She moved on into the office, taking in old familiar surroundings made suddenly disconcerting by the overlay of things which were new and unfamiliar. BZ Gundhalinu, Chief Justice of Tiamat, sat waiting for her behind the smooth, modular form of a desk/terminal—its electronic systems all fully alive and functional, and still just as startling, to some perverse part of her mind, as the strangers who were its new purveyors. She wondered how long it would be before native and offworlder stopped seeming alien to one another . . . whether they ever would.

BZ's eyes touched her face, alive with surprise and pleasure. As she saw his expression her sense of uncertainty vanished, along with all sense that she was looking at the face of a stranger. He smiled; she felt the sudden, painful constriction of her heart, something she had grown so used to that she kept all sign of it from showing in her response. She forced herself to remember why she had come, that it had nothing to do with the sight of him; and that he would understand that, all too soon.

He pushed up from his seat. "Lady," he said, bowing his head in acknowledgment, the formality of his speech belying what she had seen in his eyes, as he found her standing before him alone. "This is an unexpected pleasure. Welcome to my office." His smile widened as he started around the corner of his desk to greet her.

"You are welcome to my office, Justice Gundhalinu," she said, holding out her hand in a way that forced him to shake it, like a Tiamatan. He took her hand; his grip was gentle and strong, keeping the contact slightly longer than was necessary. She closed her fingers over the lingering warmth in her palm as he let it go; lowered her hand to her side. He looked at her quizzically, and her own smile turned wry. "This was my office, when the Sibyl College met here . . . as it did for all the years while you were gone." The College met in the palace now.

"Ah," he said, and his smile caught slightly. He glanced away at the aide, who was still waiting in the doorway. "Thank you, Stathis. . . . No interruptions, while I'm meeting with the Queen." The aide saluted and left the room; the door closed behind him, granting them privacy. BZ remained where he was, motionless, for a moment longer; she became acutely aware of his sudden sense of awkwardness, and her own. "Please, sit down." He gestured toward a low, wing-form chair, and retreated behind his desk.

"This is the first time you've come . . . here"—barely avoiding *"to my office"*—"to meet with me. It must be an important matter, Lady. What can I do for you?" In all their previous encounters he had gone to the palace, at her request. He had usually attended those meetings surrounded by a shield of advisors, just as she had. She had wondered whether it was for the same reason, as she lay sleepless at night after every meeting, replaying in her memory his every word, his every gesture. They had not been alone together once, since his arrival; and until today, she had never met with him on the Hegemony's ground. He leaned forward across the safe barrier of his desktop, his body asking her for an answer she could not give.

"I've come to you . . ." she began; broke off, looking away from his intent gaze. "I want to know why you've changed your mind about the mers," she said, bluntly, because there was no other way to ask it.

Comprehension, frustration, and something that could have been resignation showed in his eyes, and faded again so swiftly that she wasn't certain she had seen them at all. "I see," he said.

"Why have you lifted the ban on hunting them? You know that I forbid it—the mers are under Summer's protection. You have no right, no jurisdiction—"

His mouth tightened; suddenly his face looked drawn and tired. "I had to."

She frowned. "It isn't true." She heard the cold anger of betrayal come into her voice. "You know what I've told you about them . . . you know what the Transfer itself says about the mers: that they're sentient." She had demonstrated it to him, and to his advisors using BZ himself as the sibyl, asking the question of him, and hearing him speak the answer, in front of them all. "Everyone has heard it!"

He looked down, at his hands on the desk surface, and up at her again. "The truth wasn't enough to stop the hunts, before. And it isn't now." He shook his head. "Moon, I've postponed the inevitable as long as I can. I've sent out research teams, had them process and analyze your data. I know there's something there—but I can't make my people, or the Central Coordinating Committee, see it. They only see what they want to see. And the sibyl mind can claim the mers are sentient until the end of time, but damn it, the mers don't *do* anything that supports it, at least not in the way human beings have always defined 'intelligent behavior.' They don't give us any help in this; they don't even understand the question. Their society is too subtle—or too alien. The independent studies don't give enough corroboration to stop the kind of people who want the water of life. Even if it is true—"

"If—?" she began, her knuckles whitening.

"They want the water of life, and they want it now!" He met her anger with sudden heat. "And too many of them are in positions of power back home."

Home. She realized that he meant *Kharemough.* "But it isn't simply about the mers' right to live—not simply about genocide," she said bitterly. "If the mer population is decimated, then the entire Hegemony will suffer—all the worlds that were the Old Empire—"

He looked at her, uncomprehendingly. "Why?" he said. "Simply because they've lost the mers? It doesn't *matter* to them, don't you understand me?"

"No!" She rose from her seat, shaking her head. "You don't understand. It's more than that—it's much more. It would matter to them, if they could only be told—"

"Told what?" His voice hardened with exasperation. He leaned forward across his desk again. "Is there something else? What do you know that you haven't said, what do you know that you haven't told me?"

"I know that . . . that . . ." Her throat closed, her eyes, her hands, tightening into fists. She shook her head, fighting it with all her strength, but it would not yield. "I know what I know," she whispered, dropping back into her chair, still unable even to look at him.

"Gods . . ." he murmured, rubbing his face, leaning back in his seat. "Father of all my grandfathers, Moon, I've been doing everything I humanly can for you—your world. I've restructured the quotas on the number of mers that can be taken, I've made them as low as I possibly can. I've argued myself blue with my advisors. At least they accept that there have to be *some* limits, or the mers will disappear, soon—even their logic can get that far. And I'll continue to give you all the resources I can toward your research. I've already got my own people working on ways to increase the mers' birthrate, or ways to take the water of life without actually killing them."

She looked up at him, finally, with a hard knot of disgust in her throat.

"This is the real world, damn it!" he said, and she heard his own self-disgust. "We live by compromise and concession, or we don't survive. We have no choice."

"We always have a choice," she said. But her own despair sank through her like a stone, at the knowledge of what lay inside her, the secret eating her alive that she would never be able to share.

"Moon," he said softly, "I was given a choice: to sacrifice the mers . . . or to sacrifice you."

She stared at him, feeling her face sting with sudden disbelief.

"Certain factions among your people—among the Winters—have been pushing the Hegemony for an official return of Winter to power at the Festival, when the Assembly arrives. They wanted you thrown into the sea. Certain factions among my people—including the representative from the Central Committee—wanted the same thing. I tried to warn you that I couldn't hold out on this forever. I had to choose, your life or the mers. . . . I chose you."

"Mother of Us All," Moon murmured, almost a prayer. She looked down; a tremor passed through her. "How can this have happened—?"

"Moon," he said, "we are walking across the Pit, don't you understand that? If we move too fast or too slowly, if we don't sound exactly the right note in exactly the right sequence, the winds of change will sweep us both away. They nearly did at that meeting yesterday. The Hegemony hasn't crushed the technological development you've begun here, because I've been laying groundwork since I was still on Kharemough to make them accept that it's too late to go back. Now that they know the secret is out about sibyls, I've begun to make them believe that it's smarter economically and politically to give Tiamat's people what they want. But there's a price for that, there's a price for everything— The Hegemony came back to Tiamat for one reason, the water of life. They're going to take it whether we like it or not. Tiamat can get something in return for that, or it can get nothing. For gods' sakes, Moon, I'm doing the best I can for you! Tell me you understand that—"

She raised her head, her mind filled with her own helpless anger until she could not think. She stared at him across an eternity of time and distance and aching doubt: seeing in his face both past and present, a stranger and a lover; seeing the trefoil's light against the stark blackness of his uniform. She pressed her hand to her eyes; let her hand fall away, as she was finally able to see clearly again. "Yes," she murmured at last, "I do understand. . . . I know all you've done for—for us, since the Return. I understand."

He nodded, and looked down; the urgency left his eyes, the tension left his body, leaving him drained.

She rose slowly from her chair, understanding now that there was nothing either of them could humanly do to stop the Hunt, if she could not tell him the true reason why it mattered. And she could not. She could not.

She turned away, staring at the picture on the wall behind her—a strangely sensuous mingling of colors, static and yet somehow alive, solid but ephemeral, like a frozen moment in the slow swirling dance of oil on water. It was like nothing she had ever seen; it had not been there when this office was hers.

She heard BZ get up from his seat, felt him cross the room to where she stood. She was suddenly aware of her own heartbeat; wondering if even he could hear it, because it was so loud.

"We've never had a chance to really talk to one another since—I came back," he said, and his Tiamatan became oddly stilted and clumsy. She glanced at him, curious. He raised his hand, pointing at the picture. "My wife did that. She's an artist."

Moon turned from studying the painting again to stare at him. "Oh—?" she said. A rush of heat filled her face. "Oh." She looked at the painting for what seemed like an eternity, clutching her elbows. "Have—have you been married long?" She wondered if he was telling her, now, in this way, to pay her back for coming here in anger to accuse him about the mers . . . or whether there had simply been no easy way for him to tell her this, either. She felt a deep, wounding pain, suddenly angry again—at him for the way his eyes had belonged only to her, at their every meeting since his return; at herself, because she had no right even to think—

"About three years."

"Oh," she said again, inanely; groping for something more to say, anything. "Do you . . . have children?"

He hesitated, staring at the picture. "I have a son; he's about six months old. My wife sent me a holo of him not long ago. He looks very handsome." His mouth curved up in a rueful smile, but his eyes filled with regret. "It was a marriage of convenience," he said softly, at last. "I had to do something to ensure that my family estates would be taken care of after I left for Tiamat. People who are in the Foreign Service often make such arrangements." He glanced at her, away again.

"Oh." She looked at the picture, feeling its sensuality like a wave of heat. *But did you love her?* She swallowed the question like a lump of bitter bread. "You'll never see your child?" she asked, instead.

"I don't know," he murmured, almost inaudibly, as if his own throat had suddenly constricted. "Moon—" He ran his hand through his hair. "Tammis and Ariele . . . Sparks isn't their father, is he?"

She turned back to him, feeling something like panic rise in her.

"They're mine, aren't they?" he said roughly. "Sparks was using the water of life, he couldn't have gotten you pregnant."

She stared at him. "Is that true? That the water of life made it impossible—?"

He nodded. "They're mine," he said again, the words soft and almost wondering, this time. "They're ours—"

It was what she had wondered for years; what Sparks must have wondered as well. But she had never been sure, never wanted to be, any more than he had—until the moment when BZ had stood before her again and she had seen his face. "Yes." Finally, absolutely certain, after so long. She looked at his face now, remembering it then, seeing the ways in which it had changed. He had been several years older than she was, when they had met; now, through the vagaries of fate and spacetime, their ages were nearly the same. "Thank you," she said finally, her voice still strained, "for our children."

"Does Sparks know?"

"I . . . Yes. He knows. He knows. . . ." She looked down, at her hands twining, finger into finger, twisting against the smooth, imported bluegreen cloth of her robes. They had not slept in the same bed since the day that Sparks had found her watching his rival through the secret window, like Arienrhod. . . .

"How is he taking it?" BZ asked.

"Not well." She kept her eyes averted. Even during the days she rarely saw him. He did not work with her, with the College, with anyone she knew, anymore. He locked himself away in his own rooms, lost in his studies and calculations, barricaded behind a wall of new technology. Or he went out. *I'm going out,* he said, and never said where. She had heard that he spent most of his time in the Maze . . . that he spent it in the company of the Winter nobles he had turned his back on, along with the past; the ones who wanted her sacrificed. He was not turning his back on them anymore.

"How are you getting along?" BZ asked; pushing, as if he couldn't help himself, when she did not say anything else.

"Not well," she only said, again; but this time she looked at him.

"I'm sorry." He sighed, shaking his head. "I truly didn't come here to cause you grief, Moon. I . . . ." He broke off. He lifted his hand, tentatively, to touch her arm; she saw sudden hope in his eyes.

"I know," she whispered. She could not move away, as if his touch had paralyzed her. Her own hand rose, of its own will, moving toward him. She forced it down to her side. "Don't," she whispered. "Please don't."

His hand dropped away. He looked at it, shaking his head again, as if he didn't know what had come over him, or what to do now. "What about Ariele and Tammis?" he asked, after a long moment.

"What do you mean?" she said uncertainly.

"Do they know . . . do they realize . . . ?"

She glanced away. "I don't . . . I don't even know how to talk to them about it. I don't know how to talk to them at all. Any of them." She shook her head, seeing Tammis's troubled eyes, seeing him turn away and avoid her when she tried to ask him what was wrong; watching Ariele's defiant behavior mimic the behavior of the only father she had ever known, more and more, as he withdrew completely from them all. . . . She never had known how to talk to them, any of them, she realized suddenly; and now it was too late.

"If I tried—" BZ began.

"No." She looked away, toward the door.

"You don't think I have the right, after so long? If I'd known you were pregnant, Moon, I'd never have left you—"

"It isn't that." She shook her head. *But what was it, then?* She pressed her mouth together. "Sparks is still my husband. It's something we have to work out on our own." Realizing, as she said it, how the words excluded him. She looked up at him again. "Tell me . . . tell me that you understand."

He grimaced, and nodded. He turned away abruptly, striding back to his desk. He made a swift pass of his hands over the terminal's touchboard.

"What are you doing?" she asked.

He looked up. "Deleting this conversation from the record."

She started, realizing all at once that nothing which went on in this room was private from the Hegemony, unless BZ chose to make it so; remembering again, painfully, that this was no longer her ground, or safe ground. She stood where she was, looking at him for a long moment. "I have to be going."

He nodded again. But she stood motionless for another span of heartbeats, unable to make herself move toward the door. She turned away at last, when he said nothing more, and went out without looking back.

TIAMAT: Carbuncle

Tammis made his way through the halls of Carbuncle's city medical center, more aware of the knot of tension in his chest than of anything in his physical surroundings. He did not look anyone in the eye as he passed them; glad that Merovy had shown him around the complex enough times that he could find his way to her without having to ask directions.

Most of the staff moving past him through the halls were still offworlders, strangers to him; just as virtually all of the mostly unidentifiable medical equipment that he glimpsed everywhere was imported from offworld. The offworlders seemed to have a horror of finding themselves stranded here, so far from home, without the technology to save them from any imaginable disease or emergency . . . although, he thought sourly, it had not hurt their consciences any to leave the people of Tiamat without it, whenever they had left this world in the past, for all the long centuries.

At least his people would have permanent access to it now, and from now on. He thought of his father-in-law's bad back, and tried to be grateful, for Danaquil Lu's sake. And the new Chief Justice had established the medtech training program that Merovy had joined. It was partly pragmatism, he was sure—the hospital had been severely understaffed almost from the moment the offworlders had returned.

But it had also seemed to be part of a genuine effort by the Chief Justice to create goodwill. He wondered briefly, bleakly, if the Chief Justice was doing it all only to please the Summer Queen . . . if what Elco Teel and the others said behind his back was true, that BZ Gundhalinu was his mother's former lover who had returned after so many years. If it was true that when he looked into the Chief Justice's dark, foreign face, he actually saw an echo of his own face. . . .

His sister had stalked off furiously when he had mentioned it to her; his mother had murmured evasions, looking pale and distracted, when he tried to ask her. He had not asked his father, because his father would barely even look at him, since the incident at his wedding feast. Merovy had said she saw no resemblance between his face and the Chief Justice's . . . but she had looked away from him as she said it.

Merovy. His eyes registered the halls of the medical complex again; he made his way past the shining, ascetic form of some machine whose function Merovy had explained to him once, but which he no longer remembered. *Merovy* . . . Suddenly nothing was on his mind but the reason he had come here: to see Merovy, to ask her *why*—? Why he had come home last night to an empty house, to a handwritten message on a page still damp with tears, which said she was leaving him; that he could come and speak to her here today. No further explanation, no other words. Although, sick at heart, he had known her leaving needed no explanation.

Someone greeted him by name—an offworlder, one of the technicians who were Merovy's supervisors here at the hospital. "Your wife's in 212."

He murmured thanks, keeping his head down—sure that anyone who got a look into his eyes would read his guilt and know exactly why he had come here, why she had left him, why . . .

He reached the lab where Merovy was working; saw her sitting at a terminal, her thick brown hair trapped in a neat braid at her back. He saw a data model flicker and change in the air before her, watched her control its metamorphosis with deft skill and perfect concentration. Having seen her father's suffering through most of her childhood, and seeing how the offworlders' medicine had ended it, she had wanted to have a place in the new medical technology more than he ever remembered her wanting anything . . . except, once upon a time, him. "Merovy," he said softly.

She turned in her seat, startled but not surprised. "I'm glad you came," she said, but the words were empty.

"You asked me to." He held out his hands, half shrug, half placating gesture. "Why couldn't we have done this at home?"

"Because you didn't come home last night. I waited and waited for you. Again."

"I had work to do—"

"Don't lie about it!" She rose from her seat, her face flushed. "We've tried to talk about it there, too many times. It never does any good."

"Merovy . . . I'm sorry." He shook his head, looking down. "This time it will be different, I swear to you."

"You always say that! And it never changes." Her eyes filled with tears of anger, overflowed with tears of grief. "I'm not what you want, I'm only what you need, to hide behind. But I know everyone laughs at me when I'm not there, when you leave me behind—even to my face. Why do you want me to come back? I'm not a boy—I'd be anything you want, but I can't be that. I wish I could change myself, if it would make you love me as much as I love you—"

"I don't want you to change!" His hands tightened into fists with the need to hold her—knowing that to touch her would be the worst thing he could do.

"You don't know what you want." She turned away, crossing the room to the storage cabinets along the walls. She queried one, and took something out. She came back across the room, and held the thing out to him in her hand—a sheet with what looked like medicine patches on it. "Here," she said, her voice strained. "Take this, and wear one patch every day for a week. You have a venereal disease."

He felt his face redden. He took the sheet from her with numb fingers. "How do you know?" he whispered incredulously.

Her eyes turned cold and clear. "Because you gave it to me."

He shut his eyes.

"If you ever really decide what you want, then we can talk about it again. Not until then." Her mouth quivered, but he saw the utter conviction in her face, and knew that she would not change her mind.

He turned away, his throat choked with grief, and left the room.

TIAMAT: Carbuncle

Moon Dawntreader stood alone, waiting, among the docks that drifted like seaweed on the smooth surface of the sea below Carbuncle. She looked down at the green-black water moving below the interstices of the pier, the secret instability beneath her feet. Oil slicks and stranger, less definable secretions made iridescent patterns on the impenetrable darkness between the moored ships. She watched them shift and re-form, hypnotized by their deliberate motion, by the familiar shouting and clangor, the smells of the sea and ships that filled the dockyards, filling her with nostalgia.

She no longer felt the kind of yearning for the past that had once made her ache to return to the places of her childhood; she no longer had the sense that her life in the city was only a long dream. That other world was gone now, not just because of the changing climate or shifting populations, but because of the years themselves, the thousand thousand separate moments that had settled over her memories like windblown sand. She could no longer clearly see the girl she had once been, who could not have imagined a life spent in a place such as this, when she didn't feel the wind or the sun or the rain for weeks at a time, and never thought of the Sea Mother, let alone believed that She watched over every action, heard every prayer. In time it had all faded, until the life she lived now had grown to seem natural.

She looked up, feeling Carbuncle's presence above her, not reassuring and protecting, but heavy and threatening, like a storm. Her restless gaze searched the ramp leading down to the harbor, this time finding what she had been searching for, the familiar form of Capella Goodventure. She suddenly remembered standing here half a lifetime ago, the newly chosen Queen, needing desperately to have time alone to make her peace with Sparks, and the sea . . . feeling Capella Goodventure's presence shadowing them, as the Goodventures followed her everywhere, spying on her, judging her. . . .

But now it was Capella Goodventure she needed to see, privately, intimately; just the two of them and the sea, in this public place that was more private now than anywhere in the city above, even the palace. Her bodyguards, who were always nearby since the offworlders' return, stood a respectful distance away, with their attention fixed intently on their surroundings.

Capella Goodventure reached her side and nodded in acknowledgment. There was respect, and, almost, warmth, in her gaze as their eyes met. "What is it you need, Lady?" There was also curiosity, about why they were meeting here, like this.

"It isn't for me, but for the mers, that I need your help. The Chief Justice has lifted the ban on hunting them."

Capella Goodventure's mouth thinned. "I knew it would come to that. He is nothing but an offworlder, for all his pretenses."

Moon bit her tongue against the need to explain, to justify, to argue against prejudices that had risen too easily in her own mind as she had made her way through the streets of the city today. She had come to respect Capella Goodventure, even to appreciate her. But the woman was unyielding in her beliefs, and her distrust of the offworlders was as complete as her conviction that they were not a government but an infestation. Looking into that face, with its lines of hard and pitiless judgment, she was suddenly afraid that if things continued, someday she would find her own face reflected there. And so she made no attempt to argue, but only said, "I don't have the power to stop them. But I intend to impede them, in every way possible."

Capella Goodventure's eyes came alive. "What do you want us to do?"

"I want you to spread the word among the Summers—to ask their help, when they're out on the sea, to mark the presence of offworlders hunting for the mers, and do anything in their power to disrupt the hunt, without endangering themselves. You can interfere with the Hegemony's ships and equipment, or better, disperse mer colonies when hunters are approaching." They had never been able to make the mers understand the threat of an attack by hunters. The mers seemed incapable of comprehending the brutal unpredictability of human nature.

"Of course," Capella Goodventure said. "But it will be hard. The offworlders have their technology—" The word grated like a curse. "It will be hard to get around them."

"I know." Moon nodded. "I'll get you equipment of your own that can show you their locations and interfere with their tracking devices. I can get sonics that will panic the mers and drive them into the sea, to force them to save themselves. I don't like the idea of that either—" she insisted, as Capella Goodventure frowned. "But I'd rather use the offworlders' equipment against them than see the mers slaughtered. Wouldn't you?"

Capella Goodventure pulled irritably at the heavy cloth of her scarf. "I don't like anything to do with the offworlders' technology, as you well know," she said. "Learning how to use their equipment, even if it is to use it against them, goes against everything I believe to be right."

Moon tensed at the other woman's threat of refusal. But Capella Goodventure shrugged, her hands knotting deep in the pockets of her loose trousers. "But for the mers—only for them, this has nothing to do with you, and don't you take credit for forcing me—I accept your offer. Equipment will go on the ships and be used for the purpose intended, to defy its masters and protect the Sea's Children, if that is the Lady's will. And I am sure She will let us know whether it is Her will, or not. . . ." She leaned over the rail and spat three times, reverently, into the water listening below. It was only then that Moon realized Capella Goodventure was speaking not to her, but to the Sea Mother Herself.

"Thank you, Capella Goodventure." Moon smiled, satisfied. "The Lady is well-pleased with your dedication." Not sure, herself, which one of them she spoke for, or of, she offered her own prayer of resolution and dedication to the nameless, lifeless thing they both served.

TIAMAT: Carbuncle

"Damn it, boss, you're late—"

Reede jerked to a stop at the entrance to Starhiker's as he was unexpectedly accosted by Niburu. "So what?" he said. He had almost not come at all, knowing that Ariele Dawntreader would be here, waiting for him, with that look in her eyes. He had come anyway, finally, telling himself that it was only to break off this lie of a relationship. He had to make sure that she stayed away from him from now on—absolutely sure. It had gotten them noticed, gotten him in trouble, made him vulnerable . . . and her. He couldn't afford that, couldn't afford to let anybody get close to him ever, while he wore the Source's brand.

He told himself again that she was only a habit he had gotten into. Just because she loved the mers, and talked of growing up with the sea as if it were the most natural, beautiful thing in the world . . . just because she belonged to this world, and this strange city, that seemed to touch some part of his shattered soul with exquisite, inexplicable déjà vu . . . that was no reason to think he felt anything real about her. Just because when he talked of those things with her he knew peace, and a sense of his own humanity; just because she looked at him with longing, as if he were really a man, whole and sane. . . . Habits were made to be broken.

None of it meant shit, he told himself fiercely. It couldn't; it was suicide, murder. She had saved his life. Now he would save hers, by never seeing her again.

"Ariele—" Niburu said.

"What about her?" Reede demanded. He caught Niburu by the shoulder, making the shorter man wince.

"She just left—" Niburu gestured down the Street.

Reede let him go, glancing away into the crowds. He thought he caught a glimpse of silver-white, wasn't sure. "So what?" he repeated, oddly relieved that fate had granted him a delay. He started to push past Niburu, heading into the club.

"Reede!" Niburu shouted, in sudden exasperation. "Listen to me, you bastard!"

Reede turned back, mildly incredulous.

"I think maybe she's in trouble."

Reede came back to him. "What do you mean?"

"She was waiting for you like usual, and that kid Elco Teel started hassling her, trying to get her to go to some party with him, and she wouldn't. And then all of a sudden she changed. It was night and day, suddenly she was all over him, and then they went out together."

Reede frowned. "So she went to a party." He gave a grunt of disgust. "You expect me to give a damn?"

Niburu caught his sleeve, holding him when he would have turned away again. "I said she *changed*. It wasn't like she changed her mind, it was like something happened to her. Tor saw it too, she says Elco Teel slipped Ariele something."

Tor—the woman who ran the club. He remembered that Niburu was having an affair with her. "She was practically eating him, right there in public, boss. It didn't look right to me either. Tor said if you care anything about her, you ought to check it out."

Reede swore, searching the crowd again, not seeing anyone now who might have been Ariele. "Which way did they go?"

"I sent Ananke to follow her. You can track him by remote."

Reede looked down at him, with abrupt surprise. "Good." He nodded. He touched Niburu's shoulder briefly, as he switched on the tracer and found Ananke's signal.

"You want me to go with you, boss?"

He shook his head. "No," he said.

"I can keep up. If there's trouble—"

"If there's trouble it's not your legs that get in my way. It's your fucking conscience." Reede turned on his heel and started off into the crowd.

The trail led him down the Street's languid spiral; not up it like he'd expected, toward the townhouses that belonged to the rich Winters and offworlders. Instead Ananke, and the ones he was following, were headed into rougher territory, the interface of the lower Maze and the Lower City, where most of the Summers lived, closer to the sea—where warehouse districts and processing plants took up entire alleys, and things were likely to happen that nobody wanted to talk about the next day.

He pushed himself, moving faster as he realized where they were headed, as the crowds thinned out around him. At last he reached the entrance to an alley that looked entirely deserted. He hesitated and then started down it, as the tracer told him, in an insistent monotone, that it was not as deserted as it looked.

He moved deeper down the empty throat of silence, reaching into his heavy jacket. He drew his stunner and checked the charge as he walked like a hunting cat along the looming, ancient building fronts. At last he heard something, a faint echo of voices; he slowed, entering the claustrophobic accessway between warehouses. "Ananke!" he whispered, as his eyes made out a familiar form waiting in the shadows.

Ananke jerked around and Reede saw light flash on metal; saw his face go from grim fear to stupefied relief inside of a heartbeat. "Boss—" he murmured, sagging against the wall. The dagger he always wore at his belt, that Reede had never seen him draw, was in his hand. "I was going in—"

Reede could hear other voices clearly now. He gestured Ananke aside, climbed up onto the pile of boxes so that he could see in through the spot rubbed clear on the heavy, grime-coated glass of a small, high window. There was a party going on inside; and he knew without looking closer what kind of party it was. He watched a moment longer anyway, tensely searching for a familiar face, a shock of milk-white hair. . . . *There*.

He leaped down, facing Ananke again. "That's all you've got?" he said, nodding at the dagger.

Ananke grimaced. "Sorry, boss, I—"

"Shut up. Take this." Reede pulled his own knife, and handed it over. "Don't kill anybody, for gods' sakes—at least not by accident. Is the door locked?"

"I don't know."

Reede grunted, pushing past him. The door was locked. He input an override sequence and shoved it open, ignoring its programmed alarm. They ran down a short corridor; met someone coming to check out the bleating door as they reached the end. Reede hit him in the face with the stunner's weighted butt, and he went down without a protest.

Reede stepped over him and entered the space beyond, with Ananke following. The perimeter of the warehouse was crowded with piled crates and equipment; the bleak, open space at its center had been covered with cargo mats. There was a crate topped with a variety of cheap drugs, and a crowd of maybe a dozen people, most of them offworlders, most of them men, tough-looking, laborers and brands, probably. Elco Teel stood at one side, with three other young Winters from his crowd, two girls and a boy. Reede watched them watching, pointing, tittering; his own eyes leaped to the object of their attention.

Ariele Dawntreader stood in the center of the room, on the waiting mats, surrounded by a restless cluster of men. The one strap of her long, rainbow-shaded tunic was off her shoulder, the tunic halfway down to her waist. The total stranger she was kissing, deeply and thoroughly, was fondling her breasts, as someone else moved in on her from behind, pulling the tunic farther down her half-naked body. Whistles and catcalls echoed from the hard, pitiless surfaces of the room.

Ananke swore, starting forward. Reede pushed him back again, out of the way; raised the stunner and took aim. He fired. The offworlder in the process of dropping his pants behind Ariele clutched his groin with a yelp of disbelief. He collapsed on the floor, in a sudden puddle of his own urine, as he lost control of his body functions.

"Ariele!"

Heads turned all around the room, away from the spectacle in front of them, toward him. The offworlder who was fondling Ariele let her go, pushing her away roughly as she tried to cling to him. She stumbled free, turned unsteadily to stare at Reede along with everyone else. Her eyes were glassy and uncomprehending. She looked down at herself, up at his face, away again, with a peculiar quirk of her head.

Reede came on into the room, brandishing the gun. No one moved, all of them caught somewhere between chagrin and disbelief. "Ananke," he said, and pointed toward Elco Teel, "cover the little perverts, over there. Don't let them go anywhere." He watched Ananke move forward, holding the two knives in plain sight, to stand guard in front of them. "Now," he said, to the mob of sullen, silent men who still surrounded Ariele.

One of them took a step toward him. He raised the gun and the man backed up again. But he read the speculation in their eyes as they began to realize how outnumbered he was. Ananke looked his way, uneasy.

"I'm calling the Blues," Reede said, certain that he had everyone's attention, "and reporting this gang bang. Maybe you cocksuckers want to hang around and see how much fun you can have with the Queen's daughter before they get here . . . or maybe you want to see how far away you can get instead." He touched his remote with his free hand, putting in a callcode.

The offworlders began to move, one by one—toward the door this time. He kept the gun trained on them as they passed, their steps quickening as panic began to set in. They were out of the building inside of half a minute, dragging along the piss-stinking one he'd crippled. The door slammed shut behind them. He was sure they wouldn't be back.

He moved slowly across the room to the spot where Ariele stood, her face still dazed and unfathomable as she tried to pull her clothing back into place. She stopped trying as she saw him come toward her, and held out her arms. "Reede . . ." she whispered.

Reede stuck the stunner through his belt and pushed her hands aside. He caught the strap of her tunic, keeping his eyes on her face as he pulled the soft, shining cloth up over her breasts, sliding the strap back onto her shoulder with gentle, noncommittal motions. She put her arms around him, pulling him against her. "Stop it," he said, and shook her off. "Stay there." He started back across the room to the place where Elco Teel stood; realizing, annoyed, that Ariele was following him. Reede studied Elco Teel's pouting, frightened face, his pouting, frightened companions.

"Did you really call the Blues?" Ananke murmured, staring at him.

Reede laughed. "No," he said; saw Ananke relax, and the young Winters start to relax with him. His own body stiffened as Ariele came up behind him and wrapped her arms around him again, sliding her fingers into the seal of his shirt. He pulled her hand free irritably. One of the Winter girls gave a high, nervous giggle, watching Ariele's hands crawl over his body as if they had a life of their own.

"You think it's funny?" Ananke said, suddenly. Reede looked at him, surprised by the hard bitterness of his voice. "You really think laughing at her makes you safe? Makes you one of them—?" He jerked his head at Elco Teel and the other boy. "The next time it might be your turn, sister—"

The girl glared at him, sidling closer to Elco Teel, taking hold of his arm.

Reede stepped forward, catching the expensive, diaphanous shimmercloth of her tunic at its collar. He ripped it open to her waist with a sudden, brutal motion. "And next time they might not bother to put you in the mood, first, sweeting—"

The girl cried out, shrinking away from his touch as she pulled her torn clothes together. Elco Teel's face tightened, but he made no move to stop it, to help her. The other Winters gaped, wide-eyed.

Reede turned his back on them, pushing Ariele away, maddeningly aware that he was starting to get an erection. He swung back to face Elco Teel; held his hand out to Ananke. Ananke passed him his blade silently, uneasily. Reede raised the knife until its tip was touching Elco Teel's throat. "I didn't call the Blues, because they might object to what I have in mind for you, little man," Reede said softly.

Elco Teel went white, his whole body seeming to shrivel back from the knife's point.

"This was no accident, was it, Elco Teel?" Reede murmured, tracing an infinity sign along the quivering length of Elco Teel's neck. Even Ariele was silent and still now, waiting and listening; no longer touching him, although a part of him was still aware only of her, the feel of her, the smell of her— He wrenched his attention back. "Your old man put you up to this, and the Source put him up to it, am I right?"

"I don't know," Elco gibbered. "Yes—maybe— Da gave me the drug! He said I could get back at her, at you, because you took her away from me—"

Reede's hand jerked downward in a sudden, slashing movement, and Elco Teel screamed in pain.

Reede stepped back, inspecting his work. Elco Teel swayed on his feet, making a mewling whine as he stared down at the hanging ruins of his expensive clothes; at the thin, precise line of the wound running from his throat to his navel, the spreading ribbon of red oozing out of it as he watched.

Reede caught Elco's chin, lifting his head ungently. "Now listen to me, you little turd. You tell your father . . . you tell him it didn't work. And tell him he's out of his depth. You tell him it's a closed game, between me and the Source. That this is just a warning. That next time they'll have to put the pieces of your body back together like a puzzle just to bury you. . . . And that's nothing, compared to what I'll do to him. Do you think you can remember all that?"

"Y-yes," Elco Teel whimpered. Tears leaked out of his eyes.

"Then go tell him." Reede wiped his blade on the rags of Elco Teel's shirt and stepped aside, opening a space for Elco Teel and the others to escape. They fled, Elco Teel leading the way.

Reede watched them go, listened for the heavy reverberation of the slamming door. He put his knife away.

Ananke did the same, echoing his motions. Reede saw the look on his face then, half stunned admiration and half concern. "What's going to happen now?" Ananke said finally.

"What do you mean?"

"The Source—"

Reede grimaced, realizing with an odd annoyance that the concern in Ananke's eyes had as much to do with him as it did with Ananke's own safety. He shook his head, and shrugged, all the response he could bring himself to make.

Soft hands touched him again, unexpectedly, and he started. Ariele was back beside him, caressing him, her lips brushing his cheek. Her touch was more tentative this time, but still it made his body sing like a plucked wire. "Stop it," he murmured; but this time it was harder to push her away, as if something was slowing his motions, weighing down his resolve like gravity.

Ananke stood watching them, with uncertainty coming back into his face.

"Go back to the club and find Niburu," Reede said. "Tell him everything's all right."

Ananke glanced at Ariele. "What about—?"

"She'll be all right."

"Maybe I should stay, and help you get her home. . . ."

"I'll take care of it," he snapped, when Ananke still hesitated. "Get out."

Ananke nodded, with obvious reluctance. His eyes stayed on Ariele, on her hands, her mouth, and the things they were trying to do to Reede's body, as he started for the door.

Reede jerked free of her again as Ananke went out; taking hold of her arms when she reached for him. His skin seemed to burn where she had touched it. Elco Teel must have slipped her a dose of possession. He knew that it breathed through the skin, making someone who was under its influence contagious, infecting whoever touched them with the same helpless arousal. The throbbing ache in his loins spread through his entire body, making him sweat, making him burn. He told himself that it was impossible, drugs didn't affect him at all— "Ariele," he said fiercely, shaking her. "You don't want this. Stop it!"

She struggled against his hold, her eyes filling with tears . . . her eyes that were like agate, like fog, like no eyes he had ever seen. "I didn't want *them*—I wanted *you*. I want *you*." Suddenly she was soft and yielding in his grip, candlewax touched by flame, clinging to him everywhere, warm and fragrant. Murmuring, "Please, oh please . . . Reede please . . . only you. Only you. . . ." She pressed her lips to his half-bared chest, devouring him with kisses. His own arms were suddenly strengthless as he heard her speak his name, as he saw recognition in her eyes.

"No," he said, as her arms slid around him. "No, Ariele—" His hands rose to push her away; but now his hands seemed to have gained a life of their own, fusing to her flesh, refusing to stop touching her. Helplessly he felt the silk and velvet of her skin, the pressure of her body against his, making his nerves sing as though some live circuit had closed between them when they touched . . . and he knew that the impossible had happened. His mouth found hers, in a long, deep kiss. He knew that he was lost. . . .

She sank down along his body, pulling open his clothes, kissing him everywhere; drawing him down with her onto the cargo mats as the cold, barren space around them dissolved into waves of heat.

Ariele woke out of a dream of a dream, feeling the heaviness of arousal still congesting her languid body, making every motion deliciously sensual. She ran her hands down over herself, finding that she was naked beneath bedcovers; not what she had expected to find. She opened her eyes and discovered the ceiling of a room she had never seen before, but no memory at all of how she had gotten to this place. She felt a sudden coldness drop through her as she saw herself in her mind's eye, saw a cold, echoing space in which she was surrounded by strangers, offworlders with hard hands and soulless eyes, letting them . . . letting them. . . .

But the images metamorphosed like cloudforms, and it was no stranger, but Reede Kullervo holding her, caressing her, peeling away her clothing as his kisses dissolved her mind into seafoam. . . . His hands on her, melting her very flesh from her bones as they opened and explored her. She remembered the burning sword of his manhood tracing a fiery track across her skin, its white heat driven deep into her loins, searing the soft folds below with its exquisite passage as he sought, and found, and took possession of the secret core of her being; as he buried himself souldeep in her annealing, fluid depths. . . .

She remembered a slow, deep rhythm that went on and on, filling her, fulfilling her, in a way that she had never known before, until she screamed like a sea bird with the length, the depth, the purity of sensation as her pleasure crested and fell away into blissful release . . . only to be carried upward to crest again, by the rhythm that went on and on, driving her into delirium dreams. . . .

She turned her head on the pillow, as the cascading memories dissolved into the brightness of day. Turning away from the light that filled her eyes, she searched the space beside her for a form, a face; suddenly afraid that she would not find him, not find anyone—

But he was there, to her relief and joy, lying beside her, sound asleep. She studied his face, turned toward her; fascinated by the sight of him at rest, at peace. He never looked that way, so peaceful, so vulnerable, when he was awake; he was always like a fist full of thorns, filled with potential pain. It was what had drawn her to him, the hint of danger, the wildness in his eyes. But it was the man sleeping next to her now who had held her: the haunted, haunting stranger she caught glimpses of as they talked together about the mers. She was sure it was that man who had kept coming back to her, even while something inside him fought against it, keeping her at bay, keeping him unreachable and untouchable.

She reached out, touching his cheek, so softly that she barely proved his reality. She let her hand trace the line of his jaw, down along his throat, his shoulder. She had never been allowed to touch him, before; he had never let her. She studied the tattooing that tendriled the length of his arm, fascinated by the complexity of the designs. Someone had told her once that they meant he was some kind of criminal; the prospect had secretly excited her.

But he had denied it, when she had found the nerve to ask him about them. And now, looking at the beauty of the many-colored symmetries, patterns resolving into other patterns even as she looked at them, by the magic of their design, she did not believe it either. They made her think of secrets, transformations, messages with hidden meanings. They reminded her of the mersong . . . of the mystery of human existence, in all its richness and variety . . . things that she could contemplate forever, like these exotic patterns, and the mysteries of the man who wore them. . . .

Reede's hand came alive suddenly, under her touch; caught her own hand in a painful grip. He sat up, staring at her, while the emotions on his face changed and changed again, so quickly that she could only see his anger. Her smile died stillborn, and she shrank back from what she found in his eyes.

But he looked away from her again; sank back, to lie motionless in the bedding, with his hands covering his face. "No," he whispered. "No. . . ."

Ariele pushed herself up; dared to touch him again. He did not shake her off, and so she moved closer, to rest her head on his shoulder. He flinched, but still he did nothing to prevent her from being there.

"Oh, Reede," she murmured, against his neck. "I love you so much. You've changed everything for me."

He said something in a language she didn't know, that sounded like a curse. "You don't know anything about love, or about being changed . . . damn you," he said bitterly. But his arms went around her, pulling her to him, cradling her against him as if he were afraid she might disappear. He stroked her hair. "What am I going to do?" he said, to the ceiling, or the air.

"Are you worried about my mother?" she asked.

He looked at her blankly. "What?"

"She won't be angry with you. . . . She might even be happy with me, for once."

Something like comprehension filled his eyes; but he only grimaced. "Don't tell your mother. For gods' sakes, don't tell anyone!"

"But why not? Everyone already thinks—"

He sat up, glaring at her in furious desperation. "*You* don't even know the truth—"

She stared at him. "Then tell me."

"It's too late," he said, shaking his head. He lay down again beside her. "Too late . . ." He looked away from her eyes, down along her body. His hand reached out, uncertainly, to touch her breast, making her shiver and stretch with languorous desire. He rolled over, beginning to kiss her, beginning to make love to her again, with an urgency that took her breath away . . . and then sensation was all she knew.

TIAMAT: Hegemonic Starport

"Did you enjoy your tour of the complex, Lady?" Vhanu asked, behind him.

Gundhalinu turned away from the window wall, abruptly startled out of his reverie. He had managed to lose himself in the spectacular, eye-numbing view of the starport's landing grids; avoiding conversation, letting the incandescence twenty meters below him burn away all conscious thought for minutes at a time. Vhanu's question forced his attention back into the crowded reception hall as the Queen and her husband joined them. Jerusha PalaThion, who had accompanied the Queen on the tour, stood with them now, staring out at the grids as if her own mind were somewhere else entirely.

"Yes. It was fascinating," Moon said, her voice holding just the right amount of awe. Her glance left Vhanu's face briefly; Gundhalinu saw the wary amusement in her eyes. It was not the first time she had set foot in the complex, although Vhanu did not know that. The last time had also been the night of the Assembly's arrival on Tiamat; but then it had marked the beginning of the end, the Final Departure of the Hegemony from Tiamat, and not the Return.

She had not been an honored, invited guest then. She had been an exhausted refugee . . . and so had the young inspector Gundhalinu, missing and presumed dead. Together they had come out of the wilderness, starving, frozen, and wholly unexpected; and although the natives were forbidden to set foot in the complex, the duty sergeant had taken one look into the eyes of Inspector Gundhalinu, who had risen from the grave, and let them pass.

They had arrived in the middle of a celebration exactly like the one taking place tonight, and the pleasure and unspeakable relief he had felt, to find himself back among his own people, alive, safe, and going home, had matched the celebration of all the assembled guests in the hall that night.

He glanced at Jerusha PalaThion again, at her expressionless face, wondering what she was thinking tonight. She had been Commander of Police then; this time she was only a Chief Inspector. But her life had undergone so much change in the years between—almost as much as his own had—that he could not imagine what her reactions were. He remembered suddenly how she had smiled as she came into the infirmary room where he was being treated; how her pleasure at the sight of him had filled his beaten, shivering body with warmth and strength.

And he remembered the looks on the faces of the Assembly members who had followed her—thinking they had come to honor one of their own, a Kharemoughi Technician who had been lost in the barbaric wilderness—as they saw the scars of his failed suicide attempt on his wrists, and listened to him blurt out his forbidden feelings for the Tiamatan woman who had saved his life.

He glanced down at his wrists, as if he would suddenly find the red weals of fresh scar tissue standing out against his skin; although he had had all traces of them removed long ago, and scarcely even thought about them anymore. He felt surprise as he realized that, because once he had been so certain that a day would never pass when he would not think about them, even if they were made invisible; when he would not hate himself simply for being alive. . . .

But now, after so many years, it also surprised him to realize that although he could barely remember what he had eaten for dinner yesterday, he still remembered every stinging word of mockery and censure that had been spoken to him that night in the infirmary; how if he had had the strength left in him to do it, he would have taken the nearest sharp medical instrument and finished what he had so ineffectually started. . . .

He felt himself blinking too much; forced his mind to concentrate on the complexities of an adhani until his emotions were back under control. He glanced at Moon, wondering what she remembered of that night, so long ago for both of them, when his own people's self-righteous cruelty had driven him to turn renegade, rejecting everything he had ever believed; and by that act, helped Moon Dawntreader achieve her destiny.

She was not looking at him now, but stood listening to Vhanu discuss more details of the starport's function, with her own face carefully composed. She wore a long, fluid robe that would not have been out of place on Kharemough, although there was something about the subtle dappling of greens in the restless fabric that made him think of leaves moving in the wind, waves on the sea; something wholly Tiamatan. She wore her hair in a simple loose plait down her back, woven with golden thread, and on her head a diadem made of what looked like crystal. He had never seen her wear anything like a crown before; realized that it must be one of Arienrhod's, and worn for a calculated effect. She held herself like a queen; but that, he realized, was something she had always done. . . . He looked away from her as the ache in his chest suddenly grew too strong.

Sparks Dawntreader was listening too, his face taking on a rare animation, as if he were honestly interested in the subject Vhanu was discussing. He was dressed in an imported tunic and pants, formally cut, and there was nothing, superficially, that would have marked him as a native.

". . . but forgive me," Vhanu said, "I must be boring you, droning on about such technical matters." Gundhalinu heard the unconscious dismissal of the Queen and her husband as less than rational, educated human beings.

"Not at all," Moon said. Gundhalinu saw the brief glint of anger in her eyes, and knew that she had heard the unthinking judgment too. "This has certainly satisfied a healthy curiosity in me to know what your starport is like. It has been a restricted area for my people for so long, even though it has played such a vital part in the fate of our world. . . . Although I have to admit it really doesn't compare with the orbital cities that circle your homeworld, Commander Vhanu."

Vhanu looked at her blankly. "Have you . . . seen a tape of the starport hub, then?" he asked.

"No, I've seen the starport. I visited there when I was a girl. That was when I learned about the sibyl net." She smiled, pleasantly, in the face of Vhanu's suddenly acute discomfort.

"How did you get there and get back again?" he asked. "No one has been able to leave your world for years—and before that, I believe any Tiamatan who did leave was proscribed from returning. Isn't that right—?"

"I'm afraid I broke the law," she said simply. "But that was long ago . . . what I did is no longer illegal, under the terms of our new relationship with the Hegemony. And I am most grateful to you for your wisdom in changing the old, oppressive system. It was an unjust law . . . there were many of them in those days. Isn't that true, Justice?" She looked suddenly at Gundhalinu, as if she had felt his eyes on her.

He smiled, his own smile as guarded as the one he saw on her face now. "True justice is what we hope to establish in our relations with your people this time, Lady," he said softly. He glanced at Vhanu's face, seeing barely controlled annoyance, and at Sparks Dawntreader. Dawntreader looked at him with a cold speculation that was not the expression he had been expecting to see; one that triggered an unpleasant reaction in his gut.

Dawntreader looked away again, staring out at the landing grids, at the recently arrived ships of the Assembly in the docking bay beyond the windows, with a kind of fierce hunger. Gundhalinu wondered whether he was really wishing that he could fly away, disappear, leave this world and all its sorrows. Or maybe he was only wishing the Hegemony would disappear, instead. . . .

He heard a sudden stirring in the crowd across the room: The Prime Minister and the Assembly members were making their entrance at last. For half a second, he knew exactly the emotion Dawntreader had been feeling.

"Well, the Living Museum of Ancient History has arrived," Jerusha PalaThion said dryly, and quite clearly.

"PalaThion!" Vhanu snapped, his indignation not simply for appearance's sake. But Gundhalinu felt his own sudden paralysis disappear. A faint trace of smile pulled up the corners of his mouth as he looked at his Chief Inspector. He gave her an imperceptible nod; a *thank-you*. Moon smiled openly, behind Vhanu's back. Sparks turned away from the windows, all his attention suddenly on the doorway. Gundhalinu remembered that Dawntreader was the son of one of the Assembly members, fathered during the same Mask Night when Arienrhod had had herself cloned.

Gundhalinu started forward, a signal to the people around him to follow, knowing that the Assembly members would expect that courtesy as their due. Even though they had functioned as nothing but figureheads through virtually all of Hegemonic history—and had just become even more of an anachronism, as the stardrive transformed the nature of the Eight Worlds' real power structure—still they remained the living symbol of the Hegemony's influence. He understood Vhanu's reflexive anger at Jerusha's casual remark, even though he had long ago ceased to feel the kind of pride and reverence that the sight of Assembly had once inspired in him.

Because the Assembly members were little more than actors living a perpetual role, their arrival anywhere was generally an excuse for holidays and celebration, for remembering what was good about Kharemough's dominance as first among equals in the Hegemony. . . . He hoped suddenly, with all his heart, that it would be that way tonight.

The crowd of expectant offworlders and influential Tiamatans parted as though some word of magic had been spoken, opening a path between him and the waiting Assembly members. They were resplendent in gem-brocaded, perfectly tailored uniforms, crusted with the honors and decorations awarded to them during their endless cycle of returns to the Eight Worlds.

Gundhalinu glanced down at his own clothing, seeing the austere black uniform of a Chief Justice. Tonight its uncompromising plainness was crossed by a band of silver, on which his family crest and his own honors and decorations were displayed. He had felt disagreeably ostentatious when he put it on; but suddenly he was glad he had, as if he had remembered to put on body armor before confronting a mob of rioters.

He stopped before the Prime Minister, flanked by Vhanu and Tilhonne, with the other officials of his government gathered behind them. He made his bow as they were introduced, one by one, by the Prime Minister's protocol officer.

Prime Minister Ashwini touched Gundhalinu's upraised hand briefly, with a look of benign distraction, and murmured a polite pleasantry which Gundhalinu immediately forgot. The Prime Minister appeared to be in his mid-sixties, but his body was still youthful-looking; he was distinguished and obviously Technician in his bearing. He was only the fourth Prime Minister since the Hegemony's formation, and Gundhalinu had no idea how long ago, in the realtime history of his homeworld, Ashwini must have been born. He had probably known it once, in school, but he had long since forgotten. Given the access the Prime Minister had to the best available rejuvenating treatments, and frequent use of the water of life, he was certainly much older in actual years than he looked to be. And because he, and the rest of the Assembly, had spent most of their time in sublight travel between Gates and worlds, their memories carried back even further, a patchwork of random moments of history—most of them probably too much like this one.

"Honored, sadhu," Gundhalinu murmured, speaking Sandhi, as everyone else was now. He stepped aside to give the Prime Minister and the Assembly a clear view of the others who waited behind him. "May I present to you the Summer Queen—"

"Arienrhod!" the Prime Minister said, his face filling with surprise. "I say. . . ." He touched his nose briefly with his hand, glancing at Gundhalinu again. "Isn't she supposed to be dead? Didn't we see them drown her, a few months ago—?" He broke off, before Gundhalinu could make an answer; his eyes glazed over as if he were listening to someone speaking inside his own head. Gundhalinu realized that Ashwini was getting a datafeed from somewhere, possibly from his protocol officer, or else some file of stored information tuned to his own speech. "Oh," Ashwini said, after a brief moment that had begun to seem interminable; and then, "Of course. This is the Summer Queen. My apologies. Honored, Lady, to be sure." He stepped forward, holding out his hand like a local. Moon bowed, with equal dignity, and shook it solemnly. "Is this something new, then?" he said to her. "Do you have yourselves altered to match your predecessors, now?"

Gundhalinu saw Moon flush, and winced inwardly. "No," she said, without using titles, as one equal to another. She spoke Sandhi that was slightly stilted but perfectly clear. "We do not."

"Oh," he said, and the look of consternation filled his face again. "But what are you doing here at all? Your people weren't even permitted in the starport, the last time I was here."

"Things have changed, sadhu," Gundhalinu said, with gentle urgency. "If you recall. Because of the stardrive. Our relationship with Tiamat included."

Ashwini half frowned, and seemed to listen to his inner voice. "Of course they have," he said, blinking. "Well, of course, that makes perfect sense." He nodded to Moon again, as if they had just been introduced, before looking back at Gundhalinu. "And you are the man we have to thank for it all, are you not, Justice?" he said, with a smile that actually seemed genuine and full of appreciation. "You must tell me the whole story of it, in your own words, at dinner—"

"It would be my pleasure, sadhu." Gundhalinu returned the smile, briefly, before the Prime Minister's attention wandered. Gundhalinu exchanged glances with Vhanu as Ashwini looked away; seeing his own disconcertion reflected in Vhanu's eyes. *Gods, the man is a shufflebrain, a walking cipher.* But he went on making introductions, as if nothing had happened, presenting Sparks Dawntreader, ". . . the Queen's consort, the son of First Secretary Sirus . . ."

A murmur went through the gathered men and women of the Assembly, and he saw someone push forward for a better look—Sirus himself, if he recalled the half-remembered face correctly. The man looked no older than Sparks Dawntreader did now; but he smiled, with pride and feeling, as his eyes found his son. Gundhalinu felt Dawntreader look back at him in brief surprise, before turning to face his father.

The Prime Minister was being guided on into the room with gentle insistence, chaperoned by a handful of advisors and protectors. Gundhalinu felt his neck muscles loosen with relief as other members of the Assembly and their companions came forward to greet him and his staff, by turns blandly congenial, or unthinkingly arrogant, or seeming vaguely disoriented, as the Prime Minister had. They spent the majority of their time in their own hermetically sealed floating world, except when they left their ships to attend functions like these—an endless succession of sparkling soirees and elegant dinners among the ever-changing elite of world after world. Generally they only elected new members when someone died. He supposed it was surprising that their behaviors did not seem even stranger.

He accepted a drink from the assortment of mild drugs offered by a passing servo, as its highly burnished form wove an expert course through the flesh-and-blood bodies of the gathered guests. He swallowed down half the drink at once, disgusted at himself for needing it, for letting his memories get on his nerves so much. He had encountered the Assembly only once before, in that brief, bitter meeting at the port hospital. That meeting had been thirteen years ago for him, but these people had scarcely aged, and it seemed to him that some of their faces were familiar, too like the ones burned indelibly into his brain.

What was it, he wondered, that gave humiliation such a terrible power over the human soul, making the painful memories of half a lifetime ago more vivid than his memories of last week, let alone of all the good and worthwhile things he had accomplished in the years between? When he had returned to Kharemough with the stardrive, no one had dared mention his disgrace. Years had passed without a single disapproving stare or a cutting remark about his past. His suicide attempt had even begun to seem like ancient history to him.

But for these people, the memory of their last encounter with him was only a few months old. He had been barely twenty-five then, and looking half-dead besides; but even so he found himself praying to the shades of his ancestors that no one would remember, or make the association . . .

"Justice Gundhalinu," a voice said, too loudly, from just behind his left ear. "A great pleasure to meet you, sadhu—someone who has come to be a living symbol of what makes Kharemough great, of why we still rule the Hegemony, after so long."

Gundhalinu turned, backing up a step from the other man's uncomfortable proximity, and the overpowering scent of cologne. His stomach turned at the odor, one he had never forgotten.

"IP Quarropas," the man said, "Speaker of the Assembly."

"Honored," Gundhalinu murmured automatically, meeting the Speaker's palm as he looked down into the other man's fleshy, smiling face. The Speaker had obviously been a handsome man in his youth, but his life of ease and privilege had not worn well on him.

"I feel we've met this way before—" A strange expression came over the Speaker's face as their hands touched. "Have we?"

"No, I don't think so. . . ."

"But I remember your name, from before—" Quarropas wagged his finger, and Gundhalinu watched the answer struggling inexorably toward the surface of his mind.

Gundhalinu kept his expression neutral with an effort, as memory doubled his own vision. "Yes, Quarropas-sadhu," he said quietly, "we have met. On your last visit to Tiamat. I was a Police inspector then." And Quarropas had refused to touch his hand in greeting, because he had crippled it, in his attempt to slash his wrist.

"Inspector Gundhalinu," Quarropas murmured. "Sainted ancestors! Are you that one—the one from the wilderness? How is it possible? I'd thought that you would have done the honorable thing years ago, after so debasing your family and your class that night—" Several people near him turned around to stare, in open disbelief or scandalized curiosity. Gundhalinu heard someone whisper, "I *said* so. . . ."

Gundhalinu said nothing for a long moment, seeing Vhanu among the onlookers who were suddenly bearing witness to this confrontation. "The 'honorable thing'?" he repeated, finally, his voice perfectly even. "By that do you mean that I should be dead now?"

"You were a failed suicide," Quarropas said. The term also meant *coward*. "And with a filthy native girl for a mistress besides—"

"Do you mean Moon Dawntreader?" Gundhalinu asked, damming the flood of words. "Then you are referring to the Summer Queen—" He nodded toward Moon, who stood motionless in the crowd near them, with her expression caught somewhere between anger and pain. Sparks was with her, and there was only bleak disgust on his face. "In that case," Gundhalinu continued, with deadly calm, "you are mistaken. She was, and is, married, to First Secretary Sirus's son. Their children are here among the guests tonight. She helped me in a time of need; I did as much for her, a long time ago. That was all. There is nothing more to be said about the matter." He took a deep breath. "Except that I came to realize that to throw away my life was the real act of cowardice. The truly honorable choice was to go on living, and by my actions earn the right to forget the past."

"Well said, Gundhalinu-ken." Sirus, the First Secretary, was standing now behind Sparks Dawntreader. His dark, shrewd eyes met Gundhalinu's. "And well done, too. I daresay, Quarropas," he murmured, lowering his voice as he moved forward to stand between the Speaker and Gundhalinu, "I would sooner commit suicide myself than speak such words to this man here. We both committed an unworthy act during our last visit, to have questioned his honor even once, under circumstances we could not fully understand. To insult the honorable Gundhalinu-eshkrad twice is unforgivable." Quarropas bristled, glaring at Sirus with the shoe of attention suddenly on his own foot, and pinching.

"If it were not for the Chief Justice," Sirus went on, "I would not have the great pleasure of seeing my son again tonight, or meeting his family. His wife would not be Queen of this world . . . we would not be here at all, with a new future before us, and the water of life back in our hands, if he had not given us the stardrive. I salute you, sadhu." He looked toward Gundhalinu, and raised his enameled goblet. The crowd began to murmur again around him; but this time there was nothing hostile or mocking in the sound. Gundhalinu saw other glasses raised, and palms held up in solemn acknowledgment to him.

Gundhalinu nodded, letting Sirus read the gratitude in his eyes. Sirus smiled and turned away, and time began to flow again.

"By the Boatman, you skewered that *kortch* neatly." Jerusha PalaThion was suddenly standing beside him. She touched his arm, and he saw their shared past mirrored in her eyes.

His mouth pinched. "I've had enough years, lying awake nights, to think about what I would say this time. . . ." He shook his head, and smiled faintly. "Maybe I'm really not a coward." He looked back at her. "How are you doing?"

She shrugged. "I'll live. I've had worse receptions. But I think I need more fortification." She moved away, following the track of a servo.

Gundhalinu sipped his own drink, searching the crowd until he spotted Vhanu. Vhanu met his gaze briefly, then glanced away, his eyes filled with uncertainty.

Gundhalinu started forward, wanting to speak to him. But the Prime Minister was suddenly in front of him, between them, smiling at him with benign dignity. "A toast to Chief Justice Gundhalinu? Nothing could be more appropriate, or give me more pleasure. Few people in our history have deserved our tribute more, for their contributions to the prominence of Kharemough and the prosperity of the Hegemony."

Gundhalinu bowed his head, with the gesture avoiding having to look anyone in the eye. He wondered, in that moment, why it had to be that such an honor, which once would have meant more to him than life itself, was given to him now, when it scarcely meant anything at all.

When he raised his head again, Vhanu was nowhere in sight. Someone spoke his name, behind him, and he turned around. Moon came toward him, with Sirus, and her family around her. "Thank you, Justice Gundhalinu, for your defense of my reputation and my family," she said.

He nodded, hiding the surge of emotion he felt as he saw her face. "It was no more than what was due . . . to any of us, to set the record straight, Lady." He avoided Sparks Dawntreader's gaze, the silent watching eyes of Ariele and Tammis; turning to Sirus, instead: "My gratitude, sadhu."

Sirus's mouth quirked up in a slightly embarrassed smile. He was a tall man, large-boned for a Kharemoughi Technician; Gundhalinu remembered vaguely having been told that he was in fact half Samathan—a son of the Prime Minister's from some distant visit to Sirus's homeworld. The accident of Sirus's birth had helped him to become an important political leader on Samathe; he had been invited to fill a vacancy in the Assembly, on their next visit. "I would be grateful, Gundhalinu-sadhu, if you would consider the scales equal between us, after what must be, for you, so long."

Sirus glanced away, at Sparks and at Ariele and Tammis. Tammis stood behind his mother, beside Merovy, his own young wife. "We in the Assembly have been unstuck in time, due to our travels, for all these centuries. But now you have given me the chance to see what great things my son and his wife have accomplished . . . to see my grandchildren. It was something we put much store by, among my mother's people—something I have regretted about my choice in joining the Assembly." He put an arm around Sparks's shoulders, turning to him. "I know I have not had the chance to be any kind of father to you, Son; and perhaps my pride is presumptuous. But it is heartfelt, nonetheless. And it seems you have done extremely well with your life, in spite of my absence."

Sparks smiled briefly, looking back at his father. But the smile disappeared as quickly as it had come. Gundhalinu wondered what doubts and regrets and secrets hid behind the expression that replaced it; suddenly sure, somehow, that Dawntreader's expression hid as many secrets as his own had a few minutes past.

He stood with them, making desultory polite conversation as an excuse to go on watching them speak and interact among themselves. He knew that he should be mingling with the crowd, doing his duty, however unpleasant; and yet he was somehow unable to make himself leave Moon's side, unable to take his eyes off her, to stop watching her surrounded by her family.

Her family. He glanced at Ariele, whose face was still so much like he remembered her mother's, except for the chronic mocking smile, the restless impatience in her eyes. She had pasted a stim patch from the passing tray in the middle of her forehead like a third eye. Her cropped, cream-white hair was caught up in a cascade on top of her head; she wore a clinging dawn-colored bodysuit and loose soft trousers knotted around her slender waist, relentlessly expensive and sophisticated, as usual.

Her gaze settled momentarily on Sirus as he spoke to her mother; glanced away again, and Gundhalinu suddenly found himself being stared at. She half frowned, glancing at Sirus and back at him, and then at Sparks, the man she had always known as her father. Just for a moment Gundhalinu saw her mocking mask slip, saw the confusion of a lost child in her eyes. She turned away as she caught him still watching her, and disappeared into the crowd. He wondered if she had gone looking for that miserable little snot Elco Teel. Kirard Set Wayaways and his family were here tonight, being too influential to snub, although so far he had managed to avoid even the sight of them by some good fortune.

"It is quite remarkable, isn't it?" Sirus said to him, gesturing at Ariele's disappearing back. Gundhalinu looked over at him, only then realizing that he had been staring, and the others had noticed it. "The resemblance between her and her mother, I mean."

"Yes," he said, glad to take that as an excuse for his behavior. "I actually mistook her for the Queen, the first time I saw her." He smiled, glancing at Moon, seeing her surprise.

"Tammis here takes after his father more." Sirus's smile widened, as he turned to the young couple still standing beside him. "He has the look of a Kharemoughi about him; don't you think, Gundhalinu-sadhu?"

Gundhalinu hesitated, feeling five sets of eyes suddenly fixed on his own face. "Yes," he said softly, "he does." Tammis glanced down; Gundhalinu thought the boy was simply avoiding his gaze, until he realized that Tammis was staring at his trefoil. Tammis's hand rose, touching his own sibyl sign; dropped away again, to take and hold his wife's hand. Gundhalinu saw her try surreptitiously to avoid his touch, and then give in. He had heard that they were having marital problems.

He looked back at Sirus. The First Secretary seemed mercifully oblivious to the undercurrents of tension, caught up in the pleasure of his illusory fantasy about his son's family life. He would not have to be here for long enough to see it shattered, if he was fortunate . . . any more than he ever had to be anywhere for long enough to experience more than an illusion of life in the real world, with all its pain and pitiless imperfection.

Gundhalinu had wondered from time to time what could make someone like Sirus choose to join the Assembly, to sever his ties so completely with the life he had always known. Now, tonight, he thought that perhaps he finally understood. He was suddenly aware of the music that was playing—a limpid fuguetheme work from his homeworld. Somehow the music he had always known had never seemed as beautiful to him, or as poignantly sad.

Sirus turned back to Moon, as she spoke his name. "Please, call me Temmon—"

"Temmon," she said, nodding, with a brief smile, "you said that we might discuss the mers."

"Yes, of course; it's obviously a question that needs to be addressed. Sit with me at dinner, and we'll—" He broke off, as guests began to stir and mutter across the room.

Gundhalinu strained to see past the random motion of half a hundred heads turning toward the doorway. He made out Tilhonne, standing at the focus of a small open space, holding up something vaguely familiar. He froze as recognition hit him, hearing Moon's audible gasp: Tilhonne held a vial of the water of life.

"Sadhanu, bhai," Tilhonne announced, raising his voice to be heard above the crowd's. "Dinner waits for us. But first, thanks to the diligence of our new Hegemonic government, and the cooperation of our Tiamatan friends—" he gestured, and suddenly Kirard Set Wayaways was standing beside him, smiling and bowing, "we have a special gift for our honored visitors tonight. The first fruits of a renewed harvest. The water of life."

A murmur of surprise and eager anticipation spread through the crowd; ripples of motion followed, as the Assembly members began to press forward toward Tilhonne.

Gundhalinu stood motionless, feeling the people around him suddenly staring at him again. He looked at Moon, seeing disbelief and betrayal in her eyes.

"Well done, Gundhalinu-sadhu!" Sirus said, his face beaming. "No mere speech could have silenced the arrogant bigotry of certain fools so neatly." He clapped Gundhalinu on the shoulder. "You have given them their dream—you and the Lady." He turned to Moon, but she had looked away, watching in anguished fascination as the Assembly members passed the vial from hand to hand, lifting it to their mouths, inhaling, swallowing the spray of heavy silver droplets with an eagerness approaching lust.

"Well, come then," Sirus said, his expression turning to surprise as everyone around him remained motionless. "Surely we are all entitled to our share of this blessing? Unless of course you've already sampled it?"

"No," Moon said, her voice filled with desolation. "I don't drink blood. Mers die for every drop of the water of life you take. The Hegemony has broken our laws to slaughter them—"

He stared at her for a moment, as if it had never actually occurred to him before how the water of life was obtained.

"This was the matter concerning the mers that I wanted to talk with you about," she said, looking at him now, with pain-shadowed eyes.

"Ye gods," he murmured, chagrined. "I never imagined the two things would be related. . . . But yes, I still wish to discuss it, more than before. Dinner will run long, if I recall, and we can—"

"No." She shook her head, her face stiff and unyielding. "To attend your dinner as if nothing had happened would mean that I accept what was done here tonight, and that would make me a complete hypocrite." She looked at Gundhalinu, away from him again, before he could speak.

"Moon—" Sparks said, catching at her arm as she started to turn away.

"Stay if you want to," she answered, with both understanding and anger in her glance. She started away, with Tammis and Merovy following her wordlessly.

Sparks hesitated, looking at his father. But then he shook his head, murmuring something that Gundhalinu could not make out, before he went after them. As he passed, Sparks met Gundhalinu's eyes briefly, with a look that raked his conscience like claws. Surprised and disturbed, Gundhalinu watched until the other man disappeared through the doorway across the room.

Sirus shook his head, caught between concern and embarrassment, as they found themselves standing abruptly alone in the crowd. "Will you join me, then, at least, Gundhalinu-sadhu?" he asked, gesturing toward the water of life.

"No, sadhu," Gundhalinu said. "I'm afraid I would find it undrinkable."

Sirus stared at him a moment longer, and then looked away again at the silver vial still circulating through the crowd. He sighed. "Well, perhaps I am beginning to lose my interest in it—at least until I've heard more about this. You are staying for dinner, I hope?"

Gundhalinu smiled faintly. "Yes, Sirus-sadhu. I have no choice in that matter, unlike the Queen." He glanced toward the doorway that she had disappeared through, watching the counter-ripple of comment her abrupt departure had caused collide with the spreading excitement of the water of life. As he watched, he saw to his surprise that Ariele Dawntreader was arguing angrily with someone. He saw her turn and leave, as if she was offended like her mother by the water of life and all that it stood for.

As she disappeared from his sight, his gaze fell on Vhanu, standing near the door. "Excuse me. I have someone I have to speak with first." He left Sirus and made his way through the gossiping crowd, trying to hear as little as possible of what was said along the way.

He reached the place where Vhanu stood waiting. "Damn it, NR," he said furiously, "how the hell did this happen? This is a diplomatic slap in the face. The Queen was so angry she's left the complex. I never authorized this—"

"It was Tilhonne's idea, to have the water of life here and present it to the Assembly—"

"With Wayaways' eager cooperation, no doubt." Gundhalinu said sourly.

Vhanu shrugged, and nodded.

"How did they perform a hunt, without the Queen's cooperation? Arienrhod used her Starbuck, and dillyp hunters from Tsieh-pun to—"

"I authorized any supplies and operators they might need to get the job done."

"Gods! And it was thy doing—?" Gundhalinu repeated, feeling himself flush. "By what authority? Goddammit, NR, how could thou not bring this to me?"

"Because I knew thou would reject it out of hand." Vhanu frowned, his hands twitching at his sides. "In the name of a thousand gods, BZ, we have to make a good impression if we want the continued support of the ones who count, back on Kharemough. We have to prove we're getting the job done. That we're in control here, and not some enclave of superstitious natives. And damn it, thou were letting this obsession with 'enlightened government' get in the way of that." Gundhalinu saw his own troubled image reflected in the other man's eyes, and looked away. "Thou were cutting thy own throat. I did this thing for thee."

"You did it for yourself," Gundhalinu snapped, suddenly both angry and defensive. "Don't confuse the two things."

Vhanu's mouth tightened, at his use of the formal *you*. "Very well then. I did it for both of us—for all of us, just as Tilhonne did." His expression changed; he put his hands on Gundhalinu's shoulders with gentle insistence. "BZ, thou know I have always had the highest regard for thee. Thou are my friend. There is no one I admire more. But whatever thy reasons are for wanting to be here, I promise thee, once thou have taken the time to think it through thou will be grateful for what we did tonight."

Gundhalinu said nothing more, watching the last of the water of life disappear down the last eager Assembly member's throat. "They're going in to dinner," he said finally, turning back, meeting Vhanu's gaze. "Shall we join them?"

Vhanu nodded, and they went in together without further conversation.

The rose-colored light of dawn was showing through the storm walls at the end of Azure Alley as Gundhalinu reached his townhouse door at last, weary and alone. He glanced toward the dawn, the proof that a world, and a universe, still existed beyond the changeless walls and undimming light of Carbuncle. He looked away from the brightening sky again, without emotion, too drained to feel anything at the sight of it, to find any false symbolism in the simple light of day.

His memory of the night just past, after the appearance of the water of life and the disappearance of the Queen, was a blur: an endless meal that he had barely touched, punctuated by endless questions from the First Secretary. He had answered the questions to the best of his ability, unable to focus on anything but the knowledge that Sirus was a powerless figurehead, which Sirus knew as well as he did; that no protest anyone made, no matter how influential, would be enough . . . that Moon had left the starport without giving him a chance to explain. All that he knew clearly now, standing on his own doorstep, was that he had a headache three times the size of his head, and even the complexities of his door lock were barely within the capacity of his problem-solving.

He tripped over something that lay in the shadows of his entryway, swore as he lost his balance and banged his shoulder against the wall. He bent down, to discover a wide, flat bundle sitting on his step. He explored it cautiously with his hands. It was large but very light, and rustled faintly when he shook it. There was no note attached to it, not even his name; but for a reason he could not explain he sensed no threat about it. He picked it up, holding it under his arm as he deactivated the security lock and let himself inside. He dropped the lidded basket on a table in his living room, and went in search of a pain patch for his aching head.

He came back through the wide, arched doorway, loosening his collar, and collapsed on the earth-colored native couch. He breathed in the faint ocean-smell of the dried seahair that had been used to stuff its cushions. He sighed, realizing that he had actually begun to find the peculiar odor soothing. He put his feet up and closed his eyes, calling on music from the entertainment system across the room. The familiar strains of a Kharemoughi art song filled the silence of the house as he let the analgesic patch do its work; feeling it dull the pain until there was only a bearable heaviness behind his eyes, and he could think again.

But the thoughts that seeped back into his consciousness as his mind cleared only seemed to him to be a different kind of pain: the nagging ache of his growing frustration, of futility, isolation and regret.

He sat up, telling himself angrily that this was no more than he could have expected. Had he really become such a fool that he believed his own press—believed that the Hegemony would grant his every whim because of what he had done for them? Or that Moon Dawntreader had been secretly longing for him to return, thinking only of him all these years, as he had thought only of her—that they would fall into each other's arms like the lovers in the wretched Old Empire historicals he had been addicted to in his youth?

He pressed the heels of his hands into his eyes. Gods . . . he was exhausted, he should go to bed before he sank any deeper into this trackless bog of self-pity. He had always known what the reality of the situation here would be; he had just never wanted to believe it. He let his eyes take in the timeless, vaguely alien contours of the room, picturing the layout of the townhouse, one of the best in the city: ten rooms, their walls covered with beautiful murals of sea and mountains, in which he lived all alone, in rattling emptiness—as he would likely go on doing for years, unless he . . . unless he . . .

He stood up abruptly, and spoke the music off again. This had been his own choice. He had made his bed; he might as well lie in it.

As he started across the room, his eyes caught on the package he had brought inside, still waiting on the stolid, square-legged table beside the couch. He sat down again, taking the lidded basket into his hands, breaking the seals that held it together. He lifted off the lid and set it aside; sat staring in amazement at the thing which lay in a nest of sea grass inside.

It was a mask—a traditional Festival mask, handmade, exquisitely crafted; like the masks he remembered from his last Festival on Tiamat, and not the hurried, uninspired things he had seen cluttering shops in the Maze as this Mask Night approached. He had not bought one; had not even looked at them twice.

And yet this mask was new, not some relic that had been stored for a generation in someone's closet. . . . He touched it tentatively, wonderingly, seeing the glittering pinpoint diamonds of the stars, fragile veils of nebulosity spread across the dark silken reaches of space; the wings of midnight; the utter blackness of a Black Gate's heart, of the Transfer, of eyes without sight . . . and at its heart, a face made of light, reflecting, mirroring the world and all its variety . . . showing him his own face, looking back at him. And suddenly he knew whose hands had made this thing for him; who had sent it to him, and why.

He smiled, taking the mask in his hands, lifting it carefully out of the basket and holding it up to study it. He laid it back in its resting place again after a long moment, and got to his feet, stretching. "Tomorrow," he murmured to it, feeling his perspective restored; feeling an odd sense of peace settle over him as he climbed the stairs, in search of a resting place of his own.

TIAMAT: Carbuncle

"Jerusha." BZ Gundhalinu stood aside, letting Jerusha PalaThion enter his town-house. He closed the door again hastily on the din of Festival revelers. They had been celebrating in his alley, as they had been celebrating all through the city, for three solid days now since the Assembly's arrival. He felt his face settle into a frown of concern as he saw her expression. "What's wrong?"

The tight line of her lips curved up into an ironic smile. "I wish those didn't have to be the first words out of your mouth every time you see me unexpectedly, BZ."

He laughed, ruefully, as he led her in through the hall to the sitting room. "So do I." He settled into a chair, inviting her with a gesture to do the same. The room was lamplit; the heavy draperies drawn across the windows in the wall behind her shut out prying eyes and the city's endless artificial day, letting his body at least pretend to believe that it was night, and time to rest. He sighed, leaning back in his seat. "This had better be good. Riots? Bomb threats? Assassination attempts on the Prime Minister?"

Jerusha shook her head, glancing down. "Nothing so simple, I'm afraid." She looked up again. "There's no easy way to say this. Tammis is in trouble. He's down at the station—"

"Ye gods," Gundhalinu sat forward. "He's been arrested?"

She held up her hand. "No. He got beaten up and robbed. He was trying to pick up a male prostitute. He picked the wrong one. . . ." She shrugged.

"But he's—" *Married.* Gundhalinu didn't finish it, realizing all at once why their marriage was a troubled one.

"I'm keeping him at the station because he won't go to the medical center."

"His wife works there."

She nodded, and ran a hand through her hair. "I thought you'd want to know."

He sighed, looking away from the unspoken sympathy in her eyes. "Bring him here."

He waited. The time passed interminably, until at last there was another knock at his door. He opened it. Tammis stood in the sheltering alcove, with Jerusha hovering like a shadow at his back. He entered the townhouse at Gundhalinu's nod, moving stiffly; his lip was swollen, his eye bruised. Jerusha raised a hand in farewell and disappeared into the crowd.

"Thank you for coming," Gundhalinu said, closing the door.

"Did I have a choice?" Tammis frowned.

"No. But thank you anyway." Gundhalinu led the way to his sitting room again, offered his guest a seat again.

Tammis sat down, warily and painfully. "Why am I here, Justice Gundhalinu?" he said, and Gundhalinu saw him flush as he asked it—afraid that he already knew, afraid of the gods only knew what consequences.

Gundhalinu took a seat on the couch across from him. "Because we need to talk, about the reason why you won't go to the med center." He studied the boy's face surreptitiously, meeting his resentful stare; searching for resemblances, and finding them. He glanced at the trefoil Tammis wore, its clean light winking against the soft folds of his dirt-smudged vest; glanced down at his own trefoil.

"What makes you think that's any of your business, Justice?" Tammis said, holding himself like the son of the Queen. His voice was not as steady as he probably wished it was. "Are you doing this because you're sleeping with my mother?"

Gundhalinu stiffened; he did not answer for a moment, trying to pull his thoughts and his resolve together. "Not exactly," he murmured at last. "I'm not sleeping with your mother. But I am your father."

Tammis froze as the words registered; although there was no surprise at all in his eyes. He did not ask if it was really true. The silence continued between them, while other emotions claimed the space behind his eyes.

At last Gundhalinu got up from his seat, moving across the room to stand before the boy. He looked down into the bruised, apprehensive face, observing Tammis with a trained eye. "I expect right now you feel like bloody hell," he said, barely touching Tammis's bruised cheek. Tammis flinched away from his hand. "But I don't think it's life-threatening." Not meaning simply the obvious damage.

"How would you know?" Tammis said irritably.

"I've survived this long," he answered gently. Tammis looked up at him. "I have some first aid supplies in the bathroom, if you want them."

"No." Tammis shook his head, looking down.

Gundhalinu nodded, understanding too why he would not end his physical suffering even when he could.

"You say you're my real father, and that's why I should talk to you. But that's only what you say. You don't know anything about me. What makes you think you can understand me, if my—my own family can't?"

"Do you talk to them about the problems you're having? Can you?" Gundhalinu sat down again, this time taking a closer seat.

Tammis frowned. "You mean, that I can't decide whether I want to make love to men or women? That's why this happened to me tonight, you know."

"I know." Gundhalinu nodded.

Tammis watched him darkly. "Did you ever feel like that? Did your own father ever call you a pervert?"

Gundhalinu shook his head. "No," he said. "But he went to his grave thinking I was a coward. Everyone who mattered to me considered me a coward, once. Some of them still do, in spite of everything I've accomplished. They also called me a degenerate, for falling in love with your mother, because she wasn't a Kharemoughi."

Tammis's frown faded. For a moment Gundhalinu wasn't sure which confession had caused the surprise reflected on his face.

"There was a time when even I thought I was better off dead . . . but one special person changed my mind."

"Who?" Tammis asked sullenly.

"Your mother."

Tammis blinked suddenly, rapidly, and looked away.

"Have you tried to talk to your mother about this, or . . . or to—" *Sparks. Your Father.* He broke off

Tammis shrugged, a hopeless gesture. "She never has time to listen to anything. She hasn't for years. And she's a Summer. . . . She makes us go to the Summer clan gatherings, and study our traditions, so that we know who we are and what our people believe. For years I've heard the Summers, my people, talk about how wanting somebody you couldn't make children with went against the Lady's Way." Habitually he made the triad sign with his fingers. "They say 'the Mother loves children above all else'—even though they use childbane. They don't *have* to have children, somehow that's all right with the Lady . . . as long as they always put the right parts together." His voice turned bitter. "If my mother knew, she might . . . she might . . ."

". . . stop loving you?"

His face reddened. He pressed his lips together, and nodded. "Like Da. Da . . . saw me, once." He lifted his hands, let them drop into his lap, hopelessly. "I'm an adult, I'm a married man. I should be able to solve my own problems!" He shook his head.

"What about the Winters—your friends?"

He shrugged again. "I don't know what they really think . . . neither do they. Some of them don't like it . . . some of them don't care about anything. But that's because they're like the offworlders, they don't have strong traditions and values, the way we do—"

"You mean like Summers?"

He nodded.

Gundhalinu smiled faintly. "Oh, you'll be surprised. . . . There's an old saying we have on Kharemough: 'My gods or your gods, who knows which are stronger?' That's why we honor them all—just in case. There are more cultures even than gods in the Eight Worlds, and among them you'll find people who are willing to kill you, or each other, over any difference in belief or lifestyle or physical appearance you can imagine—and some you can't. They all think they're right. There's no Truth, Tammis, only differences of opinion. If that confuses the Tiamatans, they're not alone."

"How would they feel on Kharemough, if you wanted to make love to another man, instead of a—a woman who wasn't like you."

"Well, that would depend on his caste, and mine, probably."

Tammis looked at him uncomprehendingly.

"The varieties of prejudice are infinite." Gundhalinu shrugged. "But if social rank was not a problem, most Kharemoughis I know wouldn't care what consenting adults did with each other—as long as they did it discreetly. Public displays of affection or flesh are considered in bad taste. On the other hand, in parts of Newhaven, from what Jerusha PalaThion tells me, near-nudity is typical, because of the heat."

Tammis's eyes widened briefly, as if the idea that Jerusha PalaThion had ever been a casually naked child was more than his mind could imagine.

"Jerusha used to say she'd never get used to the cold weather here. I used to think I'd never get used to the faces—the eyes. All those pale, cold eyes." He glanced away from Tammis's eyes, which were the warm earth-brown of his own.

Tammis shifted in his seat, pulling his soft-shod feet up under him. "But I don't live in any of those places—I live here! And the people I live with, that I care about, they all hate what I am. They say even the Lady hates it—"

"Just because you're outnumbered doesn't mean you're wrong."

Tammis pressed his mouth together. "That's easy for you to say."

Gundhalinu laughed. "Much easier than it was when I left Tiamat." He touched the sibyl sign, glancing down. "As far as having judgment passed against you: You wear one of these. You'll never meet a more terrifyingly impartial judge of character than a sibyl choosing place. . . . On Kharemough every Technician child is required to go and be judged at one. When I was a boy, I was so afraid of being found unworthy that I lied to my family and said I'd failed the test, rather than go in, and actually know for sure that I was not strong or stable enough to suit it."

"Then, how—?" Tammis gestured at Gundhalinu's trefoil, touched his own.

"I'll tell you that tale another time." Gundhalinu smiled faintly. "It will prove to you that sibyls aren't saints. . . . Do you know who Vanamoinen and Ilmarinen are?"

Tammis shook his head.

"You should. They were responsible for setting up the sibyl net that's served all our worlds ever since the Old Empire fell. They were two men who were lovers. They'd been lovers for years; and I remember knowing that it was their love that made them believe they could make a difference, even in an impossible situation, when I . . . That is, one of them was my ancestor. Ilmarinen is the one my family has revered as its founder for centuries."

Tammis glanced away. "But that means . . . Did he have both men and women for lovers?"

Gundhalinu shrugged. "I only know that he found his solution. You'll have to find your own. But if you ever need to know that you have a right to be alive, just look down. Think about what sibyls mean to your people, and why."

Tammis sighed, stretching out his legs again, as if he were uncoiling a spring.

"But . . ." he said, looking away, and his fist began to rap silently on the wooden arm of his seat. "But Merovy . . ."

"What about her?" Gundhalinu asked.

"She threw me out."

"Because you were seeing other men?"

Tammis nodded. "I can't help myself. I don't want to do that to her, but then I start thinking about it, and I hate myself for it, but the more I hate myself, the more I want to—"

"You never think about wanting other women?"

"Yes, I do."

"As much as you want to be with men?"

Tammis nodded again. "But they aren't Merovy, and so I—I stop. Because I love her, there's no one else I ever felt that close to. That's why I married *her*."

"No boy or man you ever felt that close to either?"

"No. No one I really loved. Not like her."

"Then why can't you stop?"

Tammis shook his head. "I don't know. . . ." He half frowned, as if he had never thought about it.

"Would Merovy have thrown you out if you'd been seeing other women?"

Tammis looked up at him. "Probably."

Gundhalinu shifted in his chair, realizing that he had been sitting motionless for far too long. "Then maybe the problem you both have is that you've been unfaithful to her at all."

"I suppose so. . . ." Tammis rubbed his eyes, and winced. "I guess maybe it is."

"Then maybe the question you need to give some thought to is whether you really want to hate yourself more than you want to love your wife."

Tammis glanced down, staring at his trefoil, or seeming to. He looked up again, finally. "Can I go now, Justice Gundhalinu?"

Gundhalinu nodded, surprised and vaguely disappointed by the suddenness of the question. "Yes," he said.

Tammis got up from his seat slowly, wincing again, and hesitated. "Maybe . . . maybe I will take something, for—" he gestured at his bruised body, "before I go. If you don't mind."

Gundhalinu pointed. "Through there. Help yourself to anything you need."

Tammis started away across the room, stopped in the doorway, looking back. But he said nothing.

Gundhalinu listened to him rummaging through the medicinals in the bathroom, listened to him re-enter the hall and head directly for the door. At the last possible moment, before the door closed, he heard the words, "Thank you."

TIAMAT: Carbuncle

Moon Dawntreader stood alone in the center of a hundred glittering revelers in the Great Hall of the palace. Around her they ate and drank, laughed and gossiped and danced and sang—Winters and Summers and offworlders, all but indistinguishable from one another for once, behind the disguises of their Festival masks and exotic clothes.

She wore a mask made for her by Fate Ravenglass—a re-creation of the mask that had crowned her Summer Queen, made of dappled green velvet and shimmering rainbow gossamer, echoing the flowers of the hills, birdwings, the blues of sky and mirroring sea, the gold of the sun. She hid behind it, gazing out through its eyeholes at the people around her like someone peering through at another world; catching only surreal glimpses of color and motion, hearing every sound as if it had reached her from a distance.

She moved to her body's own slow, instinctive music, drifting with the tide of the crowd. This Mask Night Ball was the climax to an interminable cycle of parties and banquets and functions that she had been expected to participate in as Queen during the Assembly's brief, endless visit.

She had watched the Prime Minister, and everyone around him, drink the water of life in her presence, like addicts, on the night of their arrival; and then she had left the starport and gone back to the city, making her anger plain by her absence. But she could not afford to ignore every function that had been planned, because to do so would have meant that she lost face, and endangered her position with the offworlders. So she had attended them all, or her body had, although her thoughts were far away, among the mers, trapped inside the greater vision that she was never allowed to lose sight of now.

And she was attending this final ball without pleasure, without illusion because it was required. There was hardly anyone here she recognized, and she knew that even if they wore no masks there would be hardly any faces she wanted to see. It was growing late, and already the crowd was thinning as people paired off to spend the rest of the night together—this night, when traditionally everyone was allowed, and even encouraged, to cast aside their inhibitions and put off their regrets until tomorrow, when at dawn they would symbolically cast the past into the sea.

It was considered bad luck to spend this night alone, without a lover. On the last Mask Night, she had been with Sparks, reunited after so long, and their future had seemed infinite in its promise of joy. But Sparks was not even in the room tonight; he had made excuses, saying he wanted to spend what little time was left with his father, before the Assembly departed. She supposed that much was true. But she was sure he would not return before morning, no matter how he actually spent his night.

Tammis was not here either, not even making a pretense with Merovy; they were living apart, she had heard, but neither of them had come to her to tell her about it. And Ariele . . . only the Lady knew what she was doing tonight, or who she was doing it with. There was gossip about an offworlder. Tor had seen them together, she was *just a little worried,* she'd said. . . . Ariele had not been near the palace in weeks; it had surprised Moon that she bothered to appear at the starport banquet—or that she left it with the rest of her family, when the water of life appeared. She would never understand her own daughter, never understand. . . .

The Prime Minister and several other partiers, who might or might not be any of his own people behind the mass-produced sameness of their masks, came to bid her good night. She was resolutely gracious, with relief giving her responses a sincerity that they did not deserve. She recognized the voice of Vhanu, the Police Commissioner; there were several Blues, uniformed and unmasked, with the dignitaries for security. She wondered where Jerusha was tonight. On duty for the Hegemony, she supposed; missing her old friend suddenly, painfully. *No one . . .* She lifted a hand to her face; encountered the startling textures of her mask, instead of her own flesh. She let her hand drop again.

She had searched the crowd all evening for the black uniform of the Chief Justice, the silver flash of a trefoil among the dazzling abundance of jewelry and medals. But she had not found him. BZ had appeared at every other function in the days between the disastrous arrival banquet and this masked ball; sitting beside her when it was required, but seeming to take no more pleasure in anything than she did. She had seen in his eyes both apology and resignation, and they had spoken to each other only when it was necessary. Tonight he must have left early—if he had even come at all, since with masks to hide behind anything was possible. . . . She started on, moving slowly toward the stairway at the far end of the room. The Prime Minister had gone, there was no one here anymore that she was required to wait for.

A sudden flash of reflected light caught her eye. Turning, she glimpsed a mask through the blur of colors that made her stop in sudden fascination. In the crowd of bright repetition, someone was wearing a mask as distinctive as her own. Something indefinable about it told her that, like her own, it had been made by Fate Ravenglass. But she knew all the masks that Fate had made, only a dozen or so—by hand, in the old way, after she had been given back her sight. Fate had given them to Moon and her family, to Tor, to a few other people she considered her special friends. There were other surviving maskmakers, and some of them had gone back into business, selling handmade masks to rich Tiamatans and offworlders. But Fate, who had been counted the best of them all, had said she would not be bothered this time with masks that were not gifts of friendship.

Moon wondered who it was who had received this gift, only able to tell that it was a man, from this distance. The shine of the mask caught her eye again as its wearer turned toward her, as if he felt her staring at him. The mask's face was a mirror, reflecting the light and color and motion all around him, until it became a star in the heart of the night-blackness that framed it. She stood where she was, motionless, as he began to move toward her through the crowd. She watched him come, hypnotized by her own reflection gradually becoming visible in the mirror of his face, growing clearer, more distinct, as he approached her. And suddenly she knew him, by his motion, in the same way she had recognized the workmanship of his mask.

"BZ," she said, softly and with certainty, although he was not in uniform. She lifted her hand to him.

"Moon." His voice; his eyes, looking back at her from the heart of her own bizarre, masked reflection. He took her hand in his, touching it palm to palm in a warm caress. His fingers cupped hers and did not release them.

"I thought you hadn't come," she murmured. "It's almost over."

"I almost didn't come." He shook his head; his mask rustled like soft laughter. "But Fate sent me this mask. It would dishonor her gift if I didn't use it tonight."

She looked down, at his hand still holding her own, seeing her fingers clinging to his, unable to let go. She looked up again, at his eyes, her eyes, the blackness of space and the wild profusion of spring reflected around them.

"Where's Sparks?" he asked, and she felt her heartbeat quicken suddenly. "Isn't he here?"

"He wanted to spend time with his father."

"Tonight?"

"His father won't be here after tomorrow."

"Ah," he said. "But still, it's Mask Night—"

"I know." She looked down at their hands again, still locked tightly together, holding them prisoner. She tried to pry her fingers loose.

BZ's other hand came up, to capture her free one. "Dance with me, then. There's still music, still time. . . ."

She stiffened, feeling suddenly awkward and provincial as he drew her close with gentle insistence. "I don't know your dances—"

"I taught your memory how to dance, once," he murmured. His arms went around her, guiding her body into a formless motion against his own. "It doesn't matter what we do, only that we do something, so that I can put my arms around you again and hold you against me. . . ."

Her arms had nowhere left to go, except to go around him. A shockwave of heat rose through her as her hands felt the muscles of his back beneath the fine, almost silken cloth of his shirt. "This isn't like you," she murmured, and she would have laughed if her stunned, incandescent body had been able to breathe.

He made an odd sound that was not really laughter, either. "What am I like, then? That miserable wretch who spent the last few days staring at you across crowded rooms, afraid to say more than, 'Good day, Lady'? Chief Justice Gundhalinu—not Kharemoughi anymore, and not Tiamatan, neither fish nor fowl? . . . Or a man who spent twelve years of his life dreaming about you; who went to the end of the world for you, and wrestled spacetime to a draw in order to hold you in his arms again—?" His voice was as wondering as if he were possessed, and she remembered another night, the Festival night so long ago when he had spoken words like these to her.

"Yes . . ." she said, telling him everything in that one word; giving him his answer. She reached up, touching her own reflection as she touched his face. And she remembered again that it was Mask Night, and the time of Change. . . .

"I want to get out of here," he said, almost desperately. "Let's go somewhere else—there are parties all up and down the Street, there are—"

"No," she whispered, feeling the pressure of his body along her own, exquisite, unbearable. "Come with me, instead. . . ." She broke away and took his hand, leading him the last few steps across the floor toward the stairway. She did not look back, because there was no one left in the dwindling, faceless crowd who mattered, who cared where they were going now, or why. He followed her without question, without hesitation, up the white cascade of steps. They moved through the shadowed hallways of the upper levels until at last they reached the bedchamber that had been hers alone for too long.

She stopped before the doorway, stopping him beside her. She reached up and removed his mask, with infinite care; needing to see his face before another moment passed . . . before they crossed the threshold into an unknown future. "This is the time of Change, when we cast off our sorrows—"

His hands removed her mask with equal tenderness, set it down beside his against the wall. They stood, not touching now, but only gazing at each other's faces. At last he took her in his arms, holding her as if he had never let her go, and she felt him trembling, as he had trembled on that night, not with cold but with fever heat. . . .

They entered her bedchamber, and she let go of him only for the moment it took to close the door, sealing them into a private space where the greater universe could have no hold over them. But as the door closed behind her, she felt him hesitate; saw him look toward the bed she had shared for so many years with another man. "Are you sure . . . ?" he whispered. "Moon, are you sure?" He looked back at her. "Because this time, by the gods, I won't give you up."

She glanced toward the empty bed, and felt her throat close. But she looked at him again, and as she saw his face, all doubt, all regret, vanished. She put her arms around him, drawing his head down, and kissed him deeply, passionately, with the yearning of years; keeping her eyes open all the while.

He lifted her off her feet in a sudden impulsive motion and carried her across the room. And then the wide, soft expanse of her bed was beneath her, and he was beside her on it, stroking her hair, caressing her face, his kisses like nectar as she drank the sweet draught of his soul.

They broke apart at last; were caught up short by the sudden tangle of silver in silver, the barbed spines of their trefoils tangled in an embrace of thorns. She lifted her hands to slip the chain over her head. BZ did the same, setting himself free; the trefoils dropped to the floor, still entwined. But she saw the tattoo on his throat, like her own, still marking them both.

She began to unfasten the clasps of her robes. Her fingers stumbled over her sudden, painful awareness of time: of all that lay between their first night of intimacy and this one. His eyes were to her the eyes of a stranger, to whom she was about to make her body utterly vulnerable.

He stopped the stumbling motion of her hands, moved them tenderly aside. "Let me . . ." he murmured, his voice husky. She lay back, letting her body go fallow, as he began, lovingly and gently, to remove her clothes. Every touch of his hands against her skin was like fire and ice, until she lay beside him, shivering with desire, feeling as if even her soul were laid bare. He touched her breasts, her belly, touched her softness— She caught hold of his hand, pressing it against her.

But he withdrew his hand with a gentle insistence, whispering, "Wait. . . ."

She watched him loosen his clothing, his own movements suddenly hesitant and self-conscious, as if he were afraid she would be disappointed by what she saw as he revealed himself to her. He stood before her, and she saw how quickly his breath came, how his heart beat, the smooth sheen of perspiration on his skin; how achingly eager he was.

She touched him once, gently, felt him go rigid all over, heard him gasp. He sank onto the bed beside her. She kissed the tattoo in the hollow of his throat, as all her inhibition dissipated like smoke; kissed his chest, tasting moisture and salt, kissed the dark, soft line leading downward, while he buried his hands convulsively in the silver waves of her hair. His hands opened again, falling free, circling down her back in motions that were more and more urgent, as she devoured him with her hungry mouth; as he discovered her every hidden and private place until she had no secrets left, no thoughts, nothing but desire.

She felt his arms go around her again, lifting her gently, drawing her down beside him as he laid his body against her, sliding onto her, between her, inside her, until at last their separate beings were joined into one. She sighed as he began to move inside her, with the same slow, sensual motion of their dance. The rhythm of their lovemaking was like the restless sea; they sank deeper into the waters of sensation, without fear, willing to drown in the depths of pleasure.

She cried out as orgasm swept over her like an undersea swell; he moaned softly, and shuddered with reaction. But the swell passed, and the rhythm continued, building again.

"Gods . . ." BZ murmured, his eyes stunned, his face dazed with astonishment. "Oh, gods." He murmured something more, in Sandhi, a lilting flow of words, like a prayer to something inside himself. And then his lips were on hers again, and his hands covering her breasts, and he was still inside her moving like the waves, as he had been meant to be; as he had always been, would always be.

Their lovemaking was as endless as the sea, and still she sank deeper and deeper into the golden/black waters with every surge and fall; until she knew that she had been falling forever, been born to drown in these depths, and revive, and drown again . . . that she had waited a lifetime to share her own depths, and be filled with the waters of his life; to become one being, one soul, one with his mind. It was impossible now to conceal any secret at all: not her love for him . . . the children already born of it . . . even the impossible secret that she could never share with anyone, although her tongue were to be torn from her mouth—

And in the echoing golden/blackness where nothing existed beyond the sea of their shared sensation, as all physical boundaries dissolved in the fluid heat of desire, she dreamed that she swam like the mers, the Sea's Children . . . that she felt the sensuous caress of the Sea against their silken, brindle bodies, the slow fire of their passion, of their motion through the heart of the secret machinery of the sibyl mind, which lay hidden far below the place where she lay entwined with her lover; below Carbuncle, the ancient City in the North, a pin pushed into a map of time. . . . She heard the mers singing, a rippling golden vision, how their songs brought healing and order to that secret, vulnerable, vital organ entrusted to their keeping. She saw at last why the message of the mersong had been impossible to grasp. . . . The truths that had never been revealed to anyone since its creators . . . *until now.*

Caught inside an exaltation that swept her beyond thought, beyond the boundaries of time, she was terrifyingly free. There was nothing hidden from her view, and nothing that was not his to share, inside her body, inside her mind, inside that rippling sea of lightmusic where their union was complete. . . .

And as he realized the truth, his epiphany became ecstasy, and set him free. The energy of his release cascaded back through the matrix of her body, shockwaves of light resonating through every nerve, the feel of him inside her, his lips against her throat, his inarticulate cry, her incoherent sob of joy. She held him, held him, until she was sure once more of the location of every atom of his body and her own; and that she was no longer made of fluid light.

It was a long time before she was able to speak again, a long time before he even tried; before there was any need for the superfluity of sound, when their lips, their tongues, were still preoccupied with more important tasks, while they had no breath to waste, while they still clung to one another through the slowing spiral of their return to earth.

"I understand. . . ." he said, at last, with an awe and wonder that seemed to fill his whole being. And his face changed, filling with anguish and dread as he realized what it was he knew—why she would do anything to stop the Hunt; why she had never told him the whole truth . . . why he would never be able to tell anyone else.

"It's going to be all right," he whispered, holding her. But she did not answer him, her own face stricken as she saw his eyes. Her arms tightened around him. "No," she murmured, "it will be terrible."

She felt him look back at her, felt the gentle touch of his hand against her face. But he did not deny it.

Sparks climbed the stairs from the silent, empty ballroom, still seeing in his mind the telltale detritus of the Mask Night: countless masks with their empty, patient eyes, gazing at him from doorways or steps; waiting for the dawn while their owners made merry within, all along the littered empty streets. He had worn a mask tonight, the one given to him by Fate Ravenglass, all reds and golds, glittering like the sun, as vital, as angry as fire. . . . He had spent the early part of the night talking with his father, and the rest of it wandering from party to party; but he had felt as lifeless and hollow-souled as his mask, once he and his father had said their goodbyes.

He had not gone for the night, or even for an hour, with anyone, although he had had sufficient opportunities; because he was certain that Moon was spending her night alone, faithful to the word, if not the spirit, of their long-ago vow. He had broken both the word and the spirit of their pledge, many times, since the offworlders' return, although he had sworn at their departure that he would never do it again.

But tonight he had talked with his father about memories of family and home; he had shared the loneliness and regret of a man who had had neither, for far too long. His father had told him that he planned to leave the Assembly when it next visited his homeworld; that being here, at Tiamat's time of Change, had made him realize how disillusioned he had grown with an existence that seemed ever more pointless.

Carrying his father's words, his father's sorrow, with him as he wandered the streets, he had come to realize at last that this was a time of Change for him as well, even if it was in name only; that there was still time before dawn for him to lie with the only woman he had ever truly loved, and promise her a new beginning.

He walked quietly down the hall to the bedroom he and his wife had always shared, until these last few months. He stopped, standing motionless before the closed door. Two masks lay side by side against the wall, in mute testimony to the absurdity of dreams. He stared at them for a long time. And then he turned away, and went slowly back down the hall.

TIAMAT: Carbuncle

BZ Gundhalinu took his place on the ribbon-draped platform between Vhanu and the Prime Minister, aware that all eyes were on him now—the last one sliding into place, like a guilty schoolboy, when he should have been the first one here. Below the hastily erected viewing stands the sea waited, covered by floating docks; the docks were now so crowded with the ships of Festival-time that the water itself was barely visible.

But where the pier ended below him a space of water had been deliberately left open, for the ritual to come. He watched its dark, glimmering motion, feeling its relentness rhythms begin to hypnotize him. His mind sank like a stone, drawn down into the depths by the weight of his new knowledge, the unspeakable burden of the secret that lay hidden below. . . .

He forced his eyes away, clutching the rail in front of him harder than necessary as he searched the clear space that separated the stands filled with influential offworlders from the stands which held the most influential Tiamatans—segregated, as they had always been. All the faces that he could see across the way were still hidden behind their Mask Night disguises, unlike his own people; the Tiamatans would not unmask until the ritual was completed. Two real human faces stood out against the sea of alien forms—Sparks Dawntreader and the Queen, standing side by side. They were not touching, and their own faces were as fixed and rigid as masks.

He willed Moon to lift her gaze from the sea to look at him; until at last she met his eyes. He saw her translucently pale skin blush; saw the telltale redness of her mouth, the dizzying depths of passion and hidden knowledge in her eyes. His hand rose unthinkingly to his own lips, his own unmasked face; fell away again. His whole body still moved as if he were sleepwalking, stupefied by revelations at every level of awareness, revelations that still went on and on. . . .

"BZ—" Vhanu's hand was on his arm, giving him a subtle shake; he realized that Vhanu had been trying to get his attention, and failing. "Thou must have had quite a night of it," Vhanu whispered, with amusement in his eyes. "I've never seen thou like this before."

"Yes," he murmured, understating.

"I had a most entertaining night myself," Vhanu said, his smile turning private with the memory. "Really quite an interesting custom."

"Yes, indeed," Sandrine muttered, behind them. "But barbaric that they make us get up at dawn the morning after, to stand here in this wind and watch them throw straw dummies into the sea." The others around him had already taken off their masks, as if it was beneath their dignity to be seen wearing one in their official capacity, in the light of day. He had left his own mask behind at the palace, forgotten in the bedazzlement of his waking, their leavetaking, his frantic dash back to his townhouse to change into his uniform in time for the Change ceremony.

He looked back across the open space at Moon and Sparks, away again, as a murmur of anticipation began far above them in the Police-cordoned crowds lining the ramp that led down from the city. The sound swept toward him, infecting the people in the stands, who began to murmur and point as they caught their first glimpse of the sight they had been waiting here to see.

A ship-form cart was progressing slowly down the ramp, surrounded by Summers dressed in traditional clothing, dyed in shades of green and decorated with embroidery and designs worked in polished shell. They wore wreaths and garlands of flowers, and they chanted a Tiamatan lament that fell strangely on his ears.

The cart itself carried two passengers sitting stiffly upright, wearing masks. One of the masks was the one that Moon had worn, as Summer Queen, last night. The other was a mass of fiery brilliance, like the sun—Sparks's mask, he realized suddenly. As the cart drew slowly nearer, he saw the ropes that bound the two figures to the seat.

His glance went again to the two faces in the stands across the way, proving to himself that the couple in the cart were only effigies, not human beings. Moon's gaze held his for a long moment, before she looked away again, at the cart and its masked figures. Her hands hugged her arms as if she were reassuring herself of her safety, her reality.

The cart came to a halt in the open space, just before it reached the sea. Moon left her place and made her way down to the pier, and the crowd's murmurous voice fell silent at last. Throughout the city other crowds were watching this climax of the Festival's celebration on monitor screens. Gundhalinu wondered how many of them were fantasizing that this was the real thing—that the ceremonial ship-form that had made the journey down here from the palace gates was actually about to send two living beings into the sea to drown. He wondered how many of those watching had seen the real thing, the last time.

The last time it had happened he had been in the hospital, recovering from pneumonia, the result of his ordeal among the nomads. Suddenly, staring at the effigies, he was glad that he had not been here to watch Moon give the command that had sent the Snow Queen into the sea. He wondered what she must have felt then, watching her mother, her rival, her mirror image, drown before her eyes. He wondered what she must be feeling now, what she must remember, as she presided over this harmless imitation of the real sacrifice—which would have been a real sacrifice, if he had not stopped it. She stood staring at the masked effigies before her, her own face frozen.

He felt giddy with the rush of empathy that filled him as he looked at her. He wanted to make his way down to the pier where she stood, to take her in his arms, to take her pain inside him, to hold and support her. . . . He did nothing, standing motionless at the ribbon-draped rail, the picture of official propriety and indifference.

Moon tore her eyes from the effigies, looking past them, past the waiting honor guard of Summers at the contents of the cart, which was fully laden with offerings to the Sea Mother. Her expression changed again, suddenly. He followed her gaze, seeing heaps of greenery and odd artifacts donated or tossed into the cart as it passed through the crowd. His eyes found the thing that her eyes had discovered: a Festival mask, with a mirrored face framed in midnight black—his mask, that he had left behind at the palace. Its face was shattered, the mirror a net of a thousand fractures, as if someone had deliberately smashed it in before consigning it to oblivion in the depths of the sea. . . .

Moon glanced up suddenly, looking at him, before she turned to look back at the stands behind her, at her husband, silently witnessing. She bowed her head again; gathering strength, looking at neither one of them now, turning inward. She lifted her arms to the crowd, to the Sea Mother, lifted her voice and began to play her part in the ritual prayer and process.

BZ took a deep breath, easing the constriction in his chest as he listened to her song. He looked up at the masked faces—the one unmasked, among them—as the pure, clear beauty of her voice repeating the archaic recitation washed over him like the waters of the sea, washing away the past, telling him that from this moment on everything in his life was changed. . . .

"I hate this," Ariele murmured, shifting her weight from foot to foot as her body grew impatient with standing. "This is humiliating." She lifted her hands to the mask, all rainbows and colors of the sea, that Fate had made for her. It was beautiful; even Reede had said so, as close to wondering as she had ever seen him get about anything but the mers. She had felt beautiful wearing it, shining through the countless parties, falling through the pleasures of the night with her chosen lover. . . . Until he had abandoned her at dawn, forcing her to come here alone, to endure this ceremony without him.

Already stung by Reede's refusal to stay with her, she had watched the offworlders standing in judgment on the platform across the way, every one of them unmasked, their alien faces staring back at her in curiosity and bemusement. They were watching her mother perform the traditional Change ritual as if she and all her people were some sort of animals quaintly dressed in clothing and imitating human behavior.

Now, standing here under their eyes, she felt the beauty of the mask she wore wither and die, as if their gaze was frost. Her hands tightened over the fragile form as something inside her tried to force her to take it off. But then her own face, her emotions, would be left naked to their stares. She lowered her hands again to her sides, as the Chief Justice suddenly looked directly at her.

She turned her face away so that she did not have to look at the man who claimed to be her father. She listened to the strange yet familiar patterns of her mother's recitation rise and fall, filling the air; thought about the last time her mother had performed this ritual, in earnest, drowning her true grandmother on the day her own life was begun.

She looked at her true father, his hair as bright as the sunrise, standing alone like she was here in the stands, but just beyond her reach. He was not looking at her, or her mother, or even the offworlders; he was staring out at the sea. She called to him, as loudly as she dared, but he did not respond, did not acknowledge her in any way.

She felt her eyes burn suddenly, and turned away, looking behind her at Merovy, who was also alone, because Tammis had not even had the nerve to show up here. Merovy hid her sorrows behind another of Fate's masks, this one the color of fog, the color of birds' wings. Its forms were so subtle that at a glance someone might mistake them for simple, or plain.

Ariele wondered where Tammis was. For once, in her own isolation, she felt compassion for her brother and his silent wife. She reached back, touching Merovy's hand, seeing her start in surprise. She felt Merovy's fingers close over hers, briefly and warmly.

"What is it you find humiliating about being here, Ariele?" someone asked behind her, curious and without censure.

She glanced back over her other shoulder, recognizing the voice of Clavally, tying it to another masked face; realizing that Merovy had come with her parents.

"The offworlders," she murmured. "The way they watch us. They make everything we do seem meaningless and stupid. They don't believe in anything."

"They believe in everything," Danaquil Lu said wryly. "Which is just as bad."

She shook her head irritably, and felt Clavally's light touch fall on her shoulder. "Do you believe in the Sea Mother? In the rituals?" Clavally asked.

She looked up and back, suddenly glad that her mask covered her face. She listened to her mother's voice calling on the Sea. "I don't believe the sea is some kind of god," she whispered, finally. "But neither does my mother, even though she's supposed to."

"But our beliefs and traditions are just as old as the Kharemoughis'; maybe even older," Clavally said. "And what our rituals teach us is just as true to how we've always lived as the Kharemoughis' are, or anyone else's are. They're all only variations on a theme—as your father would say—" Ariele glanced back at her again, in surprise, "each variation beautiful in its own way, even if they don't always harmonize. If there was only one song to sing, in all existence, our lives would be maddeningly dull."

"But so much more peaceful," Danaquil Lu said, putting his arm around his wife.

"Everything has its price," Clavally murmured. "That's what the Change is about."

Ariele looked away again, thinking suddenly of the mers, and the mystery of their songs . . . thinking of Reede. He was an offworlder, but his fascination with her world was passionate and real; he had made her see her people's customs, and her own life, in ways she had never seen them before. If only he would have stayed with her, to celebrate the changes he had brought into her life . . . to acknowledge that in some way she had changed his own. They were together night after night; he had even, finally, shared his body with her. But he still would not let her into his heart. He never allowed any real intimacy between them, even when they lay in each other's arms.

Sometimes, when they made love, the pleasure and the sweetness filled her until she thought she would die of it; sometimes when they made love he wept. But always he left her before dawn, as he had left her this morning, slipping away like a succubus, a shadow, before the new day's light showed at the alley's end . . .

leaving her to come here alone, stand here alone, listen to the ancient Song of Change alone. And all around her there was loneliness and regret, telling her things she did not want to hear about her desperate passion for a man as secret and unknowable as the depths of the sea.

Someone stepped into the empty space just behind her, amid a rustle and murmur of bodies. She turned, with sudden eagerness; found her brother standing behind her, in his rightful spot beside Merovy. She stared at him for a long moment, trying to make his masked figure into someone else's. She could not, and so she looked away again, out at the unchanging sea.

"Merovy . . ." Tammis whispered, "I need to talk to you. About us."

She looked up at him; he could see nothing of her face but her eyes. Her eyes told him everything that her face could not, *hope/doubt/anguish/love*—

He reached for her hand, and she did not pull away. "It's you I love," he said, oblivious to the masked faces turning toward him, turning away; to his mother's voice consigning the images of herself and her consort to the sea. "Everything you are, your body, your mind. I want to live with you, and have children, and raise them together—"

Her hand tightened convulsively over his. "It's the time of Change," she whispered, barely audible as she looked toward the ritual down below; echoing it, as the people around them were suddenly turning away, pointing, straining to see.

Tammis turned too, as Merovy drew him with her. He looked down at the place where his mother stood. She stepped aside as they watched, and the Summers thrust the cart forward, sending it into the cold, dark water. The crowd's voice roared, everyone around them cheering now, as they watched the boat-form circling, circling, riding lower and lower in the water as the holes hidden in its bed let in the sea. Tammis stared, squeezing Merovy's hand painfully, as the effigies that symbolized the two actual human beings who were his parents disappeared into the Sea Mother's embrace.

He let out his breath in a sigh as the offering-boat sank out of sight, putting his arm around Merovy almost unthinkingly. She pressed against him, her body seeking his, her mind seeking comfort from the symbolic death of the past that they had just witnessed.

"All things change . . ." his mother's voice was saying, "except the Sea. The Lady has taken our offering, and will return it ninefold. The life that was is dead—let it be cast away, like a battered mask, an outgrown shell. Rejoice now, and make a new beginning—" Having no mask of her own to take off, she raised her hands, a sign to the waiting crowd.

Tammis reached up to lift off his mask, feeling the sea wind finger his hair and cool his suddenly flushed face. Merovy removed her mask. He looked at the two strange, suddenly sightless fantasy faces gazing up at him: traditional totem figures, half bird, half fish—unreal and yet somehow full of secret meaning. The masks fell together, as his hand and hers released them, and he looked up at her face. She smiled at him, and he felt the warmth spread through his entire body.

All around them other masks were dropping away, revealing Clavally and Danaquil Lu, Fate, Tor—letting him see the release that lit the faces of the people he knew and loved and suddenly felt at one with again. And he understood, as he never had before, why the Change was necessary; how even this imitation of the true ritual could affect so many people so profoundly.

His sister turned where she stood, alone, dropping her mask as she looked up at him standing beside Merovy. Her face was quizzical for a moment, and then, as suddenly as sunlight, she smiled at them. Tammis smiled back, uncertainly. Ariele looked away again without speaking, looking toward their father's place in the stands.

Tammis followed her glance, and to his surprise saw that his father's space was empty. He looked down at the pier, where his mother stood. His father was not there, either. His mother stood facing away from her own people, gazing up into the rapt face of the Kharemoughi Chief Justice, while the mindless ululation of the crowd went on and on.

TIAMAT: Carbuncle

"Well, this time they didn't get there first, by all the gods!" the lieutenant named Ershad grinned in satisfaction as he strode into the meeting chamber, and saluted. He still wore his thermal drysuit—for effect, Gundhalinu supposed sourly—and he carried a heavy container in one gloved hand. He set it on the conference table with an audible *thud,* as the members of the Hegemonic government rapped the table surface in applause. Gundhalinu kept his own hands motionless. There were brownish-red stains on Ershad's drysuit, and on the container. Dried blood. Mer blood. "There's more where this came from," Ershad said, folding his arms. "We sent it straight to the processing plant. And we arrested those goddamned Summer dissidents and confiscated their equipment again. This time they didn't get there in time to interfere with our business, at least."

"Good work, Ershad," Vhanu said finally, when Gundhalinu's silence had begun to grow awkward. Ershad nodded and smiled again.

"What did you do with the Summers?" Jerusha PalaThion asked, with her eyes on the bucket and an edge in her voice.

"They're in the lockup, ma'am," he said. "And a couple of them are in the hospital. They resisted arrest." His mouth quirked.

PalaThion kept her expression neutral, but Gundhalinu felt his own mouth tighten at the subtle signs of pleasure he saw spreading over the other faces in the room. Jerusha got up from her seat, glancing at Vhanu. "I'll make arrangements to have them turned over to the local authorities," she said. She rose from her seat and started toward the door before he had time to object; before anyone could see the hard lines of pain that Gundhalinu knew were already forming on her face.

Ershad watched her go out too, his expression darkening.

"Justice . . ." Vhanu turned in his seat to face Gundhalinu. "These people interfere with every hunt we attempt, using sophisticated equipment to disrupt our activities. But the local police let them go again immediately. Isn't there some way we can control this adequately?" He made it a question, but Gundhalinu heard the unspoken demand.

"We can't prosecute them under our law unless they actually make a physical assault on one of our people," he answered, still frowning. "And there's no law that restricts them from using our technology on their fishing boats."

"Maybe we should just drop a few of them overboard and let them swim home next time, sir," Ershad said. "That ought to discourage them."

"Then you would be breaking Tiamatan law, Ershad," Gundhalinu remarked dryly. "And our own too. Take that container out of here and see that it's disposed of appropriately."

"Yes, sir." Ershad saluted again, and was gone.

"Maybe we should consider making some new laws," Vhanu said impatiently. "We need one that equates interfering with the mer hunts to interfering with a Police action—" There were mutterings of assent all along the table.

"This world has one thing that makes it worth the Hegemony's while, and we're still having trouble producing it," Tilhonne said. "The Coordinators are getting impatient with us again, and we all know what that means. We have to produce, or we'll be—"

"I know." Gundhalinu cut him off sharply, knowing that what he said was true. Knowing at the same time that every container of spilled blood that was transformed into the water of life not only brought the extinction of the mers closer, but also the extinction of the sibyl network itself. . . . And he could not tell them. *He could not. He could not.* "I know the matter is vital. I will give it my full attention. And now, sadhanu, I am adjourning this meeting. It's been another very long day." He pushed to his feet almost peremptorily, preventing any objections or further attempts at discussion.

Vhanu walked with him out through the crowded hallways of the government complex, through the endless sea of blue uniforms and offworld faces. Neither of them spoke until they had passed through the building's entrance and stood in the neutral ground of the alleyway.

"I hope thou will give this matter more thought, BZ," Vhanu said at last, his eyes searching Gundhalinu's face.

Gundhalinu looked away, studying the changing flow pattern of the bodies within his sight. "I will, NR." *As if I can think about anything else now, night or day.* "But I can't promise thee anything. There are no easy answers to this."

Vhanu sighed. "I know thou will do what is best," he said; clearly not certain of it at all.

"Yes." Gundhalinu nodded, for once completely certain in his own response. "That I will do."

"Will thou come down to the Survey Hall with us this evening?" Vhanu nodded at Tilhonne and Sandrine, who were just emerging from the building behind them. "There is a general meeting, and some new recreational interactives have just arrived, I understand—" He put a hand on Gundhalinu's shoulder in a placating gesture, trying to bridge the gap of their strained relations.

Gundhalinu hesitated; shook his head, glancing down. "Not tonight, NR. I'm going directly home. I have reports to catch up on, and I intend to go to bed early."

"What, again? 'Early to bed' is becoming a habit with thee. And it seems to me that on the mornings after thou appear quite exhausted. . . ." He smiled suddenly, knowingly. "Are thou still seeing that woman thou met on Mask Night?"

Gundhalinu felt himself flush, and knew that it was betraying him. "Well," he murmured, "thou've found me out, I'm afraid, NR." He smiled too, keeping his gaze averted, pushing his hands deeply into his pockets, which were empty.

Vhanu chuckled. "Father of all my grandfathers!" he said. "She must be a spellbinder, to make a Chief Justice blush like a schoolboy."

Gundhalinu glanced away in relief as Inspector Kitaro came up beside them, carrying her helmet under her arm. "Sir. Justice Gundhalinu." She saluted them, smiling. Her eyes stayed on Gundhalinu slightly longer than they needed to; he looked back at her, mildly surprised.

"Coming to the Hall tonight, Kitaro?" Vhanu asked, as Tilhonne and Sandrine came up beside him.

She glanced at him, and shook her head. "Not tonight, Commander. It's been a long day. Thought maybe I'd get to bed early, sir."

Vhanu shrugged. "By all means, get some sleep, then."

She laughed, an oddly girlish sound. "Well, I didn't say anything about sleeping. . . ." She tossed her head, her dark curls shining in the artificial light. She glanced at Gundhalinu again, and away, still smiling.

Vhanu raised an eyebrow, made mildly uncomfortable by her Nontechnician frankness. He glanced between them, and an amused smile appeared on his face. "Have a good night then, both of you. Come, sadhanu, let's not keep them from their evening's plans." He nodded to Sandrine and Tilhonne, and they started off down the alley in search of transportation.

Gundhalinu murmured his own self-conscious good-night to Kitaro, vaguely nonplussed, and started away toward the alley's entrance. She fell into step beside him, with seeming casualness. "See you to your door, sir?"

He looked at her, his curiosity and surprise deepening, along with his annoyance. "No, thank you. It's not much of a walk, and out of your way besides, I think. I don't want to make you late—"

"It's not out of my way, sir, " she said, with mild insistence. "I have to stop at the market." They passed Vhanu, Tilhonne, and Sandrine standing at the corner, waiting for the tram. Gundhalinu turned uphill, following the Street, and she went with him; he felt the eyes of the others follow them speculatively. "The Chief Inspector said she wanted to be certain there's always someone covering your ass, sir," Kitaro said, throwing a glance over her shoulder as she walked, with the pretense of looking into a shop window. "And people do like to talk."

"I see," he murmured, finally beginning to understand. He studied storefronts and doorways on his own side of the Street. "I appreciate it, then. The gods forbid that the Chief Justice ever got caught bare-assed like a normal human being." He looked back at her, with weary amusement.

"Yes, sir," she said.

They went on up the Street together, making forgettable small talk about government business. If she had heard about the successful mer hunt, she did not bring it up. He did not ask her opinion. After all this time he knew almost nothing about her, except that she was a sibyl, and she was someone KR Aspundh had trusted. She was Nontechnician, and outside of the Survey Hall she did not mingle with the people he saw the most. He had no idea what she did off-duty, or what her interests were.

He was not even certain at what level she actually functioned within Survey, although it was obviously a far higher one than most of his companions suspected. She had brought him the data on Reede Kullervo; and she had helped him solve other, less crucial problems, so unobtrusively that he only realized now how often she seemed to be there when he needed a favor. But all that guaranteed nothing about her feelings on the mer question. He did not have the strength, tonight at least, to put her opinions to the test.

Instead, he asked, "Any luck yet in arranging a meeting with our elusive friend, the Smith?" Thinking of Reede Kullervo, as he had not had time to do these past few weeks, he suddenly realized something else: *Kullervo was Vanamoinen. And Vanomoinen had created the sibyl net . . . the net that was failing.* It could not be a coincidence. It had to mean something. But only Kullervo could tell him what.

Kitaro shook her head. "We've come this close—" she lifted her hand, "but the timing has never been right. It isn't that he's hard to find; it's that he belongs to the Source. Jaakola's got eyes sewn into Reede Kullervo's pockets. Getting him out from under the Brotherhood's surveillance long enough for you to talk meaningfully to him is almost impossible."

"Almost—?" he asked.

She looked up at him, and smiled. "The difficult we do immediately. The impossible just takes a little longer."

He smiled too; his smile faded. "This meeting has to happen, Kitaro. It could be vital to us all."

"I understand," she said.

Wishing that was true, he walked on in silence.

"Good night, Kitaro," he said at last, as they reached his townhouse door. He hesitated uncomfortably, wondering whether she expected to be invited inside. The sky was dark beyond the alley's end; he hadn't realized it was so late.

But she only pressed her fist to her chest in a salute, with a fleeting smile. "Have a good night yourself, Justice," she said, and started back down the quiet alley.

He watched her out of sight, before he stepped forward into the shadows and set his fingers to the identification key on his front door. The door opened silently, letting him into the sanctuary of his home. It closed again, as silently, behind him. He pulled open the seal on his uniform jacket, sighing.

"BZ—?" She stepped out of the glow of a lamplit side room, into the darkened hall. He saw her limned with light, her hair silver, her face half in shadow, half visible.

"Moon." He felt the tightness that was half anticipation and half fear of disappointment release inside his chest. He started toward her. "I'm sorry I was late . . . the meeting ran over—"

"There was a successful Hunt," she said, still standing motionless.

He stopped moving, because she made no move toward him. "Yes," he said, his throat closing on the word. "They must have changed the scheduling code, I—"

She turned away from him, shutting her eyes, pressing her forehead against the doorjamb, murmuring something that he could not hear. ". . . offworlder butchers—!" She raised her head again, glaring at him.

"Damn it all!" he said, the explosion of anger inside him not directed at her—directed at nothing, everything, himself; because he was the Chief Justice, and he was as helpless, as powerless to stop what was happening as she was . . . and she was the Queen. "It's impossible—it's insane!"

She reached out to him, this time crossing the space between them, and he saw the anguish and the helpless desire in her eyes as she opened her arms.

He took her into his own arms, holding her close, feeling the rough homespun and wool of her clothing, the yielding warmth of her body, the softness of her skin. He kissed her hungry, demanding mouth, letting all the raging energy inside him transform into need. He had never imagined that he could feel anything with such intensity—that such feeling existed. He let his desire burn, purifying him of duty, guilt, memory, until the entirety of spacetime telescoped down to this moment, this fragile refuge, this hiding place from destiny. "Oh, gods," he whispered, "I want you right now—"

Her body gave him his answer, with her warm soft mouth silencing his own as she urged him wordlessly toward the stairs that led up to his bedroom.

TIAMAT: South Coast

"Look at them all!" Ariele raised her hands, shielding her eyes against the mirroring glare of the wet sand. The beach ran for nearly a mile along the coast, between two points where the foothills waded out into the sea. It was a rare, perfect strip of fine sand, as soft beneath her bare feet as velvet cloth. And it was covered with a shifting mass of mers—not a single colony, but several at once, sharing the same territory, the same resting place on a sudden, incomprehensible journey. "What are they doing here like this? Where are they going?"

Silky rested beside her on the beach, the merling's body pressing against her leg just enough to make pleasant contact without making her stumble. They had tracked the colony by the tracer the merling wore like an earring, which Jerusha and Miroe had given her when she was tiny; she had led them to this unexpected rendezvous on the beach. Silky had greeted them eagerly, obviously delighted to see them. She seemed content, now, in their company; but something indefinable about the way she held herself told Ariele that she was not.

"They're heading north," Reede said, pushing back the hood of his parka. "All of them. I don't know why, but they are." He wore a parka while she wore only a thin shirt and pants, and had rolled up her sleeves and pantslegs; he dressed as if it were the middle of Winter whenever he left the city, no matter how hot the day was. He looked at the merling beside her; smiled almost involuntarily as he began a series of questioning clicks and trills.

Silky cocked her head, and then suddenly lunged forward, butting him in the stomach. He sat down with a grunt of surprise in the sand. He began to laugh; climbed to his feet again, rubbing his bruised pride. "Damn. I guess that wasn't the question."

Ariele looked at him in mild amazement. She had never heard him laugh like that, easily and freely; it struck her how rarely she heard him laugh at all. "Your pitch was off," she said. He shrugged, extending his hand to her in invitation.

She repeated the run of sounds, watching Silky warily. The mer moved her head in a rhythmic series of nods, and answered with a run of tonal mer speech. Ariele frowned, repeating the sounds in her mind, breaking them down into comprehensible fragments. " '*A presence*' . . ." she translated slowly, " '*and a need*' . . ."

" '*It's there,*' " Reede murmured. He laughed again, suddenly. " 'Because it's there'—?"

She grinned and punched him in the shoulder. "You—" She broke off as Silky interrupted her with another, unexpected run of trilling. "That was mersong," she said, looking back at Reede; seeing the recognition in his eyes. "Do you think it's about that . . . that there's some kind of gathering, where they share songs—?"

"Yeah," he said, crouching down, face to face with the mer. "That may be it . . . it feels right to me." Silky nuzzled him with her lips in a brief apology, and he buried his face in the warm, dense fur of her neck. She allowed him the intimacy, snuffling his hair in unspoken affection.

Ariele smiled, knowing that she would have been jealous, except that she knew, herself, how helpless she was to resist Reede Kullervo. He sat back in the sand, locking his arms around his knees, watching the mers in motion on the sand, his face rapt. She wished again that he would come with her into the sea, dive with them, swim with them. The sea was their world, and never to be with them there was to miss the true, profound beauty of their existence. But he always refused her, brusquely, without explanation. She supposed it was his ordeal trapped among the rocks that made him so afraid.

"How far do you think they're going? Is this the gathering place?" She looked away along the beach again.

He shook his head. "They're going to Carbuncle."

"Carbuncle?" she repeated, looking down at him. "Why?"

His face clouded over. "I don't know." He picked up a handful of sand, let it slip through his fingers. "I don't know. . . ."

"Lady's Tits, Reede!" she said, exasperated. She brushed irritably at the springflies buzzing around her ear. "How do you know those things? Why do you know them? You pick them out of the air like a radio, and then you're right! I can't stand you—"

"Liar," he said. The man who loved the mers, who seemed completely real only outside the city, surprised her with a sudden grin. His arms reached out, catching her by the knees to pull her down, laughing, into the sand beside him. "You can't live without me, you told me so."

He tried to kiss her; she pushed him away suddenly, squinting out to sea. "Wait. Wait a minute. Give me your lenses, Reede." She pulled them off his head, pushed them down onto her own face. She climbed to her feet again, searching the horizon.

"What is it?" He got up, beside her.

"Something's out there—" She scrambled up the outcrop of rock beside them, stood high above him, looking out to sea, ordering the lenses to full enhancement. "Ships! It's the Hunt—can you see them? They're coming this way." She went cold in the pit of her stomach.

Reede swore. "Are they coming after us?" he demanded. "Or after the mers?" She felt him climb up to where she stood; unable to take her eyes away from the sight framed inside the lenses. "Yes," she said faintly.

He took the goggles from her as he reached her side, slipping them back onto his own head. "Anything flying out there—?" She squinted into the sun, shielding her eyes with her hands. "No. They only use ships. The hovercraft look too alien; sometimes they make the mers uneasy." She could see them clearly without the lenses' enhancement, now that she knew. A mer's singsong demand reached her; she looked down, the motion giving her vertigo, to see Silky peering up at her in curiosity from below. "Reede—" She caught his arm, shaking him. "They're coming! What are we going to do?"

He looked around at her, pushing the goggles up again. "We're going to get the hell out of here. If they catch us trespassing we'll be in shit up to our necks."

"They can't do anything to us," she said, startled and angry. "My mother is the Queen."

"Mine isn't," Reede said. "They'll kick my ass off the planet."

"But you work for my mother. She'll—"

"Don't argue, damn it!" He took hold of her arm, urging her to climb down.

She jerked free. "Reede, they'll kill Silky!" Even though the hunting had begun again, the mers continued to live as if they had nothing in this world to fear. Reede had told her that it was because their lives were so long: they felt no urgency, and so they had no fear of death, no desire to compete, no need for the kind of material culture that humans were driven to create as a lasting monument to their fleeting existence. They lacked even the vocabulary to warn each other about the kind of mortal danger they were in now. "Lady's Eyes," she cried, "they'll kill them all!"

Reede looked away along the beach. His mouth pulled back in a grimace. "Shit," he said, "shit!" clenching his hands. "Come on, then, help me!" He clambered back down the rocks; she followed him, skinning her exposed flesh raw. He reached into his equipment pack, pulled something out and began to program it.

"What—?" she gasped.

"A sonic. It'll panic them into the sea. It's what the hunters use, but it'll save them if we use it first. Except it's not enough to affect this many of them—" He pitched it with all his strength out into the mass of bodies. Mers began to stir and shrill in complaint.

"Silky!" Ariele called out, called to the merling again with trills a mother would use to call its child. She ran toward Silky, waving her arms, grimacing, trying to spread her own growing panic any way she could. Behind her Reede shouted out something in the mer speech that she couldn't make out. Silky jerked up short, staring at them. She turned, suddenly, and floundered away down the beach toward the water. Reede went on shouting, running at the mers, his sudden erratic behavior driving them reluctantly into the waves.

Ariele looked up again, as more brindle bodies disappeared into the sea. "Something's happening—" She pointed at the horizon, trying to make out a clear image. Reede pulled his goggles down, and stopped short to watch. He laughed once, in triumphant relief. "The Lady heard your prayers," he muttered, peeling the glasses off. He pushed them at her. "The Summers have come."

She grabbed the lenses, watched through them with her blood singing as the handful of Summer fishing boats intersected the course of the larger offworlder fleet. They were still too far away for her to see the action clearly, but she knew about Capella Goodventure's holy war, knew that her mother's support lay behind it, making it possible. She felt a sudden pride and purpose, as if she were looking through her mother's eyes; and she realized all at once that there was something they shared, something far more important than any superficial physical resemblance.

Reede jogged her arm, silently demanding the goggles back. She gave them to him, with a crow of delight. "They'll stop it," she said. "They've done it before. My mother protects them from the offworlders—"

Reede swore, suddenly and viciously. "No! No, damn it—!"

"What? What?" she cried, straining to see.

"Those Blue fuckers! They rammed a boat. They're boarding her. . . . Gods, that's another one. It's breached—"

"No! Lady and all the gods—" Ariele turned, looking away along the beach again in desperation. She crouched down, picking up stones until her arms were loaded. She ran toward the uncomprehending mers, hurling rocks at them, shouting.

"Ariele!" Reede called. "Get back to the flyer! Come on!" He started after her.

"No!" she shrieked. "I won't leave them!"

"Listen to me, damn you!" He caught her, jerked her to a stop. "You said a hovercraft might spook them. We've got one; let's use it, for gods' sakes! Come on—"

She nodded and turned back without further protest, running toward the cliffs and their waiting craft.

Reede flung himself into the pilot's seat, barely waiting for her to clear the door before he sealed it. She collapsed into the seat beside him, felt its emergency restraints lock in place around her as the hovercraft lifted precipitously and soared down over the edge of the cliff, skimming the heads of the astounded mers. They looked up, their long, graceful necks stretching almost comically as Reede buzzed the beach. And then, already unnerved by the presence of the sonic, they began to move. She watched the dark rippling mass of their bodies begin to flow toward the edge of the sea like the current of a riptide, as Reede reached the end of the strand and banked sharply, returning for another pass just above their heads. He shouted, a wild cry of elation, as he saw them respond.

Something hit the hovercraft broadside, like an invisible fist. The craft lurched and plunged sickeningly, barely restabilizing before it would have hit the beach; alarms sang.

"They're firing on us, those bastards!" Reede ordered the hovercraft to climb, taking them up and away from the beach in another stomach-dropping, unexpected change of momentum. Ariele huddled in her seat, held there by acceleration, abruptly seeing nothing anywhere but sky.

"We've got to get clear," Reede said, looking at her now, and she saw the pain in his eyes. "We're unarmed and unshielded. That was a warnoff; if the Blues hit us again we're scrapmetal. We've done all we can do, most of them will get clear—" And, when she did not answer, "Do you believe me?"

She nodded, closing her eyes; seeing her eyelids blood red against the sun. At last she opened her eyes again, filling them with blue and white. "Thank you," she whispered.

"Don't thank me." He looked away, frowning out at the sky. "Shit . . . This isn't going to be the end of it for us, either. If they hit us, they got a reading on this craft. They'll be able to track us back to the city."

"The hovercraft belongs to my mother," Ariele said, feeling a slow, cold smile creep over her face. "The Chief Justice gave it to her as a gift." She looked back at him. "No one knows you came out here with me. No one has to know. You won't have any trouble. And if the Chief Inspector wants to question me—" she looked ahead again, "she isn't going to like the answers."

TIAMAT: Carbuncle

BZ Gundhalinu paced restlessly in the quiet confines of his townhouse sitting room, unable to remain sitting any longer. The music he had called on did not suit his mood, and no amount of attempted meditation seemed to have the slightest effect on his heartbeat or his impatience.

Gods . . . he thought, feeling the hot ache spreading, deep inside him, as he pushed aside the heavy drapes to look out the window once more. *I'm too old to feel like this.* Like a lovesick boy, like a character out of the Old Empire romances he had read in his youth. He had never felt this way then; never believed that anyone actually did, that anyone actually counted seconds that seemed hours long, waiting for a knock at the door, the first glimpse of his lover's face as she arrived in the night for a secret tryst. . . .

There was a knock at his door, barely audible. He stepped into the hallway, and the security system's monitor showed him the face he had been waiting to see. He deactivated the system and went to the door, lightfooted; opened it.

She stood there, dressed in the heavy, shapeless clothing of a Summer worker, her hair hidden beneath a scarf, carrying a delivery basket. He stood aside to let her come in, and closed the door behind her—barely in time, as she dropped the basket at her feet and put her arms around him. He laughed in startled pleasure to find she was as eager for this moment as he was. He kissed her long and deeply. "Gods help me," he murmured, "you were all I could think about, all day." They had managed to meet this way a dozen times in the months since Mask Night; but still every time seemed like the first time, because the stolen hours they had together were never enough, would never be enough, until they could spend every night together, freely. And he knew that would never happen.

He loosened her shirt, sliding his hands up beneath it, feeling the silken curves of her breasts, the heat that radiated from that contact, suddenly filling her, filling him. Still kissing her, he pressed her back against the wall, feeling the urgent pressure straining against his pants, the sweet yearning of her body arched against his as she unfastened his uniform shirt and began to stroke his skin. "Mother of Us All," she breathed, against his neck, "I love you. . . ."

"Moon—" He broke off, as another knock sounded at his door. Moon let go of him, her eyes startled.

"Justice Gundhalinu!" a voice called, muffled but clearly audible beyond the door.

"Capella Goodventure," Moon said, her surprise deepening.

"Justice Gundhalinu!" The Goodventure elder's voice reached them again, louder and more demanding. "I know you're in there."

"There was another hunt today," Moon said, her expression turning distant and gray. "Wasn't there? She's come about the mers."

"Yes." He looked down, away from the grief in her eyes, toward the door.

"I think you should speak to her."

He nodded, resigned, the burning need inside him suddenly gone to ashes. He refastened his shirt; went to the door and opened it, revealing Capella Goodventure's startled, angry face. Her disbelief at seeing him face to face would have been laughable, under other circumstances. "Come in," he said wearily, standing aside.

She pushed her way past him, as if he had tried to bar her way; stopped dead, as she discovered Moon Dawntreader waiting in the hall behind him. The Goodventure elder stared at the Summer Queen, at her clothing; turned back to look at him, at his own disheveled clothes. "You—?" she said softly, shaking her head.

Capella Goodventure hugged her arms against her chest, beneath the loose folds of her cloak, as she moved toward Moon. "I thought I would find him dallying with some foolish, empty-headed market girl. But you, and him— This is why the hunts go on, why nothing we do is enough. You—and him!" Her head jerked in his direction.

"No," Moon said, swallowing her chagrin. "He is with us, Capella. He wants to save the mers. He is doing all he can for them, just as he has for our people."

"He controls policy for the Hegemony. He controls what his people here can or cannot do; or so he claims—" Capella Goodventure looked back at him, her eyes like searchlights. "And today not only did they slaughter the Lady's sacred children, but they also sank the ships of our people who tried to stop it. Three people drowned— one was my own grandchild! Is that how you intended to help us, Justice?"

Moon murmured something under her breath, a prayer or a curse.

"Three people dead?" BZ repeated. "No one gave them orders to do that. They'll be punished to the full—"

"No!" Capella Goodventure's voice was shrill with hysteria. "No, the punishment is the Lady's, by right. It is my duty as Her hand, to deal it out to those who are guilty—" She withdrew her hands from beneath her cloak.

BZ froze as he saw the gleam of metal in both her fists. He threw himself forward, trying to knock her off balance as she lunged at Moon. As he caught her, she swung around, bringing up one of the blades. He felt a sickening pain lance through him as his own momentum drove the blade into his side. He caught her other arm as it flailed wildly at his face; her eyes were blind with frenzy, and her strength was incredible. Moon's hands locked over the older woman's wrist, dragging her back away from him. She let go of the knife handle, setting him free; he staggered two steps and fell to his knees, as his body suddenly refused to obey him. He dragged himself up again, as Moon cried out; he saw blood on the other blade, as the two women struggled against the wall.

"Justice!" Abruptly there was a fourth person in the hallway. He saw a blur of blue uniform, realized it was Kitaro who had somehow appeared there. She pushed past him, her drawn stunner useless in the cramped space. She caught Capella Goodventure from behind with an arm lock and dragged her away from Moon, still screaming, still swinging the knife wildly. "Lady! Get out of here! Out!" Kitaro gasped. "I called for help—"

"BZ—" Moon hesitated, turning back to him, clutching her bloodsoaked sleeve. Her eyes filled with frantic concern.

"I'm all right," he said roughly. "Go now, before somebody comes."

She nodded, ashen-faced, tight-lipped. He watched her go out the door, disappearing from his sight. Kitaro turned, glancing at him. "Justice—"

"No!" He lurched forward as Capella Goodventure twisted suddenly, with insane fury, blind to her own pain as she drove the remaining knife into Kitaro's chest, once, twice. Kitaro screamed, and fell. The Goodventure woman turned back to him, and there was nothing human in her eyes. She started toward him with the knife.

His hands tightened over the slippery hilt protruding from his side; he jerked it free, cursing with agony. He held it ready in his fist, pressed back against the wall.

"Freeze!"

The hall behind him suddenly filled with uniforms, patrolmen answering Kitaro's summons.

Capella Goodventure stared at them, her eyes wild and unreadable, the knife still in her hand. They had their stunners out, trained on her as they eased into the hallway, surrounding her. "Drop it," someone said grimly. "Come on, let it go—"

She looked back at Gundhalinu with something like despair, her trembling hands tightening harder and harder around the knife she held, as if it were a precious treasure. And then, suddenly, she drove the blade into her own chest, into her heart, with a wail of anguish that made him shudder. She dropped like a stone to the floor, and lay still.

They were all around him then, supporting him, seeing to his wound, trying to staunch the river of blood that seemed to be welling out of him, as if he contained an endless source of it. He watched it defy them, watched it flow, watched blue figures working over the two motionless bodies that lay at his feet. He heard the rushing of the river in his ears, as his vision slowly became a tapestry of golden static, golden/blackness, until blackness swallowed them all.

"Gods, how could this happen?"

Jerusha PalaThion glanced up from where she sat at Gundhalinu's bedside, as

Vhanu murmured the question for the third or fourth time since he had entered the hospital room. He turned away restlessly from the bed where Gundhalinu lay, still unconscious.

"He is going to be all right—?" He asked that for the second time, of the medtech who stood studying the displays on the monitor above the bed.

The technician nodded. "He'll be all right, Commander. He lost a lot of blood, but we put it back. The knife didn't hit anything critical. In fact, he's showing signs of increasing brain activity. He should wake up any time now."

"Thank the gods," Vhanu said. "How could he have let that woman into his home, armed with knives?" He faced Jerusha at last, finally speaking the doubts she had read in his eyes. "Why didn't his security system warn him she was armed?"

"He'd just had another caller," Jerusha said, glancing at BZ's face, seeing a random muscle twitch in his cheek. "He must have forgotten to reset it."

Vhanu grunted. "Was it Kitaro?"

"Yes, sir," she said. "Looks like it."

He shook his head again, and muttered a curse. "Gods, what a pointless tragedy." He swung around, staring at the closed door as if he could see through walls. "What in the name of a thousand ancestors made that woman suddenly go berserk and try to assassinate the Chief Justice?"

Jerusha shrugged. "It probably had something to do with the mer hunts," she said, carefully noncommittal. "The mers are considered sacred by the Summers, you know." He glanced at her, frowning, looking for criticism. "Capella Goodventure was an extremely conservative woman," she finished, keeping her expression neutral. "Even fanatical."

"These miserable *dashtanu*," he muttered. "After all we've done for them. Nothing makes any sense here, nothing seems to go right here! What is it about this place—?" He broke off, as Gundhalinu stirred beside her.

She looked back at Gundhalinu's face, saw his eyes flicker open and stare blindly, as if he had been looking into the sun. He murmured something; she could not make out the words. "BZ—" she said softly, and his head turned toward her. Vhanu crossed the room in three strides, and stopped beside her.

"Jerusha," BZ whispered, half in surprise, and half in relief. He tried to push himself up, getting nowhere; went limp again, with a spasm of pain. "Moon . . . is she all right? Is she safe, did she get away?"

Jerusha froze; nodded imperceptibly, before she glanced at Vhanu, trying to carry BZ's attention with her.

"What did he say?" Vhanu asked sharply. "He said 'Moon.' "

"No, he didn't," she answered.

"Yes he did. He said 'Moon.' Is he talking about the Summer Queen?"

"He's disoriented," she insisted. "I couldn't tell what he was saying. Justice—" She put a hand on Gundhalinu's shoulder, in comfort, in warning. "The Commander is here with me, sir."

Gundhalinu blinked and grimaced. "You're Commander now, ma'am," he whispered, almost inaudible. "No . . . I mean I am . . ." He shook his head, barely, and made a sound that might have been a laugh. "Vhanu," he said, with real recognition this time. "You are." He smiled; the smile disappeared as quickly as it had formed. "Is she all right?"

"Who?" Vhanu said flatly.

BZ looked up at him, clear-eyed. "Kitaro," he said. "Is she all right—?"

Vhanu's face changed. He looked down. "She's dead, BZ."

"No . . ." Gundhalinu shut his eyes; she saw a tremor pass through him. "Oh, no. Oh gods, no."

"There was nothing they could do for her, Justice," Jerusha said, as gently as she could; resenting the fact that Vhanu called him by his given name, as a friend would, and would not permit her to do the same. "She died instantly."

"It was my fault . . ." he said.

"No."

"If we hadn't been—" He broke off.

She glanced at Vhanu again, unable to tell what his expression was.

"May I see him?" a voice asked unexpectedly, from the doorway.

Vhanu turned, startled by the sudden presence of someone else behind him.

The Queen. Jerusha pushed to her feet, staring in surprise.

"Yes . . . of course, Lady," Vhanu murmured. He bowed formally; Jerusha rose and did the same, as Moon entered the room.

"I came as soon as I heard," she said, her attention already abandoning them for the man lying in the bed.

"He just regained consciousness, Lady," Vhanu said, intersecting her course. "This isn't the best time for you to speak to him—"

She stopped, glancing at him, and away again. Jerusha noticed that one of her hands was clenched whitely at her side; the other hung loose-fingered and oddly still against the folds of her cloak.

"I'm all right—" BZ's own voice, thready but resolute, cut off Vhanu's attempt to stop her. He pushed himself up onto an elbow; Jerusha saw in his eyes what the effort cost him.

"I am so glad to hear it, from your own lips, Justice Gundhalinu," Moon said softly. She bowed her head, in a gesture of relief, barely concealing the other emotion that reddened her cheeks.

"You know that it was one of your own people who tried to kill the Chief Justice?" Vhanu said. "And who murdered a Police inspector—?"

"Yes." She lifted her head. "And killed herself, as well. . . . Words are useless to express my sorrow that such a terrible thing has happened here." She looked toward Gundhalinu, turning away from Vhanu; the anguish and helpless longing on her face were suddenly, perfectly clear from where Jerusha sat. "I feel . . . responsible." Jerusha watched her one hand tighten again. "Tell me if there is anything I can do to help—"

By the Boatman, Jerusha thought, with a sinking feeling. *She was there with him.* Kitaro had not been having an affair with him, as she'd let everyone on the force think she was. She'd been covering for him. It was Moon he'd been seeing. Jerusha swore silently. She should have guessed it sooner; she should have known. But she rarely even saw BZ, lately. If she'd still been working for the Queen she would have sensed it—even if she hadn't been told, she knew the woman too well, after so many years. She would have seen the truth long before now. If only she'd known . . .

"You can start by keeping your Summers out of our way when we hunt the mers, instead of encouraging them," Vhanu said, to Moon's turned back. "You set off dangerous fanatics like that Goodventure woman—"

Moon faced him again. "What 'set her off,' " she said, her voice hard with pain, "was that your hunters attacked Summer vessels. Three people drowned, including her own grandchild."

Jerusha stiffened, looking toward Vhanu. Gundhalinu pushed himself up in the bed.

"Where did you hear that, Lady?" Vhanu asked, his eyes suddenly as cold as the icebound peaks of the inland.

"From one of my people," she said, her own eyes like ice. "Is it true?"

His frown deepened.

"Is it, Vhanu?" Gundhalinu asked, supporting himself on one elbow.

"For gods' sakes," Vhanu snapped, looking at the Queen. "This is hardly the time or place to be making such accusations, with the Chief Justice barely recovered from an attack on his life—"

"Vhanu—" Gundhalinu said, angrily. "Is it?"

Vhanu turned back, and Jerusha saw his eyes. "Summers interfered with our hunt, as usual, sir. We warned them off. No casualties were recorded." *He's lying,* she thought. *Ye gods, he's lying.*

"Look into it," BZ said.

"Yes, BZ," Vhanu murmured. "But I doubt there's any truth to—"

"Look into it immediately, Commander."

Vhanu's eyes flickered. "Yes, sir," he said. He turned away, abruptly colliding with the Queen. Moon made a small guttural sound, not of surprise, but pain.

"Forgive me. . . . Did I hurt you, Lady?" Vhanu asked, with just enough solicitude, just enough surprise. He laid a hand on her arm, as if reaching out to support her. Jerusha saw her wince involuntarily. "Do you have an injury?"

Moon moved away from his hand. "I strained my arm lifting crates, Commander Vhanu."

"Lifting crates?" he said incredulously.

"I like to work alongside my own people sometimes, when I can, to remind myself of who I am and where I came from, Commander. And what their problems really are." She touched her arm briefly with her good hand. "Perhaps you should try it some time."

His mouth pulled taut. "It sounds too dangerous for my taste." He turned away again, without any kind of farewell, and left the room.

Moon watched him go, and then moved quietly to close the door. She came back to the bed and settled carefully onto it, her good hand touching BZ's face, his hair, with infinite tenderness. His own hand rose unsteadily to cover hers, as she leaned to kiss the hollows of his temples and murmured something that Jerusha couldn't hear.

Moon straightened up again, shrugging back her cloak with an awkward motion, her uninjured hand still closed inside his. "Now you know," she said, looking at Jerusha.

Jerusha nodded, seeing the same light, the same darkness in both their faces. Slowly she got to her feet, stood looking down at them with an odd longing. "And now I've forgotten it," she said, with a fleeting smile. "Rest well, my friends." She shook her head, looking away from them as they began to smile. She crossed the room, and went out without looking back.

TIAMAT: Carbuncle

Ariele Dawntreader stopped in the hallway, looking toward the hospital room door where uniformed offworlders stood guard; feeling herself pushed forward by anger, held back by doubt. At Police headquarters they had told her she would find Jerusha PalaThion here, with the Chief Justice, who had barely survived an assassination attempt. Some part of her mind tried to tell her that she wished Capella Goodventure had been successful. She found that the thought sickened her.

She pushed it out of her mind, feeling guilty, as if the guards standing watch down the hall from her could hear her thoughts. The Chief Justice was alive; then let him listen to what she had come to say to Jerusha PalaThion. She started to walk again, seeing the Police turn their heads like twins to watch her approach. Their wariness decreased slightly as they recognized her.

"I need to speak with Commander PalaThion," she said.

One of the guards murmured something half-audible, as if he were talking to himself. He hesitated a moment, and nodded at her. "You can go in."

She moved past them, trying to enter the room as though she were perfectly confident of what she would do next.

Jerusha stood waiting for her in the middle of the room, in the stranger's gray-blue uniform that Ariele had finally come to accept as a normal part of the other woman's appearance. Behind her, sitting up in the hospital bed, was the Chief Justice. It was the first time she could remember that she had not seen him in uniform.

She looked at him for a long moment, feeling as if she saw his face for the first time; seeing a human being, and not an arrogant Kharemoughi martinet. She thought of her brother suddenly, as she looked into his eyes; suddenly imagining the face of a much younger man, who was passionately in love with her mother, willing to give up his career, even his life, for her mother's sake. She remembered the look he had given her once, meeting her in the Street, and how she had responded.

"Ariele," Jerusha said, and there was something in her voice that was both surprise and wariness. "What is it?"

"I came to . . ." She broke off. "I came to wish the Chief Justice a swift recovery," she said, glancing down.

"Thank you, Ariele Dawntreader," Gundhalinu said. "Please tell your mother that I'm doing well—"

"My mother didn't send me here, Justice," she said sharply. "I haven't even spoken to her in over a week. I moved out of the palace months ago."

"In that case, thank you for coming at all." He smiled, uncertainly.

"Actually," she said, her hands rubbing the silken cloth of her shirtsleeves, "actually I came here because I wanted to talk to—Aunt Jerusha about something. But it has to do with you too, Justice. Your people. And . . . what happened to you." She glanced up at him again, trying to read his reaction. "Do you blame the Summers for what happened?" she asked, baldly. "And . . . do you believe what Capella Goodventure said your hunters did?"

"No, I don't blame your people," he said, and she was surprised to find that she believed him. "And no. I don't believe what she said."

"Ariele," Jerusha said, "she must have heard distorted rumors. There's no evidence."

Ariele closed her mouth over the angry response lying ready on her tongue. "Capella Goodventure was right about what happened with the Summer ships. I saw it." She had spent two days waiting for a summons, for the Blues to come after her, as Reede had sworn they would. But it hadn't happened, until finally she had been forced to come here herself like this. And now, suddenly, she knew why.

"You saw it?" Jerusha repeated. Her face changed. "How?"

Ariele looked down again, watching the memory replay across the polished surface of the floor. "I was there. I tracked Silky up the coast—"

"Silky?" Jerusha interrupted. "Is she all right?"

Ariele nodded, seeing relief in the other woman's eyes; seeing the woman she had always known, the woman she had loved once like her own kin, suddenly looking back at her. She told that woman everything, calling up every detail; but editing every word in her mind before she spoke it, to keep from mentioning Reede.

"What was Silky doing, so far from the colony's territory? Were any of the others with her?" Jerusha asked, half frowning.

Ariele nodded. "There were hundreds of mers on the beach. It was as if they're all gathering for something."

Jerusha shook her head, glancing at Gundhalinu. "What the hell could make them do that—after all the time Miroe and I spent trying to show them that they had to stay clear of humans. Was it all useless?"

"I think maybe they're coming to a kind of Festival—"

Jerusha looked back at her, and for a moment she saw the other woman's mind try to dismiss the idea. But then Jerusha's face changed. She looked at Gundhalinu again. "What do you think, BZ? Would there be any record of something like this ever happening before?"

He shrugged, his eyes thoughtful. "If it only happens during Summer, probably not, unless it was preserved somewhere in their folk tradition."

"Maybe it is . . ." Jerusha murmured. "Maybe that's exactly what the Festival is."

"Then they're coming to Carbuncle," Gundhalinu said, and his voice was as sure as if he suddenly *knew,* the way that Reede seemed to know things about the mers.

Jerusha looked at him oddly, but she did not question him either. "Ye gods, BZ—if that's true, they'll be sitting targets for the hunters."

"If it's true, then the hunts will stop," he said, and his hand made a fist on the bedding. "I want observation data on the mers' movements."

Jerusha nodded, turning to Ariele. "And you saw the hunters attack the Summers who were trying to interfere?"

Ariele nodded again. "We saw them ram two ships—"

"We?" Jerusha asked.

"Silky and I. I was with Silky." She glanced down, cursing herself silently, but Jerusha did not ask her about it.

"Did you see anyone go into the sea?"

She shook her head. "It was too far away. But they deliberately sank at least one."

"Capella Goodventure believed someone died," Gundhalinu said, frowning, but not at her. "Enough to want to kill me in revenge. Something stinks, Jerusha."

"Smells like a cover-up to me," she said.

He swore softly; his body jerked with agitation under the blankets. "Start an investigation. See what you can find out, if all the evidence isn't sunk already."

"Do you think Vhanu knows about this?" she asked.

He looked up abruptly. "No. Of course not." He leaned forward, holding himself in place with his arms locked around his knees. "Ariele, you say there were hundreds of mers on the beach . . . but according to the report I was given, the hunt was relatively poor. How did the mers get away? Did you warn them off?"

She stiffened, uncertain; glanced at Jerusha, who nodded. She told them, carefully, the truth but not the whole truth. "They fired at me too—at my mother's hovercraft. I had to get away before . . . before all the mers were off the beach." Her face burned with remembered frustration and rage.

"And you're sure that Silky was gone?" Jerusha repeated, coming across the room.

She nodded.

Jerusha rested warm hands on her shoulders. "Thank you, Ari. Silky doesn't belong to me anymore—any more than you belong to your mother. But the gods help anybody that ever hurt either one of you." Her hands tightened gently, in a fond gesture that they had not made for many years, and then released her.

Ariele smiled, hesitating, wanting suddenly to say more; to tell her everything. But she only turned away toward the door.

"Ariele—" Gundhalinu called.

She turned back, reluctantly, compelled by the fragility of his voice, and not the sudden command.

"Who was there with you?" he asked quietly.

She half frowned. "I told you—" She broke off, seeing the expression on his face. *Certainty.* He knew she'd been lying to them, as surely as if he had been reading her emotions from some offworlder machine. She looked at Jerusha, and saw the same certainty in her eyes; knew that it was their experience that had betrayed her, and her own inexperience. "I don't have to tell you," she said. "I didn't even have to come here. Your own people are afraid to tell you what I was doing there, because they know I saw what they did."

"What's this other person afraid of?" Gundhalinu asked.

"You," she answered. "The Police. He's an offworlder. If the Police know he saw, and tried to stop it, he's afraid they'll deport him."

"What was he doing there?"

She tossed her head. "He was with me. He works for my mother, studying the mers."

"Your mother doesn't have any offworlders working for her, studying the mers," Jerusha said.

Ariele felt her frown deepen. "Yes, she does. She has Reede, and he's brilliant. No one knows the mers like—"

Gundhalinu's face froze. "Reede?" he said. "Reede Kullervo?"

She looked back at him. "Yes."

"I know him," Gundhalinu murmured. "He is brilliant. But he doesn't work for your mother."

Jerusha was staring at him. "That one?" she said softly.

He nodded. His eyes, still on Ariele, were suddenly dark with understanding. "He isn't what you think he is, Ariele. . . . But he can trust me. You tell him that. He wants to save the mers. We can do it, together. I can protect him, I can help him, if he'll trust me. Will you tell him that?"

She went on looking at him for a long moment, at the intentness and the desperate weariness in his face. She nodded, at last. "I'll tell him," she said.

TIAMAT: Carbuncle

"Reede Kullervo!" The voice that called his name seemed to come at him from everywhere at once, out of the shadowed doorways of the midnight-quiet alley. The streets of Carbuncle were never completely dark, but the nights grew shadows in places where none survived by day.

Reede stopped in his tracks, his hand reaching for his gun as shadow-forms detached from the larger darkness of doorways and passageways.

"Son of a bitch—" Niburu muttered in disbelief, reaching for his own weapon as Ananke spun around behind him. Suddenly they were surrounded by half a dozen Blues, in the middle of an alley that had gone from sparsely inhabited to a no-man's-land in less than a heartbeat.

"Drop the weapons," the voice said, behind him now, and he saw that the Blues already had their own weapons out, trained on him. They wore the flash shields of their helmets down, making them all into faceless, unidentifiable clones. He let his gun drop, slowly and deliberately stripping himself of weapons, as his men did the same.

"The knife in your boot too," the voice directed mildly, and he realized they were being scanned. He tossed out the knife, and held his hands high. "What do you want with me?" he said, feeling more disbelief than fear. Vigilantism wasn't the Blues' style. "I haven't done anything." *Gods, he hadn't had his fix; he needed the water of death. What if they locked him up, how long would he last—?* And suddenly he was afraid. He clenched his teeth.

Beside him Niburu was muttering, "Holy hands of Edhu, holy hands of Edhu . . ." like an incantation. Ananke was as silent as a wall, staring at the shielded faces all around him. Two minutes ago the pair of them had been bitching about waiting at the bar in Starhiker's for hours, because he didn't show up on time. He figured he knew where they wished they were right now. He thought about where he'd been. *Between a rock and a hard place.* "Fuck—" he whispered; repeated it over and over under his breath, like Niburu, like an adhani.

"You're a stranger far from home, Kullervo," somebody said. "Another stranger far from home wants to talk to you about old times."

"No—" he said, starting to turn around. But something brushed the back of his neck like a wet mouth, and then there was only blackness.

He came to again, what seemed to be a moment later, although it probably wasn't. He sat up slowly, cautiously, on a perfectly ordinary couch in a neat, austerely furnished sitting room. It was not so different from his own, could almost have been his own. He shook what might have been a dream of somebody else's life out of his head, like a dog shaking off water. He looked down at himself—recognized his own clothing, his tattooed arms . . . realized that the dream was reality, and felt a kind of hopeless fatalism settle over him.

"Hello, Kullervo-*eshkrad*," a familiar voice said.

He jerked around, startled, to find BZ Gundhalinu, Chief Justice of Tiamat, leaning against the doorframe at the entrance to the room. "What are you doing here?" Reede said stupidly.

"I live here," Gundhalinu said. He wore a pair of hastily pulled-on pants and a loose robe hanging open, baring his chest and an expanse of bandageskin. His hair was rumpled. He looked like a man who had been rousted out of bed; as if he had not been expecting this meeting any more than Reede had himself. But the expression on Gundhalinu's face said that he had been anticipating it for a long time.

Reede leaned forward, with his hands tightening over his knees. "Where are my men?"

"Niburu and Ananke?" Gundhalinu half smiled, almost as if he remembered them more fondly than he remembered the man who was his guest. "Waiting for you," he said simply. But his eyes changed as he went on looking at Reede, and for a brief moment his smile was real. "It's good to see you again," he murmured, as if the truth surprised him. He looked down suddenly.

Reede stared at him, remembering in abrupt, vivid detail the moment of their parting at Fire Lake. And yet he felt his disbelief become something truer and far more unsettling, as more memories began to rise. His hand rose to his mouth, touching his lips; dropped away again. He leaned back into the comforting embrace of the native-made couch and forced himself to relax. "What do you want, Gundhalinu?"

Gundhalinu came on into the room, moving as though it hurt, and settled heavily into a wooden chair. He glanced at the display on his house system, checking the time, and grimaced, before he looked at Reede again. "It's about what I'm doing here, Kullervo—and what you're doing here."

Reede's mouth quirked; his grip on his knees eased. "Congratulations. How do you like being Chief Justice of Tiamat?"

Gundhalinu shrugged, shaking his head. "It's not my occupation of choice. It's not like research. In politics there aren't any right answers, so you never win."

"That's because you have a conscience." Reede smiled faintly. "Lose that, and you'll start winning again."

Gundhalinu's mouth turned up in an ironic echo of Reede's own smile. He pulled his robe closer across his chest, covering the bandages, and fastened the seal. His hand stayed there, unobtrusively holding his wounded side. "If only life was that simple," he murmured. He looked up again. "How do you like working for the Brotherhood?"

Reede glanced away. "Same as always."

"Becoming the Source's brand hasn't changed anything for you?"

Reede looked back at him abruptly.

"Jaakola has a bad reputation, even for someone in his line of work. And what shows in the real world is barely the surface. He goes deep, doesn't he?"

Reede frowned. "Did you pick me up to bleed me about the Source? I can't tell you anything you don't already know."

"I know."

"Am I under arrest?"

"You haven't done anything illegal here on Tiamat, that I know of." Gundhalinu reached into a shallow ceramic bowl sitting on the table beside him, picked up a piece of fruit, and put it back again.

Reede laughed incredulously. "Then what the hell do you want from me?"

"You're on Tiamat to synthesize the water of life for the Source, aren't you?"

Reede didn't answer.

"Why did you set up that clue pointing it out to me, at the Survey Hall?"

Reede shrugged, and shook his head, still frowning. "I don't know. . . . Just for the hell of it. To see if you were still smart enough to get it."

"Were you warning me off? Or asking me for help?"

Reede's hands fisted silently on his thighs. "You're the one who needs help, from what I see." He gestured at Gundhalinu's wound, at the fatigue and discomfort obvious on his face. "What is it with you and the mers? I know you—you don't want the water of life back, you're afraid of it. But you're studying them like you want what I want. And at the same time you say you don't want anybody killing them, but they're killing them all the same, and trying to kill you too."

"Politics," Gundhalinu murmured.

"Love," Reede whispered, leaning forward. "The rumors are true. . . . It's the Queen, that's why your policy doesn't make sense worth a damn. She's the one you told me about, back on Four. That you'd change the future of the entire fucking galaxy to get back to her." He laughed once. "And I thought you were making a joke."

"We both underestimated each other, I think," Gundhalinu said, a little sourly.

Reede laughed again, with more feeling. "You could say that." He met Gundhalinu's half frown, saw it transform into something that looked strangely like regret. Gundhalinu glanced away, his fingers moving restlessly over the geometries of his robe's sleeve. "I hope she's worth it," Reede said.

Gundhalinu smiled, looking back at him, and nodded. Reede felt the image of a face he had forbidden himself to see begin to form inside his own eyes: dark, luminous, veiled in sensual mystery . . . *her* face. *Stop it—!*

"I'm sorry about your wife," Gundhalinu said, as if he had read Reede's mind, and not just his expression.

"What do you know about it?" Reede snapped, stung.

"We know what happened when you were transferred from Mundilfoere to Jaakola, Reede; when you lost her." He hesitated. "We even know what you really are."

Reede felt his face flush. *Mundilfoere's meat. A brainwipe. A lunatic—* He pushed to his feet.

"—*Vanamoinen,*" Gundhalinu said softly.

Reede's knees went weak, and he sat down again. "What?" he said.

"Vanamoinen. You are Vanamoinen. We lost you to the Brotherhood. We've been searching for you ever since."

Reede sat frozen, listening, as something inside him paralyzed his tongue, stopping his stream of questions and protest. He put his hands up to his face, touching its contours, so familiar, and yet so strange. He felt himself starting to sweat. "They called me that—'the new Vanamoinen,'" he murmured, remembering. "They knew, they all knew something. . . . But I don't know Vanamoinen. Vanamoinen's two thousand years dead! More! My name . . . *my name* is Reede Kullervo—" His fingers dug into his flesh.

"You're two people, using one body," Gundhalinu said, sitting forward, forcing Reede to look at him. "Not even separate signals, but scrambled. The Brotherhood got hold of a brainscan of the real Vanamoinen, made thousands of years ago. And they used you to bring him back. But you weren't braindead when they fed his memories into your circuits: It must have been like a head-on collision when it happened. It caused a lot of damage."

"Like holograms colliding," Reede murmured, staring. "Shufflebrain . . ." He let his hands fall away, focusing on the image, feeling the act of concentration stabilize him. "How was it done?" he asked, hearing his voice come back to something like normal. "I've never heard of that being done to anybody."

Gundhalinu shook his head. "I don't know how they preserved Vanamoinen's . . . your—soul, for so long. If you don't know, I doubt if anybody does, now."

"My soul . . ." Reede looked down at his body, not protesting the intimations. He seemed to be seeing himself from a great height suddenly; his mind spun and fell away. "I don't remember . . ." he mumbled, "but it could be possible. . . ." He frowned, and glanced up again. "But why?"

"You tell me," Gundhalinu urged softly. "Why you're back, here, now, after thousands of years."

"The mers," Reede said automatically. He broke off, abruptly, staring. "By the All—yes, I think that . . . that I . . . I'm here for the mers. I know them. . . ." He looked back at Gundhalinu again, in astonishment. "But it's not about the water of life. The water of life will never work perfectly in a human body, because human bodies are genetically imperfect." He shook his head, dazed and elated and appalled by the revelation. "That's a fool's errand. The mers are . . ." He reached out, groping in the air; his fingers closed over nothing.

Gundhalinu was staring at him, in that old, slightly incredulous way. Reede looked back at him, realizing that he had missed that expression; that it reminded him . . . reminded him of . . . His train of thought derailed. "Shit—" he muttered, pressing the heels of his hands into his eyes until he saw explosions of light. "Why? Gods . . . why me?"

"I don't know that either, Reede," Gundhalinu murmured. "There's some evidence you may have been a mistake."

Reede laughed, a tight, painful sound. His hand reached inside his shirt, and pulled out the pendant, the ring, chained together. "That's always a danger, when you're a stranger far from home."

Gundhalinu's eyes filled with sudden compassion. "But you're here, now . . . Vanamoinen. You were brought back because your knowledge was needed. You're here, and so am I, and I need your help. And I don't believe that's an accident. We were meant to work together again, on this—" He leaned forward, shining with urgency and hope.

"What?" Reede said thickly.

"You're right, the water of life isn't what's important about the mers. It's their survival. It's what they were created to do—for . . . for . . . you know what I mean. You know what I'm trying to tell you—"

Reede looked at him blankly. "No. I don't. What the hell are you talking about?"

Gundhalinu swore softly, in anger or frustration. "Damn it . . . Vanamoinen! You know why it matters. You put the mers here. You have to remember why, for gods' sakes!"

Reede felt his mind tumble and spin, fragments of shattered mirror shaken inside a bag of living flesh, a bowl of bone, until he bled. "I don't know what you're talking about! I'm not Vanamoinen. I'm *Reede*! And I don't know shit about it, just shut up about it! Leave me alone!" He pushed to his feet, starting toward the door.

He stopped, as another figure appeared suddenly before him, blocking his way. For a brief moment he thought that it was Ariele standing there, pale-haired, wrapped in a man's robe. But the hair was wrong, long, a cloud of white . . . the face was wrong, grown older— *The Queen*. He looked back at Gundhalinu, in sudden surprise, sudden understanding.

"Reede Kullervo—" the Queen said, coming forward, the robe whispering softly around her as she held out her hand to him.

He stared at her, not knowing what to do. He took her hand automatically, bobbed his head in an awkward obeisance. "Lady," he murmured, remembering the proper form of address, and let her hand go as if it were burning hot. He saw Ariele again in his mind, wondering what the Queen knew, if she knew— He looked down.

"You're the one who helped BZ recreate the stardrive, aren't you?" she asked, and her voice seemed to ground him, draining the energy of his sudden panic, letting him stand still. She studied him a moment longer, with an intentness that was somehow oddly comforting.

"Yes," he said, shifting from foot to foot. He glanced at Gundhalinu again, saw him nod.

"We've been trying to find a way to save the mers from the Hegemony," she said. "We know they are intelligent, but it's not enough. We think that their songs contain a—some kind of coded data. But it's incomplete; the slaughter has decimated them to the point where they've lost their past, and they don't even realize what they've lost. And the songs are . . . important, somehow, to—to the well-being of the Hegemony. If we can just understand their purpose, we may be able to save them. But we can't . . . we can't . . . ."

Reede stared at her, seeing her suddenly afflicted with the same inability to say what she meant that had struck Gundhalinu. "What's the matter with you?" he said, half frowning.

She shook her head, and her agate-colored eyes closed in frustration. "I can't tell you," she murmured, as if the words filled her mouth like gall. "He can't—"

"Literally," Gundhalinu broke in, rubbing his face. "It's protecting itself. . . ."

Reede felt something gleam in the depths of his mind, a spark of comprehension threatening to catch fire. He lunged after a memory; it squirted out of his grasp. "Survey—?" he whispered, empty-handed, empty-eyed. "You mean Survey?"

Gundhalinu shook his head, like a man who'd had his tongue cut out.

Reede laughed harshly. "Gods, aren't we a set!" His hands jerked. "What the hell is happening here, is this catching—?" He hit himself viciously on the side of the head.

"It doesn't matter—" The Queen reached out, taking hold of his arm. "You don't have to understand—just believe that it's important. That's enough. Work with us on the mersong; let your mind do what it was meant to do. Then maybe it will all come back to you. . . ."

Reede blinked suddenly, looking down at her hand; his free hand rose to cover it where it rested on his sleeve, closed over it almost convulsively.

"Reede." Gundhalinu got up from his seat, moving toward them painfully, and almost reluctantly. "I know the Source has some hold over you. If you want to get away from him, we can help you. Any hold can be broken. Just tell us what you need."

Reede's hand pried the Queen's fingers loose from his arm. He took a deep, ragged breath, feeling the skeleton's fist of the truth close around his throat. "You can't help me, Gundhalinu." He shook his head. "Nobody can."

"At least tell me what kind of trouble you're in." Gundhalinu held out his hands. "You know me," he said, meeting Reede's gaze with an odd intensity. "You know you can trust me with your life. And I need your help—"

Reede shook his head, turned away. "Can't. I can't help you—!"

"It's your whole reason for existence!"

Reede turned back; the turning motion made him giddy. He felt as if his entire life had begun to strobe. "I'll think it over . . . got to think about it. Got to go now, and think about it." Unsure of the consequences, unsure of himself, he started toward the door. He glanced back once as he reached it. "Ask your husband about the mers, Lady," he said sourly. "He knows some things he hasn't told *you*, too. . . ." They made no move to stop him as he went out.

Moon stood beside BZ, feeling his arm draw her close as they watched the tall, slender, unsteady figure of Reede Kullervo go out of the room.

"Gods," BZ murmured, hearing the door slam. "I hope this is the right thing." His hand tightened at his side.

"Why didn't you stop him?" she asked.

He looked back at her, his face troubled. "I can't force him, Moon. He's barely holding it together now. If he breaks we'll lose Vanamoinen forever." He shook his head. "We can't risk that. We have to believe that he'll come back on his own."

"He's only a boy, BZ," she said softly, still seeing the despair, the knowledge of something more terrible than her own deepest fears, that lay in Reede's eyes. "He's so afraid." She put her arms around him, holding on.

"He should be." BZ sighed, stroking her hair, kissing her. "He has every right to be, may the gods help him. . . . Come back to bed with me."

She nodded, letting him lead the way, setting his own pace as they climbed the stairs. "What kind of hold does the Source have on him? Is it drugs?"

BZ glanced at her in surprise. "Yes, probably. How did you know?

"I remember the Source." She followed him into his bedroom, holding on to his hand. "Arienrhod used the water of life to buy virals from him, at Winter's end—"

He grimaced, remembering, and nodded. "That's what he does best. But I don't know what he has Reede chained with. It's nothing ordinary, or Reede could get it somewhere else." He shrugged out of his robe, unfastened his pants and sat down carefully on the edge of the bed to pull them off.

Moon let her own borrowed robe slip from her shoulders, the smooth warmth of its imported fabric like the caress of his hands along her skin. She lay down in his bed, sliding beneath the covers as if she were entering the sea, as if she belonged there. He lay down beside her, and for a moment she forgot the aching weariness of her body as he settled next to it. She watched the lines of pain and weariness disappear from his face as his fingers brushed her cheek, touched the bandageskin still covering her arm. She smiled; her smile faded.

"BZ," she said, "who were you talking about, when you said 'we'? 'We know,' you said, 'we suspect'— You said that more than once, and you weren't talking about you and me."

He looked away as if he were suddenly chagrined, or conflicted. He looked back at her again, finally; touched the sibyl tattoo at her throat with a gentle finger. "I was talking about Survey."

"Survey?" she repeated, with mild incredulity. "You mean that nest of Kharemoughi snobs who meet in what you refer to as a 'social club,' to discuss Tiamat's endless shortcomings?"

He laughed. "So that's why you wouldn't come to the initiation, when I made them admit Tiamatans?"

She pushed up onto an elbow, feeling her hair slip down across her shoulder. "I have more pressing things to do with my time than spend it that way," she said irritably.

"There's more to Survey than there seems. The Survey you've seen is only the surface—there are depths, layers within layers . . . even I don't know how many."

Her sudden urge to laughter died stillborn as she saw his expression, and realized that he was completely serious.

"I shouldn't be telling you this." He pressed his hand against his eyes. "But gods, if anyone has the right to know the truth about this, you do. I'm staking my life on it. . . ." He shook his head. "The real Survey is a secret organization that dates back to the end of the Old Empire. It has its roots in the Empire's colonization guild. I told you that there was a man named Vanamoinen. . . ."

Moon listened silently as he told her everything, feeling her understanding of the strange conversation that had passed between himself and Reede grow, feeling her vision of the universe transformed by a secret almost as profound as the one that they shared together. "But Survey doesn't control everything that happens in the Hegemony . . . does it?" she said, finally.

He shook his head, and laughed once. "Human nature being what it is, no. They try . . . but as often as not they meet themselves coming the other way, on any given level, in any given situation. Even at the highest level Survey can only influence, never control."

"And Reede Kullervo belongs to Survey, and the Source does—?"

BZ nodded, resting his head on his arm. "There is a faction of Survey that calls itself the Brotherhood, and their goal is no longer the greater good, but their own good. They follow the same road, but to a different destination. The Brotherhood sees the Hegemony as prey. Their interests are in anything that upsets the stability of the status quo—drugs, political corruption, war—because whenever the balance is off, they profit from the suffering. Reede was one of their minions . . . and now he's their tool. Kitaro—" He broke off. "Kitaro had been trying to arrange this meeting between us for months; but he's so closely watched that I'd begun to think it would never happen." He fell silent, as if he were contemplating the strange legacy of Reede's unexpected visit.

"And who do you belong to?" Moon asked, at last. She settled back onto the yielding surface of the mattress, feeling it mold itself to her body. "If Reede belongs to the Brotherhood."

"The status quo. Or I did." He looked up, at the ceiling draped with shadows in the half light. "They sometimes call it the Golden Mean; they claim to carry on the work of Survey by maintaining the Hegemony's balance of order—which, to them, means that Kharemough keeps control of this segment of the Old Empire. For a while I hoped it was really that simple. . . ." His eyes darkened.

"Was it coming here that made you change your mind?" She put her hand on his shoulder.

"It only finished a process. Nothing is ever that simple . . . not right, not wrong." He looked back at her and smiled, with sorry and irony. "Without Order, Chaos would have no reason for existing . . . and without Chaos, there's no reason for Order. They need each other, they feed on each other. They're only whole together. Survey calls it 'the Great Game,' in their vanity."

"What—or who—is really at the center . . . the top, then?"

"I don't know." He shrugged. "However high I get, there are always levels above me."

"Then how do you know who to trust?"

"I don't." His smile turned rueful. "Maybe it doesn't even matter, to the Great Game. The sibyl network needed Vanamoinen back, and on Tiamat. Every faction tried to control him, manipulate him—and everyone's failed. And yet he's here. . . . That's why I believe that he'll help us. That's why I believe we can't force it, that we have to let it happen as it will."

"But you can't be certain," she said softly.

"No," he murmured, glancing away. "I can't be certain of anything."

"When I was small, my grandmother taught me that the mers were the Sea's children, blessed and protected by Her. And that I was, too. . . ." She felt her throat clog with sudden grief.

He pulled her into his arms, holding her, kissing her forehead, as if she were a child. "And once I believed that my life was over," he whispered, closing his eyes as he kissed her lips. "Gods, I do love you. . . ."

She closed her own eyes, felt tears slip out and down her face, onto his skin, burning hot. Astonished at how, in the center of this storm, his arms around her could still create an eye of calm; could make her believe that everything would turn out as it should. . . . "There isn't much night left," she said, taking his face in her hands, kissing his eyelids, feeling her weariness burn away. She kissed his lips, letting her hands slide down his chest, moving with exquisite care past the bandages on his side; moving lower, feeling him come alive at her touch.

"Then let morning wait for us," he murmured, sighing. "Let it wait."

Reede Kullervo lay awake in his bed, staring up into the cage of darkness that was his room, his world. He had lain awake half the night, every night, for as long as he could remember; but not like this. Not knowing the name of the other he held prisoner inside his brain—who held him prisoner, in a shellshocked nightmare landscape, taking revenge on him for a crime he had not even been to blame for. . . . *He was Vanamoinen.* He knew it was true, everything Gundhalinu had told him, even though he couldn't remember. . . . Vanamoinen knew it.

Reede swore, rolling onto his stomach, burying his face in the pillow. *What am I doing here? What do I want—?* "This is your reason for existence," Gundhalinu had shouted at him. *The mers. Tiamat.* But not the water of life. *If he helped them, he would understand,* the Queen had said. And he wanted to help them, needed to understand; the need was like a fire burning in his gut. . . .

But they couldn't help him. They couldn't give him the water of death; only the Source could do that. Even if Gundhalinu gave him lab space and all the equipment he asked for, he couldn't recreate the water of death in time; he had to have his steady supply. He was already feeling the effects of his missed fix, because being waylaid by Gundhalinu tonight had made him too late to meet with TerFauw.

Somehow he would have to get TerFauw to give him another chance, make up some lie in the morning. . . . If he didn't get what he needed he wouldn't be able to work. He had to have it, and the next one, and the next one. . . . If he didn't get it he would die, and then he would be no use to anybody. But what use was living anyway, when everything was impossible? Even he was impossible: a man with two brains. Maybe he'd liked it better when he'd only thought he was insane. . . .

"*Reede.*" A voice like corroded iron spoke his name in the darkness.

Reede stopped breathing.

"Reede—"

He pushed himself up. "Who's there?" There was nothing in front of him but darkness, subtle layerings of deep gray on black, the vague, familiar presences of the furniture in his room. Was something really there, at the foot of his bed, a shadow-form darker than the night, an impossible glimmer of red—?

"You know who it is, Reede," the insinuating voice whispered.

A hologram. A projection, he told himself futilely. *A nightmare . . .* but he wasn't dreaming. The Source had never done this to him before, invading the sanctuary of his own room, violating the one final place where he could pretend to himself that he was still a free man—

"Say it," the Source murmured. "Tell me who I am."

"Master," Reede mumbled, spitting out the word. He clutched the blankets against his chest as every muscle in his body knotted with impotent fury. "What do you want—?" He cursed himself, helplessly, hearing his voice tremble.

"You had a midnight audience tonight, I understand, Reede—? With the Chief Justice, and the Queen?"

Oh, gods. Reede swallowed his heart. "It wasn't my idea."

"When were you planning to inform me about this?"

"Nothing happened," he said hoarsely.

"Nothing," the Source echoed, with heavy sarcasm. "The Great Enemy sweeps you away to a secret meeting, where nothing happens. They tell you that you really *are* the new Vanamoinen. They ask you to betray the Brotherhood, and work with them . . . but nothing happens."

Reede's mouth twisted. "You know I'm not going anywhere. Where could I go? I'd be a rotting corpse inside a couple of days."

"You told them it was impossible to create a stable form of the water of life," the Source chided. "But nothing happened—"

"It was a lie! I just said it to throw them off. That's all." He felt cold sweat crawl down his back as he stared into the darkness. He prayed that the Source couldn't sense it, couldn't really read his every thought and feeling—

"Then you could be lying to me."

"I'm not lying to you!" Reede shouted. "What would it get me?"

"What, indeed? If you fail me, you'll be a rotting corpse anyway, and Vanamoinen's brain will die with you, no matter what you do, no matter what you say."

Reede licked his lips. "It's going to take time to recreate the water of life. I told you. You don't want any mistakes—" his voice hardened, "like I made before."

"No." The Source made a disgusted noise. "You'll have time enough. . . . But in the meantime, there is another thing the Brotherhood requires from you. Evidently the Queen's obsession with the mers is not just that of a religious fanatic. Gundhalinu and the Queen know something important about the mers, something so secret that apparently no one else even suspects it—not even the Golden Mean. You're going to help us find out what it is."

"How?" Reede said irritably. "They wouldn't tell me tonight . . . it was almost like they *couldn't* tell me—" He broke off. "What do you want me to do?" he asked, shielding the sudden flicker of hope inside him. "You want me to pretend to go along with them, until I find out—?"

The Source laughed, and Reede's hope guttered out. "You'd like that, wouldn't you? But no. You belong to me; Vanamoinen's brain belongs to the Brotherhood. . . . I see that your love affair with Ariele Dawntreader has flowered and borne sweet fruit, despite your thorns, Kullervo—"

Reede shut his eyes; his fists strangled the bedclothes. "I did what you wanted me to," he said.

"And you've done it with all your heart, it seems. The foolish young thing is besotted with you. She tells her friends that you make her feel she will die of ecstasy. I think she would even take you home to mother, if you asked."

Reede's eyes came open. "You want me to marry her?" he asked incredulously.
"No . . ." the blackness hissed. "I want you to give her the water of death."
A strangled sound of disbelief caught in Reede's throat. *"Why?"*
"To complete our hold on her. The Queen is her mother . . . Gundhalinu is
her father. When they see what begins to happen to her when the water of death is
withheld, they'll share their secrets with us."
"What if they can't—?"
There was only silence to answer him, and the sound of labored breathing.
"What if I won't?"
Only silence.
"Jaakola—!"
Only silence, and his own heart beating.

TIAMAT: Carbuncle

"Ariele," he whispered, leaning over her bed in the darkness like a shadow, covering
her mouth with his lips, waking her with a kiss.

Her eyes opened, blinking in wild incomprehension, and she struggled against
him, for the moment it took her to wake fully. "Ariele," he said again, and she went
limp beneath him.

"Reede?" she whispered, in amazement, because he had never been inside her
apartment before, always refused to come anywhere near it.

He did not speak again, but used his mouth to go on kissing her—her face, her
throat, while his hands fumbled with the fastenings of her sleepshirt. Finally he
jerked it open, hearing cloth rip with his impatience, beyond caring. He pulled it
down her body, hearing her sound of half-protest, half-surprise as he bared her. But
she clung to him as he covered her nakedness with his kisses, stripped off his own
clothes in a frenzy of desperate need and laid his body down on hers. She wrapped
herself around him, welcoming him, eager for him, taking him inside her; sheltering
him as he possessed her, giving her the only gift he knew how to give, until she cried
out in astonished pleasure and release, setting his own need free inside her.

They lay together, their legs tangled, their bodies still joined, their hearts
beating each to each, for a long time before he spoke her name again.

"I'm leaving," he said, and he pressed his lips to her warm, shining skin, with
infinite gentleness this time, before he slid off of her and sat up. "I want you to come
with me." His hand slipped down along her arm until he was holding her fingers
closed inside his own.

She sat up too, suddenly wide awake in the darkness. "Tonight?"

"Yes."

"Where are you going? Offworld?"

"No, I'd never get away with that. . . . Into the outback. You have to come with me."

"Why?" she asked softly.

"Because I'm tired of living, and because you're not."

"I don't understand. . . ."

"You don't have to. You just have to trust me. Do you trust me, Ariele?"

Slowly she nodded.

He took her hand, drawing her up. "Then let's go."

They headed south along the coast in the Queen's hovercraft, into the sheltering darkness. Dawn found them still traveling southward above the infinite fields of the sea. Ariele had not spoken more than two words to him all the while as they flew, only huddling against him in the seat, with her head on his shoulder, drifting in and out of sleep. The pressure of her weight against him began to hurt him as his nerve endings grew hypersensitive. His mind magnified every symptom of his systemic deterioration through the long, silent hours, making his awareness of his growing discomfort infinitely more unpleasant; but he did not wake her.

The night seemed to go on forever; and yet the new day's dawn peered over his shoulder too soon, telling him that their time of stolen peace together was running out.

Ariele stirred at last, as the hot light of the steadily rising suns beat in through the side window, falling on her face. She sat up again, rubbing her eyes, and looked out at the bleak unfamiliarity of the distant coastline. They were turning away from it now, heading out across the open sea. "Where are we?"

"Far away," he said. "Down the coast about as far as there's still any habitation. I'm going to drop you off at the last Summer village I can find, and then I'm ditching the hovercraft."

She looked at him as if he had gone insane. "Why, Reede? Why are we out here? Is it about the mers?"

"No," he said grimly. "Not directly. I want you to listen to me, really listen. I don't work for your mother—"

"I know," she said softly.

He looked at her, half frowning. But he only said, "Don't interrupt. I work for somebody called the Source. I do research for him, he brought me here to study the mers so I could make him a supply of the water of life." She stared at him, silent now. "He—owns me." He held up his palm, showing her the scar. He had seen her looking at it from time to time, but she had never dared to ask him what it was. "He tells me to do things, and I do them, or he cuts off my drugs. If I can't get my fix, I'll die."

"He—he addicted you?"

"No," he said harshly. "I did it to myself. But he controls my supply—" pushing on before she could ask more. "I brought you out here because now he wants me to give the drug to you."

Her breath stopped; he saw sudden fear in her eyes.

"I brought you out here because I won't do it!" he said angrily. "He told me to get close to you; he told me to sleep with you, he made me—made me do everything. Except this. By the Render—" His hands knotted over the controls.

"Everything . . . ?" Ariele said, her voice thin and tremulous, her cheeks reddening with humiliation. "I don't believe that. Not everything." Her fingers touched her lips, her breast. "Not last night—" She looked back at him, her eyes burning his flesh.

He kept his own gaze fixed on the endless bluegreen of the sea. At last, looking out, he found what he had been searching for. He pointed ahead. "There. The Outermost islands. They're as far south as anybody still lives, from what I can tell. There's a Summer village on one of the islands in the chain. It's so remote they've barely even heard of Carbuncle. It's habitable through Tiamat's whole climate cycle, so they never have to leave it. You can tell them your boat was swept off course by a storm, and you washed up on their beach."

"Alone—?" she asked faintly. He answered her with his silence. She looked away from the sea, from the distant specks of purple-gray that marred its perfect surface, into his eyes. She looked down again abruptly, with her hands clenching in her lap. "And then what? You expect me to live with them, like a—a *dashtu* in a stone hut?"

"It's how the Dawntreaders lived for generations," he snapped. "Even Arien-rhod lived like that before the Change. It's in your blood; you'll get used to it."

"How long do I have to do this?"

He took a deep breath. "Maybe for the rest of your life."

She turned in her seat. "Forever—?"

"If you know what's good for you. The Source wants to use you against your mother and Gundhalinu. He thinks they have something that he wants, and he'll use you to get it. He'll hook you on the water of death and then he'll let it work on you; he figures when the Queen and Gundhalinu see their own child dying by inches, they'll give it to him. But they can't, even if they want to. And I can't stop him. Nobody can. Except you. You can disappear, completely."

"All this . . . because I love you?" she said, her voice falling apart. "That's why all this is happening to me? I'll never see Carbuncle again? Never see my family, or . . ." Her anguish and betrayal, her helpless rage, filled him until he could not breathe, as he watched her realize all she had lost in the space of a dozen heartbeats; all he had done to her, in the space of a dozen words. She pressed her hands against her face, her fingers whitening. Her eyes welled with tears of fury, of hatred . . . of shame, and unrelenting hunger, as she murmured, "Or you—?"

He took a deep, ragged breath, feeling the same desperate rage against impossible fate fill him the way the air filled his lungs. He had never wanted this, never wanted her— She had been forced on him, against his will, used like an instrument of torture by the man who had made an exquisite art of torturing him. He should hate her. And yet . . . He looked away from her blindly, before she could see the same unrelenting hunger in his eyes.

He began to check readouts and systems obsessively, things whose prepro-grammed functions needed no adjusting; trying to insulate himself from her inescapable nearness. But his traitorous senses registered her presence through every fiber of his body, as if her every breath and movement was an extension of his own . . . until he was not even sure how he had come to be touching her, kissing her, holding her against him. He groaned softly as his degenerating nerve synapses shocked him like live wires, the pain intensifying his arousal with exquisite perversity. He held her closer, savoring every sensation as if it were his last.

"Are you . . . are you going back to him—?" she murmured, her lips soft and warm against his throat. *To the Source.*

"No," he said, shaking his head. "I'm letting the hovercraft take me down. No more. Let him think we died together." A wave of terror inundated him, as he imagined the cold waters of the sea closing over his head, filling his lungs, possessing him at last. He forced himself to remember that it would be quick, it could be over in seconds if he canceled the emergency safeguards and hit the water just right. He forced himself to remember the alternative.

He felt her stiffen against him. "Take me with you, then," she murmured. "Let me go with you. I don't care, I don't want to live without you—"

He pulled away from her, his hands tightening over her arms until she winced in pain. "No. Then he'll win, that fucking, diseased bastard! You've got to live!" He shook her. "If you love me, it's what you've got to do."

"Why can't we both live, then?" she demanded. "The Chief Justice will help us. Gundhalinu said he knew you, and he could help you. It isn't too late—"

"It is for me! He can't get me what I need. And he can't protect you. I'm going to die, Ariele, don't you fucking hear me? Unless I crawl back to the Source on my belly and beg him like a dog to give me what I need, I'm dead. And he won't give it to me unless I give him you."

"But if it's only a drug—"

He gave a sharp laugh, the sound of disbelief a man being impaled might make, at the moment of first penetration. He turned away from her in bleak disgust. "The Summer village is the next island down the chain. You're getting off there."

"No—" She moved suddenly, unexpectedly, reaching past him. Her hands attacked the instruments, fighting him, fighting them, unlocking the system and putting it under manual control. The craft bucked and plunged as he shoved her away, hard, against the door. He struggled to get it back under his control, but she flung herself on him again, wedging her body against the panel. He felt the hovercraft drop precipitously out from under them. "Ariele!" he shouted; he struck her open-handed across the face in desperate panic. She fell back into her seat, held there by acceleration as they plummeted headlong toward the bluegreen water that was suddenly all he could see.

He shouted frantic voice commands at the craft's guidance system, pulling back on the manual controls with all his strength, trying to stop their fatal arc with his own strength. He was not an experienced pilot, he had always had others to do the job for him. Now, when it was too late, he cursed himself for it.

But abruptly he saw a line of pale ocher, a vision of rust-red and green-gray filling his view; giving him just time to realize that they had reached land, before they struck it.

The hovercraft hit with a grinding crunch and spun like a plate, heaving and pitching, across the rock-strewn surface of the plateau. It slammed to a halt inside a grove of tree-ferns. Greenery rained down on them, covering the windshield with fronds.

Reede hung against the emergency restraints of his seat, gasping. Ariele stirred beside him, shaking her head, making a thin whimpering protest. The sound stopped abruptly, and she turned her face toward him, holding her hand against her cheek.

Between her fingers he could see the print of his own hand like a red brand on her pale skin. "Why didn't you let us crash?" she cried fiercely, her voice in rags.

He rested his gibbering, pain-filled body against the solidness of the seatback, watching her out of the corner of his eye. He felt bruises beginning to form, too easily, felt a telltale dribble of blood run out of one nostril, sliding down his lip. He wiped his nose on his sleeve.

"You don't want to die," she said, "any more than I do! We can radio for help—"

"Get out," he said, and when she didn't move, shouted, "I said get out!" He waited for her to push aside the crash restraints and obey, before he climbed out on his own side. Not trusting her, he ordered the doors sealed when they were both outside, on opposite sides of the craft. He looked at the hovercraft, seeing its battered undercarriage, the wake of debris its slide along the ground had left behind. One look told him that its ruined repeller grid would never lift them again.

He looked away, taking in the rest of their view. This was not the island he had been heading for; he could see that one still in the distance, looming out of the sea. He could see the entirety of the island they were on, turning where he stood; some miserable, nameless rock barely keeping its head above water. *Stranded.* He felt his stomach cramp with sickness; swallowed convulsively, barely able to stop himself from retching. At least the hovercraft had ended up beneath the trees. The small stand of giant ferns was the only shelter he could see; the trees were probably the only living things on the island besides the two of them, and random flights of birds. The grove would conceal the craft from an aerial search well enough; if all they were using was visual, anyway. At least it might buy them a little more time.

He turned back to Ariele. "The village is on that next island, the big one." He pointed. "You're a strong swimmer. Find something that floats; you'll reach it in a few hours."

She stared at him for a long moment. "No," she said.

"Damn it, Ariele—!" He took a step toward her, his hands tightening into fists.

"I won't leave you." Her own hands twisted together like a lover's-knot on the hovercraft's sloping hood. "I won't leave you." She was weeping now, silently.

He stopped moving and stared at her; watching her weep, for him, for them. He felt as if his body were swarming with invisible worms, until he wanted to scream. "All right, then," he said bitterly, "stay if you want. You think it's 'just a drug' that's making me sweat? Stay and watch it happen then, if that's what you want. Watch what's going to happen to you, if you ever go back to Carbuncle. Stay and be damned!" He hit the craft's door with his clenched fist, sending shockwaves of pain through his body. He swore again, blinking his vision clear. "Get away from the hovercraft!" He waved her back. "Stay away from me," he said furiously, when she would have come close to him. "Stay where I can see you, over there, under the trees."

She backed away, uncertainly, until she had gone far enough to suit him. She settled at the base of one of the tree-ferns, wrapping her arms around her knees, hugging herself. She watched him, her eyes like dark pools in the shadows.

He slid down the side of the hovercraft, sat on the hard, sand-gritty surface of the ground, blocking access to the door at his back. He pulled his stunner out of his belt and laid it on the ground beside him with exaggerated care. He knew what she was thinking; she would be waiting for a chance to get access to the craft's radio. She didn't believe him. He could see it in her eyes, she still thought there was a way out of this. He hoped he could hold her off until she'd seen enough to understand; that when she did, she'd leave him here and never look back.

He rested against the hovercraft's curving side. Everywhere that his flesh came in contact with anything, the pain was a bed of nails; but he was too weary even to bother holding his head up any longer. The metal grew warm, as the sunlight shafting through the broken foliage touched his resting place. The sunlight warmed his skin too, and the rust-red ground he sat on. *Gods, it was actually hot, here—* Not like back on Ondinee, although it probably would be before High Summer reached its midpoint; but hot compared to the northern coast, where Carbuncle lay. He let the Twins' heat comfort him, although it made his flesh burn as if he were a bug under a magnifying glass. His veins seemed to be filled with icewater, not blood, or filled with acid, or sludge.

The hours passed. Sunlight and shadows made a slow promenade through the quiet grove. Ariele sat unmoving; so did he. Birds flitted intermittently across his vision making it strobe; the sound of rustling fronds merged into the sound of the sea. The soft, incessant whispering seemed to grow louder the longer he listened; as if the sea were creeping closer, closing in on him where he waited, helpless, to drown him. . . .

He struggled to his feet with a cry as water struck his face—found himself standing in the rain, staring up at a sky as blue-black as a bruise, while the clouds of the passing squall wept overhead. Raindrops pelted him like pearls, hard and smooth, melting with his fever heat, flowing into his sweat, drenching him. He stood gaping up at the rain as the dream sea subsided; felt his legs go out from under him suddenly as reality dragged him back down.

He slid down the rain-slick door of the hovercraft until he was sitting again in the red mud. Mud oozed between his fingers, soothingly warm/cool. He looked down at his hands, seeing them swollen and purplish; like someone else's hands attached to him, not his own hands at all. He looked up again, saw Ariele still huddled miserably beneath the tree-fern's inadequate shelter. She called his name, seeing him look at her.

He did not answer. He let his head drop back, until he was staring up into the sky, letting the rain fall into his parched mouth. His face shed the sky's tears; he waited for its grief to pass.

The rainsquall departed as swiftly as it had come, swept on across the sea by a freshening wind. The Twins emerged, midway down the sky toward sunset, firing the clouds with rainbows and sundogs, doubling, splintering, painting the sky with watercolor visions. He watched them form and fade and re-form, the way his awareness of his pain-wracked body faded and re-formed now; awed and grief-stricken as he watched them. Somewhere, in a place lost in the infinite reaches of space and time, he had seen stars in a night sky illuminated like stained glass. . . . He could not remember anything else in all his memories that had touched him with such terrifying beauty. He had never really had a moment like that since. He wondered whether he simply hadn't bothered to notice the beauty all around him; or whether it was only the closing hand of death that let him see clearly.

At sunset Ariele got up from her sitting-place at last, and came toward him. He picked the stunner up in clumsy hands, and trained it on her.

She looked at him, her forehead furrowing, her face so devoid of expression that it was perfectly transparent. He saw her made of glass, waiting to shatter. But she only said, "I'm hungry."

"There's no food," he said.

"There are emergency supplies in the back of the hovercraft."

"All right . . . get them," he mumbled. "Keep away from the radio." She nodded, her face reddening. Slowly and painfully he moved aside, giving her access to the craft; his joints resisted motion like rusting hinges. He watched her find the food and bring it out, and then he moved back again.

She crouched down, a little away from him, making certain that every movement of her own was deliberate and open. She offered him food—rations in self-warming cans. The smell made his stomach turn over. He shook his head. She offered him water. He gulped it down greedily, feeling as if he could drink the sea dry and still want more. He held the cup out for her to refill it; vomited, suddenly and violently, spewing the scant remains of his last meal down the front of his clothes.

She moved forward to help him. He threw the cup at her, swearing and spitting. She scrambled to her feet, catching up the food containers, dropping them again; leaving a trail behind her as she retreated to her place under the trees.

Reede sat in his own vomit without the strength to move, until the smell of it made him sick again, his stomach heaving until there was nothing left to expel. He went on sitting, wet and stinking and exhausted, staring at her, while the shadows deepened. She ate nothing while he watched her.

At last he could no longer make out her form in the darkness beneath the trees. He thought once that he heard weeping, but he wasn't sure. She made no movements that he could detect, above the sounds of the sea and the sighing trees, the wheezing rattle deep in his chest that seemed louder with every breath. He wondered whether she was sleeping, or whether she still sat there, equally sleepless, equally alone, equally afraid. He wanted to call out to her, so that she would come to him, comfort him, hold him in her arms through this final night of his life.

His guts loosened and he knew he was going to shit in his pants, helpless to stop it from happening. He did not call out to her. He told himself that he was glad night had come, to hide what was happening to him from her sight . . . from his own. Gods spare them both vision, for these next few hours. Morning would come soon enough, and then she would believe him. Then she would understand.

Muscles spasmed in his legs. He cried out involuntarily; bit down on the cloth of his sleeve as he forced them straight again, inch by inch. He no longer knew whether the air was warm or cold; his body burned with fever, shook with chills. Through the trees he could see a band of night sky, glowing like embers with the light of countless suns, like the countless atoms of his body, burning with the fire of his self-immolation. He watched the new moon rise, vast and dark against the stars, like a hole in the night. Like a black hole, like the singularity that existed inside him where his mind should have been, swallowing all meaning, never surrendering its secrets to him, even now. . . .

He shut his eyes, his lids scraping his corneas like sand, making tears flow out and down, salt water like the sea. The voice of the sea called to him, through the rushing of his own blood inside his ears. In the sound he thought he heard the voices of the mers; although the mers were long gone from here, moving north toward a goal he would never know the secret of now . . . or to a fate that would silence them forever.

He felt his consciousness slipping, and let it go; drifting out on the tide, away from his suffering. Ariele had told him of how she would swim with the mers . . . he let himself dream that he was one with them, one of them—weaving his voice into their sacred songs, following the almost mystical urge that compelled them as they moved through the seas, traveling northward to Carbuncle, toward the soul of the ocean. He saw a vision of it now, ahead of him through the green-shadowed, blue-shafted aether of his world; felt it breathing, in and out, the subsonic rumble of its mighty voice calling him in through gates of death that shone like the flashing teeth of the Render, ready to strip his flesh from his bones, and grind his bones to sand.

And yet as they neared, the voice fell silent, as he had known it would; all motion ceased, the jaws gaped wide, welcoming the mers in to offer up their songs of renewal, and receive in turn a blessing for yet another lifetime spent in peace. It was as he had always intended it to be. . . .

Shadows darkened the watercolors of his dreamworld. Suddenly figures, alien but recognizable in form, were dropping out of the heights, spreading a net between them, to snare his kind, to drag them down to drown and die, and then to lay them out on deck or shore and slash their shining throats, collect their blood, and turn it into a precious obscenity; destroying them with all their secrets. . . .

But I'm a man, he cried, as the net dropped over him like a shroud. *Not a mer—a man!* But he had forgotten that, forgotten that he was not one with them, that the sea was death, waiting to claim him; forgotten to be afraid. He wore no suit, no mask, no breather feeding him air— He was naked and drowning, a living corpse who watched as they cut his throat, and he was drowning again in his own blood—

Reede came awake with a strangled gasp, with blood filling his nose and mouth, spilling down his face from the hemorrhaging membranes inside his head. He fell forward, coughing and spitting, struggling convulsively to breathe. At last the bleeding subsided. He slumped onto his side, unable to push himself up again. He lay still, feeling his muscles stiffen and draw, forcing him slowly into a fetal huddle; feeling his body's systems failing one by one, stretching him one notch further on the rack. He drifted in and out of delirium dreams—images of heartbreaking beauty, exquisite passion, always mutating like his flesh into nightmares of agony and corruption. But still he was grateful for them; because they kept him from ever knowing what was real, and happening to him now.

Dawn drove the reluctant night from the grove with spears of fire; drove burning needles into his flesh, pried open his eyelids, searching for signs of life. Reede moaned, looking into the face of the new day with eyes that had swollen to slits. Disbelief kept them open as he discovered Ariele, lying beside him on the ground, asleep. He wondered how long she had been there. He was filled with a sense of strange euphoria and peace for the moment it took him to realize that this was not a dream.

The gun. Where was the gun? He pushed himself up in blind panic, wrenched his spasm-locked muscles into motion with an animal snarl of suffering. The stunner was on the ground where he had dropped it; he had been lying on top of it. He reached for it—saw his hand, blackened and swollen, like a lump of burned meat quivering at the end of his sleeve. He swore thickly, shutting his eyes. His flesh felt spongy, yielding, like warm wax. Before the day was done it would be dropping from his bones like a leper's.

He opened his eyes again as Ariele stirred beside him. She sat up, rubbing her face, looking out at the sea; looking stupefied, like someone who had wakened out of a dream, only to find that she was still dreaming. Her eyes were red and puffy, as if she had been awake and crying most of the night.

She turned slowly, blinking too much, until she was facing him. Her mouth fell open and she stopped moving; stopped breathing, forgetting her own existence in the horror of encountering his. She sat frozen, for what seemed to him an eternity, not breathing, while his own tortured body stubbornly went on inhaling and exhaling, in wheezing, labored gasps. At last she took a breath; a sob of grief and terror shook her. "Lady and all the gods," she said tremulously. "Reede—?" As if she could not force herself to believe that he was the thing she found in front of her.

He nodded.

She pressed her hands against her mouth. "Mother of Us All, what's happening? What is it? Why—?"

"Warned you . . ." he whispered. "It's the water of death."

She made a sound deep in her throat, as if for a moment his agony had invaded her own body. She understood . . . now, finally, she understood.

He smiled; watched her horror deepen as she realized what his expression was.

She pushed to her feet, her face changing. "You can't do this! I'm going to call Gundhalinu—" She started past him, reaching for the hovercraft's door, calling out the code that would unseal the locks.

He lunged for the stunner, still on the ground beside him. He swung it up and around in both hands, and fired. Ariele cried out in shock and rage and despair. She sprawled, helpless, onto the red earth, as the hovercraft's door rose over her like a birdwing.

Reede turned his head slowly, seeing her legs, her back; unable to see her face where she lay, unable to see him now. He heard his own voice keening mindlessly, helpless to stop it as aftershocks of pain from his sudden motion rolled through him, wave upon wave. *Drowning . . . the sea . . . the mers . . . drowning in pain . . . death . . . Help me, help me, please help me. . . .* Someone was screaming inside his head, someone else, he didn't know who, the prisoner, screaming. . . . *Vanamoinen—*

He shook his head, trying to clear it. By the time the stunshock wore off, he would be unable to stop Ariele from calling anyone. She still didn't believe him—that no one could protect her from the Source. Damn her to hell, making everything worse for him, everything harder— Why hadn't she listened to him? He'd wanted to end it cleanly. He'd never wanted anyone to see him like this; and it had to be her, watching him puke and rot and die . . . because she loved him. He dropped the stunner, lifted a hand to his throbbing head; brought it down again with a fistful of his own hair trapped between his swollen, necrotic fingers. He stared at it for a long time.

He should disable the radio. He had to do that. If he could only find the strength to do that, then he could rest, then he could let it finish. Everything would end, his suffering . . . the mers . . . *everything would be lost, futile, pointless. . . .*

He dragged himself around and up somehow, ignoring the sounds he made as the fires of hell consumed his flesh. He crawled into the cabin, lay across the pilot's seat, sobbing, coughing up blood, unable to see, to think, but only to feel pain. At last he reached out, fumbling toward the comm link on the instrument panel beside him. His hand crossed the range of his vision; he saw the bones of a finger protruding through the half-dead flesh.

His hand jerked back, without his willing it, as if he were suddenly controlled by a puppeteer. And somewhere inside his shattered brain, the prisoner exulted, holding the keys. *You are my vessel. You have no choice,* the Other said. *I have to live. I have to live.*

His cry of fury and betrayal died stillborn. His broken voice called the panel to life, as the Other squeezed words from his throat, and spat them out of his mouth, dripping red. He had to repeat himself twice before the instruments understood him and responded.

"Jaakola . . ." he whispered into the open comm, weeping tears of blood. "I have her. I'll do anything you want. Help me. . . ."

TIAMAT: Carbuncle

"Ho, Dawntreader—"

Sparks looked up from his blank-eyed scrutiny of the empty tabletop, to see Kirard Set Wayaways picking a path toward him across the crowded dance floor of Starhiker's.

"I was hoping I'd find you here." Kirard Set smiled, stopping in front of the table with the knowing look that Sparks had begun to grow tired of.

"What is it?" Sparks asked, leaning back in his seat.

Wayaways slid into the booth across from him. "I have a message to deliver . . . and so do you."

Sparks raised his eyebrows, more than a little surprised. "Is this a Brotherhood matter?"

"Of course." Kirard Set rubbed his chin, glancing idly into the crowd. "The Source has been called away; business back on Ondinee. He expects to return to Tiamat soon—"

"The heady joys of hyperlight transit," Sparks muttered, feeling envy stir the sediment of his long-ago dreams.

"We should drink a toast to progress," Kirard Set said wryly, "but we have no drinks." He gestured at the empty table surface, his face inviting explanation, or invitation.

Sparks shrugged, without making either. "What's the Source's leaving got to do with me?"

Kirard Set's congeniality faded, replaced by an equally unsettling directness.

"We are to continue our present activities with the processing laboratories, and diverting of supplies. . . . The Newhavener, TerFauw, is in charge at Persiponë's until Jaakola returns."

"You said there was a message to deliver."

Kirard Set hesitated, in a way that only made Sparks's unease intensify. "It's a message for your wife. About Ariele, and the Source's man Kullervo."

"What about them?" he said, too sharply.

Kirard Set leaned back, as if he were getting out of range. "You already know they've been seeing each other. . . . What you may not know is that Kullervo is an addict—addicted to a drug he created himself, a kind of bastard form of the water of life. He calls it the 'water of death.' It's fatal. And he's given it to Ariele."

Sparks jerked upright, gripping the table edge with his hands. "What?" he whispered.

Wayaways suddenly had trouble looking at him. "The Source wants something from the Queen, or Gundhalinu," he muttered. "He wants them to understand that unless they provide it, he will cut off Ariele's supply of the drug." He reached into his overshirt. "Here. This is a tape of what happens to the . . . addict. I wouldn't watch it if I were you." He tossed the tape button onto the tabletop.

Sparks picked it up, held it between nerveless fingers. He looked at Wayaways again. "Where are they?" he said. His hand fisted over the tape. "Where's he got her? By all the gods—"

"It's not your problem, for gods' sakes!" Kirard Set hissed. "You belong to the Brotherhood now! Your wife is cuckolding you with the father of her bastard children—Ariele isn't even your child, you said it yourself. Get a grip on things, man. Everything's that's happening is to your gain—*your* gain, if you play your part in this well. All you have to do is give the Queen the message. Claim you were accosted by faceless strangers, act as distraught as you need to; but always remember that it's got to be an act—"

Remember. Sparks sat rigidly, forcing himself to remember the hard, useful lessons that time and the Brotherhood had taught him. He inhaled deeply, concentrating on control. "Only an act," he repeated, without expression. He looked down at his hand, lying loose and open now on the table surface. He put the tape bead into his belt pouch, before he looked up again at Kirard Set. "What does the Source think they have, that no one else does? Besides each other, I mean?" His mouth twisted sardonically.

A faint, relieved smile pulled at the corners of Kirard Set's lips. "It's something about the mers."

Sparks frowned. "They don't know anything about the mers that I don't know."

"Maybe Survey has given them new information."

He shook his head. "Jaakola has Survey connections all over the Hegemony. He could find out something like that without having to—" *to kill my daughter*—"resort to blackmail, for gods' sakes."

"Then maybe they really do know something that no one else knows." Kirard Set shrugged. "That's not our problem. Be glad."

"What proof is there that he actually has Ariele? That there's really such a drug?" Sparks said, not quite casually. "They'll want more proof than this tape."

"Have you seen Ariele around the city lately? Or Kullervo?"

"No," he said, his mouth tightening.

"No one has. Jaakola's taken them with him back to Ondinee, to give the concerned parties here sufficient time to realize that they have no alternatives. That there's no way to save her except to do what he wants. When the time is right, he'll bring her back."

Sparks looked away, searching the crowd, willing himself to see a shock of silver hair, a poignantly familiar smile; to hear Ariele's laughter, even her voice raised in anger, denying him as he had denied her. . . . But he found only random motion and meaningless noise: the face of chaos, in a crowd of strangers. . . .

"The sooner the message is delivered, the better," Kirard Set said quietly. "For everyone's sake." He rose from his seat and started away without any farewell, disappearing into the crowd.

Sparks sat for a long moment staring at the empty tabletop. And then, unable to help himself, he took the tape button out of his belt pouch and dropped it into the player at the edge of the table. A three-dimensional image flickered to life in the air before him. He began to watch . . . went on watching, paralyzed by disbelief. At last he forced his hand to move, unable to tear his eyes away from the agonizing images even as his fist came down on the viewer's touchboard, cutting off the flow of obscene horror.

"Excuse me, Sparks Dawntreader—"

He looked up, dazed, into the non-face of Tor's hired servo unit.

"We do not permit public use of such visuals in the club," it said tonelessly. "Please take a private room for future viewing, out of consideration for the club's other patrons."

He nodded wordlessly, unable even to respond to the droning solicitude of its speech.

"May I bring you something to calm your nerves, sir. A pack of iestas, a bowl of pickled fish?" Its twin vision sensors studied him with inhuman forbearance, like insect eyes.

"Bring me a drink. A strong one. Bring me six," he said. It looked at him. "I'm expecting friends," he added irritably.

The servo bobbed politely and moved away. It returned with six drinks in less time than he expected. He drank them all, in less time than he would have thought possible. They had no discernible effect on what was happening inside his head. He sat with the empty glasses in a line before him, as the tape replayed over and over in his memory; sure that he would never be able to see anything clearly again, without that overlying vision.

The servo returned to his table after a time. He felt it regard the line of empty glasses, the empty seats around him, and himself, with silent speculation. "Your guests were detained, Sparks Dawntreader?"

"Bring me six more," he said.

"Yes, sir," it responded, and went away. He went on studying the six empties, rearranging them with his hands into one futile geometric configuration after another. *I have no children. She's not my daughter.* He had actually said that, aloud, in front of strangers . . . he had actually believed that he meant it. He had turned away from his children, in their confusion and grief; turned his back on them because, knowing the truth, he suddenly could not bear to look at them. . . .

He swore softly, as the obscene hallucination filling his mind surrendered to memories of his children . . . his children laughing, clinging to his legs, building castles out of sand; with sunlight in their hair, and hands filled with shells and colored stones: precious treasures. . . . He remembered them playing at games through the halls of the palace, bringing life and joy to that cold tomb where his own youth had died. He remembered their delight, their tears, their tantrums; the music of flutes, the crash of a shattered bowl—the eyes looking up into his own with unquestioning love, asking only that he love them without reservation.

Their lives, their youth, their hearts had been his. Gundhalinu might have planted the seed, but Gundhalinu had not watched them grow. They were *his*. . . .

Visions of hideous death suffocated his memories suddenly: but this time it was Ariele he saw, suffering, dying, her flesh dropping from her bones before his horrified eyes. . . .

"Sparks—"

He looked up again, startled, knocking over glasses. Tor Starhiker stood beside his table, with the Pollux unit behind her, staring down at him. "Thanks, Polly." She sent it away and settled, uninvited, onto the seat across from him. She counted the disarray of empty glasses, and grimaced. "Pollux told me you were drinking the sea tonight," she said, "and that's not like you." She glanced down, away from his sudden frown. "You want to drink some more, or would you like to talk about it?"

He opened his mouth; shook his head, glancing at the tape viewer.

"This have anything to do with the tape you were watching? That isn't like you, either." He looked back at her, and she shrugged. "Pollux sees all, Tor knows all. . . ." She touched his hand lightly, with unexpected concern. "Someone you knew?" she murmured.

"No," he said; his hand made a fist. He cleared the congestion out of his throat. "Tor . . . have you seen Ariele, the last week or so? Or Reede Kullervo?"

Her own hand closed suddenly. "Wait here," she said, getting up. "I'll be right back. You wait—" She pointed at him, her face urgent.

He waited. She returned with two men . . . Kullervo's men, he realized; he remembered the striking contrast between them. He felt hope and relief sing through him, until he saw their faces. They slid into the booth across from him, the short man lifting himself onto the bench with the agility of long practice. Tor sat down with Sparks, but her hand reached across the table unexpectedly, to meet the short man's blunt fingers in a brief, sensual twining. Sparks noticed that his face was a twilight landscape of cuts and bruises.

The other brand, the Ondinean, removed some kind of animal from his clothes and set it on the table in front of him, stroking its back. Watching his expression, Sparks wondered which of them, the man or the animal, was more in need of the reassurance. The creature made a strange chuckling noise, like gentle laughter, as the Ondinean's fingers ruffled its fur.

"Niburu and Ananke." Tor introduced the two men as if they were a unit. "They—"

"—work for Kullervo. I know," Sparks murmured.

"This is Sparks Dawntreader Summer," she said, to them.

"We know," the short man answered, looking wary. Sparks realized he was better known to them for his dealings with the Source than he was for his relationship to the Queen.

"You need to talk," Tor said. She leaned back and folded her arms.

"Where's Kullervo?" Sparks asked flatly.

The two brands glanced at each other, uncertain.

"By the Lady and all the gods, Kedalion," Tor urged impatiently, "tell him what you know."

"Reede's on Ondinee," Niburu said, glancing down at his palm. "At least, that's what I heard."

"Then what are you doing still here?" Sparks said, frowning.

Niburu looked up again, his eyes bleak. "I don't know. . . . TerFauw just ordered us back there."

"Why did Kullervo leave without you? I thought you were his crew?"

"We are." Niburu nodded. "I don't know. Something happened . . . we went to meet him one morning, and he was gone from his place. He wasn't anywhere. TerFauw beat the crap out of me before I could convince him we weren't in on it." He touched his jaw, wincing. "Nobody'd tell us anything, after that. And then today, TerFauw calls us in and tells us the Source took Reede back to Ondinee. We're to follow. That's all. I didn't expect it; he was still working on his mer research. I figured . . ." He shook his head. "From the kind of questions TerFauw asked me, I think maybe Reede tried to run, and they got him back. But I can't figure what could be bad enough to drive him to that. The Source treats him like shit, but Reede knows there's no way out." He pressed his branded palm flat on the tabletop, like he was squashing a bug.

"Do you know anything about . . . my daughter?" Sparks felt Tor turn to stare at him.

Niburu looked blank for a moment, and then sudden comprehension showed on his face. "Reede's been—" He glanced at Sparks. "Uh, they spend a lot of time together." He shook his head. "I haven't seen her for . . . since Reede—" He broke off.

"I was told tonight . . ." Sparks took a deep breath, holding an empty glass in his hands, in fragile balance. "I was told to give a message to my wife, the Queen, from the Source. To say that . . . our daughter has been taken to Ondinee. That Reede Kullervo has addicted her to a drug he invented, something called the water of death. I was given a tape of what it does . . . what it will do to Ariele if my wife and the Chief Justice don't give him something. . . ."

"Give him what?" Ananke asked.

"I don't know!" he said, and the glass fell, clattering on the table. "Don't you think I'd give it to him myself, if I knew?"

Ananke grimaced; his pet disappeared under his arm. He glanced at Niburu, and Sparks saw something unspoken pass between them. "You think that's what he's on?" Ananke asked. Niburu nodded, frowning.

"What is it—the 'water of death'?" Tor asked. Her own face constricted as she waited for the answer, as if she were waiting for a blow.

"Kirard Set told me it was a bastard form of the water of life," Sparks said.

She shook her head slightly. "What does it do to you?"

He reached out and touched the tape player; the image materialized like a poisonous fog in the space between them. He watched, helplessly, hearing the others around him suck in their breath, hearing their curses of disbelief.

"Shut if off," Tor said. "Shut it off, damn you!"

He reached out, extinguishing the image as she tried to reach past him and do it herself.

She hit him in the shoulder with her clenched fist; hit him again. "Damn it! Damn it!" He said nothing, did nothing, as she pulled back again, going limp against the dark, mirroring wall of the booth. She struck the tabletop once, with her open hand. Niburu and Ananke sat like stunned bookends, staring at each other.

Tor looked at him, finally, with apology in her eyes. "To Ariele—?" she whispered. "To Ariele?" Suddenly her eyes were empty.

Sparks nodded, slumped in the corner. "Yes."

"And Reede . . ." Niburu muttered.

"He gave it to her—" Tor said, her eyes coming alive again as she turned back to Niburu. "You bastard! You told me he was safe! You said he wouldn't hurt her—"

"He wouldn't—" Niburu began.

"Reede wouldn't do something like that to her, he's in love with her," Ananke protested, running over the words.

Niburu put a hand on his arm. "He wouldn't, if he was getting his fixes on time. But we don't how long he was missing. What would you do, to stop that—?" He gestured at the empty space between them, the air still haunted by what they had seen moments before.

Ananke looked away, shaking his head.

Niburu turned back to Sparks. "I'm sorry," he murmured. He rested his head in his hands. "I'm sorry, Tor. Gods, I never imagined something like this would happen. . . ." He looked up again. "Shit—I don't want to leave like this. I don't want this to be why you remember me. . . ."

Her faced eased as she let go of her useless anger. "I know," she said, and sighed. "Sparks, did you say Kirard Set told you about the water of death? What's he got to do with it?"

"He has . . . business dealings with the Source." Sparks shifted glasses into a new pattern. "And so do I."

Tor stared at him, while her incredulity turned slowly to understanding, and then to resignation. She glanced at Niburu; back at him. "Kind of like a disease, isn't it? . . . Gods, what are kind hearts like us doing in a cesspit like this?" She shook her head. "Is there anybody in the Motherloving galaxy who doesn't work for the Source?"

"Moon," Sparks said bitterly. "And Gundhalinu."

"Not yet," Niburu muttered.

"I know something else about Kirard Set," Ananke said, leaning forward as his pet wandered across the table, snuffling in glasses. "You remember that night: Ariele, and Elco Teel—?" Niburu and Tor nodded, with sudden frowns. Tor pulled the animal back from the edge of the table, and began to scratch it behind the ears.

"What night?" Sparks said.

"Elco Teel slipped Ariele some kind of sex drug and took her to a—a—" Ananke broke off, looking down.

"A gang bang," Niburu said bluntly, for him.

"Reede rescued her—" Tor put her hand on Sparks's arm, holding him back until the words registered. "Reede. He risked getting himself killed to get her out of there in time. She was all right," Tor insisted gently. "She was orbiting so high up, I don't think she even remembered what happened. But they've been lovers, ever since."

Sparks shook his head, feeling his images of Reede and his daughter and himself shift and flow like oil in water.

"Reede was like a *pashayan*—a flaming sword," Ananke said, his eyes shining suddenly. "There were a dozen men, but he faced them down and they ran like rats. And then he made that little dungeater Elco Teel sweat blood. I thought he was going to have a heart attack when Reede took a knife to him—"

"Yeah, I've seen Reede like that," Kedalion said, nodding. "A *pashayan*. That night in Ravien's, when we met him . . ."

Ananke smiled, weaving a thin braid between his dark fingers. A peculiar expression came over his face, half fond and half chagrined. It faded, as his thoughts slid back into the present.

"What's this got to do with Kirard Set?" Sparks said impatiently.

They looked back at him, almost resentful, as if he had interrupted a private reminiscence between mourners. But Ananke said, "Kirard Set gave Elco the drug that he gave to Ariele. And the Source gave it to Kirard Set. Reede said . . ." He pressed his forehead, half frowning as he tried to remember the words. "He said for Elco Teel to tell his father that it was a closed game, between him and the Source. That if they didn't stay out of it, he'd kill them both." He looked up again.

"You never told me that part of it," Niburu said.

"I didn't?" Ananke shrugged.

"Why in seven hells would Kirard Set want to do a thing like that?" Tor asked. "He was always mouthing it around that Elco Teel was going to marry Ariele someday, and she was going to be the next Summer Queen. I never liked him, the vicious motherfucker, he's got a smile like a skule. But why—? Was he looking for favors from the Source? Or is he just that much of a human pustule?"

Sparks glanced at the tape player, and away again. "Yes," he murmured. "All of that . . . but there's more. It's more complicated. The Source isn't just a narco, he's involved in dimensions of corruption you or I can't even imagine. . . ." He broke off, needing to say more; afraid to, for their sakes, for his own.

Something clattered onto the tabletop in front of him. He picked it up—a chain, dangling two ornaments. He held them closer, seeing a ring with two soliis set into a band of white metal. A pendant clinked silverly against the ring; its form caught in his brain like a fishhook. *The Brotherhood.* He looked up again; met Niburu's gaze waiting for him. "Is this yours?" he asked.

"It was Reede's," Niburu answered. "He always wore it, always. But I found it in his room, after he disappeared. Reede used to call it his good luck charm. . . ." He glanced away. "He lost it once before, a long time ago. When I went to give it back to him, he was in a meeting with about a dozen people who would've gutted each other if they'd met out on the street. They would have gutted me, but Reede stopped them. He said get out, and forget I ever saw them. . . . It's some kind of secret society, isn't it? Something bigger and more powerful than any cartel. That's what you're talking about, isn't it?"

"Close enough." Sparks's hand closed over the metal and jewels, feeling their coldness bite his flesh. "They're behind everything that's happening here, I'm sure of it. And only somebody with the same kind of resources and power has even a hope of getting Ariele back from him. Gundhalinu's got that kind of power. That must be why the Source took her offworld." He rubbed his head, his fingers tangled in his hair. "That means he's not completely confident, at least."

"If she's in the Source's citadel, nobody can get her out alive," Niburu said flatly.

Sparks looked up at him. "Did you say TerFauw ordered you back to Ondinee?" Niburu nodded, looking uneasy.

"You're being sent back to join Reede, at the citadel?"

"That's what he said."

"Take me with you."

Niburu shook his head. "No way. That's impossible. We can't smuggle you in."

"If I have this, it's possible." Sparks held up the pendant, let it dangle in the air before them.

"You don't have this." Niburu held his hand up, palm out, showing Sparks the same brand that Kullervo wore. "Even that pendant won't protect you. It didn't protect Reede. Nobody much looks at brands, as long as they've got the Source's mark on them. But you haven't got it."

Sparks studied the eye-shaped scar, imprinting it on his memory. "I can take care of that," he said.

Niburu grimaced, and was silent for a long moment. "No," he said finally. The fingers of his hand closed over the eye in his palm. "I'm sorry. I can't. The rule I live by is 'Keep your head down, and hope the Dark Ones overlook you.'"

"The Dark Ones have already noticed you," Sparks said. He gestured at Niburu's battered face. "Do you like being the Source's property?"

Niburu frowned, glancing at his partner. "No," he muttered. "But I like it better than being a corpse. I think I speak for both of us." Ananke nodded, unsmiling.

"What about Reede?"

"What about him?"

"I've seen how the Source treats him. Do you care anything about what happens to him?" Sparks asked, remembering what he'd seen pass between them, when he showed them what the water of death could do.

The moment stretched like an impossibly sustained note, before Niburu said roughly, "Yeah. I guess we do," and Ananke nodded again. "I guess it matters a lot. . . ." Niburu looked surprised.

Sparks took a deep breath. "When the Source gets what he wants—or even if he doesn't—he'll probably kill them both."

"He won't kill Reede," Niburu protested. "Reede's too valuable."

"Maybe," Sparks said, with relentless logic. "Maybe you'll all live to a ripe old age, and you'll spend the rest of your lives in slavery, watching the Source break your friend's spirit and destroy his soul. Or maybe not— If the Source decides to kill Reede, what do you think he'll want to do with both of you?"

They looked at him.

"Reede wants out of there, doesn't he?"

"Yeah. Oh, yeah. . . ." Niburu nodded. "We all do. But it's like you said: the Source is too powerful."

"They'll be expecting Gundhalinu to try something. They won't be expecting this. If Reede loves my daughter the way you say he does, I think he'll help us once we're in, even if he wouldn't try it on his own."

Niburu rubbed his face. "By the Holy Hands," he said. "You know you'd be committing suicide—? And you're asking me to do it too."

"It's my daughter," he said. "And it's your choice."

Niburu and Ananke put their heads together, muttering, while Tor stroked the Ondinean's pet, staring at the tabletop. Life went on, entirely meaningless, in the room beyond her half-frowning profile. "Sparks," Tor said, glancing at him suddenly, "even if you get them out and survive, what'll you do then?"

"Bring them back here."

"But they weren't safe here, in the first place—" She broke off.

"They will be if Gundhalinu has enough warning. Will you go to him—go to Moon? Give them the message Kirard Set gave me . . . tell them everything you know about him, while you're at it," Sparks said sourly. "Then tell them the rest of it: where I've gone. Tell him they have to be ready to protect us all, when we get back. Gundhalinu will understand what he has to do. Give him this—" He handed her Reede's pendant.

"And the tape?" she murmured, taking the pendant.

He looked down. "Use your judgment," he said finally. "She's their daughter too."

"What?" She stared at him; he watched her disbelief fade. "Oh," she said.

He looked back at Niburu and Ananke.

"What about the water of death?" Niburu said. "What about when it runs out?"

"We'll get a sample. We'll make more. There must be a way to keep them alive until we can; we'll find it. If we can get in and get them out, we'll have all the backup we need to stay free, and stay alive. Are you willing to try it?"

They glanced at each other again. At last Niburu nodded, and then Ananke did. "We'll take you to Ondinee," Niburu said. "After that . . ." He shrugged. "We'll see. We leave tomorrow." He glanced at Tor, with sudden melancholy coming into his eyes. He sighed.

Sparks nodded. "I'll be waiting, wherever and whenever you say."

"Tor?" Ananke said hesitantly. Tor looked away from Niburu, facing him. "Keep the quoll for me, will you . . . until we come back," he added, self-consciously. "You know what they like. . . ." He began to take off the sling he wore over his shoulder.

Tor studied him. "Yeah," she murmured. "Sure. I'll take good care of it for you . . . until you get back. Until you all get back." She looked at Niburu again, with a smile that held nothing but sorrow. She gathered the quoll up in her arms, the pendant still clutched in her fist. She slipped out of the booth and left them, without another word.

TIAMAT: Carbuncle

"Father of all my grandfathers! You cannot do this, BZ. You cannot continue this new ban on hunting mers. It's political suicide!"

Gundhalinu looked at the time, got up from his seat, leaving the security of his desk/terminal behind as he started toward the door. He stopped, midway across the office, face to face with his Commander of Police. "I have no choice, Vhanu."

"The Judiciate is livid. The Central Committee is demanding—"

"I know what they are demanding," he said evenly.

"We'll be replaced. The entire government, just as I warned you—" Vhanu's hands jerked with frustration.

"Then so be it."

"Why are you doing this?" Vhanu demanded. "I don't understand it!"

"As I told the Judiciate—the mers are migrating toward the city. It makes them completely vulnerable to us. Until I know why they are doing that, the hunts must stop." He started for the door.

"I mean *why*, BZ?" Vhanu said, lapsing from Tiamatan into Sandhi. "Why? Thou're not the same person I came to this world with. What has this place done to three? Thou're acting like a madman—" Vhanu caught his arm.

"I have no choice," he repeated, not making eye contact. "Use Tiamatan when you speak, please, NR. I've asked you before to remember that." He removed his arm from the other's man's grasp, and went on across the office.

"Where are you going?" Vhanu asked, as Gundhalinu opened the door.

"I have some personal business to attend to." He heard the coldness in his own voice, unable to feel anything as he said it, as if all the heat of anger and frustration and hope had finally died inside him, and let him freeze to death. He left the office without even regret.

He made his way down the Street into the heart of the Maze, seeing its once-empty stores filled with local and imported goods, its alleys bright with fresh paint. It was not as he remembered it from his youth, yet: hung with colored lights and pennants, with music and street entertainers and gambling hells on every corner—a never-ending feast for the senses. Then, when the Black Gates had ruled the Hegemony's interstellar travel, Tiamat's proximity to its Gate had made Carbuncle a crossroads and a stopover. It would probably never have that kind of importance, or notoriety, again; no doubt it was just as well. But it would have its fair share of the Hegemony's benefits. He had kept that promise to himself, at least. He had brought the future back to Tiamat, and he had brought justice with it; he could be—he should be—proud of himself for that.

He glanced into a shop window as he stepped off of the tram, and found his reflection there, superimposed on a display of electronics equipment. He looked away again, suddenly feeling as formless and empty as his reflection. The problems he had come here ready to solve had not been that difficult, after all. The real problem was one he had never dreamed of, and he knew now that the potential consequences were even more terrible than he had realized when he first learned the truth.

The more he thought about the failure of the sibyl mind, the more he realized that he had been witnessing its symptoms for years: the increase in obscure or flawed responses, answers that were incomplete or actually wrong. He had initiated a datasearch for similar incidents; it had taken him months to get all the relevant reports. But as the data began to pile up, he had been stunned by the number of recorded failures; stunned by their geometric increase just within his lifetime.

And his search had revealed something completely unexpected, and far more frightening: reports of the sibyls themselves being affected—failing to go into Transfer, being stricken by seizures. It was only then that he had understood what the complete failure of the sibyl net would do, not just to the process and comfort of the civilizations that relied on it, but to the thousands, or possibly millions, of sibyls whose minds and bodies functioned as the neurons of its star-spanning brain. They would be doomed along with it, to death or madness. . . .

He looked down at his trefoil, away again, feeling cold in the pit of his stomach. The sibyls were carriers for a form of smartmatter, and so were the mers. The artificial intelligence that controlled the sibyl net was almost certainly smartmatter too. He had seen what failed smartmatter had done to World's End . . . he knew what it had done to his mother, who had found it buried like a time bomb in ancient ruins. If the sibyl computer failed, he knew what smartmatter would do to Carbuncle. There would be no Carbuncle anymore, only a seething, nightmare landscape—and perhaps no Tiamat either, as far as human habitation was concerned.

He had not confided his worst fears even to Moon. He had not revealed his data to anyone else. He could not. He could not explain why it meant anything, without sounding like he was deranged. He was sure that Vanamoinen was the key they needed to unlock the secret of the mers . . . but Kullervo still had not contacted him. He no longer had Kitaro to rely on; if Reede didn't come back on his own, soon, he did not know how they would find a solution before it was too late, and everything Vhanu had predicted came to pass. And that would be only the beginning of the end. . . .

He stopped walking as he found himself at his destination, the entrance to the club called Starhiker's. He stared up at the gaudy, gaming-hell facade, trying to shake off his mood; unable to stop reading its invitation to mindless pleasure as the punchline of a monstrous cosmic joke.

He looked down again, feeling suddenly self-conscious as he forced himself to go on inside. He had never had any interest in gaming clubs, except in his former capacity as a Blue. He did not especially like losing, and he did not much enjoy activities that did not add to the sum of his knowledge or produce some tangible finished product. Now, in the full uniform of a Chief Justice, in the full light of day, he felt more out of place than he would have thought possible.

Business was slow, because it was still only midafternoon; people noticed as he came in. Customers glanced up from their drinks, away from the simulations, with vague apprehension, as if they imagined that he had come to close the place down. When he did nothing but stand motionless inside the entrance, they gradually went back to minding their own business.

A heavy-duty work servo approached him, and said, "Good day, Justice Gundhalinu. If you will follow me, Tor Starhiker is waiting to see you." It started away again.

He followed, keeping his surprise to himself. He supposed that it must be employed as some kind of bouncer; it was not the sort of servomech one generally found acting as a greeter in a club. It led him through a bangle-curtained doorway into a narrow, empty hall; up a flight of stairs to Tor Starhiker's private apartment.

"Hello, Justice." She was sitting on a reclining couch, an offworld relic from the old days. She leaned on the ornate headrest with casual insouciance—doing her best, he thought, not to look as if his presence made her uncomfortable. She had an animal on the pillows beside her. She stroked it gently, while it regarded him with black, shiny eyes. "I'm glad you could make it." Something passed over her face like a shadow, as if she had suddenly remembered why she had asked him to come.

He nodded, feeling an unpleasant tightness in his chest. He glanced away, searching the room, taking in its bizarre contrasts, shelves and tabletops cluttered with mementos that ranged from the exquisite to the awful, a visual history of their owner's ironic and unpredictable journey through life. Another time he would have enjoyed looking at them, he realized; a little regretful, a little surprised at himself. But not today. "Is the Queen here?" Tor's note, delivered to him at home by a hand messenger, had said that she needed to see them both, urgently, today. Nothing about why. The very unexpectedness of it had been enough to make him come.

"I'm here, BZ."

He turned to see Moon step through the doorway from the next room; was surprised as she came to him and kissed him, in full view of Tor Starhiker. He raised his head, looking at Tor, checking her reaction.

She smiled at the look on his face. "Seeing you two together twenty years ago shocked me, Justice. It doesn't anymore. . . . I used to run Persiponë's for the Source."

He started, not with recognition, but with memory. He looked back at Moon, who nodded, with a rueful smile of her own.

He shook his head, resigned. "But still—" he murmured, looking again at Tor.

"It's too late for discretion, BZ," Moon said quietly. "What's between us is the reason for our being here."

He nodded, suddenly apprehensive again. "What's this about?"

"You'd better sit down," Tor said.

He took a seat beside Moon on the brocade cushions of an aging, imported loveseat. He put his arm around her, feeling her body drawn tight with tension.

Tor rose from her own seat; her pet wheeped in protest, but sat unmoving, watching her.

"Is that a quoll?" BZ asked, as its voice registered its identity in his brain at last.

"Yes," Tor said, from across the room.

"Where did you get it?" He had not seen one since he had left Four.

"From an Ondinean," Tor answered, standing by a small table with her back turned.

"Named Ananke—?" BZ said, with sudden prescience.

She looked up. "Yes," she said again, and he stiffened. She took something out of a hidden drawer, and came back to put it in his hands. "You know what this is?" It was a solii pendant on a chain: the sign of the Brotherhood. Beside it was a ring, bearing two more soliis side by side. He remembered abruptly where he had seen that peculiar combination before; who had been wearing it. His heart sank. "It's Reede's," he said to Moon. Her face froze. "Where did you get this?" he asked, looking back at Tor.

"From Sparks."

"What's happened to Reede?" he demanded.

She told them, everything. ". . . And Sparks said to tell you, that you've got to be ready to protect them, if—when they get back. That you'd know what he meant, and why."

BZ stirred, not sure whether he had moved through the entire telling. Moon sat beside him like a porcelain statue. Only her eyes were alive, searching the air for some answer, for some escape; for something that did not exist. "Gods," he said at last, pressing his hand to his own eyes. He should never have let Reede leave his house that night. He had miscalculated, Reede had lost control anyway, panicked and run. Now the Source had him—and Ariele.

He looked up again. "Sparks is gone? He's already gone after them?" Tor nodded. He swore, and sank back in his seat. "He said he was going to try to get them both out?"

"That's what he said." Tor nodded again.

"Damnation—!" It was too late even to tell Dawntreader who he was really going after, how high the stakes really were.

"Where is this . . . this tape, of what the water of death does to you?" Moon asked, her voice toneless, her hands tightening over her knees.

Tor glanced away. "It's gone. I saw part of it. Somebody was . . . coming apart. Pieces of flesh . . ." She blanched. "It's worse than anything you can imagine. You don't need to see it. You don't want to see it. You don't." She shook her head.

Moon's eyes brimmed suddenly, but the tears did not fall. "Reede Kullervo wasn't dying when we saw him," she said, almost angrily. "I don't understand. How does this 'water of death' work?"

"It's what happens when it stops working, probably," BZ murmured. "There's no drug I know of called the water of death. But it could be something Reede created himself, trying to make the water of life, from the name. An unstable form of smartmatter." *A nightmare.* He swore. "No wonder he thought we couldn't save him, if the Source holds his supply."

"You mean, there's no other place he can get it?" Tor asked. "Nobody else makes it?"

"No. And I don't even have a sample." He shook his head. Turning back, he saw Moon's stricken look. He touched her arm. "He's got to bring some out with him . . . he's smart enough to realize that. I can get it analyzed and reproduced, if necessary. They can have all they need—"

"If they come back," Moon said faintly. "There must be some way we can help them. You have contacts, BZ—"

"Sparks said that's what the Source would expect," Tor interrupted. "That your—uh, contacts would try to save them. He said the Source would be expecting that. He wanted to be the unexpected."

BZ nodded reluctantly. "But there may still be things that can be done to help him. Our friend Aspundh," he said to Moon. He flexed his hands, which wanted desperately to close around someone's neck.

"But if . . . if he fails—? We can't give the Source what he wants." She looked back at Tor. Her face was starkly, unnaturally calm, as if she had passed completely beyond fear and grief.

"You mean, you don't know what he wants? You don't have it?"

Moon shook her head. "We know what he wants. We're the only ones who do. But we can't give it to him. We *can't*. That's the hell of it. . . ." She shut her eyes.

Tor looked at Moon, uncomprehending. She looked back at Gundhalinu, meeting the same hopeless knowledge in his eyes. He saw compassion, if not understanding, fill her own.

Moon rose from the seat beside him. He stood up, realizing as she did that there was no more to say that could be said here; that there was no point in remaining longer. Tor rose from her own seat, and moved across the room to put her hands on Moon's shoulders. He was surprised to see tears in the woman's eyes. "He'll save her," Tor murmured. "I know he will."

Moon lifted her head, as Tor let her hands fall away. "Or die trying," she whispered. Her own arms hung strengthless at her sides. "Thank you, Tor."

Tor shook her head fiercely. "Don't thank me for this! Spit at me, curse me if you want to, for telling you this—but for gods' sakes, Moon, don't thank me."

Moon smiled, crookedly, and reached up to touch the wetness on Tor's cheek. "Not for that," she said gently. "You know what I mean." She turned away, her head down.

"What are you going to do about Kirard Set?" Tor asked suddenly.

Moon turned back.

"I'll have him arrested," BZ said.

"No." Moon shook her head. Her eyes turned cold. "No. Let me."

"What are you going to do to him?" Tor asked.

Moon hesitated. "The Sea will judge him," she said finally, "by the traditional laws of our people."

Tor nodded, her satisfaction tinged with sudden unease. "Do it," she whispered at last.

They went out of the club together, oblivious to the blaring noise, to the stares of its patrons as they passed.

"BZ—" Moon turned to him, blinking in the sudden brightness of the alley. "Do you remember what Reede said to us, about Sparks?"

BZ shook his head, his mind caught in an endless loop of frustration. He had been sure the next round in the Game that had assembled them all here would move Reede's piece to their side . . . not that Reede would be snatched from the board. He had believed Reede's midnight visit was the safe meeting Kitaro had promised. But it had not been safe—and now the Brotherhood held the key to the riddle of the mers, and the only ransom that might bring Kullervo back was the answer to an impossible question.

Gods, how had it gone so wrong? Had the shielded figures who brought Reede to his door simply bungled Kitaro's orders, because she was no longer there to guide them? Or had it been enemy action, an unexpected move by some unknown player, throwing the crucial game piece back into the hands of Chaos—?

"BZ?" Moon said again.

"No," he murmured distractedly. "I don't know. . . ."

"Reede said that Sparks had been keeping things from us, too. He said, 'Ask him about the mers.' We can't ask him now. But maybe we should search his files."

He looked at her, realizing that her thoughts had been following the same course as his own, without ending up in a blind alley. But he shook his head again. "Sparks has no formal technical training; there's nothing that he could have discovered that would be of any real use."

"Sparks is a very intelligent man," Moon said, looking at him steadily. "He's spent half a lifetime studying the mers. Most of what we know about their speech comes from his work. Don't underestimate him. He's one-quarter Kharemoughi, after all."

BZ's mouth quirked. He looked down. "All right then."

"Come to the palace with me. All his work is there, at the Sibyl College."

He nodded. They made their way back through the city until they reached the palace. Moon led him to the rooms that had become Sparks's living quarters as well as his private office. BZ surveyed the makeshift sleeping area in one corner of the large room, which was already filled nearly to capacity with books and electronics gear. Clothing and personal possessions were piled haphazardly into wooden chests, or shared uneasy shelf space with Sparks's study materials. He felt a sudden guilty empathy for the man whose private life he had already intruded on so profoundly. "Where do we begin?"

Moon hesitated, looking around her as he had; as if she had never seen this room before, or did not recognize what had become of it. "I think maybe you should search his datafiles for information. I'll—I'll search through his things." She looked away from him again at the room, her hands pressing her sides.

He nodded, understanding both her acknowledgment of his particular expertise, and her need to grant her missing husband the dignity of not having his personal possessions picked through by the rival who had replaced him.

He sat down at the terminal, calling it on, requesting a review of its contents, file by file. Occasionally he ordered it to transfer something to his own private files, for more detailed study, but there was nothing he saw that surprised him. Moon moved around and past him quietly, searching through heaps of printouts with scribbled notations, glancing through books and recordings and tapes, separating them into coherent piles of her own making. A part of his mind followed her as she moved, always aware of her, even as another part of him scanned the flow of data passing in front of his eyes. She moved with obsessive single-mindedness through her search, holding her emotions at bay. But every now and then he registered her hesitation, as she came upon something that caught her painfully. He tried at those moments especially not to look at her.

The last of the summary overfiles slid into view before him, finally. He sat up straighter in his seat as the port's synthetic voice informed him, emotionlessly, that the file was code-sealed. "Damn," he murmured.

"What is it?" Moon looked up, across the room.

"There's a file here that's locked."

"And there's a drawer here that's locked—" she said. He watched her pry at it with the curved blade of a scaling knife she found on the desktop. She gave a sudden exclamation as the drawer jumped out at her. Sitting down at the desk, she picked through its contents, which were not visible to him. She held something up; a small handmade pouch, beaded and embroidered, some sort of native crasftsmanship. She laid it on the table; not looking at him, seeming even to have forgotten his presence.

She lifted something else out—a pendant of silver metal on a chain, the perfect match to the one that Reede had worn. This time she looked over her shoulder, holding up the sign of the Brotherhood.

He watched all the kinds of darkness that moved through her eyes as she saw it spinning in the air, knowing now what it symbolized. She let it go; the clatter as it hit the floor was loud in the quiet room. She turned back again, away from his eyes, picking other objects out of the drawer: an offworlder medal, a string of bright glass beads, an ancient calibrator, a child's wooden top. She held the last object a little longer than the rest, before she put it down.

She reached into the drawer again, and removed something hesitantly, as if it were fragile. He saw a lock of pale hair, like the foam on the crest of a wave, sealed in a blown-glass vial. She stared at it, holding it cupped in her hands.

"Yours?" he asked.

She shook her head. "No."

"Arienrhod?" he said gently.

She placed the glass bottle on the desk with exaggerated care. "It could be. It could be Ariele's. . . ." Suddenly the tears that she had refused to let fall were overflowing. Her shoulders shook with silent sobs as she turned away, leaning on the desktop, burying her face in her hands. "I didn't even know she was seeing him." *Reede.* "I could have stopped it! I never really knew her, she was my own child. . . ."

BZ rose from his seat and crossed the room, kneeling down beside her where she sat weeping. "I never knew her at all. . . ." His own sudden grief left him speechless, and he only held her, his head bowed against her shoulder. Her arms moved spasmodically, to tighten around him, and he felt her tears soak his uniform jacket. "I should have stopped him. I had him in my hands!"

"It's not your fault—"

"It's not yours." He lifted his head, forcing her to look at him. "It isn't over yet," he said, somehow keeping his voice steady. "We can't let this paralyze us, we need every minute. . . ."

She nodded, wiping her face on her sleeve, taking a long, tremulous breath. "I know," she murmured. She moved away, out of his arms, straightening her shoulders. She took one more item out of the drawer and laid it on the desk—a book, its cover so worn with use and time that he could not read its title.

Surprised, he picked it up, unable to resist such a curiosity, as he always was. In his youth he had loved books, fascinated by the primitive but profound nature of their information storage, by their ability to cross all technological barriers, by their portability, by their feel and smell. He had read endless Old Empire romances, addicted to the flow of words—the way they let his imagination create its own fantasies of that lost time, instead of forcefeeding him a prepackaged reality created by someone else.

But then he had come to Tiamat, to ancient, mysterious Carbuncle, trying to make his fantasies come true; and for a long time after that, he had had no stomach for reading. And then he had had no time. . . . He flipped the book open, glancing at the title page. It was in Tiamatan, laid out in the universal phonetic alphabet: a book about fugue theory. He thumbed through the soft-edged pages, seeing notes scrawled along the margins in an unfamiliar, unembellished hand. There were mathematical formulas and musical notations side by side, with arrows and question marks and scribbled abbreviations he could not decode. But holding the book, he felt something resonate in the hidden levels of his brain where pure reason met pure inspiration. He closed the book again, looking at Moon. "May I take this?"

"Do you think it's what we've been looking for?" she asked.

"I don't know. But it's worth more study." He glanced away at the terminal's unblinking eye. "Do you know the key codes Sparks used to lock his personal files?"

"I didn't even know he had any files that weren't freely accessible—" She broke off. "I knew so little about them all." She rubbed her eyes distractedly. "He turned his back on all of us, not just me, when he learned . . . It hurt him so much, it took everything away from him. He always loved her more than anyone, I think." *Ariele*. "But he wouldn't even speak to her, anymore." She shook her head. "And now he's gone after her. . . ."

BZ was silent, looking down. He laid his hand gently on her shoulder; she pressed her face against it, closing her eyes.

Someone entered the room, and stopped in surprise. They looked up together, startled, to find Tammis in the doorway staring back at him. BZ withdrew his hand hastily, self-consciously; stood not touching Moon, as their son came into the room.

Tammis stopped again, looking at BZ and back at his mother in unspoken empathy. "They told me you were here," he said. "I have some news—" Moon stiffened. But then his somber expression broke into smiles. The pride and pleasure that filled his face touched them both. "Merovy and I are going to have a baby."

A small sound of disbelief escaped BZ's throat, as Moon's face emptied of all expression.

Tammis took in his mother's stunned expression uncertainly, before he turned to BZ. "We're back together," he said. "We're working it out. And I owe it to you—" He broke off, not saying "Justice," not saying "father." He held out his hand.

"Congratulations." BZ shook his hand; wanting to reach out and embrace him, but not able to . . . suddenly feeling as much of a stranger to his son as his own father had always seemed to him. "I'm honored to hear it," he said.

Tammis smiled, with a fleeting regret that matched his own, before he turned back to his mother. His face fell. "What's wrong—?"

She pressed the back of her hand against her mouth, shaking her head in mute apology; her eyes filled again, suddenly, with tears.

"Sit down, Tammis," BZ said quietly. He explained, keeping his eyes averted, unable to watch either one of them react to the words.

"Mother of Us All—" Tammis murmured, when he was finished.

"I'm sorry, Tammis," Moon whispered, "to ruin your wonderful news." She got up from her seat and crossed the room to him. BZ saw apology for far too many moments like this one fill her face, as she gazed down at her son. But she smiled all at once, the smile that BZ had always remembered. "I can hardly believe it," she said, her smile widening. "Thank you for bringing hope back into this day." Tammis rose from his chair; BZ watched them hold each other in the unselfconscious, loving way he had longed to hold the son he barely knew, as he saw the endless pattern of life unfold before his eyes. A child, he thought, was hope's laughter in the face of existence.

"Do you think Da will be able to bring Ariele back?" Tammis asked, as she let him go at last.

"I don't know." Moon shook her head slightly, glancing at BZ.

"Can you help them?" Tammis said, looking at him too, following her gaze. "Can you send the Police?"

"It isn't that easy," BZ answered. "But by all my ancestors, I'll do everything I can." He glanced away, at the open port in the waiting desk/terminal, and the secrets it refused to give up. "Tammis, do you now anything about—your father's private file codes?" Asking, although he knew it was a futile question, knowing that Tammis and Sparks had never been close.

But Tammis nodded, looking curious. "He used to use runs of mersong." He shrugged, at BZ's look of surprise. "The only time we ever talked much was when I had something new I'd learned about the mers. . . ." He took a flute from the pouch at his belt; BZ realized that he always carried one with him, just as Sparks did. Tammis looked at the fragile shell for a moment, his gaze suddenly distant.

"What is it, Tammis?" Moon said softly.

He looked up at her. "I just wondered," he said, almost inaudibly, "if Da would have gone after me." He lifted his flute, coming toward the place where BZ sat now in front of the unresponding terminal. Tammis played a brief run of notes on the flute; there was no change. He tried another, and another. At last, after he had tried nearly a dozen, the empty face of the port suddenly came alive. The program opened its invisible gates, and data began to pour through.

BZ grinned in triumph, shared his smile for a moment with the boy standing beside him. He looked back at the screen, taking in its flood of symbols, using the techniques Survey had taught him to absorb a visual datafeed almost as rapidly as a direct link. *The mersong as strands of fugue . . .*

Music filled the air around him, as Sparks's program reproduced the strands of a musical web and began to interweave them, while the mathematical equations defining the ever-changing ratios of sounds to one another filled the visuals, expressing relationships within the system. BZ sat, rapt, only vaguely aware of Moon and Tammis behind him as they spoke softly together, and then moved away to go on searching through Sparks's possessions.

When he had witnessed the entire contents of the file, he requested it again, haunted by its configurations. Sparks had found a clue, he was sure of it . . . the mathematical structure of the music was a code, one that resonated in some part of his own brain, in the nonverbal depths of thought where the root of all music and mathematical perception lay.

He watched and listened to the webs of relationship form again on the screen, in the air, inside his mind; beginning to feel a kind of awe take hold of him at the subtle artistry of their creator. And he realized, suddenly, watching the screen, that the music itself was only a carrier: the mathematical information it contained was the critical element. And he knew the significance of those equations, those relationships flashing across the screen . . . he had worked every day for months on similar problems with Reede Kullervo, as they struggled to bring the stardrive plasma under control. The mathematics within the music had to do with the manipulation of smartmatter.

But there were gaping holes in the logic flow, where critical elements had been lost, destroyed along with the mersongs that had contained them. He saw Sparks's tentative attempts to reconstruct the missing elements—the valiant efforts of an intelligent, resourceful mind that lacked the formal mathematical and programming experience to complete the revelation it had begun. An admiration for the accomplishments of Sparks Dawntreader that was not at all grudging filled him. He queried the computer, gave it another set of commands; sending the data into his own computer system with instructions to begin a series of transformational functions on it, to ask it the right questions . . .

"You've found something," Moon said, behind him, and he became aware suddenly that she and Tammis had been standing there, watching him watch the screen for some time. "What is it?"

He looked up at them, letting her see the admiration still in his eyes. "Sparks found it," he said. "The key to the mersong. It's based in fugue theory—" He gestured at the book lying on the desk next to him. "The fabric of the music has mathematical equations woven into it. There is a pure mathematics to music, at the most basic level," he said, seeing the uncomprehending looks on their faces. "Every tone lies in a precise, unchanging relationship to all others. Complex mathematical relationships can be expressed within the structure of a musical composition like a fugue, as if it were a sort of code. Sparks has laid out the basic structures—it's all here. It deals with smartmatter manipulation. I've instructed my own computer system to run a program on it that should be able to recreate the missing segments, and then maybe we'll finally be able to see what problem it exists to solve. . . ."

He looked back at the screen, as the haunting sounds of the mers' calling voices, synthesized but uncannily realistic, filled the air around him.

"You already know the answer," Moon murmured, her voice barely audible above the music.

He turned to look up at her, saw her eyes shining with astonished vision. "What . . . ?"

"The mers are coming toward the city," she said. "There can be only one reason—" She broke off, her eyes finishing the thought her lips could not speak. *It needs them.*

His mouth fell open, as a circuit closed suddenly inside his brain, filling his mind with the light of revelation. "Smartmatter status maintenance . . ." he whispered. "Yes, by all the gods!" *It needs them.* He stumbled up out of his seat and took her in his arms. "It fits together!"

"What are you talking about?" Tammis asked. BZ looked at him, as Moon did, with useless apology. "We can't explain it to you, Tammis," Moon said, looking down. "Not yet."

"But you think it will help Ariele?" he asked.

She looked back at BZ, and now it was her doubt and sudden desolation that were reflected in his own face. "I don't know," he said at last. "We have to believe it will."

Moon shook off her mood, letting him go as she faced Tammis again. "It's late. . . . Go home to Merovy, and give her my congratulations, and my love." She smiled; the smile stopped. "But don't tell her what we did here today, or why. Don't tell anyone; please, Tammis."

He nodded, his face intent. He embraced her one last time, in farewell.

"Thank you for your help," BZ said, as the boy looked at him.

Tammis nodded again. "And thank you for yours," he said, his voice husky. He turned away, starting toward the door.

Moon watched him go, with a forlorn, wondering expression. "Lady bless them," she said, almost absently. She sighed, closing her eyes. "They say . . . they say the Mother loves children above all else. . . ." Her voice faded. "Lady help them all: my children, and Yours." She opened her eyes again; but there was no hope in them. She looked up at him. "Why did Tammis thank you?"

BZ shrugged. "For being an outside observer," he said, glancing away. He put his arms around her, because that at least was once again his right. He smiled down at her suddenly, ruefully. "I'm too young to be a grandfather," he said.

She looked back at him, with a smile as sudden and as bittersweet. "Not on this world," she said. "You're on Tiamat now, you know." She looked down again. "Stay with me tonight, BZ." She pressed her face against the cloth of his jacket.

He nodded, knowing that he should not, but knowing that he could no more bear to spend this night alone with his hope and his fears than she could.

She led him through the cold, rococo halls of the palace to her bedroom, neither of them having any appetite for a late supper. He lay down beside her in the bed, sighing as the bird-down mattress embraced him like his lover's arms. Having no strength left for lovemaking, either, they only held each other, for a long time, saying little, trying to think of even less. Moon left a lamp burning on their bedside table, unable to bear the oppressive power of utter darkness.

She slept, finally, finding peace in his arms. And watching over her, with the breathing warmth of her body pressed close against his own, he felt his own eyes grow heavy, and at last he slept.

He did not know whether it was hours or only minutes later when the doors of the room burst open with an unceremonious crash, jolting him awake. He sat up in bed, sleep-fogged and befuddled. Moon pushed up onto her elbow beside him, pulling the covers over her breasts as they confronted half a dozen men in blue Police uniforms.

"Vhanu—?" BZ said incredulously, shielding his eyes with his arm as the lights came up in the room. "What the hell are you doing here? What in the name of a thousand gods is the meaning of this!"

Vhanu stood looking down at them where they lay, side by side. What Gundhalinu saw then in the eyes of his former friend—the pity, the unforgiving censure, the desperate resolve—were all the answer he needed. Vhanu straightened his shoulders as if he were about to salute, but he did not. "Justice Gundhalinu, I have come to arrest you."

"On what charges?" BZ asked, still not entirely certain that he was not having a nightmare.

Vhanu's mouth pulled down. "It is my . . . difficult and painful duty, Justice, to inform you that you are charged with treason."

TIAMAT: Carbuncle

Moon followed the taciturn officer through the blur of motion that was the interior of Police headquarters, staring straight ahead at his uniformed back. All around her she sensed the surprise spreading outward, like the wash from a ship's prow—the gossip, the speculation, the curious stares: *It's the Queen. She's come to see Gundhalinu, come to see her lover. Caught them bare-assed together, committing treasonable acts . . . Gundhalinu the hero, Gundhalinu the traitor: What does the Mother-lovers' Queen want with him now that he's locked up? . . .*

She had asked the duty sergeant to let her see Chief Justice Gundhalinu. He had shaken his head and said, "No one is permitted to see the prisoner." *The prisoner.* No indication of what he had been, until yesterday; what he had meant to his people, all he had done for the Hegemony. She had demanded to see the Chief Inspector. He had handed her over to one of his officers, and sent her through this gauntlet of smirking gossip.

She passed through it, scarcely even registering the unwanted attention, her mind preoccupied with losses and questions of such magnitude that the mockery of the strangers surrounding her was reduced to the meaningless noise that it was; until the voices began to fall silent, as if they realized it too, and she passed beyond them.

"The Queen to see you, ma'am." Her guide showed her into an office, saluted, and left, shutting the door behind him.

Jerusha PalaThion looked up at her in surprise, over an armload of supplies. Jerusha dropped the supplies unceremoniously into an empty crate.

Moon hesitated, half-frowning. "What are you doing?" she said. There were other boxes piled up beside the desk/terminal, already filled; the shelves and storage units of the office were virtually empty.

"I'm clearing out my desk," Jerusha answered, her voice heavy with irony. "The Commander of Police informed me this morning that he had charged BZ with treason, and declared martial law. And that after today is over I will no longer be serving as Chief Inspector."

"Lady's Tits!" Moon struck the closed door with her fist, as the memory of last night filled her. She sagged against the ancient, unyielding surface, suddenly strengthless. "Damn him! May he rot in any hell he chooses." She looked up again, to find complete agreement in the other woman's eyes. "Have you seen BZ—have you spoken with him? Is he all right?"

Jerusha shook her head. "Vhanu won't let anyone near him; particularly not anyone who might be tempted to help him. By the Boatman, I've tried." She sat down in her desk chair, resting her forehead on her hands.

Moon crossed the room. "You said he's declared martial law? What gives him that right?"

"He's second in the power structure after the Chief Justice. With BZ stripped of his office, Vhanu's in charge. He's calling it a state of emergency, until he receives orders from the Central Committee, or they send a new Chief Justice. It basically empowers him to do anything." Jerusha's face turned grim.

"And if I object—?" Moon broke off, turning as the office door opened suddenly behind her.

"Then I have the power to enforce my decisions," the Commander of Police said evenly. He made a small, correct bow. "Lady." He looked away from her, toward Jerusha. Jerusha rose from her seat, and saluted stiffly. He returned the salute, expressionless.

Moon felt her face burn. "Are you threatening to attack my people?" she said, shaken by anger.

"Not unless you give me cause." His eyes were as impenetrable as obsidian.

"And what do you mean by that?" She stood away from the desk, her arms rigidly at her sides.

"I intend to resume hunting the mers. If you or your people give me trouble over it, I will retaliate. Needless to say, your people will be the ones on the losing end of any conflict, not the Hegemony."

"Is this what 'autonomy' means to the Hegemony, then?" Moon said. "That you don't interfere in our internal affairs, unless you feel like it? Unless we don't put your right to exploit our world before our culture and beliefs or even the right of the mers—who have more claim to this world than any of us—simply to live and not die?"

"A state of emergency, and martial law, are justified in a situation of extreme civil unrest or strife," Vhanu said tonelessly. "Our purpose here is to keep the peace."

"I have been told that your people value honor above everything else. I see that I was misinformed," Moon murmured. She felt more than heard Jerusha draw a sudden breath; saw Vhanu's eyes flicker, and knew that she had stung him.

Vhanu's mouth thinned. "I would walk softly, if I were you, Lady. Your much-prized autonomy is the only thing that protects you from the same charges I brought against the Chief Justice."

She flushed. "You had no right—"

"I had no right—?" His hand jerked, fisted. "You had no right to seduce him, to use your body to make him give you anything you wanted! He had no right, to turn his back on his own people! He had no right to be so weak. Someone had to stop this madness, before he ruined everything we had here. I was his best friend, damn you—!" A tremor shook him, as if he had to restrain himself from laying hands on her.

"But only for as long as he gave you everything you wanted," she said, softly, coldly. "He loves me, and I love him. But he made the choices he did not because he is my lover, but because he is an honorable man."

Vhanu looked at her, his lips twitching, for a long moment. He muttered something in Sandhi, finally, glancing away. She translated the sour words: *barbarian whore*.

In Sandhi, she said, "Would you prefer to speak your own language, Commander Vhanu? I understand it fairly well."

He looked back at her; the scattering of pale freckles across his brown face flushed blood-red. He took a deep breath. "I think there is very little left for us to say, in any language, Lady," he answered, in Tiamatan. He began to turn away.

"I want to see him," Moon said. "You can't deny me the right to see him."

He turned back to her. "I'm afraid that's impossible. He's no longer here."

She froze. "What?"

"He's gone." Vhanu shrugged. "Back to Kharemough, to face charges before the High Court. If he remained here, there was too much threat of strife, so I had him deported immediately."

She felt his satisfaction tighten around her throat, as if it were his hands. "You mean," she forced the words out, "that there was too much risk that he was right; that his voice would be heard, and everyone who heard it would know."

"Walk softly, Lady," he repeated, frowning more deeply. He bowed to her again, with perfect grace. He turned away, opening the door; stopped, turning back. "By the way," he said. "I know now that your fanatical predictions about our decimating the mer population were not only superstitious rubbish but complete lies. My people tell me that the waters are teeming with mers. Their numbers are far from depleted."

"No!" She started forward. "That isn't the truth, there are no more mers— Search further, search all the seas; you have the means. The seas will be empty."

He shook his head, and his eyes pitied her, as if she were beneath contempt. He went out the door without answering.

Moon stood motionless in the center of the room, until her moment of desperate rage passed. She turned back, then, to face Jerusha.

Jerusha sat down again behind her desk, her dark eyes filled with questions, none of them reassuring. She reached into her pocket for a pack of iestas, put a handful into her mouth, chewing them to quiet her nerves.

Moon moved to a seat and dropped heavily into it. "BZ can't be gone," she said, studying her hands, which lay in her lap like dying insects. "How can it have happened? It's impossible."

"Nothing is impossible," Jerusha murmured tonelessly.

"This is." Moon raised her head. "He had to be here. He was meant to be. They both were. . . . We were all in place. And suddenly, just when we were ready—they're gone." She shook her head, feeling as if she had been beaten, as if she were bleeding inside.

Jerusha looked at her, and Moon saw an expression on the other woman's face that she had not seen in years. "Gods," Jerusha said. "It's been speaking to you again, hasn't it—the sibyl mind? The way it did when you told me you were going to become Queen."

She nodded, mute.

"Who is the third person?"

"Reede . . . Reede Kullervo."

Jerusha's eyes widened; she looked away, frowning. "He works for the Source.

BZ wanted him picked up . . . wanted it done unofficially. Kitaro was handling it, before she . . ." Her gaze came back to Moon. "What happened?"

Moon told her how it had begun, pulling her raveled thoughts back together.

"And what were the three of you supposed to do?" Jerusha asked, when she was finished.

"It—has to do with saving the mers." Moon shook her head. "But that's all I can tell you. Except that they're the key to something. If that merkiller Vhanu—" She broke off. "If he only knew what he's done, not just to the mers, not just to us, but to himself. . . ."

Jerusha sighed. "So the Hedge has Gundhalinu hostage, and the Source has Reede—"

"And Ariele." She forced the words out.

"Ariele?" Jerusha paled. "Why, by all the gods?"

"She was involved with Reede. I didn't even know. . . . The Source took them both. Because of . . . what I know that I can't tell." She told the rest of it, numbed by the words as she spoke them, until finally her voice held no emotion at all. "They're all gone. . . . And I don't know if any of them will ever come back."

Jerusha sat back in her chair and dropped a remote into a box; looked up again, bleak-eyed. "Is there anything at all that we can do, right now?"

"Nothing." Moon shook her head. "Nothing even makes sense to me, right now." Her body seemed to have turned to stone as she sat there, until now it was too heavy, too inert, ever to rise from her seat again. "Nothing will make any difference."

Jerusha leaned forward abruptly, and switched on her comm. "Prawer! In my office. Immediately."

Inspector Prawer appeared in the doorway bare seconds later. He saluted. "Ma'am?" He made a brief bow in Moon's direction; she looked away from his glance.

"You're in charge here, until the Commander names a new Chief Inspector. Have my belongings sent to my . . ." she glanced at Moon, "to the local constabulary headquarters." Moon looked up, suddenly feeling something stir inside her that was not another tentacle of despair. "I want my old job back," Jerusha said.

"It's yours." Moon pushed to her feet, glancing at Prawer, and back at Jerusha.

Jerusha came around the corner of her desk, tossing Prawer a packet of keycards. "Here. Tell Commander Vhanu . . ." She paused, and spat an iesta pod into the trash basket. Moon saw Prawer's mouth twitch. "Tell him . . . he's *mekrittu*. Like all his ancestors before him, back to the first."

Prawer looked disbelief at her. "Gods, I can't say that to the Commander—"

"Quote me," she said. "That's a direct order." She hesitated. "And tell the force that Gundhalinu's gone."

"He's gone?" Prawer repeated, his face going slack. She nodded. "Yes, Ma'am." He drew himself up and saluted again. "Consider it done."

She returned his salute; he passed them, heading toward her desk, as she walked with Moon toward the door.

Jerusha took a deep breath as they stood outside Police Headquarters at last. "It feels good to get the stink of that place out of my head." She looked behind her at the building entrance, at the sign above it in both Tiamatan script and Sandhi hieroglyphics.

"What is *mekrittu*?" Moon asked finally.

Jerusha smiled, the line of her mouth sweet-and-sour. "It's the lowest of the lower classes, on Kharemough. It's like calling a Summer 'merkiller,' raised to the tenth." Her face hardened again. "The only real mistake Gundhalinu ever made was thinking that tunnel-visioned bigot Vhanu was his equal." She looked down, spat out another seed pod, and followed Moon, who was already moving on toward the alley's entrance. "Moon, do you want to know what I think?"

"Yes." Moon kept her own eyes fixed on the way ahead, knowing that it was her only choice: to keep moving, to keep ahead of the fate that was closing in on her, trying to bring her down. "Tell me. I need a parallax view. Every way out I see is blocked by a wall of fire—" She looked up, remembering Vhanu's threat, and the fire in the sky that could destroy her world if she pushed the Hegemony too far.

"Then slow down." Jerusha's hand fell on her arm, holding her back. "Slow down." Moon slowed, looking at her. "Wait, until we learn more," Jerusha said. "BZ has friends—not just here, but also on Kharemough. He could come back to us on his own. . . ." But her voice doubted it. Moon remembered the levels of Survey, the schisms hidden within its seeming unity. "Or if Sparks comes back with Kullervo and Ariele, Kullervo may be the key . . . the fire to fight fire with."

"I need water, to put it out forever." Moon rubbed her arms. She began to walk again toward the brightness of the Street, feeling her mind slowly beginning to unlock and function. "Either way, it will be weeks—it could be months, before we'll know. And all the while mers will die." And with every mer's death, the sibyl mind would die by inches. . . . She shook her head. "I know you're right; I can only wait and see. But I'm not an empty shell. BZ was going to run an analysis of data Sparks had developed on the mersong. I can analyze that data myself."

"Your systems are interfaced with the Hegemony's governmental computer net, aren't they?" Jerusha asked.

"Yes." Moon looked over at her. "Why?"

"Martial law. I don't know what that's going to do to your access. Vhanu could restrict your usage, if he wants to make your life difficult. He can probably monitor anything you do with it, in any case."

Moon looked away; touched the spines of the trefoil she wore with wary fingers. "I have access to a far better system than the one in this city; Vhanu doesn't control my use of the sibyl net. And I think that I know now what questions I have to ask it, to get the answers I need. I'm going to call a session of the Sibyl College, and explain what I can to them about this . . . situation." Her throat closed over the word. "Jerusha, what will they do to BZ, if—"

Jerusha glanced at her. "The Hegemony doesn't have a death penalty," she said, looking straight ahead again. "But they have some prisons that make their occupants wish there was one. . . . But it won't be one of those, for him," she went on hastily. "He has a lot of influence."

"He has a lot of enemies, then," Moon said softly. She glanced over her shoulder, down Blue Alley. "I'll get him back. By the Lady and all their gods . . . I'll make them pay, if it takes me the rest of my life." She looked ahead again. "And if I fail, everyone will pay. . . ."

Jerusha looked at her, and said nothing more.

They reached the alley's end, where her escort of constables waited. She informed them of Jerusha's return; they greeted the news with smiling nods. "Gives us somebody to talk to the Blues in their own tongue again, eh?" the constable named Clearwater murmured. "It's all Sandhi to me, Commander," he said to Jerusha, and laughed.

Her own mouth pulled up in a wry smile. She turned to Moon, her eyes intent. "Is there anything I can do for you, now that I'm back in your service, Lady? Anything at all—"

Moon hesitated, searching through the images that filled her mind, searching for one that she could alter. "Yes," she said finally. "I want you to arrest Kirard Set Wayaways."

Jerusha started, and then nodded. "I'll see to it," she said. "Immediately. I'll take Clearwater with me, if that's all right with you."

Moon nodded. She held out her hand, and Jerusha shook it, in the traditional way. "Welcome home." Moon smiled, at last.

Jerusha made her way to Kirard Set Wayaways' townhouse, followed by Clearwater, who didn't ask any questions although she could see that he wanted to. She was sure Wayaways was in the city; she had seen him just yesterday, window-shopping in the Maze.

She knocked on his front door, waited, suddenly seeing in her mind an unexpected image from the time when Arienrhod had ruled—seeing Kirard Set Wayaways, as he stood waiting by the Pit, when the winds had still moaned hungrily; waiting for Police Inspector PalaThion and Sergeant Gundhalinu with a wind-taming bone whistle in his hand. She still remembered, after all these years, the smile on his youthful, perfect face as he saw the anxiety on their own faces; how he had laughed at them behind his eyes, letting the wind nip their heels as he led them across the span to their audience with the Snow Queen. She realized suddenly that she wanted to see their positions reversed; still wanted it, needed it, after all these years.

The door opened. But it was not Kirard Set who greeted her, it was his wife, Tirady Graymount. Jerusha felt surprise at the depth of her own disappointment.

"Chief Inspector PalaThion . . ." Tirady Graymount murmured, leaning against the jamb of the open door a little unsteadily. Her pupils seemed abnormally dilated; Jerusha wondered what kind of drugs she had been taking. She glanced past Jerusha's shoulder at the constable, and her sour expression turned quizzical. "What do you want?"

"I've come to arrest your husband, Tirady Graymount," Jerusha said.

The woman blinked, as if she were having a hard time processing the information. "The Hegemony is arresting him?"

"Not the Hegemony." Jerusha glanced down at the blue uniform she still wore. She looked up again, and shrugged. "I work for the Queen now."

"Oh," Tirady Graymount said, as if that explained everything. "Well, my husband isn't home. I'm sorry you missed him. . . ." She smiled oddly.

"I don't suppose you'd have any idea where I can find him?" Jerusha asked, already anticipating the predictable response.

But Tirady Graymount pushed away from the doorframe, in a motion like windblown grass. "Why, yes, I do." She smoothed back her fair, gray-salted hair. "He's gone down to Persiponë's—the club. On business," she added, and her smile this time was one of surpassing cruelty. "You know where it is. If you hurry, you'll catch him there."

"Thank you for your cooperation." Jerusha kept the irony and surprise out of her voice.

"It's my pleasure," Tirady Graymount murmured, as they turned away. "Good day to you." Her door closed sharply behind them.

Jerusha wasted no time getting to Persiponë's, and few thoughts along the way on the state of Wayaways' marriage. She held more than enough reasons in her own mind why Kirard Set could drive someone to drugs, or acts of petty revenge.

They entered Persiponë's calculated mouth of darkness, stood blinking on the threshold, as everyone else did. She felt another odd frisson as the past whispered through her present like a fever-spirit. Persiponë's Hell looked exactly as it had looked during Arienrhod's reign. It was like something that existed outside of time; appearing, disappearing, reappearing again. Then, as now, it had been a front for the Source, the drug boss Arienrhod had turned to when she had tried to commit genocide on the Summers. The Blues had stopped it—Jerusha had stopped the Source, herself. But somehow the Source had slipped through their grasp, folded himself up into his own personal singularity and disappeared.

And now he was back in business on Tiamat, and he was holding Moon's child, for a ransom nobody could even name. If she had stopped him then, for good, this wouldn't be happening. But she had failed, and she was powerless, this time, to do anything at all about it. But there was still Kirard Set.

A woman in a slit-backed black gown was coming toward them, wearing a black wig netted with silver, her face so ornately painted that it was impossible to tell who she actually was. She was called Persiponë, and she looked the same as she had twenty years ago—except that twenty years ago it had been Tor Starhiker beneath the paint, fronting for the club's real owner. But the Summer Queen did not offer them protection from the Blues, and this was not Tor Starhiker, only some anonymous hireling playing at hostess.

"Welcome, Chief Inspector. How may I serve you?" Persiponë smiled, her face glowing with eerie phosphorescence.

"Bring me Kirard Set Wayaways," Jerusha said flatly.

Persiponë nodded, pressing her hands together like a gesture of worship, and disappeared into the depths of the club. Jerusha waited, unmoving and unmoved; at her side, Clearwater whistled in awe as he watched the action unfold around them. "I've been wasting my pay in the wrong places," he said.

After a few moments Jerusha saw someone coming purposefully toward them; not Persiponë, and not Wayaways. *TerFauw.* Her brain put a name to him. He was the one who actually oversaw the club's functions; one of the Source's lieutenants. He was Newhavenese, from her homeworld, though from the look of him he hadn't been back there in a long time either.

"What do you want here?" he said, without even the pretense of civility.

"I want Kirard Set Wayaways," she answered, looking up at him. She was tall enough that she didn't look up to meet a man's eyes often, but he was considerably taller, and massive. It made her feel uncomfortable, vulnerable, especially when she considered that this was how most women were forced to feel whenever they confronted a man.

"What makes you think I know where he is? He could be anywhere on the Street," TerFauw said, in thickly accented Tiamatan. He gestured away into the crowd.

"His wife said he was here. On business." She pointed back the way TerFauw had come, toward the hidden rooms and secret activities she knew lay behind him.

"He could be gone already."

"Uh-uh." She shook her head. "If he was, you'd say so. Bring him out."

TerFauw grunted. "Tell me why the Hedge wants him," he said.

"Not the Hedge. The Queen. His own people."

He pushed his twisted lip into an unpleasant smile. "Then what does she want him for?"

"Take a guess," Jerusha said.

He nodded, thoughtful. "That's good enough." He glanced over his shoulder, lifting his hand. "Bring him out," he said, speaking to the air.

As she watched, three men appeared out of a shadow-black opening in the wall; the one in the middle was Wayaways, and he didn't look happy to be there. The others were armed; she couldn't see their weapons, but she read it in the way they moved.

"The Summer Queen wants to see you," TerFauw said tonelessly, as Wayaways and his escort joined them.

"The Queen—?" Wayaways broke off, and Jerusha saw the look she had waited to see slowly forming on his face.

"Let's go," she said, smiling the smile she remembered.

"No—" He turned to TerFauw, grabbing him by the front of his jerkin. "You can't let them take me away! I'm one of you, for gods' sakes! I'm a stranger far from home, I'm a Brother, the Source promised me the Brotherhoo—"

TerFauw drove his fist into Wayaways' stomach, as casually as another man might have shaken hands, doubling him up. He gestured again, and his two men dragged Wayaways upright. "You go to your Queen, Motherlover," he whispered, into the face of Wayaways' stricken betrayal. "And you better beg her not to let you come back here again. Ever." His finger flicked Wayaways suddenly, excruciatingly, in the eye; Wayaways shrieked, covering it with his hands.

Jerusha took a deep breath. She forced her hand to move away from her own weapon and hang loose at her side, as TerFauw turned his back on them and strode away. Wayaways' guards followed him, wordlessly.

Jerusha waited until Wayaways' screaming had subsided, until his hands had dropped away from his streaming eye. "Come on," she said, to his colorless face and vacant stare. "Let's go."

He went with her, without protest.

KHAREMOUGH: Orbital Hub #1

"Your visitor is waiting, Gundhalinu-ken."

"Thank you." Gundhalinu moved past the guard through the doorway to the visitor's room. They addressed him as "Gundhalinu-ken" here, because it was the only title he had which was not in limbo since his arrest. The sibyl tattoo was clearly visible above the loose neck of his detention-center coveralls, although they had taken away his trefoil: *It could be used as a weapon.*

The room was small and brightly lit, with calm green walls and a single table positioned at its center. There was carpeting under his feet as he walked forward, there were pictures on the walls. And running across the center of the room, through the middle of the table, there was an invisible force barrier separating him from the woman who stood waiting at the other side.

"Dhara—" he said. The full impact of all that had happened to him in the past weeks hit him like a blow, leaving him dazed. He stopped, staring back at her, at the child she held in her arms. He realized suddenly that he had gone numb since his arrest; that he had been in a state of shock, unable to face the reality of his situation or his reaction to it, until now.

"BZ?" she murmured, and he saw in her eyes the depths of uncertainty that he remembered, always hiding beneath the surface of her bright calm when she came near him. Her hesitation goaded him forward to take a seat at the table, encouraging her to do the same.

She sat down across from him, conservatively dressed in a long robe and slacks, her hair caught up with clips into graceful wings, the way he had liked it best. She settled the baby on the table with a sackful of toys; the baby reached eagerly for the bag, dumping out its contents. "Mine!" he said.

BZ watched in fascination as the child sat among the toys like someone who had just discovered treasure. The baby tried them on, twisted them, banged them on the table surface, oblivious to the absurd and tender smiles suddenly on the faces of the two people watching him at play.

"How do thou like thy son?" Pandhara said at last. She reached out, stroking the little boy's hair; he glanced up at her, distracted, and offered her a bright, star-filled rattle. "BT Gundhalinu. . . . But it's so stuffy. I call him Little Bit," she said. The baby looked up again, hearing his name. "Big Little Bit . . ." she said, touching the tip of his nose with her finger. He smiled and put his own small, stubby-fingered hands up in the air. "So big," he said.

"He's beautiful," BZ murmured. "Even more beautiful than the holos thou sent me. Gods, how he's changed—"

"Babies do that," she said, softly and a little sadly.

"And so do our fortunes," he murmured, not meaning to.

She looked up at him, away again quickly.

"It's not as if we didn't know this could happen."

She nodded, keeping his gaze this time. "He has thy eyes."

BZ took a deep breath, remembering another boy with the same eyes, half a galaxy away. "Yes," he said. "I think he does."

She nudged the baby toward him across the table. "See," she whispered. "It's thy father." BZ leaned forward, reaching out until his hands encountered the barrier. The baby cocked his head, seeming to notice him for the first time. He clung to his mother's arm for a moment, peering reluctantly over his shoulder. And then he smiled, his face filling with delight again. He held out his own hands, until they met the invisible wall. He batted them against the tingling surface, butted it with his head, trying to reach his father. BZ pressed his own hands against the faintly yielding barrier, feeling joy and longing fill his chest until he could scarcely breathe.

"Move away from the barrier."

BZ jerked his hands away as a mild shock stung them. The baby fell back, wailing; Pandhara scooped him up in her arms, comforting him.

"There was no need for that!" BZ pushed up out of his seat furiously, shouting at the walls. He sat back down again, answered only by the echo of his own voice, mocking him.

Pandhara stared at him as the baby quieted. "Are we being monitored?" she asked incredulously, her eyes dark with impotent anger. "They said we would have privacy—"

"It was probably just an automatic response," he said, not at all certain that it had been. He watched the baby turn in her arms, struggling to get free, reaching out to him, calling, "Ba! Ba!" His hands rose; he lowered them, clenching them into fists below the table's edge. Pandhara picked up a ball filled with colored lights and waved it in front of the baby; he took it in his arms, biting it, and settled reluctantly into her lap. "How . . . how are things at the estates?"

"Fine," she said, her voice strained. "Truly. Everything is fine."

"And how is thy work? Has BT let thee get anything done since his birth?"

She smiled. "Well . . . less. But I asked Ochi—my youngest sister, thou remember her—to stay with us while she completes her study course. She watches him part days while I work. He would be into everything otherwise, wouldn't thou, my Little Bit—?" She looked down at him. He held up the ball. "Pretty ball," she said.

"Pitty baw," he echoed, and nodded.

"And how has thy social life been?" BZ asked, not quite casually. "I hope thou've been able to see thy friends, and not felt too . . . isolated there."

She looked at him for a long moment. "No," she said finally, "I'm not lonely. My friends come often, someone is almost always there; they love the beauty of the place as much as I do." She glanced down. "I see Therenan Jumilhac quite often these days . . . thou met him that afternoon at the café. . . . BT adores him, he's very good with children."

"I'm glad," BZ said, and smiled.

She looked up again. "BZ, I wanted to come sooner. I tried. They wouldn't even let me see thee, until KR Aspundh intervened, somehow. He sends thou his highest regards, and regrets that he could not come with us. His health is poor right now, and he isn't permitted to leave the surface. He said to tell thee that he is doing all he can to help thy cause, that he knows these charges are unjust."

"Tell him I'm grateful, and wish him a swift recovery." BZ nodded and smiled. "My attorneys tell me that the Central Committee is trying to suppress what happened on Tiamat, calling it a matter of Hegemonic Security, in order to keep my side of it from the people. They can't afford to let me have any kind of access to the public record. But Pernatte himself sent assurances that when my trial comes up there will be Hegemony-wide media coverage. He's the head of the Secretariat, and he's always been one of my strongest supporters."

Pandhara opened her mouth; closed it again, with an odd frown working the muscles of her face. "I don't even know, myself, what happened on Tiamat, BZ. They would not even tell me what thou had been charged with."

He felt his own mouth tighten. "With treason. 'Secretly working to undermine the Hegemony's security.'"

Pandhara looked stunned—exactly the way he had looked, when he had heard the full charges. "But that carries a sentence of life imprisonment, if thou're found guilty."

Without reprieve. He nodded, glancing away. "At least I'll still be alive; we're civilized, after all. . . . And it's not like I'll be sent to the Cinder Camps. Wherever I am, I'll be able to work to change their minds. They won't send me anywhere too unpleasant," he repeated, trying to reassure her. "They owe me that much." He forced himself to smile, and shrug. "Let's take it as it comes, Dhara. I haven't even been tried yet. If I make my case well enough, I'll be exonerated."

The stricken look did not leave her face; but she nodded, controlling herself with a visible effort. "How did it happen, BZ? Who brought the charges?"

"It was Vhanu," he said.

"Vhanu?" She leaned forward in disbelief; the baby squeaked, and dropped his ball. She reached down to pick it up, and he knocked it out of her hands. She handed him a flutterstick, her eyes still on her husband. "But Vhanu was like a brother to . . . to thee. . . ." She broke off, biting her lip.

"Yes," BZ whispered. "Like a brother." He shook his head. "From the day we arrived on Tiamat—long before that, really, but I didn't want to believe it—we didn't agree on anything about the way the Hegemony should be running things. I should have seen it coming . . . but I couldn't afford to. The irony is that the real problem wasn't even the one I thought I was going there to deal with. That was no problem at all, in the end. Instead it was the water of life. . . . Gods." He leaned back in his chair, drained. "It can't have been meant to happen like this."

"And what about the Queen?" Pandhara asked, her voice betraying only the slightest hesitation. "Was she involved in what happened?"

He looked up, to see both regret and understanding fill her eyes. "Yes," he said. "Our—relationship was the thing that turned the situation critical." He looked down again, remembering the humiliation of his arrest, of being dragged from Moon's bed in the middle of the night and taken away. He forced the memory out of his thoughts. "Dhara, I . . . I have two children on Tiamat, too. Moon was pregnant, when I left there before. I didn't know it. They were grown, by the time I got back." He looked at the child in her arms, beyond his reach, and was filled with a vast, aching emptiness. He sat very still, afraid that any motion would make him lose control. He could not afford to do that to her now, or to himself. *He could not, he could not. . . .*

She was silent too, watching him watch their child. "I'm so sorry," she murmured, at last.

"Don't," he whispered, shaking his head. "The—the worst part of it was—" he forced himself to go on speaking, clearly and evenly, "that I would have had to make the same choices, even if I hadn't still been in love with her. It was true, I was needed there. I had to go back, I had to do what I did. I wasn't crazy, I wasn't wrong. Tiamat is far more important to the Hegemony than anyone knows, and the mers are more vital. . . . And yet it came to this." It was his love for Moon that had driven him to return to Tiamat. It was only their passion for each other that had revealed the truth of his purpose there to him. And yet, the only mistake he could see that he had made was to love her, to consummate that love. It was flouting the restrictions of his position, and the sensibilities of his people, that had made him vulnerable and brought him down, leaving Moon there alone to bear the inescapable geas that had been laid upon them both. "Damn it, I'm ready for this trial! Maybe that's why I'm back here, to challenge everyone's perceptions about the situation, to tell the truth—"

"BZ," Pandhara said, in sudden anguish, "there isn't going to be a trial."

"What?" he said.

"They're not going to give thee a trial, they won't let thee be heard."

"No, they will, Dhara. I've been assured—"

"They're lying to thee!" she said. "KR told me that the Secretariat is passing judgment on thee itself."

"That's impossible—"

"Everyone has been lying to thee, even Pernatte, even thy own attorneys." She turned, looking back over her shoulder, as the doors on both sides of the room burst open, and uniformed guards came in. "They were watching!" she blurted. "They lied about everything!"

He pushed to his feet. "Go to Aspundh! Tell him no one knows the real truth but Moon. He has to contact her—" The guards reached him first, dragged him back away from the barrier.

"BZ!" she cried, but suddenly he couldn't hear her voice anymore; the guards reached her, seizing her by the arms. She pulled away as they tried to force her toward the door. The baby began to wail, soundlessly; she stopped resisting, and let them lead her out, still looking back.

"Tell him—!" BZ shouted. The guards forced him through the doorway; the door closed behind him, and that was the last he saw of her.

TIAMAT: Carbuncle

First light seeped into the restless underworld below Carbuncle, limning the black-on-gray silhouettes of rigging and hoists, decks and docks, painting the human forms silently waiting there with a sullen glow. The sky brightened with every heartbeat as Moon watched it. A road of molten light formed on the surface of the sea, leading out from the place where she stood on the final length of pier, toward the shimmering disk of the emerging sun. "Now is the time," she said, with the cold wind of dawn blowing through her soul. "Bring him forward."

Jerusha PalaThion and the squad of constables led Kirard Set Wayaways through the taut silence of the small crowd of witnesses, to stand before her. Below the pier a boat waited, with two more constables aboard, both Summers. "Kirard Set Wayaways," Moon said, meeting the empty terror in his eyes without remorse, "you stand before us accused of acts of violence and betrayal, both witnessed and suspected, against your own people. I do not have the power to judge you—" her voice cut him like wire, "for I am not the true Lady, but only a vessel for Her Will. Therefore, I commend you to the Sea's judgment, under the traditional laws of our people."

"You're insane!" Kirard Set snarled. "Your rituals have nothing to do with me. I'm a Winter, you can't do this to me—"

"Tell that to Arienrhod," Moon said softly, feeling as if she would strangle on the words, "when you see her—"

She looked away, hearing a murmur of noise ripple through the crowd behind her. Jerusha touched her arm, pointing.

A squad of Hegemonic Police was making its way toward them through the maze of docks and moorings. She saw their leader raise a hand, stopping his men a short distance away.

"Thank the gods—" Kirard Set mumbled. "I knew they'd come. I knew they wouldn't let you do this to me, you insane bitch— Help!" he shouted. "Help me! They're trying to drown me! Stop them!"

Moon saw weapons show among the constables, all of them Summers, at Jerusha's signal.

The officer left his squad and came toward them, his hands peaceably at his sides. "Lady." He nodded respectfully in Moon's direction, before turning to Jerusha. "Good morning, uh, Commander PalaThion." He saluted, as if in apology for stumbling over her new rank.

She returned the salute, with a faint smile of acknowledgement. "Good morning, Lieutenant Devu. What's a patrol doing down here on the docks, at this early hour? Not standard procedure, is it?"

"No, Commander," he said, giving Moon, and the crowd surrounding her, a slightly uncertain glance. "Commander Vhanu ordered us to hunt mers. We're about to board our ship and do that." He gestured behind him at the waiting Blues. Moon realized that they were carrying different equipment than she had ever seen on them before; realized suddenly what the equipment was intended for. She saw Jerusha stiffen; felt her own body go rigid. "But first, Ma'am, maybe you'd explain to me what's happening here? You know that under the rules of martial law assemblies of more than ten people are restricted." He jerked his head at the crowd. "What are you doing to this citizen?"

"It's a trial," Jerusha said. "He's being tried on charges including kidnapping and drug dealing."

Devu frowned. "Here? Now?" he said. "Like this?"

"According to the laws of Summer, Lieutenant," Moon said. "He is going to be judged by the Sea."

"They're going to drown me!" Kirard Set shouted. "Help me—"

"You're going to drown him?" Devu asked, his frown deepening.

"He will be taken out into the open sea, until the shoreline is no longer visible," Moon said evenly, "and left there to swim ashore. Whether he drowns or not depends on him. The Sea Mother will judge him. That has been the law of our people, for centuries."

"It's obscene!" Kirard Set said. "You can't let them do this to me—you're a Kharemoughi, a civilized man, for gods' sakes!"

"And I am the autonomous ruler of my people." Moon lifted her head. "He is one of us, and he has broken our laws, not yours, Lieutenant."

"What's his name?" Devu asked, glancing at Jerusha.

"Kirard Set Wayaways Winter," Jerusha said, shifting her weight from foot to foot, with her stun rifle cradled casually in the crook of her arm. "A Tiamatan native."

"Wayaways?" The lieutenant rubbed his chin. "Hm," he said, and nodded, with an odd, random smile. "Not our jurisdiction." He began to turn away.

"Stay if you want to," Moon said. "Watch our system of laws in action. Watch how the Sea deals with those people who offend Her sense of justice—"

Lieutenant Devu looked abruptly uncomfortable again. "Some other time, perhaps. We have to get going."

"Give the Commander my greetings," she said, fixing him with a stare. He bowed, nodded to Jerusha, and was gone, walking rapidly.

"No—!" Kirard Set wailed, but he did not look back.

Moon waited, watching the offworlders until they disappeared into the geometry of masts and machinery. Finally she turned back to Kirard Set, who stood silent now, glowering at her. "The Mother of Us All is waiting," she said. She nodded toward the ladder behind him, that led down to the boat riding at low tide beside the floating pier.

"I'll be back—" he said, with defiance and desperation.

"If the Sea wills it," Moon answered steadily. "But if you live, don't return to the city. She may forgive you, but I never will."

He turned away from her, his face livid with impotent rage; he glanced out into the crowd, as if he were searching for someone. Whoever it was, he did not find them. He turned back again, and moved slowly to where the ladder waited; went slowly down it. "The hell with all of you," he said, before his face disappeared.

Moon moved to stand at the rail as the small boat with its Summer crew and Winter prisoner unfurled its crab-claw sail and started outward along the golden road. "Arienrhod!" Kirard Set screamed suddenly, looking back at her with eyes like coals, and she did not know what he meant by it.

As she watched the boat grow smaller in the distance, she realized that someone else had come to stand beside her at the rail. She turned her head, wondering whether Danaquil Lu Wayaways had decided at the last moment to attend, and witness his cousin's ordeal. But it was Tirady Graymount, Kirard Set's wife, who stood beside her, and their son Elco Teel. Moon realized that she had not seen them in the crowd before this moment, either. The woman's face was pale and hollow-eyed—with anguish, Moon thought. But her mouth, as if it had a life of its own, was smiling. She held an empty liquor bottle in her clenched fist; her other arm was around her son, holding on to him possessively as she watched her husband sail out toward the horizon. She raised her fist with the empty bottle in it suddenly; hurled the bottle with all her strength out into the sea. "I hope you drown!" she shouted.

Elco Teel put his arm around her shoulders, turning her away from the rail again. There was no expression at all on his face, as he led her back through the crowd.

Moon watched them go, feeling neither surprise nor compassion. She saw the astonishment on some of the faces around her; saw Jerusha shake her head. Standing alone, she looked out to sea again, watching the boat grow smaller. On its stern she could still read the name she had painted there with her own hand: *Ariele*. Behind her the crowd began to separate and drift away. She did not leave the rail until she had watched the boat out of sight.

Moon took her place at the head of the meeting table in what had once been yet another of the palace's echoing, unused chambers. When she first came to live in the palace had reminded her of the countless ornaments it held: a jeweled shell, empty and without purpose. She had been afraid of it, frightened by its immensity and the power of all it represented—Arienrhod's past, a kind of desire that seemed completely alien to her, yet which must exist somewhere inside her, too.

But the secret sentience that had compelled her to succeed its Queen had compelled her to remain here, within reach. In time she had come to accept the palace and all it held as simply a part of the greater pattern of her life. The palace itself was neither good nor evil, no more a matter of her choice or lack of choice than anything else, in a world that had seemed more and more random and beyond her control.

And as more time passed, adversity had freed her to see everything she looked at in new ways. The offworlders had forced her to house the Sibyl College within the palace's walls, and the College had filled the rattling emptiness of its chambers with activity and purpose.

Now, when she looked around her at the beauty of the sculpted detail along the ancient ceiling line, the newly painted murals, even the graceful forms of the aging, imported furniture, she saw the artistry of the human minds and hands that had created them. They had become a symbol of the potential that existed in her, around her, within the women and men—Summers, Winters, and offworlders—who had helped her to build the future that she had been driven to seek. She realized that seeing longtime friends and trusted companions against the setting of this place had become one of the few things in her life that brought her pleasure.

And now, she thought, as the image of the *Ariele* disappearing into the sunrise overlaid her vision, they were her only hope. She glanced down at the recorder in front of her and the pile of printout data that she had had laboriously hand-copied, after Vhanu had shut down her computer system. She looked up again, at Tammis beside her, his eyes filled with concern—seeing in his eyes three lives: his own, his father's, the life of the unborn child that Merovy carried. By right there should have been nothing but joy in her as she looked at him, seeing the future and the past; but she could not feel anything, not even grief. A clear, impenetrable wall seemed to rise between her and all emotion, allowing her to see what remained that was right and good in her life, but not to take any comfort in it.

She looked on around the circle, seeing the intent, worried faces of Clavally and Danaquil Lu, Fate Ravenglass with her vision sensor like a shining crown, the two dozen other sibyls who were waiting expectantly. She could not tell them everything; but she knew that at least she could trust them to give her the data she needed without a full explanation.

She called the recorder on, and the eerie chorale of the mersong filled the air. She watched their expressions change: the peace, pleasure, surprise and incomprehension that overtook them as they listened.

And then she told them all she could, explaining the part they must play to complete the fragmented mathematical sequences hidden inside the songs. She passed them the copies of the data she had collected from Sparks's files—thinking of him suddenly and painfully, thinking about the strangeness of the parallel lives they had come to lead. She described his work to the assembled sibyls, wondering as she spoke what would come of the journey he had taken alone; whether he would bring their daughter back from the place the Ondineans called the Land of Death, or be lost there forever with her. There were few questions from the people listening around her; none that she could not answer.

With a few final words about urgency and secrecy, she left them to their work. She made her way back through the halls into the upper levels of the palace; offices, libraries, studies passed in a pale blur of exhaustion. She had not slept at all last night, lying rigid and alone in her bed through the interminable hours before the ritual at dawn. Now that she had done all she could, about everything over which she had any control, the last of the momentum that her fury had given her had spent itself.

She saw again in her mind the *Ariele* carrying Kirard Set Wayaways out to sea—the only one of her tormentors on whom she had been able to take revenge. She let herself imagine him reaching shore, half-drowned, exhausted, pulling himself onto the docks below the city . . . saw herself waiting for him there, with a knife in her hand, to keep her final promise to him. . . .

Sickened, she pressed her hand to her face; pain throbbed in her head with every heartbeat, as the headache that had been threatening her since she rose this morning burst into blinding life. She had eaten nothing all day, but the very thought of food repulsed her. She reached her own bedroom and stopped, leaning against the doorframe, unable to force herself to go inside.

She went on along the hall, until at last she reached the doorway to the room that had been Arienrhod's. The bedchamber waited as Arienrhod had left it, over twenty years ago, and had not been slept in by anyone since she had died. Moon opened the door, and stood gazing inside.

"Do you need anything, Lady?" A servant passing in the hall hesitated, inclining her head.

Moon looked at the woman, pressing her mouth to stop its sudden urge to ridiculous laughter. *Need anything—?* "I need to rest," she said finally, her voice thick. "I don't want to be disturbed for a long time. . . ."

"Yes, Lady." The woman nodded respectfully. She glanced at the open doorway and hesitated, as if she wanted to say more, before she went on down the hall.

Moon went into the room, retreating into its silence. Its wide windows were hidden by heavy curtains; it was entirely self-contained, a womb into which she could withdraw. She undressed and lay down in the nacreous, shellform bed, wrapping the bedclothes around her, her arms and legs embracing the softness and emptiness. No memory lay waiting for her here, no phantom arms to reach out to her, no whisper of gentle words, the remembered heat of no one else's body to warm her own. . . .

She darkened the bedside lights, throwing the ghost-haunted shadows of the room into utter blackness, so that it did not matter whether her eyes were open or closed. Utterly alone at last, she folded her arms around her shivering flesh and began to weep, silently at first, and then wrackingly, because there was no one to hear her, no one to comfort her, no one to forgive her.

She wept until she had no strength left, until she could only lie still, closer to sleep than to waking. She waited there, her body unresisting, her mind surrendering, ready to be taken by oblivion.

But instead she felt something else seize hold of her—an irresistible force drawing her down into a darkness even more complete. . . . *The Transfer.*

She let go, let herself fall, through the darkness and into the corruscating light/sound of a place she remembered, feeling hope come alive inside her, almost unbearably. (BZ—?) she called, seeing her voice go out from her in ripple-rings of harmonic light. (BZ, where are you?)

(No . . .) the answer came, and the touch of it against her mind was a stranger's.

(Who—?) she thought, because there was something almost familiar about the disembodied patterns of the other's contact.

(KR Aspundh—)

(KR—?) Her disbelief rippled out from her like tolling bells.

(Yes, my dear. . . .) His thought turned fond and gentle, like the feathery touch of an old man's hand against her cheek. (After so long. BZ told me what had become of you, all that you have become. . . .)

(BZ—where is he, KR? How is he? How can I reach him?)

(Slowly,) he whispered. (Go slowly, Moon—though I should address you properly as Lady—my strength is not what it was, even when you knew me. This is difficult for me. . . . BZ is being held by the Hegemonic government. He will be sentenced without trial, the Golden Mean will see to it, because they fear his popularity. They mean to be rid of him, because of his opposition to the water of life . . . to send him somewhere he will never return from. He told me to contact you. Why has all this happened, Moon? He said that you could tell me.)

(Lady's Eyes— I can't, KR. . . .) She felt her desperation and fear grow blinding, making her thoughts incoherent, drowning his contact. She forced the heart of ice that had formed within her these past weeks to cool her blood, letting her see clearly, and think dispassionately. (It's impossible. I can't explain it, any more than he can, even like this, even to you. I can only tell you that if I fail in what I was meant to do, every world on which there are still sibyls will suffer . . . including Kharemough. And there are only two people who can help me—BZ, and a man named Reede Kullervo. But something called the Brotherhood has taken Kullervo, and my daughter. I don't know how to save them. My husband went after them to Ondinee . . . BZ believed you might be able to help them. But how can we save them, KR, how can we save BZ, if even the ones he trusted have betrayed us—?)

His thoughts enfolded her like warm hands. (The Golden Mean is only one facet of Survey's hidden structure, as the Brotherhood is another. . . . I am taking a chance in assuming you understand that. There are others, they are all like mirrors within a kaleidoscope. There is still hope—there is always hope. I will see what can be done to help save your daughter, and bring Kullervo back to you. But beyond that . . . a balance was thrown off when Kitaro-*ken* was killed. She was a counterweight: with her support BZ might have held his own against his formidable opposition . . . Reede Kullervo and your daughter might not have been lost. The Golden Mean controls the water of life completely now, and we who see further than they know enough to see that they must be stopped.)

(Yes,) she thought. (Yes. The water of life has everything to do with what is wrong, what went wrong. . . . The sibyl net is in danger, because the mers are in danger . . . the mers. . . .) Strident waves of interference beat back against her brain, drowning her thoughts in undertow. (It has to stop! They must stop hunting the mers.)

There was silence, shimmering like a reflection on water through a moment's eternity. (Very well, then. But what will make them stop?) Aspundh asked finally. (We must find something that will make them stop. Something that they desire even more than the water of life. . . .)

(I don't believe anything exists that they want more,) Moon thought bitterly.

(It exists, somewhere . . .) Aspundh replied, with a faint ripple of pained amusement. (But it is nothing easily discovered, or they would have it already, like the water of life.)

(The stardrive plasma,) she thought. (But they have that, because BZ gave it to them.)

(Perhaps that was his mistake,) Aspundh murmured. (But then, we are all only human—none of us can see the future, and see it clearly. There must be something else they want.)

She thought of the secret of the computer itself; if they knew of its existence they would never touch another mer. But they could never be allowed to possess that knowledge, after having proved so profoundly how little they could be trusted with power. Even if she could give it to them . . . (I don't know. I don't know.)

(Nor do I. But we must not give up hope, or give up searching—)

(But where else can I search?) she thought, despairing. (Where can I go? I have no options.)

(You have all of spacetime,) he answered. (You are adrift in it now. You are what you are for a reason; I have never been more certain of it than now. I can send outward, through the network of contacts Survey has provided me. But you have the greater resource—the sibyl mind speaks to you, it opens itself to you in a way it does for no one else I know; this is something I had only heard tales of, before I met you. There are secrets the sibyl net hides even from its most trusted servants . . . but clearly not from you.)

She made no answer, suffused with the radiance of his words, and the vision they created in her mind.

(We are doing what we can for BZ. But the Golden Mean is powerful in the Hegemony. You may be the only real hope BZ has. He needs a force strong enough to turn back the tide . . . perhaps it is why you are called Moon,) KR thought gently, as strands of golden light began to unravel all around her. (May the gods of your ancestors help you . . .) Her mind sang with his final benediction.

But she was alone in the darkness again, without an answer.

ONDINEE: Tuo Ne'el

"There it is," Kedalion said, pointing ahead over the blasted heath of the Land of Death as the citadel became visible. He called up enhancement, and a segment of the displays leaped into magnification, showing them more detail.

"By'r Lady . . ." Sparks murmured, beside him. "It's huge. It must be bigger than Carbuncle."

"They're entire self-contained city-states," Kedalion said, remembering the citadel's labyrinthine streets and levels with sudden vividness. A part of him was still casually amused by Sparks Dawntreader's tireless wonder, even while another, separate part of his brain felt sick with dread as he watched their final destination fill the screens.

It had been difficult to believe Dawntreader had never been offworld, when they were back in Carbuncle. He belonged to the same secret organization that Reede belonged to, and his single-minded obsession with getting to Ondinee made his confidence seem utterly unshakable. He even had a fair amount of knowledge about starships and how their systems worked; but it was all textbook knowledge. He had never set foot on an actual ship, and on board the *Prajna* he had been like a dumbstruck boy. It had reminded Kedalion of Ananke's first transit; but Dawntreader was at least his own age.

Dawntreader had asked them endless questions about their past lives and homeworlds, and how they had come to be here, in these bizarre circumstances. He had not even complained about the cramped quarters—which had been designed to suit Kedalion's size requirements, and not those of his passengers or crew. Dawntreader had tried everything, learned every task, no matter how tedious or unpleasant, aboard the ship; and for the most part, he had done them well. "I've waited my entire life for this," he said once, when Ananke had asked him why he wanted so badly to scrub down the control room floor. There had been a desperate passion in his eyes when he said it; but the emotion had turned to ashes, as he remembered what had finally driven him to break the chains that had bound him to his homeworld.

Now Kedalion watched Dawntreader's amazement slowly change, darkening, as he realized that this was the stronghold of the enemy, the place he had to bring his daughter out of. "Lady and all the gods. . . ." Dawntreader murmured, and Kedalion read the rest of the thought in his eyes: *How—?*

"Nobody told you it would be easy," Kedalion said, expressionless. "You want to go to Razuma starport, instead? The citadel might still let us turn around . . ." He gestured at the image on the screen.

Dawntreader glanced over at him, and frowned. "No," he said.

"Just asking." Kedalion shrugged. He looked over his shoulder at Ananke, sitting in the back, brooding in silence with his arms folded across his chest. He looked naked somehow, without the quoll; seemed to feel naked, from the way he held himself. Every time Kedalion looked at him, the quoll's absence was like a shout, reminding him of what they were planning to do here, shouting at him that they were insane, and going to die. Or maybe it was only his own common sense that he heard screaming. He sighed, and began the approach codes; listening to the answering signal burst tell him that he was doomed, they were all doomed now. . . .

The citadel beckoned them into its waiting mouth, on down its throat into the designated docking bay. They climbed out as their craft locked down, and were met by a reception committee of armed men.

"We were only expecting two of you," the leader, a man named Samir, said, holding his stun rifle at roughly Kedalion's eye level.

Kedalion felt sweat burn unpleasantly down his back, as he began the speech he had rehearsed in his mind a thousand times over on the way from Tiamat. "TerFauw ordered us to bring this man with us, because he has important data for Kullervo. He's been cleared. Show him your hand," he said, nudging Dawntreader.

Dawntreader held up his palm. He had learned to speak Trade on the way here, using an enhancer, practicing it on them. He showed off the eye he had burned into his own flesh, a reasonable facsimile of the Source's mark; or at least Kedalion hoped so.

Samir stared at the brand, frowned. "Nobody told me about that," he said flatly.

"How could they?" Kedalion answered, his tension giving it the snap of impatience. "I'm telling you now. Kullervo needs to see this man, he's got special information, he's a local expert on the mers. If Kullervo doesn't get to see him, somebody's going to be real pissed off."

Samir looked at the scar. He looked back at Kedalion, his stare long and hard. At last he shrugged, and nodded. "All right," he said, and waved them on.

They made their way through the maze of tunnels that led into the heart of the citadel complex, where transportation waited that would take them to Reede. Kedalion pushed his hands into his coat pockets, feeling for his huskball; hating the prospect of being a passenger and not a pilot, especially now, when he felt so powerless. The huskball was not much more than a rough nub in a nest of loose shavings now; he had nearly worn it out, with years of nervous fiddling. He wished he knew where to find another one; even though he knew a new one would never be the same, would be like encountering a stranger in his pocket. "Well, here we are," he said, with relentless banality, as they reached a transport stop.

"That was great, Kedalion," Ananke said suddenly, glancing over his shoulder. "The way you— Gods, I thought I was going to puke when Samir stuck his gun in your face. Reede couldn't have backed him down better."

"Actually," Kedalion said, with a slow smile, "I was thinking how Gundhalinu would have done it, back on Four. Gods, he was slick."

Sparks looked at him with a sudden frown, as if he had unintentionally hit a nerve.

"Sorry," Kedalion murmured, realizing what lay behind the look. "I was also thinking about when I was a kid, and we used to go drafting, off the cliffs. If you didn't keep your glider in balance, you'd kill yourself. You knew if you failed you'd die. So you didn't fail." His smile faded. "Actually, I'm still thinking about that."

"Yeah," Ananke muttered, as they sat down on a metal bench to wait for transportation; he tugged at his leather-gloved foot as he looked out over the scene. Dawntreader leaned back in his seat, silent, staring straight ahead.

"Reede—?"

Reede pushed back in his seat as Ariele's voice reached him from the entrance to his lab. He shook his head, shaking off his stupor of fatigue. He had been resting here with his head on his arms for what seemed like hours, sleepless, while she still slept on in their bed, escaping reality a while longer. He wondered what her dreams had been like. Not like his own, he hoped.

"Reede? Where are you?" He heard panic starting in her voice.

"Here." He got up from his seat, moving through the maze of equipment and imagers to find her, to reassure her. He did not want her to see him as he had been, wallowing in useless self-loathing, unable to work, or even to think. He should have killed her, should have killed himself, when he had the chance. But something incomprehensible had stopped him; had made him choose to live, when the only sane choice had been to die. *Lunatic. Coward. Masochist.* The litany repeated again in his mind, as it had been repeating ever since he had regained consciousness, and found himself back in the Source's hands. He looked down at his own hands, still clumsy with bandages.

But the water of death was alive inside him again, invading and controlling every cell in his body, healing him with a vengeance. He did not really need the bandages anymore, but they were an excuse for stalling his research work that much longer. Because it was not his hands that he couldn't control; it was his mind. He couldn't even pretend anymore that he could do what was required of him, do the Source's dirty work. He could only think about the mers, and the mystery of their existence. The patterns of the mersong, and the profound secrets he had discovered hidden within it, haunted him day and night: so alien, and yet so familiar. He could not think of the mers only as receptacles for the water of life: to think of them that way was an obscenity, to think of the water of life at all was futility, it was—

He met Ariele, felt her trembling through the layered silken cloth of her Ondinean-style robe as she came into his arms. "What's wrong?"

"I couldn't find you. . . . Reede—" She looked up at him, with terror echoing in the depths of her eyes. "Am I all right? Do I look . . . *changed*? I don't feel well. . . ."

He caught her arms with his bandaged hands, shook her, insistently. "You're all right. You're fine." He touched her cheek, keeping his touch gentle although he could barely feel her flesh. He turned her so that she could see herself in the reflective surface of a cabinet. "Look. Look at yourself. . . . See?"

She shut her eyes; opened them, stared at her reflection. Slowly she nodded, her body going soft and yielding in his arms.

"You feel fine," he went on, with calm reassurance. "So do I."

"I had a dream—" Her voice was unsteady.

"It was only a dream. You have hours to go still before you even have to think about the next dose."

She looked back at him suddenly.

"I have it," he murmured. "I have it here already. Don't worry." He stroked her hair.

She clung to him, sighing. "I don't feel bad. I feel good . . . I've never felt better. It's true. You're so good and strong and wise. I love you, Reede. I love you. I love you. . . ."

He put his arms around her again, feeling bile rise in his throat. He controlled the tremor that ran through his body, kept her from feeling it pass through her own. She was the one thing that could drive the mers from his mind; but seeing her, being with her, only filled him with suicidal guilt, as he watched her moods swing from euphoria to terror, and back again. He had been too sick for them to force him to commit the act—but he had been forced to watch, as they made her drink the water of death, starting the irreversible process of her dependency, not simply on the drug, but on him. He was to blame, and yet she did not cower or rage at him. She did this to him—she loved him.

And so he had tried his best, as soon as he was able, to make it up to her; to give her stability and courage and reassurance. They were strengths he had not known existed in him, but he had found them somewhere, somehow, for her sake. But he was not certain how much longer he would be able to go on this way, barely holding their lives together, day after day.

And even if he was able to stay sane, keep them both sane, the gods only knew what would become of them. If he didn't produce fast enough to please the Source, then Jaakola could cut off her supply, use her against him, make her suffer for it, causing him pain but keeping him intact. . . . Even if he did produce, Jaakola could hurt her anyway, do anything he wanted to her, any time he felt like it, simply on a whim. Jaakola enjoyed keeping him on a short drug supply, stringing him out just to let him know how powerless he really was. Now that he had Ariele to be afraid for too, whole new dimensions of potential cruelty opened like bloody jaws, waiting. Whatever happened to Jaakola's plans to force secrets out of the Summer Queen and Gundhalinu, he was sure they'd never get their daughter back alive. . . . Even if they did, it would only be to watch her die. And there was nothing he could do about it. Nothing.

He let go of her, fumbling in his pockets. His sense-deadened fingers barely recognized what they had been searching for when they found it. He pulled it out: his ring, the mate to the one he had given Mundilfoere. He had worn it all these years alone. He took hold of her hand and slipped the ring over her thumb. Her hands were large for a woman's, long-fingered, but her fingers were slim, and the ring rested precariously against her translucent skin. She closed her hand over it. Looking up at him, she took his hand in hers, and kissed his bandaged, open palm.

He led her wordlessly back through the lab, into his apartment—their apartment, now, at least for a time. "Are you hungry?" he asked. "Do you want some breakfast? Maybe some music—?"

She nodded, opening her mouth to speak; turned, startled, as the apartment door suddenly opened.

Reede froze; went weak with relief as he saw Niburu come through it, followed by Ananke. He stared at them, suddenly feeling the way a man who had been lost at sea would feel, sighting land. "What took you so long to get here?" he snapped, frowning.

Niburu shook his head. His mouth formed a quirky, uncertain smile. "You forgot to leave a forwarding address, boss." He shrugged. "So, you missed us?"

It was Reede's turn to look at him oddly. "Missed you?" he repeated. Something like a laugh caught in his throat; something like a piece of glass, so that for a moment he could not speak. "Yeah," he muttered, finally. "I can't figure out how to use the fucking kitchen system."

Niburu's smile stabilized. "Right, boss," he said, with an expression that looked strangely like contentment. "TerFauw sent us back. He said . . . said you needed us." He glanced abruptly at Reede's bandaged hands; Reede saw the discomfort in his eyes as he looked up again. Reede turned away from it, keeping his rictus hold on Ariele.

"We brought somebody with us," Niburu said, suddenly uneasy again. He gestured toward the open doorway behind him. A third man entered the room. Reede stopped in disbelief.

"Da—!" Ariele cried, starting forward.

"Shh." Reede caught her arm, pulling her up short; his eyes warned Dawn-treader to stay where he was. "What's he doing here?" He asked the obvious question, letting Niburu and the others read the one he could not speak aloud in the burning-glass of his stare.

Niburu hesitated, knowing as well as he did that the walls had eyes and ears. "He . . . has important data for you. About the mers—"

"Oh?" Reede glanced at Dawntreader, trying to keep his response neutral. Dawntreader was staring at Ariele; Ariele was trembling in his grip. He didn't know how much longer he could keep either one of them silent with nothing but willpower. "Let me have a look at what you brought. In there—" He jerked his head toward the waiting lab; led them through its doorway and sealed the door behind them with a brusque command.

He let go of Ariele. "All right. Now we can talk." Niburu shot him a surprised glance; he nodded. "I control the systems here," he said, with bitter satisfaction. It was the one place where he was given free access to enough sophisticated hardware and software that he actually had the power to manipulate his environment.

Ariele ran to Dawntreader. He met her halfway, held her in his arms; and if he wasn't really her father, Reede couldn't tell the difference in that moment. "You're all right," Dawntreader kept repeating, mindlessly, while she murmured, "You came for me . . ." over and over.

"No she's not," Reede snapped. "You're too late. She's taken the water of death."

Dawntreader looked up, and a knowledge of horror that he should not have possessed was suddenly in his eyes. He looked back at Ariele, at Reede again. "Then maybe I came here to kill you, instead of save you—"

"Kill me?" Reede sneered, waving his bandaged hands. "I'm already dead. Save me? Don't be an ass. If you try to take either of us away from here, you'll only kill us both. You might as well pick up a gun and do it cleanly. Or else give up now, and admit you've walked empty-handed into hell, and you'll never get out alive. Become a brand for the Source. Then we can all be one big happy family—" His hand slammed down painfully on the counter surface beside him.

Dawntreader winced. He tore his gaze from Ariele's pale, despairing face to look at Reede again. Slowly his gaze cooled. "All right," he murmured. "I was prepared for this. . . . You'll have to forgive me if it's still hard to take. But hear me out before you tell me I'm an ass. I know about the water of death, and everything else . . . so do Moon and Gundhalinu, by now. Gundhalinu can recreate the drug for you, he can protect you, and he'll be willing to do it, if only for Ariele's sake." He glanced at her again, missing Reede's sudden ironic smile. "I'm taking my daughter out of here. Will you come with us?"

Reede remembered Gundhalinu's desperate attempt to haul his unwilling cooperation into the Golden Mean's net. He thought about being Gundhalinu's drug-dependent lackey, instead of the Source's. He thought about the mers. He frowned, refusing to listen with more than half an ear; refusing to hope. "You're missing the point. We'd still be dead before we even got back to Tiamat. It takes too long—"

"Do you have a sample of the drug we can take with us?"

"Yes." Reede shrugged. "So what?"

"Then we can keep you both suspended in stasis until we have a safe supply."

"How the fuck are you going to do that?" Reede felt his anger rise as Dawntreader kept attacking his defenses.

"We came down in an LB from the ship, boss," Niburu said. "We can use the emergency pods to put you in stass."

Reede turned to look at him. "Gods . . ." he murmured. The emergency units for injured passengers on a ship's lifeboats had a limited suspension cycle, but it might be enough.

"You don't have to be there at all, until Gundhalinu has what you need, once we get out of here," Dawntreader said.

"That's fucking brilliant," Reede muttered, with a grudging shake of his head.

"Niburu thought of the lifeboats," Dawntreader said.

Reede glanced back at Niburu, who shrugged self-consciously. It struck him then what Niburu and Ananke had risked, were risking, even to have smuggled Dawntreader in here. He realized at last that they had not done it for Ariele's sake, or out of loyalty to the Hegemony, or simply because Dawntreader had asked them to. And that left only one reason, that he could think of. "You must all be crazy," he said thickly.

Niburu burst into unexpected laughter. "A man doesn't have to be crazy to work for you; but it helps," he said. "What do you say, boss? Will you do it? We could get free of this place, forever—"

"Gundhalinu will help us if we can just get back to Tiamat," Dawntreader repeated. He looked at Reede expectantly, with Ariele at his side.

"You really intend to do this, don't you? You've got it all worked out." Reede looked at them, his mouth twisting. "Except for how we're going to cover that first few hundred meters through the citadel's security to get ourselves out of here." He watched the rest of them look at each other. "That's what I thought," he said sourly. And then he smiled. "All right," he murmured. "That's the kind of odds I like—suicidal." They all looked at him, now, their expressions turning even grimmer.

"And I have something I've been working on for a long time, a little private exercise. I've been waiting for the right moment to try it out." He turned away, striding back to the closest terminal. He sat down, stripping the bandage material from his hands with his teeth. He murmured a sequence of keycodes as his fingers passed over the touchboard. The sensation of the tingling board against the barely healed skin of his hands was exquisitely intense, like his mood was suddenly, as the buried datafile emerged from his secret storage and appeared before him in all its virulent perfection. "Go," he whispered to it, "and destroy." He spread his fingers and flattened his branded palm across the touchboard. The image vanished again, leaving the screen empty.

He turned in his seat, to see the others gathered around him in silent incomprehension.

"What did you do?" Dawntreader asked.

Reede let his smile spread. "I released a computer virus I designed into the citadel's central operating system. Soon everything will start to slow down. In a matter of hours the entire citadel will be completely defenseless. When the rest of Tuo Ne'el discovers that, they'll do to this place what the Source did to Humbaba." He saw Niburu and Ananke start. "That might give us the chance we need to get clear. At least it'll take us all out together, cleanly, if we don't make it. . . . Either way, it's for the best. And it's already done," he finished, ending their protests before they could begin.

"Thank you, Gundhalinu-*eshkrad*. . . ." He leaned against the desktop, his finger caressing the touchboard like a lover's skin. "One night," he murmured, "when we were back on Four, Gundhalinu walked out through that research complex's security system with a container of stardrive, like he was taking out the garbage. The system would let him do anything, because he'd programmed it himself. The man is a fucking genius, and he doesn't even know it. And you know why? It's not because he's brilliant—he's smart enough, but his real strength is that he's got common sense. He sees the *point* of things. The parallax view, the practical application; when to push, and when to pull back . . . the human fuckup factor. Gods, I envied him that night; I wanted to have his mind, instead of mine—" He broke off, glancing down. "I've been trying to think like that ever since. It's not generally something I'm good at."

"Neither am I," Dawntreader murmured. "Maybe that's why I'm here, and he's with my wife."

Reede looked up at him. "And you still trust him to take care of us if we get back there?"

Dawntreader sighed. "Completely," he said.

"You know him that well?" Reede asked, skeptical.

Dawntreader looked at Ariele, squeezed her shoulder gently, before he looked back at Reede. "I don't know him at all," he said. "I don't want to."

Reede nodded, and glanced away. "Tell me, did you really have data for me about the mers?"

Dawntreader looked surprised by the change of subject, but he nodded. "I thought it would be a good idea, in case anybody asked for proof."

"You brought your work on mersong and fugue theory," Reede said, and knew from Dawntreader's face that he was right. "That took real vision. You have a gift, Dawntreader."

Sparks frowned, ignoring the compliment. "How did you get that? I didn't give you that."

Reede smiled. "I knew you were at least smart enough that you wouldn't trust the Source completely when he ordered you to give us your data. So I raided your files. That's something Gundhalinu taught me too . . . if you want it done right, you have to do it yourself." He laughed humorlessly, glancing at the terminal. "He showed me that if you control the system, you become a god. Well, I'm the Render now, I'm the God of Death—" He wove his fingers together, and squeezed.

"You've had that all along?" Niburu asked, in something like disbelief. "You could have used it?"

"No. . . ." Reede shook his head. "It took a long time to learn the system, find its weaknesses, perfect my approach. . . . I had to find the perfect moment for my revenge. And now it's here." He got up from his seat, moving restlessly past them. They stepped out of his way, as if they saw something in his eyes, as if they believed in his godhood, his powers of destruction.

He went to the system that contained his work on the water of life, the sample he had been going through the motions with since before his last meeting with Gundhalinu. He toyed with the structure of the three-dimensional data model he called up into the screen. He altered it slightly, here and there; implementing the changes that he had tried over and over in his mind, frustrated by their perversity until his conversation with Gundhalinu had given him his sudden, terrible insight. He finished his alterations; ordered the system to copy them and produce a sample.

The others waited uncertainly as he retrieved the maintenance doses of the water of death already waiting in one of the sealed cabinets. The Source had been unusually prompt in releasing his supply while he had been recuperating from his ordeal.

He handed the combined dose to Dawntreader, explaining tersely about what it was. "Don't lose this, for gods' sakes, whatever you do." Dawntreader nodded, putting the small container into his belt pouch.

"All right," Reede said. "Niburu, I want you to take everybody on a little tour of the citadel. Lose yourselves." Niburu stared at him. "End up back near the entrance to the docking bays, and wait. Wait for the confusion to start, and pick your moment to ride it. I'll meet you there."

"What the hell are you going to be doing?" Niburu demanded.

Reede looked away. "I have unfinished business. . . . I have something the Source wants. I'm going to let him have it."

"Reede, no—" Ariele said, pulling away from Dawntreader and coming to his side.

"Boss, you can't—" Niburu protested.

"By the Lady and all the gods!" Dawntreader said. "If you've really set this entire citadel up to be destroyed, you'll get all the revenge you need against the Source, for whatever he's done to you. That's enough."

"No," Reede whispered. "It isn't enough." He jerked his head toward the way out. "You think they won't check up on your unexpected arrival, Dawntreader? You think they're not asking a lot of questions about you right now? Jaakola's not stupid—he knows who you are. I've got to give him something else to think about for the next couple of hours, or we'll never make it out of here alive. I said I'll meet you later. Get out." He took a step toward them, and they retreated—all of them except Ariele. Dawntreader took hold of her arms, gently but firmly, and forced her away from him. She followed her father out, looking back over her shoulder as he led her away. Reede saw fear for him in her eyes—and, suddenly, a red hunger for vengeance that matched his own.

"The LB's in Docking Bay Three, boss. On the lower level," Niburu called. "Just in case you're late—"

"Hurry—" Ariele cried.

He nodded, watching her go, watching them disappear one by one through the doorway and back into the outer world. He listened until they were gone. And then, moving as if there were all the time in the world, he sent a message to the Source to expect him soon. "Tell him I have what he wants," he said, and cut contact.

He went back, alone, through the echoing lab to check the displays on the molecular cookers. He settled onto a stool, sat motionless watching the progress of his program. At last the screen went blank, replacing its run of data sequences with two luminous words: SEQUENCE COMPLETED. Reede smiled. He got up again, and went to the place where his weapon waited for him. He picked up the clear vial, studying its contents—the heavy, silver fluid that moved like memory within its walls.

He took the vial and left the lab, made his way through the sprawling citadel complex, observing its workings, its inhabitants, its perfect, hermetic universe with an odd detachment. He noticed with satisfaction the unusual number of cursing, confused workers of all kinds who were suddenly having difficulties with their operating systems.

It took him longer to reach his destination than he had expected, because he was delayed for nearly half an hour when a shuttle was unexpectedly rerouted. His satisfaction at the error was tinged with unease by the time he finally arrived at the outer perimeter of the Source's private sector and requested his audience with the Master. The virus seemed to be spreading through the system even faster than he had anticipated. He prayed the others would be watching the signs, or they'd never time their return to the docks right. He had to trust them to play their part; just as they had to trust him to do this. . . .

Reede forced himself to stop looking everywhere, stop twitching, frowning, tapping his foot as the guard cursed and repeated his unanswered request for a fourth time, and then a fifth. A desperate voice inside of him tried to tell him that what he was doing was insane; that he was taking an insane risk coming here. But he had to do this, he had to keep the Source looking only at him, thinking about him, or the others would never escape. He would only get out of here alive if they did. *He needed to do this.* . . . He had to trust himself.

"Goddammit—" the guard said.

The Source's voice answered them abruptly, a shower of words falling out of the air, completely unintelligible.

The guard looked up, frowning. "What did he say—?"

"He said, 'Come on up,'" Reede snapped. He pushed through the yielding barrier of the security shieldwall, and when it did not stop him, the guard didn't either. "Go on," the guard said, resigned. "You know the way."

He knew the way. The lift took a very long time getting there. He thought about how often, since his first, forced, visit to the Source, he had had nightmares of being trapped in one of these fucking things. Almost as often as he had dreamed about drowning. . . .

The lift let him out at last, in the deceptively ordinary reception area before the unmarked doors that opened on darkness. He glanced at his watch, checking the time again as he crossed the open space. He had to make this take long enough, just long enough. . . . The guards, human and electronic, let him pass without comment; the doors welcomed him.

Reede stopped just inside, as the doors sealed shut behind him; feeling his heart miss a beat. His sweating hands tightened around the precious vial of silver fluid. *I am the god of death.* . . . "Master," he said, straining in the blackness for an almost undetectable glimmer of red. "I have it."

"Kullervo," the Source's voice whispered, perfectly clear to him now. *Yes. He saw it now, the faint glow of ember-light.* "The water of life? Bring it to me. Bring it here. . . ."

He started forward, shuffling his feet, moving cautiously despite the eagerness in the Source's voice. He reached the seat in which he was always forced to sit, finding it abruptly in the darkness. He began to grope his way around it.

"Come here," the Source said. "Come closer. Give it to me—"

Reede obeyed, moving like a man working his way through a minefield as he approached the dim, indefinable silhouette. He had never been permitted to approach this closely before. For all he knew, this could be another illusion, another projection—for all he knew, he could be here alone. But he thought not.

He collided with the impenetrable edge of something that abruptly stopped his forward momentum. He fumbled in front of him with his hands, finding a flat, cold surface that stung the hypersensitive skin of his fingers. "Here it is, Master." He set the vial down on it, working by touch, and began to back away.

"Stop," the Source said. "Come forward again."

Reede unlocked his muscles and moved forward again, until he encountered the hard edge of the obstacle between them. He folded his fingers over the edge, clung to it, grateful that it was still there, separating them.

A sudden beam of blue-violet light struck him, falling on him from above, bathing him in blinding brilliance. He shut his eyes against the glare, his shirt fluorescing like a strange flower in the darkness. *For you, Mundilfoere.* . . . He let his hands drop to his sides, letting her memory form a sublime and exalted space within him, an adhani of perfect calm in which he endured whatever perverse scrutiny was being inflicted on his body and his soul. The light went out again, abruptly. He waited, motionless.

"So, you've actually done it . . ." the Source whispered. "You've synthesized a form of the water of life which we can reproduce, and sell—"

"Yes, Master."

"You told Gundhalinu it was impossible."

"I said I lied about that."

"But you wouldn't lie to me," the Source whispered. "Would you—?"

"No, Master," he said.

"You told me it would take a long time to find the answer. But you've found it already?"

"I had a lot of time to think, while I was recovering." Somehow he kept the words uninflected.

"I'm sure you did. I hope you have given a lot of thought to humility, and futility."

"Yes, Master."

"And if I take this, I will find it to be as good as the original."

"Better," Reede said softly. "It's better."

There was a moment of silence. "In what way?" the Source asked.

"It's stable. Just what you asked for. I found a way to extend its life outside of the mer's body. Makes it easier to produce, and ship, and sell—"

A beam of blinding light struck the invisible surface in front of him like a sword, focused on the vial he had set there. He shut his eyes again against the brilliance; he could see its line of brightness through his closed lids.

And then, as suddenly, there was only darkness again. He opened his dazzled eyes, blinking uselessly.

"Well?" the Source demanded suddenly, his voice disintegrating with impatience. "What is it?"

"What—?" Reede broke off, as he realized the Source was not speaking to him now, but instead demanding an answer from the hidden data system that had just run an analysis on the contents of his vial.

He heard a sudden rustling in the darkness, as if something had moved abruptly, and a guttural noise that might have been a curse. He waited; invisible, implacable.

"Congratulations, Reede . . ." the Source's voice murmured at last. "Or should I congratulate Vanamoinen? It is what you say it is . . . perfect. Better than before. You truly are a genius—" Something in his voice made Reede freeze with the sudden fear that his usefulness had ended, and he was about to die. But the Source chuckled unexpectedly, and muttered, "Who knows what new worlds you will conquer for me?"

Reede did not answer. *Drink it,* he thought. *Come on, take it, you putrescent bastard. Drink it.* "The first dose is yours, Master," he said finally, trying to keep the urgent need out of his voice. "That's why I brought it straight to you. So you could be the first."

"What?" the Source said, with faint mockery. "You didn't try it first on yourself, like you did with the water of death?"

"What's the point?" Reede said harshly. "It wouldn't do me any good. It's yours, Master . . ." adding just the right note of bitterness, "just like I am."

"Yes," the Source murmured. "Yes, that's fitting."

Reede heard another rustling sound, as if someone had shifted his weight. He stared at the spot where he imagined he had set down the vial on the surface that separated them, stared so intently that he almost thought he could really make it out, limned with a faint corona of red; that he could really see a dark, shapeless form come down on it, covering it, taking it away. There was more rustling; he was sure now that the glow was brighter, that he could see clearly the misshapen lump that pretended to be a human form somewhere in front of him, when before he had not even been sure of that. *It was happening, even here.*

He heard a sigh of satisfaction. "At last," the Source whispered. "It feels right. . . . Yes—it feels the way I remember it."

Elation sang through him. *At last . . .* And there was still enough time: he had enough time to twist the knife. "There's something I forgot to tell you," he said. "Something else about the water of life. It isn't just stable outside the body of a mer. It's stable in the host."

"What do you mean?" the Source rasped. "Stable for how long—?"

"Decades, at least. I'm not really sure. It's working right now, taking the measure of your DNA, preserving every system and function in your body just the way it finds them at this exact moment. Nothing will change, everything will remain the same from now on. . . ."

"Then no one will need it more than once over decades," the Source snarled. "There's no profit in that—"

"I suppose not," Reede murmured. "But that's not the real problem."

"What do you mean?"

"The real problem is what it does to you."

"What—?" the Source breathed.

"The water of life was designed to produce longevity in mers, not human beings. The mers were bioengineered—their genetic makeup is far simpler than ours, far more streamlined. Our bodies were designed by trial and error; we're a crude, inefficient mess by comparison." Reede let a smile start; let the Source feel it grow, cancerous. "The water of life has a very narrow definition of 'normal function' for any given biological system. The only reason that human beings were able to use it to slow their own aging was because it was always breaking down. It never imposed limits on a human body for more than a day without interruption. It allowed the body the freedom it needed to change . . . to vary its natural cycles, its rhythms, its randomness. Chaos—" he said savagely, "versus Order."

He pressed forward, on the cutting-edge of darkness. He could see a silhouette clearly now, as the space before him flickered, momentarily brightening. He could not tell what it was the silhouette of; but he was beyond caring. "Pretty soon your short-term memory is going to start failing. Pretty soon you'll be living in isolation, because your immune system won't be able to respond to an attack. . . . Pretty soon you'll be perfection. The Old Empire thought they'd found perfection. That's what destroyed them. They say perfection makes the gods jealous. . . ." He pushed away from the hard edge of the night, laughing as he heard the Source swear again, a guttural, viscous sound. He realized that he could see the shadow outlines of his own hands, his body, now.

"I don't believe you," the Source snarled, and he heard fear in it. "You wouldn't dare."

Reede's mouth twisted. " 'Things change.' Do you remember when you said that to me? I do. Now the power is in my hands. You told me Mundilfoere took a long time to die. . . . How long do you think you'll take—?"

"Why is it so bright in here?" the Source shouted in sudden fury, into the air. "It's too bright in here!"

"Blame me," Reede said. "It's my fault. It's my doing, Jaakola. My virals are taking over your body and they're taking over your entire citadel too. Soon you'll have no defenses at all."

"It isn't possible—"

"Then why is it happening?" Reede whispered. Only silence answered him. "Would you like me to stop it? What if I could still stop it, would you give me anything I wanted? Everything? How much do you really control, how long is your reach? What secrets do you know . . . what's enough to buy back your life?"

"What do you want?" the Source grated, the words like chains dragging. "What—?"

"I want you to beg. You made me beg for Mundilfoere's life, you stinking, sadistic bastard . . . I want you to beg me for yours."

"Stop it. . . ."

"What?"

"Stop it! Stop, stop it, by the Unspoken Name, I'll give you anything you want, you lunatic, everything, name anything you want, just tell me there's a way to stop it!"

Reede began to laugh. "You can't stop it—there isn't any way."

He heard a strangled sound of disbelief, or rage. "You brain-dead puppet! You madman!" Something lunged at him across the barrier between them; he danced backward, still laughing, untouched. "You're killing yourself too!" the Source bellowed. "You fucking lunatic, you'll kill us all!"

"That's the idea," Reede said softly. "That's what I'm here for." He began to back away. "Your enemies are coming, Jaakola. I'd run, if I was you. I'd hide. . . . Not that it'll do you any good." He turned, moving toward the doors, able to see them now, a faint outline in darker gray.

"Kullervo!" The ruined voice shrieked obscenities somewhere behind him. The room brightened, graying like fog at sunrise, revealing the featureless wall, the doors, growing closer with every step. If he turned back, he knew he would be able to see it now—the face of his nightmares, still screaming impotently. He did not look back.

He reached the doors, and flung himself against them with all his strength. They gave way, dissolving under his impact, so that he sprawled through into the daylight beyond.

Jaakola was screaming at the guards now, screaming for them to cut him down. Reede scrambled up and lunged into the closest of them, catching him in the stomach, knocking him flat. He grabbed the man's fallen stun rifle; even as he rolled for it seeing the other guard raise his own gun, knowing that it would be too late.

A wall of white fire blotted out the blue expanse of sky, as the meter-thick ceramic of the window behind the guard blew inward with a blinding roar. Reede flung up his arms, covering his head as a hurricane of transparent shrapnel hurtled through the space around him. He was slammed back against the wall beside the guard he had sent down, lacerated in a dozen places at once as the fragments kept falling, as time itself seemed to go into slow motion. *Already*—the citadel's defenses were failing already, and somehow everybody already knew it. *Gods—it was happening too fast.*

He staggered to his feet, bleeding, deafened. He saw the eyes of the man who lay beside him staring up at him, wide and unblinking; saw the dagger of shattered ceralloy protruding from his skull. There was no sign at all of the other guard; as his vision cleared he saw a spray of red splattered across the far wall like graffiti. He heard more explosions in the distance, dimly; felt them through the floor as the entire structure shuddered. There was no more shouting, no screaming, no sound at all now coming from the room he had just escaped. It was dark again in there, as he looked through the doorway.

He turned back in stunned disbelief to the gaping breach in the wall, the blue vastness of the sky beyond it; saw smoke tendriling upward as the thorn forest caught fire below. Smoke stung his eyes and throat as he stooped down to pick up the guard's rifle. He turned away again, stumbling toward the lift. He beat his fist on the callplate; laughed incredulously as the doors opened to him and he found the lift waiting.

He gave it an override command, preventing it from stopping until he had reached his destination. He slumped against the wall, sliding down to sit on the floor as the lift dropped him level after level, its velocity varying from sluggish to precipitous. He stared at his bloody, stupefied reflection gaping back at him from the polished metal, wondering whether Niburu and the others were still waiting, or had gotten clear and gone up already.

If they weren't crazy they'd gone, they'd saved themselves. If they hadn't, he cursed them for fools; if they had he cursed them for abandoning him when he suddenly wanted so badly to live . . . *wanted to live, had to live, to get back to Tiamat—because he had unfinished business there. What he had left undone there was more important than life itself, even his own life—*

And he knew all at once that he would not die here like this—would not, could not. That if he had to murder and maim and crawl over broken glass, he would do it, because this was not his destiny; his destiny lay on Tiamat and he had to go home. . . .

The lift car slammed to a stop, jarring every bone in his body; its doors opened halfway, jammed. He squeezed through, cursing, into a bedlam of panic-stricken workers, soldiers bellowing futile orders, falling masonry and the stench of burning plastic. He saw a mob off to one side; saw that they were fighting over a hovercraft. He sprayed them with the stun rifle, clearing a path to it; dodged over helpless fallen bodies and squeezed into its cab.

He sent it spiraling up through the vast inner column, like a leaf caught in an updraft; through the access canyons toward the docking bay where Niburu and the others would be waiting for him, *had to be,* had to be crazy if they were still there, *had to be still there. . . .*

He landed on a loading platform, seeing barricades ahead. He fought his way out through the instant mob that formed around the hovercraft, wondering where the hell anybody thought they were going to go in it. Just away from where they were, maybe— He staggered as the citadel shuddered around him; ran on toward the barricade, with his heart in his throat. The guards blockading the access swung their weapons toward him.

He slowed, and dropped his own weapon. "I'm Kullervo!" he shouted. "I've got clearance, I've got to get through, they need me inside!"

They hesitated, staring at him. "Something came through about Kullervo—" the man in charge said.

"Couldn't make it out, sergeant," someone said. "Garbled, like everything else—"

The sergeant frowned, then gestured. "Go on," he said. The other guard shouted, and the sergeant ducked aside as something smashed down between them. "What the fuck is happening here?" he bellowed.

Reede ran on, not sure the question was meant for him; certain that he didn't want to answer it.

The access corridor to Docking Bay Three was filled with acrid smoke and armed men. Reede shoved his way through them, half afraid that by the time he reached the end there would be nothing left to find. At last he emerged inside the bay's lower level, seeing the vast chamber still intact, its docks rising and falling away for stories on all sides.

There was motion everywhere, noise and smoke, the looming hulls of freighters cutting off his view, until it was impossible to make sense of anything his eyes and ears fed to his brain. He swore, looking left and right, up and down. All the citadel's systems must be choked with the poison of his virus program by now; there would be no way he could call up the LB's location or communicate with its onboard systems—no way to find out whether they were even still here.

He found a ladder, began to climb the scaffolding, hoping it might give him a better line of sight.

"Kullervo!" A voice called his name as he pulled himself up onto the platform. He turned, saw Sparks Dawntreader pushing toward him through the mass of semi-rational human bodies that lay between them. Dawntreader gestured frantically. "This way!"

He shouted in acknowledgment and relief, began to run toward the half-visible beacon of Dawntreader's red hair, dodging workers and soldiers.

"Kullervo!" Someone else shouted his name, behind him; a hand clamped over his arm, jerking him around. He was face to face with the sergeant from the barricade. The sergeant's eyes were black with fury. A gunbutt came at him out of nowhere, struck him in the side of the head, clubbing him to his knees. "The Master wants you back, you miserable fuck." The guard's fist closed over the front of his shirt, dragging him to his feet. "They said you did this! I ought to kill you myself—"

Reede swayed, his hands pressing the side of his face; he was knocked reeling into the metal wall of the bay as someone else slammed between them.

Dawntreader. Sparks collided with the guard, knocking him off-balance. The guard pitched backward down the ladder-well with a strangled cry, and disappeared from sight.

"Are you all right?" Dawntreader was beside him now, supporting him with an arm around his waist.

"Yeah," Reede muttered, wiping blood from his eye. "Come on—" Dawntreader led him on along the echoing platform through what seemed to be an endless game of human carom. Reede thought he heard shouting behind them, someone calling his name again. "How far—?" he gasped, as they started out across the scaffolding between two looming transport hulls.

"Other side," Dawntreader panted, gesturing ahead. "See it, right there—?"

Reede wiped his eye again, nodded. "Are they all—?" Something shook the catwalk like a giant's fist, jerking it out from under him. He went down, with Dawntreader sprawling on top of him, as gouts of fire exploded through the wall of the bay high above. He watched helplessly as enormous chunks of twisted metal came hurtling out of the sky, falling toward them like deadly leaves. "Hang on—!" He shut his eyes, sinking his fingers into the grillwork beneath him.

A sheet of metal larger than both their bodies slammed down on the catwalk half a meter behind his foot, shearing away the alloy as if it were cardboard; the metal platform under his body shrieked and bucked. More falling metal roared past him, and on top of him Dawntreader screamed once, a brief, raw paincry.

Reede swore, shaking his head as he pushed himself up at last, trying to lever himself out from under the dead weight of Dawntreader's unresponsive body without dislodging either of them from the broken platform. He heard shouting again, behind him; sure this time that the voices called his name. He looked back across the sudden chasm, saw the line of armed men barely visible beyond the still-intact hull of a cargo freighter, inching their way out onto the ruined scaffolding, trying to reach a point where they could get a clear shot.

Reede struggled to his knees, pulling at Dawntreader's arm. Blood matted Dawntreader's hair, red on red. He couldn't tell anything about the wound or how bad it was. "Come on," he shouted, barely aware that he was shouting uselessly. "Come on, damn it, get up, get up—!"

Dawntreader's body shifted, slid; he saw Dawntreader's legs go over the side of the catwalk, felt the other man's body try to follow. He caught the back of Dawntreader's tunic with both hands, digging in his heels, stopping their slide. But his own exhausted body refused to give him anything more. He swore, watching the progress of his pursuers toward them.

Suddenly someone was behind him, beside him; he caught a glimpse of midnight skin and hair. "Here, boss—"

"Ananke—" he gasped, "get him!"

Ananke slid past, going out over the edge of the twisted walkway as if it were flat on the ground, not a hundred meters in the air. Ananke clung with an acrobat's skill to the broken superstructure, levering Dawntreader's unresponding limbs back onto the grid as Reede hauled with all his remaining strength. Something gave, and Dawntreader's body slid forward suddenly. Reede pulled him onto the catwalk with a final heave.

"Boss—!" Ananke shouted, pointing down. Reede followed his pointing hand, seeing Dawntreader's belt, the thing that had tangled in the grid and trapped him until it had come apart. It hung from a claw of twisted metal below the catwalk; the pouch dangling from it was the pouch in which Dawntreader had carried the water of death.

Reede flung himself down with a curse, pushing precariously over the edge, his hand flailing. But the pouch was impossibly beyond reach. Ananke crouched beside him, steadying him, until he came up again, white-faced, shaking his head.

Ananke looked down through the grid, and up at him. Suddenly he disappeared over the edge, swinging out and down until only his feet showed. Reede watched through the grid as he pulled himself underneath the platform. In a moment he was back on top again, grinning, as if there were no gravity. He held something in his hands, held it out . . . the belt and pouch.

Reede pushed up onto his knees, staring in speechless gratitude. He slung the belt around his neck as Ananke passed it to him, and moved to help him lift Dawntreader's body.

"We've got to hurry, boss—"

"Kullervo!"

Ananke straightened, looking back; screamed, falling, as the blinding beam of an energy weapon licked him.

Reede grabbed him, pulled him close with furious desperation. "Move!" he shouted, willing sense back into Ananke's shock-glazed eyes, willing Ananke's brain to ignite with the urge for survival. "Run, crawl, get to the LB, goddammit!" He pushed Ananke forward, propelling him as he dragged Dawntreader's body along behind.

They made it to the far end of the catwalk, sheltered by the hulls of the big transports. He saw the LB lying like a toy in their shadow, heard more explosions echo through the bay, and more screams.

Ariele was waiting, her voice lost in the cacophony, her face frantic. She ran forward to help him get the two men to the ship and drag them inside. Niburu was in the pilot's seat, his face shining with an intensity of relief that should have been laughable. "Go!" Reede shouted, dumping Dawntreader into an acceleration couch, as Ariele pushed Ananke into a seat behind him.

"Ananke, get up here!" Niburu called.

Reede fell into the copilot's seat, as Ariele dropped into the couch beside her father's. "Ananke's hit. He's out of it."

Niburu turned, looking over his shoulder. "How bad?"

"Don't know." Reede shook his head. "Won't matter, if you don't get us the hell out of here. Go. Go!" Niburu took them up before he had finished the words, the LB shooting down the length of the bay and out into the open sky like a beam of light.

Beams of light slashed the air all around them, licking the crippled citadel from every direction including the top of the sky; taking it down millimeter by millimeter. The LB shuddered as raw energy glanced off its shields; Niburu swore. "Gods, shit, I can't handle this alone. We'll never make it through this crossfire—"

He broke off, as the view ahead of them suddenly cleared of lightning; the images on the LB's screens showed them a column of inviolate air, their trajectory rising out of the atmosphere, toward the *Prajna*'s orbit. Their way lay open, and as they arced toward the sky, behind them the citadel's shattered spire immolated like a star gone nova.

They flew on in utter silence, as if even a spoken word might break the spell and destroy them; their arc steepened, acceleration pressed Reede into his seat with a heavy hand. There was no pursuit, and no more random energy pulses struck their shields. Reede watched the sky, the only thing he could do; watched its serene blue slowly deepening toward black, watched the sun rise, a vast scintillating jewel, radiant against the starry night as they left Ondinee's atmosphere behind. Reede wiped blood out of his eye again, and sighed.

"Clear." Niburu cut their acceleration. The LB's momentum ceased, and Reede felt himself begin to drift up from his seat, weightless, beyond the reach even of the planet's gravity. He caught the seat's restraining straps, laughing out loud as he pulled himself down again, and locked himself into place.

"Copy. Free and clear," a voice said, suddenly and unexpectedly from the comm speaker on the panel. "Congratulations, survivors. Good luck." And then silence.

"That was Sandhi!" Niburu looked at him, stupefied. "What just happened?" he said.

Reede felt a weary smile pull up the corners of his mouth. "I think we met some strangers far from home."

Niburu shook his head, looking out at the empty sky, at the curve of Ondinee's surface far below, its atmosphere limned by sunlight. He murmured commands to the LB's computer as his hands touched the instruments almost absently. Reede felt himself settle back into his seat, regaining substantiality as the LB's drive kicked in again. "We'll intersect the *Prajna*'s orbit in about six hours," Niburu said. "The medical supplies are down there." He pointed.

Reede nodded, already rising from his seat, moving cautiously as he got a feel for what kind of gravity they were functioning in now. He pulled the supply box from its stash.

Ariele was on her feet beside Dawntreader, mopping blood from his ashen face with the sleeve of her robe. "Da . . ." she murmured. "Da—?"

Reede edged her aside, gently, as Niburu pushed past them to see to Ananke. "Let me look." He used his own shirtsleeve to wipe away more blood, seeing the deep gash in the side of Dawntreader's head. Scalp wounds bled like hell, his own blood was still getting in his eyes. The blood didn't mean anything; he only had to get it stopped. But a blow that hard probably meant a fractured skull, could mean something worse; he had no way of telling. He pushed back Dawntreader's eyelids; one pupil was wide open, the other narrowed reflexively as the light hit it. "Shit . . ." he breathed.

Ariele passed him coagulant and a compression bandage from the medical supplies as he asked for them; he got the bleeding stopped and the wound bandaged. Dawntreader did not stir or make a sound all the while; his breathing was shallow and not quite regular. But as Reede finished working on him, he moaned, and his eyes opened, staring glassily. He mumbled something; Reede couldn't make out the slurring words.

"What—?" Reede leaned closer as Dawntreader repeated them, with painful effort, reaching up to catch the front of Reede's shirt in a spasmodic grip.

". . . Promise me," he whispered. "Promise it."

"Yeah. All right," Reede said softly. "I will. I promise it."

Dawntreader released him; his hand fell away, lay motionless across his chest. His eyes closed.

"Is he going to be all right?" Ariele asked anxiously, as Reede straightened away from Dawntreader's limp body.

"Can't tell," he muttered, blocking her view. He touched the activator on the arm of Dawntreader's seat, and the translucent gray shield suspended above it began to lower. "This will suspend his body functions until we can reach Tiamat, and get real medical treatment," he said quickly, seeing her face begin to fall apart. "His condition won't change. It's the best we can do." He took hold of her arms, drawing her away as they watched the stasis unit seal. He checked the readouts. "Okay," he said softly. "That's as safe as anyone gets." He turned, looking into her eyes. "You're next. And then me. We'll all sleep, suspended, until Niburu gets us to Tiamat."

Her mouth trembled; she pressed it together. "A magic nap," she whispered. "Da used to say, when I was little, 'It's such a long way, Ari . . . why don't you take a magic nap? When you wake up, you'll be home. . . .'" Her voice disappeared.

"Yeah," he murmured, holding her, "we'll be home." He kissed her hair, looked up again as Niburu came forward to get something from the medical kit.

"How is he?" Reede jerked his head toward the seat where Ananke lay, half-hidden from his view.

"He's—" Niburu broke off, with a strange expression on his face. "He'll be all right. A bad burn, but it's superficial. I can treat it with what's here."

Reede nodded, relieved, wiping the blood from his own face with a leftover strip of bandage. He tied the bandage around his head and stuck on a painkiller patch, feeling his wounds as he finally had time to think about them. Dawntreader's belt and pouch were still slung around his neck. He pulled them down, opened the pouch and looked at the vial of the water of death. He sealed it shut again, and fastened the belt around his waist. He glanced at Ananke, able to see nothing but his face, eyes shut, mouth slack, and part of his shoulder.

Reede turned back, drawing Ariele toward her seat again. He kissed her as she settled in; she put her arms around his neck, keeping his mouth on hers a last long, sweet moment before she let him go. He reached down to activate the controls.

"Is it like suffocation?" she whispered. "Is it like freezing—?"

"No," he said, and smiled. "It's like peace." He watched the dome come down; she held his hand until the last moment. He let her go, the unit sealed. He could still see her face through the translucent shield; knew that she could see his. He saw the apprehension in her eyes, watched it fade. She smiled. Her eyes closed, and she slept.

He checked the readouts, and then made his way silently to the final seat, which lay waiting for him. He settled into it. He felt no painful pressure anywhere along his battered body; it was as if he were lying down on clouds. He looked over as Niburu approached him, face to face with his pilot for once.

"I can handle it from here, boss," Niburu said, answering his unspoken question. "The hard part's done."

Reede grimaced. "Don't say that. Gods, don't ever say that!" But he smiled again, faintly; touched Niburu's arm. "What the hell would I do without you, Niburu?"

Niburu grinned. "Stay in one place for a while, maybe."

Reede laughed. "They can put that on my grave. . . ." He reached down, triggering the shield that hung above his head. It began to descend. "Wake me up as soon as we reach Tiamat. I need to talk to Gundhalinu."

Niburu nodded, as the shield's smoky gray came down like fog between them. Reede felt a moment's panic, the same panic he had seen in Ariele's eyes, as the shield sealed in place. His eyes clung to the dim image of Niburu's face as he struggled to keep his body under control. But a cool, tingling vapor was already filling the air, and as he breathed it in his apprehension faded, along with his vision. He smelled fresh wind and sunlight and exotic spices, pleasure and release . . . silence . . . peace. . . .

Kedalion watched Reede's eyes close, saw his blood-streaked face become young again as his consciousness slipped away.

Kedalion checked the readouts, satisfying himself that the unit was functioning properly. He turned away in the sudden, clicking silence, back to where Ananke lay passed out in the other seat. He pushed aside the charred cloth of Ananke's coveralls, that he had cut open for better access to the livid burn that ran from shoulder to hip down his side. He saw the stretch of blistered flesh again, and grimaced. And then he pushed the ruined cloth farther aside on Ananke's chest, slowly, almost reluctantly, needing to confirm to himself that he had not imagined what he had glimpsed in one harried, distracted moment in the middle of chaos.

He pushed the cloth aside. He stared, for a long moment, at what lay revealed beneath it: the smooth, gentle curve of a young woman's breast.

Carefully he drew the cloth down over Ananke's breast again, hiding her secret, covering her painful vulnerability. And then, as calmly as he could, he treated her burns, sealed them with a protective film of bandageskin, and applied a line of anesthetic patches up the length of her spine, to deaden the pain when she woke again.

At last he went forward to the pilot's seat, climbed up into it; leaned back, staring out at the stars. Reaction caught him then, finally, overwhelming him with an exhaustion that was both physical and mental. He felt his eyes closing, against his will. He couldn't remember how long it had been since he had felt safe enough, certain enough, to sleep for long, and he no longer had the strength to fight it. The LB was synchronizing orbits on autopilot; it would wake him when they eventually caught up with the *Prajna*. He could let himself sleep now, finally, for a few hours, if he wanted to . . . he could sleep. . . .

"Kedalion . . . ?"

Kedalion opened his eyes, groggy and uncertain even of what had wakened him. Ananke stood beside him; he started in surprise. "What—?" he said, not meaning to say anything.

"Sorry to wake you up. I . . ." Ananke settled into the copilot's seat with elaborate care, tight-lipped, wincing. "Sorry."

"S'all right." Kedalion straightened up in his own seat, shaking himself out, abruptly wide awake. He glanced at the displays, out at the night, habitually reassuring himself that everything was still going according to plan. He looked back at Ananke—the same face, the same eyes, the same body he had seen every day for years—trying to detect a difference in what he saw; perversely trying not to. "What is it? You all right? You need anything?"

"I'm all right." Ananke shook his—her—head, gazing at him out of blue-black, slightly dazed eyes. "Did you . . . did you dress my wound?"

He nodded. "Yeah. Probably makes you feel like hell right now. But it'll heal fine."

She nodded, glancing away, biting her lip. "Hurts some, even with the pain stuff. Thanks, Kedalion, for—"

"No thanks needed." He smiled, shaking his head.

She looked back at him, and he knew she was trying to guess what he'd seen, *if* he'd seen—if she dared to ask him . . .

"Yeah," he said, ending her suspense. "I know. I saw . . . I couldn't help it. Why the hell didn't you tell me you were a woman?" Half a hundred small anomalies over the years suddenly fell into place in his mind, making perfect sense in hindsight. The pathological shyness, the sidelong looks whenever he'd mentioned sex . . . "Why?"

"Because you're a man," she said, as if that explained everything. Her arms rose unsteadily, one bandaged, one safely hidden by heavy clothing, to cover her breasts, as if they were exposed again, simply by his knowing they were there.

"Anyway," she looked away from him again, "you would never have hired me on if you'd known. Would you?" Her voice turned accusing.

"Well . . . I don't know," he said frankly.

"And Reede would never have let me stay."

"Maybe not . . . not then. Now—" He shrugged.

She looked back at him, stiffening. "Does he know?"

"No," Kedalion murmured. He shook his head. "Nobody knows but me. And you."

She sank back into her seat, her body trembling visibly with the effort of having held herself upright. "Hallowed Calavre . . ." she whispered, her hands clenching and unclenching on the cloth of her coveralls. "Why did this have to happen?"

"Why did you do it in the first place?" he asked. "Did you hate it that much, being a woman on Ondinee?"

Her eyes opened again, black with memory. "Yes," she muttered, looking down at her body. Her voice took on the faintly singsong Ondinean accent that he had not heard in her speech in years, as she slid deeper into memory. "On Ondinee, men are everything, and women are nothing—like animals in the marketplace, bought and traded. Some, the rich ones, are lucky enough to be like pampered pets, dressed in jewels and fine cloth, taught to read, so that they have the illusion that they are human."

Her head came up again. "We weren't rich. My father was a day laborer. My mother had been a dancer once, she taught me a little how to dance. . . . But my father wanted money, he wanted to sell me to the priests to be used in the temple rites. My brother . . . my brother was always trying to get me alone, touching me, and making me touch him—he told me what happens in the rites, how all the men can come and use you after . . . what the priests do, how they mutilate you, so that you can't even feel any pleasure, because women are not even allowed that—" Her voice rose, and broke; tears poured down her face, blurring it with wetness, reflecting the instrument lights in alien traceries of color.

She was not looking at him, not seeing even the night, blind with tears of rage and betrayal. "And he laughed at my tears, and he pushed me down, calling me a whore, and he tried—tried to rape me. But I took his knife and I stabbed him! And I stole his clothes and I ran away. And I went as a boy after that, just so I could live, so I could work, so I could be human. . . . I thought someday, somewhere, I would be able to stop, but I can't stop, because nowhere is safe, and whenever I look at a man and remember that I am a woman I'm always afraid. . . ." She wiped her face fiercely on her sleeve; a small sound, a sob or a noise of pain, escaped her.

Kedalion shut his eyes. He opened them again, looking over at her. He put out his hand, offering it tentatively, in comfort.

"Don't," she whispered, shaking her head. "Don't touch me. Please, Kedalion."

He withdrew his hand, sat looking at it for another moment that seemed endless. "When I was a boy, on Samathe, we used to go drafting off the cliffs, with a glidewing—it was like a big kite. You could fly for hours, if you were good, riding the updrafts like a bird. The stilts—the tall ones—from the other villages used to come and try it; but we were the best at it, because we were small. Some of them hated that. It didn't matter that they could run faster or jump farther or make our lives miserable on the ground . . . they hated seeing us in the air."

He looked out at the stars. "One day when I was drafting, a stilt started shooting at me with his pellet gun. The son of a bitch shot holes in my wing; it ripped, and I went down. It scared the hell out of me, I thought I was going to die. But I was lucky, I just landed hard, cuts and bruises, broke a couple of fingers. . . . But some of my friends saw it, they went after the stilt and they got him. They put my wing on him and pushed him off the cliff. He fell . . . he broke half the bones in his body. They just left him there. I called the rescue service. . . . After that day I swore I was getting out of that place, if it was the last thing I ever did." He shook his head. "One thing that you find out when you leave somewhere is which of your problems belong to where you are, and which of them belong to what you are. . . ." He sighed, looking back at her at last.

"Why did you call the rescue service?" she said faintly.

He glanced away. "Because I saw my friends' faces when they pushed him over the edge. And I was afraid the same look was on my face."

She sat staring at him for a long time, without saying anything. She looked down at her body again, still silent.

"It doesn't matter," he said at last. "You do your job. You do it right, and you don't complain. You can go on doing it, like you always have, if you want to. I don't care what you do with your private life. It's none of my business, as far as I can see."

She lifted her head slowly. "What about Reede?"

He shrugged. "If you do your job, it's none of his business either."

She went on staring at him, her eyes clouded, her face clenched.

"Look," he said, "after all this time, I think I know you. I know I can trust you. Does that mean anything to you? Can you trust me that much, enough to go on working for me now that I know the truth?"

She smiled, in an acknowledgment as uncertain as the offer of his hand had been. And then, slowly, painfully, she offered her hand to him.

BIG BLUE: Syllagong, Men's Camp #7

"There it is."

Gundhalinu pressed his face against the narrow window slit in the transport's vibrating wall, as the guard's voice announced their destination from somewhere up in front. He saw nothing that he had not seen before, glancing out the window in nervous anticipation every few minutes during their flight: the purple murk of the sky, like a massive bruise filling his limited view—the color never changing, brightening or deepening, because the world they called Big Blue was tidally locked, and the penal colonies they called the Cinder Camps existed in the marginally habitable twilight zone on the perimeter of the night side.

A twilight existence. He looked away again from the desolate, shadow-ridden landscape below him. The land below seemed never to change, like the sky above. Someone pushed against him, trying to look out; pressing him back into his seat.

The Cinder Camps. Gods . . . For a moment the sense of overwhelming betrayal that had filled him from the day he had learned that he would not even be allowed a trial crushed all his ability for coherent thought. He saw Survey's hand behind this—the Golden Mean's hand, the one that he had bitten, as Chief Justice of Tiamat. They had made certain that he would be buried alive—not allowed to serve his life sentence in the kind of humane minimum security institution he had expected, where he might have the opportunity to go on fighting to change his situation. Instead he had been spirited away without warning or explanation, taken halfway across the galaxy to this place—sentenced to the Camps. He did not know whether anyone he mattered to had even been told where he was; he doubted that they had.

He had heard of the Cinder Camps, again and again, while he served in the Police; it was the place they sent the worst dregs of human existence, the ones Hegemonic justice considered unsalvageable or incorrigible. *And how many other political prisoners had that included, over the centuries?* He had no idea, although he had an idea about how long most of them had lived, after they got here. He was grateful that he had been a Police officer, that he was trained in hand-to-hand combat, at least . . . as long as no one ever found out where he had gotten the training. He had heard the stories about what they did to ex-Blues, here.

He took a deep breath, as the man next to him leaned away with an inarticulate grunt that might have been disgust. He saw the heavy collar locked around the man's thick neck; reached up to touch the one around his own: *A block,* they called it. It made the use of any kind of charged weapon impossible. If he so much as tried to fire a stunner while wearing one, the block would explode and blow his head off. They had taken away his trefoil, and locked this on him, instead. His fingers clung to it, like the fingers of a man dangling from a cliff, as he felt the transport begin to settle toward the landing field.

He pulled on the pack filled with his survival gear—which had suddenly become the sum total of his worldly possessions—as the guard ordered them out. The pack was not very heavy. Like the other prisoners, he wore gray coveralls of some material as thick and stiff as the hide of an animal, and a hooded parka. He went out with the others as the hatch dropped, not waiting for anyone to urge him to it; trying to remain as unobtrusive as possible. The wind was cold, and smelled of sulfur. Ash blew into his eyes.

The guards fanned out in a ring around the craft, which was already heavily armed, ensuring that unwelcome approaches by anyone waiting there would be instantly fatal. Gundhalinu saw the shadowy figures who stood just beyond the boundaries they allowed, gathered in tight claustrophobic groups, watching for a sign. Behind them, like a surreal painted backdrop, he saw the vast arc of the far larger planet this world circled, the gas giant which was the real Big Blue. Its presence in the sky colored the smoky mauve with a swath of violet-blue. The ground shuddered, faintly but perceptibly, under him where he stood.

"Anybody going back?" one of the guards shouted; the words sounded strangely flat and uninflected, as if the desolation swallowed them whole. But a restless whisper of shuffling feet stirred the silent bodies beyond the ring of guards, as one man came limping forward, moving as though it took the last of his strength. His face was gaunt, but his eyes shone like the eyes of a man who had seen a vision of his god.

The other convicts let him pass, and then the ring of guards opened to let him through, as if he were a holy man. Gundhalinu saw the green light glowing like a beacon on his collar as he came on toward the transport. "He's served his time," the prisoner beside Gundhalinu muttered. "Lucky bastard." Gundhalinu touched his own collar again, silently.

The guards ordered the new arrivals to begin unloading the supplies that had been crammed into the transport's belly along with them. The crates and sacks were stamped with the numbers of work gangs. He worked without complaint, silently cursing himself with each strained muscle for not having kept in better shape.

As his vision adjusted to the dim light, he began to make out more detail in the landscape around him. At first he saw only the utter lifelessness of the plain, nothing but an unending undulation of the same ash-gray cinders that crunched under his heavy, chemical-sealed boots. His eyes kept searching for something more, until he noticed that the cinder desert was pockmarked here and there by an odd extrusion— small craters, their puckered mouths smeared with something black and tarry.

Near the transport there was a cairn heaped up from slabs of stone; probably the sign marking the landing-place. He saw no structures of any kind; but scattered over the surface of the ground, three or four meters apart for as far as he could see, there were poles—wooden, metal, he couldn't be sure—the size of felled trees, and always laid out in a direction he guessed was east to west.

When the offloading was finished, the ring of guards moved inward, passing through the dozen men being left there like so much extra baggage among the supplies. The last guard to pass him paused, looking at him with hard, knowing eyes. "Good luck, Commander," the guard said. "You're going to need it."

Gundhalinu froze, stared at him, trying to make the guard's face into the face of someone he knew, one of the men who had once served under him. But the man was a stranger. *A stranger far from home.*

The guard grinned, and turned back to the transport. The hatch gaping in its underbelly took him in and sealed. The ship rose into the purple twilight with the heavy throbbing of a heartbeat, and rapidly dwindled in the distance.

Gundhalinu dropped the sack he was somehow still holding, feeling the stares of the small knot of strangers around him penetrate his flesh like needles. He said nothing, not acknowledging them, as he looked toward the men on the perimeter who had been waiting for the transport's departure as patiently as hungry carnivores.

The work gangs came forward, each one a coherent unit, the solidarity of their members a show of strength, an act of defiance intended to keep the other gangs at bay as they came in to collect their supplies.

The men around Gundhalinu pressed closer together, instinctively, as the gangs approached and began to go through the supplies. They picked out their own shipments until the ground around the new convicts was completely empty. And then one man broke away from each pack, coming in from their territory to study the newcomers. Gundhalinu guessed that they were the gang leaders, coming to choose recruits.

He held his breath, his tension a physical pain in his stomach as he waited for someone to denounce him. But no one around him said anything, all of them suddenly preoccupied with their own fates. He realized what it would mean to be left on your own in this wasteland. At least as part of a work gang there was some chance of survival.

The gang bosses who came to pick and choose among the new arrivals were ragged and bitter; pale-skinned, dark-skinned, and everything in between. He endured, with the other new men, being inspected like an animal or a slave. The three or four biggest, strongest-looking men went first; he began to smell desperation among the ones who remained.

"Show me your hands." The words were in Trade, the bastard tongue that was probably the only language most of them had in common.

He glanced up into the hard, emotionless stare of one more set of eyes. He held out his hands; the other man's heavy, callused fingers touched his smooth palms. The man snorted and shook his head. "Bureaucrat."

"I can fix things," Gundhalinu said, in Trade. "I'm good at fixing things."

"Got nothing to fix," the man said, "and you're not pretty enough." He moved on.

Someone else stepped into his place. "You say you can fix things?" Gundhalinu nodded, studying the other man, as he was being studied. The gang boss was about his own height, gaunt and raw-boned, not an imposing figure. His face was dark, layered with grime; his eyes were gray and deep-set. Gundhalinu couldn't guess his homeworld, but he recognized the measuring intelligence that looked him over, still holding back judgment. "Kharemoughi?" the man said.

Gundhalinu nodded.

"Tech?"

Gundhalinu nodded again, reluctantly; sensing that the other man would know when he was being lied to.

"What was your crime?"

Surprised, he said, "Treason."

The man grimaced, and shook his head. "I think you're too smart," he said. "Politicals aren't worth the trouble."

Gundhalinu moved suddenly, as the other man started to turn away; used a Police move to pull him off-balance. The other man went down flat on his back, taken totally off-guard. Gundhalinu stood looking down at him. "I can take care of myself," he said.

The man got slowly to his feet, his expression a mix of self-disgust and grudging amusement. "Okay," he said, and shrugged. "I'm Piracy. Come on, Treason." He turned, starting away.

"But he's a Blue!"

Piracy spun back as the prisoner still standing unclaimed beside Gundhalinu shouted out the words. There were razors in his stare. "Is that right, Treason?" Piracy asked softly. "Is it?"

"The guard called him 'Commander.' 'Good luck, Commander,' he said, 'you're going to need it.' . . ."

"Oh, yeah?" The gang boss who had rejected Gundhalinu first pushed toward him again. At the perimeters of his vision, Gundhalinu saw heads turning, the sudden ripple of bodies starting into motion, starting inexorably in his direction, as if he had suddenly developed a magnetic field. The big man shoved him, hitting him hard in the center of his chest, so that he staggered back into the waiting arms of half a dozen other men behind him. He struggled free, kicking and elbowing, as their hands tried to get a hold on him.

He stood in the center of the small open space that was suddenly all that was left to him; ringed in now by a wall of convicts. "I'm a sibyl!" he said, hearing his voice break. "Keep away from me—!" He lifted a hand to his throat, to bare the tattoo that was also a warning sign, that meant *biohazard* to anyone who saw it. His fingers brushed the cold metal of the block; he remembered suddenly that the collar completely covered his tattoo.

"Where's your proof?" somebody called.

"He's got no proof. He's lying."

"Come any closer, and I'll prove it on you!" Gundhalinu shouted.

"You want to bite me, Blue?" Someone else laughed. "You can bite my big one, you Kharemoughi cocksucker."

"I never believed that 'death to kill a sibyl' shit, anyhow—"

Gundhalinu heard the catcalls starting, the muttered threats and curses in half a dozen languages—the hungry sounds of a mob starved for entertainment, for release, for a victim. He turned, slowly, balancing on the balls of his feet as the trap of human flesh closed on him.

They came at him first in ones and twos, and he held them off, sent them back into the mob again, crippled, or laid them out on the cinder field. At first his mind barely registered the blows his own body took; he had not fought, even in practice, for a long time, but the adrenaline rush of his fear honed his reflexes and deadened his pain.

And then they began to come at him in twos and threes, threes and fours, pinioning his arms, tripping him, falling on top of his struggling limbs and body. Someone's hands were at his neck, crushing the metal collar into his throat, choking him into submission. He twisted his head, opening his mouth, and used the only weapon left to him. He sank his teeth into the man's wrist. The strangler bellowed; the pressure on his throat eased, and then came back doubled, sent the universe of stars reeling across his sight.

And then, as suddenly, the crushing pressure was gone again; the weight slid from his chest. He lifted his head, as his vision came back, to see the convict who had been trying to strangle him sprawled on the ground beside him, twitching and white-eyed, as if he were having a seizure. And then the maddened eyes closed, and the body beside his own lay still.

Gundhalinu pushed himself up onto his elbows, gasping, every breath like acid going down his ruined throat. He heard the shouts and laughter fade away into murmurs of disbelief, questions, angry demands: *"What happened?" "What did he do to him—?"*

"I'm a sibyl." He spat the words out, with the taste of a stranger's blood. "I warned you."

For a long moment there was near-silence. He got to his feet somehow, stood swaying. He saw Piracy, at the edge of the crowd, shaking his head. *"Too much trouble,"* Piracy mouthed silently. No one moved around him.

The ground shuddered suddenly; Gundhalinu lost his balance and fell. And then the inner wall closed in on him in a rush, like one creature with a dozen heads, half a hundred arms and legs, a thousand hands, knees, feet and fists. They stuffed his mouth with ash and gagged him with a strip of cloth, bound his hands and feet. He was pulled up, beaten, kicked, and dragged; passed from hand to hand, buried alive inside a moving mass of bodies until at last he came down hard on the blackened rim of a crater he had glimpsed from the landing field. He only had time to realize what he saw before he was forced, face down, into it. Black, reeking ooze covered his head, filled his eyes, his nostrils, his ears. He held his breath, praying to all the gods of his ancestors and the Eight Worlds as he felt himself sink deeper, as they did not pull him up and did not let him breathe and did not stop and did nothing at all but let him die. . . .

". . . come on, now, come on, come on you ungrateful shit, come back. Come on. . . ."

Gundhalinu felt a tremor run through him, and was aware, with a kind of dreamer's perversity, that he still existed inside the mass of bleeding, helpless flesh the mob had made of what had once been his body. He could not see, it was still as black as the foul drowning pool that was his final memory, and yet he heard someone speaking to him, a vaguely familiar voice reciting a kind of abusive singsong chant. It went on and on, as if the chanter believed he had the power to bring souls back from the Other Side. Gundhalinu moaned, realizing with the sound that he could, that he was no longer gagged or—he lifted trembling hands to his face—bound.

"Hey—" Hands closed over his as he would have touched his eyes. He fought, cursing, flailing blindly, until they forced his own hands back to his sides and held them there, strengthless. "You're all right," the voice said. "It's safe now. Nobody's going to hurt you—"

Gundhalinu went limp, lying as still as death again when the hands released him. He felt them move inward along his arms, setting off more pain at every touch; down his body, along the length of his legs. He was beyond caring whether it was meant as torture or molestation, or even a primitive medical exam; only caring that all he saw was blackness. "My eyes," he whispered at last, when he found the courage to speak.

The hands moved abruptly to his head in response, lifting it slightly; fingers brushed his cheeks, his forehead, like birdwings. And suddenly there was light, dim and gray, more light, orange, white, agonizing light. He put up his hands again, with a cry; no one interfered with his movement this time as he covered his eyes with his hands, letting the light back in a millimeter at a time. Still the pain grew with the light, but he forced his eyes open, flooded with tears, to confront whoever held him now.

Piracy's face swam into focus above him. Recognizing the face, he realized that he had recognized the voice too, all along, with some random fragment of his consciousness. He wiped his eyes, swearing in frustration as the tears went on streaming down his face.

"Let 'em come," Piracy said. "Helps clean that shit out of your eyes. They'll heal up in two, three days, if no infection sets in."

Gundhalinu let his hands fall again. He moved his head, the only voluntary motion he had the strength for; able to make out his own body, lying on a pallet bed, stripped of clothing, half covered by a rough blanket, covered with tar and bruises and cuts. His body was one continuous throbbing ache; he was glad that he could not see more clearly what they had done to him.

"You're fucking lucky," Piracy said; Gundhalinu gave a grunt of disbelief. "You look like death warmed over, but you got no broken bones, nothing that won't heal. They were gentle with you, considering what you are. Guess the blood virus scared them just enough, after all. . . . Not that they didn't intend to kill you—"

"You saved me?" Gundhalinu asked. Every word seemed to take the effort of an entire sentence.

"Not me, Treason." Piracy shook his head, his mouth curving up in a sardonic smile. "I told you you were too much trouble. It was him." He gestured over his shoulder.

Gundhalinu blinked his eyes clear, forcing them to see beyond Piracy's face, to make a second human shape take form in the shadows behind him. He realized that they were inside some sort of shelter, its walls reflecting the incandescent glow of a small radiant heater somewhere on the other side of where he lay. The second man moved forward, his massive bulk looming over Piracy until he seemed to fill the entire space of Gundhalinu's vision. "This is Bluekiller. He saved you."

Gundhalinu stared at the man. Bluekiller's enormous, black-bearded face smiled, revealing yellow teeth. His eyes were like small jet beads, almost lost in the narrow space between the filthy snarls of his beard and hair. Gundhalinu could tell nothing at all about his expression. "Why?" Gundhalinu whispered.

A guttural mumbling emerged from the lips hidden inside the beard.

Gundhalinu shook his head, closing his eyes, unable to understand the man's speech. He was not even certain what language the man was speaking.

"Because you're a sibyl," Piracy said.

Gundhalinu felt a sudden pang of gratitude, honed sharper by the brutal memory of the mob's hatred. "Tell him I—"

"He can understand you." Piracy cut him off. "He's hard to make out because he's only got half a tongue. It doesn't mean he's stupid. Don't make that mistake."

Gundhalinu opened his eyes, looking at Piracy, back at Bluekiller. "I learned . . . not to make that mistake . . . a long time ago." He smiled warily, wearily.

Bluekiller muttered something, with an unpleasant laugh.

"That makes you unusual, for a Tech," Piracy said. "Or for a Blue. I figured you'd have certain blind spots that don't stop with your eyes. . . . But he doesn't want your gratitude. He wants you to answer a question."

Gundhalinu met Bluekiller's inscrutable stare again, still reading nothing in it. But the man leaned forward, catching his jaw in the vise-grip of a hand nearly as large as his face, making him cry out involuntarily. Bluekiller held his face immobile; more unintelligible speech poured out of the other man's mouth.

"He wants to know about his family," Piracy said, tonelessly. "He left two wives and eleven kids behind in Rishon City, over on the dayside, when they sent him here. He wants to know what happened to his family. He wants to know now."

Gundhalinu shut his eyes again, not knowing where he would find the strength to begin a Transfer; knowing that he had to, somehow. If he could only begin it, the inexorable energy of the sibyl net would carry him through. "Give me names. . . . *Input*—" he whispered, forcing his mind to focus on the response. He felt the sudden, vertiginous fall begin, as the bottom dropped out of his consciousness, and he fell away thankfully into the waiting darkness. . . .

"No further analysis."

He heard the words that ended Transfer echoing inside his head, knew that he had spoken them himself, as he came back into his own pain-filled body, his own inescapable existence . . . realizing as he did that he had no memory at all of where the Transfer had sent him. He wondered if he had actually blacked out; wondered, with sudden, sickening uncertainty, if he had failed to get an answer.

He turned his head toward Bluekiller and Piracy, gazing up at them through burning, weeping eyes.

Bluekiller cocked his own head, muttering, reached out with his hand. Gundhalinu cringed, but Bluekiller only laid the hand on his forehead, with surprising gentleness. He took his hand away again, and pushed to his feet. Moving stooped over through the cramped interior of the shack, he reached its entrance and went out through the ragged curtain that was its door, disappearing into the twilight.

Gundhalinu looked at Piracy, asking with his eyes; wondering suddenly whether he had been allowed to live only long enough to answer one question.

Piracy reached behind him, brought something forward—a cup filled with dark liquid. "They're all right," Piracy said. He smiled, and there was no mockery in it this time. "And so are you, Treason." He took a sip from the cup, a gesture of good faith, and held it out. Gundhalinu pushed himself up, propping his back against the packing-crate wall behind him. He took the cup in his hands; Piracy helped him guide it to his mouth. He sipped it, tasting a strong bitter flavor of unidentifiable spices, an afterburn like alcohol. He sipped some more, cautiously, feeling it warm him from the inside.

"I guess you belong to Gang Six now," Piracy said. "Bluekiller will spread the word about what you did for him. Everybody respects him. And you put up a good fight. They'll remember that. Pull your weight, and they'll play you fair. How long is your sentence?"

"Life . . ." Gundhalinu whispered. "That shouldn't be more than a week or so." He looked away.

"We'll watch your back," Piracy said. "It comes with the package. Lot of us here have got urgent questions, of one kind or another. . . . If you're not too particular about what you get asked, word will get around. They'll forget you're anything but a sibyl, in time."

Gundhalinu looked back at him, lifted the cup to his lips and drank, so that he did not have to speak. "Where do you get something like this?" he asked finally, nodding at the dark, pungent liquid, feeling it work.

"The perimeter outposts." Piracy poured himself a cup, with infinite care, and took a sip. "When we have a full harvest, we trek it to the nearest post, and trade it in for a few luxuries—" He laughed, gesturing at the naked patchwork walls of the hovel they sat in.

"Harvest?" Gundhalinu said, wondering what living thing could possibly exist in the desolation he had witnessed.

"You remember that crater they tried to feed you to?"

Gundhalinu felt his face freeze. He lifted a hand to his cheek. His face was still caked with a tarry crust of filth; he brought his hand away, blackened and sticky.

"Don't touch it. You can't get the rest off without ripping your skin off too. It'll wear off on its own," Piracy said. Gundhalinu nodded, folding his hand into a fist. "What we're out here to do is find those craters as they come up, and wait for the tar to breed and go crystalline when it crawls out over the rim. We harvest the crystals—that's what they want."

"Is it alive?" Gundhalinu asked, incredulous.

Piracy shrugged. "Semi-alive. A crystaline life-form; about the most primitive kind of thing you can imagine."

"What do they do with it?"

"Who knows?" Piracy turned his face away and spat. "Doesn't matter to me. I just survive, that's what I do, and wait for the green light." He touched the block he wore around his own throat. Gundhalinu remembered the man he had seen getting on the transport, as he was getting off. Piracy looked back at him; Gundhalinu saw the other man's eyes glance off his own collar, where no green light would ever show.

"What happened to the man I infected?" Gundhalinu asked.

Piracy finished his drink. "Somebody smashed his head in with a rock. One thing we don't need out here is a raving lunatic."

Gundhalinu put his empty cup down carefully on the cinder floor. The ground seemed to shudder as he touched it; he jerked his hand back.

"Earth tremors," Piracy said. "We get 'em all the time."

"Tidal stress," Gundhalinu murmured, glancing up as if he could catch sight of the gas giant whose moon this world was, whose violet arc lay across the sky. Its gravitational pull held this lesser world prisoner, with one hemisphere perpetually facing the parent planet, and one forever facing away. The gravitational stresses caused by the slight orbital drift of the two worlds caused this twilight zone to shudder like shaken gelatin, a solid forced to behave like a liquid.

"Whatever." Piracy shrugged.

"Do you get any real earthquakes here?"

Piracy laughed. "You see those logs spread out over the ground when you came in?"

"Yes."

"They're out there because sometimes the ground shakes so hard it splits open, and we fall into the cracks. They usually open up north-south. We lay out the logs east-west like bridges, and hope to hell we're lucky enough to grab one if the ground drops out from under us."

Gundhalinu shook his head, made dizzy by the motion; he felt his body begin to slide down the wall. He struggled to push himself upright again, failed.

"Get some rest," Piracy said. "You can stay here till you can get up and work. It ain't much, but it's better than nothing. I'll take up a collection; the men'll help you put up your own shelter when you're on your feet."

Gundhalinu nodded, his throat working, suddenly unable to speak as he lay down again.

Piracy pulled the ragged blanket up over Gundhalinu's shoulder, hiding his bruised flesh from his sight. "Get some sleep, Treason. Everything always seems better after you sleep." He grinned, wolfishly. "Except, of course, you always wake up here."

TIAMAT: Carbuncle

Jerusha PalaThion stood on the deck of the ship that had once been her husband's, trying to adjust to the unfamiliar roll of its deck, which she had once been so accustomed to. Around her were all the ships her plantation—which had also once been his—could spare, and dozens of other craft, both Winter and Summer, bobbing on the gray ocean surface beneath the sullen gray sky. They covered the water for as far as she could see, ringing Carbuncle. Tiamat's people had come, at the request of their Queen, to witness the miracle of the mers' gathering . . . and, not coincidentally, to impede the offworlders' attacks on them.

Because the mers were here as well, making the sea boil with their restless motion, like an impatient crowd gathered at a gate—but gathered for what purpose she could not imagine; no one here could. She felt the thrumming vibration of mersong in the water all around her, carried up through the very timbers of the ship and into her feet as she stood on its deck.

She wondered what Miroe would have made of this, whether he would have had some insight she lacked. He had been in her thoughts constantly, since she had turned her back again on the betraying Hegemony, and become once more wholly Tiamatan. His memory was with her now, here—in every breath of sea air, in the motion of the deck beneath her feet, the sound of Tiamatan voices calling and speaking around her.

She had barely let herself think of him in all the time she had served as Gundhalinu's Chief Inspector, keeping herself endlessly busy with the details of her work. She felt his absence from her life so profoundly that to remember his presence in it had been unbearable. She had walled herself off from her grief, she realized now; shut away her personal needs behind a barrier of official business, as she had done all her life before she met him.

To be here today in the middle of this strange sea was a kind of catharsis, giving her emotions an outward focus, and a meaningful goal. *He should have been here today*, she thought. And, thinking it, she knew that he was; because she had become the keeper of all that he had believed in, not just under the law but in her soul.

She looked down over the catamaran's rail, checking again on the position of Silky, who had been ranging farther and farther from their position in the water, disappearing but always returning just as she began to grow concerned. Silky blew spray, sneezing noisily in the ship's shadow just below her, and submerged again as she watched. It reassured her to see the merling in the flesh, even though she could track Silky's location any time with the ship's instruments, from the sonic tag the young mer wore.

She had had dreams—nightmares—of the Hunt every night for weeks, even though she had had plantation hands following the colony's course by boat ever since she had learned that the mers were traveling north; trying in the only way she knew to protect her adopted child from Vhanu's hunters. So far she had been successful.

But now the mers had gathered here at Carbuncle, just as BZ had predicted. She had no way of knowing how long they would choose to remain here, any more than she could say why they did it, or how long Moon would be able to maintain this level of support from her people. The offworlder's threats and restrictions had only made the Tiamatans more stubborn; but soon the real pressure would come from the need of people to get on with their work and their daily lives.

The comm bug in her ear came alive suddenly, and a voice said, "Commander, this is Fairhaven. Commander Vainoo is coming your way, in a hovercraft; just so you know."

"Thanks, Fairhaven," she murmured, with an involuntary chuckle. The common local mispronounciation of Vhanu's name had rapidly become the only one, since he had declared martial law. She shrugged at the curious stare of one of her deckhands. "Prepare to repel boarders," she said.

"Commander?" The woman's expression grew even more uncomprehending.

"A joke." Jerusha shook her head, looking out across the sea. She watched mers ripple the water surface off to starboard; saw them submerge, as a hovercraft passed over their heads, just above wave height, heading directly for her ship.

She stood where she was, leaning against the rail, feeling a fine mist that was part cloud, part sea, clinging to her face as she waited for Vhanu to come. The hovercraft slowed, settling with uncanny precision until its door was directly beside her. The bug in her ear came alive again, on the Police frequency this time. "Permission to come aboard, Commander PalaThion?"

"Granted," she said. She smiled, with an irony she knew would not be missed by the watchers behind the mirrored windshield that loomed like a predator's eye above her.

The door rose and Vhanu climbed out, landing awkwardly on the pitching surface of the deck. The hovercraft remained protectively beside him as he saluted her, punctiliously correct, as always. "Commander PalaThion." She heard in his voice how it annoyed him to have to address her by a rank equal to his own, when in his mind she was no more than the head of a local constabulary.

"What can I do for you, Commander Vhanu?" she said, not returning his salute; refusing to participate in his charade of Technician propriety.

He frowned. "You can tell me what you're doing here, in the middle of this unlawful assembly, to begin with," he said.

She raised her eyebrows. "To begin with, this is not an unlawful assembly. Your restrictions only specified gatherings of more than ten people within the city. It said nothing about boats on the open sea. As for my part, professionally I'm ensuring that order is maintained, while at the same time, as a private citizen, I'm observing the Lady's miracle, like everyone else."

"You don't believe that rubbish," he said flatly.

She stared at him. "What I believe, or don't believe, is no business of yours."

His frown deepened; she saw him searching for a trace of sarcasm in her voice, a hint of it in her eyes. She showed him nothing. "You and the Queen have strained my patience long enough with this harassment," he said, his own eyes turning cold. "The Police are beginning a sweep even as we speak. I have ordered my people to arrest everyone who refuses to disperse and remain outside of a five-kilometer radius of the city, and to sink their ships. That includes you, PalaThion, if you remain here."

"More people will take their places," Jerusha said.

His mouth twisted. "Then we'll go on arresting them. You can't keep it up for long. This miserable world doesn't have enough population." He hesitated, as her expression did not change. "And what population it has is extremely centralized," he said slowly. "These ignorant technophobes have no idea what kind of position that puts them in strategically. But I don't have to tell you what we could do to you, if you give us any real trouble. I've been lenient so far. You know that—"

"Commander Vhanu! Sir—" The voice of the hovercraft's pilot came over her own comm link, even as she saw Vhanu react. "Carbuncle has just lost all power."

"What?" Vhanu said.

"Everything has gone down there, sir. It's like someone threw the master switch. They have no lights, no power—nothing."

Vhanu swore, looking toward the city, his face suddenly naked. Jerusha had never seen him show an emotion as spontaneous as the disbelief, and then the fear, that filled his eyes. The fear frightened her more than any threat. "Take me back to the city," he muttered, into his own link. He turned away as if he had forgotten that she existed, and climbed into the hovercraft.

Jerusha watched the craft rise, bank sharply, and soar away toward Carbuncle. The city looked unchanged to her, from where she stood, in broad daylight. But that was the thing about Carbuncle—it held its secrets well. She wondered what would happen when night came . . . wondered if Moon had done this, somehow. She was certain that was what Vhanu must be thinking. Her hands tightened on the rail as she remembered the look in his eyes.

She called on her link, alerting the constables who were out on the sea with the locals, ordering them back to the city. She tried to raise her headquarters in Carbuncle, getting only static; her skin prickled suddenly, as if the sound had invaded her very flesh.

She glanced down over the rail again, searching the water beside her for Silky. The mers nearby had scattered as the hovercraft came down; some of them were returning to fill that gray, restless space now, although suddenly the entire surface of the sea seemed to have grown almost empty of them. "Atwater," she called, glancing into the ship's cabin. "Get me a reading on Silky, will you?" She waited, her hands tapping a silent rhythm on the rail as the time stretched and still she got no answer. "Atwater—?" she demanded.

"I'm sorry, ma'am," Atwater said, at last. "I can't trace her beacon. It's gone."

Hegemonic Police Commander NR Vhanu was met at the gates of the Summer Queen's palace by an escort of two city constables, carrying lanterns. They studied him and his escort with guarded expressions, saying only, "Come with us, sir," as they led the way back through the heavy doors. He felt their hostility like a wave of heat as soon as they turned their backs on him.

He followed them along the hallway, catching fleeting glimpses of the primitive murals that defaced its walls; struck more profoundly by the complete darkness that surrounded him. He had never even thought about what an immense, dark tomb this city was, without the artificial light and life support that the Old Empire's technology had given it. The storm walls at the end of every alley had opened, as if in some strange, programmed ritual, letting in the chill breath of the open air, so that Carbuncle did not become uninhabitable when its systems failed—only massively inconvenient. As if someone had planned it that way.

They reached the Hall of the Winds. It was brighter here, because there were windows to let in the bleak silver light of day—although, he realized with some surprise, these windows had remained closed. He remembered suddenly being told how once only these windows remained perpetually open, so that the winds interacted with the sail-like curtains high above, making what was now simply a rather nerve-wracking passage over the city's open access well into a trial by air.

According to the story, the Summer Queen had caused the windows to close, controlling the city's arcane, self-perpetuating machinery in a way that no one seemed to understand. . . . He crossed the bridge almost without being aware that he did, for once; looking up, studying the sealed windows, and wondering.

They climbed the wide stairway on the other side, and entered what was still called the throne room, although its once-elegant decor had been usurped by rude examples of Tiamatan arts and crafts until it looked to his eye more like a village marketplace. He was always secretly surprised that he did not find live animals wandering among the visitors there.

Today, in the unexpected darkness, he felt as if he were entering a cave. It had never struck him before that this room had no natural light source. The Queen was waiting for him, sitting on the crystal throne which was the only surviving relic of Winter's reign. He had wondered before why she had not had that single striking piece of furniture replaced with some crude native-made chair. Perhaps even she had been awed by the exquisite workmanship of its gleaming convolutions. It seemed almost beyond human design; as if it were a creation spun from ice by the forces of wind and sun.

And now, led by lamplight as he entered the shadow-hung chamber, he saw the throne illuminated by candles and oil lanterns. In the flickering light, it shone as if it held a fire of its own: the patterns of reflection flowing along its undulant surfaces reminded him of the aurora that filled the night sky of his homeworld. The play of light and shadow gave the anemic paleness of the Queen's face, the whiteness of her hair, a strange, almost unearthly luminosity that his startled eyes persisted in finding sensuous. The Queen's eyes were no color that he had ever seen before, no color that he could put a name to; they watched his approach with smoldering hostility.

He felt a moment of vertiginous uncertainty as he stopped before the throne; as he found her beautiful in spite of himself, and remembered the silent air in the Hall of Winds. What was it that Gundhalinu had been unable to resist about her, that had transformed a friend into a stranger, a hero into a traitor? For a moment, remembering Gundhalinu and seeing her before him, shining like aurora-glow, he wanted to find out for himself what it was about her, what it was she had made Gundhalinu feel; how it would feel to possess her, to be possessed by such an obsession. . . .

His sudden guilt and shame suffocated the images filling his mind. He drew himself up, making a perfectly controlled bow. "Lady," he said, his voice flat.

She nodded, a barely visible acknowledgment in return. "Commander Vhanu. What is it you want now?"

"Two things," he said harshly. "I want you to order your citizens to clear the waters around Carbuncle. And I want the city's power restored."

She raised her eyebrows; her expression was surprised to the point of mockery, but he saw her hands tighten over the arms of the throne, her fingers searching its convolutions. "What makes you think that I can control either of those situations, Commander?" she said softly.

He took a deep breath. "You are the leader of this world's people, or so you claim. You ordered them out there."

"I am 'technically only a religious leader, with no real authority to rule,' I believe you said, to justify yourself when you declared martial law. I spread the word among my people about the gathering of the mers, because it is a religious matter to them. They chose to make pilgrimages, to witness for themselves this marvel of the Lady's blessing. How do you expect me to order them not to do that?"

He saw in her eyes that she did not believe anything she said, any more than he did. He had always taken her for a religious fanatic; it shocked him to realize suddenly that she was an exquisite hypocrite, mouthing religious platitudes about the Lady as an excuse to exercise secular powers to which she had no legal claim. He swore under his breath as the once solid ground beneath his convictions crumbled further. "Then you leave me no choice but to control your people for you, Lady," he said.

But it was an empty threat. He had had to pull the force back from their task of arresting the protestors to maintain order in the paralyzed city. And there were disturbing reports that the mers were suddenly disappearing from the seas around Carbuncle.

If this went on too long, he would lose his opportunity to show the tribunal the kind of productivity and control he had been so sure he could demonstrate to them. If he could not find out how to get the city's power functioning again, he would lose everything.

He was a rational man, not a man who liked to take risks. He had gambled on what seemed to be a sure thing; he had put his judgment, his political prowess, his honor, on the line to secure the water of life. If he failed, he would have sacrificed Gundhalinu's trust and friendship, Gundhalinu's distinguished career, his own career—all for nothing. All of them would be brought to ruin by this damnable enigma of a world, and its elusive, seductive Queen.

"I suppose you will tell me next that you had nothing to do with what's happened to the city?" He gestured at the shadows around them.

"I had nothing to do with it," she said, shaking back her long, silver-lit hair.

"They say you stopped the winds, in the Hall down below. You know things about this place that no one else does—" he thought she stiffened imperceptibly, "and how to control them."

"I control nothing about Carbuncle," she murmured. "Any more than you do."

He felt his chest constrict, as her blind dart struck too close to home. "I may not control the power source for Carbuncle," he said, "but I control far greater powers, as you know. We have weapons capable of destroying this city completely—there would be nothing left of it, do you understand me?" He thrust the words at her. "No structure, not even wreckage, no human beings left alive. A crater, filled with the sea."

Her face flushed. "You don't have the authority. You wouldn't dare do such a thing. Why would you—?"

"Perhaps because you left me no alternative. Perhaps simply because I could." His anger fed on her sudden reaction like fire on air. "But if it happens, your last thought will be that you could have prevented it from happening . . . that you drove me to it—" He forced his voice back under control. "A tribunal committee from Kharemough is coming here to investigate the situation that led to my removing the Chief Justice from office. There will be an inquiry, and it will involve your part in his dishonor—"

"There was no dishonor—" she began.

"—And if things continue here unchanged from how they now stand, the tribunal committee will undoubtedly back any measures I am forced to take against your people."

The Queen was silent for a long moment, looking back at him with her changeable eyes. "It strikes me, Commander Vhanu," she said at last, "that we have more in common than simply our roles in bringing a good man to undeserved grief. Gundhalinu is gone because you and I both possess a certain amount of power, which comes to us from some greater source; and we both try to use it to further ends we believe in. Whether we succeed is not always our choice. But it remains our choice how we go about it. I was taught, when I became a sibyl, that my duty was to serve all who needed the power that passed through me; not to use it to serve my own selfish ends. . . . I am simply a conduit, Commander, which is why I cannot give you what you want. I am a vessel. And you are a hollow man." She rose from the throne in a motion as fluid as water, and stepped down off the dais into the protective gathering of her advisors and lightbearers, who had waited for her as silently as shadows. She started away toward the far door, leaving him behind without acknowledgment.

But she stopped at the door, turned back to look at him. "Anything you do to this world or any of its people will come back to you threefold in misery," she said. The stagnant, lifeless air of the throne room gave an unnerving quality to her voice, as if something else were speaking through her. *Only a vessel . . .* She turned away, and did not look back again before she disappeared.

He turned, frowning, and pushed a path through the silent stares of his own retinue. He started back the way he had come, forcing the lantern-bearing constables to hurry after him through the unchanged darkness.

TIAMAT: *Prajna,* Planetary Orbit

Reede Kullervo opened his eyes with the confusion of a man wakened after too little sleep; heard his own slurred voice mouthing sounds that should have been questions, or demands.

"Boss . . ." someone else's voice was saying, with more effect than his own. "Boss—?" *Niburu.* His last memory was of Niburu, fog-gray, melting away. Niburu's face was perfectly clear in front of him now; his hand crossed Reede's line of vision to shake his shoulder with hesitant insistence.

"We're there—?" Reede asked, managing somehow to speak intelligible words this time. He sat up, surprised that his body would obey him; clutched the seat-arms as he began to float upward, until he saw that restraining straps held him in. "Tiamat space?"

Niburu nodded; Reede filled in the slim, silent shadow of Ananke behind him, wearing a headset. "What about—?" He jerked his chin at Ariele's seat, where the smoke-gray shield still rested undisturbed.

Niburu shrugged, and nodded.

"They've closed with us, Kedalion," Ananke said suddenly. "They're locking on to our hatch."

Reede released his restraint harness and pushed up from his seat unsteadily. He clung to the solid support of the seatback until his sense of balance stabilized. "What is it? Have we been contacted?"

"More than that," Niburu said grimly. "We're being boarded. They barely gave us time to set orbit before they were on our backs; they must've been tracking us since the minute we came out of the last jump. The Hedge's nearspace security wasn't this paranoid before we left."

"Move—" Reede gestured them aft with sudden vehemence. "Clear out of the LB, and seal it up. I don't want them snooping around in here, fucking with those stasis units and asking a lot of questions. Hurry up!"

They followed him without protest; Niburu sealed the hatch behind them and led the way out of the *Prajna*'s holds toward the passenger area. Reede worked his way through the serpentine corridors that Niburu had filled with extra cargo storage so that there was barely space for a normal-sized man to pass through without banging his head on something. He swore under his breath, watching Ananke swimming lithely along the passageway ahead of him. His own sluggish body was made dizzy by his every movement. "Damn it, Niburu, why didn't you turn on the gravity?"

"Sorry, boss," Niburu said, looking back/down/up at him. "I move faster this way."

Reede grunted. He had commented, complained, and finally ordered Niburu to get the interior of the ship refitted so that it was more comfortable to a man his own height. Niburu had ignored him, stalled, and finally, standing eye to eye with him from the height of a raised access in the systems center, told him to fuck off. "This is my ship," Niburu had said. "It has to be my way." And to his own surprise as much as Niburu's, Reede had let it go.

He looked down/in as they passed the empty room that was the ship's real heart, where Niburu navigated and they all endured the brutal passage through Black Gate transits. Its passenger cocoons gave them some protection against the stresses of hyperlight as well, now that the ship was outfitted with a jury-rigged stardrive unit, and the past and the future were fused into one imperfect present.

He went on without stopping through the cramped maze of dayroom, commons, and private sleeping cubicles, with nothing worse than bruises and curses. They arrived in the systems center just as the access at the other end filled with a cluster of armed troopers in spacesuits.

Niburu and Ananke raised their hands, drifting free, at the sight of the guns trained on them. Reede did the same, reflexively, kept his hands up reluctantly.

"Who are you? Why are you on my ship?" Niburu demanded, the indignation in his voice belying the submission gesture. "We had clearance when we left. You've got no reason to board us, let alone threaten us. I'm going to report this—"

"You can report it to me." The front man in the group of intruders pushed toward them; banged his head on a piece of suspended equipment and pulled himself up short. He swore under his breath, his eyes threatening death to anyone who cracked a smile. "Lieutenant Rimonne, Hegemonic Navy. Tiamat is under martial law, and we are investigating the arrival of all unscheduled ships."

"Martial law?" Niburu said blankly. "Look, I'm a free trader. I get shipments where I can; I don't run on a schedule."

"Our records show you claim to be arriving with the same cargo you were carrying when you left Tiamat. Would you like to explain that?"

Niburu shrugged. "A deal fell through. It's a hard life."

"Nice try." The lieutenant gestured at his men. "We're taking you aboard our vessel for questioning, and probably detention."

"Wait a minute," Reede said, moving forward cautiously, his hands still high. "I'm their return cargo. They brought me here to see Gundhalinu. I have to see Gundhalinu, as soon as possible."

Rimonne raised his eyebrows, taking in Reede's bandaged head and torn, bloodied clothing. "The Chief Justice? That's going to be difficult."

Reede glanced down at himself, realizing that his appearance didn't help his credibility any. "Take me down to the surface. Contact him, tell him I'm here, he'll see me. My name is Reede Kullervo."

The lieutenant looked unimpressed. "It doesn't matter—"

"Maybe you've heard of me. They call me the Smith."

Everyone's eyes were on him suddenly, staring. "The Smith?" Rimonne laughed. "There's no such person. The Smith is a legend; he doesn't exist."

"What if you're wrong?" Reede said, staring back at him.

Rimonne hesitated. His face pulled into a frown. "What kind of business would the Smith have with the Chief Justice of Tiamat—if the Smith existed?" He held his gun aimed more precisely at Reede's chest.

"It's about the water of life," Reede said steadily. "He needs what I know. I have to see him."

"That's unfortunate, because he's gone," the lieutenant said. He smiled sourly. "And you're under arrest."

"Gone? What do you mean he's gone?" Reede said, feeling his mind stop functioning. *Ilmarinen, you can't abandon me again.*

"He was sent back to Kharemough, charged with treason. Police Commander Vhanu has declared martial law; he's in charge now."

"No," Reede said fiercely. "He can't be, that goddamn son of a bitch—" He looked at the guns trained on his heart, as the full realization of what he had done to himself hit him. He turned suddenly, shoving Ananke aside as he pushed toward the doorway.

Someone fired; the stunshock caught him full in the back, deadening his entire body. He drifted, helpless, as they hauled him ignominiously into the systems center again. They locked his hands together behind him; did the same to Ananke and Niburu. They searched him; he watched in numb despair, unable even to protest as they took the vial containing the water of death from his belt pouch.

"He's sick," Niburu protested, as the marines confiscated the drug. "He needs that. It's medicine, let him keep it."

The lieutenant shook his head. "That's not what it looks like to me." He glanced at the man holding the vial. "Send it down with them. Have the Police check it out."

Reede shut his eyes, unable to make any sound at all; feeling as if the frustration and rage inside his brain would explode his skull like shrapnel.

The lieutenant pointed toward the access behind him. "Take them out. Contact the Police." He looked back at Reede. "Too bad the Chief Justice can't see you, Kullervo. But Commander Vhanu's going to be overjoyed."

By the time they reached dirtside his voluntary nervous system had come alive again, letting him stand and walk on his own feet as the marines turned them over, with the water of death, to the waiting squad of Blues.

The Blues took them back through the umbilical tunnel that connected the starport to Carbuncle. Reede slumped in his seat, saying nothing, staring straight ahead into the blackness shot with light.

They did not take the usual lift ride, up through the hollow core of one of the city's pylons to an exit somewhere along the Street. Instead, the Blues forced them on into the twilit docks below the city, toward the main access ramp the Tiamatans used to get to and from their ships.

"Why are we going this way?" Reede snapped, breaking his silence at last, irritable with tension and fear.

One of the Blues glanced at him. "Lift's not functioning," he said.

Reede looked at him in disbelief. He looked away again, already too aware of the crawling itch beneath his skin, the burn of his soles as the ground pressed against them, the separate exquisite pain of every cut and laceration on his battered body, as his nerve endings became hypersensitized. He tried not to think about how much longer their journey would take this way, how much more effort it would take, how much less time and strength he would have at the end of it.

The Blues halted him at the foot of the ramp, as another cluster of patrolmen came toward them, carrying what looked like a corpse in a body bag.

The sergeant in charge of his squad moved forward, his face tight. "Who is it?" he asked.

"Not one of ours," the woman leading the other detail said. "Some local."

The sergeant's expression eased. "One of those Motherloving Summers fall overboard again?" His mouth turned up in a hopeful smile.

She shook her head. "A Winter. One Kirard Set Wayaways. We're turning him over to the city constables."

Reede stiffened. "What happened to him?" he demanded.

The female Blue looked toward him, surprised. "The Queen's justice," she said sourly. "Guess he wasn't much of a swimmer."

Reede felt his own face form a smile more like a rictus. "Out of his depth . . ." he murmured. His guards urged him forward again, and he began to climb.

As they ascended the ramp he realized that something else was wrong with the city: it was growing darker instead of lighter as they climbed. Carbuncle had always been filled with light, day and night—he had never even thought about it, taking it for granted, like the automatic climate control of the city's self-contained system. It had existed that way since before the Hegemony's recorded time, a product, a relic, of the Old Empire. He had been told that Carbuncle ran on tidal power, that there were immense turbines in caves somewhere deep in the rock below the city. He had been told that it always ran perfectly, self-maintaining, self-perpetuating.

But there was no such thing as perpetual motion. The city's darkness, waiting above to swallow him, filled him with a strange emotion, that was as much urgency as it was fear. "What the hell happened?" he asked. *But he knew what had happened; he knew, these signs were important, he had to act now. If he could only remember what he had to do—*

"The lights went out," the Blue walking beside him said. "Everything went out. The city's stopped working."

"Why?" Reede asked.

"I don't know." The Blue shrugged, frowning.

"How long ago?"

"Two days," the Blue said.

"Three days," Reede murmured. "Two gone . . ."

"What?" The Blue stopped him.

"I have to see the Summer Queen," Reede said. "I have to see the Queen."

"You know something about this?" the Blue asked. His hand struck Reede's shoulder, when Reede did not answer. "Do you—?"

"He doesn't know anything, for gods' sakes," another man said. "He's trying to jerk us around. Get moving—" A hand caught Reede between the shoulder blades, propelling him forward.

Reede went on without protest, stupefied by the seething mental energy that the darkened city had set loose inside his brain. *Yes,* he thought, looking left and right at the batteries of portable lights, at the flickering dance of candles being carried along the night-filled alleys of the Lower City, where mostly Summers lived. *Yes. I've come home. . . .* But he did not know why he thought it, and the thought only filled him with desolation.

They went on, circling slowly, ever upward, the helmet lights of the Police surrounding him like glowflies, showing him the way ahead. The few other lights he saw passed them by like the motion of strange creatures in the black depths of the sea. Most of the citizens seemed to be staying at home, by choice or otherwise. The air felt stagnant to him, although the transparent storm shutters at the ends of every alleyway stood open now, letting Carbuncle's human hive breathe on its own. His face ran with sweat; he could not wipe it away, with his hands locked behind him.

They went on, through the Maze, although he had difficulty even recognizing it with so much of it in darkness. Even Persiponë's Hell was closed down and dark. Behind him Kedalion swore, breathless from trying to keep up. He had not realized that he was slowing down too, until someone shoved him again from behind. He stumbled into Ananke, who was ahead of him now. Ananke lurched sideways, with a clumsiness Reede only recognized as intentional when Ananke collided with the Blue shadowing his own steps. The Blue went down with a grunt of surprise, in a sudden lightstorm of intersecting headlamp beams.

"Reede, run—!" Ananke's voice shouted, as Reede dodged groping arms and flailing legs. Reede broke away from their struggling bodies, looking back as he heard Ananke cry out in pain behind him. *Run*— He ran, with no choice but to abandon them. *He had to make it to Street's End, to the palace*— A random stunshot grazed his arm; he felt it go numb and tingling.

He ran faster up the black, nearly empty street, knowing that he still had a third of the city to go, all of it uphill through the darkness. He wondered if the Blues were able to call for reinforcements. The darkness must be crawling with Police, out doing their job, harassing potential thieves and troublemakers. *Thieves and troublemakers; gods*—

The way ahead was still a tunnel with no light at its end; but as he passed one more alley entrance, light flooded around him suddenly, and voices shouted at him to stop.

He jerked to a halt; trapped in the sudden crisscross of beams like an insect, as dark figures swarmed around him.

"We've got him! Commander!" someone called behind him, catching hold of the binders that still trapped his wrists. He jerked free, but there was nowhere left for him to go. He stood still, his exhausted body trembling, humiliating him. Someone stepped in front of him; he was blinded as another helmet light shone directly into his face. He swore, squinting; opened his eyes again as the light unexpectedly dimmed to a bearable level. Blinking his sight back, he tried to make out the face of Vhanu, BZ Gundhalinu's right-hand man, the ass-kissing martinet Gundhalinu had stupidly made Commander of Police.

But it was a woman's face he saw—middle-aged, cinnamon-skinned; New-havenese, not even Kharemoughi. The Chief Inspector . . . PalaThion, that was her name. But they'd called her *Commander*. He peered at her, seeing that she was not wearing a Police uniform; realizing that the people surrounding her, and him, were all Tiamatan—the local constabulary, not the Blues. "Huh—" he said, half in confusion and half in disbelief. And then, like a mindless recording, he said, "I have to see the Queen."

PalaThion's eyes narrowed as she looked at his face, until she was almost frowning. "Who are you?"

"Reede Kullervo. I need to see the Queen."

"Yes—" she whispered, but for a moment she wasn't seeing him. "Thank you, gods!" she murmured. Uncertainty filled him as she looked at him again, at his pinioned hands. She turned away as the sound of running feet closed with them, and more lights joined their pool of illumination.

"You got him?" a voice demanded. He saw blue uniforms gathering in the light of the constables' lanterns; recognized the voice of the sergeant who had been in charge of him.

"Don't let them take me back," he muttered, holding PalaThion's gaze. "Don't."

She nodded, a barely perceptible movement of her head, before she stepped past him to face the Blues. Reede turned, squinting again as their lights picked him out inside the ring of constables. "This man is in our custody now. We have a prior claim on him."

"He's an offworlder," the sergeant said. "He's under our jurisdiction."

"What's he charged with?"

The sergeant hesitated. "He says he's the Smith."

"Do you have any proof of it?"

The Blue glanced at his men, back at her. "No. Not until we run an ID check on him. What does the Queen want him for?"

"He kidnapped the Queen's daughter," PalaThion said, her voice deadly. "He's in our custody, and he stays with us. If Vhanu wants him, let Vhanu come to the palace, and discuss it with the Queen. Although I don't expect he'll get much cooperation, as long as we're under martial law."

The sergeant's face twisted; Reede watched him assessing the situation, the fact that the Tiamatans outnumbered his own men. He must have left part of his patrol behind with Niburu and Ananke. Finally he jerked his head. "Keep him, then. And tell the Queen if she wants to talk about an end to martial law, she'd damn well better turn the lights back on!" He gestured at the others; they followed him away down the Street.

"Did the Queen really shut down the city?" Reede asked, when they had gone.

PalaThion shook her head. "But Vhanu's ready to blame it on her. Are you really the Smith?"

Reede looked away. "I thought you worked for Vhanu," he said, ignoring the question. "I thought you were Chief Inspector."

She shook her head again. "I worked for Gundhalinu. But he's gone."

"I know," Reede murmured. "I know." He felt a sudden wave of nausea hit him, and realized that he was shivering again, as if it were cold. It was not cold. "Shit!" He jerked his head. "Take me to the Queen, damn it, I don't have much time!"

"Ease off, boy," she said, putting a restraining hand on his pinioned arm. "We'll get you there soon enough."

He glared at her; pulled away from her grasp and started on up the hill at a jog trot, forcing them to follow.

At last they reached Street's End, the plaza before the palace entrance. Its white alabaster expanse was ringed with lanterns. PalaThion took the lead now, speaking to the guards who stood as they always did near the heavy doors. The doors opened to let them pass, and Reede entered the Summer Queen's palace for the first time. He followed PalaThion down a long, echoing corridor, his eyes disturbed by the dance of light around him, the glimpses of painted pastoral scenes—green hills, water and sky, illuminated by the restless motion of lantern beams.

Up ahead the hall finally ended, opening out into a vast, high chamber. The air smelled suddenly, surprisingly, of the sea. Far above him were more windows like the storm walls at the end of every alley along the Street. But these were shut, unlike all the rest. Beyond the windows the night sky burned with the light of a million stars.

Reede looked down again, seeing another cluster of lights across the chamber. Someone was waiting there. "It's the Queen," PalaThion murmured.

But between the Queen and where he stood, there was something else . . . a strand of darkness arcing across a well of eerily glowing green light. Reede moved past PalaThion, starting toward it with a sense of premonition, a sudden urgency.

"Kullervo!" PalaThion called sharply, catching hold of his arm. "Wait a minute, that's the Pit. You can't cross this room in the dark; there's no floor."

"It isn't dark," Reede murmured.

"It's pitch black," she said. "What are you talking about?"

"Let me go." He jerked against her hold, starting forward again. "I see perfectly. I have to go there . . ."

She released him, wordlessly; he saw the look in her eyes. *She doesn't see it.* He felt his skin prickle with sudden terror, felt his entrails knot up inside him. But he went on, alone, drawn toward the glow like an insect, helplessly, instinctively. He reached the spot where the railless span bridged the Pit, and stopped again. *Now, here, at last, all his questions would be answered. . . . He had finally come to the place where he had been meant to be.*

He held his breath as compulsion locked his muscles and forced him to step out onto the bridge, over the well of bottomless light. He was dimly aware that PalaThion had followed him, but was keeping her distance. He took another step, trembling with awe and fear, feeling the green light reach up to caress him like a lover, engulfing his senses in the most beautiful music, the sensation of silk and velvet, the smell of the ocean wind. . . . "No," he whispered, like a child, as he went on into the light, "no, I don't want to, I'm afraid . . ." as his consciousness dissolved into the sea of sensation and compulsion. He sank to his knees at the center of the bridge, as he sank deeper and deeper under its spell. . . .

Vanamoinen. It reverberated in his brain, a demand, an affirmation. *Yes. . . . He was Vanamoinen,* not the other, the receptacle of flesh and blood, the stranger who huddled on the span now in pathetic human misery. *He remembered . . .* how he had chosen this world, created this city, an ornate, incomprehensible jewel that would haunt humankind for generations after he was gone. They would preserve and protect it, because it was unique, never guessing that it existed to be the pin in the map, marking the secret place where lay his real gift to future generations: the databanks that preserved all that he could gather of human knowledge—the nexus of the sibyl mind, the mirror of his soul.

But not his soul alone—*Ilmarinen's.* It would never have existed, he could never have realized his dream . . . he would never have had those dreams, if it had not been for Ilmarinen, whom he loved. Whose calm rationality and understanding of human weakness amazed him, whose dark eyes were deeper than infinity, whose sudden, unexpected smile had come to mean more to him than a hundred honors, a thousand empty gestures of praise from the corporeal gods of the Interface. Ilmarinen, who had been the other half of him, of his genius; whose soul was joined with his forever in the design and programming of the sibyl system. The system born of their mutual vision and sacrifice had survived the generations since their deaths, doing good, spreading knowledge freely; the symbol of all they had been to each other, all they had believed in. *Ilmarinen . . .* he called. *Ilmarinen—?*

But Ilmarinen was dead, laid to rest millennia ago, as he thought he himself had been. He should not be here now, like this, awakened from his centuries of peace, brought back to life as a total stranger in this strange and terrifying existence.

Except . . . He remembered it now, remembered everything that had been denied to him for so long: He remembered that he had willed this himself. After Ilmarinen's death, he had made the arrangements, had recorded his brainscan and hidden it in a secret place remembered only by the sibyl mind, in case the net should ever need him in some future time.

And now that time had come. He had been called back to life, and he did not need anyone to tell him what had happened. There had been no crucial errors in the system's design or programming; there had been no mistakes in the genetic design when they had played god and created the mers. Their only failure had been in underestimating human greed. Giving human beings indefinitely extended lives had never been their desire, or their point. But someone had taken notice of the mers' longevity, someone had unlocked their secret, and the Hunts had begun.

And because, over the centuries, they had slaughtered the mers, the sibyl mind was failing. Now it had called him back, to save it if he could. *If he could . . .*

Come with me, the voice said. *Help me. . . .*

"Come with me. . . ."

He raised his head, looking up into the face of the Summer Queen. He realized slowly that he was down on his knees, crouched fetally on the fragile span above the glowing Pit, his body shaken by tremors as though he were having a seizure.

"Help me," the Queen murmured, her hands lifting him, gently but firmly. "Help me get you away from here, to somewhere you'll be safe."

"Nowhere . . ." he mumbled. "Nowhere I'm safe."

"Yes," she whispered, with soft conviction. "With me."

He got clumsily to his feet, drawn by something in her gaze, and let her lead him on across the bridge, to the safety of the far rim. She carried no light; she did not seem to need one. PalaThion followed them; when they stood on solid ground she breathed a sigh of relief, and released the binders he still wore.

Reede brought his hands up; pressing his eyes, trying to burn away the suffocating echoes of green. He let his hands drop again, and found the Queen's steady, searching gaze still on his face. He saw other figures standing behind her, but registered only one—thinking, for a brief, heart-stopping moment, that he saw Gundhalinu waiting in the shadows. But it was only the Queen's son, Tammis, with his wife standing beside him, her expression guarded and fearful.

Tammis was not looking at him, but past him; staring at the Pit. *He sees it too.* Reede moved slightly, for a better view; saw the glint of a trefoil against the boy's tunic. *Does he know—?* He let them lead him away, on up the wide stairway into the palace's heart; gazing in fascination at the glimpses of form and decoration illuminated by their passage. He recognized nothing, and yet he knew, with an indefinable sense of space, exactly where he was, as if he were a traveler returning home after an absence of many years.

They brought him into a small room that had been made into a library, filled with varieties of information storage from primitive to state-of-the-art. One wall opened on the city's silver-lit silhouette, on the sky and the sea. He looked around him, only remembering to sit down because his body abruptly insisted on collapsing. The Queen herself brought him something to drink. He accepted the cup without comment and sipped the cool, bitter liquid, feeling its pungency begin to clear his head.

"Where is my daughter?" the Queen asked, as he raised his head again. "Where is my pledged?" Reede saw how she looked at him, taking in the bloodstains, his ruined clothes, his face.

"Ariele's safe, for now," he said. "On board my ship, in stasis. Your husband . . . your husband died." He looked down, away from her stricken face. "He caught a bad one, getting us out. He died. I'm sorry. . . ."

The Queen made a small, wordless noise as grief choked her. She turned away from him, moving toward the windows. She stood there alone looking out at the stars; no one around him moved, granting her the illusion of solitude. Reede set his cup down roughly on the opalescent table surface beside his seat; wanting to shout at her that there wasn't time for grief, there wasn't time— He kept his silence, like the rest of them, until at last she turned back again.

"What about the drug?" she said to him. Her body gave an involuntary spasm. "The water of death?"

"The Blues got all I had." He shook his head. "I thought Gundhalinu would be here, damn it! I thought he'd be able to help us—"

The Queen was silent again for a long moment; fighting for control, he realized, when he looked back at her at last. "He will come back," she said finally. "When we've done what we have to do."

"It'll be too late," he whispered. He felt giddy suddenly, as if his head were lighter than air. He swore under his breath.

"Vanamoinen," the Queen said softly. "Do you know why you're here? Did it tell you—?"

He raised his eyes again, studying the strange paleness of her hair, the porcelain translucency of her skin. "Yes," he murmured.

The Queen glanced at the others waiting behind her. "We need to speak alone." They nodded, starting one by one toward the door. PalaThion hesitated, her eyes asking a question. The Queen nodded, and she followed the others out.

"Not you," Reede said suddenly, as Tammis moved away from his mother's side. "You stay."

Tammis hesitated, half frowning with doubt or surprise. His wife closed her hand over his, trying to pull him after her without seeming to. Reede recognized the slight swelling of her belly, and wondered if that was what made her try to change his mind. But Reede held the boy's gaze with unrelenting insistence. "You saw something," he said to Tammis. "You know something."

Tammis nodded, and urged his wife silently, apologetically, away from him. She went out, and her doleful stare was the last thing they saw as she shut the door.

When they were completely alone, he said, "I need two sibyls—the sibyl net picked you," he gestured at the Queen, "and Gundhalinu. But Gundhalinu's gone." He turned back to Tammis. "I think you're here to replace him. Can you swim? Use underwater gear?"

Tammis nodded, settling into an ornate corner chair. "What's this about?"

The Queen took a seat on the long couch where Reede was already sitting, and he saw the dubious glance she threw his way. She was prevented from explaining; the sibyl mind controlled her, as it had controlled Gundhalinu. But it didn't control him, and it was too late now for second thoughts. "The artificial intelligence that runs the sibyl net—the entire database, and the programming that controls it—is located here, below Carbuncle," he said.

Tammis stared at him. "How do you know that?" he asked. "I thought nobody knew where it was."

"Your mother knows." Reede glanced at her. "And Gundhalinu. And I know it, because I put it here."

Tammis laughed in disbelief. "There's been a sibyl net for millennia! Even the Snow Queen didn't live that long."

"I'm not just someone named Kullervo. I'm something more now. My name was—is—Vanamoinen. The real Vanamoinen died long ago; I'm a construct, a database . . . his avatar, for want of a better word. I'm using Reede Kullervo to do what I have to do, here, now. The network I helped design brought me back because it's failing. The mers are part of the system, they were meant to interact with and maintain the sibyl network: it's a technogenetic system with two radically different substrates—" He broke off, seeing the incomprehension on their faces. He tried again, groping for terms that they would have some chance of understanding. "The mersongs contain information that the smartmatter of the computer requires, and certain chemicals released during the mers' mating cycle also trigger self-maintenance sequences, allowing the computer to purge itself of errors, and restructure any drift in its logic functions."

"Their—mating?" Tammis said. "I thought they mated at sea."

"It's a two-stage process." Reede shrugged. The initial stage occurred when the mers were actually within the computer; all of them together. Their communion with the sibyl nexus primed them biologically, so that when they did mate, they could conceive. He had intended for it to keep their population stable, because they were so long-lived. And he had intended for it to bring them pleasure, so that they would be glad to return, for their own sakes, as well as the sake of the net.

He shook his head, with a smile that held as much pain as irony. "We thought we had it all planned perfectly. We never imagined the people the net was meant to serve would begin killing them off. . . . We never realized what forces would work on a system that survived this long, through so much history." He looked up at them, and his smile became self-mocking. "*You* try inventing a fault-tolerant system with superhuman intelligence that has to survive forever. . . ." He laughed once. "We made a mistake; we were only human, after all—"

They were both staring at him now, in wonder and fascination. He felt an unexpected tenderness fill him, as he looked back at them—the descendants, the survivors, the people for whom he had created all of this. Seeing the trefoils they wore, the same symbol he had worn, so long ago; knowing that they carried in their blood the same transforming technoviral that he had been the first to carry. He had designed the choosing places to seek out people like these, counted on people like these to go on seeking out the choosing places; and after more than two millennia, even with all that had gone wrong, it was still happening as he had planned.

He smiled, even as Reede Kullervo's body twisted and shifted position, made restless by the growing discomfort of its failing systems. He wiped his sweating face on his sleeve, and wished suddenly that he had not drunk whatever it was they had given him. Even the thought of drinking or eating made his stomach rise into his throat. He swallowed hard, feeling panic start inside him, not certain whose it was, who he was. . . . "What—?" he said, as he realized the Queen had asked him something.

"Is there . . . is there anything I can get for you?" she repeated, her eyes troubled.

He shook his head, and stretched his cramping hands. "Just listen. We don't have a lot of time. Do you know why the city's gone dark?"

"No," the Queen said, her gaze sharpening. "Do you?"

"Yes." He glanced away, looking out at the sky and its reflection in the sea below. For a moment he remembered another darkness, with only the faintest whisper of ruddy light, so fragile he might almost be imagining it, to make its dark heart all the more terrible. He looked down again, focusing on the fractal patterns of the rug beneath his feet. "Because it's time—the right time, the only time when anything can be changed. The turbines that provide the city's power—and power for the sibyl nexus—shut down once during every High Year, at the time when the mers return to the city. At all other times, the turbines make the passage in to where the computer lies completely inaccessible. Anyone who tried to get past them would be killed. But for those three days the way is clear, to let the mers pass inside. When the turbines start up again, the computer will be unreachable for another two and a half centuries. Any attempt to get at it any other way will fail, or destroy it."

"Why?" Tammis asked.

"Because I had to be sure that it would never become the possession of a single faction in any human power games. That's why I made absolutely certain that its location would remain unknown. That's why your mother and Gundhalinu could never explain what they were doing."

Tammis glanced at his mother. "Then how did you find out?"

"Once, as I was crossing the Pit, it called up to me . . ." the Queen said, her voice growing faint. "It . . . chose me, to help it. And all these years, I've tried—" Reede saw the terrible weariness in her eyes. "Tried to understand what it needed from me . . . why it chose me."

"It chose you because you were in the right place at the right time." He hesitated. "I'm not saying it was an accident. . . ." He touched his own head. "I'm not saying it was entirely predestined, either. But you're Arienrhod's clone for a reason." He saw her flinch. "Arienrhod proved she had the strength and the intelligence to get what she wanted from her own people and the offworlders, whether they liked it or not. You are what you are, Moon Dawntreader. . . . But you're also the Lady," he added gently, "the holder of this world's trust. You are what Arienrhod should have been. Because you were raised by the Summers, who kept—kept peace with the sibyl net, and protected the mers, you have the ability to see the long view. Arienrhod couldn't have done that. You understand why it matters, why it *really* matters—" He broke off. "You are the future I wanted to believe in."

She looked down; looked up at him again, with gratitude shining in her eyes. But then her expression changed. "You said there would be access to the computer for only three days. More than two of them are gone."

He nodded. "That's why we can't wait. One reason." He glanced down at his unsteady hands. "Your husband had data on the lost elements of the mersong. I have to reconstruct them—" He realized, with a sudden sinking feeling, that there was probably not a functional computer with the kind of database he required anywhere in the city.

"It's already been done for you," the Queen said.

He looked back at her. "Gundhalinu? Did he do it before his arrest?"

"No," she said, with a faint smile. "The Sibyl College finished his work." She touched the trefoil she wore. "I can get the tapes for you—we reproduced the mersong, inserting the missing passages."

He smiled too, in spite of himself. "I'll need underwater gear for two people—him, and me." He gestured at Tammis.

She half frowned. "What are you going to do?"

"We've got to go down into the . . . into the—" He broke off, found himself with his hand pressed to his mouth, like a man about to be sick. He forced his hand down to his side again. "Into the sea, through the turbines, into the computer with the mers. I have to check out the system myself, to see what's gone wrong with it, and reprogram. . . . We have to give the right songs back to the mers."

Into the sea, under the water . . . drowning, death, blackness. The images filled his mind, and again he did not know whose fear filled him, who had always been terrified of death by water, who had always known that it would be his destiny. . . . He swore under his breath, wanting to cry out. *You're damned anyway, you miserable bastard,* he thought, with furious self-loathing. *Death by water, or the water of death. It doesn't matter how you die!* But it did. . . . He looked out at the night, so that he would not have to look into the eyes of the two people watching him.

"Why does Tammis have to go with you?" the Queen demanded, and he heard fear for her son in her voice. "I'm a sibyl; the sibyl net chose me."

"That's why. You have to remain clear, where you're protected. You're going to be in deep Transfer, for hours, inside its mind . . . it will show you, and you're going to tell me, what's wrong. I need you to guide me, let me know when the healing is done. That's going to be dangerous enough." He felt the heat of her resistance, her uncertainty as she searched the face of the man who had poisoned her only other child. "You won't be functional, damn it! I need someone who can work with me—and it has to be another sibyl who can act as go-between for us." He gestured at Tammis.

"But I thought you were a sibyl," she said, still frowning, even though there was the beginning of understanding in her eyes now.

He laughed, with another man's bitter terror. "No, Lady," he whispered, with another man's voice. "I am not a sibyl. Sibyls are sacred. I am a human sacrifice. . . ." Tammis shuddered, staring at him.

The Queen's face changed. She reached out slowly, as if she were afraid he might bolt, and touched his cheek, as gently as she might have touched her own child. The barest contact of her fingers sent a shock jittering through the nerve endings in his face. But he did not pull away.

He felt her withdraw her hand, after a moment. "I'll get the data and underwater equipment for you as quickly as I can," she said. "But how will you reach the computer? You can't go into the city; you can't get to the sea without Vhanu's patrols seeing you."

"Yes, we can." He rubbed his eyes, forcing himself to concentrate again, to stay focused, to function as one human being. "The Pit is an access well, it goes down to the sea. It goes exactly where we need to be."

"But there's no power—even the well is shut down."

"Not for us," he said gently. "It knows about us. I want you to come with us down into the well. We can't risk being interrupted. Even Vhanu can't reach us once we're down there." He hesitated, seeing her face change. "Have you ever experienced an extended Transfer?"

She nodded. "Once. It was—" She broke off, and he saw the memory of an endless absence that still haunted her. *Like drowning . . .*

"It won't be like that, this time," he murmured. "It will be—nothing like anything you've ever known. But it will still be difficult. . . ."

"I know." She looked up at him with a weary, sorrow-filled smile. "Isn't everything?" She rose from the couch. "I'll see to things," she said, looking away again, suddenly distracted. For a moment she gazed at Tammis, and then she went silently out of the room.

Moon entered the room that had become her husband's entire world within the palace, before his journey to Ondinee . . . to the Land of Death. She moved slowly about its perimeter, her eyes taking in every detail of its contents . . . the study materials, the imported electronics equipment, the makeshift bed to which he had exiled himself, after she had driven him away. He had never allowed servants to enter his private workspace; she had not allowed it either, since his disappearance.

She sat down on the edge of his cot, picking up a rumpled shirt that he had carelessly thrown aside. She pressed it to her face, inhaling the familiar scent of his skin until her mind filled with images of lying beside him in the sweet abandonment of love . . . memories of all that they had meant to each other, for so many years. Even knowing all that they had done to each other, all that they had thrown away or let slip through their hands, still in this moment she could remember only the good things. Because there was no need now to remember anything else. Because he was dead. He was dead. . . .

She dropped the shirt and rose from his bed again, moving on around the room, passing the terminal, remembering the work he had done, alone and unappreciated: the hidden secrets of the mersong he had discovered, the difference that his discoveries were about to make, which no one would ever be able to thank him for, now.

She stopped again before the small table whose private drawer she had forced, seeing its contents still scattered on the tabletop where she had left them, thoughtlessly, on the day she had lost the only other man she had ever loved. The sign of the Brotherhood still lay on the floor where she had dropped it: the symbol of Survey, in all its endless permutations of treachery and betrayal—yet with a gemstone as beautiful as the sun, the symbol of enlightenment, glowing at its heart.

She looked away from it, kicking it aside with her foot. She sat down by the table, picking up the objects that lay on its surface, one by one . . . the wooden top that Sparks had played with when he was a boy . . . the lock of someone's hair, as pale as milk, inside a blown-glass vial . . . the embroidered love-token that she had made for him, when they had first pledged their lives to each other. . . . *Why had no one ever warned them about how long the years would seem . . . about how they would end, without warning?* She fastened the small embroidered pouch to the inside of her shirt, next to her heart, as Sparks had always worn it in his youth. She wiped the wetness from her face with the edge of her sleeve.

And then she rose from her seat, dry-eyed, and went out of the room; because the sibyl mind was waiting, and her life was not her own.

TIAMAT: Carbuncle

Moon followed her son and Reede Kullervo down into the transport car that waited below the rim of the Pit. She looked up at the last moment at Jerusha, who stood watch over her here, now, as it seemed she had always done. She saw the memory that haunted Jerusha's eyes, the way memory had always haunted her own vision, here in this place. She had told Jerusha only that Reede believed he could find a way to reactivate the city's silent core, and give them a bargaining point in their war of nerves with the offworlders . . . all that she could tell anyone, but it had seemed to be enough.

"The gods—the Lady—go with you," Jerusha murmured. She glanced past Moon at Tammis's pale, upturned face below them, his own eyes clouded with memory. She looked at Reede. Her concern turned suddenly to doubt, and she frowned.

"We may be gone a long time," Moon said. "Maybe for hours. We won't be able to communicate with you from down there."

"I'll be waiting," Jerusha said. "For as long as it takes." She gripped Moon's arm tightly, as if she could send her own energy, her own spirit, with them, before Moon let herself down into the space below.

Moon saw instrument lights scattered like gems across the dim faces of the equipment around her, more and more of them winking on as she watched, just as Reede had predicted. The hatch sealed above them, sealing them in. Beyond the expanse of the viewing window the walls of the Pit remained dark and dead, revealing no sign of active response. But Reede stood at the window beside Tammis, gazing down, the two of them equally still and intent.

Moon slipped in between them, holding on to a support rail along the instrument panel as they began to move down the spiral course into the well's depths. Looking out as they did, she did not find utter blackness, but instead the green light waiting, intensifying as her mind accepted its presence.

A sourceless joy filled her, as she remembered that distant time and place in the islands of her youth where she had been drawn irresistibly into such light, hearing a music no instrument had ever made, calling her on, calling her away, calling. . . .

She looked over at Tammis. His silhouetted body bristled with the equipment of his diver's drysuit; its helmet rested forgotten in his arms. She saw the same rapture on his face, the anticipation, the joy . . . and the shadow of misery, the pain inextricably bound up in the memory of his choosing, Miroe's death, the sacrifice that had been required in return for the gift of his sibylhood.

She felt her memories of her own choosing darken: she remembered Sparks . . . remembered how he had tried to follow her through the darkness of the cave that had been their choosing place, into the light that only she could see. She remembered his face, blind and despairing, at the moment when she had realized that she was being chosen and he was not. He had begged her not to go on; clung to her, trying to hold her back.

But she had pushed him away, frantic with need, and gone on alone into the embrace of the irresistible light, sacrificing their love, his trust, her heart. . . . She put an arm around her son. He started, turning toward her; seeing what lay in her eyes. He nodded, moving closer as he looked out again at the light.

She looked away at Reede/Vanamoinen, who stood at her other side, his body rigid, his attention fixed on what lay below with a kind of fierce obsession. But the face of the man whose body was physically beside her, who had been made an unwilling host for the mind of someone thousands of years dead, was filled with helpless resignation. Reede was not much older than her son, and there was a wildness about him, as if he had never known peace.

She felt a sudden, profound pity for both the men who inhabited him now; but more for Reede Kullervo, whose staring, wide-pupiled eyes saw nothing but darkness, she was sure. He was not a sibyl, even if Vanamoinen had been the first. How much of what was happening did he even grasp, how much of his fear did Vanamoinen feel . . . where did one begin and the other end? Which one loved her daughter—or did they both?

She looked away from him again, watching the illumination grow stronger around them, feeling its pull on her mind increase. She closed her eyes, still seeing it, hearing it. It streamed through her like sunlight through windowglass. She felt it illuminate her from within, felt all other thoughts, concerns, emotions fading; compelled to leave behind the world she had known, and become one with this calling wonder. She was neither afraid, nor reluctant; she went willingly, eagerly to this union with the unknown for which she had been preparing all her life. . . .

She realized at last that their motion had stopped; that Reede was speaking to her. She pulled her thoughts together, like someone caught naked, and saw a brief flash of understanding in his eyes. "Lady . . ." he said again, his voice uncertain, "it's time. We're going out . . . down." He wiped his sweating face on his sleeve. "You have to—to—"

"Yes." She felt as though she could see them both even through closed eyelids, as if her body had become transparent, ephemeral, consumed by the radiance within her. "I know what to do," she said quietly. "Tammis—" She reached out, catching his hand, as he began to put on his helmet. "Be careful. Ask, when you need me, and I will answer." She spoke the ritual promise, watching the doubt in his eyes fade.

He nodded; she saw him letting go, letting himself surrender to the siren call of the force that was alive around them. "Goodbye, Mama," he whispered, and settled the helmet over his head.

"I'll be with you," she said, as much to comfort herself as him. She turned back to Reede. "I'll be with you," she repeated, to the man whose eyes looking back at her were at once as old as time, and as vacant as a blind man's. Reede looked away from her, putting on his own helmet without speaking, his movements abrupt and unsteady.

An access lay open in the wall behind them, where none had been before. Reede pushed by her, heading out. Tammis followed, glancing back as he passed through the opening. "I love you," she said, but she did not know if he heard her.

She went back to the port, looking out. Below her, below the car's final resting place, lay the sea. She saw its surface rise with the surge of the unseen tide. The water seemed alive with a strange phosphorescence, glimmering greenly, eddying in an unnatural, hypnotic dance with itself. She could smell it now, the raw, poignant ocean-smell, the flavor of green light. . . . She saw two forms climbing down, making their way slowly along what might have been hidden footholds, or only random crevices in the wall of machinery.

She watched Tammis let go and plunge into the waiting water, saw him re-emerge. Vanamoinen—Reede—still clung like a fly to his precarious hold on the wall; until at last he fell free, dropping like a stone into the phosphorescent sea. He did not come up again, and Tammis's head disappeared beneath the surface.

She stood a moment longer, staring down at the water surface, its state of ceaseless change unbroken now by any intrusive human form. Holding tightly to the panel's edge in front of her, she attempted to close her eyes again, only to realize that they were already closed, that she was poised on the brink of what waited for her alone, and the time had come now for her to let go. . . . *"Input,"* she whispered, and felt her own body fall away through the darkness of Transfer, into a sea far stranger than the one below her . . . than any she had ever known. . . .

Darkness became light/music, a sensory symphony that was to the stimuli she had just known as the energy of a sun was to a candle flame. Its intensity spread her consciousness into a spectrum: She was all the colors of light, her mind was a myriad net of pearls borne on the crest of an infinite wave . . . she was the wave, rising and falling through a motion that was eternally without momentum, flowing and folding into and through itself, in progressions of colors for which there were no names; flows of ice, waves of fluid crystal as satin-folded as flesh, colored gems, polished, perfect, flowing like tears. . . .

And she knew now that when she had entered this other plane as a sibyl only, she had entered it as a blind woman, seeing only darkness. When she had been called deeper into its hidden heart by BZ, raised to a higher level of awareness by the guardian knowledge of Survey, she had still glimpsed only the golden reflections of its infinite surfaces with her mind's eye. But now all mirrors had shattered, all barriers, physical and mental, of space and time, had fallen away, and she was here inside the impossible. *She saw. She existed within. She was . . .*

. . . in a place beyond spacetime, beside it, and even within it, where lay access to all times and places; where time itself was not a river, but a sea. And She was the sibyl mind, burningly aware of the nexus, the focus-point, the timebound physical plant hidden beneath sea and stone on a tiny, marginal world: the artificial intelligence that held Her identity and all of humanity's gathered knowledge programmed into its technoviral cells; that anchored Her to the fleeting, hapless lives of the creatures who were both Her progenitors and Her progeny . . . the brain that was failing because Her children were, in the short-sightedness of their timebound lives, feeding on Her, destroying the one thing that tied Her to their universe.

Her nervous system—luminous broadcast nets of particle waves, sensors and receivers of sentient flesh—spread its tendrils across the reaches of the human-occupied galaxy, listening, responding, answering the questions and tending to the needs of countless supplicants; always, through the willing service of the sibyls, seeking ways to lessen strife, to increase understanding.

But Her ability to respond was being destroyed, as human depredation snapped the strands of Her memory one by one. The interference in Her process, the crippling mutations occurring at Her center, were making Her always oblique relationship to the lives of mortals ever more tenuous and unpredictable. Soon, unless the pattern was altered, the drift would become so profound that She would cease to remember the reason for Her existence, and cease to function in their spacetime plane.

And when that happened, the chaos and suffering She would leave behind Her would be terrible and far-reaching. The nexus of smartmatter that held Her core memory would decompose, destroying the ancient city of Carbuncle. The land around it would become a seething, deadly wound of transmogrified matter, distorting reality, making what little of Tiamat was inhabitable now into a wasteland where nothing survived. Every choosing place, on every world where they existed, would become a separate festering sore, as the Old Empire's legacy became the Old Empire's curse, reaching up through time to breathe decay on the civilizations that were its inheritors. And every sibyl who existed would go insane and die, as the sibyl technovirus in their own bodies malfunctioned. . . .

And so She had used what free will She had evolved, employed what resources and influence She dared, trying to create the living, breathing tools that might save Her. She had scattered the seeds of Her soul into the winds of measurable time, watched over them as they grew and bore fruit, transplanted them by whatever means lay open to Her. This was the moment She had been working toward with all of Her failing energies. She had called awake the avatar of Vanamoinen, She had brought him here, given him the healing hands and willing minds She had created to help him. . . . She had done all that was within Her power to do. If they failed, it would be the end of her interface with them, the end of their ability to reach Her, and each other; the end of the sibyl mind.

Now was the right time, the only time, the last time that Her destroyers could again become healers, and bring life out of death. She focused in, drawing together the scattered motes of Her consciousness with a will as inevitable as gravity; drawing them down into the physical matrix of Her core, the restless presence of the smartmatter plasma. She felt the seething heat of its random fever dreams, which bred more and more misdirection and error into the circuitry of the net; saw the spreading disease of its drift that had gone unchecked because the mers had been unable to weave their songs, to balance the equation. She witnessed all these things, knew them, became them . . . and She waited now, for them to change.

Reede sank through the black water, drawn down and down by the relentless undertow of hidden currents, with his own scream still rattling inside his ears from the moment when he had lost his grip and fallen into the sea. The moment of impact had nearly undone him; but now that the sea had him in its grasp he felt almost calm, as if he had gone beyond terror into some emotion that was off any scale he knew.

The light of his helmet showed him the black, amorphous walls of the well, and Tammis Dawntreader's suited figure drifting through its beam, his own headlamp sometimes visible, sometimes not. And there was another kind of light, indescribable, that he felt more than saw: a strange radiation streaming into his brain that had never passed through his eyes. It was the same light he had seen flowing out of the Pit; but he only realized now that he had not actually seen it at all. The vision of the Other saw it for him—Vanamoinen, with the eyes of a sibyl, revealing to him the larger form of the space through which they traveled.   \

The water current shifted abruptly, tumbling him, sucking him down and around through a moment of giddy panic into a new direction of flow. He righted himself, letting the water's momentum carry him; preserving his failing strength. *This was right,* the Other inside him insisted; *this was proceeding as it should.*

"What's happening?" Tammis's voice surprised him from the speakers inside his helmet.

"We've entered the conduit." He spoke the words that someone else's knowledge poured into his mouth, obediently, like the puppet he was. He had no illusions now. He knew at last why he had gone on living, no matter how profoundly he had hated his life, how desperately he had wanted to end it. He knew whose obsession had forced him to survive until he arrived at this singular place, at this pivotal moment in time. And at last he even knew why. . . ."This is the tunnel that feeds sea water into the caves below the city."

"What caves?" Tammis's voice asked, eerily, in his ears.

"We cut them out of the bedrock below the place where we built Carbuncle. Look, up there—" He pointed with his helmet's beam, illuminating something that loomed ahead of them, the sheen of alloy, the smooth gleam of ceramics—the bladed battlements of an alien city beneath the sea, its heights and expanse unimaginable, its purpose unfathomable. "There are the turbines—" He swore in surprise as something winked through his lights; came back again, whirling past his face in a curious rush.

A mer. Two, three of them—already on their way out. He wondered how many others were already gone, believing they had finished their part in the broken ritual. "We've got to hurry," he said. "Or they'll be gone before we even reach them. When the tide begins to turn again, the turbines will reactivate. Any mer that isn't clear by then will be trapped inside, or torn to shreds trying to leave."

"Or any human?" Tammis said.

Reede glanced over, seeing the boy's pale face behind helmet glass, illuminated by his lights. "Or any human," he said, and looked ahead again. He forced his aching body to propel him faster, feeling the water of death punish him for his exertion. Sweat ran into his eyes; he blinked them clear, and ordered his suit's life support to lower its internal temperature, cooling his fevered flesh, numbing the bone-deep ache of his piecemeal disintegration.

They approached the gap between the turbine blades, swept on more urgently as the undersea current flowed faster, forcing its way through the narrowed access. Reede looked up as he was carried past; felt his brain paralyzed by the sight of the naked blades, row upon row—executioner's blades, poised to punish the damned, in the claustrophobic darkness of a place whose heights and depths were a vision of hell . . . *blood, pain, death by water. . . .*

A surge of panic broke through the walls of his control, as he realized suddenly that he knew, had always known, what his fate would be when the question of his existence was finally answered . . . *death by water* . . . *drowning*. . . . He was drowning in terror . . . drowning in the green light that was suddenly everywhere inside him, as the Other answered its call with a rapture against which his terror, his panic, and finally his consciousness, could no longer hold. . . .

He was Vanamoinen, and somewhere inside him he heard the other's cry of despair fade into static as Reede Kullervo disappeared into the depths of his own mind. He was completely free, and completely in control, for the first time since he had awakened in this prison of flesh he shared with a tormented stranger. The brutal years as Kullervo's silent prisoner had been a nightmare . . . and yet he knew now that in the end his own struggle for survival had inflicted on Kullervo acts of cruelty and betrayal far greater than any Reede himself had ever committed.

Vanamoinen felt a guilty compassion for the man fate had chosen as an unwilling sacrifice to the greater good. But he could not let Kullervo's fear, or even his own, keep him from what he must do; or else they would both have lived, and died, in vain.

They were past the turbines now, and the undersea caves opened out before him, glowing with a radiance that let him see perfectly. And all around him, in motion everywhere, he saw the mers, their bodies shimmering and shadowed. Their abandoned motion through the liquid gravity of the chamber was like joy and passion given living form. He called on his helmet's outside sound pickups; the haunting voices of the mersong filled his head, completing his vision. "By the All . . ." he whispered, as he was granted at last a fulfillment that had been denied him for a hundred lifetimes.

He heard countless variations on a set of crucial recurring themes: each colony with its separate fragment of song that rose and fell, sighing, chittering echo echoing, in a choir that seemed, for all its heartbreaking beauty, to be as random as their motions. And yet their motions were not really random. As they moved the many strands wove a fragile web, with a pattern visible to a mind that had been born capable of following them, trained in logic's secrets; just as the illumination of this chamber by the radiant energy of the sibyl nexus was visible only to a perception altered by the sibyl virus, or the water of life.

And yet, listening with the part of his mind that had always, almost mystically, perceived the structure within chaos, the randomness underlying order, he sensed the silences of lost songs, heard the broken threads of songs irrevocably altered as entire colonies of mers were slaughtered. The interplay of those songs, preserved and shared, passed down through the millennia, had been intended to transmit to the smartmatter of the sibyl nexus a series of messages in hierarchical code, allowing it to correct and recalibrate any changes within its system.

Because of the sibyl mind's volatile semisentience and the complexity of its function, he had known that slippage and error would be inevitable. And so he had created a system that united the self-contained hardware of the nexus, and the bioengineered lifeform of the mers. He had taken two potentially faulty systems, one designed for the greatest flexibility of function, and one for the greatest stability, and combined them. A pride as pure as light filled him: There had never been anything like this system before, in scope, in function—and he had done this thing. He had given it life. . . .

They had been intended to work together to create an extremely fault-tolerant whole, its long-term reliability guaranteed because its parts were capable of healing each other. He had given the nexus the mers, to monitor and correct its drift; he had given the mers this gathering, where the nexus would monitor and correct the stability programming of the water of life, allowing them to adapt to any changes in their environment . . . and at the same time reward them with the gift of latent fertility . . . through the interaction of the radiation that illuminated the waters around him now. A giving and taking, a sharing of vital gifts. But his best-laid plans had still gone awry, because in the end, like his beloved Ilmarinen, he had been only human. . . .

And so now, awakened from the oblivion of centuries, this artificial construct of himself (though he felt far more real, trapped inside this aching prison of flesh, than he had ever felt when he really existed) must set things right, and he had only now in which to do it.

"They're magnificent . . ." Tammis murmured, beside him. "I've never seen them like this, heard them sing all together. . . ."

"No one has," Vanamoinen said softly. "No one ever has. Now you've got to sing with them—start the recordings of the completed songs, and swim with them. If they hear new song, they'll learn it—they'll understand that something is incomplete. I'm going to be checking out the computer's functions. If things go right, what you do will aid the recalibration. But I've got to work with it, because the slippage is severe and we haven't got much time left. When I call you, you come back to me."

Tammis nodded. "Where is the . . . the computer," he asked, glancing around him, his voice suddenly faint with awe as he realized the magnitude of the knowledge that he had been entrusted with. "I don't see any machinery."

"It's all around you." Vanamoinen gestured, raising his own head, letting the radiance fill his vision. "The technoviral 'brain tissue' is matrixed into the rock of the cavern's walls." Tammis was looking at him with a mixture of incredulity and wonder. He smiled and put out a hand, touching the boy's shoulder. "Just do your part. That's all." He pointed toward the ballet of mers, their music filling his head again like a draught of sweet water. Tammis started away, glancing over his shoulder once before he lost himself inside their dance.

Vanamoinen turned back, swimming upward through the glowing reaches of the cavern toward a single unremarkable undulation in the cave's fluted wall, where the interface controls lay waiting for him.

He found the place, recognizing the exact convolution of stone from the image he had memorized only yesterday, more than two millennia ago. He pulled off his heavy insulated gloves, feeling the cold fluid kiss his bare flesh, feeling it try to creep into the sleeves of his drysuit as they sealed around his wrists. He ran his hands over the wall, groping like a blind man, until suddenly he encountered the interface, and the machine welcomed him: a burst of electronic stimuli shot up his arms, through his body and into his brain. He gasped, almost losing his contact as the shock burned his degenerating synapses like liquid fire.

He kept his hands in place with an effort of will, letting the interface confirm his identity from the pattern of his brainwaves. The space behind his eyes filled suddenly with a flood of data, blazing across his mind's vision as the computer's safeguards came down, granting him access to the original operating system that he and Ilmarinen had designed together. *Ilmarinen.* An overwhelming sense of isolation, of loss and discontinuity, filled him suddenly, as he looked down into the depths of time that separated him from Ilmarinen's life and death, and his own. He told himself fiercely that the emotions were phantoms, mere memories of regret, pointless and worse—dangerous to his work. He had been pitiless about Reede Kullervo's suffering; he must be pitiless with himself. He must succeed.

He refocused on the data filling his mind; utterly dispassionate now, feeling only the chagrin of a systems engineer who had discovered that he had been his own worst enemy. He queried, studied, compared, his brain sliding into an altered state where nothing existed but the purity of pattern; guiding his mind into the ultimate reality of communication, processors, and algorithms—universalities unaffected by the ebb and flow of time's tide, by human weakness or the restlessness of an artificial intelligence only tenuously loyal to one single place and time, in one single universe. He gathered data, processing it laboriously with only the raw skill of his human brain; grateful that Kullervo had been born with the gift for mathematical thought that made it possible to do what he had to do this way, but cursing his drug-ridden, failing body.

Hours passed here in this inevitable timebound present, as they did not pass within the singularity where the sibyl mind existed, while he completed his measurement of its rate of drift away into that cosmic sea. He thought of the stardrive plasma lying at the heart of World's End, remembering what its collapse into randomness had done to the world around it; remembering how he had ended its suffering—he, and Gundhalinu.

He never would have imagined someone like Gundhalinu would lose everything, rebel against his own people and the rule of order he had been raised to worship . . . and all out of passion—passion for the Summer Queen, and passion for the greater good. *Ilmarinen,* he thought again, unable to stop himself. It had been Ilmarinen's passion and compassion that had led to the creation of this system. He could never have conceived of the need for it, without Ilmarinen's vision. He had always been a systems man, more at home with machines than human beings, lost in the labyrinths of theoretical thought. But Ilmarinen's irresistible humanity had drawn him out of his hiding places, and made him real. They had been opposites attracting, and the sum of their joined lives was greater than its separate parts.

He had not had Ilmarinen with him at Fire Lake—but he had had Gundhalinu. He realized now that the sibyl mind had perceived depths in Gundhalinu that Kullervo's paranoia had always been blind to. And he realized that, even seeing Gundhalinu through Kullervo's eyes, he had been drawn to the man with an inchoate longing. His own eyes had always seen something of Ilmarinen's hidden fire in Gundhalinu. Gundhalinu's presence had steadied and comforted him—and, strangely, Kullervo—even through the static of Kullervo's suspicion and fear.

He wondered where Gundhalinu was now, what Survey had done to him; how the Survey he remembered had developed into this maze of deceit and lies. . . . And yet, for all its separate hands, each reaching toward what it believed to be a separate goal, the Great Game had still delivered him to his intended destination. Survey's members had sworn to serve and protect the sibyl net . . . and he realized that, from the viewpoint of the sibyl mind, they had done their duty. Human perceptions of good and evil became irrelevant, on this plane. The Brotherhood and the Golden Mean saw themselves as opposing forces, embodying Chaos and Order; and yet their realities were far more limited, complex, and self-deluded than they themselves would ever know. They had followed separate roads, leading to the same destination. And the road was destined to be long and hard for the sibyl mind's chosen tools, no matter what choices brought them here. . . .

He suddenly felt sick with pain. Pain rolled through his mind, forcing him to realize that it was not simply grief or memory that filled him, making his hands spasm and tremble, his body run with sweat. "Tammis!" he shouted, turning to look at the mers.

Slowly, after what seemed to be an eternity, he saw Tammis rising toward him through the shifting cloud of bodies, still carrying the recorder. He saw the look of serenity and pleasure that filled the boy's face; saw it fade, as Tammis got close enough to see his own face. Belatedly, he realized that one of the mers had followed Tammis up from below. He recognized Silky, Ariele's companion, and felt a sudden rush of relief that she had been spared by the Blues' hunt.

"Give her the recorder," he said to Tammis, ignoring the look on the boy's face and the sound of his own voice. "Send her back down."

Tammis did as he was told, unfastening his equipment belt with the recorder attached and looping it around her neck. Vanamoinen ordered her away with sharp urgency; watched her spiral down into the depths again, leaving them behind with a darkly curious stare.

"It's time for you to go into Transfer," he said to Tammis. "I'm going to give the AI system the feedback it needs to perform the recalibration. With any luck, the mers will be able to maintain it that way. This could take a while; have you ever been in an extended Transfer?"

Tammis shook his head. "But I'm ready," he said. His eyes were confident, full of the trusting optimism of youth.

Vanamoinen thought again of Ilmarinen; thought of Gundhalinu's love for Moon Dawntreader . . . of their daughter, whom he had loved, and their son, here before him: a strong, handsome boy with an entire life ahead of him, a wife, a child on the way, everything to live for. . . . He remembered Ilmarinen's love for Mede, in the time before they had met. Ilmarinen and Mede had had children of their own, to give them a sense of continuity. He had envied Ilmarinen that; always regretted that he had never had any children himself. *The mers are your children,* Ilmarinen had said. *Every sibyl born will be your son or daughter.* But it wasn't the same. He thought of Ariele again, suddenly, hopelessly, and a wave of hot longing surged through Reede Kullervo's shivering body, life struggling against death.

Vanamoinen blinked sweat out of his eyes, and swallowed the sorrow that clogged his throat. "What you'll see . . . see when you go into Transfer is like nothing you've ever seen before. Don't resist it . . . it's very beautiful there, I remember. Question, sibyl—"

"Input," Tammis said, his face tensing, his gaze steady. Vanamoinen saw his eyes glaze, watched the boy slide into Transfer as he spoke words in his own tongue that would give him access to the artificial intelligence's other reality, filtered through Moon Dawntreader's perception.

Tammis twitched and began to drift as two minds interchanged inside his body, leaving it helpless. Vanamoinen reached out with one hand, catching him by his suit front, pulling him into a crevice in the wall and lodging him in its embrace. He pressed his cold-numbed, nearly senseless hands back against the interface's contacts, watching Tammis's eyes as someone/something else was suddenly there, looking back at him.

"Moon Dawntreader?" he asked softly, in Tiamatan.

"Yes," she said, with her son's voice.

He asked again, speaking in his own tongue, and heard another presence respond through her. When he was certain that they could both respond to him, he began to input his correctional instructions to the matrix through the interface. He was doing here, now, in a precise but oblique way, what Gundhalinu had done in a crudely direct way, when he vaccinated Fire Lake: setting in motion the agonizingly painstaking process of healing.

Moon felt Her focus shift and slide, responding to Vanamoinen's input, which moved through the slowly shifting flow of Her awareness like a burning wind. The matrix around Her subtly changed, and changed again, like the diffracted colors inside a slowly turning prism.

She felt the compulsion seize Her to compress Her focus, to reach down through one glowing pearl among the million jewels that were Her eyes, drawn through its surface into the wormhole in spacetime that led Her to her son's mind. She looked out through his eyes, witnessing the activities of Reede-who-was-Vanamoinen, answering his questions, compelled to describe changes in what was to her an indescribable state of flux, responding to him in a language that she did not understand.

And again, when She had described the indescribable, She was released into the flux, becoming infinite, seeing into the farthest reaches of the Old Empire, touching random jewels that opened on the minds of sibyls on all the worlds where sibyls still existed, of which the worlds she knew were only a tiny fraction. She saw half a thousand worlds, half a million sibyls on them; knew their identities, their access to special knowledge that augmented the store of data contained within Her nexus memory. She knew the past, the present, the future of them all—and yet She could not put a name to any action, a direction to any motion, knowing that they were all one, here in this place, all a part of Her, as She was all of them. . . . Her existence folded through itself, making connections between them in ways that to a timebound mortal mind were meaningless.

Her own existence here seemed timeless, as if She had always been this way, expanding into the infinite, contracting into the narrow space of a hidden matrix, where a semiliving system was changing, altering its perceptual structure, mutating around Her, within Her, so that every time she came back into herself, and looked out through the eyes of her son at Vanamoinen's labors, her vision was clearer. . . .

Until at last Moon saw him perfectly, with the mers moving like a watercolor painting behind him: his haggard face, his desperate eyes shining with a triumph that was almost the light of madness. "Go free—" he said to her, in her language and then his own, lifting his hands as if she were a water spirit, and he an island conjuror.

Moon felt herself flow back into the omnipresent lightmusic, the heart of time, which the sibyl mind's transforming power allowed her access to; feeling herself become one with time, feeling Her power, Her freedom, the utter clarity of Her vision, Her sense of higher order. And yet she remained timebound, dutybound to return to her own body, her own ephemeral form . . . to become again a mortal woman surrounded by enemies, without weapons to defeat them.

She looked down at her from an unimaginable height, seeing clearly at last the nature of Her chosen tool, touching her existence as if She toyed with a child's puzzle. And as She saw clearly the desperation of Her other fragile, solitary self, She was filled with compassion. She embraced her mind with the fluid motion of an omnipresent sea; She was the gratitude and the tenderness in that touch. . . .

And Moon saw, like a flower opening in the depth of her soul, that she had always been the Lady's vessel, Her willing servant, just as the traditions of her people had promised she would be. The Lady existed, the Lady watched over Her chosen world; those who peopled its lands and seas and kept Her peace were truly Her beloved children. And among them all She had chosen Moon Dawntreader as Her eyes, Her hands, Her champion; to be guided, to be relied on, to help Her in Her need. They were one, and their needs were bound together, as they had been from the beginning of her life.

And she realized that there were secrets here in this shifting eternal now that She had never revealed to those who sought Her with their questions. Even the innermost circles of hidden Survey, all of them sibyls, who named themselves Her servants and protectors, had never known where the ultimate circle lay, or whom to trust completely. Because at the heart of Survey lay the sibyl mind itself, whose secrets only Moon Dawntreader, out of all the people since the days of its creators, had seen and shared: she who had had the strength and the resourcefulness of a sibyl, the heritage of her world behind her, and no ties binding her to the secret web of Survey, which had become both a blessing and a curse to the system it protected.

She had given her life to the sibyl mind, done its work, done everything in her power to bring about its renaissance and the survival of the mers—willingly, although she had had no choice. And still she had no choice but to go on, because she saw suddenly, that the struggle was still not over. The net's deterioration had been reversed, but the mers still were not safe, and without them, everything that She had caused to be done would become meaningless. But now, here, while she was for this eternal moment She, Her mind was infinite, filled with knowledge that even Survey could not possess; and She knew that somewhere here lay the answer to all Her questions, all Her trials.

She searched the reaches of the galaxy . . . seeing where every cluster of luminous pearls, each pearl marking the mind of a sibyl, charted the farflung worlds that were still inhabited by survivors of the Old Empire. She studied the starmap that She had never made accessible to humankind for as long as humans had failed to learn the lessons of time and of the Old Empire's fall; for as long as they had gone on hunting the mers. And, guided by a perception that was at last both clear enough and human enough to realize that even She must risk something in order to gain something, She saw that She had always possessed both a threat and a promise sufficient to Her needs. . . .

She reached out, seeing the pearls of individual human minds like foam on the crest of a standing wave. . . . She reached through, to touch the mind that lay at the other end of one of those umbilicals of shining energy, the mind of KR Aspundh. She drew him up, into the sea of light, calling to him with the voice of the woman he had once known:

(KR . . .)

(Moon—?) She felt his stunned surprise ripple upward through the luminous strand of contact. (What is it? What has happened?)

(I have the key, KR. The key to saving the mers . . . to helping BZ. The key to unlock the universe.)

(By all my ancestors—) His thoughts sang with light. (Then what must we do?)

(You must take this key, and turn it in Survey's lock. Take this information from me, to those you know and trust in the Inner Circles. They must pass it on in turn to the Golden Mean. . . . Tell them that unless the mer hunts stop, the sibyl net will cease to function. This genocide must end, or all the sibyls will die, all their choosing places will be destroyed—)

(Is this true?) Aspundh thought, his mind strobing with disbelief. (It can't be—)

(The errors, the seizures, the failures in the net that they experienced were a warning: the data is there, just as the truth about the mers is. Let them look at it and see!) She touched him with the truth, gently, but it was enough: His sudden terror was like heat lightning. (And promise them this . . . as evidence of good will . . .) she murmured, letting his fear diminish. (If the hunts cease, they will be given the location coordinates of one world of the Old Empire, relatively near in space to a world of the Hegemony, enabling them to reestablish contact. Over time, if their contact with this world proves peaceful and mutually beneficial—and as long as the mers are protected—other coordinates will be revealed to them. If they agree, they can pursue their empire dreams. If they do not, they will having nothing—less than nothing.)

(Gods . . .) he thought, the word shimmering through her vision. (You can do that?)

(Yes,) she answered.

(Yes . . .) he echoed, (yes, I will tell them, immediately—)

(KR—)

(What is it, Moon?)

(Where is BZ? How is he—?)

(We think he is on Big Blue. As to how he is . . . I don't know. Surviving, I pray.)

She made no answer, feeling the pressure of the emotion inside her expand, until at last, unable to hold back her anger, she demanded, (Why haven't you helped him? You, and those he trusted?)

(We tried, but we could not—)

(Then what good are you?) she thought, her bitterness flowing like acid, burning her, burning him. (All of you—forcing him to do what he must, then leaving him to suffer alone, while you hide and mutter your secret words like the sanctimonious cowards you are—) She began to withdraw her contact, letting the static grow into blinding waves of gold-blackness.

(Moon—) he called after her, his anguish strobing. (For gods' sakes, I'm an old man!)

She pushed toward him through the filament of light again, strengthening her contact for the fleeting moment it took to form the words. (You tell them Gundhalinu will have his honor restored. He will come back to Tiamat as Chief Justice, or by the All there will be no new worlds, as long as I exist—) not certain now even if it was only she who spoke the promise, or She. (And nothing at all, if I die.) She felt the power of her own words on fire with truth; felt him recoil from it before she broke contact.

Alone in the limitless sea, she was suddenly aware again of the soul-deep need still calling her back to her own timebound reality. Somewhere time still flowed forward, carrying her with it, and her body's strength was waning, its need growing irresistible. But she expanded her vision, once more, for the final time, searching frantically across the thousand thousand radiant droplets of sentience in Her singular sea, each one with a name, a mind, a soul of its own. . . .

(BZ . . .) She sank through the mirroring brightness into the warm heart of his lifeforce, her relief and joy at finding him safe flaming around her like the energies of a star. (BZ,) she called again, softly, inside his thoughts.

She felt his mind move restlessly, buffeting her with random colors as something somewhere deep inside it struggled to wake and respond. *To wake* . . . He slept, she realized—a sleep so deep and exhausted that she could not penetrate it. (Sleep, my beloved,) she thought, and the tenderness she felt was a song of surpassing beauty. (Soon,) she whispered, seeing her promise spread in golden ripples through the restive currents of his brain, (soonsoonsoon. . . .)

She let him go, slipping back into the music and light, the embrace of the Lady, still and eternally waiting, for her, for all of humanity, the sibyls that were Her own flesh and blood, the minds that She served and shaped, both created and creator in the Great Game of human survival. And within Her mind she set one last, small wheel in motion.

(Now—) she thought, gathering herself, reaching and falling away, out of the everywhere, into the here. . . .

Vanamoinen saw the alien light fade from Tammis's eyes, saw awareness and control come back into his body with a shudder.

Tammis clung to the wall, still dazzled by the vision of the place where his mind had taken and held him. He shook his head, clearing out his sight. He stared at the face he found abruptly in front of him, Reede Kullervo's face. Vanamoinen saw Tammis's expression change. "What's wrong?" Tammis asked. "Reede—?" He broke off, as something jarred them from below.

Looking down, Vanamoinen found Silky butting their drifting feet with hard insistence.

"Look—" Tammis waved his arm. "They're gone! The mers are gone."

"It's over," Vanamoinen whispered hoarsely. "The tide's turning. . . ."

"Then we have to get out."

Vanamoinen nodded, clenching his teeth over the sudden, desperate need to vomit. He shoved Tammis in answer, propelling him down and away toward the opening through which they had entered the cave. Tammis began to swim, the mer circling him in absurdly graceful corkscrew motions, urging him on. But Tammis hesitated, looking back as Vanamoinen let his own pain-wracked body begin to fall through the water, making no effort to follow. "Reede?" Tammis called. "Lady's Tits, come on! We'll be trapped!"

Vanamoinen felt Reede Kullervo's terror fling itself against the iron cage of his restraint like a berserk animal, begging him to *move, move*—even though he was doomed anyway, even though it had all been meant to end here, and his fate was unfolding as it should. . . .

"Reede!" Tammis shouted again, his voice rattling inside Vanamoinen's helmet.

Reede's body swung toward him, kicking its legs, forcing itself into motion. Vanamoinen surrendered to Kullervo's frantic desperation, granting him the dignity of choice, no matter how quixotic . . . realizing that if he did not follow, Tammis would not leave.

Reede forced his arms and legs to propel him forward, his mind fighting its way up through a cloud of disorientation, his body floundering through the liquid atmosphere in Tammis's wake. The cavern seemed endless. Only the last straggling handful of mers were still departing, barely visible far ahead. The direction of the water's flow had begun to change now, as the fluid driven into the system of hollowed-out chambers by the action of the tide began its return to the sea. The changing tide did not oppose him, at least, sweeping him in slow motion toward the entrance, through the eerie incomplete darkness that the other in his mind still saw as filled with light. He pushed on, feeling with every forced movement as if some muscle would tear loose from bone, feeling as if a knife went through his chest with every breath.

Silky swept back from her circling of Tammis to butt him impatiently onward as the gap between their swimming bodies began to widen. He swore in agony, the ungentle collisions driving him to more speed in his efforts to escape her.

Up ahead, the last of the other mers had already disappeared through the narrow passage where the turbines waited; he saw Tammis reach it, saw the dark, impossible gleam of metal—

"Hurry!" Tammis called, his voice rising. "I see movement. Reede, come on—"

"Go through!" Reede shouted, hearing his voice corrode. "Go on, damn you, go on!" Tammis swam on into the passage. Reede struck Silky hard across the nose with his fist, driving her away, ahead. He watched her follow Tammis. The water was beginning to surge unnaturally around him; he felt the throb of heavy machinery vibrate through the caverns, as the turbines began to take up their work once more. The blades had begun to turn, slowly coming together to seal the access their brief rest had created, for another two and a half centuries.

Gods . . . He prayed, not sure to what he was praying, or even for whom, as he watched the shaft of Tammis's helmet light spear the darkness of the tunnel ahead of him. But somewhere he found the madman's courage to start his own journey into the blackness where the Render's jaws were closing. He swam blindly, his eyes shut against the sight of what lay ahead of him, his nose filling with blood from a sudden hemorrhage.

The water was becoming more turbulent, making his progress harder; forcing him to open his eyes and search the way ahead. In the distance he saw Tammis's headlamp, through the maelstrom of the waters; saw its light turn back toward him, searching the closing passage.

"We're through!" Tammis called. "Reede? Reede! You can make it—"

Reede coughed and spat; blood blurred the inside of his helmet. "I can't. . . ." He gasped out the words, barely intelligible even to himself. He could see the distance between them expanding, the gap through which he passed shrinking. The heavy heartbeat of the turbines filled his head; the liquid through which he moved seemed to thicken as its churning violence increased. *He was not going to make it.*

He felt the last of his strength leave him, along with all resistance; let the water possess his body, binding him for sacrifice. He watched the blades rising, falling . . . his mind filled with the epiphany of death. The turbulent water battered his body, forcing him to acknowledge every agonizing symptom of his deterioration; forcing him to admit, in his terror, that he welcomed this end, the moment of blinding pain when his body was torn to pieces and his soul at last set free.

"Reede!" Something collided with him—someone. Tammis's arms were around him, pulling him frantically toward the tunnel's end, the mer pushing him from behind, urging him to try to struggle, move—

"No!" he cried, half a paincry and half a warning, as they wrenched his body in their insane determination to save him. "Leave me, damn you, you'll kill us all!" He beat at Tammis's faceplate with his fists. "Get out!"

"No," Tammis gasped, locking an arm around his neck, pulling him through the white vortex as if he were a panic-stricken drowning victim. "You don't know what you're saying."

"It was meant to end this way!" Reede shouted. "Let me die."

"No!" Tammis's voice rang inside his helmet. "Not again, I won't let someone else die down here because of me—"

Reede felt his body twisted and heaved forward through the maelstrom of metal and white water, spewed helplessly out of the tunnel by a final spasm, into the emptiness beyond.

Something collided with him, spinning him. He reached out, groping frantically. "Tammis—?" But it was the mer's face his hands found. He turned back, fighting the current's momentum. "Tammis!" he shouted, seeing the boy suddenly in the beam of his headlamp, the glare of metal; reaching frantically toward the hands flung out to him. He caught them, pulling—felt them jerked from his grip. He thought he heard his name in the scream that pierced his soul, as Tammis was sucked down into the churning whiteness.

His own raw cry of denial drove through his senses as he lunged toward the turbines. But Silky was there in front of him, colliding with his body, driving him away, against all his efforts, herding him on through the tunnel.

Reede surrendered, as the last of his frenzy died like the echoes of Tammis's death scream, which should have been his own. . . . He was helpless against her singsong bullying; he closed his arms around her long, sinuous neck, feeling the shock of her warmth, the softness of her fur under his numb, cramping fingers. He let her carry him away from the white waters of death, borne on her back; away from the heartbeat pulse of the turbines, into silence and darkness, and finally upward toward the waiting air.

TIAMAT: Carbuncle

Moon stirred, pushing herself up from the floor of the car as sounds rose echoing from the well below. Stupefied with exhaustion, she was not certain if she had slept or fainted, or how long she had lain there. Her mind reeled as awareness came back to her, and with it the visions of all she had done, and been, through the hours past; the vision of Her . . . until she felt herself slipping away again, back down the fluid corridors into the dark mansions of memory.

She pulled herself to her feet, clinging to the panel, clinging to consciousness with an equally relentless grip. She peered out and down. Far below in the green-lit water she saw a figure—thought at first that it was human. But it was not, it was a mer. A human figure was struggling up the wall below her, clinging to the footholds she could not even see among the outcrops of equipment. Only one figure. She looked out again, trying to make the mer's form into a second human being. But she could not, and still there was only one man climbing the wall. She remembered her last sight of Reede's tortured face, as she had looked out at him through Tammis's eyes, there in the hidden caves: the face of a man with pride, but without hope . . . the face of a dying man.

She turned away from the instrument panel to the car's access opening; staggering, as if she had forgotten how to use her physical body in the time that she had been incorporeal and infinite. She stepped out onto the narrow catwalk beyond the exit, holding on to the edge of the doorway, pressing a hand against the solid support of the wall as she edged forward.

A helmeted head pushed up over the lip of the platform in front of her. She jerked back, startled; leaned forward, her weakness and giddiness forgotten as she caught his arms. "Tammis!" She helped him drag himself onto the platform and stumble with her back inside the car. He collapsed inside the doorway, falling to his knees as if all his strength were gone. His faceplate was smeared inside with something that obscured her view of him. She dropped to her knees beside him as he fumbled with the helmet's seals. Pushing his useless hands aside, she unfastened his helmet and pulled it off.

She fell back, from the smell of sickness, the sight of blood. Eyes as clear and pure a blue as the skies of summer gazed back at her from a face that was an unrecognizable mask of vomit, runneled with red. "Reede." She felt her heart stop.

He nodded, swaying unsteadily. "Lady . . ." he whispered, his voice barely recognizable. He broke off, trying futilely to wipe his face clean on the sleeve of his suit.

"Where is Tammis?" She caught him by the shoulders; he cried out as she jerked him upright. Sick at heart, she shook him, forcing him to give her an answer. "Where is he! What happened?"

Reede focused on her again, finally responding to the anguish in her voice. "He's gone . . ." he mumbled, and she felt a spasm wrench his body. "The turbines—"

"No," she whispered. "What? How? No—" mouthing words without meaning. "Why—?"

"It was supposed to be me! I had to stay alive, I had to survive, until the sibyl net was healed. . . . And then I had to die." Reede sagged forward, his hands knotting. "He wouldn't let me. He saved my life, the bastard, for what—? He was safe! He had everything . . . everything to live for. But instead he died, for me. It should have been me. . . ."

She let him go, let him slide down into the puddle of seawater pooling around her on the floor. She closed her eyes against the sight of him; seeing Miroe suddenly, his death reflected in Tammis's eyes. *Tammis. Tammis* . . . "Tammis. . . ." She became aware of a thin keening, realized that it came from her own throat.

When she could bear to open her eyes again, Reede lay motionless, staring up at her. He raised a hand, clutching at her sleeve. "Sorry . . ." he whispered, "I'm sorry I'm sorry I'm sorry. . . . What I did to you—your daughter, your son. Should have been me. Me—" His voice broke down into sobbing. "Me! Me!"

She leaned forward, lifting him up, her weary arms trembling with the effort. She ordered the car to take them to the surface; held the clumsy dead-weight of him close against her as she watched the access door close, merging seamlessly into the wall. The car started into motion again, carrying them upward this time through the still-darkened well. She went on holding him, pretending for that brief space of time that there was no time, that she was still inside the outside, within that epiphany where everything was always happening . . . that this was really her own child, held safely in her arms, and not the half-mad stranger who had destroyed her family in the name of the sibyl mind. . . .

But in time their motion ceased, and the ceiling hatch opened silently above her. She looked up, without the strength to do more, heard voices calling down to her—Jerusha's, Merovy's. She looked down again, unable to bear the sight of their faces, their reaction to what they were about to find.

Reede stirred as he heard them; he had not moved or spoken during their entire journey upward. Now, he struggled upright until he was sitting alone. He looked at her, with dazed incomprehension; looked away wordlessly.

"Moon—?" Jerusha's voice came again, more demanding, with more concern.

"Here . . ." she answered, barely able to force herself to speak that acknowledgment. She heard someone climb down through the access, glanced up again as Jerusha dropped to the floor beside them.

Jerusha's gaze flickered from one of them to the other; the lines of her face deepened with her sudden frown, as she saw what had become of them. "Tammis," she said, not really a question; her eyes were back on Moon's face.

Moon shook her head.

"Gods . . ." Jerusha breathed. She moved forward, giving Moon the strength of her arms, pulling her to her feet. She looked at Reede, back at Moon. "Nothing's changed, up here." It was half a question, half a statement of fact. "The city is still dark. Moon what happened? Can you tell me?"

Moon only shook her head again. "Get me . . . get us out, Jerusha. Out of here."

Jerusha nodded, helping Moon toward the ladder, and up. Moon caught the hands waiting for her up above, was pulled free from the reeking prison of the car. She stood inside a lamplit circle of familiar faces, the arms around her reaffirming her existence in the world to which she had finally found her way home.

Clavally and Danaquil Lu supported her as Merovy brought her strong medicinal tea. She took it in her hands and drank it down, her eyes on the figures emerging now from the car's glowing interior. Jerusha came first, reaching back to pull Reede up the final few feet of the ladder, half-dragging him out onto solid ground at the Pit's rim. He collapsed as she let him go; she left him like a broken doll at the edge of the well. The others turned expectantly, looking past him. "Tammis?" Merovy called, her anticipation turning to concern as no one else appeared.

"Merovy," Moon said, her voice as thick as treacle in her throat. "He isn't coming."

Merovy turned to look at her, looked toward the Pit again, with an expression that Moon felt in her bones. "Yes, he is," she insisted, with mindless conviction. "He went with you. He's coming—"

"He's not coming," Moon whispered, feeling her own eyes brim. "He's dead, Merovy." Her hands closed over the heavy stuff of her sweater, twisting the sodden yarn. "He's dead."

Merovy's face emptied; her hands pressed the gentle swell of her belly. "How—?" Her voice squeaked like an unoiled hinge.

"I killed him."

Reede's voice made them all turn. Moon saw him stagger to his feet, a man climbing out of his own grave to stand before them. She heard Merovy's guttural cry of anguish. Jerusha looked back at him, staring.

Merovy started forward, her face contorted with rage and loss; her mother caught her, holding her back. "Why?" she screamed.

"It was an accident," Moon said; the words lacerated her throat. "Tammis saved his life."

"Why? Who is *he*?" Merovy cried, and there was no answer that Moon or anyone could give her. "It isn't fair, we have a *child*—"

Her mother held her close, pinioning her struggles. "*You* have a child . . ." Clavally murmured, holding her tighter. "You have his child, my heart; take care of the child. . . ." hushing her as she began to sob. The sound of Merovy's grief magnified in the vastness of the room until it seemed to Moon as if the entire world wept. Clavally and Danaquil Lu looked up at her over their daughter's hidden face, in sudden, terrible understanding.

Moon turned away, unable to face their compassion, afraid of breaking down. She looked toward the Pit. "I saved the world," she murmured, with sudden bitterness, "but I lost my children."

She saw Reede move, out of the corner of her eye; saw him starting for the Pit's rim. "Stop him!"

Jerusha caught him in two strides, knocked him aside as he reached the edge and tried to fling himself over. She subdued him without effort, forced him away from the rim, back toward the people who stood in silent judgment of him.

He fell to his knees. Her hands stayed on his shoulders, holding him there; but Moon could see that she needn't have bothered. He glared at them, his face lurid with fresh blood, his eyes wells of despair. "You want to watch me die?" he spat. "Watch it happen then, damn you!"

Moon moved toward him, feeling as if her own body had become the body of an old woman, stiff and slow and full of pain. She stopped, looking down at him. "Who are you?" she asked.

He lifted his head; let it fall again, without speaking, when she had seen the impossible truth still in his eyes.

"I don't want you to die," she said softly. She put her hands against his face as he tried to turn away, her touch as gentle as if she held snow. "I want to help you. Tell me how."

He shook his head slowly, wetting her hands with blood, staring up at her again in utter confusion. But he only said, "You can't. I can't."

"You said that the Police took all the water of death you had, when they arrested you?"

"Yes," he muttered wearily.

She glanced at Jerusha. "Would they still have it?"

Jerusha shrugged. "Maybe. But it's not likely they'd hand it over to us."

"On humanitarian grounds—?"

Jerusha laughed humorlessly. "To save the life of a criminal you're sheltering from the Hegemony? Under the circumstances, I'd say it's bloody unlikely."

Moon moved away from Reede's side. "Send a messenger to Vhanu, Jerusha. Tell him that if he wants the lights on in this city again, he'll send the drug to me, no questions asked."

Jerusha stared at her. "I thought you had nothing to do with the city's power going out."

"I didn't," Moon said.

"But now you can bring it back?"

Moon glanced away, into the dark reaches of the Hall of the Winds. "Yes," she said.

Jerusha stared at her. "I'll send someone right away," she murmured, "Lady." She bowed, and went quickly from the hall.

Moon turned back, to face Merovy and her parents, still waiting like mourners at a funeral. "Clavally, Dana, will you help me get Reede to a bed? I want him made as comfortable as possible." They nodded, with doubt as plain on their faces as anguish, and their hands still on their daughter's quivering shoulders. "Merovy," Moon said quietly, "you have medical training. Will you see what you can do to help him? He's in considerable pain."

Merovy blinked; the white, dumbstruck emptiness of her face slowly regained a suffusion of color, and for a moment Moon thought it was fresh anger, and refusal. But Merovy turned, forcing herself to look at Reede, and her expression wavered. "Yes," she said finally, almost inaudibly, her eyes downcast. She came forward with her parents; still looking down, her hand pressing her stomach.

Reede lifted his head, watching them warily as they approached. But he allowed himself to be half-led, half-carried up the curving flight of stairs, and back into the palace.

Moon made certain that he was settled into a bed, used a cool cloth to wipe vomit and blood from his face with her own hands. She watched Merovy tend him as best she could with what medical supplies they had. Merovy's face eased, her movements grew calm and sure as she worked, as contact with his flesh forced her to acknowledge his humanity.

Reede lay with his eyes closed, breathing shallowly, as though he were unconscious. But Moon knew from the rigidness of his muscles, the stark whiteness of his clenched fists, that he was only trying to ignore their presence, their unasked-for intrusion into his suffering.

At last, satisfied that she had done everything for him that she could, she left him in their care and went back through the dimly lit palace halls, down through the throne room and back to the Hall of the Winds. She stepped out onto the bridge above the Pit, feeling its siren light call up to her. She felt only a distant echo now of the many-colored splendor she remembered in her mind, but still it made her senses sing with yearning. *The Lady* . . .

She breathed in the smell of the sea that rose up the well to fill the air here; a constant reminder of the presence of an unseen power, one that she had believed in profoundly in her island youth. Then there had been a goddess incarnate in the waters of the sea, who spoke through the lips of every sibyl, granting the special gift of Her wisdom only to the Summers, Her chosen people.

That belief had been destroyed by her head-on collision with the ways of the offworlders, their far vaster and more sophisticated web of knowledge and deception. She had learned what she believed was the real truth about the sibyl net, and lost her innocence in the same moment. There had been no Lady any longer, except as the empty source of curses, through all the years since; only the ache of loss, whenever she had needed the strength of belief.

But now at last she had seen the greater truth hidden within the lesser one of the offworlders' cynical self-deception. The intelligence that guided the sibyl net was not a supernatural force, but it was something more than human—*other* than human, although affected by human needs and desires. It was itself partly created of minds like her own, and it lay at the heart of Survey, influencing the fate of countless beings on countless worlds she would never even hear the names of.

And the two separate but uniquely joined peoples of this world were its chosen ones in a way that was both natural and profound. She had not been insane, she had not been deluded, obsessed with power, driven by ambition—she had not been Arienrhod. She had been right. And all that she had believed had, in some way, been true after all.

She looked down, unafraid, into the green light; and looking down, felt her mind recoil like a spring as she remembered her son . . . remembered suddenly what price she had paid to be Her chosen one, to serve the needs of the true Lady. A tremor shook her. She went on across the bridge, moving now by the strength of her own will, her own need and urgency, no longer controlled by any compulsion. She did not stop until she reached the other side. And there she stood alone, in the empty silence beyond the Pit's rim, with the heels of her hands pressed into her eyes until the only light she saw was a burning brilliance of phosphenes.

At last she raised her head, picking up her lantern, hearing the hollow echo of footsteps coming toward her. She saw another light appear ahead; saw Jerusha leading Vhanu himself into the Hall.

She wiped her face hastily, lowered her hands to her sides. She read the unease that Vhanu could not entirely disguise at being in the palace without any escort; saw it turn to surprise as he found her waiting here for him, equally alone.

"Lady." Jerusha bowed. "The Commander has what you asked for."

"I am surprised to see that you brought it yourself, Commander," Moon said, raising her eyebrows, hearing the coldness in her voice answer the coldness of his eyes.

He made a brief bow in return. "Your offer was—sufficiently unusual, Lady, that I wanted to know for myself what lay behind it. And see for myself that you could keep your part of the bargain."

"I, for my part, never make promises I do not intend to honor," she said. She felt Jerusha glance at her.

Vhanu moved forward slowly, flanking her, until he stood beside her at the rim of the Pit. He stayed within the glow of her light but beyond her easy reach. Slowly again, he removed a small, silver-metal vial from his clothing. "I have what you want." He held it out—suspended over the edge of the well. "Now tell me why you want it."

Moon's breath caught; she saw the faint gleam of satisfaction come into his eyes. His glance took in her drab native clothing with a flicker of disgust. She realized that she had forgotten even to change, that she still wore what she had worn into the Pit, that her clothes were wet and stained and reeking of Reede's sickness.

She felt her sudden fear catalyze into anger at the touch of his eyes. "What I want to do with it is not your concern, Commander," she said.

"Your constables took a prisoner away from my Police yesterday: the man this drug belongs to. What you intend to do with it—and him—very much concerns me."

Moon took a deep breath. "He is an addict. So is my daughter. They need that drug to stay alive."

He glanced at the vial. "There isn't that much of it." He looked back at her without compassion, and her brief impulse to ask him for help in synthesizing it died unspoken.

"That is my problem to solve, Commander," she said, perversely glad that he had given her a reason not to beg him. "Your problem is getting the city's power back. I can do that for you, if you give me what I want."

He arched his neck in an odd, craning gesture, as if he were trying to look behind her words somehow, and see if they were true. "What about the Smith?" he asked warily.

"Who?" she said, before she could realize who he meant. "You mean Reede Kullervo."

He nodded, half frowning. "I want him back."

"He addicted my daughter. He caused my husband's death," she said flatly. "He—he drowned my son. He's mine to deal with." She felt Jerusha's eyes on her again, their uncertainty unchanged.

Vhanu's frown deepened, but this time a fleeting, reluctant comprehension showed in his gaze. Finally he lowered the hand that held the vial out over the Pit. "I want him back," he said, "and I want him back alive. He's too important to us—" He broke off. "His apprehension is important to the Hegemony." *To Survey.* She felt the hidden reach, the relentless hold of the secret order he served more faithfully than he served his government. She saw Reede, who had been the pawn of the Brotherhood, becoming the pawn of the Golden Mean; knew they must want possession of him, want to exploit his brilliant, stolen mind, as much as their rivals had.

"You can keep him until the tribunal arrives, Lady." Vhanu's expression altered subtly. "Punish him in whatever way you choose. Just see that he lives. . . ." *Barbarian,* his eyes said, filled with contempt. "Will that satisfy you?" He held the vial out again, toward her this time, but still beyond her reach. "Bearing in mind that we could come and take him any time we wanted to, if we chose. So far I have tried to respect your sovereignty to the extent you allow me to—since I expect to be named the new Chief Justice soon." His mouth imitated a smile.

She folded her arms, clutching her elbows with her hands until the pressure was greater than that of the anger inside her. "I would be ungrateful to refuse your offer, since you show such consideration of our traditions," she said, her voice toneless. "I will keep him, until there is a new Chief Justice. And then—" She shrugged.

A fleeting unease touched him. He shook it off. "Restore the city's power, Lady. Then you get this." He gestured with the vial.

She hesitated, seeing how close he stood to the rim of the Pit. She shook her head. "Give it to me first." She held out her hand, saw him stiffen with refusal. "Give it to me. Or you get nothing." Her hand fisted.

His own hand tightened around the vial; his eyes were as black as obsidian. She held his gaze, unmoving, unyielding.

He looked toward the Pit. After an endless moment he looked back at her, and nodded. But his expression held something more unexpected, and more disturbing, than simple capitulation. "All right, then," he murmured. "But I want to watch; I want to see you do it."

She nodded slowly, surprised and uncertain. She held out her hand again, and he put the vial into it. She closed her hand and turned her back on him, stepping out onto the bridge. She moved without hesitation now, with no space left inside her for grief or doubt. Turning back to face him, suspended above what to him was darkness but to her was light, she saw his skepticism and barely concealed scorn . . . his dark, obsessive fascination. She closed her eyes, murmuring, *"Input."* And although the only request was spoken inside her own silence, she felt the sibyl mind stir in answer, as she had left it waiting to do. For a moment she glimpsed infinity rolling like an endless sea. . . .

She fell back into the present, swaying, catching her breath. She looked down, into the Pit; saw far below in the darkness a rising pattern of light—real light, not the secret radiance that she had moved through. The swell of energy spiraled upward like a licking flame, bringing the machinery alive, until it reached the rim and overflowed, filling the dark hall with incandescent light.

She moved forward toward the illuminated faces, the motionless forms of the two people waiting in the sudden, unnatural day before her. "I have kept my part of the bargain, Commander Vhanu."

He backed away as she approached, staring at her, his pupils still dilated even though he was looking into the light. A tremor ran through him. She read disbelief in his eyes now, and fear. *How?* they asked. *How—?* She did not answer him, holding his gaze as steadily as if she could actually have told him the answer.

He shook himself out of his gaping trance; looked at the vial still in her keeping. He forced all expression from his voice, but there was an electric tension in his movements, a drawn tightness to his face, as he murmured, "And I have kept mine."

She tightened her fist over the vial, feeling an electric ripple of triumph.

"By the way," he said, his voice strained, "I have been told that the mers are being sighted again, in the waters around the city. Nothing else has changed. If the power goes out this time, I'll know who to blame. And tell your people to keep out of our way, or they will suffer the consequences. Lady—" He bowed stiffly again, gave a brusque nod to Jerusha, and went quickly from the Hall.

Moon bit her lips, looking down at the vial in her hands. She raised her head, called out to his retreating back, "It will come back on you threefold!"

He spun around to stare at her, and she saw his expression clearly before he went on his way.

Jerusha watched him go, making no effort to see him out. She turned back to Moon, her eyes troubled. "How?" she said. "You said you had nothing to do with the power outage."

"That was true," Moon murmured, still seeing Vhanu's haunted face inside her mind's eye.

"But you brought it back."

She shrugged, drained of strength and thought; searching for a way to explain honestly without telling the truth.

"Was that what you did when you went down into the Pit?"

"Yes," she said gratefully, and let it go.

"Moon. . . ." Jerusha hesitated. "What else happened down there? You were gone for hours. Tammis . . . was it an accident? Or did Kullervo—?"

Moon shook her head. "No. Not Kullervo. Tammis . . . Tammis stood in the way of fate. It was his goodness that killed him, Jerusha." *And Miroe's memory.* But she did not say that. "I can't . . . I can't talk about it. Mother of us All—" Her hand tightened around the vial, trembling. "I can't."

Jerusha held herself tautly, as if she were uncertain of what move to make, afraid to make the wrong one . . . afraid.

Moon saw the shadow of doubt that had clung to the other woman ever since the moment when they had begun their descent into the Pit. "Jerusha, are you afraid of me?" she murmured.

Jerusha looked at her for a long moment; shook her head, finally. "I'm only afraid that Vhanu won't rest until he knows how you did that." She gestured toward the glowing well.

Moon looked behind her, and away again, without answering.

"What about the mers?" Jerusha asked. "Is the return of the city's power all you brought back?"

Moon hesitated. "No. . . . But it was all I had that I could use as leverage with Vhanu."

Jerusha frowned, and Moon saw her doubt deepen into frustration. "Then maybe we would have been better served if you'd driven a harder bargain," she said. She gestured at the vial. "Reede Kullervo hardly seems worth what you've just paid for his life."

Moon felt a pressure growing in her chest. "It isn't just his life—it's Ariele's. Reede Kullervo may be able to save my daughter."

Jerusha grimaced apologetically, and nodded.

"And beyond that, he doesn't deserve to die—and he doesn't deserve to be used any longer, by anyone. I intend to see that he is not." Moon turned away, starting back across the bridge toward the heart of the palace.

Jerusha followed her wordlessly as they traveled back through the endless halls and chambers to the room where she had left Reede.

Clavally and Danaquil Lu looked up as she entered, with Jerusha behind her. Merovy sat beside Clavally, her eyes closed, her head on her mother's shoulder, while Clavally stroked her hair with soothing, rhythmic fingers.

Moon went to Reede's bedside. His eyes were closed too, and he did not acknowledge her presence when she spoke his name. "Reede," she said again, afraid that this time he actually did not hear her. "I have the water of death." Speaking its name left a bitterness in her mouth.

His eyes opened; he looked up at her face, down at the vial she held in her hand.

"Can you make more of this?" she asked, kneeling down beside him. "I'll find laboratory space for you—"

He shook his head. "Can't."

"If you drink it—" She held it out to him, her heart beating too hard. "If you drink this, you'll have the strength to make more."

His swollen hand twitched on the bedclothes, lifted—dropped. "No good," he whispered. "Start from scratch, takes too long, two doses won't buy enough time. Save it. Save it for Gundhalinu. If he makes it back he can help you . . . save her." *Ariele.* He shut his eyes again, as if the sight of the vial was a kind of torture.

"It's not too late. There has to be a way to help *you*—" She put her hand on his arm.

He swore, gasping; she jerked her hand away. "Cut my throat," he said, his eyes filled with hatred.

She pushed to her feet, holding the vial; hesitated. "How much do you love my daughter?" she asked softly, and saw his face tighten with pain. She looked down at the vial. Slowly, as if she were moving underwater, she lifted her free hand and broke its seal.

"No!" Reede said. "Stop her—"

"Moon!" Jerusha leaped forward, catching her arm. "By the Lady and all the gods, what are you doing?"

Moon held her gaze, until Jerusha's hand dropped away. "BZ said that the water of death is a failed form of the water of life. That means it uses a kind of smartmatter as its base—isn't that right?" She looked toward Reede.

"Yes, but . . ." He pushed himself up onto an elbow, swearing with the effort. "It's defective. I didn't have . . . the right control environment . . . or equipment, when I made it. There's no way to fix it. I tried, and tried . . . I couldn't find a way."

"The sibyl virus is also a form of smartmatter, isn't it?" Moon asked. "All the existing forms are related."

He nodded, frowning.

"BZ told me that you and he found a way together to reprogram the stardrive plasma when it was damaged . . . to 'vaccinate' it, he said, to alter its function."

"Yeah," he murmured. "What's the point?"

"There is a perfectly functioning form of smartmatter in my body, and the sibyl mind acts through it. If I take the water of death, and go into Transfer, I will be the laboratory—the net can interact with the drug through me to alter its function."

"Moon!" Danaquil Lu rose from his seat. "He said it's not possible. You can't know whether this will even work—"

"Unless I try it," she finished for him. She turned back to Reede. "Do you think your . . . the sibyl net's AI can do that?"

"Gods. I don't know. . . ." He groaned faintly, falling back onto the bed as his strength gave out. "Maybe . . . maybe it could. But if you're wrong," his eyes found hers again, "this is how you'll die."

She looked away from his face, at the innocuous silver metal vial, open now in her hand.

Jerusha's hand fell on her arm again. "By the Bastard Boatman, Moon—" Jerusha whispered. "Your son is dead, and Reede Kullervo is not going to take his place! He's the man who addicted your daughter to a fatal drug! You can't take a chance like this for a man like that. What if you both die?"

"Then you will bury us at sea, I suppose," Moon murmured.

"What about the Hegemony, and the mers—?"

"What about them?" she said, her voice raw. "For years, the sibyl net has made me give it what it wants, no matter what it cost me. It's stolen half my life from me. And his too." She looked at Reede, feeling the uncomprehending stares of the people around her. They had done everything for the sibyl mind that it had been humanly possible to do. "Now it's time for it to give us something back, something *we* need. Or else it will get nothing from me ever again." *Lady, hear my prayer. . . .* She felt a sense of impossible freedom and terrifying resolve, and she realized that the geas that had controlled her for so long had finally, truly, released her. She raised the vial to her lips and swallowed half its contents, so quickly that no one could stop her—not even herself. She pressed the vial with the remaining sample into Jerusha's waiting hands. *"Input—"*

She fell away down the hidden well inside her mind, the access into another dimension, where once she had seen only the blackness and utter silence the sibyls called the Nothing Place. But now that she knew how to listen, how to see, her vision revealed to her the corridor of light that bound her to Her, to the mated minds of the net's creators, joined with Her own, the past and the future combined, the Dreaming Place. *Lady, help us,* she thought, prayed, demanded. *For the love of Vanamoinen, give us back what is only our right. Give us back our lives. Heal me.* Gazing backward through the golden filament that bound her to the sibyl mind, she saw her own body as a glittering network, each cell winking briefly as the multiplying water of death invaded and seized control of it, death imitating life.

And what she saw, She saw . . . forced to look back through the eyes of Her timebound avatar at the fragile, fleeting lives of Her servants, Her nerve endings, Her tools, witnessing their pain with inescapably human vision. She saw Reede Kullervo: the expendable vessel who had carried the essence of Vanamoinen's mind. The vessel meant to shatter, once Vanamoinen had completed the task he had returned to do; because for Vanamoinen's mind to go on existing, sharing the same continuum with Her enemies, was a danger to Her. . . . And yet her human eyes bore witness to his human suffering, forcing Her to see that in Her desperate effort to survive and be healed, She had violated the reason for Her own existence. She had betrayed the servants whom She had been created to serve; in Her suffering She had wounded the very parts of Herself that had been called upon to heal Her wounds.

But because they healed Her, She could see clearly at last: could see Reede/Vanamoinen's desperate hunger to survive, to claim his own brief moment in time, now that his will had been set free. And She could see, in the timeless sea of Her own existence, that the survival or death of Reede/Vanamoinen had been/was- /would be no more than a ripple-ring of randomness. . . .

And She could see the fatal error spreading like poison through the body of Her avatar, as clearly as She could see the pitiless chains of Her own making that had driven Moon Dawntreader to an act of defiant self-destruction that was also a prayer. But She was no longer pitiless, or soulless, or blind. A vast compassion filled Her, and She knew that because She had been healed, She must heal their wounds, if She could. . . .

And Moon saw that with her entrance into the hidden nexus, and her awareness as she had guided Her reprogramming, she had cast a reflection on Her soul, just as Vanamoinen and Ilmarinen had done in their original act of creation. She was not even certain now whether she looked back on her existence with her own mind, or the sibyl mind's mirror image of it. But she knew that it did not matter. For this moment she was all things, she could grant her own wishes, anything that lay within Her power. If there was an answer to be found in the uncharted depths of Her knowledge, she would find it.

She looked in through the open windows of the sibyl virus, which existed already in every cell of her body . . . knowing that in each of those already-altered cells lay a potential trap for the new invader, if she could only find the trigger. With vision that could simultaneously track every alteration in the activity of all of those cells as precisely as if she were threading a needle, she analyzed the schematic of the water of death, noting its similarities to the programmed structure of the real smartmatter; recording its minute, fatal structural flaws.

With free access to the full spectrum of the Old Empire's technological knowledge, and the processing power of a computer that spanned worlds, she searched for secrets hidden since the Fall; knowledge judged better forgotten by the individuals who had brought it to its highest form. Manipulating the interactions within her body, she tried key after key in the lock of the water of death. But each time, it defied her.

She searched deeper and deeper into the heart of Her existence, into the workings of the technovirus that was Her very essence, Her own key to open the locked doors of the universe . . . into the uncharted depths of wisdom and unwisdom of her long-dead ancestors. . . .

And at last she found it: the transformation process that would render the deadly invader of her body step by step harmlessly inert, to be swept away by the normal processes of her restored body functions. But her elation colored with grief, as in that same moment she saw that even a miracle had its price. And she had no choice but to pay it. . . . She sent the electrochemical sequence to the waiting interactive network, the flesh and blood computer, the living laboratory that was her body, waiting at the end of the bright strand which bound her to Her. . . .

And as the sequence was completed, she felt herself called, as inexorably as before, as unwillingly, back into her own existence at the Transfer's end. But she carried with her the echo of lightmusic, like a mother's blessing, as her contact faded, rippling, and turned inside out. . . .

"Moon. . . ." Voices surrounded her, too solid, too real, like the hands restraining her body, as the colors of an infinite spectrum became the colorless light of day. "Mother . . ." she whispered, "thank you, Mother. . . ." She was on her knees; she let herself fall forward, felt the soft, hand-tied fibers of the rug press her cheek.

Something was still happening inside of her, the residue of changes at the molecular level as profound as those that had occurred when she had first been infected with the sibyl virus, and changed so irrevocably. . . .

She pushed up again, dizzy and faint; found herself face to face with Merovy's concerned, uncertain eyes.

"Are you all right, Ama?" Merovy murmured, touching her shoulder gently, almost hesitantly.

She nodded, sitting upright, rubbing her face, her eyes. "Ah, Lady . . ." she whispered, incapable of anything more, as realization followed realization, out of the realm of formless radiance and into the spectrum of coherent thought. Slowly she allowed herself the knowledge that she would live, that she had been spared, that she had answered her own prayers . . . more slowly she began to see what remained to be done; and to comprehend what the cost had been. She sat, strengthless and motionless, a moment longer, pulling her thoughts together enough for speech. "Merovy . . . bring your medical kit here."

Merovy brought the kit to her. Clavally and Danaquil Lu were behind her back, supporting her now. "Do you have a syringe?" Moon asked. "A large one, for drawing blood." Merovy nodded. "I want you to draw some of my blood. Inject it into Reede's vein. The water of death is dead."

Moon got to her feet, feeling giddy, feeling her own veins burn as if her blood were superheated. Clavally and Danaquil Lu rose with her, still supporting her. "Reede," she said; saw his pain-filled eyes already on her, saw him afraid to hope.

Merovy looked up from her medical supplies, "But—"

"Moon," Clavally said, "if you do that you'll infect him with the sibyl virus."

Moon shook her head, turning to look at them. "It won't happen," she said faintly. "I'm not a sibyl anymore."

"Not a sibyl—" Danaquil Lu broke off.

Clavally's eyes widened. "But I thought that was impossible," she murmured.

"No," Moon said, with tremulous laughter. "There is a place where everything is possible." She moved to Reede's bedside. Merovy followed her, and took blood from her arm. Moon watched it flow, deep red, with an odd detachment, almost disappointed that it did not show gleams of a strange light.

Merovy turned to Reede, with the syringe in her hand; Moon saw her hand tremble slightly as she looked at him. Merovy glanced up again, her eyes reminding Moon that no one had been able to bring their son and husband back from the dead.

Moon looked away.

"Lady . . ." Reede whispered. "It's true—?" He lifted a hand, reaching out to her.

"Yes." Her fists tightened at her side, as something grieving inside her balked at taking his hand. But she reached out, folding her fingers gently around the swollen flesh of his own. She held his arm steady as Merovy, taking a deep breath to steady herself, injected the blood serum into the lurid track of a vein dying by poison.

Reede stiffened, making a sound that made her shudder. He murmured something in a language she did not know, as the needle came out of his arm. And then his body went slack; his grip loosened, his fingers slid from her grasp.

Moon glanced at Merovy, watched her check for a pulse. "He's still alive, Ama . . ." Merovy murmured. She laughed once, a chirrup, half of relief, half of bitter irony.

Moon took Reede's limp, dangling arm, settled it gently at his side on the bed. She turned away; swayed suddenly, as reaction struck her. She took a step forward. Jerusha's waiting arms caught her as she fell, and that was the last she remembered.

BIG BLUE: Syllagong, Men's Camp #7

"You look too cheerful," Bluekiller said, as Gundhalinu emerged from his creaking hovel, dragging his equipment pack after him.

Gundhalinu climbed stiffly to his feet, bracing himself against the full impact of the wind, shielding his eyes from the swirl of ash and cinders, the blinding brilliance of the setting sun. This workshift he barely noticed the bite of the cold air, the sting of grit against his skin. He could feel himself smiling, unable to stop it. "I had a good dream last night," he said. He still thought of the time he slept, habitually, as "night," although in fact it was this world's day: during most of it the sun was eclipsing behind Big Blue, making their days as black as pitch and freezing cold. They worked at night, in the endless twilight of Big Blue's reflected planetshine. The only time they saw real daylight was for a few brief minutes at sunrise and sunset. He looked toward the sun, as a vision of golden light enfolded him, and her voice, whispering, *Sleep, my beloved . . . soon. . . .* "A good dream," he murmured.

"Musta been," Bluekiller muttered, scratching his beard. As the days passed Gundhalinu had grown used to the other man's distorted speech, until now he understood it without much trouble. "Otherwise I think you lost your mind, Treason. Only a shufflebrain smiles when it's workshift here. Or when it's not. . . ." He shrugged. "Good dreams are maybe good omens. Maybe we find a fresh harvest today."

Gundhalinu sighed, pulling on his pack. "Nice thought," he said, stuffing a ration biscuit into his mouth. Usually he was the first one up, ready and waiting, wanting to avoid Bluekiller's volatile temper, or Piracy's unfavorable notice. But today he had slept late, warmed and eased by the dream's hallucinogenic reality, for once not wanting workshift to come and end the cold, interminable hours that passed for his time of rest.

He chewed and swallowed while Bluekiller watched impassively. It could have been a cake of pressed sawdust he was eating, from the flavor and consistency; but it kept him alive, and so he assumed it was nutritious. He washed it down with a gulp of water from his canteen. Most days the act of eating only left him feeling hungrier, just as waking from a dream left him feeling emptier. "Let's go."

Bluekiller picked up the rope of their sledge and yanked it into motion, as Gundhalinu shoved it from behind. The sledge's runners made a high whining, an endless protest, as they moved out through camp toward the lifeless plain. Gundhalinu glanced at Piracy's hovel as they passed, as he did every workshift; seeing the dead plant that sat beside its door, a withered seedling in a container filled with ash. Piracy had smuggled the seeds in from a trip to the perimeter fort; had tried to make them grow. They had sprouted, like hope . . . and like hope they had withered and died. There was not enough light to support photosynthesis. The only things that survived here were the bacteria and parasites within a living human body.

"You dream about your woman?" Bluekiller asked, just when Gundhalinu had begun to think he was not going to. Gundhalinu seldom spoke unless spoken to; still half afraid, after what had been done to him when he arrived, that even Bluekiller might suddenly turn on him and break his neck over some casual remark.

"Yes," he said, feeling the sound of her voice fill his vision again with colors he had almost forgotten the names of, here in this monochromatic twilight. He had not seen her face, but somehow she had seemed more real to him than he had ever felt her to be, except when they had made love together on Mask Night, reunited at last in the extraordinary union of souls that had carried them outside the bounds of time. "She said I'd be free, soon. . . ."

"Those stop, after a while," Bluekiller said, looking back at him with a mix of disgust and pity. "Better when they do."

Gundhalinu said nothing, holding on to his inner vision. He squinted his eyes against the stinging reality of windblown sand.

They wandered for unmeasured hours through the shifting hills and valleys, over the cinder-strewn plains of their territory, finding meager scrapings at the round of pits they already knew. He had not yet developed the uncannily precise sense of time the other men in the work gang seemed to possess, that told them when to start work, when to eat, when to sleep. The human body had rhythms of its own, Piracy had told him; but he had never been forced to pay attention to them.

"Stop pushing," Bluekiller said abruptly. "I need to take a piss."

Gundhalinu stopped in his tracks, more than happy to take a break, although he made a point of never requesting one. But this time, instead of sliding down to sit, he began to climb the rise above them, still driven by the restlessness that had filled him since he woke. The luminous arc of Big Blue hung above him like a giant's eye, watching his every move the way he had watched insects struggle over the gray stone of the estate grounds when he was a boy on Kharemough. A surveillance craft passed through his line of sight as he looked up, its running lights like stars in the gloom far overhead.

He looked down, shielding his eyes as he searched the horizon beyond the hill's crest. In the distance he saw the plume of dust that marked the track of another sledge, another work team scouring their ground, probably Piracy and Contract.

The ground shuddered under his feet. He staggered, staying upright by sheer luck. His vision fell to his own footing, until he was sure he was safe again. Glancing on down the slope into the rift below him he froze, as he saw the telltale black-lipped mouth of a crater where he had never seen one before. He stared for a long moment before he was sure he believed his eyes, and then he turned back. "Bluekiller!" he shouted. "I found one! I found one!"

Bluekiller came scrambling up the ridge, slipping and sliding, until they stood side by side. "Sonuvabitch," Bluekiller said. "You did." He laughed, a sound Gundhalinu had never heard him make before.

They slid down the far side of the hill, cinders and dirt cascading into their boots with every step, until they reached the blackened mouth of the new crater. "Maybe this is your lucky day, Treason," Bluekiller said. "Look at that—it's got teeth. Big time! After you—" He gestured.

Gundhalinu kneeled down, reaching into his equipment pack. The unharvested crystals lay like a strange bouquet before him; he had never seen untouched growth like this. The crystals had a peculiar asymmetrical grace that was as close to beauty as anything he had seen in this bitter landscape. He pulled on his protective gloves, and reached out to pluck the first spine.

The ground shuddered. He lost his balance and fell forward; his hand smashed into the growth of spines, snapping them and sending them into the maw of the pit. A second, harder shock almost sent him headlong after them; he flung himself backward frantically.

He heard Bluekiller shout something unintelligible, saw him stagger and fall as the shaking did not stop. A rumbling so deep and omnipresent that at first he had not even recognized it as sound vibrated through the ground, the air, every atom of his body. He lay paralyzed by disbelief and fear, until Bluekiller crawled to him, shoving him roughly. "Up!" Bluekiller bellowed. "Climb! Up! Nothing to hold on to here—"

Gundhalinu felt his instincts take over, pushing him to his knees. His body sent him scrambling up the hill as if he were inside a machine that he did not control.

The hillside rose and fell, undulating beneath him as if he were a ship on the sea, throwing him flat on the cruel ground. He swore as he felt himself begin to slide back down the slope.

He heard Bluekiller shout, behind and below him. He rolled over for a clear view of the other man, just in time to see the tortured earth split open along the bottom of the ravine, spewing fumes and ash, swallowing up their prize crater. And Bluekiller, sliding downward toward the sudden rip in reality.

Gundhalinu flopped onto his stomach, slithered down the smoking slope until he caught hold of Bluekiller's ankle. He lay spread-eagled, digging into the surface of the heaving ground with his feet and one free hand. "Hang on!" he shouted, not knowing whether Bluekiller could hear him, not sure that he even heard himself.

He shut his eyes, gritting his teeth, fusing his body with the slope's surface, stopping their downward slide, while the entire planet seemed to convulse with gigantic seizures beneath and above and around them.

At last, after what seemed to have been all of eternity, he realized that the ground beneath him was still, that there was no roaring like the voice of a chthonic deity in his ears; that what still seemed to him to be noise and motion were only aftershocks in his mind. That only his fear was real. He lay there, too spent even to raise his head, feeling Bluekiller's leg clamped inside the rictus-grip of his gloved fist, until even his fear faded, leaving his mind a white wilderness like fields of snow. And he saw her hair, like fields of snow, falling around her face, along her shoulders, her skin as translucent as moonglow, her eyes like mist and moss agate. . . .

"Treason!" Someone was shaking him, calling his name—or what had come to be his name, now, as if he had never been someone else; as if there had never been any other existence. He shook his head, not certain of anything now, except that Bluekiller was beside him, pulling him up, trying to make him react. He grunted, spitting out cinders and ash, feeling the rawness of lacerated skin as he rubbed his face. "Gods . . ." he croaked. "You all right?"

Bluekiller nodded, jerked his head at the gaping wound in the surface of the ground, barely two meters beyond them. "Yeah. . . ." He wiped his forehead on his sleeve. "The Hidden One set a good trap that time, by Hanu!" His voice turned sour as he gazed at the spot where minutes, or centuries, ago, they had had in their hands the closet thing to treasure that this benighted land could offer. "Damn it to hell!" Bluekiller flung away a handful of ash, and then he looked back at Gundhalinu. He went on staring, for a long moment, and Gundhalinu heard in his silence the words that some unhealed memory would not let him speak.

Gundhalinu nodded once. "Better see if we've still got a sledge," he murmured, looking away up the hill. He forced himself to begin climbing, sliding back as often as he made real progress, his body rubbery with shock. Bluekiller climbed after him, until they reached the top of the rise together. The sledge with their day's take and most of their important supplies still lay below, tumbled onto its side but intact. He sighed.

Bluekiller grunted in satisfaction, straightening upright. He turned, glancing back down the slope; looked at Gundhalinu again. "Do me a favor, Treason. Don't have any more dreams." He shook his head, and started on down the hill.

Gundhalinu looked over his shoulder one last time. Then, silently, he followed Bluekiller down.

TIAMAT: Carbuncle

Falling. . . .

Moon opened her eyes, her cry of terror choking off as she found herself in her own world, her own room, her own bed. She sat up, pressing her chest, as her fall from an impossible height ceased in midair, ceased to exist.

She sagged forward, supporting her head in her hands, breathing deeply . . . piercingly glad to be awake, and alive, in the brief moment before she remembered who she was.

She shifted her body to the edge of the wide bed, pushed away the covers and dropped her feet over the side, driven to a kind of mindless urgency by the sudden, overwhelming return of memory. She froze there, staring, with one foot settled on the fur rug at her bedside.

Reede Kullervo sat in a chair across the room, watching her silently. She glanced away from him, searching the room for the presence of someone else.

He shook his head, with the ghost of a smile. "It's only me, Lady. And I haven't got the strength to get myself in trouble, or PalaThion would have tied me to the chair." He shrugged, lifting his hands. "I wanted to be here when you woke up. So you'd know."

Moon pressed her own hands against her body, through the cloth of her sleep gown. "How are you feeling?" she asked faintly. He was wearing a loose, handspun overshirt and shapeless pants; it surprised her how much like a Tiamatan he looked. He could have passed for an islander.

"I feel like shit," he said, his smile turning rueful. "But that's a hell of a lot better than I felt yesterday. Your vaccine stopped the deterioration in my cells. Now I've got to heal what's left, without its help. I've got to heal a lot of things. . . ." He looked down suddenly. "Some of it'll never be right." He looked up again, his gaze as clear and deep as the sky. "I don't understand why . . . why you did this for me. Gods, even I thought I deserved to die! The sibyl mind—" He broke off.

"—has changed its mind," Moon said gently. "And perhaps its perspective."

Reede ran an unsteady hand through his hair. "And you? PalaThion said Vhanu wants me handed over to him." She saw a haunted knowledge come into his eyes. "She said it's up to you, whether I stay or go."

"Your coming has released me from a geas, Vanamoinen," she murmured. "That's the last time I'll ever call you that—" she added, as he looked up in protest. "You have given me a kind of freedom. And so I would like to give you what freedom I can, I suppose. You may stay here, under my protection, for as long as you want to." She twined her fingers together in her lap, stared at them.

"Thank you," he whispered. She did not look up. After a moment he asked, "Is it true, that you're no longer a sibyl?"

She nodded, feeling oddly insubstantial as she admitted it, as if she had lost her moorings and was drifting with the tide.

"Can you forgive me?" he asked, barely audible.

"To be a sibyl was all I ever wanted from my life." She raised her head. "But it's a kind of freedom. . . ." And within her the memories were still alive, would always be, of what she had done, and seen, beyond the gates of time. She had been allowed that much, a gift of parting. "Ariele is the one you'll have to ask forgiveness of."

He grimaced, and nodded. She pictured Ariele, adrift in space far above them in a stasis coffin, in a ship tethered to this world by an invisible cord of gravity; her life tethered by something far more fragile. "Reede, how soon can we get to Ariele, so that we can—heal her?"

He shook his head. "You can't, Lady. Not now. Vhanu's got my ship. If we're lucky he won't search it again, while he knows where I am. If he found out about her. . . ." He did not finish it.

Moon took a deep breath. "Goddess!" She heard her voice turn tremulous, felt her precarious control slipping. "When does this stop—?"

He looked up at her, and she realized that the man behind his eyes suddenly was seeing her with an unimaginable parallax view. "It never stops . . ." he murmured. "It isn't meant to. That's what we're all about, you and I. We took the frayed ends of time and rejoined them, inside the sibyl mind. Its circle is complete again, because of us. Think of it, Lady! Think of what we've done together, what we've already accomplished. We've healed the net! I started a process, millennia ago; and thanks to you and . . . me . . ." he glanced down at himself, "it will continue as it was meant to. We've already performed a miracle. Two. . . ." He touched his face. His eyes shone, willing her to remember, and believe. "The wheel is still turning," he said softly. "Be patient. Have faith. We have to give it time."

She nodded, and sighed, feeling belief struggle toward the light inside her as he held her gaze.

He looked away at last. "You contacted the inner circles of Survey, didn't you, while you were in Transfer, in symbiosis with the matrix?"

She started. "Yes," she said. "I—the net—threatened them with what would happen if the slaughter of mers goes on, and promised them access to the starmap, if they stop the Hunt. I think it will turn the tide; but I don't know how long it will take—"

"Then we wait." He shook his head. "That's all we can do."

She sat up straighter, her eyes going to the window behind him, its view of the sea hidden by drawn drapes. "The mers are in the waters around the city again; Vhanu was going after them. Did Jersuha call out ships—?" She pushed to her feet.

"No need," Reede said. He rose from his chair and moved stiffly to pull aside the heavy, brocaded cloth. "They're protected."

Moon stopped where she was, staring without comprehension at the expanse of boundaryless gray that met her eyes. There was no ocean, no sky; only storm, merging one into the other, a rippling ferocity of wind and water pounding the unbreakable window surface with a rage that made it tremble.

"The sea lung . . ." Moon murmured, clutching a table for support. Reede looked back at her. "It's what the Winters call a storm like this, when there is no difference between the sea and sky." She had never experienced it, but she knew Winters who had. "The Summers say it's the Sea Mother's fury."

Reede smiled strangely, and went on looking at her. After a moment he glanced back out the window at the storm. "I wonder . . ." he said.

"We heard reports that a storm was moving up the coast, for days," she said. "A bad storm. But they said it would move out to sea and miss the city."

"It's come inland directly over Carbuncle, instead."

She found herself for the first time in years, making the triad sign of the Mother with complete sincerity. She thought of Capella Goodventure suddenly— remembered her without pain for the first time. "Vhanu won't be able to send out his hunters until it's over. By then the mers will have gained some distance at least."

He nodded, looking at the storm again. Her own eyes went to it as if she were hypnotized.

The door to the room opened suddenly, and one of the palace servants came in. "Lady!" she gasped, bobbing her head in apology. "The offworlders are in the palace! We couldn't stop them—"

Blue-uniformed figures appeared in the space behind her, carrying weapons. Moon looked toward Reede, where he stood frozen beside the window, still holding back a sweep of curtain.

She looked down again, at the tray of food someone had left by her bedside. She picked it up, moved to Reede's side without a backward glance of acknowledgment for the intruders who had forced their way into the room. She held the tray out to Reede, pressed it into his unresponsive hands. "That will be all. You may go," she said, urging him with her eyes.

He came alive, taking the tray from her without too much awkwardness. "Yes, Lady . . ." he murmured, bowing his head. Carrying the tray, he went toward the door, moving lamely, his shoulders knotted with tension. The Police edged aside, letting him pass. The woman who had brought the warning crept out in his wake, followed by their baleful stares.

Their stares turned back to her. Curiosity and faint amusement crept into the men's expressions at they saw her standing before them, disheveled, exhausted, in her nightgown. "Commander Vhanu wants you—" the sergeant in charge began.

She felt her sudden self-consciousness turn to anger. "You will wait outside, and allow me to dress," she said, lifting her hand. "Now."

They hesitated, glancing at each other, suddenly uncertain. And then, lowering their guns, they went one by one back out the door, closing it behind them.

She took her time, having no eagerness for whatever came next. She dressed pragmatically, in trousers and a robe cut Kharemoughi-fashion, but made of cloth in the shades of green that always soothed her eyes. She reached for her trefoil where it lay on the bedside table; hesitated, and left it behind.

When she opened the door they were waiting, nearly a dozen of them. She ignored the raised weapons, and said in a voice like glass. "What do you want? If it's Reede Kullervo, your Commander gave me his word that—"

"No, Lady," the sergeant in charge said. "It's you he wants brought to him."

"Where is Jersuha PalaThion?" she asked sharply.

The sergeant looked down, up again. "Under arrest. For obstructing justice."

"Justice," Moon murmured. She held out her hands. "Does Commander Vhanu want me bound?"

The sergeant grimaced, and nodded. They were all looking at her again, at her throat. Even without her trefoil, her tattoo was still visible. One of the men stepped forward at the sergeant's abrupt order. He drew her hands behind her, locking them into binders. She felt suddenly giddy; she had not believed they would actually do it.

They led her away through the halls, past the stunned, uncertain stares of the palace staff. She did not see Reede anywhere. She did not ask where they were taking her.

The sergeant and two of his men transported her in a hovercraft down through the city; she watched in surprise and half-fear as they passed by Police headquarters and kept going—through the Maze, down through the Lower City, without explanation. She remembered Arienrhod: her mother, her other self; remembered the final journey she had made down through the city to her death. Arienrhod had tried to change her world, defied the offworlders . . . and it had ended in a journey like this. There was only one imaginable destination they could be heading for now . . . and a storm was raging outside Carbuncle's walls.

They stopped at last at the head of the ramp which led down to the docks, and she was urged out as the craft's doors rose. She obeyed, moving awkwardly with her hands pinned behind her. The wind struck her and she staggered; one of the patrolman caught her, steadying her. The wind's fist drove them back against the side of the hovercraft with another blow. The impact knocked the breath out of her; she heard him swear in surprise and pain. She was drenched to the skin, without even realizing how it had happened.

The others gathered around her; they pulled her forward together, moving into the wind's teeth with arms linked, as if they were facing an angry mob. She could see nothing, blinded by pelting rain; but she heard the wind screaming, the thud and boom of storm-driven waves crashing over the docks far below her feet. She felt the city itself shudder with the blows. Her feet were suddenly in water up to her ankles as the sea swept up the ramp, flooding the pavement, and poured back down it again.

Vhanu was waiting for them, flanked by half a dozen more Police, in the security watchpost to one side of the ramp. The men around her crowded inside eagerly, dragging her with them out of the direct force of the wind. But even here the wind found them, drenching them with fresh volleys of rain and spray, whipping her hair loose, blowing it into her eyes maddeningly.

Vhanu pushed between his men until he stood face to face with her, and there was something in his eyes that made her want to shrink away.

She held her ground, even as he violated her space, pressing too close to her, intimidating her physically under the pretense of making himself heard. "What do you want?" she demanded, shouting over the wind's screaming moan. "Why am I here?"

"This!" he shouted. He caught her painfully by the arm, turning her, pushing her between bodies toward the watchroom's wide window. She caught a blurred glimpse of the causeway leading down, into what appeared to be nothing but the ocean. There were no moorings, no ships at all visible—only the sea, swirling with unidentifiable wreckage. As she watched, another wave broke against the city's pylons; its crest barely cleared Carbuncle's understructure, which was fifty feet above the normal high tide. She felt the city shudder again with the impact; saw water surging up the ramp into the city's open throat, before windblown spray struck the window in front of her, obscuring her view. She felt cold water lap her ankles again and withdraw.

She turned away, into the fanatical fury of Vhanu's gaze, shaken more by the sight of his face than by the power of the storm.

"I want you to stop it!" he shouted, gesturing at the storm's elemental madness behind her.

She stared at him, feeling the attention of the guards around her suddenly riveted on the two of them. "What—?" she cried.

"Make it stop!" He pulled her back to the watchroom's door; she felt the full force of the storm tease her, caress her, trying to coax her body out into the arms of its rage. She tried to turn back, but he held her there, letting the storm half-drown and abuse them both. "You heard me! Do it now!"

She twisted her head, trying to see his face clearly. "I can't!"

"Don't lie to me!" he said furiously. "You control the city's power supply at will! You turned Gundhalinu into a traitor! They even say you're the old queen reincarnated— And now you've turned the storm, to keep me away from the mers! You've ruined your own people's livelihood. Damn you, the city will be in chaos when the tribunal arrives! They're in orbit now, but they can't even land. What are you, some kind of witch? How do you do it? Where does it come from?"

She shook her head, shaking back her sodden hair, and took a deep, sobbing breath as the wind sucked the air from her lungs. She would have laughed, her disbelief was so utter; except that she knew he meant every word. *Oh, Lady,* she thought, *Lady, Lady* . . . But there was no response inside her. "No one can stop the storm!" she cried. "It has to run its course!"

"Then you admit you caused it?"

"No!" she shouted.

He gripped her arms again, hard enough to bruise her. "Stop the storm, or I'll order an orbital strike on the city!"

You can't! She choked back the words that came to her lips, seeing something like panic in his face. "You can't—" she said, and it was not a protest, but a threat.

His own angry response died in his throat. "What do you mean?" he shouted, his hands still bruising her arms. He shook her; the city shuddered beneath them, cold water climbed their legs and withdrew, leaving a trail of flotsam.

"Your weapons won't function," she said, holding his gaze with sudden ferocity. "Their aim will be off. If you try to fire on Carbuncle, you might miss. You might hit the starport complex instead, or one of your own ships, or—"

He swore. His hand came at her out of nowhere, striking her across the face, knocking her to the pavement in the wind and rain.

She struggled to get her feet under her and rise, without hands to help her; stunned with pain, battered down again by the storm. Behind her she heard unintelligible voices exchanging angry words. Two of the patrolmen were suddenly beside her, dragging her back again into the relative shelter of the watch station.

She gasped for breath, tasting blood in her mouth as she was supported between the two men. Two others held Vhanu away from her. The city trembled under another blow. An officer spoke urgently to Vhanu, in their own tongue; she could not hear what he said. But slowly the fury went out of Vhanu's straining body. The two guards let him go and stood back. He glared at her, immolating her with his eyes as he tugged at the soaked, unyielding cloth of his uniform sleeves. "Take her away," he said tonelessly. "Lock her up."

The three patrolmen led her to the hovercraft, and it carried them back up the street to Police headquarters. They did not speak to her, but their treatment of her was cautious, almost apologetic. She leaned against the window at the corner of her seat, dazed and strengthless, avoiding their eyes. The streets were almost deserted. She wondered whether it was martial law or the terrifying presence of the storm rattling the transparent walls at the end of every alley that kept her people indoors. She wondered, wearily, what their reaction would have been to see her like this . . . could not carry the thought any further. She was invisible to the few people who did venture out, hidden behind the reflective windows of the Police craft.

They reached Blue Alley at last. She was led through the station house, past half a hundred uncomprehending stares, and into a cell somewhere deep in its heart. There were other cells around hers; she searched them, looking for Jerusha. But the other cells were all empty. The guards removed the binders from her aching wrists and left her alone, sealed in by a clear wall that gave off sparks when she touched it.

The cell was cold; she began to tremble, from reaction as much as from the clammy embrace of her wet clothing. She wiped blood from the corner of her mouth with her hand; stood staring at the sticky redness, uncertain what to do with it. There was a narrow cot along the wall, with a single blanket folded at its foot. She wrapped the blanket around her and lay down, stupefied by exhaustion, her thoughts as empty as the space around her. She closed her eyes, letting her mind and body escape into oblivion.

She woke from restless, nightmarish sleep, to push the blanket away; woke again after more fever dreams to cover herself, shivering with chills. Time passed in a measureless flow, and gradually her sleep became deeper, more peaceful, less troubled by dreams.

At last she woke again, and her mind was clear. She sat up, shaking off the covers, leaning back against the wall as her body's sudden weakness took her by surprise. Her mouth was parched and dry, and she realized that her weakness was partly hunger and thirst. There was a plate of food on the floor just inside the barrier at the front of the cell. She wondered how long it had been waiting for her; she had nothing with her to tell her how much time had passed.

She got up from the cot, managed to retrieve the plate and a cup filled with some unfamiliar drink. She sat down with them again before dizziness overwhelmed her, and waited, motionless, while her heart hammered against the walls of her chest. And then she ate, slowly, savoring every bite of the plainly prepared native food; delaying for that much longer the need to think beyond the present moment.

By the time she had finished, her mind had begun to function again. Her clothes were completely dry; she pulled them into something like order. She drew back the tangled mass of her hair, braiding it again into a long neat plait. She noticed that there were two blankets on her bed now, where there had only been one before. Someone had been here, checking on her while she slept.

She got up again and went to the front of the cell, calling out. Only echoes answered. She suspected that she was being watched, remembering Vhanu's pathological fear of her; but there seemed to be no other human being in the cell block. The isolation must be intentional. Vhanu would want even her exact location kept from anyone who might try to find her.

She touched the bruise on her cheek where he had struck her, and felt a coldness fill her that had nothing to do with the air. Why was she here? What did he intend to do with her? Would he have her deported, without anyone even knowing it, the way he had done to BZ? But if that was what he intended, surely he would have done it already—

She went back to the cot and sat down, controlling the sudden frustration and anger that overwhelmed her as she realized her helplessness. She thought of Ariele . . . tried not to, as pain blinded her. She wondered whether Jerusha was still held prisoner here, somewhere; whether Vhanu had had the palace searched, whether they had taken Reede away. Without Jerusha free, there was no one who would be able to change anything, stop anything, help her get free from here. . . . She rocked slowly back and forth, her fists clenched over buried folds of cloth on her robe.

She thought suddenly of the tribunal that Vhanu had said was coming to pass judgment on his version of the truth against her own. What was it he had said, in the flood of his accusations, there in the storm—? *They're here, but they can't land.*

Was he holding her to display to them as an enemy of the Hegemony, the cause of Gundhalinu's downfall? Or would she simply be kept here, locked away—not even given a chance to speak, until they had come and gone again, leaving him in charge? What would happen to her if he tried to force the truth from her . . . ? She let the thoughts come, every futile, fearful vision; let her mind fill with possible scenarios. She fingered them like beads in a necklace, trying to find some solution to each of them, because thought was the only thing left over which she had any control.

At last she heard the echoes of voices and footsteps, and knew that whichever way her fate was falling, she would know the outcome very soon.

She stood up, pulling her rumpled clothing straight again, as the guards came to take her out of her cell—different men this time, not the ones who had seen their Commander strike a defenseless prisoner.

"Where are you taking me?" she asked, keeping her voice even as they locked her hands behind her.

"To the starport," one of the guards said.

"Why?" she asked.

"Commander's orders," he said. They led her back through the dreary corridors and out of the station without further explanation.

The sea lung had passed; she could see clear daylight through the storm walls at the alley's end. She wondered bleakly how her people were coping with this disaster—how many had been caught outside the safety of the city's walls, injured or lost in the wild waters. She remembered the sight of the moorage below the city, nothing left to see but the impossible storm surge of the water, and swirling wreckage. She imagined that people would be down there already, below the city and along the shore, searching through what the sea had left them, sorting out their lives. She wondered what they would make of her disappearance, in the middle of all this. People at the palace knew she had been taken by the Police; the constabulary must know that Jerusha was the Hegemony's prisoner. Word would spread—

But the storm that had saved the mers and driven Vhanu to this act of vengeance might work to his advantage after all, as recovery diffused the energy of any protest the Tiamatans might make. She had no illusions, either, that Vhanu would not move swiftly to put someone in her place, probably a Winter. Kirard Set was gone to the Mother, but there were too many of his old acquaintances still in the city, waiting for their opportunity to regain Winter's lost power. And there was no one left who had the authority or influence to protect Summer's interests against them. . . .

They were in the transit tunnel already, on a shuttle threading rings of light like a needle through the darkness. She knew from experience that they would be inside the starport in a matter of minutes. And then . . . "Am I being deported?" she asked, suddenly unable to endure the pressure of the unknown any longer. "Am I going to disappear, like the Chief Justice? Where are you taking me? I am the Queen. I have a right to know. I want to know where you're taking me!"

The squad of guards surrounding her in the otherwise empty car looked at each other. "The Commander said bring you to the starport, Lady. He didn't say why." The patrolman who had spoken to her before shrugged, and glanced away. No one else spoke; they avoided looking at her.

The shuttle reached its terminus, and they took her up through the starport's interior, leading her finally to the reception hall in which she had once met the Prime Minister and the Hegemonic Assembly. The wide window-wall at the far side of the room showed her the glowing grids of the landing field, below and beyond it.

She entered the room, surprised; saw Vhanu turn to stare at her, across the expanse of deep blue carpet. He was surrounded by a small cluster of government officials, most of whom she recognized. He kept watching as she approached; his gaze lay somewhere between unease and satisfaction. The other faces around him watched her too, wearing a mixture of expressions.

Her instinctive reaction, as she saw them there, was relief. If Vhanu meant to deport her secretly, this was not how he would do it. But if that was not what he intended, then she suddenly had no idea what her presence here meant.

The guards halted her beside Vhanu, and he returned their salutes. Looking away from his eyes, she stiffened as she saw someone enter the hall from the other side.

Vhanu turned, seeing her stare. The others turned with him, as the new arrivals were escorted into the room: a dozen more Kharemoughis, of varying ages and both sexes, all of them with the aristocratic features and unconsciously arrogant manner of Technicians. Some wore uniforms, others wore the discreetly sophisticated, sexless clothing of highborn citizens. One, she saw, wore a trefoil. She knew without being told that this was the tribunal Vhanu had been waiting for.

They looked, in varying degrees, relieved and weary and glad to find themselves finally at the end of their journey. They all looked pleased, and somewhat curious, at the size of their welcoming committee.

Moon glanced again at Vhanu. She saw recognition and sudden pleasure fill his face. "Pernatte-sadhu!" he exclaimed, starting forward to greet the leader of the group. The man he called out to smiled, and held up his hand. Vhanu touched it in a greeting between equals. They spoke together in rapid Sandhi; she heard them use the informal *thou,* and realized that they were friends, possibly even related somehow.

She waited, understanding her function here at last; feeling her hope gutter as Vhanu led the tribunal members forward. She had been brought here to be displayed as a scapegoat. But Vhanu had not dared to have her gagged; she could still speak for herself. She gathered her thoughts, watching them come.

"—I say, Vhanu, couldn't we perhaps delay these matters for a bit? We're all extremely fatigued," Pernatte was protesting, his initial animation fading rapidly.

"Forgive me for pressing thee," Vhanu said. "But a series of events have occurred since our last communication that have made it vital for us talk now, before we enter the city." He looked toward Moon, his face hardening.

"Oh?" Pernatte said, with overtones of annoyance. He followed Vhanu's glance until his eyes reached Moon's face. "What's this?" he asked, his frown deepening.

"This woman," Vhanu gestured at her, "is the reason I must inconvenience thee."

Pernatte stopped in front of her. "This pale, bedraggled creature? Is she Tiamatan? She hardly looks capable of inconveniencing anyone—"

"She speaks Sandhi," Vhanu said.

"Oh." Pernatte looked back at her.

"She's the Summer Queen."

"Indeed?"

"Yes," Moon said stiffly. "And I do not need Commander Vhanu to speak for me."

Pernatte frowned again, glancing at Vhanu. "And thou've brought her here as a prisoner? This is a drastic step. What in the name of a thousand ancestors is happening here?"

"That is what I need to explain to thee," Vhanu said, grim-faced.

Pernatte nodded, finally. "I trust thou will be brief and to the point." He did not look at Moon again, or acknowledge her presence further. The other members of the tribunal committee fanned out behind him, watching and listening in weary resignation.

"Yes, sadhu, I shall." Vhanu drew himself up. The tension radiating from him, and from the officials grouped behind him, was almost a physical heat.

"This is the woman with whom Gundhalinu is accused of committing treason?" Pernatte asked, as if he still found it hard to believe.

Vhanu nodded. "She is more than she seems. I consider it imperative that she be removed from Tiamat as quickly as possible, and never allowed to return. She should be taken to Kharemough, where she can be intensively questioned and investigated. Not only did she cause Gundhalinu to forsake his background and commit miscegenation, she led him to pervert Hegemonic policy to suit her own superstitious, primitive beliefs—"

Moon stiffened, taking a step forward; the guards forced her back, as Pernatte said, "Yes, yes, all that was in the report. But she is the sovereign ruler of an independent government, and however repugnant we may find her actions to be, making her our hostage is hardly justified by—"

"That isn't all," Vhanu said, with a sharpness that made heads turn. "This woman controls—powers, some hidden energy source we don't know about, that enables her to do things that should be impossible."

Pernatte looked mildly incredulous. "Such as—?"

"She controls Carbuncle's power supply at will. She controls storms. She has taken control of our own orbital weapons systems, so that I didn't dare to use them—"

"What?" Pernatte's disbelief was plain now.

"The city is in . . . disarray," Vhanu said, his voice catching. "I have not been able to obtain the quotas of the water of life that I promised to deliver, even though—and here again, she lied—the seas are teeming with mers. She seduced Gundhalinu to make him stop the mer hunts; and when I took control from him she turned her people against us. And when even that wasn't enough, she shut down the city's power, so that it was all we could do to maintain order. After I forced her to restore the power, she called up a storm at sea that destroyed virtually every vessel in the city's harbor. When I threatened to turn our weapons on Carbuncle unless she stopped the storm, she said that they would not function, that we would strike our own starport instead—" He broke off, as Pernatte's expression, and the rising murmurs of the people behind him, began to register. "I know, this seems absurd to thee, I know it sounds impossible; but it happened!"

Pernatte took a deep breath, as if someone had been holding his head under water. "This is . . . quite unexpected, Vhanu-sadhu." He glanced away from Vhanu, at the tense, tentative faces of the other officials behind him. "Do you all share this interpretation of events—?"

"We did not actually witness all the incidents that Commander Vhanu related to thee, uncle," Tilhonne said cautiously. "But what we do know about the Queen proves unquestionably that she is to blame for our difficulties in obtaining the water of life, and that Gundhalinu was involved in a liaison with her that compromised his judgment as Chief Justice, especially regarding the mers."

"I see." Pernatte pursed his lips. He turned slowly, as if his body were resisting the motion, until he faced Moon again. Meeting her eyes directly this time, he asked, "And what is your response to these questions? Do you have one—?"

"—Lady," she finished for him, in Sandhi, seeing that he did not have the faintest idea even of how to address her. "I have many responses, Citizen Pernatte," she said; addressing him as foreigners on his homeworld were expected to do. "Where shall I begin?" She felt the blood rise into her face as her existence suddenly became real to the others who surrounded her. Her gaze glanced off Vhanu's frozen hatred, back to Pernatte's reluctant attention, as Pernatte said, "I have always been told that Carbuncle's power supply was completely self-contained. Do you actually have a secret way of controlling it?"

"No," she said.

"Then how do you explain a blackout that lasted for three full days?" Tilhonne demanded. "There is no record of such a thing ever happening before."

"Once in every High Year, Carbuncle shuts down," she said carefully, "because it has to renew its systems. That only happens during High Summer; the Hegemony has never been on Tiamat during High Summer before."

"Then how do you know about it," Pernatte said, "if it only happens once in two hundred and fifty years?"

"The traditions of my people tell of it, going back for centuries."

"I saw you restore power to the city with my own eyes!" Vhanu said.

She did not take her eyes off Pernatte. "I knew that it was due to happen. It would have happened anyway. I pretended to do it myself. It was an act."

"And there was a storm that struck the city?" Pernatte said.

She nodded. "But that was the will of the Sea Mother . . . an act of the gods, you would say."

His frown came back. "And do you actually have some means of controlling our orbital weapons system?"

She smiled, as she looked toward Vhanu at last; it was not a smile she remembered ever touching her face before. "That was a lie."

"What—?" Vhanu started forward, stopped himself. "No! She said—"

"Did you actually test the system, Vhanu?" Pernatte asked.

"No, I was afraid to. I—"

"You believed what you wanted to believe, Commander," Moon said, letting the disgust she felt for him fill her words. "You wanted to believe that I was—what was it, a witch? That the only way that BZ Gundhalinu could have fallen in love with me was because I had somehow . . . magicked him into a sexual obsession. That the only reason he could possibly have for resisting the slaughter of the mers was that I had him in my thrall. That the only motive I could have for protecting them was superstition . . . that the only reason I could have for taking him into my bed was to use and control him. Nothing—" She broke off, taking a deep breath. She looked back at Pernatte. "Nothing," she said softly, "could be further from the truth."

Pernatte stared at her for a long moment, and she found no understanding in his eyes. But, to her surprise, she found belief. "So you are saying, then, that everything you did, and Gundhalinu did, was for the purpose of protecting the mers, which you claimed were an intelligent alien race, and not merely animals?"

"Yes," she said.

He looked down, away, restlessly. "Frankly," he said at last, "I have found the idea that the mers could be intelligent almost impossible to accept."

Moon opened her mouth.

"But—" Pernatte held up his hand. "I have been forced to accept it . . . we all have." He indicated the tribunal members around him.

She did not know whether the disbelief on Vhanu's face or her own was more complete. "What are you saying?" Vhanu demanded. "That you accept what this foreign woman has told you, over my own testimony—?"

"No." Pernatte looked at him with troubled eyes. "I am saying that we have been—made aware of certain relevant new data, new *discoveries,* by sources which are above question." He emphasized the words carefully. "This has resulted in a change in Hegemonic policy. The Central Coordinating Committee has reversed its position on the status of the mers. It has declared them to be a separate intelligent race. They will no longer be hunted and killed; there will be no more water of life." His eyes turned bleak as he spoke the final words.

"What?" Vhanu said. "That's impossible! Father of all my grandfathers, I don't believe this!"

Pernatte's dour expression deepened into disapproval. "I know this comes as a blow to thee, as it does to all of us. Thou may verify it, if thou wish—we have a sibyl here." He gestured at the tribunal member who wore a trefoil.

Vhanu shook his head, taking a deep breath. "No. That will not be necessary. Thy word is sufficient, Pernatte-sadhu. . . . But if there is to be no more water of life, then what purpose is there even in maintaining contact with a world like this one?"

"Not much, perhaps," Pernatte answered. "Although it has been pointed out that, given the scarcity of habitable worlds, no world on which humans survive successfully is beneath our attention. Even before Gundhalinu became Chief Justice, he documented in extensive reports that the cooperative long-term development of Tiamat's natural resources is not a pointless—or necessarily unprofitable—project. And considering that we now have no alternative . . ." He turned back to Moon. "In light of these new events, Lady, it appears that your defiance of Hegemonic law was justifiable. Some might even call it honorable." He lifted his hand. "Release her," he said to the guards.

They looked toward Vhanu, waiting for confirmation. Moon looked at him too, as betrayal distorted his face. "No!" he said. "By all the gods, this is not going to happen! This woman must be stripped of her influence and position. She must be investigated, taken back to Kharemough. She is in collusion with some group, or some power—"

Pernatte stepped forward and seized Vhanu's spasmodically gesturing hand. "Vhanu . . ." he said, his voice low but impossible to ignore. "Thou have been under a great deal of strain, I know. Thou have been faced with many difficult decisions in recent months, and thou have tried to behave honorably. But thou must let this obsession go. The situation has changed here. This woman is not only a sibyl, but the leader of her people."

"She has to be replaced!" Vhanu insisted.

"But not by thou—not by us," Pernatte said, his jaw tightening. "Vhanu, to find that a man like Gundhalinu could willingly let himself become so infatuated with a—" he glanced at Moon, "with a foreign woman, is as incomprehensible and distasteful to my beliefs as it is to thine. And yet suddenly everything has changed, black has become white. What he did is no longer treasonable, but instead . . ." he shook his head, "preternaturally wise. How can we explain the changes a man goes through, who is a stranger far from home—?"

Vhanu froze, and suddenly all the resistance went out of him.

"I think it would be prudent for thou to return to Kharemough with me, Vhanu-sadhu," Pernatte said, lowering his voice again. "Thou are in need of a rest and a chance to regain thy perspective. I'm sure there is a less taxing position somewhere, for which thou would be better suited."

Vhanu gazed at Pernatte in stricken silence. And then, tight-lipped, he turned toward Moon. He did not acknowledge her with his eyes as he gave the signal to release her.

Moon stepped forward, massaging her wrists. Pernatte bowed to her, a full obeisance. "Forgive me, Lady, for the hardships and humiliation my government's unjust accusations have caused you to endure," he said, with perfect poise and transparency. "Be assured we shall make whatever reparations are necessary to reestablish our previous relationship of trust and goodwill with your people."

Moon took a breath, held it until her lungs ached; until she was able to say, with equal conviction, "I accept your apology, Citizen Pernatte . . . on the condition that the charges against Chief Justice Gundhalinu are dropped, and he is restored to his former position as the leader of the Hegemonic government on Tiamat."

He nodded, without showing the least surprise, "Your request will be accomplished as swiftly as stardrive technology can make it possible, Lady. I'm sure it is a request that will meet with the complete approval of all parties." Only the barely perceptible tic of an eyebrow betrayed any emotion.

"Thank you," Moon said, and smiled with complete sincerity. "Perhaps you and your committee members would be my guests, then, at a dinner in your honor at the palace tomorrow . . . and we can discuss further policy changes in more pleasant surroundings."

Pernatte smiled too, slowly and almost grudgingly. "It would be our pleasure," he said. He turned back to Vhanu. "And now, Vhanu, if you would kindly show us to our proper quarters, we can all finally get some well-deserved rest."

Vhanu nodded stiffly. His face was a mask of highborn propriety, and his eyes were completely empty as he turned his back on them and led the way out of the hall.

BIG BLUE: Syllagong, Men's Camp #7

"That's it?" Piracy said, as Gundhalinu and Bluekiller dropped their day's take into the cache-pit.

Bluekiller shrugged, his brows furrowing. "Treason twisted his ankle. Slowed us down."

Gundhalinu reached into his coverall pocket and pulled out a small wad of janka wrapped in a rag. He held it up. "Here," he said. "Somebody from Gang Four paid me for a question with this." He took barter now for any equipment he fixed and any questions he answered. He had not wanted to put a price on answers he gave as a sibyl, but Piracy had insisted.

He heard grunts of interest from some of the men around him; aware of no warmth, but at least of acceptance, as he tossed the wad of janka to Piracy. Janka was a mild narcotic some of the men chewed, when they could get it.

"You take a cut?" Piracy asked.

He shook his head. "No, I . . . Yes." He sat down cross-legged on the ground, suddenly too weary to go on standing. "Yes, I'll take a cut." Maybe it would help him sleep. The longer he was here, the worse he slept.

Piracy glanced up at him in brief curiosity, looked down again. "Okay—" he said. "You heard Treason. Anybody else wants a chew, ante up."

Half a dozen scabbed, filthy hands tossed offerings from their scant rations onto the ground in front of Piracy. He split up the wad of janka scrupulously with his knife, passing it around. Solemnly he pushed the final piece, and the small pile of rations, toward Gundhalinu.

Gundhalinu gathered them in, his battered hands indistinguishable from anyone else's. He began to eat without ceremony, not caring what it was that filled his stomach, barely even tasting it. The sun's burning face pushed up over the horizon, making him squint. The other men who weren't already sitting sat down now, taking out their own food, as Piracy resealed the lock box, kicking ash and cinders over it.

They ate in near silence, as they did at the end of every workshift; having little left to say, and no energy to say it. But they ate together, still hungry for human contact, although none of them would admit it. This had come to be the most important moment of his own day, the one thing that he looked forward to: sitting on the ground in the cold wind among these men who made his barely tolerated existence possible.

Sometimes Piracy even held up the other end of a conversation with him. Piracy's mind possessed an odd, eclectic accumulation of knowledge, most of it self-taught. They had talked for hours while Gundhalinu recovered from his beating, sharing the other man's hut. But even Piracy did not risk talking to him often now, and sent him out with Bluekiller, not as his own partner; afraid that getting too friendly with an ex-Blue would undermine his position with the others.

The ground trembled; Gundhalinu swallowed convulsively, and coughed.

"We got almost a full cache, Piracy," someone said, after a time. "We could make a trek to the post soon."

Piracy glanced up over the mouth of his canteen. He grinned, setting it down. "Yeah," he said. "I guess that's true. Maybe it's time we choose who gets to go." A charged field seemed to build around him as he groped in a pocket, drew out the cracked, ancient gaming piece he guarded as if it were a jewel. "Three closest guesses take it, as usual. Whoever went last two times is out of the game."

Gundhalinu had been told the rules of this choosing, but he had never actually witnessed it. He watched as the exhausted, dull-eyed men around him suddenly came alive, leaning forward, calling out numbers with an eagerness he had never seen them show about anything before. The three who won got a break from the grueling drudgery of their work routine, and the chance to spend a night in a place that actually resembled civilization, with beds, showers, and real food, while they traded in the harvest they had brought for the small rewards that made their lives bearable until the time when they were set free from this living death.

"Treason?" Piracy said. "You got a number?"

Gundhalinu looked up, startled; realizing that he had not said anything, as usual. He had not even been sure they would let him play. Sudden excitement and hope filled him until he shone like the rest. He licked his cracked lips, and said, "Twenty-three."

Piracy nodded, and pushed up onto his knees. He held the game piece cupped between his hands, shaking it, prolonging the ecstatic moment when anything was possible for the men around him. And in that moment Gundhalinu understood what had made him their leader. When the game piece fell, three men would not only have the journey itself as a reward—they would have the days in between of looking forward to it. Even the losers would win those days of pleasant anticipation, of deciding what small, precious item not tied to their own survival that they would put in a request for. . . .

Piracy held his hands out, bathed in golden light, and let the game piece drop.

Whoops of triumph and curses of frustration made a deafening cacophony in Gundhalinu's ears, which had grown too used to silence. He pushed forward, seeing the number face up in the sand, seeing that it made him a loser. The loss caught in his chest like a barb; he swore. The others shrugged and shook their heads, accepting defeat like they accepted everything else. But he felt stunned as he realized how much the sudden, real hope of winning had meant to him, now that it had suddenly been taken away.

He tried to focus on an adhani; unable even to remember one, as Piracy announced the winners. They were congratulated by the losers, more roughly than was necessary, but taking it with smug good humor. He felt bodies begin to move, jarring him as they rose and went their separate ways back to their huts to sleep. There was more conversation than usual, more animation, even laughter. He forced his own unwilling body to get up, suddenly aware of every ache and strained muscle; not understanding why only he felt worse, not better. Maybe because the rest of them knew this would all end for them someday; only he had no other hope that he still dared to believe in.

"Hey," somebody said. "Look at Treason."

Gundhalinu stiffened, and turned toward Accessory, who was pointing at him.

"He's got the green light," Accessory said. "Look!"

The others began to turn back, staring in curiosity, as Gundhalinu suddenly lunged at him, knocking him to the ground.

Gundhalinu sat on Accessory's chest with his hands around the other man's neck. "Joke about that again, you bastard, and I'll stuff your lying tongue down your throat—"

"I'm not lying!" Accessory squealed, prying at his hands. More hands were on him, dragging him off of Accessory, holding him back.

"He's not lying, Treason," Piracy said. He stepped in front of Gundhalinu, meeting his furious stare. He held up a fragment of polished metal, let Gundhalinu see his reflection in a sudden blaze of sunlight, and the green light on his collar shining like a star.

Gundhalinu stopped struggling, seeing his own mouth fall open. His hands rose to the collar around his throat, as the men holding him let him go; as the rest clustered behind Piracy, staring at him.

"You said he was a term," Accessory muttered, getting to his feet. "I thought he only got the green light the hard way."

"I was . . . I am," Gundhalinu whispered, still gazing at his reflection, seeing a man he barely recognized press grimy fingers to his throat; detecting the faint warmth given off by the light on his collar.

"Maybe it's a mistake," someone said. Gundhalinu spun around, glaring at him.

Piracy put a hand on Gundhalinu's shoulder. "They don't make mistakes like that around here, Treason," he said quietly. "I'll radio the post. Guess you're going along this trip after all. One way." His mouth quirked slightly. "Congratulations. We might even miss you, a little. . . ."

Gundhalinu nodded, barely, meeting his eyes. "I won't forget you, either. I won't forget any of this."

Piracy gave him a long stare, and shrugged. "Better if you do, Treason," he said. "It's better if you do."

Gundhalinu shook his head, looking down. "I couldn't if I wanted to," he whispered.

"Guess your dream was true, Treason," Bluekiller said.

Gundhalinu glanced up. "I guess it was," he murmured, with a strained laugh.

He took a step, suddenly afraid that he was still moving through a dream. They parted ranks for him, the way the convicts had parted ranks for a man with a green light on the day he had arrived. He passed through them, his shadow walking a golden road through the dawn. He reached his hut and crawled inside, still followed by the benediction of their stares, as if he had become a peculiar sort of hero. He lay down on his pallet of rags with a sigh. And then, against all odds, he went to sleep.

TIAMAT: Carbuncle

Reede Kullervo stood on the hidden balcony that overlooked the reception hall, leaning against the rail in voyeuristic fascination, watching the gathering below as he had watched it for hours, all-seeing but unseen. This was only one of many hidden rooms and secret observations points in the palace; he had been shown them all, after the Queen's arrest, by members of the Sibyl College. The aging blind woman who was the College's head had ordered them to protect him when the Blues arrived to flush him out; and they had, even the two whose pregnant daughter was Tammis Dawntreader's widow. He remembered Merovy Bluestone's quiet, pragmatic manner as she had treated his illness; he remembered her eyes. . . .

He sighed, filling up his vision with the motion and color of the crowded hall below. He could not remember now whether he had created these quirks of design when he had dreamed of what Carbuncle would be, or whether they had been added later, somewhere in the long, lost centuries between his once-and-future lives.

He was grateful for them, whether it had been foresight or not; because they had saved his life, and because now they let him observe the closing of a circle which he had helped to bring about. The party below, where offworlder officials and Tiamatans mingled in a fragile dance of diplomacy, celebrated the return of Chief Justice BZ Gundhalinu.

He did not dare show himself down there while a single Kharemoughi lingered, afraid that his face, or some random response, might reveal the Smith to the unwanted attention of the Golden Mean. And so he had watched from here as the hall slowly filled, studying the variegated colors of skin and hair and clothing, the varieties of ostentation, sophistication, and simplicity; savoring the sensuous pleasure of the patterns they inscribed on his mind.

The Queen had moved among them, her movements seemingly random except to his observation. His eyes told him that she drifted near the entrance to the hall too often, looked toward it too much, smoothed back her hair and checked the time repeatedly, with restless impatience.

Until the moment they had both been waiting for, without entirely realizing it, had come at last—Gundhalinu had arrived. The music, and all motion, had stopped in the hall: dancing, eating, gossiping, politicking, all suddenly frozen into a magnificent tableau.

Gundhalinu had entered the room, accompanied by Jerusha PalaThion, who wore the uniform and insignia of her position as the new Commander of Police, and the endless silence was broken by applause. Gundhalinu had stopped moving, in the small space left open to him inside the entrance, as if the noise of sudden adulation had taken him aback. He stood, his head up, not acknowledging the welcome, seeming after a moment hardly even to hear it, as his eyes searched the crowd around him.

And then he had found what he was searching for—the Queen, coming toward him as the crowd parted to let her pass through, her hair like snow, her robes made of whispering moss greens, the diaphanous flowing blues of the summer sky. She glittered with crystal beads like stars, like tears of the sea. She wore no crown, but only a simple garland of flowers, as she approached him with her hands held out in welcome.

Gundhalinu moved at last, stepping forward to take her outstretched hands. They stood face to face, daring to embrace only with their fingertips; but in the moment of contact, the unbearably intimate entwining, there was an ecstasy as pure as if the crowd's witnessing eyes were a sacrament, and not an intrusion.

Their hands released and fell away at last, as slowly as if gravity had ceased to function in the space around them. Gundhalinu turned briefly and said something to Jerusha PalaThion, gesturing toward the far side of the room. PalaThion nodded, moving away through the crowd as the Queen led Gundhalinu into the tide of congratulations and well-wishers, former enemies and friends who were now indistinguishable, at least for the next few hours. Pernatte and the other members of the Hegemonic tribunal were the first to greet him; Vhanu, the former Commander, was conspicuous by his absence.

All at once the hired musicians, who had held their silence since his arrival, began to play again, an exquisite song Reede did not know, but Gundhalinu seemed to have been waiting for. Gundhalinu's face, which except for his eyes had shown no readable expression until now, suddenly smiled. He leaned over, murmuring something in the Queen's ear. She turned toward him, her surprise plain. He took the gesture as acceptance, taking her hand again, drawing her toward him, leading her into the motions of a dance.

The crowd fell away around them, watching and murmuring as they moved gracefully to the music through a widening gyre across the floor. Reede watched too, thinking that the most hidebound Kharemoughi Tech in the hall below could not possibly feel an astonishment any more profound than his own as he watched Gundhalinu dance openly with the woman he loved. One by one, other dancers began to take to the floor, until they were adrift in a sea of bright motion.

Reede watched them dance together, with eyes for no one else in the room: seeing in their faces the poignant contrasts, the painful dichotomies that separated their two worlds . . . seeing in their eyes the only truth he knew.

And he remembered Mundilfoere, letting the midnight beauty of her face fill his mind . . . remembering all that she had been to him, and done to him, and sacrificed for him. And he remembered Ilmarinen, whom he had loved . . . And he wept, in his solitary space, alone.

And when the dance was done, he watched Gundhalinu and the Queen eat and speak and move through the crowd, always together, forcing all witnesses to recognize and acknowledge their unspoken union.

At last the guests began to depart, disappearing like beads from a broken string. The Hegemony's elite left first, as soon as it was graciously possible to do so; only Gundhalinu showed no signs of restlessness. Reede shifted position as he watched the last Blue leave the hall, suddenly restless himself, as if he had been freed of some oppressive weight.

A sound made him start and turn. He looked behind him, his back pressing the rail. "Ariele?" he said, as she materialized silently in front of him. She was not wearing the clothes he had last seen her in: she had changed her strobe-colored, defiantly sensual offworlder clingsuit for a long, shapeless native robe, its sleeves and neckline covered with smocking. Strings of heavy beads hung around her neck, made of carbuncles and agates and polished shell.

She hesitated, uncertain all at once, and he was abruptly aware of his own reaction, how he stood clutching the railing as if he were expecting attackers . . . or a ghost.

He straightened away, letting go. "Where were you?" he asked, half frowning in concern, half frowning at himself as he saw her face. "I saw you in the hall when they started arriving; and then you disappeared."

She looked down, coming to stand beside him in the alcove as he put out his hand. She kept her face averted as he slipped his arm around her; staring at the scene below, as he had done. He felt her hand cover his, tentative but warm. She had seemed somehow insubstantial since her awakening, since her mother had brought her back from the dead. "I did what was required of me," she murmured. "I greeted the offworlders with the proper hypocritical solicitude. And then I went to my old playroom, and I looked at all the toys that used to be mine, and—and Tammis's. . . ." Her voice faded. She was silent for a long moment. "I read some books, and had warm tea and honeycakes, as if I was a little girl again. It was very peaceful, there in my room." She looked up at him. "Did you watch from here the whole evening?"

"I'm an offworlder," he said, touching her face, and it was not an answer to her question.

"You're not like them." She jerked her head disdainfully, at the Kharemoughis who were no longer in the room below, but whose shadows remained, clouding their future.

"Your father is," he said, making her turn back again in anger and grief. "Or your father was," he amended, more gently. He glanced over the hidden railing, seeing the Queen and Gundhalinu still side by side, bound together by an invisible cord of need. She followed his gaze, and he saw her frown. "Let them be happy. . . . It's what he wanted them to be. It's what they deserve."

She stood motionless, watching them together, her frown slowly fading until her face held no expression at all. Finally she nodded.

"Here." Reede took his arm from around her, reaching into his belt pouch for something he had carried there, forgotten, until now. "He wanted you to . . . have this back." He passed her Dawntreader's shell flute, its fragile, spiral form traced with hairline fractures, anciently mended.

Her mouth opened; nothing came out of it. She took the flute, held it, pressed it against her cheek, closing her eyes. "I want to go away from here—from the city—and never come back. Aunt Jerusha said that we can live at her plantation. We can be alone, with just the mers. . . ."

"She said that?" His hands tightened over the rail again, as his body suddenly seemed weightless. "We could do that," he whispered. "We could. Yeah, that would be good . . . that would be just fine."

She looked up at him again, with a bloom of color coming into her ashen cheeks, a smile ripening the full softness of her mouth.

He took her hand, looking at her long, slender fingers, pale even against his own, and the solii ring that she wore, the mate to his own. His throat closed over the words that he tried to say, and he took her into his arms, holding her against his heart, breathing in the sweet, warm scent of her, and the musty, ancient smell of the walls. After a time he asked, "Why did you come up here?"

She broke away from him, to look up at him with a smile, as the music suddenly began again below. It was a completely different kind of music from what had been played before, the refined measures intended to lull hypercritical Technician sensibilities. Reede glanced over the rail, proving to himself that it was really the same group of musicians he heard, suddenly playing the lilting, whimsical melody of a traditional Summer dance tune. "This is the real party, beginning now," Ariele said. "I wanted you to come and be with me, down there—" She reached for his hand, hesitated; smiled, as he came with her willingly, almost eagerly.

They went down the stairs side by side, entering the sea of bodies and faces, their arrival barely making a ripple. Most of the people around him looked completely unfamiliar; here and there among them he saw someone he had met before. He saw Merovy Bluestone; their eyes locked, before he could look away again. He had lost track of Gundhalinu and the Queen as he reached the level of the ballroom.

Ariele brought him to an open space where people were dancing now in a way that was as spontaneous as the music was. She pulled him into the motion of the dance, making him dance with her. The steps were simple and he obeyed; feeling clumsy and frustrated, because he still had not completely accepted that his body was no longer the perfect machine the water of death had made of it. He kept on, gamely, and he began to discover that his body liked to dance—had always liked to dance, he realized, although he could not clearly remember ever having done it. They danced together, not simply with each other but within the embracing motion of all the other dancers, to music that was alternately lively and plangent, until Ariele's face was flushed and laughing, like his own.

But his once-tireless body forced them to the sidelines, to eat pickled fish and drink strangely flavored wine until his senses began to buzz. "I remember this . . ." he murmured, with unsteady laughter, as the wine went to his head.

Ariele looked up at him. "What?" she asked.

Someone calling his name saved him from having to answer. He looked away through the crowd, seeing three figures moving toward them, in an unexpected juxtaposition of forms: The Tiamatan woman who ran Starhiker's, and with her his pilot and crew.

"Hey, boss," Niburu said, and his sudden grin told Reede that he'd probably been drinking too much too.

"Gods," Reede said, looking from one of them to the other, feeling his face doing odd things. "Where the hell have you been?"

They had been in jail, until PalaThion had finally been named Police Commander and set them free. Since then he had scarcely seen them; something which, he could only admit now, drunk with wine and fatigue, had bothered him considerably.

Niburu looked at him, with a wry glance past his shoulder at Ariele. "Around the city, helping clean up the storm wreckage," he said. He put an arm familiarly around Tor Starhiker's waist. Her own arm snaked across his shoulders, rubbing his chest.

Reede raised his eyebrows. "I guess virtue has its rewards."

Niburu shrugged, and grinned. "She likes my cooking."

Tor smiled. "It's plain," she said, "but it's very filling. . . ." Niburu turned red. Ananke stood behind them, wearing the quoll in its sling, smiling and silent; always the cryptic shadow. "You haven't had much need for a ferryman lately," Niburu said.

"That's true," Reede murmured, glancing at Ariele. "Guess not." His hand touched hers.

"So," Niburu said, finally, "what do we do now?"

Reede looked back at him. "Eat. Dance. Have a good time," he said.

Niburu shook his head. "I mean, after that. Tomorrow. Next week. A couple months from now?"

Reede hesitated, staring at the three of them, at the variety of expressions on their faces, that were somehow all the same expression. "We—Ariele and I," he glanced down, "are going down south, along the coast. We're going to try . . ." He broke off. *To find forgiveness.* "To find . . . something we lost."

Niburu nodded—as if he was satisfied, Reede thought. "Then you still won't be needing a pilot," he said.

"Guess not," Reede repeated, looking away again. "You like boats?" He looked back.

"I don't like boats," Niburu said. "They sink. I didn't like them on Samathe. I still don't like them. He doesn't like them either." He gestured to Ananke.

Reede looked at them oddly. "You want to go," he said. "You're leaving."

"You've got somebody to take care of you now, boss." Niburu smiled. "You don't need us anymore." He hesitated. "It's been a long time. Maybe we all miss something."

Tor looked down at him. "You sound like you're never coming back," she said.

"Well, love, I didn't say that." He looked up at her, with his faint smile widening. "I never say never. If I learned one thing from him—" he gestured at Reede, and his smile turned sweet-sour, "it's never say 'never.' . . ." She kissed the top of his head. He kissed her exposed navel. Ananke rolled his eyes.

And Reede felt a sourceless pain strike his gut. He put his drink down on the table behind him, blaming it. "So when are you leaving?" he asked, without looking up again.

Niburu didn't answer, for a moment; as if he were waiting for something else, or had expected a different response. "Soon as I can get our cargo set. A few days."

"A few nights?" Tor asked, running her fingers through his hair.

"That too," he said, glancing up. "Well," he murmured, as Reede finally faced him again. "I guess we'll stop off before we go, and say goodbye. . . ."

"I hate long goodbyes," Reede said, blinking. "Don't do that." He realized that his nose was running, and wiped it on his sleeve. "Got a cold," he muttered, and coughed.

"Better take care of that," Niburu said, his eyes filled with both disbelief and a kind of wonder.

"Take care of yourselves." Reede offered his hand, and Niburu took it, covering the identical brands on their palms.

Niburu's smile spread to his mouth again. "That'll be easy, now that we don't work for you."

Reede laughed. "Thanks . . ." he muttered, and knew that Niburu understood what he was really being thanked for. He reached past Niburu to Ananke; touched the quoll where it lay, contented as usual in its sling. He stroked it for the first time since the day he had fished it out of the well, back on Ondinee. The quoll burbled in congenial surprise, watching him with a black, bead-bright eye. "Take care of that thing, too. You saved its life, you're responsible for its life, forever; you know the rules."

Ananke looked up at him, stroking the quoll, so that their fingers touched briefly. "I know, boss," he said, his voice soft but strained. "Goodbye," he said, and there was something in his face that Reede might have taken for longing, except that that wouldn't have made any sense.

The music changed again, making them all look up. Another song was beginning, and floating above the blend of native and offworld instruments was a new sound, high and haunting, unlike anything he had heard before, but reminding him suddenly, achingly, of the mersong.

He turned, looking for Ariele as he realized that she was no longer standing beside him.

Tor touched his arm, pointing toward the music. He lifted his head, following her gesture, to find Ariele among the musicians; realized then that it was the sound of her father's flute he heard. He had known she had a gift for music and mimicry, but he had not known that she played.

The music, and his own surprise, held him captive for a long moment. When he turned back, he found the others were already drifting away, out of his reach, across the dance floor. Ananke lifted a hand in farewell, looking back, and then they were gone.

Reede started on through the crowd, trying to make his way closer to the place where Ariele and the musicians were playing. He saw Merovy Bluestone again, standing beside the Queen. Moon's arm was around her; the two women were motionless, listening, with the same astonishment and grief filling their faces. He remembered that Tammis had carried a flute; that probably he had played it, just as his sister had . . . just as Sparks Dawntreader had. He considered the strange patterns woven by heredity and environment, by love and grief; and he wished that he were drunker, or not so much so.

"Kullervo," a voice said. He looked up, and saw Gundhalinu, who had been standing at the Queen's other side. Gundhalinu moved away from her, coming toward him.

"Welcome back," Reede said, without a smile. "To the land of the living."

Gundhalinu looked surprised at him, as if he had said something completely incomprehensible. But then he nodded, not smiling either. "Yes . . ." he said quietly. "Thank you. Thank you for your part in it."

Reede shrugged slightly. Seeing Gundhalinu up close at last, he was startled by the drawn weariness of the other man's face, the way its lines had deepened—the marks that Gundhalinu's ordeal in the Camps had left on him, that his sudden reprieve had not begun to erase. The stark black and silver uniform, the reflected light of badges and medals, the cruel curved spines of a trefoil among them, only echoed the hard disillusionment in Gundhalinu's eyes. "Maybe it makes us even," Reede said.

Gundhalinu smiled then, barely; as if his mouth had almost forgotten how to form the expression.

The Queen turned, hearing their voices behind her. Merovy had disappeared; Reede suspected that his presence was the reason. As the Queen moved toward him, stopping beside Gundhalinu, Reede was struck by the sight of them: They were like mirrors, each reflecting the other's suffering, their separate ordeals that had only been manifestations of the same ordeal. He realized that he had not even been aware of how the Queen had changed, until this moment; he had been too preoccupied with his own sea-change. He wondered what they saw in his face.

"I didn't know she could play," he said, looking away from them toward Ariele, who was still lost in the rapture of her music. He felt a sudden, unexpected yearning fill him, like the sweet, sorrowful gaiety of her song rising into the air.

"Neither did I," Gundhalinu murmured, a little sadly.

"Neither did I. . . ." The Queen's voice was an echo of the music's joy and plangency. Gundhalinu put his arm around her, drawing her close.

She looked up at him and nodded, as if he had spoken; as if there was no real need for words between them anymore. She looked at Reede again; her eyes were wells of memory. Reede stepped aside to let them pass. He watched as they made their way through the dwindling crowd, heading toward the stairway that he had come down. He watched them go out as he had watched them come in, completing the circle.

He turned his back on the empty stairs, granting them their privacy; looking toward the music, and Ariele. He let his thoughts dissolve into the fluid melody, letting Reede Kullervo become lost in the crowd.

Moon led BZ along the quiet hall, up another stairway, through more corridors, hand in hand. He did not question her, following her with a yielding compliance—as if he were still a prisoner. She looked back at him, aching inside. She had thought she was leading him to her bedroom; but they went on, passing its door. BZ glanced at her in silent curiosity, but still asked her no questions.

She had spent every day of the interminable weeks between the tribunal's arrival and his return working from dawn until far into the night, pressed on all sides by the demands of renegotiating Tiamat's relationship with the Hegemony and overseeing the city's recovery from the storm's disastrous passing. But every night, when she lay in her bed at last, alone, she had imagined him lying beside her: the sound of his breathing, his heartbeat; the warmth of his touch bringing her cold, grief-wracked body back to life.

And yet here, now, when they were alone at last, she knew that it was not what she wanted, or needed. The first giddy rush of joy they had felt at the sight of one another had carried them gracefully, painlessly through the party's public eye. But here in these empty halls, that bright, thoughtless moment of pleasure was fading, letting memory overtake her, letting in ghosts and shadows. And looking up at his shadowed, weary face, she knew that it was not what he needed, either, to be hurried into intimacy.

And so she led him on through the halls and up the final spiral stair, leading him to her private room at the palace's, and the city's, peak. The night sky opened out around them, glowing with the fire of countless stars. The cool, blue-silver face of Tiamat's single large moon was a luminous mystery rising over the sea.

She heard BZ draw a breath of astonishment, as he saw what lay before and below him. "I had no idea this existed . . ." he whispered, and she did not know whether he meant this secret room, or a view of such beauty. She rested her head against his shoulder as they stood together, looking out; holding one another but perfectly still, forgetting their own existence.

Something broke the water's surface, far out on the placid dark-bright mirror of the sea: one silhouette and then another and another, stitching tracks of blackness across its shimmering surface; a reminder of all that lay hidden beneath its illusion of calm. "Are those mers?" he asked.

"I think so," she said softly. "I can't be sure, at this distance."

He sighed. "I thought I'd never live to see this world again," he said. "I thought I'd never see your face—" He looked away from the ocean, into her eyes; touched her face tentatively, with a work-scarred hand. "They tried to kill me . . ." he murmured, at last.

"Who?" She would have held his gaze, but he looked out at the sea again. "The same ones who wanted to kill the mers." His face hardened like a fist. "The same ones who were congratulating me on my return, and licking my boots downstairs tonight, probably. They didn't have the influence—or the courage—to kill me outright. So they sent me to that place. . . ." He broke off. "And hoped time would take care of things. Except that you saved my life, again." His expression eased, and he kissed her hair, a tender, passionless kiss.

She did not answer, did not move, her body insensate and unresponsive: remembering how thin a membrane lay between life and death, remembering all the things that could not be changed, ever.

"Moon . . ." He closed her in his arms in sudden compassion. "I'm sorry. I'm so sorry. . . ." And in his broken voice she heard the memory of sounds torn from her throat by her own mourning.

She shook her head, feeling her flushed cheek brush the cool, impersonal cloth of his uniform jacket; feeling the armor of hard-edged medals he wore press into her back, her neck, as he held her. Feeling no comfort. "Mother of Us All," she whispered, gazing out at the sea, "I would rather have died than have had my heart torn out of me." She thought of Arienrhod then—of her bones rolled eternally in the dark depths of the sea—with pity and terror.

He had no answer, this time; only went on holding her, until she began to feel the warmth of his body penetrate her skin like a soothing balm. "Look," he said at last. "Those are mers. You can see it clearly now." His arms still held her tightly; his voice insisted that she look.

She raised her head, to see them, a whole colony rejoicing in the night at the interface between worlds. Their lives were complete again, their reason for existence secure again; although she saw in the hidden forms of their abandoned motion, their courting dance, that in their timeless world, existence itself could be reason enough. They had far more in common with the sibyl mind than they had with the human servants who shared their spiritual bondage to it. She watched them appear and disappear, leaving the subtle patterns of their passing imprinted on her mind as they winked in and out of sight on the star-filled surface of the water. "I envy them . . ." she whispered. "They live without regret."

"Their lives will never again come to an unnatural end, because of us," Gundhalinu murmured, against her hair. "And no human lives will ever again be unnaturally prolonged by their deaths. A balance has been restored. . . . Maybe now we can get on with our own lives. With our life together. We've lost so much time that we can never get back—"

Moon closed her eyes, remembering an eternity where time's arrow had lost its way, and pointed all ways at once. She opened them again, looking out at the sea and sky on fire with stars. She could not find the line where one ended and the other began; it was as if there were no separation, but instead a single continuum flowing from the depths of the sea into the depths of space. " 'Time will take care of things,' " she repeated softly, remembering his bitter words. "It has . . . it will. It owes that much to us." She looked up at him again, seeing the night reflected in his dark eyes.

He smiled at last and nodded, holding her, warming her. "I look forward," he said, "to growing old with you."

TIAMAT: Prajua, Planetary Orbit

"Gods," Kedalion said, stretching his fingers until his knuckles cracked, as he leaned back in the command seat of the *Prajna*. "I'm still half afraid I'm going to wake up from this dream." He looked over at Ananke. "Tell me I'm not dreaming."

Ananke smiled. "You're not dreaming. Unless I'm having the same one." She shrugged, stroking the quoll's bulbous nose as she studied the readouts on the control room wall. "Drive systems, check. Cargo, check. Life support systems, check. Clearances are all in, and departure window has not changed. We're free, Kedalion. We're really free to go." She settled comfortably into the copilot's seat, dropping the quoll into its nesting box, secured underneath the instrument panel in front of her.

"Ready to leave Tiamat space?" Kedalion spoke the ritual question, looking up at her again from his own boards.

"Ready," she answered, without hesitation.

Kedalion glanced back over his shoulder. "Ready, Dawntreader?"

Sparks Dawntreader looked up at him, and nodded his bandage-wrapped head imperceptibly. But his eyes still searched the display screens, still clinging to the final view of his homeworld passing by, grandly, thousands of kilometers below them. "Am I doing the right thing, Niburu?" he murmured.

"I don't know," Kedalion said. "But you're doing a good thing. . . . Are you ready?" he asked again, after a moment. At his touch the image on the screens became a field of stars.

Dawntreader drew a deep breath. "I'm ready," he said, and this time he was looking at the future. He smiled, lifting a hand in a gesture that might have been meant as reassurance, or only as a farewell.

Kedalion settled back into his seat. He spoke to the port orbiting far below; spoke to the ship's computer, activating the departure sequence.

And then, in the sublime grip of anticipation, he waited, while the *Prajna* came alive around him, and fell away into the night.